C. S. JOHNSON

THE ORDER

of

THE CRYSTAL DAGGERS

A HISTORICAL SPY ROMANCE SERIES

◊   ◊   ◊   ◊

Kingdom of Ash and Soot, Book 1
Prince of Secrets and Shadows, Book 2
Night of Blood and Beauty, A Companion Novella
Heart of Hope and Fear, Book 3
City of Light and Sun, A Companion Novella

C. S. Johnson

C. S. JOHNSON

Box Set Collector Edition
ebook ISBN: 978-1-948464-72-7
Book ISBN: 978-1-948464-73-4

SPECIAL COLLECTOR SET DEDICATION

There are always so many people to whom I owe so much, and I always feel it when it is time for me to write my dedications. But this one, I can confidently say, is easy.

This series is for Terri Rand, who I am blessed to count as one of my best friends.

Like so many things, I could not have made it through this book without you beside me. To me, you are more than a friend; you are a hero. I am so proud and humbled to be able to walk with you in this life and in the next.

C. S. JOHNSON

KINGDOM

of

ASH and SOOT

BOOK ONE OF *THE ORDER OF THE CRYSTAL DAGGERS*

◊ ◊ ◊ ◊

C. S. Johnson

C. S. JOHNSON

DEDICATION

First and foremost, this is for my darling children. The world needs more brotherly love and sisterly affection such as yours, and you are my inspirations.

Second, as always, this is for Sam. I have never forgotten your questions or our conversations, and I hope in some small way, you'll read this and allow them to live on.

And finally, this is for all my favorite people I fangirl over.

To my favorite podcasters: Ben, Michael, and Drew. I love you all. And my video playlists are filled with Ravi, Dinesh, David, Dennis, and Nabeel. Thank God for you! I would not be anywhere close to who I am without all of you, and I am tremendously grateful for your wit, wisdom, and insight over the years.

As a special note, I would like to add Michelle and Ayah to my list. I am sorry for the late tribute to Nabeel, but I am grateful you are able to carry on his life's work.

For the translation help, I must thank Riad El-Choueiry. Small as it is, your words have helped me so much.

C. S. JOHNSON

Prologue

◊

My father's hands, stained with darkened sunlight and roughened sores, were cold as I touched them for the last time.

As he lay still in his coffin, I rubbed my small hands over his, much as he had done to mine before I went to sleep each night when he was home.

"Night-night, *Táta*." I said my final goodbye softly, my lips barely moving to form the words. Not even my hair stirred, the ebony curls stilled out of solemnity.

My gaze turned to his face, as the church's robed pallbearers, silently but surely, came up beside me. I felt them surround my father's body more than I saw them, as I continued to watch his face, searching for any sign his eyes might open and wink up at me once more.

A sleeve tickled my neck. "It's time to let go, miss," one of the pallbearers whispered into my ear.

"Not yet!" I objected.

"Eleanora." The sharp voice of my stepmother, Cecilia—officially Baroness Cecilia Haberecht Chotek Svobodová of Bohemia—snapped loudly and harshly against the quiet sea of silence inside the church. "Let the men do their job."

Only after I turned to face her did her hard expression melt into one of concern.

"Please," she added more sympathetically, but I knew from the hard line of her jaw she was more concerned I would make a scene in front of the whole kingdom.

How impudent it would be of me to embarrass her with my grief.

"But Ben didn't get a final chance to say goodbye," I said, my nostrils flaring.

At the sound of his name, my brother, at twelve years of age, shifted uncomfortably on the hard pew bench. In the last few days, Ben had transformed from the smart and silly, fun-loving boy I grew up with into a cynical, unrecognizable man.

I did only what I could—I waited for his response. There was a long moment where the crowded church returned to its stifled silence, before finally, *finally*, Ben coughed discreetly, and spoke.

"It's fine, Nora. I've already said my farewells to *Otec*."

I grimaced at his tone; it was brusque and formal, and nothing about it suggested Ben was as heartbroken as I was.

"Come sit down, Eleanora," Cecilia insisted once more. "Father Mueller is waiting to perform the last rites."

1

THE ORDER OF THE CRYSTAL DAGGERS

"I'll not come down until Ben comes and says a proper goodbye to our father."

"You are embarrassing yourself in front of our family and neighbors. Even His Grace has come from Moravia to be here at your father's Mass." Her voice was low and deadly.

Briefly, I glanced over at the stern-faced man who was standing next to Cecilia. The Duke of Moravia, Lord Franz Maximillian Chotek, was a cousin to both the Emperor and my stepmother. His thin, dark mustache twitched in irritation as Cecilia and I battled over the right to grieve.

"It is the honorable thing to do," I argued.

My brother sighed. In his lap, I could see his fingers clench into a fist.

"Benedict, go. If it will let us move on before Adolf's body starts to smell, then by all means, appease your sister."

I held my breath, wondering what I would do if he did leave me to send *Táta* off all by myself.

I relaxed a moment later when he reached over, almost as if he was mentally reconsidering his reluctance, and grabbed his crutch; glaring angrily at me, he hobbled less than gracefully up to the altar. I was relieved when no one muttered anything about my brother's crippled right leg.

"I can't believe you're making me do this," he whispered to me. "You of all people know how I feel about *Otec*."

I frowned. "*Táta* was a good man. Even the king said he was a good man who protected him during the Revolution."

"Kings are quick to reward those who would die for them."

"Not all of them."

"Nora, what do you know of war or any soldier's duty?" Ben hung his head at my childishness. "It doesn't matter anyway, does it? The Germans are still in control of the Diet, and the Emperor is in his palace in Vienna, while King Ferdinand is playing with his posies all day long."

My brother was clever. In ducking his head, it looked from behind as though he was sad or even crying. The church's audience murmured a quiet approval as Ben grasped onto his crutch with one hand and put his other hand over mine, while I continued to rest it on *Táta's*.

As we stood there, I saw there was a bluish tint to my father's stiffened hands, and I wondered if death had chilled him even in the afterlife, so much that his veins had swelled. I looked back up at his face, surprised to see there were similar lines around his lips, although his beard and mustache helped to hide the unsightly marks.

"There." Ben squeezed my hand. "Are you satisfied?"

2

"Yes." I nearly choked out a response. "He was all we had, Ben, no matter what you say."

I slowly released my father's hands and whispered one last prayer toward the heavens for his soul as I headed back to my seat in the pew.

But when I turned around, I suddenly stopped, as a flurry of sound and movement in the back of the church caught my attention. Ben, with his uneven steps, bumped into me from behind, and I heard his mumbled curse.

Fortunately for Ben, everyone else, including Father Mueller, was too busy staring at the back of the church to chastise him.

My own mouth dropped open as I saw a kingly procession entering the chapel. Men wearing fine livery made from shining threads, woven with the proud red and white colors of Bohemia, dotted the small crowd.

It was only when they parted that I saw the king.

King Ferdinand V, the former leader of the Austria-Hungarian Empire and King of Bohemia, and a string of several other titles, had arrived.

"His Majesty!" Cecilia gasped. I might have laughed at her expression at any other time, but she was right to be surprised.

The king did not come out in public very often, and at once I could see why. My eyes took in his large forehead, his wide-set eyes, and his aged, enlarged face. His robes were grand, and his jewelry ornate, but there was nothing ostentatious enough to hide his shaking discomfort. He walked slowly, with a cane in hand and two young attendants immediately behind him for support. I, along with everyone else stared as the elderly figure proceeded toward the front, where my father's casket was waiting.

I had heard the rumors of the king's precarious mental state—of his simplemindedness, his mental fits. I wondered as he passed, only giving me a light glance, if he was here against his doctor's wishes.

King Ferdinand V used to be our king. In 1848, the same year Ben was born, Ferdinand had been forced to abdicate his throne to his nephew, the current Emperor, Franz Joseph I.

But, as the king bowed down before the altar and made the Holy Cross over my father's corpse, I remembered King Ferdinand's informal title, Ferdinand *Dobrotivý*, or "Ferdinand the Good."

It seemed to suit him.

I blinked back tears, remembering *Táta* telling me that even kings had to bow to something greater than themselves in the end. Many of them submitted to God, in life and in death, while King Ferdinand had submitted to the power of the people. My father had remained at the king's side, protecting him from physical harm during the Revolution of 1848, when King Ferdinand's power was revoked.

3

Maybe that's why the king decided to come down out of his castle in the city to see him.

Father Mueller continued with the Funeral Mass, reciting the familiar lines of liturgy, along with the occasion's additions for the deceased. I barely listened to the service for my father. While grief was not preferred, it was familiar; Ben, *Táta*, and I had all been through it four years prior, when my mother was lost at sea.

As we responded to Father Mueller's reading of the twenty-third Psalm, I glanced back over at the king. My grief was great, but my curiosity was proving itself the more demanding of the two.

"I can't believe the king came," I whispered to Ben.

"He didn't come for *Máma's* funeral," he whispered, "and she was the better one between the two."

"*Táta* is with *Máma* now. They are together again at last."

"If *Otec* even made it to heaven," Ben retorted.

"Ben! That's terrible to say."

"He was a terrible man."

"To you, maybe."

"Exactly."

At the bitterness in his tone, I decided to discontinue the conversation.

But I stopped for other reasons as well—two of them, to be more precise. Priscilla, my stepsister, was earnestly tugging on her mother's skirts as she glanced over in our direction, and my stepbrother, Alexander, glared menacingly at Ben.

How can they be the same age as us, but act like such little children?

It was not hard for me to make that deduction; they had never known pain as Ben and I had. It seemed that for every burden my family had borne, our stepsiblings had only brushed theirs aside.

In addition to our mother's death, there was Ben's injury. *Táta* never forgave Ben for getting crippled two summers past, falling off the stable roof after trying to fetch one of my cats for me.

Priscilla and Alex's father, Cecilia's second husband and the one before my father, had died serving in the armed forces abroad. Even at our first meeting, Alex had been eager to boast of how his father's shield had saved the baby prince, Leopold, and his mother, Queen Victoria, and subsequently, the entire kingdom of Britain, from death and destruction. When I asked if his father was acting as a nursemaid, he nearly cried.

I think that was the moment when he began to hate me.

Quickly, so Cecilia would not see, I stuck my tongue out at Alex and glared a warning to Priscilla, before turning away from them completely.

Ben shifted in his seat uncomfortably again. I looked up to see he was giving silent warnings to our stepsiblings himself. Their derision toward us since the day we had met had never been more inappropriate. Some part of me blamed Ben for that; he had been angry, angrier than ever, the winter after his accident, and gaining a new family was the last thing that could have cheered him up.

"Stop fretting, Ben," I told him, placing my hands over his as I had done to *Táta's* just moments before.

"I can't. I have to watch out for you now."

I wrinkled my nose. "Cecilia's *children* don't scare me."

"Lucky you," he said. "There is no one to stop them from taking our inheritance now. Indeed, Cecilia has already begun raiding *Otec's* estate. How else do you think she was able to get such a fancy dress made up from the seamstress before his funeral? And how else do you think she was able to get clothes and shoes for Alex and Priscilla? I also overheard her ordering a new carriage in the English style. She fancies herself to be Queen Victoria or Empress Elisabeth, cast out to far and foreign lands."

I glanced over to see Ben was right; Cecilia's dress was indeed much finer than my own. The gown was cut in a fashionable style, though from what I remembered of *Máma's* wardrobe, I would have said it was French rather than British. The stitching was fine, and even from where we were sitting, I could easily make out the sheen of expensive silk.

"We didn't get any new clothes," I said.

"Clothes are one thing, Nora. But how will you be able to get married? You have no dowry to your name now."

"I'm not even ten years old yet."

"I knew after my accident I would never marry," Ben said. His words were stilted, as though he had to chisel them off his chest. "But you, Nora. You could have had any suitor in the kingdom, just as *Otec* said *Máma* did."

"I *did* inherit *Máma's* looks," I said, straightening my posture, momentarily forgetting my pain as pride took over.

"You dream of a family."

"No." I shook my head firmly. "*You* are my family. It is enough for me. I need no husband to be content."

"I would not let you be alone with me if you could do better."

"For all your trouble, there is no one better than you," I said. "You have always watched out for me, even before Cecilia and the demon twins came to live with us."

A small chuckle was smothered in his throat, but I heard its echo nonetheless.

"You've got *Máma's* humor too, it seems. Hopefully you'll have her strength as well," Ben said. "Because these next few years may be hard."

"*Máma* taught me to be brave, Ben. As long as you'll face them with me, we will survive." My hands tightened in his.

"We may survive, but we will not be free."

"One day we will," I vowed. "You'll see."

He could only grip my hand back in reply before Father Mueller, finished with the eulogy, harkened us once more to prayer.

" ... And so, let us pray for Adolf Svoboda, a regal nobleman in the court of His Imperial and Royal Apostolic Majesty, the Emperor of Austria, Apostolic King of Hungary Emperor Franz Joseph I, of the House of Hapsburg-Lorraine, his kind and generous legacy in service to His Majesty King Ferdinand V of Bohemia ... "

Upon hearing his name, I glanced over at the king once more. He had his one hand resting on his walking stick, and the other nudged between his legs underneath a thick blanket.

I tilted my head, watching him. Was he cold? I wondered. It was getting close to the end of summer.

When he began to twitch and moan a moment later, I felt my own body go still. "Ben, look!"

The congregation began to whisper voraciously as the king fell over in his pew, convulsing fitfully. Father Mueller faltered mid-prayer, and I saw another man, one I recognized as my father's friend and medical doctor, Dr. Sigmund Artha, hurry forward to help.

"Your Highness," Dr. Artha said. He patted down his bushy wave of gray-streaked hair, and I wondered if he had only just remembered he was in the presence of the former king of Bohemia. The faded, familiar rosary beads from the Church of St. Nicholas, the *Kostel svatého Mikuláše*, jangled against his small medical bag as I watched him hastily make a quick bow. "Let me assist you."

I had seen Dr. Artha in our manor enough to know that he was deathly afraid of the silliest things, from spiders and dusty books to messy rooms and babies. On several of his visits with my father, he would excuse himself to go to wash his hands, and he would rub down his hair in both a nervous and necessary habit. I found it amusing and endearing that Dr. Artha had no fear of approaching King Ferdinand.

"We're here, too, sir." One of the young attendants, the shorter one, behind the king, stepped forward.

The first attendant, the one with black hair, began to issue orders to the king's men. Meanwhile, the other one who had spoken with Dr. Artha, a slightly shorter boy with copper hair, stepped up beside the king and began to tend to him, whispering into his ear. I saw he had a small decanter in his hand.

6

"Stay calm, Nora," Ben whispered beside me, as the king let out a loud moan.

"Father." The second assistant suddenly yelped as the king fell to the side.

I frowned. King Ferdinand had no children.

"Father Mueller," the black-haired boy called, his voice more confident and urgent, and I quickly realized my misunderstanding. He was calling for the priest. "Please, continue on. His Imperial Highness would benefit from your godly prayers."

The other boy nodded, and the reverend complied. I saw Father Mueller's face was white with slight panic as he stepped back up to the pulpit.

As the normal prayer resumed, this time louder and clearly more strained, I kept glancing over at the king.

"Oh, merciful infant Jesus! I know of your miraculous deeds for the sick. How many diseases you cured during your blessed life on earth … "

I made the sign of the cross over me, still watching as the king slowly reverted to his previous state; there was less jolting and gasping, and his eyes, even though they were still blinking fast, seemed more alert. He watched the copper-haired attendant with a tepid smile on his face.

That was when the attendant boy caught my eye. He was dabbing the king's head with a handkerchief, carefully and calmly, almost lovingly, before the king whispered something. Then the boy turned to see me staring at him.

Remembering my father's affection for the disposed king, I gave the boy a kind smile.

He went still, staring at me.

I stared back.

Just as I noticed he seemed to be close to Ben's age, the other attendant stepped in front of him.

"Guard," I heard him call. "Prepare His Highness' coach for departure. We will be leaving shortly. The king needs his rest."

A guard saluted him and headed down the back of the small church.

The dark-haired boy suddenly narrowed his gray eyes in my direction. From his expression, I could tell he expected me to turn away or bow my head in feigned prayer.

Rather than submit to his wishes, I stared back at him, arching my brow at him, letting him know, in my own small way, he had no moral authority to shame me. As a citizen, I had just as much concern for our king's health, even if he was no longer our ruler.

Our imagined conversation did not seem to be going as smoothly as he might have hoped. The boy at least seemed unnerved by my response, blushing quickly and then turning back to say something to Dr. Artha, who seemed to be asking him a question.

"Nora," Ben whispered. "Stop causing trouble."

"I didn't do anything," I said.

"Just be quiet and focus on the ceremony, would you, ségra? Maybe it was nice of the king to come, but it seriously doesn't matter."

I was tempted to pinch him for his flippancy, but hearing his pet name for me softened my resolve. It had been awhile since he had called me ségra, and I was glad to hear it again. I took his hand in mine, holding it as I returned my focus to Father Mueller.

" … Extend your most holy hands, and by your power take away all pain and infirmity, so that our recovery may be due, not to natural remedies, but to you alone … "

I sighed. Father Mueller's prayers were appropriate, I supposed, but they were as dead to my ears as the words were to my heart. I knew they were for my father's heavenly ascent, but I felt Ben and I needed prayers more than our father did.

I tightened my grip on Ben's hand and prayed. *Please, Holy Father, help Ben and me. Help us to find a way to be happy once more. Please keep us together and keep us safe.*

As my father's casket was finally removed from the church, as Cecilia wept loudly, kneeling before the benign king of Bohemia, as I sat helplessly next to my brother, I beseeched God again with a barrage of earnest prayers.

It would be many years before I believed God had heard me—and even more before I realized that he had bigger plans than I could have ever imagined, and he had already set them in motion.

1
◊

"Nora."

The call to wake up was never a pleasant one. Ben's voice, though it had grown deeper over the years and changed according to his moods each day, was constant throughout the last decade of our lives; it was the precursor to the endless rounds of chores and errands.

It was a comfortable kind of discomfort.

My slumbering barrier against the real world was breached again, this time more urgently.

"Come on, Nora, wake up."

I could hear the mix of impatience and compassion in his tone as Ben sighed.

"Cecilia's coming."

At that, I shot up, sitting upright on my small pallet. I groaned as I pushed back the loose tresses of my hair, allowing my eyes to find sunlight. It was a wasted effort; the sun had not yet risen. "Already?" I asked, rubbing my eyes. "Why is she even up this early? You'd think that after so many evenings of dancing till dawn she would never again rise from sleep before noon."

"Why else?" Ben asked. "She and Priscilla have rounded up more treasures that used to belong to our father, and she wants us to trade or sell them at the market before the neighbors can see how shabby they look."

"Oh, no. Not more of *Táta's* things!" I turned my face away from my brother and flopped back onto the small, soft bag I had stuffed with cotton and feathers to use as a pillow. "I thought she'd finished searching for his stuff years ago."

"*Otec* collected a lot of junk from his travels for the king," Ben said. His formal use of "*Otec*" snapped in the air between us, also reminding me of his animosity toward our father. "*Máma's* stuff is nearly gone, too. Including all her lovely books from Paris."

From the look on his face, Ben mourned the loss of those books more than I did, and it was likely only a little less than either of us missed our mother.

"I know, but still. It's been over ten years since *Táta* died," I moaned. "Cecilia wasn't married to him that long."

Ben gave me a small smile. "I know it hasn't helped Cecilia that we've hidden some of *Otec's* things. And there is her party tonight, don't forget."

"How in the world could I forget about the party?" I held up my hands. "My palms have been raw all week from the extra scrubbings she's had me and the other maids do."

9

"That's probably how she managed to find some more of *Otec's* collectibles."

"She didn't find anything under the floor in the pantry, did she?" I asked, my eyes suddenly wide with fear. "I put *Máma's* locket there, along with *Táta's* pocket watch."

"I'm sure we'll find out," Ben said. "I just saw her hanging out the east tower window, yelling at the gardeners, and when I went to go pilfer some bread earlier, Betsy told me 'Her Ladyship' has to check on the barn's repairs on her way over here to us. She'll come for us last."

"Of course."

"*Of course.*" Ben mocked my tone. "So you'll have time to shake the soot out of your skirts."

"Huh?" I looked down and sighed. I had stayed up late reading by the fireplace, and my skirts were covered in a light coating of soot.

Why was it so hard to find the time to read, and then to have the joy of reading itself tampered with the cost of Cecilia's anger?

"Ben, help me." I began jumping up and batting the ashen dust off my apron. "She'll kill me if she sees my dress like this. She hates doing laundry any more than she has to."

"You mean she hates it when *we* have to do laundry any more than she wants us to. It's laughable to think she does any real work herself."

"She does all the accounting work. I've seen her doing it, even very late into the night in the library." I suddenly laughed. "Oh! I forgot to tell you. The other night, I actually saw her wearing her spectacles."

Ben smiled as he pushed my pallet and homemade pillow inside a small chest and grabbed a broom while using his crutch to push aside the rug. "I'll bet that was a sight," he said. "What did they look like?"

"They were wire frames," I said, "and they were perched on her nose like a chained bird, trying desperately to fly free. They made her nose look so big! I'd never noticed how long it is."

"We'll have to keep that in mind if we ever need emotional blackmail," Ben said.

"Yes, most definitely—"

"Ouch!"

I flinched as Ben's weak leg tripped over the book I had managed to hide under my pallet; once I recovered, I hurried over and picked it up, quickly thrusting it behind my back.

"I see you were in the library looking for books again," Ben said.

"I can't help it," I insisted. "Life is so dull without books."

"Life also gets much worse when Cecilia realizes you're reading these by the fire, getting them dirty, and demands we work more to earn back the cost."

I lowered my eyes. "We only have each other, Ben. Can't we have books, too?"

"Not while they're technically hers, and we have to pay for them."

The door snapped open with a melodramatic creak. "Pay for what?"

Instantly, we snapped to attention before our stepmother. While ten years had passed since our father died, and it had been eleven years since her marriage to him, Cecilia's face was nearly as fresh and fair as it had been on their wedding day.

Unless, of course, she was frowning, as she usually was when she looked at us.

After the long years of working as her servants, Ben and I were well acquainted with the flash of her temper and the guilt of her sermons.

"Good morning, my lady," I murmured delicately, curtsying in the fine manner *Máma* had taught me.

"Save your curtsies," Cecilia snapped. "I have no time for your disruptions today. Tell me, what are you going to pay for?"

"A new dress," I said. I did not think God would mind the small misdirection. "I heard that Madame Balthazar down at the market has a bolt of new silk in from the East, and I'd like to try to earn some money to pay for it."

Between dresses and books, I was more than happy to let Cecilia think I wanted the dresses more. She was appalled at the thought of servants knowing how to read, let alone actually reading.

Her nose reflexively sniffed. "I doubt you'd be able to afford it, Eleanora. It would be a poor investment besides, considering you ruin the dresses you have now by sleeping close to the fire." She prowled around the room as she shook her head. She let out a disapproving *tsk, tsk* as she looked up and down at my servant's outfit.

I turned along with her, keeping the book behind me and out of sight.

Ben coughed, effectively distracting her.

She turned her gaze on him. "Benedict, are you ill?"

"No, ma'am," he said, bowing his head down to her ever so slightly.

"I have some items I need you to take to the market." Her eyes narrowed. "I'd like for you and Eleanora to take them today, and quickly. I also have a list of things you will need to pick up before His Grace arrives for the party tonight."

"Yes, ma'am," he said.

"See to it that you are both back in time to help with the dinner preparations," she said. "Betsy and Mavis are going to be extra busy, and we need all the hands we have to make sure the day is sufferable."

"Yes, ma'am."

"Stop that," Cecilia barked. "Don't use that tone with me."

Ben said nothing.

Part of me waited to see if Cecilia was going to give the same old lines to Ben:

You're lucky I am able to keep you, as a cripple wouldn't last long in the market streets or out in the fields.

I am more than willing to do my Christian duty to your father's memory, but you're enough of a man to know I could turn you out if you would ever indicate that was your desire.

You have no place here anymore; it is fortunate for you that you can be of some help, given your regrettable condition.

I should think you would be grateful to me, to keep you here with your sister, rather than thinking you deserve more.

Life does not guarantee you anything, and it's time to stop acting like I should feel sorry for you, rather than embracing what my good choices have brought me.

It was almost as if she had branded those words on Ben, deforming his heart as much as his leg. A moment passed, and from the small smirk on Cecilia's face, just barely peeking out from the thin layer of wrinkles, I knew we were all thinking the same thing.

I guess she knows that she doesn't have to say it anymore.

Still, I held my breath as she turned to face me. Over the years, I had learned to stop flinching; the one time I stopped her, back when she was more apologetic about the state of "poverty" my father left her in, she had me flogged. "As a servant girl should be," were her exact words on the issue.

"See to it that you have at least one clean outfit to wear tonight, Eleanora," she said. "I will need you to help with our guests."

Her impressive skirts swept around her, and before I could ask her who else besides the Duke was coming to dinner, Ben cut me off with a stern look.

I shut my mouth and nodded to him.

"You'll find the items to trade gathered in the back of the main house," she called back. "Go, and hurry now."

I finally allowed myself to wince. "She's getting shrilly," I said to myself.

"Old age comes to us all," Ben said. "Hopefully, we won't have to deal with her too much longer."

"How is our goal coming?" I lowered my voice by several degrees. "Are we any closer to Liberté?"

"Nora." Ben sighed. "We will need another year, at least."

I wanted to pout. But I gave Ben my best smile. "Only a year doesn't sound so bad." I almost hid my roughened hands in my skirts, before I recalled I was hiding the book I had taken from the library.

"Do you want me to return it for you?"

There was a playfulness behind his grin, and seeing it, I could not help but give in to the temptation to run and pretend I was far away from home. "I'll race you," I said. "Just let me get my shoes."

"If I win, you have to go to town yourself," he said. "I want to stay and help with the cooking."

"Help yourself to the cooking, more likely."

"The rich and fancy have people taste their food before they eat it," Ben said. "They aren't like us, Nora."

I ignored the part about the fancy. Ben and I had known our share of a comfortable world, before *Máma* was lost at sea and *Táta* died. "Are you hoping you'll get the job?"

"No, and that's a shame. It might help us get to Liberté faster."

"Ha!" I rolled my eyes. "I doubt Cecilia would let you be hired, even if it was the Duke of Moravia that wanted you as his personal food taster."

"Yes, where would she be without us?" Ben rolled his eyes. "She wouldn't be able to get on her high horse and claim she's doing her duty to our father's memory."

"I can't imagine her on any horse at all," I said, trying to add some levity. "Not in those gowns, with those horribly voluminous skirts. It's worth it to be a servant just so I can walk without falling over and drowning in a puddle."

Ben laughed, and I cheered at his mirth as I grabbed my shoes and laced them up. My brother knew little of joy in his life, outside of caring for me and working on his machines. It was only right that I tried to provide him with as much happiness as I could.

Especially since Cecilia seemed so determined to take it away, just as she had taken our inheritance away.

"Ow," I muttered.

"What is it?" Ben asked.

"My shoe." I held up the small slipper. "It has a hole in the bottom."

"I'll see if I can repair it while you're out on the town, you klutz." The smirk on his face might have made me mad if I did not know we relied on making each other laugh and keeping each other fighting.

"Ha!" I stood up. "You really think you'll beat me to the library?"

13

THE ORDER OF THE CRYSTAL DAGGERS

"*While* I'm holding the book." He lifted up his right pant leg to show me the latest brace he had designed for his crooked leg. "This model helps my balance a lot more. I used some spare iron from the blacksmith's shed. I don't even need my crutch to run."

"Run, maybe," I said, "but I'll still be able to beat you climbing into the kitchen windows!"

And before he could stop me, I tore out of the small servant's house and headed for the main house, laughing all the way.

Ben quickly managed to catch up to me. I could see his twisted leg moving with a straightened limp, and he had been right; his balance was kept in place as he ran.

As soon as I could feel him catching me, I twisted about, skipping through the pig's pen.

The mud and muck would surely slow him down, I thought, not too thrilled to be so competitive that it made me less than compassionate.

Ben did not seem to mind.

"Ha, nice try, Nora!"

As I watched, he pulled out the feeding trough and used it to slide through the muck. The pigs did not even see him.

And I did not really see them. I stumbled right into one, only managing to jump over him at the last moment.

Furious Ben had found a way to beat me, I grappled with the ivy vines, thick from years of growth in the Bohemian clime, and pulled myself up to the second floor of my father's mansion.

"Ha, yourself!" I called back, teasingly waving as I headed down the stone battlement.

Ben grunted in response, but I saw the smirk on his face as he trotted up a small tower of hay bales and hurried into a nearby window, only catching his leg briefly on the outer trim.

"Hey!" I rushed toward the door.

Only to be immediately stopped by my stepbrother.

"Where are you rushing off to?" he asked, as he lazed about in the doorway to the inner keep.

"I'm just going inside, Alex," I murmured, avoiding his eyes.

He looked too much like Cecilia that I did not like to look at him in general, but he had inherited her vanity along with her looks.

As I glanced up at him, waiting for him to move, I caught sight of the leer on his face, and I felt the sudden urge to hit him. He was looking down his nose at me, as though I was beneath him.

Which, considering my role in his household, even I had a hard enough time doubting. But I was a lady, a true one, just as my mother had been, and my father made me a knight's daughter.

"That's Lord Alex to you."

"Well, then it's Lady Eleanora to you," I spat back.

"I'd hardly bow to a servant, especially a hoyden such as you," he countered. "What kind of lady romps around on the battlements just before breakfast? One returning from an illicit, romantic tryst, maybe?" His gaze wandered down my dress, and I gave in to my hateful temptation.

My fist balled, and I struck him in the stomach before he could move.

"*Ack.*" He gasped before doubling over in pain.

"Serves you right," I said, kneeing him in the face. I could feel the stark bluntness of the impact, and I was not surprised a moment later to see droplets of red slam against the stony walkway.

"You'll pay for that," he vowed, as his nose began to bleed.

"Oh, what are you ever going to do? Tell your mommy on me? She'll hardly think you're man enough to marry that countess then."

"I'll find a way to make you pay," Alex grunted, "if it's the last thing I do."

"I would gladly let you try, if it was indeed the last thing you would ever do," I yelled back, already moving past him and out the door of the next room.

It was no secret my stepbrother was a monster; Ben and I had caught him trying to coerce Betsy and some of the other younger maids into dark corners of the house a few years ago, and ever since then we made sure he was constantly watched.

All of *Táta's* playing around when we were younger looked more and more like a wise investment, I thought, as I arrived at my destination. Ben and I had learned to hit and fight as well as any siblings who shared the ups and downs of our lives, mostly thanks to each other, but plenty of others as well.

The halls around me were quiet and still. I burst through the double doors of the library and threw up my arms in triumph.

"Take that, Ben!" I twirled around and flopped into a chair. I decided it was the perfect place to greet him as he entered and found himself in second place.

There was just one problem with that.

"Take what?" Ben asked, all too innocently, from behind me.

I jumped up and swiveled around, the mud on my shoes making my feet more slick. "Oh, no."

"Yep, that's right. I'm the winner." The innocence was gone, and the arrogance had come.

My shoulders slumped over. "I guess this means I have to go into town by myself."

"You know it." Ben grinned. A moment later, he softened. "It might be for the best," he said. "If you go by yourself, you'll take longer. That'll give me some time to get the work done around here."

I sighed. "Anything to get away from Alex. I ran into him out on the battlements. That's why I lost."

"Then it is better you go," Ben said. "So when I beat him, you won't be around to take the blame."

"I already took care of it," I said, before diving into the details, telling Ben the story of how I had fought off our wicked stepbrother.

"In all seriousness, we need to practice your fighting some more," Ben said when I was done, and he was done laughing. "He'll be the master here soon, Nora."

"Not for some time, surely. Even if he gets this manor when he's married, they're only announcing the engagement tonight. It'll be at least another year before they get married and move in. That's plenty of time for us to get the funds we need for Liberté and then get out of here."

"I hope so. But that also gives him plenty of time to terrorize us." He came up and patted me on the shoulder. "I don't want anything happening to you, *ségra*."

Since I coveted his approval and affection, I quickly hugged him, before brushing off his concern. "We'll be fine, *brácha*," I assured him, using my own endearment for him in return. "Now, let me go. If I'm supposed to be back from town before tonight, I'd better get going. Alex might be a terror, but he's still nothing compared to his mother."

2

◊

If I had any other reason to be there, going into the city would have been my favorite chore. Over the last few years, I had grown accustomed to the sadness I felt when I sold my father's possessions, but I never tired of the wonder I felt when I wandered into the city.

As I packed up the small carriage and flicked the horse's reins, I breathed in deeply, tasting freedom's forbidden elixir. I had nothing of my own, except the time that was given to me, and I was reminded of this nearly every day since my father's passing. Going into the city was a respite from my reality, and like anyone who hungered after something so secretly and desperately, the tendency to hoard it and hide it came naturally.

It doesn't come senselessly, though.

That was why I pulled on Dox's reins, stopping at a small cottage not far from my home.

I hopped down from the carriage perch and knocked on the door. After waiting patiently for a long moment, I cupped my hands against my cheeks and hollered, "Tulia! It's me!"

The door creaked open, and one-half of a half-wrinkled face appeared before me. Despite her annoyed look, I grinned at the surly figure. "*Dobré ráno*, Tulia. I need a companion today."

Tulia rolled her pretty topaz eyes, gesturing toward the sun and curling her fingers, making a motion like she was checking the time.

"I know it's early," I said. "Cecilia's party is tonight, remember? She is on a tirade, preparing for His Grace's arrival."

Tulia had worked for my mother as a nursemaid and companion for several years. After *Máma* died, she took up residence at her cottage, keeping watch over Ben and me as best as she could. I was sure it was hard for her, especially because Tulia was never permitted inside our manor after Cecilia moved in. Cecilia hated "crippled folk," as she called them, and she seemed to have a particular animosity toward Tulia, who was a mute.

But Tulia was like a second mother to me—or maybe because of her age, more like a grandmother—and I sought her company as much as I could, even if it meant trouble.

From her doorway, Tulia shot me another bitter look, and I gave her my best smile.

"I'll bring you more tea next time," I promised, as she came over to the carriage, finally ready to head toward the heart of Prague.

17

Tulia climbed up beside me on the wagon's perch, bumped against me companionably, and waved her arms toward Dox. It was her way of signaling to me she was all ready to go, and there was no need to keep her waiting now that I no longer had to wait for her.

At her spirited movements, I laughed; Tulia was perpetually silent, but she had a way of speaking that left me in little doubt of her exact thoughts.

I jostled Dox's reins, and together we set off for the city.

Prague was the crown jewel of the whole kingdom of Bohemia, and I did not need to travel great distances to see that reality. The city skyline misted over with clouds, keeping itself steady on the edge of my dreams while it remained grounded in the roots of my blood.

The November fog cleared as the sun rose, leaving the city sharp at its edges and shimmering at its core. I breathed in the fresh air deeply as I surveyed my surroundings. The mishmash of newer housing clashed with the cramped townhouses in color as much as in design, further juxtaposed against the darkness of the old city walls. It was a strangely beautiful thing, ugly but still mesmerizing, to see the city growing even as it remained the same.

I knew convenience and change came with a cost, just like the new sewage system that was installed a few years after the Revolution. I did not know if it was always a fair exchange, and I did not know if the Lords and lawmakers always acted in the best interest of anyone but themselves. The political wars between the Bohemian Diet and the German Diet were legendary, and I considered myself too young and too poor to care as much as I might have.

When I had been younger, my father mentioned once that there used to be much more violence in Prague, but more effort was culled into political maneuvering than anything else. When I told *Táta* that sounded like a good thing, he said the expended effort was better going into the arts.

"Always remember, art is upstream from politics," he had once told me at bedtime, before pulling out a new book for us to read.

"What do you mean?" I asked.

"Art is supposed to inspire the highest level humankind has to offer. Politics is only agreeing on rules that one might use to engage with others, and slowly changing them with the hopes no one else will notice."

"Is that really how politics work?"

He cupped my cheek and smoothed back my hair lovingly, in that way he had always had with me. "Always so curious," he said. "Just like your mother."

Then he would kiss me goodnight, before reading to me until I fell asleep.

Tulia suddenly clapped her hands, and I blinked. "What is it?" I asked.

She nodded toward the city, urging me to go faster.

THE ORDER OF THE CRYSTAL DAGGERS

"Dox can only go so fast," I said, briefly reaching forward to pat my faithful steed. "Besides, you're the one who took her time this morning. Are you getting older and slower naturally, or were you just moving slowly on purpose?"

Tulia flicked her nose at me.

"Careful. God still knows you're cursing at me."

In reply, Tulia made even more obscene gestures at me, and I laughed. I was pleased to have had inherited her friendship.

Tulia waved her hand again, and I looked to see she was greeting a man with his own *leiterwagen* full of grain. She gestured to me, cupping her hands and rounding them out in a small oval.

"I should have enough to get some bread from the baker's." I glanced back at the goods in the carriage. "There's enough here that Cecilia won't miss a *koruna* or two."

Tulia gave a silent cheer, and my stomach concurred with her, giving a hungry rumble of its own.

I knew I should have eaten more, especially after fighting with Alex and racing with Ben.

"Alex is just terrible," I told Tulia, recounting my earlier tale of bravery and triumph. Even though I had lost the race to Ben, I held my head up high. I had stood up to my terrible stepbrother, and that was no easy task. Over the past ten years, Alex had grown much taller and with his schooling at Oxford complete, he had become even more insufferable.

And Alex was barely human before he went to London. Ben was right to worry about him.

"I can't wait until the day Alex goes too far," I told Tulia. "I'd really love to see him squirm."

Tulia grinned, and I could see her full smile, complete with its gaps of missing teeth.

My hands tightened carefully on the reins while Dox's feet hit the bridge stones hard and steady as we headed over the river.

"I wonder if this is how Aeneas felt," I mused aloud, "crossing into the Underworld."

Tulia pretended to yawn; she knew of my love for books, but she always insisted I read too much.

As soon as we entered into the heart of the city, heavy traffic and crowded streets forced us to a momentary stop. Carefully, I stood up on the coach box, only to see there was a funeral procession heading down Kaprova Street.

Tulia tugged on my skirt. "There's a funeral," I explained, surprised when she stood up herself. As she looked down the street, her expression changed from one of interest to something much darker.

"What is it?" I asked.

She held up a hand to me, telling me to wait. It was strange of her to be so blunt with me.

I heard angry yelling, the words mixed with German and Prussian. From the little German I knew, the man was yelling about the funeral.

"Sounds like a politician died," I said as we passed by, heading deeper toward the heart of Prague, where the markets were located.

Beside me, Tulia nodded. She was a mute, but I had a feeling she knew six or seven languages herself. When I was younger, she had caught me trying to learn how to swear in Italian, and when I switched over to Slovak and then Spanish, she had still known what I was saying.

Then, like any good mother figure, she had me learn to curse in French properly, telling me in her own way that if I was going to curse, I was going to curse like a lady.

"Who was it?" I asked her, and she used her secret language to spell out the man's name.

"Sigmund Artha?"

Tulia nodded again, and I was shocked I recognized his name. "He was *Táta's* doctor. He was close with the king, too. He came to my father's funeral. How sad that he died."

Tulia frowned angrily. I saw her fists clench and her eyes narrow with dangerous tears. When I asked her what was wrong, she responded with a vitriolic message.

He did not deserve to die.

"What happened?" I asked. Something was unusual about her demeanor, and I was suddenly worried. "Tulia?"

Tulia did not respond, as she was still looking over her shoulder, distraught at the sad scene. As we passed by the *Betlěmskěnàm* church, I saw Leopold Artha, Dr. Artha's brother, the former Minister-President of Austria. He wore his finest clothes and a stoic expression, but, even from where we were, I could see his eyes were blurry with tears and tiredness.

"He was a good man," I said. From what I remembered, Dr. Artha had been a polite man, even with all his strange idiosyncrasies. I could not imagine him as a politician, but his brother had likely compelled him to accept such a position.

Tulia was obviously upset about it.

"I will pray for his soul's peace." I made the sign of the cross over my heart, silently sending love to my mother and father as well.

Tulia joined me in the motions, but much more slowly. She kept her eye on the funeral as we turned down the street and headed for Old Town Square.

As we approached the market, I forgot the funeral and Tulia's frustration.

I was not indifferent to her confusion and pain, it was just very easy to get lost in the city and its beauty. Prague Castle dominated the background as we rode through the crowded city streets. We passed by the Old Town Hall, where the *Pražský orloj*, the Prague Astronomical Clock, continued to push the shadow of its dial around its concentric faces in an age-old dance. The *Kostel Matky Boží před Týnem* church, flanked with its high twin steeples, sounded with echoes of pipe organ music, mixing with the angry shouts, the hurried people, and the busy, face-freckled crowds. The city radiated a life and heart of its own.

I looked back at the goods Cecilia had ordered me to sell, the ones that let me reach back into my past, when my father was alive. I was carrying out a hellish task in the middle of my imaginary heaven, and I suddenly felt the weariness of the world sink into me even more at the irony.

"Well, Tulia," I said with a heavy sigh, "I hope this doesn't take too long."

◊   ◊   ◊   ◊

I worked my way through the various traders and sellers, negotiating deals for hours as the sun passed overhead. It took no more than a couple of hours to find buyers for the things my father had spent his life collecting.

As I passed the last of the furniture pieces to their buyer, Tulia tossed me a warm roll.

"You did pay for this, right?" I asked.

She rolled her eyes again, but nodded. As she took a bite out of her own loaf, I saw the earlier sadness I had witnessed was not completely gone, just hidden.

Is she upset at Dr. Artha's death because he was friends with my parents?

It was possible Tulia had known him, although I could not remember ever seeing them together.

Still musing over her strange reaction, I took a bite of my bread. The warmth ran over my tongue and I felt a spiritual sense of strength return to me. "This is great. Who made it?"

Tulia nodded toward a baker delivery cart, and I frowned. *No wonder this is so good. French bread is expensive.*

21

THE ORDER OF THE CRYSTAL DAGGERS

"How much was it?" I asked, and Tulia made a few gestures.

It took me a few moments longer to realize what she was saying, and then I blushed. "You didn't have to trade your ... amorous favors for the bread. I could have paid for it."

She grinned before she puckered up her lips and blew a few kisses toward me in reply. It was her way of saying that she did not mind having to allow a merchant a stolen kiss or two, knowing it was a gift for me.

"Still," I mumbled, embarrassed, "*Máma* would be upset with you for teaching me such behavior."

Tulia shrugged, and it was as if I could hear her tart reply. *You asked, didn't you?*

As much as I hated to give her credit, I ate the rest of the bread.

When I was finished, I turned back to the carriage. There was a small chest left, and that was it. Despite the nourishment of the bread, I felt my spirits plummet once more. There were only a handful of things that could be in the chest.

As I opened it, I saw my hunch had been correct. Two books, editions in prime condition, were carefully placed inside, and I despaired at the sight.

Táta's books were each small pinnacles of civilization, and only a bookstore could give me a good price for their treasured contents. I wept when Cecilia sold his first edition copy of *Le Morte d'Arthur*.

I carefully pried the two books out of the soft velvet lining. One book I recognized easily; it was one of my father's favorites, *The Prelude*, by William Wordsworth.

The other made me pause. It was an intricately carved book, with a strange symbol on the front. I opened it up to see a script written in unusual, foreign scrawl.

I sighed. My father's books were very precious, and very expensive. He would not have kept these two side by side if they were not of high value, but I hated to have to haggle with a bookseller not knowing what I was trying to sell.

"Well, I hope Cecilia's not hoping for a fortune," I said, noticing the small notes along some of the margins. "I'm not sure if I'll be able to sell this at all."

We approached the small bookshop, Wickward Bookseller and Publisher, with its name branded in golden gilt across the top of the building. I could only sigh at the oncoming headache.

I jumped down to the ground, eager to get the business over and done with. In my haste, I landed hard on the stony streets, and the small chest I had held went crashing down to the ground and fell open at the feet of a man.

"*Prominte*," I said quickly, rushing to hide my embarrassment. "I'm so sorry ... " I felt my voice trail off as the man turned around.

I felt bad for staring, but there was something about him that demanded my full attention. Beneath his white turban, I saw his glossy black hair was combed back in the London fashion, and he had a trimmed mustache that would not have been out of place in a Spanish court. His skin was a deep tan with a bronze undertone, hinting at his Turkish blood and bringing out the darker chestnut of his irises. From his own stare, he seemed just as surprised to see me, although I had to wonder why. I was perfectly average in Prague.

"*Naděžda,*" he whispered, and I had to wonder what language he was speaking.

"*Pardonnez-moi,*" I tried again, hoping the French would work. The Ottomans and the Turks had significant trade deals with France, and I could only hope he would know enough French to realize what I was saying.

I was gratified when he replied, "*Je vous pardonne, mademoiselle.*"

At that, I smiled, and then hurried forward to grab my fallen books. "*Merde.* They're covered in dirt now. Wickward better still give me a good price on these, or I'm going to be upset."

I hurried to wipe the books off with my skirt, making a face when I could not get a scuffmark off *The Prelude.* I caught sight of the man's Hessians as I stooped on the ground.

Why is he just standing there? He was still staring at me with a shocked look on his face.

Realizing I was staring at him again, he suddenly knelt down next to me. He produced a handkerchief, and when he held out his hand, I realized that he was offering to clean it. I handed him *The Prelude*, and he kindly wiped it off.

Behind me, Tulia was throwing a fit, pointing at him and waving her arms.

"Wait a moment, Tulia," I said to her, glancing over my shoulder. I had to wonder if she was afraid of him, or if she suspected him to be dangerous because he was a Turk. "He's almost done. He has the other book now."

As I turned around, there was suddenly a small, curved dagger in my face.

"*Merde,*" I cursed again, this time much more loudly, as he lunged forward. I was terrified he was going to hit me, so I put my hands up. I felt something pound against my chest, and I ended up falling into Dox.

I saw the Turk's dagger slice through one of the reins. At the sudden movement, Dox reared, almost sending the carriage toppling over.

"Tulia!" I called, but I watched as she leaped down and grabbed a hold of Dox's bridle.

I looked down to see *The Prelude* in my hands.

The other book was gone.

Meanwhile, the Turk headed down the streets. Anger suddenly boiled within me. "Stay here, Tulia! See if you can fix the wagon. I'm going to get my father's book back."

Before Tulia could signal to me not to go, I went.

As I was chasing the Turk through the crowded city streets, I mentally cried out to Ben, hoping he had managed to find someone to fix my shoes for me. The ones that I had borrowed from Betsy seemed to pinch more with every step.

"Come back!" I raked my mind for the German, French, English, and Czech words for "thief," as I began to pant.

I saw him round a corner ahead of me and instantly brightened.

I've got you now. There's a shortcut ahead.

I ducked through a small alleyway, skirting around sludge, piles of trash, and fallen laundry from one of the upper floor apartments.

When I came out on the other side, I pressed against the crowd.

I had taken a risk, and I was rewarded.

The Turk came barreling right into me. The second before he collided with me, I saw his eyes go wide.

My own face might have betrayed my fear, because a moment later, I felt him latch onto me. Together, we whipped around, and a second later, I saw we were back in the small alleyway, pressed between the buildings and in a fight.

"Give me my book back," I demanded, punching him hard. My left hand burrowed into his side, and he fell back against the wall.

"I just want my book." I stood over him, panting quietly. "I won't report you if you just give it back."

The curved dagger glinted off the small light of the alleyway. I could not say if I stood my ground out of bravery or fear.

"*Non, mademoiselle,*" the Turk replied, before he jumped up.

He feinted, and I lashed out a quick kick. He managed to land a quick blow to my leg.

"Whoa!" I lost my footing and stumbled, desperately trying to keep my balance.

Just as I managed to steady myself, I felt the chill of his blade next to my throat. In the seconds I had been distracted, he wound his arm around me and held me at his mercy.

"If you're going to take the book from me and threaten my life over it, I should at least be told why you want it so badly, shouldn't I?" I snapped, unable to stop myself from fighting even if I was only left with words.

THE ORDER OF THE CRYSTAL DAGGERS

He sighed. "'*Anti la tafhamin.*"

I frowned, angry and flustered, frustrated and embarrassed. "That's not telling me anything," I said. "I don't understand what you're saying."

Before he could respond, a new voice stepped into the conversation.

"*Ma aldhy yajrī?*"

The Turk stilled behind me, shifting his focus from me to the young man who stood in front of us, blocking the entrance to the alleyway. I sighed. From his clothes, I could see this young man was clearly a street urchin, possibly homeless.

I was wondering if he would try to rob me too when he gave the Turk a quick bow, pulling off his cap in a gesture of respect. "*Ymknny musaeadatuk fi dhalik.*"

The Turk shook his head and said something else. The boy nodded and responded easily, and I grew more frustrated as their conversation continued.

"I don't understand either of you," I said. "But I will scream until someone comes to help if you don't let me go and if he doesn't give me my book back."

The street urchin smiled at me, before giving me a quick wink. "I'm sorry, my lady," he said. His voice was unusually calm and cheerful, despite the tense situation, and I was loathe to trust him.

"What is he saying?"

"It seems this gentleman believes that book to be his."

"It's not," I snapped. "It was my father's. I want it back."

He nodded in understanding before he talked to the Turk some more, who shook his head. Their arguments grew more terse, before finally the Turk seemed to give in.

The street urchin smiled as he turned to me again. "He will let you go. He wasn't expecting you to give chase."

I wrinkled my nose, ready to respond with a tongue-lashing that would have replaced any public execution when the Turk pushed me away, hard. My pinching shoe caught on the cobblestones, and I fell forward.

My scream was late, and because it was late, it was muffled. The other man jumped to my rescue, catching me close to his chest. I tasted the streets on his scarf as I gripped onto him. Behind us, the Turk disappeared.

"*Merde,*" I shouted.

3

◊

I stood there, paralyzed with simultaneous shock and rage, as the young man tightened his grip on me. He seemed to be steadying himself as much as he was helping me.

"Let me go!" I insisted, suddenly realizing he was keeping me from any chance of pursuit. "He took my book."

"I rather think you should be grateful you survived the encounter, even if you lost the book."

I thought of the book, of how my father must have cared for it, protecting it after he procured it. "You don't understand."

"Why? It's just a book. And from how you dropped it earlier, it was a dirty one at that. I doubt you would get much for it, especially if you were going to see Wickward. He would have been unwilling to buy it, and he would have lauded every defect as he looked it over."

It was too tempting to hate him for the blatant superiority in his words at that moment.

"You wretch!" I finally came to my full senses and shoved myself out of his arms. "My father is dead. His books are among the last things I have of his."

I was a little infuriated to see the young man smile.

"Your father would be happier, I think, that you are still alive. So it was good that I saved you."

"What was the point in saving my life if you just made it harder?" I glared at my so-called rescuer, and I only grew more upset as he began to laugh.

"What's so amusing?" I asked through gritted teeth.

"Your logic. A hard life is still better than death."

Cecilia briefly came to mind. I did not know whether or not to agree with him.

He saw my hesitation, and I stopped to study him. Under his sloppy hat, he had darkish brown hair, with kind eyes the color of lightened shadows, a strange but lovely gray layered with silver. I was still unsure whether or not he was going to rob me, too; I was glad I had given *The Prelude* to Tulia. As his hand reached out for mine, I eyed him suspiciously.

"Well, if that is not enough to convince you that I have done you a service, perhaps I can make your life easier in another way."

When I did not allow him to take my hand, he gave me a deep bow instead, and I softened ever so slightly at his manners. A thief did not need to use manners.

THE ORDER OF THE CRYSTAL DAGGERS

As far as I know, at least.

"It only seems fair I help you once more, since I made your life harder, after all."

He did not push for me to accept his offer, but his politeness seemed to insist upon it.

"You can call me Ferdy," he added, as he straightened.

"Ferdy?" I wrinkled my nose. "That's a strange name."

Ferdy did not seem to take any offense. He laughed, before giving me a slightly crooked smile. It was, despite my attempts not to notice, quite charming. His whole face seemed to light up, and I was momentarily dazzled.

I was suddenly aware that we were still very close, standing in the small alleyway.

"You can blame both Bohemia and my family for that one, although 'Ferdy' seems more fitting for a poor man such as myself, rather than my proper name," he said, ignoring my discomfort. "'Ferdinand' is a Bohemian favorite, thanks to the king, and in my family, we have the same two or three names that get used again and again, and each generation is expected to surpass the greatness of the previous one."

I looked down at his slovenly clothes again, reliving the smell of what I suspected was tobacco smoke on his scarf. "I wish you the best of luck in that regard, then."

"Well, I have proven my worth for today at least," he said, looking back to the far end of the alleyway, where my assailant had slipped away. "After all, I saved a damsel in distress."

I could not stop myself from scowling at him. I had been protecting myself for the last decade, only occasionally with Ben's help, and I did not appreciate being reminded of my failure.

But he was obviously poor, and he was right; he had stepped in to protect me. If I let myself, I could still feel the cool edge of the Turk's curved blade held against my neck. Pushing that thought aside, I decided that Ferdy had earned some merit.

"Well, then." I gave him a grand curtsy, mimicking his own introduction. "You have my thanks. I'll remember you in my prayers tonight. Surely the Lord himself will repay you for your trouble. Now, if you will pardon me, I must go."

"God might reward me later, but I'd prefer to collect now, if you please."

I knew it! I felt a rush of vindication. He was just after a reward.

I steeled myself against him. "So you would have me reward you?"

"*Absolument.*" The cheeky smile was back, and I was suddenly aware that he was flirting with me. I did not know whether to blush or scoff. While I was a servant in my home, I was still born a lady, and I knew better, even if he did not.

"Well, unfortunately, Mr. Ferdy," I said, emphasizing his name with all the power to dismiss him, "I do not have anything with which to pay you—"

"Ferdy, please."

"—so you will have to leave it up to providence for your remittance. Good day." I turned away from him and headed down the street. Already, I could see Tulia maneuvering Dox toward me. She waved eagerly, placing her hand on her heart and taking a deep breath.

"I was not talking about money," Ferdy said from behind me. "In return for my services, I request only to know your name, my lady."

Groaning silently, I turned to face him once more. "Why?"

"Why not?"

"It hardly seems proper." Tulia arrived behind me, and upon seeing Ferdy arguing with me, immediately leaned down to better hear our conversation.

"I imagine it's very improper in some circles to interrupt a thief about his business, too," Ferdy pointed out. "But here we are."

I turned back to Tulia, frustrated and confused. I needed to get home soon or Cecilia would have me beaten again, although she would probably do that anyway.

The thought disappeared as I realized Tulia was suddenly smiling sweetly at Ferdy. She nodded her head toward me in that manner of hers, compelling me to give in.

No, I thought, recalling the kisses she had given earlier to the baker as payment for our bread. *She cannot possibly be on his side in this matter.*

"My lady?"

Glancing back, I eyed Ferdy suspiciously. He did not seem to be sorry in the least for making me uncomfortable. And while there was nothing inherently wrong with him, something did not seem right. I could not explain what it was. Behind me, I heard Tulia start to fuss.

I resigned myself to my fate. *I cannot believe I am doing this.* My hands tightened around my skirt.

But before I could properly introduce myself to Ferdy, he nodded to the book lying beside Tulia on the perch. "What book is that?" he asked. "It seems that you still have some left after all."

"That one? It's a first edition of *The Prelude*, by Wordsworth." I almost told him it was my one of my father's favorite books, but I decided not to mention that. While Ferdy had saved me, there was no need to pretend we were close.

"I can get you a good price on that, if you're interested in selling it," Ferdy said.

His offer briefly distracted me from my suspicion. I arched my brow delicately. "Do you even know who Wordsworth was?"

"I happen to know what 'first edition' means, if that is what you really want to know," Ferdy replied. "And that if it's a book, Clavan will probably like it."

"Who's Clavan?"

"A friend of mine. He collects rare books. Including first editions. I can assure you, he pays much better than Wickward, too. Wickward is as tight as a drum, but Clavan's especially cheerful, especially if you get him full of liquor first."

"Does your friend perchance have a drinking problem?"

"Why, yes he does," Ferdy said, so guilelessly I almost laughed. He straightened his cap. "But he's familiar enough with me that I think I can use that to your advantage."

I bit my lip. I needed a good price on the book, especially since the other one was gone. Cecilia would be upset if she thought I did a poor job selling our goods. "Where is his shop?" I asked. "Is it near?"

"It's further east of the bridge, down by the Vltava."

"In the Jewish Quarter?" I asked.

For the first time, I caught him off guard. His eyebrows raised a little, but he nodded. "Yes, my lady. Clavan works out by the *Josefská*, the Jewish Quarter."

"I see." It was a little further than I would have liked to go; I had to get back to the manor soon.

"Does this offend you?" Ferdy asked. His voice was careful and his tone was casual, but he was suddenly less at ease.

"Oh, no, that's not it," I said, blushing. "I was just worried about the time. I have to return home soon."

"Well, let us not waste any more time on it," Ferdy said, his quick smile returning. "I'll take you there, and Clavan will buy your book, and then you can head back to your home. Here, let me help you up."

He held out his hand to help me back up into the carriage.

After all the trouble I had gone through, I was tired. Tulia was nodding at me, giving me her stern looks to tell me to accept. And I needed a good price on *The Prelude*.

That is why I allowed Ferdy to take my hand—or so I told myself. But I laid it down gently in his, intending to suffer through it, his hand wrapped protectively around mine, and I found myself unable to resist twining my fingers into his.

As I sat down on the carriage box, I looked down at him again, suddenly nervous. "My name is Eleanora."

Ferdy bowed properly once more. "It is a great pleasure to meet you, Lady Eleanora." He gave me a thoughtful look, before he frowned.

"What is it?"

"Your name is too long."

"Hey!" I objected. "It is not."

"You're the one who said mine was strange. I can say yours is too long."

Beside me, I could tell Tulia was amused. She seemed even more amused when I scowled at him and he laughed.

"I'll call you Ella instead. It's a lovely name for a lady—suitable for a princess, in fact. Now, give me the reins. I'll lead the way to Clavan's shop."

I decided not to bother to tell Ferdy that my family called me Nora as Tulia eagerly tossed him Dox's hastily repaired bridle. He intrigued me, but that did not mean I had to give him any intimate details.

"If you are too lazy to say my name properly," I said, "it's unlikely you'll be able to accompany us to the Jewish Quarter. It is several blocks away."

"Maybe I am trying to conserve my energy so I can make the effort. Besides, it is only proper for a lady to be escorted. And you are very concerned with what is proper, aren't you, Lady Ella?"

Tulia nudged me with her arm. She wanted to hear the details of what happened, but I said nothing as we made our way through the various streets. Ferdy did not need to hear how angry and frightened I had been during the whole encounter with the Turk, and I did not want to admit I was still skeptical of Ferdy himself. Several minutes passed as I watched him, more curious than I wanted to admit.

It was only as we came upon the Vltava that I began to ask him questions.

"How did you know I was a lady?" I asked, scooting forward on my seat as we faced the edge of the Jewish Quarter. "I'm dressed like a servant."

In front of me, Ferdy shrugged. "Everyone lies about something. Once you figure that out, it's easier to figure people out."

"Oh."

He glanced over his shoulder, his eyes sparkling like lightning across stormy clouds. "Don't worry, Ella. Your secrets are safe with me."

I was about to assure him I did not need him to keep any of my secrets when he added, "Clavan's place is just up ahead. I'll pull over here. Does your grandmother want to stay with the cart?"

"Grandmother?" I suddenly realized he meant Tulia. I was surprised to see the amused look on her face, but I was glad she was not insulted. "Oh. She's not my grandmother. She's my companion. And she is going to come with me."

"My apologies." He held out his hand, waiting for me to take it.

My stomach suddenly twisted into knots. I jumped down on my own, brushing passed him, ducking my face away from his. I told myself that if he was going to call me by half of my given name, he could not expect me to take his gestures of gallantry seriously. But, as I watched him help Tulia down in the same manner of a gentleman attending to a proper lady, I felt a layer of shame settle on me.

Tulia handed me *The Prelude* firmly; it was her way of reminding me to be brave and kind, as my mother would have wanted, and that sometimes it required more bravery to be kind.

"Clavan works here," Ferdy said, pointing to the sign above us. "The Cabal."

"The Cabal?"

Ferdy nodded. "He enjoys the absurd and the eccentric, like all the elites. But he is a good man, and you'll see what I mean, the more you get to know him."

Ferdy led us into the tavern, and at once, a new world reached out to welcome me. It was dark inside, with homey colors and elegant fixtures; the air clashed with a battle of smells and moods, with food cooking and foreign spices, the taste of fine alcohol, and the distinct cloud of tobacco smoke—all of it converged together to give a strange and immersive sense of otherworldliness.

As Ferdy led me to the bar, a dark and rich oak, polished to a shine, I felt my eyes wander around, trying to take in the small tables and plush chairs, the silk wallpaper, and the quiet rattling of newspapers.

"Josef Clavan, you old kook," Ferdy called. "Where are you? In the kitchen, busy under your wife's skirts, looking for something to do?"

I blushed at his insolence and intimate joking. I felt Tulia twitch with silent laughter beside me.

"If you're distracting Helen from her cooking, your customers are going to be upset."

Seconds after Ferdy's taunting, a door opened and a man walked out. The lights of the tavern glistened on his bald head and twinkled off the small, round glasses on his slightly crooked nose. He rolled up his shirtsleeves as he walked over to us. "Well, if it isn't Ferdy," he said. "Should I even count you as a customer, since you have yet to settle your tab?"

"You know my word is as good as gold," Ferdy said with a friendly chortle. "And speaking of my tab, I'm going to help take care of it with your help today."

Clavan cocked an eyebrow and gave Ferdy a smirk. "Is that so? Enlighten me, you knucklehead."

"Let me start by introducing you to Ella here." Ferdy reached out and took my arm, pulling me forward. "She's a lady I rescued earlier today, when a thief was after her books."

31

"Well then, it sounds like she's had a hard day." Clavan took my hand in his over the bar and bowed over it. "Lady Ella, is it?" he asked. "I can't imagine which was worse for you—dealing with the thief or getting stuck with this rogue as your hero." He gestured toward Ferdy, and I could not help but laugh.

"I'm not done deciding," I replied, and Clavan nodded approvingly.

"Smart lady, Ferdy," he said. "You're already not worthy of her."

"Don't I know it," Ferdy agreed. "Which is why I can at least buy her a drink. Put it on my tab, won't you? And one for her companion, too."

"I would say it's only appropriate." Clavan hurried to get us our drinks. "Perhaps too appropriate."

"And yet, not proper at all," I muttered, before Tulia nudged me.

Clavan handed me a small glass of beer, and it struck me just how inappropriate this whole scene was. I was a lady, I was not supposed to sup with my vendors, I was not supposed to allow myself to be led around by a street urchin, and I was not supposed to visit any taverns.

I was not supposed to chase down any thieves, either.

For all Ferdy captivated me, I finally allowed myself to see the absurdity of my situation with a smile.

Tulia put her hand on my arm, giving me a reassuring pat. I was not comforted as Clavan handed her a shot of French whiskey, telling her he knew a connoisseur when he saw one, but I decided I could relax.

Not senselessly, though. I put my glass down after a small sip, just in case. I recalled Ferdy saying that Clavan had a drinking problem—and indeed, he probably did, working in an establishment such as his, with temptation all around. I was not going to lose my wits as Ferdy attempted to coax Clavan free of his.

If Ferdy was actually going to do that at all. I was already starting to see Ferdy joked about any number of things, and it was hard to tell what he was serious about and what he was not. His irreverence was as dizzying as it was fascinating.

"Where's Jarl?" Ferdy asked, looking around. "I was hoping to see him today. I found a new pipe merchant he might like, one that trades with a plantation in San Salvador."

"Jarl's working, since he has a steady job, unlike you," Clavan said, sitting down across a table from us.

"Only because that was your requirement for him."

"Well, if he's going to marry my Faye, and Faye says he is, and since she and her mother are their usual, insistent selves on the matter, he has to keep a job. I won't have him standing out on the streets, waving a sign around, asking for a new job every other day."

"That means you're allowing some poor businessman to take the risk and employ him, though."

"Is that why you have yet to get a job and keep it?"

As Clavan and Ferdy talked and laughed together, I tightened my grip on *The Prelude*. Was this really worth the trouble?

Before I could wonder too long, Ferdy said my name, and I became the focus of the conversation.

"We're boring Ella with our discussion," Ferdy said. "And since it was hard enough to get her to come here, let's talk business, Clavan."

Clavan gave me a smile—a genuine one, not the smirk he had given to Ferdy. "Well, Lady Ella, if I did not know Ferdy here as well as I did, I would wonder what kind of woman would associate herself with him. But I'm sure I can help you free yourself from him if needed."

I eyed Ferdy carefully. "Well, I'll be sure to hold you to that then, Mr. Clavan."

He chuckled. "Ferdy mentioned books earlier. I assume he's brought you to me in order to see if I am interested?"

"I gather that is the reason. He said you collect rare books, as my father did before he died. This is the latest book in his collection I've been ordered to sell." I carefully reached out and handed him the copy of *The Prelude*.

He shifted his glasses up to the bald crown of his head as he studied it. "Beautiful etching," he observed, and I decided I already liked him.

As if Ferdy read my mind, he nodded. "See, Ella? I told you Clavan was a better buyer than Wickward."

"Wickward?" Clavan huffed. "I'm surprised that ancient blowhard is still in business, considering how well he treats his customers. Not to mention his books."

"I admire any man who has the courage to make his love of writing and books into a business," I said softly, thinking of my own dreams of Liberté, the small bookshop Ben and I wanted to open once we made enough money to escape from Cecilia. "Even Wickward."

"True enough," Ferdy declared. "What else would the alcoholics and addicts do to relieve themselves from the stress of their addiction, if not write? It's best that we keep them in business, so Clavan can stay here in business, too."

Clavan put his glasses back down on his nose. "You're in a rare mood today, Ferdy. I see Lady Ella is acting as a tonic for your own addiction to trouble."

"A tonic to which I might well find myself newly addicted," Ferdy agreed, and I blushed. He glanced over at me, suddenly thoughtful and sincere, as he added, "If for no other reason than she's too easy to tease."

33

I decided to ignore him. He was unsettling me, and I did not like it. Or at least, I did not like that I liked it so much.

"Well, Mr. Clavan, what do you think of the book?" I asked, shifting my focus back to sales.

"I'd love to add it to my collection. And as I'm partial to Wordsworth, I'll even settle Ferdy's account here at the bar as his finder's fee."

"Much obliged, my good man," Ferdy cheered, lifting his cup in celebration. His eyes met mine over the rim of his glass. "And my good lady, too."

Moments later, Clavan handed me a small pouch of *koruna*, and upon feeling the weight, I felt much better about my decision to follow Ferdy to the Cabal.

"Thank you, Mr. Clavan," I said. "I hope next time I will be able to bring you another work you will like."

"I do not merely like Wordsworth. His work is among the most prized in my collection. His wisdom and insight are too keen to miss, for all the poetry he hides even in his prose." He glanced over at me. "Have you read his work?"

"Some," I said. "More of his poetry than his prose."

"There's magic to be had in his poetry," Clavan said. "But there is more freedom in his prose."

I saw the reverence he held for the book and its writer, and smiled. *Táta* would be happy with my choice of buyer. And Cecilia would be happy with the money, even if it came from a Jew.

"Then I will have to read his other work," I replied, and Clavan's eyes twinkled warmly at me.

"You long to be free?" he asked, and it was almost as if he had spoken into my soul.

I nodded. "Yes."

"From what, if I might ask?"

"My stepmother would be a good start," I admitted, half-watching as Ferdy chatted away at Tulia, trying to figure out some of her silent signals. "She is the one making me sell my father's books in the first place."

"I wish you luck in that regard," Clavan said. "I know the pain that comes with dealing with a tyrant, especially one who is a parent. But freedom is found in truth and the struggle for it, and if you are as determined as you seem, I believe you will find it one day."

"Thank you," I said, touched and humbled. Clavan had a way of speaking that seemed to release calmness and hope into the world.

THE ORDER OF THE CRYSTAL DAGGERS

"You're welcome. It was a pleasure meeting you, Lady Ella. Take care—especially if you're going to go around with this *schlemiel*." He nodded toward Ferdy, and I laughed again.

"There are far worse people than me running around Prague." Ferdy grinned. "And you know it, Clavan."

"Speaking of which, did you hear anything new about the Artha case? Eliezer sent me a message asking for more details."

Behind me, Tulia went still. I caught her concern and quickly leaned in closer.

Ferdy sighed. "A runner saw him leaving the Church of Our Lady of the Snows after taking confession. He was stabbed by a man wearing a servant's coat as he was leaving and then left for dead."

Dr. Artha was murdered? My eyes, wide with shock, met Tulia's. She did not seem surprised at all to hear the news.

"Hmm. That doesn't give a thief a lot of time to ask for money." Clavan frowned. "Anything else?"

"I've talked to a few sources, but nothing else odd or suspicious," Ferdy said, his voice grim. "The former Minister-President blames the Jews for his brother's death, but the king's guard suspects the Nationalists."

"You are talking about the politician who was buried today, aren't you?" I asked.

"My apologies, ladies," Clavan said. "I forgot it is hardly proper conversation."

I waved my hand, brushing it aside, knowing Tulia would appreciate the chance to hear more. "No, no. I am interested in hearing about what happened. What can you tell me?"

Clavan and Ferdy exchanged a quick glance, before Clavan shrugged. "Sigmund Artha was a medical consultant for the king before his brother promoted him to a political advisor. He and I were friends, since we shared several interests. He sent a message to me a few days ago, declining his weekly invitation to the Cabal. He mentioned he had reason to believe he was being followed. He was killed only a day later."

"This is not entirely unexpected, unfortunately," Ferdy said. "Several politicians in Prague have been threatened of late. Even Dr. Artha's brother received a threat, which is rumored to be the real reason he stepped down from his position as Minister-President. There have been two murders like his in the last several months, where it appears to be a hasty mugging or a gruesome accident, and the Jews have been blamed. Others have died, too, but under less unusual circumstances."

"Less unusual circumstances that seem much odder when considered who gains from their death, anyway," Clavan murmured thoughtfully.

THE ORDER OF THE CRYSTAL DAGGERS

"That sounds terrible," I said, suddenly very glad I was a servant in my own home, rather than one to the lords of Bohemia. As much as Cecilia could rail and wail, I doubted she would ever try to kill me.

God forbid she would have to do her own laundry or hire someone else to do it for her.

"It is terrible." Ferdy gestured toward the Cabal. "Eliezer, our other friend, has been gathering information on the cases. If the murderer is Jewish, he wants the Jews to see to it that this person is caught and tried. But so far, we have not found any solid leads."

Clavan sighed. "When something like this happens, the Jews need to be the ones to take care of it, or our silence will be seen as support."

"Why would a Jew kill Dr. Artha?" I asked. "Was it because he was Catholic?"

"Jews and Catholics do have a terrible history. However, Sigmund was good friends with me and Eliezer. That is why others, like his brother, condemn us in this matter," Clavan said with a shrug. "Sigmund also worked with Eliezer's wife, who is a midwife, several times. He was her source for a lot of her herbs and medicinal supplies."

"That is hardly fair for the Minister-President to blame the Jews."

"Many things in life are not fair," Clavan reminded me. "With increased tensions between the German Diet and the Bohemian Diet, many prefer it that the Jews are to blame for things like this. I am not surprised to hear that the king's guard actually suspects the Bohemian Nationalists."

"It is a sad story all around," Ferdy said. "The runner said Dr. Artha died calling for Father Novak, one of the priests at the church."

I thought of the rosary beads Dr. Artha had kept on his bag. "I'm sure he had enough patients who requested the same thing."

Beside me, Tulia was rigid with muted anger. I pressed against her, offering a small gesture of comfort while we said our farewells.

Clavan saw us out, inviting us to come again as he gave us a kind smile and a small wave, before disappearing behind his doorway.

As we made our way to the carriage, Ferdy grinned. "Well, that was a nice visit, even with that last little bit."

I nodded. "Yes, it was very nice. I enjoyed coming to the Cabal."

"See, Ella? You sold your book. I've made your life much easier now."

"According to your friend, that's quite a risk I took." I had been suspicious of Ferdy's kindness before, but after the visit to the Cabal, I knew that it was quite genuine. I gave him a smile of my own and allowed him to take my arm as we walked toward Dox and the carriage.

"Any lady who would follow after an armed thief can surely summon the nerve to gamble every once in a while." Ferdy offered Tulia his hand and helped her up to the carriage perch.

"Gambling is a sin."

"Well, that's why it's so fun then, right?" Ferdy laughed. "But you know that some would say it is just misplaced hope and faith. Sometimes it is occasionally rewarded."

"Are you one of those people?"

"It was a gamble earlier, stepping between you and your book thief." Ferdy leaned against Dox comfortably, taking a long moment to stare at me.

I stared back, before I felt the unbearable heat of my blush. "Ever the charmer, aren't you?"

"I would be happy to give you a further chance to see just how charming I can be," Ferdy said. "Next time you come to the city, ask for me. Most of the merchants in Old Town Square know of me and can point you in the right direction."

I saw Tulia heave a silent sigh at my hesitation.

"You should come back here when the others are around," Ferdy said. "Between Jarl and Faye, and Helen and Eliezer and Eliezer's wife, it is always a riot."

"It was very enjoyable meeting your friend, Mr. Clavan." I had never planned for this kind of conversation, and it was frustrating that I liked it.

"We can see each other again, then?"

I bit my lip. I knew Cecilia would only be too happy to forbid me to go into the city if she found out about Ferdy.

He took my hand again. "Come on, Ella. Be brave and take a risk."

There was something about him, I thought. Something that made me nervous and excited, somehow certain and completely unsure at the same time.

"Sometimes when you gamble, you lose," I said quietly.

"I haven't lost yet, where you're concerned." Ferdy leaned closer to me. "Will you come and see me again?"

I could not refuse him—or myself.

"I'd like to," I finally admitted. "But I really must be going for now. I have to go home and help get ready for tonight. My stepmother is throwing a party for a special guest."

"So, you like parties? Are you going to the Advent Ball this year, then?"

"Advent Ball?" I shook my head. "I've never heard of that one."

"Empress Maria Anna celebrates the Advent each year. A lot of the nobility and aristocracy come to the castle to join her for mass and celebrate afterward. It is the only ball that the royal family still hosts every year for Bohemia."

"That sounds lovely, but I have never been to one before."

"Here." Ferdy pulled a scroll out of his pocket. He jerked the wax seal off the letter and tore off the heading. "Take it. I'm sure your stepmother would love to be invited."

I glanced down at the crinkled sheet of vellum. It was indeed an invitation to the Advent Ball, hosted by their imperial highnesses at Prague Castle.

"How did you get this?" I asked.

Ferdy smiled. "Sometimes I work as a runner, which is why Clavan still lets me come in out of the cold every once in a while."

"Then won't someone else be missing an invitation?" I ran the torn stationary between my fingers where the recipient's information had been ripped away. There was an ugliness to the frayed edges, but I could not tear my eyes away from the fine lettering. "You'll get in trouble for this, won't you?"

"It will be worth it all if you will come."

"But—"

"Just take it, Ella, please. And come."

"But I wasn't invited."

"They won't turn you away. You're a lady, Ella," he insisted. He gave me an assessing gaze. "Aren't you? You weren't lying before?"

"Well, no, I am a lady, but—"

"Excellent. And since that is the case, I swear on my life, and all of my honor, you will not be turned away. So, come. I will see to it that you have fun."

"Will you be there?" I asked.

"Yes. I've also worked as a server before, at different soirees."

"I thought Clavan said you didn't have a job."

"I don't have a job. I have several."

As much as Ferdy intrigued me, I still felt unsure. "I know we have met under unusual circumstances, Mr. Ferdy—"

"Ferdy, please, Ella." He flashed me one of his charming smiles, and I was distracted enough to stop talking.

Despite his impudence and relentless flirting, something about him made me look twice and still left me curious. I stared at him in the dimming sunlight, transfixed and mesmerized, and I felt angry I was not free to enjoy myself, that I was not free to allow myself to feel happy at his attentions.

As the clock tower struck the hour in the distance, Tulia tapped me on the arm, letting me know it was time to go. She probably thought she was saving me from embarrassing myself—or from Cecilia's wrath, should I be late in returning.

I sighed. "I have to go," I said.

Ferdy nodded. There was an understanding, if unsatisfactory, look in his silver eyes. "It was truly my great pleasure in meeting you, my lady." He gave my hand a final squeeze before stepping back. Ferdy bowed gallantly as I flicked the reins and we headed off.

As we were about to turn back toward the bridge, I glanced over my shoulder to look at him once more.

Ferdy was gone, and I already missed his cocky grin.

Sighing, I rolled up the torn scroll in my hand and pressed it deeply into the hidden pockets beneath my skirt. Tulia left me to my thoughts, and it was only as we pulled up to her cottage that I wondered if she was still upset at Dr. Artha's passing.

As much as the day felt like a very strange dream, I needed to focus in order to get through Cecilia's party. The Duke of Moravia was coming back into town for the first time since my father's funeral, in order to finalize the engagement between his daughter and Alex. Of all nights I would have to be prepared, it was this one.

4

◊

Hours later, I was still mulling over the events at the market. Mostly, I kept reliving my time with Ferdy. Part of me hated how much I thought of him and his irresistible, irreverent smile.

But thinking of Ferdy was a welcome distraction. My feet were aching in the newly repaired shoes Ben had brought me, my back was sore from walking all over the castle, and I could feel my hair falling out of its pins as I changed out linens, scooped up laundry, and mopped up messes.

I was just about to head to the kitchens to check on dinner when Ben came up beside me in the hall.

"I heard Cecilia was pleased with the money from the market," he said as he matched his pace to mine. "Even though she was upset it took us so long."

"It's money. Why would she be upset at all, other than when there's too little?" I asked, blinking away Ferdy's face from my thoughts. "Wait. Did she know you were home while I was gone?"

"No." Ben grinned. "I've been running around the castle, gathering information."

"You've known the Duke of Moravia was coming since Alex finished his last semester at Oxford," I reminded him. "What more do we care? What more *should* we care?"

"If we're going to survive here with Alex in charge, I thought it would be best to make sure we have the upper hand. And a lot of that includes collecting information that is not readily shared with us—or anyone else."

"You only make people angry when it comes to blackmail. Cecilia's glasses are one thing. Business with the manor is another."

"We have both been spying on Cecilia's movements for years, between your unauthorized trips to father's dwindling library and my midnight forays into the kitchen. Besides, how did you think I found out Cecilia was happy enough with the money you brought back that she didn't question how long it took?"

"I told her that there were some new vendors I met who were willing to pay more for certain items."

"Lying is a sin, Nora."

"So is extortion, Ben." I stuck my tongue out at him playfully. "The difference between us is that I am telling the truth, as that is more or less what happened."

We came to a full stop as I told Ben the story of my adventures in the heart of Prague. It was a respite from work, and even though I maintained a serious expression throughout, I was decidedly amused by Ben's reaction. He was not surprised I chased after the thief, but he was angry when I told him about Ferdy.

"You should stay away from men like him," Ben said. "He was not interested in helping you just to be a good Samaritan. He wanted rewarded, an in a more ... *intimate* way, clearly."

"I have stayed away from men like him," I said carefully. "But Ferdy was a gentleman. Or enough of one, anyway. Besides, I told you, I'd lost one of our father's books, and I needed to get a good price. You know how Wickward is. It was very nice meeting Mr. Clavan, and if we do have to sell more of *Táta's* books for Cecilia, I will be more assuredly going back to see him."

Ben snorted, and I knew he had no argument against me.

"Ben! Nora!"

We turned around to see Betsy, one of the English maids Cecilia hired on her last trip to London, as she trotted up beside us. Along with her sister, Mavis, they made a good pair of friends as well as workers.

"What is it, Betsy?" Ben asked.

"Her Ladyship is going mad," Betsy said, ignoring some of her golden curls as they bobbed out of her pins and into her face. "His Grace has arrived early. She wants everything ready at once."

"Did she slap you?" I asked, noticing Betsy's cheeks were very red.

Betsy lowered her gaze and shook her head. "No, but she tried," she admitted. "She's very upset, Nora."

"If she's on one of her tirades, we'd better hurry, then." Ben gave me another meaningful look. "Be careful, Nora."

I nodded. "You take care, too." They hurried off to prepare for His Grace's arrival, while I stayed at the entrance to the kitchens, watching as Lord Franz Maximillian Chotek, the Duke of Moravia, walked into the great hall wearing his fur-lined greatcoat, supple leather boots, and a fine traveling suit.

The Duke had a mix of the Czech and Slavic features that marked him as a proud Bohemian. His nose was pointy and hard, with his narrow face and dark, coal-colored eyes. From what I was able to remember of him, standing next to Cecilia at my father's funeral, it did not seem as though he had changed much in the last decade, although the fashionably rounded curls of his imposing mustache now had more of a black and white mix creeping around his mouth. But other than that, Lord Maximillian was still clearly a man that believed in destiny, provided that his destiny involved prestige and creature comforts.

His daughter, Lady Teresa Marie, trotted after him like a prize foal at a horse auction. She had amber hair, a shade or two darker than Betsy's, that was combed back and held up with ribbons. It made her look childish, and the pastel colors that were currently popular in London heightened this impression. But then, I

41

remembered, Ben had mentioned she was only fifteen. She was supposed to wed Alex just a few days after her sixteenth birthday. In many ways, she really was just a child.

A rush of unexpected sympathy overcame me, as I thought how Teresa Marie was just like me, a young woman who was caught up in the plans of all the people surrounding her.

I sighed, thinking of how I felt when Mr. Clavan spoke of freedom with me. That strange mix of longing and sadness briefly settled on me, and wistfully I yearned for the day when my destiny would become my own.

"Eleanora." Cecilia appeared behind me like an apparition, and I nearly jumped.

"Yes, madam?"

"Everything needs to be ready for His Grace and his daughter. Go and see that it is taken care of."

I gave Cecilia a small, flippant curtsy. "Of course."

"You can dispose of your mockery as well." Cecilia clapped her hands together angrily. "I will not tolerate *any* mishaps tonight, Eleanora. I will hold you personally responsible if anything—*anything at all*—goes wrong."

I gulped but said nothing as she dictated more chores for me to attend to later on, listing everything from sweeping the floors to dusting to laundry to serving tea after supper.

By the time she was done, I was surprised she had neglected to tell me to offer an animal sacrifice to God to make sure it did not rain. As much as I was sure she would keep her promise to punish me, I would have refused to do so. I liked to think God would have ignored her as well, since it began to rain almost as soon as the butler announced dinner.

Personally, I was glad for it. The rain was another reminder that reality was bigger than what was before me, and there were things even Cecilia could not spoil.

Not that she will hesitate in finding a way to blame me anyway.

I tried my best not to worry, but when Betsy called for me once more, I could only groan at her anxious tone. Any sign of trouble meant more trouble for me.

"Is something wrong, Betsy?" I asked. "Did Priscilla complain about her food again? If she did, I will force it down her throat myself—"

"No, that's not it, Nora. The housekeeper just told me another coach has just pulled up to the front."

"And?" I shrugged. "It's likely more of His Grace's luggage."

"It's a very grand coach," Betsy said. "Much more grand than the one His Grace arrived in."

THE ORDER OF THE CRYSTAL DAGGERS

That was surprising.

"Were we expecting any more guests? Did Cecilia say anything to Graves or the housekeeper?"

"No, I already talked with Graves." Betsy shook her head fiercely, her curls swinging back and forth in pretty protest. "He didn't know anything, and he's the butler. Please, Nora, come and see."

Recalling Cecilia's threat, I knew I had no choice but to investigate.

"Don't fret; I'm coming." It was hard for me to put the bread aside and follow her out to the front hallway.

As we watched through the window, several liveried footmen descended from the coach's box and then hurried to open the carriage door.

A veiled woman, wearing a long, black dress stepped down out of the coach. She stepped confidently onto the cobblestones that surrounded the front of our estate. I watched as she surveyed our manor, looking up and down the east and west wings, before finally looking toward the main entrance.

Even from where I was, even with the rain and fog between us, I could tell this was a lady of great power.

"Cecilia's not going to like this." I stayed transfixed, as the woman made her way to our front door. She was going straight in, I realized, and I had to admire her for her forthright manner as much as her steadfastness.

"She's from London," Betsy whispered. "Astounding."

"How do you know?" I asked.

"The coach. It's got the crest of the House of Wellesley on the side, look."

I glanced over to see that Betsy was right. There was a coat of arms that was familiar in many ways, even though I could not place it. "Wellesley?"

Betsy giggled, seeing my apparent confusion. "It's the family of the general who defeated Napoleon."

"Oh. Yes, I see."

"They're a prominent family in England, thanks to the Duke of Wellington's service to the Crown," Betsy said. "I wonder why they've come."

The question of their arrival stumped me as well. I watched as others alighted from the carriage. Among them were two men wearing greatcoats and hats. Because of the rain and shadows, I could not make out their features much more than to know they were gentlemen.

I tapped my fingers together thoughtfully as Graves opened the door. From the angle I was watching, I saw they entered with very little hindrance, despite the butler's attempts to prove himself one.

"What do you think?" Betsy whispered.

"Nora, what's going on?" Mavis asked. Her brown eyes, the same shape as Betsy's, blinked back unshed tears. "Her Ladyship never told us she had more guests arriving. What do we do?"

"Do only as you are told," I said in a hushed voice. "I don't think these are guests of Cecilia's."

"She's going to be so upset with us!" Mavis pouted. "She's going to punish us severely after this."

"You will be fine," I assured her. "The responsibility is mine."

"I don't think we can be sure," another maid said softly. "Madame Cecilia is very clearly upset by the sight of the new arrivals."

Scooting toward the hall entrance, I saw that she was right; the hall was chittering with the small talk between my stepfamily and our guests one moment, and in the next, everyone went silent and still.

I watched as Cecilia stood up, prepared to do battle. "Who do you think you are, coming here without an invitation? And you, Graves, how could you let them in?"

As far away as I was, I could still see Graves' throat convulse with stress.

Before he could answer, the lady reached up and removed her dark veil. Her gray hair was piled up onto her head in an intricate style, and I could see her high forehead and classic British features; her heart-shaped face became an ironic quality as I watched her. She had the face of a lady, but wore the smile of a viper. And when she spoke, I felt the vibrations of her words echo throughout the whole castle.

"Perhaps the better question, Lady Cecilia, is who do you think you are, and what makes you think you can keep me from entering at all?"

The small party began to murmur uneasily amongst themselves once more. I slipped out of the kitchen another step, careful to stay in the shadows of the servants' entrance.

I could not stop watching Cecilia attempt to stare down her uninvited guest. She was fighting a battle she would never win, and I found myself looking forward to the coming spectacle.

"I am the mistress of this manor," Cecilia insisted. "My husband died and left it to me. It is mine by right of inheritance."

The lady's smile curved, suddenly even more dangerous than before. "Well, if that is what you think, let me answer your first question and introduce myself properly."

She inclined her head, only by mere degrees. "I am the Dowager Duchess of Wellington, Penelope Ollerton-Wellesley, in service of Her Majesty, Victoria, by the

Grace of God, of the United Kingdom of Great Britain and Ireland Queen and Defender of the Faith."

"That means very little to me." Cecilia looked to the Duke of Moravia in a hurried manner. Her sallow cheeks brightened with fury. From Lord Maximillian's expression, I could see he was no longer annoyed by the interruption. Rather, he was now looking at Lady Penelope with undeniable interest and curiosity.

"Wellesley, did you say?" he asked, and Lady Penelope gave him a shrewd nod.

I put my hand over my mouth, trying to hide my smile. I did not know why a dowager duchess from the other side of Europe would come and visit Cecilia, but it was nice to see someone displace her.

"Well," Lady Penelope said, her voice tight, "it meant considerably more to my son-in-law, who was your husband as well as the husband of my daughter."

My world began to crumble at that moment, as I realized who Lady Penelope was.

"Grandmother?" My mouth dropped open in shock as I heard myself speak.

Behind me, I could feel the stares of Betsy, Mavis, and the other maids all turned on me, while Lady Penelope shifted her gaze in the direction of my hiding spot.

A memory of my mother, back when I was only five, came back to me. I remembered her as she worked through brushing my hair, lamenting my knots, even as she awed over my Bohemian curls. "Grandmother would adore you, just for your curls," she whispered, before telling me stories of how her mother would always brush her hair, long and straight, each Sunday before church.

The memory faded, and I found myself still concealed in the shadows of the servant entrance. My grandmother was searching for me, and I suddenly felt completely trapped as her eyes slid over the darkness around me.

"Who is there?" she asked.

My hand covered my mouth. I felt foolish, I felt trapped; I was unsure of what to do, or if indeed, I should do anything at all.

I was not the only one who seemed beyond words. Cecilia stared at her, the wrinkles on her forehead piled with stress lines and her mouth flapping open and closed, as though she was trying to say something, but God in his goodness was refusing to let her words sully the earth and its atmosphere.

It was only when Cecilia finally found her voice again that I was released from my indecision.

"That's no matter. You are trespassing in my home, and I will deal with you."

"Unfortunately, you are wrong on both accounts," Lady Penelope replied. "This is not your home, and my man of affairs shall take business with your man of affairs. In the meantime, while we settle the details that have been neglected since the death of my daughter, I will take up residence in the manor's west wing."

45

Cecilia sputtered, unable to form a coherent response.

Dismissing Cecilia, Lady Penelope turned to Lord Maximillian. "It is a pleasure to make your acquaintance, Your Grace. I apologize for the intrusion. Perhaps over the next few hours we will be become better acquainted as you begin to search for new lodgings."

Lord Maximillian blinked. "Beg pardon, Your Grace," he began, "but is this a very opportune moment to make your acquaint—"

Cecilia found her voice in time to object. "Max, I beg your patience in this matter."

"You cannot expect one such as His Grace to stay here while the ownership of this estate is being debated by men of law," Lady Penelope said. She added enough abhorrence to her voice to suggest that it was among the most scandalous of activities. "Why, the very thought is appalling. Indeed, it would be very unfortunate for His Grace. I imagine the rumors alone would destroy his reputation among his business partners and his daughter's potential suitors."

"My son is his daughter's suitor!"

"But surely that was before the integrity of his estate was questioned?" Lord Maximillian said, and I almost laughed at the sputtering rage on Cecilia's face.

It made me wonder if the Duke was looking for a way out of their agreement on his own.

Lady Penelope shook her head, before turning back to her two guards—companions?—behind her. "I fear we are indeed a long way from London, if this is the sort of practice we find in these places. And I remember Prague as such a refined city, too; it is a shame how its stock has fallen since I last visited."

Cecilia's face burned. She turned back to the Duke. "I seem to have some unexpected business I need to see to immediately, Max. Pray, continue with the celebration while I handle these *unfortunate* matters. Then we will discuss our arrangement."

"Nothing would please me more, Cecilia. It seems we will have to renegotiate."

With her nostrils flaring, Cecilia beckoned Lady Penelope to follow her out of the great hall.

I was not surprised when Lady Penelope remained where she was. "I believe I will be the one to dismiss you," Lady Penelope said. "I will confer with you in tomorrow morning, in the library in the west wing."

Cecilia scowled, so furious her face was twitching. "You assume too much, Lady Penelope."

"And you are playing a very dangerous game," Lady Penelope replied. She took a menacing step toward Cecilia, and Cecilia immediately backed down.

THE ORDER OF THE CRYSTAL DAGGERS

Priscilla, my stepsister, finally decided it was her turn to speak up. "Does this mean our party is over?"

I groaned, but I knew that if Prissy said anything, it was sure to be something ill-timed or completely ignorant. She was Cecilia's doted daughter, and I never knew her to take anything serious except for her food intake and daily exercise routine. Like Empress Elisabeth, she often spent days fasting. If we could have afforded it, Cecilia would have set up a gymnasium right next to Prissy's room. It was the only thing I had ever heard Cecilia deny her.

"It is very unfortunate that I did arrive in the middle of your celebration," Lady Penelope said, talking more to everyone in the great hall rather than just Priscilla. "By all means, continue on. The good Lord knows that there might not be anything at all to celebrate tomorrow."

"Is that a threat?" Cecilia hissed.

Lady Penelope gave her a dazzling, devious smile. "Of course it is, Lady Cecilia. And a very credible one, would you not agree?"

"We could have you arrested for that!" Alex finally stood, angry and ready to fight.

Lady Penelope turned her eye to him. "I see I have been too quick to assume that Lady Cecilia was the lady of the household. My apologies. You have my attention, young sir."

I saw him wince at her wry tone, but Alex held his ground. "You should leave immediately, Madame."

"You have my apologies for my assumptions," Lady Penelope said, "but hardly for my logic. The orders I have issued will go observed, despite your bravado, young man."

"You cannot—"

"You would be most wise not to tell a lady what she can or cannot do. Consider that lesson a welcome gift. Now, sit down and return to your silence. I would hate for you to embarrass yourself even further."

Alex was not used to having his wishes denied, let alone his intelligence or authority questioned. Like a dog with his tail tucked between his legs, he sat down and slumped over in his seat.

"My son is right," Cecilia said.

"Hardly. I assure you, Madame, I have come well prepared for any amount of force, legal or otherwise, that you could possibly muster against me."

"No one can verify who you are," Cecilia insisted.

Lady Penelope walked up to her. Each step was a slow, deliberate act of pure intimidation. Cecilia flinched as Lady Penelope reached into her cloak.

I watched, unblinking, as she produced a letter, shut with an elaborate wax seal.

"No one less than Her Imperial Highness, Queen Victoria, can provide the details of my person." Lady Penelope handed the letter to Cecilia. "She was kind enough to ask for your willing assistance in settling our legal matters. She recalls your previous husband's kindness to her and her son, Leopold. She remembers how, during the week of German and Prussian reception, he once caught Leopold as he fell out of a tree, no doubt saving him grave injury, and she wishes you well."

Cecilia's fists were shaking as she tore open the letter and read it. When she was done, I could tell she was having a hard time not screaming.

It's true.

The murmurings continued, more awkwardly. Lord Maximillian looked over to Cecilia, uncertain, as Teresa Marie asked about her marriage contract to Alex, and Alex only looked viciously appalled.

"If you are satisfied, take your seat and finish entertaining your guests, before I relieve you of that duty as well." Lady Penelope waved her hand, and slowly, ever so slowly, Cecilia backed away, her resolve as neutered as Alex's bluster.

Lady Penelope nodded approvingly, her contempt apparent even as she remained calm. "Now, I will excuse myself and see to the details of my stay."

Before I could do anything else, Cecilia turned and stormed out of the great hall, headed right for me. Her fluffy skirts whipped against me as she passed, and fury suddenly boiled into her eyes.

"Eleanora, this is unacceptable!"

"It is hardly my fault that the grandmother I did not even know existed came to call tonight," I said.

"You mark my words," she bit back, wagging her finger at me, practically mad with rage. "You will pay for what you have done tonight."

Anger simmered inside me. "But I didn't do anything!"

"That's enough." I looked over and saw Lady Penelope standing just behind Cecilia. "You have been dismissed to your room. I can have a guard escort you, if you insist on making this more difficult."

Cecilia cursed before flying down the hall.

Lady Penelope looked at me, and for the first time she seemed visibly discomforted. "Eleanor."

"Eleanora," I corrected her.

She winced. "Apologies … Eleanora. You … you look so much like your mother."

I could only nod. *What else am I supposed to do? Curtsy?*

Lady Penelope also seemed at a loss for what to do, as all of her earlier gusto disappeared. It was not a look that suited her, and she seemed to agree; a moment later, she cleared her throat. "I request you join me in the library in the west wing shortly."

"Should I bring Ben, too?" I asked.

"Ben?"

"Benedict. My older brother."

Her somber expression further saddened. "I see. Yes, bring him as well. We will talk then."

Lady Penelope turned away and headed off, and I heard small footsteps as they shuffled behind me. "Are you feeling well, Nora?" Betsy asked, putting her hand on my arm.

Almost as a reflex, I patted her hand, comforting her even though I was the one who needed it more. "I have to go and get Ben," I said, deflecting her question. "Excuse me."

I have to tell Ben about this.

That thought was the only thing that propelled me forward. As I headed toward the stables, where Ben would likely be, I felt another strange sense of absurdity take hold of me, much as I had felt earlier in the Cabal with Clavan and Ferdy. Only this time there were so many more questions I had—questions that hurt to even think, let alone ask.

Why is our grandmother coming to see us now?

Táta had been gone for ten years. She had not come to the funeral. I thought of that day in the church, with Father Mueller, with Cecilia, Priscilla, and Alex. Even Lord Maximillian had been there, along with Ben and me.

Ben was truly the only family I had left. Our father had no other siblings, and he was the last of his line. I knew that well enough—that was the reason Cecilia was able to gain control of his estate so well. Ben was neither old enough, nor deemed fit enough to challenge her.

In all that time between the funeral and now, I had never even thought of our mother's family. But *Máma* had been gone for even longer than *Táta*, and it was possible I never thought of her family because no one from her family came to her funeral mass.

Of course, she had been lost at sea, so there was no burial. It was possible that Lady Penelope had received the news too late.

I had so many questions, and there was so much I did not know if I was ready to face. I did the only thing I could, which was the same thing I had done all those years ago, on the day of my father's funeral in the small church.

My steps slowed to a stop, and I leaned against the hallway wall for support. I clasped my hands together, bowing my head down to my chest. "Please, Lord," I prayed softly, "help me."

Tears threatened to come, and despair momentarily choked me as I stood there, surrounded by uncertainty and darkness.

But the moment, like all moments before it, passed, and I was able to take comfort in my faith. It was a bedrock of my life, having sustained me through the loss of my family. It kept me going through the hard times, silent during Cecilia's floggings, and hopeful that Ben and I would one day find our freedom.

Maybe this was the day. Maybe this was the day my life would change forever.

At the thought, the memory of my mother's bright laughter sang through me. *"Dear Eleanora, my lovely one, your life can change at any moment; you need only be brave enough to let it."*

I clung to that thought—that wish—as I continued onward, looking for my brother.

5

◊

Seemingly hours later, I watched Ben as he mindlessly picked at the dirt underneath his fingernails. We were stationed outside of the library, both of us silent.

I had a feeling Ben was going through the same emotional turmoil as I was; as I gave him an overview of what happened in the dining hall, his expressions shifted constantly, ranging from amused to angry to suspicious.

"Do you think she's really our grandmother?" I finally asked Ben.

"No one with that kind of coach and team would come to our manor in Bohemia if it were not for real," Ben said. "Besides, it makes sense. She is British, as *Máma* was, and she's clearly a member of the higher social circles. And remember, when *Máma* left us, she was headed for London."

"And then her ship went down," I remembered. "*Táta* was devastated."

"We were *all* devastated, Nora. *Táta* wasn't the only one."

The door opened behind us, held open by one of Lady Penelope's companions wearing a long cloak. He shuffled back, keeping his face hidden under the hood, and I was just about to ask him what he wanted when I heard Lady Penelope call out from inside the room.

"You may enter."

Ben and I exchanged a quick glance, and then the two of us walked into the room.

The doors shut quickly behind us, and my attention was immediately focused on the lady sitting at my father's desk.

Up close, Lady Penelope had even more formidable features. The wrinkles around her eyes complimented her resolve, while her high forehead suggested intelligence and insight. Her lips, though they were thin with age, curled into a small, somewhat welcoming smile as she looked at us. "It is good to see you."

Ben and I bowed and curtsied respectively, unsure of what else to do.

She waved her hand, brushing our formalities aside. "There's no need for that. Now, I imagine you have a lot of questions for me."

"Yes," I said, unable to resist. "It is not every day that one is introduced to one's own grandmother."

"Especially when our mother has been dead for over ten years," Ben added.

Lady Penelope frowned at his surly tone. "I apologize if you are somewhat inconvenienced by my arrival," she began, and then I cut her off.

51

"As Lady Cecilia might have failed to mention to you, we have been more inconvenienced by your absence, Madame."

"She did not need to mention it," Lady Penelope assured me, her voice still calm and level despite the anger within my words. "I have two perfectly good eyes; I can see it for myself. Cecilia is like a slow-acting poison; sweet at first, and then sickly, and finally too painful to hope for anything but a quick death. Your father must have been mad to have married her."

I looked over at Ben. He shifted his weight onto his straight leg entirely, hiding his begrudging agreement. I was suddenly glad he had left his crutch in the stables. I did not want to see our maternal grandmother cringe at the sight of it.

"I can assure you, your stepmother will be paid back for all the pain she has caused, down to the last little prick."

"She should," Ben muttered. "With interest."

"On that, we agree." With her gray hair and her frosty face, Lady Penelope suddenly radiated a chilly aura. But as she softened her smile, warmth suddenly shone in her blue eyes—eyes that mirrored my own.

Máma *had eyes like that, too.*

I nodded, barely able to contain my delight, but Ben huffed. "I would have preferred it ten years ago."

Lady Penelope looked at him, taking in every detail. Her eyes raked him up and down, before she let out a tired sigh. "And I would have preferred it that your mother stay at home, rather than cross the sea to come to London."

As Lady Penelope made her way over to us, walking around my father's desk, there was a small shuffling noise behind me. I glanced back to see the same man as before, straightening his shoulders and pulling at his cloak.

"Well," Lady Penelope said, "there is no point in questioning what happened back then. What is important is what we can do about the here and now."

"And … you will be staying with us, then?" I asked.

"Nora," Ben hissed.

Lady Penelope eyed him carefully. I watched her lips purse tightly, pinching her face into a scowl. "There is no need to be so hostile, Benedict. I am, after all, your grandmother. And you are correct. It is time I take up the duty my daughter's departure has left me. I intend to not only pay Lady Cecilia back for her trouble, but I will do what I can to make it up to you."

"Really?" My heart beat faster as she nodded. Ben and I exchanged a glance. I was hopeful; he was distrustful.

"What do you want in return?" Ben asked.

THE ORDER OF THE CRYSTAL DAGGERS

I was about to assure Ben there was nothing we could possibly give Lady Penelope when she gave him a wry smile "You're a clever young man, aren't you?"

My heart sank. "But we can't give you anything. "We have no money to offer."

"I'm not after money, am I?" Lady Penelope stood tall as she looked back at me. "You are so much like your mother, Eleanora. And I believe I may yet have a use for you."

"Pepé."

A guard spoke up and stepped forward. Ben and I watched as Lady Penelope frowned at him.

The man removed the hood of his cloak, revealing his tan face. He was a man who had clearly traveled the world, all the way from his home in the East Indies to the streets of London. From his crown of bright white hair, I would have said he was close to Lady Penelope's age, though there was something about him that seemed ageless.

"Pepé, I must object," he said. "These are your grandchildren."

Lady Penelope shrugged. "Then it's not your concern, is it, Harshad?"

"It is my concern if we are compromised."

"We need not worry about what might be."

"Your duty has higher demands," Harshad said.

"Is there any higher demand than family?"

Harshad's eyes narrowed. "You swore your life over to a different ideal."

"I made my vow to God, and God himself has given us the blessing of family. Fealty to one cause does not preclude another."

Up until that moment, I had only seen Lady Penelope calmly and coolly dismiss any arguments or objections at Cecilia's hysteria and Ben's distrustful sneering. As she battled against Harshad, she quickly lost her calm and fire replaced it.

At my inquiring gaze, she immediately switched to another language, still bitterly exchanging verbal blows with Harshad. Even as they spoke in what I guessed was an Indian tongue, I could tell they were nowhere close to a compromise.

Taking the opportunity, I took a moment to study Harshad; I saw he was slightly shorter than Lady Penelope, only a little taller than myself. His accent was distinct, and even when he had spoken in English, his heritage seemed to carry the essence of his past. From his tone, I could tell he was a stubborn man, deeply rooted in his beliefs.

Why is she traveling with an Indian? And what are they talking about?

When I heard Lady Penelope say "Artha," in her mix of lilted language, my heart jumped.

Why is my grandmother arguing about a dead man?

A second later, I frowned. That did not make sense. Was it possible I had heard her incorrectly?

Lady Penelope went back to ignoring Harshad. She returned her focus to us, and somehow she gave the impression that the argument with Harshad had never happened.

"Well, Eleanora, Benedict, there is no need to worry about all the details tonight. Now, I will need you to go and collect your things and bring them back to this wing of the house. You will have new rooms while I am here, and my servants will see to your needs."

Ben and I remained unmoved, and she seemed to be at the end of her patience.

"Go," she instructed. "It is for the best, after all. Your stepmother will be tempted to take her anger out on you, especially since she knows she cannot touch me. We should at least agree that for now, you will be safer with me."

Ben clenched his fists, and I had to wonder if he was upset at Lady Penelope for successfully making her point.

"You have already had a long night. Nothing good comes from talking business or making deals when you are tired."

We filed out of the room, passing the other guard. I watched as he shifted, burying even further into his cloak as I passed.

I was confused, but Lady Penelope and Harshad once more began to talk, and I forgot the strangeness of it all.

Remembering my time in the city, watching Dr. Artha's funeral procession, meeting with Ferdy and Mr. Clavan, fighting with the Turkish thief, and seeing Lord Maximillian and Teresa Marie, I decided there was a lot that was extraordinary about the day. Lady Penelope—my estranged grandmother—suddenly did not seem so unusual.

Unable to help myself, I let out a tired giggle.

"What are you laughing for?" Ben snapped. "There is nothing funny about this, Nora."

"You didn't see her battling with Cecilia and Alex." I wrapped my arm around his. "Come now, Ben, it might not be funny, maybe, but it is still not bad. Cecilia's angry, and there is nothing she can do about it."

"There doesn't seem to be much we can do, either," Ben pointed out. "We are dependent on Lady Penelope now."

I thought about the letter Lady Penelope had in her hands, the one she had given to Cecilia. She was clearly here on some kind of business. What it could be, and what it was, I was not sure. But she was our family, and I told Ben as much. "Surely there is nothing inherently dangerous about that."

"I don't know, Nora." Ben sighed. "Did you hear her, at the end? She's talking about making business deals. That hardly seems like the terms you would use to describe family matters."

He did have a point.

I hated how he had a point.

"But she promised us she would take care of us." I nearly jumped in excitement. "Just think of it, Ben. If nothing else, Liberté could be ours at last!"

"The devil always offers you everything you want," Ben said darkly. "But there is always a price to pay. Always."

"We have already paid it. All these years of serving in our own household, under a tyrant of a woman and a beast of our stepbrother, and not to mention the pampered princess who masquerades as our stepsister."

"Only to now find ourselves dealing with an even more dangerous woman." Ben sighed. "Our dream of opening our own bookshop and lending library is not worth the cost, as far as I can see right now. Liberté will have to wait, so long as we know there are invisible strings attached to anything Lady Penelope has to offer us."

"You certainly have a way of dampening my spirits," I muttered.

"I'm allowed to do that, since I am the only one who cares enough to raise them," he said. "Now, as much as I hate to agree with Lady Penelope on something, she was likely right about Cecilia. Go and get your things and come back here quickly. If Lady Penelope is interested in making a deal with us, she is unlikely to harm us."

I rolled my eyes. "How does it feel to be suspicious of people all the time? To always feel like everyone is going to treat you horribly?"

"I find it is easier to live with their derision than my disappointment. Being a cripple in a society that has no use for you will remind you of that every day."

"Oh, Ben. Please don't think that. You know I was only teasing … " Before I could embrace him, he twisted out of my grip and headed down the dark hall toward his own room.

I watched him until his shadow disappeared around the corner, and then I hurried out to the barn to collect my things. Ben was right to be worried, but I still believed I was right to be hopeful.

Wasn't I?

I glanced up at the ceiling, ignoring the fine craftsmanship of the stonework to look for the face of God behind the darkness. "Well, Lord, this certainly has been a long day," I said with a tired sigh. "I can only pray for your peace in the night."

6

◊

By the time I woke up the next morning, having barely slept at all, nothing had happened that made things seem any less surreal.

I doubted Cecilia felt any different. I did not know the specific details of Cecilia's pain, but through the stone walls of the castle, her muffled cries and disparaging howls rang out from the midmorning hour until noon. Even from my new room two hallways down, I could hear her constant wailing and gnashing of the teeth as she fought with Lady Penelope.

Sometime after Lady Penelope's servant brought a plate to me for lunch, there was another knock at my door.

"Who is it?" I called, quickly stuffing the book I had been reading behind one of the larger pillows of my bed. I frowned at my practiced movement; it was an old habit, but I was not sure if I would be able to break it.

"It's me." Ben entered, his own lunch tray in hand, and I hurriedly took it from him as he moved toward the window seat in my room. "I can take care of it myself," he said, annoyed by my help.

"I know you can. I'm just being polite, Ben."

"We're family. There's no need to be polite."

"Then choke on your food and see if I care."

It felt good to have things back to normal between us.

Ben grinned. "That's better. But if I do, you better hope I choke only after I finish telling you all the gory details of Cecilia and Lady Penelope's argument."

"You were eavesdropping?"

"This is my house, and I'm allowed to go where I want within it," Ben said. "Even if Cecilia and Lady POW are arguing over it, *Otec* was supposed to leave it to me, and Lady POW will leave it to me when she's gone."

"Lady POW?"

"Her full name is Lady Penelope Ollerton-Wellesley. I shortened it to Lady POW, for her initials. Her name's too long." Ben shrugged.

I smiled, nearly laughing as I recalled Ferdy telling me my name was too long, too. "Maybe it's a family trait."

"Huh?"

"Never mind," I said, brushing it aside. "Lady POW seems like a good name for her, anyway. She seems quite powerful as a lady, and one who is used to getting her way."

Ben nodded. "I'll give her that. She could most likely walk into Market Square and convince the vendors to give her their goods for free."

"From all the disruption I heard this morning, I'll bet Cecilia experienced something like that."

"She did." Ben chuckled. "Among other things, the engagement is off between Alex and Lady Teresa Marie."

"What?"

"His Grace was clearly much happier about it than Cecilia. He was still trying to curry favor with Lady POW as he left the library. He is going to stay with us another day or two, and then I believe he will leave."

"I can't believe it. That was all Cecilia had worked for these past ten years."

"Lord Maximillian told her to write to him if it became acceptable to discuss marriage at a later date."

"What did Cecilia say?"

"Nothing. Lady Penelope interrupted and told him that I was allowed to choose my own bride."

Ben's face was stoic and stubborn; he would not allow me to know how he felt about that particular topic. I thought about how he had believed, all those years before, that he would never marry because of his leg, and because he had no inheritance.

After a long moment of silence, I finally giggled softly. "Well, you said we were at her mercy, but it seems she will allow you to make that decision on your own at least."

Ben snorted. "Lady POW also said she intends to give you a Season or two before she will consider marriage a priority."

I was the one who ended up choking. "What?" I sputtered, sending a cloud of crumbs flying all over the floor. Ben thumped me hard between my shoulders before I was able to articulate my surprise better. "What did you say?"

"She's intent on giving you a Season," Ben said. "She's going to buy you a whole new wardrobe and send you out to the marriage mart."

I groaned.

"Calm down. You're already a lady. Now you just have to act like one."

"I guess," I said slowly, "with Lady POW as my example, that does not appear to be as bad as it sounds. If I can give scathing lectures to my stepmother in public, at a party she is throwing herself no less, that would make it worth it."

It was Ben's turn to scowl.

I flicked my nose at him, using one of Tulia's silent insults. "Come on, Ben, I don't think she's bad," I said, putting my lunch tray aside. I paused for a moment before I added, "And I don't know if she knew about us before, either. She called me 'Eleanor,' like *Máma*, when she first saw me. She did not seem to know about you, either, when I asked."

"She's still dangerous, even if she didn't purposefully neglect us. I overheard one her servants call her the Iron Dowager. Apparently, she is formidable, in addition to her impressive wealth and prestige."

"You say that like it's a bad thing."

"Of course it is bad for us. We are at her mercy."

"Not entirely. Cecilia's been banished back to half of the manor's rooms, right? She told the Duke I was going to have a Season, so that means she really does want to do something for us. And if you are worried about it, we just need to assert our compliance comes with a price, too."

When he said nothing, I tugged at his arm. "Come on. Let's go and talk with her. We're rested, and she's done with Cecilia. Surely we can discuss everything now."

Ben groaned, but he walked with me toward the library. From his dragging foot, I could tell Ben was only going along with my wishes. I scowled at him, silently reminding him the only other option we had was to do nothing.

Neither Ben nor I had ever been any good at doing nothing if we could help it.

As we passed by the doors to Lady POW's bedchamber, we could hear her arguing with Harshad again. Immediately, Ben quieted his footstep and shuffled up against the door.

I gave him a disapproving look, but he only rolled his eyes. Before I could tell Ben to ignore her and that everyone should have a right to some privacy, I heard my name.

"—Eleanora is clearly a fine young lady with spirit, just like her mother," Lady Penelope said. "She's just the element we need as a new cover."

Ben's eyes snapped to mine, and I knew he was silently telling me he had been right to mistrust her.

"Pepé, stop this nonsense. Dezda did not tell you about them, remember?"

"So?" I could almost see the angry snarl on Lady POW's face through the door.

"She likely thought it was for the best," Harshad said.

THE ORDER OF THE CRYSTAL DAGGERS

"Well, now she is dead, and it is up to me what we will do—both in regard to my grandchildren, and to the mission."

Mission? What mission? Ben and I exchanged a quick glance, before Lady POW and Harshad started arguing again.

"Amir was right," Lady Penelope said. "It *is* her. He was right about Eleanora. And I must honor my role as a grandmother, to both her and her brother."

"This will disrupt our mission."

"Hardly. This helps us, if anything. Dr. Artha was our lead contact, Harshad, and now he is dead. Lady Cecilia is in no position to be of any help. This is not the time to question the gifts of providence."

The world seemed to shift unexpectedly, as I realized my grandmother was interested in the death of my father's former doctor—and she was interested in us, for some reason. Before I could voice my concerns to Ben, Harshad began to speak once more.

"What will you tell them about their mother? And even if you tell them the truth, who is to say they will accept her legacy? They could easily reject us and leave us with a heavy liability."

"And what if they do accept our offer?" Lady Penelope countered. "It will be wonderful."

"It will be terrible."

"Likely a bit of both. Which will be all the better, if you ask me."

"Pepé, it will still be a liability."

"We've had worse!"

"But what would you have me do? Teach them? That will take time away from our inquiries. We do not have time for this. More lives are at risk, as Dr. Artha has shown us."

"Then we will just have make time for it. That is an order, and you will follow it, Harshad."

Harshad sighed, and I could hear his reluctant defeat. "The League is already not happy with you, Pepé, and this decision will call for a special council. The Order will not be able to help you this time."

"You can make the arrangements for that, then." Lady Penelope paused. "Assuming you have enough time."

"You cannot just alter our plans."

"The plans were already altered, long before we arrived."

"Dezda would not approve of this!" Harshad hissed.

"It matters not. She is not here. For now, I have heard your arguments, and I will take them into serious consideration, no matter how much I disagree with you."

"Your grief is blinding you to the truth," Harshad said.

"And your pride and arrogance have always blinded you," Lady Penelope shot back. "That is why we work so well together, despite our past. We know each other's weaknesses too well."

"Then you should consider listening to me more."

"What an appalling thought," Lady Penelope said. "As I've already listened to you for quite some time, and I've found no such reason to bend to your wishes."

"You should still let them choose. Dezda regretted it in the end."

"She did not regret anything. She just wanted more. And as we now know, she was able to get it, clearly. But we will not argue over that now. I am the appointed leader here, and what I say will go through in the end. Send a summons to Eleanora and Benedict. I will meet them in the library."

"You have always been too stubborn," Harshad said. "You are free to ruin your life, but I will not let you ruin theirs."

"It is *their* choice if I will ruin it or not. Besides, what would their alternative truly be? Cecilia seems to have done quite enough damage. Do you really think it is better that they stay here, under her authority? As I see it, better they are with us, than with her. And much better with us than being out on the streets."

Secretly, I agreed with her. I knew how terrible Cecilia was, and that alone was enough for me to hope for a better future with my increasingly odd, estranged grandmother.

"You are not the only one who owes Dezda," Harshad said.

At his icy tone, a shiver went down my spine. I tugged Ben's arm. "Come on," I whispered. "Let's just go to the library and wait for them."

It was clear Lady Penelope and Harshad would still need several moments to bark at each other. Their voices gradually faded as Ben and I approached the library.

"Well, that was intense," I said. "Even through the door."

Ben nodded. "What do you think their mission is?"

"I don't know for sure, but I have a feeling I know what part of it involves," I said, thinking of Dr. Artha. Before I could tell Ben what I suspected, I tugged open the door to the library. There was a shuffling noise and a grunt of surprise.

That was when I saw him again.

My eyes went wide and then narrowed in anger as I suddenly found myself staring at the Turk, the one who had stolen my father's book.

"You!" My mouth fell open in shock. There was no mistaking him. He had the same eyes, the same nose, even the same expression of registered surprise as he saw me.

"Nora, what's wrong?"

I barely heard Ben's question as I raced across the room to the bookshelf, lunging an attack at the man. In the brief seconds before contact, I saw that while his turban was missing today, his black hair was still elegantly combed back, his mustache was still immaculately trimmed, and he was still astonished that I would attack him at all.

My fist managed to strike his torso with enough force to send him slamming into the bookshelves behind him; I was gratified to see I managed to land a successful blow once more. He groaned in pain before falling to the ground.

"What are you doing here?" I demanded, preparing to strike again. "This is my home, and I will not let you steal anything else from me."

The man sighed. "Please," he said. His English was without inflection, and I stopped.

"You know English?" I asked.

"Yes, much better than I know Czech. But I can switch to French, if you would like." The Turk fell back on his bended knee in apparent surrender. I was disgusted to see there was a hesitant smile on his face as he looked at me, and I gritted my teeth at his gall.

"Nora, who is this?" Ben asked. "What are you doing?"

I pointed at the Turk accusingly. "This is the man who took our father's book from me yesterday."

"The one who accosted you?" Ben looked down at the Turk and frowned. "With the knife?"

"My apologies," the man said. He pulled out his curved dagger from underneath his cloak, presenting it before us as proof of who he was. "Yes, I am the man you saw yesterday."

"Why did you come here?" I asked again, my voice angry and loud. "Who do you think you are, to be here—"

"Eleanora, that's enough."

Lady POW's voice cut through my vicious triumph, severing its full life force with the power of her words.

I swiveled around to see her enter the library, with Harshad at her heels.

"Lady Penelope," I exclaimed, "this man is—"

THE ORDER OF THE CRYSTAL DAGGERS

The Turk reached out and took my hand, squeezing it firmly. "I am not an intruder," he interrupted. He moved quickly, standing up with my forced assistance. "I do believe I have startled Lady Eleanora."

"Well, you are a Turk, and I've heard there have been more Turkish thieves in the city of late."

"Eleanora, do not allow prejudices to cloud your vision," Lady Penelope said. "Skin and race are no more proper judges of character than wealth, health, or wisdom. The devil believes in oversimplifications, but I do not."

I blushed at her comments, knowing I agreed with her in principle. If the man had not stolen from me, I would not have said anything at all, let alone attacked him.

"Amir here is harmless, Eleanora, and I have good reason to trust him with nothing less than my life."

The Turk glimpsed over at Lady Penelope, rubbing his side where I had managed to hit him. "She has an impressive left hook, Lady Penelope."

"Does she?" Lady POW moved gracefully into the room, making herself home at my father's desk, just as she had the previous night. She sat down and smoothed out her skirts. "Well, I guess some good came out of her attacking you, then."

I had no doubt there was a befuddled look on my face as Lady POW tapped her fingers together. "Eleanora, this is Amir Qureshi, my medical consultant and confidant. He has been in my service for the last thirteen years, although we have known each other for much longer. What is it now, Amir? Nearly thirty years?"

"Twenty-five, Madame."

For the first time, I noticed the small threads of silver at the sides of his temples. Before, I would have easily guessed he was in his thirties, but it was clear he was at least forty. "*Enchanté*," I muttered, the barest amount above polite I could muster.

"Amir, allow me to properly introduce my granddaughter."

Harshad scowled beside her. "As you might have already seen, she is Dezda's daughter to the bone."

Dezda? I frowned. Was she talking about my mother?

Suddenly, the earlier conversation Ben and I had overheard made a lot more sense. And it made me a lot more suspicious.

"I have seen it is so," Amir agreed, "although there are several hints of her father."

I sneered at his too-proper tone.

"I'm hoping not too much," Lady Penelope said, making me further frustrated. I hated how she talked over me, as if I was not present. "Now that I've found my grandchildren here, I see it was a needless errand to send a servant for them."

THE ORDER OF THE CRYSTAL DAGGERS

"I'll attend to rescinding the order." Amir turned to me. "Will you see me out of the room, mademoiselle? So you may see I am not a philistine or mongrel of sorts?"

I glowered at him but took his outstretched arm. As we approached the doorway, he whispered, "Please, do not tell Lady Penelope about yesterday. I will explain myself at a later time, if you will only let me. You have my word."

"Your word means nothing to me. You took my father's book."

"Your father's book?" He frowned, and then shook his head. "Never mind. I will explain myself and my actions to you, and this I swear on the soul of your mother."

As he made his vow, Amir covered my hands with his, and that was when I noticed the burning white scribble seared into the skin of his right hand.

The stark white of the scar, a large half-loop dotted with a searing square, winked at me against the library light.

"Please, mademoiselle," he whispered. "There is much more going on than you realize."

I looked into his eyes and then back down at his hand. Seeing the crispy outline of the mark against his knuckles made me soften. It was an older scar, but it hid a deeper pain. I thought the shape of it looked vaguely familiar, but I had trouble recalling where I had seen it. "Fine," I said through clenched teeth. "But I will hold it against you if you give me any trouble."

"Not only your mother's daughter, but your grandmother's granddaughter as well, I see." The smile on his face was a sad, rueful one.

"Eleanora," Lady POW called. "What is taking so long?"

Amir's hands slipped out of mine. "She just wanted to make sure I was feeling well, Lady Penelope," he replied.

"Did I ask you something, Amir? I believe I was talking to Eleanora."

"My apologies, Madame." Amir's smile turned wry as he looked back at me. "Excuse me."

I watched him for a long moment as he left, eyeing the small outline of his dagger from beneath his cloak.

He had better keep his promise.

I was intrigued, if somewhat repulsed, by the man my grandmother trusted so much.

As I walked back toward Lady POW and Ben, I glanced over at Harshad. He was quiet and still, and he did not look back at me, even though I had a feeling he was still taking in everything from around the room.

"Now, then," Lady Penelope said. "To business."

Ben narrowed his eyes at me.

I pretended not to notice. He had been right, but the earlier conversation we overheard only added more mystery. I was interested, even if family came after business.

"I will start by suggesting you stay in this half of the manor for your own safety while Cecilia and I settle our legal disputes."

I briefly thought of *Máma's* locket and *Táta's* watch, still tucked away under the pantry floor. *I will have to go and retrieve them soon if I want to keep them safe.*

"What happens to us after that?" Ben asked.

"That is the question, is it not?" Lady Penelope mused. "I know I have neglected my duties as your grandmother for far too long. I know there is much hurt between us—"

"The hurt seems to just be with us," Ben interrupted.

"Not all pain is seen, Benedict." Her tone was distinctly soft, and I felt a hint of the feeling behind it.

Whether or not I believed it was a different story, however. I knew Ben was likely unsure of her sincerity. He grumbled and crossed his arms, but he went silent.

"I would first seek to make amends—should you choose to allow me. I have coerced Cecilia into allowing you to make that choice," Lady Penelope said.

I was not as interested in making amends as I was getting answers to my questions, which seemed to be accumulating by the moment. It was time to do something. "We heard you need us for something," I said. "You said I would make a good cover. What were you talking about?"

Harshad's mouth dropped open, before he glared at Lady POW. She shot him a smug look before turning to me. I was expecting her to explain herself, but even though she was clearly pleased by my admission, she waved the matter aside.

"You will see later," she said briskly.

Did she want *me to overhear their conversation?* I wondered. *Or is she just happy that I did?*

Before I could ask, Lady POW turned toward a stack of papers on the desk. "Now, Lady Cecilia was kind enough not to test my patience—much. She has shown me her budgets for the last several years, and I am prepared to restore your inheritance."

"Thank you," I said. "But—"

"That will include a new wardrobe for you, Eleanora. If you are in agreement, I will make arrangements for your introduction to Society at once. While we are here, waiting for my man of affairs to make settlements with your stepmother, we can

THE ORDER OF THE CRYSTAL DAGGERS

send you out on several social calls. It is the perfect time, too, as the Diets are in session and the elites of Prague will be ripe for entertainment."

"But I'm not an entertainer," I cut in, tired of letting her interrupt me.

"You may not be an entertainer, but you will be a sensation. I will see to your wardrobe and your manners, and then we will go out and introduce you to the town. Even his Imperial Highness King Ferdinand V will be eager to meet you once I am finished with you."

"What? Why—?"

"It will be an adventure," Lady Penelope insisted. "And we can make up for our lost time."

I hesitated to object; I did not want to dampen Lady POW's spirits. She seemed much happier than she had the previous evening, and some part of me was secretly thrilled. All my years of yearning for my mother came rushing at me, and it pushed back against my fears and questions.

"Harshad is right—you are clearly Dezda's daughter," Lady Penelope said, flicking another snippy gaze over at her colleague. "She was a beauty."

"I do remember *Táta* saying so," I whispered. I glanced over at Ben, and my resolve found itself again. "What about Ben?"

"Yes, indeed. What is it that you want, Benedict?" Lady Penelope asked.

Ben stilled beside me. "I will have to think about it."

"What is there to think about?" Lady Penelope scoffed.

"It doesn't matter," Ben muttered. "If there is anything I want for sure, it's just Nora to be happy."

I was touched by my brother's concern, but Lady POW bristled.

"Believing that your own happiness is not feasible does have a tendency to limit it. You might already know that, from what I have seen."

Ben scowled. "What's that supposed to mean?"

"It's easy to be altruistic when there is no real sacrifice involved."

"I—"

"It's clear that you believe your life is meaningless," Lady Penelope said. "Is it because of your leg? Do you think you've become useless because of it? Or do you just want to be unhappy?"

Ben stared at her, speechless. I tried to speak up and defend Ben, but Lady POW stopped me. She held up her hand, making me think of Tulia briefly. "Stop, Eleanora," she barked. "This is not about you, despite what your brother thinks. This is about his pride, his damaged sense of honor, and how he can overcome his shame."

"I have no shame in who I am," Ben retorted.

"Not in who, but in what."

"This isn't something you should talk about," I interrupted. "Ben doesn't like—"

"The truth?" Lady Penelope turned back to me. "He doesn't like the truth, Eleanora? Is that what you were going to say?"

"No." I blushed. "I was going to say he doesn't like to talk about his injury, that's all."

"If only the world could work in such a way that everything we did not like would go away if we would only cease to talk about it." Lady Penelope threw Harshad a wry look over her shoulder. "That would do wonders for us, would it not, Harshad?"

Harshad continued to say nothing, even though I could tell there was nothing more he wanted in that moment than to speak up.

Lady POW shook her head at Ben. "I am asking you to allow me to make your life better. It is time I rectify my mistakes after all these years."

"Mistakes?" I asked.

Lady Penelope's lips suddenly tightened into a twisted grimace, and I blinked in shock, realizing I had caught her slip up before she did.

"Yes. My mistakes."

"Pepé, stop." Harshad lunged forward with a speedy grace that belied his age, gripping her wrist as she reached for something at her side.

"Enough," Ben objected. "We already know you're hiding something from us. If she is going to tell us what it is, I want to hear it. *That's* what I want."

"Me, too." I reached out and took Ben's arm in support. "Tell us why you are here. And tell us what it has to do with Dr. Artha's death."

Lady POW's eyebrows raised, while Ben and Harshad both whirled to face me.

"So, you know of Dr. Artha's murder?" Lady Penelope asked.

"I heard rumors in the city," I said, suddenly determined to keep Ferdy and Clavan out of any of my explanations. Her casual tone was disconcerting.

"Rumors are one thing, but truth is another."

"Then tell us the truth," Ben grumbled.

Lady POW sat down and folded her hands together in careful consideration. "Is that what you really want?" She briefly narrowed her eyes at Harshad, and I saw his face sour even more as he saw me look at him.

"Yes," Ben insisted.

Lady Penelope ignored the fury in his gaze. She turned to me. "What of you, Eleanora? You will not be able to go back to not knowing, once you learn the truth. Do you still want to know?"

Sudden fear and solid certainty took hold of me. "Yes," I said, unsure if I had the bravery to match my sudden bravado.

Lady Penelope cast another quick, triumphant look over at Harshad, who pursed his lips in further displeasure. A silent battle continued between them, but he stepped back.

"Very well then, Benedict, Eleanora," Lady Penelope said. "I will tell you the truth. But it does not start, nor stop, with me. I must tell you about your mother and the Order of the Crystal Daggers."

7

◊

Lady POW clasped her hands together. I scooted forward on my seat, dreading and anticipating what she would reveal. If hearing the truth was the price for our freedom, I knew telling us the truth also required a price from her.

"My Eleanor, your mother, was a member of an elite, secret society once known as the Order of the Crystal Daggers," Lady Penelope said. "Before she died, she handled several delicate assignments on behalf of certain kingdoms and governments."

Ben and I only looked at her, torn between reactions, as we waited for her to go on.

What could I really say? *Máma* had died many years ago. I remembered her the way one might recall a strange and vivid dream; sometimes I would forget about her for days at a time, and then I would smell a familiar scent, or recall a certain memory, and I would long for her embrace. Before Cecilia came to the manor, I would walk past the portrait *Táta* had commissioned of her, truly seeing her face stilled in the dried oil; at those moments, I would be caught back in that feeling of wondering where she was, and how I missed her.

To imagine her as a government worker, as someone who did not spend her days taking care of our family or seeing to our needs, was not beyond my capability; it just seemed beyond believability.

It seemed to be beyond Ben's, too.

"*Otec* never mentioned anything like that," Ben said. "And I never saw anything to indicate you are telling the truth."

"Your father was part of her last assignment," Lady Penelope said. "She was supposed to come down here with some others and take care of King Ferdinand V during the Revolution of 1848."

Ben and I exchanged glances. From his eyes, I could tell he was frustrated—and afraid. I was surprised to realize I was, too. The beautiful lady in that portrait had always been a loving, maternal memory, and it was troubling to hear she had led such a contrasting life prior to my birth. My childhood innocence had long been gone, thanks to Cecilia's callousness and my father's death, but I felt a secret pillar of my heart splinter as my memory of my mother, a relic born of ignorance and illusion, began to crumble.

"This was not an unusual task for a member of the Order to handle," Lady Penelope continued. "The Order goes back several hundred years, starting with the warriors of Constantine. When he converted to Christianity, there were several more threats on his life from those in the kingdom he had displeased. Everyone from the pagans to the Jews were upset at his conversion and his success as a leader. There were others, of course, who were upset with him long before that."

"Saint Constantine?" I asked, briefly recalling the church's Latin rites. "That is who you mean, correct?"

"Yes. Forgive my confusion. The Church of England does put a barrier between me and Catholicism. But Constantine had a particularly sharp intuition for betrayal," Lady Penelope said. "Under his rule, the Byzantine Empire commissioned a small, secret group of elite members to protect him. As time went on, and the empire collapsed in on itself, the last of the rulers, in a desperate attempt to gain allies, pushed the Order to protect more allies of the surrounding nations. The group decentralized, and loyalties shifted. Today, the Order itself spans many nations. Queen Victoria herself sent us out here to investigate the situation and keep the status quo."

"Why is the British Empire sending you out here?" Ben asked.

"Her Imperial Majesty wants to ensure the safety of the trade routes to the Orient and the Indies."

"Many consider her to be a powerful ruler, even in my home country," Harshad added. "Her vocal support has kept these lands, and others, stable during growing political divides. But not all are happy with her support."

"Is that who sent *Máma* out here the first time?" I asked. "Queen Victoria?"

"No." Lady Penelope shook her head. "Back then, it was the papal state government, under His Holiness Pope Pius IX himself, that requested aid, for Savoy's sake."

"Empress Maria Anna," Ben said. "King Ferdinand's wife."

I thought of the lady I'd only seen in small pamphlets, the one who had once ruled as my country's queen as well as the Empress of Austria and Hungary. She was rumored to be devoted to the church and her husband, with her only other love reserved for traveling throughout Bohemia during the summer and decorating Prague Castle in abundant Christmas decorations every year.

Briefly, I thought of the half-torn invitation to the Advent Ball Ferdy had handed me. Despite all the confusion of our present situation, I could not stop wondering if I would be able to go to the Empress' ball, now that I had the chance to be free from Cecilia. I clasped my hands together tightly, trying to keep the sudden excitement inside of me to myself.

Lady Penelope, oblivious to my inner delight, nodded. "Yes."

"The former empress was concerned about the revolution, and she had a right to be, in hindsight. That is why your mother came here. Dezda was very eager for another mission at the time," Harshad said.

"When she met her Dolf," Lady Penelope said, "she decided to stay and marry him."

69

There was something in her tone that told me she had been displeased by my mother's choice.

"And then she had us," I said.

The terse brunt of her response left me breathless. "Yes."

There was a long pause, before Ben finally said, "I do not understand why this information matters. Our mother has been gone for fourteen years now. What does an old society and Dr. Artha's death have to do with why you are here?"

"The society for whom she worked is still around," Lady Penelope said. She cocked her head to the side, glancing back at Harshad. "Mostly."

Realization dawned on me as I looked from her to Harshad. "And you are part of it," I said. "You're a member of the same society as *Máma* was, aren't you?"

"Excellent, Eleanora. The good Lord gave logical faculties to both male and female, and I am proud to see you use yours so well."

"Since you are here then," Ben said, "that must mean the society sent you on another assignment."

"Also very astute," Lady Penelope said. "You are correct. Harshad and I, along with the others under our command, have been ordered to come here on a special mission."

"Did they send you out here to investigate Dr. Artha's murder?" I asked. "Does this mean Ben and I will help with your assignment?"

There was no mistaking the satisfaction on Lady POW's face. "I hope so. I have a plan, and it includes you both."

Harshad cleared his throat. "Lady Penelope sees this as an opportunity to be with her family as well as serve the kingdom of Bohemia and discover the truth."

His tone was resigned, but it was how he used Lady POW's proper name that made me shudder. I wondered if it was an insult of sorts between them.

"What good would a cripple do this society of yours?" Ben asked.

I saw the small amount of fear in his eyes as he stared at Lady POW. Breathlessly, I waited for her response.

She smirked. "Plenty, given your spying abilities," she said. "Harshad and I were aware you were listening in on the conversation Cecilia and I had in the library this morning."

For the first time, Ben dropped his guard. "Really?"

Between Ben and Lady POW, I could suddenly see a lot more similarity.

Ben's earlier warning whispered through me; Lady Penelope was our grandmother, but she was clearly more dangerous than either of us had anticipated.

What she was asking of us was not clear, and as I watched she and Ben began to discuss more about the Order, and I felt myself pulling away as Ben was pulled in.

"So we would be spies?" I asked, interrupting her. "That hardly seems proper."

"It is hardly proper for you, as a rightful lady, to be subjected to preparing an engagement dinner for your stepbrother, or selling your father's heirlooms at the market. Spying is not an honorable task, but that has never negated the necessity of it at critical times like these."

Lady Penelope's tone was sharp and shaming, and I blushed at her remarks.

"Protecting others is a calling, but each has to answer it. Some do not. That is what even God himself offered to man."

"So the Order protects people?" I said, still hesitant.

"Yes." Lady Penelope nodded firmly. "We serve truth. And the truth is, rulers are needed in order to keep the peace. We protect them at great cost. We investigate on their behalf. We seek to overcome and control chaos. We serve others in love and in hopes of peace. Is peace for our time not a noble enough endeavor for you?"

"It is a good goal," I agreed, "but—"

"—and just think, you would be taking up the banner of your mother's legacy in helping us. She worked hard to maintain peace here in Bohemia, before you were born. Wouldn't you like to honor her memory by helping us now?"

At the mention of my mother, all the wispy memories I had of her flooded into my mind. I heard her words, I saw her smile. I wanted to run to her and embrace her, to feel her heart beat against mine; I thought about what she loved, including my father, and about how she was proud of him for protecting the king during the revolution all those years ago.

The illusions of my mother were gone, but I could still know her in a real way, to walk through the steps of her life on my own.

"You do not have to help, of course," Lady Penelope said, her sudden flippancy repulsive to my pride. "You know the truth about your mother, and now it is up to you what you will do with it. Even those set free by the truth often choose to remain enslaved. And I know Cecilia would love the chance to remain your guardian, if you would let her."

"I want to be free." The words came rushing out of me before I could think through their implications and consequences.

"There are two things you need to know about yourself if you want to be free— what you stand for, and what you stand against." Lady Penelope held up her hands, brandishing a pair of daggers that had been hidden in her skirts. "This world lives enslaved to its destruction, and so long as you are living, as long as you are fighting, you will be free."

I gazed at the daggers, transfixed. Each blade was clothed in a leather scabbard, but the silver and obsidian of the daggers' hilts winked at me, as though it was calling for me.

Lady Penelope pulled the daggers free, revealing a pair of gleaming blades; each were an unusual shade of violet, one that held other spots of blue and green, and other colors, even as it encompassed them. The gemlike mosaic added to the overall power of the weapon.

"Beautiful, aren't they?" Lady Penelope ran her gaze down her blades, following the elegant curve of the daggers. Her fingers lightly stroked the weapons as she held them. "The motto of the Order is *In Hoc Signo Vinces*, or 'With this sign, you shall win.' It was the same message Constantine heard from God."

"What are they … " My own voice trailed off, hushed and full of awe as I looked on the mysterious weapons.

"This is the weapon of a member of the Order," Lady Penelope continued. "You bow to God alone, but the rest of your life will be a fight, in which you alone will have the choice of victor. It was my privilege to free you from ignorance. Now, it is my duty to teach you how to stand, and remain standing, even when you are tempted to fall."

I looked back at the daggers in her hand and swallowed hard. Lady Penelope was clearly offering me a choice between different lives of servitude, but only one offered meaning and redemption in the end.

My life would mean nothing, my mother's life would mean nothing, if I wasted my efforts to serve Cecilia and her household. I already knew I was insignificant in the eyes of the world, but I suddenly had a chance where my life would be about something greater. And I did want that.

So I reached forward and made my choice. It was the one I wanted.

Ben put his hand on my shoulder protectively as I took hold of a dagger. From the look in his blue-green eyes, I knew he was ready to stand with me. "We accept your offer."

Lady Penelope clasped her hands together. "Then it is time to get to work."

At her determined smile, I could not stop the rush of anxious excitement that washed over me.

8
◊

To my dismay, I soon found out my excitement was unwarranted.

"Are we finished yet?" I asked, grumbling as I stood on the small pedestal. "I've been here for hours."

"Let Jaqueline finish," Lady POW barked. "This is hardly difficult, Eleanora."

I groaned. For hours, I had been standing in the middle of a large parlor room, one that had been closed off to the other parts of the wing, all while three of Lady POW's maidservants worked to measure every inch of my body. Jaqueline, Amelia, and Marguerite doubled as seamstresses, and they were making me different outfits to wear.

"I don't see why a new outfit is necessary. I can work fine in my current skirts. Ben and I have been brawling with each other and battling our way around the manor since we were born."

"You have been wearing that oversized maid's outfit for far too long, Eleanora." Lady POW sat at a small writing desk in the corner of the room, jotting down notes and, from the looks of it, keeping up with her correspondence. "I thought you were much bigger than you actually are."

I bit my lip, irritated. It was bad enough I was naked except for my chemise and stockings, but Lady POW made the whole experience much worse. Every ten minutes or so, she would glance over at me, narrow her eyes, and call out some condescending judgment or shake her head with a sigh. Occasionally, she would come over to me and circle me, wearing a look of cold professionalism that unnerved me.

While it was tempting to whirl around to face her, if for no other reason than to remind her that she had flaws, too, I was stuck holding my arms out straight while Amelia wrapped them in rolls of a range of different fabrics, from velvet and silk to leather and suede. If I moved even the slightest, her pins would dig into my arm. I discovered this for the second time when I glanced behind me, surprised by another one of Lady POW's comments.

"You have good hips for birthing, Eleanora," Lady Penelope observed. "We will have to be careful, though; it seems one is a little higher than the other. It's not ideal for fighting."

I was just about to ask her what my hips had to do with fighting when she continued.

"Men like hips like yours; they make it easier to grab onto during intercourse."

My face went dark red instantly.

73

"It will likely be easy to coerce information from your opponents and informants if you use your bodily charms, should the occasion call for it."

"What?" My voice nearly squeaked.

Lady POW grimaced. "Oh, dear. It has been a long time since I have dealt with the sexually inexperienced. Marguerite? Add that to the list, please."

It was suddenly much easier to worry about fighting.

"Lady Penelope," I said, "I would rather learn how to beat the answers out of my opponents, please. I don't ... I don't want to ... " My voice trailed off as I felt the heat in my face rise.

"Spoken like a true innocent." Lady Penelope sighed. "In that case, consider yourself fortunate that we don't have time for a full review of the curriculum."

I did. I considered myself very, very fortunate.

"I will go over the basics, and that should be enough to suffice for our current mission," Lady Penelope said.

"Now?" My eyes went wide with horror at the thought.

"Come now, Eleanora, don't tell me you have never even thought of sex before?"

"I know what it is," I shot back through gritted teeth. "If that is what you mean."

"Any simpleton can look at a painting or sculpture and know that it is art. But only a true and trained master knows how to create such a splendid pleasure."

I squirmed. "This is hardly appropriate."

"One does what one must, Eleanora; propriety be damned." Lady Penelope returned to her desk.

"What do you think I will be doing that requires such ... explicit ... knowledge? I thought I was just to be a cover."

"And you will be," Lady Penelope agreed. "We will begin introducing you to everyone in Prague tomorrow, ordering clothes for you so you can attend socials and breakfasts and balls. Hopefully, it will not be too much longer before we can launch you into Society properly." She reached over and took a sip from her teacup. "God, I miss England. London is so wonderful this time of year."

"None of what you listed seems like it would require a discourse on manipulative sexuality," I said, ignoring my own stomach's grumbling as I suddenly wanted some tea for myself.

"There is more to your introduction to Society that we need to concern ourselves with," Lady Penelope said.

"You're not secretly auctioning me off to the marriage mart, are you? I can already tell you that I would reject such a fate."

"Hearing that relieves my nerves like nothing else." Lady POW rolled her eyes. "The Order takes its business seriously. There is no time for real romance in these instances. Relationships just cause problems."

For some reason, Ferdy's face flashed in my mind, and I felt sad at the thought of never seeing him again.

"Take it from me, Eleanor. It is best to use people as much as you can and then forget them."

At my mother's name, I winced, but that was not the only reason her statement shook me. From the harshness of her voice, I could tell it was a personal lesson she had learned.

"Eleanora," I corrected.

Lady Penelope did not seem to hear me. "Jaqueline, make sure we have enough material to hide Eleanora's hips, *s'il vous plait.*"

As Jaqueline filled in my corset with extra padding, giving me more of a boyish figure, I decided I would do my best to make sure that, even if I did learn how to use my bosom to get what I wanted, I never needed to employ it.

"What kind of outfit is this?" I glanced down at the full ensemble. It was made of all black, with different shades and different materials. As Amelia allowed me to lower my arms, I felt the smoothness of the leather as it hugged my body. My legs were nearly bare, with only short pants reaching to my knees. It felt like a long pair of delicates, even though I had on a pair underneath it. I felt better that there was a leather skirt hanging over my legs, secured at the waist with a belt.

"This is your stealth habit," Lady Penelope said. "The leather is sturdy and able to provide some protection. The lining is infused with silk, to provide comfort as well as smooth movement, and the linen wraps are there to provide padding."

"Padding for my hips?" I asked her, still annoyed by her earlier comments.

"Yes. Although the wraps are typically there more for your wrists and knuckles."

Marguerite came up to me. "Here, mademoiselle. This is a hood for you."

"A hood?" Before I could ask for specifics, she pushed the material over my head, briefly catching on my hair.

"It has a mask sewn into it." Amelia said, reaching toward my face. She wrestled with the material as I tried not to groan. When I could see properly again, I saw Jaqueline had brought a small hand mirror over for me.

I gazed into it and briefly wondered if everyone else could see how uncomfortable I felt. My eyes were a stormy blue, and my face was clearly pale. My hair had been shuffled free from my pins, so some of my disheveled curls were sticking out from under my hood.

"You and your brother both have such beautiful black hair," Marguerite said. "It matches the outfit perfectly."

"Put the mask on," Amelia said, before she did it for me.

A strip of thick, dark cloth suddenly pressed against my nose and mouth, and I coughed at the sudden interruption of fresh air into my lungs. No one else voiced any objection; the seamstresses all smiled and gasped, delighted to see my semi-finished self.

I had to admit, I liked it. The long tunic over the leggings made it much easier to move, and my arms were loose enough that I could move without tearing at my seams.

"*C'est parfait*," Marguerite cheered.

"Wonderful!" Amelia beamed.

I had to wonder what I was supposed to be doing in an outfit like that.

Lady POW made her way over to me once more. "It'll do. Now, ladies, we do not have much time. Please see to it that this is finished first."

"*Oui*, Madame." Their choral response was amusing, and it cheered me up some as they began to slide the outfit off me.

"Madame, what about the rest of her attire?" Amelia asked. "Should we get started on that as well?"

"We will need a walking dress for her; make it in the Parisian style." Lady Penelope looked thoughtful. "I will take Eleanora out to the city tomorrow and order other clothes. As much as I know you ladies are the finest talents with a needle and thread this side of the globe, I need to make Eleanora a sensation."

She turned to me. "Which means we will need to go over etiquette next."

I drew myself up proudly—or as proudly as I could, as Jaqueline, Amelia, and Marguerite were peeling away the pinned fabric. When my mouth was free of the mask, I said, "I remember a good bit of what *Máma* taught me."

I did not add the additional insight Tulia had provided me, considering most of it was counterproductive to acting like a true lady.

"You were only a child." Lady Penelope dismissed my concern. "I doubt Eleanor taught you how to flirt outrageously with a man and get away with it under the guise of innocence, or how to waltz, or any number of other important skills you will need to learn in order to stand out."

I could have used that chance to ask her about the mission, and why I would need to learn all of that, but something else bothered me more about what she said.

"Why does Harshad call *Máma* Dezda?" I asked. "My father always introduced her as Lady Eleanor."

"Your mother's first name was Eleanor, but Harshad and I often called her Dezda, for her middle name. It is not that unusual a practice; Queen Victoria's first name is actually Alexandrina." Lady Penelope waved her hand. "It is hardly a matter of concern."

"So it is a British tradition to call people by their middle names?"

"Do not be foolish, Eleanora. People often have names that are specific to their loved ones. Your own brother calls you Nora, after all."

I thought of Ferdy calling me "Ella," and smiled. I smiled even more as I faced the temptation to ask Lady POW if Harshad's name for her, Pepé, was an endearment.

But a long, thoughtful moment later, I decided since Lady Penelope had the power to make me suffer, it would be best not to provoke her—especially when I was already tired from the past several hours of wardrobe demands. "I suppose that is true."

"Of course it is. Now, stay still. Do not cause my lovely seamstresses any duress. One more dress for today, a riding habit for later this week, and then we will be finished here."

I kept my groan to myself and prepared to feel another hours-long session of aches and stiffness as I was prodded and poked and measured.

Watching her scribble notes on a small tablet of stationary, I realized Lady POW had yet to tell me anything specific about her special assignment—or why she was concerned with Dr. Artha's death.

"What is the stealth habit for, exactly?" I asked. "I can't imagine I will need to wear this while I'm dancing and flirting outrageously out in Society."

"You're so inquisitive, Eleanora."

"I wouldn't be, if you would answer my questions."

Lady POW gave me a sly smirk. "True. I don't know yet what this assignment will demand of you. I was not expecting you at all, and now that you are here, I feel as though I have our Dezda back."

Lady POW's gaze moved across my face and over my messy curls. I saw her sadness, and I mourned for my mother's loss once more. This time, it was not just for my own loss, however; I saw more than ever that her absence had removed me from an entire life I could have known, and one in which there were more people to embrace.

"But," Lady Penelope said, her voice snapping back to its professional tone, "luck favors the prepared. You might need such a suit if we need information or reconnaissance."

"You mean espionage?"

"You would be surprised at how often the right information has saved lives," Lady Penelope said. "It is easier to save lives with the right information than to simply take out threats."

I nodded. My only real experience with a threat seemed to be Alex, with his pretentious and licentious expressions. Kicking him and occasionally bloodying him up was simple, but then, he was really a simple villain.

"Will we begin looking into Dr. Artha's death?"

"You will not be worried about that," Lady Penelope said. "I will handle that. I have contacts sending me information. For your end of the mission, we will go out to shop and socialize. We will need to make arrangements to be invited to different houses and parties throughout the season."

"Dr. Artha's death seems like a bigger concern," I said. "Especially since he was your lead contact and he was murdered."

"You would do well to remember that murder is always a serious business. I will not involve you in this aspect of my mission, Eleanora. It is risky, even for an experienced spy."

"Dr. Artha was my father's friend," I said. "I remember him from when I was younger. If he was murdered, and there is something I can do, I should do it, should I not?"

"That question is now mine to answer, both as your grandmother and your direct leader, and I have told you what you will do about it."

"But skipping around Society seems … " I searched for the right word, knowing that Lady POW would likely not care if I feared boredom or vanity, especially compared to the threat of murder. "Inefficient."

"It is actually very efficient, in terms of my inquiries. Remember, the Diets will be meeting again before the year is out," Lady Penelope said. "We will need to keep the elites entertained to avoid suspicion. With my arrival, we will have plenty of it already. Especially since I will not be able to manipulate Cecilia into helping me as I had originally planned."

"Suspicion?" I frowned. "What are you talking about? There's no need to worry about anyone being suspicious of us. Unless it's possible you were lying about my father's will?"

Lady POW clapped her hands together. I had a feeling she was getting impatient herself, considering my previous concern for efficiency was marred by my own arguments. "You do not have to worry about Cecilia anymore, Eleanora. As I have said, you are free from her. You are under my protection now."

I stood there, wrapped in pins and measuring tape, wearing only my undergarments. I had to wonder if this was truly freedom, or if it was only a different kind of cage.

But there was one thing I wanted to know for certain.

"You had a message from Queen Victoria for Cecilia, but nothing for Ben or for me."

"Yes. When your mother moved out here, she married Dolf. He was almost bankrupt, and I bought the manor's property, as I said before, in order to help them out. When she died, I largely left it to my man of affairs. He had years in between her letters, as he was inquiring if she wanted to buy the property back. She never seemed to have the money for it. When Queen Victoria requested my presence here, I came with the intent to befriend her and settle our accounts."

"You are not going to do that now." There was no question behind my statement.

"Heavens, no. Now I will see she suffers in any way I can imagine. And I will stay here, overseeing your entrance to Society and Benedict's education. I will look for a new house in the city, but this one is suitable for now."

I felt my breath catch as I asked the question I had wanted to ask since she had revealed herself. "You really did not know about me or Ben, did you?"

"I see your powers of observation and deduction are well-honed. This is to our benefit. Even if you will have nothing to do with the murder, you will need to pay close attention to what you see and observe as you go about your role," Lady Penelope replied.

She was right about my powers of observation. That was proven once more as I noticed she did not answer my question. "When did you find out about us?" I tried again.

"It wasn't me, initially. Amir was the one who found you." She sighed. "When he saw you in town yesterday, he came rushing back to our hotel and told me he had discovered something of critical importance. I thought it was something related to the mission, but then … "

Suddenly, I would have given almost anything to have been there, to see the look on Lady POW's face, when Amir told her about me.

"And Ben?" I asked.

"You told me about Ben, just after I saw you myself for the first time."

"I remember that."

"Good. You will need to have a good memory," Lady Penelope said, trying to switch topics.

I did not let her. "*Máma* never wrote to you about me and Ben at all?"

She shook her head.

My throat was suddenly dry as I remembered meeting Amir. Briefly, I was torn between disgust at his thieving and my despondence over my mother's secretiveness; it was hard to decide which one felt worse.

"You mustn't hold it against her," Lady Penelope said. "Believe me, I could hold it against her enough for the two of us."

"Why did she—?"

"Everyone has secrets, Eleanora." Lady Penelope sat down at her small desk again, looking glum. "Everyone lies, everyone has secrets, and everyone has regrets. In the end, the truth cannot hide forever. But if you are to take your mother's place in the Order, you must accept you may never know some things. You will spend your life searching for truth, but there is no guarantee you will find it."

"I will," I insisted.

Lady POW gave me a rueful look. "Careful. Your naïve illusions will get the better of you if you let them. Thankfully, you will be following my lead on this mission."

"But surely that doesn't mean I will be running around and following your orders blindly?"

She gave me a look, and I knew at once that Lady POW was expecting *exactly* that.

I grimaced. "Really?"

"You've followed Cecilia's orders for years, from what the staff and others have told me," Lady Penelope pointed out. "And I know you do your best to follow the teachings of the church."

"My faith in God is not blind, and neither is my fear of Cecilia's wrath," I argued.

"True. But in regards to Lady Cecilia, I will say that you will need to unlearn what she has taught you. Being under another's authority is not necessarily something to abhor. A bad master, yes. But not mastery itself. She is not to be feared."

"I know you have taken care of her for the meantime," I said slowly, "but it might be a long time before I trust in it."

"And you have that right. But I would request you speed it up as much as possible. And not just for your own sake, but for your brother's, too. It is clear she has managed to do more damage to him than you."

There was no denying she was right about that. "You are correct. But that does not mean I will follow your orders without explanation."

"I am the leader of the Order, Eleanora. It is your job to follow my orders, whether you know why or not. My goodness, do you want me to put a formal request, as though I was petitioning the House of Lords? I will never understand your generation's comfort in bureaucracy." She gave me an assessing gaze. "But ..."

"But what?"

"But you and I must find a way to work together. So I will tell you this much. I was telling you the truth that I have been sent to Prague by the request of Queen

Victoria. She wants to make sure this area is secure, especially with all the trouble she is facing in India right now."

As Amelia began to pull the newer set of sleeves off my arms, I asked, "What's happening in India?"

"Trouble," Lady Penelope replied. "There are several in the government who are making an appeal to the queen to become their ruler."

"But India is on the other side of the world," I said. "How would she be able to rule it from England?"

"The same way she rules her other land holdings in the Americas and in Australia," Lady Penelope said with a sharp smile. "By good and gracious force, and the goodwill of God."

I frowned. "I guess that's quite an accomplishment. The Bohemians here cannot even rule themselves. The German Diet has been in power for so long. I do not know much about politics, but even I know their stalemates are legendary."

"Which is another reason why I have been asked to come," Lady Penelope said. "There are always people who look for something to be discontent over, and there are always people who seek to make their discontent the government's problem. The rule of law is precarious enough in this region, and the recent causes for alarm are particularly unsettling. If Prague was not experiencing an economic boom thanks to Bohemia's coal industry, we would see much more of a political uprising."

"I guess if the death of Dr. Artha was enough to disrupt the country, it is something to be concerned about."

"It is not just his death. The other two similar deaths were members of the Upper House of the Lords, who had a lot of influence in the *Reichsrat*, the German-speaking Parliament of Bohemia and Austria. The representatives from Mlada and Beroun were killed, supposedly by Jews."

I frowned. The death of Dr. Artha, and the other deaths that Ferdy and Clavan discussed the other night suddenly seemed even more sad.

A new thought struck me as I stood there. *I have a reason to go and see Ferdy again!*

My body prickled with excitement as I cheered silently, while Lady POW paced around the room.

"Of course, it is possible they are using the Jews as a scapegoat. Still, this is discomforting. There have been other deaths, too, where the Parliament members have likely been poisoned."

"Poison." I shuddered. "That sounds awful."

"It is. Especially since the Order has identified the poison in question. It makes it look like the individual has had a heart attack. It is only hours afterward that the skin turns blue at the fingers."

"If it works so well, why did they kill Dr. Artha in the street?" I asked. "And the others, too?"

"It is possible, though very unlikely, that the two Lords had a natural immunity to the poison," Lady Penelope said. "Thus, a different means of disposal would be required."

"And Dr. Artha?"

"We don't know yet if he was killed by the same people. That is one thing we are looking at in this investigation. But just because something looks a certain way, does not mean it is true. Once you see that, you begin to see everything else."

A small smile flitted to my lips as I recalled Ferdy's similar observations. "I suppose you're right, even though I have yet to see it."

"Then you must understand why this is too important for you to go about untested," Lady Penelope said. "There is more than your comfort at risk, Eleanora."

I snorted. "It's been years since I've had a life of comfort."

"Even in your life under your stepmother's cruelty," Lady Penelope said, "you have been sheltered from the world's pain. Do not think pain only takes something away from you. You have experienced things being taken away, but you have also been given things as a result."

I suddenly felt very small, as the world around me grew and I shrank.

In that moment, I did not know what was more overwhelming to me; the idea that my pain, as great as it was some days, was small compared to the world's, or the idea that the world's problems were much bigger and much more complex compared to mine.

As if she sensed my displacement, Lady Penelope nodded prudently. "You have lived your life here, on the outskirts of Prague and across the Vltava. As you grow older, you see more of the world and its politics, its hypocrisy, and its illusions. The trick is not to allow it to drag you down."

I was uncomfortable with the bitterness in her voice, but it was not enough to stop me from seeing that, despite her cynicism, Lady POW was still determined to accomplish her goal. "Yes, Lady Penelope."

She gave me an approving look, no doubt at my humble tone. "Whatever our association comes to be, Eleanora, I will always be your grandmother, and I am very proud to have that title. When Eleanor died, I thought all was lost. Now I know that I was wrong. Of all things I could have been wrong about, I am very glad it was that."

Looking me up and down with a critical eye once more, she added, "Which is why I am going to tell you now that you will need to go on a diet and begin an exercise regime as we make our way into Prague's Society. You are much too soft around your middle to be considered fashionable. The empress would be frightened if she ever met you in this state."

I groaned. "Empress Elisabeth is much too thin," I said with a shudder. "I have heard the rumors that she has a thirteen-inch waist, and if my hips are good for birthing, I doubt I will ever have her proportions."

"If you are going to add to your stepmother's comeuppance, we must make you a sensation, yes?"

She must have expected me to nod or voice my agreement, but my accommodating disposition was gone. "A sensation is more feasible than a stick, Madame."

Lady POW chuckled. "Oh, Eleanora. You do remind me so much of Eleanor. You will be a legend among the town within a fortnight."

Pudgy hips and all, I thought with a smirk.

9

◊

Before long, I had the distinct feeling that if I was going to be a sensation in less than a fortnight, I was going to spend at least half that time deprived of sleep and food.

"Come along, Eleanora," Lady Penelope called. "We have several more appointments to keep yet."

"Surely you are jesting," I muttered under my breath, as I hurried after Lady POW. We had just come from a milliner's shop, and I was certain I had seen enough hats and bonnets and caps to last me a lifetime.

I yawned as I caught up to my grandmother's spritely steps and decided to be grateful we were at least out in the city. Lady Penelope had spent the previous evening drilling pure boredom into my flesh in the form of etiquette review. I had been astonished to find whole books dedicated to discussing how a lady should walk and laugh and fold her hands and a million other useless things.

My mind felt so stuffed, I had several nightmares surrounding *The Ladies' Guide to Excellence and Etiquette*, easily the most loquacious offender. I decided once I learned enough for Lady POW, I would burn that hideous book.

"This has been a wonderful day for shopping, Eleanora." Lady Penelope glanced around Prague's crowded streets. I had to agree; there had been some snowfall over the past couple of days, preventing us from heading out for any significant errands, but today the sun was out, and the chill in the air added a shine to the whole city. "By the time we are finished here, all of Prague will know who you are and how much you are worth. No one will be able to resist talking about you."

"I hope it is not because you have paid them to do so," I said as a coachman offered me his hand. I climbed up into the coach and settled in the cushions across from Lady POW, while another one loaded some of our new purchases into the back.

"I guess this is the cover part of your plan?" I glanced outside, peeking through the silken coach curtains. As we passed by, heads turned, eyes widened, and mouths dropped.

Lady POW chuckled as I buried my backside even more into the seat cushions. "You will need to get used to this, Eleanora," she said. "You will need to command their attention, and not only keep it, but manipulate it to achieve your ends."

"I'll go ahead and write that down."

Lady POW only nodded curtly at my supposed diligence before starting another lecture of some sort.

THE ORDER OF THE CRYSTAL DAGGERS

Another reason to envy Ben, I thought. He was allowed to stay home in the shadows, while I was forced into the limelight. I did not get a chance to talk with him earlier, before Lady POW summoned me to try on my new walking dress, but I knew he was starting his own form of training with Harshad and Amir.

At the thought of Lady POW's associates—the sympathetic thief and the angry colleague—I decided not to envy Ben after all. Instead, I focused on my own good fortune.

It is rather nice to be in the city without having to worry about selling anything.

As we passed by the Old Town Square, I leaned closer to the window again, suddenly wondering if I would be able to spot Ferdy's faded hat among the crowds.

"Have you heard from any of your contacts here?" I asked Lady POW, unable to resist looking for my own.

"The Minister-President, Count Potocki, is unusually busy," Lady Penelope said. "He has not returned my inquiries, but I have secured invitations to a ball he is hosting for the political elite at Queen Anne's Royal Summerhouse."

"We are going to see him there, then?"

"Yes." Lady Penelope's eyes gleamed. "He is the newly promoted Minister-President, and lately he has been seen in the company of Karl Marcelin, a young man making waves in society because of his disdain for the Emperor."

"I see," I replied neutrally, beginning to realize just how little I knew of politics. "Should we be concerned with Mr. Marcelin? Did he know Dr. Artha?"

"I have not yet discovered an association with Dr. Artha. From what my informants have told me, Marcelin is highly educated, having gone to Oxford in London, and then studying at the university here in Prague. He is close to Benedict's age, but his ambition would suit a much older man."

"And that is a bad thing?"

"Not necessarily," Lady Penelope said. "He is ambitious, but he is looking for funding for his various campaigns. I am curious as to why. From what I have seen, he has always been able to afford quality items, including his education. I wonder if his family is not supportive of his political career. There is not much else I have heard."

"Are not politicians always concerned with money?" I said.

"True. But Marcelin returned to Prague a month ago, and that is when other political figures began dying mysterious deaths," Lady Penelope said. "Dr. Artha is just the latest, and Count Potocki is my best lead. Thus, we will investigate this new young friend of his."

"Do you believe Count Potocki will back Mr. Marcelin's career in politics financially?"

"Possibly, but it would reflect poorly on him as an active agent. His vocal support is enough. In regard to finances, Marcelin is single, and rumors have said he is looking for an heiress to marry." Her eyes glittered. "Which is where you will come in."

"You don't want me to marry him, do you?" I asked, suddenly frightened and appalled.

"Heavens no, Eleanora." Lady POW shook her head. "For now, I plan on collecting several invitations for various dinners, social calls, and balls in the coming weeks. I am sure you will get your chance to playfully ignore him, drive him mad, and then make him spill all his secrets."

"What?" I sputtered.

"Calm down," Lady Penelope said. "We are working with a short window of time, and we cannot wait for a full, fashionable courtship and wedding."

"Oh." I was relieved.

"A quick seduction might be all we need, should it come to that."

I started coughing.

"Oh, do grow up, Eleanora," Lady Penelope scolded. "I have no patience for this."

"But—"

"But what?" Lady Penelope looked down her nose at me. "You know I need the cover, Eleanora, and the cover I will have. But in the meantime, you will just have to trust me."

"Fine," I growled. "But I don't want to talk about intercourse."

"For now, you must focus on the task at hand. If you want to help, pay attention to the things you see, and what the people say. Learn your lessons well. Observation is a dying art, Eleanora, and you will never gain the upper hand on your opponent if you are too concerned with yourself." She glared at me. "Especially if you are worried I will auction you off to a suitor of my choosing."

I desperately wanted to roll my eyes, but I only gave her a contrite look. It seemed to be the quickest way to appease her. "Apologies, Lady Penelope."

My hands curled in the walking dress I was wearing. The bright yellow material had turned several heads as I walked through the various shops with Lady POW at my side. I had to give credit to her seamstresses, and of course to Lady POW herself. If she wanted me to stir up rumors and draw attention, she had certainly succeeded.

"That color is splendid on you, Eleanora," Lady Penelope had said, when I was unnerved at the thought of wearing it. "It brings out the blue of your eyes and complements your dark hair very nicely."

I was still unsure, but I felt better after she told me my mother favored yellow.

"So far things are going according to plan," Lady Penelope said. "You have captured the attention of Prague beautifully today. Even your slipups have been seen as endearing. I thought Madame Bourgeois was going to kick us out of her shop after you insisted on the roomier sleeves for your gowns, and then you convinced her that you intend to set the trends rather than follow them."

I laughed nervously. "Persuading others must be a family trait, since you were able to convince Cecilia to let me go."

"It was not persuasion that won over the dressmaker," Lady Penelope said. "It was sensibility mixed with charm and tact. I was impressed myself, Eleanora."

It was the first time I could remember her praising me for something I had not struggled to learn, and I allowed myself to savor my first taste of success.

"Convincing Madame Bourgeois to mix in classic Bohemian style with French influence was good for us, too, I think," I said.

Lady Penelope nodded, as her coach came to a stop at Market Square. "I am going to check with some of the vendors. Use this chance to buy whatever else you'd like, and have the bill sent to your stepmother."

"What?" All of my previous purchases ran through my mind. We had to have spent at least two years' worth of income from my father's tenants. "You didn't charge everything to her, did you?"

"Don't worry about the money, Eleanora. It is only to give Cecilia a good scare. That is all."

I laughed a moment later, remembering to do it that musical, charming way *The Ladies' Guide to Excellence and Etiquette* instructed, with a high pitch and my hand covering my mouth in a delicate manner.

As Lady POW strode through the flanks of people, her steps sure and direct as she headed away from me, I felt free once more.

I roamed slowly through the market, ignoring several gazes and open stares more easily, knowing I was supposed to command attention. It helped that I knew there was a footman trailing me, and Lady POW was nearby if I needed her.

I went up to Madame Balthazar's shop, and she greeted me with a confused and happy look.

"My dear Miss Eleanora. My, you look so lovely today!"

"Thank you, Madame," I said, giving her a small curtsy, despite remembering *The Ladies' Guide to Excellence and Etiquette* forbade such posturing to my economic and social inferiors. "I have come into an inheritance from my, um, grandmother," I said. "The Dowager Duchess of Wellington."

"I heard Lord Wellington had multiple affairs," Madame Balthazar said. "I did not realize he married again."

"Well, the title and the land all went to his sons," I said, glad Lady POW had prepared me for such questions. "It seems he married my grandmother and settled a handsome portion on her, as his second wife, when he died. They were not married for a long time."

Madame Balthazar looked impressed as I reiterated all the details Lady POW told me about her scandalous courtship and marriage to one of London's most renowned rakes. She also told me to make things up if I did not remember all of it, because people remembered general stories and key details, but never the full story.

"If you want to be remembered," she had said, "be clear in your speech and emphasize your talking points."

It sounded nice, but I was not sure reality agreed with her.

"This red silk will look lovely on you," Madame Balthazar said, as I began to look at her displays. "It is perfect for you, Miss. You must wear it to a fancy ball and tell all your new friends to come and see me."

It did not take much for me to agree with her. As she totaled up my expenses, the mention of a fancy ball stirred my memory. I thought about the ripped invitation Ferdy had given me to the Advent Ball hosted by Empress Maria Anna.

I wonder if Lady POW knows about the ball.

Thinking it over, I decided I would keep my invitation from Ferdy a secret, but I would talk to Lady POW about the ball. I did not think she would appreciate Ferdy's insistence any more than she would enjoy the ripped letter.

"Madame Balthazar," I said slowly, "do you know of a street urchin named Ferdy? He says he knows a lot of vendors around here."

"Oh, of course," she said. "He brokered a trade between me and a midwife just a few weeks ago, when my daughter became feverish after delivering her twins."

"He seems to be good at making deals," I said.

She laughed. "That he is, Miss. But he is, too, a very kind young man."

"Do you know where I might find him?" I asked, trying not to blush. "I … I actually had him help me sell something before, and I wanted to see about giving him his full pay."

"I have not seen him in a few days," she said. "He has probably been down by the riverbanks again. There are fights there every week, and there are plenty of men who enjoy watching a good fight and having a good gamble."

"Fighting?"

Madame Balthazar chuckled. "Young men easily get bored. If you are fond of him, be grateful the worst thing he does is attend fights down by the riverbanks. Well," she said, wrinkling her nose in distaste. "I suppose he does hang around the Jewish Quarter a lot, too."

"I see." After a quick moment, I decided to risk her scorn. "Why is it bad he associates with the Jews?"

"Oh, poor dear. The Jews cause trouble wherever they go," Madame Balthazar said. "Rumors have been circulating that they are starting to form their own political group here in Prague. And that is the last thing Prague needs now—another group of people who feel entitled to dictate our laws just because they live here."

"Aren't you a migra—never mind." I brushed the matter aside. "How much are my purchases?"

I walked out of the vendor after instructing Madame Balthazar to send the bill to the castle with a bad taste in my mouth. I did not like Madame Balthazar's opinion on the Jews, especially after meeting Mr. Clavan.

My heart swelled at the thought of Ferdy's kindness. He was clearly a man who refused to look down on any person, no matter their ethnicity, culture, religion, or even their social status.

Thinking of him proved to be an enjoyable distraction. I made my way through the market, glancing around, hoping to see Ferdy's cheeky grin and silver eyes light up in mine.

I hope he wasn't lying about wanting to see me again.

The sudden thought made my face flush with heat, and I struggled to dismiss the sudden mix of hope and fear inside of me.

I shook my head, trying to clear my thoughts. Even if he had been lying, I still needed to see him. He was the one who had information on Dr. Artha's death, and Lady POW and I needed it.

My steps came to a slow stop as my hands felt clammy. The footman who had been following me bumped into me as I stopped short, abruptly frightened. What if the reason I was not able to find Ferdy was because he was in trouble? He was the one who told me the details of Dr. Artha's death.

Suddenly, there was more than one reason I wanted to find him.

"Hurry. We need to get back," I ordered the footman, and we began to head toward the coach again, where Lady POW was waiting with a triumphant gleam in her eye.

"We have just been invited to several events," Lady Penelope told me. "A concert, a picnic, a house party, and more! We will be booked from dusk till dawn for the next several days, and I have an invite from Lady Hohenwart herself! This is excellent—"

"Lady Penelope, we need to talk."

"What is it?"

THE ORDER OF THE CRYSTAL DAGGERS

"I have some information," I said, and Lady Penelope quickly ushered me into the carriage.

"What is it?" she asked.

I quickly told her everything that Ferdy and Clavan had told me, desperately raking my mind for the smallest details. As I spoke, I left out their names, hoping she would not ask for them.

"I have received that information already." But then she paused for a moment, looking thoughtful. "You said he came out of the Church of Our Lady of the Snows?" she asked. "That is unusual. He was a patron of St. Nicholas for years."

"Yes, that was the church where he was," I said. "Or something like that, anyway. But I am more worried that the people who told me this are in danger."

"That is the nature of the job," Lady Penelope replied.

"I still think we should go and find the people who told me," I said, keeping my tone careful so I would not reveal anything. "We should warn them. What if we go over to the Jewish Quarter, around where I heard the news, just to see if everything is okay?"

I did not think it was possible to surprise Lady POW, but she blinked twice before she said anything. "There is a line between eccentricity and impropriety you do not cross, Eleanora," she began. "You hint and tease, but never promise anything—no stolen kisses in the gardens, no getting caught *in flagrante delicto*. Going to the Jewish Quarter is not a breach of propriety in Prague, but it promises only the worst sort of trouble for your reputation."

"But it would make people talk, and we might be able to find out more for me as a cover."

"That is a job for your brother and Amir to handle. It would be good practice for Benedict. I will assign them to take care of the task."

"But—"

"Enough, Eleanora." She shook her head. "There is no reason to believe that your source is in trouble. You are concerned for the well-being of others, which is a natural inclination you have, from what I have seen in how you care for Benedict. But you cannot—I repeat, you cannot—allow your feelings to cloud your judgment. For now, as you learn about the Order and work on developing your skills, just follow my orders."

Slowly, I nodded, even though I disagreed with her. As I sat there, I was strongly reminded of Cecilia's way of ordering me around.

I stared down at my folded hands, imagining Ferdy attacked or running from trouble, picturing the Cabal burning to the ground as the neighborhood screamed in panic.

My fingers tightened into fists as I made a decision.

If Lady POW was going to act like a spymaster version of Cecilia, I would do what I had done in the past. I would agree with her to her face, and then when she was not paying attention, I would do what I wanted.

And I will get Ben to help me. If it is his job to help gather information now, he should be able to take care of it for me.

"I am glad that is settled. Now, Eleanora, let us go over our upcoming schedule," Lady Penelope said. "The Hohenwart Ball is tomorrow, and this is our first chance to mingle among the political elites. We will have to make sure your gown is ready, your hair is washed, your shoes are … "

As Lady POW went through the details of the ball, I smiled and nodded. Inside, my mind was only thinking of Ferdy and our adventure into the *Josefskà*. I desperately wanted him to appear in the streets as we passed, even though I knew I could not step out and see him without causing a tidal wave of whispers.

But his smile would have brightened my mood considerably.

10

◊

The Hohenwart Ball was to be my official introduction into Prague's Society, and if I was going to move up in Lady Penelope's limited measurement, everything had to be perfect.

Where have I heard that before?

As Lady POW's carriage cheerfully rolled down the city streets as the moon made its appearance on the horizon, I remembered Cecilia's warning the night of the Duke's arrival. I had a feeling, especially after hearing the Duke of Moravia had left to stay at a friend's townhouse, she still would find a way to make good on her promise.

"Come now, Eleanora, make haste," Lady Penelope hissed. "This is your first ball, and I want it to go perfectly."

We arrived at the Hohenwart house in Lady POW's grand coach. I nervously gripped at my skirts as we stepped down and headed toward the grand manor.

As Lady POW began to list the various social niceties I had to remember, I grumbled to myself, swearing in French under my breath the way Tulia had taught me.

Lady POW likely heard me, because a second later she stopped short, whirling around to confront me. "Listen to me now, Eleanora," she said. "If there is any doubt—any whatsoever—that you are going to be able to do this, I will offer you this chance now. We will turn around, claim an illness, and opt for a soft launch at another ball. But if you stay the course, after tonight, there is no going back. You will reap the consequences of your choice."

She had not even finished speaking before I knew the truth, and I knew my answer.

It was already too late to turn back. Ferdy could be in danger. I had to find a way to make sure he was safe.

After all, Dr. Artha and many others were already dead. How could I go back to knowing nothing but my life under Cecilia? And even with Lady POW allowing me to be free of her, what was the point of being free if I used it to only serve myself?

"I'm ready," I said.

"Are you sure?" Lady Penelope arched her brow. "Last chance."

"I already said I was ready." I whipped out my fan and flapped it furiously. "Now, don't make me repeat it, or I might just change my mind."

At my show of spirit, Lady POW smirked. "Good. Now, we do not want to disappoint Lady Hohenwart. Hurry."

Easy for her to say. My toes were squeezed inside small-heeled shoes, and I had been stuffed into a tight corset. I wondered how my dancing would be affected, with all the petticoats and bindings and fluffy things I was wearing; my gown had to be at least a good fifty pounds by itself.

My hair was pulled back for the evening, while several of my curls playfully slipped free from their pins. I had a small amount of rouge on my face, and even with the little bit I had on, I knew why rouge was supposed to be scandalous. I felt like a mask had been painted on my face. I was literally wearing a lie.

The analogy worked in more ways than one, since my smile was blatantly false as I made my way up the entrance to the Hohenwart Ball.

It was a magnificent house. It stood on a small hill just outside of Prague, on the opposite side from my father's manor; it had taken Lady POW's coach a long time to weave through the city streets. While I had enjoyed the sight of Prague and its glowing nightlife, Lady POW relished the chance to give me one last session of etiquette review.

When I asked about being late, Lady Penelope had replied, "*Psh*. We are fashionably late, and I intend for us to only be fashionable tonight, Eleanora."

It seemed she was no longer content for that, I noticed, as she cajoled me up the stairs.

"Walk gracefully," she murmured.

This was my first big test, and I wanted to show Lady POW I could handle my part. But her orders, while I imagine she thought they would be helpful, were only making my nerves worse. I arched my brow as I glanced down at her feet. "Are you wearing heels?"

"Watch your manners, Eleanora."

"I'm so sorry, I forgot old people can't hear as well," I said more loudly. Another lady and her companion glanced over my way, clearly trying not to laugh at my assentation.

Lady POW frowned, but she said nothing.

I turned my attention to the grand house once more. Several glowing chandeliers and candelabras were scattered throughout; in the grand, gothic windows, I could see billions of lights shining like stars against the night.

I hope it will not be this cold inside, I thought, snuggling into my cloak.

"The red looks wonderful on you," Lady Penelope said. "Be sure to stay away from red wine tonight."

I rolled my eyes when I was sure she was not looking. When she whacked me with her fan lightly a moment later, I knew I had failed.

There is just no sneaking around her, is there?

"Get it out of your system before we get in. Remember your main objective tonight, Eleanora. Go in there and make people talk. I will be watching, but I will also be working. Now, do not fail me."

"I won't."

As the footman came and took our cloaks, I took a deep breath, trying to calm myself.

It was not just Lady POW I wanted to impress. I hoped to make my mother proud, and I wanted to protect my country. It was frustrating that my stomach was turning in knots, my feet were sore, and I was secretly worried for a street urchin who managed to charm his way into my life.

As I stepped into the house, seeing the throngs of people before me, I was relieved to be here in service to my country. *I could be here actually looking for entertainment, rather than here on a mission.*

"Over here," Lady Penelope whispered. "We will enter the greeting line and introduce you to Lady Hohenwart."

I followed her gaze to see our hostess for the evening. Lady Hohenwart was matronly, wearing a fashionable turban covering her whitening hair and a dress even more heavy-looking than my own. She wore the deep purple gown well, even though she was quite thick around the middle. Even with the corset, her gown was pulled too tightly across her bosom.

When she greeted my grandmother, Lady POW gave her a slight bow of the head, and she began giggling like a schoolgirl.

"Oh, Penelope," she crooned. "I'm honored, absolutely honored, that you decided to come. Imagine! The Iron Dowager in my ballroom tonight."

"We thought it was a prudent stop on our way around the city tonight," Lady Penelope replied, before turning to me. "Now that I have been reunited with my lovely granddaughter, nothing will make me so happy as to share the sights with her. May I introduce my Eleanora?"

"Madame," I said, giving her a perfect curtsy.

Lady Hohenwart giggled again. "Oh, you are just lovely, Lady Eleanora," she said. "Please, stay beside me. I simply must introduce you to my guests. We have some of the nation's finest coming tonight."

Lady Penelope pulled out her fan. "If you insist."

We stood there for the next hour, as more people began to gravitate toward us. Lady POW was practically radiating joy as I was introduced to several members of the Upper and Lower House of Lords. Soon after we joined Lady Hohenwart, I noticed that more and more young men were coming up to pay their respects.

I soon found myself surrounded by lords and ladies, members of the militia and the Diets, all of them asking me questions and telling me stories and fawning over me or my gown or anything witty I happened to say.

The attention was intoxicating at first; as I laughed and smiled with them, and as I made them laugh and smile back, I almost forgot why I was supposed to be there.

When I noticed how comfortable I was, it was as if a spell had broken. Thankfully, the crowds around us gradually thinned, as more people sought drinks and dancing, and others made their way to the gardens.

I learned too many names and saw too many faces, and I definitely had my hand kissed more than I would have ever liked.

Thank you, Lord, for allowing me to wear gloves.

Several of the gentlemen asked for me to dance, and Lady POW, despite all her trouble, declined all of them.

Until he arrived.

Long moments passed, and eventually several of the other men began to part the crowd. I looked over to see who was causing the disorganized shuffle.

It was a man; he was tall, with hair the color of night, with just a hint of brown mixed in. His features seemed a little hawkish, but not in a necessarily unattractive way. I could tell from the storms in his eyes he was a man of great passion, and he controlled himself with an iron will. If that alone was not enough to make me look twice, I saw he wore the elegant clothes of a traveled man, with the confidence to match. He stood out among the others instantly as a man who was walking among the world in hopes of leading it.

Even Lady POW seemed to straighten as he came before us.

"Mr. Marcelin," Lady Hohenwart said. Her voice was so squeaky with excitement I had a feeling this was going to be the climax of her night.

"That's Karl Marcelin," Lady POW whispered as she nudged me, and I nodded. I was supposed to see what I could find out about him.

"Lady Hohenwart," he replied. He took her hand and bowed over it reverently. "It is wonderful to be in your company again."

As he bowed, I saw he was glancing at me from the corner of his eye, studying me. I used my fan to hide my blush; so far, the other dandies had been overtly delighted by my appearance and charm, but none of them had seemed so intentional in their attentions. I took the moment to study him back, letting him know in my own way I would not allow him an easy conquest.

Lady Hohenwart also noticed his interest. "May I introduce my dear friend, Lady Penelope Ollerton-Wellesley, and her granddaughter, Lady Eleanora of Bohemia?"

"Enchanté," I murmured, as he held my hand. Even through my gloves, I could feel the solid quality behind his strength. "It is a pleasure to meet you, Mr. Marcelin."

"Karl here is a personal friend of Count Potocki and my husband," Lady Hohenwart said. "He has become a very prominent figure among the Diets since returning from London."

"The only reason I was invited tonight, I assure you," Karl replied.

"Oh, Karl, you are too much." Lady Hohenwart laughed before turning to me. "Is he not, Eleanora?"

"I confess, I am not certain," I replied, with just a hint of ennui. "I have only just met Mr. Marcelin."

"You have excellent judgment in such matters, my lady," Karl said, and at once, he was ready to meet my own challenge with one of his own.

I never lost his gaze as I gave him a small, thoughtful smile. "You have only met me just now yourself."

"Then you simply must get more acquainted with Karl, Eleanora," Lady Hohenwart insisted.

"He seems like a gentleman, but he is hardly duty bound to insist on my company."

"I only wish that I could," Karl replied, "but that would hardly allow me to be a true gentleman."

At his remark, I could almost feel Lady POW's excitement beside me. I knew he was on her list, and his acceptance of me proved my exhausting efforts to impress the right people worked well enough to give me a preliminary acceptance into their circles.

"If you want to convince me," I said, still playing coy, "perhaps a compliment or two would help?"

"Lady Eleanora," Karl said. "May I say, you are the most enchanting of flowers in this garden of beauty tonight?"

"I suppose," I said, "since you have just said it, it would be best for me to allow it."

Lady POW and Lady Hohenwart laughed.

"What spirit she has," Lady Hohenwart cheered.

"Indeed," Karl replied. He reached out for my hand once more. "May I then request the honor of your next dance?"

THE ORDER OF THE CRYSTAL DAGGERS

I looked to Lady POW modestly, even though I already knew what her answer would be. Still, it made me look like a dutiful heir, and one who was not necessarily impressed by manners or the man himself.

"Go on, Eleanora," Lady Penelope said. "You have my permission."

There was enough of a sneer in her smile that I decided she was really saying, *"You have my permission to make a fool of yourself."*

I hated to admit, it was possible she was right. I told Lady POW before that I had learned to dance several years ago, when Priscilla was taught. The instructor, Mr. Binghamton, had caught me watching them several times, and after my stepsister retired for the day, he would allow me to match her success.

After all the shopping around and reviewing etiquette with Lady POW, I had not wanted to review dancing, too.

Lady Penelope pushed me forward, playfully laughing as a cover. "My Eleanora is so modest."

"Karl here has a wondrous reputation as a dancer." Lady Hohenwart glowed with such motherly approval, I wondered if she thought she was helping Lady POW play matchmaker tonight. "She will be in good hands."

"Yes," Karl agreed. "She will."

Grinning broadly to hide my discomfort, I finally allowed him to lead me down the stairs to the dance floor.

God, please help me. Knowing that while my grandmother was content to ignore my silent pleas, God had promised never to do so.

Whispers started immediately. The hushed tones and the soft words licked at my skin, sliding over me with their own sense of grotesque pleasure and perverse delight. The crowd's collective leering and gossip was inescapable; I had to focus hard on Karl's supportive arm as we made our way down to the ballroom dancefloor.

Everyone else seemed to fade as I stepped out onto the marble. As we walked toward the middle of the ballroom, I smiled up at Karl, remembering what Ferdy had told me when we first met.

"Everyone lies about something."

Lady POW wanted me to be a sensation. That meant I had to command attention and control the situation, just as she had taught me.

"Well, sir, I will give you credit," I said. "You do not seem to be overly upset at all the gossip you're sure to inspire."

"I might inspire the gossip," he said, "but you will inspire the poetry."

I laughed, tapping him with my fan playfully, hating myself every step of the way. "What an outrageous thing to say. After all, we haven't even danced yet. For all you know, I could wind up stepping on your feet for the next several moments."

He likely had no idea how much of a possibility it was.

Karl gave me a slow smile. "I'd still risk it."

"Well, quite the gambler, are you?" I needled him. "This is hardly a proper topic for conversation, sir."

"It is entirely proper for a man to be frightened by asking the most vibrant and lovely lady in the room to dance," Karl said. "Especially when you are the loveliest lady in any room I've seen in Prague."

"Well, thank you," I murmured, humbled more than amused. I prayed desperately I would not cripple his toes. While I was trying to decide if he had anything to do with a murder, I had to admit he did not seem like the type.

As the music began and we talked more, I saw he was very sensible, smart, and graceful on his feet. Even as he talked, he led me through the steps of a waltz perfectly. Karl lived up to his reputation as a stellar dancer, and the two or three times I tripped, he caught me with an easy grace I was sure even Lady POW would admire. I fumbled along after him, but I still felt graceful as he caught me.

The waltz was scandalous in many London drawing rooms, and even more so outside of the city. It was said to inspire the worst sort of sin, and as I allowed Karl to lead me, I realized it was very easy to slip into daydreams and lose sight of the task at hand.

Lady POW wanted me to be a sensation, but I wanted to find the truth. I had to protect Ferdy and his friends, after all, and others like Dr. Artha deserved justice.

"So, what brings you to Prague, sir?" I asked. "I might be the loveliest lady here by your judgement, but I cannot imagine I hold a candle to the ladies of Paris or London, or even Rome."

"Most assuredly, my lady, you need not fish for compliments. Especially when you do it in such a manner that it makes it hard for me to assure you I came here just for you."

"It would be hard to do that regardless," I said. "Especially when it is well known you are great friends with Count Potocki."

"Do you know of him?" Karl asked, giving me a dazzling smile.

For some reason, I suddenly had a much harder time concentrating. His smile seemed to tug at me, and I wondered suddenly if we had met before.

I quickly dismissed the possibility. Lady POW told me that he had just come back from his studies abroad, like Alex. If I thought he was familiar, it was likely because Lady POW had reviewed the politics of Prague for hours before so I

THE ORDER OF THE CRYSTAL DAGGERS

would have something engaging to discuss, but I was hoping Karl would have other interests. I doubted it, as he warmed to the subject.

"I'm afraid I have not had the pleasure of meeting him yet," I said, realizing Karl was still waiting for an answer.

"Alfred—the Minister-President—is indeed a good friend and mentor of mine."

At least Karl is not hard to look at, I noticed, recalling that Minister-President Potocki was easily forty years my senior. I was not certain of Karl's age, but I doubted he was much older than Ben. If he had just finished his schooling abroad, he would be in his early twenties. Entertaining Karl, and digging down to his secrets, would be easier and likely more interesting.

"So you are here to amuse yourself with the Diets, perhaps?" I asked.

"Are you interested in politics, Lady Eleanora?"

"Only minimally," I said, wanting to keep the focus on him. "But surely that is not the case for you?"

He gave me a smile, one that was both rueful and playful. "Well, my lady, you are indeed correct. I am very interested in what is happening in Prague."

"I did not realize there were so many interesting things happening in Prague's politics. Enlighten me," I pressed, glad Ben was nowhere around to see me. Either he would be disgusted by my performance, or he would have laughed me off the dance floor.

Or he would have hit Karl, for the look on his face as he stared at me.

"I am here as an elected orator," he said. "I will be serving directly under Count Potocki while his successor is elected. He is set on retiring in the new year, due to his health and his interests."

"Are you hoping you will be on the ballot to replace him?"

"It would be the greatest honor of my life to serve Bohemia," he said, his words weighted with passion.

It sounded nice, but I wished he were less vague in his response. "So that is a yes?"

"It is of little consequence," he said, ducking my question once again. "I will say, as of now, I am merely attempting to fulfill the role I was born for. It remains to be seen if God should grant me such a privilege. I have great hope that I can broker deals that would fundamentally change the course of Bohemia's future."

"You must have a lot of connections," I said. "In politics, it is not what you know, so much as who you know."

"I do have the connections," Karl agreed. "But I am always open to more."

I knew he was flirting with me, but his words were infused with such intent that I could only laugh. Otherwise, I would have been frightened. "Are you proposing to me, Mr. Marcelin?"

"Karl, please," he said, this time more easily. "If you are so curious about my intentions, I insist you call me by my given name."

"Surely one cannot fault me for wondering, Mr. Marcelin," I said, intentionally addressing him formally as he spun me around once more. "My grandmother is searching for a husband for me, and she would be remiss in her duty if she did not see to my welfare."

"She is looking, then?" Karl gave me an eager smile. "I heard rumors that she would allow you a Season or two."

"She may be the one looking," I said carefully, "but I am the one who will do the finding."

"You are certainly clever. I must admit, that makes conversation with you all the more engaging."

The music fell to a close, and the audience applauded. I gave Karl a quick curtsy, but before I could excuse myself, he reached for my arm.

"Allow me to escort you back to Lady Wellington," he said. He tucked my hand around his arm and kept it there. "I would ask you for another dance, but I have a feeling your grandmother would object at the gossip."

I hid a smile; Karl's assumption was dead wrong.

"So many people are here, and this is such a beautiful place," I said, as we weaved our way through the crowded room.

"The view from the garden balcony is wonderful," Karl said. "You can see all the city's lights, even the ones down by the Vltava."

"I will have to see it for myself."

I looked back over toward the stairs, hoping Lady POW would give me some idea of what to do next. I blinked in surprise, watching as Lord Maximillian began talking to her.

"I wonder what His Grace is doing here," I said.

"Oh, you mean Lord Maximillian?" Karl followed my gaze. "I imagine he was invited, since he is staying with at the Hohenwart estate for the rest of the year. Lord Hohenwart is a close friend of his."

"He is?"

"Of a sort. Lord Hohenwart, along with Alfred—excuse me, Count Potocki—are avid beer enthusiasts. Both of them have stock in distilleries. But Lord Maximillian is from Moravia, with several estate vineyards. They have argued for

THE ORDER OF THE CRYSTAL DAGGERS

years over which is better, but they also exchange bottles and harvesting information every so often."

"Do you also have an interest in such topics?" I asked.

Karl shook his head. "I have little interest in where my beer and wine come from, so long as it is enjoyable."

"I see." I started to feel a slight panic. We were getting closer to Lady POW and Lord Maximillian, and I still had nothing on Karl that seemed to help our investigation much.

"Lord Maximillian has generously gifted His Imperial Majesty with a full shipment of wine this year," Karl said. "It will arrive just in time for the Advent Ball Empress Maria Anna is hosting this year. I know she is most pleased. Several other representatives from around Bohemia are acquainted with his estate's reputation."

The Advent Ball? I thought of the ripped invitation Ferdy had handed me days ago.

"Will you be attending the Advent Ball this year?" I asked. "I have heard it is wonderful."

"I have attended it before, though it has been some years since my last attendance," Karl said. "It is indeed quite wonderful. Her Imperial Majesty the former Empress does an incredible job each year."

"You have attended it before, so that must mean you are from Prague, then?"

"Yes," Karl replied. "I have been many places, but I was born here, and I relish the chance to be back."

"Where are you staying?" I asked. "With your family?"

"I am staying with a friend," Karl replied. "Perhaps you have heard of him? Roman Szapira of Slavuta is hosting me for the first part of the season, until after the Advent Ball. He is a friend and confidant of the count's, and one of the most well-known architects in Prague. He is currently being commissioned to renovate Prague Castle's wine cellar."

"His name sounds familiar," I lied. "Who else does he know?"

"He would likely know of your grandmother," Karl answered. "She is quite famous."

I laughed in that fake, overly charming way. "Of course Lady PO—I mean, my grandmother—is well known. She is very rich and very difficult to ignore. Would she know your friend, Mr. Szapira?"

"I am not certain. Roman is very well known in other respects. Like Lord Maximillian, he has a large vineyard, and I know he and the count argue over the virtues of the vine quite frequently."

I will have to ask Lady POW about him.

As if she knew I was longing for her counsel, Lady POW suddenly stood before me—on the arm of Lord Maximillian. The Duke looked down his pepper and salt mustache at me with curious eyes.

"Eleanora," Lady Penelope said. "I have accepted His Grace's invitation to dance. Please wait for me with Lady Hohenwart."

"I shall watch over her for you, Madame." Karl patted my arm gallantly. "I am greatly enjoying her company."

I almost rolled my eyes as Lady POW profusely thanked him. What did Karl really think he was doing for me? Taking on a dragon? Slaying a witch? Rescuing me? Keeping me company as I stood with the hostess of the evening hardly seemed like something worthy of a grand announcement.

"I hope you are not enjoying her too much," Lady Penelope told Karl. "I have heard you are in the market for a bride, and I fear I cannot part with my Eleanora so easily, now that we have been reunited."

Karl smirked. "I assure you, I am up for the job of convincing you, should it be necessary, Madame."

Pardon me? I was too shocked to say anything. Was he joking? I wondered. Who really decided they were going to marry someone after one dance?

Before I could make my own statement on the matter, Lord Maximillian turned to me. "Perhaps you will say hello to my daughter, Lady Eleanora," Lord Maximillian suggested. "I do not believe you had much time to converse the last time our paths crossed."

It took no effort to remember Teresa Marie's entitled self-absorption and her churlish display at Cecilia's dinner party.

"Perhaps I will, Your Grace." I gave him a quick curtsy before Karl and I headed over to stand next to Lady Hohenwart and Teresa Marie.

It was hard not to feel like a novice standing next to her. Teresa Marie was expertly dressed, with her hair piled up on her head, with a few stray curls twisting free. Her amber hair gleamed under the chandelier and the pastel colors of her dress seemed to make her skin glow, while a string of ruffled flowers winded around her bodice like a vine, looping itself under her bustle.

In my bright red dress, with its simple French silhouette and lace trim at the sleeves, I easily saw the contrast between us. I had a feeling that, as we stood there, others did, too.

"Well, well, Lady Eleanora," Teresa Marie said. Her lips were tight across her teeth, and I knew at once she would have sold her soul for the chance to spew venom at me. "So nice to see you again. And what a lovely dress you have on. It is so … different … from the one you were wearing the last time we met. You must give me the direction of your new modiste."

THE ORDER OF THE CRYSTAL DAGGERS

Karl reached for her hand. "I do not believe we have been introduced," he said. "But any friend of Lady Eleanora's surely has the highest of recommendations."

Teresa Marie smiled much more warmly. "Lady Eleanora is too kind to introduce us," she said, shooting me a dirty look behind her flower-covered fan.

She cornered me into an introduction. Even though I was not interested in marrying Karl, I hated her for her deceit. "Mr. Marcelin, this is Lady Teresa Marie, Countess of Moravia."

Karl introduced himself as a new song began. I glanced back to see Lady POW and Lord Maximillian dance. From Lady POW's form and frigid smile, I could tell she was less than delighted with her choice, but there was a determination on her face that seemed to suggest she had a good reason for making herself suffer.

Karl saw me watching them and cleared his throat. "I must thank you once more for the earlier dance, Lady Eleanora," he said. "One account of thanks hardly seems appropriate for such pleasure."

"You're welcome." I gave him a teasing smile. "I will forgive your lapse of manners, and I am happy to have a chance to talk with you without worrying I will step on your toes. I fear I am not as experienced with the waltz as you are, sir." I used my fan to hide my face with graceful contrition.

Teresa Marie cleared her throat. "Perhaps you would find another dancing partner that is equally as charming, Mr. Marcelin?"

"I sincerely doubt it." Karl brushed her subtle suggestion aside and kept his attention on me. "Might I ask to share another dance with you later this evening, Lady Eleanora? Your grandmother had given me permission before, so I do not see why it would not be allowed."

"I have often been complimented on my own skill at the promenade and even the Scottish Reel," Teresa Marie remarked. "Perhaps you would be interested one of those?"

Karl did not seem to hear her at all this time. "Well, Lady Eleanora?"

I hesitated for only a second, before begrudgingly deciding that if I was going to talk to him more, it was best I accept his invitation. "I would be—"

"Excuse me, sir."

Karl whipped around to see a footman behind him, and I breathed a quick sigh of relief. I was getting tired of smiling, and I was glad for the break. I was also better able to enjoy seeing Teresa Marie, as she silently fumed at Karl for neglecting her. Given her churlishness, I felt my own delight at her anger was a forgivable offense.

I turned my attention back to Karl when I heard him snap at the footman. "What is it? Can't you see I am busy?"

I winced at his tone. His polite demeanor dimmed as he glared at the servant.

"Beggin' your pardon, sir," the footman said. "But a message of grave importance has come for you." He held out a small note.

Karl grabbed it and turned to read it in the small lamplight beside us. When he cursed under his breath and crumbled the note, I knew it was not good news.

"Thank you," he said, waving the footman away. He turned back to me. "I must profoundly apologize, Lady Eleanora. I find I must depart for tonight."

"Is something wrong?" I asked. "Where are you going?"

Inside his dark gray eyes, an angry storm was brewing. "Nothing you need concern yourself with." Karl took my hand and bowed, before kissing it gallantly. "I hope I will see you at other balls in the future."

"I have been invited to the Advent Ball," I said. "Perhaps I will see you there?"

"Yes, you will," he said. "I have been invited along with several of the other nobles and aristocracy. But I hope to see you much sooner than the Advent Ball. That is still a week away."

"My grandmother and I have been invited to several events."

"I will see to finding you again soon, then," Karl said. "So we might enjoy another dance. Farewell, my lady."

"It was a pleasure, Mr. Marcelin." I curtsied, and then I watched him go. I nearly laughed at Teresa Marie's pout when he forgot to give her his goodbyes.

Lady Hohenwart seemed to forget about Teresa Marie, too, since she patted my shoulder in a motherly manner. "Do not fret, dear. He seems most enchanted by you."

I nodded. Before I could respond by saying something witty and amusing and completely forgettable, another footman caught my eye.

I saw his shadow in the hallway behind us. His hand waved at me, motioning for me to come over. I could not see his face, but there was something familiar about him. Curious, I decided to investigate.

"Excuse me, Lady Hohenwart," I said. "I am going to … the ladies' withdrawing room."

After Lady Hohenwart's quick directions, I slithered off and then twisted around, ducking into the dark hallway.

The footman was no longer there. I continued deeper into the corridor, cautious, but still determined.

Several steps later, I realized I was in a private hallway used for servants. There were no decorations along the wall, and the dimmed lights hid a good deal of the poor cleaning.

"What that was all about?" I wondered if my imagination was getting the better of me. Silent seconds ticked by, and I suddenly felt foolish.

I sighed. "I should have stayed with Lady Hohenwart after Karl left."

"I hope you will excuse his impromptu exit," a voice said from behind me. "He received a note that his brother was down in the center of town, making a fool of himself with an actress."

I stopped short, turning back toward the source of the voice. "Who's there?"

"Over here."

I watched as a man came out of a darkened corner of the hallway. His roguish grin caught the small glimmer of the moonlight. There was no denying that smile, and I gave him one of my own. "Ferdy?"

"At your service, Lady Ella."

11

◊

Ferdy shifted out of the shadows, and I was unable to stop the rush of happiness inside of me. Before I remembered myself, I ran over and embraced him. I was so happy to see him, after wondering if he had gotten into trouble over Dr. Artha's murder.

"What are you doing here?" I backed away from him, noticing he was dressed in livery identical to the footman who had delivered the note to Karl, but as he stood before me, I saw he was missing the matching hat and his outfit seemed much too loose.

He bowed over my hand, and as much as I expected him to kiss it, I was disappointed when he did not. He kept himself at a respectful distance, and I found myself more irritated than relieved at his propriety.

I wonder if Ferdy has read The Ladies Guide to Excellence and Etiquette *too?*

He gestured down his clothes. "I'm working, clearly. But I've decided to take a break, now that I know you are here."

"Is that how you know what was in the note Karl received?" I asked.

"It's not too hard to figure out the secrets footmen carry. They're only too happy to share interesting tidbits of information between themselves."

"Is this another one of your jobs?"

"You ask a lot of questions," Ferdy said, and I blushed again. "But I don't mind answering them. This is not usually one of my jobs. They've hired some additional staff for the party tonight."

That would explain the ill-fitting garments. Extra hires don't have much time for proper fittings.

"But when I heard you had asked about me from some of the vendors in Market Square, I wanted to come and find you. Lately you have been the talk of the city, it seems, so it was not hard to find you tonight."

"So you decided to come and work here, all to see me?" I was flattered and embarrassed, but still pleased. "Don't you think one of your superiors will notice you are missing?"

"Someone will likely notice *you* missing before they miss me."

"That's true. My grandmother will likely be worried if I am not back with Lady Hohenwart soon."

"I actually meant that other guests would miss you. I certainly would, were I among them."

THE ORDER OF THE CRYSTAL DAGGERS

"We have a little time to talk," I said, daring myself to forget Lady POW would be upset with me for spending time away from the ballroom.

Ferdy reached out his arm, just as gallantly as Karl had moments ago. "Shall we take a quick stroll through the corridors, my lady?"

I took his arm with no regrets. "I am actually glad you are here," I admitted as we walked. "It is nice to see a familiar face."

"Familiar and fun," Ferdy reminded me. "Who else here would save you from a thief and take you through the city's forbidden haunts, all to find a new home for your lovely book?"

I tapped his arm with my fan at his teasing. "How is Mr. Clavan enjoying *The Prelude?*"

"He loves it. He devoted a whole hour to it at our last meeting," Ferdy said.

"It sounds like a job or club when you say it like that, instead of a friendly visit."

"It is more of a meeting, in actuality. Clavan and Eliezer are business associates," Ferdy said. "Clavan is the owner of the Cabal, but with Eliezer, he helps run a small publication company dedicated to discussing politics and current events. They hold meetings every week where they talk over different things, and I enjoy listening to them."

"Are they a political group?" I asked, remembering what Madame Balthazar had said.

Ferdy laughed. "No, but they discuss politics often. My friend Jarl works for them on the side, writing up pamphlets and articles that they submit to different newspapers and distribute to interested parties."

"I see."

"You should come. To one of their meetings, I mean," Ferdy said. "If you like books, you will like it."

"I am curious about it. Mr. Clavan seems like a good man."

"He certainly is," Ferdy agreed. "But never let him know I agreed with you. Clavan knows nearly everything that goes on in Prague, as it all filters through the Cabal sooner or later."

"Even news about specific people, like Karl Marcelin?" I asked, and Ferdy's smile suddenly waned.

"I suppose." His voice was still cheery but suddenly hollow. "Are you interested in him? Is that why you danced with him?"

"Do you know him?" I asked.

Ferdy scoffed. "Oh, I know him," he said. "But I don't like him. We have very little in common, and even the little we do, I'm sure he would be willing to argue."

"So you know him? Personally?"

"We've met," Ferdy said, his lips pursed with unpleasantness. "I know a lot of people myself, from working in some of the top social circles."

"He seemed very nice to me."

"That's because he likes you, clearly." Ferdy looked glum. "But he does not think much of people who disagree with him and people who inconvenience him."

I thought about how Karl had snapped at the other footman when he had come to deliver the note.

"He's very smart," Ferdy said. "He can make himself sound as though he agrees with you, even if he doesn't. He can quote a thousand and a half philosophers and poets, and even some Americans, but he can't see the wisdom behind all of his knowledge."

"So you do not agree with him in anything? Not even on politics?"

"Definitely not there," Ferdy said. "I'll admit I enjoy Clavan and his Cabal for the politics. There is something about a government that can't sign a whole country over to an Empire at the stroke of a pen. Even Empress Elisabeth has sympathetic leanings toward democracy. Karl's views on the matter are vastly different. He wants to return Bohemia to a full sovereignty."

"He seems to be quite popular," I said, even as I remembered Lady POW mentioning he disliked the current Emperor.

"The Federalists fear him, but they keep it polite, on the chance he actually will be elected to the Bohemian Diet or assigned to the Minister-President position when Count Potocki steps down," Ferdy explained. "The socialists on both sides can tolerate him, when they are not fighting amongst themselves. They think he is a nice enough man on his own. That will allow many people to tolerate his policies for some time, even if they are failures in the end. And the Nationalists, of course, love him. They are so happy to see some youth and energy coming into Bohemian politics."

"What of Germany and Prussia, and the Austria-Hungarians?"

"What of them? The Emperor has demonstrated time and again that Bohemia is hardly his concern," Ferdy said. "Other nations are too worried about their own to worry about us."

"That's interesting." I wondered if anything had to do with Lady POW and the recent murders.

"You're strange," Ferdy said. "Why so interested in politics?"

I shrugged, and then decided to turn the tables on him. "You seem interested in it as well. That is strange, for a street urchin such as yourself."

Ferdy grinned just as I realized I had insulted him. "First, I'm not polite enough to keep myself from talking to you about anything, even if we are talking about something as indecent as politics. And second, I know enough about politics that it amuses me," he said. "The world will never be a better place with people just talking about it, whether they try to shape the world into their vision, or they scrape their words out of the clay of the world itself."

"I don't know about politics much," I said. "Just a little, mostly from what my father taught me. But I like learning what I can from others."

Especially if they are going to help me solve a murder.

"Governments, according to the Americans, were made to secure the natural, inalienable rights from God," Ferdy said. "It gets to be a bigger deal when there is a government who is preventing the people from their rights."

"Did Mr. Clavan tell you that?" I giggled.

"Why, yes he did," Ferdy said with his usual guilelessness, and I laughed even harder.

"Good, I've made you laugh, and for real," Ferdy said. "None of that fake, flirty chittering you did earlier."

"How did you know that was fake? And how long were you spying on me and Karl?"

"Long enough to wait for the footman to deliver the message," Ferdy said. "And that took him enough time, to be sure. I should have waited until afterward to pay him."

Realization struck me. "You sent Karl the message?"

"Of course." Ferdy gave me his charming grin. "You know I would never miss the chance to rescue you if I could, Ella."

Mild shock sank into me, and I was just as surprised to find I was pleased. My steps slowed, eventually coming to a stop near a window.

"I know him well enough to get him to leave, and I would not have missed the chance to steal you away for even a few moments this evening."

I suddenly realized that we were all alone. There were no other people around, and the last warmth of the ballroom had long since been whisked away.

"Are you angry?" Ferdy asked. "I didn't want to upset you."

"No." I shook my head. "I'm fine. I am just surprised at—"

"—how much you missed me."

Despite being interrupted, I could only laugh. But after a moment, I had to admit Ferdy was right. Everyone else out in public was someone to lie to or someone to manipulate. Ferdy still knew me as the lady who was forced to do her stepmother's shopping, dressed in a maidservant's dress and accompanied by her muted neighbor.

"Well, I have been worried for you," I said. "My grandmother was concerned of all the dead politicians turning up, and I thought you would be in trouble since Mr. Clavan asked you about it."

"I see." Ferdy squeezed my hand. "There's no need to worry about me. I have been out in the city long enough to know how to take care of myself and cover my tracks."

"That's a relief, but I want you to promise me that you will be careful."

"I would never deny you anything." Ferdy stood beside me, and as I looked out over the view, I had a new appreciation for how peaceful and robust the city looked. The simple happenings during the day, and the darker stains of murder and intrigue of the shadows, seemed to whisk away into the light of its magic.

Prague had stood for hundreds of years, and the blood of my father's ancestors ran through me, bringing me to this moment in time, in all its vastness and mystery, watching as the kingdom and its housed traditions continued to stand against time's ebb and flow. The richness and the endurance of it all added something mystical to everything, and I wondered, glancing over at Ferdy, if there were things that really did last forever. The warmth of his arm brushed against my shoulder, and I was strongly tempted to lean into him.

"I must admit," Ferdy said, "that I have been worried for you, too. I was happy to hear of your grandmother's arrival, but I thought maybe you would forget about me once she came and took you out on all those fancy shopping adventures."

"I didn't," I said with a laugh. "If anything, I will need you more in the coming days, to remind me who I was before she came. I feel almost like a different person in all these fancy clothes."

"You are different. You are more beautiful than ever." Ferdy waited until it was clear I was too embarrassed to reply before adding, "But if it will make you feel better, I can steal something from you. I'm willing to bet you would chase me down, just like you did to the Turkish man."

I smiled at the thought of Ferdy running from me, clutching something against his chest as I tried to steal it back.

Looking up into his eyes, I suddenly had to wonder if he was not already stealing something from me; my heart seemed to beat faster as I stood there.

"You seem to like gambling," I said, keeping the conversation light as I pondered the depths of my heart, and what it held for the pleasant street urchin and job hopper I'd met only days ago.

"Some things are worth the risk," Ferdy replied, stepping even closer to me.

"Always the charmer," I whispered, before Ferdy tightened his fingers around mine and he drew my hand to his lips.

"And you, Ella, are always the enchanter," Ferdy replied. "But your spells would be even more irresistible if you were to only stop lying."

THE ORDER OF THE CRYSTAL DAGGERS

"Lying? About what?" I asked. His remark caught me off guard, and suddenly I wondered if he had found out about me, Lady POW, and the Order of the Crystal Daggers. I momentarily pictured Lady POW bursting into flames, angry with me for my carelessness.

Ferdy grinned. "How much you want to kiss me, of course."

I nearly laughed in relief, but then his eyes caught mine in the moonlight. Nerves of a different sort twisted inside of me as I saw his gaze slip down to my lips.

He was only a breath away from me. My heart began to beat faster, racing like a jubilant melody. In the distance, Prague Castle glowed with a mix of light from the moon and stars. Everything seemed to overwhelm me in that moment. I could smell the fragrance of the gardens below us; I could sense the barest edge of the wind … feel the tremor of my hand in his.

Ferdy's silver eyes were bright as he waited for my response, his breath warm against my cheek. My hand was still on his arm, and his other hand covered it gently.

I knew we were alone. It was a moment where I could be free to do as I pleased, and, as hard as it was for me to admit, Ferdy was right.

I liked him, a lot more than I should, and I did want to kiss him. That was why I stayed where I was, daring myself to be brave, daring myself to allow him so close to me—even as my logic warned me, and the expectations placed on me by others cried out bitterly.

He was a street lad, someone who was fast and loose with the truth, and he had just admitted to me that he had tricked one of the most well-known political stars of Prague in order to steal some time with me.

Everything seemed so strange. Even a week ago, Ferdy was someone I never would have expected, someone I never would have even dared to dream was real.

But here he was, standing next to me—and here I was, letting him, hoping he would close the distance between us. I could take half a step and find my body pressed against his. Our breath mingled together as I was overrun with confusion and curious longing.

"I won't force you to tell me the truth, Ella," Ferdy whispered. "I know better than most that some lies are preferable to the truth. But I can't keep aching for you like this."

Heat fluttered to my cheeks. "Do you really want to kiss me?"

He laughed and stepped back from me, making me miss the shadow of his warmth. "Oh, Ella, it's no wonder why I am enchanted by you. Of course I do. I might be the bigger liar between us, but I could never lie about that."

"Why?" I asked. Another thought struck me at his words. "What are you lying about?"

THE ORDER OF THE CRYSTAL DAGGERS

"Plenty," he said. "But not about wanting to kiss you. Even if I were to say otherwise on that matter, you would find the truth out easily enough. I am sure it is written on my face at this point."

My brain was limpid mush as I tried to focus. "Were you lying about your friends earlier?" I asked. "About Mr. Clavan and the others?"

"Why would I need to lie about that?" Ferdy asked. "No, they are intellectual, and yes, a little scary, especially considering how fast Eliezer talks, but they have nothing to do with this part of our conversation."

"I suppose you have a point. You're right."

Ferdy grinned. "About you wanting to kiss me?"

I blushed again, before glancing back down the darkened corridors of the Hohenwart house. "I should probably head back. My grandmother will be worried by now, I think. It probably does not take anyone this long to find a powder room, even if they are lost."

"Your chaperone will likely need her vinaigrette, especially since Karl left."

"Hardly," I scoffed, but I smiled at the thought of Lady POW fainting.

We walked for several moments in silence, retracing our steps back to the ballroom. All too quickly, the music grew louder and I felt my freedom shrink as my time with Ferdy ended.

"I would love it if you could come and see me again," Ferdy said.

"This time, you were the one who came to see me," I pointed out. "You seem to have better luck in finding me than I do in finding you."

He laughed again, but softly this time, as we were approaching the edge of the shadows.

"That's true," he said. "But come to one of Clavan's Cabal meetings. They're on Thursdays and Mondays, in the evenings. I'll be there. And you'll be able to see for yourself what the Cabal is all about."

It was so tempting to say yes.

So I did.

"I'll make arrangements," I promised, even though I had no idea how I was going to make it work.

"Good." Ferdy finally pressed his lips against my knuckles, and then against my palm, and I felt my legs go weak with strange wanting. "Next time, Ella, I will find a way to get you to admit you want to kiss me."

Unable to resist giving him a challenge, I arched my brow at him. "We will see, won't we?"

"You're not denying it," he pointed out, and I felt my heart flutter as he blew me a kiss.

I headed back toward the ballroom, sighing and smiling, unexplainably happy. Ferdy was safe, and I would see him again soon. And, I thought, feeling a little guilty, if I did go to the Cabal, I might be able to see if there was any more news on Dr. Artha's death.

My happiness was immediately interrupted by my grandmother, almost as if she could sense how forbidden it was.

"Eleanora."

I snapped to attention as I saw her in the doorway to the ballroom. "Lady Penelope."

"Where have you been?" she asked. "I have been waiting for you to reappear for the last thirty minutes."

"Um ... I was looking for the withdrawing room," I said. "I had to take care of some ... personal needs. I was lost."

Lady Penelope groaned. "I knew I should not have danced with Lord Maximillian. Leaving you on your own was clearly a mistake this early in the game."

"You could have refused Lord Maximillian," I said. "What did he want to dance with you for, anyway? Did he want a chance to ruffle your petticoats after you ruined his plans with Alex and Teresa Marie?"

"No." Lady Penelope frowned. "He seemed very thankful I gave him a way out of that arrangement. His daughter will be able to find someone in higher circles now."

"If she's charming enough," I said, thinking of how she had failed to take Karl's attention away from me.

"Lord Maximillian took the time to check up on you, to see how you were adapting to life outside of Cecilia. He said he was shocked and appalled to find out that you and Benedict were being treated so horrifically."

I crossed my arms over my chest. "I do not believe him."

"He also assured me that he and his daughter would refrain from speaking of your time as a servant."

"I don't care about that," I said. "If anything, maybe it would be better for people to know the truth. He is likely only refraining from saying anything to keep Cecilia from looking bad, and himself by extension."

"That is true," Lady Penelope said. "But you are smart enough to know that you are the entertainment for society, Eleanora. No one wants to feel guilty in seeing you as entertainment, either. Revealing the truth is counteractive to your efforts to enchant them."

THE ORDER OF THE CRYSTAL DAGGERS

I thought of Ferdy, and how he had called me an enchanter. Was it possible he felt sorry for me? A moment later, I decided he did not. He lived on the streets, working for a living. He was not the same as the rest of society.

Besides, I thought with a quick blush, it was clear he had other feelings for me than pity.

"Eleanora? What is it?"

"Karl told me that Lord Maximillian is a guest at the Hohenwart house," I said, changing the topic. I did not want to think of my role in society.

"Karl?"

"Mr. Marcelin."

"You were supposed to get him to like you, Eleanora, but there is no need for you to like him when we speak face to face, as we are now."

"Well, he was nice enough, especially to me," I said, remembering his kindness and patience with me and my subpar waltzing skills. "He mentioned several things to me about his high hopes for his political career and how Count Potocki shares an interest in wine with Lord Hohenwart and the Duke of Moravia. That was when he told me His Grace was a guest at the Hohenwart estate."

"Lady Hohenwart did not mention that to me," Lady Penelope replied in an irritated tone. "But it sounds like you have some information we might be able to use. We will discuss it later with Amir and Harshad."

"And Ben."

"Yes, of course."

"Does this mean I passed your test?" I asked. I thought of the crystalline blades of Lady POW's daggers, the chosen weapons of the Order of the Crystal Daggers.

Will I get the chance to wield them one day soon?

Lady POW sighed. "Now is not the time for this, Eleanora."

"But I did *some* good tonight. And if it's not good enough, you know as much as I do that it's hardly fair to test me when I don't even know what I am being tested on."

"On the contrary. It is the perfect time to test you."

"It's still not fair."

"Life is not fair, Eleanora, in case you haven't noticed."

"I assumed it would be at least somewhat better after you came and assumed responsibility of me from Cecilia. Her chores were harder on my body, maybe, but yours are completely mad on the mind."

"As I said, enough of this." She took my hand. "Come. We are leaving."

114

THE ORDER OF THE CRYSTAL DAGGERS

"Do we have permission from the social betters to do so?" I scoffed. "Or is this one of your orders that I must follow blindly?"

"None of that, Eleanora. If you must know, another murder happened earlier tonight. Amir and Ben are waiting for us outside. We must hurry."

Shame and silence weighed heavily on me as we made our exit.

12

"Where are we headed?" I asked, as I settled into the carriage cushions. I pulled my cloak more tightly around my shoulders, regretting that I had to be in my evening gown the first time I joined Ben on a mission.

"We are going to the Church of Our Lady of the Snows." Lady Penelope pulled the carriage curtains shut and began tugging at the lacings and hooks of her gown.

"What are you doing?" I asked.

"Changing." She reached down under her seat and lifted up the cushion. I was amazed to see there was a secret drawer there, and I was even more confounded as she tossed me a pair of breeches. "Which is what you should be doing."

I gripped the soft material hesitantly, noticing it was cut in an older style. "Do I just change … in here?"

"Now is not the time for modesty, Eleanora. We only have a few blocks."

Carefully, I pulled off my own gown, alternatively cringing and sighing over the next several long moments. It was a simple ball gown, but it was so fine I hated the thought of ruining it. As the carriage jostled, I stumbled and shifted uncomfortably in the small space I had to change.

"You'll get accustomed to this," Lady Penelope assured me, before she pulled a shirt on over her own chemise. She seemed to all but slip out of her own gown.

I tried to ignore her, considering she had a critical gaze set on my middle, where I was trying to squeeze myself flat as I squirmed in my petticoats.

Finally, several more uncomfortable moments later, I bundled up my chemise and tucked it into the pants. My gown bubbled up on the empty seats, and as much as it irritated me, I regretted rolling it up into a ball and shoving it into the newly empty drawer. I winced as I shut the top down on its soft fabric.

"Amelia and the others will be able to tend to it," Lady Penelope told me, and I was grateful for her concern, even if I hated to give her seamstresses more work.

I looked over to see Lady POW was dressed all in black. She had on her slacks, a shirt, and even a greatcoat and hessians. She bundled up her gray hair and tucked it under a hat, before pulling out a walking stick and sitting down once more.

"You don't happen to have shoes for me, too, do you?" I asked.

She quickly tossed me an identical set of clothes and a fine walking stick of my own. "Pull up your collar to help hide your hair."

Moments later, I was wearing a set of man's clothes, and I felt deliciously sinful in doing so. I kept moving my legs, crossing them over each other, reveling in the freedom to move.

"This is great," I said, pulling the black greatcoat over my stays. "This is almost as good as my stealth habit. And it fits so well."

Lady POW smiled. "I had a feeling it would. You are close to your mother's size the last time she wore it."

My eyes went moist. I felt the soft material surround me in a new way, almost as if I now saw it as my mother's embrace.

"Oh, if only Harshad could see you, Eleanor."

"Eleanora," I muttered.

She waved my correction aside, quickly and meaninglessly apologizing before moving onto the next topic. That was when I realized I had not seen Harshad since the day Lady POW initiated Ben and me into the Order. I wondered why. Maybe it was because he was busy with Ben, or maybe it was because of something Lady POW had said.

Those seemed like good reasons.

But why would Lady POW get such delight at the thought of torturing him?

Eleanor.

It was jarring to realize Harshad had known my mother, too. If Lady POW was looking at me, and seeing my mother, she knew Harshad would likely see her, too.

I shuddered inside the large greatcoat. How much did Lady POW have to hate Harshad to enjoy torturing him that way?

"You will need to make sure you follow my lead when you wear those clothes," Lady Penelope was saying, as I drifted back into the moment. "Men are different from women in form and function. We walk differently, we carry ourselves differently, we even think differently. And we must adapt if we are to convince others of the truth of our charade."

"It's dark enough out I don't think people will notice much," I said.

"No need to be sloppy about these things, Eleanora."

The carriage rolled to a stop in a darkened street, and we alighted into the night.

Since we were still several blocks away from the church, we made our way through the dark alleys. During this time, Lady POW tutored me on my walk and using my hat and walking stick as a metaphorical sword and shield.

As a kind of game, I used the stick to hit different piles of garbage until I struck a pile of horse manure. After that, I stopped. I kept my frustration to myself as I watched Lady POW lead the way. I saw the twin hilts of her crystal daggers sticking out by her side.

Our earlier debate, just before we left the Hohenwart Ball, momentarily slipped back into my thoughts. *I hope she doesn't think she made a mistake in allowing me to join the Order.*

"I checked into your earlier information," Lady Penelope said. "You were right. Dr. Artha was last seen coming out of this church. But he has been a patron of St. Nicolas for years."

"It is possible he was meeting someone here," I said. "He seems to have a lot of friends who are not members of St. Nicholas."

"That is correct. He was meeting with Father Novak, who is now dead."

I said nothing. It was slowly dawning on me that Lady Penelope was comfortable with death and other uncomfortable topics, and if I wanted to prove myself to her, I would have to become accustomed to them, too.

That did not mean, of course, that I had to approve of them.

"Here we are," Lady Penelope called, as I attempted to fling the manure off the stick. "The Church of Our Lady of the Snows."

I looked at the building, marveling at its construction. It was constructed over two hundred years before, and its beauty was restored over the various generations.

"Admiring the scene, are you?"

"Hey!" I whirled around, and there was Ben, standing right behind me. "You scared me."

"Eleanora, hush. And Benedict, control yourself. This is no time to scare your sister."

"Apologies, Madame," Ben muttered. It was a little unnerving how much he sounded like Lady POW when she apologized to me for calling me by my mother's name.

"I don't even know how I missed your approach," I grumbled.

Ben pointed down at his misshapen leg, where I saw the gleam of new metal brackets sticking out from the bottom of his breeches. "Between my mechanical skills and Amir's knowledge of anatomy, we were able to design a new brace that's much more light and quiet than my previous ones. It's still a little harder for me to move around than others, but I am improving."

"Well, if anyone is up for a harder task, it's you," I said.

"I would say the same of you," Ben whispered, and I marveled at his genuine cheerfulness. I was glad it had nothing to do with keeping our stepsiblings in line or pilfering pastries from the kitchen.

"Mademoiselle."

THE ORDER OF THE CRYSTAL DAGGERS

I looked over to see Amir as he came up beside the rest of us. As my gaze met his, all the hardness of his face from our previous meeting melted away, and a look of frightful terror took its place. "What is it?"

He seemed to realize he was staring and quickly lowered his gaze. "Lady Eleanora." He quickly gave me a proper bow.

I curtsied in return, before I remembered I was supposed to be acting like a man. I attempted a bow instead. "Mr. Qureshi."

My voice was dull and hard, and Amir seemed grateful for the reminder that I disliked him.

"Amir, I am waiting," Lady Penelope called.

Amir nodded and began talking to her at once, making me scowl. I had wanted to remind him of his promise to me.

I nudged Ben. "Where's Harshad?" I asked. "Is he here, too?"

"No, he's not. He does not go with Amir when I am here. He says Amir draws too much attention as it is, and with my limp, we are already having trouble blending in. He goes by himself if he wants to make rounds."

"Oh." I wondered if Harshad was telling Ben the truth. "I thought maybe he was avoiding us. He doesn't seem to like us that much."

At Ben's sudden grimace, I frowned. "You're hiding something. Tell me."

Ben sighed. "He is not happy about having to train you. I overheard him arguing with Lady POW over it. That's actually why she probably brought you from your ball, since he is refusing to do anything for now."

"What?" Anger burst through me. "So he's not going to train me? How can I do a good job at this stuff if someone isn't going to teach me?"

"Calm down." Ben glanced over at the others. "This is business, Nora, and if it's one thing you should know from watching Lady POW by now, it's that business does not mean people need to get along to work together."

I snorted. "That's true. But still, Harshad can't just deny me the right to—"

"Eleanora. Benedict. This way," Lady Penelope called. "We are going to inspect the body."

"We can talk about it later." As Amir led the way into the side of the church, Ben gave me a smirk. "I don't know what is stranger, seeing you in a lady's gown or a gentleman's clothes."

"Hush, Ben." I smiled at his teasing, but I was still upset hearing Harshad did not want to teach me. What kind of person wanted his colleagues to fail? How could I trust him after hearing this?

How could I really trust any of them?

Lady Penelope changed from leader to grandmother and back again when it suited her. Harshad was aloof and distant, and even Amir had been careful to avoid me for the last week since our meeting in the library.

Walking behind them, I studied Lady POW and Amir.

What reason do I really have to trust them at all? I thought.

I glanced over at Ben, and suddenly I had an answer. Despite the darkness of our mission, my brother had lost the desire for pleasure in the pursuit of purpose. I thought about the past few days where we had quietly exchanged updates, discussing everything from Lady POW's too-literal translation of a Hungarian vendor's cursing to Harshad's questions.

Ben not only seemed more alive, he was a better man.

I knew I could risk trusting Lady POW and her cohorts for a little longer if it made Ben happy. If he trusted them, I knew I could trust them, too.

"You should prepare yourself," Ben said. "This is going to be unpleasant for you. It's nothing like my other ventures into the city with Amir."

From our stolen moments of brief conversation over the past week, I knew Amir had been taking him to meet with runners and traders recently; Ben had mostly been meeting with people who bought and sold information as much as goods or services around Prague. I doubted he had come across a murder since he had been exploring the city at night.

"Half of what I have been doing is smiling and nodding and laughing at things that are not funny," I said. I decided not to tell Ben about Ferdy. Karl's amorous interest alone would be enough to get my brother riled, I thought.

"You sound jealous."

"Well, I am, even if you are forced to work with Amir."

"Amir's not so bad, Nora. You might actually like him if you gave him a chance."

Amir and Harshad could not be that *different.* I wrinkled my nose. "I doubt it."

"Don't be so stubborn," Ben said. "He's really smart, and he has a good sense of humor. And he knows where all the best food is in Prague."

"Oh, so that's why you like him. Well, in that case—"

"You two need to keep it down," Lady Penelope hissed, as we walked through the winding hallways under the chapel.

"We're almost there," Amir said, leading us up a small staircase before entering main chapel.

Flickering lights greeted us as we made our way through the large chapel. The beautiful vaulted ceiling crisscrossed above us as I looked to the altar with wonder.

THE ORDER OF THE CRYSTAL DAGGERS

The contrasting shine of gold and black on the portal spoke of so much more than worldly worship, calling back to the ancient battle of good and evil, and the resounding reward only goodness brought.

"This place is magnificent," I whispered.

"Yes," Lady Penelope agreed. "It is too bad Father Novak died in here. But then, perhaps it was a good place for such a fate. One last glimpse of worldly beauty, and then death's release."

I looked over at her, shocked by the simple horror of her words.

But then I looked past her; a limp body was lying at her feet, half-hidden behind the confessionals. The gray-streaked hair covering the sides of his head fluttered softly at our arrival, as our small group surrounded his prostrate form.

Amir knelt down at his feet. "He was sitting in the booth as he died. I pulled him out to examine him."

"It doesn't look like murder," I said. I stared down at the dead man, taking in the sad details of his form as I contemplated his fate. I felt a tenderness for the man, for even though I had never met him, I wondered at the sadness of dying alone. "There's no blood and no wound."

Táta's death was similar, I remembered. He died in his study, sitting at his desk, with his cup of wine from dinner still half-full. Dr. Artha had been called at once, and Ben later told me that he said *Táta* had likely died from a fit of apoplexy.

"You are correct," Amir said, surprising me. "But that does not mean it wasn't. Look at the tips of his fingers and the corners of his mouth. You'll see there is a small, blue tint, and it is a simple explanation."

Lady POW sighed. "Poison."

I looked over at Ben, who was staring at the body with his mouth gaping open in silence.

Amir sighed. "From the blue markings, it is safe to say it contained elements of the silver thallis. Likely a hefty dose, too, if its effects are already showing up on the corpse."

"Are you sure?" Lady Penelope asked.

"Yes. Xiana taught me well."

"Who is Xiana?" I asked, desperate to find anything that would keep me from shuddering. If Harshad did not want to teach me, it did nothing for me to show my weakness in other areas.

"One of the Order's other members. She is a trained herbalist who studied under Harshad. I know it will be a few weeks before she arrives."

"She might be too late," Lady Penelope said. "Poison, especially of this sort, is powerful. We can have Xiana mix an antidote when she gets here. I will have Harshad send her a message. If anyone can reach her, it will be him."

"Why, though?" I asked. "Why would someone kill him? Was Father Novak the one that Dr. Artha met with before he wound up dead, too?"

"From what one of the altar boys was able to tell me, he was," Amir said. "And that means trouble. Father Novak was one of our regular informants. He knew of the Order of the Crystal Daggers, just like Dr. Artha."

"That is not good news," Lady Penelope said. "That gives the murderer another motive."

"It does?" I asked.

Lady Penelope ignored my question. "Do we have time to search the church? I know the other monks and priests have given us a small block of time before they will need to summon the city authorities and see about disposing of the body."

Lady POW began searching through the priest's pockets. As Amir began to search the nearby confessionals, I turned to see Ben was still staring at Father Novak's body.

"What is it, Ben?" I asked quietly. "Are you well? You're the one who warned me it would be unpleasant."

"I thought it would be hard to see it," he said slowly, "because I am not used to death. But … I recognize this."

"What are you talking about?"

"His blue fingertips," Ben said. "The small tinges around his mouth. I saw the same things on *Otec's* body at the funeral."

"What are you … " My voice trailed off as I remembered that moment, at *Táta's* funeral, where I had seen the bluish skin of his fingers and the azure veins of his knuckles. I looked down at the dead reverend, seeing the evidence of his death in a new light.

"You know what I am talking about, don't you?" Ben asked.

I nodded slowly. "Do you think … does this mean … ?" I looked at Ben, unable to finish my sentence, though I was unable to say if it was due to shock or rage.

"I think so," Ben said. "*Otec* was poisoned."

"But why? And by who?" I was not able to stop looking at the poisoned priest. I watched through half-glazed eyes as Lady POW picked up his fallen rosary. "Do you think it was by the same person?"

"It is possible, but doubtful," Lady Penelope said, as she took hold of the large printed Bible beside the priest.

I gripped Ben's arm, though whether it was for his comfort or my own, I could not say. "What does this mean?"

"It means," Lady Penelope said, standing up and wiping her hands off on a handkerchief, "that this goes back much further and deeper than Queen Victoria suspected. If it goes back as far as your father's death, this is a political coup."

"No political party advocates for killing priests," I said. "Dr. Artha was a good man, too. The Federalists and Nationalists both agreed he was a good man."

"A good man is nothing compared to a man who will get you what you want."

"Well," I said, "at least there will be no way for someone to blame the Jews for this one."

"The Jews make a good political scapegoat, because there are plenty who would believe the worst of them," Amir said, as he came out of one of the confession booths. "I do not think this was a calculated death. Father Novak was collateral."

"So someone decided to kill him after Dr. Artha's death," Ben said.

"Good, Benedict. I agree." Lady POW nodded. "Dr. Artha's death was intentional. If it was poison, and one that he would have been familiar with, that is why he was stabbed."

"It could also be a strategy of misdirection," Amir said. "If a priest were to die with the same circumstances as the other politicians, it would likely reveal too much about the murderer's intent. Because we can link Father Novak with Dr. Artha, we are better able to discern their intent."

"Not to mention their identities," I added.

"Yes," Amir agreed. "Misdirection can be a powerful tool. Especially if this is something that goes back more than ten years. And it looks like it might."

"What did you find, Amir?" Lady Penelope asked.

Amir handed her a small note. "Father Novak had Dr. Artha's last message tucked away. Here you are, Madame."

Lady Penelope tore open the note and read it. Her eyes shifted along with the script, and I waited for her to react. She went still.

"What does it say?" Ben asked.

When Lady POW said nothing, Ben jerked the paper out of her hands. "It's in French," he said. "I can't read it."

"Let me look," I said.

Lady POW regained her composure. "I warned her. I warned her something like this would happen if she decided to stay."

I glanced down at the paper, looking over the words. "She?"

"It's a quick note. Translated, it read, 'Sent for the Light, made arrangements with my sweet *Mira*,'" Lady Penelope read. "It also mentions he is praying for protection and hopes this note is an unnecessary precaution."

"It is unfortunate for him that proved not to be the case," Ben said sadly, looking down at the corpse again.

"But not for us," Amir said. "He made arrangements."

"And Lady Penelope knows who it is." I turned to see her angrily pacing once more. I had seen this expression on her before, when she was facing unavoidable inconveniences.

Amir nodded. "*Mira* is a codename. She is a woman who was once your mother's companion. Her real name is—"

"Tulia?" A strange sense of foreboding took hold of me, as I realized another illusion of my lifetime was about to come crumbling down. "Tulia wasn't just my mother's companion. She was her assistant. Wasn't she?"

"So, you know where she is?" Lady Penelope turned on me, and I felt the fire and brimstone from her gaze.

"Yes," I said. "I've visited her frequently since my father's death, actually."

For a long moment, Lady POW seemed unable to process what I had said. Then she shook her head. "That lying witch." Lady Penelope let out a string of muttered curses, prompting me to make the sign of the cross. "I should have known she would be fine with betraying me, too."

Ben and I exchanged glances, and we both looked to Amir as Lady POW stomped away.

"What's her problem?" Ben asked. From the expression on his face, I could tell he was as concerned for Tulia as I was.

"You must forgive Madame," Amir said. "She has been somewhat disconcerted by the fact you both have managed to be hidden from her for so long. Your mother's companion would have known about you, so Lady Penelope is distraught over her deception. Now we have this concern to look into as well."

"Everyone lies, and everyone has secrets," I said.

"It is wonderful to hear you are taking our lessons seriously, Eleanora." Lady Penelope made her way over to us once more. She appeared much more calm, even if her tone was bitter.

"But just as there are secrets and lies, there are those who will strive to find the truth. I will summon Tulia in the morning," she said.

"Are you going to punish her somehow?" I asked, more curious than worried in that moment. Tulia was tough. She would not submit to Lady POW without a fight.

THE ORDER OF THE CRYSTAL DAGGERS

Lady POW smirked. "Somehow," she replied. "But for now, you need to make another round of appearances, Eleanora. There is still plenty of time to drop in on one or two balls tonight."

"But we'll be out until dawn."

"That is the point of Society."

"Can't we just go and see Tulia ourselves?" I asked. "If we can figure out who murdered Dr. Artha and now Father Novak, and the others as well, we might be able stop them."

"It is not just about stopping the murders," Lady Penelope said. "This is a matter of kingdom security. If these same people poisoned your father, whoever they are, there is a long-awaited *coup d'état* underway. Taking down one man is not enough. This is a coordinated effort against the Empire."

"Ideologues do not usually murder people," Amir said.

"But their adherents might," Ben said. "Just look at the Revolution of 1848. The protestors were willing to kill King Ferdinand. He abdicated rather than face their wrath, and my father was poisoned by someone who would undo his work."

"I thought you hated *Otec*," I said.

Ben glared at me. "I hated him, but I will not allow the little good he did in his life be disregarded, especially by someone who thinks killing politicians and priests is some kind of worthy game, like four-dimensional chess."

"That's enough for now," Lady Penelope said. "We must return to the social scene, Eleanora. I will discuss things with Tulia tomorrow."

"Good," I said. "I want to hear what she has to say myself."

"You will be busy." Lady Penelope brushed me aside with the wave of her hand. "I will take care of it."

"What do I possibly have to do that is more important than talking with Tulia?"

"You'll have plenty to do," Lady Penelope insisted. "You'll see."

13

◊

Much to my chagrin, Lady POW was right; I was busy the next day. But it was not until later that I realized being busy did not mean I would be doing something important.

By the time Ben came to my room with the lunch tray, I was desperate for relief from my assigned task.

"Oh, thank God you are here," I said, as I reached for a new cup of tea.

"Are you talking about me, or the tea?" Ben asked,

"Give me a few moments and I'll let you know." I saw him smile before he sat down and relaxed into a chair. For the next several moments, the two of us indulged in our grand lunches, allowing me to reconsider the annoyance I felt at Lady POW.

Even if I was not good enough to be trusted to help more in her assignments, I was grateful for what I did have; I had good food and I was free to read anything I wished, and Ben and I still had the comfort of each other's company.

He sat with me, sighing happily as he poured more tea for himself. "Sundays are the best. No training today."

"Not for you." I wrinkled my nose. "Lady Penelope accompanied me to church today, and it was a miracle God did not strike me naked for all the attention I was stealing away from him."

"I'm sure if he did that, he would have lost a lot more attention."

I laughed. "True. I'd be crowned a saint on the spot."

"Or condemned as a witch, since you would have been showing your unholy flesh in church. The Pope would have had a fit of apoplexy reading that letter from the bishop."

"That is also true."

"So that was Lady POW's big assignment for you?" Ben asked. "Going to church today?"

"No. These are." I gestured toward my desk and the area surrounding it. Several arrangements of flowers, including a large bouquet of roses from Karl, cluttered the desktop and mixed with various calling cards and other notes from admirers. "I have to send thank you missives to everyone who sent one. And I can't just say something vague or polite. I have to be specific and elusive. She says that will increase my popularity."

"And help with her cover."

I huffed indignantly. "*Our* cover, you mean."

"So you've just been writing letters all morning?" Ben arched his brow. "Why didn't you just go and see if Betsy and Mavis would be able to help you?"

Irritation and inspiration struck me at the same time. "That would have been a good idea. It would have given them a chance to practice their Czech. I wonder if Lady POW would let them come over here? Or would Cecilia's wrath be too great?"

"I guess I don't know if it would actually work," Ben said with a shrug. "They are Cecilia's servants, after all. Lady POW has no claim on them."

"I hope they are doing well." I thought of Betsy's frailty and Mavis' hesitancy. "Alex will be a handful for them if he is not watched carefully."

"Amir told me Alex and Priscilla are both under watch from Lady POW, in addition to Cecilia herself."

"That's a wise move."

Ben nodded. "I suppose it is better she is wise. If she's dangerous, I mean."

I agreed with him, and I would have cheerfully commiserated over that topic until nightfall. But there was something I wanted from Ben, and I finally had the chance for the perfect opening. "Speaking of dangerous, Ben … I have a favor to ask."

"Why do I get the feeling that this is something you'd rather not discuss with Lady POW?"

"Because you know me so well, obviously."

Ben crossed his arms. "Well, now I know I should be worried. What do you want, Nora?"

I bit my lip, before forcing myself to follow through. "I wanted to see if you could meet me in the city tomorrow night and take me somewhere."

"Without Lady POW?"

I nodded. "Yes. Lady POW told me Count Potocki is throwing a ball at Queen Anne's Royal Summerhouse tomorrow night. It is supposed to be packed with the aristocrats and nobles. I'm sure I can slip away before she realizes it."

"I don't know about this. You really don't have a lot of practice at reconnaissance, Nora," Ben said. "Maybe you should practice some this week and try some other day."

"What about all those years dodging work from Cecilia and bullying from Alex?" I objected. "I know how to sneak around."

"That's not quite the same thing."

"But I don't want to wait," I said. Ferdy told me the Cabal held its meetings on Monday and Thursday, and I wanted to go and see him again sooner. The thought of waiting was worse than even the thought of Lady POW's wrath. "Come on, Ben, help me. Please."

"Why do you want to go so badly?"

Quickly, I turned my gaze away from Ben. "It is ... mostly for a private reason."

It was true, even if it was a reason I did not even fully understand. I liked Ferdy. I envied him, even. He was free to be himself and do what he liked, and I was touched and even excited that he wanted to spend time with me. And despite all his joking and his lying, I could tell he was a good man. He was poor and homeless maybe, but he was someone who could understand me in ways that no one, especially men like Karl Marcelin, ever could.

"Now I know this is not a good idea," Ben said. "How can a reason be 'mostly private,' Nora?"

"Well ... " My fingers curled into fists, tightening around my skirt. "You remember that boy who helped me sell *Táta's* book?"

"Now I especially don't like where this is going." Ben shifted forward in his seat.

Despite his vacillation, I told Ben about Ferdy—specifically, about how he worked with Mr. Clavan and the newspaper, and how he had been investigating Dr. Artha's murder when we first met.

I did not mention how I felt about Ferdy, or about how he felt about me.

Ben was quiet as I told him about Clavan and the Cabal, and Ferdy's other friends. When I mentioned their meetings on Mondays and Thursdays could possibly help us, giving us clues as to who was behind the recent string of murders in Prague, Ben finally interrupted me.

"So this is for the mission?" he asked. "How is that a private reason, Nora?"

"Just think about it." I ignored his question. Misdirection could work in my favor, just as it could for others. "We could find more information on our own, and Lady POW would see that we were serious about being part of the Order."

"When you put it that way, it sounds like you want to prove her wrong."

"Can you blame me?" I asked. "Harshad has yet to teach me anything. And as much as you like Amir, I don't want to go begging him for anything."

"I don't think you would have to beg him," Ben said, his voice hardened and sad at the same time.

"Either way, I'd rather ignore him. Besides," I said, nodding toward the wardrobe, which was overflowing with dresses and hats and accessories of all sorts. I reached under a nearby pillow and pulled out the gentleman's clothes Lady POW had given to me in the carriage the night before. "I'd much rather get another chance to go around the city wearing these instead."

128

THE ORDER OF THE CRYSTAL DAGGERS

"I can't fault you for that," Ben said with a small chuckle. "Some of those contraptions look like a nightmare. I'm glad I don't have to worry about such matters."

"Another reason you'd rather not get married?" I teased, hoping the small amount of levity would further distract him from asking about my feelings for Ferdy.

Ben snorted. When he said nothing else, I decided to risk his wrath with my prodding. "Don't you want a wife of your own, now that Lady POW can provide an inheritance for you?"

"Please, Nora. No woman would want me," Ben said. "I am not fit to provide for her. As much as I hate to say it, Cecilia was right—"

"No! Never say that! She is wrong on every account when it comes to you."

"Be fair, Nora. You and I know the truth. A beautiful woman would never look my way, except out of pity or amusement."

"That's not true," I insisted. "You deserve someone to love you. You watch, the most beautiful woman in the world will find you and beg you to marry her. I will pray for just that to happen. If for no other reason than to make you recant your awful words." I wrinkled my nose. "Imagine, Cecilia being right. Ha!"

"Well, if you believe that God will hear your prayers," Ben said, "I'd rather not have a beautiful wife."

"Why not?"

"Beauty fades and often hides the hollowness behind it. Give me a wife who is unique. As the years go by and the beautiful fade into the background, my wife will only grow more vibrant."

I stuck my tongue out at him. "You'd better hope she isn't mad then."

"I've had plenty of experience with that, between our stepmother and Prissy and Alex."

"True enough," I agreed. In that moment, it was hard not to wonder if my father had lived—if he had not been poisoned—how he and Cecilia would have gotten along.

Would things still be this bad? Would I still be this desperate for my own independence, my own freedom?

I could never know the answer to that. But I was grateful, despite all her thoughtless comments and insistent prodding, that Lady POW had come into our lives. Even if *Táta* had lived, I would have wanted something more of *Máma*.

As Ben shifted his leg restlessly, I shrugged. "I'm glad we haven't had to worry much about marriage until now."

"But you are, indeed, thinking about it now?" Ben asked.

It crushed me to see the somber look on his face, and even more when I realized I was blushing. "Not really, Ben, but Lady POW has mentioned it as a ploy enough to make me worried."

"It's fine, you know, if you want to get married, Nora," Ben said. "I'm glad that you are thinking about it, at least. I don't want you to end up alone and hating me for it."

"I won't end up alone if you are with me. And if I do end up hating you, it will be for other reasons. You have my word on that, *brácha.*"

"You won't hate me if I decline to participate in your desired venture, will you?"

I gave Ben a rueful smirk. I had to admit, he was good at catching me at my own game. He had distracted me enough that I did not see his counterargument coming. "I never thought you would decline, so we will have to see. Would you risk that fate?"

"I've never been much of a gambler." Ben sighed. "So it appears to be in my better interest to take you. If for no other reason than if I do not accompany you, I have a feeling you would try to do it yourself."

"Yes!" I bounced over and gave him a hug. "Thank you."

"But when we get there, I want to meet your new friends," Ben warned. "Especially the one you're pining for."

Before I could vehemently deny that, there was a knock at the door. We both turned and watched as Amir appeared.

I groaned to myself. His mustache twitched, and I had to wonder how much of our conversation he might have heard.

Amir looked much the same as he had when I first saw him, with a formal shirt and pressed pants. His shoes gleamed, and the dagger at his side was tucked behind the folds of his coat. "Ben. Mademoiselle," he said, greeting each of us with a polite nod.

I gave a cool, polite curtsey. "Mr. Qureshi."

He caught my tone and straightened. "Lady Penelope has requested mademoiselle's presence in the west parlor. She sent me to find you."

"Why?" I asked.

"She said after the Hohenwart Ball, she needs you to practice the waltz."

I did not know why, but the way Amir said it made me feel even more foolish. I had been hoping Harshad was ready to teach me, or that I would begin to learn more about surveillance or reconnaissance.

No, instead I would be dancing. Dancing, when murders were happening all over the city and Bohemia's political situation grew more precarious.

THE ORDER OF THE CRYSTAL DAGGERS

"No," I grumbled, "I meant, why did she send you?"

Amir's patience never faltered, even as Ben gave me a blunt kick in the shin.

"Because it was efficient, no doubt," Amir replied. "But one does not question Lady Penelope's decisions too often, of course."

His response was perfectly polite. But I was certain he knew of my reluctance to follow orders without asking questions. If he really was Lady POW's trusted confidant, there was no telling how many hours she had complained about me to him.

Ben nudged me with his leg, this time more gently. "Go, Nora," he said, with a teasing smirk. "We'll talk later. I have some relaxation to tend to."

I nearly whimpered at Ben's good fortune, but I settled for pouting as Amir escorted me to the west parlor. I gave my brother one last angry look, and then I brushed past Amir.

Leaving the room when I was with Ben was already hard enough, but I was appalled when Amir followed me. He caught up to me quickly, his long steps shortening into an easy rhythm as we headed for the library. He started to offer me his arm but backed down when I glared at him.

A few moments passed in silence, save for our footsteps, before Amir spoke. "I have heard Lady Penelope is pleased with your performance so far," Amir said, as we walked through the hallways of the castle.

"So far? Does that mean you think I'll fail at some point?"

Amir pursed his lips. "No," he said. "Although it is a possibility, and one that should be considered in its proper context."

"How about we consider the context of other things?" I purposefully provoked him. "Such as when you attacked me and stole my father's book?"

Finally, I saw a quick flash of emotion on his face. He said nothing and silently turned away from me.

"Lady Penelope is waiting for you, mademoiselle. We do not have the proper time to spend on such … an enlightening tale."

"Well, when are you going to tell me about that day? Are you going to go back on your promise?" I asked, as a cloud of thick tension increasingly surrounded us. "Or are you hoping I will just forget about it entirely?"

"We have other things to concern ourselves with, mademoiselle."

"Such as?"

"Miss Tulia has refused to answer Lady Penelope's summons. She is not in good humor today," Amir said quietly, and I had to wonder if he thought he was being slightly treasonous in saying so.

"Tulia's smart enough to know not to come here if Lady POW is upset at her."

Amir cleared his throat, as if he was holding back a laugh. "Lady POW? Oh. I see Ben's endearing nickname for Lady Penelope is catching."

"It is an appropriate one," I argued. "And it is much easier to say her name that way. I don't care if she hates it."

"I don't know if she does. She's never said anything about it to me. But it would not surprise me to find out she enjoys it. She has a fondness for pet names."

"I still wish she would stop calling me Eleanor." I wrinkled my nose in irritation.

Amir went quiet. I saw he was staring straight ahead with a faraway look in his eyes. His expression seemed to suggest he was suddenly no longer there.

As his eyes cleared and he looked back at me, it was almost as if we shared the same, single thought.

"Naděžda."

At that moment, I finally understood. He had known my mother, too. Amir had called out her name when he saw me for the first time, face to face. When he first saw me, he recognized her.

I stumbled a little and stooped for a moment to fix my shoe, struggling to think through everything.

Lady POW had mentioned that to Harshad, I recalled, thinking of the conversation Ben and I overheard before any of this began. Harshad called my mother "Dezda," and Amir had met my mother. Clearly, he called her by her full middle name.

It was strange to think that my mother had been so much to so many people.

I was still stunned as we walked into the west parlor. Lady Penelope called out to me, and I was immensely grateful for the distraction. "Ah, there you are, Eleanora."

"You sent your servant here to find me," I said, pointing my thumb at Amir. "Why wouldn't I be here?"

Lady Penelope frowned. "I know better than most the complexities of sarcasm and wit, Eleanora. It is best to keep your good humor out of the former and concentrated on the latter. There is no need to insult anyone. You know Amir is not my servant. We are on the same side here."

Yes, the side of espionage. How comforting.

"Thank you, Amir," Lady Penelope said. "Please await us in the ballroom. We will be there shortly."

"Ballroom? We?"

"Your gown for tonight's ball is here," Lady Penelope said. "We need to be sure that you can dance properly in it. As much as Karl Marcelin might have found your clumsy footwork attractive, I prefer we stir the pot with your exceptional skills."

For a long moment, as she went on about social politics, I felt a new sense of weariness come over me. There was nothing that exceptional about me. Not really. If I had been smarter, I might have found a way to be free before Lady Penelope's arrival. If I had been stronger, I might have found a way to stand up to Cecilia. If I had been more aware of the world surrounding me, I might have been able to find my place in it. And if I had been more faithful, maybe God would have erased all my doubt of who I was and what I was put in this world to do.

I was none of those things. I was a simple girl playing dress up, chasing after my mother's shadow, longing to be free when I was not brave enough, strong enough, smart enough, or sure enough to face freedom's cost.

"Come, Eleanora. You will be practicing with Amir." Lady POW looked me squarely in the eye, demanding my full attention, before she put her hands on her hips. "And while you are practicing your dancing, you can also practice being a proper lady. That includes *not* insulting your dancing partner, and pretending to be civilized."

I gritted my teeth angrily, saying nothing as Amelia, Marguerite, and Jaqueline began suiting me up inside my new gown.

It took longer than I expected, but at the end of their frittering, my hair was combed back, my feet were placed into small silk dancing slippers—I thanked God for his goodness that they were not heels—and I had the stays around my waist groaning as my figure was pulled in place.

"Eleanor, you look lovely," Lady Penelope said as I twirled for her final inspection.

"Eleanora."

"Yes. Apologies, once more."

"Maybe it would help if you called my mother 'Dezda,' like Harshad does," I said. *Or Naděžda, like Amir.*

Her gaze softened, ever so slightly and ever so briefly, and I felt guilty, as though I had struck her. "I don't like to call her that as much as he does," Lady Penelope said quietly, before the hard, stoic mask came down again. "That was always his name for her when she was … "

Lady POW let her voice trail off, and before she could say anything else, I took her hand. I did not know if I was trying to comfort her or not.

"I'm sorry," I said. It was part of who I was, to be curious, but I would not want to impose her with my questions if it pained her.

She seemed to understand as she nodded. "Yes. Of course." Then she marched forward, as if our quiet moment had never happened. Soon we reached the ballroom, where Amir was waiting for us.

He was in the middle of the empty ballroom, standing tall and awkwardly straight. As I approached him, he held out his hand. "Will you do me the honor to dance with me?"

"I don't know that I should give it to you." I was aware of Lady POW's standards, but I decided I did not have to be cheerful when I was forced to be polite. I gave Amir a gritty smile. "But my grandmother demands it of me, doesn't she?"

"She demands it of both of us, I'm sure," Amir replied, and I was close enough I could hear the bitterness he was hiding in his voice.

At his tone, I knew Lady POW was watching us intently, waiting for me to accept Amir's hand. I could already hear her voice in my head, reminding me of *The Ladies' Guide to Excellence and Etiquette*, telling me it was not polite to refuse when a gentleman asked for a dance.

It did nothing for me that I did not consider Amir a gentleman, no matter how much he had insisted before that he was not a mongrel.

Reaching out, I settled my hand into Amir's.

An old memory of my father came to the forefront of my mind. He would dance with me when I was younger, before he died. *Táta* loved to indulge me with his kindness and his kisses, and as Amir's hand swallowed mine, I could not help but feel sad and nostalgic for those days.

"Just follow me," Amir said as he stepped closer to me.

I had practiced the waltz with Karl at the Hohenwart Ball, so I was not surprised by the steps that followed. But I was grateful the speed had slowed as I relearned how to anticipate direction and center my balance. Amir led me around the room in slow, lulling steps, and his gentleness never faltered.

I was more surprised that all the details of the room disappeared as Amir guided me through the slides and twirls of different dances. As I shifted my gaze from my feet to Amir's eyes—a glittering brown, with speckles of gold peeking out near the edge of his irises—I felt an unusual rush of compassion and warmth, and I did not like it.

"What is it?" I asked him, noticing that he was staring back at me.

"It seems you have remembered your dancing quite well," he said, and I shook my head at once, keeping my forced smile steady as we passed by Lady POW.

"The practice helps," I replied neutrally. "And it did help that Karl was a good dancer last night. Some of the others I danced with were not as good, but fortunately they blamed it on their own poor performance."

"They were likely distracted by your beauty."

"You don't have to talk to me like that." I rolled my eyes. "Besides, you might distract me now with your false flattery."

"Flattery is always false, mademoiselle. I was speaking truth." Amir smiled. "You may have that problem in the future, when other men are dancing with you."

"I can learn to handle it later, then."

"You can also learn it now. There is nothing efficient about wasting time, after all."

"I'd rather not, thank you very much. There is no need for you to continue talking to me." My tone was frosty and bitter, every part a perfect complement to the kindness in his eyes. "Unless, of course, you'd like to tell me why you stole my father's book from me when we unfortunately met?"

"I would not say it was unfortunate."

"What would you say it was, then?"

Amir's mustache curled around the corners of his mouth. "God's humor at work."

"What's that supposed to mean?" I asked, frustrated and infuriated. "Are you insulting me?"

"Never, mademoiselle."

Before I could accuse him of lying in addition to insulting me, or before I could "accidentally" begin stepping on his toes, Lady POW began calling out instructions, making me feel even more insulted and infuriated—and even worse, isolated, and unable to do anything to escape.

"Hands up, Eleanora," she called. "Yes, take a step closer. Now, remember to smile. Watch your timing; men are supposed to lead. And show your interest. Pretend you are dancing with a prince!"

Between Amir's dancing and Lady Penelope's snappy judgements, I felt trapped in a world of soft tyranny. It was a world where the truth was too impolite to be spoken, and even if it had to be, it had to be dressed up in clothes as strange and as ornate as the ones I was wearing, and it was likely as unrecognizable as I was in the end.

I certainly felt nothing like my usual self.

The others did not seem to believe it was me, either.

Amir held me at a polite distance as we danced, but I was still close enough I could see the pained delight in his eyes as he watched me, and recalling Lady POW's earlier mistake of calling me by my mother's name, I suddenly wondered if he was thinking of her, too.

The last note of the waltz rang out, and we finally slowed to a stop.

"Why did you take my father's book?" This time, my question was quiet but harsh against the growing silence. Amir seemed surprised, but he did not refrain from responding.

"It was not your father's book, mademoiselle."

I slowly dropped my hands from his.

Already, I knew what he was going to say.

"When I saw you, it was like falling into a portal to the past, twenty-six years ago. I saw the book, and I knew it could only belong to my Naděžda."

"You knew my mother." The words were chunky and foreign to me as they came out of my mouth. I knew I had no reason to accuse him of something I already knew to be true.

"Yes. She was my dearest friend for many years before … " Amir said quietly. I saw his gaze lower to the scar on his right hand. "And when she … left … I was angry."

It plagued me, knowing that Lady POW was not the only one who seemed to prefer my mother to me.

"When she left the Order, you mean?"

"She did not leave the Order," Amir whispered. "She left me."

It took me a long moment to process everything. Amir and I were still standing in the middle of the room. Somewhere, a thousand moments and a million miles away, Lady POW clapped and praised us, telling us I was already much better at the waltz than before. She was calling for another song, but I barely heard any of it, as I watched while Amir's eyes swam over with memories and emotion.

There was suddenly no denying the full truth of the matter.

Amir had been in love with my mother.

As his eyes cleared and his mind returned to the present moment, I did the only thing I could think to do.

I reached out and slapped him.

The smack of my palm on his cheek echoed through the now-quiet room. My hand seemed to fall against his face with much more force than I had meant, but it was over all too quickly just the same.

He just stood there, looking at me. And when he looked at me, he saw her—and his own heartbreak.

"Eleanora!" Lady Penelope gaped at me in shock.

I fumed as Lady POW stepped forward. I was too angry and confused and frustrated to care. I ignored her and stood my ground in front of Amir, who did not say anything as he only gave me a wounded look.

"Stop," I hissed at Amir. "I am not my mother, and you had no right to steal what I did have of her away from me."

Before Amir could say anything, I already knew there was nothing I wanted to hear from him.

So I ran away.

I brushed past Lady POW without any regard, throwing her off balance by my sudden and ardent desperation to escape.

"Eleanora!"

I struggled not to show my regret and confused rage; I did not want to show Lady Penelope my own weakness any more than I wanted to admit it to myself.

So I ran away.

I ran away from her, I ran away from Amir, and I ran away from the truth, as another one of my childhood illusions was stripped away from me.

"Eleanora, get back here at once, young lady!" Lady Penelope called. She was no longer surprised, but now she was angry. I heard her start to run after me, but Amir called after her.

"Let her go, Lady Penelope," I heard Amir say. "Please. I made her uncomfortable."

"We have to be ready for tonight. This is no time for her to be fighting with you over trivial matters."

There is nothing trivial about this. I stopped for a quick moment, leaning against the wall outside the door. My breath came quick and shallow while I forced myself to hold in my tears as I listened to Amir's response.

"I fear that is not all she found offensive," Amir replied. "You must forgive her, as I do, Madame."

Lady Penelope huffed. "But you did nothing wrong."

"Even so, my lady, I am not without my shortcomings."

At his insufferable forgiveness, I took off once more, hoping that his little speech would be enough to keep Lady POW from breathing hellfire and damnation down my neck the next time she saw me.

For now, I decided, it was enough just to run away and be free from them, even if it was for only a few moments.

Even if it was ultimately futile in the end.

I could not run from the truth.

My mother and Amir had been friends—and he had been in love with her. Had she been in love with him, too? And if so, why did she leave him? Did she even care for my father at all? I was surrounded with more and more questions, and everything I had grown up never questioning seemed to fall apart as I made my way to my room.

Outside the window, a strange midday fog rolled in. The outline of Prague and its proud castle had become more mysterious and ethereal, and I wondered if it was truly real, too. Before, everything about the city had a celestial touch to it, as if I could walk down a street and suddenly find myself in Heaven.

In that moment, I could not say that; my paradise was suddenly full of poison, and I had to wonder what parts of my life it had touched.

I entered my room, confronted with the terrible sadness of this reality. I flopped onto my bed, burying myself in the covers, letting my eyes swell over with tears.

It was only then that I allowed myself to admit the deepest part of my pain.

"*Máma*," I whispered into the silken sheets. "I miss you."

While I missed her because I loved her, I missed her more for the questions I had, the ones I knew could never be fully answered.

I missed her, and I had missed her whole life. How would things be different had she lived? Would I have known Lady POW sooner? Would Amir still be a strange man on the streets, thieving books, or would he be a friendly visitor of sorts?

Would anyone look at me and just see me? Would I be able to find my mother and not lose myself in the process?

"*Máma*." I curled up in the bed, feeling small and alone and silly.

I missed her, but I could never be her. I did not have her strength, and the strength I did have was only there because of all the pain I had endured without her.

14

◊

I gradually fell asleep in my bed. No one came to bother me, and later I would wonder if Amir had interfered, since Lady POW apparently canceled our evening entertainments. I slept so deeply that nothing woke me up until the earliest hours of the morning.

It was the rain that woke me up, long after the night had saturated itself in gloominess. I awoke feeling rested, more rested than I had felt since Lady Penelope's arrival. Sleep had renewed me, and my questions as well. I sat up in bed, curling my legs under my chin as my thoughts, as varied and complicated and deliberating as they were, kept me preoccupied.

I glanced at my door. I did not have to open it to know there was a heavy silence about the manor.

I felt surrounded in darkness in more ways than one.

I wondered, briefly, if Lady POW would be upset with me when she woke up, or if she would be relieved we were not out on the town while it was raining. We lived on the city outskirts, close enough to see the city skyline, but she would be upset if her coach was stuck in the muddy lanes that surrounded my family's farmland.

I rubbed my face, wincing at the scratchy tearstains. They were rough patches on my skin, hinting at the previous, ongoing pain in my heart.

I knew very little of *Máma's* life before Ben and I had come along, and from what Lady Penelope told me about her time with the Order of the Crystal Daggers, the little I did know was likely a cover of sorts.

My mind settled on another memory of *Máma*. I saw her wearing the locket she had worn each Sunday to church. She would brush my hair, and I would tug at it. She would open it and show me the miniatures of Ben and me, and the one of my father on the opposite side.

I thought about the locket as Ben's earlier comment came back to me. *"You really don't have a lot of practice at reconnaissance. Maybe you should practice some."*

That was what I should do, I thought. *I should go and retrieve it from under the pantry floor.*

Giving myself a task, even as it was nothing that would put me back in Lady Penelope's good graces—if indeed, such a thing was possible—helped me immensely.

I slipped out of my sheets and put on the breeches I had pilfered from the previous night. If I was going to sneak off to meet with Ferdy, I had to prepare myself. Retrieving my mother's locket and my father's pocket watch was a secondary pleasure to my ultimate purpose.

139

Thinking of Ferdy energized me, even if I knew I would be risking Lady Penelope's temper once more. I began to undress as I pushed that concern out of my mind, reaching for memories of *Máma* and Ferdy instead. I stuffed my chemise into the pants and bundled up, pulling the coat tightly across my body to hide any slits of white that might be visible. Pulling on the men's shoes, I felt free again, in a new way.

Women did not have as much power as Queen Victoria made it appear. Even in Prague, where there were artists and inventors and people of all backgrounds, the ways of London and Paris led us to be slaves to fashion, and fashion did not stop with our constraining clothes.

I made my way through the halls of my home, working my way to the end of the west wing with ease, trying not to feel a sense of despair. I had tumbled throughout the manor before my mother's death, reigning free as a queen in training and a princess in my own place. I was free because of my security, in my parents' love and our titles and income. Once Cecilia moved in and *Táta* died, I found a new sort of freedom, hiding in the shadows of the servants' quarters and their assigned hallways. Now, even though Lady POW had freed Ben and me from Cecilia's charge, I knew my freedom was limited.

I had learned, after the long years, that freedom was a precious, fragile thing, and easily overturned by power. That did not stop me from wanting it; in fact, I was certain I was even more anxious to secure it.

As I made my way toward the kitchens, I heard footsteps dashing about in different rhythms, according to the early morning routines. The cooks were preparing breakfast, mixing up ingredients for meals and gathering tools they would need; the laundry had to be prepared, and the stables had to be cleaned and the horses and other animals fed.

I was just calculating my odds of being able to get some freshly baked bread when I heard new footsteps start to come down the adjacent hallway in loud, angry stomps.

"I can't believe this!" Cecilia's screeching rubbed my ears raw. It seemed that no matter how long it had been since I'd heard her say anything, her voice was still shrilly enough to make me cringe.

I stopped short, hoping she would not pass by me on her obvious tirade.

"That bastard! How could he do this to me? To all of our plans?"

"Isn't there anything that we can do?" Alex was walking behind her, keeping up with her infuriated pace.

At the sound of his voice, I scurried to a nearby doorway and smooshed myself as flat as I could. I did not want another confrontation with Alex for more than one reason.

"What can we do?" Cecilia's voice dropped to a quiet whisper, but in the night, I was able to hear each word clearly. "The only thing would be to turn him in. Tell

THE ORDER OF THE CRYSTAL DAGGERS

the king everything, destroy any chance of bettering our lives and ruining the little we do have."

"Surely the king would be grateful?"

"Grateful for what?" Cecilia spat. "Planning his overthrow? Funding it with our investments over the last twenty years?"

My heart began to pound inside my chest, so loudly I could feel the pulse behind my ears. Their footsteps began to move away, and I tiptoed closer to the edge of the corridor, hoping to keep up with them as they carried on their conversation. I was also glad to see they were heading toward the kitchens. I would be able to make an easy detour and head back to my room.

"I meant he would be grateful for your information. Why not place the blame on His Grace?" Alex asked. "Tell him he tricked you, forced you into it. Maybe we can say he even blackmailed and threatened you?"

"Have you seen King Ferdinand at all since he was forced from the throne? He is ignorant and simple-minded, and his only power remains because of the benevolence of his nephew. He will not be able to protect us from Max."

"What of the people?" Alex asked. "Surely their benevolence is also necessary?"

"The people are fools as a collective. They can do nothing, other than what their betters tell them to," Cecilia muttered. I could hear her cursing that followed. "I will need to contact Max's foreign benefactors. But I don't know what to tell them yet."

"Mother," Alex said. "Maybe instead of stopping the plan, we should be ready to act if it succeeds. The others are already dead, remember? What is one more body, especially if everything else is in place?"

I held my breath, waiting for her to respond. There was something going on, and Cecilia was part of it.

When she said nothing, Alex pressed her. "His Grace has extended us his fullest regrets about Teresa Marie. There is no harm in playing along for now."

"He will discard us. If we turn on him, he will find a way to assign us the blame. He has all the advantage now, Alex."

"We do not need to just sit here," Alex hissed. "This is what got us here in the first place. You allowed that British lady to destroy my marriage contract! If she had not come, none of this would have happened."

I smiled. It was good to see Lady POW, for all her trouble, was living up to her promise. She had clearly ruined plenty of Cecilia's plans by dissolving the engagement between Alex and Teresa Marie.

"Don't you see? Max found what he was looking for all those years ago. He would have broken the engagement himself, now that he's found King Ferdinand's son and heir."

My eyes went wide. *King Ferdinand has a son?*

"There's no need to be obtuse about this, Alex," Cecilia continued, as my world kept reeling from the news.

"We have to do something," Alex insisted. "I will not let your inaction stop us from getting what we want."

"We have already lost." Cecilia shook her head. "Max has what he wants. He has the advantage. There's nothing we can do, and if we oppose him, he will come after us."

"What can he really do to us?" Alex scoffed.

"People have died, if I might remind you. You've asked what one more body would cost. It costs something entirely differently when it is your own."

Alex went mostly silent as they turned around another corner. I heard their muffled argument continue as they walked further away from the kitchens.

Before I could trail after them, I heard an exclaimed gasp from behind me.

"Nora!"

I jerked around to see Betsy, her apron full of apples. It was the first time in more than a week I had seen her, and even though I knew Lady POW would be upset at me for shirking my spying duties, even if they were unassigned and impromptu, I raced toward Betsy with open arms.

"Betsy," I said, hugging her. "I'm so glad to see you."

The apples fell from her apron as she hugged me back. "It's wonderful to see you, too," she said. "Mavis and I have been lonely without you and Ben around."

"How are you and your sister? Are you faring well?" I glared back toward the shadows, where Alex and Cecilia had disappeared only a moment earlier.

"Her Ladyship has been in a rage," Betsy said, as we began to pick up her fallen apples. "She seems unsure of doing anything, however. Her Grace's servants pass us in the halls when we do chores, so she knows if she takes any of her anger out on us, she will be the one in trouble."

"Thank God for Lady Penelope," I said with a small laugh.

"Oh, I do, Nora. I'm so happy you and Ben have escaped her Ladyship's claws."

"Even if you are still her prisoner?" I asked, shaking my head. "You are too kind, Betsy."

"Your stepmother was cruel to you," Betsy said. "But believe it or not, she saved me. And Mavis, too. She hired me as an orphan with a younger sister and brought me here. She is cruel, sometimes, but she has saved me from a greater cruelty."

"That's still not good."

Before I could say anything else, Betsy noticed my outfit for the first time. I enjoyed the surprise in her eyes as she looked me up and down.

"Oh, my! What are you wearing?"

"It's one of Ben's outfits," I lied. "I thought it would be easier to sneak down here and see you. And I wanted to get something from the pantry while I was here."

"Your mother's locket?" Betsy asked.

When I gave her a quizzical look, she giggled. "You told me about it before. Come on. I need to take these apples to the pantry myself. I'll help you in."

"Thank you," I said, grateful to have a friend by my side once more.

It was strange to see Betsy, and even stranger to have her remind me I once was able to share secrets with her. Ever since Lady Penelope told me about the Order of the Crystal Daggers, I had felt like a new person. I had secrets of my own now, and I would not be able to tell them to her. As I watched Betsy help me duck around other servants and sneak into the pantry unnoticed, I mourned for the loss of our sisterly bond.

When Betsy handed me my hidden treasures, I forced myself to smile. My mother's golden locket gleamed in the dull pantry light, and *Táta's* pocket watch shined as I opened it up. The clockwork screws were still, but I could see the familiar, delicate design.

"Thank you for helping me," I said to Betsy, sincerely and somberly, knowing it was likely one of our last adventures together, if not *the* last one.

"Oh, it's no trouble," Betsy said. She gave me a friendly smile. "I am glad you were able to sneak down here and talk with me. I know from the other rumors I've heard you have been busy, dancing in all them fancy ballrooms with proper gentlemen and dining all over Prague."

I laughed nervously. "It's not as fun as it sounds."

"It sure sounds wonderful."

"It is," I said, and as Betsy's eyes lit up with dazzling interest, I decided to tuck more secrets into my heart. I wanted to tell her so much about how the polite world was beautiful but hollow, and how I knew that I did not belong there.

Instead, as we walked back toward the west wing, I told her of the Hohenwart Ball, and the different parks around the city, all the new buildings that were being built. I allowed her to think it was a magical sort of world, like the one I used to believe it to be.

When we came to the last hallway before the west wing, I gave her a hug and wished her well.

"Please tell Mavis I miss her, too," I said.

THE ORDER OF THE CRYSTAL DAGGERS

"Will do, miss."

I smiled. "It'll always be Nora to you, Betsy."

Betsy giggled and headed off, and even as I waved goodbye, I wondered if I was not a hollow person, too.

My old life as a servant had never felt comfortable, but I missed it enough to mourn it as Betsy's bubbly shadow scurried back to the kitchens.

Entering the west wing was almost like stepping into a new world. The darkness, while it was still silent and heavy, seemed to carry more vulnerability and hope. I gripped my mother's locket and my father's watch closer to me. I prayed for God to hear me once more, to fill my heart with comfort, and, if he would, to send me a new friend—someone with whom I could share my new life without reservations.

It seemed like a reasonable request. After all, I had enough reservations about things. After Lady Penelope largely dismissed my theories about Lord Maximillian earlier, I had stumbled into a reality that would have seemed even less plausible only an hour earlier.

I felt a strong urge to go and wake Ben up, just so I would have someone to tell. But before I could turn back and head to his room, I saw that there was someone waiting for me beside the library door.

My feet stayed put as I tried to make out the features of the dark figure before me. I was just wondering if Alex had spotted me after all and had come to ensure my silence when the shadow spoke.

"I was wondering when you would return, mademoiselle."

15

◊

My eyes squinted at the darkness, before they found the familiar shape of Amir before me. He was standing upright, with his hands clasped together behind him, so unnaturally I wondered if it was a military stance. As I took a tentative step closer, he stepped back into a sliver of light peeking out from the library. He seemed to have been waiting patiently, although I had no idea how long he had been there.

"Amir. I mean, Mr. Qureshi. What are you doing here?" My fingers curled into fists, tightening around my parents' trinkets.

"I was just waiting on you to return from your outing."

"Why?" I frowned. Was he going to tell Lady POW? I could not say if she would be happy or not, but if I had to bet on it, I would have said she would have been less than pleased. Especially since Amir had caught me.

"I was on my way to return this to you." He pulled out the small book from behind his back. "I am somewhat surprised—but not entirely—to find you coming back from an unauthorized outing."

"It wasn't like I left the house." I shoved my father's watch into my greatcoat pocket before reaching for the book.

It was the same book, of course. The etching of the book's cover was clear, with its elegant and intricate design carved into the leather. I held it between my hands as my mother's locket dangled from my fingers, and for a moment, I wondered if I would feel closer to her by merely holding it, in just seeing it as something she had once owned.

Nothing staggering or supernatural happened as I stood there—as far as I could see, anyway. But as the moment passed, slowly and quietly, I remembered I had asked God for a friend before, and I wondered if this was God's way of convicting me as well as answering my prayers.

He would do this to me.

I looked back at Amir.

"You have my sincerest apologies over the matter of its theft," Amir said softly. "As you no doubt know, from our earlier encounter, I loved your mother very much. Seeing you—and her book—brought out the worst part of me that day. I pray you will forgive my lapse in manners and judgment."

I looked back at the book, opening it up, only to see scrawls of finely shaped letters, written in nearly perfect lines. It was my mother's handwriting, though I did not recognize the language or the words she had written. My eyes lingered over the preciseness of her hand, before looking up once more at Amir.

145

I do not want to like you.

"If it makes you feel better, your mother did not like me at first, either."

"Huh?" I blinked, and I blushed, realizing I had spoken my thoughts aloud. I sighed. "Oh."

"I cannot imagine Lady POW tells you a lot of stories of Naděžda," he said. "Would you like to hear one?"

"Lady POW?" I arched my brow appreciatively. "You are calling her that, too?"

"You were right. It is more efficient."

"You don't have to call her that so I will like you." I slipped my mother's locket into the other pocket of my coat.

"I was not doing so with that intention. I had to work to win your mother over, too, you know. If you talk with me, I'll tell you the story of how we first met."

I said nothing, and even in the dim lighting, I could see Amir was smiling, letting that mustache of his curl upward along his upper lip.

"I know you are very curious about her, mademoiselle. You need not allow your pride to get in the way of your happiness."

"Do you want me to talk with you or not?" I scoffed. "You shouldn't tell me how you are going to make me do what you want if you want me to do what you want."

"I only want you to do what you want."

I wanted that, too.

"Fine," I said, before pushing open the library door. The room was lit to full brightness, with candelabras flickering at me as I walked toward my father's desk. The fireplace was full of dying light, the dulling embers offering more comfort despite less warmth.

"Your mother loved books," Amir said. "It was one of the reasons she wrote as much as she did. Some of the books she read have notes along the margins. I found a few the other day when I was in here."

"The second time we met?"

He nodded. "The book you have now was the last journal she wrote before … before she passed."

I opened the book, looking down at the written lines. Just like before, I was not able to decipher the writing. "I can't read it."

"I was up all night with it," Amir admitted. "I wanted to give it back after earlier. But I could not tear myself away from it without finishing it. I hope you will forgive me this intrusion, too."

THE ORDER OF THE CRYSTAL DAGGERS

"It is written in a language and script I don't recognize. I didn't even realize it was written instead of printed before." I thumbed through the pages, carefully at first and then more comfortably, as I looked for numbers or any sign that I would be able to translate some part of the message. "I do not know why my stepmother thought I would be able to sell it if it was her journal."

Amir came up beside me, looking over my shoulder. "It is written in Arabic, but it reads from front to back. It was an odd system of compromise Naděžda and I worked out when we became friends. She would work on her Arabic while I learned to read books from left to right."

"So you've read all of it?" I asked, looking back up at him accusingly.

"Not all of it." He shook his head. "I know I stole the book from you, and I know stealing is wrong. I'm here to make amends. But before you get angry, you should remember that you are not the only one who feels robbed since her death."

Amir's sadness suddenly reminded me of my father. When my mother came up in conversations, the rare times that she did after her death, he wore the same downcast expression as Amir, right down to the same glittering eyes and softened gaze.

I leaned back against the desk. "I wasn't about to get angry," I lied.

"You were, too." Amir crossed his arms. "I've known you now for close to a fortnight. Your nostrils flare open and you clench your fists when you are angry."

"I can do that for other reasons." I held up my hand in protest, and it was then I noticed it was indeed curled into a fist.

Amir was kind enough not to laugh at me, although it might have made me feel better. I was grateful that I did not have a mirror to show me what my nose looked like.

"Naděžda had similar foibles. She would also stamp her foot and tap her toe if she was impatient. When we worked together on her business for the Order, we had more than one captive who would complain. One even broke down at what he called the torture of her incessant nature."

"You worked with her and the Order of the Crystal Daggers?"

Amir nodded. "That was originally how we met. She was fifteen and visiting India with Lady POW and Harshad—"

"How long have they known each other, anyway?" I asked. "How old is he? Seventy?"

"Seventy-two, next spring," Amir said. "Lady Penelope is only a few years younger. They have known each other since at least 1825, when your mother was born."

"Forty-five years is a long time to hate someone."

"This likely has more to do with love than hate."

The familiar turn of phrase took me back into the world of *The Tragedy of Romeo and Juliet*. I thought of all my trips into the library. "You have read Shakespeare?"

Amir smiled. "I have lived in London for many years, under the service of Lady Penelope and the League of Ungentlemanly Warfare. Yes, mademoiselle, I know my Shakespeare."

"The League of Ungentlemanly Warfare." I frowned at the foreign name. "So you are not actually part of the Order of the Crystal Daggers?"

"No, I am not. But I remain Lady Penelope's fiercest ally." He put his hand on the curved dagger at his side. "This is a *Wahabite Jambiya*, a special dagger that comes from my homeland. It is our choice of weapon, when it is needed."

"Such as when we first met?" I asked, cracking my knuckles. I decided to circle the conversation around to the League again later.

"Yes, mademoiselle." Amir took the dagger out of the wooden sheath and held it out to me, hilt first. Curiosity compelled me to take it.

"When Lady Penelope succeeds in making Harshad teach you, weapons such as this will be among the first ones you master. A sword is commonplace, and while a rapier might serve you best, they are often cumbersome for the spy and subtle attacker."

"It's beautiful." Studying it, I saw the inscription down the side, in foreign letters and unusual markings. Some of them were similar to the writing in my mother's journal.

"Arabic," he explained. "This is the language I was speaking with your beloved, when we first met."

"My beloved?"

"The boy who interrupted our battle, back in the alley."

At the mention of Ferdy, I forced myself not to blush. "He's not my beloved."

"He seemed to think he was," Amir said, making me frown.

What did Ferdy say to Amir?

As much as I wondered, I decided to worry about that another day. I turned back to the dagger. "What does it say?"

"A blessing for the wielder's protection from Allah."

"Allah?"

"The Arabic word for God, although there are significant differences between the religious views on God himself. Many in the Ottoman Empire follow Mohammadism."

"Oh," I said. "Bohemia is mostly Catholic, although there is more Protestantism here in recent decades. And there is the Jewish population, too, across the Vltava."

Amir nodded. "I've become very familiar with the Anglican Church, serving Lady Penelope. And you are right. In the Western world, there are not many Muslims."

"Are you a Muslim?" I asked, before realizing I was being more than a little too upfront.

"Not anymore." He shook his head. "I once was lost, but now I am found."

Another familiar phrase. "John Newton."

Amir nodded. "I grew up with an affinity for music, despite my father's disdain for it. Never has my soul been so gratified than by Handel's *Messiah*. But that story is for another day, as I have this one to tell first."

"Sorry," I murmured. "I did not mean to interrupt."

"It is no trouble. But this story is more enjoyable than that one, I can assure you, and it is less complicated. The differences between Eastern and Western minds are extraordinary."

"So tell me then." I wanted to hear about my mother.

"When I was much younger, even younger than you, I was working near Constantinople as a medical student, under my father," Amir said. "My Abba, my father, met Harshad as he cared for some of Harshad's … sources, most of whom were not so willing to tell their secrets."

"You mean after Harshad beat them, he sent for your father." I smiled at the thought as he nodded. "And you followed your father in medicine."

"I followed my father in every aspect of my life, until I met Naděžda."

I said nothing. His tone said it all. My mother had driven a deep wedge between Amir and his father, and Amir had chosen *Máma* in the end.

"The day I met her, my life changed." He looked over at me, and I did not have to guess that he was thinking the same thing of meeting me. "I had never seen such blue eyes before. And she was so spirited, unlike any other woman I had met before. She could argue with me in a way that was smart and charming, and even after I admitted my infatuation with her, her arguments still stood better than mine in a way that was uncomfortable."

"I don't remember her like that at all," I said, looking around the library as if I was suddenly in search of her ghost. "She was very gentle and soft. She taught me how to read, and she would spend long days with me while Ben was off with my father. He probably followed him around like you did yours."

"That is why I think your brother and I get along so well," Amir said. "Both of us understand the pain of a father's rejection over something we could not help."

I saw his gaze fall to the looped scar on his hand, and I wondered if that injury had been what had turned Amir's father away from him. Glancing down at the book in my hand, I saw that Amir's scar was the same shape as the design on the cover.

Amir cleared his throat a moment later. "But we were talking about your mother," he said. "I met her in Agra, a city in the northern part of India. Harshad had asked my father to join him as his medic when he returned to India for a business trip of sorts. I doubt my father would have accepted his offer, if it was not for the political unrest facing the Sultan at the time."

"But he did accept, and you went along with him."

"My father learned his trade from the Ottoman Army. After he retired, he was a devout man of faith. When he heard Harshad was going to Agra, he was eager to go and see the Taj Mahal so he could worship in its legendary mosque."

"I've seen some drawings and maps of the Taj Mahal," I said. "It is beautiful. I did not know it was also a place of worship. I thought it was just a tomb."

"It is that and more. And it is beautiful, but I barely noticed it at the time, of course." Amir's eyes looked off into the distance, and I wondered if he was somehow meeting my mother all over again.

"Harshad was introducing me and my father to his business partner there. By then, my father was devoted to Harshad. He was a good man, if not a Muslim, and a rich one, too. Abba was hoping to convince them to pay for my remaining medical education. He had known Harshad long enough to know our family could earn much more if I was trained in Western and Eastern medication."

"It did not go as planned, I take it."

"No." Amir smiled. "Abba was annoyed to find Harshad's business partner was a woman, and a British one at that. I only found that out later, of course. When you are young, the complicated nature of politics, and what it does to people, is elusive. I did not understand my father's concern over the British Empire at the time; I was taught they were the enemy, but one that we could get along with, if they would only play by the rules."

"I take it Lady POW made her usual impression."

"She did. She has her own rules."

I laughed. "That's for sure."

"When they met, Naděžda and I also met. She was angry with me quickly enough, just as you were."

"Did you steal a book from her, too?" I asked, this time with a small, teasing smile.

"No." He laughed. "I'm afraid the reason is much worse. My manners were somewhat lacking, especially in British terms. This was her first trip into the East, and from what she told me, it was to get away from her father. Lady POW

THE ORDER OF THE CRYSTAL DAGGERS

corrected her behavior, but Naděžda was unsettled by my 'mongrel ways,' and the moment our parents were distracted, she did not hesitate to tell me so."

"I don't know why you even liked her." I thought of all the diverse communities in Prague. If I were offended at every little slip in manners, I would have had to stay home.

"I am not sure I did like her, at first," Amir admitted. "But there was something about her that … something I recognized. Eventually, we grew on each other and became inseparable, especially when I was done with my education and she was initiated into the Order."

"Did you go on adventures together?"

"That is one way to say it." Amir smiled, and from his expression, I knew he would refrain from telling me the whole story. I was not sure I wanted to hear it, either, from the sad joy I saw in his eyes.

"We worked through London and Germany, protecting emissaries and investigating murders and other crimes. We did this for many years, before we … before she left for her last mission to Prague."

I hugged the book in hands to my chest. I wanted to ask him why she left, but there was something too cruel about that question. "You don't have to tell me anymore."

"Yes, I do." He nodded toward the book again. "I owe you the truth."

I could not argue with him, even though I wanted to.

"She left at the end of 1847, and I never heard from her after that. It was only after the Revolution concluded the following year that I heard from Lady POW. Your grandmother told me that Naděžda had married and resigned her position from the Order. That was all."

"She did not even tell you why she stayed in Prague?"

"Another reason I was more eager to steal the book," he admitted. "We did not end our friendship on a cordial note."

I was not able to stop myself from putting my hand on his arm. "I'm so sorry. I hope whatever is in here has given you peace."

"Thank you."

I waited for him to tell me what he had found, but he said nothing more.

As I looked at Amir, I no longer saw a Turkish book thief. I saw a man who was desperately in love and unable to stop himself from any act of depravity if it would bring him closer to the answers he sought. In some ways, we were both searching for her; I was looking to find the woman that she had been, and he was determined to find out the woman she had become.

"Thank you for telling me," I said quietly, trying to give him a brave smile.

There was a rustling sound outside the door, and Amir reached out for my hand. "It seems that the morning has come. We should get you back to your room, mademoiselle."

"That's true." As I took his arm, I saw the scar on his hand and stared at it. "I suppose you can call me Eleanora now. There's no need for formalities, right?"

"Are you saying you prefer the casualties?"

I gave him a small smile, grateful for his levity. "Maybe. We'll have to see how it goes when Harshad and Lady POW allow me to begin fighting."

"As much as it is something you might want, I hope you will not rush into it too eagerly. Death is not something to be eager for."

"I think it is more that I want their approval," I admitted, somewhat surprised I said it aloud. But after a moment, I decided it was not so strange.

In some ways, it is much easier to be honest with another person than it is to admit things to even yourself.

"Do not allow your desire to acquire that get in your way of being free. If you want to be free, truly free, you should know that you answer to the truth, not to Lady Penelope or Harshad. Not even yourself at times."

I thought about that for a long moment, before deciding Amir was right.

"If you do want to progress in this field, I believe you are doing the right thing by practicing. I have studied many years as a medical student, but I would not have learned even half of what I know if I had not been paying attention to the condition around me, and if I had not been proactive in seeking out new knowledge."

Amir's logic impressed itself on me in that moment. He was right. Whether I failed or succeeded was not up to my teachers; it was up to me, and I had to take that responsibility seriously.

And, I thought, that was what I was doing earlier this morning. And that reminded me of my own discoveries.

"Wait." I gripped Amir's hand under my own. "That reminds me. I did actually learn something helpful today, and it is very important. It's about our mission."

I quickly told Amir what I had heard from Cecilia and Alex, about how Lord Maximillian knew there was a secret heir to the throne of Bohemia, about how he was threatening Cecilia, and how Alex and Cecilia were likely plotting something in revenge.

When I was done, Amir looked back at the fireplace.

"Well then, I will send for tea. Lady POW and Harshad will want to hear this news for sure."

"You don't seem surprised by this," I said.

Amir nodded to the book in my hands. "Your mother detailed her last mission in her journal, among other things. It seems Empress Maria Anna was pregnant when she arrived, which is why she worked so hard to persuade your father to protect the king."

"She would have done that." I thought of my mother, how gentle and wonderful she had been with me when I was a child. "She always wanted children."

"I know." There was something new and broken in Amir's voice. He cleared his throat a moment later. "I was going to inform Harshad and Madame when they awoke this morning."

Before I could ask him another question or say anything else, he slipped his hand free from mine. "Go and change, Eleanora. I will summon the others."

"Wait." I slowly held out my mother's journal to Amir. "I can't read this anyway. You might as well have it."

"Are you certain?" he asked.

"I have other things of hers," I said, gripping my mother's locket inside my coat as he took the book from me. The design on the book and his scar seemed to align as he held it. "And if there is proof in her journal that what Cecilia said is true about the king's son, maybe we can use that to find him."

"Thank you." Amir clutched the book to his chest, and, as much as it hurt, I knew I was doing the right thing. "If it is agreeable, I would rather keep the matter of her book between us. Your grandmother will be willing to investigate Lady Cecilia's claim, just by virtue of her saying it."

"Maybe you should say by vice instead of virtue." I wrinkled my nose.

Amir smiled. "This does mean that you will have to tell Lady POW of your nighttime adventure."

I bit my lip. If Lady POW learned of my adventure, it was possible that it would be harder for Ben to sneak me away from the Royal Summerhouse. I did not want to miss meeting Ferdy and his friends. "Maybe we should wait to tell her then."

"Are you worried about Lady POW's response?" Amir asked. "There is nothing to worry about. She will be pleased once she learns of your information. Tulia has still refused to meet with us, and Harshad is still looking for a doctor or apothecary who sells the silver thallis herb in Prague."

"I will tell you why I'd like to wait, but I want your word that you will not say anything to Lady POW about it."

Amir's mustache twitched in amusement. "You really are your mother's daughter, Eleanora. Tell me what your plan is, and I will find a way to help you."

16

◊

"You're in fine spirits tonight, Eleanora." Lady Penelope handed me a glass of lemonade. One of my many dance partners had recently fetched them for us, and I was grateful for it as I returned from the ballroom floor.

We had arrived at the ball only an hour before, and I had stepped into dancing almost at once. I had to cause a stir, and from the way the Royal Summerhouse was set up for the evening, the dance floor took me to the middle of everyone's attention.

"You're the one who insisted I would become a sensation," I said. I took a long drink, hoping she would not notice my extra enthusiasm. "This is a good place to do it, with Count Potocki here."

"Are you trying to make Mr. Marcelin jealous?" Lady Penelope asked.

"He can have my next free dance, if he is interested," I said. "Assuming I have any open dances at all."

I glanced over to where Karl was standing. Underneath a brightly lit chandelier, he stood talking with Lord Maximillian and some other gentlemen, including Count Potocki and Lord Hohenwart. I saw that Teresa Marie was standing with them, too, but Karl was not paying attention to her.

Almost as if I had whispered in his ear, he turned.

From across the room, our eyes met. At first I blushed, embarrassed to be caught staring, but I boldly stared back. From where I was, I could see his gray eyes were stormy and somehow sad. I nodded toward Teresa Marie, giving Karl a look that clearly asked him if she was the reason for his displeasure.

He gave me a rueful smile and a small shrug, before Teresa Marie tugged his arm and forced his attention back to her. I felt a twinge of sympathy for him, and in more ways than one. I was also a little afraid for him, as I knew Lord Maximillian was up to no good.

"It seems he is otherwise preoccupied," I told Lady POW, watching Teresa Marie scowl at me from behind his back.

"Count Potocki is a good friend of his, and if we want the Minister-President to pay attention to us, we should give him good cause," Lady Penelope replied.

"I agree, but Count Potocki is the one who invited you. You don't need me to get his attention."

There was no denying I had a lot of success in that chore. I heard the whispers— all of them, ranging from hushed awe to snippy criticism. The crowd questioned each other about everything from my hair to my shoes to my dancing partner; they

154

would discuss my dowry and make bets over who would be the first to be rejected as my suitor.

"I was invited out of courtesy by his office," Lady Penelope said, drawing my attention from the glittering room before me. "I will not be able to ask him about his safety or anything relevant to our mission if I don't have an excuse for a private meeting with him."

"I've been dancing and smiling and flirting tirelessly since we arrived. I think I can survive long enough on my own for you to go and make your introductions," I said. "And if you wanted, I could do something that would give you more time."

"Is that so?" She gave me a thoughtful look, tapping her fan against her chin. "What is your plan?"

Quickly, I told her my idea. I did not tell her I had thought of it hours ago, with Amir's help. It sounded strange as it came out of my mouth, even though I had rehearsed my plan to myself so many times.

For a long moment, I was worried I had overplayed my hand, but when Lady Penelope arched her brow at me, I could tell she was genuinely interested in my proposal. "Are you serious in your offer?"

"What's wrong with that? I'm supposed to be a fast learner."

"You are also a troublemaker."

The way she said it, I had to wonder if Amir had broken his promise and told her about my plan to leave early. Though I had not informed him of the specifics of my intended destination, I stressed that it was a mission to collect more information and Lady Penelope did not need to know about it. The more I talked to Amir, the more I felt like I was trying to convince myself I was not asking for anything unreasonably outlandish.

Maybe I was. But I did really want to see Ferdy, and I wanted to prove to Lady POW that I was a good investigator. If I could manage to do both at the same time, it was only efficient.

Amir and I could agree on efficiency.

That was probably a large part of the reason he agreed to keep his silence. He also offered to help Ben smuggle me out of the Royal Summerhouse. They were waiting for me outside, near the carriages. Ben would escort me while Amir waited to inform Lady POW of my departure.

Giving him that book was the right thing to do.

Although I had to wonder if giving him a fair chance was also the right thing to do.

I glanced up at the clock. If I was going to make my move, it would have to be soon. It was time to move forward with my plan.

"If I am a troublemaker, it only goes to show that I am truly your family," I said, watching Karl intently as I whispered in soft tones.

He seemed to realize I wanted to dance with him, playing right along with my plan as he unlatched himself from Teresa Marie.

"Just watch and get ready to abduct Count Potocki. I'll take care of the rest. I'll head out to the carriage when I'm done so you'll have plenty of time."

"You have a good plan," Lady Penelope said. "Let's see if it works."

The approving smile on Lady Penelope's face was gratifying, even if her comment was irritating. Both elements gave me the courage I needed as Karl came up beside us. I could sense his delight as he bowed over my hand.

"Mr. Marcelin, we meet again," I said coyly. "What did you say to Lady Teresa Marie that allowed you to slip away from her?"

"I lied to her, naturally." Karl confessed his sin with an ease that almost reminded me of Ferdy. "I wanted a dance with you."

"So you will get your penance for your sin after all," I replied, and he laughed.

"I would gladly pay it. I regret I was not able to locate you last night for another dance."

"Oh, you know how it is, running from one place to the next," Lady Penelope said. "But we have missed you as well, Mr. Marcelin."

Karl seemed to have not heard her, as his eyes held mine. "Not as much as I have missed you."

I felt bad he seemed so sincere in his efforts. Other gentlemen had expressed their pleasure at my acquaintance, but Karl's admiration seemed starkly genuine compared to theirs.

"It is to your good fortune that I am free to dance then," I said. We joined hands, and thanks to all the practice I had with Amir and at the previous ball, we easily slipped into a comfortable waltz. I gave Lady POW a quick nod, telling her to make her move, and then turned back to Karl, batting my eyelashes.

"You were right, of course. It is indeed my good fortune that you were free to dance," Karl replied.

"I agree." I almost giggled, seeing the boyish enthusiasm that lit up his face before he squashed it back under a mask of austerity and regality. "But there is no need to be so serious about the matter, sir."

"This is an honor and should be treated as such."

"But it is fun and one should treat it as such, too."

His gray eyes twinkled. "You are indeed very clever, my lady."

THE ORDER OF THE CRYSTAL DAGGERS

"I can't imagine why you would think otherwise." I whirled around in a spin, and then came up next to him again. "I am dancing with you, after all. I suspect many other young ladies have been clambering after you for such an honor."

"If they have, I have only noticed you."

I tapped his arm with my fan. "I do not think I am doing what can be described as 'clambering.'"

"Then I shall make it my mission to convince you to do so in the future." Karl offered a smile, one full of genuine appreciation and admiration. For a moment, the innocent eagerness in his expression almost reminded me of Ferdy. I nearly tripped at the thought, but Karl caught and steadied me.

Too early! I yelled at myself.

"Are you well, my lady?"

"I'm fine," I assured him, squeezing his arm more tightly. He seemed to brighten even more at my closeness.

As we danced, I wondered if I would have been able to stay above the seas of Karl's spell if Ferdy had not stolen my attentions. Karl was handsome and intelligent, and his passionate nature was dominated by a strong will. He was serious and grounded, but it was not hard to see that Karl would make an excellent husband.

"I suppose I should not blame all of those ladies calling for your attentions, sir," I said, giving him a flirtatious smile. "You are among the better dancers here, as your reputation stated."

"Thank you. I have always been a conscientious student. Since my father was less inclined to indulge her, my mother used me as her dancing partner quite frequently as a child."

"That's sweet." I imagined a small version of Karl prancing around with his mother. "Is your mother in town?"

"She is, though she is busy. She is preparing for the Advent Ball this week."

"That is another reason for you to go, if your mother is excited for it."

"Yes. You and your grandmother will also attend, will you not? I fear it will not be fun at all without you there."

"I am certain my grandmother would be willing to go."

"I hope you will come. I do not want to be left alone with Lady Teresa Marie's attentions."

"Lady Teresa Marie?" I asked.

"She is here, and her father is, too."

"Do you suspect they are following you, sir?" I asked, curious, even though I kept my tone blasé.

"Oh, I doubt that," Karl said, "but Lord Maximillian has expressed interest in furthering my political career. He is a new friend of Alfred's and he is eager to support me."

I wondered if that meant that Lord Maximillian also hated Emperor Franz Joseph's neglect of Bohemia.

Does this mean Karl knows who the king's son is? Does His Grace see Karl's leadership as a step in taking over Bohemia's government?

I needed more answers.

"Lord Maximillian is a wealthy duke. His support would help you in your aspirations, surely."

Before I could remark on the Duke's vision of the future, I realized Karl was blushing, ever so slightly. "What is it?"

"I was rather hoping you would be more interested," Karl admitted, and I realized his flirting was taking on a more serious tone.

In all of my trappings of apparent wealth, and even Lady POW's actual wealth, I knew that there were plenty of men interested in pursuing courtship. I was my mother's daughter, after all, and I was a great beauty among the crowds.

I wanted to scream in frustration. My charm was an act and my grace was the result of education, and my reasons for indulging the crowded ballrooms of Prague were part of my quest for answers in a murder.

I did not really want to worry about relationships. Not like this, anyway, I thought, as Karl continued talking, mentioning marriage in the most obscure ways.

I wondered how my mother had faired when she came to Prague. Was this what she had experienced? Did my father fall in love with her at first sight? Did he fawn over her, dance with her, compliment her, treat her the way Karl treated me? Or was he more like Ferdy, hiding out in the shadows, waiting for the moment to come and rescue her from boredom, offering her real moments of laughter and truth, even if it was cloaked in secret?

At the thought of Ferdy, I turned and glanced along the ballroom walls, wondering if he would come and rescue me from Karl again.

"What is it?" Karl asked. "Is something wrong?"

"Oh, uh, no," I stammered. "I just … was curious where my grandmother went. That's all." I glimpsed back to where I had left her, only to catch sight of her talking with Count Potocki.

At least she got that far.

THE ORDER OF THE CRYSTAL DAGGERS

"Oh, I see." Karl nodded. "I would want to discuss matters with her as well, but I believe it is better that we are in agreement ourselves, first."

"Matters?"

"Marriage." For once, he hesitated. "I have not explained myself very well, have I?"

"Why would you want to discuss marriage?" I asked, genuinely curious. "We have only danced a few times. We barely know each other."

"I know you better than you think," Karl said. "Lady Teresa Marie told me some of the ... the more unpleasant aspects of your life."

I arched my brow. Of all things, I had not expected that. "Shouldn't that disqualify me as a future Minister-President's wife?" I asked bluntly. "I can't imagine it would make good press for you."

"No," Karl blustered. "Of course not. If anything, I was ... inspired, to be honest. Even before I found out about that, I have always known of your kindness to your brother, and to others, and of your bravery in facing your parents' death."

I faltered, nearly falling on accident. *How did he know about Ben? Lady Penelope had never said much about him to anyone.*

"I don't know what to say. I still don't know you very well."

"But you like me, don't you?" Karl asked.

"I think you are a very fine gentleman. And a good dancer. But ... "

As I stood there, I felt strange. I should have been thrilled or touched to have Karl's affections, especially since he knew the truth about me serving under Cecilia. But all I could think of was the Order, and Ferdy, and how this was all very strange.

"You will not completely dismiss me, will you?" Karl asked, the hope fading from his eyes.

I smiled, forcing myself to play along. "Of course not."

"I'm glad to hear that." Karl pulled me close and held me tight. I shivered against him, surprised at his gentleness. I took a moment to look up at him, and I felt myself caught off guard.

"Perhaps I am not used to how society arranges marriage. My parents had a marriage based on mutual feelings," I said.

However, now that I think of it ... I don't really know that, do I?

Karl nodded. "Thank you for your honesty, my lady."

At that point, the music began to swell into its ending crescendo. I was ready to leave Karl's side. The whole dance had been lovely, but the dialogue had been awkward and unsettling.

THE ORDER OF THE CRYSTAL DAGGERS

As I stepped back, I slipped my foot halfway from my one shoe and twisted it into my skirt.

"Oh, my!" I shrieked as I fell over, finding every way I could to make a scene.

Ben had taught me at a younger age how to duck and roll. Admittedly, it was harder to fall gracefully in a ballroom surrounded by other dancing couples, but when I landed on my backside with only a small bump, I knew I had achieved my goal.

From the stunned look on Karl's face, I could tell his reaction would be the perfect way to garner sympathy and concern.

I hurried to rearrange my skirts, but my stockings were still sticking out as other dancers stopped and hurried over to help—or just stare, which is what the majority of them did, as Karl and a few other gentlemen offered me their hands, and other ladies called out asking me about my condition.

When asked if I was well, I answered, "I will be, once I manage to get back up on my feet."

The crowd laughed nervously. I took Karl's hand, but reached for others' support as I worked to find my balance.

As I began to brush the wrinkles out of my gown, I glanced over the crowds to see Lady Penelope steering an astounded Count Potocki out of the ballroom.

"Are you hurt, Eleanora?" Karl asked.

For the moment, I ignored his use of my first name. Instead, I slowly pretended to put weight on my foot.

"Ouch!" I whimpered. "I do believe I have twisted my ankle, sir."

"Allow me to escort you," Karl said, as several other gentlemen reached out and offered me their hands as well.

"Thank you." I looped my arm around Karl's neck as I pretended to limp. We walked through the hoard of people together. I felt simultaneously guilty and grateful, glad my intended trickery had not led to actual injury.

"I apologize for this. I should not have startled you in such a manner."

"It's not so bad. But I doubt I will be able to dance for the rest of the evening," I said. "I believe I will head to my carriage, so I might return home and rest for the evening. If you would be so kind as to escort me?"

"Of course." Karl patted my hand. "If I cannot prove my affections to you on the dancefloor, I will be content to do so in other manners."

I barely heard him, as others we passed began asking questions about my injury. Once we were out of the Royal Summerhouse, we made our way through the large pillars of the building to where I knew Ben and Amir were waiting.

THE ORDER OF THE CRYSTAL DAGGERS

"As much as I am sorry for your injury," Karl said slowly, "I am grateful for the chance to speak with you alone and without everyone watching."

"Oh, I'm sure we have plenty of people who are watching," I said, looking back toward the entrance where more people had gathered.

"They love you."

"They love a good story," I scoffed.

"No, it's more than that. They really do admire you."

"I know you want to make a name for yourself in politics, but there is no need to presume the masses are so adamantly—"

"It is true that I am versed in politics, my lady," Karl said. "And that is how I know they truly adore you."

Between the way he said it and the way he looked at me, I almost believed him.

I shrugged. "Well, it's no matter now. Tell me, what was it that you wanted to say to me that you cannot say in public?"

Karl sighed. "Lord Maximillian has offered to support my political ambitions. He and Count Potocki are supportive of my election as the next Minister-President."

You already told me that.

I gave him a brilliant smile. "That's wonderful. You are so young, too. This must be very exciting for you."

"It is," he agreed. "But there is a condition to accepting Lord Maximillian's endowment. He has requested that I marry his daughter."

"Lord Maximillian wants you to marry his daughter?" I repeated his words slowly, and it was at that moment that the pieces all began to fall into place. "How old are you, exactly?"

"I am two and twenty."

"You were born in 1848?"

"Yes." Karl frowned. "Why do you ask?"

My mother's mission, Cecilia's screechy outburst—everything seemed to run through my memory all at once.

"Max found what he was looking for all those years ago. He would have broken the engagement himself, now that he's found King Ferdinand's son and heir."

The Empress had been pregnant when my mother arrived in early 1848.

Karl was determined to fulfill his duty to Bohemia, and thanks to Ferdy, I knew Karl wanted to return the kingdom to its own sovereignty, free from the Emperor.

Karl is King Ferdinand's son.

161

I stared at him, studying his face in the moonlight, as if I was seeing him for the first time. I did not recall much about King Ferdinand's face, or Empress Maria Anna, but nothing caused me to question the notion he was their son. With his dark hair and narrow chin, combined with the Hapsburg eyes and straight nose, I suddenly wondered at how others had missed this for so long.

In any other reality, he would one day be my nation's king.

"Does it bother you that I am so young?" Karl asked, interrupting my mental spasm. "I was rather certain you enjoyed my company and the closeness of our ages."

He slowed to a stop, as we drew near to my carriage. I saw Ben disguised as a footman, and Amir settled comfortably on the perch.

"I have enjoyed our dancing," I replied, my voice struggling not to betray my astonishment, "and your company as well, sir."

"I am relieved to hear that. I was rather hoping I could convince you to marry me instead."

At that, I stopped moving completely.

"I apologize if it is improper," Karl swiftly amended. "But I could not marry Teresa Marie without the hope I could convince you to marry me instead."

"I ... don't know what to say."

For a long moment, I was flattered. Karl was the rightful heir to the Bohemian throne, or he would have been, if it were not for the Revolution of 1848. And here he was, telling me that he wanted to marry *me*.

Me—someone who had been a servant in her own home for the last ten years of her life, someone who longed for books and freedom, someone who spent her days dreaming dreams and commiserating miseries with her brother.

But as I thought through it, I was suddenly curious. "Why do you even like me?"

Why did he like me enough to have him turn his back on Teresa Marie and her father's significant financial support? If he wanted the Minister-President position so badly, why was he willing to risk it all for me?

Karl seemed as surprised by my question as I was. "Because I do. I do like you. And plenty of others do, too. You're clever, and funny, and you're beautiful. I ... think you would make an excellent wife and mother. You are a true lady, in every sense."

"Oh." I nodded slowly. "I see."

"Please, Ella, consider my offer. I have a promising career, and significant holdings I am to inherit from my family one day."

He started listing other reasons I should marry him, and all I could concentrate on was how he called me Ella.

THE ORDER OF THE CRYSTAL DAGGERS

"My name is Eleanora," I said, still stiff with remaining shock.

Karl blushed. "I apologize. Your name is quite long." He bowed gallantly over my hand. "I don't have much time before Teresa Marie and her father demand that notice be sent to the papers. Unfortunately, I need to know your answer soon. I would not put you in this position otherwise, I swear. Count Potocki is to announce his support for me to become the next Minister-President at the Advent Ball. I need to know I will have your support by then."

"I see." I chewed on my bottom lip, thinking it over. If Karl was the heir to the throne, but he needed financial support, I suspected he did not have his family's support, as Lady POW had said before.

Another thought struck me. Was Karl somehow connected to all the strange murders that had happened? Had he needed to dispose of Dr. Artha and Father Novak?

"I would be happy to come and call upon you and your grandmother to formally ask for your hand. But I would not want to do so without knowing you are in agreement."

I had to stop myself from flinching. "Thank you." Karl was more mercenary than I liked, but he was polite about it.

"Please," Karl said. "I like you. Very much."

Quietly, I detached myself from Karl. "I will think about it," I promised.

I knew I could say that honestly, too. I would think about why someone like Karl would pledge his lifetime to someone who was smart and clever and funny, especially when I was sure that Teresa Marie would be more than willing to act the part of the perfect wife and mother for him. I appreciated he knew the truth of who I was, and my background, but I was still too shocked to do anything but curtsy.

"Send me word through a messenger when you make a decision," he said. "I will call upon you and your grandmother and we can discuss this more."

"As you wish, Mr. Marcelin."

"Karl, please." He kissed my hand. "Farewell … Ella."

I nodded tepidly as Ben came over beside me. Together, we watched Karl walk away. He was as confident as ever, with his head held high and his eyes remaining forward.

"I told you," Ben said, "you have *Máma's* charm and beauty. It was only a matter of time before gentlemen all around started to propose to you."

I would have laughed and agreed if there was less riding on the situation.

"Karl is not just any gentleman," I said. "He is King Ferdinand's son."

"What?" Ben blinked. "Are you sure?"

THE ORDER OF THE CRYSTAL DAGGERS

I nodded. "I'm fairly certain."

"But the king was declared medically unfit to have children," Ben said. "This is … that's not … how?"

Amir came up beside him. "What did you learn, Eleanora?"

"Karl has to be the king's son," I told him. "Lord Maximillian is offering him money for his political career in exchange for marrying Teresa Marie. From what I overheard Cecilia say, and given Karl's age, that means he has to be the true heir to the throne of Bohemia."

"Wait, what? What did Cecilia say? When did this happen?" Ben asked. "Did Marcelin tell you this when he asked you to marry him?"

"He asked you to marry him?" Amir repeated. "Well, this has certainly been quite a night for you already, Eleanora."

"She was asked by the king's son," Ben said.

"Is he the one?" Amir glanced over his shoulder, looking back at the entrance to the Summerhouse.

"I'm almost completely positive it's him," I said. "From what I know about him and what others have said, he's the right age, and he has the right connections. And it makes sense. His family—his mother and father—would not support an uprising against Emperor Franz Joseph. They are happy in their retirement, by all accounts."

"Do you have proof?" Amir asked.

"I can't even believe you think he's really the king's son," Ben said.

"I'll explain everything I know to you, Ben. But first, we have other plans. Lady POW is distracted for now. I managed to secure her an extremely private session with the Minister-President, and now I want to get to the Jewish Quarter before it's too late."

The Royal Summerhouse still swelled with music behind us. The early evening moon was shining on the alabaster of the columns behind us. I shivered at the touch of wind, even as it sifted through my hair like a loving hand. I turned away from Ben and Amir, looking out across the city. Prague was starting to light up with little flickers of light, and I felt it call to me.

"I can't believe you still want to go." Ben crossed his arms. "If what you're saying is true, we need to talk to Lady Penelope right away."

"Of course I still want to go." I threw up my hands in exasperation. "Besides, Amir is right; we need proof. And if anyone would know the truth about Karl, it is Mr. Clavan. Ferdy himself told me that everything filters through the Cabal sooner or later."

Ben still looked skeptical.

I tugged on his arm. "Please, Ben. Amir will be staying here and he can fill her in on the details. I don't want to disappoint Ferdy, and we might be able to learn more to help us. Besides, you promised."

"Fine, Nora." Ben sighed. "Come on. If nothing else, I want to meet this Ferdy person. If you're so enamored of him, especially when it appears a prince is asking for your hand, it is my duty as your brother to make sure he is worthy of you."

I flushed red, but I said nothing. Ben had a way of ruining my good mood, and I knew I would only get in trouble if we ended up arguing over Ferdy. Karl might have liked me very much, but I knew without even thinking that I liked Ferdy much more. Even if Ferdy had lied to me about things before, I had a feeling he would never lie to me about wanting to marry me for my dowry.

THE ORDER OF THE CRYSTAL DAGGERS

17

◊

Ben and I made our way through the evening streets of Prague swiftly, crossing the Vltava and sneaking our way through the tighter streets of the Jewish Quarter.

Clavan had said it right; there was a sad history between the Christians and Jews, and I felt the truth of the segregation's pains as Ben and I headed for the Cabal.

The streets of the *Josefská* were cluttered with tiny townhouses and small rooms. In the darkness, the shuttered windows and the chipping paint made the neighborhoods collectively dreary. I gripped my old maidservant skirts. I had changed into them in the carriage, before stuffing my hair under a simple bonnet and pulling on my old work shoes. The rough stitching was already foreign to me, but I had a feeling that the downtrodden figures shuffling into the alleyways to avoid my gaze would have welcomed their itchy warmth.

"I've never been here at night," I said. "Is it always like this?"

"Like what?" Ben asked.

"I don't know. Quiet. A little sad. A little strange. It's hard to describe."

"The Jews have always been foreigners outside of the Promised Land," Ben reminded me. "Just as Christians are aliens this side of Heaven. You shouldn't be so surprised to feel like you are out of place, and that this place is, too."

"I suppose. But it seemed a lot more welcoming in the daytime the last time I was here."

"That's just an effect of night," Ben assured me with a laugh. "You don't go onto the streets of a city like Prague unless it's for balls or parties. Now that you can see past the gilded cover, you'll see poverty and other trials that exist in the city's crevices."

Ben was right. As we skimmed across shadows toward the Cabal, I saw the city was not just a wonder of light and magic; it was a place of darkness and sin, crying for deliverance.

My heart softened, witnessing plight of so many others, the ones I could see now that the daytime crowds had dispersed and the night had called out society's undesirables. "I wish we could help more people."

"That's part of the reason I like working for the Order," Ben admitted. "With Amir's help, and Lady POW's income, I've been able to see the world more for what it is than what I thought it would be."

"I know what you mean. Quite a few things have changed since they've come into our lives."

"I've noticed you've warmed up to Amir."

THE ORDER OF THE CRYSTAL DAGGERS

"He apologized and brought me back the book he stole," I said. "It was *Máma's* journal."

Ben nodded. "He told me about it when I asked, the first days we worked together."

"Why didn't you tell me?" I asked, slighted. "You're the one who wanted me to get along with him."

"He said it would be better if you asked, so I said I wouldn't say anything. And … "

"And what?"

"And you were younger than me when *Máma's* ship was lost at sea," Ben said. "You probably don't remember her the same way I do. She loved us, and even *Otec*, too. But there were days when she would disappear, locking herself in her room. I found out later she suffered from bouts of melancholy."

"Where did you hear that?" I asked.

"Cecilia mentioned it once or twice in her list of reasons I should be glad to be alive, even if I had to work in the manor." Ben shrugged. "Amir said that *Máma* and Lady POW had quite a falling out. He said he was certain that at least one of the reasons she left Prague to go to London was to apologize to her. I didn't say anything to you earlier because I didn't want to tell you anything you weren't ready to hear."

I did not tell Ben that as much as I was grateful for his earlier consideration, it almost prevented me from finding out the truth. I knew that was a large part of growing and learning, and I did not want to be left behind because of childish matters. Thanks to Lady POW, and now Ben, I knew that the woman I remembered as my mother was as wispy and insubstantial as the wind.

We said nothing else until we caught sight of the Cabal. Torches flickered at either side of the doorway. Through the windows, I saw clusters of friends and family gathered together.

We made our way to them. As Ben shuffled beside me, I took his arm. "Ben?"

"What is it?"

"Promise me that we won't let anything come between us like *Máma* and Lady POW did."

Ben took my hand and squeezed it affectionately. "I promise that won't happen to us."

"Are you sure?"

"I'm certain, *ségra*." Ben sighed and looked back at the Cabal. "But I'm warning you, if this Ferdy character is as much of a charlatan as I think he is, the limits of my patience and your forgiveness will be tested."

"It's better that way," a voice said from behind us. "Such things become more precious in the end when they are tested."

Ben and I whirled around to see Ferdy walking toward us. He had his cap on over his hair, and his scarf looped around his neck in a poor attempt to ward off the chill in the air. In the evening darkness, I might not have realized it was Ferdy at all, if I had not seen his slightly crooked grin.

Everything seemed instantly more vivid. My heart raced and my stomach twisted with happy nerves.

"Ferdy." I smiled and waved, and it was hard to quell the joy—and relief—inside of me.

"I'm glad to see you've made it to the Cabal tonight," he said, taking my hand and bowing over it before turning toward my brother. "And you've brought a friend?"

"This is my brother, Ben."

"I'll admit I'm relieved," Ferdy said as he bowed to Ben. "I've heard Ella's quite the sensation on the dancefloor—even if she falls over."

I laughed. "How did you hear about that already?"

"I know a few people," Ferdy teased. "And some of those people were very excited to see your stockings."

"Excuse me." Ben coughed. "Do you want to repeat that?"

"Later, my new friend," Ferdy said, giving me a quick wink. "But only if you insist. I know from Elie and Clavan that the news cycle can get quite dull."

Ben cracked his knuckles. "Is that so?"

"And this is one of the reasons I vastly prefer a brother to an admirer." Ferdy slapped Ben on the back in a friendly manner, ignoring Ben's threatening posture. "If I am going to fight someone for her, it's better that it's her brother than an admirer. That way, if we end up broken and bleeding, I can at least gain your respect in the end, if not your friendship."

Ben glanced over at me, and I could tell he was unsure of what to say.

Ferdy reached out to me and offered me his arm. "Well, Lady Ella, why don't you come in and see what's going on? Jarl is here with his Faye, and Helen cooked up a mutton stew that will keep you warm until next month."

"Sure. Come on, Ben."

"Yes, Ben, you too," Ferdy said with a smile.

"Ella?" Ben whispered behind me.

THE ORDER OF THE CRYSTAL DAGGERS

"That's what Ferdy calls me. He said Eleanora was too long." I thought about telling him that Karl had said the same thing, but Ferdy opened the door and the inside warmth called to us.

"I still like Nora better," Ben grumbled.

"I think both have their charm." I could tell he did not like my answer.

He frowned, but the atmosphere of the Cabal instantly overwhelmed our senses. I smothered a laugh as I looked at Ben's face. Right away, I saw he was impressed with the surroundings; after telling him how Ferdy had brought me here the first time, Ben had likely expected it to be a seedy place, full of drunks and criminals.

Candles decorated all the small tables as circles of friends surrounded them. The air was full of pockets of smoke and brandy, all layered with a warm ambiance coming from the kitchen at the back.

Looking around, I saw there were a lot of men and women in pairs, the men wearing their dark suits, and the women wearing long skirts and scarves. Most of the men wore hats or yarmulkes, but some had no caps at all. I was surprised there was a priest. He was sitting at a table near the bar, reading a Bible.

"Jarl," Ferdy called, waving toward a table tucked into the corner beside the bar.

"There you are, Ferdy. Where have you been?" A German man with dark hair and a smoking pipe gave Ferdy a brotherly hug, before he blew a stream of smoke out in greeting. "Faye and I have been here for hours."

"We have not." The young woman sitting beside him rolled her eyes before she laughed. "We just got here."

"They don't need to know that, Faye. I was hoping to leverage that into getting Ferdy to buy me another round."

"Oh, so you're not in your cups already?" Ferdy pulled over two more chairs for Ben and me.

"Of course not. Dad's been keeping his eye on him," Faye said. She looked behind her chair, where I saw Clavan scowling down at Jarl. I was glad to see Clavan gave Faye a wink a second later, and I realized he was in on the joke.

Ferdy laughed and then introduced us. "This is Ella, and her brother Ben," he said. "They're new to the Cabal."

"So you brought them over to meet us first, so we'd scare them off?" Jarl asked.

"If anyone could do it, I figured it would be you."

"Don't forget about Eliezer," Clavan said from behind us. He was carrying a tray full of beers, and when he sat it down on our table, he turned to Ferdy. "I've got a new tab started for you."

"Excellent," Ferdy said. "I didn't even have to tell you. Sometimes I think you can read minds, Clavan."

THE ORDER OF THE CRYSTAL DAGGERS

"It's a mark of a good businessman," Ben said, as Ferdy handed him his glass.

Ferdy and Ben seemed to get along after that. I smiled into my own glass as they began talking, Ben asking some questions and Ferdy jokingly answering them. I was introduced to Jarl and Faye, and even Clavan's wife, Helen, when she came out of the kitchen to meet us. It was clear there was an air of comradery and familiarity to the group that seemed to add to the open warmth of the atmosphere.

"So, Ella," Jarl spoke up, "Ferdy tells us that he rescued you. Is this true?"

"Ferdy has a reputation for being quite a liar," Faye said. "But he insists he is telling the truth this time."

"He is right to do so." I began to recount the tale of how I met Ferdy. I did not mention that I found out who Amir was later on, nor did I say anything about the book. Jarl was still skeptical of Ferdy's account, but Faye had misty eyes as I told her how he brought me to the Cabal and treated me like a princess.

As Jarl and Ben began talking about cigars, and Faye, Ferdy, and I all discussed Prague's latest social season, I lost track of time. The sounds of friendship and comradery around me blurred into a single confection of comfort and welcome, and I tasted the opportunity with relish.

It was only when the door opened and another man walked in that the atmosphere changed into one of business. He was wearing the dark suit of an Orthodox Jew. His yarmulke sat atop his head, the dark, loopy ringlets of a devout man framing his bearded face. As he entered, several men lifted their glasses to him.

"Elie!" they cheered, and the man waved their praises down.

"It's fine, folks," Eliezer said, greeting the crowds. "It's fine. I'm here, you can all settle in."

"Any good news this week?" a man called.

"If there was only good news, there wouldn't be news at all," Eliezer replied. "That's the way the news works. There's only news if it's bad."

"So the bad news is that there's news? That's good news to me!"

The crowd laughed, and I chuckled at their banter as it continued.

"Eliezer runs a news network of his own throughout the city," Ferdy explained to Ben and me. "I get to be part of it from time to time, passing along information I hear. I enjoy it. Jarl helps with the printing, when he's not working at the factory down the river, and Faye even helps by cleaning the bar here. Clavan provides the beer and offers his own insight, while Elie usually interrupts him."

Faye smiled. "I also help with some of the pamphlets," she said. "I take notes every meeting and help Jarl with the deliveries."

"That's wonderful," I said. "I'm looking forward to hearing the news tonight."

"It's mostly about politics now," Faye said, "since the Diets are in session. But Christmas is coming, so we might have something more religious, too."

"Most of the people in here are Jewish," I said. "Why do they want to hear about Christmas?"

"There are plenty of Jews here," Faye said. "But my father has friends who work as artists and writers who come in to hear the political and cultural commentary. And Elie studied law before he went into business. With his political analysis and Dad's cultural insight, there are plenty of Christians who come to hear them. As it should be. It's not good for people to focus on the little things that they forget about the greater calling around us."

"And they do this every week?"

Faye nodded. "Maybe one day politics will be so engrossing that there will need to be daily meetings, but so far politics is just a small sliver of our lives."

"So, folks, let's begin," Eliezer called. "Thanks to the end of the American Civil War, it seems that there is chance that republics will become more commonplace among the nations of the future. This could be either good or bad for Bohemia, but likely there will be a lot of good and bad that comes with this. As the Americans have proven in the last five years, revolutions are not bloodless, and settling disputes can take generations."

Over the next hour, Eliezer continued to talk about the life of empires, and how the Bohemian people were recklessly embracing nationalism at the oppression of the German Diet; Clavan talked about art and freedom, and the struggle for beauty despite the ugliness of the battle. Even Jarl, an artist of sorts when he was not at his job, chimed in with insights and occasionally insults.

Ben was mesmerized by Eliezer, as he began talking about a shipment of wine that, somehow, had exploded on its way from Hradiště, a small town in Moravia. When Ben called out a question, Eliezer answered him, never losing any of his enthusiasm.

I was about to congratulate Ben when I looked over and saw Ferdy, who was just staring at me.

I stared back, silently trying to remind him to pay attention.

He gave me a smirk and turned back to watch Eliezer and Clavan discuss the failure of the Minister-President to bring the German and Bohemian Diets to any meaningful compromise or agreement regarding regional transportation laws. But not even a moment later, Ferdy took hold of my hand.

And I let him.

There was no hesitation in me as I laced my fingers with his under the table.

After that, it was difficult to remember the rest of the meeting. The heat of our hands distracted me; excitement ran through my whole body, and I kept reminding myself not to blush as the discussion continued.

Eventually I gave up, deciding I would ask Faye if she would have a pamphlet sent to my house so I could hear what I missed.

Sitting here and holding hands with Ferdy was a relief my heart never seemed to know it needed. I thought of how intently Karl had looked at me while we danced and talked, remembering how I had wondered how someone could be so sure of wanting another so quickly.

But here I was, sitting here, slowly but surely allowing myself closer to someone I had really only met, someone who was a mystery and an adventure, a jokester by all accounts and a liar by his own.

When Clavan finished a reading from Wordsworth's *Lyrical Ballads*, discussing Edmund Burke's influence, and mentioning a slew of other names I did not recognize, the crowd clapped.

Ferdy and I exchanged a secret glance before he let me go, and we both clapped along with the rest of the crowd.

"That was brilliant," Ben whispered to me, almost making me jump. I had nearly forgotten he was there with me.

"Yes," I hastily agreed. "It was."

"I can see why you wanted to come. I'm not sure if there's anything that will help us, but it is good to be informed of local sentiments."

"Maybe we can ask for specific details. It's better we ask in secret anyway."

Ben leaned closer to me. "You go and try then. You know Clavan better than I do."

"Was there something you wanted, Ella?" Ferdy asked. "Or you, Ben?"

"Nothing," Ben and I said at the same time. When Ferdy arched his brow at us, I took a drink and smiled up at him. "I was just wondering if Mr. Clavan would give me another beer."

"Oh. Of course. He's already gone back to manning the bar," Ferdy said. "Maybe I'll tell him to bring a cup of coffee here to Jarl. He looks tired."

"I'm not tired," Jarl objected. "I've been working all day, not running around the streets like you."

"See, I would think that work would *make* you tired," Ferdy said. "Running around the streets means I can take breaks. From the sound of it, you also have to fight off some jealousy, since you can't come and join me."

As Ferdy and Jarl continued to argue the semantics of a full day's work, I slipped away and stepped up to the bar.

Clavan came up beside me, already pouring me a new drink. "Well, Lady Ella, what did you think?"

"I loved it," I said, trying not to let him see I had been distracted through most of it. "I especially thought your reading was wonderful."

"Well, as you know, Wordsworth is a favorite of mine," Clavan said. "Maybe next time I'll read something from *The Prelude*."

"Can I ask you a question about something else?"

"It seems you already have." He picked up a bottle of whiskey and poured himself a small shot. "What is your question?"

"Ferdy mentioned that you know everything about Prague," I said. "Is that true?"

"It depends, not on me, but on my information." He gave me a roguish grin. "What do you want to know?"

"I was wondering if you had heard rumors about King Ferdinand and Empress Maria Anna having a son," I said. I kept my gaze on his face, watching as his eyes shifted from interested to wary and then back to speculative.

"A son?" he asked.

"Yes." I frowned, wondering if he was trying to buy some time to respond. He seemed strangely uncomfortable all of a sudden. "You know something, don't you?"

"There were whispers of the Empress and King having a son a long time ago, back in the 1850s," he said quietly. "So I would not be surprised to see if it were true."

I nodded. "I was wondering, with the Nationalists fighting with the other parties, if they were trying to reinstate the monarchy."

"On the surface, it would seem like a good goal for them," Clavan said, "but the people like having power. That was proven in '67, when the Emperor reorganized the Minister-President's office. The Bohemian Diet is here to stay, even with a new monarch and a new governmental structure."

"Even if it's constantly deadlocked by the German Diet?" I asked, unable to stop myself from glancing at Jarl. It was strange to see a German getting along with so many Bohemians, and even more to hear him discuss the growing economy in Prague, now that the Diets were moving onto other matters in their sessions.

"Most certainly. The Nationalists would gain nothing," Clavan said. "And the other parties, and the Minister-President, might agree with a new king like that in the short-term. But in the long-term, it would fail."

"What do you mean?" I asked.

"The Nationalists are happy with the progress they've made, even if it is small. The other main parties are not as happy, but they are learning how to use the system to gain more power."

"So no one would like it if there was a new king on the throne of Bohemia."

"Not long enough for it to matter." Clavan shook his head. "The Revolution of 1848 brought an end to that line's power. Even if it were true, he would need to be elected to the throne now, and even that would take a large disaster to set in motion."

"But if the king's son wanted to get elected to the throne," I mused, "he would need the votes."

"For starters. He would also likely need a full-scale disaster, or an act of war from the Emperor himself, in order to make his argument." Clavan shook his head. "I don't see Franz Joseph allowing that to happen. He has his weaknesses as a ruler, but he is smart and sharp when he needs to be."

I nodded and took another sip of beer.

"Why so interested in the topic?" Clavan asked.

I looked at him, and then back at Ferdy and Ben as they struggled through an arm-wrestling match. "I heard the rumors while I was out at a party," I lied. "I thought, perhaps in light of the murders of Dr. Artha and the others, something was going on."

Clavan said nothing for a long moment. And then he took another swig of his whiskey, draining the small cup before refilling it. "It's strange that you did hear such rumors. Most who talk of that particular nature end up dead."

"Really?" My eyes went wide. "Why aren't you, then?"

"I only listen to those rumors." He took another drink of whiskey and gave me a small smile. "I don't report on them. Officially."

"I did enjoy the reports. Eliezer is a good lawyer, from the sound of it," I said, switching topics. "I enjoyed his analysis of the Diets and Bohemia politics, especially in light of events happening around the country."

"He's my brother in all but blood." Clavan nodded toward Faye and Jarl. "And that will be my son, after my daughter marries him next year. He's a knucklehead with charm. Not unlike your own admirer."

"I've noticed," I said.

"Ferdy's good at moving when he has to," Clavan said. "Which is why I will tell you, when he gets your brother to argue with Jarl over something inconsequential, he will slip away to see if you want to go on a walk with him."

I glanced back to see Ferdy was still watching me.

"If you like him, go with him," Clavan said. "Jarl takes Faye down by the Vltava and I've been assured by Helen I don't have to worry. And seeing how your brother watches over you, you won't have too much time alone with Ferdy."

I laughed. "I'll be surprised if he manages that," I said. "Ben is pretty smart—"

THE ORDER OF THE CRYSTAL DAGGERS

Before I could assure Clavan that Ben would not fall for such tricks, Ferdy was suddenly standing directly beside me, close enough I could feel the warmth of his body. "Ella," he said, "I hope Clavan here isn't boring you."

"I certainly am," Clavan said with a small chuckle. "Ah, I see Hermann Kavka has arrived. I have business I want to discuss with him. Excuse me."

As he had predicted, or warned, I was left alone with Ferdy.

"You aren't going to seriously ask me to go on a walk, are you?" I looked back to see Clavan pull Helen into a quick twirl as she came out from the kitchen, before greeting a robust man at the other end of the bar. "Mr. Clavan already warned me."

Ferdy laughed. "Of course not," he said. "I'm here to rescue you. If that involves walking outside for a little while, that's not the same thing."

"I don't exactly need to be rescued," I pointed out.

"If you don't exactly need to be rescued, and I'm not exactly rescuing you, then you can come with me for a few moments." Ferdy offered me his arm. Seemingly sensing my hesitation, he stilled, waiting for me with a gentle expectancy on his face.

After only a second's worth of uncertainty, and seeing Faye was now battling with Ben and Jarl as they discussed values and the finer points of the news, I laughed. "Maybe I need more rescuing than I thought."

"At this point, you would be rescuing both of us, Ella." Ferdy grinned.

THE ORDER OF THE CRYSTAL DAGGERS

18
◊

Winter was only a few weeks away, and I felt the chill in the night as we stepped into the small alleyway behind the Cabal.

"Well?" Ferdy asked. "What do you think? You can see why I come here."

"You were right," I said. "It's fun, even if it is a little more than I am used to. It's almost like going to school, I imagine."

"Oh, Eliezer would love to hear that. Keeping up with him as he talks is more than half the battle, but we love him for it." Ferdy wrapped my hand more tightly in his, pulling it into his coat as he led me down the alleyway.

"Are we headed toward the Vltava?" I asked.

"We can go anywhere you'd like," Ferdy assured me. "I'm just happy to be with you."

I thought of Karl once more, and I decided if I could be blunt with anyone, it was Ferdy. "Why?"

"Why what?"

"What is so special about me?" I asked. "Do I look that different in my usual clothes, without the gown and dancing slippers?"

"It's not that." Ferdy playfully batted at my bonnet. "You're beautiful no matter what you wear. I've been waiting for another chance to be alone with you again."

I laughed. "I can't imagine why."

"Can't you?"

He stopped in front of me, and I went silent as I met his gaze.

It was just like before, I thought, remembering those stolen moments at the Hohenwart Ball.

It was just like before, only everything felt even more vivid. The warmth between us, and the coldness of the wintery world around us; the dark of the night, and the light of the stars; the comradery of the pub beside us, and the world only we shared before us.

"I believe I made a promise last time," Ferdy said, "to get you to admit you wanted to kiss me."

Terror and hope, that odd combination of emotion and feelings I always felt when it came to Ferdy—all of it leapt at me at once, and I took a moment to enjoy the rush before the inevitable hesitation came rushing in.

"Mr. Clavan told me that you would do this," I said, pulling my hand free and crossing my arms. "So I assume you've done this before, possibly more than once. And I don't know you very well. After all, I just met you."

Ferdy did not step back from my objection. "That is a fallacy, you know. Time never plays as much a factor as people think when it comes to situations like this." He met my gaze in the moonlight, and I felt vulnerable and exposed.

"Like this?" I stiffened, and he continued.

"Haven't you heard the tales of love at first sight? The stories of friendships that suddenly turned into love?"

"I have. But those are just stories. Things like that don't happen in real life."

"There is no such thing as 'just stories,'" Ferdy said. "Behind each story is truth, feeling, and experience." His gaze dropped to my mouth. "Just as the magic of a kiss is not in the kiss itself, but in the heart behind it."

"You just met me," I insisted, but my inner resolve was crumbling. There was something inside of me that wanted to respond to him, something that wanted to believe his words—and something that already agreed with him.

"No," Ferdy said. "I did not just meet you. I recognized you."

At his words, I felt my breathing falter. The beauty of the night fell away from me, and the last of the cold was whisked away as his hand reached out and cupped my cheek. Instinctively, I leaned into his touch. My mind was racing with incoherent thoughts, but the sound of my pounding heart drowned out any possible argument or objection.

"How brave would you be tonight?" he asked. His silver eyes held mine, and I could not help myself from leaning into their brilliance. "Brave enough to glimpse at the heart of a man who sees into yours?"

I thought of my mother. "I am nothing if not brave," I whispered softly.

"Good. I don't think I can wait any longer to kiss you." And then his lips pressed against mine, and what was left of my defenses shattered.

His kiss was at first warm and soft; he tasted like freedom and fun, just a little roguish and rebellious, both dangerous and safe. Ferdy reached up and pushed back my bonnet, letting his fingers find my hair. I fell into him, unable to fully process the pleasure running through me, as the warmth burned into searing heat.

We fell into a desperate rhythm of kissing and being kissed, a dance as old as time itself. The strangeness of the experience transformed into a welcome rush, as my arms wrapped around him and drew him closer to me. I heard him whisper my name and I felt my knees weaken.

It could have been hours or moments later when he finally pulled back. The chill of the night caught our heavy breathing, and I was tempted to laugh.

Ferdy beat me to it. "I'm not laughing at you, I promise," he said. "I'm just so happy. I can't seem to stop myself." He pulled me closer to him, trying to protect me from the chilly air.

"I know," I whispered back, unable to stop myself from winding my arms around his neck, forcing our bodies even closer. "I know how you feel."

He kissed my cheek before I curled into the crook of his shoulder. "You've always been kind," he whispered. "Tough, but kind. I'm glad you understand."

"I do, even if I don't." I leaned over and kissed him again.

I could not explain it. I could not explain why I was so drawn to him. I did not know him well, even after glimpsing at his heart. He was flippant but serious, teasing but friendly. He was caring in a way that made perfect sense, even if it seemed selfish. He was insightful and astute, always polite even as he was passionate. He knew me for who I was, not what I was nor how much money I had or how much beauty I displayed.

I attempted to think through everything, but I knew the individual reasons were not enough to account for the reality. It was terrifying but freeing, and I desperately wanted to embrace freedom.

Ferdy pulled back from me. "I was right, then?" he asked, his voice too husky to take as one of his usual taunts. "You did want to kiss me."

I had to drag myself away from him in order to reply. "*Absolument*," I murmured, teasing him back.

"Now all I have to do is get you to admit you love me," Ferdy said with another laugh.

At his words, I went still, staring at him for a long moment. My hands brushed against his cheeks, feeling the small stubble on them. I was enthralled and elated, and the heat between us added an edge to every emotion I could process. "You admitted you wanted to kiss me first. Maybe that strategy will work again."

He leaned into my palm before kissing it smoothly. "Oh, Ella, I've already told you how I feel."

"You did?" I pulled back from him, suddenly terrified I had insulted him.

"I did." He kissed me again. "And there, I just did it again."

I giggled. "You can hardly expect me to answer your kisses with words. Besides, you seem content with my kisses in return."

"I would be a fool to be anything other than content with the time I have been given with you." Ferdy loosened his grip on me and sighed. "Which means I'd better get you back inside. I'd hate for your brother to be upset with me already."

"Ben would be upset. But I don't think he would hurt you, if that is what you are concerned about. At least, he wouldn't hurt you too badly."

"I'd suffer any trouble in the world for another taste of you," Ferdy said, as he leaned in and kissed me once more. "But it is early yet. I'll take the pleasure of testing your brother's limits over time, rather than pushing him past the point of no return right in the beginning."

"Maybe I should have let you kiss me before, back at the Hohenwart Ball," I said, sad to see our time together end already. The hesitation I felt earlier had transformed; No longer was I unsure of meeting Ferdy—now I was unwilling to leave him.

Even if he was right about Ben.

"It won't be long before I do it again," Ferdy assured me with his characteristic aplomb as he led me back up toward the Cabal door. "Now that I know what I'm missing, I can promise you it's taking a good deal of self-preservation to take you back inside."

"Just how many other hearts have you looked at like that?" I asked, realizing he never denied coming outside the Cabal with other girls.

"Plenty," he admitted with his guileless grin. "But yours is the only one I have been searching for, and it is the only one that has proven irresistible."

I felt like a fool for smiling, but Ferdy had a way of making me feel incredibly happy. I barely noticed as the door opened before us.

It was only when I saw Ben in the doorway, glaring at us with an irritated look on his face that I snapped back to attention.

"There you are, Nora," Ben said, clearly aggravated. "I've been wondering where you were."

"We just took a little walk," I said, blushing again.

"It's getting late," Ben said. "We need to head back now."

Somewhere in the distance, I heard the *Pražský orloj* chime. It was midnight. Somehow, the long hours of the evening in the Royal Summerhouse had shortened once we arrived at the Cabal.

I glanced back at Ferdy ruefully. "Thank you for the lovely stroll." I reached for him once more.

Ferdy nodded and took my hand. He kissed it gallantly, keeping his usual respectful distance from me as Ben watched him. Despite all the confusion and strangeness, I missed his closeness; but in seeing the scowl on my brother's face, I understood Ferdy's reservations.

"Will you come back again soon?" Ferdy asked, as Ben steered me away from the Cabal.

Quickly, I looked at Ben, who gave me careless shrug. It was a small, silent movement, but I knew Ferdy had earned Ben's initial approval.

THE ORDER OF THE CRYSTAL DAGGERS

"*Absolument.*" I smiled as we said our last goodbyes.

"*C'est parfait, ma chérie.*" Ferdy leaned back against the wall of the Cabal before blowing me a kiss. "I will wait for you."

"Not too long, I hope."

Ben groaned. "Please stop, before you make me change my mind."

"Are you angry with me?" I asked Ben as we walked across the bridge, heading out over the Vltava.

"I feel better knowing that Lady POW will likely scold you enough for the two of us," Ben admitted.

"Does this mean that you like Ferdy?"

"You like him enough for both of us."

"I still want your approval," I said, unable to stop the heat from rising to my cheeks.

"If you like him enough, my approval shouldn't matter."

"If your ambivalence is punishment me for walking with him for a few moments, you have made your point."

Ben stopped. "I didn't mean it like that, Nora," he said. He gave me a small smile. "Maybe I should start calling you 'Ella,' too, huh?"

I took his arm. "Ben—"

"Don't worry about it," he said. "I know you are growing up, and things have changed. Things will always change, but I will always be here for you. And if you like Ferdy, you really should not let me get in your way. I know you well enough to know that's not going to happen anyway. But you don't need my permission to love someone else."

I stood there, quietly amazed. My brother was right, and I knew he was telling me the truth. But I did not expect the sudden sadness that came with it.

"Besides," Ben said, tweaking my nose. "I know you'll punish him enough for loving you."

"Hey!"

Ben laughed and took off running. I heard the click of his brace as he hopped over the bridge cobblestones, and I hurried to keep up after him. It was a game we had played more than a million times, it seemed; by the time I came close to catching him, we were both laughing.

We reached the end of the bridge, and then he stopped.

"Ah-ha!" I cried, nearly tackling him, before I realized there was a familiar coach.

The door opened swiftly, as though it had been kicked open, and I found myself looking at the flaring nostrils of Lady POW.

Briefly, I wondered if that was what Amir saw when I was angry, too.

"I should have known you would be doing something inappropriate." Lady Penelope stared down at me.

Ben stepped in front of me. "It was my—"

"None of that, Benedict. I know Eleanora is responsible for this. Get in, both of you, before anyone sees you."

Despite his earlier teasing, Ben gave me a sympathetic look as we complied. We both knew Lady POW was anything but happy. And just in case we did not realize this on our own, she said so as soon as the coach began moving again.

"I am not happy about this, Eleanora," Lady Penelope fumed. "I cannot believe you thought it would be good for you to sneak away from the Summerhouse Ball. I felt like a fool, trying to find you and introduce you to Count Potocki."

"My apologies, Madame." I did not like that I had disappointed her, but I refused to regret stealing away. Besides having fun at the Cabal, Mr. Clavan had given me enough hope to believe that my instincts were correct.

"I had enough of a struggle in talking with him," she said, ignoring my apologies. "He asked about you, but was interested in little else."

"Karl is the son of King Ferdinand," I blurted out, angry she was not listening to me. When I managed to shock her into silence, I continued. "If Count Potocki knows the truth about Karl, that might be why he was concerned about me."

Lady POW just stared at me, blinking.

"Karl likes me," I said. "He is upset that Lord Maximillian is willing to sponsor his bid for Potocki's position only in exchange for Lady Teresa Marie's hand in marriage. I heard Lady Cecilia complaining that the Duke of Moravia was happy to end his daughter's engagement to Alex because he had found the heir to the Bohemian throne."

There was another long moment of silence, before Lady POW cleared her throat.

"Amir?" Lady Penelope turned to Amir, who was sitting beside her in silence. "What do you say to this?"

"We can easily get proof, Madame," he said. "But Eleanora's logic is sound. And it would not be unheard of to keep an heir a secret."

"Karl was born just after the Revolution of 1848," I said. "My mother would have known."

"Tulia." Lady POW nearly spit out her name in disgust.

"That is one way to know for sure," I said, grateful Amir would not have to reveal my mother's journal. As much as I knew Lady POW loved my mother, I wanted to keep that a secret; for once, it was nice to share a secret with someone, and in many ways, I felt that I owed Amir for the trouble I had caused him earlier.

THE ORDER OF THE CRYSTAL DAGGERS

"Tulia is also the one who Father Novak alerted," Ben said. "She might be able to tell us more about what happened to Dr. Artha."

"I think it is time we made a stop at her cottage, then," Lady Penelope said through pursed lips. She tapped on the roof of the coach, calling for the driver. "She cannot avoid me forever. Amir, you might have to restrain me. I suggest you prepare yourself."

"I am always prepared, Madame." He gave me a smile, and I felt a sense of relief as we headed for Tulia's house.

Several moments passed while Lady POW settled into deep thought, a disgusted look on her face. Amir and Ben were also silent. Both of them were content to stare out into the darkness.

It appeared only I was restless. I tapped my foot on the floor, agitated, until Amir looked over at me. He raised his brow at my foot, and I did not know whether to be insulted or delighted I was reminding him of my mother.

"Why don't you like Tulia?" I finally asked Lady POW.

Her answer came at once, much more quickly than I would have expected.

"Do I have to remind you that she kept you and Ben from me for over a decade?" Lady Penelope scowled. "She could have stopped Cecilia's reign of terror in your lives. If anyone should be angry, it should be you, Eleanora."

I thought of Tulia's silliness and her silent kindness, of how she had stayed close to watch over us for the past years. It was hard to imagine that she had refrained from contacting Lady POW for so many years out of malice.

"Maybe she had her own reasons for failing to do so," I said. I could not think of anything else to defend her, but I was determined to do as much as I could.

Beside me, Ben crossed his arms over his chest. "I'd like to know what they were, if that is true."

"Maybe *Máma* did not want her to say anything," I said.

"But after your mother died, there was nothing stopping her from doing just that, was there?" Lady Penelope bristled in her seat. "Of course, there are likely other reasons for her silence on the matter."

"If you're talking about how she is a mute," I snapped, "let me be the one to assure you I will be the one to give you an answer myself."

"I did not mean silence literally. Goodness, Eleanora, calm down—"

Outside, there was a large popping sound.

The coach rumbled to a quick stop, but not before we were all jumbled together. I grabbed onto the cushions for support, while Ben slipped onto the floor between the seats.

Lady Penelope groaned. "What is it, John?" she called, pushing open the coach window.

"There's been an explosion, Madame." I heard the muffled reply of the coachman as I moved closer to Lady POW. "Straight ahead."

The instant I heard the news, I pushed past Lady POW and opened the door. I hopped out of the coach, struggling with my skirts to keep from falling on my knees.

"That's Tulia's house." Ben came down after me, landing hard on his feet. In the dark of the night, with the small moon in the sky, I saw he was right. Tulia's small cottage, perched on the horizon, was alight with fire.

"Get back inside," Lady Penelope called.

"We have to go help," I argued.

"It will be easier to get there and help if you are inside the carriage!"

"Come on, Nora." Ben helped me up, and I was grateful all over again that I had changed back into my maidservant's outfit as the driver clicked on the reins and hurried toward Tulia's house.

I was already moving when the carriage came to a stop several yards from Tulia's house.

"Tulia!" I called, hurrying toward the cottage. I saw the roof flickering with flames and felt fear choke me as much as the soot in the air.

"Stay back," Amir said, reaching in front of me.

"We have to make sure she's safe." Before I could argue more, Amir pushed me down on the ground as a shadow jumped out of a window. There was a weapon held high in his hand.

My eyes adjusted to the inconsistent light, watching as a gleaming blade appeared before Amir, who had already unsheathed his curved dagger.

There was a small clash of the metal on metal. The noise of the battle faded into the crackling fire, as flames consumed Tulia's cottage.

I struggled to move out of the muddy grass, watching as the attacker met Amir in battle. In the firelight, I could see Amir's adversary was no taller than Ben, and he was wearing a footman's uniform, along with a black mask that hid the bottom half of his face. Seeing it, I was reminded of the mask on my own stealth habit.

Behind me, Lady POW jumped down from the carriage, and her drivers pulled out a pair of pistols.

Ben grabbed me from behind and lifted me up. "We have to help," he said. "We've got to see if Tulia is inside."

I did not hesitate at his words.

184

THE ORDER OF THE CRYSTAL DAGGERS

"When we get in, watch your skirts," Ben ordered, as he slammed his shoulder into the front door. It shuddered against his force but did not budge. I could feel the heat behind it as we pushed together, bashing our bodies against it in hurried desperation.

It did not move.

"Tulia!" I cried again, hoping for any sign that she was alive.

Ben tapped my shoulder, nodding at my hair. "Give me two of your pins. I can pick the lock."

I hurriedly plucked two longer pins from my hair. My curls bobbed free and added to the heat on my cheeks. "Here. Hurry."

Never had I ever been more grateful for Ben as he fiddled with the lock. He had learned to do some smithing work in order to build his leg brace, and I felt like all of his pain was suddenly worth it in that moment as I watched him, amazed at his calmness as much as his skill. Just as he turned the knob, Amir cried out behind us.

"Watch out!"

I whirled around, just in time to see Amir ram the attacker into the house beside us. The attacker's head smashed into the cottage hard, and Amir used the chance to drive his dagger deep into the man's shoulder.

I screamed, covering my eyes. "Did you kill him?"

"It's fine, Nora," Ben said. "Amir just got his coat. The man is fine."

"Really?" I peeked out from behind my fingers, only to see Ben was right. Amir's blade had snagged the man's jacket.

As I watched, the attacker narrowed his glazed eyes at Amir. He launched out a kick, and Amir responded by punching his face.

A dark wet spot began forming at the side of the man's mask. Behind the cloth, I could hear him sputter and squeak with pain.

"Nora," Ben called. "I got the door."

"Stop!"

I whirled around as Amir hollered. His opponent had slipped free from his jacket, renewing the battle between them once more.

He lunged toward me.

My instincts kicked in, and I was already stepping back as another dagger came rushing through the air between us. I heard the attacker cry out in anguish as Lady Penelope's dagger slit through his shoulder. I watched as the purple-tinted blade splashed with crimson blood.

The dagger of the Order.

I hurried forward and kicked him, tearing Lady POW's dagger free from him. He yelled again, lashing out at me.

Hurriedly, I stepped back; from the momentum of my movements, I fell; the attacker brushed past my skirts, before slipping around me. We were both caught off balance long enough that Amir and Lady Penelope both came forward, shielding me from him.

"Here," I said to Lady POW. "Here's your dagger."

She took it from me quickly. As it passed from my hand to hers, I already missed the comfort its legacy of strength and protection offered.

"Go and get Tulia." Lady Penelope held up the blade again, looking deadly as she aimed for the attacker once more.

Before I could object, Ben tugged on my sleeve

"Come on," Ben yelled at me. "You've got to focus now!"

"Sorry." I knew he was right. We had to save Tulia.

I allowed him to pull me after him as we hurried into the burning cottage with nothing to protect me but a prayer.

Immediately, I was flooded with the burning shadows of the fire. I coughed, breathing in the sooty air, and put my hand over my mouth to stop my tongue from tasting the ash.

"Tulia!" Ben called, as he made his way around the small house.

"Do you see her?" I asked, my mouth suddenly very dry. The wooden beams around me cracked, and I jumped closer to Ben at the sound.

"Ouch." He grimaced, grasping at his leg briefly. "My brace might need some adjustments after this." His latest model had metal springs, and I wondered if he would be able to manage in the heat.

"Can you move?" I asked.

"I'm fine. You check over that way," Ben said. "I'll look over here."

I was proud to see Ben was taking his role seriously. I held my hand over my mouth as I headed deeper into the house, heading toward the heart of the flames.

Outside, I heard a gunshot go off, and I gasped.

"Keep looking," Ben called. "Don't stop unless you're hurt. And even then, keep going if you can."

I hurried through the house, carefully sidestepping flames and broken boards. I frowned. The house was a mess. As I jumped over a toppled table in her parlor, I realized that the house had been ransacked.

That man must have attacked her and then lit the house on fire to cover his tracks. He must have been looking for something. We would not know whether he found it unless we caught him.

I desperately hoped we would catch him.

As I was heading out of the room once more, circling back to the front of the house, I caught sight of Tulia's hand.

Then I saw the rest of her. I moaned at the sight, and quickly called to Ben.

"Ben!" I called. "Over here; I found her."

Tulia was tucked behind a fallen chair, passed out on her stomach. Seeing her unconscious on the floor made me feel sick, but I forced my sudden queasiness down as Ben arrived. Together, we pushed the chair out of our way and Ben began checking for signs of life.

As we carefully turned her over, my mouth dropped open. There were several shards sticking out of her hands and face, gleaming in the firelight. Little trickles of blood and sweat ran together from the numerous tiny cuts in her skin.

"Tulia," I wept.

"Keep your focus," Ben snapped, and I tried to stifle myself. I knew he was feeling poorly too, or he would not have been so curt with me.

I lowered my gaze in shame, realizing this was not a situation where a member of the Order would get emotionally sloppy. As I glanced down, I saw a trail of glass shards spanning out on the floor all around, with several more small pieces littering the nearby area in a strange circular pattern.

Had Tulia been drinking? I gently touched two fingers to her forehead, where one particularly large shard was laced into her wrinkles. It was searing to the touch, and I almost gasped at the sudden burn on my fingertips.

"Eleanora! Benedict!"

From outside, Lady Penelope was calling for us. She might as well have been calling from the opposite side of the world, rather than from the other side of the door.

I wanted to yell back, but I inhaled too quickly and felt the smoke gather inside of my mouth. I ended up coughing before Ben knelt beside me.

"Take her right arm."

Carefully, I knelt at Tulia's side and hauled her up, suddenly grateful for all the years Cecilia had forced me to work with my hands so much. Despite the dizzying heat and the sharp sweat drops running down my face, I was able to balance her weight against my own and Ben's.

"I have her." I nodded as another loud crackle of fire whipped around us. I coughed and began to feel choked by the sweltering atmosphere.

Together, Ben and I managed to make it to the doorway. Amir was quick to relieve me of duty, and Lady POW breathed a sigh of relief. I felt her exhale rush past my cheeks, still warm against the chilly winter air that soon settled on me once more.

"What happened?" I asked, my voice croaking and cracking as I breathed in all the fresh air I could. "Where is the attacker?"

"He slipped away while Lady Penelope and I were calling for you," Amir told me. He looked away. "Lady Penelope managed to injure his arm and I took his weapon. That will be enough of a victory for us tonight."

"I'm surprised," I said. "I thought for sure you would win. Aren't the good guys always supposed to win?"

"This is not a play or a novel. You will find, in real life, there are more times than we would like that failure finds us."

Hearing his words, I almost wondered if Ben had been keeping him company too much lately. Ben was more likely to be the pessimist.

"Besides," Amir added with a small smile, "Lady Penelope had one of the footmen take off and follow him. With any luck, we will be able to find his local haunt and his boss while we are at it."

That was more like Lady Penelope, I thought with a grin. "Good."

"We already have some clues. Here, Eleanora," Lady Penelope said, as she stuffed a handkerchief into my hand. "Use this to help you breathe some."

All I could do was nod, before coughing some more. I looked down at myself, smelling of decay. *Well, now I am* really *glad I changed outfits.*

"What kind of clues did you find?" Amir asked.

"A handkerchief of his own," Lady Penelope said, pulling out a soot-covered scrap of fabric. "It's been embroidered with a coat of arms. I do not recognize it, but I will see what Harshad says."

I studied it, and I was glad to know Harshad would be analyzing it later. I did not recognize the loopy 'S' that marked it, any more than I could identify the wavy lines or the prancing horse embroidered into the fine cloth.

"What about Tulia?" I asked.

"She needs medical attention," Ben called. "Amir!"

Amir and I hurried over, and I realized Ben had blood on his hands.

"Don't try to move her." Amir came running up to us. He tore at his shirt, hurriedly making bandages for Tulia. "Let me stop the bleeding first."

"She is going to get better, right?" I asked. Behind me, the fire burned brighter as the house began to collapse.

"We will need to get some better bandages," Amir said, "and I will have to sew her up."

"I will make room in the coach," Lady Penelope offered. "Eleanora, come along and assist me."

I nodded dumbly, otherwise frozen by fear. Glancing back at the scene, I watched Ben and Amir grapple with blood and glass; as the house behind me burned to the ground; watched as my world became intensely more intimate with fear and all its oppressive power.

The next several minutes—perhaps hours—seemed to pass by in a feverish dream. As we transported Tulia to the manor and settled her into her own room, I struggled with all the powers around me and inside me. I felt helpless to curb the anxiety and its accompanying trials that crippled me. My mind raced quickly, running from Tulia's kindness to the world's ugliness, jumping from the realization I could do so little to stop the world's bleeding, before finally crashing at the aching hatred that the world should be so full of evil in the first place.

Why, God? Why? Why give me a problem I can't solve, a burden I can't bear?

I did not know how life could go on without Tulia.

Once she was settled into her bed, with the fireplace roaring and the dawn breaking through the windows, I took hold of her hand and grasped it tightly. Amir carefully removed many of the glass shards in her face and hands, while Ben reapplied new bandages, and Lady Penelope and Harshad worked on finding out who was behind everything.

All of this happened while I sat there, holding her hand, watching her sleep. I felt useless, needless. I did not know if there was anything else I could do, or if I would be able to do anything anyway.

20

◊

I was dreaming.

In my dreams I was flying, and then I was falling, and then I was flailing.

And then I slammed into the waking world.

"Huh?" I woke up, nearly shooting out of my chair. At once, I noticed the uncomfortable ache in my back and my neck; the smell of soot shot across my senses and pain pierced through my forehead. I was unable to process how much time had passed since I had fallen asleep.

Blinking, I looked around and steadied myself. I had fallen asleep in a chair next to Tulia's bed after we had brought her back to the house.

At the small tapping on my knee, I rubbed my eyes clear of the morning blur to see Tulia looking up at me.

The speckles of dots across her face had scarred over, but I saw no signs of permanent trauma in her eyes.

"Tulia!" I cheered, carefully reaching over to embrace her. "You're awake."

She smiled weakly, rolling her eyes, as if to say with all of her regular spunk, *"I'm alive."*

"I'm so glad. We were worried for you."

The eyes crinkled again, this time with curiosity.

"We, including Ben and … Lady Penelope, too," I said, answering her unspoken question. "My grandmother."

Her eyebrows crinkled again, and then she exhaled, defeated.

"I won't let her hurt you," I promised.

Her fingers, stiff with bandages mixed with dried blood and healing herbs, flicked at me. She was not afraid of Lady POW.

I hesitated for a long moment. Part of me knew I should go and call for Amir and let the others know Tulia was awake. We needed to know what happened to her, and who was behind it.

But …

"Why didn't you tell me about her?" I asked.

Tulia reached over and took my hand, gently squeezing it. Our eyes met, and for the first time in a long time, I had to guess at what she was trying to tell me.

"Did my mother want you to keep us from her?" I asked.

190

THE ORDER OF THE CRYSTAL DAGGERS

She nodded.

"Why?" I asked. "Was it because of Lady POW—er, Lady Penelope? Or because of the Order?"

Her expression gave me the answer long before she did. Tulia knew about the Order; I did not have to explain it to her. As I mentioned it, she closed her eyes, as though to stop any tears she might shed.

She nodded again. Her hand tightened in mine, as she slowly signaled her answer to me.

"The Order has many enemies."

"Enemies? You mean like the person who attacked you last night?" I bit my lip. "And the people who killed Dr. Artha?"

For a quick second, I saw the surprise on her face, and then I saw it transform into tired resignation. Tulia nodded again.

I sat back in the chair, slumping over with a sigh. It was easy to see what had channeled *Máma's* decision to keep her children a secret from her mother, especially if Lady POW was as relentless a leader back then as she was now.

Tulia slowly moved her hand, placing her palm over her heart. She patted it twice, before nodding to me.

"I am sorry."

"I know." I closed my eyes and sighed. I would forgive her, of course, just as I had forgiven my mother. It was hard to say if Lady Penelope would forgive her, and I was petty enough to hope she would not. Lady Penelope's anger seemed to be more of a punishment than my rejection.

I jolted upright in my chair as the door opened behind us.

"Well, you're awake." Lady Penelope's voice was as sharp as ever, leaving me to wonder if she was talking to Tulia or me.

Tulia's speckled face twisted into a grimace.

"I was hoping that we would not meet again, either. Family reunions have never been pleasant for us."

"Family?" I asked.

"Just how much have you kept from them, Tulia? Were you just acting under Dezda's orders? Or maybe Jakub's?"

"Who's Jakub?" I asked.

"Your grandfather," Lady Penelope replied with a disdainful snort. "Tulia is his half-sister."

Tulia nodded as I looked at her. She gave me a small, rueful smile. Her fingers moved over mine. *"A bastard child."*

I said nothing. And nothing happened. I did not ask any questions, nor did I start spewing accusations or lashing out in anger. I was getting tired of being surprised, but I continued to sit there, still and silent, somehow waiting for more surprises to come along.

"Which is why I'm not terribly surprised that she has betrayed us, come to think of it," Lady Penelope continued.

Tulia rolled her eyes, and I just stared blankly between the two of them. I was numb to the tension around us, even though I could sense it.

"Since she has neglected to tell you our wonderful family history, it would be better for you to wait with the others in the library. Your curiosity, Eleanora, as endearing as it can be when it is not inconvenient, would only keep us from getting down to business."

"But if she is family," I objected, "then I should be here for her."

"Operating like a business is better, when your family is full of secrets and lies."

"I'm part of the business, too, now that I am a member of the Order." I stood up, facing her, prepared to fight her objections.

"And as such, you should listen to my commands." She crossed her arms in front of her and shook her head. "Your anger right now is exactly the reason you should leave. You struggle to keep your focus enough."

Tulia brushed her fingers against my skirt. I turned and watched her nod, telling me she would be fine, and it was true that I should go.

"I want Amir in here first," I said slowly. "He needs to check her injuries."

"Go and send for him, then. I can trust him to remain silent."

Tulia made a small movement, telling me she was still tired and wanted to rest longer. I began to translate for Lady POW, but she shook her head.

"There's no need. I know what she is saying. It has been many years, but we have not forgotten how to communicate."

"Fine. I won't bother trying to help you again," I muttered, irritated at her lack of graciousness.

As if to prove it, Tulia signed a vicious insult, and Lady Penelope scowled. For a long moment, they stared daggers at each other.

When they finished their silent battle, Lady POW turned back to me. "Go and get Amir. He might as well tend to her for a few hours, and then we can ask her our questions. I will stay here until he arrives."

I frowned.

THE ORDER OF THE CRYSTAL DAGGERS

"There are a few questions I have for her." Lady POW arched her brow at me. "And besides, we will need her for our investigation, Eleanora, so you need not worry that I will allow any further harm to come to her."

"I didn't think you would," I said with a sigh, before moving around her and heading out the door. "But when she has rested enough, I am coming back with Ben. We both deserve to know the truth, especially after last night."

Lady POW scowled, but she said nothing. I had to wonder if she was more frustrated I refused to do what she wanted or if she was more upset she could not bring herself to correct me.

I took comfort in the opportunity to escape. My body ached from sleeping poorly, my mind was fuzzy and full of too many possibilities to worry exclusively about one reality. My clothes smelled of pungent smoke, and my hair was falling from the last of its pins.

But most of all, I was weary.

It seemed everything that had changed since the night of Lady POW's arrival ran up to me, catching me all at once. Since then, I had a completely new life; I struggled to imagine what life would have been like if Alex and Teresa Marie were still to be married, if I had never been freed from Cecilia's servanthood, and if I had never learned the truth about my mother, my work, and my home. My life.

All I knew was things were different, and there was no going back. There was only going forward, and there was no guarantee that there would be any rest or renewal.

The magic of Prague's far away city had dimmed, and in my disillusionment, I encountered a terrible plot to overthrow the kingdom. I had watched as one of my dearest companions almost burned and bled to death, and I saw that same companion turned into an unrecognizable family member. I was constantly being pulled in all sorts of directions.

Sighing, I shook my head. I was not just tired of being surprised. I was tired of being disappointed.

◊   ◊   ◊   ◊

Hours later, we were still waiting for Tulia to wake up again. Despite the delay in the investigation, I was glad for the break. I was able to get a bath and wash my hair, change my clothes, and take a proper nap. I was also glad that Lady Penelope sent out our regrets for the evening, citing my twisted ankle from the previous night as the reason I would not be in attendance for Society's delight.

She informed me of her decision when we were in the library together, still waiting to hear from Tulia.

"Thank you," I replied, clutching the book in my lap. I was ignoring it as Lady POW worked at my father's desk, but it helped to feel I had some protection from her direct study.

"That was good thinking on your part last night, you know." She gave me a reluctant smile. "It gives us an excuse to stay away, and it will still make people talk. Perhaps their pity will be even more useful than your presence."

"I'm glad it helped. At least I am good at something, even if it is lying."

Lady Penelope's hands tightened together. "I suppose I should apologize to you, Eleanora."

The book dropped to the floor. "What?"

Lady Penelope smirked. "I know. Shocking, isn't it? And you have already had quite a few surprises lately."

"That is an understatement," I agreed. "But not one worth your apology."

"I do not want to apologize for the truth," Lady Penelope corrected. "You are doing well as a member of the Order, and I am proud of what you have done so far. If I do not express it, it is usually because I am not accustomed to surprises, either."

"Is it a family trait?" I asked with a small smile.

"Probably," she replied. "Just as curiosity is, no doubt. But my apology is more for the matter of our instruction. You are family first, and it has been a very, very long time since I have had to worry about family before work, if, in all fairness, I have ever done so."

I watched her as she said it, and it was hard to fault her as anything less than genuinely repentant.

Ben had said before that everyone was devastated by *Máma's* death, and it looked like the truth; but much like the truth, I did not realize it affected others as much as it did me.

"I'm just glad I am not a failure," I said.

Lady Penelope cleared her throat again, clearly uncomfortable. "These are early days between us, Eleanora," she said. "Our time will stretch out into eternity, and we must make it count. If there is any failure between the two of us, it is with me."

Lady Penelope met my gaze, and I felt a small ripple of approval from her. "Thank you. I did not want you to be angry with me."

"You should never fear my anger," Lady Penelope said. "Not as long as we are on the same side."

I nodded.

THE ORDER OF THE CRYSTAL DAGGERS

"From what Amir told me about your adventure earlier," Lady Penelope continued, "I can understand the reasons for it. I am glad to hear that you have good friends in the city. I cannot imagine Cecilia has made it easy for you to meet with them since your father's death."

Was she talking about Ferdy? I frowned, wondering if Amir had embellished our relationship in order to protect me. Lady POW would not fault loyalty, especially if there was good cause for it. Amir did not know the exact nature of my interest in Ferdy. Was it possible he had misread my interest when I told him? Or maybe I had given too much of my affection away?

I shrugged. "Oh, well, I really just met—"

"And it does help that they are apparently well informed of the city's secrets and news. Imagine the surprise when people find out there is an actual heir to the Bohemian throne. Tulia confirmed the report."

When she saw my troubled look, she added, "I told you earlier, Eleanora, I had a few questions for her. When you left, I asked them."

"So you know the truth, then?"

"Yes. Empress Maria Anna was pregnant when your mother arrived in Prague. That was the reason she was worried about the kingdom, primarily. She did not want the Revolution to claim her son's life, even if he could not inherit the throne."

"It also makes sense that she called for the Pope then," I said. "She would have been very concerned about her situation, as a Catholic mother."

Lady Penelope shrugged. "All mothers worry for their children. I know your mother must have worried for you."

There was no doubt in my mind that Lady POW was right. I was not happy with Tulia and my mother's deception and secrecy, but I was sure of their love for me.

"You suspect Karl Marcelin is the heir," Lady Penelope said, changing the subject.

"He is the right age, and Lord Maximillian, the Duke of Moravia, is interested in working with him. Karl told me that His Grace wants him to marry Lady Teresa Marie. And it makes sense, from what I heard, if their plot is to free the kingdom from the empire."

Lady Penelope snorted. "Freedom from the empire would only lead to its death. But I commend them on their vision. It is a noble goal, even if it carries great risk and flawed methods."

"If Karl does get the position of Minister-President," I said, "he would be able to push for his election as King of Bohemia, wouldn't he?"

"In theory." Lady Penelope looked down at the scribbled mess before her. "The king would have to be ratified by the constitution of Bohemia, which would require acceptance by the Upper and Lower Houses, including the Bohemian and German Diets, and by the *Reichsrat*. That is a lot of votes."

"Is there any way he could do it without all those?" I asked. Karl did not seem like someone who would worry about defeat when it came to getting what he wanted.

"Only if the majority of them were killed," Lady Penelope said. "Many people have died in the recent string of murders, but it is unlikely he would be able to continue using that method. If, indeed, he is behind the murders at all."

"If he is the heir, and working toward the crown, it is something to consider."

"To consider? Absolutely. To accuse? Maybe. But judgment at this point is early. We would need something that directly links him to the killings."

The door to the library swung open, and I was surprised to see Harshad enter. I had not seen him much over the past few weeks, and when I did, it was only for moments, if not seconds, at a time.

"Well, Pepé, you know what the Scriptures say," Harshad said, as he made his way over to the desk. He held out a small square of linen before her. "Ask and you shall receive."

"You know who it belongs to," Lady Penelope cheered. She stood up in triumph, snatching the handkerchief out of his hand. "Tell me who the unlucky bastard is."

"The man in question was a worker in the household of Mr. Roman Szapira," Harshad said. "While John was not able to follow your enemy into the house, he did see our culprit go into the servant's entrance at the Szapira mansion across town."

"Szapira?" I repeated. The name sounded familiar. Only a second passed before I remembered where I had heard it. "That's where Karl is staying for the season, until the Advent Ball."

"Well, then, we have our proof." Lady Penelope smirked. She clapped her hands together eagerly. "It seems that Mr. Marcelin is determined to gain his throne, no matter what he has to do."

"I don't think he is like that," I said, suddenly flushing over as I thought of his sincerity and eagerness in wanting to dance with me. There was nothing sinister about him that I had seen. "Maybe there is another reason why our attacker was at Mr. Szapira's house."

"I do not believe in coincidences," Lady Penelope said. "And that is not just because of location. There is timing to consider, too, and opportunity."

Harshad met her gaze, and rather than switching to another language, I watched as they communicated with their eyes. I saw the thrill of discovery in Lady Penelope's, and the grim hesitation in Harshad's eyes.

"I give up," I groaned. "I can't read your minds, as you two apparently can."

"Roman Szapira has recently completed renovation of Prague Castle's wine cellar," Harshad said. "He would know his way around the castle very well. And he would be able to infiltrate it. Marcelin has only recently struck up a good friendship with him since he returned to Prague."

"That minimizes Szapira's role," Lady Penelope said. "Marcelin must have a plan to take care of his adversaries at the Advent Ball. That is when Count Potocki is supposed to announce his official last day as Minister-President. He told me so himself at the Summerhouse Ball."

I had been wondering if Count Potocki gave Lady Penelope any useful information after Karl escorted me out of the ballroom.

"We have received more than one invitation for the Advent Ball," Harshad said. "So we will be there without cause for suspicion."

"Good." Lady Penelope pursed her lips together. "Now we just have to plan what we will do once we are there."

That is also when Lord Maximillian wants to announce Karl's engagement to Lady Teresa Marie. I thought about what Karl told me when he had escorted me out to my carriage the previous night.

As Lady POW and Harshad continued to discuss the likely scenarios, I was briefly taken aback, realizing it had been less than a day since I found out Karl was the heir to the Bohemian throne, and that he was infatuated with me to the point he was almost risking his political future.

It had also been less than a day since I had seen Ferdy—and less than a day since I had kissed him. My cheeks burned at the thought of him and my heart began to beat faster inside my chest.

Then, just as quickly, all color and blood drained from my face as I realized that if Karl did do something at the Advent Ball, Ferdy would be there, too. He was going to be in danger.

I can't let anything happen to him.

My heart lurched, imagining Ferdy poisoned, his body still like Father Novak's, surrounded by any number of other corpses. Or maybe it was possible he would be stabbed, I thought, thinking of Dr. Artha.

I stood abruptly, so fast even Lady POW and Harshad turned to face me.

"What's wrong, Eleanora?" Lady Penelope asked. "You have a strange look on your face."

"It's … it's … " I stammered, trying to put my thoughts into words properly.

Before I could manage, there was another knock at the door, and Ben poked his head inside. "Tulia's awake," he said. "She's ready to answer more of our questions."

Ours, not yours.

Lady POW looked at me once more, silently asking me if I was going to say anything. She wanted to know what concerned me, and I did not want to share with her the newfound fear in my heart.

While she had just commended me for my quick thinking, I did not want her to see me as weak for caring so ardently for a boy like Ferdy. From what I had seen of her, she would only see it as an unnecessary complication.

I could not risk losing him to Lady POW any more than I could willingly risk his life at the Advent Ball.

I shook my head, and Lady Penelope allowed me to keep my silence on the matter. As we walked toward Tulia's room, I decided to talk to Ben once we were able to learn more from Tulia. Between the two of us, I knew we would be able to come up with a plan to save Ferdy.

21

If Tulia was upset at the small crowd of people that appeared in her bedroom an hour later, she handled the situation with enough grace I did not notice.

It was possible I did not want to notice. I was too distracted by other things; I was worried for Ferdy, for one, and I was also concerned for Karl. As much as Lady Penelope was ready to believe he was involved, I was still hesitant to think he would murder anyone, let alone his own parents and colleagues.

If Tulia had any information that could save Ferdy and distance Karl from suspicion, I wanted to hear it.

She was propped up on her pillows, sitting up. There were new bandages around her arms, but those on her fingers were unraveled. I could see several cuts and scrapes sticking out from the strips.

"Let's start this from the beginning," Lady Penelope said. She narrowed her cold gaze at Tulia. "Feel free to chime in when something comes up you can contribute."

"Please, Madame, have mercy," Amir said. "I have not yet removed all the wine bottle shards from her skin. She is still in a great amount of pain."

"The laudanum should be enough for that," Lady Penelope insisted, although her tone softened ever so slightly. "She has already proven she can handle—"

"Enough, Pepé," Harshad interrupted. "The beginning, if you please. Or I can start, if you prefer."

Lady POW turned her ire on him, while I said nothing. I was content to watch out for Tulia, but I was beginning to enjoy watching Lady POW and Harshad torment each other. It was a poetic sort of justice, and it made me feel better about all the irritation the two of them caused me.

"Let me begin," Amir said, before either Lady POW or Harshad could start a new argument. "We were called here by Her Imperial Majesty, Queen Victoria, when she asked the Order of the Crystal Daggers to secure this area. There were rumors of deep political division, and there were enough mysterious occurrences to give her cause for concern."

"You're not part of the Order," I said, remembering what he had told me before. "Why did you come along?"

"He is my confidant and medical advisor, even if he is not part of the Order," Lady Penelope replied. "Amir has proven himself to the Queen separately, so he is an honorary member of the League of Ungentlemanly Warfare in her kingdom."

"The Order has more of an international reach," Amir said. "And it is fitting for me, as I will never be a citizen, nor a gentleman, in Her Imperial Majesty's court."

I felt the sadness in his words, before Lady POW let out an impatient groan.

"I am also a member of the League, Eleanora," Lady Penelope said. "It often works with the Order for assignments such as these."

"Oh. I see."

"It probably makes it easier for Queen Victoria to fund you if you work in both," Ben said.

Lady POW nodded, giving Ben a smile.

I still did not know a lot about politics, but I knew money was at the heart of a lot of debate in the Bohemian government. The Diets especially fought over budget deals and spending, and the only thing they could consistently agree on was increasing their own fortunes. Ben's explanation gave me a good idea of why Amir and Lady Penelope had both come.

"Her Majesty is more concerned about unrest in India," Harshad said, "but she does not want this area to collapse while she pursues other international settlements. When we agreed to investigate, we headed for Prague, where several of our contacts were able to provide information."

Tulia flicked her fingers, signing out a name. I saw the letters she made and deciphered it for the others.

"Dr. Artha included," I said.

"Yes. Sigmund was very well informed of political division, being an instigator of sorts," Lady Penelope said. "He had great friendships with all parties, and even collaborated with the Jews from time to time. Needless to say, the Bohemians and the Germans did not like this, even if they liked him."

Tulia nodded in agreement.

"And then he was murdered," I said. "And that led to Father Novak's murder, too, at the Church of Our Lady of the Snows."

"What information did he have that made him a target?" Lady Penelope asked, turning to Tulia.

For several long moments, I watched her as her fingers and facial expressions spelled out her story.

"He was working on creating the antidote recently, especially after discovering the herb had been used for political deaths in the past."

"Did he find out who was purchasing it?" Lady Penelope asked.

Tulia shook her head, before running her fingers over my hand.

"There is another seller, but not an enemy of the Order."

"Who is it?" Lady Penelope's eyes glittered. "Tell us."

THE ORDER OF THE CRYSTAL DAGGERS

Tulia shook her head, shrugging, and Lady POW let out a frustrated groan. "You should know this, Tulia!"

She gave a few more signs, and I knew that she did not have a name for us.

Our clues were leading us nowhere.

I thought of what Ferdy had said. "Dr. Artha was stabbed by a man outside of the church, dressed in a servant's coat. Some people thought it was a thief, but it wasn't."

"I wonder if that was our fire starter last night?" Lady Penelope looked back at Tulia, who exhaled slowly.

"After Dr. Artha was murdered, Father Novak was, too," I said. "Someone knew he had left a trail of information that led to you. It makes sense it would be the same person."

"The attacker was young," Amir said. "Youthful and energetic. He is a good fighter, which is why he was able to slip away. But he is not a seasoned fighter. I landed several blows of my own before he escaped."

"If he is that agile, it would explain why he was able to get such good information, too," Ben said. "It would have to be someone who was used to finding information. Especially since we were the only ones who could make the connection to Tulia."

"He might have other sources," Lady Penelope said, and Tulia nodded.

While the others debated the identity of the attacker, Tulia met my gaze. She peered at me intently, and I remembered what she had told me earlier.

The Order of the Crystal Daggers has many enemies.

"So if Dr. Artha is dead," Amir said, "we must find the new source of the silver thallis herb. Whoever it is, he will be able to lead us to the people trying to kill off the politicians with it."

"We have tried to find someone all over town," Ben said. "Harshad did not find anything, either."

"Xiana has contacted me," Harshad said. "She is coming here to help investigate, as this is her area of expertise. But she will not be here for another week at best. She did tell me that Dr. Artha was our only contact with the silver thallis in his reserve. He told her that there was only one other person in Prague who would sell it."

"If he was able to tell her that, it must be true," Lady Penelope said. "Benedict, this is a good task for you."

"What I want to know is how this connects to Lord Maximillian and Karl Marcelin," Ben said. "Lord Maximillian would have known about the silver thallis from my father's funeral. He does not live in Prague now. He is just visiting."

"Visiting while he arranges for Lady Teresa Marie to marry the heir to the throne of Bohemia," I added.

"Karl Marcelin's ambition does play an interesting role as a catalyst," Lady Penelope said. "He finished his schooling in the summer, before he headed back here. That is when the politicians began to die strange deaths and others were elected."

"He does appear to be the mastermind," Harshad said, remaining still as Lady POW moved around the room restlessly.

"What do you mean?" I asked. "How is Karl the one behind the murders?"

Amir cleared his throat. "I have received some information from a source," he said. "He is a fellow league member. He contacted me regarding this matter. Apparently, Mr. Marcelin has made contact with others to help him work to free Bohemia from the empire."

"What?" My throat went dry.

"This makes sense," Harshad said, "given that we know from your own information from Lady Cecilia that Lord Maximillian has foreign contacts. We believe these foreign influences put the two of them in contact with each other."

"There is still no way to be sure who is the mastermind, then." But even as I spoke the words, the narrative began to come together in my mind. Lord Maximillian had been in contact with others for years. Karl wanted the throne. There were foreigners who were coordinating with them. The timing even seemed to make sense, I realized, thinking of how Karl told me of Lord Maximillian's friendships built over vineyards.

"Lord Maximillian would not have known about Karl until he came here, correct?" Ben asked. "Why murder other politicians beforehand?"

"Maybe he found out about Karl later on," I said. "He could have been considering a political career before. Karl told me he was a good friend of Count Potocki's, and he is staying with Lord Hohenwart right now."

"If he found out about Karl this season," Lady Penelope said, "he could have made some adjustments to his plans."

"Yes, precisely!" I said. "I don't think Karl would actually murder anyone."

"And Lord Maximillian would?" Ben scoffed. "Come on, don't tell me you're serious? You can't let feelings influence your opinions on Karl and this case, no matter how much you might like him."

"I don't like him," I insisted, blushing slightly. Of all people, Ben should have been the one to know that I did not like him. At least, not in *that* way. "But I'm the one who knows Karl the best out of all of us."

"You know the image that he has striven to project to society best," Lady Penelope said.

THE ORDER OF THE CRYSTAL DAGGERS

"It doesn't matter. He wouldn't have done that. And we just agreed the murders and threats started before he returned to Prague."

"So that means he's paying someone to do it," Ben said darkly.

"Maybe Lord Maximillian is doing it. He's the one with the money, remember?" I fought back.

"That's enough, you two," Lady Penelope interrupted. "There is no need to fight about it. We need proof."

"Lady Cecilia should be enough proof," I said. "She was the one I overheard talking about how Lord Maximillian found King Ferdinand's son."

"Maybe we should go and get her," Lady Penelope murmured. She tapped her fingertips together thoughtfully.

"We would be better to watch her," Harshad said. "There is no telling if she would tell the duke of our interest if we question her."

"That is true." Lady Penelope frowned, drawing her frosty eyebrows together in thoughtful consideration. "The Advent Ball is at the end of this week. That gives us four days to find out how they plan on massacring the masses. They still need a disaster to spark a revolution, and the timing is too convenient to ignore."

As Lady Penelope, Amir, and Harshad began to trade theories and suggest different routes of action, Tulia signaled to me again.

She gave me a secretive look, and I took her hand, pretending to comfort her while she used her stiffened fingers.

The attacker came as a messenger. He had a gift for me.

"What was it?" I whispered.

She cupped her hands and twitched it, moving like it was a shot glass. I saw the gleam of the glass shards, some of them still stuck in her flesh.

"Wine?" I asked, and she nodded.

Her hand tightened around mine.

He said it was from the Cabal.

I felt my heart drop and my breath catch in my throat. Was it possible … Mr. Clavan and Eliezer, all of them … was it possible they were working for the enemy? Was it possible they *were* the enemy?

Or were they in as much danger as we were?

Tulia pinched my palms. *He smashed the bottle, attacked me, and started the fire.*

I nodded again, before squeezing her hand. "I'm so glad you are safe," I said. "You are my family, and you always have been."

She smiled, and at that moment—as the plans were being made and the tasks were being assigned, as Lady POW and Harshad argued while Amir injected logic into the conversation, as Ben and I exchanged worried glances and Tulia fell back asleep—I resolved to protect the ones I loved, no matter what I had to do.

22
◊

While I was determined to do whatever I had to do to protect my friends and family, I was faced with any number of impossible challenges. As the Advent Ball crept closer, I was certain I would go mad before it was all over.

The first problem I ran into was Ferdy.

Or rather, I thought bitterly, the problem was that I was not able to run into him.

In keeping with my earlier excuse, Lady Penelope made it known throughout all of Europe I would be attending the ball, but I had to rest up if I was going to be able to dance and enjoy myself. I had an enormous pile of cards come to the house wishing me well, and little notes from different ladies and gentlemen, all ranging from friendly to flirty.

I was stuck at the manor, unable to escape the house. There was no way I could go and warn him. The whole world seemed to conspire against me, because even when I sent Ben out on his own investigations, he was unable to find Ferdy.

"Even Clavan and the others at the Cabal have not seen him this week," Ben said when I came around the morning before the Ball. He handed me my note, the one I had written days before. The paper was still carefully folded, as though my prayers for its protection were so effective it had failed to be delivered.

"You went there?" I asked carefully. "To the Cabal, I mean?"

"Yes." Ben shrugged. "Jarl and Faye are there most nights, and they are able to answer some of my questions. I never ask them directly or tell them why I want to know. They are closer to my age so I think they think I am there to be their friend more than I am trying to get them to be my source."

"What about the wine from them? The one that Tulia's attacker used to get her to open the door?" I asked.

"It was obviously a ruse, Nora," Ben said. "Do you really think they are part of the plan to free the country from the Emperor?"

I thought about what Clavan had told me before, about how freedom was found in the struggle. "I ... don't know what to think," I admitted.

"But you're ready to leave Karl Marcelin out of everything, but Ferdy and his friends are not above suspicion?" Ben asked.

His words cut into me as I realized he was right.

"You're right," I said. "I don't know what is wrong with me."

"Tulia's going to be fine," Ben said. The look in his blue-green eyes softened, and I was briefly reminded of our father as he reached out and patted my shoulder. "You have a soft heart, Nora. If I worry for you, it is only because that's something that can be easily bruised. That's why I was worried about Ferdy, and that's honestly why I am worried about Karl."

"You think he is innocent, too?"

"Not exactly." Ben crossed his arms over his chest. "I meant more how I worry that you like him more than you might want to admit."

I felt myself flush. "I don't like him. At least, not the way I like Ferdy."

It was a rare moment of vulnerability as I admitted I cared for Ferdy to my brother. Of all the people in the world, I loved Ben the most, and I did not want to face a world where I would have to choose between him and someone else.

"That's fine," Ben said briskly. "And that's even more cause for worry for me, frankly. I know you like Ferdy. He's fun and exciting and immensely distracting. He can tell a story that will make you forget about everything else, and he can argue with you until you are mad with rage. All while he just sits there, laughing at you. Or," Ben added thoughtfully, "he gets his friends to."

I might have smiled at the reference to Ben's own experience with Ferdy's friends and their collective craftiness, but I had a feeling more was coming. "But?"

"But it is hard to say if there is anything meaningful about him," Ben said. "Is Ferdy serious about anything? If not, he's not someone who would make you a good match in the long run. At least, not from what I have seen."

I said nothing, wondering if Ben was right.

I thought about why I liked Ferdy. He had rescued me from Amir before, that was true. Ferdy was sweet and goodhearted, even if he was too much of a jokester sometimes. He was clearly able to support himself, or at least enough so that he could rely on Clavan to open a tab for him, so he was clever as well as charming.

And he claimed me as his, even if I had yet to give him permission to do so.

Karl would never have charmed a kiss out of me, or called me out on my own secrets.

Karl might as well have been Ferdy's polar opposite. He was still charming, but he was dignified and intelligent, passionate about making the future a better place, fighting to get what he wanted.

"When you danced with Karl," Ben said, "and I saw you talk with him, I thought you might like him. He is someone you would have been able to meet properly, if our parents had lived. He would have been the kind of man you would marry, if our lives had been different."

I did not know what to say. Ben, as always, had solid reasoning. He was right on so many things.

Sighing, I crumbled up the note I had written, the one I had written warning Ferdy to stay away from the Advent Ball.

THE ORDER OF THE CRYSTAL DAGGERS

"I still do not want Ferdy to get hurt," I insisted. "If Karl is trying to kill everyone between himself and the throne, he will have to find a way to survive the party. I don't want Ferdy caught up in that."

"And if Lord Maximillian is the one behind everything, as you'd prefer," Ben said, teasing me some, "he will find a way to protect Karl."

"Exactly. Karl is safe no matter what. I need to make sure Ferdy is, too." I leaned against the wall behind me. "We only have hours left before the Ball."

"Once we arrive, I promise I will go and find Ferdy and tell him," Ben said. "If that will make you feel better, *ségra*."

I reached out and embraced him, letting myself breathe in his warm strength like a tonic.

"Thank you," I whispered into his shoulder. "It would make me feel better. It seems I have done nothing this week but pace through the manor. I can't sleep well, or for very long, thinking about it. Even Cecilia's part of the house has gone quiet by the sound of it."

"I'm surprised Lady POW did not make you work on something," Ben said.

I scowled. "She said I should learn how to wait. Can you believe that? Amir lets me help him tend to Tulia's wounds, and that is the only reprieve I have had from worrying for the last several days."

"You mean talking with me is not enough to ease your mind?" Ben gave me a grin. "It will be all right, Nora. Or maybe I should call you Ella, since Ferdy and Karl both refer to you as such?"

I shook my head. "I will always be Nora to you," I said. "No matter what happens."

"We will see," Ben said. "You can't stop some things from changing."

"Yes, you can," I argued. "And even if you're right, there's no need to change how we react to it."

"Well, your resolve relieves me," Ben said, patting my shoulder, "as it always has."

He gave me a quick kiss on the forehead, much like *Táta* used to do. "Be safe tonight. I have faith in you, but don't take any unnecessary risks if you don't have to."

"You, too." I gave him a brave smile. As he walked away, heading to his room to change for the night, I found that his faith in me gave me peace.

I clasped my hands together, as though I was trying to hold onto that moment and that feeling, letting it submerge me in its comfort. "Thank you, Lord."

As if he had granted my prayer, I felt the fullness of that moment settle on me. Even as I slid into my stealth habit, even as Jaqueline, Amelia, and Marguerite sewed my gown on top of it; the scarlet silk was just dark enough to hide the black suit underneath, and it was loose enough I could move easily. Several ruffles and an elaborate sash of ribbon hid the seam at the side, the one I could easily rip if I needed to make a quick wardrobe change. Jaqueline instructed me carefully on how to slip out of my stays, and I went over it twice, just to make sure I was ready.

Even as my hair was curled and piled onto my head; even as I faced myself in the mirror, getting one last look of myself before we disembarked, I knew I was going into battle, and I knew I would face it with resolve. My blue eyes were clear, and I swore I could almost see my mother looking back at me and through me.

"You look beautiful, Eleanora."

I turned away from the mirror to see Lady Penelope behind me. She was dressed in resplendent holiday colors, with fur lining her gown layers and her neckline.

"Not Eleanor?" I asked, only teasing her slightly.

She shook her head. "No."

I felt a twinge of guilt at her saddened expression. "I'm sorry," I said. "I shouldn't have said that."

"We are family." Lady Penelope stepped closer to me. Her tone was brusque, but I knew from the look in her eyes she was still concerned for me. "And as such, the pains and pleasures we give each other will always be interconnected. Besides, it is much better to remember Eleanor than to allow her memory to slip into the darkness."

I nodded. "You are right."

"Of course I am." She gave me one of her haughty smiles, and I gave her one right back.

"I am not just Dezda's daughter," I said, remembering what Amir had said before. "I'm your granddaughter, too."

"Which is why I have two things for you tonight," Lady Penelope said. She came over to me and held out her hands.

Inside of her outstretched palms sat a dagger, sheathed in black leather.

"This is the first," she said, while I just stared at it, my eyes wide with reverence and disbelief. "I think you have earned the right to carry it."

"Really?" I asked, reaching for it.

"Well, not entirely. I still have to insist that Harshad will instruct you. After tonight, we will have more time to devote to such matters."

I did not trust myself to say anything. I was upset Harshad had to be forced to do what I saw as largely his job, but I had been waiting for this moment, the moment I would gain the right to bear my mother's weapon and legacy. I was overjoyed and fearful, eager to please and terrified to fail. My inner mix of

THE ORDER OF THE CRYSTAL DAGGERS

emotions only settled as I took the dagger from Lady Penelope. I pulled it out of its snug pocket, allowing the violet blade to shimmer in the evening light.

"Honesty is better than lying in matters such as this," Lady Penelope said. "You don't know how to use it, I might remind you. And you know this, too. You would not believe me if I said you were ready for it. But you are ready to embrace the responsibilities of the Order of the Crystal Daggers."

I curled my fingers around the hilt, the old weapon full of ancient strength, tense with passion from its previous wielders.

"If there comes a time tonight," Lady Penelope said, "where you must reveal yourself and the Order, the King will recognize this as a symbol of your authority."

"He will?" I asked.

Lady Penelope nodded. "We do not reveal ourselves unless the situation calls for it, when death or defeat are the only other options."

I studied the blade again, testing it in my handling. I believed in destiny; I believed in God, and I knew he had his plans for me. At that moment, it struck me as odd how right this seemed, to be here, standing on a precipice, standing before a moment when I had the chance to do something greater than I could have ever imagined. It was humbling and awing, and I was floored with the tension between looking up in faith and glancing down in fear.

Lady Penelope watched while I looked at my eyes as they reflected darkly in the blade.

"What is it?" I asked.

"You should know this is your mother's dagger," she said. "I have carried it beside mine all these years, since she resigned her position. It is not something I would pass to you lightly, but I welcome the chance to share her legacy with you."

I felt my throat clog as I tried to imagine my mother holding her dagger for the first time. I could see her rising to the challenge, sharing her adventures with Amir by her side, looking for approval from her mother with fiery determination.

"Which is why you must listen carefully now," Lady Penelope said. "As the following information is the most important thing for a lady in the Order to know."

"What is it?" I asked, eager to hear.

"Eleanora, when you fall in love with someone," Lady Penelope began, "it is important that you do not lose your head in the process of letting go of your heart."

I nodded. "I think I can remember that."

"That's not it," Lady Penelope said. "I'm telling you that when you decide to have sexual intercourse, you must remember to indulge in it according to your monthly courses."

209

THE ORDER OF THE CRYSTAL DAGGERS

"What?" My voice squeaked.

"This is the rule of twos. You can have as much sex as you want in the two weeks following the end of your monthly cycle, but you cannot have sex in the two weeks before. If you engage in intercourse two weeks before your period, you can get pregnant." She arched her brow at me, intently staring into my soul, as though instilling inside of me a permanent sense of discomfort. "Do you understand this?"

My voice was gone. I only nodded.

"Good. When was the last time you had your monthly courses?"

At her intrusive question, I balked. "I'm not going to have sex tonight," I sputtered. "There's no reason to ask that."

"I have plenty of reasons," Lady Penelope snorted. "The Order is sworn to serve the truth and protect the innocent. That includes our children. I would hate to have you live up to our family's reputation in this matter."

"This matter?"

She grimaced, realizing her mistake. "Never mind," she said. "But you should start keeping track of your monthly courses. We can't afford any slip ups."

Lady Penelope turned and walked away as another round of questions came rushing up from inside of me.

"What do you mean by family reputation?" I asked. "Did you—"

Lady Penelope glared at me. "That's enough on the subject. Amir and I do not wish to discuss such things. Now, finish getting ready and hurry downstairs. We need to make sure we arrive early tonight. We will need the extra time to secure the castle."

She shut the door to my room hard enough that the dagger in my hand quivered, and I sighed.

Was that the reason my mother had resigned from the Order? That did not make sense; at least, not to me. Lady POW had not known about Ben or me before she came here. Was it possible she was talking about herself? Had my mother been an "unnecessary surprise?"

And why mention Amir? I stared back down at the dagger. I could only wonder for now.

Other things needed to be done.

Tucking the dagger into the hidden pockets under my gown, allowing the sheath to sit around my stealth habit, I felt an old sense of comfort.

It seemed that I was used to the stress of fulfilling my intended role at parties, I thought with a smirk. As much as that was true, I was glad to be armed with more than my wit and beauty this time.

23
◊

The crystal dagger was a gift that seemed to christen the night, giving me a supernatural sense of purpose and preparation.

It also helped keep my stomach from turning over into knots. As I sat up straight in Lady Penelope's coach, the hilt leaned into my side, giving me something to focus on, something other than how if I failed tonight, the majority of Prague's aristocracy and nobility would be dead, along with me and likely everyone I ever cared for.

Ben, dressed up in a footman's livery, squeezed my hand as he helped me descend from the carriage.

"Remember your promise," I whispered to him.

"I will," he assured me, and then he quickly let me go.

Lady Penelope and I hiked up our skirts and headed up into the entrance to Prague Castle.

If I had been there under any other circumstances, I would have thought I had died and gone to heaven. A heaven, I thought with a smile, where it was Christmastime all the time.

Since Queen Victoria had taken up the tradition of decorating trees for the season, many others had followed in her example. Empress Maria Anna had gone further, hanging wreaths and silk all over, presenting many images of the infant Jesus, surrounded by his holy mother and the shepherds who gathered at his birth. At the front of the room, there was even a mock manger scene, complete with sculptures of angels and shepherds. Tall trees lined the walls of the room, each of them lit with small candles and decorative ribbons and other little ornaments.

The ballroom was filled with light, so brilliant it was hard for me to look up at any of the chandeliers without shielding my eyes. I stood atop the staircase before it, wondering if it was wrong to feel as though I was descending into Elysium rather than Hades.

The dagger at my side, underneath all my skirts, slanted against me, even though the rest of my outfit seemed weightless all of a sudden.

It was as though I was an actual princess in this moment, and I smiled at the thought of seeing Karl. The voice at the back of my mind reminded me that if I wanted, I could be a *real* princess.

"Remember our plan," Lady Penelope hissed at me, as she walked down the stairs beside me.

I glanced around at the footmen, wondering if Ferdy was already working. "I remember," I said, hoping she would not realize how I intended to add some small changes to what we agreed upon earlier.

"I see Lord Maximillian is here already." Lady POW pointed to the receiving line, where he stood before King Ferdinand and Empress Maria Anna.

I was shocked to see the king. I had not seen him since my father's funeral, but he seemed to be the very same as I looked at him. He had the high forehead, the uncertain gaze, and the kind, weak smile. I studied him for a few moments, as Lady Penelope was surrounded by her friends—or at least, the people who were familiar with her.

I stepped back to look over at Empress Maria Anna. Her black hair had grayed over the many years, and I saw she was wearing a large crucifix among all her pearls. She seemed like such a little old lady, one who seemed content to look down as if she was in perpetual prayer. She was so different from Lady POW, who had very little jewelry but still carried herself with a regal sense of being, despite her older years.

A soft whisper of footsteps approached me from behind. "Would you allow me the honor of your first dance tonight, my lady?"

I whirled around in disbelief to see Ferdy behind me. But this time, he was not wearing a footman's uniform. He was wearing a fine suit and pressed pants, paired with boots that gleamed with a shine and a simple cravat. I barely recognized him, with his hair combed back and the shy stubble of his beard gone from his face.

Seeing Lady Penelope was busy receiving effusive praise from Lady Hohenwart, I grabbed him by the wrist and whisked him away quickly, before anyone else could see him.

"What are you doing?" I hissed at him. "This is not the time to pretend that you're a lord or something."

He grinned at me. "How could I resist?" he asked, testing the limits of my patience as he took over my lead and turned me toward the marble dancing floor.

Ben's earlier comments came back to me, and I felt another round of frustration. "Don't you take anything seriously?"

Ferdy took a step closer to me, closer than he should have been. "Of course I take some things seriously," he said. His eyes twinkled under the ballroom lights. "I have wanted to dance with you ever since I rescued you from the Hohenwart Ball."

"Enough to steal some royal's clothes?"

"I can assure you, the royal in question is close enough to my size that he won't notice, and he won't miss one of his suits. Though he will be upset, if he ever figures out what I've done."

I gaped at him incredulously. "Why would you do this?"

THE ORDER OF THE CRYSTAL DAGGERS

"Does it make you mad to see me risk so much for you?" Ferdy asked quietly as the music began. I was too shocked at his daring to realize that he was a confident dancer.

"Yes," I admitted, too brazen to care. "I need you to leave here at once, Ferdy. You're in danger."

"I know."

"What?" I glared at him. "What do you mean, you know?"

"I know that I'm in danger," Ferdy said. "But I have been in danger for a long time, Ella. From the moment I first saw you, I've been in love with you."

It was then that I noticed Ferdy was indeed a good dancer, since he caught me as I tripped.

"Have you fallen for me, too, then?" Ferdy asked, holding me too close as he looked into my eyes.

I was so tempted to scream in frustration. I wanted to so badly. Ferdy was wonderful. I cared for him deeply, more than I knew why, and here he was, dressing up like a noble, stealing me away from my grandmother, and passionately declaring that his heart was mine, all in the middle of my imaginary kingdom, where heaven touched the earth and flooded me with pure wonder.

I would have given anything, anything at all, to have been able to respond with more than a stunned look and a rush of heat running through my body as it pressed into his.

"Ella?" For the first time that night, Ferdy frowned. "What's wrong?"

"I need some air." I flushed, silently cursing myself for my befuddlement.

Ferdy quickly obliged me, twirling me toward the back of the ballroom. Together, we slipped into the shadows of a dark hallway, and I was reminded of the time that we shared before at the Hohenwart manor.

"Better?" he asked, the eagerness waning from his voice.

"Yes, thank you." I leaned against the coolness of the walls. "I'm sorry."

"Sorry for what?" Ferdy asked. He gave me a friendly pat on the shoulder. "I did not mean to take your breath away."

"No, that's not it," I said, shaking my head. "I need you to leave now, please."

"Will you come with me?" he asked, and at his flippancy, my patience broke.

"Enough," I snapped. "I need you to be serious about this, Ferdy. There's danger here. Something is going to happen here later, and I don't want you to be around when it does."

"What is it?" Ferdy asked. To his credit, he did look more serious all of a sudden.

"I can't tell you," I said. And that was the truth. I did not know what was supposed to happen tonight. All I knew was that something was supposed to happen, something that could possibly kill people, and no stretch of my imagination allowed me to believe Ferdy would be safe just by virtue of his humble status.

"You can tell me anything, Ella," he whispered.

I grabbed his coat and tugged him closer to me. "We don't have much time here. Right now, I just need to know you're not here. That you'll be safe, please. I care for you too much to let anything happen to you."

"So you do love me, then?"

"Of course I do," I snapped. "But this is—"

He cut me off, along with all my complaints and concerns, as he kissed me.

The taste of him was lightning across my senses. I felt the shock of our lips pressed together, the ache in my heart as I wanted him. I closed my eyes, unable to resist, as the longing inside of me stood strong, and all my feelings came rushing out, pushing reason to the side.

I had been so worried for him over the past few days, and I was suddenly more desperate than ever to cling to him. I was so worried the Cabal was in danger, and I was so worried when Ben could not find him and warn him. I had been prowling around the manor like a caged animal, and now that I was with him again, I was free.

Ferdy's hands trapped me next to him, and I could only revel in the chaos, clinging to it as I claimed his heart as my own.

He is freedom, I thought, as I let out a small moan. Ben was right; Ferdy was flippant and fun, but he was freedom, and he was more than able to frustrate me. Karl might have proven to be the more stable one, but I would never feel such power and passion.

Ferdy pressed against me, driving me into the wall behind us. The solid coolness of it sent another shockwave of pleasure behind me, as the space between us collapsed and my body melted against his.

It was only as his hands slid down my body, roaming over my side where the crystal dagger was tucked away, that my mind insisted on reorienting itself.

He seemed to sense the change and slowly pulled back from me, breathing heavily. "I cannot tell you how long I have waited for you," he whispered. "I knew you were meant to be mine."

I breathed in deeply, letting my hands run through his hair and down his face. I was shaking. I did care for him. I did love him. I did not want him to be hurt. I did not want to think about what my life would be like if he was gone.

How could the world exist if he was gone?

THE ORDER OF THE CRYSTAL DAGGERS

"Then," I said, still breathing irregularly, "please, promise me that you will leave this ball now."

"I would not worry about anything if I were you. If there is any danger, we will face it together," Ferdy said. "Besides, I think I might be able to help you, if you let me stay."

"No!" I shook my head. "Please, no—"

"Do you think after all these years of searching for you, I'd risk losing you now that I've found you again?" He gave me a grin, and I was suddenly aware of how odd his words were.

I frowned. "What are you talking—"

A new voice called out from down the darkened hall. "Ella?"

"Ella?" Ferdy frowned. "Who else calls you Ella? That's my name for you."

I groaned. This was a whole evening of poor timing. "It's Karl Marcelin," I said. "He likes me. He said my name was too long, too."

Ferdy began to growl. "Why—"

"Please go," I said. "He can get you in trouble. I don't want anything to happen to you."

"But, Ella—"

As Karl made his way closer to us, I shoved Ferdy behind a nearby corner. "Stay here and don't say anything," I hissed. Even though there was very little light in the corridor, I hoped he would be able to see the grim look on my face.

After he remained quiet for a long moment, I hurried away, determined to meet Karl halfway.

"Ella. I thought that was you," Karl said. "I'm pleased to have found you here. I did not see you in the ballroom."

"Oh, I was … looking for the ladies' withdrawing room." I made a mental note to find a new excuse as I thought I heard Ferdy smother a laugh. It would not be long before someone noticed I was apparently going to the bathroom too often to be normal.

"I can give you directions, if you still need … " Karl's voice trailed off politely and I quickly shook my head.

"Oh, I am perfectly well."

He offered me his arm. "Then might I request the pleasure of your company?"

"Yes, you may." Under the guise of tucking in a loose curl, I glanced back to see Ferdy was still out of sight. I sighed, glad I had found him, even though I was still worried he was going to refuse to leave.

"It's a pleasant night," Karl said. "The Advent season is always magical."

"Yes," I agreed. "And the castle is so lovely. Her Imperial Majesty has clearly done a wonderful job decorating."

Karl beamed, and I wondered if part of it was familial pride. "She always does an excellent job," he said. "But this year, nothing compares to your presence."

We were walking down the hallway toward the ballroom when Karl veered off to the opposite side.

"Come this way," he said. "This is one of the king's gardens."

With Ferdy out of immediate danger, I was hoping I would find a way to escape from Karl soon enough. But as he opened the door and I was able to see the indoor gardens, I momentarily forgot the mission.

Large windows glowed with opaque lighting. Outside it was winter, but inside it was the height of spring.

It was an indoor garden, where several rows of plants were crawling with vines and blossoms. Walls held pots full of draping ferns and cluttered flowers. In the moonlight, it felt like walking into the Garden of Eden, just before its twilight.

"This is beautiful," I said, my voice hushed with awe.

"The king is very fond of his botanicals." Karl led me through an aisle of planted blooms. I was grateful to feel the warmth of the room. "He is in here a lot of the time, experimenting with different crops and planting methods."

"It sounds like you know him very well," I said, doing my best to keep my tone unsuspecting.

Karl smiled. "I do. It is a shame he is not as supportive of me as Count Potocki is, in terms of politics," he said. "But His Imperial Majesty has been most kind on other accounts."

"That is his name among the people," I recalled. "Ferdinand the Good."

I eyed Karl carefully out of the corner of my eye. "It is a shame he did not have any children of his own," I said. "Bohemia is poorer for it."

"I could not agree more," Karl said, startling me with his tone. It was a mix of anger and longing, and it was one I could recognize myself. I knew what it was like to live with the feeling life was not what it was supposed to be.

"How is your situation with Lord Maximillian coming along?" I asked, changing the subject as I moved away and glancing down at a bed of orchids. "He would be upset if he knew you were with me in here, wouldn't he?"

"He would," Karl agreed. "But it is worth the risk. Especially if you have thought about what we talked about before."

I sighed. "I must be blunt, sir," I said, pretending I was trying to be brave. "I do not wish to marry for anything but love."

"Have I not confessed to my love for you?" Karl asked.

I shook my head. "No."

"Then I love you."

There was the chime of the clock in the distance, and I was taken back to the night when Ferdy had kissed me for the first time. That night had been over far too early for me.

And this one could be over at any moment. As long as Karl is here in the castle, nothing can happen.

"Thank you, sir," I replied quietly. "But I fear your love for me is quite shallow compared to your ambition."

"Others are depending on me, Ella. Lord Maximillian is ready to announce my engagement to his daughter tonight if I tell him to. He has plans for us, and I won't be able to go forward with any of them if I am not completely dedicated to my calling." His tone was much harsher all of a sudden.

And then I had an idea. If Lord Maximillian did not have Karl's agreement, maybe the rest of their plans would fall through.

Is it possible?

"If your love for me is true," I said carefully, "then go and tell His Grace that you will not marry his daughter. Tell him that you want to marry me instead."

"He is very insistent on supporting me. I do not feel it would be wise to upset him."

"You cannot have me as a bride if you are already betrothed," I pointed out.

Karl raised his eyebrows. "So you will marry me, then?"

"If you love me, you will go and tell him the engagement between you and Lady Teresa Marie is off," I said, sidestepping the question. I did not want to commit to anything. Lady POW's warning came back to me.

"You hint and tease, but never promise anything—no stolen kisses in the gardens, no getting caught in flagrante delicto."

Karl reached over and kissed my hand. "I will do as you say, my lady. You have made me the happiest man on earth."

Before I could stop him, he drew me close and kissed me.

Karl's kiss was soft and gentle, completely polite, both passionate and restrained. I went still, paralyzed by the unexpected tenderness as much as the unanticipated guilt. I had not wanted him to kiss me, but I felt like if I stopped him, it would be impolite.

THE ORDER OF THE CRYSTAL DAGGERS

After all, he might have kissed me out of excitement, but I was the one who was lying to him. I did not want to marry him, and I did not want to kiss him, either. I felt nothing of the fire I felt for another, and only my desire for Ferdy's safety kept me from pushing him away.

Karl pulled back, oblivious to my disenchantment, with a satisfied look on his face.

I gave him a bland smile back, unable to do anything else, before he stepped back, bowed, and headed toward the door.

"After I am finished talking with the Duke," he said, "I want to introduce you to my parents."

I nodded, waving as he headed out of the room. "I'll meet you back in the ballroom."

Karl was still grinning when the door finally closed between us.

I squeezed my eyes shut and sighed. For the first time, I felt the excitement of being a member of the Order transform into poison.

My love for Ferdy, in all its innocence and purity, made me feel wretched. Kissing Karl had not been altogether unpleasant, but I felt more like a mistress of politics, a member of the demimonde who sold her time, body, and mind to the preservation of the state.

I reached down toward my dagger, wondering if my mother had ever experienced a similar feeling. *Maybe that was why she quit.* If she was in love with Amir, she would have been unwilling to do certain things for the sake of information.

I rubbed my eyes and temples, grateful I had succeeded. I had agreed to nothing, technically, and Karl was off to buy us more time before Lord Maximillian could execute his plan. "Thank God that's over."

"Yes, I couldn't agree more."

Ferdy's voice echoed in the spaces between us as he appeared behind me, and I jumped, my heart beating with sudden fear and adrenaline.

"Oh, my God. Don't scare me like that." I was angry at his sudden appearance, but then I saw the look on his face and forgot everything else.

I did not have to ask him to know he had overheard everything. *Everything.*

My head fell into my hands. "Oh, no."

THE ORDER OF THE CRYSTAL DAGGERS

24
◊

A long moment passed before I felt like I would be able to withstand the shame. When I looked up, Ferdy met my gaze squarely.

The shame was hard and fast and left me breathless, and even worse, it stripped Ferdy of all the fun and joy I loved about him.

"Well, I guess you were right."

"What do you mean?" I asked.

"Something terrible was going to happen tonight." The harshness of his tone was unbearable, and I heard every splinter of his heartbreak in each syllable.

"I can explain," I said, trying to find my bearings.

"You can explain," Ferdy said. "But I don't think I will wait around to hear it."

"Ferdy, please—"

"Good day to you, mademoiselle," he said, giving me a quick bow. "I hope you'll be very happy in your engagement. Mr. Marcelin offers you such wonderful prospects, much more than I could ever hope to offer you—"

"That's not it!" I stepped up in front of him, trying to stop him as he made for the door. "I'm trying to save people's lives—"

"By destroying others'?"

"That's not what I meant." I took a hold of his arm. "Ferdy, Karl is King Ferdinand's son."

Ferdy finally stopped. "You know?"

"You know, too?" I blinked. "I found out a few days ago."

"After he talked about marrying you before, at the Summerhouse Ball?"

"Yes," I said. "He is—"

"So that is why you want to marry him?" Ferdy asked. "Because he's a prince?"

"What? No," I argued. "Listen to me, I'm trying to tell you—"

"I'm not going to listen to you," Ferdy said, struggling to free himself from me. When I would not let go, he pulled his arm away even more, pushing me away with his other arm. "Let me go!"

I felt the last of my strength leave me at his bark, and I ended up tripping before slamming into the wall behind me.

"Ouch." My shoulder scraped hard against the brick wall behind me. I sucked in my breath as a small trickle of blood oozed out from my skin.

219

I glanced up from my blood-speckled fingers to Ferdy's face. He looked shocked and apologetic, and for a long second, I was certain he was going to run back and embrace me.

But a moment later, he pulled out a handkerchief from one of his pockets and tossed it my way. "My apologies. I must return to the streets for the night. It is for the best. That's where I belong."

His words cut into me deeply and the second he left, I slipped down to the floor, trying not to cry. My fingers were shaking, this time out of grief, as I reached for the handkerchief he had left behind, resting the soft silk against my cheek. The cut on my shoulder hissed with softly searing pain, but I ignored it. It felt better to bleed.

I knew I only had a limited amount of time to myself. Even if Karl did manage to convince Lord Maximillian to change their arrangement, there was still a chance that something was going to happen. I knew from our plans that Lady Penelope was keeping an eye on the King and Queen, and I knew that Ben was searching the castle for any signs of suspicious activity, especially from the Szapira household.

I was supposed to be the distraction, keeping an eye on Karl.

"For all the good it did." I pulled out my mother's dagger and looked at it again.

Now that he was leaving, I knew Ferdy was safe, even if he hated me. I managed to get Karl to discuss terms with Lord Maximillian. I did not know if the assassination plot was foiled, but if nothing else, I had bought time.

Even if I had broken Ferdy's heart and my own in the process.

The door opened again, and I nearly jumped. "Ferdy?" I was unable to stop myself from hoping he would come back for me.

"Nora?" Ben's voice was a welcome one, and if it had to be someone other than Ferdy, I was glad it was Ben. He was a friendly face I could count on.

"I'm over here," I said, hurriedly wiping my eyes once more. It was time for me to find something more useful to do than cry over my pain.

"Lady POW was looking for you," he said. "She just saw Karl Marcelin leave."

"Why? He told me he was going to go talk to Lord Maximillian."

"He's gone, too."

I felt fear seize hold of me and determination move to cut through it. "Then something must be happening somewhere."

Ben sighed. "I'm not sure where. But I followed a footman from the Szapira household down this way when I thought I saw Ferdy storm out of this door and head toward the kitchens."

"That was probably where he came in."

THE ORDER OF THE CRYSTAL DAGGERS

"So it was Ferdy?" Ben asked. "I saw his face, but I wasn't sure when I saw he was wearing those clothes."

"That's the way he sneaked inside the castle," I said. "He danced with me for a song, and then ... " I waved my hands, unable to say anything else. It was better to let Ben assume things.

"Is something wrong?" Ben asked.

I shook my head. "Nothing that can't wait. We need to get to work. If Karl and Lord Maximillian are both gone, we have to work quickly to make sure nothing will happen to all the people here."

Standing up, I stripped off my gown, tearing at the stays and ripping the fine fabric, just as Jaqueline had taught me. I stuffed the gown into a fireplace before quickly lighting it. The simple but thick layer of the dress began to burn, and while I was sorry to see such finery be destroyed, I felt much more like myself.

The smell of burning fabric, too similar to the aroma of Tulia's house, chased me away. But I jerked my mask up and readied my dagger at my side.

"Are you finished?" Ben asked.

I nodded, reminding myself to be brave. "I'm ready."

Ben and I made our way to the hallway, and then I sighed. "Wait," I said. "Give me one moment."

"Hurry," Ben said with a quick nod. "I'll head for the kitchens. Amir might be there already, checking for signs of the silver thallis herb."

"If nothing else, the head chef will be able to tell if there's something wrong with the food. We could warn them that way."

I turned back to the fireplace, now smoking with the remnants of my dress. Taking the handkerchief Ferdy had thrown at me, I prepared to settle it on top of the pile. I would talk to him later, so there was no need to be so sentimental over his souvenir.

But just as I was about to let it go, the embroidery in the corner caught my eye.

The trotting horse, and the squiggles symbolizing wheat and waves were all too familiar.

He got this from the Szapira household.

I froze.

Is it possible ... ?

All those moments of Ferdy telling me he was a liar fell through my mind. He was well informed. He knew how to sneak around. He had a variety of jobs that allowed him to find out information on different people, sometimes very quickly.

He knew about the Cabal, and he would know that Tulia would recognize it if he talked to her about it.

Was it possible Ferdy was the one who attacked Tulia?

Surely not. I shook my head. *But ...*

"But if it was, I'll kill him myself," I muttered, before I turned around and hurried to catch up to Ben.

25
◊

"What's wrong?" Ben asked, as I crept up beside him. He was standing in the shadows, just outside the main entrance to the kitchen. As we watched, several lines of servers and maids rushed about, working on preparing plates and refilling drinks.

We had been careful to sneak quietly through the servant corridors. Prague Castle was known throughout the kingdom for its intricate hallways, and I was surprisingly relieved at the reality. Combined with the busyness of the Advent Ball, Ben and I were able to keep the shadows without much trouble, and any serious scrutiny we might have faced was negated by the event's demands.

"Nothing." I peeked out over his shoulder, watching for any hint of Ferdy.

"You're really not going to convince me nothing's wrong if you use that tone."

"Be quiet," I muttered. "I'll tell you later, when we have more time to worry about killing people rather than saving them."

Ben raised his brow in surprise, more likely at my temper than at my words, but said nothing. We both turned and watched.

"There." Ben pointed at a taller figure, who was slinking toward the far end of the kitchen. "I'm certain that's the missing footman."

"How can you tell?" I asked, looking him over carefully. He was dressed in a large coat, and it was hard to make out his features from where we were standing. I could not tell if he was the same height as Ferdy or not.

"Remember what Lady POW did?" Ben asked. "She managed to slice through his arm. If you look, there's a slight bulge just under his right shoulder."

"That could be his shirt," I said.

"I saw him earlier in a different outer coat, and the same thing."

"I still don't know."

"He's going into the wine cellar. That should be proof enough, as far as I'm concerned."

"Why?"

"Because Roman Szapira's the one who renovated the wine cellar here," Ben reminded me. "He would be the one who knows how to get into it and how to use it. They have been planning this party for months, so there is no telling how easy it would be to hide it."

"The wine."

223

The words left my mouth before the idea had fully formed inside of my mind, but there was no stopping it. I grabbed Ben's arm. "Ben, it's the wine."

"Yes, I just said that's where it might be."

"No, not in the wine cellar, it's the wine. It has to be. Karl told me before that the wine had been shipped in from Lord Maximillian's vineyards for this year. He was supposed to be in town and attending the Advent Ball."

"He poisoned the wine?" Ben asked. "If that's the case, we have a major problem on our hands, because it's been pouring steadily since the guests started arriving. Some of them are already tipsy from what I've seen."

"That can't be it then, I guess," I said.

But it had to be something like that, I thought. There was the wine cellar designed and renovated by Karl's host; a footman from his house was linked to Tulia, and even she had mentioned the wine before the fire exploded …

"It *exploded*."

"What is it?" Ben asked.

Buried inside my mind, cloistered between the moments of Ferdy holding my hand and holding me close, another memory called for my attention.

"It's the wine," I said.

"We just had this discussion." Ben rolled his eyes.

"No, remember what Eliezer said at the Cabal? There had been a shipment of wine that had exploded," I said. "It was coming from Hradiště. It's close to the border of Bohemia, and Lord Maximillian owns several vineyards throughout Moravia. That's got to be it!"

"So the wine is supposed to explode?" Ben glanced around nervously.

"I don't know how," I said. "But that's got to be the plan. Think about it. What better way to say the Emperor is incapable of leading Bohemia? He's already ignored us. With a major attack escaping his notice, especially after he paid for the renovation of the wine cellar? His project would literally blow up."

"And Karl's role?"

"He's the heir. He could offer leadership to a revolution, like Harshad and Lady POW said."

"But he's supposed to be set on getting the Minister-President position."

"Maybe that's a front." I thought about the way he was eager to marry me instead of Teresa Marie. He needed the support to look good. Was it possible he did not actually want the position?

"I don't know," Ben said. "That sounds like circumstantial evidence to me. There might be another clue down in the wine cellar."

"Come this way," I said, tugging Ben's arm toward the left. "This is the kitchen area. We're close to the wine cellar."

"If you say so."

Together, we headed down the stairs, slowly and quietly making our way through the empty corridors. Ben's brace tapped noticeably on the stone stairwell as we moved through the underground halls.

"Where are we?" I whispered.

"Probably underneath the kitchens," Ben said. "Look. There's a door up ahead. The wine would not be too far away from the kitchen. They would need it for cooking as much as serving."

I wrinkled my nose. "True enough. I remember all too well some of Cecilia's cooking needs."

"I try very hard to forget everything I can about her," Ben replied, and despite the enormous amount of fear we were facing, I smiled at his remark.

"Good," I said, as we stepped into the wine cellar entrance. "Hopefully, we will never have to worry about her—"

"Watch out!"

Ben pushed me aside as the shadow of the footman came rushing out the wine cellar door at us. Our attacker had his mask back on, but I could see his dark eyes widen in surprise as Ben fought with him.

He quickly threw my brother off him, but I stepped in to distract him before he could attack Ben again.

"Here," I called, pulling out my dagger before I remembered that I had not been trained to use it properly.

The attacker took the bait, regardless. He had his own knife in his hand, and I felt all of my breath rush out of me as he slashed through the air, barely missing me. If I had been wearing my fancy clothes, my petticoats would have been sliced open. My stealth habit's short skirt managed to whip around him as I dodged his attacks.

Ben stood up behind him and hurried over to help me.

I heard a small crackle; Ben's brace caught on the uneven floor. He went skidding across the stone floor, managing to trip just behind the footman.

"Ben!" I lashed out a quick kick. Triumph shot through me as my aim proved true, hitting the footman in the groin.

The footman fell over and yelled in pain. His mask covered his mouth, so I was unable to tell if I recognized his voice or not. Ben knocked him down and he fell, hard, before I held my dagger in line with his heart and Ben pinned him to the ground.

"Got him?" I asked Ben, my own voice muffled through my mask.

When he nodded, I carefully reached down and pulled off the attacker's mask.

And then let out a sigh of relief.

It was not Ferdy.

"Who are you?" I asked.

The attacker glared up at me in the darkness. "It's not your concern."

"We captured you," Ben insisted, tightening his grip on the footman's arms. "Tell us who you are."

"I don't think so," our enemy declared. "All I'm going to tell you is that it's too late. I've done my job, and this place is going to be destroyed in a matter of moments."

Ben and I exchanged worried glances.

"That's right," the footman said. "And if you were smart enough, you would let me go and get out of here as fast as you can."

Ben thrust a knee into the man's back. "Tell how to stop it."

"You can't." The footman smirked. "That's the power of fire. It's destructive, breaking everything down until there is nothing left. Once the wine cellar explodes, it will take half of the castle with it. And then the rest of it will fall, too."

For the first time, I noticed that there was a large cloud of smoke flowing from the wine cellar door. "Ben," I hissed. "Look."

As Ben turned to look, the attacker launched another punch. His fist caught Ben in the stomach, but I launched myself at him.

The impact was harder than I would have ever expected, but when our attacker slumped over, unconscious, I did not feel the least bit sorry for him.

"Thanks," Ben huffed, trying to breathe properly. He wavered as he stood up and grabbed my hand for support. "Let's go see if there's a way to stop the fire—"

Boom!

A burst of fire and noise poured through the wall and covered the stone halls with fire around us. Ben and I struggled against the fire, coughing in the smoke and debris. Behind us, I squinted through the fire to see our attacker was writhing around in pain as he screamed.

I felt sick as Ben pulled me to the staircase and pushed me forward.

"We need to get out of here, and fast. This is bad, Nora," Ben said. "That had to be enhanced gunpowder. Maybe even nitroglycerin."

"What is that?" I asked.

"It's an ingredient found in a lot of explosives." Ben glanced around us uneasily, looking down at the large barrels of wine and the walls lined with countless bottles. "This is bad. The alcohol in the wine will only make the fire more difficult to put out."

So I was right, I thought. *It was the wine, even if it is not directly the cause of the explosion.*

"So there is no stopping it?" I asked.

"I wouldn't even know where to begin. But maybe if I can take a—"

"No!" I argued. "No, we have to get the others out of the castle, and fast. There's no way of telling how much time we have."

"I'm guessing that the footman was the one who was supposed to set the trigger."

"We don't know for sure," I said. "You need to go outside and get Amir. I'll go and get Lady POW and then we will get everyone else out of the castle."

"You go get Amir. I'll retrieve Lady POW."

"No." I shook my head. "I'm the better runner."

Ben paused for only the slightest second before he nodded. "Well, you know I don't gamble with risks—"

Another explosion rocked the floor around us. I felt pure fear as the ceiling began to crack and the castle walls next to me suddenly shifted.

"Go, Nora," Ben yelled at me. "We will do it your way. Go and get Lady POW. I will get Amir. I'll see you outside."

His tone was hard and unyielding, and I squeezed my eyes shut as in a second of frustrated, fervent prayer.

And then slowly, I nodded. I did not want to leave him, but Ben was right. We had to get the people out of here, and we would do better if we split up.

I put a hand on my dagger. I needed to go and find Lady POW, and we would have to save King Ferdinand and the Empress. *I guess it's time for me to go and meet Karl's parents. Although I doubt this is what he had in mind.*

"Be careful, Ben!" I called back, as I made a run for the ballroom.

◊   ◊   ◊   ◊

Making my exit from the wine cellar was much easier and quicker than getting in. I gripped my dagger, holding the hilt in my left hand as I eagerly charged through the hallways, telling everyone I could to get out of the castle.

227

THE ORDER OF THE CRYSTAL DAGGERS

The cook looked confused, but when I explained to her that it was the king's wishes to protect his people, everyone seemed to follow much more smoothly.

I raced through the halls, only mixing up my location once. I struggled not to think of Ben. I hoped he was not lying to me about getting Amir. I did not want him trying to enter the wine cellar, even if he thought he might be able to stop more explosions.

I prayed for him fervently as I headed up the steps and worked my way back to the ballroom.

I pulled my mask up more tightly around my face before I entered the room of glittering light.

The ladies and gentlemen all turned to stare at me, but I was thankful once more for the mask. I had pulled the hood over my hair, and it was a relief to hear their concern. I saw several back away from me, and some left the room entirely.

"Halt!" A guard blocked me, but I skirted around him. For all his armor, he moved slowly, and I was able to dodge him much more easily than I anticipated.

I came to a stop before King Ferdinand and Empress Maria Anna, before I bowed. At that moment, I gave them the full view of the purple blade in my hand.

There were whispers and shrieks behind me, but I ignored them as I waited for the king's response.

I felt rather than saw Lady Penelope as she came up behind me, shielding me from the others' scrutiny.

"Your Imperial Highnesses," I said. "I will need a private audience with you. And quickly," I added, daring to look up. "Everyone here is in danger."

After he exchanged a quick glance with his wife, King Ferdinand ducked his head toward mine. "Come … with me," he stuttered.

Immediately, several guards beckoned me toward a large tapestry. Behind it, I saw there was another hidden hallway. I thought briefly of Ferdy, desperately afraid I would never see him again all of a sudden.

I barely noticed Lady Penelope had made her way to my side.

"What happened?" Lady POW hissed beside me. "There's no need for you to reveal yourself to an entire ballroom of guests."

I gritted my teeth as I told her what had happened. "The other guests did not see my face, and it was important to get here as quickly as possible. I don't know how much time we have."

It disturbed me that Lady POW went quiet all of a sudden.

"Please tell me you have a plan," I whispered back. Hearing my voice was an attempt to hold onto my sanity. We were likely moments away from disaster, and I had no way of knowing if I would make it out alive or not.

THE ORDER OF THE CRYSTAL DAGGERS

"Are you worried for your life?" Empress Maria Anna turned around to face me.

"No," I lied. But I thought of Ferdy again, and I decided I could die happy knowing he was safe, even if he hated me. Even if he would never believe the truth about me.

"I see." The Empress' dark eyes glittered, and I thought I saw a hint of Karl as she smiled.

The room we came to was open and large, almost like a hidden coronation room. There was a pair of thrones at the forefront, and I tried not to fidget too much while King Ferdinand and Empress Maria Anna sat down.

Why do they still worry about all these formalities at a time like this?

"Now, what is all of this?" King Ferdinand asked me.

I took off my hood and pulled down my mask. "Your Imperial Highness. I am sorry to report this, but you must order everyone out of the castle at once. There is an assassin here who prepared an explosion in the wine cellar. This wing of the castle will be likely destroyed, and all the people in it could suffer greatly."

Lady Penelope nudged me. "Show him your dagger again, Eleanora."

I reached out, but King Ferdinand waved it away. "Eleanora?"

"Yes, Majesty. I am Eleanora Svobodová, of Bohemia."

"Adolf's daughter."

It felt strange, hearing my father's name, but I nodded affirmatively, praying the king would not go into a lengthy dialogue of my father's deeds or something similar.

I was surprised when he chuckled. "What is it?"

"You're the one my son is in love with." The king's small chuckle blossomed into a throaty laugh.

"I understand he has feelings for me," I said slowly, "but this is not the time to discuss it. We have to get everyone out of the castle now."

"I will send the guards." The king clapped his hands. "But you must go and retrieve my son for me. I know he was upset about something. He is likely moping around the library in the east wing. Go get him, please, Lady Ella."

Lady Penelope stepped up beside me. "There is no need to worry about him, sire. I saw him follow the Duke of Moravia when he left earlier."

"I know Karl wanted to talk to him about his engagement to the Duke's daughter," I said. "So he is safe. There was an assassin dressed in black running around the castle earlier, but Karl left before the assassin made his way to the wine cellar."

"Karl?" King Ferdinand repeated. Then he laughed. "No, not Karl."

"What?" I frowned. "What do you—"

Before I could finish asking him, a strange look suddenly appeared on the king's face. It was a look I recognized, and instantly I could see it all once more inside of my mind. I remembered my father's funeral, when the king had experienced a seizure, and I saw him beginning to flail back and forth.

"He's having a spell," Empress Maria Anna cried. "Come help, quickly, Heinrich."

"Yes, Your Imperial Highness." A tall attendant appeared at the king's side as the other guards were dismissed to carry out the king's orders. Lady Penelope took off after them.

"Eleanora," Lady Penelope hissed, pushing me out the door. "You heard the king. I will alert Amir and help the other guests evacuate."

But I stayed where I was, watching the attendant as he tended to the king, much like the other two assistants had all those years ago, trying to give him medicine and pinning him down to the chair while the spasm continued.

It suddenly struck me as very odd that the king had brought two young assistants with him to my father's funeral. They would not have been able to keep the king pinned down while he had an episode.

I remembered the dark gaze of the one boy as he glared at me, telling me in his own way to mind my own business while the king was experiencing an episode.

Karl.

"Oh."

The king continued to fall apart before me as I stood there. Empress Maria Anna took charge. "Heinrich, please call another guard, so we can escort the king out of the castle," she said. "Lady Eleanora, I must ask you to go and retrieve my other son. His father is right; he is likely in the library further down toward the east wing. He has recently come home from Silesia to celebrate with us, but he does not enjoy social events."

I could only nod, already hurrying off.

◊　　◊　　◊　　◊

The pounding in my heart might as well have been a doomsday clock of sorts as I hurried through the complicated maze of hallways around the castle. With each moment that passed and I found myself not only still alive and the castle intact, I found reason to hope.

As I made my way in the direction of the east wing, all I could think of was Karl and the king.

Karl had been at my father's funeral. He would have known who I was, and he would have recognized my name when he was introduced to me. The king remembered my own father well enough, and the Empress had met with my mother at least once, to the point where my mother knew she was pregnant with an heir.

Or another *heir,* I thought, as the focus on my memories shifted to the other little boy who attended the king at *Táta's* funeral. He had been shorter than Karl, I remembered, and his hair was more brown, and he had different eyes.

It was so hard to remember that, but it had been over ten years since that awful day. And it was not like I wanted to remember that day so well in the first place.

I turned down another hall and saw a door ajar. A light was on, and I could see glimpses of bookcases inside. *That must be it.*

As I watched, a young man came out of the room. He was about the same height as Karl, with brownish hair. As I got closer to him, he jumped in surprise, and I could see freckles dotted his cheeks.

That must be him, I thought, suddenly realizing I did not know the other prince's name. "Your Highness," I called, waving my dagger high, hoping he would recognize it.

He apparently did not, because he pulled out his sword a moment later.

"There were rumors that there was an assassin dressed in black in the castle," the man said. "I see they were correct."

"Your Highness, please," I said, skidding to a stop. "I am not the assassin, that was—"

"No one would admit to being an assassin." The man lunged at me with his sword.

I almost smiled. In many ways, the young man reminded me of Alex. I ducked and jumped, landing a quick blow to his knee. He yelped in surprise, before I punched him across the face and elbowed him in the side.

"Oy!" He fell back against the wall, gripping himself, winded from his injury. His sword fell out of his hand as he fell over.

Certain I was safe, I hurried over to him and quickly bowed. "I'm so sorry, Your Highness," I said. "But we must go. I was sent here by your mother, Empress Maria Anna. I am a member of the Order of the Crystal Daggers. I'm here to protect you."

"I'm—"

"I'm sorry," I said again, as an expression of pain flashed across his young features. "I promise we can get some bandages for you if you need it. I have a friend who's really good at fixing people up."

The man shook his head. "I'm not ... "

231

"Not what?" I asked, starting to get irritated. I quickly sheathed my dagger and tried to pull him upright.

It was only when he stood that he took a deep breath and tried again.

"I'm not the prince," he said.

My mouth dropped open. "You're not?"

"No, he's not."

The voice behind me was too familiar.

While everyone was clambering to safety outside, I had been sent to find the king's second son. Little did I know, I had already found him.

I had already found him, and I had already fallen in love with him.

And when we finally met this time, I found myself staring at him, unable to take my eyes off him, as he held a sword up between us. His silver eyes no longer gleamed with stars, but instead held a dangerous mix of lightning and sadness. The light of the grand hallway teased out the copper-colored undertones in his chestnut hair. He stood prepared to fight, the princely attire no longer a costume he wore but a sign of his true self.

I could only stand there, as my mind put it all together. The Hapsburg features, the straight nose and the defiant chin … I had seen Karl's sharp features transform into the face of a prince, and this time, it was even harder for me to acknowledge my ignorant blindness.

"Ferdy."

His name was a whisper on my lips, but I knew he heard me; he flinched and faltered in his stance ever so slightly.

"Ella." I could tell from the grim look on his face that he was deadly serious. The sword held steady. He glanced at the dagger I had at my side. Recognition flashed through his eyes, but his gaze only hardened. "You've already managed to wound me enough tonight. There's no need to try to kill me, too."

"I'm not here to kill you," I said, trying to regain my focus. It was hard to move; of all the surprises I had faced in recent weeks, I had never imagined this one was possible. "I came to save you."

Ferdy arched his brow. "And why should I believe you?"

It was the wrong thing to say.

"Excuse me?" I snapped. "You're the one who always insisted he was the better liar between us. And clearly you were telling the truth about that, *Your Highness.*"

"There's no need for formalities," Ferdy muttered as a small blush came over his cheeks. "I am a prince in name only."

"Just like your brother?" I asked, my voice even more acerbic.

THE ORDER OF THE CRYSTAL DAGGERS

"Exactly," Ferdy said. "Although I am the one who is more content to keep it that way."

I took a step toward him. Beside me, the servant I had initially mistaken for the prince stepped back.

"Philip," Ferdy called. "Stay where you are. There is no trouble here."

"You're wrong," I said. "We have to leave the castle. You are in danger here. Someone is trying to destroy the castle."

"Oh, is that so?" Ferdy narrowed his eyes. "Who is it? Would it be Karl? Do you really think he would go so far as to claim the throne from our cousin?"

"I'm not sure about him," I grumbled, tightening my grip on the hilt of my dagger. "You're the one who's been carrying around an assassin's handkerchief. For all I know, you could be behind everything."

"You really think so poorly of me?" Ferdy asked, genuinely surprised.

"You lied to me about being a prince!" My hands were suddenly shaking as I relived every interaction I had ever had with him, trying to figure out how I had missed something as important as this.

Every single encounter only proved to make me more frustrated with myself. I saw Ferdy as a young boy, not even a year younger than Ben, at my father's funeral as he looked over at me, staring as he tried to control his father's seizure; I heard him speaking fluent Arabic to Amir in the streets; I saw the quickly borrowed footman's clothes at the Hohenwart Ball; I felt the learned grace of his dancing from back in Prague Castle's ballroom.

How did I miss so much?

Ferdy lowered the sword to his side.

I looked at him now, realizing *this* was who he truly was. He was a prince.

I tried to shove my memories aside, but seeing the distrust in his eyes, I found myself unable to bear his derision. But I did not want to admit how deeply he still affected me.

Lying to me would not have been so bad, if I had not fallen in love with him.

"Surely lying about being a prince is different from lying about being an assassin." Ferdy met my gaze with a challenge, much as I had done to him the first time he had seen me.

"That's not the only thing you've lied to me about." I put my hands on my hips. "You never told me that you saw me at my father's funeral."

Ferdy frowned. "I'd rather not discuss that. Obviously, falling in love with you was a mistake, and at this point, I'm allowed to keep my pride."

His words were sharp, like a slap to the face.

"Especially if you're going to stand there and accuse me of being a killer," he added, seemingly out of spite. "We've heard the rumors of an assassin running around in black."

"I'm not the assassin," I nearly shouted. I held out my dagger. "I am a member of the Order of the Crystal Daggers, and I have pledged my allegiance to your protection."

"You freely admit to being part of the Order?" Ferdy arched his brow. "That gives you even less credibility. From what I know, they've done more than their own share of murders."

"That's not true," I said, but my voice was suddenly much weaker. I did not know much about the Order, other than what Lady POW had told me. It was not enough to deny such charges, and I felt, impossibly, even more foolish.

"Are you going to kill Karl, too?" Ferdy asked.

"Right now, you're the one who is putting us in more danger," I shot back. "You're standing here, arguing with me, when we could be escaping the castle."

"You're not answering the question, I see."

"Sire," Philip, the servant behind me, spoke up. Both Ferdy and I seemed to jump at his voice; it was clear we had both forgotten the servant who was watching us.

"Perhaps she is right, sir," Philip said. "Maybe we should leave, especially if your life is in danger as she says. There is an assassin that is rumored to be here, after all."

"Yes, thank you!" I grumbled, before turning back to Ferdy.

"I do not fear death," he said. He walked up to me and looked me directly in the eye. "Or little girls, no matter what weapons they might wield against me."

"So far I have only managed to wound you with the truth," I said quietly. "It might not have hurt so much, if you had simply given it to me earlier."

We stood inches apart, while there were so many worlds between us; but even in that small moment in time, I felt as though I had the faith to bridge the distance, if only he would meet me in the middle. As we stood there, face to face, unable to ignore the truth between us, I silently begged Ferdy to trust me, to let me keep him safe this one last time. As much as I knew we could never be together, I knew I still could not imagine a world without him.

I could not stop myself from gazing at his mouth, remembering the soft texture of his lips against mine. "Please," I whispered, suddenly unsure of what it was I was asking of him.

As if he sensed my thoughts, Ferdy relented. "Ella," he murmured, so softly only I could hear.

There was a rumbling noise behind us, but I was already lost.

The explosion began to crescendo. A storm of breaking walls and crashing stones exploded, rippling into a tidal wave of sound and wind.

In those precious seconds, I launched myself into Ferdy, grasping onto him tightly. No matter how much he had hurt me, no matter how much he had lied to me, I was still determined to protect him.

We were thrown back at the impact. Seconds passed before I realized I had screamed.

I felt a sharp pain against my head before everything started to slip away.

In those moments, I felt the entire kingdom's heart break along with my own. I screamed and yelled, even as I was jolted and pressed on all sides. The power from the eruption burst out like a tidal wave of stones and dust, stripping me of the last of my illusions and innocence, crashing down all around me before burning up into piles of ash and soot.

In the last seconds of my consciousness, I thought I heard Ferdy call to me again.

I did not know if I responded or not.

Everything, I thought as darkness fell, *everything had been a lie all along.*

AUTHOR'S NOTE

Dear Reader,

Welcome to another new world of mine. Once more, it is a world that has stewed inside of me much longer than it would have liked, and like a demon being exorcised, I am relieved to finally have freed it for you.

Freedom really is at the core of this novel, and will continue to play out as a core part of the series. As it is in real life, it is an idea that is bound to much more than itself. Ella wants to be free, but under her stepmother's authority, she really has no idea what it means to be free. Under the state, she has no certainty of maintaining freedom. Under the Order, she has the tools to fight for it, but they are given to her in exchange for responsibilities.

I've been wondering about freedom and liberty myself lately, and what it means for growing up. Is there such a thing as true freedom? I am continually dependent on air and food, and even coffee, no matter what my doctor tells me not to consume. I've found, after all my "philosophical reflection," which is what my one professor in college referred to it as, that there is freedom, and it is real, but it is not something we can see as we might see an object. It is an idea, and it is something that my life will spell out for others through my actions and reactions, unbound by time and unguided by circumstance.

What that means more practically, really, is that I'll write stories about it. And that is, for me, proof of my own freedom. I know it does not come free. Writing these stories provides me an outlet of freedom, but it still takes time and effort from others in order to come to life. And that is the great lesson for me in all this. Trust, love, and freedom are all interdependent on each other. That is why I must thank all of the people who have dedicated such care to my work, including my (Almost) Famous Readers, my "book doctor" team, and my family.

Ultimately, true freedom has always been found in Christ. We are shown the Truth, and the Truth has set us free. We are able to recognize our chains for what they are—our inner fears, the power struggles around us, the individual forces, both natural and spiritual, interacting around us—and we are, through that recognition, able to choose the right ways to struggle for our freedom. We can, like Ella, choose to be brave, to be kind, and to be determined to fight for what we love.

THE ORDER OF THE CRYSTAL DAGGERS

I hope you have enjoyed your introduction into Eleanora's life, and all the complicated quests and inquiries that it has presented. Please look for the next book in this trilogy, *Prince of Secrets and Shadows*, where Ella must face the reality that truth has shown her—despite all the pain it brings.

Until We Meet Again,

C. S. Johnson

THE ORDER OF THE CRYSTAL DAGGERS

THE ORDER OF THE CRYSTAL DAGGERS

PRINCE

of

SECRETS and SHADOWS

BOOK TWO OF *THE ORDER OF THE CRYSTAL DAGGERS*

◊   ◊   ◊   ◊

C. S. Johnson

THE ORDER OF THE CRYSTAL DAGGERS

DEDICATION

First off, this is dedicated to my incredible family. My love of reading and fun and functional dysfunction comes from you.

Second, to Sam. Wherever you are, you are always in my heart, mind, and prayers. I still hope to see you again one day.

Third, to the wonderful people who made my writing time possible: Ryan, my beloved; Gabby, our new friend; Joy, our special aunt; Dr. Jon and company, down at my local coffee shop; and to Barry and Joann Benningfield. Every word I write, I write with the joy, wisdom, and time afforded to me.

And finally, to my fans. I can't believe I am lucky enough to have you as fans, and I am certain your generosity in being my friends, too, is even a less warranted miracle.

THE ORDER OF THE CRYSTAL DAGGERS

1

◊

"Ella."

The whisper of his voice inside my mind was enough to jolt me free from any dreams and propel me into the waking world.

I gasped as I woke, gripping the fine sheets I found surrounding me. The silken softness beneath my fingers was a foreign feeling, one that became clearer as I sat upright on the bed. I blinked, glancing around as moonlight glowed outside the window in front of me.

Squinting, I saw the view was completely unfamiliar.

Where am I?

My nose wrinkled, as the scent of lavender and mint wafted around me, and I began to feel a pounding pain in the back of my head. Reaching under my loosened curls, I felt a small bump.

The pain seemed to spread as I became aware of it; my muscles were sore, and my body ached. I took careful inventory of myself, finding a bandage wrapped around my right leg, just above my knee, and another around my shoulder. I was still in my stealth habit, with its short skirt, black bodice, and armored sleeves, tucked between fine sheets in a bed that was not mine.

As my eyes finally adjusted to the night, I could make out my surroundings.

My hand covered my mouth in shock.

I was in a bedroom, alone, seemingly surrounded by every creature comfort imaginable. The bed was grand, with intricate carvings and covered in delicate drapery. There were rugs on the floor from the East Indies, and a messy bookshelf tucked beside a window seat. Other items—chests and chairs and lamps of all sizes—dotted the room, shining in the retreating moonlight.

Despite the glory of the room around me, my gaze went immediately back to the window.

The dwindling starlight reflected through the glass as morning rapidly approached. Outside, the remaining walls of Prague Castle gleamed, taunting me with their unmoving stasis as my last memories trickled into my mind.

"The fire," I whispered hoarsely, struggling to orient myself to reality's bitter welcome. I did not know if the sound of my voice against the emptiness of the room would keep me from going mad or send me there sooner. There was a singed quality to my throat, and the taste of smoke was suddenly on my tongue.

I licked my lips and cleared my throat. Then I shifted out of the bedsheets and forced myself to find a cognizant starting place.

The last I remembered, I had been at the Advent Ball, the yearly event hosted by King Ferdinand V and his wife, Empress Maria Anna. It was the first time in over a decade I had seen the former rulers of the Austria-Hungarian Empire, which included my home nation of Bohemia, and it proved to be just as devastating as the last time.

"If not more so," I whispered, as my head fell into my hands. I rubbed my forehead and raked back my hair, the dark curls feeling frayed and knotted between my fingers.

It was almost like a bad dream, and my current surroundings did nothing to make it less surreal. The room I was in was crowned with high ceilings, the walls were decorated with splendid paintings and lined with silk wallpaper, and books of all sorts were scattered around, while a half-open wardrobe and several unlit, half-melted candelabras leered at me from the shadows.

On a nearby table, there was a basin filled with lavender-scented water. The fragrance caught my attention before I saw the folded dress beside it.

After only a second's hesitation, I went over and picked up the gown. The fabric felt as soft and pliant as liquid when I held it up to me, surprised to find it was my size. There was even a new set of matching combs on the table beside it.

Is this for me?

It was too much. Everything about the room was too much, I thought, spying a copy of *Morte d'Arthur* on the floor, splayed upside down, carelessly forgotten. I picked it up, briefly noting it was a different copy than the one my father used to own before I clutched it to my chest and looked around again.

The elegance of the castle room was something my stepmother would have sold her soul to have, even if it was just for a day.

I looked back at the dress, noting the fine stitching and the ornate design. My fingers fiddled with some of the ruffles, marveling at the elegance.

THE ORDER OF THE CRYSTAL DAGGERS

Cecilia would probably sell the souls of both her children for this dress.

Not that the devil would take them, I added, allowing myself a small giggle despite my uncertainty.

As I made my way back to the bed, my eyes scourged over everything; the room was elegant and beautiful, resplendent with treasures I had never seen and could never earn. But it was a kind of illusion—just like the heavenly city of Prague outside my window.

The room was still a prison, and I was its prisoner.

I was *his* prisoner.

I slumped back against the pillows as the onslaught of memories ran through me. I relived those last moments of terror all over again. In many ways, they kept me captive more than the sturdy locks on my door.

Fresh wounds scraped against the flesh of my heart, as I drifted back to that night, to that moment—the last moment before everything fell apart, and nothing seemed like it would ever be the same again.

I remembered running as fast as I could through the hallways of the castle, my breath coming in small pants. I knew I only had a limited amount of time before the walls would fall, thanks to the wine cellar collapsing. The castle's cellar had been set afire, and it was only a matter of time before it spread and wrecked its way through the castle.

It was an act of treachery courtesy of Lord Maximillian, the Duke of Moravia, his nefarious henchman, and possibly Karl Marcelin, the secret heir to the throne of Bohemia.

On the other side of the ballroom, guests were quickly evacuating the castle under the orders of the King, aided by the oversight of my grandmother, Lady Penelope Ollerton-Wellesley, the Dowager Duchess of Wellington and the leader of the Order of the Crystal Daggers. My brother, Ben, and our small team of spies were working to save as many people as possible.

I had been sent to find the second heir to the kingdom—only to discover I already knew him.

"Ferdy."

In my mind, I heard myself speak his name. I saw him, standing in the hallway outside the ballroom. He was regal and serious, nothing like the boy I had fallen in love with. We sparred verbally, fighting with our feelings, arguing over secrets and lies, before the castle rooms behind me echoed with oncoming destruction.

THE ORDER OF THE CRYSTAL DAGGERS

The last thing I remembered was grabbing onto him and trying to pull him away from danger.

There was a small part of me that felt him grip me back, that heard him call my name.

I clutched my arms, trying to force myself to distinguish between dreams and reality after that. It was too much to hope for that he would call to me, after everything else that had happened.

My shoulder shifted against the pillows. I saw it taped up, covered with medical bandages. Carefully, I reached up and began to unwrap the wound, flinching as the bandage tugged at my skin.

I was prepared for the worst, so I was surprised when, underneath it, I only saw a small cut across my skin. Immediately, my eyes squeezed shut, trying to ward off the memory.

It was hard—there were a million moments I wanted to forget, but they were all still there.

Ferdy dancing with me in the ballroom. He had worn a lord's jacket and combed back his coppery hair. There had been a distinctive shine on his boots and a twinkle in his eye. He was utterly irresistible, and never more so when he told me he was in love with me.

Ferdy kissing me with grand and growing passion as I unremarkably admitted I loved him, too.

Ferdy overhearing me discuss marriage with his brother, before confronting me, assuming I was only after Karl because he was a prince.

Ferdy trying to run from me before I could explain. Then him struggling as I tried to speak before he finally pushed himself free of me. I had scraped my shoulder at the time, causing it to bleed.

I barely registered the pain then, and now there was none left as I carefully touched the clotted blood scabbing over in a thin line and a patch of red, roughened skin.

But the bandage was soaked with herbs and medicine, and it had been tied back with care so evident it could have been a silent apology.

Does this mean he still loves me?

I could not stop myself from hoping he did.

For several moments, I allowed myself to indulge in my feeble hopes. I wondered if he would come and see me again. As the eerie light of dying night transformed into blossoming day, I finally shook my head.

THE ORDER OF THE CRYSTAL DAGGERS

I was being foolish—a lovesick servant girl and spy, pining for a prince.

"I shouldn't even want to see him," I said to myself. "He *lied* to me! And about so many things. Who's to say he was even telling me the truth about loving me?"

My memory tried to contradict me, and it was at its rebellion that I pushed myself out of bed and began to get ready to leave.

I *had* to find a way out of there.

"I still have a job to do," I reminded myself.

I needed to find out what happened to Ben and Amir, and the others, too. Admittedly, I was not as worried about Lady Penelope. My grand-mother was a spymaster, no doubt one used to dangerous situations. She was probably used to finding a way out of a mission's complications, even ones like half of a castle collapsing. She might have been used to losing people, too.

After all, she had lost my mother.

Deep down, I knew it was possible Lady Penelope would be happy to see me when I returned to my father's manor. But I could already hear her chiding me for even needing to recover as I washed my face and brushed out the knots in my hair.

As I contemplated changing into the new gown, the locks behind me chimed, and the door opened.

A shadow stepped forward. "Good morning, my lady."

Disappointment crushed me. It was Philip, the servant I had originally believed to be the Prince of Bohemia. For the first time, I recognized the smothered accent of the streets, the hidden Bohemian harmony, tucked underneath his proper tone.

There were other things I noticed now, too; Philip was close to Ferdy's height, only a little taller than myself. He had a similar color of hair, but his eyes were brown rather than silver, and even in the darkness of the morning hours I could see the string of light freckles on his face.

I could also see the hesitation in his gaze as he looked at me.

Carefully balancing a silver tray in his hands, he cleared his throat, clearly embarrassed to be caught staring. "How are you feeling, my lady?"

It was hard to give him an answer when I did not know myself. "What is today?" I sidestepped the question altogether.

"It's the seventh of December," he said. "Two days after the Feast of St. Nicholas."

Two days since the attack on the castle.

"How did I get here?"

"His Highness and I brought you here after you fell unconscious," Philip replied. He cautiously made his way to a bedside table and set down the small tray. My stomach grumbled at the smell of freshly baked bread and herbal tea.

"Can you tell me what happened?"

"After you found us and argued with His Highness," Philip began slowly, "the floor in the ballroom collapsed in on the castle's underground hallways while some of the nearby walls and ceilings fell."

He looked up me, clearly overwhelmed with gratitude. "You pushed His Highness out of the way and protected him. Some debris fell on your head."

The small bump on my head twanged with remembered pain, as if in agreement.

"I see. So then you brought me here."

"Yes, my lady."

One of the lessons Lady POW had taught me was to observe things, and knowing how traumatized I was by Ferdy's deceit—how I failed to realize he was a prince in disguise, I would never fully understand—I vowed to be extra careful in the future. As I watched Philip, eyeing his quick and careful movements, I saw no immediate reason to distrust the freckled servant who apparently served as Ferdy's royal stand-in.

Admittedly, I was not willing to distrust him when I was as desperate as I was for news.

"What happened to my brother? And what about the ballroom? Did everyone… survive?"

Philip stood, straight and rigid, as he informed me of what he knew. There was no way for him to answer some questions, but even then, I already knew some of the answers.

As Philip remarked on the damage, the Empress' pain, and the king's proclamation of sorrow regarding the loss of life, worry for Ben started to override my concern for Ferdy. I had to get back to my home, find Ben,

THE ORDER OF THE CRYSTAL DAGGERS

Lady POW, and my other friends. Then, if I was still allowed to help after all of my mistakes, we had to find out what to do next.

Lady Penelope will be upset with me when I see her again.

I decided I would welcome her ire, if it meant Ben was alive and the Order would allow me a chance to redeem myself. And then Lord Maximillian would pay, I vowed, gripping my fingers into fists as my failure tormented me.

"Please," Philip said, stepping forward as I began to pull on my boots. "You are not well."

"I'm fine," I insisted. It was at that moment I realized my dagger, the one that marked me as a member of the Order of the Crystal Daggers, was missing. "Where is my dagger?"

Philip hesitated again. "Please, just rest for now, my lady. His Highness only wishes for you to recover."

"I am feeling fine," I repeated angrily, shooting him a threatening glance. "Give me back my things. I need to be on my way, and I won't let you—or him—stop me."

Philip did not seem to be very brave—or at least, he was not willing to anger me. As displaced and determined as I was, I supposed I could not fault him for that. He gulped and nodded slowly. "As you wish, my lady. I shall return."

He paused briefly when he opened the door. "I know I should not tell you this," he said quietly, "but His Highness wishes for you to stay here. You are safe, and so are your secrets. We are indebted to you for what you have done."

Heat poured through me. As Philip left, relocking the doors, I finally caught sight of myself in the mirror. My cheeks burned bright crimson as my heart began to beat faster inside my chest.

He wants me to stay.

But a long moment later, I forced myself to move. I could not stay. I had my family to find, my work to finish.

My dignity to salvage, my honor to restore.

I grabbed at the dress left out for me and tugged it over my head. With the stays laced loosely, I could easily wear it over my stealth habit. I hurried to secure it, grateful it would be a suitable disguise. Just as I was contemplating how to get home, even if it meant walking the whole way there, the lock clicked again.

The door opened as I pulled my hair free and tucked my hood down beneath a line of ruffles.

"You can put my dagger down on the table, Philip." I tugged the sleeves down off my shoulders, grimacing as the lower neckline brushed over the small cut. "I'll get it in a moment."

"I suppose it shouldn't surprise me that you hardly pay attention to me when we meet like this."

My spine tingled with sudden awareness, and my heart began to race at the sound of his voice. It was not Philip who had come.

It was Ferdy.

THE ORDER OF THE CRYSTAL DAGGERS

2

◊

Ferdy's voice stilled me. My body felt paralyzed as he moved behind me.

"But then," he drawled, "you've never seemed to recognize me for who I am."

I whirled around to face him. He was leaning against the door, dressed in a new ensemble of princely clothes. His brown hair was brushed back and styled so I could not see any of the hidden red, although there were hints of it in the shadow of a beard on his cheeks. There was a faint smirk on his face as I studied him, trying to see the Ferdy I knew: the street urchin who had set out to save me from trouble, the footman who stole me away from ballrooms … the simple boy who had loved me as a simple girl.

"You look well." Nervously, I fiddled with my sleeves, smoothing out all the wrinkles as I called on my failing courage. I could feel Ferdy's eyes linger on my bare shoulder, the one he had bruised. "Are you going to Mass?"

"As a matter of fact, I am. Mother has called for special masses this week for the victims of the incident, and I am to attend them with her."

"I suppose Karl will be there, too," I said. "He assured me that he was dedicated to your mother's happiness."

Ferdy's breath released sharply. "I was hoping we could avoid talking about him."

"Why should we?" I snapped. All my courage and patience was gone, and only my anger was left. "You *lied* to me. About *everything*."

"Not everything."

A new thought struck me as I stood there. "I don't even know your real name!"

His confidence faltered, ever so slightly. "My name *is* Ferdy. Well, Ferdinand. I was named after my father and the king. I wasn't lying about that. I only … neglected … to mention that my father and the king were the same person."

251

When I crossed my arms over my chest, he gave me a sheepish look. "The name goes back several generations," he murmured, still attempting to defend himself.

My chin jutted forward defiantly. "I suppose Karl's does, too?"

"Even you should know Bohemia's history." Ferdy shifted his stance, moving away from the door to stand tall, his temper kindling in response to my own. "Karl was named after the first crowned king of our people. I was named after the last crowned king, which, thanks to my cousin, is still my father."

"You should have told me Karl was your brother."

"I told you enough about him!" Ferdy argued. "I even said he had a brother, the night I tricked him with the note from the footman. Remember?"

It took me a moment, to recall the scene at the Hohenwart Ball, where Ferdy had appeared out of the shadows to come and see me. The scene became clear in my mind as I stood there, still attempting to rein in my remaining arguments. Underneath all my inner fury, I saw that night. I remembered Ferdy telling me Karl had been summoned away to go and retrieve his brother.

"You were the one fooling around with an actress?" I arched my brow at him.

"I did not know how accurate it was at the time." Ferdy's eyes roamed down my body, unable to hide his appreciation. "You clearly had some secrets yourself."

"Secrets are one thing," I said, blushing. "Lies are another."

"I agree." He glowered at me. "There's enough of an overlap in this case that I find it offensive."

"Offensive enough when it's done to you, but you don't seem to have any trouble offending me."

"I also hate accusations."

"This from the man that has lied to me from the beginning!" I waved my arm around, gesturing toward the room around us. "Should I be flattered or insulted that after all your lies and secrets, you've kept me here like a prisoner of war?"

"You were the one who accused me of being an assassin before. But you saved me, so I think we should consider ourselves even," Ferdy said.

THE ORDER OF THE CRYSTAL DAGGERS

"You had a handkerchief from the assassin's place of employ," I said.

I thought of the handkerchief Ferdy had handed to me, the one he offered to me to stop the bleeding on my shoulder. It was just after he left me at the Advent Ball after Karl had run off, trying to find Lord Maximillian, in hopes of renegotiating their terms for the kingdom takeover. Ferdy had carried the handkerchief in his pocket.

"There was a man who worked for the Szapira household who attacked Tulia," I said. My head throbbed as I tried to keep my focus, but I was not going to let Ferdy see me cry.

Never, I vowed.

"Tulia was attacked?" Ferdy's anger quickly transformed into surprise.

I barely noticed his concern or heard his question. "Why else would you have it, if you were not in league with him?"

"I had to borrow the ensemble from Karl, if you must know," Ferdy said. "The handkerchief must have been a mix-up. He has been staying at the Szapira household since he returned to Prague. A simple mistake, that's all."

"Your lies are no 'simple mistake.'" I put my hand to my forehead, rubbing it in irritation. "You let me think you were nobody!"

"You kissed my brother."

"*He* kissed *me*."

"You didn't stop it."

"I was trying to stop him from possibly killing a bunch of people. It seemed like a decent gamble at the time." I turned away again, looking for some way to distance myself from him.

"That's all you have to say about it?" He came up to me and put his hand on my arm.

"Of all people, you should know that when you gamble, sometimes you lose," I said, sullen at my own poor luck.

"You told me that you loved me."

This time, Ferdy's words came across as an accusation more than a reminder, and they cut deeply into my already floundering heart.

His hands took hold of my shoulders and forced me to face him. I refused to look at his face; I did not want to witness the fun-loving Ferdy I had fallen in love with fade into nothingness.

THE ORDER OF THE CRYSTAL DAGGERS

Another illusion, I told myself bitterly. "After all the lies you've told me, I'm sure we can forget about that."

"I never lied about how I felt about you."

"Well, I never did, either," I snapped, trying to step back from him. I came up against a wall, and suddenly I was trapped.

"Prove it." He pulled me close, and I felt helpless as the angry heat between us transformed into desire.

My arms were already twining around his neck as his mouth came crashing down on mine.

There were endless lies surrounding us, but as he embraced me, I knew there was also one very important truth between us: I wanted him, and he wanted me.

I almost laughed as Ferdy held me tightly, his hands pressing on the small of my back; I remembered Lady POW telling me once before that men liked to grab onto hips during intercourse. Then his body pressed even more into mine, and I stopped thinking altogether.

Our kisses grew hotter and harder as I gripped onto him, unable to stop myself from wanting the moment to go on, even though I knew it had to stop.

"We can't do this," I whispered, nearly out of breath.

"I want to," Ferdy murmured, as his lips found my throat, and then my shoulder, where he lovingly lingered over the cut he had caused. My former pain was replaced by pleasure, and a small moan escaped me, as if to give him absolution.

"I know." I hugged him, gripping him for balance as much as to keep him close. "But we can't."

"Why not?" His eyes had clouded over with passion.

"You know why not." I waved my arm toward the window, gesturing at the broken kingdom outside the room. "You're a prince."

"I'm not a real prince."

"Yes, you are," I said. "And you just can't be with someone like me." I wanted to burst into tears, telling him that he could hardly marry someone who used to scrub the floors of her own home, let alone someone who was part of secret order of spies and protectors.

It was just not proper.

THE ORDER OF THE CRYSTAL DAGGERS

I pushed him away from me, determined to put a safe distance between us. "That's why I have to go."

"Ella."

The vulnerability in his voice made my knees weaken. "The kingdom needs both of us," I murmured, forcing myself to keep moving. "You have a duty to the kingdom, and I ... I have to protect you."

"But—"

Outside of the room, the church bells rang. We went silent in the room, letting the solemn joy of the music interrupt us for the moment.

When the bells quieted, I shook my head. "Your mother will be worried for you. You should get to Mass."

"My mother can wait," Ferdy said with a dismissive snort as he turned to look out the window. "She thinks I've been in Silesia for the past several months and that I came home to celebrate Christmas with the family. Do you remember the invitation to the Advent Ball? The one I gave you?"

The one I had used as a bookmark for my reading as well as marker for my daydreams. The one I had run my fingers over many times, even the ragged, ripped edges at the top, where Ferdy had torn off the official greeting. Yes, I remembered it.

"That was the invitation she sent out for me," Ferdy said. "I stole it from the mail carrier one day while Jarl distracted him. Philip is the one who has been serving as the prince in my place, staying with the Duke of Silesia, disguised as a cousin to the Empress. He came back to report to me this past week. When he is gone, I will be free to go into the city while he goes back to studying and attending lectures in my place."

"So your mother thinks you've been at school instead of running around the streets of Prague dressed like a homeless person?"

For a brief second, Ferdy grinned, and I had my beloved rascal back. "*Absolument.*"

I grinned in reply, and we stared at each other for a long moment. It was so strange, I thought. I knew him so well, even though I knew nothing about him at all.

The moment between us passed, and then he came up to me, threading his fingers into my hair before he kissed me again, softly and sweetly.

No, I thought. There was one thing I knew for sure. We could not be together. Not now—not when there was nothing lasting between us, no

THE ORDER OF THE CRYSTAL DAGGERS

real truth, and certainly no trust. Without that, the tidal wave of our passion, a tumultuous and rapturous thing, would end up destroying both of us.

"Ferdy," I whispered, with both wanting and warning.

"You're safe here, in my room," he whispered back. "Let me keep you."

I knew what he wanted. I knew I wanted it, too. Already, half of my mind was mentally calculating the days of my monthly courses, anything to give me a reason to stay, while the other half was scolding me for even considering it.

"How do I know you're telling me the truth?" The last thing I wanted to do was hurt him, but if I did not find a way to break free of him, I would risk doing even more harm.

Ferdy met my gaze with his. "I promise you this, Ella, that as of now, I will never lie to you again." He leaned forward and kissed me again, and I stood there, letting him, desperately debating whether I could trust him or not. His promise burned through me, his words scorched into my being. It was so tempting to believe him, more tempting than anything else I had ever faced in all my life.

Freedom was only freedom if I could trust it to be true.

"Will you let me keep you?" Ferdy whispered against my lips.

I was floored. The pleading in his voice, though disguised by pride, was clear; Ferdy was begging me to stay. He was a prince. Even while he played a beggar on the street, he never had to worry about his next meal or fear that he would be denied anything he wanted. But as he kissed me, I could feel the raw, burning desperation inside of him, the kind that only came with true risk. He knew he could make me stay. But he also knew it would mean nothing if I did not want to.

"I have to go back to my family." His humility, juxtaposed against my own humiliation, allowed me to pull back once more. "I don't know what happened to my brother or the rest of them. Ben is too important to me."

Ferdy held onto me more tightly, and I felt my breath catch. I did not want to have to remind him there was a murderer on the loose.

But as he held me in his arms, still and unmoving, I had a feeling we both knew he could convince me to stay, and I would not object so long as I had his kisses to keep me content.

THE ORDER OF THE CRYSTAL DAGGERS

It seemed both too long and too short of a time had passed before he nodded, letting me slide out of his embrace. "You saved my life, despite my attempts to negate it, perhaps. I am indebted to you. And I know what your brother means to you, even if my own brotherly affections have been stymied over the last years."

I bit my lip, curious all of a sudden. "Why don't you and Karl get along?" I asked. "He seemed nice enough to me. I know Ben and I have our differences, but we still love and care for each other."

"It takes an extraordinary amount of kindness and courage to love someone who hates you. Karl and I don't appear to have much patience for that." Ferdy smiled at me. "That's something I've always loved about you. Your kindness and bravery were endearing to me, even at the beginning."

"The beginning?"

"The first time I saw you, at your father's funeral." Ferdy looked out the window again, where dawn was starting to peek through Prague's elaborate streets. "When the king heard about your father's death, he was unusually determined to go. He said he never owed a man more of a debt than he did Adolf Svoboda."

It felt strange to hear Ferdy speak of my father. "*Táta* served as one of his bodyguards during the Revolution of 1848."

"While my mother was pregnant with Karl, and later after he was born," Ferdy said with a nod. "I know. My father made your father a knight and gave him land before my cousin took over as Emperor."

"That's the only real reason I'm a lady," I said. "Is that how you knew who I was, the day we met in Prague?"

Once more, the flirtatious grin appeared. "Among other things. It wasn't the first time I'd seen you in the city. I know you were upset at losing your book, but I was quite glad for the excuse to rescue you."

I did not tell Ferdy that Amir had been the one behind the theft, and I had forgiven him for that day.

"I remembered the funeral," I said. "I didn't realize you and Karl were there until… "

Until I learned the truth. Until I learned the truth about the secret heirs of Bohemia.

THE ORDER OF THE CRYSTAL DAGGERS

"Karl would have gladly neglected the funeral. I am the younger heir, but I am my father's favorite. That is a large reason for the animosity between us. I doubt Karl has ever forgiven Father for such an insult."

I bit my lip, tempted to tell Ferdy he was my favorite, too. I kept to the relevant topic instead. "That is hardly your fault."

He paused for a moment, studying me closely.

"You were your father's favorite, too, weren't you?" Ferdy asked, startling me with the abrupt question. "You don't know what it is like, to feel the pain of being rejected by a parent."

I thought of how *Táta* had treated me, and then how he had treated Ben. Even before Ben fell off the barn roof and shattered his right leg, our father had been less affectionate toward him.

I have never thought about that before.

Was it possible I had ruined his life even before I had caused him to break his leg?

"I don't think Ben hates me for that," I said, forcing myself to focus on Ferdy.

"He has likely thought about it, even if he does not hate you for it." Ferdy shrugged. "Karl and I have many differences, but most of them come from our father's favoritism. He hates that he is still ordered to watch out for me, too."

I nodded blithely. From what I knew of him, Karl was a proud man.

When Ferdy had tricked Karl into leaving the Hohenwart Ball, Karl reacted furiously. He was irritated at the interruption of our time together, but it was also clear he hated the task he was called to perform. It would anger him to be obligated to chase after his younger brother, especially while facing the neglect of his father. Such a slight would have been devastating.

No wonder Karl was so accomplished for his age, I thought. He would have wanted to stand out in other ways, almost as a way to punish his father for his lack of faith and favor.

"When I said I wanted to go to your father's funeral with him, Karl changed his mind," Ferdy said, continuing with his tale.

"Why did you want to go?" I asked. "You couldn't be much younger than Ben. Even *he* didn't want to go."

THE ORDER OF THE CRYSTAL DAGGERS

"Any boy who has ever wanted to be a man looks to his father first," Ferdy replied.

I thought about Ben's own disdain for our father's memory, but how quickly he would defend *Táta's* legacy as a soldier for the kingdom. Ferdy was right, as much as I might have wished to disagree with him.

"I know my father has his mental limitations and he is not what anyone might consider a prize. But as a child, none of that mattered quite as much to me as it did to others."

I knew that still did not matter to Ferdy. He had always been the one who saw the worth of others before he saw their capabilities or labels. He acknowledged his father's shortcomings, but clearly, he did not see them as a barrier to a relationship.

"When I found out what going to the funeral would mean to my father, I was determined to go."

"That must be why we get along so well," I said. "We are both determined creatures at heart."

"You more than me. When I saw you—when you smiled at me as I helped my father through another one of his seizures at your father's funeral—I felt unusually uncomfortable. I was there because I wanted my father to be proud of me. You were there because of your father's death, and even in your sadness, you had enough goodness to offer a child your kindness."

He came up to me again, clasping my hand in his and caressing it affectionately.

"So you must know, Ella," he whispered, "this idea that you are not of my station is true. But you have it wrong. I do not deserve you."

I shook my head. I did not believe him.

"There are other reasons we can't," I whispered, looking down at my new dress, the one that covered the stealth habit Lady POW had commissioned for me. "It's too dangerous."

Ferdy straightened and took a small step back from me, allowing the tension between us to lapse ever so slightly.

"That reminds me." He reached behind himself and pulled out my sheathed dagger. "I kept it safe for you. Here."

"Thank you."

"I have heard of the Order of the Crystal Daggers," Ferdy said. "I'll admit, I do not know how I feel about you being part of that assassination group."

"It's not an assassination group," I insisted.

He ignored me. "I feel better knowing you're a beginner."

My eyes narrowed at him. "What makes you think I'm a beginner?"

"You've had the younger prince of Bohemia in front of you for weeks now, and you only learned the truth two nights ago," Ferdy said pointedly, clearly trying to hide a smirk.

My fists clenched angrily at his remark, as true as it might have been.

Before I could defend myself, he shook his head. "I will not fight you on this now. You saved me when the ballroom walls fell, so I know, for the moment, you are on my side. I know that might change, but I do not feel like that should preclude you from my attentions."

There was nothing I could say. There was just too much between us, and that moment, the moment back in the castle, right before everything was destroyed, only proved our fate. We were too far away, and even if we were to work to bridge the chasm between us, one of us—or both of us—would end up hurt.

And I did not want to hurt him. I was not willing to risk his life or safety, even if it meant we would be together.

I glanced back at the door, eager to escape.

"If you are determined to leave me, I've already said I would let you go," Ferdy said in a resigned voice.

He knew I was not going to choose him. His voice was too much like before when I first met him, and he asked if we could see each other again.

Too much had separated us back then. Even more kept us apart now.

"Thank you," I said. That was the only thing I could think to say. I put my hand over his before I added, "Your Highness."

He frowned, before leaning close to me. I thought for sure he was going to kiss me again, and I could not stop myself from wanting him to do so.

But he only touched his forehead to mine, lightly and softly, staying there for the most bittersweet moment of my life. "Goodbye, Ella."

The way he said it, I wondered if he would ever call me that again.

Before I could find the courage to ask, he turned around and left the room, leaving me alone with my many scrambled thoughts.

The door was left open for me.

I did not move as I listened to the sound of Ferdy's footsteps fade across the castle hallways. I was finally free to leave; I did not know if I had ever been free to stay.

3

◊

The journey home felt painfully interminable.

Philip arranged for me to travel by coach, so I did not have to sneak through the city. Even in my state of sadness, I could see why Ferdy trusted him; Philip took care of everything, down to the smallest details. He even brushed my hair, pinning it back with new combs. When I commended him on his work, he lightheartedly confessed that men could be even more difficult than women when it came to styling hair.

It was only when I promised to send the combs back to the palace after I arrived home that he refused to accommodate me.

"His Highness gave them to you as a gift." A slight flush peeked out from under Philip's freckles, and I had the feeling he was telling me the truth against his better judgment. "The prince would like you to keep them."

It broke my heart, but I allowed it. If it was Ferdy's gift to me, and I turned it away, he would be even more hurt.

As Philip drove me home, I looked out from the coach windows and saw the small portion of Prague Castle that had caved in and fallen over.

I felt as though my heart had done the same.

What could I do in the face of such evil?

The rest of the city seemed just as wounded. The people, usually so jubilant and colorful, wore heavy-hearted, careworn expressions as they wandered through the wintery streets. The church bells chimed, but this time there was a bleak, tinny quality to their music.

The sun was shining through the last layer of morning fog as we pulled up to my family's manor. I looked back at the city skyline long enough to see that nothing had changed from this far away. The dullness of the buildings struck me as strange; the heart of the kingdom seemed wearier than ever as it stood against the passage of time.

What could I do against such sadness?

"Thank you for the escort, Philip," I said, as he helped me out of the coach.

"It was an honor, my lady. The prince and I are glad you are safe."

262

THE ORDER OF THE CRYSTAL DAGGERS

I sighed, looking around my family's home. It was a smaller manor, made of stone and wood. It had been built and refurbished over the many years, starting as a small keep itself and then, as peaceful times came, it blossomed out into a home instead of a fortress. Hallways were added even as the battlements were maintained. It was surrounded by plenty of farmland, and even a few tenant cottages dotted the edge of our property.

Thankfully, there was no one outside; no one was there to witness my shameful entrance. "I don't know if I will get to see you again, but please tell Ferdy—I mean, His Highness—that I am grateful."

"Thank you. I know he will be very pleased."

Recalling Ferdy's earlier sadness, I doubted that. Ferdy would be happy to hear I kept his gift, but he would have preferred that I let him keep me.

I did not even know what he meant by that, exactly.

"My lady."

The sudden look of worry on Philip's face surprised me. "What is it?"

"You won't tell anyone else about His Highness, will you?"

It was the first time I had even thought about that. Lady Penelope would have known about Ferdy, wouldn't she? I thought of the night of the Advent Ball when Empress Maria Anna sent me off to find Ferdy. It was possible, I realized, Lady POW would not have known about him. She had gone off to help others escape the castle before the empress said anything about her younger son.

I have to find out, and I have to be careful.

I did not want to think about what Ben or Lady POW would say about Ferdy, especially since I had fallen in love with him without knowing his real identity. It would only make my failure even worse in their eyes.

I shook my head. "No."

"Thank you." Philip smiled. "Empress Maria Anna has spent a good deal of the younger prince's life hiding him from others, including those in the Order of the Crystal Daggers and the League of Ungentlemanly Warfare. Now that you know the truth, she will be glad when I tell her you have given your oath of silence."

"Why would it be a problem if they knew?" My hands curled around the dagger I kept at my side. Surely the Order would have protected Ferdy if they had known the truth.

"Years ago, the Spring Revolutions brought change, but there is much corruption and self-service among the aristocracy. This is not something unique to Bohemia, but if another upset comes, it may lead to bloodshed, as it nearly did last time. Both King Ferdinand and Empress Maria Anna know it could just as easily come from within our own borders as it could the outside."

My mind wandered back to the Cabal, where Ferdy had taken me. It was a small tavern beside the Jewish Quarter that housed a small group, one that met to discuss everything from local news to culture, religion, and politics.

Maybe that was the real reason Ferdy became friends with them—to make sure he was safe.

But as I thought of his carefree smile, of the friendliness shared between Ferdy and Clavan, Jarl, and Faye, I quickly discarded the idea. It might have been a benefit, but Ferdy did not stay with them to protect himself; he clearly enjoyed them as much as they enjoyed him.

"Currently, there are certain parties—more than most would prefer to believe—that are very glad for His Highness' brother speaking up against Emperor Franz Joseph," Philip continued. "The princes have taken on their mother's family name to ensure they are hidden."

"Is Ferdy in danger?" I asked, suddenly afraid for him.

"He easily could be," Philip said. "Fewer know of Prince Ferdinand than his brother, but with Prince Karl's political ambitions, Empress Maria Anna is worried he will cause the wrong attention. Especially since, as Bohemia's history will tell, we have only survived so long because of the benevolence of God and the friendships we have with our foreign neighbors, as precarious as they are at times."

It was at that moment I realized how little I actually knew about Ferdy. Why would he be running around Prague disguised as a homeless person? Was he hiding? Did he have a plan of his own?

There were suddenly a million questions I had never allowed myself to ask, and even more, I did not know if I would ever have the chance to ask him.

The former empress had been willing for me to go and protect Ferdy. She could have sent someone else. *Why send me? Why admit to me at all that she had a second child?*

When I asked Philip, he smiled at me. "From what I understand, your mother made quite an impression on her. Lady Eleanor and the other gentlemen who came to her aid during the Revolution of 1848 vowed to keep their silence."

Other gentlemen?

Was Philip talking about my father? The League? Or someone else?

It seemed I would have to figure that out, too. It would not be an easy task, especially where Lady POW was concerned.

"Her Imperial Highness no doubt trusts you will live up to your mother's legacy," Philip said.

"I will," I promised. "I'll protect him."

Even if I cannot trust him.

"Thank you. Prince Ferdinand is a good man, and Bohemia would certainly suffer at his loss."

I agreed with Philip. Bohemia would never be the same without Ferdy. Neither would I.

Philip said his goodbyes again, bowing before he climbed up to the carriage perch once more. He flicked the reins and then sped off, leaving me all alone, standing before my childhood home.

My family's manor seemed different. The same farmland still surrounded it, the same morning sky watched over it. But the world had changed, and so had I.

I looked toward the city again. The world would have to move on, and so would I.

The entrance opened, and I heard a familiar voice cry out to me.

"Nora!"

Ben's greeting welcomed me like nothing else could have, and I hurried toward him at once. "Ben!"

He ran up to me, his crooked leg perfectly balanced in its brace, and we collided into each other as he gripped me in a tight hug. He was as strong and solid as he had ever been, smelling of home and mischief and a familiarity that absolutely blindsided me in all of its mysterious wonder.

It was such a contrast to the lavender and mint of Ferdy's room, and such a departure from the careless mix of fun and longing I found in Ferdy's embrace.

Tears started to swell behind my eyes.

"We were so worried for you," Ben said.

"I'm so glad to be back." I whimpered out solemn worries and my apologies as Ben wrapped his arms around me, whispering back assurances that everyone else was fine. But I ignored him, and soon he realized I was crying for other reasons.

"What is it, *ségra?*"

At his old endearment for me, I felt so young and helpless; I would have wished for my mother if she was still alive. I swallowed the rest of my tears, taking a deep breath, desperately forcing myself to regain control.

"It's nothing," I managed to choke out.

Ben knew me well enough to know I was lying. "Nora."

For the first time, hearing Ben call me "Nora," shocked me. It was so strangely different from Ferdy calling me "Ella," and it was unnerving to realize how odd I felt at the distinction.

"What is it?" Ben pressed.

"It's Ferdy," I mumbled. I breathed deeply and swallowed the rest of my sobs. I had hoped to distract Ben away from my weakness, but saying Ferdy's name proved to reveal it even more.

It was bad enough I had failed in so many ways to prevent disaster, but it was even more embarrassing to admit I had made a complete fool of myself in the process.

"Did something happen to him?" Ben asked. I shook my head, and then he pulled himself back from me, allowing me to see the sudden spark of fury in his blue-green eyes. "Did he hurt you?"

By his tone, I knew Ben was ready to defend my honor. "Not exactly," I admitted. "But I shouldn't see him anymore."

"Why not?"

"Just because," I muttered. I took a deep breath, trying to steady myself. "There are plenty of other things demanding our attention now. We can worry about him later."

"Tell me."

I sniffed again. "Later."

"Does he know about the Order?"

THE ORDER OF THE CRYSTAL DAGGERS

All of my bravado left me as Ben guessed a significant part of the truth. I nodded and looked away, hoping that would end the conversation.

"Well, if he thinks that you're beneath him for that, he was never worth your time to begin with."

At his anger, I wanted to cry all over again. I could not tell Ben that it was not because Ferdy did not want me that I was upset; it was more upsetting that Ferdy wanted me anyway.

Thankfully, Ben only patted down my curls and kept me close. "I'm sorry."

Ben was the one person who knew me, the one person I could trust without hesitation. I leaned into him, briefly glad he did not have to carry his crutch any longer; since Amir had come, Ben had designed a new brace using our new companion's medical expertise, and he was able to go for longer periods of time without using it.

As I stepped back from him, I knew I was not willing to trust him with the full truth. I did not want to admit I had fallen in love with Ferdy, thinking him to be a pauper, only to find out he was a prince, and I did not want my brother to know how damaged my pride was despite all the desire Ferdy and I felt for each other.

Ferdy was mine, and that meant my heartbreak was mine, too.

Sniffing loudly, I wiped my eyes again, determined to show strength. "I'm glad to be home."

"You might not say that after you see Lady POW." Ben's voice was soft and playful, and I knew he was trying to make me feel better. I was glad for his support, especially since his joking meant he was not asking for more answers.

Together we made our way toward the library. While we walked, Ben told me how, back at the castle, he had hurried to meet up with Amir before the ballroom, and the adjoining wings caved in. Several hallways, the kitchen, and two more sections of the castle had imploded, including the hallway beside the east library. They both helped guide people to safety and even rescued a few people caught under some of the debris afterward.

"Not that they were that grateful for our efforts," Ben said. "They were more upset at their fancy clothes being ruined than they were happy to be alive."

My laugh was dry, too bogged down with despair.

"Some of the king's guards have told us that the fires are still burning underneath all the rubble in the wine cellar," Ben said. "They have been working to account for as many people as possible while they try to extinguish them. Harshad is waiting to hear the final count of casualties. The latest estimate was six."

I hung my head. "This is entirely my fault."

"Please." A new voice broke through our conversation. "There's no need to be so narcissistic and melodramatic about the whole situation, Eleanora."

Glancing up, I saw Lady Penelope standing in front of the library. The look in her eyes, the same deep blue as my own, suggested she was relieved to see me, but her arms were crossed, and her face was pinched into a disapproving frown.

A small bubble of pride swelled up inside of me; I had been right about her reaction. She was glad to see me, but she was rightfully suspicious of my sins. She was likely just as eager to expose them to the rest of the world, too.

I swallowed hard. "Lady PO—I mean, Lady Penelope."

"We have been waiting for you, Eleanora. You're late."

"Apologies, Madame," I murmured humbly, knowing it was the best way to irritate as well as appease her.

Her frowned deepened, before she whirled around, her dark skirts snapping in the air as she walked into the library.

My grandmother is definitely unique, I thought. In all my life, I had never met anyone so inclined to win, yet so irritated when she won without a fight.

Ben nudged me in his brotherly manner as we entered the room behind her. "She hasn't rested much since we heard you were missing."

"I knew she would be difficult about seeing me again."

"She is difficult with nearly everything."

Amir, Lady POW's medical consultant and an honorary member of the League of Ungentlemanly Warfare, looked up at me first. In his chestnut eyes, I could see his visible relief, and I welcomed it.

Harshad, my grandmother's other colleague, also glanced over at me. I was not sure what to expect from him, but when he only turned away, unaffected, I felt that was a logical response.

THE ORDER OF THE CRYSTAL DAGGERS

Briefly, I had to wonder if the two of them were thinking of *Máma* instead of me. Both Amir and Harshad had known my mother, Lady Eleanor Svobodová, for many years. She had been a member of the Order of the Crystal Daggers before she resigned her post and married my father. She never contacted them again after her last mission in Prague.

Amir admitted to me before that he had been in love with *Máma*, but Harshad's exact feelings were harder to deduce.

I only knew for sure he objected to Lady Penelope's orders to train me; of course, he objected to plenty of her other decisions, too, but this was the only order he had successfully managed to avoid. Seeing how he turned away from me now, I wondered if the nature of his objection was rooted in my mother's memory.

"So." Harshad's attention remained on the papers strewn across my father's desk. "You are back."

Amir inclined his head. "It is good to see you, Eleanora."

"Thank you," I said, giving Amir a quick curtsy. I ignored Harshad. I never thought he was impressed with me, and I never expected him to change his mind—least of all now, as I returned from a failed mission.

Before they could ask me any questions, Ben cleared his throat. "What is the latest news?"

Amir and Harshad looked to Lady POW as she settled herself behind the desk.

It was such a simple movement, but it was one that summed up my life since Lady Penelope, and her small group of spies and secret guards, had arrived in my father's manor in Prague. It not only changed my present and my future but my past, too. Thanks to learning the truth about my mother and the Order of the Crystal Daggers, the ideas I had about my family and my childhood had faded into illusions.

"Well, what has happened?" I asked. "Were we able to catch Lord Maximillian?"

Lady POW wrinkled her nose. "Unfortunately, no."

"What?" I put my hands on my hips, allowing my right hand to rest just above my dagger. Having it so close lent me courage, and I knew I would need it in standing up to my grandmother. She was not called the Iron Dowager for nothing. "He orchestrated the attack on the castle."

Ben gave me a rueful look. "Since the man who attacked us by the wine cellar is dead, there is no way to prove Lord Maximillian was involved."

My breath left my body in a rush. I did not know why I was surprised to hear our attacker was dead.

From the sympathetic look on Ben's face, he had been anticipating my reaction. He knew I was not prepared for death, let alone one I might have caused.

"We are back to where we started, with Dr. Artha's unresolved murder," Lady Penelope said, as Amir slipped around the desk and made his way to stand beside Ben and me.

At the mention of Dr. Artha—my father's former doctor and a consult to King Ferdinand V, as well as a former politician—another wave of weariness washed over me. A lifetime had passed since the Order's arrival, and I was still reeling from my losses.

It seemed like just yesterday when Ben and I had been working to prepare a grand engagement celebration for my stepbrother, Alex, and Lady Teresa Marie, Lord Maximillian's daughter. I remembered that night vividly—Lady Penelope, my indomitable grandmother, commanding the entire dining hall as I floundered in the kitchens with my friends and fellow-servants; Cecilia, my stepmother, unable to whine her way out from Lady POW's thumb. There was also Ben's initial disgust at meeting our spymaster grandmother, my early arguments with the reserved but determined Amir, and hearing Harshad speak with such daring against my grandmother, even while going along with her wishes.

Everything about that night became a fixed anchor in my life, a point where time stopped, and the direction of my life forever altered.

"That is not entirely true, Pepé," Harshad insisted. "We know that the political system has been compromised by a powerful coup, with foreign players and native members alike. The doctor's death has allowed us to discover this connection."

We knew Dr. Artha had been murdered just outside the Church of Our Lady of the Snows. as he researched the mysterious deaths that were happening around Bohemia, especially after finding out several had been poisoned.

Upon arriving in Prague, Lady Penelope had set out to find out why. Then she found Ben and me, and she began to train us as members of the Order. As we slowly uncovered an organized plot to take over the kingdom, we discovered the truth about King Ferdinand's secret heir.

Heirs, I silently corrected myself.

THE ORDER OF THE CRYSTAL DAGGERS

"Eleanora, I knew you were caught in the castle when you did not return here after the ball." Her eyes looked up and down my dress before she narrowed her eyes at the combs in my hair. "I heard Karl Marcelin was at *Tynem* today with the empress and King Ferdinand. Did you see him at all after the wine cellar collapsed?"

I shook my head. "No."

"The empress sent you after him, did she not? And you were unable to find him?"

"No, I didn't see him. He had left earlier, remember?"

"I remember." Lady Penelope's eyes flicked over me again before her brow furrowed. "Are you quite certain that you did not meet with him?"

There was something almost sadistic in her voice, strangely threatening. She knew I was keeping secrets from her.

"Anything at all could help," she added slowly, as if she knew each second her gaze burned into me left me more anxious than the last. "Bohemia's heir could still be in danger."

Ferdy.

Recalling what Philip had said earlier, I blanched. "Why do you think that?"

"Karl Marcelin is at the center of the coup," Lady Penelope said. "He might have initiated it, but it could easily get out of hand. Despite what fairy tales might tell you, there is no honor among thieves. I know that well enough from my own experiences."

I was confused for a moment before I realized Lady Penelope did not know about Ferdy.

Thank you, Lord.

One of my biggest questions had been answered, and one of my biggest fears had been allayed. While I was happy she did not know the extent of my humiliation and failure, there was something else that kept me back from trusting Lady Penelope with the truth about Ferdy. I did not know what it was, or at least, I did not know how to describe it; maybe it was because of my promise to Philip, and by extension, Empress Maria Anna, or maybe it was because of Lady Penelope's own reluctance to share her past. Either way, my nerves rattled as her eyes stared at me, watching me with her cool, unblinking gaze.

"Well, Eleanora? Is there anything else?"

"No." I shook my head fiercely. It was time to ask my own questions. "Why do you want to know? Do you think Dr. Artha was the one who told Lord Maximillian about Karl? Would he have known about him?"

"We do not know that for sure," Lady Penelope admitted. "I am not inclined to think so, but there is no way to verify that now."

Amir cleared his throat. "There are others who could have informed Lord Maximillian of the Bohemian heir. The League has a history in Prague."

"I have already considered that, Amir," Lady Penelope snapped brusquely. "I do not wish to discuss it. We are discussing Dr. Artha's death, not the Revolution, and not heir to the Bohemian—"

"I fear there are other connections to the past we cannot ignore, Madame," Amir interrupted his voice oddly laced with impatience.

At the abrupt interruption, I blinked. For the entire time I had known him, Amir had always allowed Lady POW an impressive amount of deference, even when she did not reciprocate. His hardened tone caught me off guard as much as it did Lady POW.

Amir glanced my way as he added, "And you well know."

Lady Penelope's jaw tensed, and Amir remained steadfast as he weathered her wrath. As they glared at each other, silence paralyzed the room. I dared not even breathe as Amir, and Lady POW faced off against each other in wordless rage.

Finally, Lady Penelope sighed. "Jakub is dead."

"Jakub?" Harshad repeated. "Dezda's father? He died fifteen years ago, shortly after he retired from the League."

"One does not merely 'retire' from the League." Lady POW's lips pursed, wrinkling her face and souring her whole demeanor like a slow poison.

"Wait." I stepped forward. "You mean my grandfather is a member of the League of Ungentlemanly Warfare?"

"He *was*." Lady POW could not hold back her small, cruel smile. "He is dead now, likely fighting the devil for his throne in hell."

"After being dead for fifteen years, it is unlikely he has influenced our current situation significantly," Harshad said.

"But he had friends and contacts," Amir said. "Tulia is one of them. Her codename is *Mira*. And there are others. I reached out to some of

THE ORDER OF THE CRYSTAL DAGGERS

them for information last week, and that was how we discovered Mr. Marcelin and Lord Maximillian were working together."

Lady POW shot up out of her seat. Her anger was palpable as she faced down Amir. I worried for him, but his face remained calm. He was not afraid of her.

That did not comfort me as much as I hoped.

"Jakub is dead," Lady Penelope repeated, briefly narrowing her gaze at Ben and me. "He was a liar from the start, and I was a fool to believe anything he said. You would do well to do the same, Amir."

"Amir, you know Pepé, and I do not agree on much," Harshad said, "but there is no telling how much, if any, of his old followers can be trusted."

If Amir interrupting Lady POW had been a surprise, it was nothing compared to seeing him shake his head at Harshad. I had never seen the two of them disagree about anything, especially something this important.

"I believe there are some we can trust," he said. I watched as he clasped his hands together before him, his fingers curling over the bright white scar on his fist. "Our current information from my source has been proven true."

Lady POW snorted disdainfully. "They always give you some truth so the lies will be more easily believed. In the future, Amir, you will cease contact with your sources from Jakub's councilors. We are in a tenuous enough situation."

"There is no need to make it worse, Madame."

"I am glad you agree with me, then. You should have no trouble ceasing your communications with them. Even Tulia was reluctant to give me more information. I cannot imagine what would compel them to make our jobs easier."

"I know there are friendly—"

"You're fortunate enough that I can trust Harshad and you, Amir, but I do not trust your so-called friends." Lady POW glowered at him, and Amir, in realizing he would not win, fell into a disgruntled silence.

I found myself wishing Lady POW would argue with him in another language, like she usually did with Harshad. At least then I would have some idea of the level of vitriol between them. Both of them seemed to accept the impasse between them, but neither regarded it as a good

THE ORDER OF THE CRYSTAL DAGGERS

position. It was too quiet for Lady POW to bow out of a fight, and it was unusual that Amir stood up to her in such a direct and disrespectful manner.

A knock at the door interrupted us. A footman materialized in the doorway with a note in his hand. Lady POW broke off her taciturn war with Amir as she took the message, allowing the rest of us a moment of peaceable reprieve.

When I first met Amir, Lady POW had expressed the utmost confidence in him. Now, he wore a deadly expression, one that marked him as a man who was very capable of hurting others, and one who was possibly eager to do so. I saw his fingers twitch before curling around the hilt of his curved dagger, the one he always carried at his side.

Beside me, Ben looked worried as Lady POW returned.

"It seems that we have some more complications to deal with in addition to figuring out Lord Maximillian's next steps," Lady Penelope said. She had a tired look in her eyes as she sighed. "John has just informed me that Lady Cecilia has completely disappeared."

I wrinkled my nose in disdain at the mention of my stepmother. "I don't know if I would call that a complication."

"It is still suspicious," Harshad said. His brusque tone made me flinch. "She is Lord Maximillian's cousin, and, by your own admission, one of the only few who knew of his plans."

"It is even more suspicious because she knows we are here," Lady Penelope said. "She and her offspring have refrained from going out into Society since our arrival. But she could easily do much damage in undermining my authority and our reputation."

"But she doesn't know about the Order," I said. "Does she?"

"Not to my knowledge. But she has always been trouble, and she sees us as her enemies. You know this better than anyone."

I did not want that to be true; it was too uncomfortable. I looked away and straightened my skirts, brushing some imaginary dust off the finery Ferdy had given me.

"If she has been kidnapped," Amir added somberly, "her life could be in danger, too."

I wrung my hands, torn because I did not care much that Cecilia was in danger, but I felt like if I were a better person, I might have felt more sympathy for her.

274

THE ORDER OF THE CRYSTAL DAGGERS

"I have instructed my footmen to keep searching for clues to their whereabouts," Lady Penelope said. "There is no one here to tell us where she might be."

"I'm still happy she is gone," I muttered, more to myself than anyone else.

Amir reached out and put a hand on my shoulder, unsettling me. "I know you did not get along, and I even know to say that is an extremely poor understatement. But Cecilia is also a source, one who might be able to give us the connection between your father's murder and the current political killings."

His remarks made me curious. "Why would my father's death matter after all this time, Amir? Lady Penelope said before it was unlikely that it was the same person," I reminded him.

"It was not likely the same person." Lady Penelope interrupted our quieted conversation through gritted teeth. "But it was clearly done under the same direction."

I frowned at my grandmother, who shot an angry glare at Amir. "What do you mean?" I asked.

Before Lady POW could dismiss the issue, Amir cleared his throat. "The Order of the Crystal Daggers has a disturbing connection to these murders, Eleanora, and not just because they threaten to upset the political order and possibly damage the British relations with India," he explained. "The silver thallis herb was a mixture that was originally concocted by a member of the Order. Since the Justinian era, the Order has used it as a silent killer."

"Our secret weapon is poison? Not our daggers?" My hand involuntarily went to my own weapon, hidden in the pockets between my stealth habit and my new dress.

Lady Penelope groaned loudly. "You see, Harshad? This is why you need to instruct her!"

I felt my cheeks flush over in embarrassment. "What is it? What did I say?"

"Daggers are a poor choice of weapons," Ben told me in a hushed voice, as Harshad and Lady POW began one of their famous fights. "They can do quite a lot of damage in skilled hands, but it is easier to kill with a sword or a pistol."

"Or poison," Amir added.

I nodded slowly. "Oh."

"Poison is not considered an honorable weapon." Despite his avid disagreement with Lady Penelope, Amir gave me a kind smile, one that tugged at the ends of his neatly trimmed mustache. "It is not a topic Society would consider proper."

"Propriety be damned, right?" I replied, making a small laugh break free from him.

At the sound, Lady POW broke off her argument with Harshad to turn and snap at me. "You would not know such things, Eleanora, because Harshad has been reluctant to teach you anything."

"I have been learning other things," I said. Harshad had made it clear he wanted very little to do with me, and I doubted he wanted to instruct me any more than I wanted to learn from him. "Surely it takes more than a fortnight to learn everything."

"It takes a lifetime." Harshad scowled as he looked at me. "And even your mother stopped well before then. Perhaps she gave up even before she left."

I felt my mouth drop open in surprise, but before I could say anything, Lady Penelope shook her head.

"Harshad." Lady Penelope stepped between us, as I tried to recover from my shock. "That is enough. Eleanora is young yet. She questions these things out of ignorance, not impudence."

Harshad tucked his hands behind his back and turned to face the fireplace. There was no evidence of remorse in his demeanor.

"We have let enough time go by, Harshad. Especially now that we will have to locate Cecilia and her household."

"The whole household is gone?" I asked, surprised.

"Of course." Lady Penelope arched her brow at me. "Did you fail to notice there is no one in the stables? All of the servants and your stepsiblings are gone, too."

"That is … strange." I blushed at my mistake; while I did not care much for Cecilia, Alex, or Priscilla, several of the other servants, including Betsy and Mavis, were friends of mine.

What could have happened to them?

Another concern rose up from inside of me. "Is Tulia still here?"

THE ORDER OF THE CRYSTAL DAGGERS

Silence once more descended on the room as no one stepped up to answer me. From the stoic expressions on Harshad and Lady Penelope's faces, to Amir's sympathetic look, and even Ben's clear resignation, I knew the answer.

She was gone.

My breath rushed out of me in a huff, as though I had been kicked in the stomach. My mother's companion was gone. My head fell into my hands as another part of my heart collapsed.

"We have to find her." Tulia had been attacked the previous week and was making a slow recovery. She was older, too, and I knew she would not be able to last long without proper care.

The sickness inside my stomach transformed into anger. When I looked back up, I saw everyone quickly divert their gazes.

"We will do our best," Lady Penelope said, surprising me with her patient tone. "It is not an easy situation in which we find ourselves."

"Do not forget," Amir said, "they disappeared under our watch, too."

My fingers clasped around the hilt of my dagger. "Lord Maximillian must be behind it. We may not be able to prove he was behind the attack on the castle, but we know he was the one who supplied the wine. Cecilia would have known of his guilt. Maybe he took her to live with him."

"He has been staying with the Hohenwart family," Lady Penelope reminded me. "He does not need servants for a household."

"Perhaps he is moving?" I suggested. "Surely staying with them is temporary."

She considered the idea, tapping her fingers together as she thought it over. "We will need to investigate."

"I don't think that will be too difficult," I said. "When can I go back out into Society? Surely someone will be able to tell us something."

Ignoring my question, Lady Penelope began her habitual pacing. "Since the Advent Ball, King Ferdinand and Empress Maria Anna have let it be known that there was an accident that started the fire, which in turn destroyed different parts of the castle."

"But we know it wasn't an accident," Ben said. "The king knows that there's danger, and the Order was sent to protect the kingdom."

"He might know that, but the royal family doesn't want the people to know the truth," Lady Penelope said. "Which is why I did not appreciate your appearance in the ballroom that night, Eleanora. Others have seen you, and now there will be whispers about a secret coup."

"I had my mask up," I argued.

"That might work to our advantage." Amir picked up a sheet of parchment off my father's desk. "If there are rumors of a coup, our enemies will be on high alert and more inclined to make mistakes."

Lady POW waltzed around the library in moving thought. "It is still not ideal."

Harshad gave her an uncharacteristic smile. "What other choice do we have, Pepé?"

I was a little surprised to see Lady Penelope smile coyishly at his words. There were likely years of shared moments between them, and at any given second, any random memory could manifest itself between them.

"The same one we always do, of course. But giving up has never been our style," Lady Penelope replied.

"We can spread other rumors about the coup to make it more confusing if that will help," Ben offered, clearly cheered by the thought of making his rounds.

"Or more convincing," Amir added.

Lady Penelope glanced over at Ben. "You can take care of that, Benedict, while you are out looking for the other seller of the silver thallis herb. We still need to find the merchant if we are to make an antidote and possibly find out more about Dr. Artha's murder."

"I can help with that, too," I said. "It would give me something else to talk about at any parties. I have been introduced to quite a few gossips. If we head out tonight, we might even be able to learn about Lord Maximillian."

I was not excited about the thought of dancing again—especially knowing that Ferdy was unlikely to come and "rescue" me as he had before—but I was eager to prove myself again.

Lady POW shook her head. "You will be staying here, Eleanora."

"Why?" I put my hands on my hips, and from Amir's sudden smirk, I had a feeling my nostrils were flaring. He had told me before that *Máma* used to do the same thing when she was angry. I ignored him as I tried to stare down my grandmother.

THE ORDER OF THE CRYSTAL DAGGERS

Lady Penelope was not about to let me win, any more than she had been willing to let Amir defeat her earlier. "Calm down. You can use some time off from Society while Harshad starts training you."

"Excuse me?" Harshad whirled around and frowned at her. "Pepé, I must object."

"I do, too!" I stepped forward angrily, cringing as my leg, the one Ferdy had bandaged so carefully, ached with momentary pain. "If you remove me from Society, people will talk."

"People *always* talk." Lady Penelope sniffed. "If you do one thing, they'll talk, and if you do another, they'll talk. And if you do nothing or speak out or anything, they will talk. There is no stopping it. The trick is to get them to talk about what you *want* them to talk about."

"So what would you have them say about me?"

"I will tell them you were injured in the castle incident. We can say your leg was injured—which appears to be true." She looked down at my leg. There was nothing preventing me from applying pressure to it, but Lady Penelope had apparently noticed my injury. "It is a decent excuse, and it will give Harshad the chance to train you in basic fighting techniques."

"What about Cecilia?" I asked. "And the others? How am I going to find them if I stay here?"

"And how are you going to stop an assassin or prevent a castle from imploding if you don't have the correct training?"

Shame instantly silenced me, while Lady POW turned to Harshad. "There are times when expediency allows for flexibility. This is not one of those times. We have a responsibility to Eleanora. No objections, Harshad. We have made too many mistakes already. The coup is clearly very astute, and we need to make sure Eleanora is ready to face them next time. You will begin her training in the morning. No excuses."

She glanced over her shoulder at me, as though she was daring me to object. There was a familiar, critical look in her eye, and I knew she was analyzing me for weakness.

Remembering my failure again, I knew it was not a hard calculation to make.

Harshad and I exchanged glances and then briskly looked away.

"Amir," Lady Penelope called. "You will continue with your assignments."

"Yes, Madame." Amir nodded, but at his bitter exasperation, I realized Lady POW was punishing him. As Lady Penelope issued Ben his orders, Amir gave me an enigmatic glance.

When I arched my brow in return, he shook his head, but I saw his fingers twirl and flick, just the way Tulia did when she wanted to tell me something.

Later.

A rush of curiosity and dread ran through me at his signal. As Ben left the library, trotting at Lady Penelope's heels and Amir excused himself, I realized I was not the only one who was keeping secrets.

4

◊

Much to my dismay, Amir was gone for the rest of the day. It seemed I would be left wondering how long it would take to hear what he wanted to say in addition to wondering what it would be.

I could not say if my ignorance made it easier or harder to fall asleep, as a hundred little things kept turning over inside my mind. Everything from leaving Ferdy, to Lord Maximillian's success, to Amir fighting with Lady POW—all of it shifted through my mind as I lay in bed, waiting for sleep to come and free me.

I learned too late it was a false freedom. When I slipped into sleep, I dreamed of *Máma*. I saw her, I ran for her; my arms were wide open. I desperately wanted to embrace her, but I somehow managed to run right past her, before she faded away entirely. I was despondent, left with my father as he lay dying in his study. *Táta* looked over at me as he cried, and I wondered if he saw me as a ghost of sorts—a shade of my mother, always present but never there.

A loud knock at the door sounded behind me, and I blinked awake. My eyes opened to see my bedroom, and I was instantly torn between what was real and what was true, unable to see the difference. My dreams were filled with terror and longing, and so was my reality.

"Wake up, Nora. Harshad sent me to collect you. He expects us in the west wing parlor at once. You're already late for your first lesson."

Ben.

His voice pushed back the fog inside my mind, reminding me of our former lives—days full of chores, ranging from frivolous to dangerous to monotonous, evenings together as Ben toiled away with his tools and I fled reality with the help of my stolen books. I could have been happy with that life, if it were not for Alex. Over the years, my stepbrother's leering grew more licentious, and I began to feel more nervous. While she was intolerably proud, I welcomed my stepsister Prissy's haughtiness to Alex's predatory gaze.

"Harshad is waiting," Ben called from the other side of my bedroom door. There was more impatience in his voice this time.

How long has it been since he came to wake me up? It could not have been more than a minute or two.

"You don't want him to give Lady POW a poor report, do you?"

"Of course not." I finally sat up in bed, reluctant to leave my bed even if I was eager to run from my dreams.

"We should be there already."

I rubbed my eyes, slightly irritated by his persistence. "Why are you coming?"

281

THE ORDER OF THE CRYSTAL DAGGERS

"Harshad asked me to help with your lesson today. Lady POW thought it was a good idea for us to train together."

It took me a moment of consideration, but I eventually decided the decision made sense to me, even if it caught me off guard; after all, Ben always did his best to make sure I could protect myself, whether I was fighting against Alex or my own doubts and despair.

That was how Liberté was born.

I smiled at the thought of our old dream. By the time Lady Penelope had arrived in our lives, Ben and I had a fully-conceived plan to own a bookshop, and we only needed a little more time to get the money to finance it. We were going to name it Liberté, all in hopes it would bring us the freedom to escape Cecilia.

There were many times, I remembered when Liberté was my only light in the darkness of my life.

Ben knocked on my door again, calling me back to the present. "Harshad is a demanding teacher. You don't want to do anything to make it worse."

"Tell him I will be down shortly," I said as I got out of bed and reached for my stockings.

There was no reply, but I could hear Ben's uneven footsteps echoing softly down the hall; there was an eagerness in them that made me pause. My brother had a good deal of respect for Harshad. When Cecilia called us to work, Ben would only hurry if we were going to be punished. He never did more than he had to for her.

If Lady Penelope had not shown up the night of Alex's engagement, what would Ben and I be planning now?

Not getting dressed for an early morning training session with the most surly man on this side of the empire, that was for sure, I thought. I pulled back my hair with a tie before taking a quick moment to examine myself in the mirror.

My breath caught at the sight of the twinkling gold and glimmering gems behind me.

The combs Ferdy had given me for my hair were lying on my night table, next to my mother's locket and my father's pocket watch. I had pulled them out last night, clinging to them like talismans as I let myself mourn over my losses.

At the sight of them, shining so innocently in the small light of my room, I hurried to put them away.

I did not want to lose the ones I loved or the treasures they left behind. But for now, there was nothing I could do. I shut them inside my drawer firmly, reminding myself of that truth before I made my way down to the west parlor.

THE ORDER OF THE CRYSTAL DAGGERS

The west parlor was a room usually kept for the master of the house and, as far as I knew, his brandy collection. When I was much younger, Ben and I used it as a place to play on rainy days, wrestling with each other and climbing on the tabletops, pretending they were mountains, while our father watched.

After *Táta* died, I never returned to that room, or to the idea that life could be carefree and fun.

When I arrived for my lesson, I did not recognize the room at all. From the strange rearrangement of the furniture and the potent smell of sweat and leather, nothing fit with my previous memories except the small fire crackling cheerfully in the fireplace. I stared at it, seeing the light was unable to penetrate into the farthest reaches of the room, slinking around the strange equipment.

"Good morning, Miss Eleanora."

Harshad was seated on the floor in front of the fireplace, his back facing me, sitting so still I had missed him entirely. He was wearing a loose shirt and a strange pair of pants, ones that were printed with bright colors and stitched with golden thread. His feet were covered with tight leather shoes, vastly different from the Hessians he usually wore.

At his tone, I could not tell if he was irritated or not, so I decided if he could be matter of fact, I could too.

"My apologies for the delay, Mr. Harshad, sir."

"Allow me to formally introduce myself to you." He stood up. "My name is Harshad Prasad, and I am a longstanding member of the Order of the Crystal Daggers, as well as an honorary member of the League of Ungentlemanly Warfare under Her Imperial Majesty Queen Victoria."

At his introduction, I started to curtsy to Harshad, offering a proper greeting, more out of habit and manners than anything else. "How do you—"

"You need to work on your observation skills, Miss Eleanora," he continued. "Lady Penelope has never properly addressed me in your company. If you are going to work with us, you must do better."

"I noticed that you call Lady Penelope 'Pepé,'" I said. From the other side of the room, I thought I heard Ben chuckle softly.

Harshad arched his brow, seeming to hide a smile. "What good does that do you?"

I felt my cheeks flush over in embarrassment. "I know you are friends that way," I said, attempting to salvage my pride.

Ben signaled to me from the corner of the room. I did not know what he wanted to say, but Harshad did not give me time to figure it out.

"'Friends' is hardly the proper term," he scoffed. "Colleagues, yes. Friends? We have known each other too long for that."

"But—"

"But nothing. You will need to pay very close attention to what I am saying and what I am doing, starting with two basic skills. As you know, your brother is here to help in these matters."

Ben gave me a quick, self-assured smile. I thought about giving him one back when I caught sight of a small, empty plate on the desk. The sight of it made my stomach rumble uncomfortably.

Someone had his morning tea already, I thought, torn between hunger and jealousy.

As if he knew I was already distracted, Harshad cleared his throat. "You're not dressed properly. Where is your stealth habit?"

"I didn't see why it would be necessary," I replied, unable to stop my cheeks from burning. I had not thought of what I would need to wear before I left my room, but Harshad had already made me feel uncomfortably hapless. I tried to dismiss his worries. "I can work fine in skirts. Ben and I have been brawling with each other and battling our way around the manor since we were born."

"That's true," Ben said. "She has a lot of promise as a fighter."

Harshad glared at Ben. My brother fell silent, but I was heartened that he did not recant his words.

"For our first area of instruction, Miss Eleanora," Harshad began, "what I will be teaching you includes different techniques and styles of fighting."

"Will we work with weapons, too?" I asked, pulling out my dagger. It was still in its sheath, the violet blade hidden by the ancient leather.

Harshad took it out of my hands so fast I only blinked and then it was gone. "Pay attention to what I am telling you now."

"But—"

"You would have been able to move better if you had been in your habit. If you are going to work with the Order, you should know right now, you will face opposition. If you are to stand for something, you will find yourself standing against something else."

"That sounds like one of Newton's Laws," I murmured, thinking back to one of my father's books on science I had once stolen from the library.

"It is similar," Harshad agreed with a small sigh, and I felt a small spark of hope inside of me that I might be able to impress him, if only a little. "You will find it is easier to fight the more you prepare for to face backlash on multiple fronts. You will find it is necessary to stand for something, because other people will not only stand against you, but their ideas will come up against yours. Ideas cannot be destroyed—they can only be controlled."

I nodded in easy agreement. What he was saying seemed to make sense. As much as I might have loathed the instructor, I lauded the content.

"Chaos is never as chaotic as it seems. You will see that in each struggle. And that is where we will begin."

THE ORDER OF THE CRYSTAL DAGGERS

"How is Ben going to help?" I looked over at my brother, watching him as he stepped forward.

Harshad frowned. "I thought I made myself clear earlier. Do not interrupt me when I am talking, Miss Eleanora."

I narrowed my eyes at him; I had a feeling I was not going to like Harshad any more than he appeared to like Lady POW.

"You must focus your mind and learn to balance your body. Where your attention is, where your focus lies, that is where the rest of you will follow."

"Why would that help—"

"Following that," Harshad continued, interrupting me, "you will learn to direct your strength in mind, body, and spirit in order to fight effectively.

"Not all battles are physical. Many are fought in the worlds beyond this one, and many are fought inside of us—in our need for purpose, to understand, to be loved and accepted and understood. The heavenly and hellish wars, we cannot do much for; but the battles inside of us we must learn to fight, especially if we are to win."

I nodded, figuring there was no way he could object to that, so long as I remained silent. Before I could find out, the door opened.

"Amir," Harshad barked. "You are late."

"My apologies, sir." Amir stayed at the edge of the room, standing with his arms folded, serving as a guard and silent audience. In the bleak harshness of the early morning light, I could see the weariness etched into his face, which made him look much older.

What is Amir doing here? Does Harshad think I will need medical treatment after this morning?

I sincerely hoped that was not the reason.

From the expression on Ben's face, I knew he was curious as to why Amir had come, too.

"It seems you are working well enough with the first rule, Miss Eleanora," Harshad said, forcing my attention to return to him. "Now, let us begin. We will be working with a form of western boxing, mixed in with more eastern martial arts."

"What is the difference between the East and the West?"

"It is the same difference between power and persuasion, between truth and authority," Harshad murmured, clearly pleased by his own mercurial answer. "Both have their advantages and disadvantages. They start at the same point—your form."

With Harshad's instructions and Ben's help, I began to work through different fighting stances. Before long, I forgot about Amir, and a good deal of the rest of my troubles, as my mind was overrun with descriptions and positions and reasons, exceptions and metaphysical meanings, all while my body was tasked with working through several motions and movements.

"From now on," Harshad muttered, as I wobbled around on the balls of my now-bare feet, "when you come to train with me, you will wear the outfit Lady Penelope has commissioned for you. Skirts are hardly advantageous for these sessions. I would send you back to change, but Lady Penelope insists on hastening your instruction."

In other words, he is content to make me suffer from my own poor choices.

Beside me, Ben worked at a steady pace. The more tired I felt, the more calm he looked. In many ways, he reminded me of Amir, and I both envied and hated him for that.

Eventually my legs, unaccustomed to the peculiar exercise, began to twinge in pain. It had been several weeks since I worked as a servant, and my muscles resisted the old, familiar movements of chores, even those of a different sort.

At least Harshad is still someone I can trust more than Cecilia, even if he is less hospitable.

So far as I knew.

"Your brother never complained at the pain," Harshad said, catching me secretly trying to massage my leg cramps.

"I didn't say anything," I said, as I noticed Ben straighten with pride.

"One does not need to say something in order to communicate."

"I wasn't thinking of physical pain," I lied. My fists clenched, and my chin shot forward defiantly. "I was thinking of what my mother would say. These sessions are hardly proper."

"I taught your mother, too, if that makes you feel less improper." Harshad waved away my dishonest objection while Ben raised an eyebrow at me.

At their simultaneous dismissal, I sighed. "I did not mean to insult you, Mr. Prasad."

There was nothing reverent or polite in my tone, but I thought an apology might help smooth over our relationship—that approach usually worked with Lady POW—and, as much as I might have hated to admit it, I owed it to him. I had already learned from my time with the Order that I would be expected to do any number of inappropriate actions. Society's civilized manners were maintained through sacrifice. I did not have to think of anything other than Advent Ball to know this, where my attempts at saving everyone had done nothing to prevent disaster.

"I do not need your false apologies," Harshad replied dismissively. "And for the sake of time, you should just refer to me as Harshad."

He was right about the fake apology. Every time I opened my mouth, I only seemed to get into more trouble.

I shouldn't have said anything at all.

THE ORDER OF THE CRYSTAL DAGGERS

The time passed more slowly as I remained silent. Ben joined in with me, always careful to show more dedication and discipline. As I watched Ben work, I sincerely hoped Lady Penelope did not want him to come train with me because he was behind in his own espionage instruction.

Ben had already had close to a month of training with Harshad and Amir, but he had been at the castle when its ballroom walls collapsed, and Lady POW would likely blame him for the destruction as much as she blamed me.

Well, she likely blamed me more.

But I could see where Ben would have trouble. His right leg was crooked, and his stance was still uneven. With the special brace he had built with Amir, he wobbled without his crutch on occasion.

Twelve years had gone by since his accident. I was only a little over seven years old when it happened. *Máma* had been gone for two years, lost at sea, and *Táta* was just starting to come out of perpetual mourning, staying at home for longer periods of time. Tulia admitted to me a few years later that my father found it easier to pretend my mother was still alive while he was away.

The day Ben broke his leg, *Táta* had just arrived home from Vienna. He often reported between the king and Emperor Franz Joseph, passing along information and making requests to politicians from the different branches of the empire. One of my kittens had found a way to slink through the barn rafters, and I had cried for help. The maids were sympathetic but unwilling to leave their work; the stable hands dismissed my needs; my father was exhausted and ordered no one to pay me any mind.

But Ben came to my rescue. He patted down my curls, gave me a brotherly hug, and headed up to the top of the barn to rescue my kitty.

She was such a sweet little kitten, with her large green eyes and black fur. I loved her as my own, and I was terrified when she ran away from me and seemed to be stuck on the roof.

Ben quickly climbed up next to her; I cheered as he reached for her and scooped her into his arms, only to end my celebration in horror as she wriggled free and Ben lost his balance.

I squeezed my eyes shut against the memory of my ten-year-old brother's scream and the distinctive *crack!* of his leg snapping.

"Miss Eleanora, are you paying attention?"

"What?" I blinked, only to see Harshad in front of me, staring down at me from below his thick, pristine-white eyebrows. I blushed, feeling the drops of sweat on my forehead simmer. "What were you saying?"

"We were discussing the breath. Breathing is very important."

I nodded blandly, following through Harshad's orders as I tried to focus. Ben stood beside me, working through the same fighting motions, and I gave him a smile.

He gave me a worried look, glancing back at Harshad. In his own way, he was telling me Harshad was serious, and it was best if I adopted a similar demeanor.

I resisted the urge to roll my eyes, but only barely. If Ben knew I had been distracted by the memory of his accident, he would be angry. Ben had forgiven me, but he never wanted me to feel sorry for him.

"You will be able to sense your body through your breath," Harshad intoned, drawing my wandering attention back to the present moment. "It moves through your blood and touches every part of you. As you move between your inner self and your full self, breathing will help you focus. It can also ease your pain as you stretch."

As I reached down for my toes, I exhaled, and the tension inside of me broke. I did not know why I was so surprised that Harshad's advice continued to prove itself true.

"You will need to breathe while you keep your stance; for balance, always find something to focus on in the distance. Your focus will determine your perception, and your perception will influence your decisions."

Breathing while balancing was difficult, but it did allow me to forget about Ben and my other troubles.

"The world presses into us at every moment." Harshad's lilted words poured over me like a waterfall, both soothing and terrifying as they spouted down wisdom and beauty.

"You must learn to quiet your mind as it takes in everything around you. Once you quiet your mind, you will be able to better pinpoint the exact issues you need to consider."

My legs varied between numb and cramped from all the stretching and standing. I said nothing still, allowing myself to cheer at the ease of this part of my instruction. I had grown up in church, where prayer and meditation were encouraged, and it had a similar process; my weakness was in collecting all the right information, not in determining what to do once I made up my mind.

"Whether it is a matter of belief, action, or destiny," Harshad said, "you will only be open to answers when all of your questions have ceased."

At that, I was done being submissive. "That doesn't make any sense."

"Discipline, Miss Eleanora," Harshad remarked, making me squeeze my eyes shut in irritation and shame.

"Eleanora is fine," I said. "If I don't have to use formalities with you, you don't have to use them with me."

"How very democratic of you, Miss Eleanora."

I did not like the annoyance in his voice. "Are you going to call Ben, 'Mr. Ben?'"

Harshad was momentarily stunned by my question. "My logic makes sense," he finally replied, ignoring my interruption, "because questions do not answer themselves."

THE ORDER OF THE CRYSTAL DAGGERS

"But you're still asking questions."

"Nora, be quiet," Ben hissed. "You need to—"

"There will always be questions, Miss Eleanora," Harshad interrupted, "and only once you are done asking them will you be able to receive answers."

I mumbled out a wordless reply, unhappy he was right.

"It seems suffering in silence is not your strength, Miss Eleanora."

It seemed he was just as capable as Lady POW was when it came to hearing my inward thoughts.

I frowned. "I guess suffering is easier for you and Ben."

"Being a cripple does not tend to make life easier, no matter the task," Ben grunted, and I flushed over in shame. I silently vowed to say nothing further.

Ben's life was much harder, and I knew it. Whether it was because he loved me enough to go and retrieve my kitten off the barn roof, or because of our father's scorn, there was nothing noble about wondering if he had an easier time at training than I did.

"Envy ruins everything, Miss Eleanora," Harshad said. "That I know far too well."

His words echoed Lady Penelope's own words from the day before, and I suddenly wondered what Harshad's past was like, what made him play the spymaster alongside my grandmother. His sentiment seemed very personal. I stared at him for a long moment, trying to imagine the sort of life he had lived, the things that led him to make the choices that he did.

He cleared his throat, and I blushed, realizing I was caught up in my own imagination. I must have made him uncomfortable because his footsteps were very distinct against the floor. "If silence will not stay with you, maybe it is time for you to show me your fighting."

The room fell quiet. I heard only the rapid beating of my heart, the slick dripping of my sweat, and the faraway crackle of the fire.

5

◊

"Fighting?" I repeated cautiously, hoping I would still be able to talk my way out of it.

Much to my displeasure, Harshad ignored me and turned to face Ben. "Are you ready?"

Ben hesitated for only a second before he nodded.

"Wait, Ben is going to fight me?" I stood up, forcing myself not to scream as my numbed legs swayed. "Why?"

"It is just a beginner's battle," Ben said. He gave me one of his friendlier smiles, his earlier frustration still there but buried. "I won't hurt you."

"I'm not worried about that," I said, fighting off the urge to rub my legs again. I managed to give Ben a teasing look. "I'm more concerned with how easily I'll win."

Harshad sighed at our verbal sparring before he began snapping out orders and directions.

"This is a test," he told me, "to see what you can do with what you know and what you've learned."

"Ben and I already defeated the assassin at the castle," I reminded him.

"But it was not enough to stop the henchman from carrying out his work. You will have other enemies, and you will need to learn how to stop them more quickly."

I went back to stewing silently, angered at his remark and frustrated with myself once more. Harshad talked with Ben, discussing their previous instruction on different stances, attacks, and counterattacks.

"Why are you helping Ben?" I crossed my arms. "That's not fair."

"Life is not fair," Ben reminded me.

"Your brother is the better trained between you," Harshad said, stepping between us. "This is unavoidable for now, and there are two potential issues. One is that his affection for you will affect his performance. The second is, as the better trained fighter, he will be in a position to protect you, should he feel the need to do so."

"The second part is negating the first," I said.

"Contradictions are not the same thing as paradoxes, Miss Eleanora."

Before I could say anything else—likely an objection—I heard a small cough from the other side of the room.

THE ORDER OF THE CRYSTAL DAGGERS

Amir caught my gaze with his own using Tulia's gestures to sign his message.

Go along.

I traced a few of my fingers in the air, asking a question of my own, and he nodded. I relaxed at his response. In his silent response, Amir promised he would help me later.

Ben let out a small grunt, and I was surprised to see him glare angrily at Amir. I did not know what Ben was so upset over; he worked with Amir all the time, and Harshad was the one helping him now.

"Ready?" Harshad called the two of us to attention. After checking our stances and listing some rules, he nodded, and Ben and I faced each other.

It was at that second that it all seemed too strange to me, to be fighting Ben. I did not like it—not like this. Ben was my brother, after all, and the one person in the world I would never want to hurt.

"Work on your focus, Eleanora," Harshad called, as I brushed a few stray hairs out of my eyes.

At his words, Ben lunged forward; I caught his attack with a block, before twisting my left arm and hitting him back.

He retreated, and I gave him an apologetic look. "Sorry."

"It's fine, Nora," Ben said, giving me an aggravated look. "We have done this before, remember?"

"Not properly," I murmured, and Ben sighed. He glanced back at Harshad, who was watching us with his hawkish gaze. Ben moved in front of him, blocking Harshad from my view.

"Why are you always so worried about propriety?" he asked, launching out a series of punches. "It's not like you will ever truly be accepted into the polite world."

I ducked and twirled away, frowning in concentration as much as frustration. "I still have to pretend to fit in with them, if I'm going to help the Order."

Ben caught my arm and pulled me in close, trapping me with a headlock. "If you really want to help the Order, you're going to have to fight me. I can handle your attacks, Nora."

I said nothing, partially because I was struggling to breathe, and partly because I knew Ben was right. I would have to learn how to fight, and

Harshad was going to see to it that I did it, regardless of how emotionally difficult it was going to be.

"Would it help you if I pretended I was Alex?" Ben asked. I laughed as I slipped out of his hold.

"We can try," I said, stepping back. "But I don't think you could ever be as evil as Alex. Or Lord Maximillian, come to think of it."

"What about Ferdy?" His voice was soft enough that I knew Harshad could not hear.

I stumbled, nearly falling over as my heart skipped a beat. "Leave Ferdy out of this."

Ben groaned. "You can't be opposed to hurting him, after all he put you through."

"Balance, Miss Eleanora," Harshad snapped.

"Yes, Harshad," I muttered back, suddenly angry he was here at all. I turned back to Ben. "I don't want to talk about him, Ben."

"Why? Afraid Ferdy will keep you from winning?" Ben ducked down and managed to land a blow to my legs, sending me crumbling down to my knees.

I forced myself to swallow my heartbreak. I did not want to think of Ferdy any more than I wanted to fight Ben.

"Good, Ben," Harshad said. "Find the weakness and use it."

A flicker of sympathy crossed Ben's face. "Please, Nora," he whispered as we locked blows again. "Fight me."

"I am," I insisted.

"Do it better, then. I don't want to have to bring up Ferdy every time I need you to attack." Ben shook his head. "You don't still love him, do you?"

The question struck me hard, leaving me stunned and still. My hand flew to my chest, pressing into my heart as it beat furiously. Ben's words cut like an accusation, containing such a level of vitriol and disgust.

I knew that Ferdy and I could not be together. He was a prince, after all, and he would be expected to marry someone politically beneficial— someone with a standing well above my own, someone whose life was not tainted by abuse and poverty, not to mention the scandal of espionage.

THE ORDER OF THE CRYSTAL DAGGERS

But I was not able to completely forget Ferdy. Not yet. The worst part was I did not know if I wanted to forget him, either. It was a legitimate weakness.

I fell to my knees, slumping over as I shook my head. "I give up. Ben wins."

At the long sigh, I looked up to see the disappointment on Harshad's face. I expected to see it on Amir's, too, and I was right—but he was looking at Ben, not me.

"That is enough for today." Harshad scowled at me. "I have seen what you and your brother can do. From your years of service under your stepmother, it is clear you have a good deal of flexibility and endurance. Your balance and focus need work in addition to your fighting form. We will spend the next weeks working on building up your strength and then work on technique."

"I told you Nora would be a good fighter." Ben reached down a hand to help me up.

The self-satisfaction in his demeanor was repugnant, and even more so because I was suffering. Before I could stop myself, I reached out and jerked him hard, forcing him off-balance. His brace clattered as he fell to the ground in front of me.

"Ouch!" Ben grabbed his right leg, hurrying to check on his brace.

For the first time in a long time, I could see the terrible bend in his limb; his lower leg jutted out to the side from the knee, more curved than crooked from where he had grown over the years. There was a small indent in his calf where the temporary splint had cut into his skin for weeks after the fall.

A spring had shaken loose, and there were several shimmers of metal on the floor beside us as the other parts began to bend and twist out of sync.

"Well, that is one way to use weakness," Harshad said. "A point for Miss Eleanora."

"I didn't mean to do it," I sputtered, feeling sick as Ben glared at me. "I didn't, I promise. It was just an accident. I didn't mean—"

"Stop it," Ben snapped, already retreating from me. "It's over. There's no need to pretend anymore."

THE ORDER OF THE CRYSTAL DAGGERS

He found a way to stand using his other leg. Without the brace, I could see his limp was much more exaggerated and painful. As he stood, I hurried up next to him, grabbing his arm to help.

"Get away from me." Hatred burned in his blue-green eyes. "I can do this myself."

My hands fell to the side as my mouth dropped open, stricken as if he had struck me across the face. "Ben—"

"That's enough," Harshad said. "It appears that you both have significant work to do. While you are strong, you must work on your weaknesses."

"Ben doesn't have a weakness," I insisted. "He can use his leg to fight just fine. I caught him off guard, that's all."

Ben huffed. He exchanged a few words with Amir before he left, but I was too far away to hear. All I could see was Ben's deepening scowl and Amir's hardened expression.

Harshad had me clean up the room as my final task. I had to put the equipment away, mop up the floor, and wipe down the room.

I did not want to; it was something that reminded me of my days as a servant, something I was as eager to escape for my dignity as much as my bitterness. Eventually, I resigned myself to the task, taking it on as a punishment for hurting Ben.

Amir stayed behind to help. We worked in silent harmony, our movements smoothly synchronized, as if we were working on our waltzing.

It was only after Harshad left the room that Amir finally said anything. "You did well for your first lesson, Eleanora."

I shook my head. "It doesn't feel like it."

"You are not the judge of this matter. Harshad is, and I can tell he was satisfied."

"If this is what it is like to win his approval, I'm not sure I want it." I hid my gaze, focusing on scrubbing scuff marks off the floor. "I did not want to hurt Ben."

"His weakness is not his leg."

"I know." I lifted my chin proudly. "It's not going to stop him from being a good fighter. He can do anything he wants, just like anyone else."

"That is not quite true," Amir said. "If he is to be a good fighter, he has to acknowledge his shortcomings. That includes his physical ones as well

294

THE ORDER OF THE CRYSTAL DAGGERS

as his emotional ones. Ben is able to compensate for his injured leg. He has done it for years, and he is able to work through our exercises with accommodations."

"You just said that his leg was not a weakness."

"And it is not. *You* are."

I stopped moving, my eyes wide. "I am?"

"He loves you, as much as a brother can love his sister, and he cannot easily forget that connection." Amir gave me a wistful smile. "I know that from my own sister."

"You have a sister?"

He nodded, and I blinked in surprise. It was not just Ferdy who I did not know as well as I should have.

"There is a reason that Lady POW requested that he fight you. He is clearly worried for you, but he did not say why."

"Lady POW wanted him to fight me?" My voice raised in anger and surprise. "I can't believe—"

Amir gave me a warning glance. "Things are not always as they seem. She talked with him after your return."

"I know that. I thought she was sending him out to find Tulia and others."

"Your grandmother is not worried about Tulia. She was injured, but she has lived a long life, and she knows how to take care of herself." Amir crossed his arms. "Lady POW wants to know more about you. She knows you are keeping something from her."

I wrinkled my nose. "Well, that would upset Lady POW. She does not mind keeping her own secrets, but she is quick to seek out others'."

"Is your brother right to worry for you, Eleanora?"

Before I could think through it, I shook my head. I had promised to keep Ferdy's secret safe, and I did not know yet if telling my brother was a good idea or not. He would be furious that Ferdy had lied to me, and then there was the fact that Ferdy knew more about Karl than he had revealed.

With no substantial proof leading us to Lord Maximillian and our only other leads missing, Ben would not hesitate to confront Ferdy.

"Are you certain?"

At the note of sympathy in his voice, I was unable to brush aside his concern. Lying to Ben to keep Ferdy safe was necessary, and lying to Lady POW, knowing she had her own secrets, was nothing. But lying to Amir, a man my mother had loved and trusted, felt very different.

I will have to tell him something.

I sighed. "I'm coming to the conclusion that I will have to let my friends go if I am going to succeed as a member of the Order."

It was not the complete truth, but it was not a complete lie, either.

"Knowing what I do know of you, Eleanora, I would suspect it is more than that." He gave me a small smile. "What about your beloved?"

I blushed at his perceptiveness. "I don't want to talk about that."

"I already know about him, and I've kept that information from the others," Amir reminded me gently.

"Why?" I narrowed my eyes.

"Because I know firsthand how difficult it is to face scorn from your grandmother for young love." He shifted his stance, clearly uncomfortable. "You have my sympathies, Eleanora. Heartbreak is never easy. It was not meant to be, for either side."

He was likely right; I knew Ferdy was not happy with the situation between us. My chest constricted at the thought of him, alone and hurting, and all the more so knowing it was my fault.

I shook my head, clearing away all the images of Ferdy suffering. He had his friends from both the Cabal and the castle to help stave off his loneliness and disappointment.

Glancing up at Amir, I saw his eyes had blurred over with memories, too.

"What are you thinking about? My mother?"

Amir shrugged, a crimson color lighting his amber cheeks. "It is hard not to, with you around. But there are others who I have caused to suffer. Your mother is not alone in that regard."

"You had another beloved beside *Máma*?"

"I have had some passing fancies in my lifetime. I promise Naděžda was the only true love of my life, but there were others who were heartbroken by my devotion to her."

THE ORDER OF THE CRYSTAL DAGGERS

Other women would have loved Amir, I thought. While we had been at odds the first several times we met, I knew he was a gentle, virtuous man, one who was knowledgeable and insightful, and even after all these years, he remained loyal to my mother's memory.

"Of course," Amir continued with a small smile, "no one was more disappointed in me for loving Naděžda than my father. That one continues to sting the most."

He glanced down at his right hand, where his old scar scorched through the warm brown of his skin, an inch above his knuckles.

"Does it hurt?" I asked the question before remembering it was not proper to do so.

Amir did not seem to notice. "The scar itself? No. The pain of rejection it represents? That is a different matter."

"What happened? My mother didn't do that, did she?"

"Harshad was right. You do ask a lot of questions."

I could feel my nostrils flare as I made a face at him, but Amir only laughed.

"You did say before you would tell me more about her. Why not tell me now? It'll give me something else to think about while we clean. I could use the distraction." I held up my rag. "This brings up bad memories. I hated cleaning for Cecilia."

"If you make it a point that I owe you for the years of your pain, it is a poor argument."

"I have been told I am quite determined. Ben, Tulia, and plenty of others have said so."

Even Ferdy had noticed that, seeing my determination and kindness at my father's funeral. I faltered for a moment, wondering if it was as much of a gift as he thought it was. My determination to find truth and protect others seemed to erode my kindness of late, and I could not say if it was a good thing or not.

Maybe I was more kind when I was a child.

"Tulia was the one who could have told Lady POW about you and your brother. She is more at fault for your pain."

"I have forgiven Tulia for that."

"Have you not forgiven me, then?" Amir's voice was slightly teasing, but I worried that he was sincere. Before I could say anything, he nodded

297

THE ORDER OF THE CRYSTAL DAGGERS

slowly. "I suppose you are right. I did say I would tell you more. I will start by saying Nadĕžda was not the one who gave me the scar, but she was part of the reason for it."

He turned away and went back to helping me clean. I saw the scar, a strange, dotted loop on his hand, gleaming white against the warm tan of his skin.

I had seen the shape of it before, and I said so. "That's the same symbol that's on the journal you have—the one you took from me when we first met in Prague."

I saw his mustache twitch at the mention of the journal. "What is it?" I asked.

"There is another reason Lady POW is not afraid for Tulia," Amir admitted. "She thinks she is the one behind the disappearance of your stepmother and the rest of the household."

"What?" My mouth dropped open in surprise. "Why?"

"Tulia is Jakub's half-sister. She had connections to the League, even if she was not a full member. Dr. Artha's priest sent out a message to her, remember?"

To Míra, and the Light.

"He sent word out about the threat to the League then," I said. "But Dr. Artha was one of the Order's correspondents."

"Yes." Amir's forehead creased with worried lines. "There are plenty of us who work for both the League and the Order, but it seems strange he would send for only them."

"Perhaps it was because they were close friends?" I suggested, remembering the endearment from the letter, saying word had been sent to "my sweet *Míra.*"

"That would confound Lady POW," Amir agreed wryly.

"What does this have to do with the journal?" I wondered why the mention of my mother's journal had sparked the change in topic. As I waited for him to say something, I knew it could only be something bad.

"The journal is missing," he admitted. "I have not seen it since the ball."

"It's gone? Where? Did someone take it?" I was stunned. I could well believe others would want to read my mother's journal, but I was not sure who would have recognized it.

"Those are my questions, too, I can assure you."

"Did you finish reading it?" I asked. "Before it disappeared?"

"I finished reading up to where your mother admitted to running into Jakub while she was on her mission, and that is it." Amir gave me an apologetic shrug. "I would have read it faster, but seeing Naděžda's writing again is a joyful sort of pain."

I decided not to chastise him for that. I would have lingered over every word myself if I knew how to read Arabic.

Instead, I shook my head. "This is terrible. We have to get it back."

"I would appreciate your continued silence to Lady POW in this manner," Amir said. "She might have taken it too, but Tulia is the more likely culprit."

I did not know what to say. Tulia was hardly a thief, that I knew of, even if she did not like my grandmother. But I was coming to trust Amir.

I did not know what to think.

"Finish telling me about your scar," I said. We could worry about the journal when we found Tulia. "What does that symbol mean?"

"It is an Arabic letter, the *noon*, one that marks the *nassara*, the Nazarenes," Amir said. He paused for a long moment as if he was trying to calm himself, before he finally continued. "One of my cousins gave it to me at my father's orders, after I told him of my conversion to Christianity."

"Your father had you marked for converting?" My mouth dropped open in surprise.

"It is the mark of the deepest betrayal, for a Muslim to convert," Amir replied. "We do not only betray our upbringing, we dishonor our families and taint all the good we have been given in the name of Allah and his prophet. Religion is a way to understand and demonstrate the best life has to offer, from honor and truth and compassion, and for both the Muslim and Christian, rejecting it cuts sorely into the heart of those who believe.

"I was my father's only son, so my cousins took on the task of restoring honor to the family. My father gave them this dagger to take care of it. They carved it into my skin and then prepared to kill me."

He reached down to his side where his dagger, the *Wahabite Jambiya*, was carefully secured.

Eying the mark once more, I grimaced. "It must have been painful."

"It was," Amir said with a nod. "Your mother was working with Xiana at the time, and it took both of their skills to stop me from bleeding out or losing full function in my hand."

"Xiana?" I barely managed to recall her name, horrified by Amir's experience. "Oh, the lady who taught you about herbs?"

"Yes. She is part of the Order, too, and hopefully you will get to meet her soon. Harshad has sent for her to join us here in Prague."

"If she helped save you, I am sure I will like her. It was fortunate that she was there with my mother so they could save you."

"My sister was not so fortunate."

At his remark, I did want to know what happened. As I had learned before, there was a cost to knowing the truth, and I was quickly finding out that cost was both freeing and sobering.

"Halal was my older sister. She distracted my family so Xiana and your mother could smuggle me out of my family's estate, so I could escape. Halal did not want me to die. She tried to understand why I did this to our family, even if she did not agree with my decision. She worked hard to foster peace between me and my parents. But when I escaped, she was killed."

"She was killed because she did not want them to kill you?" I barely felt my lips move at the question. I felt my heart ache in pain for Amir and his sister.

I knew Ben was angry at me, but I suddenly wanted to go and hug him, reassuring him, and myself, of our affection for each other.

"You are young yet, but even you know there are things worth dying for."

"Dying for something is different than killing for something," I said slowly.

"The first time I killed a man, I did it to protect your mother." Amir tried to give me a small smile. "I considered that a matter of deep honor and love, even though it was gruesome. But that is another story, of course."

Amir slipped into silence. I reached over and patted his hand, covering his scar with my hand.

"I'm so sorry," I whispered.

THE ORDER OF THE CRYSTAL DAGGERS

"Do not be sorry for me. I ask that you do not judge my family. I have known deeper betrayals than theirs, but it is good of me to forgive them."

"Who could betray you more than family?"

Amir's lips twitched into a wry smirk. "Those who would become family, of course."

I wondered if he was talking about my mother, but he shook his head before I could ask. "Forgive my grievances, Eleanora. It was one of the hardest things I ever had to do, to first leave my family, and then forgive them. In spite of the pain between us, I still love them, and there are many values we still share. There is much good we can affirm."

"You are a better person than me. It is too easy to hate people." I thought of Cecilia, and how she had treated both me and Ben over the years. As cruel as it was, it was nothing compared to Amir's sorrow. I clenched my fist, struggling not to hate Amir's family for him. "I'm sorry I asked you about it."

"It is better to remember," Amir said. He turned his hand over and patted my hand gently, the same way my father used to. "We must remember, too, that blessed are those who mourn, for they shall be comforted. And we can only mourn properly when we remember the depths of our losses."

At his own words, I thought of my own faith, and how much it was a cornerstone of my own life. I had been born into it, but Amir had given up his entire childhood and his family to gain it. I silently prayed for his comfort, but I already felt like he had been further cheated with the loss of my mother.

As if he knew what I was thinking, Amir said, "It is much better for me to remember Naděžda than forget her, too."

It was hard to speak at the sudden lump in my throat. "I wish she was still with us."

"She is," Amir replied. "She is here, even if she is not. We will see her again one day, Eleanora. Some people say that religion only causes pain, but there is much pain tied to goodness. If all truth is God's truth, then all goodness is his, too."

When we first met, I had envied Amir's time with my mother. Now, as we stood there, having lost so much, I wondered if I had been strangely spared from missing her even more than I already did. I clung to Amir's certainty that he would see her again, with the further hope I would, too.

"I should have asked a question about fighting instead," I said, resuming my cleaning.

"Religion and fighting share something very significant, and that is why it is actually good to consider matters of faith and its practices alongside battles."

"What do they share?" I asked.

"Truth." Amir gave me a smile. "And, by extension, love."

"Love?" The word might as well have been one of the Arabic words inscribed on his dagger. "What does that have to do with truth?"

"True truth is unable to be separated from love, and you know as well as I do, that God is love. If I were allowed to guess, Lady Penelope and Harshad's teachings have failed to serve you because they have lost that connection."

I snorted. "You are likely correct. I didn't know love had anything to do with any of this."

"They are set in their ways, and they are not used to having their authority, or their intentions questioned, let alone by you."

"Me?"

"You look so much like your mother," Amir said. "When they look at you, with your dark locks and your bright eyes, I would not be surprised to find they see her looking back at them. It is a hard thing, to live between times."

"You said before I looked like my father."

"You have the narrow facial structure of a Bohemian, as well as the curls your mother wished for all the days of her life." Amir shrugged. "But your expressions, and even the way you flaunt authority, surely reminds them of happier... of the past."

I did not disagree with him. Lady POW had called me "Eleanor" several times before, and it always seemed hard for her to acknowledge her mistake. I suddenly wondered if Lady Penelope had offered me the chance to join the Order of the Crystal Daggers to relive her days with my mother as much as I had accepted in hopes of connecting with my mother's memory.

"I suppose it is hard to live between times, but it is even more difficult being a conduit for it," Amir added.

I profoundly appreciated the sympathy in his voice, but only nodded at his conclusions.

"I am glad she has convinced Harshad to work with you. His lessons will serve you well in the weeks to come."

Amir changed the subject, and I let him.

"I might need your help understanding them," I said, laughing a little.

"They are a good distraction from thinking of your beloved, too," Amir added, making me cough. "And if they do not, and you need someone to talk to, I would—"

"I'll come and find you." I cleared my throat. "Hopefully, my heart will be all mended before too long."

Even though I doubt it.

"Thank you. But that is not what I was going to say," Amir said, his voice quiet and grave. "I was going to say, I would not say anything to Ben. Do not forget, he wants to prove himself too."

We did not say anything else after that. Amir and I finished cleaning the training room, working together in amicable silence.

After he left, I thought there was likely another reason Amir kept his knowledge of Ferdy to himself. Undoubtedly, he wanted me on his side as much as I wanted him on mine.

6

◊

"Eleanora."

At the sound of my name, I looked up from the book in my hands, only to see Lady POW standing in the doorway before me.

A week had passed since the Advent Ball, and I had finally made it back to the library. Cecilia had forbidden me from using the library after discovering my love of books, and I found peace in having full access to them once more—even if I was consistently distracted. For the last hour, I had been looking past the words while my mind drifted off to other places in search of comfort.

"What is it?" I asked. "Ben and I finished with Harshad today. He said I could rest up for tomorrow."

"I am not here about Harshad's lessons. You and I have things to discuss. Come with me."

From the tone of her voice, I had a feeling I was in trouble. As Lady Penelope guided me out of the library and propelled me down the hallways of my home, I mentally prepared myself for another lecture and stinging letdown. It had to come, did it not? After all, I had already woken up to a world filled to the brim with disappointment last week. Why would Lady POW refuse to add her own distinct flavor to my sadness? Her displeasure was not a question of what, it was a matter of when.

So I was surprised, after several hallways of silence, she pulled out a chatelain and used one of the dangling keys to unlock a door.

"Go inside."

Her tone was still frigid. I walked inside, unsure if I would be locked in the room as a punishment. It would not have been unearned, I thought sadly.

The room was dark and musty; I wrinkled my nose at the smell. There were only little strings of light slipping through the curtains to brighten the room.

"What is this place?" My voice echoed into the dark shadows.

I almost expected Lady POW to snap at me for daring to ask a question. Instead, she struck a light and walked around the room, lighting some candles.

THE ORDER OF THE CRYSTAL DAGGERS

Slowly, the outline of another broad desk, several bookshelves full of books, scrolls, and papers, came into quiet view. In the other corner, I could see a large chair covered in mothballs, and a large globe tucked awkwardly behind the entrance.

"This room was your father's study."

I went cold at her words.

This is worse than a punishment.

"Why are we here?" I asked, unable to stop myself from gaping at the room around me.

My father had died there, alone, sitting at his desk. At the time, there had been no reason to suspect anything other than natural causes.

But now, Ben and I knew the truth. Our father had been poisoned by someone using the same silver thallis herb mixture that was unique to the Order of the Crystal Daggers.

My fingers tingled as I remembered touching *Táta's* hands at the funeral, unwilling to believe that he was truly gone.

"I wanted to ask you what you know about your father." Lady POW waved her arm out. "I understand you were quite young when he died. After Eleanor married her Dolf, I did not hear much from her. Of course, I did receive her dagger, and the later request for money to buy out the manor's debt. But I did not endeavor to know him on a personal level. Eleanor could take care of herself, after all."

The bite in my grandmother's words reminded me my mother had left on unpleasant terms with Lady POW.

"So you did not know my father at all?" I pressed, hoping to find out more from her reaction.

"I did not try to learn much about her life after she left the Order. Eleanor left for her last mission to Prague at the end of 1847," Lady Penelope admitted. "I knew there was a certain risk in sending her. Bohemia was her first home, but because of her talent for taking care of delicate matters, I decided to allow her to go. I never met your father in person. What I know is what she told me, and even that was limited enough."

From the way she spoke, so carefully precise, I knew there was something she was keeping from me.

Everyone lies. Everyone has secrets.

Lady Penelope's own teachings were working against her.

Ben had warned me about this at the beginning, I thought, remembering his own apprehension and disgust at the thought of being at our grandmother's mercy. After meeting her, he had seen her as a woman who put business over family, a relentless fighter in pursuit of her preferences.

Thinking of my brother's current eagerness to please her, I almost groaned at his complete reversal.

"Ben would be the better person to talk to," I said slowly, keeping an eye on Lady Penelope. "He was older when *Táta* died."

"I have already talked with him. He has seen this room, too."

"Why do you want to know what I think?"

"Because you are different from your brother, and you might know something that will allow me to see him in a different light." Lady Penelope held herself steady, keeping her eyes focused on me. "I want to know why someone would want to kill him."

My father was almost as elusive in my mind as mother was, but it was hard to dispel his ghost when I stood in his study. I thought about the reasons he had to die, and I could not think of personal ones.

"He worked for the king, mostly as a court ambassador and then later as a soldier," I said. "He was knighted at the end of the Revolution, before King Ferdinand abdicated in December."

"Your mother would have been in Prague for about a year at the time," Lady Penelope said. "Thanks to Tulia, we know that your mother knew about the king's son. They helped hide and protect him."

"They?"

Lady Penelope grimaced, ever so slightly. "Tulia and your mother, of course."

There it was—she was lying. There was someone else who had been helping my mother. Philip's earlier comments echoed in my memory, and at Lady POW's irritated hesitation, I wondered if my grandfather had worked with my mother on her mission.

Why would Lady POW hide that from me? He was dead, after all, even if she did not want to remember him.

Looking at her now, and recalling her vehemence before, I decided I would ask Amir. He had contacts from the League who might be able to tell us what happened when my mother came to Prague.

THE ORDER OF THE CRYSTAL DAGGERS

That was not the only thing she did not want to discuss, I thought. Lady POW had been loath to admit the Order of the Crystal Daggers used the silver thallis poison, and someone was using it now to poison politicians, and someone had used it to kill my father.

A new thought suddenly struck me. *Was it possible the Order was responsible for* Táta's *death?*

Ferdy's voice, the one voice I tried to muffle more than any other, called to me at that moment. His assertion that the Order of the Crystal Daggers was a group of assassins ran through my mind. While I did not agree with his perspective, I was suddenly very aware that I was floundering in a sea of confusion and distrust.

If I was going to protect my kingdom, save others, and restore my honor, I would have to find out the truth about the past, and how it connected to the present, and I would have to do it before anyone else was injured or killed.

"Well?" Lady POW put her hands on her hips, clearly irritated I had slipped away into my own world. "What do you think?"

"My apologies." I glanced around the room, trying to think of how to describe my father. "Well … *Táta* was a very kind man—to me, at least. He would travel for long weeks, but he always came home. Before *Máma* died, he would hold small parties here occasionally."

I had been too young to understand many things; I was only five when *Máma* had been lost at sea, and nine when my father followed her to the grave.

"What was his temperament like?"

"He was a quiet, studious man, but still very tough. He always had time for me. He would dance with me sometimes, and he read to me at night." I lowered my eyes to the ground. "He was very upset when Ben broke his leg. He had been training Ben to be a soldier for about two years when it happened. After that, they were never close."

"I see." Lady POW frowned. "So you were his favorite, then?"

Hearing her echo Ferdy's earlier observation made me even more uncomfortable.

"I think so," I admitted softly. "But I'm not sure it was because of my own merit. He told me once I was proof of *Máma's* love, since I looked so much like her. He said he could enjoy her for two lifetimes instead of just one."

The room seemed to settle from our earlier intrusion. I stood there, watching the last of the dust dance around in the dim lighting, waiting for Lady Penelope's next question.

"I can understand his feelings on that particular matter," she finally said, a small smile forming on her wrinkled face.

I looked around the room again, eying the framed items on the wall. There were maps and a few documents, but no pictures. "There was a portrait of my mother hanging in the library when I was younger. I remember after she died, he looked at it quite frequently. Cecilia removed it after she married him."

"It was in here when Benedict came in with me," Lady Penelope said. "I am having it restored by one of the footmen. Hopefully you will see it again in the library soon, where it belongs."

"Really?"

She nodded, and I beamed with pleasure. "Thank you. I appreciate that."

I had agreed to work with Lady POW because I wanted to know my mother more. Having her portrait restored was an added blessing, one that would help exorcize Cecilia's harsh memory from the manor.

"Nonsense, Eleanora. You should know I loved your mother, too, even if ... " Her voice trailed off, and then she sighed. "What else do you remember about your father?"

Renewed by her revelation, I looked around the room once more. "He had dark eyes," I murmured, sinking into my own past, shocked at how much I had let myself forget. "I think they were hazel. He was a tall man, too. Or so it seemed, from the shortness of my age. I knew he collected a lot of things from the different places that he went for the king."

"Books?"

"Most of the ones I remember are books," I said. "Cecilia has made me trade them or sell them off over the years. The day I met you, I had just sold his copy of *The Prelude*."

I did not mention that Cecilia had wanted me to sell my mother's journal, too. Amir had stolen it from me, and I was more grateful than ever that he had. Not only had I met him, and by extension Lady Penelope and the Order, but that was how I met Ferdy, too.

"Ella."

Impossible yearning momentarily devastated me. It seemed in allowing his voice to speak inside of me, there was no longer any hope of suppressing it. I would go from suffering of one sort and then slide into another too easily, all while I was compelled to further hide my true self from everyone around me.

"What is it?" Lady Penelope asked. "Do you remember something else?"

I had to force myself back into the moment, back into my father's study, facing my grandmother as she watched me along with the rest of the room.

"He has been gone for several years now, and I knew him as a daughter, not as an equal. Maybe when we find Cecilia, she will be able to help you answer more questions about him."

"I'd rather not rely on her completely, given the choice." Lady Penelope shuffled her skirts toward the desk. "But you are right. She will be a good source. You can really only trust the people you don't trust at all."

"That can't be right." The absurdity of her statement almost made me laugh. "That's irrational."

"Haven't you realized it yet, Eleanora?" Lady Penelope hissed. "People are far more irrational than rational. You can't trust *anyone*. We are loyal to our mission, but our allegiance is to the truth alone, and that includes the realization that other people will fail you—sometimes purposefully."

At her temper, I felt my own anger stir. "Is that why you and Harshad work together?"

"Yes." Lady POW's lips pursed, souring her expression even more than her tone. "We know each other's worst traits, and we are well aware of our capacity to betray each other. That means he will be prepared to make sure I stay in line, and I him."

I gaped at her. "That is madness! How could anyone ever have any normal relationship?"

"Why do you think your mother left?" Lady Penelope shook her head. "This is part of the price you pay to protect others, Eleanora. You only trust people you know well enough, and once you know someone well enough, you know exactly how they will fail you in the end."

"That's not true," I insisted.

"If you truly believe that," Lady Penelope warned, "you will only be more disappointed when it happens."

THE ORDER OF THE CRYSTAL DAGGERS

Another chill ran through me at her words.

"Right now, we must work to find Lady Cecilia," Lady Penelope continued. "We know the disaster at the Advent Ball was meant to inflame
the public. The former king has managed to quell a lot of conflicts. Since
it failed, we can be sure that there will be another attempt to upset the
kingdom."

I thought of waking up in Prague Castle, in Ferdy's room, seeing the
damage done to the city; a sense of determination renewed inside of me. I
was allowed to mourn, but there was still work to do.

"While you are training, I will keep making my rounds in the city. It
likely won't be long before there is another plan we will have to foil.
Christmastime and the weather may offer politicians a break, but there is
no vacation for insurgents."

"What else would you like me to work on?" I asked, crossing my arms
over my chest. If there was danger, and Lady POW wanted to keep me at
home, I would place the blame for any incident on her.

"Keep focusing on your lessons with Harshad for now. We are still
working to find more information, but the weather and Society's stag-
nancy has slowed our resources in that regard." She paused. "You should
know Benedict is worried about you."

I squared my shoulders at the sudden change in subject. "Ben knows I
am sad that we failed to protect the people at the castle."

"Forget about that." Lady POW snorted delicately. "People die all the
time. We do what we can. You clearly did what you could, and it did not
save everyone. That happens. Now we must work to prevent it from happening again."

I said nothing, stunned by her brusque tone. Lady Penelope had been
quite adamant before that we had to do something to stop the kingdom
from crumbling. Now that it had fallen apart, she seemed much more cav-
alier.

"Ben does not think that there are other reasons you might be distracted, does he?"

I thought of Ben's antagonism toward Ferdy and quickly shook my
head.

"I don't know what he thinks," I said, unable to disguise the growing irritation in my voice.

THE ORDER OF THE CRYSTAL DAGGERS

"Perhaps Ben is the one who is distracted in his observations, then?" Lady POW shook her head. "And here I was, thinking he was doing so well, too."

"I think Ben is doing an excellent job." I knew from just looking at my brother how much he had changed in the last several weeks. I had to credit the Order, and even Lady Penelope's own efforts, for Ben's happiness.

"Maybe I should make him step down from the Order for now. If he is wrong about you, then there is no telling how wrong he is about other things. He knows you so much better than the rest of us, after all."

"No." I balled my fingers into a frustrated fist. "He really likes working with you. He would be upset if he had to stop."

"Should I put the rest of our team in danger, all to spare his feelings?" Lady Penelope asked. "There is much more at risk than one person's comfort, if I need to remind you."

She was not just talking about Ben. She was talking about me, too.

I tried to relax and succeeded only in the smallest degree. I did not want Ben's position with the Order to be jeopardized. After my father's rejection of him as heir, Ben had carried such a burden. I did not want to be the reason, again, that he would suffer.

"Ben is just overprotective of me," I insisted. "Even when we were fighting the assassin in the wine cellar, Ben was more concerned with me."

"I see. I will note your thoughts on the matter." Lady POW folded her hands together thoughtfully. "Very well, then. Get some rest, Eleanora. Harshad will send for you in the morning."

"Where are you going?"

"I will continue making my own inquiries. Before Tulia disappeared, she gave me some information, and I must check her reports."

I felt another chill at her words. *Tulia knows about me and Ferdy.*

Even if Tulia did not know he was the younger Prince of Bohemia, she might have been able to tell Lady Penelope about the boy I loved. "What did she tell you?"

"Always so curious," Lady Penelope murmured crossly. "You will find out when you need to know. For now, go and rest. I'd hate to think I've spent a good deal of time harassing Harshad to instruct you only to find he was correct about what a poor student you would make."

My fingernails scraped into my palms as my fists clenched, and I watched her disappear down the hall. I fought the urge to scream.

Instead, my hand went to the dagger at my side. I had earned the right to carry it, even if I did not know how to wield it. I was a member of the Order, and I was only loyal to the truth.

And the truth was, I had little to no idea of what that could be. I only knew for sure that the illusions I had grown up with were gone, and I had to monitor their remaining influence.

Visions of those lies passed before me as I made my way to my bedroom. I saw my mother's life and my father's death; I saw my grandmother and her colleagues; I saw Prague in all of its glory, stained by the sadness I was now intimately acquainted with. I even saw Tulia for who she was, as my grandfather's half-sister; and there was Ferdy, too, with his roguish grin and his princely stature.

What do I have left?

I clasped my hands together, no longer able to carry my anger and frustration. "I still have you, Lord," I whispered, leaning my head down in prayer. I begged for his help, for his patience, for his comfort. "Please help me."

After several long moments, my heart steadied. I still had my faith, and I still had Ben. I could trust Ben.

I bit my lip, looking at the door to my father's study one last time.

I can trust Ben ... can't I?

7

◊

As much as I worried about Lady Penelope, I did listen to her advice and focus on my work. As the days passed, I worked on becoming a more skilled warrior, learning how to be invisible, to move in silence and stealth. The effort was demanding but engrossing, and I was largely able to hide my worry from myself.

That was part of the real trick—finding a way to put fear aside for the moment, before forgetting it altogether.

Of course, just because fear is silenced, that does not mean it truly goes away. It bides its time, waiting for a moment of weakness, before it pounces again, twisting itself into sudden sickness.

I discovered this the hard way when Lady Penelope called for me the following week.

"Eleanora!"

Ben and I had just finished up another session with Harshad. When I heard her voice, I jumped, whirling around to face the door to the west parlor as my sweat-soaked towel whipped through the air after me.

"Careful." Ben ducked around the sudden movement.

I glanced over at him apologetically, but he only gave me a spiteful look in return. He was absent the last few days of Harshad's lessons, but I had not missed him much.

Perhaps it was because of his festering irritation I only noticed at the end of our session that his one eye was shadowed by darkened puffiness.

Immediately, I forgot all about Lady POW.

"Ben!" Examining his injury, I could tell he had been hit very hard, and very recently. "What happened to you? Your eye—"

"I don't want to answer any questions, Nora," he hissed. "Amir already told me I would be fine. He even assured me that I was deserving of it, thanks to you."

"What?" I tried to reach for him, but he slipped away from me. "What are you talking about?"

"Eleanora!"

313

Lady Penelope's voice cut through the air between us, this time much more sharply. Ben wrinkled his nose at me. "Lady POW is calling. You should see what she wants."

"Ben—"

He shook his head and left the room, leaving me with my mouth open in hurt shock.

Why was he being so harsh? I knew Lady Penelope was trying to get him to tell her my secrets, but for the first time, I was more angry than hurt by Ben's attitude.

Ben should be on my side, not hers.

Ben did not tell me about Lady Penelope's inquiries regarding my secrets, but he should have, just as she should have talked about the League or about the past. I had my own secrets, but I had good reasons for keeping them. I could see no reason Ben would hide something from me.

Something has to be done.

My fists clenched angrily. Over the past weeks, I had focused solely on my work with Harshad with very limited interruptions and manageable relapses. In many ways, it was necessary. What else could I do to stop myself from thinking of my failures? Between Ferdy's loss, Ben's antagonism, and the Order's demands, I was overwhelmed with pain, sorrow, and shame.

I knew in coming home from Prague Castle, I would need to redeem myself. That meant becoming a better fighter. My fighting, while still rudimentary, was now more nuanced and fluid; my muscles were stronger, my endurance increased, and, no doubt much to Lady Penelope's glee, my midsection was even flatter. I could do several rounds of pushups, lunges, and sit-ups; I ran and jumped, moving until my breathing came in erratic patterns as I panted, feeling sticky in my stealth habit.

There was no hint of Lord Maximillian's next move, or Karl's, or anything else suspicious. There were no more murders for us to solve or activities to investigate. We were still stuck at the same unanswered questions, and I was tired of waiting for an absolution that might never come.

As I stood there, watching my brother willingly ignore me after an uneventful Christmas, after weeks of no word of Cecilia's whereabouts or Tulia's fate, my resolve only strengthened. Being a better fighter was obviously important, but it was only part of what was required of me. I had worked through my pain only to find more pain waiting for me when I was finished.

THE ORDER OF THE CRYSTAL DAGGERS

It was time to change my focus. It was time to go look for answers myself.

"Eleanora!" Lady Penelope's voice was much louder as she burst into the room. "There you are. Thank the Lord I've found you."

"What is it?" My voice was edged with bitterness, but I was genuinely curious at her overwhelming pleasure.

"Something has happened, at last," Lady Penelope cheered. "You have a visitor."

"I do?"

"Yes, and we need to hurry!" Lady Penelope grabbed me by the wrist and pulled me out of the room, nearly running into Amir. She brightened at the sight of him. "You should come, too, Amir."

"Yes, Madame," he replied, careful to keep his tone respectful. But as we headed out, I caught the glimmer of defiance in his eyes and knew he was still frustrated with her, despite his façade.

It seemed that Amir was growing tired of playing along with Lady POW's lead as much as I was.

"I heard you did well enough in your sessions this week. I am glad to hear the mostly positive results." Lady Penelope in exuded an excited energy as she pulled me along, belying the seventy-some years old she had to be.

But then, maybe I was just too tired by comparison.

"Should I say thank you?" I almost pulled myself free before noticing Lady POW forcing me to move was actually a reprieve from my own efforts.

"Training with Harshad has been very good for you, Eleanora." I saw her glance down at my midsection for a quick second. "It has helped significantly with your figure."

Normally, I would have said something at her condescending remark, but I was too tired, and I did not want my rudeness to give her a reason to further reprimand me. Beside me, Amir gave me a silent look of teasing approval.

"Who is here to visit me?" I asked, deciding it was time to change the topic.

"A certain gentleman has come to call," Lady Penelope replied with a cheery grin. "He gave me his card."

THE ORDER OF THE CRYSTAL DAGGERS

"Let me have it," I said, snatching it out of her grasp. *It can't be …*

My heart sank as I read the card. Karl's name stood out in bold lettering. I crumpled up the paper in my hand, angry at myself more than anything.

Of course Ferdy is not going to come and see me.

Ferdy could play the gentleman, as I now knew thanks to the Advent Ball. But that did not mean he would. He had let me go, and it was not like he was going to show up at my home and demand I change my mind about us.

Even if I might want him to.

"Eleanora?" As we stopped in front of my bedroom door, Lady Penelope cleared her throat. "What is it?"

"It's Karl," I said. "Karl Marcelin. He's here."

"I know that. Why do you think I went to go and find you? What is wrong? After these last few weeks, I thought you would be happy to see him."

"It's nothing," I murmured. "I am just too tired to be surprised, pleasantly or otherwise."

Another thought hit me hard. What if the empress or King Ferdinand had said something to Karl about my role as a member of the Order? Was he here to confront me?

The earlier, unpleasant feeling in my stomach morphed into pure dread.

"I was hoping he would visit sooner, but now I am just glad he is here at all." Excitement laced Lady Penelope's words as she burst into my room, opened my wardrobe, and began tossing me towels. "Amir, you stay outside. Eleanora, come. Karl is expecting you."

"What?" I gestured down my body, where my sweat-soaked outfit hung limply and my body odor eagerly announced itself. "I can't see him."

I did not want to mention that I did not have any strength left to fight Karl in the event he attacked me for my deception.

"Amelia and the others will take care of you while I distract him," Lady Penelope promised. "I heard some interesting rumors a few days ago, and I would love to hear them confirmed."

"What rumors?"

316

THE ORDER OF THE CRYSTAL DAGGERS

"Just hurry. Mr. Marcelin is our remaining link to Lord Maximillian, and we cannot alienate him. Not yet, anyway. We must use charm to get information, and that means you need to be ready."

"If Karl and Lord Maximillian are working together, why don't we just confront Karl?" I asked.

"Karl is the king's son, and Lord Maximillian has significant status as a duke, and we can't forget he is a cousin to Emperor Franz Joseph," Lady Penelope reminded me. "In our position, we need proof, not just what appears to be a coerced confession, and that means we need to find out who is financing their nefarious deeds if we are going to protect Bohemia and the surrounding nations from further danger."

"Oh."

"They are never going to admit to murder, let alone attempting to take over the kingdom, without damning evidence," Lady Penelope said. "We are fortunate that the empress trusts us, or we could easily be imprisoned ourselves."

Lady Penelope gathered her skirts as she bustled out the door. "So that is why you cannot fail us now. Change your clothes, fix your hair, and wash up. In ten minutes, Amir will carry you into the front room and you will sit there, like the invalid I've reported you as being. No objections."

"Ten minutes?" My mouth dropped open in disbelief.

"Did I not just say you were to have no objections?" She sighed heavily as she left the room, brushing past Amir. "I am pleased with your progress this week, Eleanora, but you must realize this does not make up for your mistakes at the castle."

I nearly stopped breathing at her words, chilled at the edge of disappointment in her voice.

"Go and do what she says." Amir broke through my momentary despair as he reached over to close my door. "The rest of us are here to help you."

Even if Karl knows about me and the Order.

I relaxed, but only by the slightest degree. "I'm going."

"Not eagerly," Amir replied, attempting to coax a smile out of me; I obliged, if only a little. It was hard to resist Amir's kindness. Before I could say anything else, Amelia, Jaqueline, and Marguerite appeared to take charge of the situation.

Lady POW's seamstresses were a team of frightening efficiency. Their movements blurred together, perfectly synchronized as they pushed me into a new outfit and cleaned up all evidence of my training session.

"Your hair needs work," Marguerite said. "Here. Let me put it up in turban so we can hide it."

"No, leave it down," Jaqueline said. "It is much more intimate, *non*? The gentleman will appreciate it."

"If we leave it down, we will need to comb it with oils. That will help cover up the smell of the sweat. I think it is better if we put it up." Amelia spoke with a kind smile on her face, but I forced down a grimace before letting the three of them take over.

"Here you are, miss," Marguerite said, as she handed me a large swath of bandages.

"What is this for?"

"Your leg. Madame instructed us to wrap your leg in extra bandages. The rumor is that you've injured it."

"Oh. Well, it's not broken." Before I could say anything else, new bandages were drawn tight and warm against my skin, firm against where the bruise on my leg had once been. I tried not to compare the sense of cold detachment to how I felt before, when my leg was wrapped in Ferdy's kindness.

When everything was done—when I was dressed in a modest house gown, my hair was clean and pulled back into an ornate bun, and my body was covered in multiple layers of soap and perfumes—Amelia, Jaqueline, and Marguerite handed me over to Amir.

I saw Amelia grab a thick blanket. "Hurry, sir," she said. "Madame will be waiting for us."

"What are you doing?" I asked as Amir picked me up, surprising me. His strong, gentle embrace, combined with his careworn expression, reminded me of my father.

"No need to worry, Eleanora," Amir said. "I have you."

"This seems unnecessary."

"It is all part of the plan. There is no telling what Karl will see while he is here. It is better we give him a show."

I sighed as I hooked my arm over his shoulder, embarrassed more than anything else. I felt like a little girl again—and in some ways, I reveled in it. The world had seemed like such a different place when *Táta* was alive, and it had been so long since I relied on someone to take care of me. The death of my mother had ripped the world out from underneath me, but the loss of my father had left me without any sunshine in my skies.

I shrugged off my yearning as we entered the front room from the back way. I could hear Lady POW talking with Karl in the adjacent room. Amir set me down on the couch, while Amelia and Jaqueline hurried to tuck the blanket around my skirt. Marguerite appeared with a wet rag to lay on my forehead a moment later.

"For added effect," she explained quickly.

The instant she turned away, I let it fall to the side. I already felt silly, like a bedridden child or an overly-dressed grandmother. "I'm glad it's winter. This is getting hot."

"You should be fine while Mr. Marcelin is here." Amir tucked the cover in around me. "Lady POW will likely only bring him here for a few moments to talk to you. She'll need you to get as much information from him as possible."

"I'll try. I don't think he will confess to anything." I thought of my brother, too. He did not want to tell me about his injury, and he had managed to keep that hidden from me. What were the chances that Karl would confess anything important?

I glanced up at Amir. "Do you know why Ben has a black eye?"

Amir must have been expecting that question, because he waved it aside. "He has other orders from Lady Penelope. That is all he told me."

The answer was vague enough to make me suspicious. "He is still angry with me. If he didn't tell you what he was doing, he might be upset with you, too."

"I am certain he is," Amir admitted. "He was not happy with me the other day, after your fight."

I remembered that day Ben fought with me, after Harshad's first lesson with me. "What was it that you said to Ben on his way out of the parlor?"

"Nothing of importance."

"If it's nothing of importance, you should have no issue telling me."

"There is no stopping you, is there?" Amir sighed. "That day, I told him that he deserved it when you knocked him down."

"What? Why?" I slapped his arm. "That's awful."

319

"He was proud of his victory when you gave up," Amir said. "That's not right, Eleanora. Ben has his own struggles to overcome. You are a weakness of his, but you are not the only one. He needs to watch for his own flaws, and winning can show them as much as losing."

"That's still cruel."

"The truth is often upsetting. If Ben is to improve, he must understand the difference between not only failures and victory, but victory and false victory." His eyes met mine as he added, "It is the same for you. There is a difference between freedom and false freedom."

It was hard to push my sudden discomfort away, almost as hard as it was to hide my fear. "I suppose you are right."

"Well, if you say so," Amir replied, and I saw the smirk under his mustache appear briefly.

"Thank you for telling me." I folded my hands, unsure of what else I could say. I was not happy with the truth, but there was nothing I could do to change it.

"You are welcome, Eleanora. I'll look forward to seeing what you can find out from Mr. Marcelin."

"I just hope we can discover something that will help. I know we haven't been able to discover much since the castle incident."

"I hope so, too." He gave my hand an affectionate squeeze, allowing me another look at the scar on his fist before he left the room.

I bit my lip. Obviously, Amir had known his share of suffering. I did not want to add more anguish to his life. But as I heard Lady Penelope's formal remarks and eager footsteps coming closer, I had a feeling that neither of us would be able to avoid it.

"Ben told me that we have to find a physical connection to Lord Maximillian and the castle's attack," Marguerite said as she pulled one of my curls out of its pin. "So please, Nora, see if you can find a connection."

"Why were you talking to my brother?" I asked, frowning.

"We are all concerned about the mission, miss." Marguerite blushed, no doubt sensing she had overstepped herself.

"I'm sorry," I said. "I was just curious, that's all."

It did not make me feel good knowing I had gotten better at hiding the truth in the last few weeks. Deceit might be required for a spy, but it was disheartening to see myself fall so easily into sin.

THE ORDER OF THE CRYSTAL DAGGERS

"Of course. Hopefully this will not take long," she replied. "It is not proper for a gentleman to be in a lady's presence when she has taken ill or if she is injured. But Lady POW wants to give him the chance to slip up, and this is a clever way to surprise him."

"Surprise him?"

"Yes. When you surprise an unsuspecting foe, he will have a harder time hiding the truth." Marguerite patted my hand in a friendly way, while I just sat there, dumbfounded.

I had never been very good at asking Karl to give me information. It did not help that he was as much of a liar as Ferdy was.

If not more so.

Secretly, I hoped Karl would decline an audience with me. He knew I was indisposed, and I did not think he would push to make me even more uncomfortable. When he came through the door a moment later, I stifled back a groan.

It's really a good thing I never learned to like gambling. Ferdy would be appalled at my luck.

"Eleanora is, of course, delighted to have you as a visitor," Lady Penelope was saying, and I had to bite my cheek to keep from arguing with her. "Goodness knows the poor dear needs something to lift her spirits. She has been rather down since the accident."

"I am pleased to be of service to my lady."

I had to bite down even harder at the sound of Karl's voice. I had never noticed before how much he had the same lyrical undertones as Ferdy, the same cadence to his proper tone. All that was missing was the heart of a rogue beating underneath it.

My cheeks grew hot as he took my hand.

In truth, Karl looked very little like his younger brother. They were of similar height, and they shared the same jawline and pointed nose, but Karl's eyes were a darker gray, giving him a more hawkish face. And while I could nearly always make out a smattering of fuzz on Ferdy's cheeks, Karl was cleanshaven. His ebony hair was brushed back from his face, emphasizing his steadfast demeanor. He was clearly a man with a serious and settled nature, strong willed and focused. While I had witnessed Ferdy's temper before, I did not want to know what Karl's was like; I had a feeling it was just as resolute as the rest of him.

"Mr. Marcelin." My voice was low and weak as I greeted him, and I suddenly wondered if Ferdy also used Marcelin as his surname. My eyes watered at the thought.

"My lady," Karl replied. He bowed over my hand and kissed it, just as gallantly as he had the night of the Hohenwart Ball. There was nothing in his demeanor to suggest he thought I was a traitor and a liar; if anything, I could feel his eagerness beneath my palm. "I am glad to see you again."

Empress Maria Anna did not tell him.

The thought struck me hard and fast, and I was relieved and disappointed at the same time. What kind of mother did not tell her son he was courting a spy?

Then again, what kind of mother *was* a spy? Philip had said *Máma* had impressed the former empress, and I was starting to see why. They must have had a lot in common.

Karl sat down on a chair close to me. I gave him a teasing look. "Even if it is in this condition?"

To his credit, he blushed a little at my banter. Karl had impeccable manners. "I heard the tragic news of your injury, but I did not want to inconvenience you or hinder your recuperation. Lady Penelope was kind enough to allow me to see you."

"You are most welcome, Mr. Marcelin." Lady POW held her position at the doorway as Amelia, Marguerite, and Jaqueline all filed out of the room. When they were gone, only Lady Penelope loomed over us, as any proper companion would.

Of course, the situation was already inappropriate, since I was supposed to be indisposed. We were courting scandal as it was.

"I am glad to see you are being taken care of so well. I miss you dreadfully, and I fear I will continue to do so while you recover," Karl said.

"I am sure there are other ladies who would be willing to dance with you in my stead."

"There is no one like you, Ella." His words were soft and quiet, hushed enough to hide the intimacy from Lady Penelope.

"Eleanora, you should know that you need not worry much about that," Lady Penelope said. "There is not much amusement to be had in the city with weather such as this."

She looked toward the windows, where a small layer of powdery snow was lying on the grounds.

THE ORDER OF THE CRYSTAL DAGGERS

"That is correct, Madame." Karl nodded. "While Emperor is in Vienna, he has granted Empress Maria Anna's request for a political recess while the castle undergoes repairs."

"It seems that we must continually suffer boredom as well as inconvenience because of the incident." Lady Penelope narrowed her gaze. "What a shame anything happened at all. And those poor souls who died. I am so fortunate that my Eleanora only injured her leg."

Karl nodded solemnly. "I should have stayed with you that night."

"Forgive my upset, Mr. Marcelin," Lady Penelope replied. "It is not as though you caused the ballroom walls to collapse."

Karl clenched his jaw at the sudden silence between us.

"I did not hear much of the official story while I have been recovering," I said, feigning delicacy, drawing Karl's attention back to me. "Do you know happened at the Advent Ball?"

"There was a fire in the wine cellar of the castle that night." The smoothness of his voice made me wonder if it was practiced.

But then, I thought, Karl was an excellent politician.

"Roman is very upset by the news. As the architect who restored the wine cellar, he feels responsible for the design's failure. He is offering to oversee the rebuilding and repair of the castle."

"I see."

"I have also offered to help. In fact, I have moved out of Roman's house to stay in the castle itself while it is repaired." Karl straightened, clearly eager to share his news.

I nodded and smiled. "So you are staying with the king?"

"Yes," Karl said, clearly enjoying the prestige of his position. He would welcome the attention, and I had to admit, it was a nice cover story for staying with his parents. "From the castle, I will be easily able to attend to the needs of the Bohemian Diet and the *Reichsrat* Congress as sessions resume. The Minister-President is also not far away, should he require my attention."

"I have heard that Count Potocki has decided against retiring his position," Lady Penelope spoke up from behind us.

Karl's subdued expression further soured. "Yes, Madame. That is true. Since the accident, Alfred has decided to stay on until the repairs are organized and Emperor Franz Joseph has taken care of Bohemia. Should the emperor decide to do anything about it at all, of course."

"If Count Potocki is not retiring, what will you do?" I asked. "Will you campaign for his position while he remains in office?"

"Such a venture is risky," Karl murmured, clearly flustered. "It is not polite or honorable."

"It would be a political move." I almost expected Karl to laugh at my observation, but he did not.

"I have not conferred with Alfred about the matter," he said. From his serious tone, I would have said he was lying, but there was no way to know for sure. "I am, for now, content to remain where I am."

At that, I *knew* he was lying. Since I had met him, Karl had talked eagerly of moving into the count's position, and now he was trying to come across as a man with solid connections. I commended Karl on his attempts at humility, and even his success at deception, but I did not believe him.

"If you are not running for his office, is Lord Maximillian still insistent on your arrangement with Lady Teresa Marie?" I asked.

It was too hard to sound hopeful.

"The immediacy of our mutual discussions has stalled for now, if not indefinitely," Karl replied. His eyes went dark as he looked away from me. "However, I believe this gives us some time to discuss our own future, my lady, especially considering our last conversation."

"Oh." I thought of the Advent Ball again, remembering he was in agreement to marry me. Panic nearly choked me, as I remembered I never gave my own specific approval, but I had allowed him to think that I was in agreement. We had shared a private moment, even a kiss, and Karl had run off to make arrangements.

I could not even remember Karl's kiss; all I could think of was Ferdy, and the taste of his lips on mine as we grasped onto each other in his room, each breath between us crying out with fervent desperation.

Lady Penelope cleared her throat, making me blush even more. "Mr. Marcelin has informed me of his intentions, Eleanora. For now, I have only consented to consider his offer. My life experience with husbands has brought me a fortuitous amount of wisdom when it comes to arranging a marriage, and I feel it is appropriate to exercise it in this regard."

Karl cocked an eyebrow at me, and I nearly laughed. He was no doubt recalling Lady Penelope's hasty wedding and short marriage to the Duke of Wellington before he passed away several years ago. They had been rumored to have a scandalous affair and a difficult marriage.

Thinking of the Order, I could not stop myself from wondering if he had been poisoned, too.

"I would also prefer to wait for your full recovery to give my final answer." Lady Penelope's condition seemed to give Karl a renewed sense of hope, and he cheered at once.

"I am certain of your knowledge in this matter, Madame, and I am glad for the opportunity to embrace it," Karl said. If I did not know him so well, I would have believed his sincerity.

"Well," I said, "you know what happened to me the night of the Advent Ball. What happened to you?"

"I went looking for the Duke of Moravia as soon as we parted," he said. "I was hoping to renegotiate the terms of our agreement, as you know. I was informed that he had left. The footman I spoke with told me that one of his business associates had summoned him."

"Business associates?"

"The Duke is a very wealthy man with many connections," Karl said. "He no doubt had to discuss his latest investment pools or company stock. He is quite diligent in personally overseeing these matters. From what Alfred and Lord Hohenwart have told me, he does not follow the accepted practice of hiring a man of affairs for such activities."

So Lord Maximillian is personally involved in the scheme to take over Bohemia, I thought. It made sense, from what I had heard Cecilia say before. He had several foreign backers that were invested in his project, too.

"Grandmother?" I nearly gagged at the strange title. While Lady Penelope was indeed my grandmother, it was difficult to think of her as such. If it was not for her blue eyes, the blue eyes shared by both my mother and me, I would hardly believe we were related.

"Yes, Eleanora?" Lady Penelope's eyebrow twitched in irritation. I did not think she liked the title either.

"Would you call for some tea?" I asked. "Please?"

I saw her gaze from me to Karl in that calculating way of hers.

"I shall return momentarily." She narrowed her gaze at Karl in warning, but I knew she was secretly pleased.

"Thank you, mum," I said, making her smile even more twisted.

The second she was gone, I turned my full attention on Karl. "I am so glad to see you, Karl. Thank you for coming."

Pleasure radiated from Karl's face. "It is hard talking candidly with your chaperone present."

I nodded. I was ready to ask him my questions when he slipped down on his knees in front of me.

"Ella, I know your grandmother has denied me consent to marry you for the time being, but might I at least ask a promise of your fidelity?"

"My fidelity?" I stared at him blankly.

"I understand a formal engagement is a big step, especially for your grandmother," Karl said. "But the matter of a pending engagement is different."

As he explained the nature of differences between this—which I did not understand at all, thanks to my ignorance in Society's demands—I felt my stomach twist into several knots. A pending engagement between Karl and me would allow people to believe he was courting me, with the intent to marry. Those people would believe that I was in agreement as we appeared in public together.

In other words, I thought glumly, it was the engagement without the announcement.

I would be lying every step of the way.

Everyone lies about something.

Ferdy's words, so close to Lady Penelope's, skipped cheerfully across my mind, and I hated Ferdy in that moment. I hated that he could not be mine, that I was too proud in my rags to have him, that he would too easily discard his worth to gain me.

I hated that everything had happened in such a way that I could not trust him to stay beside me, nor could I assume I would not push him away.

And Karl, whether he realized it or not, was just making me feel worse. The one thing I never wanted to do when I started working for the Order was marry for the sake of a mission. I clearly remembered fighting with Lady POW about it.

And yet, here I was, about to lie and sacrifice everything for my kingdom and my heart's desire for answers.

THE ORDER OF THE CRYSTAL DAGGERS

But, true to form, I would not do it senselessly.

"I will agree to this," I said slowly, hating myself for every word, "if you make me a promise in return."

"What is it?" Karl asked impatiently, clearly startled and displeased by my request. He cleared his throat and corrected his tone. "Anything for you, my lady."

"I want you to promise me that you will not ever lie to me."

"Done."

"About anything," I emphasized the words very carefully, and Karl narrowed his eyes. I knew he had his own secrets, and he would not enjoy sharing them with me.

But a moment later, as he met my gaze with his own, I saw him relent. His gray eyes softened, and I felt a sting of shame at my manipulative demands. I had to remind myself that Karl, no matter how nice he might have been to me, was working with Lord Maximillian to take the Bohemian monarchy, that he was connected to a plot to kill people, and that no matter how noble he thought he was, Karl had to pay for his unhealthy ambition.

"You have my word, Ella," Karl took my hand again and bowed over it. "I was so worried you would completely retreat from me."

Not while I have a murder mystery to solve and a coup to uncover.

"I will not allow myself to keep anything from you that would hinder our relationship," he said, standing up straight and puffing out his chest proudly once more. "And I will begin working on a way to change your grandmother's mind immediately."

"Thank you," I said. "I believe your oath. Now, I would like you to tell me about your brother."

He dropped my hand, reeling back on his heels as his face blanched and his cheeks burned with fury. "What?"

The disbelief on his face was almost amusing. I doubted I could have said anything else that would have made him feel less surprised, even if I accused him of blowing up the castle himself.

"I apologize for my impudence," I said, feigning sudden discomfort. "But since you knew about my brother, I thought it would be nice to know about yours. After all, my brother is my closest family, and I am glad to know we have such a blessing in common."

There was a long moment of silence as Karl's expression became more embittered. I said nothing, holding my breath nervously.

"I regret I will not be able to share in your joy. My brother is a nuisance and a plague to my family's legacy. I prefer to forget about him altogether if possible."

"Oh?" My hands folded in my lap, as I watched him with sudden curiosity. "Why is that?"

"My brother has been suspended from any number of schools across Europe. He spent several years in Paris, and some in London with me, and I can attest to his brawling, his gambling, his … numerous indiscretions."

I blushed, thinking of Ferdy with other women. Anger flared inside of me, even as a very small part of me held onto that memory of our first kiss.

"I see," I said very quietly. "I can see why such a reputation would upset you."

"All I have worked for is the future of Bohemia," Karl said. "My brother has spent his life dedicated to fun and frivolity. He is not anything like me."

"Not by the sound of it," I said. "Where is he now?"

"He is currently staying in Prague, but just for a little while longer," Karl admitted. "He is finishing up his education in Silesia. Until his return, I will keep watch over him and make sure he does not get himself into trouble."

"It sounds like he has a talent for it." I had to muffle a giggle. Ferdy was much more trouble than Karl could have ever guessed. "Would I be able to meet him?"

"No." Karl's sharp tone was quick and fierce, and it took the rest of my daring to ask him another question. "Please, Ella, he's hardly proper. My family prefers I do not tell anyone about him."

I could believe that, from what Philip and Ferdy had both mentioned before. "What is his name?"

"I'd rather not tell you, if it would keep you from finding out his trouble," Karl said. "I know I promised to tell you the truth, but this is something you are better off not knowing."

THE ORDER OF THE CRYSTAL DAGGERS

"I am only curious," I insisted. "If I wish to know you better, it would be best to do it on more intimate terms. Indeed, I would like to know more about your family."

Karl's mouth twisted again, and I could see he was getting more frustrated with me. "His name is Ferdinand. He was named after the king, of course."

I pretended to brush a stray curl out of my eyes as I smirked. "Of course."

"May I ask how you learned about him?" Karl asked, suddenly rounding on me. "No one knows of him here in Prague, not even my closest companions."

"I learned about him the night of the Hohenwart Ball," I said. "Was that not what was written on the note the footman gave you? That you had to go and attend to your brother?"

Ferdy had thrown that in my face before, and as I watched Karl for a negative reaction, I suddenly wondered if that was what the note truly said.

No, Ferdy would not have lied about that.

He was too pleased at his cleverness, that he had told me the truth without me realizing it.

Before I could say something else, Karl's fists clenched at his side. "I did not realize that footmen could be bribed so easily. You are correct. I was called to go and extract him from another potential scandal."

"I am sorry for my curiosity," I said once more, noting his frustration. "I did not mean to make you upset. I would prefer to have no lies between us."

Outside my room, I could hear Lady POW approaching, and I was relieved my time alone with Karl was nearly over. As much as I was excited to learn what I could, there was still nothing to prove that he was behind the attack on Prague Castle—at least, not that I could see.

"It is understandable that you are curious." Karl gave me a hardened look. "And I am happy to satisfy your need for answers, so long as your loyalty is to me."

He certainly did not look happy. My earlier concerns resurfaced in my stomach, and I felt it twist into more uncomfortable contortions. Had I just risked Karl's favor, in order to find out about Ferdy?

THE ORDER OF THE CRYSTAL DAGGERS

"Of course my loyalty is to you," I lied. "I did not mean to cause trouble. What a burden you must bear over this. After all, you are an honorable man."

If my flattery was excessive, Karl did not seem to notice. He took my pity in stride, only nodding. "Thank you. Ferdinand has long been a thorn in my side. Maybe it is good you know about him. There are not many I can admit my frustrations to when it comes to him."

"If he is as deplorable as you say, I can certainly sympathize."

"It is not just his personal choices, Ella. It is his whole approach to life. When one is blessed with privilege and opportunity, one is responsible for the betterment of other people."

At his remark, I was intrigued enough to risk a daring question. "Even if the people don't want it?"

"Of course," Karl said. "It is the best way to ensure only good choices are made. When there are too many options, a man chooses whatever one benefits himself first. What of others? Ferdinand believes that freedom matters more than order, nobility, and education. His own choices in these matters have led to his life of chaos, a disregard for the Bohemian aristocracy, and a disdain for the knowledge found in the best universities."

He sighed. "It is better that those who know best lead the way, even if compulsion is necessary. This is the only way for civilization to progress."

As Karl stood there, I felt a little afraid of him. He was a proud man, and he would not take being found a fool lightly. I did not know how he would react in discovering I was attempting to use him to find connections between several recent murders and an ongoing political coup.

It would be even worse when he realized I was in love with his brother.

"Here is the tea, Eleanora," Lady Penelope called, entering the room with Jaqueline close behind her. Thankfully, Karl quickly resumed his respectful demeanor.

"Thank you, Grandmother," I called, straightening up against the couch. "Would you like a cup, too, Karl—I mean, Mr. Marcelin?"

I gave him a sheepish look as I said his name. It was proof enough that I was becoming closer to him. He gave me a small smile before he shook his head. Behind me, Lady POW frowned. She seemed to understand I did not find out anything relating to our mission.

It was hard to feel bad about that. I did want to find a way to trap Lord Maximillian. We needed to understand his role and Karl was our best lead. But just as Karl felt some relief in confiding to me the truth, however reluctantly, I was pleased to hear Ferdy was alive and well, even if he was annoying his brother.

"I must decline for now, Madame. I believe I must be going. I have numerous meetings to attend today, some of which I have forgotten. But I would love to call upon you in the near future." Karl's hand tightened in mine almost painfully, and I knew he was looking for reassurance from me that I would receive him again.

I gave him a brilliant but false smile back. "I would certainly hope so."

"Would you be well enough to attend a concert this week, my lady?"

I glanced over at Lady POW, looking for her permission. I already knew she would want me to go, but I was still disappointed when she nodded her approval.

"A concert would be lovely, though I regret we will not be able to dance." I gave him a small, modest smile. "It would be an honor to join you, sir."

"Thank you. I will send out the formal invitations after the arrangements are made," Karl promised before he turned to Lady Penelope. "A pleasure, as always, Madame."

"I will see you out," Lady Penelope offered.

Jaqueline handed me a cup of tea as Karl gave me one last lingering gaze. I smiled brightly at him as he left, pretending to believe a lifetime of bliss was before us.

The bliss only came when he was gone.

"Well, miss?" Jaqueline asked. Her eyes, a light mix of green and brown, glittered with excitement. "Were you able to find out his secrets?"

"No," I said, thinking of Karl briefly before turning my thoughts to Ferdy. "But I at least had him admit to a few of them."

Lady Penelope poured her own cup of tea. "Well, then, tell me what you learned. I hope you didn't disappoint me."

I sipped my tea carefully, hiding a snort of laughter. I was already a disappointment. While I wanted to redeem myself to Lady POW, I knew I could not do it at the expense of Ferdy's safety, and I was not willing to lose Ben over it.

I stirred the spoon in my tea slowly. I decided I could keep Lady Penelope distracted while I tried to fix everything.

So I gave her a short summary of what had transpired between Karl and me—leaving out any mention of Ferdy. At the end, I was surprised to see Lady Penelope smile.

"Excellent," she said. "We can expect to see him more in the near future. And in the meantime, he sounds like he genuinely likes you."

"He barely knows me."

"He knows about Ben," Lady Penelope pointed out. "And there is no telling what Teresa Marie might have told him. Nobody can give you information like a scorned rival."

"That still doesn't mean much." I sniffed, thinking of Lady Teresa Marie, Lord Maximillian's spoiled daughter. It was not hard to picture her, shaking her amber locks back from her young face.

One of the conditions of Karl getting financial support from Lord Maximillian had been agreeing to marry her. Karl was not interested in that, even though he wanted the support for the Minister-President position. Lady Teresa Marie, who had been previously set up to marry Alex, was not happy the secret heir to the Bohemian throne had turned her down.

She was especially not happy he had snubbed her in favor of me, especially since I was Lady Cecilia's stepdaughter and former servant.

"Ben is not a dark secret of our family," I said. "There's a perfectly good reason he is not moving in Society. He has chosen to stay away because of his leg. And he seems to be good at working for the Order."

"Amir has been doing well with him."

I was glad to hear her compliment both Amir and Ben. My brother's progress meant a lot to him, and it was nice to see Lady POW held Amir in high esteem, even if they could not entirely trust each other.

"One hopes," Lady Penelope murmured, "that you will one day do as well with Harshad."

I nearly dropped my tea, cut deeply at her sudden derision.

She excused herself before I could say anything in return.

As she marched away from me, I glared at her back, hoping she would be able to feel my displeasure. "One hopes that one day I will be able to prove you wrong," I muttered, knowing she was unable to hear me.

THE ORDER OF THE CRYSTAL DAGGERS

8

◇

The rest of the week passed uneventfully, as if it was allowing me time to recover from Karl's visit. After he left, I did not think much of anything again, allowing myself to fall into a daily routine of working instead of waiting. Ben was still avoiding me, Amir was never around, and Harshad was his usual quiet self. Lady Penelope was moody and distant, and I did not know whether I preferred her that way or not.

Days later, I was lying on my bed, staring up at the ceiling, when I finally decided I had waited long enough.

Previously, after working with Ben and Harshad, I would retire to my room, throw myself onto my pillows, and allow rest to come. My body screamed for relief, and sleep was usually kind enough to answer it at the end of each day.

Until now.

There was a sadness inside of me, one I both recognized and did not recognize. I could have blamed Karl for my troubles, but I decided more responsibility belonged to Lady POW. She had interrupted my session with Harshad earlier, barging into the room only to announce Karl's formal invitation had arrived.

"Karl Marcelin has sent a personal invitation for you," Lady Penelope told me. "He requests your attendance at a concert at the *Stavovské divadlo* tomorrow night."

"Why is it such big news?" I asked, using her arrival as an excuse to catch my breath—for all the good it did. As if he knew, Harshad motioned for me to finish the various fighting sequences before giving Lady Penelope my full attention. "He said he was going to send out an invitation."

"That was *two days* ago." She emphasized the words carefully and slowly, as if I was struggling to learn a new language or understand basic arithmetic.

When I frowned and kept punching the bag in front of me, she only sighed.

"You still don't know much about Society, do you?" Lady POW shook her head. "If his interest in you wanes, we will have a harder time finding information. There is also the matter of your reputation."

I stopped moving as Harshad gave me a nod of approval. I was finished with his assigned work. "I don't care about that."

"You might want to. The *Stavovské divadlo*, the Estates Theatre, is hosting a special concert to celebrate the new year. If Karl shows up with you, especially for your triumphant return to Society, he will be showing the people that Prague can return from disaster. He will be seen as an inspiration, and he can use that to transform into a leader."

"I think you are giving him too much credit. I can't imagine why that would be inspiring." I wiped the dripping sweat off my forehead with the leather of my stealth habit's small skirt. "But it will be nice to get out of the manor."

Even if I have to join Karl for the evening.

"I will send out your acceptance and get Marguerite to prepare your dress at once," Lady Penelope said, already skipping out the door.

Once she was gone, Ben snorted. "She sure can be frustrating at times."

"I know." I gave Ben a smile, but he ignored me and went back to working on another round of fighting sequences. I looked over at Harshad.

He wore his usual unreadable face, the stoic expression more enigmatic than ever as he turned away from me, looking toward the window. Harshad was content to ignore Lady Penelope, and at the time, I wished I could, too.

Hours had passed since then, but my sadness only increased. I glanced over at the drawer where Ferdy's combs and my parents' heirlooms were tucked away.

I missed him.

I missed all of them.

My life was very different from the previous year. Last Christmas, Ben and I had been ordered to help Cecilia prepare for an extravagant dinner for several of our rich neighbors. I was certain that, while she believed Alex's marriage arrangements were settled, she was hoping to find someone for Prissy to marry, too.

At the last moment, a large winter storm had come over the area, and no one was able to come. Rather than allow the staff to celebrate the holidays, we were ordered to throw out the food and stay in our rooms.

But despite Cecilia's anger, Betsy and Mavis, my closest friends, had made little gifts for me and Ben. We celebrated together in the barn. It was freezing but huddled around the fire, we were content. Ben and I took turns reading from the books I had pilfered from the library, and Betsy, at Ben's prodding, brought us food she had saved from being thrown out.

This year, Betsy and Mavis were gone, Ben was ignoring me, and I spent my free time working with Harshad and pretending to read. I barely noticed the cold winter days as snow began to fall and accumulate.

I am alone.

I wondered, briefly, what Ferdy would think of me if he saw me at that moment. At the thought of his gloating, or more likely the thought of his sympathy, I sat up.

There was no reason I had to lie here and wait for things to happen, I decided. It was time to go and make things right, starting with Ben.

Squaring my shoulders, I made my way out of my room and headed toward Ben's. My brother had ignored me for long enough. I had apologized and given him some time alone, and he was still begrudgingly diffident.

Thankfully, we had a mission, just as Amir and Lady POW did, and if he would not reconcile with me in one area of our lives, he would still work with me on another. I could certainly force him using that leverage.

Still, I said a silent, desperate prayer as I knocked on his door.

"I'm coming!" he called enthusiastically.

I was about to tell him it was me when he opened the door. His excitement faded at once. "What are you doing here?"

"Who did you expect?" I pushed past him, walking into the room.

Before I could press for an answer, Ben groaned.

"Why are you here?"

I gave him my best smile. "I have a favor to ask of you, *brácha.*"

"My answer is no."

"I didn't even tell you what I wanted," I objected.

"I know you, Nora. I'm not helping you go see Ferdy." He crossed his arms. He narrowed his eyes at me; his black eye, still slightly puffy, made his acerbic expression more comical than aggravating. "I'm a cripple, not your caretaker."

"You're both," I snapped back before I remembered I was here to make amends. I did not appreciate his attitude, but we were not going to be able to get along if I reciprocated.

"I'm sorry." I took a deep breath. "I came here to say I'm sorry, about everything. I was upset the other week, and you were right. I still … I still don't want to think about Ferdy."

"Then why do you want to go see him?" Ben asked.

"I'm not here to go see him. I wanted to go to the Cabal. I thought if we can go see Clavan and Eliezer, we might be able to find a lead on where Cecilia and everyone else is."

"I've already been there a few times. I didn't learn anything. Why don't you go with Amir, since you're his favorite now?"

"His favorite?" I paused for a moment, and then I shook my head. "That's not true, and Amir is friends with both of us. Even if it was true, that has nothing to do with this."

"So you say." Ben rolled his eyes. "Either way, I'm not going with you."

"It's been a few weeks," I pressed. "Surely there's something new for us to find. Come on, please? I'm tired of just training. You've been able to see our friends there and I haven't, and we do need to find out what we can. Even if we don't find anything, we can at least say we tried."

There was a long minute of silence before Ben softened and sighed, ever so slightly. "Harshad will be upset if we are tired in the morning."

"Maybe Clavan can give us some tea to take home." I smiled brightly. "I know you want to find Betsy and Mavis as much as I do. I'm worried, especially since they disappeared with Alex. There is no telling what happened to them with him around."

"That is true. I haven't thought about what might have happened to Alex." He shook his head. "I'll go with you, but you have to follow my lead. If we do run into Ferdy while we're out, I don't want you causing trouble."

"Me?" I laughed. "You were the one who looked like you wanted to kill him the other day."

"He hurt you."

Ben's voice was conflicted, and I paused. All of my life, my brother had been the one to protect me. Even though I knew he was angry at me, I knew he would have felt responsible for my pain—even if it had nothing to do with him and everything to do with a roguish prince.

THE ORDER OF THE CRYSTAL DAGGERS

"That doesn't matter now," I said quietly. "Betsy and Mavis, Tulia, and the others all need our help. And as for Ferdy … I don't think we will have to worry about him at the Cabal."

"Why?" Ben asked.

Amir had warned me Lady POW was pressuring Ben for my secrets, but it would have been amusing to tell him that Ferdy was Karl's younger brother, playing the part of the good prince with his family for the holidays, instead of running around Prague dressed like a pauper. I could picture Ben's reaction—the initial shock, the eventual anger, and then the list of questions I would not be able to answer.

The thought of those questions, and the certainty of my complete humiliation, prevented me from saying anything.

Instead, I turned toward a window. "It's cold outside. He's probably not going to be walking out in the winter this late at night."

Ben's gaze followed mine, where the ground was still sprinkled with a small layer of white powder. "You have a point, but you could just as easily be wrong. What if we do run into him?"

If Ferdy did dare to show his face to me, knowing my heart was tender and my mission was dangerous, I would likely kill him out of frustration. I might have wanted him, but I still wanted him to be safe more.

I did not tell Ben what I was thinking. Instead, I shrugged. "Thanks to all of Harshad's training, I can take care of him."

When Ben laughed, even though it was a small one, I knew I had won.

"I don't want to tell Lady POW about this," I added, as Ben reached for his shoes.

"You might as well tell her," Ben said. "She finds things out anyway. Remember how she caught us coming back from the Cabal last time?"

"I know, but she's got secrets of her own. I should be entitled to a few myself." I reached out and took his hand. "And, for now, Ferdy is one of them. I don't want her to know about him."

"What happened with him, exactly?" Ben asked. "I know you saw him at the castle."

"He knows about the Order," I said. That was the truth.

"And?"

"And he did not want anything to do with me after that."

THE ORDER OF THE CRYSTAL DAGGERS

That was a lie. My mind taunted me with the memory of Ferdy's embrace, the beautiful horror of our fiery passion, a self-sentenced penance far worse than any I could have been given.

Once we made it to the stables, I watched as Ben made a few adjustments on his brace. "Is that new?"

"Yes." Ben did not look at me. "After it broke the other day, I decided to try out a few ideas to help with our new activities. See? I added some padding at the joints to help with the clacking sound, and it fits inside my boot better."

"Can you ride using it?"

"I can, but since we're going to go into the city tonight, we should walk."

"Walk? It's going to take more than an hour to do that," I groaned.

"Lady POW is more likely to notice we are gone if there's a horse missing," Ben said. "And Dox is getting old. Let him rest."

"He's not that old. *Táta* bought him the summer before *Máma* died," I remembered. "He called him 'Dox,' for doxology since it was a miracle he had gotten such a good price on a horse in his prime."

"That was fifteen years ago. See? He is old."

I said nothing in reply. Although Ben was right, even though I was attempting to get along with him, I did not want to give him more accolades than he needed.

"*Otec* did always have a strange way with names," Ben added, almost as if he sensed my reluctant concession. "'Benedict' was short for 'benediction.'"

"It seems to be appropriate, on both accounts."

Ben brushed off my teasing. "Well, I suppose it's a miracle now that Dox has managed to survive this long."

"We survived, too," I reminded Ben gently. If I had been younger, I might have reached over and hugged him in comfort. As it was, I was still tempted to reach for him.

Instead, I buried myself into my cloak, already blistering against the chill as we made our way toward the heart of Prague.

The city was not far from our home. Riding in the carriage or up on Dox, I could cross the Vltava within thirty minutes, and that usually included a stop at Tulia's cottage. We passed by her former home, and I

THE ORDER OF THE CRYSTAL DAGGERS

could still see a few of the remaining walls. The fire had devoured the small house weeks before, and now the snow covered a good portion of the scorched wood.

In the background, Prague's city skyline glowed with lamplight from within and moonlight from without. From where we were, I could not see the broken, collapsed castle walls, nor could I hear the city's chatter.

As I studied the castle walls, I saw a few rooms lit up with light, and I wondered if Ferdy was there. Karl was staying there, too, I recalled, and I chuckled at the thought of them forced to dine together. I knew it was wrong to laugh at another's misery, but if I could find no joy in my own despair, laughing at someone else's did not seem so unnatural.

"What is it?" Ben asked. "What is so amusing?"

"Oh … I was thinking of Karl," I said, scrambling to think of something else. "He said he was staying at the castle. I thought … I was thinking it would be amusing if we just kidnapped him."

"We could do that." Ben's tone was serious as he considered my jest. "You know him, so we would be able to get close enough. If he is there without Lord Maximillian, he would not be able to call for help. And we could likely get around the guards. King Ferdinand already knows about the Order."

"I do know that Empress Maria Anna trusts me, at least enough she did not tell Karl about me," I added. Philip had told me that before, and Lady Penelope confirmed it. "You know, she trusted *Máma*, too, during the Revolution."

"Did she?"

"*Máma* was the one who protected her, along with *Táta*." I glanced back at the castle, thinking of Karl. "She was pregnant at the time."

"Well, I was born just after the Revolution," Ben said.

"I meant the Empress, not *Máma*."

"Well, she was pregnant, because I was born just before 1849." Ben shrugged. "I guess they were both pregnant at the same time."

It was strange to think that. I had never thought about it before, but Ben was right. My mother and the former empress had both been pregnant at the same time.

Maybe that was the real reason they were able to trust each other, I thought. There had to be something to motherhood that bound women together, the same way that my life was connected to Karl and Ferdy, in that I could understand the uniqueness of a sibling's love, or the lack thereof.

"Ben?" My voice dropped to a whisper, as though I knew it was treachery to even think such a thing. "Do you think we made the right decision to join the Order?"

"Of course." Ben's answer was immediate and certain, and I could not stop myself from envying him. He had all of his doubts answered at the beginning.

"Why do you ask that?" Ben pressed, stepping closer to me as we crossed the Vltava, heading toward the Jewish Quarter where the Cabal was located. "Don't you like it?"

"Well, I've failed at it," I said. "And … what about *Táta*? He was poisoned with the Order's secret weapon. Who could have done that, other than a member of the Order?"

"There are always traitors on every side."

His answer did not give me comfort. It sounded too much like a scripted answer, something he had overheard and decided to believe until a better theory or certain proof came along.

"I've been thinking … maybe we should find out what happened when *Máma* was here before," I said. "I know Lady POW does not want to talk about it, but she says she knows that our father's murder and the current political coup are related."

Ben sighed, his steps slowing down as we came up to the entrance of the Cabal. "I don't know, Nora. If Lady POW does not want to reach out to the League, she likely has a good reason."

"Amir and Harshad are both part of the League, as is Lady Penelope herself," I pointed out.

"She would know firsthand how treacherous some of the members are then."

"Stop making excuses for her. We should learn about that ourselves. And besides, if Lady POW is keeping secrets, she might be lying to us as well."

"She's been a good leader so far. What could she be lying about?"

"Plenty. She's a woman who puts business before family, remember?" I bit my lip, not sure what else I could say. Ben's disinterest made me worry that I could not trust him with my doubts, and as much as I knew it was

THE ORDER OF THE CRYSTAL DAGGERS

true, I hated to think that I was right to keep Ferdy's secrets from him, too.

"Maybe we can learn some things about the past when we get back," Ben said, clearly conflicted. I saw him avoid my gaze as I looked over at him. "But first, we are here to look for Betsy and Mavis."

I sighed. He was right about that. We could worry about multiple things at one time, but we could only do one thing at a time, too.

"I feel so useless sometimes, Ben," I confessed. "There is so much evil in the world, so many questions that will always be unanswered. And there are so many other people who don't seem to care."

He gave me a scrutinizing look. "Do you want to quit the Order?"

I bristled, feeling like he had missed my point. "*Máma* did."

And she kept her own mother from learning about us, too—maybe to protect us.

Philip said before that Ferdy had been kept a secret from the Order and the others who protected the king during the Revolution. Was it possible that in joining the Order, while I was able to learn more about my mother and who she truly was, I was actually working against her wishes?

"Nora." Ben tugged on my cloak. "We can't leave the Order now. There are people we need to save."

Even if I did not feel good about it, I knew Ben was right. I could almost hear Harshad's voice inside my head, telling me to focus. We were here to find information on Betsy and Mavis, and the rest of our former household.

I did not have time for doubts.

But … but there would likely *always* be people to save, countries to help, maybe even rulers to protect.

"I don't know if we will ever be able to leave," I whispered. "Do you think we can?"

"Why would you want to?" Ben said. When I only shrugged, he sighed. "Leaving is one thing that Lady POW never did mention to us. We know she has been doing this for decades now. I suppose it's possible she doesn't know how to quit herself."

That was a distinct possibility, I thought. Lady POW did not seem to give up, and she would see quitting as giving up.

We fell into silence, as the Cabal came into sight.

THE ORDER OF THE CRYSTAL DAGGERS

It was time to see if we could find some answers to my many questions. I straightened my shoulders, determined to remain hopeful.

9
◊

The Cabal seemed different as Ben and I entered. Last time, the warmth of the atmosphere had leaped out to greet me, to pull me in and absorb me into its setting. This time, I felt more like a stranger, as though I had walked into the wrong building by mistake.

It was mostly empty, like it had been the day Tulia and I visited for the first time, and I could not stop myself from wondering if I had imagined it differently with Ferdy by my side.

The long, wooden bar at the back of the room was polished to a shine. Several tables cluttered the room in front of it, while a few large chairs were arranged in front of a fireplace. The embers burned low, already spent from the cold weather; I saw the small fires blink at me from among the soot, like demon eyes pulled out of the past.

Ben hesitated more than once as we made our way through the pub. My stomach briefly clenched, wondering if it was possible Ferdy would come. I could easily see him stealing away to see Clavan and his other friends, breaking away from his time at the castle with his family.

But as I walked closer to the bar, I knew Ferdy was nowhere to be found; his absence was as noticeable and as tangible as his presence.

"Ben." A familiar voice, coupled with a cloud of pipe smoke, called out in greeting from the far end of the room.

"Jarl." My brother instantly cheered. We shuffled over to his table, where I could see he was reading a book and sipping from a glass of beer. With his smoker's coat and a pair of thick, half-moon spectacles perched on his nose, Jarl looked much older than me and Ben, even though he was in his late twenties.

"I cannot tell you how delighted I am to see you," Jarl said. "Faye is working with her mother, and Clavan is seeing to the business side of things tonight."

"There are not a lot of people here," I said.

"Which is good for me, and possibly bad for you." Jarl stood politely, giving Ben a nod.

I glanced around. There was a priest reading his Bible alone, and a pair of travelers who settled into a corner at the far end of the bar.

343

One of them caught my gaze and gave me a brilliant smile. He was wearing a greatcoat, while his bright blonde hair, curled and styled high, twinkled under the bar lights. I was first embarrassed at the exchange, and Ben, seeing my discomfort, stepped between us. But when Ben turned his full attention to Jarl, I saw the man's piercing green eyes settle and stay on me.

I tried to shake off the ominous feeling of being watched. It was only when Jarl pulled out my chair that I managed to forget about the man at the bar.

"Thank you for joining me," Jarl said.

"Of course." Ben gave him a friendly clap on the shoulder before he took his seat. "I know you enjoy having an audience, and the options are limited tonight."

"Usually Ferdy helps me out in that regard, but he hasn't been here for a few days."

At Ferdy's name, spoken so casually, my world broke. My previous embarrassment shifted into something more morose; I felt the fear of upcoming mortification, the terror of a confrontation I did not want, and the fervent wish for a divine reprieve.

"Where is he?" Ben gripped his hands together, and I could hear him cracking his knuckles. I frowned at him, hoping he would calm down. I did not want to make a scene, and this was the wrong place for Ben and me to hold a rematch to our earlier battle with Harshad.

"He frequents the Cabal but goes missing from time to time." Jarl took off his glasses and tucked them into a pocket on the front of his coat. "But since you're here, I can assume he is coming? He owes me some money from our last bet."

I shook my head. "I haven't seen him lately, either. My apologies."

Jarl waved away my regret. "If I didn't know he was good for it, I'd hunt him down. But no matter. Now, keep me from perishing from boredom. Tell me of the excitement around town. Working as much as I do, you always hear the good gossip last."

"We are quite bored ourselves," I said. "We were hoping Clavan and Eliezer would be here."

"Clavan's in the back, and Elie might be here later. My Uncle Rhys came into town, and the two of them can talk for days, if they can find the time, and I know Elie would be quick to do just that. Zipporah's been keeping Elie busy with all the babies she's been tending to of late."

THE ORDER OF THE CRYSTAL DAGGERS

"Zipporah?"

"Elie's wife is a midwife." Jarl took a long puff from his pipe before grinning. "I'm surprised you didn't know. Eliezer repeats it quite frequently during our meetings. I think he wants to remind us that at some point in our lives, the difference between life and death might come down to how nicely we've treated him over the years."

I had heard that before, I realized. But it was not because of Eliezer; Clavan was the one who had mentioned it. Eliezer's wife had worked with Dr. Artha before.

Inspiration struck. "Has she seen a lot more patients because of Dr. Artha's death earlier this year?" I asked.

Ben glanced over at me in surprise, while Jarl merely nodded. "I don't imagine it is much different. They worked well together, but some patients do not want to be tended to by a Jewess. She is more than a midwife, working with herbs and other medicines."

"That reminds me," Ben spoke up. His voice had an eager tone to it, one I shared as much as I recognized. "I need to buy some special herbs for our companion, Tulia."

"Zipporah's likely got it," Jarl said. He chuckled. "She has everything. Ferdy's been looking for better pipe tobacco for me for weeks, trying to prove she doesn't have better connections than he does."

"Did he prove himself the victor in that bet?" I asked, unable to stop myself.

Laughing, Jarl blew out a stream of smoke thick enough I had to swallow back a cough. "Honestly, I'm not keeping score. He gives me plenty for free, while Eliezer insists Zipporah keeps raising her prices so I will stop smoking in here. He insists it is not kosher and I only laugh at him, knowing Clavan would easily smoke one along with me."

"Would she happen to be around?" Ben asked, drawing the focus back to our mission. "I'd love to see about buying some of her stock."

"She only comes in here every once in a while, but Clavan can always send word if you need an order filled."

At that moment, the door behind the bar opened. A bald man came out, carrying a pair of cups in each hand. The light reflected off his head and the small pair of rimmed glasses precariously balanced on his slightly crooked nose. He smiled in greeting as he made his way to our table.

"My ears are burning more than my eyes, so I am not surprised to hear my name, and I am especially not surprised to find it coming out of this knucklehead," Clavan said, nodding his regards to Jarl. "What lies is he spreading about me now?"

Ben and I laughed congenially as Jarl and Clavan chatted, exchanging barbs and insults with the familiarity of a close-knit family. Their easy conversation reminded me of Ferdy even more. It was not until Jarl mentioned him again that I remembered I was supposed to forget about him.

"Ella's wondering where Ferdy has been lately," Jarl said.

Clavan turned and glanced at Ben. Before he could say anything, Ben shook his head.

"She doesn't want to talk about Ferdy," Ben insisted. A second later, he winced as I stomped on his foot. With Harshad's training, I knew it had to hurt, but he really did not need to announce to everyone that I was upset.

"I'd much rather talk about the local gossip," I declared, struggling to put on a brave face. "What news can you tell us? Are any important things happening? Any more murders?"

"The weather has slowed the trickle of news somewhat," Clavan said, giving me a smirk as he adjusted his glasses. "Surely you can't be so bored that you want to hear about murder, Lady Ella?"

I ignored his question. "Were you able to find the man who murdered Dr. Artha, Mr. Clavan?"

He stared at me for a few seconds, likely weighing out whether or not I should be indulged. But he relaxed a moment later with a shrug. "No."

At his solemn expression, I felt a rush of shame at my insensitivity. Dr. Artha had known my father, just as he had known Clavan. I remembered Dr. Artha as a decent man, and even if I was uncomfortable at my own loss, I did not have a right to cause further despair. "I'm sorry. I was hoping for better news."

"He was a good man, and he made peace with God and his life," Clavan said. "There is no better news than that."

"It would be better knowing justice has been done," Ben said.

"Better for us, maybe, but not much different for Sigmund." Jarl puffed his pipe a few more times with a tepid smile.

We dipped into a remorseful silence. Ben took a sip of the drink Clavan had brought him, and I just stared at the table top, briefly noting the title of Jarl's book. From the small amount of German I knew, I saw it was *The Evils of Revolution.*

If revolution was evil, I thought, it was good to prevent it as much as possible.

I glanced back at Clavan. "Jarl mentioned that your friend's wife sells herbs and medicine. Do you know if she is around? My companion, Tulia, is in need of some for her health."

I did not like lying to Clavan. He turned to me with that ageless look on his face, the one that made me wonder if he could listen to my mind as well as speak to my most ardent desires.

"She is not here right now, but I can arrange an introduction for you. If you leave me your direction, I will send word when I can to you."

"That would be wonderful."

"Do you know what you need? I can give her a list. Sickness waits for no one in this world." Clavan pulled out his glasses and put them on, the small round frames adding a touch of whimsy to his character.

Ben began rambling off a varied list, starting with sage and rosemary. He slipped the silver thallis in along with thyme and nutmeg and cinnamon.

Clavan paused as he wrote. He said nothing until he was done, and then he looked over at Ben's eye. "She should have all of this. None of this is because of your fight, is it?"

"No." Ben's reply was too quick. When I looked over at him, concerned, Clavan only laughed.

"I know Ferdy suffered some damage, too," he said. "Elie told me he came by his house and interrupted their Hanukkah celebration after you were finished with him."

"Fight?" I repeated.

Ben groaned, and at once, everything became clear: Ben had gone into the city, found Ferdy, and they ended up fighting.

I grabbed Ben's arm and hauled him up out of his chair. "Excuse us," I said, my teeth ground together forcefully as I struggled to maintain my manners. I pinched Ben's arm to keep him from saying anything. He likely already knew I would refuse to let him escape my anger, whether we left or not. "I do believe we must be going now. I will look for your note."

I did not wait for Clavan and Jarl to extend their own well-wishes or wave goodbye, but as I passed by the bar, the man with the green eyes spoke to me.

"I'd go easy on him, *chérie*. Why, Society would be horrified to see a temper such as yours unrestrained."

I whirled around to face him, watching as he laughed. For the first time, I noticed his companion. While Prague held its share of traveling foreigners, I had only ever seen a few dark-skinned men before, and I faltered at the sight of them together.

"Oh, dear, I do believe you've shocked her, Didier." The man with the green eyes shook his head, still smirking. "No need to worry, *chérie*, we are just strangers in town having a bit of fun. I mean, of course we are having fun at your expense now, but still, we are quite harmless, I can assure you. You can run along home in peace."

At his teasing, Ben shuffled free of my grip. "Don't talk to my sister."

The man cheered even further at his new audience. "You're a gem of a brother, I'm sure, and a handsome one at that. But you need not worry about me, good sir. If anything, I was on your side, was I not? I'd hate to see her beat you. Women with incorrigible tempers are such nasty creatures, aren't they, Didier?"

The man beside him gave him a disapproving look, and I took the moment of silence to grab Ben's arm again. I tugged him out of the Cabal.

The men had disrupted my anger, but the minute Ben and I were outside, I felt it return in full force.

"What was that all about?"

"I don't know," Ben said. "I've never noticed that man before."

"I'm not talking about him!" I put my hands on my hips. "And you know it. Why did you attack Ferdy?"

"That's none of your business."

"Of course it's my business!"

"It's my job to take care of you, whether you like it or not. That's why I stood up to that obnoxious man in there for you, too."

"It's *my* job to take care of myself."

"Please. You couldn't even fight me before. At the mere mention of Ferdy, you lost."

THE ORDER OF THE CRYSTAL DAGGERS

I glared at him. "So you went to take care of him for me?"

"Yes." Ben returned my glare with one of his own, one without any hint of remorse. "Sort of. I didn't know I would run into him."

I turned away and started walking back home, struggling to keep my voice down. "I can't believe you did that. I wish you would've just left him alone. I didn't want you to hurt him!"

A new thought struck me hard and fast. What if Ben had hurt Ferdy, and that was why he had stayed away from the Cabal? *How can Ferdy ever forgive me for this?*

"He hurt you," Ben said.

"Well, now you've hurt me, too, all because you stuck your nose in my business where it doesn't belong," I snapped. "I didn't want you to bother with him at all. Now he probably hates me."

"What does that matter? You told me he hated you before, because of the Order."

My cheeks flushed red. "No, he didn't. Oh, goodness. Did he say something to you? What did you tell him?"

The thought of Ferdy admitting the truth terrified me. I did not want him to be in danger, and I did not want the former empress to lose her faith in me. I was supposed to be protecting him, and thanks to my brother, I had failed once more to do my duty.

"Tell me what he said!" I gripped Ben's collar hard, astonished at the sudden rush accompanying my strength and fury.

"Oh, now you want to fight me?" Ben shook his head.

"I will," I warned. "I will, and I won't stop until you tell me everything."

Ben and I stared down at each other for a long moment, and I felt the world crumble between us. If my mother had been my sunshine, and my father the earth, Ben was my moon, and I felt darkness fully overtake me in that moment.

Lady Penelope was right. She was right. I can't believe she was right.

Ben had failed me. He had failed me, and I had never seen it coming.

I stepped back from him, shaking my head. "I can't believe this."

Behind me, Ben shrugged. "If you must know, and I suppose you must, he didn't say anything useful. He commended me on being a good brother. Even after we fought, he tried to make nice with me. He said he never meant to hurt you, but that's what anyone would say after a fight."

I did not think Ferdy would tell Ben the truth; it was good to hear it confirmed, even if I still hated Ben's role in the whole situation.

"If you want to be a good brother," I said, "just stay away from him from now on."

"Why do you even care? Ferdy doesn't care about you."

Ben's words were soft but angry. I gave him the only answer I could.

"It doesn't matter what I feel. He knows about the Order, Ben, and scuffling with him in the back of an alley is not going to make him stay quiet. If we want him to keep our secret, it's best to leave him alone. Don't tell me you didn't think of that."

Ben said nothing, and I scoffed. "You didn't think anything through at all, did you?"

"I'm not the only one with weaknesses," Ben shot back.

I crossed my arms over my chest. "I'll work on mine by myself, and you can work on yours alone, too."

We fell into a bitter silence as we made our way home. The journey back seemed so much longer and harder. There was much less of a chill in the air, or maybe I had grown accustomed to it. It was also possible that I was just numb from everything. That I was too afraid to let myself feel anything.

It was only when I fell back onto my bed that I allowed myself the freedom to cry, to let the tidal waves of my loneliness and sadness flood over me.

350

THE ORDER OF THE CRYSTAL DAGGERS

10

◊

I had been hoping that the trip into the city would close the rift between me and Ben, but it only made it worse. That night, I did not sleep well at all. Getting up for Harshad's training sessions the following morning went against every natural instinct I possessed. Dread crept through me as I made my way down to the parlor.

But when I entered the room, Ben was nowhere to be found. I did not know whether I was more grateful or upset, and if I was upset, I did not know if it was more because of Ben or because of myself.

It was almost as though he suspected my thoughts on the matter, I thought bitterly. Especially since Ben was the one who had been so concerned we would upset Harshad with our late-night outing.

"There you are, Eleanora," Harshad said. True to his usual self, he was sitting at the desk in the corner of the room, working on some notes in a foreign scrawl. "I have been waiting for you."

I studied him, watching as his aged hands moved his pen swiftly across the stationary, transforming his thoughts into symbols I could not decipher any more clearly. With Ben's absence, I had a sudden appreciation for Harshad's consistency. I might have had reservations about him, but I could see why he would stay with someone like Lady POW for so long; he was a man who knew how to dismantle chaos, and it was possible he even looked forward to the job.

Before I could ask Harshad if Ben was out on assignment for Lady POW again, I saw there was a new presence in the parlor.

The figure stood in front of the fireplace, wearing a hooded cloak, much like the ones I had seen Harshad and Amir wear when I first met them. Before I could say anything, Harshad looked up from his desk.

"Eleanora, I am pleased to introduce you to another member of the Order."

The hood fell away, revealing another foreign face, this one of a warrior maiden. A looped braid of pure black hair settled on her head before it fell away, hanging down her back. Her slanted eyes were dark, closer to black than brown, as she watched me. It was impossible to guess her age; she seemed timeless, too wise and watchful, too still to be a part of our world.

351

"This is Xiana," Harshad said. "She is the Order's leading expert on herbs and medicines, as well as one of our best fighters. She has agreed to come here and assist us with our inquiries."

"You make it sound as though I had a choice," Xiana murmured, and I was astounded to see Harshad smile.

"Xiana, this is Miss Eleanora Svobodová, Dezda's daughter." Harshad cleared his throat, quickly wiping away any trace of emotion. "She is our newest member."

Xiana gave me a bow, bending her body forward. She was clearly from the Orient, and I wondered if that was really how they were allowed to address each other. I curtsied in reply. At Xiana's wry smile, I knew I had amused her with my manners.

"A daughter for Eleanor at last, I see, along with her son," Xiana murmured. Her voice was so precise, almost as if it were constrained to each perfect syllable. Her gaze never wavered as she smiled. "How wonderful it was that she was able to keep you."

"I certainly think so," I replied, mustering up a smile at the mention of my mother and Ben.

I saw a glitter of laughter in her gaze. "It is nice to meet you, Eleanora. I am sure I will enjoy teaching you while I am here."

"You're going to be teaching me?" I glanced around the room. "And Ben, too?"

"Benedict has been given a new assignment by Lady Penelope," Harshad said, and I knew at once it was no coincidence that Ben was not here. After we had returned home, Ben went to see Lady Penelope. I could understand why he would ask her to be free from me, but I hated that he had severed more ties between us.

Xiana cleared her throat delicately. "I understand you need a new sparring partner."

"Xiana is a fine tutor," Harshad replied behind me. "She will allow me to help you with some more complicated moves, Eleanora. She will begin to assist us tomorrow since she has only arrived."

"What about Ben?" I asked. "Will I still have to fight him? What is he supposed to do now?"

"Lady Penelope has reassigned him, and that is all you need to know for now," Harshad said.

"Why?"

THE ORDER OF THE CRYSTAL DAGGERS

Harshad's brow furrowed in irritation, but he answered me nonetheless. "Do not forget, we are still looking for Lady Cecilia and the others. Amir has not been able to find any leads in this regard."

"Amir? Amir Qureshi?" Xiana asked.

Harshad and I both turned to see the startled look appear briefly on her face.

"Yes," Harshad answered. "Yes, Amir Qureshi. He will be glad to see you again. I am surprised he is not here already."

The point of her chin jutted out a second later. "I did not realize he was here, too. It has been many years since I have last seen him," she murmured, her tone shifting toward apologetic.

I remembered Amir's story from before. *So this is Xiana, the woman who helped my mother save him from his family.*

Amir had spoken of Xiana highly, especially her expertise with herbs and plants, and I told her so.

She nodded once, firmly. "It is good to hear he remembers me."

"We will get reacquainted in good time," Harshad said. "Eleanora is working on the basics of fighting."

"Not that I've mastered them, of course." It was better that I told her the truth than allow him to, I thought.

"All masters begin the same as the student, and eventually return to their beginnings," Xiana said, coming up beside me. She pushed back her cloak a little, enough to where I could see she was clad in a close-fitted outfit, one with long black pants and sleeves allowing her to blend into the shadows completely. From what I could see, the fabric reminded me of my own stealth habit, only her set was cut differently.

Her mouth curled into a smile as she caught me staring. "I was never very good at fighting in any skirt, even one as short as yours."

"I can understand that," I said. I liked my habit, but I did not think I would ever get used to the thin, short skirt that went down to my knees.

I was just about to ask Xiana more questions when the door opened. Amir slipped inside, clearly arriving from his nightly rounds of collecting and dispersing information in the city. He never faltered as he saw Xiana, but I saw her balance shift ever so slightly.

"Amir."

"Xiana. It is lovely to see you again." Amir gave her a quick but respectful nod. I knew him well enough to know there was nothing in his movements to suggest he was being false. He was glad to see her.

Amir gave me a quick smile. "Are you going to be fighting with Xiana today, Eleanora?"

"We will start tomorrow, as I have only just arrived in Prague." Xiana straightened. "I wonder if she will give me as much of a fight as Naděžda used to?"

I did not pay attention to them too much as they talked; I was too surprised to her Xiana use Amir's name for my mother. She had allowed Harshad to call my mother "Dezda," but she herself had called me Eleanor's daughter. I glanced over at Harshad, remembering what he had taught me about names, and the names people give each other.

At my glance, his mouth hardened into a straight line, one I could not be entirely certain of, but it almost made me smile. Harshad had noticed the change in my mother's names, too, and it seemed as though I was growing in his esteem.

I was glad for that. It was not just physical battles I was supposed to learn how to navigate.

Harshad cleared his throat a moment later, interrupting Xiana as she mentioned her recent trip to Paris. "Amir, would you show Xiana to her quarters? She just arrived this morning and I imagine she is eager to settle in."

"Yes, Master." Xiana gave him another nod and then turned to face me. "It was nice meeting you, Eleanora. I look forward to seeing what you have learned."

When Amir and Xiana were gone, I glanced over at Harshad. He waited for several long moments before he nodded to me.

"Thank you for your patience, Eleanora," he said. "Welcome to your first official day of training."

"What?" My mouth dropped open. "What do you mean? I've been in here working nearly every morning since the Advent Ball."

"You have been learning how to fight, how to protect and prepare yourself," he conceded. "I did not think you would agree to continue for so long and I applaud you for your efforts."

"I don't think I should thank you for that, by the sound of it," I grumbled.

354

THE ORDER OF THE CRYSTAL DAGGERS

He did not seem to hear me. After all our time working together, he was likely used to ignoring me. "But what I have taught you so far, any street fighter could have. Now that your brother has been reassigned, it is time for us to officially begin."

"Why did you teach me to fight at all, if it was not for real?"

"Because Ben has to learn, and he thrives when faced with a competitor. You were our only option, and indeed, the best option."

"He's been mad at me ever since we began," I said. My cheeks burned, and I struggled to hold back my tears. "You destroyed the trust between us, and on purpose!"

"Of course. Life does this, on a regular basis," Harshad said, his flattened tone somehow much more harrowing than any anger could have been. "You were instructed to find your weaknesses."

"Which is apparently trusting the wrong people, and failing to trust the ones I should," I muttered.

"Trust was already a weakness of yours," Harshad said. "Your parents have both died and you were left with your stepmother to raise you. But she did not do that, did she? She used and abused you and your brother. While Lady Penelope and I are now here, we cannot undo her damage. We can only work you through it, and that is often times more painful."

"Well, what else is my weakness, then?" I put my hands on my hips and frowned. "If you're going to be torturing me to teach me, I might as well be prepared for it."

"You are too stubborn and too easily distracted. You are far more compassionate than you should be. You lie quite a bit, possibly for the wrong reasons. You have trouble with authority, and you are concerned with appearances much more than realities."

He clasped his hands behind his back. "That is just a preliminary list, Eleanora, and as we work on diminishing those, others will appear. It is the nature of things."

I did not know what to say. There were plenty of things I would not argue with him, if only he had been a little nicer about presenting my flaws.

Harshad turned his back toward me. "We will also work on your strengths, if that is any comfort to you. You are a stubborn, curious soul, and that is something we can harness as a strength as much as a weakness."

THE ORDER OF THE CRYSTAL DAGGERS

I wonder what my other strengths are. I tried to think of what else Harshad would say, but recalling that he had just dismissed me as too easily distracted, I tucked the question away for another time. I consoled myself with the knowledge that even if he did tell me my strengths, he would do it in the same backhanded manner Lady POW did.

A new idea popped into my head. Lady Penelope's teachings had worked against her, and I wanted to know if Harshad's had that same capability.

"Harshad?" Despite his teaching, and all the time we had spent together in the recent weeks, his name felt strange coming out of my mouth.

Perhaps that was why he did not reprimand me right away.

"What is it?" he asked.

"What is your weakness?"

He was silent for a long moment, and I was sure he was going to refrain from answering. But then he sighed. "Several of your own," he admitted. "But there are others, too."

I put my hands on my hips, a sinful sense of satisfaction coursing through me. "It is good to know you're not perfect."

"Your mother is one."

At the mention of my mother and his admission, I froze. I had not been expecting him to admit any specific weaknesses, let alone one that seemed so personal.

"Amir says you are curious about her most of all," Harshad said. "Is that true?"

It was suddenly very hard for me to swallow. "Yes," I whispered.

"I thought as much." Harshad's eyes lost their hardened quality, and he seemed much older all of a sudden. "If you do well with your sessions, I will tell you more about her."

I pursed my lips. "Does that mean you'll tell me something about her today?"

"I have already admitted she was a weakness of mine," he reminded me. "That is enough for today, is it not?"

"Well, you said she was a weakness, but you didn't explain how." I crossed my arms over my chest. "That seems like a fair follow-up question."

THE ORDER OF THE CRYSTAL DAGGERS

"Fair, but foul as well."

"Paradoxes are not the same thing as contradictions," I reminded him.

"It is good to see your wit is quite a weapon." Harshad nodded. "But it also shows that I was right. When you want something, you are much more focused."

I blushed, unsure as always if it was a compliment or an insult or even both. Harshad had been merciless in forcing Ben to admit to his hidden resentments and his insecurities, and now I was sure he was going to do the same with me. Harshad was focused, too, and I had to give him credit for it. I saw now that he was willing to do anything to see that I became a better fighter.

He sat down, crossing his legs on the floor. He motioned for me to follow, and I did.

"Why did you join the Order, Eleanora?"

"To help save others," I answered.

Nothing changed on his face, but his tone softened ever so slightly. He closed his eyes and breathed in deeply. "There is more to it than that."

"Well, I wanted to be free from Cecilia," I admitted. "And I thought ... my mother ..."

My voice trailed off as I thought about my mother. *Máma* had been a beautiful ghost of sorts, a memory never real enough to satisfy me. I wanted to grow up to be a true lady, as she was, and make her proud; I had no idea how to do that. In meeting Lady Penelope, I had been hoping for some way to capture that ghost, to make the memory more real, to resurrect the dead long enough to find my way in life.

How did someone admit to that? How could I put into words that I was on a strange, illogical quest for my mother, looking for approval and acceptance I feared I would never find in anyone else?

"I met Dezda for the first time when she was very small," Harshad said, jolting me out of my introspections. I blinked to see he was watching me intently, and I wondered if he was able to make sense of my own confusion. "Your grandmother was still working with Jakub and his best friend, Louis Valoris, at the time."

"You knew my grandfather, too?"

"I knew him before I met Pepé," he said. "She was his mistress when I met him."

THE ORDER OF THE CRYSTAL DAGGERS

An involuntary blush heated my cheeks and I coughed, choking on air.

Harshad sighed. "You are old enough to not be surprised."

"According to Society, I'm supposed to be horrified," I said. "Surprised is much more mild."

"Society is so strict with youth. And in many ways, I can understand it. So many people suffer needlessly when people are careless. Rules are there for reasons, even if those reasons might seem strange to others. But there are exceptions in every case, and you need to watch for them."

"I've already noticed Lady Penelope makes up her own rules," I said. "You don't need to tell me that."

I was surprised to see the smile on his face. The little lines on either side of his lips tightened together in little batches, wrinkling his face as much as humanizing it.

"Exactly. But that was something she picked up from Jakub, and something that she only enacted when he grew increasingly uncomfortable with her involvement with the Order. She had an aunt who was a member of the Order before her, who ran a brothel in the streets of London. When Pepé's father died, she was sent there to work, learning how to coerce gentlemen into giving up their secrets."

I did not say anything, this time too shocked and horrified. The truth seemed too awful for words, even though I was suddenly very glad Lady POW did not teach me the full curriculum on sexual manipulation. I had a feeling it was even larger than I originally feared.

"Dezda, by Lady Penelope's own words, was a … miscalculation," Harshad continued. "But … But I certainly never saw her as such, and as Her Majesty Queen Victoria took more interest in my work and Pepé became her close acquaintance, I made it my mission to convince Pepé that Dezda was a blessing to us. She was the next generation of our legacy, working for the Crown and helping maintain the order of the world."

The rest of the story's outline fell into place as I listened to him. Amir had told me before that he had met my mother in Agra, in India, when he was on business with his father. They were there with Harshad. Lady Penelope and my mother had come along with him in order to escape Jakub and begin a new life.

Lady Penelope had been irrevocably disillusioned with men and relationships, and as proud as she was, she would not allow Harshad to rescue her from her disappointments. My mother might have been repulsed by

Amir at first, but when she fell in love with him, she found there was nothing she wanted more.

Well, almost nothing, I recalled. *Máma* wanted her freedom, and she wanted a family of her own.

"Do you know why I am telling you this, Eleanora?" Harshad's voice, always so strict and brusque, was almost calming.

I shook my head. "No."

"I have two reasons for doing so. The first is practical in our lesson. Your mother is the key to your focus. I was hoping she could also lend some help with your balance."

"I'm not sure how learning about her would help with balance."

"Balance must be inward as much as outward," Harshad explained. "There are too many lies and too many secrets that surround us."

"You could just get Lady POW to admit to her secrets," I pointed out. "That would help."

"That is the second reason for my explanation. Secrets are different from lies," Harshad said. "When we lie, that is when we inflict damage to ourselves and others. Secrets, even the ones we keep from ourselves, sometimes protect us as much as they can hurt us. It is much harder to calculate the risk when it comes to secrets."

"But they hurt others, too," I said. "Just look at Lord Maximillian and Karl. And even Tulia, too. She kept me and Ben a secret from Lady Penelope for all these years. We have a duty to find out the truth."

"Sharing secrets is a sign of trust," Harshad said. "Your duties for the Order do not need to supersede your relationships; the wisdom you learn should inform your decisions, not dictate them. And that is the slippery part of free will."

He gave me a knowing look. "You have your own secrets, Eleanora. You know this is true. Secrets offer us freedom from the world, but they can enslave us, too. They let us draw close to some and push us farther away from others."

I did not say anything, slipping into a thoughtful silence as Harshad gave me another assessing look. "That is why the search for truth must be an ongoing process."

"What do you mean?"

"Do you know what will be even more perfect than our first day in Heaven, Eleanora?"

The question was unusual and seemed to be misplaced, but luckily, Harshad did not wait for my answer.

"Our second day."

I understood. "You can't have something 'more perfect,'" I said. "Perfect is perfect."

"I both agree and disagree. This seeming complication did not stop the Americans from putting it in their Constitution," Harshad said. "But it is not poor learning as I assumed before. Perfection is not a state of stagnation, though we use the word as such."

I thought about what Lady POW had said before, about not trusting anyone, especially the people who would fail her. I realized before that it was an absurd premise, but she was not seeing the same thing I was. She was looking at the paradox as stagnant, and I had known, instinctively, that it was malleable.

"I told you the truth about your grandmother's past, including some of the secrets she carries," Harshad said. "But you are still not any more inclined to trust her with your secrets, are you?"

I blushed at his perception and shook my head. "No."

He nodded. "I thought as much. Trust is a process, especially in a fallen world."

Perhaps for once, I understood why Harshad wanted me to remain silent while he talked. Everything he said was intentional, designed to tantalize the mind. I was suddenly appalled when I realized how much I had likely missed in our sessions before.

I hoped I would be able to make up for it, after our mission was over.

When he did speak again, it seemed as though ages had passed. "You really are so much like Dezda. I wanted to see for myself how different you are, and that required time." His voice was much more of a whisper, and I knew he was taking a risk, and letting me know one of his secrets. "I know you are different enough that I can freely admit that I came to regret training Dezda. I did not want to make the same mistake with you."

"This is not a mistake," I said, but I felt my resolve weaken. I remembered how Ferdy told me that the Order of the Crystal Daggers was full of assassins, and I had nothing to say in return. He was likely right. I did not know if I was comfortable having the talent to kill someone.

THE ORDER OF THE CRYSTAL DAGGERS

Harshad seemed to agree with my unspoken concerns. "Fighting is contrary to your nature."

"Being stubborn and contrary is not." A wry grin appeared on my face, and I was suddenly determined to change the subject. "Besides, Lady Penelope says that Society can only exist when people do things that are unacceptable to save it."

"That does not mean you must be such a person."

"I do not agree," I said. "I am free to see the truth of such a calling, even if it is uncomfortable."

"This is not what you want."

I did not know how to respond; Harshad was right. I had my doubts about the Order, about working with people who, as Lady POW said, would fail me.

But I was at the castle when Karl and Lord Maximillian's attack commenced. If I had done nothing at all, if I had backed away from Lady Penelope's offer, if I had jumped at the chance to travel abroad and find a husband, or if I had taken enough of her money to start up Liberté with Ben, I would not have been able to save Ferdy.

And he was worth it. Protecting Ferdy was worth it.

As if to prove myself, I stood up and moved back toward the center of the room and took a fighting stance. "If you're going to help me win against Xiana, I'm going to need to learn more advanced moves than you've been having me and Ben go over."

Harshad turned around, reverting back to his solemn, unreadable self as we remained content to let the topic drop. "You are correct; Xiana is quite the skilled fighter. That is certainly no secret."

11

◊

Later that evening, I stepped down from Lady Penelope's coach and made my way into the *Stavovské divadlo*. I was dressed in the extravagant gown of a socialite, a member of Society. The weight of the gown surprised me, after days of working in my stealth habit and loose clothing, but I had to admit, it was beautiful. My dress was a deep amethyst lined with mink, with matching ruffles of silk and muslin. I had a matching fur stole and even some jeweled combs in my hair. I was tempted to wear the ones Ferdy had given me, but when Marguerite had shown up with silver combs, dazzling with tiny diamonds, I made no objection. Because I loved my outfit, the inconvenient frivolity of it was much more enjoyable. I was happy enough that I had an assignment that would allow me to sit down for several hours, even if I had to entertain Society and spend time with Karl.

Underneath my gown, I wore a new pair of kid boots. The soft covering of winter snow had slushed over near the theatre, and the boots protected me from the cold as much as the mixture of horse manure and other dirt from the streets.

Not that I was thinking about that when I arrived; I was ready to observe my environment, pick up on all the important details, and search for the information I needed. I was still here on a mission.

This thought marched through me, almost skipping to the sound of music as it poured out of the *Stavovské divadlo*, the Estates Theatre, as Lady Penelope and I walked inside.

Even Lady POW was in brighter spirits. I learned from Amir that Ben told her about Zipporah, and they were waiting for Clavan's summons from the Cabal.

Any progress was progress, and after weeks of wintery solitude and monotonous training, we were both excited to be back, looking for clues while we dazzled the crowds.

"This is wonderful," Lady Penelope murmured as we arrived. I could practically feel her enthusiasm beside me as we were escorted to a box at the side of the theatre. "I have missed the theatre quite a bit since we left England. I wish we were here to see a play, but this is lovely, too."

"Aren't you always a player on the stage, as a spy?" I asked. "Why would you miss something you have to live through every day?"

"Watching others perform is much more enjoyable."

She is a complicated woman, I thought, *but she is right.*

I sat down in my seat with my own sense of wonder, mostly awed that I was able to be seen as much as I was able to see everyone else. There were several lords and ladies all around us, enjoying the concert—or pretending to enjoy the concert, while they indulged in gossip.

Even a month ago, such a sight would have been unimaginable to me. The golden gilt of the theatre shined, the warmth washing over the audience along with the sound of music. The silk-covered walls and the velvet stage curtains hinted at their highest glory, adding to the magic of the performance as I sat there.

The magic did not last long.

I glanced over to see Karl come into the box. He made his formal greetings, both to me and Lady POW, and then he took the seat beside me, a rare privilege allowed to a gentleman. Lady Penelope, resplendent in her own gown behind me, waved her fan of feathers, signaling to me to get to it.

I could almost hear her thoughts.

Get on with it, Eleanora! We need information.

We might be enjoying ourselves, I thought with a smile, but we were still working, too. "This is a wonderful performance. Don't you think so, Karl?"

"I am eager for the finale," he said, but I wondered if he was telling me the truth. Karl was dressed elegantly for the evening. He watched the crowds, as if waiting for his cues to wave or appear deeply invested in the music. I saw him nod gallantly to several others who were looking our way. He seemed to enjoy the attention he was receiving, and he loved to have the chance to gain more later.

"Well, I am glad to see you are eager to leave me," I teased, batting my eyelashes at him. My stomach twisted, and I decided I did not like flirting with Karl.

"It's not that," Karl quickly assured me. He reached for my hand, and I allowed him to take it. "I requested a special number in your honor."

"My honor?"

"Of course. You have enchanted all of society, Ella."

I did not know what it was, but suddenly hearing him call me "Ella," Ferdy's name for me, made me feel sick. Maybe it was because of Ben, fighting with Ferdy over a misunderstanding or maybe it was realizing I would likely never see him again. Ultimately, I did not want to be reminded of Ferdy anymore.

"Eleanora, if you please," I murmured, pulling my hand out of his. I glanced back to see Lady POW frown at me and hurriedly set about adjusting a hairpin to cover for my quick movements.

I hoped she would not question it. I did not need her snooping into my personal life. I counted it as a blessing that I did not have to reveal anything to her at all about Ferdy, romantic or otherwise, and I was praying I never had to. I did not want to admit I had a broken heart, and I desperately missed someone I had no business loving in the first place.

"My apologies ... Eleanora." Karl took my hand again, and I relented.

As the music continued, I looked down at the crowds where Karl was watching.

"Are you looking for Lady Teresa Marie?" I asked. "I don't believe I see her here tonight."

"She and her father have been busy of late, moving into their new townhouse," Karl said. "My parents were able to help get them a residence in the city for the rest of the Season."

"Oh?" I arched my brow. "Does this mean he is still interested in supporting your political ambitions?"

"Yes. Lord Maximillian and I have reached an understanding. He has been preoccupied these last few weeks, but in the meantime, I am free to attend to you."

He glanced over at me, giving me an affectionate look. "Not that I have much of a choice, of course. One look and you are enough to enchant even the hardest of hearts."

"Thank you," I mumbled, trying to hide my irritation under the guise of pleased modesty. "It is good your parents approve of Lord Maximillian, especially if His Grace is still supportive of you."

Which was strange, when I thought about it. Empress Maria Anna was very concerned for Karl and Ferdy. Why would they help Lord Maximillian set up a household here, especially when he had been behind the fire at the castle?

Maybe they were watching him, I thought. That made sense.

364

THE ORDER OF THE CRYSTAL DAGGERS

"Max is grateful, too," Karl said. "He has some extended family in the area, and he is eager to spend more time with them."

"I see." I was getting tired of trying to find ways to circle around to information I wanted, without seeming suspicious.

Before I could find a way to see if Lord Maximillian had been talking about Cecilia, there was a shuffle of movement behind us.

The curtain parted, and a footman stepped forward.

My heart clenched. I peered closely at the footman's face, half-hoping, half-dreading that Ferdy was up to his old tricks. When I saw the footman's young face, clearly several years younger than myself, I exhaled. I was still not sure if I was more disappointed or relieved.

"A note for you, m'lady," the footman said, bowing to Lady Penelope. "From Lady Hohenwart. She is visiting Lord Taafte's box and has requested you come and join them."

"I see," Lady Penelope replied. She glanced over at Karl. "I shall return shortly, Mr. Marcelin. Do take care of my darling granddaughter for me until then."

"As you wish, Madame," Karl replied with a grin.

He waited until Lady POW was out of our box before he inched closer to me.

"I am greatly honored you were able to come tonight," Karl said.

I mostly ignored him, waving out into the crowd. I was hoping some of the many people who came to fawn over me at balls and parties would wave back. I got my wish and smiled, noticing Karl was suitably impressed. But it also helped to remind Karl we had an audience.

"Things have been rather lonely since I have returned from London," Karl said, surprising me. "Now that I am staying in the castle, I am, of course, very grateful, but I have not had much time with the people I love."

"I imagine you have more friends abroad, considering you studied there."

Karl nodded. "I am hoping some of them will come and visit."

"Will you have time for them when they do?" I pressed. "I mean, you have your duties to the Diets, after all."

"I am certain once our sessions resume, there will be more time for revelry."

For the next several moments, I half-listened as Karl laid out his plans to introduce new bills for the Diets to consider.

"If you can see that Emperor Franz Joseph has no concern for us, even after the fire incident at the castle, then surely others do, too."

I did not have to feign ennui anymore; I had to hide it. "I'm sure."

"He should not be allowed to ignore us," Karl said, his jaw hardening in anger. "He is supposed to take pride in his empire, and he has not even come to Bohemia for a formal coronation. Don't you think that the nation feels his neglect? And we still suffer for it, too."

"But it's not so bad, is it?" I thought of what I had learned at the Cabal. "The Bohemian Diet remains in power, and the German Diet has allowed us to celebrate our roots to a much more liberal degree of late. The people are more free than ever, and we have hopes for more representation."

"The German Confederacy has fallen in stature since the time of King Ferdinand," Karl replied. The bitterness was creeping into his voice as he railed against the established governments. "And the Bohemians should be represented properly with a king, not one of these republics the Americans are celebrating. Look at what that brought them. Only civil war. Millions have died for a republic that will one day fall, too, and all because they could not trust in their leaders."

"Plenty of kingdoms have experienced that," I reminded him. "Even King Ferdinand was forced to abdicate because he was unable to lead his people. I do not think you would be able to convince the people that separating Bohemia from the empire would be good for us."

"They only need a strong leader who is unafraid to stand up for his nation," Karl said. He tightened his fingers around mine. "Not one like Franz Joseph."

"What about the people?"

Karl frowned. "I know Empress Elisabeth has made democracy look attractive, but it only leads to mob leadership in the end. And if there is a stalemate, war comes without mercy, Ella."

"Eleanora, please."

"Why?"

I blinked. "Why what?"

"Why do you prefer I call you Eleanora?" He frowned, and for the first time, I saw the two little stress lines in the middle of his forehead, as he

THE ORDER OF THE CRYSTAL DAGGERS

crinkled his face into an angry, thoughtful expression. "Ella is a perfectly lovely name."

"I just do," I said, trying not to grit my teeth. "A name is very important, after all. Ella sounds like a silly girl's name. Eleanora is my proper name, and propriety is very important, as you well know, sir."

When his frown only deepened, I tapped my fingers against his arm playfully. "It is no different for you and Bohemia, is it not? You wish to give it a leader and a vision with a good name, so it can have a prosperous future."

Karl brightened at my comparison. "Yes, I do. I want to make Bohemia a great nation once more. Even if it means breaking free from Austria and Hungary."

"That would be treason," I said, exaggerating my shock.

"Treason against slavery," Karl argued. "Surely you know of the freedom of which I speak."

I thought of my own freedom from Cecilia. I had wanted that freedom, to determine my own life's course.

"There is freedom," I said, "and there are false freedoms, Karl. It is important to know the difference."

He did not seem to realize I was looking past him, seeing if I could find a glimpse of Ferdy in his gaze.

Karl reached out and took a hold of my other hand. "Which is why I am very glad you are here with me. It is no small task to turn the tide of history, to fundamentally change a nation. A man who wishes to do just that needs a strong woman behind him."

I did not know what to say to that. I did not think I was that strong, and I knew as a member of the Order, my missions were to be carried out in the shadows.

"Speaking of the country," Karl said, "there is a special dedication ceremony this week most of the Diet members will be attending. It is at the *Nàrodni muzuem.*"

"I see. Does this mean the Diets are resuming their sessions?"

"Not quite. There is still a little more time before that. But I would love to have you accompany me to the ceremony." Karl gave me a smile. "I want to show them a vision of a brighter future."

THE ORDER OF THE CRYSTAL DAGGERS

"I will be happy to join you," I said, "but I don't see what your vision for Bohemia's future has to do with me."

"You're the daughter of Adolf Svoboda, a man who saved King Ferdinand from certain death at a critical time," Karl said. "You're beautiful and charming, and everyone here loves you. Just look around at all the people who are watching us."

I hated that Karl had a point. Society in Prague was small, and many had seemed to approve of me. Or at least, they approved of the picture I made. Between Lady Penelope's dowry, and my own performance, several spyglasses settled on our theatre box throughout the evening.

"You are the embodiment of everything I could hope for," Karl said, his voice softening. "A lady who was fashioned from adversity, one who is determined to make her way in the world while making it more blessed along the way. There is nothing that could make Bohemia greater than you."

I blushed at Karl's praise, even if it stung. The first time he had wanted me, it was for my money, and now, it was for my influence. He might have liked me enough to believe I was perfect for him, but I almost wished he would just marry Lady Teresa Marie. Her father wanted power and the throne, and it seemed that they were so well-suited to each other in that goal that they would be reasonably happy together—but, I thought, only if they succeeded.

"Thank you, Karl," I murmured, suddenly desperate to get away. "You must also thank my grandmother. She is my inspiration. She was married to the Duke of Wellington."

"I know that," Karl agreed, "but—"

"My goodness. I did not realize until this very moment how thirsty I am. Would you be kind enough to fetch me a glass of lemonade?"

Karl narrowed his eyes at me as he stood up. My attempt to distract him was not smooth, and even he knew I was uncomfortable. "I will alert a footman at once, my lady."

He knew I was uncomfortable, and he did not like it. I let out a sigh as he walked away, feeling a reprieve for the moment, even as I knew Karl would make me pay for it later. If he wanted me to be his wife, and a perfectly enchanting one for all of Society to see, he would have to find a way to get me to agree with him.

Isn't it bad enough that he got me to agree to a pending engagement?

THE ORDER OF THE CRYSTAL DAGGERS

The other side of the curtain fluttered, and I heard Karl's voice rise briefly.

I frowned. *What happened?*

"Karl?" I called. The music from the stage made it difficult to know if my voice was loud enough for him to hear me. "Is something wrong?"

He had stepped outside the box, out of my sight. I sighed and went after him, hoping I could sneak away with an excuse. Maybe I could tell him that my grandmother had signaled to me from the Taafte's box—anything that would allow me to escape that conversation.

All of my plans disappeared as I pulled back the curtain.

Karl was standing there, arguing in an angry, hushed voice. His back was turned to me, and I was just about to interrupt him when I saw who he was talking to.

It was Ferdy.

12

◊

I never considered myself to be the type of lady who was prone to fainting. After years of serving as Cecilia's chimney sweep, I was used to more difficult and dangerous situations than the delicate ladies of the city's social circles, and the idea of fainting at the least provocation was laughable. But at that moment, watching Ferdy as he stood there, I felt my knees wobble, and my heart stop. A lightheaded feeling took over me, and I could not tell if I was dizzy from pain or pleasure, or some heady mix of both.

Ferdy, by contrast, seemed undeniably pleased at the sight of me. He was dressed in his proper gentlemen's attire, down to the ruffled shirt and the fitted coat, formal enough to make me feel underdressed, even in my elaborate gown. His hair was brushed back properly, and he wore a smug smile on his face. He stood at ease as Karl faced him, meeting his brother eye to eye, deliberately being as provocative as possible. His insufferable self-satisfaction and the resulting anger it stirred inside of me were the only reasons I did not swoon.

"Why do you insist on making things difficult?" Karl's tone was harsh against the musical background. I might have even felt badly for Ferdy if I did not want to ask him the same thing.

Karl's authoritarian tone did nothing to deter Ferdy. He heaved a large, dismissive sigh. "Why, brother dear, we only have so much time before I will be on my way back to Silesia. I thought it prudent to spend *some* time with you. When I found out you had gone to the theatre, I could hardly resist, now could I?"

"Do not call me 'brother,'" Karl hissed back.

"Oh, would you prefer 'cousin,' then? I remember that is how all of your teachers described our relationship back at Oxford, especially as they lectured me on dishonoring my family's heritage and denigrating its obvious potential."

"It is not my fault you insisted on wasting your years of education causing nothing but trouble for your headmasters."

"A man is not a true leader unless he can get others to follow him," Ferdy replied. Then he glanced over at me, and it was then that I realized my mouth had dropped open in surprise and outrage. My heart raced with fear and a sudden desire for revenge. "Isn't that right, Ella?"

Karl whirled around. I heard him inhale sharply as he caught sight of me.

I froze. *Why is Ferdy jeopardizing himself, and me, too?*

Did he hate me that much? Was this revenge for Ben's attack?

"Eleanora," Karl said. "I must beg your pardon. Please, do not concern yourself with … this unfortunate interruption to our evening."

Ferdy rolled his eyes at Karl's attempt to dismiss him. My own anger flared again, but my curiosity compelled me to speak up. "What is going on?"

Karl scowled. "Nothing."

I arched my brow at Karl, silently attempting to remind him he had promised not to lie to me.

While I could not tell if he was able to decipher my thoughts, Karl relented a moment later. "Fine. May I introduce you to my brother, Ferdinand? He has decided to grace us with his presence. Much to my dismay, of course."

Ferdy stepped around Karl swiftly, knocking him out of my direct path. Ferdy reached for my hand and kissed it gallantly, letting his fingers slip into mine.

I was unable to stop the flush on my cheeks, remembering our more intimate kisses. An unstoppable wave of longing flooded through me.

"It is a pleasure to meet you, Miss Eleanora," Ferdy said. "You must be the one that my brother calls 'Ella,' even though it is more of a name for a silly girl, don't you think?"

All my embarrassment transmuted into rage.

So, he has been listening to us, waiting to make a move.

My fingers gripped his in warning. I knew Ferdy loved to play games and take risks, but I was in no mood to join in on his fun.

"A pleasure to make your acquaintance, Mr. Marcelin," I said through gritted teeth. "Karl has told me much about you."

"I can assure you all of it is true, even the worst of it. Karl would never lie to you, my lady. I doubt you would allow him, either. You are clearly as smart, charming, and beautiful as he says." Ferdy's voice dropped to a softer, more seductive tone. "Even without the introduction, I recognized you."

371

At his tender, familiar words, I dropped my hand from his, breathless at the wound as much as I was with wanting.

"When exactly are you leaving to go back to Silesia, Ferdinand?" Karl asked. "I would hate for you to miss Eleanora and I announcing our engagement."

I did not want to look at Ferdy in that moment; I forced myself to remain still. I tried to let him know it was part of the game, but I saw the pain flicker across his face.

"So good to know that Lord Maximillian has allowed you to step out of your previous arrangement with his daughter, brother dear," Ferdy said, recovering quickly. "I assume he has made other plans, too?"

"Who told you about that?" Karl scowled before he stood tall. "And why would you even care? Are you looking for a bride yourself?"

"I'm sure it would be something to consider, even though you know I am a dedicated bachelor." Ferdy's smile went cold as he looked at me. "I would not want a wife to worry while I make my rounds about the city, looking for all sorts of lively entertainment. And I am sure Ella here would not want to be such a wife, either."

"I'm sure your wife would search the streets just to make sure you were safe," I retorted. "Not that you would ever know of her sacrifice."

He arched his brow playfully. "It is almost worth kidnapping Karl, just to see if you would come after him."

"From what I have heard of you, it is better that I not come if he was with you. I shudder to think of where he would end up with you at his side," I snapped.

Karl cleared his throat. "I believe it is time to end this conversation. Ferdinand, please, you are causing Eleanora undue duress with your … impropriety."

Karl was right about that, even if his reasoning was wrong.

"Eleanora, let us return to enjoying the concert, if you please," Karl said.

As much as Ferdy was upsetting me, I felt everything inside of me call out to him as I was forced to retreat. The past weeks' worth of missing him broke through me, and I could only look over my shoulder at him as Karl pushed the curtain aside.

Karl turned back to face Ferdy. "I trust you will find someone else to bother? Ella and I are presently occupied."

THE ORDER OF THE CRYSTAL DAGGERS

"Eleanora," I whispered.

Karl halted his departure to glare at me, and I flinched at his impatient frustration. "My apologies, my lady."

Ferdy cleared his throat. When we looked back at him, I saw he had finally stopped smiling.

"I will be leaving for Silesia in the morning, Karl," Ferdy said. "It appears you will be in better company until then."

"Allow me to extend my heartfelt wishes for a safe journey." Karl held out his hand, solemn but still disdainful. "The Diets resume their sessions this week, and I have other commitments. I regret I will be unlikely to meet with you before your departure."

"Unwilling, or unlikely?" Ferdy stepped forward and shook Karl's hand, though there was no evidence of brotherly affection or goodwill between them. "Never mind. Farewell, *brother*."

At his taunting, Karl swung around, angry, and brushed past me. Ferdy gave me one last look, nodding down the hall; it was a signal of sorts, letting me know he wanted me to find a way to follow him before he disappeared into the crowds.

It took everything I had not to run after him at that moment—I could not honestly say if I wanted to kiss him or strangle him more—but I knew I had to see to Karl first.

I headed back over to my seat next to Karl.

"Well, you were obviously correct. It was a waste of time to meet your brother," I said, forcing myself to say something. I knew he would like the reassurance I was not enchanted by Ferdy, and that I was on his side.

"I call him my cousin to help with the embarrassment," Karl admitted. "I do not know how we are brothers at all."

"Of course. You care about Bohemia's future, and he only cares if he is having fun."

Karl took my hand, clutching it affectionately with a flooding sense of relief. "I am glad you see the differences, my dear. They are quite stark, I assure you."

I nodded, even though I disagreed. Ben had made similar remarks regarding both of them before, noting Ferdy's carelessness and Karl's ruthlessness. I held onto Karl's hand, thinking how his deep devotion to the country had led to destruction, and how Ferdy's careless lies had left me broken.

373

THE ORDER OF THE CRYSTAL DAGGERS

"Did you know, Eleanora, in some countries they execute family members who bring dishonor to their families?" Karl sighed remorsefully. "What a shame that we do not adopt that custom. Disownment will only go so far in certain circles here. Fortunately, my parents are supportive of our estrangement."

Karl's statement jolted me out of the stupor of my own thoughts and ignited my rage.

He was obviously upset. I watched him as he anxiously tugged at his collar, straightened his cravat, and smoothed out his jacket. He was fidgeting, and Ferdy had rattled him to the point he was making lighthearted comments about situations like the one Amir faced, comparing Ferdy's embarrassment to an act of family dishonor punishable by death.

Karl always seemed very refined, always very courteous—a gentleman to his fingertips. But his remark, as careless and thoughtless as it was, revealed the more grotesque truth inside.

Disgust ran through me, and I knew it was time for me to escape. My heart felt hollow at the thought of staying where I was, for so many reasons, and there really was nothing I wanted more than to go and find Ferdy again.

"I do believe my grandmother is signaling to me from Lady Hohenwart's box," I said, struggling to keep my voice from breaking. "Please excuse me. I will return shortly."

Before Karl could offer to escort me, or worse, question my decision, I hurried away. I pushed past the velvet curtain and made for the stairs, heading in the direction Ferdy had indicated before.

"Where did he go?" I muttered, frustrated as I had to smile and weave through the crowds. I caught sight of a darkened staircase at the far end of the hall and hurried onward. Navigating the stairs in my gown slowed me some, but I finally found an exit.

Just as I slipped outside, a hand reached out and took hold of me from behind. I almost fought back, but then I heard his voice.

"I was wondering if you were going to come at all."

Ferdy.

My knees buckled, and I fell back against him briefly. Then I remembered how upset he had made me by showing up and pretending we had never met before.

"And miss getting the chance to chastise you for your impudence? Never." I turned to face him. "What were you thinking, showing up here? Were you trying to make me upset?"

"You cannot make me feel guilty over making you upset," Ferdy replied tartly. He drew me back against the side of building. The alleyway behind the theatre was dark, but we were safe and out of sight. "Especially after promising Karl you would consider an engagement."

"I only did it to see if I could trap him," I said with a huff. "He promised me if I agreed to it, he would never lie, and I was trying to get him to by asking about you. I didn't think he would admit to being your brother."

"We need to work on your gambling skills."

Despite my anger, I almost laughed. "I've been too busy learning how to fight to worry about gambling."

"I am relieved to hear that. Philip and I agreed that your injured leg was an exaggerated excuse to stay out of Society while Karl figured out what to do next."

"How is he? You'll have to give Philip my regards." I crossed my arms over my chest. "And speaking of Society, why are you here?"

"Why, to see you, of course." My eyes were gradually adjusting to the darkness in the alleyway, and I could see his smile against the shadows. "Karl is not the only one who has missed you."

"Ferdy—"

"Don't worry," he said. "We don't have time for a proper reunion right now. I am here because I wanted to see you, but I also wanted to give you this." He reached inside of his coat and pulled out a folded sheet of paper.

"This isn't another invitation, is it?" I asked, taking the paper.

"No, it's not," Ferdy replied with a quick grin. "It's a letter my brother sent out to Lord Maximillian, the Duke of Moravia, this morning. I had one of my informants intercept it."

"You have informants?"

"Of course I do. I've been running around the streets for nearly a year, and since then I've come to learn the value of having the right information." A sly glimmer appeared in his gaze. "How else do you think I knew to come and rescue you tonight, *chérie?*"

I refrained from slapping him at his teasing remarks, but only barely. Instead, I unrolled the paper, but it was too dark to read it. "What does it say?"

"He was formally rejecting Lady Teresa Marie as his future wife," Ferdy said. "He says that he is pursuing you instead, since you have expressed your interest, and his friends in the League would approve of his choice because of your father, and of course, your other 'most excellent qualities.' Karl also offered the Duke a seat on his council and considered it a 'gracious' and 'generous' act, considering the nature of their recent disagreements."

"The League? The only league I can think of is the League of Ungentlemanly Warfare," I said. "But that's based in London, and Lady POW is a member. I don't know why they would care what Karl was planning."

"I was more surprised to see your name," Ferdy said. "I am sure you've noticed I am disgusted by your position."

"You can take heart in knowing that it's a lie." I did not want to tell Ferdy, but I agreed with him. I crossed my arms, remembering I was supposed to be upset with him. "You're pretty familiar with those, if I recall."

"I'm working on making it up to you. Since you told me you only allowed Karl to get close to you in order to save people the night of the Advent Ball, I am keeping a closer watch on my brother."

"Ferdy." I felt my earlier ire soften as I shook my head. "The Order knows Karl has reached out to Lord Maximillian and they are trying to restore Bohemia to a full monarchy. They were going to use the death of the politicians and aristocracy back at the castle to leverage Karl back onto the throne."

"Fortunately, their plans were foiled by a clever young lady." He brushed his hand against my chin, and I hurriedly turned away.

"I still failed," I murmured, torn between shame and pride at his remark. "The Order suspects there are contingency plans."

"You are right to do so. I've known Karl has wanted to free Bohemia from the empire for some time. But I did not realize until recently he was intent on following through." His gaze dropped to the ground. "I should have."

"It's not your fault," I assured him, surprised by the amount of guilt I heard in his voice. "You were the one who told me he is very smart."

"He is," Ferdy said, "but I should have known something was wrong. With the Duke of Moravia and now the League of Ungentlemanly

Warfare, he has the right connections, and after the Advent Ball, he no longer seems to exhibit any moral restraint."

I bit my lip momentarily. I did not want to encourage him, but I did not want to miss out on any important information, either. Finally, I gave in. "What do you know?"

"Enough to know we have to stop him."

We?

The day that I left him at the castle, I thought Ferdy was letting me go. But now, as I held the letter he had given me, as he looked at me with such concern, I saw he wanted to help me and the Order—even though he believed we could turn on him.

That was not the only risk he faced, either. Going up against Karl would mean that he was putting himself at risk from his brother's ire and possible retaliation.

"Ferdy." I took his arm. "Your mother is worried for you."

Ferdy balked. "What does that have to do with this?"

"I appreciate the help. I really do," I said. "This letter is a good clue. Maybe Lord Maximillian's foreign backers include members of the League. But I can't have you looking into this. You need to stop. This is dangerous."

"You told me that the kingdom needs me," he said, and I felt a rush of anger; he was trying to use my own reasoning against me. Before I could object and fight back, he stepped even closer to me, trapping me between his body and the building. "And as much as you might not like it, I need you."

His hands cradled my face, and I ached for him. My heart was thundering loudly between my ears as we stood there. All of my being was torn inside—duty and love fought a dizzying battle inside of me, leaving me unable to move.

"You need me, too." Ferdy's voice was soft and full of wonder, sending shivers down my spine. "I can tell."

"This is madness," I whispered.

"Madness or magic?" Ferdy's gaze fell to my lips, and I felt my heart fall out of my chest and into his hands all over again.

I barely managed to find my resolve. "My life is nothing, Ferdy. You have to be protected. I can't have you involved in this."

THE ORDER OF THE CRYSTAL DAGGERS

"It's not your job to take care of me," he said. "I can protect myself. What do you think I've been doing for the last year, playing the pauper for all of Prague to witness?"

"I'm not sure how that helps." I eyed him curiously. "Why were you living on the streets, exactly?"

"I may not be a true prince—"

"Yes, you are." I jutted my chin forward. I did not want to debate the technicalities of his title, but I would if I had to. "That is the truth, and you promised me you would only tell me the truth."

"Fine." The reluctance in his voice was palpable as he drew back from me. "I am a prince. But my father was king and emperor, and eventually, he was forced from his throne because he did not know his people. He was lucky he wasn't killed. And now, Karl is following in his steps to the same end. He is too focused on his own ambition to see that the people simply will not support him."

"There is a strong Nationalist movement. And he could easily garner support after the fire, even claiming it was an accident."

"The Nationalist support will disappear when they see Karl wants power for himself. The people want to be free, as free as they can be in a fallen world. Karl doesn't think they are smart enough to know the difference, but I know they are."

I felt my own heart push back at me, telling me Ferdy was right. Clavan had recognized it in me, too—the desire for freedom, for liberty. That was another reason I had agreed to join Lady POW, too. Freedom required power.

"I have chosen to live among the people, as one of them, so I could know them again," Ferdy said. "I can assure you, it was more educational than going off to school, too, especially considering what Clavan and Eliezer have taught me."

"I can imagine," I said. "But Karl—"

"Karl doesn't know Bohemia the way I do. If there is a way to stop him from destroying himself and the kingdom, I will find it."

"Even if you're the one who is destroyed in the end?"

He shrugged. "He has protected me my whole life, and while we disagree on many issues, I would not have him killed. Mother would be more than distraught, especially after the hell she went through to have us."

"Ferdy ..."

Ferdy gripped my hands. "And I can't have you in danger, either. I know of the League, and the Order, Ella. So does Karl. We heard about it years ago, first from our mother and then while we were at school. Karl might not know that your grandmother is a member or that you are part of it, but we both know of its deadlier capabilities."

"We're not assassins."

"Your enemies would not agree," Ferdy argued, giving me a pointed look. "And that might include Karl's friends in the League."

My breath caught in my throat. I thought of my mother's mission and my father's murder. Amir, Harshad, and Lady POW were not enemies of the Order. But there were other members, too—like my grandfather— and Lady POW was against utilizing them, even to help our mission.

"Do you think it's possible there are members of the League who would want to betray the Order?" I asked.

"There are always traitors on every side."

His answer unnerved me, both at its truth and timeliness.

Ferdy did not seem to notice my discomfort as he continued. "I'm sure it's possible, just as I am sure it is possible that the League is using Karl as much as his thinks he is using them. And that's why I won't let you face this alone."

"I'm not alone."

"Oh, yes, I've almost forgotten your brother." Ferdy laughed as he patted the right side of his torso, just above his hip. "He bruised me up quite a bit the other day."

"I'm so sorry about that," I murmured, embarrassed. I reached out and touched him, feeling him shiver through the layers of clothes. "I did not tell him to go find you."

"Oh, I know. You've never been one to have other people fight your battles." He placed his hand over mine, tracing his fingers over my knuckles, where days of Harshad's instruction had left them red and slightly swollen. "I was wondering if you were learning how to box. Maybe one day I'll get a chance to show you how to fight like a beggar."

I blushed. "We aren't discussing that now."

"Of course not," he said, giving me one of his irreverent smiles. "If it makes you feel better, I was actually glad to see Ben. Even fighting him was worth it."

THE ORDER OF THE CRYSTAL DAGGERS

"You gave him a black eye. Why would it make you happy?"

"Because it meant you were upset." He pulled my hand up to his cheek before grazing his lips across my palm. Even through my glove, the sudden, searing heat between us taunted me, urging me closer even though I knew it would burn me in the end. "Over me."

"I'm nearly always upset over you," I whispered, unable to stop myself from leaning closer, basking in the smothered scent of mint and lavender on his formal jacket.

"So you have missed me, too?"

The playful tone reminded me of how much I did not know him, of how I had allowed myself to be dazzled by him before—of how I wanted him anyway.

I stepped back from him and smiled, even as I felt his disappointment. "*Absolument.*"

For a long moment, one of those moments that burns through time more sweetly, we stared at each other, and I was allowed to bask in the wonder that I loved him, and he loved me. Even if there was no trust between us, even if there was only danger ahead—I loved him, and there was nothing more freeing than feeling secure in that love.

In the distance, the *Pražský orloj* chimed, and the magic of the moment was gone.

"I will have to wait until next time to kiss you," Ferdy said, making me both angry and grateful. "Karl and your grandmother will be worried for you if you don't return soon."

The thought of Lady Penelope and Karl waiting around for me anxiously was enough to break the spell surrounding us. I swallowed hard. "You're right. I have to go."

With a quick nod, I started back toward the entrance of the concert hall. Just before I turned the corner, Ferdy called out to me again.

"Ella."

I turned around. "What is it?"

Even in the shadows, I could see the sparkle of silver in his eyes. "It gets harder to leave you, every time."

I felt the lump in my throat return before I tried to smile. "Parting is such sweet sorrow," I reminded him.

THE ORDER OF THE CRYSTAL DAGGERS

"With all due respect to the Bard, Shakespeare was never so wrong as he was about that," Ferdy said. "I don't feel any sweetness in my sorrow. Desperation, anxiety, and longing—even anger and suffering—but no sweetness."

"It's supposed to be sweet in knowing it won't be long before a reunion."

"Do I know that we will ever meet again?"

I laughed. "Of course we will. How else will you kiss me?"

His sad smile came back briefly. "Will you let me keep you?"

"Ferdy." I took a step toward him, unsure of what I could say, or even what I would do, but he shook his head.

"No. We do not have time right now. My brother will ask you too many questions as it is."

I patted my pocket where the letter he had given me was safely tucked away. "Thank you."

"*Absolument, chérie.*" The cheeky grin fluttered on his face, and then he sank further back into the shadows, disappearing completely.

After the past weeks of trying to forget Ferdy, it was clear I had failed spectacularly. I headed back inside, making my way back to the theatre box, completely overwhelmed.

I could not stop seeing his face inside my mind. His eyes swam before me, silver seas of emotion and intelligence. He was broken by our separation, and I seemed beyond repair without him.

It was only when I bumped into a man that I returned to the world once more.

"Pardon me," I murmured. I glanced up to offer an apologetic curtsy, but as I saw the man's face, I stopped and stared.

It was the man from the Cabal—not the obnoxious green-eyed man, but his companion, Didier. He was wearing the formal suit of an aristocrat, with his black hair cut short, the same shade of ebony as his boots, and a few shades lighter than his skin. He smiled kindly at me; even in the shadows of the theatre hall, I could see his gentleness. "All is forgiven, Lady Ella."

It was the first time I heard his voice, and it startled me. He offered me his gloved hand, and I blinked again. Even with the name and outfit of a

Frenchmen, his manners and accent were distinctly American. I glanced at his coat, where a small revolver was peeking out from his inner pocket.

"There she is!"

I nearly jumped at the sound of Lady Penelope's voice. She came up to me, and I briefly saw Karl was not far behind her, before she smothered me into an awkward hug, smooshing me up against her bosom. I saw Karl behind her, looking frustrated.

"What is wrong with you?" Lady Penelope hissed in my ear. "Where did you go?"

"Uh …" I glanced back and saw Didier was gone. He had slipped away, falling back into the shadows, much as Ferdy had done only moments before. "I was just looking for the ladies' withdrawing room."

"I still can't believe you got lost on your way to see me, Eleanora," Lady Penelope nearly shouted, as she turned to smile at Karl. "Can you imagine!"

She held me tight against her once more. "There's no need for you to go to the withdrawing room if you told Karl you were going down to join me."

"I was trying to escape the marriage talk," I muttered back, hoping she would not inspect my reasons for leaving too closely.

"We will have another discussion about this later," she hissed before Karl stepped up next to us.

"I am just as glad as you are, Madame, that we have found her," Karl said.

He might have been trying to reclaim the kingdom as his own, but I was grateful for Karl's interruption in that moment. It was very fortunate timing, and I could only hope and pray Lady Penelope would forget all about discussing anything later with me.

"The finale is coming," Karl said. "Please, Eleanora, we need to get back to your box. At my request, *Kde domov müji?* Is the last song of the night. The song and its composer have ties to the theatre and remind Bohemia we are united in this place we know as home."

I eagerly abandoned Lady Penelope's false affection, practically leaping onto his arm; we just made it back to our seats as the music began to play.

Karl's eyes widened in excitement as the music began to swell; the crowd was full of mixed reactions, but many people seemed unsure. Some of them stood up to cheer, and some began to leave.

But then, the music stopped, and trumpets began to sound from behind the crowds.

"What is going on?" Karl asked. Over the blaring horns, I could not hear him very well, but I heard him enough to know he was furious. "This is not part of the concert."

I stood up, angling myself over the railing in front of me. Down in the center of the crowd, two lines of servants, strangely dressed figures in bright French livery, touted out on trumpets.

At the sight of them, I turned to Lady POW. Her jaw was rigid with anger, and I did not know what to make of that; I could only hope this had nothing to do with Ferdy.

The trumpets continued, as a pair of dark-skinned performers suddenly appeared between them. I quickly looked away; they were dressed in grass skirts and flowered ornaments, hardly what I would call clothes. Their chests were bare, and their faces were covered with masks as they juggled sticks.

From around the concert hall, I could see half of the ladies in the theatre boxes scrambling to get away while the other half tried to look demure and embarrassed as they secretly stared at the spectacle.

It was a strange sight, the sort of thing I always pictured when I tried to imagine Vauxhall Gardens in London. I almost smiled at the performance before I noticed Lady Penelope's face crinkled with disapproval. Before I could ask what was wrong, the trumpets went silent, and a man's voice called out to the crowd.

"Good evening, my lords and ladies! As God said, 'Let there be light,' it was so, and he saw that the light was very good. I am Lumiere Valoris, and as I was named for the light, I can say, it is very good that I am here!"

The voice was coming from a pallet, carried by six more muscular men, as it made its way in front of the room. There was a man at its center, sitting on an ornate chair, as though he were a king; surrounding his feet were brightly colored flowers and a large array of peacock feathers. Flames flickered up from hollowed-out coconuts.

Fully fledged rage lined Karl's every feature as he turned to me. "Excuse me, my lady," he said, bowing over my hand quickly. "I do believe I must depart for tonight. I will send a formal invitation for you for the ceremony at the *Nàrodni muzuem.*"

He left before I could say anything else, and I was more than a little relieved. Karl had been upset at me when I left him to go after Ferdy. If he

THE ORDER OF THE CRYSTAL DAGGERS

was too distracted to ask questions about my earlier disappearance, I was content.

I turned my attention back down to the man who had usurped the concert finale, watching as he descended from his throne, shook hands, and nodded cordially to all the ladies. I was confused at his performance, but I did enjoy it much more than the rest of the concert.

But then the man looked up at me directly, catching my eye, and I felt my skin grow cold.

It was the man from the Cabal, the one with the green eyes and the sneering smirk. And while I did not know him, he clearly knew me.

13

Lumiere seemed to be in his natural element, though whether it was chaos or the spotlight, I could not say. Several of the theatre's musicians ceased their playing, and it appeared Lumiere had anticipated their response. His own small troupe of footmen took up the lapse, using an array of different instruments to send out a stream of music I had never heard before. Judging by the small drums and hollowed flutes, I would have said it would have been at home on an island, perhaps on in the Caribbean or among the more distant East Indies, perhaps as far as the island of Hawaii.

"What's going on?" I whispered to Lady Penelope. "Who is that?"

"Lumiere," she muttered. "I haven't seen him in years. I always assumed he would die on some island, hung for his deviant crimes or incessant foolishness. It is a testament to his cunning he's still alive, just as it is sign of his immaturity that he's still undertaking obscene spectacles like this one."

"I heard his name. I was wondering who he was that you would know him."

Lady POW did not seem to hear me. The crowd in the theatre was undergoing a mass exodus at this point, while only a few lingered behind, including me and Lady POW.

"This is all Louis' fault," she whispered, shaking her head. "Come, Eleanora. We should return to the manor. I have things I need to discuss with Harshad."

"I'm a member of the Order, too," I objected, watching as some of the policemen attempted to get near Lumiere. Up on his pallet, he only smiled and signaled to the officers that he did not hear them. "Tell me who he is."

She pursed her lips together thoughtfully, before she sighed. "Years ago, before Eleanor was born, your grandfather was the leader of the Eastern division of the League. Lumiere's father, Louis, then the Viscount de Beaumont, was his second in command. Until Jakub met me."

I remembered what Harshad had told me before; Lady POW would have known Louis while she was still my grandfather's mistress.

"So?" I frowned, frustrated. "Why are you worried?"

385

THE ORDER OF THE CRYSTAL DAGGERS

"If you're going to stop the destruction of civilization, you should be worried," Lady Penelope snapped lightly, her eyes never leaving Lumiere's dawdling figure.

I had a feeling she was more upset I had witnessed her worry than she was perturbed by Lumiere's appearance. She did not say anything else to me; instead, she remained focused on moving through the crowds, her ageless grace suggesting none of her irritation.

We were near the theatre's main entrance when she slowed. I nearly ran into her at the sudden change of pace, but before I could ask her what was wrong this time, I saw the answer in front of us.

Lord Maximillian was at the entrance to the theatre. I could hardly believe it. He was standing there so effortlessly, even though he was the man behind all the plotting and all the disaster that had run through my home and my city.

He was dressed in his usual finery, with a golden sash and a pristine white vest, underneath an elegant coat. While I had met him several times before, I had never seen him so meticulously sadistic in his appearance. His mustache, thick and full of black and white hairs, twitched with perverse delight as he saw Lady Penelope, and the toes of his shined boots seemed to tap with anticipation. I stumbled as we approached him, but she only met his gaze with cool interest.

"Lady Wellington." He reached for her hand. She eagerly stepped forward. So, Lady POW did not want to avoid him as much as I did.

"Your Grace," she said, inclining her head in an elderly curtsy. I wanted to ask her why she insisted on using manners, why we did not just capture him there and demand answers, but I knew she would not welcome such a question.

"It is lovely to make your acquaintance once more." Lord Maximillian's gaze went to me. "I have heard of your recent upset, and I am relieved to see Miss Eleanora has made her recovery. I am one of the many who are celebrating her return to Society tonight."

"Yes, we have just had the pleasure of your friend's company," I said. "Mr. Marcelin speaks very highly of you, sir."

"I am flattered to hear so." Lord Maximillian's eyes narrowed only slightly. "I know he is beholden to you."

"Yes, he certainly is," Lady Penelope agreed. "I have heard he was considering marrying your own lovely daughter before he met my Eleanora, so you must know Mr. Marcelin has excellent judgment."

Lord Maximillian might have been a leader in a coup determined to overthrow the empire, but he was still able to be flustered by a matchmaking grandmother. I watched as his cheeks fluttered with a rosy glow as he narrowed his eyes at Lady POW.

"It may be unfortunate for me and my daughter that we did not act quickly enough," Lord Maximillian said, "but that does not mean we will not get another chance in the future."

Lady Penelope and I both caught the underlying threat, and she was just about to reply when Lumiere's voice once more rang throughout the theatre.

"Max!"

We all turned at once, only to see Lumiere break away from a team of police. He hurried forward toward us. Now that he was standing, I was able to see his outfit more clearly, and I had a hard time not staring. He had a cloak trimmed in ermine and peacock feathers hanging on his back like a robe, while his suit was cut in classic lines. There were several watch fobs hanging on off the chain of his pocket watch. The little glimmering fobs caught my eye, and I noticed the watch looked very similar to my father's.

Glancing back up at Lumiere's face, I suddenly wondered how old he was. He seemed young and foolish, as Lady Penelope had asserted earlier, but his jovial milieu, along with carefully placed makeup, only hid his age better.

I need to get better about estimating ages.

After another careful look, I realized he likely had to be close to Amir's age, though perhaps a little older. Early-to-mid forties, at most.

"Max!" His voice carried a distorted amusement, as if he knew he was causing trouble. Lumiere came up and placed a greeting kiss on each side of Lord Maximillian's cheeks, before he shamelessly embraced the man in a hug.

Lord Maximillian was clearly not expecting that. "Come, now, Lumiere," he grunted. "That is enough."

"*Tsk, tsk.* Ever so straight-laced, *mon ami.*" Lumiere ran a hand through his golden hair, letting the theatre lights catch on his many rings. "God gave us everything for our pleasure, remember? It is only sin that keeps it from being so."

He glanced at me with a smile. "Speaking of pleasure, mademoiselle, may I introduce myself?"

"I do believe you have already done so, back in the theatre, Mr. Valoris."

At my wry tone, I saw I earned his respect, though whether or not it was a good thing, I could not say.

"Your mother would be pleased to see you have become a woman who pays attention to 'the least of these,'" he said, quoting the gospel of Matthew in such dulcet tones that it made me wonder if he was the devil himself in human form. "The daughter of such a lady deserves the proper introduction."

I stiffened at the mention of my mother, and I turned to see Lady Penelope was appalled as well. She clamped her lips together tightly, as if she was too outraged to risk allowing herself to speak.

"You needn't worry about my sensibilities when it comes to propriety at this point, sir." I stepped forward and reached out my hand, allowing my grandmother a moment to collect herself.

For that small, pitiful, prideful moment, it heartened me to see Lady Penelope had to recover from a secondary attack. I had come to notice Lady Penelope was a superb fighter, but on occasion, she still needed time to switch tactics.

"Oh, of course not, mademoiselle. But I would be remiss if I treated you in such a nasty manner, especially in such a public place, with the finer members of Society around to witness. Perhaps another place would be better for informalities."

At his provocative gaze and his deliberate choice of words, I knew he was referencing our first encounter back at the Cabal.

"I would have you call me Lumi, if we are to be friends," he continued, taking my hand. "It is my pleasure to formally meet you, Lady Eleanora. After all, any previous meetings are not official until names are honorably given, *ne c'est pas?*"

"The 'honorable' aspect would be the part in question," Lord Maximillian interrupted. "It seems the police are still waiting for you to leave after your disruption tonight."

I turned to see he was right. The police were looking on our small group, waiting anxiously. They knew they could not do much, not with the higher-ranking members of Society around Lumiere, but they seemed prepared to wait.

"You and my father know very well that I have always been good at inconveniencing people with my mere existence," Lumiere replied with an

THE ORDER OF THE CRYSTAL DAGGERS

impish grin. "Undoubtedly you remember him well, do you not, Lady Penelope?"

It was an interesting sight to see Lady Penelope's cheeks fluster over. She composed herself quickly, but I still saw the glimpse of irritation in her eyes.

"Who could ever forget your father?" Lady Penelope's tone turned deadly as she gritted her teeth behind her snakelike smile. "Is he joining you in town?"

"Shortly." Lumiere grinned. "I consider myself playing John the Baptist to his Jesus, of course. Quite an honor, you know."

"If you are comparing your father to Jesus, it must be a high honor indeed." Lady Penelope arched a brow. "Should I expect to see him arriving on an ass?"

Lumiere laughed uproariously, drawing even more uncomfortable attention to us. "He's more likely to part the waters, considering our recent acquisition of a fleet of clippers. They're sadly going out of style, but now is the time to buy. I've just had the loveliest time on the Vltava in one of my own. I'm sure Max here can tell you how hard and time consuming it is to find good accommodations when traveling. Of course, you know how I jump at the chance to take on any hard task I can."

Lord Maximillian's face blotched over in annoyance. "Give my regards to him, please. For now, if you will excuse me, ladies, I do believe I will retire for the evening."

"Wonderful. I will accompany you, as we have business to discuss," Lumiere said.

Lord Maximillian, finally out of patience, blinked and frowned. "I beg your pardon?"

"Come, Max. We might have had our differences the last time we met, but I insist on the chance to make amends." Lumiere gave me a wink. "Business is so unfashionable, and even more so on holidays. I was unable to make the Advent Ball because of you before, and I was much saddened to hear I missed the excitement. Surely you owe me for that. Or perhaps I owe you?"

He turned to Lady Penelope again, and then nodded to me. "If you will excuse us, Madame. It was so lovely, so absolutely lovely to meet you again. Your daughter spoke highly of you before, and I am glad to see after all these years, her assessment remains astute."

"I'll kindly ask you to refrain from discussing my beloved Eleanor," Lady Penelope snapped. "She has passed, and I would not have my grand-daughter's sensibilities maligned by your thoughtlessness."

For the first time, Lumiere looked somewhat contrite. "A thousand apologies," he said, bowing to me. Behind him, Lord Maximillian was try-ing to slink away unnoticed. Lumiere gave me the same self-satisfied smile he had worn before, when I saw him at the Cabal. "Perhaps I will see you again soon. Perhaps in a more quiet environment, one that allows for thoughtful discussion? There are so many good places to meet in Prague, after all."

"Perhaps," I muttered, unable to say anything else. I did not want him to mention the Cabal to Lady POW. "Good night, Mr. Valoris."

"Lumi, please, *chérie*. There is no need for us to be strangers."

He might have thought that, but I was not convinced. My fingers clenched into a fist as he walked away. He stepped up beside Lord Maxi-millian.

If he was a friend of Lord Maximillian's, and the son of a League mem-ber, he was somehow connected to our mission.

"What do you know about him?" I asked Lady Penelope. "He's part of this. He more or less just admitted to it."

"Come, Eleanora," Lady Penelope hissed. "We must get back to the manor quickly."

"Why?" I glanced around into the night, wondering briefly if I would be able to find Ferdy among the crowds. I did not see him, but I did see a shadow slinking around the columns of the theatre, and it reminded me of Didier. Was Lumiere's companion following us, too?

"Just hurry," Lady Penelope snapped, waiting on me as I climbed up behind her into the coach. I heard her give directions to the footmen, and I had only just sat down when she rapped on the roof and we sped off.

"I don't see why you're in such a hurry," I said, rubbing my knee. The sudden lurch forward had sent me tumbling, and I banged my knee on the hard edge of the seat.

"Now that Lumiere has made his appearance, I have a feeling I know who attacked Tulia."

"What?" I glanced out the window, watching as the city's twilight scene rushed past us. "You think Lumiere did it?"

THE ORDER OF THE CRYSTAL DAGGERS

"I'm almost certain of it," Lady Penelope said. "Lumiere is Louis Valoris' son—and he is a trickster to the very end. The fact that he was meeting with Lord Maximillian before only makes everything more precarious. I have no idea what kind of trouble he has managed to create."

"Are you going to tell me and Ben about Louis now?" I thought of what Harshad had said to me before, about Louis working alongside my grandfather. "And Grandfather Jakub, too?"

"There is no need to know all the details of the past," Lady Penelope insisted. Even in the soft moonlight, I could tell she was blushing. I did not know my grandmother was still capable of shame. If I was not as curious as I was, I might have laughed. "Suffice it to say, you only need to know Louis was a troublemaker then, and he has clearly remained one after all these years."

"You were the one who told me before that there is a cost to learning the truth," I nearly shouted, irritated beyond measure. "Why are you trying to protect me now?"

She ignored me. "Thank the good Lord that Xiana is here. Now that I know Lumiere is in Prague, we must be even more cautious. I must speak with Harshad, and I will have to find Amir, too. We need to see everything all over again, starting with Dr. Artha's death."

"What about Ben?" I asked, suddenly curious as to what my brother was doing. While Harshad had mentioned he had a new assignment, I still did not know the exact nature of it.

"Ben is working," Lady Penelope said. "I'm having him spy on a few people in the city, if you must know."

"Why?"

"He needs the practice." She waved her hand through the air, brushing the matter aside. "As you will learn, if you haven't already, there are many tasks one must master in order to protect others. Stealth, fighting, understanding strategy, and finding the right information are all imperative skills in our line of business."

"And keeping secrets, too?" I crossed my arms.

Lady Penelope wrinkled her nose. "Partially. But we are more concerned with discovering others' secrets than keeping them. Tonight, you will get a full demonstration of just such a skill."

I gulped, immediately trying to hide any trace of guilt. "I will?"

"Yes." Lady Penelope steepled her fingers together, while a sadistic form of pleasure came over her face. "My patience is at an end, and there is too much riding on this, now that the reasons are becoming clear. I have been waiting for this day, really."

"You have?" I tried not to let my voice crack. Lady POW was a forceful presence, but after all the hard work she had put me through, and the anguish she had caused between Ben and me, I hated to think she would try to find another way to break me.

"Oh, yes. I knew he was just waiting for the right moment to betray me." She seemed to be talking to herself more than me. "Now that he has found Eleanor's children, it was only a matter of time."

"What?" My skin began to hum with eerie uncertainty.

"What are you talking about?"

"Tell me, Eleanora," Lady Penelope said, her voice deadly and dangerous.

For a second, I worried she was going to ask me about Ferdy, and I would be unable to face her. But her next words sent an even deeper chill through my blood.

"Tell me what Amir has been keeping from me."

"What? I don't know of anything." I shook my head, somewhat relieved before I remembered that Amir had agreed not to mention Ferdy to Lady POW.

"This is not the time to be playing favorites," Lady Penelope snapped. "Your mother never won against me either, not even when it came to him."

"Clearly," I replied bitterly. "But Amir has nothing to do with Dr. Artha's murder. You weren't even here when it happened, were you? Frankly, I fail to see what Amir has to do with the rest of the coup, either."

"That is not something you would know. Lumiere is the missing piece in all of this, and his father is behind it. There is not just a coup that is happening in Bohemia, but one happening within the League of Ungentlemanly Warfare. Everything makes sense now."

I twisted my hands into my skirts, trying to force myself to remain strong against Lady Penelope's reasoning. The letter Ferdy had given to me earlier brushed against my hand. My earlier question about the League called to me, and I was beginning to realize the danger of our situation.

THE ORDER OF THE CRYSTAL DAGGERS

If I am going to protect Ferdy, I need to be careful.

I took a deep breath. "I still don't see how Lumi fits into all of this."

"But you know he *is* a part of this. You just said the same thing only moments ago!" Lady Penelope shook her head. "Do not allow your stubbornness or your loyalty to Amir blind you."

"Tell me how Amir's betrayal fits into everything, then." I covered my hidden pocket, shielding Ferdy's letter further from detection. "If you think I know some of Amir's important secrets, then you'll have to do better to convince me to part with them than just because you order me to."

"Insolent child," Lady Penelope roared. "Need I remind you that I am your leader?"

"Trust is earned, not forced." I glared at her. "And you're in no position to order me around in this regard. You won't tell me any of your secrets, either."

"There is a difference between us. I am not obligated to tell you anything. I am charged with keeping certain secrets of history, for the kingdom of Britain and for others as well. You accepted me as your authority. You owe me your allegiance."

"My allegiance is only to the truth!"

It was hard to remember the last time I rendered Lady Penelope speechless, if it had ever happened. But as she stared at me, her expression aghast, I gloried in a small victory against her.

I reveled in it even more when she sighed in defeat.

"It seems I have taught you too well," she murmured. "Well done, Eleanora. You have managed to learn your lessons, and much more proficiently than I thought."

I bristled at her reluctant praise. "It doesn't do me any good if you won't tell me the whole truth."

"The whole truth is not yet known," Lady Penelope admitted. "But there is no denying Lumiere's presence, and I must consider the evidence. And I need your help to do that."

"I can only help you if you tell me what you know."

Lady POW's eyes went soft. "We will have to compromise."

"Then you can go first. You need more practice with humility."

She dropped the sympathetic act. "I should have known you would avenge Eleanor, too."

I took a deep breath, inhaling sharply. I did not know if Lady Penelope had been meaning to insult me or not, but I knew *Máma* had always called me to be brave, and that meant being brave enough to be kind, too.

We were discussing delicate matters, and it was easy to see kindness as a sort of cowardice in this case.

I did not want to fight my grandmother, and as much as I doubted Lady Penelope was anything like the average grandmother, that was who she was. We were both disillusioned and damaged by the world, and it was my duty—my freedom, my choice, but my duty nonetheless—to help bind up the broken wounds inside of us.

"She would not need to be avenged if things had worked out differently," I pointed out quietly. "But it's like you said before, about the fallen castle walls. There is nothing to be done about it now. We can only go forward."

"Yes." The terseness of her voice suggested Lady Penelope was, indeed, ready to move on. I almost smiled; she was as uncomfortable with my mercy as she had been with the idea of my mother's justice.

My grandmother was a woman who would never be satisfied until she let herself be satisfied, and even in the short time I had known her, I had a feeling she would never completely allow for that.

"I still have to coordinate information with Harshad," Lady Penelope said, "but we must start at the beginning."

I nodded. "I'm listening."

"You know as I have told you before that I was sent here by Queen Victoria," she began. "This region has experienced plenty of upheavals in the last several years, including the Revolution of 1848 and the polarization of the main political aristocracy. When there were several deaths of representatives, especially by those who favored working with Emperor Franz Joseph, it was a signal to Her Royal Majesty to investigate. She sent me and Harshad, along with our small team, to come here and assess the situation. She is further concerned that Indian leadership shows signs of destabilizing."

"I remember that part. You came to talk with Dr. Artha and found that he was murdered."

"Dr. Artha was an informant of mine, and one of the few in the region familiar the Order. He also knew of the League."

THE ORDER OF THE CRYSTAL DAGGERS

"You said before they were the same."

"They have the same goal," Lady Penelope said. "When it comes to much of our work, anyway. But there are some more nuanced differences. We have worked together in the past, but there are some personal issues that remain between us. When Dr. Artha sent notice to Tulia, I did not realize they were such close friends. He also sent notice, through Father Novak, to the Light."

Understanding dawned. "Lumiere."

"Yes. 'Light' is his codename." She nodded. "I was so caught up in Tulia's reappearance that I forgot all about him."

That was understandable; Tulia had worked with my mother as a nurse-maid and companion, but she was also Jakub's half-sister. The surface animosity between Tulia and Lady Penelope was clear, even if I was uncertain at its depth.

"If Dr. Artha sent for Lumiere, I doubt Lumiere would be the one who killed him," I said.

"Dr. Artha was the one who knew of the Order, and he knew of the deaths of the politicians, and the others who were getting threatened," Lady Penelope reminded me. "He would have recognized the Order's poison where it was used. That is likely the reason he reached out to the League as well as the Order."

I did not know what to say. It was hard to remember everything that was going on. There were murders and threats, whispers of coups and now, Amir, whom I had believed to be my ally, was getting accused of betraying Lady POW.

Lady Penelope glanced out the window of the coach. "Lumiere is the son of Louis Valoris, now the Minister of the League. He and I have never been friendly, exactly."

"So he is working against you?"

"Likely." She snorted. "He was very good friends with Jakub, your grandfather. We were his closest confidants several decades ago. After our relationship soured and I escaped from him, Louis naturally blamed me."

I thought of what Harshad had told me before about Jakub. Harshad was the one who had really rescued Lady Penelope, even if she did not credit him.

Despite the seriousness of the situation, I smiled. Harshad had been right about Lady POW; they had known each other long enough to know they could never truly be friends.

My thoughts turned to Ferdy and the letter he had given me. If I let him help the Order, was it possible we would be the same as Lady POW and Harshad? Would we be unable to be friends through our lives, even if we were able to work together?

But Ferdy already has helped me. I curled my fingers around the letter again, thinking of the League.

"So Louis is trying to help Lord Maximillian and Karl restore the Bohemian monarchy," I said, "and he knows he can expect a fight from you."

"That is likely why Lumiere has come, yes." Lady Penelope gazed out the window. "Louis always romanticized power, but he was a realist about it, too. The most powerful position for him, in his estimation, was always to be at the right hand of the devil instead of the devil himself."

"I suppose he liked my grandfather quite a bit then, from your earlier remarks."

She smirked. "He did. Louis has a point; the one holding the title of power is easily different from the one actually in power, and it makes for a great excuse and disguise, in the event something goes wrong."

"Like the French Revolution."

"It's humorous that you should mention France. Louis always dreamed of helping Napoleon."

"Well, it's no wonder he didn't like you," I said. "Not after you married the Duke of Wellington."

Lady Penelope laughed, a crusty sound that emanated from deep inside of her, almost as if she had forgotten how to do it. "I married Arthur more to ensure my escape from Jakub, but you are right. It would have been something Jakub and Louis would have hated. They were already leery of my British heritage, even though the Order transcends nationalities."

"Why didn't you just marry Harshad?"

As soon as the question left my mouth, I knew I had overstepped myself. I hurriedly shook my head, but Lady Penelope did not seem to notice.

"Harshad was a merchant trader before he came to work with the League," she replied. There was a vague practicality in her voice that made

THE ORDER OF THE CRYSTAL DAGGERS

me cringe. She had clearly thought through this possibility more than once.

Before everything else, I knew for certain that everyone lied about something. As I watched Lady Penelope recount her earlier adventures, I saw that she was lying to herself as much as others. I could not say if she knew the *real* truth or not, but she was certainly against admitting it aloud.

"Harshad suffered quite a bit when he went up against Jakub, freeing me and Eleanor from him. I left him thinking it would help him if I stayed away. He was upset with me for trying to protect him further, and once I was certain I was safe and in a position to resume my duties for the Order, I understood why. He loved Eleanor dearly, as his own daughter. Harshad is the only one who called her Dezda, and she called him 'Uncle' affectionately."

"I think he might have loved you, too." My voice was a whisper against the darkness of the carriage; my words seemed to echo past the windows filling the night sky with their heaviness while the stars twinkled.

Lady Penelope shrugged, letting me see only the smallest degree of doubt. It was possible she knew she was lying to herself. "It does not matter now. Relationships only complicate things, especially when you work in the espionage business. Harshad might have wanted me to stay, but I know I made the right decision. Later on, I was able to reach out to him and secure his position as an honorary member of the League. We began working together, and we have been the same ever since."

"If you were just trying to protect Harshad," I said slowly, "I can understand why you would distance yourself from him."

I did not want to tell her just how much I understood her decision, and how much I envied her certainty. Ferdy's face once more came into my mind. I knew it was only my concern for his safety, and possibly my pride, that kept me from seeking him out.

"Well, that does not matter so much now." Lady POW straightened in her chair. "Louis has found himself a puppet in Lord Maximillian and an ally in Karl, and Lumiere has been sent to prevent me from stopping him. Louis is likely behind the death of Dr. Artha."

"But Louis is not here."

"Logic, Eleanora. He has resources. There are any number of henchmen and mercenaries he could employ, such as the one who died the night the castle walls fell. I would not be surprised to learn he was acting under Lumiere's orders, even if he was paid by Lord Maximillian or Karl."

It seemed like years had passed since that night, when Ben and I were on the same team, fighting for our lives and the lives of others in the underground walls of the castle's wine cellar. I could only see a blurry face when I thought about the man who had died in the blaze.

Lady POW gazed back at me. "Now, it is your turn, Eleanora. Tell me what Amir has been keeping from me. I know he and Lumiere are old friends. How long has he been talking with him?"

I blinked. "Amir is friends with Lumiere?"

"You heard him in there," Lady Penelope reminded me. "He knew your mother and held her in high esteem. Of course he would have been friends with Amir."

"I didn't know about that." I felt my mouth go dry. Lumiere was the enemy, and Amir was his friend? It did not make sense in my mind. "I know he mentioned before he had contacts with other League members, but I heard it straight from him, the same as you did, that day in the library."

"You're not cooperating with me. Don't lie."

"I'm not involved," I said. "He did not tell me about Lumiere. I've never met him before today."

That's not true. My mind conjured up the memory of seeing him in the Cabal, and I faltered as I tried not to show my weakness.

"I can tell you are hiding something. What did Amir tell you then?" Lady Penelope asked. "There must be something."

"He told me how he got his scar, the one on his hand," I admitted. Surely there was nothing wrong in admitting that. "He said his family tried to kill him and he would have died if it weren't for *Máma* and Xiana."

There were other things he told me, too. He told me the journal, the one my mother had kept during her last mission, was missing. He told me Lady Penelope was looking for my weakness, and she was putting pressure on Ben to find out my secrets.

I mentally ran through the list of things I had learned from him, only to realize Lady POW was still waiting for more of a response from me when I reached the end.

She looked at me, irritated and expectant. "What else, Eleanora? What else did he tell you about the scar on his hand? Did he tell you what it meant?"

Slowly, I nodded. "He said it was the mark of the *nassara*, the Christian converts."

"That's all he told you?"

"Yes. There was nothing else."

"You're certain? You were paying attention to what he said, correct?"

"Yes." I frowned at her, upset at her insinuation, and still sore at her accusation against Amir.

"What is it?" Lady Penelope asked. "Did you remember something else?"

There was one other thing I could remember.

Amir had mentioned the *noon*, the symbol of the *nassara*, when he told me about his scar. It was the mark on his hand, but it was also the mark on my mother's journal.

After he told me his story, the use of the same mark had not seemed so unusual, considering Amir and *Máma's* history together.

If Lady POW thought Amir was keeping secrets from her—secrets that would affect our mission—it was likely that it had something to do with my mother. And that meant that it was possible it was tied to even more of the past than I had originally suspected.

The coach pulled up to a stop in front of the manor a moment later. We were home, and I saw a way to get out from Lady Penelope's grasp.

"Eleanora." Lady Penelope's voice was impatient, but my resolve was firm and final.

I shook my head. "I have nothing else to tell you."

She snorted disdainfully. "We will see about that, won't we? Come. Join me and the others in the library."

Regretfully, I gathered my skirts, keeping Ferdy's letter wrapped in my hand. In some ways, I gripped it in hopes of comfort; I did not like the foreboding feeling suddenly unraveling in my stomach.

The thought of Amir working against Lady POW, of him betraying the Order in favor of the League—all of it seemed too impossible at first. But I thought through his disagreements with both Harshad and Lady Penelope, how he protected me against Ben, and how he found a way to befriend me despite our difficult beginning.

Was it possible?

I hated asking myself that question. I walked into the house, heading toward the library. It was here, I thought, that Amir had told me himself that he was Lady Penelope's most loyal ally. Had he been lying to me?

It was only when Harshad spoke to me that I awoke from my troubling thoughts.

"Eleanora, what is it? What is wrong?"

His voice seemed to call to me from far beyond me. When I looked up at him, he frowned. Before either of us could say anything—before I could answer his question or before he could ask it again—Lady POW interrupted us.

"Harshad, where is Amir?" Her voice was brittle and sharp, and even Harshad knew it was best not to keep her waiting.

He looked at me, somewhat apologetically, before he said, "He has already left for his rounds tonight. He will be back in the morning."

Lady Penelope narrowed her eyes at me before the two of them began to speak in another language. I listened closely, hoping I would discover some clues. I caught "Valoris" and "Amir," and even "Ben," but I was not able to deduce the meaning behind their words.

Quietly, I sighed and took a seat. It was going to be a long night.

14
◊

The next morning my fingers were cold, even as I gripped the cup of tea in my hands. Mindlessly, I blew on the contents, watching as the force of my breath rippled across the hot drink and the steam wafted away from me. I did not know what else to do but sit there and stare off into space. It was too tempting and too easy to get lost in my own thoughts, jumbled as they were. Only one seemed insistent on repeating itself, and it was the one I hated the most.

Amir had not returned to the manor.

Harshad and Lady Penelope had discussed things long into the night, leaving me to sit on the couch, silent and watchful. I had fallen asleep, still in my evening gown, and it was only hours later when I woke up, alone and cold.

After trading my gown out for a housedress, I went to the kitchens for some breakfast, even though I could hardly eat. The events of the past evening were too mysterious. Between Karl's anger, Ferdy's determination, and Amir's disappearance, I was tired of trying to figure everything out.

All of a sudden, nothing in my life seemed to be the same.

"Nora."

I blew on my tea again as Ben came into the small kitchen behind me. He was wearing a loose-fitting pair of pants and a tunic, one of the many training outfits Harshad had ordered for him. He even wore similar shoes, I noticed, seeing the soft woven coverings on his feet.

"What is it?" I turned to him and tried to keep down a yawn. It was past the usual time I woke up when I was working with Harshad, but no one had come to get me that morning. At the sight of Ben, I wondered if that was the reason he sought me out. "Have you come to get me for a lesson?"

With everything that was going on, I was hoping that the chilliness between me and Ben would disperse some. When I saw him shake his head, I felt the last of my hope shrivel and die.

"No." He moved around me, reaching for his own cup. I heard him sigh softly. "I heard what happened last night."

I said nothing, only taking a small sip of my tea.

401

"Lady Penelope and Harshad have been awake for hours. They've headed out of the manor, both of them, so they can go and see if they can find Amir," Ben said. He hesitated before adding, "I am not sure they ever sleep, to be honest."

I liked that he was trying to be nice, bringing me tea and speaking kindly to me, even though I was upset about Amir. "Have you heard anything?"

"He's not here."

"I know that much. Do you think he is in trouble?" I asked. "I know he usually comes home by the time we're working with Harshad."

"By the time *you're* working with Harshad," Ben corrected.

I decided to let his barb slide this time, especially when I noticed Ben's expression was grim. "What is it?"

"Lady POW and Harshad are upset," Ben said. "And I think they have good reason to be."

I frowned but said nothing.

"I have been thinking it over," he said slowly, "and after talking with both of them earlier, I think they are right to be worried about him."

"Why would you say that?" I asked. "I mean, I am worried for Amir, too. He could be in trouble, or there could be some information that is causing his delay. There is no real reason to question his loyalty to Lady Penelope over a delay."

"It's not a delay."

My skin chilled over at the edge in his voice as much as the condemnation in his words.

"I saw him last night," Ben said. "I saw him as I was watching Karl's movements last night."

"You were watching Karl?"

"Yes. Lady POW wanted me to find out as much as I could about him, and she thought sending me would be a good idea." Ben shrugged. "She said if he caught me spying on him, all I had to do was tell him that I was worried for you, as your older brother."

"Makes sense," I murmured. I thought about Ferdy last night. *Did Ben see him while we were at the concert?*

THE ORDER OF THE CRYSTAL DAGGERS

"I nearly missed Karl as he stormed out of the *Stavovské divadlo*," Ben said. "He was angry and upset. I followed him to a new address, and then I saw Lord Maximillian come with a stranger."

"The man from the Cabal. Lumiere Valoris."

"Yes, that's who it was," Ben said. "How did you know?"

"I met him last night. He was the one who interrupted the concert and made Karl so angry. Karl had arranged for the last piece of the evening to be a tribute to Bohemia, and Lumiere ruined it for him."

Ben did not ask for details on Lumiere, so I knew he had discussed him with Lady Penelope before. I wondered if she had told him the same things that she told me, or if this was another way to see if she could get me to reveal my secrets.

"Lumiere is connected to Lord Maximillian and Karl," Ben continued. "I know from Lady Penelope that he is a member of the League, but she doesn't trust him. When he was done with his meeting, Lumiere went back to the castle with Karl. I decided to follow Lumiere after that. I didn't know who he was at the time, but I felt like it would be good to have some information on him since he talked with both Karl and Lord Maximillian."

"That was a good idea," I said, making Ben smile.

"I thought so, too," he admitted. "He didn't get far before I saw Amir."

"So Amir was near the castle last night?"

"Not exactly," Ben said. "I followed the carriage as well as I could. It wasn't too hard, since the winter weather has kept a lot of people from heading out. Eventually, Lumiere stopped at the church where Father Novak was murdered."

"Our Lady of the Snows."

He nodded. "He went inside for just a few moments, and then Amir stepped out of the shadows and greeted him."

I thought about what Lady POW had said before. "I know they were friends when *Máma* was alive."

Ben wrinkled his nose. "It seems they are still quite good friends," he said. "Lumiere was ecstatic to see him. Amir got into the carriage, and then they rode together for a few blocks before Amir slipped out."

"What happened then?" I asked. "Did you follow Amir?"

Ben took a long sip of his tea before he shook his head. "No."

"Did you keep following Lumiere then?" I asked.

Ben was suddenly much more reluctant to talk. I saw him glance back at the kitchen door, nervous and bitter.

He wants to leave now.

Which meant he had done something.

I stood up and put my teacup down on the small table. "Tell me," I said. "I might be able to help."

"I doubt that," Ben muttered. "You're Amir's favorite. You don't think he's a traitor."

"Of course not," I said. "He told me before he was Lady Penelope's most loyal follower. Even Lady POW told us that she would trust him with her life."

"That's exactly what a traitor would want you to think," Ben said. "Come on, Nora. Think about it. Something's happened to us in the last few weeks. Amir has been causing problems between us."

"Amir?" I slammed my teacup against the table. "Amir is not the one who has been using you to try to find out my secrets."

"Are you really that blind? He's the one who made you suspicious of me in the first place," Ben insisted.

"You didn't help by going out and beating Ferdy up."

"I told you why I did that." Ben stood up now, too, only to look down at me.

"Please, Ben," I said, grabbing his sleeve. "Even if you think Amir is the one behind the trouble between us, you have to at least face the truth that it only remains there because you keep it there."

"That's not true."

"Yes, it is," I insisted. "This is the first time in weeks we've spoken plainly to each other."

"Because you won't tell me the truth!"

I was taken aback. My hand dropped from his arm. "Is that really what you think? That I won't tell you all my secrets? That you can't trust me?"

"It's true." Ben shook his head. "You know it's the truth."

I felt my heart clench. Once more, I was tempted to tell him. But the thought of Ferdy's safety, of how wrong Ben was about Amir, and even

Empress Maria Anna's concern stopped me, and that was when I realized something important. I did not want my brother's ire, but I did want his trust. I would not always be able to tell him things. I knew he had secrets of his own from me, starting with his own feelings about our father playing favorites between us.

The same thing was true of Ferdy, of Lady Penelope, of Harshad and Amir and even Tulia. I did not need to know all their secrets. I just needed to know I could trust them.

Lady POW had been adamant before that it was necessary to know that people would fail me. She warned me that I had to be on my guard at all times, and that it was important to pay attention to everything so I would not be surprised at betrayals, and that I would be able to know how to manipulate people to do what I wanted and get the results I wanted.

I had balked at the idea then. I realized now that she might have had a point, but there was a price too great for me to pay.

I wanted to be able to trust people, so that even if we failed in the end, we would be together.

I did not know if that was more important or not, but it was important enough to me right now that I knew I had to say something to Ben.

"Some secrets are not just mine, Ben," I said. "I can't tell you everything. Other people are counting on me to keep silent."

"I knew you were lying before." He did not sound smug; he sounded relieved, which made me soften, even if I did not want him to worry about it at all.

"I'm sorry. I don't do it to hurt you. I'm trying to protect others. Maybe I'm even trying to protect myself," I said quietly. "But there are bigger things happening here, things that are bigger than you and me."

"I know that," Ben insisted. "I'm worried you don't."

"I do know it. I'm still trying to figure it out some, but I do know there's a lot at stake. But you do know I love you. And I would never want to hurt you." I looked up at him. His blue-green eyes were just a little lighter than mine, and for some reason, it was so hard to explain to Ben how much I did love him. He was my family, my only family, and someone who had suffered so much at my hand, yet someone who still fought to protect me. I sighed. "I guess it's unavoidable that I will hurt you, but I don't want to lose your love. Or your trust."

I looked down at the floor, unsure of what else to do. Ben and I had always had a common enemy with Alex and Cecilia, and we had always had

THE ORDER OF THE CRYSTAL DAGGERS

a common dream in Liberté. This was the first time in recent years we had different loyalties and different pursuits.

Finally, Ben sighed. He shifted his feet and put his hands in his pockets.

"I suppose you're right." Ben's voice was more gentle this time. "We are going to have to trust each other if we're going to succeed. And that includes trusting each other with our silence as much as our secrets."

Hope renewed inside of me. I almost cheered at his reply, but I stopped myself. Ferdy's earlier restraint had clearly been against his wishes, but he knew he could only have my trust if he could earn it. I would do the same with Ben; I would have to wait to see that I had earned Ben's trust back.

At the thought of Ferdy, my smile brightened even more. I loved him, and I knew I could trust him. He wanted me to trust him, and he had earned it.

I nearly squealed with delight, thinking of the next time I would see him. There would still be trouble between us, but if we trusted each other, we could find a way.

Ben sighed. "I still think it is fair to question Amir's loyalty," he said. "I talked with Lady POW this morning after I met with him, and she's certain that he is working to betray her. And possibly us, too."

"You met with Amir?" I frowned and waited for Ben to provide further information. I could already guess what happened.

Ben had confronted Amir, wanting information on Lumiere, and Amir told him something that made Ben and Lady POW suspicious.

When Ben finished his story, I was disappointed with how much of it I had guessed.

"He said he had to go and take care of something," Ben said. "He said that Lumiere was his friend and he wanted Amir to help him with something. He said it had to do with Lord Maximillian and Karl, and that was all he could tell me."

"Did he say when he was coming back?" I asked.

Ben shook his head. "But it's not a coincidence, is it, that Lady Penelope thinks he's betrayed her? The timing is suspicious."

What could Amir be doing to help Lumiere?

I could not think of anything, but I also did not know why Amir would be helping Lumiere in the first place. I had seen him myself, chatting with Lord Maximillian. He had talked of meeting him the night of the Advent

Ball, of mending the issues between them. It did seem like Karl and Lord Maximillian had been fighting with each other, too, as I recalled what Karl had told me, and the other information Ferdy had given me.

"We can question Amir's loyalty," I said slowly, "but I think we need to question Lady POW's, too. She has reasons for her own feelings on this matter. And there is no denying her own secrets."

Ben sat down at the table again. His expression was remorseful. He picked up his cup and poured more tea. "That is fair, I suppose."

I grinned and sat down across from Ben. "If that's fair, we've found a good starting place to start asking questions."

Reaching into my pocket, I curled my hand around the letter Ferdy had given me. "I have a few more questions I'd also like to run by you, *brácha*."

"I'll see to the tea. Looks like we're going to need more."

Before I could show Ben the letter, Xiana appeared in the doorway. She appeared like a ghost, silently and gracefully, and in her dark robes, I almost felt it was too apt of a description.

"There you are," she said. "I have been looking all over for you."

"You have?" I asked, sad to see my time with Ben interrupted. It was nice to feel like his friend again.

"Yes. You've received a message," Xiana said. "It's from someone named Clavan. He says Zipporah will be able to meet with you this weekend, on Saturday night after the Shabbat."

She handed Ben the small scroll of paper. I watched as Ben read through the note, before turning to Xiana. "Have you heard anything from Lady Penelope or Harshad about Amir?"

Xiana shook her head. "No. But if I know Amir, I know if he does not want to be found, he will not be found."

"You don't think he will betray Lady POW, too, do you?" I asked, surprised.

Xiana's stoic face hardened, ever so slightly. "He is more than capable of betrayal. Remember, that is what he did to your mother." She shook her head, her long braid of hair swinging behind her. "And others as well."

Before I could ask another question, she excused herself. I watched as she left, my mouth hanging open in shock and confusion. I would not have said Amir betrayed my mother; he left her, and broke her heart maybe, but he did not betray her.

What did Xiana mean by that?

Ben, unaware of my thoughts, looked up from the note. "Eliezer's wife will have our herbs for Tulia this Saturday. That's a few days away yet. We'll have to question her carefully. I don't like the thought of getting Clavan and Jarl and their friends mixed up in our trouble."

I nodded. "I agree."

"Now we just have to get to Saturday," Ben said. He leaned back, stretching out some. "And then we'll have our answers."

"Don't forget, we'll be able to make an antidote to the Order's poison, and we'll find out if anyone else is making it, too." I took another sip of tea, then got up from the table.

Hopefully Amir will be back before then, and we can forget this betrayal nonsense.

"Are you looking for something to eat?" Ben asked.

"Yes."

"Get some for me, too."

I laughed. "I was planning on it," I assured him. As I searched the kitchen, I glanced back at the doorway where Xiana had disappeared. Amir had told before that he had made a mistake when he allowed my mother to leave. I would not have said he betrayed her, the way Xiana had.

I did not think he would betray Lady Penelope, either. Ben and I did not agree with our conclusions, but there was no point in fighting about it until we found him.

THE ORDER OF THE CRYSTAL DAGGERS

15

Three days passed, and there was no sign of Amir. I did not allow myself to despair, because if I did, I would not just wallow in my sadness, I would go mad. While time seemed to move only slightly quicker than absolute stillness, I relived our conversations, running them over and over again inside my mind, turning them over and examining them again. There were so many, from the time I had met Amir on the streets of Prague, to the time he had carried me to the front parlor. I thought about meeting him in the library the second time, knocking him down with a punch, and practicing the waltz with him. I thought about his devotion to my mother and the changing mix of pain and pleasure in his gaze as he talked with me.

It had been a struggle to pay attention to anything over the past few days; even Harshad seemed to understand my distraction. He had Xiana review the basics of stance, footwork, and technique with me before dismissing me from my sessions. Harshad said I would be too distracted to fight well, and he was right.

Ben was allowed to roam the city, searching for any sign of Amir, while Lady POW herself went to lectures and socials with other older ladies. It turns out the elderly were a wealth of gossip and information, but there was no mention of a rogue Turk wandering around the town.

We could only wait, Lady Penelope had said.

Her words were a prison sentence to my heart, but I was comforted in that she did not seem to take her own advice. I saw her as she prowled around the manor at all hours of the day, and even when we came back from our outings, I would wake up in the middle of the night to find her pacing the hallways. I had no idea where Amir's room was, but I heard her steps pass down my hallway more than once as the night dragged on. Neither of us seemed to be able to sleep well.

It's a miracle that I am able to stay awake for this, I thought, looking around at the scene before me.

The *Nàrodni muzuem* was full of aristocrats and the political elite, but it was not much different from any other ball I had seen. A large crowd had gathered in the atrium, where Karl lorded over the room from atop a twin pair of grand staircases. *The place really is beautiful,* I thought, taking note of the gothic arches and the detailed metalwork. The marble floors reflected the warm lighting, sending a ripple of sparkles through the regal crowd.

It was a fitting metaphor, as the secret prince of Bohemia reigned over the room as its crown jewel. He had been invited to make a speech, and the one he was making was full of meaningful, celebrated pauses as he impressed the masses.

As his audience broke out in another sea of applause, Lady Penelope cleared her throat behind me. "Stand up straight, Eleanora. There are a lot of important people here. We wouldn't want to look sloppy."

"Of course we wouldn't." I struggled to keep myself from yawning.

"Why are you so tired? You already fell asleep on the way here. Goodness, your hair is a mess." Lady Penelope discretely tugged on the combs in my hair, and I waved her meddling hands away at once.

"Stop it," I hissed. "I'll get it."

I did not want her fussing over me. I was already under severe scrutiny, since I was not actually a member of the political elite even if I was welcomed by Society. Many of the lords and ladies looked me over carefully as we had entered the museum, and I knew they had a right to be curious. As Karl continued to make his speech, I saw a wave of eyes turn to glance at me.

Lady POW huffed. "You should have checked yourself better before we came in."

"You should have said something sooner if they bothered you."

"Why are you even wearing these combs?" Lady Penelope asked. Her expression suddenly soured as she straightened the one behind my left ear.

I was wearing the combs Ferdy had given me. After the long days of worrying for Amir, the twinkling combs served as a talisman of sorts, with all their small emeralds, the brilliant sapphires, all decorated around golden *fleurs-di-lis*. Wearing them reminded me to remain steadfast in my determination, even if I did not feel like being brave.

And, if Ferdy did come and "rescue" me from here, he would know I had decided to trust him. I tried not to blush, thinking of the pleasure he would feel.

Lady Penelope cleared her throat. "Did Karl give you these?"

"What? No. There is no need to worry about them." I batted her hand away one last time, before twisting the combs once more into my curls. I winced at the pain, but I gave Karl my full focus. Secretly, I hoped that the rest of the room would follow my example and pay attention to him.

THE ORDER OF THE CRYSTAL DAGGERS

I already did not relish the thought of seeing Karl again.

"It's not my fault you are content to look like you've napped all the way over here," Lady Penelope muttered. "Even if it is true, there's no reason give it away."

The *Nàrodni muzuem* was on the far side of Prague from where we lived. I considered my nap a small repayment for the task I was about to face.

"I've been working with Harshad in the mornings, and I had more late nights now that we are moving in Society again," I reminded her, trying to mask my moaning. "Be grateful I do not look worse."

"I have had some late nights myself," Lady Penelope remarked, and I was amused that she would admit to her nightly discomfort. "There is no reason you should not be able to recover if I can."

I ignored her, yawning again, as Karl continued on with his speech.

He seemed very happy, much more energetic than me. His voice was booming and somewhat seductive as he heralded the courage of his fellow men and condemned the uncaring heart of the emperor.

"Ever since the disastrous fire at the castle, there have been no condolences from Emperor Franz Joseph. What can we conclude, except for the obvious?" Karl waved his arms around, exaggerating his facial expressions. "Bohemia is not his concern. Our pain is not his pain."

There were several murmurs of agreement, even if they were quiet.

"Are we not called to be free?" Karl asked, speaking with the easy grace of a practiced prodigy. "The Lord himself called the Hebrews out of Egypt, and I ask you, my countrymen, are we not in Egypt ourselves? Surrounded by an empire that is crumbling under the weight of bureaucracy, the decadency of dispassionate rulers, of taxation without representation or recompense?"

There were more cheers this time. I glanced over at Lady Penelope. She had an impressed look on her face.

"You're not agreeing with him, are you?" I asked.

She gave me her sadistic smile. "I can appreciate an honest attempt to manipulate the masses, Eleanora. That's his Oxford education coming through, right there."

"I am here to proceed over this dedication," Karl said. "But I do not want to dedicate our work to the greatness of the empire. Bohemia's greatness is in its people. We are the dreamers, we are the makers, we are the ones who carried and build greatness from the bond of our blood. We

411

are the ones who are called to represent Bohemia to the world, and it is time we took a stand and demand that we be heard, as is our due. We are the ones who make this country great, and we deserve to be properly represented on the world stage."

"He is certainly a good orator," Lady Penelope murmured, as Karl began talking about taxes and tariffs and the empire's abuse of our people. "If what he was saying was true, he would make a good ruler."

"His rhetoric could be considered treasonous in some circles," I said.

"That is good politicking," Lady Penelope reminded me. She gave me a wry smile. "Speak, strike, redress. You will be surprised how politicians use language to get you to believe what you think they mean."

"Hopefully, that will change one day." I shook my head. "That is dishonest."

"People do not want the truth. People want to be the hero of a good story, and more often than not, they want to be the hero without doing any of the work." Lady Penelope nodded toward Karl. "He is giving that to them now, and they are responding as expected. We will have to be careful."

"Will this disrupt Queen Victoria's relationship with India?"

"The worst part is that I don't know if it will or not," Lady Penelope said. "As much as it pains me to admit, many leaders do not have everything figured out. We can only act in the manner we see best, without knowing if it will work, or if it will be the best position to have taken in the end."

I knew she was talking about her own position as the leader of the Order, and I wondered if it was good for me to have doubts about trusting her. I could not seem to help my response when it came to Amir, but there were other areas in which I did not trust her.

For the moment, I did not say anything about that. "It seems there is a lot of guesswork in trying to change the future."

I gave her a response that was ambiguous and vague, hoping she would be pleased.

She nodded. "Especially for the better."

"Better for who?" I murmured, wondering aloud more to myself as Karl concluded his speech and stepped down. The audience clapped and cheered, and he waved gallantly to them.

THE ORDER OF THE CRYSTAL DAGGERS

Lady POW sighed beside me. "If he is not stopped," she warned, "he will be a formidable opponent for the emperor. He has already made some high-ranking people uncomfortable. Harshad received a message from one of our associates in Vienna that said Franz Joseph has been asking King Ferdinand for information."

"Did the king respond?" I asked as I kept my eyes on Karl, watching him grin as he met with other members of the Diet and those who were in attendance. He seemed much happier than he was the last time I saw him.

"No," Lady Penelope said. "The king and Empress Maria Anna have been ill the past few days. They have not allowed anyone to meet with them. Empress Maria Anna has canceled her plans to leave for their country estate, too."

"I have heard she likes to travel," I said, "but with Karl here, I would think she would want to make sure he was staying out of any trouble."

"Yes, I suppose. Family members do tend to make poor decisions because of love." Lady Penelope turned to me. "And while we are discussing that particular subject, there is something I need to ask you."

"What is it?"

Lady Penelope's eyes, so similar to my mother's and my own, pierced through me. "Are you falling in love with Karl? I need you to tell me now, Eleanora. This is not the time to remind you that there is no room for romance in the life of a spy, but I feel I must. I know you are worried for Amir, and I will be the first to admit that this is my fault. I thought he had forgiven me for the business with your mother."

"We don't know if you're wrong yet," I said, choosing to ignore, if only for the moment, how she downplayed my mother's unhappiness and Amir's regret. "He hasn't had the chance to explain himself."

"Either way, it does not matter now. I'm more worried for you. Falling in love has no place in this job."

"I am not in love with Karl."

"You have not been yourself recently. You have not been yourself since the concert, and it's not just worry for Amir. There is more to it, isn't there?" Her eyes darted up to my hair. "I know Karl had to give you those combs, Eleanora."

"I already told you he didn't," I hissed, suddenly afraid. I reached out and lightly brushed my fingers against the jewels of the combs. Ferdy had insisted I take them, and I wondered all of a sudden if he had tricked me.

I straightened my shoulders. I had to take care of one thing at a time, and Lady POW's temper was the more immediate. I could find a way to yell at Ferdy later, I decided.

"It does not matter now. I am not in love with Karl, and if you make me scream it, it might damage our cover."

I hoped she would not say anything else; Lady Penelope had a perfect hold on me. I had nowhere to run as we were surrounded by the public. If I left now, and suddenly, there would be whispers that could adversely affect our mission.

She glared at me. "Eleanora, don't be ridicu—"

"My lady."

I was never so happy to see Karl as I was in that moment. He came up to me, and even though I could not stop myself from wondering if Ferdy was going to follow him, there was nothing dishonest about my smile as I greeted him. "Mr. Marcelin, how lovely to see you."

I curtsied, and he bowed over my hand, kissing it reverently while I praised God for his providence in allowing me to wear gloves once more.

"I am so grateful to see you here today," Karl said. "Especially since I know our last meeting was marked with unpleasant circumstances."

"Oh, there is no need to worry about it," I murmured, hoping that Lady POW was not listening. When I saw one of her friends had come up to speak with her, I added quietly, "Unless there is some reason I should expect to see the other Mr. Marcelin here?"

This would be another event where Ferdy would be eager to "rescue" me.

Karl's smile dropped. "No."

Ferdy had said he was leaving for Silesia in the morning on the night of the concert.

But surely, he wasn't actually leaving? I suddenly wondered if he had been telling me the truth.

He did promise me before that he would not lie to me.

Carefully, I asked Karl, and he shook his head.

"Please, Eleanora," he said. "The rededication of the museum has been a lovely event, and I'd rather not discuss the tragic events of this week. Please, come with me. I will introduce you to my friends."

THE ORDER OF THE CRYSTAL DAGGERS

"Tragic?" I smiled. "I know you have your struggles with family, but tragic is hardly the right description for them."

"You haven't heard the news?" Karl sighed. He took my hand, mumbled off an excuse to Lady Penelope about taking me to see Count Potocki, and then led me toward the side of the room.

As we walked, I was suddenly overcome with a feeling of dread. My palms were clammy, and I felt sick in my stomach. "Karl?" I asked. "What is it?"

"My brother is dead."

Karl spoke quietly, wearing the same stoic expression Xiana had worn as she told me Amir was more than capable of betraying the ones he supposedly loved. I felt like I had to hear the words several times over, as if hearing them did not make sense at all. My hand covered my mouth in shock; the floor seemed to quake beneath my feet, and my whole body suddenly went numb.

Ferdy is dead? How can this be?

"I regret to tell you this now," Karl replied. "But this is a very important day. Today, I have drawn up a resolution for Emperor Franz Joseph, and with the support here, he will not be able to—"

"I don't understand." My eyes were watering over; my nose prickled with pressure, and I felt lightheaded. I pulled free from Karl, nearly tripping over the length of my gown. "What do you mean, your brother is dead?"

"Please keep calm," Karl muttered, his eyes dark and dangerous. "He was killed by a foreigner as he was on his way back to Silesia two days ago. His carriage was attacked and then doused in fire. A nearby vicar witnessed the whole thing. He nursed the coachman in his final hours and sent word to my family of the incident."

My chest constricted, and my heart stalled. Karl tried to explain the rest of my possible questions, but all I heard distinctively was how it was clear Emperor Franz Joseph did not care about his citizens, if he was going to constantly allow foreigners to come and do what they pleased.

The memory of Ferdy's question hit me hard.

"Do I know that we will ever meet again?"

I had trouble moving; I had trouble breathing. I barely noticed we were still at the *Nàrodni muzuem*, surrounded by Karl's political allies, and everyone was looking to me to smile and dance and charm my way into their hearts.

"Eleanora?"

"What is it?" I gaped as I looked around, as if my existence had suddenly taken on a form too alien to even recognize.

I am not supposed to live in a world without Ferdy.

Karl sighed, trying to soften his expression. "I know the news is very sad, but there is nothing we can do now. My parents have taken to their beds this week, and I did not blame them. But I know I must be strong, and that is why I am so glad you are here with me. I need you to be strong for me here today. Please, there is no need for you to feel badly for me."

Suddenly, I wanted to scream at him. I did not need to feel badly for Karl; I was too busy feeling bad for myself! I could not believe how selfish he was being, and how little he must have thought of me, thinking I would just take sad such news in stride.

And then there was the matter of Ferdy himself. *What could have happened? Surely he is not really gone.*

Ferdy promised me he would not lie to me, I thought. He was supposed to return to Silesia. I mean, I knew he never went, but what if he was on his way back when everything happened?

There was no denying that King Ferdinand and Empress Maria Anna had been missing their scheduled appearances, and they *had* canceled their travels. Lady Penelope had just said so.

The world swam before me, and I began to withdraw into myself.

I did not know if I could bear it if Ferdy was really dead. It seemed more likely that I was dead, and this was a preamble to hell.

"Eleanora?" Karl's voice called me again, and I had to shake my head.

"I don't know what to say," I finally managed. My voice was raspy and weak, and I felt my eyes start to water. "But I do believe I need to tend to a call of nature. Excuse me while I go to the ladies' withdrawing room."

"Ella, come back here. This is our moment, for Bohemia. I have the resolution for the Emperor to give us back our throne, since he will not bother to be crowned here. This is important." Karl reached out and snared my wrist, tugging me back toward him. Immediately, I shoved my palm forward, slamming it into his nose.

My training had taken over before I realized it.

THE ORDER OF THE CRYSTAL DAGGERS

"Ow!" He wiped his nose, which had a small smattering of blood on it. I had hit him too hard, I realized. Fortunately, it was only a little, and he was able to clean a large amount of it off without others' notice.

"I'm very sorry, sir," I muttered, ducking around him. "I must excuse myself."

"If you leave me now and make me look like a fool," Karl hissed, "you will regret it."

His angry tone stalled me for only a second, but the viciousness in his voice was not enough to overcome my sadness. If I had been thinking more clearly, I might have realized that Karl's mask had slipped again, and his lies were beginning to fall away. He was worried about his appearance, he was worried about his reputation. He was worried about what the other aristocrats would think of him; he was worried about falling out of their good political graces.

He was not worried about me, or my distress.

Karl said he wanted Bohemia's freedom, but he really meant he wanted power. He wanted his throne back. This was just all part of his plan—me included. What better queen to rule beside him than the daughter of a man who saved the last king during a revolution?

But I was too upset and too distracted to care.

I walked out of the ballroom, brushing past Karl's friends and hurrying down the large set of stairs in front of the museum. The winter breeze was mellow but sure as I made my way down the streets.

There was no clear task in my mind, no clear place to go.

But I kept walking.

I did not know what I could do. Amir was gone, I had no idea where Ben was, and I needed answers. So I went to the one place where I knew I could get them.

I had already walked for blocks when I noticed I forgot my cloak back at the *Národni muzuem*. All I could do was put one foot in front of the other as the winter weather joined me through the snow-spotted streets. My hands were numb but shaking, and my feet were pinched with cold

THE ORDER OF THE CRYSTAL DAGGERS

pain. I was more grateful than ever I had worn my new kid boots when I reached the Cabal.

I entered in, still listless but somehow more settled.

"Ella."

Faye's voice called out to me in a friendly manner as I entered her family's establishment. There were a few other people around, a couple of regulars nursing their drinks. I was surprised, for some reason, to find myself here at all. A lady did not walk the streets alone, let alone to come to a publican house.

"You look lovely." As if she knew of my own confusion, Faye came up to me carefully. I wondered if I looked as terrible as I felt. I could see her hesitation in her slow approach. Her eyes were wide with concern. "Are you well?"

"I need to speak with your father," I mumbled, unable to say anything else. It was as if there were two versions of me living inside my body, and half of me was hiding secrets from my other half. I did not know when I arrived that I was supposed to come here, and I did not know I was looking for answers until I asked for Clavan. "I'm sorry, but it's imperative. I need to speak to him or Eliezer now."

"If you're waiting for Elie's wife, I am not sure she will come here tonight," Faye said. "But you're welcome to come in and warm up. Where is your cloak? You must be freezing."

I felt my chin tremble as Faye led me to a nearby table.

"I'll call for my dad while I get you some soup and tea," she said. "Please, sit here."

"Please, I just need information," I said, even though I sat down. I did not want to tell her I was not sure if I could handle any food at all. My stomach was empty and grumbling, but my nerves stole any trace of my usual hunger. "Please. I promise that's all I need."

Faye was clearly troubled by my expression, but she nodded. I was grateful for her poise, especially as I felt the fear inside of me start to multiply.

When Clavan appeared through the door a moment later, I was too grateful to hide my desperation. "Mr. Clavan," I sputtered, standing up from my seat. The urge to run over and collapse into his arms shocked me. It hit me hard, knowing how much I wanted a father's comfort.

THE ORDER OF THE CRYSTAL DAGGERS

He took one look at me and shook his head. He grabbed a nearby bottle and a set of cups. "Patience, Lady Ella."

He sat down across from me. "I'm not surprised to find you here," he said quietly. "I know Ferdy is quite stubborn at times."

"What are you talking about?" I blubbered.

"You're here because of him, aren't you?" Clavan calmly poured a drink for me. "You're dressed up for all of Society to see, but you're in love with him. I imagine it's quite distressing on your grandmother."

"How you know my grandmother?"

"I hear the gossip from all around." Clavan gave me a small smile. His ageless eyes twinkled behind the little round glasses. "Lady Penelope Ollerton-Wellesley has been known to chase fortune and drama all her life, and I see she has not changed a bit, even after entering your life. The rumors say she has been dangling your suitors along, especially that Karl Marcelin."

"That's not why I am here." I took a sip from the cup before me, surprised to feel the burning sensation of the liquid. "What is this?"

"It's best not to ask the questions that have troubling answers," Clavan said with a kind, teasing smile. "I assumed when you came in here, you were looking for Ferdy. I know it's been a while since he's been here, but he'll be back. He always comes back."

I swallowed hard. "I wanted to know something else," I managed to say. "I heard something happened a few days ago, outside of the city. There was an attack on a carriage that was headed to Silesia. I wanted to know if you heard about it."

He raised his brows at my question but gave me a thoughtful look. "Do you mean the incident with the empress's cousin?"

My heart sank.

"The empress's cousin?" I repeated carefully. That was one of Ferdy's covers.

"Yes." Clavan nodded. "There was a carriage with the coat of arms for the Duke of Silesia that was attacked by a Turk a few days ago. He got away, but apparently no one else survived."

A Turk.

My hands fell away from my glass as I felt my heart break into two.

"The news and a mix of the gossip said that there was a fire from something the carriage was carrying with it. The vicar who saw the whole thing said it was likely wine."

"Wine," I repeated the word, as though it was as foreign to me as any of the Arabic words Amir had carved on his dagger.

I thought of the wine from before, the wine which carried the power to bring down castle walls. I fell back in my chair as Clavan told me the rest of the story, about the fire, about the futile search for the villain.

Ben had told me that Amir had talked with Lumiere before, and how Lumiere was connected to Karl and Lord Maximillian.

Was it possible?

I did not want to think about it. The idea that Amir had killed Ferdy, the idea that Ferdy was dead—those were impossible ideas.

The idea that Karl was somehow behind his brother's death, of course, was more plausible. With Lord Maximillian helping him, and Lumiere, too, all of it came together in the worst sort of way.

"Ella?" I heard Clavan's voice in the small seconds before the rest of the world slipped away and everything went dark.

THE ORDER OF THE CRYSTAL DAGGERS

16

◊

"Ella."

If there was a big difference between getting knocked out and fainting, I was not able to distinguish it. I heard Ferdy's voice calling to me as he had last time, and I woke up in just as strange a place as I had when the castle walls had come crumbling down.

"Ferdy." I sat up and opened my eyes, already searching for him as I woke up. Once more, I found myself in a foreign room, one that was not my own, and I was alone. My head fell into my hands as I collapsed forward.

I ran my hands through my hair as I looked up again. The room was far less grand than Ferdy's room in the castle, but it was neat and orderly, from the worn copy of *Jane Eyre* on the table beside me, to the impeccably embroidered pillow behind me.

Ferdy was not there. No one else was around, either.

I was in a small bed, with thin sheets and an extra quilt tucked over my gown. Through the small window behind me, I saw the sky was still colored with the white-gray sheen of a Bohemian winter afternoon. I did not know if a lot of time had passed since I was talking to Clavan. When I tried to think about it, all I could remember was the feeling of a father's love as my body was carefully carried and set down.

The door opened, and Faye walked in with a tray.

"Oh, good," she said. "You're awake."

"I'm so sorry," I mumbled, embarrassed. "I didn't mean to cause trouble."

"This is a publican house," she reminded me. "You're not the first person to pass out here, nor are you first to get what appears to be the first decent sleep you've had in days."

I felt my shame further deepen as I looked outside. As Faye indicated, it was clearly late. I suddenly did not want to know how long it had been since I had collapsed.

"You might be one of the sober ones who did, but other than that, we're very familiar with what happens."

421

"Is that how you met Jarl?" I asked, trying to smile even though I was unable to find any strength in me.

Faye laughed. "Close enough." She moved her book and put the small tray down on the table beside the bed. I saw there was the warm cup of soup and a cup of tea she had promised me earlier.

"For a moment, I was worried the brandy my father gave you was too strong," she admitted. "But when I saw you barely had any at all, I knew you would be well with some rest. Luckily, you're close to my height, and Jarl's uncle Rhys came in as Dad started to move you."

I shook my head. There was a pounding feeling behind my eyes, a pressure from the Clavan family's kindness and my own despair at Ferdy's loss. "I don't feel well at all."

"I can see if Eliezer and his wife will come," Faye said. "They usually come to see us after the Shabbat is over and she finishes her other rounds, but I know she will make exceptions for special cases."

I shook my head. "Your family has done more than enough for me. I am already indebted to you."

"We take care of our own," Faye promised. Her eyes, a pretty hazel in the dim lighting, sparkled with a benevolent mischievousness. "And sometimes others as well."

"Thank you."

"Just rest for now," Faye said, fluffing the pillow behind me. "I've been checking in on you every couple of hours. My room is small, but it'll be good for you to stay for a bit."

"This is your room?"

She nodded. "It's likely a bit smaller than yours, but—"

"It's wonderful," I said. I looked down at the finery of my dress. "I wasn't always the kind of person to wear gowns and go off to parties. I was a servant for my stepmother after my father died. He was knighted by the king before the Revolution, so I might have been born into a world of riches, but I can promise you, I envy you for your family's goodness. You are much richer than I am."

"You still have your brother."

"My brother, and my faith." I barely choked out the words. Both had been tested of late, and it felt wrong to say something was true when it did not feel that way at all.

Before Faye could do anything other than pat my hand reassuringly, Helen called for her. She quietly excused herself, and when I was alone again, I curled my knees up under my chest, letting myself sink into the sudden loneliness of the atmosphere.

I hoped I did not make Faye feel awkward. I already felt badly enough.

I had felt just as terrible when I woke up after the Advent Ball. It was mortifying to know I had been blind, to have missed Ferdy's real identity before. Now, I felt even more foolish.

What is this, God? I wondered. To have Amir's actions and motives questioned, and to have Ferdy's life ended?

Did I not believe ardently enough? Did I do something to deserve such sadness? Was he punishing me for my mother's sins?

"Is this further proof I have failed you, Lord?" I whispered, daring to ask a question of God. I did not know how I would respond to any answer I would get, if indeed I received any at all.

All I knew for sure was that there was too much sadness and too many secrets.

So many secrets.

Much as I had the day I left the castle, I looked out the window. I saw the outline of the city beyond the buildings and across the river, acutely aware there was so much brokenness in the world.

I grew up in the church, where we learned about the fall of Satan and the poison of sin in this world. As I remembered Karl's earlier speech about Bohemia's damaged pride, I thought about the magic of the city and the power it held to withstand the various foes of this world. I thought about sin and the power it had to engulf so many hearts in despair.

How did it come to this? I wondered, still lost in the cityscape before me. How did so much pain and so much destruction manage to infiltrate this world?

As I climbed out of bed and hurried to smooth out my dress, pat down my hair, and put on a presentable face, I knew I had no real answer to that question, either.

I did get an answer of sorts when I walked down the stairs and entered back into the bar, though whether it was an answer from God or Satan, I could not say.

Lumiere was back, sitting at the same spot as before, accompanied by his companion at the bar, half-hidden by the shadows. From what I could see, he was relaxed and cheerful.

In the face of Ferdy's murder, I was more than ready to kill him.

"There you are, Lady Ella," Lumiere called. His bright blond hair was wild and despite his best attempts, I could see the lines folding under his eyes.

"What are you doing here?" I hissed, as I came up beside him. Didier, as if sensing my desire to do harm, moved to protect Lumiere, reaching inside his elegant coat with one hand. Before he could pull his weapon free, Lumiere stopped him.

"She's fine, Didier," Lumiere assured him in quieted tones. "She doesn't have her dagger on her. Do you, Lady Ella?"

I stepped back, realizing he was right; and then I frowned, suddenly aware there would be no pretenses in this conversation.

I frowned. "You have some nerve to assume things about me."

"I'm very well-practiced when it comes to assuming things, I can assure you," he replied with a smile. "But I do happen to know you quite well. I knew you were Naděžda's daughter right from the beginning, even if I had doubts about how much Pepé had actually trained you."

"Pepé?" I wrinkled my nose. "Why do you use that name for Lady Penelope?"

"She was the mistress of my father's best friend for many years, and he repeatedly referred to her as such when he wanted to blame her for all his problems. I can assure you, my father believed she alone was responsible for your grandfather's excessive drinking and his incessant need to meddle in chaos. I imagine your grandfather would have been a quite a solemn priest, content to bore himself into heaven, if he had never met her."

The biting sarcasm of his words almost made me laugh, before I remembered he was the one responsible for my pain.

I glanced back at Didier. Harshad and Xiana had taught me the basics, and I did not think that would stand up well against Didier or his revolver. I was also unsure if Lumiere was armed.

"I heard about your recent departure from Karl Marcelin's brightest moment," Lumiere said. "He was quite upset you left him there alone. He was hoping to announce your engagement with you by his side, although knowing him as I do, I'm sure he enjoyed having the spotlight all to

THE ORDER OF THE CRYSTAL DAGGERS

himself. You should know the crowds cheered quite loudly at his announcement."

"But I never agreed to marry him," I objected, curling my fingers into fists. "My grandmother would never agree to it, either."

"*Au contraire*. She agreed to it after you left the museum," Lumiere told me with a smug smile, making me feel even more queasy.

What is going on? Karl and I are engaged? Why would Lady Penelope agree to this? She promised me she wouldn't do this to me!

"He will have to issue a retraction," I said, trying my hardest to maintain my composure as panic began to take hold of me.

All I needed to do was get to Lady Penelope, I told myself.

"Doubtful. He is very determined to marry you. Most ladies would be flattered. He is leading the charge for Bohemia to become its own nation, to separate itself from the Austrians and the Hungarians, and the rest of the remnant of the Holy Roman Empire."

"Well, I don't want to marry him," I snapped.

"I noticed that, *chérie*, just as I noticed it took quite a bit of acting on Pepé's part to make sure others believed you do," Lumiere said. "She even left with him. No doubt there is some sinister work afoot."

"Karl will have to make peace with my departure. I was … sick."

"Your grandmother is also quite upset. But then I would be too, if I was forcibly escorted out of a party I didn't want to leave," Lumiere cooed.

"You're the reason for it," I hissed.

"*Chérie*, I am not the one who is lying to Karl about wanting to marry him." Lumiere giggled. "And not to mention his brother is in love with you. I commend you on being brave enough to wear the royal combs. I'm sure Karl loved seeing them on you, especially since Ferdinand would be the only other person in the world who could give the crown princess jewels to you."

I reached up and touched one of the combs, then I felt another part of my soul crumble. I had unwittingly blown my cover; I heard the anger in Karl's voice as I left him in the middle of the room. He would know the truth about me now, for certain.

425

THE ORDER OF THE CRYSTAL DAGGERS

Just like Lady POW does. I thought about her strange interrogation earlier, after she noticed them. She had assumed they were from Karl, and that was how she knew I was keeping other secrets before, too.

Indignation briefly ran through me; if Ferdy was not already dead, I would have been tempted to kill him.

Ferdy gave me the princess combs for my hair, tricking me into taking them. Now as a result, I had revealed myself, and the Order's whole mission was at risk.

"No one else has seen Pepé either since then," Lumiere continued. "I do believe Karl has finally taken my advice. I did tell him to stop letting people walk all over him when it came to being in the criminal side of business. Begin as you mean to go on, I told him. If you want the crown, if you want to rule, you have to be relentless. But I do have to admit, kidnapping your grandmother was a stroke of brilliance. I just hope he can handle it. It's rather like watching a baby bird choke on snake. Ah, well, if nothing else, it is delicious entertainment …"

Lumiere rambled on, trying to be funny and provocative, but all I could think about was how Lady Penelope was now Karl's prisoner.

Or, I thought, with a perverse sense of pleasure, *he is hers.*

But still, everything seemed to spiraling out of control. Karl had announced our engagement at the party last night. He had managed to get Lady POW to agree to it, even to the point she worked to convince the crowds of its truth.

I was engaged. Karl knew my secrets. Ferdy was dead. Lady Penelope was captured.

I put my head in my hands. *Where did I go wrong?*

All I wanted to do was scream, but Lumiere distracted me as he raised his glass. "Ferdinand is an excellent match for you. He needs someone who will keep him grounded. Of course, Karl would prefer he was grounded in a different sort of way, if you would believe it."

Suddenly, there were no tears left. I felt the full measure of my temper burst free. "I knew you were involved in all of this."

"This what?" Lumiere batted his eyelashes at me, trying to look innocent. "I have no idea of what you're talking about."

"I might not know the specifics now, but I am sure Amir will tell me."

"Oh, please. Amir wouldn't tell you we were friends. You are too close to her, and he knows how Pepé feels about me, considering who I am."

THE ORDER OF THE CRYSTAL DAGGERS

"Oh? And just who is that?" I asked.

"I am the prince of secrets and shadows, of course," Lumiere said. "I am the son of Louis Valoris, the head of the League of Ungentlemanly Welfare, and heir to the power of the British and French Empires—and the Austria-Hungarian Empire, too, if my father gets his way."

Before I could respond, he guffawed with laughter. "Ah, it is so good to laugh, especially after such a trying week. Assassinations and betrayals and set-ups are all so tiring, and I've had to plan plenty in the last few days."

I blanched at his words. "You're a monster."

"Yes," he murmured, seeing my reaction. "Yes, I suppose you are right. But as my father always says, it is the mark of true power to operate in the daylight. Alas, I am not quite there, but I at least have enough power to tell you that I *am* involved in all of this, and I am truly sorry to distress Naděžda's daughter in such a way. But one day I will make it up to you, and this is my oath. Didier, take note of today's date and my promises to Lady Ella."

I clenched my fist. "I don't want your promises."

"You might one day, especially if a certain Bohemian prince is involved."

"Leave Ferdy out of this!"

"Well, you do have a point," Lumiere conceded. "After all, he is dead. It's not like there was a chance that he would survive an attack so stealthily planned by *moi*, would he?"

The last of my hope perished inside of me. "I'll kill you," I hissed, already leaping at Lumiere. Didier moved to block me as I raised my fist.

Before, I had been too conflicted to fight.

But Ferdy's fate, and Amir's role in it, and now everything else, had killed something inside of me. I was no longer bound to protect Ferdy in this world, and I owed loyalty to no one other than myself. In that moment, I lived only to inflict pain and torture on Lumiere.

Didier managed to grab a hold of me, but I heard him grunt as I hit him instead.

Before I could fight any further, a new voice called out to stop us.

"Yes, Lumiere, Miss Ella is correct. You are a monster, and you do not need to be here at all. I think it is time for you to leave."

Eliezer was suddenly standing beside me, reaching out to put a hand between me and Lumiere. I blinked at the sight of him as he appeared, and I took the time to make a second look as he positioned himself between Lumiere and me. He was not much taller than me, and I likely could have fought him and won. But there was a commanding presence about him, one that did not waver.

It was surprising to see him again, and even more to be on my side; I had never really talked to him, and he was always so busy with his listeners and other friends when I was at the Cabal. I would have expected him to ask what was going on, but as I watch his dark eyes narrow at Lumiere, I realized they had already known each other.

"Oh, look who it is. Little Eliezer, I was wondering when I would get to see you again. Imagine my surprise to find you here, and after the Sabbath has begun, too," Lumiere cheered. He ran a hand through his hair, pushing back the blond locks with a sense of showmanship and glee. "I have missed you terribly."

Eliezer wore a look of disgust as he faced Lumiere. "None of us have missed you."

"Now, now, falling leaves return to their roots." Lumiere pouted. "A Jew is always a Jew, even if he prefers the Catholic church his father raised him in. Certainly Clavan would agree with me on that, and he is the proprietor here, *non?*"

"That is not the issue. All are welcome here at the Cabal," Clavan spoke up, "but welcomes can wear out, Lumi, and you are better off leaving before yours does. We will not have you upsetting our Ella."

"Oh, such a bother." Lumiere sighed, before he stood up and bowed to me. "I was having such a lovely time, too. But then, I suppose I cannot blame you for your affections toward Ella. She is quite her mother's daughter."

Didier followed him, but instead of bowing to me, he reached for my hand to shake it. I was surprised, given my own violent response, but he gave me the same smile as he had before at the Estates Theatre. "I look forward to seeing you again soon, my lady. Perhaps even sooner than you realize."

"I don't know if I would be so delighted by our next meeting, sir," I replied. "If I have my way, our next meeting will be our last."

"With all due respect, I doubt that, my lady," Didier whispered. "But should you wish to come and find us, we are staying at the port on the *Salacia.*"

THE ORDER OF THE CRYSTAL DAGGERS

It was only when they were finally out of the door that I turned to Eliezer. The loops of hair at the side of his head were bobbling with unexpressed anger, and I could tell he had done himself a favor as much as he had helped me.

"Thank you, sir," I said, struggling to contain myself. I breathed in deeply, hating that I had been stopped even though I knew I would not have survived the fight had it been allowed to continue.

"You're welcome." Eliezer looked me over. "You should stay away from him, but I have a feeling you already know that."

"What do you know about him?"

"He is a proficient liar and good at making people believe what he wants them to believe. He is no friend of ours, even though he would like to be." Eliezer gestured to the Cabal. "He used to come here before with his father, when we were both younger."

I glanced over at Clavan. "How long have you been in business?"

"The Cabal has always been a place of entertainment," Clavan said. "My father fancied himself a performer, but thankfully my mother convinced him he should have alcohol readily available for his audiences. Our family was kicked out of the Jewish Quarter for that, but I am content to remain its neighbor. Elie has been a real help in turning it into a place of information rather than entertainment."

"Much to Jarl's displeasure, I'm sure," Eliezer said. He straightened the yarmulke on his head and excused himself as another man, one I assumed was Jarl's Uncle Rhys, called out to him.

Clavan came up beside me. "I hope you do not let Lumi's words bother you."

"It is not his words so much as his actions," I said.

The anger inside of me continued to burn without mercy, and I decided it was time to end the waiting. It was time to face Karl, Lord Maximillian, and Lumiere. It was time to confront them, to trap them, and to get them to confess to their treachery—anything to ensure that they were stopped. It was too much to wait for them to give me their trust, to allow them the space to continue when I knew they were guilty, even if it meant revealing myself and the Order to Society.

What difference did it make in the end? I had already failed.

Ferdy was dead.

THE ORDER OF THE CRYSTAL DAGGERS

I decided to start with Lumiere. He seemed to be the most deserving of my anger, and I had a feeling that, with Amir still missing, I would have less trouble convincing Lady Penelope to act.

Faye appeared once more, this time with more blankets. She insisted I stay in her room for the night, and then I could go home in the morning. I agreed only because she wanted me safe, and it was true that I was in no condition to return home on my own.

The situation did press into me the resolution that I would never leave the house without my dagger again.

17

◊

The long hour of walking home did nothing to temper the storm inside of me. I burst into the manor, my boots covered in mud and snow, my gown and Faye's cloak flowing out behind me with a mix of wind and rage.

"Eleanora? Is that you?" Harshad called out to me, but I did not stop.

I was putting everything together inside my mind as I made my way to my room. I slammed the door shut and immediately began to pull off my clothes. I paused only for an extra second as I felt the thin fabric of Faye's cloak. I knew the material was cheap and the stitching was worn, but the friendship I had with her, and the other members of the Cabal, was not deserving of anything so fine. I knew this was true, even before learning she had slept in her parents' room, while Clavan slept in a chair.

If I died avenging Ferdy and condemning Karl, I hoped they would remember me fondly.

My stealth habit was tight against my skin as I finished getting ready. My hood was up, my mask was in place, and my dagger was at my side. I would find Lumiere, I decided, starting with his ship, the *Salacia*. Ferdy's letter had shown me that they were all working together, and Lumiere had confirmed it. All I needed was some physical proof. Maybe I could find more letters from Lumiere to Karl or Lord Maximillian, and then I could take it to King Ferdinand and Empress Maria Anna. Then, they could send it off to Franz Joseph, so he could see the degree of treachery involved by his cousin and his cohorts.

"Nora? Harshad and Xiana are waiting for us in the library."

Ben's voice was full of concern and a brotherly cadence I could only marvel at, especially in light of our recent troubles. It was as if he knew I no longer had to worry about dividing my loyalty between him and anyone else.

"I'm coming," I said as I hurried to fix my hair. I tugged at the combs Ferdy had given me, the ones which always seemed so innocuous. I paused in putting them away, taking a moment to study them, thinking of how Lumiere had called them the crown princess combs.

When I had woken up in the castle after the attack, only to find myself in Ferdy's room, I was conflicted over whether or not I wanted him to love me. He was a prince, even if he was kept a secret from the rest of the kingdom.

Now, as I curled my fingers around the combs, I only felt angry with myself. I was in love with a liar. Once more, Ferdy had put himself—and me, and my mission—in danger, all so he could keep a hold on me.

No wonder Karl had him killed.

Ferdy had finally pushed his brother too far. And since he was dead, it was up to me to fix things.

"Nora." Ben knocked on the door again.

At the sound of his voice, I jolted out of my pained reverie. "I'll be there in a moment," I snapped. I was glad Ben and I had resolved some of our differences, but I wanted only a few moments all to myself, to grieve and to plan my vengeance.

I put the combs down in my drawer, lying them next to my mother's locket and my father's pocket watch. Recalling Lumiere had a similar watch, I picked it up and opened it, marveling once more at the workmanship. A pattern of gold circled its way around the clock, twisting its finery around each of the numbers. It had been many years since I had wound it to work, but I felt the comfort of my father's memory in just holding it.

Máma's locket also shimmered up at me, calling to me like a little child eager for attention. Opening it, I saw the small miniature of me and Ben on the one side, and my father's picture on the other.

From everything I remembered about her, I knew my mother loved me and Ben. I never saw her disagree with my father, and when they were together, I only ever saw her smiling. Ben had told me before she had suffered from periodic bouts of melancholy, and I supposed it was unusual to think of my mother as only ever happy. But with Ben and me, and our father, too, it was still hard to think we were not enough for her.

Studying my father's picture, I knew *Máma* had loved *Táta*. And whatever her past held, I could face it, knowing she had known true love.

I thought of Amir, and how my mother had loved him, too. He did not go with her when she wanted them to run away together, but she had loved him enough to ask.

I rubbed my thumb over my father's picture again. He looked so young in the picture. I wondered when it had been completed.

THE ORDER OF THE CRYSTAL DAGGERS

Curious, I pulled the picture out of its small frame. The miniature slipped through my fingers and fell. I was just about to reach for it when I realized it was not the only picture in the frame.

There was a smaller picture tucked away behind it, of a younger man with dark brown eyes and hair the color of a starless night. There was no mustache on his face, but I recognized him regardless.

Amir.

I pulled out his picture to study it, setting my father's portrait aside. He wore a military jacket of the Ottoman Empire, but no smile. His hair was parted differently under the strange cap. I looked it over and smiled; the picture was like a portal, linking me not just to Amir's past but a whole other person's life.

On the back of Amir's picture, I saw the same scraggly shape of his scar, next to a small drawing of a dagger.

My mother's dagger, and Amir's scar.

Beside it, there was a date listed: *April 25, 1847.* The date did not mean anything to me, but I recognized the importance of the drawings easily enough. Amir had mentioned before, I recalled, that love was connected to suffering. I could imagine my mother suffering as she held onto his memory, even as she embraced my father and their future together.

I looked back at the picture of *Táta.* Had he known of my mother's devotion to another?

Did my mother know of Amir's pain, to the point he would betray me and Lady Penelope?

After another long moment, I carefully tucked the locket and its hidden contents into my drawer, along with the combs Ferdy had given me. I loved them all—my mother, my father, and Ferdy. Yet they all held secrets, some of them I was still trying to discover.

Harshad was right, I thought. Some secrets are kept as a matter of trust, bringing two people closer, and some were destructive, forcing others apart.

I could not say which result was more true as I made my way down to the library.

As I entered the room, I was surprised to find the portrait of my mother hanging over the fireplace mantle. Lady Penelope had promised me before that she would have it restored, but it was still a shock to see my mother's blue eyes staring down at me.

"There you are," Harshad said. He looked down at my outfit and nodded. "I see you have come prepared."

"I'm more than prepared," I insisted, pulling my dagger out. The violet-colored alloy gleamed a dangerous purple in the firelight.

"Excellent. But I am not sure you understand the gravity of the situation."

"Karl has captured Lady Penelope, and Lord Maximillian and his new best friend Lumiere Valoris are preparing an assassination, a set-up, or both," I said.

I was gratified to see Ben's eyes widen. Even Harshad seemed surprised.

"We know that," Ben said. "But how did you hear?"

"Someone told me," I said, ready to tell him what happened.

But Harshad interrupted me. "Do you also know that Karl is requesting your presence at the Potocki house this evening?"

I opened my mouth and then closed it. I sighed and shook my head.

It figures that Karl would complicate my anger. His brother had a knack for it, so I shouldn't be this surprised.

"After you left the museum dedication earlier, he found a way to convince Lady Penelope to grant his request for your hand." Harshad began to pace the floor, and I started to get worried. Lady POW was the one who paced incessantly, and for Harshad to be adopting her mannerisms likely meant he was more worried than he wanted to admit, possibly even to himself.

"If he thinks capturing her will convince me to bend to his will, he's going to be surprised," I recalled Lumiere mentioning something like that earlier, but I had been too upset to notice it. I tucked my dagger back into its sheath. "We'll get her back."

"He blackmailed her," Ben said.

"At his own peril," I asserted. "Lady Penelope would not allow herself to be manipulated like that unless she knew how to control it."

"She managed to buy us time by agreeing to his schemes, I am sure, but that's all," Harshad said. "We were just about to go search for you. Lady Penelope is only able to work as a member in the Order by maintaining her cover as a respectable dowager duchess. While money does have a tendency to silence people, Karl, as the secret heir to the throne and the leader of a growing nationalist resistance, has the power to damage our reputation and diminish our ability to protect others."

"She could just kill him," I said, unapologetic in my anger. "That would solve a lot of problems."

"The last thing Queen Victoria needs is a spy who killed the son of a ruler," Xiana said. She took a step out of the shadows, her calmness and power clear. "Her Majesty is already facing a large amount of problems at home and abroad. The Order was sent in to stabilize the area. This is not official Crown business, or the League would have been sent in. While it may be a quick solution to our troubles here, killing Mr. Marcelin is not advantageous in the long run."

I clenched my fists. One heir to the throne was already dead.

"Eleanora," Harshad said. "You will go to the ball at Count Potocki's house tonight. Karl will announce your engagement, and then, as you leave the ball, we will capture him. We can bring him back here, to your family's manor."

"Karl will likely be protected," Ben said. "If he knows about the Order—"

"He does," I said. "He likely heard about it from Lumiere. He knows Lady Penelope."

Harshad shook his head. "Lumiere has always been a problem, and he enjoys it. To a fault, certainly. I warned Amir not to trust him."

Hearing Amir's name, I whirled on Harshad. "Do you know where Amir is? The last time any of us saw him was after he met with Lumiere."

"Lumiere is a friend of Amir's," Harshad explained. "They used to work on missions and carry out tasks together with your mother. But people grow older, and loyalties shift."

"I don't think Amir's have," Ben muttered.

"But your mother's did," Harshad countered softly, making me jump. "She left the Order before, and it is entirely possible, especially given Lumiere's father and his long-standing animosity toward Pepé, that Lumiere's have also changed."

I looked back at the portrait of my mother, thinking of the picture she carried of Amir close to her heart all those years after she married my father. Her loyalties did not shift, I thought. She might have married another, but she never forgot about Amir.

As for Amir, I did not know what to say. It still seemed impossible that he killed Ferdy, especially under Lumiere's direction.

"Do you know where Amir went?" I asked. I glanced over at Xiana, her calmness almost unnerving, before turning back to Harshad for an answer.

"No." Harshad shook his head. "But Amir would not disappoint me, even if he has unresolved feelings toward Lady Penelope."

I thought about Lady POW's own feelings about Amir. It was possible, I realized, that she was the one who had the unresolved guilt toward Amir. I had known both of them for such a short time, but I did not see Amir as someone who believed in vengeance.

Lady Penelope was another story.

"He always returns to me," Harshad said.

My eyes watered. Clavan had said the same thing about Ferdy.

"For now, we will have to worry about Amir later." Harshad clasped his hands together.

"I agree. We are losing our focus," Ben said. "Nora, you'll need to get dressed up for the party tonight. You'll go in and dazzle Karl, assure him you don't know what he is talking about when it comes to the Order. Xiana and Harshad can look for Lady Penelope. Once they find her, they can work out a way to kidnap Karl as you leave, and then we'll have him."

"And then I will have him at my mercy," I muttered. I gripped the hilt of my dagger. "Good."

Harshad shook his head. "I do not anticipate killing someone will be necessary in this instance. Empress Maria Anna and King Ferdinand will be able to rein in their son."

"I don't know about that," I said. "They are upset right now, and they haven't moved to stop him yet."

"With Karl working with Lord Maximillian and the League, not to mention his own support from people like Roman Szapira and Count Potocki, they are unable to confront him," Ben said. "If we can bring him down, at least to the point where he can admit he is trying to take back the throne, they will be able to report him to Emperor Franz Joseph."

"The emperor was already alerted to the plot," Harshad said. "That is why he is calling a special council in a few months."

"A council?" I asked. "What kind of council?"

THE ORDER OF THE CRYSTAL DAGGERS

"Empress Elisabeth is sympathetic to Bohemia's desire to be its own country," Harshad said. "Emperor Franz Joseph has decided to call a tri-partite council, to discuss the possibility of allowing Bohemia to be a full kingdom as part of the Empire."

"So it would be the Austria-Hungarian-Bohemian Empire instead," Ben clarified.

"Karl would love that." I pouted. He would love that, and then he would use it as a way to wedge the kingdom free from the empire entirely. "I have heard Empress Elisabeth agrees with the democratic notions of the West."

"She does, but she knows her power is little, especially in the Austrian courts. The Hapsburgs have never been kind to outsiders. Empress Elisabeth is an outsider in her own home, even if Franz Joseph loves her."

"But she is technically the emperor's second cousin," I said. "Doesn't that make her a Hapsburg, too?"

"Through her mother's side." Harshad frowned. "She has been treated better since her son, Rupert, was born, but Empress Elisabeth has gone against the royal family in getting closer to the Hungarians, and she seeks to help Bohemia, too. I imagine she is a little more hesitant, given King Ferdinand is still alive, and there is a growing Nationalist movement."

"So she is calling a council to give Bohemia more power?" I asked.

"She has convinced Franz Joseph to do so," Harshad said. "That does not mean it will come to be."

"Karl has gotten bolder with his speeches." I thought about how he had called for Bohemia's freedom the day before. I had to push back a lot of sadness to recall what he said, but I knew if there was a possibility of emancipation, his rhetoric would likely turn dangerous.

"Karl likely heard of their intention," Harshad continued. "That is why his speech yesterday was so important."

Ben chuckled. "And that's why, when Nora left, he was extraordinarily angry."

"I don't understand why," I retorted. "I'm not anyone important. I know Society enjoys me, but there are richer women Karl could marry, or even people like Teresa Marie, who has a connection to the throne her-self."

"You might be a passing fad," Ben said, "but Lady Penelope's history and her money make you very interesting. The fact that you are so talented makes people excited. And to top it off, you are *Otec's* daughter."

I was surprised to hear Ben say anything about our father. "What does *Táta* have to do with anything?"

"He protected the King during a raid on the castle," Ben said. "*Otec* refused to leave the king's side when he was attacked with a knife. He nearly died because of his wounds. That was why the king was so nice to him, remember?"

I did not remember the exact nature of my father's duty. If I had ever heard the story, it had been a long, long time before, and I had forgotten the details.

"Adolf Svoboda's role in saving the king, even though the Revolution eventually succeeded, is remembered by those who are upset by Emperor Franz Joseph's neglect of Bohemia." Xiana folded her hands together in front of her. "You carry bravery in your blood, Eleanora, and that is a legacy that Karl Marcelin seeks to preserve."

"And claim as his own." I wrinkled my nose at the thought of marrying Karl.

"We will not let him do so," Ben promised. "You're my sister, and this is exactly the sort of threat I am allowed to keep you from."

"Thanks." I did not want Ben's protection, but I was glad he was at least offering it. I sighed. "I suppose I better get ready."

"Yes," Harshad said. "I fear if we do not move quickly, we will fail to save Karl from Pepé as much as we will fail to save her from him."

18

◊

The city once more passed before me as we rode by in Lady Penelope's carriage. It did not look much different from earlier, when I had walked home from the Cabal, but I felt more tired as I looked at it. Not only was I still upset about everything that happened, but I was about to make things even more complicated.

We were on our way to Count Potocki's address, and the plan was in place. I fiddled with my skirts, ruffling the gypsy red silk with an unacknowledged wonder. I was on my way to announce and celebrate my engagement. If I was not secretly a spy trying to dismantle foreign dissents and a traitorous prince, I might have actually been excited. Assuming I would have been in love.

"Are you well?" Ben reached forward and gave me a quick pat on my arm.

Mindlessly, I nodded. I did not want to admit I was looking forward to the end of the charade.

Harshad was up on the box, disguised in a footman's livery, and Xiana was also hidden away. She had twisted herself up in ways I never imagined possible, before securing herself to back of the coach.

Ben was with me in the carriage. I appreciated his presence, even though I wished I had the time to myself. I gripped my dagger, slightly irritated it was buried underneath another one of the fine gowns Lady Penelope had ordered for me. Much like the other one, I could easily dismantle myself from it and resume my movements in my stealth habit. I was not nervous. I was out for blood.

I wanted the time to myself for other reasons. There was a wide chasm between justice and vengeance; one was a divine calling, and the other a sin. I did not want someone I loved as much as Ben to see my nature tainted, even if it was necessary to help preserve the world's good.

"Everything will be fine." Ben tried to reassure me once more.

I looked at him as he sat across from me. He was dressed in his normal clothes, the everyday clothes of a servant he had worn when Cecilia was in charge of our lives.

"I know that I can count on Harshad and Xiana to save Lady POW," I said. "What will you be doing?"

THE ORDER OF THE CRYSTAL DAGGERS

"While you attend the party at the count's house, I'll be heading into town," Ben said. "Clavan sent the notice that Zipporah would be coming into the Cabal tonight, and she has the herbs we ordered. Once I have them, I will come back to meet up with you and the others."

"Are you sure that it's a good idea to leave us?"

"I'm certain between you, Harshad, and Xiana, you will find a way to extract Lady POW from her captors," Ben replied. "Besides, we should get the herbs. Lady POW has wanted them since she came here. She wants me to find out the names of other buyers, and if Zipporah has had any trouble getting her supply."

"It seems unusual that you would worry about getting the silver thallis herb now," I said.

"Disappointed you don't have any to use on Karl?"

I snickered at Ben's teasing grin, but I had to admit he was the one who was more right between us.

"Either way, it can't be helped," Ben said. "We've waited this long, and Xiana will be able to make some of the antidote for us. We might be able to save some of the people that are dying off."

"I haven't heard of any new deaths lately."

"If you ask me, I think Karl's too busy planning for your nuptials."

Karl had talked about marriage at every occasion we had together. It was part of his plan, I assumed; gain the approval of my following, use the power of the people as leverage, secure the Bohemian throne, and reveal himself to be the true heir to the kingdom. Then all he would need would be a family to inherit his legacy, and Karl would have everything he had ever wanted.

"I would have thought Lord Maximillian would be doing more of those," I said. "He has been remarkably silent in recent weeks."

"Karl seems to have made it pretty clear he wants to marry you, and even more so since the Advent Ball."

"Lady Penelope and I did run into him at the Estates Theatre," I said. I thought of Ferdy's letter again, the one where Karl offered Lord Maximillian a role as a counselor. "Lord Maximillian tried to threaten us there. He was more than polite about it, and he would be the first to deny it, of course."

Ben frowned. "Is he coming to the ball tonight?"

THE ORDER OF THE CRYSTAL DAGGERS

"I don't know." I sighed. "I'll keep an eye out for him."

"Be sure to watch yourself most of all." Ben gripped his fingers together in his lap. "I know you can take care of yourself, but I won't be around to help."

"I'll be in good company."

"I know, or I wouldn't leave you." Ben sighed. "Amir was right. You are a weakness of mine."

I smiled. "And you are one of mine. But we can work with that, and that's the important part."

"Amir is one of your weaknesses, too, you know."

My eyes met Ben's from across the carriage bench. "I am sure he is," I admitted.

Ben was different from me in that I had been allowed to consider my weaknesses thoroughly; I was given time to work on mine. Ben had to begin his struggle right away, with our father's dismissal of him after his injury, and then Cecilia's further harm. Ben was taught to hate weakness, to get rid of it, and to condemn it. He was morally tied to the destruction of his weaknesses, while I was largely ignorant of mine. When I thought of my love for Ferdy or my admiration for Amir, I could see it as a weakness or as a strength, and I was unable to dismiss it entirely.

I looked away from Ben, turning my attention back to the city streets before me, feeling the clatter of the wheels as they turned over the cobblestone streets. "You know, if things had worked out differently, Amir would be our father instead of *Táta*."

Ben shrugged but he said nothing. I sank back into silence, too.

The coach slowed down as the traffic became thicker. The moon was just peeking out from behind the snowy clouds when Ben said his farewells and slipped out of the coach, heading off for the Cabal.

I envied him. Ben was going into a den of friends, while I was waltzing into the heart of darkness.

To be fair, it was a very grand-looking trap. Count Potocki's manor had the high arches of Gothic architect, with brightly patterned windows and elegant masonry. The coach stopped, and Harshad hurried down to assist me.

"Once you're inside," he whispered, "go and find your grandmother. Karl will likely want to rehearse his terms, so you will be able to give us time while Xiana and I look for a way to overpower any guards he might have."

"I will." I patted his hand as I stepped down. "Thank you."

His face was expressionless, but I thought I saw a twinkle in his eye as I headed toward the door.

I picked up my skirts, making sure I was able to leave my boots covered. Underneath my dress, I wore my stealth habit and the matching black boots Lady POW had ordered for me when we had set out to captivate Society. My dagger was tucked away at my side. I could grab it through a slit in my skirt, one that was usually reserved for pockets.

It was strange to think I was dressed for war, and that I was marching into battle wearing a gown.

I held my head up proudly. The fact that I was wearing a gown, yet still facing my enemy, gave me confidence. Warriors came in all sorts of outfits, and I had chosen to don a disguise worthy of a spy.

The fact that I was here to help my own grandmother, the spymaster who was tangled up in our adversary's grasp, was only slightly less relevant. Karl was not anticipating a fight, but he was going to get one.

Upon entering, a hand reached forward for my cloak. I took it off and handed it over, only to find I recognized my helper.

"Amir." His name escaped in a gasp as I stood there.

"Shh, please, Eleanora," Amir whispered, holding a finger up to his lips. He hurried to pull me off to the darker confines of the castle before anyone else noticed where we were going.

As we walked briskly through a darkened hall, I was admittedly disappointed; if I was going to be rescued from a ball, I would have preferred Ferdy had come to save me rather than Amir.

But considering Ferdy had been killed by Amir, I knew that was not going to happened.

At that thought, I tugged myself free from his grasp. "What do you think you're doing here?"

"I came to help," Amir said. "Lumi told me that Karl managed to coerce Lady Penelope into leaving the rededication ceremony with him before, but we have a problem."

Lumi. Amir called Lumiere "Lumi," as if he was a friend.

THE ORDER OF THE CRYSTAL DAGGERS

"You aren't really trying to betray Lady Penelope, are you?" I asked, suddenly very worried. I took a step back from Amir, unable to see how any of this could make sense. Was he here to finish her off?

I struggled to maintain my composure. "I didn't want to believe it when she said that was what you were doing, but I can't believe that you would consider Lumiere a friend!"

"Eleanora—"

I felt my heart clench, as if it was struggling to continue to beat. "He orchestrated everything, Amir. He made you kill Karl's brother."

"What?" Amir shook his head. "I didn't kill anyone, Eleanora."

"I know Lumiere sent you after the coach," I insisted. "Ben told me that you were talking with him, and then you left for days."

"I can explain that," Amir said. "But you need to calm down, please."

"Fine." I took another step back, digging my fingers into my skirt, reaching for my dagger. I did not want to pull it out entirely, but I needed to protect myself. "Tell me about Lumiere first, and why you would be friends with that vile creature."

"Lumi is an old friend of mine," Amir said. "He was the one who originally told me that Karl and Lord Maximillian were working together. He knew because they were also in contact with Louis, who is Lumiere's father and the leader of the League of Ungentlemanly Warfare."

"I know about Louis, and the League, too."

"Then you know Louis is dangerous," Amir said. "Lumi told me that Father Novak had sent word to him, and he decided to come, especially since his father told him Lady POW was coming to Prague."

"Lady POW said he was your friend, as well as *Máma's*," I said. "For all you are his friend, he was not very nice to me."

"He is an acquired taste." Amir smiled, unable to hide his amusement. "But I know I can trust him."

"Which is why you went to kill Karl's brother," I accused, my voice nearly breaking. "Karl and Clavan told me what happened. I know that there were witnesses to the attack on that coach heading for Silesia. You can't deny it."

"I did not kill anyone, let alone your beloved."

I went silent at his words, taking the moment to glance around to make sure we were alone. "How did you know?"

"Lumi is a friend of his, too," Amir said. "They met each other while Ferdinand—or Ferdy, if you prefer—was at school in Paris. Lumi met Karl at Oxford for his education, too."

Breathing seemed abnormally difficult all of a sudden. I felt my hand cover my mouth in shock, as my mind raced with the implications.

Ferdy? Friends with Lumiere?

Ferdy had told me before he knew of the Order and the League, and it looked like he had plenty of personal connections to the two of them.

"Your beloved has been keeping secrets, hasn't he?" Amir took a cautious step toward me. "And he has asked you to keep them, too."

"Not entirely." I sighed. "His servant did. Empress Maria Anna seems to remember *Máma*, and I did not want to disappoint her, either."

"That's why you haven't said anything, and that was what you were keeping from Lady Penelope, wasn't it? You knew Karl had a younger brother."

Frustration ate at me. "I haven't known for that long. I found out the night of the Advent Ball. Keeping silent seemed to be the most prudent thing to do. I didn't want him to get into trouble."

"It seems as though he has a talent for it, living on the streets." Amir suddenly let out a small laugh. "I'll commend him on his disguise, though now that I think of it, I should have seen it from the beginning."

"What do you mean?" I asked.

"No ordinary street urchin would just happen to know formal Arabic."

"Well, that doesn't matter now, does it? I heard about what happened. I know he's dead." I turned away. I did not want to face Amir. "And it's all your fault, isn't it?"

There was a long, uncomfortable moment of silence between us that told me everything I needed to hear.

"You said you heard the story about what happened," Amir said quietly. "It is true those men are dead."

The lump in my throat suffocated me. I ducked my head into my hands and slumped down against the wall. My gown fluttered out around me as my dagger leaned into my hip.

Amir telling me that Ferdy was gone was like losing him all over again.

THE ORDER OF THE CRYSTAL DAGGERS

"Please, believe me when I tell you I am not the true villain; I had to go to the castle and find a way to track down the coach, and then I had to catch up with it. I was warned that there was another henchman following, to ensure that everything happened according to plan. Lumi was right about that; a man attacked about half a day's journey from Prague, killing everyone in the coach. I had only managed to catch up when he attacked. Once he was finished, I saw him light the coach on fire, and a piece of luggage exploded."

"You were too late." My voice was scratchy as I looked over at him. "Did you go over to help? Is that why the story was changed where you were the one who was …"

I couldn't bring myself to finish the sentence.

Amir seemed to understand what I refused to say. "I changed the message before it was sent out."

"You criminalized yourself?"

"I had to," Amir said. "Once a nearby village saw the fire, others came to help, including a vicar. Some people noticed me, and they assumed I was the villain anyway. There is a reason I do not join you and Lady Penelope in Society, and that I am an honorary member of the League instead of a full one. My skin color cannot be changed, and others know of my heritage just by looking at me. I know the assumptions that come with it very well."

I went silent at his sadness. I knew the prejudice that existed in the world, and given that Amir was armed, he would have been arrested on the spot.

"People would have contradicted the story if they heard I was actually trying to rescue them, and there was no proof I was not the villain. You know no one would have believed it then," Amir said. "So I adopted the villain's role as I headed home. I had to watch out for those who heard and avoid the gossip. That is the reason for my delay in returning."

I said nothing again, as I attempted to right myself. I did not want Amir to think I was weak, but I was. I was devastated.

I could see Ferdy dressed up in his princely attire, waltzing around Prague Castle's ballroom, confessing his love for me in a way that infuriated me as much as it captivated me. The first time I saw him, arguing over my mother's journal with Amir. All the times I had seen him in costume—so many costumes any regular person would have wondered which was the real Ferdy, or if he existed at all.

445

But I knew him. I could see him again in my mind, dressed in proper breeches and a formal shirt. He wore boots but no cravat, and his copper hair was tousled in the wind.

And then there was a blaze of fire, and he was gone.

"Their bodies have been salvaged as much as possible," Amir said. "The Royals have been informed of their son's passing. And it is likely, since he was the king's son, they will have a funeral for him, although a private one. The king never announced his birth to the kingdom, so he was not a prince of the nation."

"I don't want to hear anything else," I said, struggling to stand up. I had to force myself to focus. There was a reason I was here, and it was not to worry about Ferdy. I could no longer worry about him. I had to let him go for now.

"I'm so sorry, Eleanora. I know it does not mean much, or even anything to hear, but if I could do anything to save him for you, I would."

Amir's apology hung in the air between us as I waited for myself to accept it.

I did not want to accept it.

It seemed like a long time later when I breathed in deeply, wiped my eyes clear of any tears, and stood up tall. "It's too late to do anything else. We're here to save Lady Penelope, and Karl's expecting me."

"Please, listen. Lumi sent me to stop Ferdy's assassination from happening," Amir said. "He also told me that Karl cornered Lady POW after the rededication ceremony and forced her to leave with him."

"So?"

"So Lumi is on our side."

I wiped my running nose unceremoniously against my shoulder. "I do not believe it."

"The information he has given me is correct."

"It is also possible he's lying, and you're too close to him to see it." I crossed my arms. "Is he a weakness of yours, Amir?"

Amir grimaced. "This is getting us nowhere. Right now, we have to find your grandmother."

"That's the only reason I am here. Although I would not say no to killing someone right now."

THE ORDER OF THE CRYSTAL DAGGERS

Amir ignored my anger. "Lumi told me Karl wanted to offer a future to the nation, especially given his age, so that is why you—as the daughter of Adolf Svoboda, the former king's most loyal servant, with your charming innocence and the wealth from your dowager Duchess grandmother who is a close friend of Queen Victoria—play such a key role in his plans."

"Good to know I'm worth something to someone." I huffed.

"Considering who we are dealing with, I would not feel bad for being a pawn if I were you." Amir's expression softened. "It does nothing, but I can tell he does genuinely like you. He could have had Lady Teresa Marie as his bride if he did not think you were the better gamble."

"Well," I said, "Karl's about to find out that sometimes when you gamble, you lose. Once I find Lady POW, I will make sure he pays for his duplicity and treachery."

Not to mention his heavy-handedness. I gripped my dagger again, remembering his warning to me back at the museum.

"That brings us back the problem we now face. Lady Penelope is not here. I have been watching for you for the last hour, trying to intercept you. You will gain nothing if you confront Karl tonight without her here."

"Where else would she be?" I asked, perplexed. Amir was right. Even with as little I did know about Society, I knew if Lady POW was not here to protect me, Karl would have an easier time getting me to agree to his terms.

"Lumi told me that she was with Karl earlier," Amir said, "but that's clearly changed. She could be anywhere. If we are going to stop Karl, we will have to find her quickly. If you do not show up here, he is in a position to use her life as leverage."

I still had trouble imagining Karl as one who would take an old lady hostage, but I had no trouble considering that Lumiere had men who would do it for him.

The whole plan we had conceived earlier was for naught. If I was going to save my grandmother, I would have to find her before Karl was able to get away from his own party.

"Do you have any thoughts on where he might have taken her?"

"Karl is staying at the castle," I said. "Is it possible she is in the dungeons there? It seems like if he was going to coerce her, he would likely find a way to make sure she stayed where he put her."

Amir nodded. "It is a logical guess."

THE ORDER OF THE CRYSTAL DAGGERS

"Where do you think he would hold her?" I glanced around. "Are you sure he's not keeping her here, in some locked room, far away from the crowds?"

"I have been here for hours," Amir said. "I have examined the servants and walked through the majority of the house."

"Harshad and Xiana are also here, looking for Lady POW," I said. "Should we try to help them before we leave?"

"You need to leave right now." Amir took my hand again and started walking down the hall. "There is a servant's entrance here. You'll be able to wait for a lull in their movements and sneak out. Once you're out, find a way to get a ride on a departing coach and head for the castle."

"If I get there, I will be able to see the former empress," I said, suddenly dreading the encounter. Empress Maria Anna had entrusted her younger son's protection to me, and I had failed her. "She will recognize me and be able to tell me if Lady Penelope is there."

"It's the best bet we have right now," Amir said.

"What if she is not there?"

He shrugged.

"If you stay here, Harshad and Xiana might be able to help you capture Karl as he is leaving still," I suggested.

"I'll go and find them, and we will work out a plan. Either way, we will meet you at the castle."

"Are you sure they will believe you?" I asked. Was I able to believe him, too, then?

In the end, I decided that I could trust him for now. It was true that Amir had kept Ferdy a secret before, and he had apologized for failing to save him. And it was nice, I had to admit, that he wanted me to leave the ball. As majestic as Count Potocki's manor was, I eagerly embraced the chance to escape.

"Give me a moment." I stopped in my tracks and pulled out my dagger.

Amir looked at me curiously, unmoving, and I wondered if he thought I was going to attack him. It might have been tempting if I did not believe him, but instead, I ran the sharp and ancient edge through the side of my gown's bodice, cutting the outer layer of my fancy clothes. When I was done, I shed the outer layers and stood ready in only my stealth habit. The dark fabrics, overlapping each other across my chest and down my legs, allowed me to sink into the shadows like an agent of the devil himself.

THE ORDER OF THE CRYSTAL DAGGERS

Amir raised his brow.

"There's no use for me to wear the gown now," I explained. I tugged my hood over my hair and pulled my mask to the bridge of my nose.

"I see your argument," Amir said, "but you should still wear your cloak on the way out. There's no need to freeze, even if you will be able to maneuver through the streets with much less notice."

It was an easy choice for me to grant his wish. I pulled on my cloak, letting the fine fabric conceal my costume.

Amir squeezed my hand before we departed. "I know we have little time, Eleanora, but I have one last question for you."

"What is it?"

He looked down at me intently. "Did you tell Lady Penelope about anything that I said to you?"

"She thought you told me more, but I only admitted you told me about your family and your scar." I looked down at his hand, where in the dim lighting, I could still see the heavy outline of the *noon* above his knuckles. "That was it."

"Did she ask about Nassara?"

At the tone of his voice, so hollow and detached, I frowned. "I did not tell her about the journal, if that's what you mean."

Amir patted my hand and stepped back from me. "Thank you, Eleanora. I appreciate your silence on the matter. *Allah yusallmak*, and I will see you later."

At the sound of the foreign words, I suddenly had a new question for him. "Amir? What did Ferdy say to you the day we met in that alleyway?"

"After he understood the problem between us, he offered to trade your life for his," Amir told me. "He said he wanted to keep you for himself."

I did not know what to say to that. Amir had always known I had a beloved. I never thought it was strange how well he seemed to know until now.

"Thank you," I mumbled, before I turned and walked away. I held my dagger tightly as I left, grateful that even if Lady POW was nowhere to be found, I would find a way to end everything soon.

19

◊

I was halfway to the castle when I realized I had forgotten something very important.

"*Merde*," I hissed at myself, stopping short as I passed by Old Town Square. "I forgot about Ben."

I glanced at the castle in the distance. The towers and walls of the ancient structure gleamed ghoulishly in the moonlight, backdropped against the dark pleasures of the city nightlife. I turned back toward the bridge, looking down the Vltava to see if I could estimate how far away the *Josefkà* was.

Should I alert Ben to the change in plans?

He was meeting with Zipporah tonight, getting herbs, including the silver thallis herb that the Order required for our special elixir. He was supposed to go over to Count Potocki's when he was finished.

It was uncertain if he was even still there, I thought. But surely it wasn't that unlikely? After all, I had left Karl's party much earlier than anticipated, and he had gotten off the coach several blocks away.

Ben would be upset with me if I did not include him, I reasoned. I remembered Lady POW telling me that she was not sure if she should allow him to continue helping out, and I made my choice.

No, I thought. *I cannot leave him out of this.*

Besides, if Lady Penelope was not at the castle, Ben and I would have a better chance at fending off Karl, in the event he came after us.

I slivered in and out of the shadows, heading toward the Cabal.

As I made my way through the cluttered streets and the alleys, I wondered if it really only had been less than a day since I had seen my friends at the Cabal. But, I figured, if the last weeks felt like a lifetime, it made sense that my temporal facilities were considerably off.

Keeping my cloak firmly against my skin, I slipped up beside the entrance to the Cabal. The wind blew my hood down, but I let it go. Without it, I could watch through the window as Ben talked with a comely woman near the bar.

At first look, I knew it was Zipporah. Eliezer's wife was nearly exactly the way I had imagined her to be. She had hair that was dark and curly like

450

THE ORDER OF THE CRYSTAL DAGGERS

my own, though hers seemed thicker. She was considerably shorter than me, and she wore the proper clothes of a mother and caretaker. I saw her apron strings sticking out from underneath her coat and almost smiled at the gentle, delicate picture she made. Everything about her suggested that she was a perfect match for her short but commanding husband.

I watched as Zipporah handed Ben a small drawstring bag, one that was puffed out and full. He offered her coins, and I was surprised at the amount, before I thought about Amir. He had managed to work his way into Count Potocki's manor, and it was likely he had bought the silence of the staff in the process.

Bribery is a trick Ben has no doubt learned from Amir. I tried not to laugh at the thought of what Lady POW would have taught him to do. She would have told him it was acceptable to rob Zipporah at gunpoint or use a weapon to inspire fear. Xiana would have used her stealth to steal it, and Harshad …

I paused, suddenly stumped. *I do not actually know how he would go about getting the herbs if Zipporah was not a friend.*

After a few moments of consideration, I could see where Harshad would pay her, too, but I did not think he would retrieve the herbs himself. As a foreigner from the East Indies, he would want to send someone with more anonymity to retrieve them—someone just like my brother, as a matter of fact.

"Miss Svobodová? Is that you?"

Hearing my name nearly made me jump. I grappled my cloak's ties, hoping against all hope the newcomer would fail to notice I was not wearing a gown.

I turned to see Madame Balthazar, one of the merchants I used to trade and do business with before Lady Penelope freed me from Cecilia's grasp.

"Madame." I greeted her as politely as I could, given that a small curtsey was all I manage without exposing my legs.

"I thought that was you," she said. Her mouth curled into a slight pout of disapproval. "What are you doing here? This is no place for a lady such as you to be."

"I am not here by myself. I was actually looking for my brother. I had only just lost him when you called to me," I lied.

"Oh, that makes sense." She looked relieved. "For a moment there, I thought you were in trouble. This is not a pleasant part of town, what with the Jews all around."

I pursed my lips and said nothing. I did not trust myself to respond in a way that did not end with me attacking her in some way, but thankfully, she kept talking.

"I wouldn't be here myself if it weren't for the fact I am desperate," she said. "I've been told that there is a midwife around here, and I need to speak with her at once. My daughter just had a baby a few weeks ago, and he has developed a terrible cough."

I was about to tell her Zipporah was inside the Cabal, but she kept fretting.

"I wish I had been able to find someone to send instead," she said. "It's so cold out tonight and I haven't had a bit of luck in finding her. Aren't you freezing, Miss?"

"I honestly did not notice."

She did not seem to hear me. "I should have called for that messenger boy. You remember him, don't you? Ferdy, that was his name. He always seemed so eager to pick up work, but not as much in recent days."

"It is probably the weather," I said softly. I did not have time to get caught up in mourning his loss anymore, and I really did not want to hear what Madame Balthazar thought of his passing.

"Perhaps, but not likely." She huffed. "I know for a fact he's been fighting again. There is a mission house that feeds those in poverty at the docks where a friend of mine works, and she says he's been causing trouble for the last few days."

I did not hear the rest of her words, as she complained about everything from the weather to the trouble that beggars and urchins caused. All I could hear was my heart beating between my ears while my skin started to prickle. I felt numb to the world, as if I had been shocked out of time's pull and then smashed back into it.

Was it possible Madame Balthazar was right? Ferdy was alive?

"You said he at the docks?" I repeated. The words tumbled off my tongue, thick and cluttered together, as though I was suddenly speaking a foreign language.

"Yes. Otherwise I would have sent him to find the midwife, of course."

"Nora? Is that you?"

Behind me, Ben appeared in the doorway. He had a confused look on his face, but I was at too much of a loss to say anything coherent.

THE ORDER OF THE CRYSTAL DAGGERS

Ferdy could be alive.

My mind reeled, first with unbelievability, and then broken with bursting, unbridled hope. It hurt to think that it could be wrong, but there was nothing I wanted to be true more ardently in that moment.

"Which dock is it?" I asked, turning back to Madame Balthazar. "Tell me where he is."

She looked shocked at my impropriety. "What? Why would—"

"Just tell me, please." I did not mean to sound like a desperate beggar, but there were any number of thoughts and feelings jumbled together inside of me, and everything from Karl, to Lady Penelope, to Lumiere and the mission—everything was lost as I suddenly had hope.

"He was at the Port of Prague, down by the riverfront." Madame Balthazar gave me the direction, and I hurriedly thanked her.

Before I could head toward the port, Ben came up beside us. I remembered the reason I had come, and hurried to usher Madame Balthazar toward the Cabal, telling her that Eliezer's wife was the midwife she needed.

The second Madame Balthazar was inside the Cabal and out of earshot, I grabbed a hold of Ben.

"Nora, what's wrong?" Ben asked. "What was that all about? Why are you here?"

"Things have changed. I need you to go to the castle," I said. There was too much to tell him, and I felt the words surge out of me like water from a broken dam. "Amir came back, and Karl is keeping Lady POW prisoner somewhere. Harshad and Xiana will be there shortly."

"What are you going to do?" Ben asked.

I was already moving as I hollered back to Ben. "Just go. I'll meet you at the castle. I have to check on something first."

"Nora!" Ben called back to me, followed by murmurs of sentences dotted with garbled phrases. Other than my name, I was not certain of what he said as I sped away.

It was likely something I ultimately did not want to hear. I knew I was already running behind schedule by stopping off to get Ben, and anything he said might have convinced me to stop my sudden quest.

But I had to know if Ferdy was alive.

◊   ◊   ◊   ◊

The Port of Prague was not welcoming to any aristocrat at night, let alone a lady. I was glad I had shed my gown earlier; I could move more freely. I even managed to use some of the stealth techniques I learned from Xiana and Harshad as I made my way through the loading port.

Weaving through the tight spaces and the winding walkways, keeping as much to the darkness as I could, I tried not to think about the passing time. I could only be grateful I had sent Ben. He would be able to help the others in my place, and that gave me a little time to pursue my own interests.

I tried not to cringe at the thought; Lady Penelope would chastise me for sure, and I would further fall from grace. It did not take much for me to imagine her boxing my ears for this, especially since the last time I went looking for the younger prince of Bohemia, I had gotten caught up in the partial collapse of the castle.

But this is worth it.

If he was here, everything would be worth it.

But, I thought, it would still be better if I could take care of this business quickly.

Fortunately, it did not take me long to find the warehouse Madame Balthazar spoke of. I crept up to the backdoor from the outside, surprised to find it was unlocked.

As I stepped inside, a flickering light whispered at the intrusion. I could feel the cold of winter much more sharply, and I held my breath as I acclimated to the putrid smell.

"Oh my, what is that?" I whispered, struggling not to choke. I had hoped the sound of my voice would comfort me, but I barely heard myself as the growing jeers and cheers from the other side of the hallway suddenly escalated.

I pulled my hood up more tightly to my face, and I secured my mask while I walked toward the sounds. I was able to see through the small sliver of the doorway.

For all the good it ended up doing.

THE ORDER OF THE CRYSTAL DAGGERS

The only thing I could see was a crowd of dock workers, many curled up in shabby clothes. Several were smoking cigarettes, and I briefly wondered if Jarl would be impressed or appalled at their choices.

After a silent, desperate prayer—was there any other kind I was offering to God of late?—I slowly opened the door and slid into the shadows.

No one noticed me on the outskirts of the crowd, and I relaxed to the slightest degree.

Until I saw why everyone was cheering.

There were two men, shirtless and covered in sweat, throwing punches, fighting with a force that shook me as I watched.

It was only as I watched the one fighter take a direct hit to the side of his torso and fall back that I recognized him.

Ferdy.

20

◊

It seemed to be a combination of shock, anger, and joy that stopped me from moving. From breathing, really.

He is alive. Oh, thank you, Lord, he is alive!

Never had I ever been so happy. Ferdy was alive and well, even if he was trying to dodge the fighter in front of him. I watched as he ducked down in pain at the blow to his side and then reached out and grappled with his opponent. I saw his hands were wrapped in leather, not unlike the ones Ben and I had used in Harshad's lessons.

I also had a really hard time ignoring his physique. Sweat rolled down his back as he moved, falling down the toned muscles. He had a very nice body, and I was not able to keep myself from blushing any more than I was able to look away.

It was only after he took another hit to the side that reality set in, and I realized he had lied to me—again.

Again!

He had lied to me about leaving for Silesia, and now he was in the middle of a needless, frivolous fight. All this while I was suffering at the thought of his death.

To make it worse, he must have known about the incident, too. And still he was here, saying nothing, reaching out to no one. Even his friends at the Cabal should have known he was here.

Were they lying to me, too?

I can't believe this! I had just decided to trust him, too.

That was the worst of it, I decided. I was in love with this selfish, privileged fool, someone who was content to waste his life on fights at the docks while his brother tried to murder him and seize the kingdom. Someone who seemed almost eager to run through my heart and make me question every decision I had ever made and every person I had ever trusted.

I watched as he feinted forward, making his opponent angry. The other man grunted loudly as he flung forward into the crowd. The men cheered even more as they pushed him back out.

THE ORDER OF THE CRYSTAL DAGGERS

Ferdy waited for a moment before the man raised his fists again. He was still his usual self, allowing even his enemy to have dignity. I saw him say something to the man, and the man shrugged it off and then spat. The wad of saliva hit the floor between them, and I could see he was more upset than anything else.

"Ew," I murmured as I tried to move closer. Ahead of me, off to the far side, there was a small gap between the front lines of the edge of their adapted boxing arena. I slipped in where I could, and if others paid me any mind, it did not stop their enthusiasm for the fight.

I will never understand men. I shook my head as another round of cheers filled up the room when Ferdy landed another punch, and the man fell down.

Another man came forward to check the man, who was struggling to get up. He seemed to be the referee, and he held up Ferdy's arm.

"Our winner for this round," he called, setting off a mix of booing and applause, along with the people calling on each other for bets to be settled.

Ferdy did not seem to care much. He nodded toward a couple of others, brushing off their comments. He was breathing hard and someone tossed him a towel.

That was when I noticed his opponent was getting up. His eyes were red, and he wore a cross expression.

He jumped up and steadied himself, wiping his long hair back from his face.

Before I knew it, he was running toward Ferdy, his fist balled and ready to attack.

And then, suddenly, I was leaping forward, entering the match grounds and bracing myself for impact. I ducked down and held my breath as he ran toward me.

I only briefly registered the man's shocked look as he tripped over me. My cloak tore free and fluttered to the ground as he went flying over my back. The fabric rolled over on the man, briefly trapping his arms as he flopped onto the ground.

The entire room was suddenly staring at me, including Ferdy. I straightened up and stared back at him. There were calls from the crowd for the man to be removed, but I only saw Ferdy's eyes widen and then narrow suspiciously.

457

Just like that night, I thought. It was the same look he had given me the night of the Advent Ball, when he recognized me as a member of the Order.

"It's a woman," one of the men shouted, and immediately the bets were announced again.

I finally glanced around, and my divided attention caught me.

My knees were swiftly knocked out from under me by my fallen foe. I tumbled down, feeling the sudden pain of a real fight at once as I landed on my back.

The man lunged over, trying to pin me down. My training with Harshad kicked in, and I hurried to block as I twisted out of his range. I rolled to my feet and held up my fists, surprised to see Ferdy with a headlock on my opponent.

"What are you doing here, Ella?" he called over the sounds of the crowd, as the room echoed with their overindulged pleasure.

"Trying to protect you!" I yelled back. I still did not know if I was more angry than relieved. "For all you deserve it, clearly."

The fighter elbowed Ferdy in the side, breaking free. He came running after me, and I used his focus to twist out of his reach. The second he ran past me, I lashed out a sidekick. His momentum carried him to the end of the arena, where the crowds were still cheering him on even as mud scrapped into his face.

"I'd like to think I deserve a better quality of protection than you can offer," Ferdy hissed as he came up beside me. From our sudden closeness, I could smell him, the faint scent of lavender and mint buried deeply under the aroma of ash and sweat. "I heard what happened."

"I did, too, and that's why I thought you were dead." I crossed my arms as I stared at him, furious.

"Why would you think I was dead?" Ferdy seemed surprised.

"You told me you were leaving for Silesia at the concert," I snapped. "What was I supposed to think?"

While I was distracted, our opponent came back up behind us. Ferdy pushed me out of the way as he threw out a hook. I could hear the *crunch* of the impact, and I watched in horror as the man flopped down onto the ground and stayed there.

Behind us, the crowd cheered again.

THE ORDER OF THE CRYSTAL DAGGERS

"Take a bow," Ferdy said, grabbing my arm and holding it up like the referee had done to him only moments before. "And then you and I are going to talk."

"Fine by me," I shot back. "I have plenty to say."

"I imagine you do." Ferdy rolled his eyes, and the two of us bowed. I had to stop myself from curtseying.

After that, Ferdy hurried to usher me out of the room. One of his friends tossed him a shirt, and he grabbed my dirt-splattered cloak on the way out. We headed back the way I had come, toward the other room in the warehouse. Once there, he found a smaller room, one I assumed to be an office, and shoved me in.

I stumbled forward, only stopping as I came up against a wooden box. There was a large pile of rope on the floor next to it. It was not an office we had entered, but a supply room.

Immediately, I whirled around to face Ferdy. I pulled down my mask and watched him lock the door. "Ferdy—"

"Shh." He glared at me in the poor lighting, listening at the door as some of the men walked by, talking loudly and possibly drunkenly about the fights.

I realized at once why Ferdy wanted me to keep silent. My eyes widened at some of their language; it was crude and coarse, enough to make even Lady Penelope blush—possibly.

When they were gone, and another round of fighting had commenced, Ferdy slipped into the shirt someone had tossed him. I was glad when he left it unbuttoned, even if I forced myself not to think about that.

"They're distracted now," he said, as another round of yelling and cheering resounded from the adjacent room. "I don't think they know we're in here."

"They seem very eager to be distracted."

"Poverty has its price. The entertainment here is brutal. I suppose you noticed that when you decided to make a spectacle of yourself. You shouldn't have done anything back there."

"That man was going to hurt you," I insisted. "It was the right thing to do, to stop him. Even if you deserved it."

"The men are just going to want more women boxers in the future after this."

THE ORDER OF THE CRYSTAL DAGGERS

"Maybe I'll give it another try after I'm done with you." I put my hands on my hips as I tried to make out his features in the darkness. The evening hours had arrived, and there was only a trickle of light coming in from the hall as we stared at each other. "Tell me why you're here in the first place, besides the fact that you've clearly gone mad."

"If I am mad for being here, what do you think that makes you for coming?"

I would not allow him to intimidate me. No matter what he had just done to that man. "You know why I'm here. I'm here for you."

"I'm not sure how your betrothed would feel about that."

I bit my lip, realizing why he was upset. Ferdy had likely heard the rumors, especially since he was taking care to watch his brother now. "I'm not going to marry Karl. You should know that. I told you before it was all a lie and part of my cover."

"Well, the morning papers are a little different," Ferdy snapped. "And besides, I didn't lie to you about Silesia, and *you* should have known about *that*."

"You told Karl that you were leaving in front of me!"

"You're lying about how you feel about him in front of me," Ferdy pointed out. He pushed back the sweaty locks of his hair. Even in the poor lighting, I could see it was still wet from his recent fight. "Why wouldn't I lie about my travel plans in front of him as well?"

"You could have told me you were lying when we met outside the theatre." I felt a rush of embarrassment, realizing he was right. But I was not going to admit it. Not now, not after I had discovered he did nothing to tell me he was alive when I thought he was dead. "At least I clarified my lies."

"I promised you I would not lie to you again," Ferdy said. He leaned back against the wall, and for the first time, I noticed there was an ugly bruise appearing on his right side, just under his ribs.

That has to be from Ben's attack. It had gotten worse with all the fighting.

"I know that I have kept important things about myself from you, and I wanted to make up for it. That is why I made you that promise—so you could trust me again." Ferdy looked disgusted. "I should have asked the same of you, but I didn't."

I crossed my arms. "If you wanted my trust, you should have told me that you were alive after the carriage exploded."

460

THE ORDER OF THE CRYSTAL DAGGERS

His fist lashed out, hard and quick, denting the wall behind him. I flinched but said nothing.

"Do you know what happened?" Ferdy asked, his voice slightly raised. I realized then how hard he was trying hard to keep himself together. "They killed Philip, and my other friends. They thought they were killing me, but they didn't."

My nose prickled with unshed tears, and my cheeks burned at my foolishness and shame as I thought about Philip and the others. Ferdy would have been devastated to learn what happened. And I was, too. Philip had taken such good care of me for him.

And my pain was only a pittance compared to Ferdy's, I thought. He had known him for years. Philip had been trusted with the kingdom's most precious secrets. My gaze lowered to the floor, thinking of the ones I loved and lost.

I already knew I could say nothing to make his pain go away.

"You know what the worst part of being a prince is?" Ferdy asked, his voice full of stinging bitterness. It was a complete departure from his energetic irreverence, and I lost all my hostility at his pain.

"No," I whispered. "Tell me."

"Other people feel the need to die for you." Ferdy narrowed his gaze at me. "People feel they need to lie to you. They feel so noble and justified in keeping secrets from you. All in the name of protecting you."

"I know that's frustrating." I knew from my own experiences with Lady POW and the others that I had plenty of others who were content to do the same thing to me.

"Damn it all to hell, of course it's frustrating." Ferdy punched the wall again, before he gripped his fist in pain. "I'm not special, Ella. No one should have to die for me."

I hurried forward and clasped my arms around his neck, holding on as he flinched. "I wouldn't die for a prince," I told him quietly. "But I would die for you."

I thought about telling him how much I wanted to kill for him, too, to punish Lumiere for his plans and Karl for his deviousness. But before I could think anything else, Ferdy reached up and pushed back my hood.

And then all of a sudden, his mouth was on mine again, and nothing else in the world mattered.

THE ORDER OF THE CRYSTAL DAGGERS

It seemed the storm inside of me was only matched by the one in him. His fingers were scratched and bloody as they tangled themselves in my hair, but I did not care. His kiss was rough and heavy, nothing like any other we had shared before. I could feel the frustration inside of him, along with the anger, but I knew it was the uncertainty that drove him to seek the solace of truth.

I was breathless as he pulled me closer to him, and then pressed into me. My back came up against the wall he had hit in frustration moments earlier. I might have been afraid, but I was too overwhelmed.

His hands were suddenly on my hips, the heat of his body burning against mine. My hands gripped onto his shoulders before slipping under his shirt, eager to feel the strength of him I had witnessed earlier, desperate to soothe the ache of his bruise. My fingers trailed down his side, seeking out his injury. I felt him shiver at my touch and I was about to ask him if I had hurt him when he pressed his hand over mine, flattening my palm even more ardently against his bruised rib. The slickness of his torso was oddly irresistible.

"Tell me what you want, Ella."

I already had my answer. "I want you to keep me," I whispered, clinging to him even more tightly as I drew his lips to mine again.

It was all too much to have him with me again. The taste of him, the feel of him—everything rushed at me all at once, and I did nothing to stop it.

I used to think being free meant an escape; I thought it meant I would be able to move away from authority and addiction, to be still against the forces of time and space. But as he held me there, pushed up against a wall, I knew freedom was not an escape, but a coming home; it was a place to run to, a star to guide all other forces of life and light, pushing back against the darkness of hopelessness and sin. Embracing it meant I was loved and cherished as myself; I could be who I was, and even more of who I was meant to be.

Ferdy's breath was ragged as he finally pulled his mouth away from mine. "This is madness."

"I thought you said it was magic before." My voice was shaking and hoarse as I whispered into the darkness.

Ferdy laughed and kissed my neck, letting the shy stubble on his cheeks rest against my skin as he caught his breath. "There is nothing magical about me wanting to make love to you inside a warehouse."

THE ORDER OF THE CRYSTAL DAGGERS

I stilled at his words, suddenly very aware we were too close. I slid away from him, only a little, but he stepped back as well. "You're right about that. Lady Penelope says there's no room for falling in love in the life of a spy."

He leaned in and kissed me once more, softly and slowly, before resting his forehead on mine, just as he had that day I woke up in Prague Castle. "You are more than a spy, just as I am more than a prince."

There was no trace of jesting or mockery in his voice. This time, he was only sincere and succinct, and if I had not fallen in love with him already, I would have done so in that second.

"What does your grandmother think about a spy getting married?" Ferdy asked.

It was too hard to tell if I was more hopeful at the question or dumbstruck at the possible answers. Lady POW had not married except to ensure her survival, and none of her other team members were married, either.

But my mother got married.

The safest answer was the one I gave him. "I don't know."

"Well, I guess we will find out when I meet her, won't we?" Ferdy took my hand and brought it to his lips, lacing his fingers into mine.

I froze. The thought of being with Ferdy no longer seemed so impossible; if death was no longer between us, I did not see why social order and kingdom security would stop us from being together. But I was genuinely unsure of what Lady Penelope would say, and I did not know if I could bear her refusal, or what we would do if she denied us.

"I'm glad you came to find me," Ferdy whispered. There was still a hint of sadness in his voice, but he seemed more hopeful than before.

"Me, too." I barely remembered what a marvel it was, that I had been able to find out about him at all. If miracles happened enough, it was too easy to see them as normal and take them for granted. I was not supposed to even be near the port, nor was I supposed to go to the Cabal, or run into Madame Balthazar ...

I am supposed to be looking for Lady Penelope and stopping Karl from announcing our engagement.

"What time is it?" I looked around and saw nothing to indicate how much time had passed. There was not even a window around to let me see if the moon had risen. "I have to go."

"Already?" Ferdy gave me a small smirk. "I thought you were going to see about another round of boxing?"

"If I do, my opponent is going to be your brother," I said. "He kidnapped Lady POW and he's holding her somewhere. That is the only reason the papers published the news about our engagement."

"Karl kidnapped your grandmother?" Ferdy frowned. "That doesn't sound like him."

"That reminds me." I scowled up at him. "He's working with your so-called friend Lumiere. He was the one who organized the attack on your coach."

"That does sound like Lumi. I wonder if he knew it was really me or not." Ferdy muttered a curse or two under his breath, and I immediately felt better. Lumiere likely wanted Ferdy to be his friend the way he wanted me to be his friend, and there was no way I could ever see that happening short of a miracle or two. "I'll have to ask him. He is very clever, but it would not be the first time his plans went awry."

"I can't believe you even would give him the benefit of the doubt there," I scoffed. It was true that I felt deeply empathetic for Ferdy and his loss, but it was no help to be ignorant of the facts.

"I did not say I would only ask him questions." Ferdy gave me a wink as he buttoned up his shirt. "I'll likely intersperse them with a few punches."

I nodded approvingly. "I would love to join you. Before we can take care of him, I need to find Lady POW."

"We can do that. What is the plan?"

"What?" I blinked up at Ferdy. "You're not part of the plan."

"I never was, *chérie*, but here I am. Are you really going to let me loose on the streets of Prague again without worrying for my life and safety?"

"You should be more worried about your life and safety if you think you're going to trick me into letting you help with my mission," I said, suddenly remembering Ferdy's other mischief. "Karl found out about us all because of you."

"What? I was extremely discreet when I came to visit you at the concert."

"It wasn't that. It was the hair combs you gave me before. He saw them."

Ferdy's hand gripped onto mine more tightly. "You mean you actually wore them out in public?"

"I didn't know they were the princess combs!"

"You really don't know anything about your kingdom's history, do you?"

"One does not need to know the history of a nation while working as a maid," I snapped. "Besides, knowing you as I do, I would say you didn't think I would recognize them. That was why you offered them in the first place."

"If Karl does know about us, that makes more sense as to why he kidnapped Lady Penelope and sent the notice to the papers," Ferdy said, clearly ignoring my point. "He had to force her hand because he knew I was pursuing you."

"You *were* pursuing me." I glanced around again, gesturing to the warehouse closet where we were located. "Or maybe I should say you were making *me* pursue you?"

"Let's call it even." He gave me a quick smile before his expression turned dark again. "Do you know where he's holding Lady Penelope?"

"Not exactly," I said. "I thought he would take her to the castle, since he's staying there, and he would be able to have someone watch her while he was busy with other things."

"I can help with that. My parents live there, after all, and all the servants are under orders to listen to me."

"I don't want you to get hurt." I hugged him close, looping my arms around his waist. "I already thought I lost you once."

"You couldn't lose me if you tried," Ferdy insisted. He tucked a stray curl of my hair behind my ear. "I am too clever for you, even if you are a spy for the Order."

"I've only just forgiven you for lying to me about being alive and blowing my cover, and you're comfortable enough to insult me?"

"They made your mission about me when they decided to try to kill me, remember?"

I was losing the battle, if I had not lost already.

"Consider this a matter of efficiency. And speaking of which, we should head out to the castle now," Ferdy said as he took my hand and opened the door. "If we're going to stop my brother, we'll need to … "

THE ORDER OF THE CRYSTAL DAGGERS

Ferdy's voice trailed off as he stopped. I glanced over his shoulder, only to see a small group of shadows stationed at the exit.

The shadows were attached to men, and all of them stared at us as we stood there. They seemed to be waiting around for something. I yanked my mask up over my nose, afraid they might have been looking for me. Ferdy inched in front of me; the same thought was likely running through his mind. He stepped forward and stretched out his arm, as if he was going to exchange greetings, but one of them pointed to Ferdy. "The boss was right. He's alive. Get him!"

Before I could do anything, Ferdy tugged me around and began running the other way. "Other way out."

"Well, hurry it up, you lazy thugs! Go get them." Another voice spoke up, and I struggled to keep running as I thought I recognized it. As carefully as I could, I turned to see the leader of the small group. While Ferdy and I had been preoccupied inside the supply closet, other lamps had been lit.

I gasped at the sight, my suspicions confirmed.

It was my stepbrother, Alex.

THE ORDER OF THE CRYSTAL DAGGERS

21
◊

The warehouse was much bigger and more complicated on the inside than what I had anticipated. Still stunned at the sight of my stepbrother, I was glad Ferdy was able to lead me through the makeshift arena and the labyrinthine halls connected to it. He would join me on my mission for sure now, but I was here to protect him as much as I was out to destroy Karl now.

We raced through the crowded halls, jumping through another round of fighters, before bursting into another storage area.

"Is this where you've been sleeping?" I asked Ferdy, looking around at a few shoddy makeshift beds and poorly constructed tents. There were several other people scattered throughout the warehouse halls, some of them sleeping, several of them smoking cigarettes, and many huddled together in close circles for extra warmth.

"It's not as bad as it looks."

I thought back to the days where Ben and I would sleep out in the barn, just to get away from Cecilia and her tyranny. Ferdy was likely right, but it did not make me feel any better. "I'm sorry."

"I could be dead," Ferdy reminded me.

"Apparently so, since there are still others trying to kill you." I glanced back to see the men were struggling to follow us. I saw them get caught up in the same crowds as we had. "My stepbrother is their leader."

"Your stepbrother?"

"Yes, Alex."

"How did he get involved in all of this?"

I was not even sure if I could describe what the whole situation was. I knew that Alex, along with the rest of Cecilia's household, had disappeared weeks ago without a trace. Now that I saw he was after Ferdy, it could only mean one thing: he was working with Lord Maximillian.

"Cecilia's a distant cousin to Lord Maximillian, the one who wanted to secure the throne for Karl," I said. "He purposefully broke off his daughter's engagement to Alex so he could get her to marry Karl."

"And then Karl suddenly decided he wanted you."

I blushed. "So did you."

467

THE ORDER OF THE CRYSTAL DAGGERS

"If you think my interest in you is sudden, you haven't been paying attention."

"You saw me more than ten years ago," I said. "I can't imagine that made any lasting impression on you, at least to the point you wanted to marry me."

"There are a few other times I've seen you in the city," Ferdy admitted. "But I still hold to my story. Something about my life changed when I saw you all those years ago."

"I appreciate that, I really do." I was panting hard as we ducked around a corner and pushed through a door. The bite of the winter night was harsh, catching my throat. "But this is not the best time for this."

"True."

"Even if your interest is not sudden, Karl's is."

"I doubt it. He knew of our father's admiration for yours," Ferdy said. "And he might have known of my feelings toward you, too."

I was panting too hard to respond.

Ferdy led me around several crates. "Stay down," he ordered, before glancing back. "I'm going to monitor them from over there."

"Be careful." I pulled out my dagger, hoping Alex and his cronies would have the good sense to give up.

"Hopefully they will lose us out here. The docks are dangerous, but especially at night," Ferdy said. "Stay here."

It was not the best time to argue with him, but I grimaced as he began issuing orders. He was the one infiltrating my mission, after all. If anything, he should have been taking orders from me.

Yards away, I heard some grunting mixed in with Alex's voice.

"Put your pistol away," I heard Alex say. "Max wants him alive. If we're going to correct the wrongs we've been dealt, we can't kill him."

It was not easy to picture Alex as I remembered him, with his bright hair brushed back and his fancy clothes, as the ringleader of mercenaries. But his words did make more sense; Lord Maximillian had hired him to find Ferdy.

Which meant that he knew of both the secret heirs of Bohemia. I was horrified to think what he would do to Ferdy if he got a hold of him. With Karl engaged to me, he might be looking for a way to usurp Karl's leadership.

THE ORDER OF THE CRYSTAL DAGGERS

A hand came down on my shoulder, and I jumped.

"It's me," Ferdy whispered. "Come this way. I think I found a way we can go around them."

"Where are we going?"

"To the Cabal. Jarl and his family are more than able to help, and Elie and Clavan might have more information for us."

Ferdy took the lead, and we began winding our way through the various lanes of shipping supplies, crates, and machinery. We were almost back on the cobblestone streets when a shot rang out behind us.

"Hurry!"

Ferdy did not need to tell me twice. I went running, recalling how Harshad had warned me before, in one of our various lessons, that it was unwise to get into a gunfight without a gun. Pistols had their drawbacks, but there was only so much I could do if I was shot.

Ferdy suddenly pushed me to the side. "You go that way," he said, pointing to a crossroad ahead of us. "I'll try to draw them back to the port."

"No," I objected. "No, you're not leaving my sight."

"It's a tactic, Ella. Divide and conquer."

I did not have a chance to point out that if we were splitting up, we would be doing their work for them. Ferdy turned around and headed for them.

"Ferdy!"

He did not pay any attention to me, and I skidded to a halt, ready to follow him. He was much quicker than me, and he turned down another lane before I could catch him.

I heard Alex call out to his men, telling them to separate.

"No," I huffed, still struggling to catch up. That was when one of Alex's henchmen began to run toward me.

A rush of fear propelled me to the side, away from where Ferdy went, and I found myself at the side of a smaller warehouse building. I could just hear the others as they cried out, and I did not know if Ferdy was able to fight them off or not.

Why in the world did he think it would be a good idea to leave me?

"Because he wanted to protect me," I realized, suddenly upset with myself. But Ferdy was not doing me a favor by endangering himself.

The henchman who followed me appeared, just yards away. I raised my fists, ready to fight.

"You're trapped now," the man said, lunging forward. "Nowhere else to go."

As I did my best to block his attack, I saw he had a handkerchief in his hand, one that held a sickly, sweet aroma.

Chloroform.

I had only ever smelled that once before, when Cecilia cut herself after yelling at one of the cooks about a year ago. She had to send Alex out for the doctor at once, while I watched from the shadows, both fascinated and horrified as she bled. When the doctor arrived, it was not long before he used chloroform to knock Cecilia out while he stitched up the gash on her leg. I would not have blamed him if it was to keep her quiet as much to keep her still, but he finished much more quickly with his work while she was unconscious.

I gulped, pressing my lips even more tightly together as we began to circle each other.

A few blows later, I was able to relax, if only in the slightest. The henchman was not as skilled as me as a fighter, but he did have a distinct advantage when it came to strength. And while I was surprised at the difference between fighting a real enemy as opposed to Harshad or Ben, I kept my focus clear. I had to get back to Ferdy.

Brushing off my blows, the man grabbed me and trapped me from behind.

He laughed, his chest rumbling with delight as he held me. "The boss will be happy to have an extra," he said as he laughed. "Might get paid more if you prove to be amusing."

I squirmed but said nothing; I did not know if he knew me or not.

The chloroform grew stronger. I held my breath, grabbing for my dagger.

My fingers looped around the hilt, and I pulled the blade free. Squeezing my eyes shut, I stabbed him in the thigh.

He screamed and let me go, just as I felt a sense of lightheadedness take over. I pulled my weapon free from him, noticing that in the moonlight, the dagger glowed a vicious purple.

THE ORDER OF THE CRYSTAL DAGGERS

There was blood dripping down the tip now. I knocked the man down to the ground and held him there, placing the blade at his throat as I stuffed his handkerchief into his face.

"I'm sorry," I whispered as his body went limp. I slowly stood up, using my skirt to wipe the sweat off my face. Glancing around, I saw I was alone.

I wiped my dagger on the man's coat, cleaning off the blood, silently thanking my mother for her help in protecting me. I knew I still needed a lot of work to master the skills, but I was glad to see I was able to hold my own against an attacker, even if my stomach twisted at the thought of harming him.

I looked down at my hands for a moment, wondering if the man's injury would lead to his death. The sickness inside of me burned even more, but I had to push it aside.

It had never bothered me to hurt Alex. He was the one who was terrorizing me, and it was worth it to hurt him in order to protect myself.

I was worth it. And so was Ferdy.

I hurried back to where he had left me—only to see the rest of Alex's crew carrying a limp form between the three of them. I slammed myself back around the corner, my hand pressed into my racing heart.

"Ferdy."

In the background, I thought I heard the city clocks chime, ringing with an ominous delight as the last of the evening passed away into night.

"Help me, Lord," I whispered. Praying was the only thing I was certain I should do at this point. Karl would be unhappy with me for failing to show up at Count Potocki's, Lady Penelope was still missing, I had no way of contacting my other colleagues, and the man I loved was in the hands of my wicked stepbrother.

Whether I was prompted by the divine or not, it took me less than half a second to follow after the men. I did not know if I could free him on my own, but I could not handle losing Ferdy, not after I had found him again.

Lady Penelope and the others would just have to wait. And if Karl did anything to any of them, I would make him suffer so much, he would wish he had never been born.

I made that silent vow as I hopped across the lane, hurrying after Alex and his minions as they made their way down toward the docks.

The men were loud and boisterous, and it was so evident I was certain that it was part of their plan. They appeared to be just another group of friends, carrying the one who managed to drink himself into a stupor.

The one carrying Ferdy on his back grunted as they began walking toward a ship. "What're you going buy with your cut, Will?"

"He can't afford to buy anything, not with his gaming habits," another man said, sending the rest of the group into a round of laughter. I could see Ferdy's body shake in their grasp, his copper hair glowing in the small sliver of moonlight.

Their banter angered me as I trailed after them. All of them, save for Alex, of course, eagerly continued to discuss what they were going to do with their reward. None of it would be appropriate in any context I could imagine. It also saddened me that, when Alex finally asked about their friend, the one I had managed to fell, the rest of them shrugged and immediately cut him out of their payment.

So much for honor among thieves. Lady Penelope had said before that everyone had their own system of honor, but she had yet to meet these people, clearly.

I looked up at the side of the ship and choked.

The name on the bow read *Salacia.*

Lumiere's ship. I pounded my fist on my chest, trying to swallow the rest of my coughing. *I should have known.*

"What was that?" A new voice from Ferdy's group of captors crackled against the calm night.

I sucked in my breath quickly, nearly sending myself into another coughing fit at the chilly air. It was much cooler down by the water. I put my hand over my mouth, noticing that my fingers were slightly numb from the cold.

"Stop getting distracted. You'll have your money soon enough," Alex said, his cultured tones much more distinct as he ordered the men onto a gangplank.

I watched as they boarded the ship, praying they would stay at the port. I did not know if they were there for long. Given my own mixed signals with Lumiere, the sense of urgency never left me as I scoured the deck, hoping to see a way to climb onboard.

As Ferdy's limp figure disappeared onto the *Salacia*, I closed my eyes and fell forward, dropping my head into my hands.

THE ORDER OF THE CRYSTAL DAGGERS

Could this night be any worse? I wondered.

Lady Penelope's sharp voice, the part that had made itself home inside my head, answered me.

It might be worse than you wanted, but you're not making it any better by standing there, moping.

I sighed as I straightened. She was right about that. It was not the time to indulge in my hopelessness.

"What would Lumiere want with Ferdy anyway?" I wondered, trying to think through everything clearly. Lumiere had told Amir he was friends with Ferdy, but Ferdy did not seem as agreeable.

I thought about Alex. His reappearance was strange and worrisome, but only because I had no idea his role in this whole situation. Glancing up at the ship's name, so proudly carved into the bow of the ship, I frowned.

"Why would Alex be helping Lumiere?" I pushed back my hood, letting my loosened curls flutter freely.

As if to provide an answer, I felt a pinch on my shoulder. There was someone else standing next to me, someone I had not noticed.

Immediately, I had to muffle a scream. My mind went reeling, wondering if I would be knocked out and taken aboard, or if I was lucky enough that Ferdy had managed to wake up and escape on his own.

Since I knew chances of that happening were nonexistent, I was in trouble.

"Who are you?" I demanded.

There was no answer as a hand reached out for mine, grabbing my wrist. But when I felt the familiar pattern of wrinkled flesh, roughed with scars and patches of peeling skin, I realized why the stranger had failed to reply.

"Tulia?" I whispered, astounded.

Immediately, I got another pinch from her other hand. As she held onto me, she moved her fingers to spell out a snarky welcome.

"Oh, thank God it's you," I said, reaching out into the darkness and hugging her. "I was so worried for you."

She patted my back patiently before I slipped free and took her other hands. I jumped eagerly, like a little child happy to be back with her mother. "I'm so glad to see you again," I said before I snickered. It was impossible to make out any of Tulia's features against the night.

She grabbed my hand again and asked me a question.

Is it?

"Of course," I said. "I thought you …"

Then it hit me; Tulia was here of her own free will. She was well enough to move, even if she was older and still recovering from the burns she had sustained before.

Tulia was here by choice—working with Lumiere. She had been called for, by Dr. Artha and Father Novak. Lumiere was here for the League. He was here to help Karl and Lord Maximillian.

Tulia was working with the League.

I backed away from her, and she followed me out of the shadows.

I saw her face highlighted in the dim lighting. Her eyes were dark as she shook her head. Her fingers flicked across my vision briefly.

I'm sorry.

And then I felt her hand around my neck, an impossible amount of pressure. I thought about screaming, but my cry was cut short as I fell into darkness once more.

THE ORDER OF THE CRYSTAL DAGGERS

22
◊

"Psst. Ella. Can you hear me?"

The sound of my name seemed to come from miles and memories away, but I jolted awake at the familiarity. I lurched forward, accidentally slamming my face into the floor. "Ouch!"

I did not have to open my eyes to know I was not at home. From the slight bow in the floor and the dry wood, I had a feeling I was on the *Salacia*, and I could only hope we were not heading out for open waters.

"You need to keep your voice down." This time, the voice was clear. "Someone might hear you."

"Ferdy?" My voice was low and quiet, but my relief was blatant.

"I'm here," he said, talking to me from the far right. "Over this way."

"I'm so glad you're here." I tried to rub my eyes, but I found that my hands were tied together. From my position on the floor, I could see a small window on the opposite side of the room. It allowed in enough light that I could just make out my surroundings.

"I'm glad you're happy now, because you likely won't be for long."

Using my shoulders and legs, I twisted around and sat upright. All of those hours sitting with Harshad going over stretches seemed much more useful. In the dim lighting, I saw Ferdy was sitting on the floor not far from me. His hands were tied behind him, too, but he was also tied to a pole behind him.

"I'm glad you're willing to get us in trouble, all for the sake of teasing me," I replied, scooting over on my knees. I grimaced as they pounded against the coarse, unforgiving floor, but I forgot all about that when I arrived in front of him.

The ropes around him were thick and rough, no doubt similar to the ones binding my hands behind my back, but I did not pay them any attention as I leaned against him.

"I'm glad you are awake," Ferdy whispered, lying his head on top of mine. We were unable to embrace, but just having him beside me was enough of a comfort for me. "I was worried when they brought you in. I wasn't sure how long it would be until the chloroform wore off."

"I wasn't knocked out with chloroform," I said. "Tulia did something. She grabbed me by the neck and that's all I remember."

"Tulia?" Ferdy pulled back and looked at me. "Your companion?"

"Yes." I groaned. "I had no idea she was on Lumiere's side. But I guess it makes sense, in a way. Father Novak was murdered after he reached out to her and Lumiere."

"How many murders are we dealing with here?" Ferdy frowned. "I remember you were interested in that doctor's death before."

"I'll tell you all about it," I promised, "but it will have to be later. There's just too much going on. Right now, we need to get out of here. You're not safe here."

"*We* are not safe here, Ella."

I barely heard him as Lady Penelope's training, coupled with Harshad's lessons and Amir's insight, began to take over, and I started to make a plan.

The first thing we have to do is get out of our ropes, I thought. I cheered at the thought of using my dagger. It was sharp, and I knew just how sturdy it was now, since I had used it to protect myself.

Guilt seeped through me as I struggled to reach for my blade. I had to push off the guilt of killing a man, especially since he would have easily killed me, too.

Or maybe he wouldn't have killed me, I thought. Maybe he and his friends would have brought me here with Ferdy just the same.

Either way, I have to stop this. Feeling bad won't change things.

I had been worried before, when Ben started to sound more like Lady POW; hearing my own thoughts echo her reasoning, I was even more frightened.

But, like my guilt and everything else, I would have to worry about it later. I had Ferdy to rescue.

I began to shuffle around the pole where Ferdy was tied. "We need to get out of our ropes. I'm going to move into a position where you can get my dagger out of the sheath. Can you feel it?"

"I can feel plenty," Ferdy replied innocently. I made a mental note to hit him later as he playfully felt around my waist and hips before latching onto the hilt of my dagger. "Got it."

THE ORDER OF THE CRYSTAL DAGGERS

"Good. Now pull it out and hold still. I'm going to rub my ropes against the blade. You have to hold it tightly, or one of us could get hurt."

"I know."

"Well, good. Then I know for sure that it'll be your fault if I cut myself." I tried to give him a warning look, but he only raised his brow at me.

A few moments passed as I pushed my bindings against the blade, sawing up and down, glad no one could see me. No doubt, I looked like a clumsy fool. It did not help that I felt like one, too.

"There." I cheered as the ropes fell from my wrists.

Gratitude poured out of me, thankful for my mother's protection once more. As I rubbed the feeling back into my wrists, I glanced down at the sharp blade, wondering all over again how it was that I was here. If my mother had lived, if she would have taught me how to wield the weapon of an Order member, or if she would have dedicated herself to being a true lady in Society's eyes?

I also wondered why I had my weapon in the first place. It struck me as odd, as I held it, that I still had it on my person. Tulia would have known about it, and it was not hidden from sight as I wore my spy costume.

Either way, it is better I have it, even if I do not understand why it wasn't taken.

I shook my head to clear my thoughts, hurrying to cut Ferdy out of his bounds. The ropes fell easily at the dagger's cut.

"Thank you, Ella." He embraced me quickly, giving me another kiss.

"We don't have time for this," I warned him, already softening against him.

"I told you when we met again, I would allow us to have a proper reunion."

I laughed. "This is hardly what I'd call proper."

"When our lives are at stake, there's nothing more proper than a man telling his beloved how he feels."

"But not at the cost of our lives."

"Better my life at stake than my heart," Ferdy argued, but he allowed me to step away from him.

"I should have known you would say something like that." I headed for the door, pressing my ear to listen. There were plenty of sounds that grew louder as I concentrated on them; the sound of soft footsteps, the movement of men as they hoisted goods aboard. I heard the clatter of dishes and the different calls of seamen between floors. Cautiously, I tried to turn the knob. It was locked.

"I've never been on a ship before," I admitted to Ferdy. "I've never had to escape one, either."

"We're likely in a spare cabin," Ferdy said, glancing around at our surroundings. He walked over to a desk, one that was tucked away in the corner of the room. "This would be one of the servants' quarters."

"Are you sure? It seems large for a servant's room." The window caught my attention again. Swiftly but silently, I walked over and examined it. It was not big enough for us to escape through.

"Lumiere has expensive tastes, but he is actually quite generous. He would keep his crew in good order." Ferdy picked up a bag from under the desk. It was full of what looked like dark-colored balls; when he pulled one out into the moonlight, I could see it was a coconut. "Especially since it seems he's been visiting the Hawaiians."

"How do you know for sure?" I asked. "It could be from the Caribbean colonies."

"There's also a wedding announcement from a few months ago." Ferdy picked up a scroll of stationary. "Archibald Cleghorn and his bride, Miriam Likelike."

"Who is that?"

"She's a princess of Hawaii," Ferdy said. "I've never met her, but I know of her. She's just a little younger than you. I'm not surprised that she invited Lumiere to her wedding. They're both rumored to be very conscious of fashion."

I thought of all the exotic dressings and decoration of Lumiere's performance at the Estates Theatre. Were those flowers and clothes from Hawaii? I decided it seemed likely, but there was something else I wanted to say. "Ferdy?"

"Yes?"

"Please don't say things like he's someone to be admired." I wrinkled my nose. "He made the arrangements to kill you earlier. I don't think I'm going to like him, even if you are friends with him."

"I would not say we were friends. I met him in Paris, in a gaming club, if you must know."

THE ORDER OF THE CRYSTAL DAGGERS

"Somehow I am not surprised."

"You don't need to be so prudent all the time," Ferdy teased. "We were playing against each other in a card game, for high stakes, and in the end, when he won, he would take none of his winnings. He said he played for the game, not for the prize."

"He was more likely playing, so he had a chance to talk to you."

"You're right—that was his real gamble, and he took it." Ferdy smiled. "Just like I took a gamble in saving you from that thief when we first met."

"If you credit Lumiere for allowing us to meet, I think I might beat you. Does it not mean anything that he is the one responsible for Philip's death, and that we're being held on his ship as captives?"

"It means a lot to me," Ferdy replied, his voice soft and deadly. "But I'm only pointing out that Lumi has his weaknesses. And we can use them to our advantage."

"Unless we're going to play cards, I'm not sure how we can use that information."

"We aren't playing cards, but we are gambling with our lives." Ferdy glanced back toward the door. "There's no chance we can get through the window. It's too small. Now that we're free, we will have to find a way to sneak off the ship."

"I wish Ben was here," I admitted. "He would know how to pick the lock."

"We could always wait until someone comes to see us."

I arched my brow. "Do you think someone will come?"

He shrugged. "They've got to feed us, don't they?"

"What if we're out to sea before then? What if they just let us starve here?"

"We could try something else." Ferdy thought for a moment before he chuckled. "Though I guess it's not likely you will be able to escape using the withdrawing room excuse."

Despite the dread growing inside of me, I giggled. "If Lumiere is working with Karl, he's likely not going to believe me if I use that one."

"Quiet." Ferdy held up a hand, and for a moment, I thought he was upset at the mention of his brother. But as we stopped talking, I realized he was paying more attention to the window. The sound of hooves accompanied with the clacking of wheels called to us.

We both pressed our noses to the glass. Through the darkness, I saw there was a grand carriage coming down the narrow lane of the docks. I tried to see if there was a crest on the coach, but there was nothing I could see that would identify its passenger.

A click of keys clattered behind us as the door opened. Ferdy and I turned around just in time to see Alex's shadow fill the entrance.

"What are you doing here?" Alex stared at me, before a sadistic smile crept on his face. "Well, if it isn't my favorite little sister. Max told me that you had to be involved in all of this, but I must confess, Eleanora, I didn't think you had it in you."

"We're not family," I objected, but he ignored me.

His hand reached into his coat and he pulled out a pistol. "You always cause more trouble than you're worth."

A renewed sense of fear tingled down through my body.

Ferdy, on the other hand, leaned back and yawned. "I don't know why you'd even bother with us. We're not worth any trouble, especially if we're only going to give you more."

"My cousin says differently," Alex said, shifting his attention to Ferdy.

"Is that who just arrived?" Ferdy nudged me with his foot, carefully, waving his arm toward the window to further distract Alex. He wanted me to move.

I did not know his game, but I followed his silent orders. I stepped to the side carefully, making it only seem I was shifting my stance as Alex continued to focus on Ferdy.

"He says you're the younger prince of Bohemia," Alex continued, "and if we're going to secure the throne for our family, we have to kill you."

"I fail to see why," Ferdy said. "My own cousin holds the throne. Karl and I have no legitimate claim to it."

"Not yet," Alex grumbled. "I've come to take you to my cousin."

"I'm not going with you."

"I didn't ask," Alex snapped, and even in the dim room, I could see a flush across his pale cheeks. "I'd hate to kill you first."

"If you're going to kill me, you might as well do it now," Ferdy said. "So go ahead. Shoot."

I felt the blood drain from my face as Alex raised the gun. Before I could think through it, I stepped in front of Ferdy. "No."

"Ella, get back," Ferdy ordered. "He can't do it. I was calling his bluff. You really don't know anything about gambling, do you?"

"Apparently, she doesn't."

I glanced back to see Alex was watching us, and I could almost see his mind putting the pieces together.

"You're in love with her," Alex said, and I knew we were doomed. He turned the gun at me, a new perverseness on his face. "Excellent. If you don't do what I want, I'll kill her instead."

Ferdy's jaw hardened. Before I could assure Alex that Ferdy meant nothing to me, that such a prince would never fall in love with a former servant girl and current spy, Ferdy held up his hands in defeat.

"I will do as you say," he said. "But you must guarantee her safety."

"I swear on my life she will live," Alex assured him. "Now, come to me, Eleanora, and give me your weapon."

It was against everything inside of me to put one foot in front of the other and approach Alex. Slowly, I held out my dagger, and he took it from me. His pistol remained pointed firmly at Ferdy as he tossed my dagger to the far side of the room. He grabbed my arm and thrust his gun just under my chin. I silently sent my mother an apology for letting go of her dagger; I had a feeling she would forgive me, knowing it was to protect Ferdy, but I felt her loss all as Alex held his weapon steady.

My nose twitched at the smell of gunpowder mixed with the metallic heat. The barrel jutted into my skin as my heart began to race in terror.

I was further alarmed as Alex locked his arm around my neck and clutched me against his body. "You always were too alluring for your own good, you know," he hissed, breathing in my scent deeply.

"Get away from her!" Ferdy yelled as he stepped forward, angered by Alex's attention to me.

"I said I wouldn't kill her, but I never said I would keep myself from her." Alex laughed, drawing me even closer to him. I began to resist, but the gun barrel dug further into my neck. I struggled to breathe at the pressure.

481

THE ORDER OF THE CRYSTAL DAGGERS

"You're here for me," Ferdy reminded him.

"Then let's get going, shall we?" Alex twisted his fingers into the ends of my curls, clearly enjoying his time incensing Ferdy as much as he was pleased to have me beside him. "It would be a pity to shoot such a pretty lady at such a close range."

Ferdy glared at him, his eyes never leaving Alex's as he walked toward us. I silently pleaded with him to do something, but I knew Ferdy would not risk me.

It is up to me, I thought. I scrambled to think of something, anything at all. I was not sure if any of the fighting techniques I knew would work.

And then a new idea struck me. I did not have to fight Alex. All I had to do was get him to think he had lost his advantage.

I gasped for air one last time, loudly, before I closed my eyes and allowed my body to go completely limp. Alex buckled under the sudden pressure of supporting me, and I felt the gun slide away from my skin.

"Hey!" Alex wrestled with the sudden extra weight, and Ferdy did not fail me. I heard his quick steps and a strange *crunch* as something flew through the air and hit Alex.

When I opened my eyes a second later, I saw a coconut rolling on the floor in front of me. I pushed out of Alex's grip and used the momentum to slam my fist into his nose. Ferdy came up beside me to further force Alex onto the ground.

I hurried over to where Alex had thrown my dagger. I'd just picked it up when the gun went off, and I heard Ferdy's cry of pain.

"No," I yelled, watching in horror as Ferdy fell back. My heart stalled at the thought of losing him. When I saw him grip his arm, gritting his teeth and struggling not to cry out in pain, I knew we had to finish this battle.

I gripped my dagger and used the hilt to bludgeon back of Alex's head. I did not feel any remorse as the dagger hit him, nor did I feel any sadness as I felt the shock of bones cracking and blood vessels breaking.

"Damn you." Alex's voice was slurred as he struggled to remain conscious, only to collapse onto the floor a second later. His breath came in uneven stints, but I was too concerned with Ferdy to care.

"Ferdy." I knelt beside him and carefully put my hands on his arm where the ruby red of his blood was leaking through his shirtsleeve.

"It's not bad," Ferdy insisted. "It was a graze, that's all."

THE ORDER OF THE CRYSTAL DAGGERS

"Let me look at it." I gently peeled his fingers away before tearing at the sleeve. A large gash, from the middle of his arm to the edge of his shoulder, glowered up at me. From what I could deduce, I agreed with Ferdy; it was a surface wound, though it looked like it had burrowed several little chunks of skin off from his arm.

"We need to get this cleaned," I said slowly.

"Just tie it up for now," Ferdy said. Sweat ran down his face as he gritted his teeth, determined to keep me from knowing how much pain he was in. "Tear some strips from my shirt. Once we get out of here, we can take care of it."

"I don't want you to be hurt."

"It's too late for that." He tried to give me a smile but was too pained for me to say anything.

I hurried to bind up the wound as he instructed, praying every step of the way he would be fine until we managed to get back to the Cabal, or even the manor. *Amir will be able to take care of this, surely.*

"Don't cry."

"Huh?"

"I can see the tears in your eyes, Ella," Ferdy said. His smile was much less pained this time. "Don't cry. You did well, especially handling that beast of a stepbrother you have."

We both glanced back at Alex's body. He was still breathing, but there was some blood coming out of his head.

"I'm glad he'll be in pain for a while," I said slowly. I did not admit the terrible truth, that I did not actually want him to die.

Well, that was not true. I did not care if he died, but I did not want to be the one who killed him.

Ferdy squeezed my hand tightly. "You can't trust someone like him to keep his word. He was going to kill you after he was finished with me."

He carefully stood up, and immediately I ran my hands down his back, clutching him. "I'm so sorry. I didn't think he would shoot you, I swear."

"It's fine, as long as you're safe." Ferdy wrapped his good arm around me, while his other bled freely. I felt him flinch and I knew he was trying to hold back his complaints as he held me. Another layer of guilt pressed into me, and I struggled not to cry at his pain. I leaned up and kissed him.

I had no words that would suffice for an apology that could be accepted, but I wanted Ferdy to know I would be there to comfort him.

"I thought you said we didn't have time for this," he murmured against my mouth.

"I will never have enough time to love you properly," I whispered back. "Especially with people like Alex trying to kill us, it seems."

"Ella." His breath tickled my ear as I burrowed into his chest, losing myself in him.

When the castle walls had collapsed, I embraced him then, too. My kingdom of illusions and innocence had fallen, and I was crushed by its destruction. This time, as Ferdy held onto me and I clutched at him, I no longer felt the same sadness. My world before had been beautiful, but with very little to offer in the way of reality. Now, having been through the darkness and having seen the meanness of this world, I knew what true beauty and virtue meant. With Ferdy beside me, we could rebuild what had been burned down, and together with the others I loved, we could strengthen every good thing for the future.

A future where we are together.

"Well, what a lovely and touching scene this is."

Ferdy and I looked over at the door simultaneously. Lumiere stood there, lounging in the doorway. I pulled out my dagger, and Ferdy balled up his fists, while Lumiere only laughed.

"There's no need to jump the gun," Lumiere said. He nudged Alex's fallen body with his toe. "I trust my associate here did not give you too much trouble?"

"I'm going to kill him after I kill you," I promised bitingly.

Lumiere shook his head and tiptoed around Alex, picking up the gun Alex had dropped during our scuffle. "*Tsk, tsk,* Lady Ella. There's no need to be so hostile. I understand you are my guest, and you have been upset with your treatment while you have been here. But please, allow me the chance to properly rectify this situation before you rob me of all ability."

Before I could ask what he meant, he held up Alex's gun and fired.

My body reacted to the movement before my mind did. Ferdy and I both grabbed onto each other, the two of us trying to shield each other. I told Ferdy before that we were both determined creatures, and it seemed we were both determined to stay in this world or leave it together.

THE ORDER OF THE CRYSTAL DAGGERS

I prayed for deliverance and squeezed my eyes shut as the shot crackled like lightning and thunder, the smack of its force whipping past us.

But when the echo of the gunshot faded, Ferdy and I were both still standing.

We had not been shot.

"What did you do?" I asked Lumiere, before I saw my answer.

Down in front of us, Alex's body was no longer twitching. It was deathly still, as a puddle of blood began to bubble up on his back and pool out from underneath him.

Beside me, Ferdy gripped onto me even more tightly. I welcomed his strange comfort as a reminder that I had to stay composed, even at the gruesome sight.

"There," Lumiere said, tossing the derringer aside once more. "I've taken care of the situation. I can assure you, *chérie*, such a grave offense to your person will never happen again from this pathetic creature. Now, I must insist that you both come with me. And, if you do not want to end up like this vile mess, you will be silent."

He paused for a moment, before looking to me. The green of his eyes seemed to glow as he gave me his cocky grin. "I suppose I do not have to warn you. I know if you truly are Naděžda's daughter, your curiosity will keep you quiet."

I gripped my dagger in my hand, ready to tell him that my mother would be upset at his treatment of me, and I refused to believe that she would be friends with him, either. But then he nodded toward my weapon, waving his gun around in a dismissive movement. "I would also tuck that away. You will not need it to get the answers you seek."

THE ORDER OF THE CRYSTAL DAGGERS

23
◊

I was telling Ferdy the truth when I said I had never been on a ship be-fore. Ever since *Máma* had been lost at sea, I did not like the thought of traveling by boat. It always loomed inside my mind like a shadow, and I did not think I would ever be comfortable sailing.

As we made our way through the small hallways of Lumiere's ship, I was further convinced my instincts were right. The deck beneath my feet tipped slowly from the right to the left, and then back to the right. My legs felt the strange pressure, almost as if walking onboard was an exercise Harshad would prescribe.

Ferdy walked behind me, and Lumiere behind him. My dagger curled into my side, further tucked into the small leather skirt of my habit.

When we immerged from the bowels of the ship and onto the upper deck, I saw there were torch lights glowing as workers hurried around, cleaning the deck and preparing to set sail. The workers were all clothed in masks, but I recognized the blond curls of a short figure as we headed toward the bow.

Betsy!

As if she heard my silent call, her eyes widened as they saw me, filling with hope and then fear. Before I could say anything, Lumiere cleared his throat behind me, and I had to refrain from action—for now.

But I knew, in seeing Betsy, what had happened.

Tulia and Lumiere had coordinated with each other, stealing away the household workers from my father's manor. They were now working on Lumiere's ship, which was kept far enough away from the dock that they risked drowning if they attempted escape. Lumiere kept them from leav-ing, and Alex worked for Lord Maximillian.

Did that mean Cecilia and Priscilla were also onboard? I wondered if that was possible, given Prissy's high standards and Cecilia's arrogance. My stepsister would not be willing to stay on a boat because of the lack of luxury, and Cecilia would be reluctant to do so without commandeering the captain's authority.

I glanced back at Lumiere for a quick second, and he continued to stare straight ahead. He did not seem like someone who would let another per-son hold power over him, no matter what Ferdy said about his card game.

THE ORDER OF THE CRYSTAL DAGGERS

"Ella."

Ferdy whispered my name and grabbed my hand. I was worried that Lumiere would not allow me to keep a hold on him, but when I looked forward again, I suddenly realized that Ferdy was the one who was worried.

Karl, Lord Maximillian, and a dozen of their bodyguards and runners stood in front of us. Karl saw me, and I blushed as he scowled. There was no hiding myself from him anymore.

"Gentlemen," Lumiere cooed. "I must apologize for the delay."

"What is going on? Where is Alexander?" Lord Maximillian's voice was harsh against the darkness. The rustling river below harmonized with it, adding an eerie quality to the atmosphere.

"Unfortunately, there was a bit of a scuffle, and I am remiss to have to announce he has passed from this world," Lumiere said. "Next time you're going to send someone after a member of the Order, you might want to consider sending someone more experienced. Or at least someone who wouldn't get shot by his own gun."

I noticed Lumiere did not tell Lord Maximillian who it was that shot the gun in question.

"I see. Yes, that is unfortunate." There was nothing in his voice to suggest that he was upset at Alex's loss, other than a minor inconvenience. "Such a shame, too. He had promise."

"As what? A mercenary?" I snapped, and Lumiere nudged his gun into my shoulder. I knew he was unhappy at my outburst.

Lord Maximillian's heavy brows furrowed as he looked at me. "So, the rumors are true. Lady Wellington is a spy, and she has trained her granddaughter in the art. I must confess, I did not think you were capable of pulling off such an elaborate ruse."

I blushed at his cutting remarks. Ferdy squeezed my hand more tightly, likely pleading with me to abstain from commenting back.

Lumiere stepped forward. "She has her charms. And that helps blind us to her, shall we say, more egregious faults, perhaps? Isn't that right, Prince Karl?"

It was Karl's turn to turn red. He opened his mouth to say something, but Lumiere cut him off.

THE ORDER OF THE CRYSTAL DAGGERS

"Maybe I should have phrased it differently. I meant to say, 'Wasn't I right when I told you that your beloved Ella was secretly in love with your own brother?'"

Karl straightened, tightening his cravat around his neck. "You have made your point, Lumiere. You have my trust."

"I should think so, and I am appalled that you should have questioned it in the first place after all we have been through," Lumiere snapped, and I saw that he was genuinely upset at having to prove himself. He ran his hand through his hair, irritated, and then smiled brightly. "But, considering it is Ella, I am more understanding. I can see why you would want to marry her."

"Yes." Karl frowned. His eyes moved away from mine, following their way down to my hand in Ferdy's, before he focused on his brother. "What a pity it is, that she does not seem to share the same opinion on that matter."

Ferdy moved to stand in front of me. I could see a line of blood dripping from his arm, but the slow trickle did nothing to deter him from facing Karl. "I would apologize for my deception on the matter, if you hadn't called for my death, brother."

"As usual, you don't understand what is at stake, Ferdinand," Karl snapped. "Your selfishness was what nearly got you killed before, not my desire for vengeance. You were interfering with my affairs, and I will not have you continue to be my stumbling block."

"You would have killed your own brother for the kingdom?" I was finally free to ask my questions, no longer bound to the silence due to my disguise.

"He was actively plotting against me and the future of Bohemia, Eleanora." Karl groaned. "Please don't tell me you foolishly believe his lies, too. Ferdinand would gladly see the people of this country rule it by mob force. That is all direct democracy is, you know, when you allow the people who have no formal education or even reading ability to help determine law. Do you want such savagery to ravage our nation? Wars among our neighbors have already done enough damage."

I said nothing, and Karl only shook his head. "When we are married, I will have to see to your education."

"I'm not marrying you," I snapped. "No matter what the morning papers say."

THE ORDER OF THE CRYSTAL DAGGERS

"You *will* marry me, Eleanora," Karl hissed. "You've humiliated me enough, both in my own family and among my friends." At his grimace, I wondered if he was thinking of earlier when I left Count Potocki's ball before making an official appearance. "It is clear you will have to learn your place in this world."

"Why would you want to marry me anyway? I don't want to marry you."

"Your actions in Society have failed to suggest otherwise," Karl accused. "Even if I failed to see through your lies, no one else needs to know. We can still marry and free the kingdom from the empire."

"You can't force me to."

"I won't let you, either," Ferdy said.

Karl scowled. "Well, I can readily believe that, *brother*. You have never allowed me any happiness, have you? Especially not when it was convenient for you. This is no exception, I see. It is the same as when you did everything you could to become our father's favorite. You stole his love for me away, and now you have Eleanora's, too. But she is mine. My plans for the kingdom are too important for Bohemia. If you do not stand down, you will be put down."

"Karl, if you don't stop, you will be the one who is stopped," Ferdy told him. "The people don't want you as their king."

"They seemed plenty happy about my decision to pledge for Count Potocki's position once he steps down. Not that you would know that, since you missed the ball."

"I told you Eleanora was there," Lord Maximillian interrupted. "She left early, which is why I had my suspicions and had her followed."

"Yes, that is true," Karl muttered, clearly upset he had been interrupted only to be corrected. "I suppose I owe you for bringing my wayward brother back to Lumiere's. I am grateful for Eleanora's return, too, even though I am surprised she did not come to see me. I would have thought her grandmother's life was more important."

I felt my breath leave me at the thought of what Karl had done to Lady POW. "I swear this now, I will pay you back for every bit of pain you inflict on her."

"What an insolent girl." Lord Maximillian sniffed, his thick salt and pepper mustache fluttering the darkness. "I told you my daughter would have been a better pick, Karl."

"And I told you both, I would take care of the two of them for you," Lumiere said, stepping out in front of Ferdy and me. "Obviously, both of them are harder to kill and persuade than we originally planned, but what is the fun in doing an easy job? I happen to like harder jobs myself."

"What do you want now, Lumiere?" Lord Maximillian turned to face him, clearly irritated.

"Need I remind you I require payment, your grace?" Lumiere shook his head. "We all must pay for our pleasures. And as I enjoy seeing to my own pleasure, I must insist you compensate me for my trouble."

"I hardly think this was any trouble for you," Lord Maximillian muttered, but he called forth one of his servants, who brought forth a large bag.

Lumiere smirked. "It was trouble enough for you to be searching for the rumored heir of Bohemia for the past several years. The fact that you failed to contact my father before wasting so much time speaks to your weakness, not mine."

I glanced at Ferdy, and I suddenly wondered what Lumiere was doing, treating Lord Maximillian with such disdain. He gave him a mocking bow as he took the bag, quickly opening it. By the light of the fires, I could see several hundred pound notes inside.

"I trust it is to your satisfaction?" Lord Maximillian asked.

"Why are you paying him?" Karl asked, his voice impatient. "I told you it was taken care of."

"Prince Karl, *mon ami*, you should know that my satisfaction can always grow," Lumiere replied, giving him a quick wink. "One only has to ask Didier if there is any doubt."

I glanced around as Lumiere continued to shuffle through the bag. Where was Didier? I wondered. I had never seen him far from Lumiere's side. Ferdy gave me a questioning look, no doubt wondering if I was planning something.

I did not know where to begin, but if we could do something, now was the time to do it. Lumiere was distracted, engrossed with his payment, and I was armed. I reached for my dagger, catching Ferdy's eye. I did not know if I could get the two of us out of there without his help, but I did not want to make his injury any worse. From the paleness of his face, I already knew I only had a little bit of time before I would have to find Amir or see if Zipporah was still at the Cabal.

Ferdy tensed up but shifted his feet, ready to pounce along with me. I took a deep breath and then stepped forward.

Only to be sidetracked at once, when Lumiere let out a stream of curses in French.

"*Mon Deus,* where is my letter, Max?"

I tripped forward as Lumiere began arguing with Lord Maximillian.

"You know I need that letter," Lumiere hollered. His face, always so serene and easy-going, was taut with boiling rage. "My father is the ambassador to the French empire, not me. I need my diplomatic immunity!"

"It is in there," Lord Maximillian argued, stepping forward. "I signed and sealed it myself."

"I *need* it, Max, I need it so badly," Lumiere bemoaned. "Otherwise everyone will know about the information from my father regarding the Order of the Crystal Daggers. How I have helped smuggle your special wine across Bohemian hills and mountains, and I have delivered to you both the second heir to the throne and ensured the proper queen would ascend to the throne."

"Calm down!" Lord Maximillian shouted, surprising me with his stern tone. "Surely it is in there. You can't find it when you're throwing a hissy fit."

"I do love a good hissy fit," Lumiere yelled, "but not when so much is at stake."

"Ella," Ferdy whispered. "Look."

I turned away from Lumiere and Lord Maximillian, only to see the familiar gleam of a purple blade as it moved behind Karl. Several moving figures slipped onto the deck behind it, and I grinned.

Lumiere slowly looked up around us. He had noticed the new arrivals, too. "Well, it seems we have some more visitors here, your grace."

"Intruders!" One of Alex's henchmen cried out as he was cut down and tossed overboard. Squinting, I saw Ben was the one who had felled him, and my smile only grew wider.

"I hope you will excuse our tardiness. The traffic between here and the castle is quite awful." Lady Penelope's voice was scratchy but certain as she called out her wry greeting. "But I am pleased to say we made it just in time for Lumiere's confession and your agreement."

24

◊

Lady Penelope had never looked deadlier as she stared at Lord Maximillian. Dressed in men's clothing, with the fitted pants and the dark jacket, she had come prepared for battle. I watched with pride and terror as her eyes narrowed in the moonlight. At her side, I saw Amir appear from the other side of the ship, and together, the two of them were focused on their foe.

I was relieved to see that they had put their differences aside. At least, they did so long enough to make sure I was safe.

From the other side of the deck, I saw the shadow of Harshad's form, and I heard him call out for Ben to follow. My friends and family were all here, and I felt an enormous wave of relief break through me.

They are all here. They've all come to rescue me.

I suddenly groaned at the thought. While I was happy to see them, I did not need another reason for Lady Penelope to think I was incompetent.

I felt even worse as I realized my cover was blown. Karl, Lord Maximillian, and everyone else knew the truth of who I was, and who I worked for. There would be no more gallivanting around Society now, and I would be shunned by the crowds, if not driven out of the city for my indecency.

Ferdy took my hand again, and I glanced at him. He gave me his cheeky smile, and I nodded.

He might have been a prince among men, I thought, just as he was the prince of my heart.

I still had to focus. There was no use worrying about Lady Penelope's disappointment and Society's rejection if I was silly enough to die tonight. I gripped Ferdy's hand in mine, resolved, even if I was still ruffled by the future's uncertainty.

Ben appeared, hopping over the side of the ship. "You're lucky we managed to find you."

I smiled brightly at the sight of my brother. "Ben."

There was a bit of swagger in his step as he greeted me. I was glad to see he was here, not only because I knew I could count on him to help

492

me, but because I knew it meant a lot to him to be included in our mission.

"You've missed a lot of action, Nora," Ben said. "Harshad, Xiana, and I met at the castle, and Amir came, too, as we were rescuing Lady Penelope from the dungeon. Amir had a message to come here for you."

He tried to explain everything to me, but Lady Penelope quickly became the center of our attention as she came up beside Karl.

"It is lovely to see you again, too, Mr. Marcelin," Lady Penelope said, giving Karl a mocking curtsy. "Let me take this quick moment to tell you I have decided to withdraw my own agreement for Eleanora's hand. It seems she is already engaged."

I glanced over at Ferdy with a raised brow, watching as he swallowed a laugh.

"I forgot about that," he said.

"Forgot about what?" I asked.

"I talked to my father about marrying you. All I needed was your approval."

"And my grandmother's." I looked back up to Lady POW, watching as she took her dagger out and pointed it at Lumiere.

I did not think it was time to ask her about it. Not when she had her intended prey nearly at her mercy.

Lumiere only laughed. "Madame, you never fail to delight me in your own right."

"Surrender, Lumiere," Lady Penelope ordered. "You are surrounded."

"We might be surrounded, but we are far from outnumbered. Remember the old adage for retirement? Death or defeat, and we fight only to the death aboard this ship, Pepé!" Lumiere pulled out his gun and fired out several shots wildly into the air. "Attack, men!"

The remaining guards, still a little confused, jumped into action. Lady Penelope and Amir quickly came to each other's rescue, fighting back to back as they were repeatedly charged.

"Ready, Ben?" I asked, glancing over at him as I widened my stance.

"It's about time we can practice Harshad's lessons in real life." Ben stepped up beside me, while I saw Karl duck where he stood as swords came out. He hurried toward the side of the ship, but a few of his guards, keen on fighting, blocked his way.

493

THE ORDER OF THE CRYSTAL DAGGERS

Ben and I stood back to back, while Ferdy tapped Ben on the shoulder. "May I join you?"

I grinned, but Ben frowned. "This isn't a game of cards," he snarled.

"Ben, stop harassing him," I muttered.

"He's been lying to us this whole time about who he is," Ben argued, before his gaze turned dark. "But then, I suppose you knew that."

I blushed, grateful another guard came up to attack me. After a few well-placed kicks, I was able to reply. "Just since the Advent Ball."

"If he wanted nothing to do with us then, he's lucky we're even here to help him now."

"I can assure you," Ferdy said as he flung another fighter away from our group, "I am happy to see you. And I apologize for my deceit. It has been a lifelong burden for me. And my brother, too, though his reasons for hating our requested silence are far different from mine."

"Which one of you had the reasons that included seducing my sister?"

"Ben!" I nearly hit him at his impropriety. He was fortunate we had other enemies that required our attention.

"I would have said romancing," Ferdy said, trying to coax a smile out of Ben. "But yes. You should know I'm in love with her, just as I know you can't blame me for it."

"Believe me, I'm more than content to blame her," Ben muttered.

I did not know if I preferred it that way or not, but before I could respond, Harshad leaped down from the upper deck. My mouth dropped, gaping as he landed squarely on the shoulders of a guard, and I could barely believe my eyes as I watched him. For a seventy-two-year-old man, he certainly had a lot of agility.

"You need to focus," Harshad said. "Lumiere is distracted. Use it to your advantage."

I did not know what he expected of us. While Lumiere was close by, we still had a few of Lord Maximillian's guards to consider. "Well, at least we've stopped fighting each other when it comes to Ferdy, and we're fighting with him beside us."

"That's not going to change my mind about him," Ben replied.

"Can I just say, I'm happy to have the chance to defend myself?" Ferdy gave Ben a quick pat on the shoulder. "And you never know. You might change your mind about me."

THE ORDER OF THE CRYSTAL DAGGERS

"You mean like how you might change your mind about Lumiere?" I asked.

"I told you, he's overstepped himself," Ferdy replied. "Badly, too, this time."

Before Ferdy, Ben, and I could argue more, I heard Lord Maximillian cry out in frustration. "What do you think you're doing? You set us up!"

He was yelling at Lumiere. For a few short seconds, I watched as Lord Maximillian pushed against Lumiere, forcing him back several steps.

With a frustrated look, Lumiere stumbled back but quickly found his balance. It was then I noticed there was an envelope in his hand.

"A setup? I am appalled by this accusation. Is this really how you would treat me, when I am saving your life?" Lumiere pushed him, handing him his gun as he took the letter. "You're lucky I can be bought, Max! Now, go and take your prince. I'll hold them off while you escape."

"No," I cried, jumping in front of Ferdy. I pulled out my dagger, ready to defend him from anything, at any cost—only to find there was no threat.

But Lord Maximillian did not pay any attention to me. Ben rushed forward. "Watch out, Nora."

Ben raced toward us, heading for Lord Maximillian. A gun gleamed in his hand, and I worried he would take a shot at Ben.

Everything seemed to happen all at once. I saw Lord Maximillian's finger tighten around the trigger. I saw Ben running toward him, oblivious to the danger.

There was no way to stop the gun, but I knew I could stop Ben. I jumped forward, hitting Ben hard as he passed us. He wobbled as I fell over, while the momentum of our impact pushed him over the railing of the upper deck.

"Ben!" I shouted, just as the gun went off. The bullet missed both of us, but I scrambled to see where my brother had gone.

I heard his scream—almost the exact same terrible scream I had heard before, all those years ago, when he fell off the barn roof—and I froze.

Every moment of my life from the moment of Ben's first accident to this one collapsed inside of me, and I felt the pressure crush me. Tears started to form in my eyes as I realized, once more, that Ben was suffering, and all because of me.

THE ORDER OF THE CRYSTAL DAGGERS

"Ella," Ferdy called from behind me, and I barely managed to turn around to make sure Ferdy was safe, too. Lord Maximillian was heading toward him.

"No." The word rushed out of me, and I began to panic—until I saw Lord Maximillian pass Ferdy and head for Karl, grabbing him and guiding him off the ship.

"Keep holding them off," Lord Maximillian called back to his guards.

At that moment, I realized why Lord Maximillian had been required to pay more. He had not come to the *Salacia* to get Ferdy. He had Ferdy and me captured in order to get at Karl.

"Prepare to set sail!" Lumiere called, and his crew members appeared in their heavily cloaked forms.

I glanced back at Lumiere as he tucked the envelope he had in his hand into his jacket pocket before turning his attention back to the bag of money. Seeing he was sufficiently distracted, I took the moment to head toward the stairs.

"Where are you going, Ella?" Ferdy called after me.

"I have to get Ben."

"What about my brother?"

"We will have to get Karl later." I was just about tell him that since Lord Maximillian had confessed, we could have him brought to the castle for a trial. Everything was nearly over, as long as we caught him.

But that was when Lumiere appeared in front of me, blocking me from the stairs, blocking me from Ben.

Anger filled me at the sight of Lumiere, coupled with the fear I felt for my brother's life.

As if he knew of my struggles, Harshad called out to me. "I'll see to Ben, Eleanora."

From where I was, I could see the top of Harshad's head, his white hair a crown around a small bald spot. He knelt in front of Ben, who was still whimpering in pain, while Lady Penelope swooped down a nearby railing to help.

I said nothing in reply, but I was eternally grateful in that moment Ben had someone to help him. I breathed out a quick sigh of relief, my breath forming a cloud against the lights along the port.

It was then that I noticed the ship was sailing away from the docks.

THE ORDER OF THE CRYSTAL DAGGERS

What is he planning for us now?

Lumiere was still onboard. He might have been buying time for Lord Maximillian to escape with Karl, but he was still stuck with us and the guards.

"You must be exhausted from all the failing you've done tonight," Lumiere said, as if to confirm my losses. I turned my attention away from the river, ready to face Lumiere at last.

Ben was injured, all because of me. We were trapped on the ship, Lord Maximillian was gone, and there was no way for us to keep up with him as he carried Karl off.

"Eleanora," Lady Penelope called. She stared up at me from beside Ben's fallen form, and it seemed hard to believe that I had forgotten how imposing she could be in the last two days. "Get to work. If he wants a fight, don't just stand there."

"I've been assured by many of my lovers how much work I can be," Lumiere warned me playfully, as Lady Penelope took off again. "Are you up for the challenge of fighting me?"

To answer him, I stepped forward with my dagger stretched out. It was true that I had failed tonight, but I was determined to see to the protection of those who were mine, and if Lumiere did not let me see my brother, I would force him out of my way.

He twirled away as I attacked, but I anticipated his movement. My dagger was high and dropped down swiftly, allowing me to cut through his coat.

The fine fabric spliced open with a loud rip, and while I did not think I drew blood, I had a feeling Lumiere was just as upset as he would have been if I had.

"This is French," he shouted, holding up the ends of his coat, clearly upset. "There is no fixing this!"

"I agree," I said, charging him again.

This time, he was more eager to engage. He grabbed my arm and elbowed me. I cried out in shock more than pain, and nearly dropped my dagger. I fully expected him to hit me; he had no weapons on his person that I could see. I was preparing myself for the eventual blow when Amir stepped in between us, pulling Lumiere away from me.

"Enough, Lumi. Leave Eleanora alone."

"Amir!" I cheered at the sight of him. "How is Ben?"

He shook his head. "I cannot examine him now, but I promise I will take care of him, right after I interrupt your fight with Lumi here."

I watched as Lumiere smiled. "I just need to occupy her attention for a little while longer, *mon frère*."

"Why don't you fight me instead?" Amir offered. "It has been ages since we last sparred."

"Don't you have more amusing targets to chase?"

Amir sneaked a quick glance over at me, one that was strangely entertained, before looking back at Lumiere. "How could anyone be more amusing than you?"

Lumiere grinned. "I've always loved your wit. A Turk with a sense of humor is indeed rare in this world."

"As is a Frenchmen with a sense of honor, if we're going to go by stereotypes."

"Ha! Honor is for those who see good and evil, not for those of us who only want to win. And I happen to like stereotypes. Personally, there is nothing quite as thrilling to me as putting someone in a box and then watching them cut their way out of it."

Despite the tension, Lumiere did not look insulted. He was talking with Amir the way that Clavan and Jarl often did, using the language of old comradery and respect, despite disagreements.

Amir slid his dagger into his sheath and took up a fighting stance to match Lumiere's. "I'm still waiting for an answer, Lumi."

Lumiere ran his hand through his hair, brushing back his ruffled locks. "You have a fight on your hands, then."

The two of them began to fight, and it was hard not to stare at them. It was a violent form of waltzing, where Amir would bob and duck and Lumiere would jab and cross.

"Ella." Ferdy appeared at my side, nearly out of breath. The bandage on his arm was leaking blood, but he seemed determined to ignore it. "That's the Turk who robbed you before. What is he doing here?"

"He's on our side," I said, as I caught sight of the new layer of sweat that had appeared on his forehead. I put my hand on his brow, discouraged to find he was terribly hot. "You need to be careful. That earlier wound is still causing you pain."

Ferdy gave me a weak smile. "I'll live. If for no other reason than I'm hungry."

His wry humor was comforting in that moment, and I could only hope we would be able to escape. While Ferdy wanted to get dinner, I just wanted him to get his arm fixed.

"Eleanora."

There was something so painfully distinctive in how Lady Penelope said my name as she appeared beside us.

"What is it?" I asked, turning to her. "Is it Ben?"

"No. No, he'll be fine, eventually. His leg is broken again."

The world went out from under my feet as all I could think was that it was my fault—*entirely* my fault. My hand went over my mouth in shock, but Lady POW did not seem to notice my dismay.

"There aren't too many guards left, but if you're just going to stand here and let other people fight your battles, I have a task for you."

I frowned at the accusation. Amir and Lumiere seemed to enjoy fighting each other. "What is it?"

"We have to stop the ship," Lady Penelope said. She pursed her lips as she nodded toward Ferdy. "See if you can get the other Mr. Marcelin to help with that, perhaps? If he does not feel like too much of a prince to help with such a lowly task?"

The bitterness of her voice was clear. She was more than a little upset with me, and possibly with Ferdy, too. I knew if she was fighting alongside Amir, she would not let her anger at us interfere with the mission, but it was only a matter of time before she said something.

"How?" I swallowed hard. "How—"

Lady Penelope shook her head. "There was a reason Karl was comfortable taking me to the castle dungeons. He accused me of the murder of his brother. At those charges, even Empress Maria Anna wanted nothing to do with me."

"I apologize if my mother has said or done anything improper," Ferdy said as he kicked at another guard, preventing another attack on us. He hurriedly wiped his hands off on his pants and extended one in greeting to Lady Penelope. "It is lovely to finally make your official acquaintance."

THE ORDER OF THE CRYSTAL DAGGERS

"The feeling is not quite mutual," Lady Penelope said, eying his bloody knuckles with a raised brow. "But if I can curry favor with the royal family, especially one who is supposedly deceased right now, I will take it."

"You can have all the favor you want, if I can only keep Ella."

"I've already figured out your earlier attempts, Prince Ferdinand, and I do not much appreciate them, given that I was put in jail because of them." Lady Penelope frowned. "But right now, I will excuse you, since we have a ship to stop and villains to catch."

"Yes, Madame." Ferdy looked more than a little deflated.

Lady Penelope paused and rolled her eyes. "If you are willing to prove your worth, help Eleanora stop the ship."

Ferdy brightened, but I only balked. "How do we do that?" I asked.

"Figure it out yourself," Lady Penelope said. She brandished her dagger in one hand while she pulled out her pistol in the other. "But try not to hurt the crew. We can use them for information later."

"That's even more difficult—"

"Just find a way to do it. I'm going to help Harshad with the last of the guards on the bow."

With that, Lady Penelope sped off. I watched as she headed for a trio of guards, firing shots and using their sudden movements to attack with her dagger.

"Come on," Ferdy said. "We've got to go."

"Go where?" I asked, looking at the port. We were already floating toward the middle of the Vltava, heading down the riverway. I wondered where Lord Maximillian had taken Karl.

"We have to stop the ship first," Ferdy said. "That means we have to get Lumiere."

He wants to get to Lumiere so we can get the rest of the crew to stop the ship.

"You're a genius," I said, following after him.

"Of course I am. I told you I was smart enough to outsmart you."

I felt irritated by his remark, but I decided not to say anything as we turned our attention back to Lumiere and Amir, who were still fighting. Ferdy and I agreed to barge into the fray from opposite ends.

But as we circled around, I stopped when I heard my mother's name.

THE ORDER OF THE CRYSTAL DAGGERS

"Naděžda would be proud of your little Eleanora," Lumi said, wiping a small amount of blood off of his lip. "She's just like her mother."

"There's no need to taunt me by mentioning Naděžda." Amir stepped back and they began circling each other again. "If you have to resort to such lows to win, it only means you lack the skill."

"It is not the individual skill that decides the victory," Lumiere argued. "It is the sum of all skills, and that should include mockery, ridicule, and insult."

They exchanged a few more blows before Amir landed another punch to Lumiere's side, driving the hilt of his weapon into Lumiere's rib. He bowed over in pain.

I met Ferdy's gaze, and between the two of us, we knew it was time. We would follow Amir in delivering the final blow, and then use our opening to capture Lumiere.

Lumiere seemed to know he was about to fall himself. His smile left his face, and he glared at Amir as a hint of genuine animosity finally came through. "Besides, Amir, if I wanted to render you helpless, we both know that Naděžda is not your greatest weakness."

"Is that so?" Amir asked.

He nodded toward Amir's hand, the one that was marked. "All I have to do is mention Nassara."

Nassara?

Amir's face suddenly contorted in the worst sort of anger. I watched as his chestnut eyes darkened with blood and rage, as his mustache twisted along with his mouth into the deepest frown. His heavy brows slanted downward. His dagger was suddenly out again and flying through the air.

That's the name of the Christian converts in the Ottoman Empire.

It was also the meaning of the symbol on Amir's hand and the inscription on my mother's journal.

I did not know how badly he did so, but it was immediately clear Lumiere had miscalculated. Lumiere fell back hard as Amir tackled him, holding his blade at Lumiere's neck hard enough to draw a fine line of blood.

Ferdy motioned to me, but I shook my head. We could not let him continue. We had to stop Amir from killing him—though I do not know if I would have objected—if we were going to use him to stop the ship.

THE ORDER OF THE CRYSTAL DAGGERS

"Amir," I said, coming up and grabbing his wrist. "We need Lumiere to live for now."

"Well, I am certainly glad to see you again, Ella." Lumiere's eyes were still wide with fear as he attempted to add levity to the situation. "I will be ecstatic to help you, if you would only tell Amir to get off of me, please."

Amir did not move. He seemed to be in shock.

Ferdy shook his head as he struggled to pull Lumiere free from under Amir. "Good God, what did you do to him, Lumi?"

Lumiere's smirk came back as he looked at me. "I suppose you'll have to excuse him, *chérie*. It has no doubt been many years since he's thought of Nassara."

Amir dropped his dagger and ducked his head. When he looked back up, there were tears in his eyes, and grief was written all over his face. "Don't mention her to me. You dishonor her like this."

I felt terrified. Even as my lips formed the question, I did not know if I wanted to know the answer. "Who's—"

"How did you know?" Amir asked, his voice cracking as he held Lumiere by the collar.

"Naděžda told me, of course," Lumiere said. "I came to see her along with my father when the League was last in Prague. She told me she lost the baby, and that was the reason why she wanted to stay with her Dolf when she wound up pregnant with their son. That is also why she decided to protect the empress."

"Baby?" My voice was a whisper, and I did not have to ask any further questions.

I could see it all play out inside my head. Amir and my mother grew up together, and then they fell in love. Lady Penelope objected to the union. My mother had been pregnant, and then she miscarried the baby.

Nassara.

The baby had been another little girl, I realized. My mother had another child before Ben and me. Amir's child.

Xiana's words to me when she arrived made much more sense. *"How wonderful it was that she was able to keep you."*

My mother had been able to keep me, after losing her previous daughter.

THE ORDER OF THE CRYSTAL DAGGERS

And when *Máma* tried to convince Amir to leave the Order with her, to start a new life, he said no. And so she left him.

The fighting and everything all around me went numb as I watched Amir wrestle with his pain. Lumiere, no longer struggling, was trying to shrug it off. It was Ferdy who reached out a hand to Amir, breaking the spell that seemed to capture the rest of us.

"If you please, sir," Ferdy said. "We need you to move. We need Lumi to order the crew to stop the ship. We can still hold his life hostage, but we need him to live."

"For now," I muttered darkly.

Amir allowed Ferdy to help him up, and I kept my guard on Lumiere.

"They already have their orders," Lumiere said to Ferdy as he stood up and began adjusting himself. "They'll finish them, and then evacuate."

I frowned at him, holding my dagger up to his face. "Evacuate?"

"Watch where you hold that thing, Ella. I don't need you ripping up my coat even further." Lumiere shook his head, running his hands through his hair again to smooth it over and flick it back in his stylish way.

"Just tell us what you've planned," Amir said. The anger was gone from his face, while the shadow of sadness remained.

"If you know me so well, you know it'll be a blast," Lumiere said with a small chuckle.

Not one of us—Ferdy, Amir, or myself—appreciated his attempt at humor.

Lumiere rolled his eyes. "Didier's been loading them into another boat, back by the stern," he explained. "I've already dislodged the anchor, so the ship is not going to stop. Besides, I've already shot through the sails, remember?"

I thought about his temper tantrum earlier, as he was calling Lord Maximillian's guards to attack. "Why did you do that?"

"For show, of course. There's no point in committing acts of high treason without some fanfare. I might as well get caught at gunpoint or go into a dark room and hang myself." He shuddered, appalled at the thought. "It's such poor showmanship, in the end."

"You're worried about showmanship?"

"I told you he was big on fashion before," Ferdy whispered. "It's not so hard to believe."

THE ORDER OF THE CRYSTAL DAGGERS

I glanced around. Harshad and Lady Penelope were still fighting. The crewmembers, true to Lumiere's assertion, were gone. They had their orders, they carried them out, and it was time to leave.

"We need to get everyone off the ship then," I said. "We will have to see if another ship can haul it in."

"No one will want to," Lumiere warned. "There's plenty of gunpowder and explosives down in the cargo holds."

Ferdy groaned. "It was a literal blast you were talking about."

"Did you think I was being facetious?" He gave Ferdy a grin. "Well, if that's all it is, I think I will leave it to you, won't I?"

Lady Penelope appeared beside us. "No, you won't. You're coming with us."

"Since I am the one who is in charge of the crew's rescue, don't you think it should be that you're the ones who are coming with me?"

Lady Penelope grabbed him and hauled him over to the side of the ship. "It would be a shame to toss you in, especially in your fine clothes, Lumiere. I know you would sink to the bottom from the weight of your jewelry alone."

Lumiere tried to fight her off. I took a step forward to help her, but Amir stopped me.

"Let her handle it now, Eleanora," he said. "Lumiere's rigged the ship to explode. It's better if it's in the middle of the river for that. We need to make sure the rest of the crew is off the ship first though."

"Can't we stop the explosion?" I asked.

"Lumiere has grown up working with the French and the Chinese," he said. "They have some of the best and most potent gunpowder in the world. If we can save everyone, it will be better. That will also get rid of Lumiere's ship, and that will force him to stay here. And we can definitely use that to our advantage."

I took his arm. "If you say so. Ferdy and I will go and check the ship."

"Stay away from the cargo hold," Amir said. "You don't want to set it off. I will go and see to it that Lumi does not escape. I have some more questions for him, it seems."

I nodded but paused before I left. A half a second later, I reached around Amir to give him a hug.

Amir stiffened under my embrace. I could not blame him for the surprise as I held onto him tightly. Rationally, it was a silly choice; we were in the middle of a fight, and there was so much at stake. We did not have the time or the luxury to console each other on our losses.

But he had lost a daughter, I had lost a sister, and we had both lost my mother. What else could I do?

"I'm so sorry," I whispered. I did not know what else to say, and honestly, I did not know if I could have said anything else. Amir's kindness to me took on a new light as I thought about how much pain he must have felt in seeing me. It was not just my mother he had lost. It was a daughter, one who would have been only a little older than me. Considering my initial hostility, and even our acknowledged silences and shared stories, I was a poor replacement for a future I knew he feverishly wanted.

"Thank you." He patted my hair, reminding me of my own father in that moment. "But you have to go. We can talk later."

I nodded and swallowed hard. I let him go and reached for Ferdy, who seemed to understand my heart was broken at another's anguish.

"Let's start down and work our way back up," he said, grounding my attention in the moment.

"Good idea." I rubbed the last remnants of tears from my eyes, using his words to focus. "I'll lead the way."

25
◊

Together, Ferdy and I ran back through the galley, heading down into the lower decks of the clipper ship.

"How are you feeling, Ella?" Ferdy asked, as we made our way down a stairwell.

"As well as can be expected." I did not sound vague intentionally, but as I thought about it, I wondered if I was still trying to figure out how broken I was. "How about you? How is your wound?"

"The bleeding seems to have stopped," Ferdy replied. He plucked at the crude bandage, trying not to wince at the resulting twinge of pain. "It still hurts to move it, though."

"I hope you haven't made it worse by all the fighting up there."

Ferdy gave me a rueful smile. "It would be considerably worse if we were dead. I can handle fighting with my left hand for now."

"Please just be careful. I know Amir can take care of it, once we get back to the manor."

"Amir is the Turk who was fighting Lumi out there, I presume?"

Quickly, as we methodically made our way through the ship, I told Ferdy about Amir. When I finished, Ferdy nodded. "I see. What a tangle, fate is."

"I'm surprised you recognized him," I said. "I did not think you would remember him after all this time."

"There are not many Ottomans in Prague. My Arabic instructor was from the Arabian Peninsula, where there are plenty of smaller coups rising up against the sultan. He taught me a lot about their culture. When I saw you that day in the city, I was worried for you, since I saw he had been branded. They brand thieves and other villains."

"Amir told me what you said to him." I stopped for a moment, glancing into a small room, similar to the one we had been held in earlier, looking for any sign of Lumiere's remaining crew. "He said you told him you would trade your life for mine."

"Of course I would, *chérie*. I told you before, I do not deserve you."

"I still say you have it wrong." I cupped his cheek. "I am the one who does not deserve you."

506

It was hard to believe I deserved anything. I had forgotten Lady POW in search of Ferdy, I had caused Ben more agony, and I had dismissed Amir and Harshad over various causes, some of them imagined and others misunderstood. And I had even thought I could abandon Ferdy if my duty called for it. It was only after I thought he was dead that my heart revealed the truth.

"It is possible, you know, that we do not deserve each other. In that case, we are perfect for each other," Ferdy said.

I smiled as he kissed my palm and took my hand in his. Maybe that was the true miracle of God in a fallen world. There were things in this world that were able to be so true that they were more than real, and when I lost my footing, I could still use them to find my way back to where I needed to be.

"Come on," I said. "Only one more level to check, and then we can get off of this ship, too."

We quickly resumed our task. It was only a matter of moments later when we came to the next floor, and I heard a small, familiar squeak. I turned and saw the same figure I had seen earlier, when I was walking on the top deck.

"Betsy!"

She was curled up behind the stairs, sitting with her knees up to her chin. She looked so small and childlike in her uniform, even though her face was gaunt and fearful. When she saw me, she stood up and hurried to embrace me.

"Nora!" she cheered. "Oh, I never thought I would see you again. And when I did, I was certain that you were going to be killed."

"What's happened to you?" I asked, watching as she pulled her hood down. "You look like a nun."

Betsy giggled, some of her girlishness coming back to her fraught face. "You look like an Amazon."

"I'm sure that's some of the inspiration." I glanced over my shoulder. "Ferdy, this is my friend, Betsy. It's a long story, but she was taken here with the rest of my stepmother's household."

I made quick introductions. Betsy was clearly tickled as he bowed and kissed her hand, just like the gentleman I knew he was.

"Can you tell us what happened? How did you get here?" I asked.

THE ORDER OF THE CRYSTAL DAGGERS

"Yes." Betsy nodded. "That man, the tall, blond one with the demon-green eyes, he came and took us the night after the Advent Ball. He had several dark, scary guards with him, so we followed him without much hassle."

"Is Cecilia here, too?"

"Yes. But Lumiere got tired of her, and Miss Priscilla, too."

"I can imagine that."

Betsy smiled at my wry tone. "The day we got here, he gave them over to your old friend Tulia. I haven't seen them since she stuffed them in the cargo hold." She blushed, her heart-shaped face burning over red.

"What is it?" I asked.

"I've heard their cries from that room," she admitted. "But I did not bother to see if there was a way to help them. I figured it was them, and I rather liked that they were out of my way. It has made my chores much more bearable."

I could understand her decision in that matter, recalling my own hours working in the manor while Cecilia was busy with paperwork or while she was asleep from the late nights before.

For now, though, I did not have time to reminisce. I took Betsy by the shoulders. "I need you to go and get into the boat at the stern. Ferdy and I will see to Cecilia and Prissy."

Betsy nodded. "Please be careful, Nora." She smiled and bobbed a quick curtsy to Ferdy, and then hurried upstairs.

"I hope Lady POW is finished taking care of the others," I said. "I wouldn't want her to run into more trouble."

"From the sound of it, your stepmother and stepsister are all that are left to get," Ferdy said.

I was about to agree, before a hunched shadow filled the hallway before us. "Tulia."

Tulia signaled her hello, and I drew out my dagger. She rolled her eyes before tapping her finger to her head.

She did not seem hostile, but I was still hesitant to trust her. "I'm doing much better, from when you knocked me out before."

She frowned at my tone and shook her head at my reaction. She signed out a repentant response.

I said I was sorry. You were able to come onto the ship and keep your dagger.

The blade at my side did seem to confirm she had only been acting in my best interest. "We don't have time for apologies," I said. "We need to get Cecilia and Prissy out of here before the ship explodes."

This time, Tulia frowned. Her hands twisted fast as she clearly objected.

"What did she say?" Ferdy whispered.

"She said that Cecilia and Prissy should be punished for how they treated me and Ben all those years ago. She's not going to help us get them out, and if we don't leave, we could end up dying."

"So …what do we do now?"

Tulia pointed to the door, flicking her wrist and then shaking her head.

"It's locked, and Tulia won't give me the key."

In some ways, I appreciated Tulia's efforts to avenge me. She was trying to help by forcing me into making the only choice that seemed rational, all so the burden of their deaths would not rest on my soul.

But my eyes fell to my dagger, and I knew if I left them to die now, I would not be worthy of the Order. It was not, as Ferdy had repeatedly told me, an assassination group. We protected people, and even though I hated Cecilia's actions toward me, I did not want her to die with my step-sister, trapped inside a ship full of explosives.

I put my dagger in my sheath. "If she's not going to help us, we need to find a new way to open this door." I faltered as I stepped forward, wishing desperately that Ben was able to be at my side. He had always been the one who tinkered with machines and mechanical ideas. The thought of him lying unconscious on the top deck stymied me, and I had to push through my sudden guilt and sadness to focus on the mission again.

Just get the mission done, and then you can tend to Ben.

Ferdy turned around and headed back down the hall. "There might be a spare key in the captain's room. I'll search around for one."

"Hurry!" I called after him, before narrowing my eyes at Tulia again. I studied the door, trying to see if I could fit the tip of my dagger in and break the lock. "Don't you do anything else."

Tulia only crossed her arms and began her silent tirade. Her hands flashed and fluttered, but I paid no mind to her. It was already tempting enough to leave Cecilia and Prissy, and if I could get away with it and not feel responsible for another person's death, I would have done so.

I knocked on the door, hard enough to bruise my knuckles. "Hello? Lady Cecilia? Priscilla?"

I waited a moment, before I heard some scurried movements on the other side. "Hello?" I called.

"What do you want?" Cecilia's voice crackled, and even from the other side of the door I felt her voice scrap at my patience and goodwill. "We're trapped in here, if you failed to notice."

"I'm trying to get you free," I called back. "Can you unlock the door?"

"What an egregiously unintelligible question. If we had been able to unlock the door, don't you think we would have left already?"

"Mother, be quiet," Prissy said. Her voice was weak and whiny, but I felt more compassion for her at once. After all, I would not want to be stuck in the cargo hold of a ship with my stepmother, either.

I examined the lock again. It was a metal one, so it would be hard to use my dagger to pick the lock. I did not have any pins in my hair, since it was tied it back with only a band.

I glared at Tulia again. "Why can't you just let me get them out?"

Why can't you just let them die?

Trying to reason with her was impossible. We went through several rounds—the Order was supposed to protect the innocent (*They are not innocent*), it was morally wrong (*It is morally wrong to let injustice remain*), they might be useful for information (*I can provide better information*)—before I was ready to give up and wait for Ferdy, hoping he would be able to find another key.

Tulia raised an eyebrow at me, her ancient face folding into wrinkled layers, and at her triumphant haughtiness, I tried again.

"It is not what my mother would want," I insisted.

You don't know have any idea of what your mother would have wanted. Tulia gestured to my outfit. *She would not have wanted you to join the Order.*

At that, it was just like before, when Ben had attacked me in Harshad's lessons. I froze, my heart aching at the stunning realization that she was right.

I had nothing to offer Tulia anymore. I shook my head. "You should go. I know Didier has the rescue boat near the stern. I have nothing more to say to you right now."

THE ORDER OF THE CRYSTAL DAGGERS

She shook her head sadly, but she left. As she walked past, I studied her features carefully. Tulia was my grandfather's half-sister, and I wondered if he had been just as unmerciful to Lady Penelope.

The moments passed, and I was stuck listening to Cecilia and Prissy's moans, repeatedly assuring them help was coming. I did not know if they believed me, but I honestly did not know if I believed me, either.

It was only when Ferdy came down the stairs carrying a bag and waving a key in his hand that I felt any gleam of hope return to my soul.

"Oh, thank you, Lord," I whispered, hurrying to unlock the door.

"And me, too, right?" Ferdy joked. "There were a lot of interesting things in the captain's room. I brought a few things to see if you wanted to look at them—"

"Not now," I said. I barely heard him protest as the door creaked open, and I ran inside to see to my stepfamily.

Inside, the room was framed in crates marked with warnings. Cecilia and Prissy were both chained to the far wall. The smell of the room was awful, flooded with the singed smell of ashes and gunpowder. I did not want to look too closely at what Lumiere kept in the hold of his ship.

Cecilia sniffed, sticking her large nose up in the air as she saw me. "Well, I would say it's about time you came for us."

"Apologies, Madame," I muttered. I knew Tulia had good reasons for wanting them to die. It was fortunate that she had plenty of bad reasons, too, or I would have left Cecilia there at her sniveling.

Prissy was much kinder. She was tired from the lack of exercise, her skin was pale, and she seemed much thinner than before. I almost wondered if she was happy with the results of her imprisonment, even if she did not like the imprisonment itself.

"Thank you, Eleanora," she whispered to me, and I pulled her arm around my neck to help her as her legs buckled under the rocking ship.

I only nodded, but I was grateful Ferdy was willing to help Cecilia. She did not recognize him as a Prince of Bohemia, and even I had to smile as she called him "urchin garbage" as we made our way to the top deck.

Lady Penelope was waiting for us. Her gun and dagger were tucked away, and she was clearly in command of the ship. Lord Maximillian's guards, Karl's attendants, and even some of Lumiere's crew were scattered around the deck. I tried not to notice some of the blood dripping along

THE ORDER OF THE CRYSTAL DAGGERS

the wooden planks of the ship's floor, but in the moonlight the crimson wash glimmered eerily.

"Excellent work, Eleanora," Lady Penelope said as we approached her. "You and your companion have done well."

Cecilia huffed. "I would beg to differ."

"I would love to see you beg to do anything," Lady Penelope snapped. "If I were you, I would keep from saying anything else until you are back at the manor, and even then, a vow of silence would be more than appropriate for you. After all, you would not want me to drag you to the castle to beg for forgiveness for treason, would you?"

Cecilia's lips opened and shut, and then she glared at Lady Penelope.

"Yes, Lord Maximillian confessed, along with the secret heir to the throne," Lady Penelope told her. "You can guarantee your name will be brought up, too. Especially since your son is dead."

"Alex?" Cecilia's voice cracked before she began to sob.

For the first time in my life, I felt truly sorry for her. I felt even more sympathetic as Lady POW waved her aside and told her to take Prissy and get off the ship before she was killed, too. There was nothing remorseful in my grandmother's gaze as she issued her commands.

Cecilia, without another word, did as she was told.

Lady Penelope turned her attention to Ferdy. "Well, Your Highness, it looks like I owe you my thanks."

Ferdy bowed his head. "Please, Madame, call me Ferdy. I would have us be friends."

"And here I thought you were more concerned with being family." Lady Penelope's tone was cool, but she seemed pleased by Ferdy's response. "Well, then, we will talk business later. Right now we have to leave."

"Is everyone else off the ship?" I asked.

She nodded. "Including Lumiere. I have him bound and just for the fun of it, gagged. He told me he would enjoy it more that way, likely thinking I would not agree with him. But I can tell you for certain, I enjoy it more."

I did not want to ask her about Ben. Lady POW was not the most compassionate of people. I worried she would tell me that he would be useless and cut out of the Order's future missions.

512

THE ORDER OF THE CRYSTAL DAGGERS

Ferdy took my hand as we boarded Didier's small boat. I could barely see it, tucked away in the shadows of the *Salacia,* with no lights on to show its presence. There were several others on the small riverboat, including Amir and Harshad, but no one—not even Cecilia—made any noise as we pushed away from Lumiere's sinking, demolished clipper.

It was only as we began to disembark back onto the docks that I heard a series of loud noises, all rippling out from the bottom of the boat. We all seemed to turn back at the same time, watching as an explosion ripped through the *Salacia,* setting it on fire.

A large spray of water washed over us, soaking us with the icy waters of the Vltava. Beside me, Ferdy laughed, while I heard Lumiere, already free of his gag, complain that his residence was gone—it was his own fault!—and Ben let out another groan. Harshad began to call for assistance, and Lady Penelope began rehearsing threats under her breath.

"Time to go home," Ferdy whispered behind me.

I reached up and hugged him, careful to watch his injured arm. I was surprised to find he had the bag from the captain's room on his back, but I said nothing as I held onto him.

I held onto him, and he held me back. It was enough.

I was with him, and it was enough.

26
◊

I do not remember much of the trip back to my father's manor. Harshad and Lady POW, as always, seemed to have the situation under control. We were able to hire several coaches to carry us back, though some of the servants, having nowhere else to go, decided to walk. Harshad issued instructions for a few of the men who were willing to give us information. With the members of the household, Lumiere, Cecilia, Prissy, and the rest of us, I imagine we could have been something out of the Wild West in America, like a kind of traveling caravan.

Ferdy tried to stay awake for as long as possible, looking to find ways to make me smile. He kept asking about dinner, wondering aloud if Clavan would be willing to send some of Helen's stew to the manor. Before I knew it, and likely before he did, too, he was leaning on my shoulder, silent at last.

I watched Ferdy sleep for several moments, thinking how serene he looked. With his jaw relaxed, the lines of his face eased into slumber, he seemed much younger. I missed the sparkle of his eyes, but as the moonlight clung to his skin, I could not stop my smile.

Even in his dirty rags and covered in blood, he was a prince.

Because we were all drenched, I curled up against him and tried to fall asleep, too. I managed to doze off and on, unable to stop replaying the scene in my mind where Ben had gotten hurt, and all because of my mistake.

My only comfort was knowing Amir was tending to Ben's leg as best as he could while we were on the road. I was glad I was not in the same curricle as they were; I did not want to hear Ben's moaning in real life any more than I knew it would haunt me inside my mind.

I helped everyone inside as we arrived. I let Harshad and Lady POW deal with the main villains of our night. Her footmen were up and ready to take care of guarding them, and I was content to know I had a break from seeing either Cecilia or Lumiere, even if it was only for a short while.

Once everyone was settled, including Ferdy, Amelia came to help me clean myself up. I was able to wash up and change, getting rid of the chill in the air.

After I finished seeing to my own care, and sending Amelia away, I made my way back to Ben's room, where Amir had gone to tend to his broken leg.

I opened the door, and Amir did not look up at me as he spoke.

"You don't have to be here, Eleanora."

I watched as he pulled out a bag that I had never seen before, one that was full of medical tools and other supplies. Amir reached inside and searched for something. A moment later, I saw he held up a syringe and a small bottle.

"I know I don't have to be here," I whispered back, trying not to cringe as Amir filled up the needle with the bottle's contents and injected it into Ben's thigh. "I just …"

My voice trailed off, and I could not say whether it was because my reasoning was too embarrassing or because I knew Amir would not agree with me regardless.

As if he sensed my thoughts, Amir shook his head. "I know why you came, and I can tell you, punishing yourself will not make Ben's leg heal faster. And if you are here to see if he will forgive you, you might be waiting for some time. The drug I gave him on the way over won't keep him asleep for long, but I can say for certain he does not want to talk to you tonight."

"I know that, too," I said. "But I want to be there for him."

"He has a long road of recovery before him," Amir told me. "I did everything I could, but there is no way to know this will not get worse yet."

"This can't possibly get worse."

Amir sighed. "I am hoping I can set and wrap it without waking him. You might as well go and get some sleep."

My brother had fallen asleep during the ride over, and I doubted Amir wanted him to wake up any more than I did.

"It might make him feel better, though," I retorted, though I did not want Ben to wake up only to curse me out.

"That won't make him *be* better in the end, either."

The fire was bright in his room. Lady POW's seamstresses apparently doubled as a small band of nurses, as they all bustled around his room while Amir worked.

"What happened, Nora?" Marguerite asked, her pretty young face worried as she looked down at Ben.

I shook my head and said nothing. I did not want to tell her that I had caused this. I might have saved him from a worse fate, but it was because of me he felt the pain of a broken leg, and it was possible he would face the life of an outcast once more.

I did not dare ask Lady Penelope if Ben would have to quit the Order. I knew it would be too painful for him.

Amir waved them away, quietly dismissing them. He did not seem eager to talk with me while they were there, and when they were gone, Amir put aside his medical tools to focus on me. "I finished sewing up Ferdy's arm for you. He's resting now in the room beside yours. He's a good patient, despite the pain he was in. He was eager to talk with me in Arabic, if you can believe it."

"I can believe it." I smiled ruefully. I wondered if most of those Arabic exchanges involved foul language or curses. "Thank you."

"He should be the one to thank you, for taking care of his wound as quickly as you did. It was good to get it wrapped up quickly. I didn't see any infection or pus, but we will have to watch it to see if there's any part of the bullet still in there."

I nodded. "I'm just glad he will be well."

"And you?"

"I don't have any injuries."

"Your heart is still tender from the many things we experienced tonight," Amir replied quietly. "You should go rest."

This time, I shook my head. "I don't think I can. I feel so terrible about what happened. If I had done things differently, Ben's leg wouldn't be broken again."

"He will likely be angry with you for a while yet, but he still loves you. He told me about how it broke the first time. I know from my own experience that the heart will win out in the long run."

I wondered if he was thinking of Nassara, or if he was thinking about my mother.

"Everything in your life will circle back around to what you love," Amir said. "Even if you deny your heart, your heart does not go away. That is why everyone lies, everyone has secrets, and everyone has regrets."

THE ORDER OF THE CRYSTAL DAGGERS

"I certainly have regrets today."

A moment passed before Amir took my hand, holding my palm against his scar. "Listen to me, Eleanora. Your mother left me, and it broke me."

The spell of my own sadness shattered as Amir knelt before me and his eyes met mine.

"I'm sorry," I said. "I'm sorry she left you. Even if I am only here because she did." I tightened my hands around his, wishing I could will away the scar on his hand and the deeper scars on his heart.

Amir surprised me by shaking his head. "No," he whispered. "I deserved it. She was right to leave me. I loved her, but I was not worthy of her. I did not stay by her side when she needed me the most—when she needed me to stand up to your grandmother."

"You don't have to tell me this," I said, unsure of how this related to anything at all.

"I am telling you this because I know Naděžda wanted a different life for you and Ben. She wanted to quit the Order and have a family and a chance at a normal life."

"That is not what happened."

"No. Your grandmother strongly objected to our relationship. She was quite furious with me for a long time." Amir looked away again. "We only reconciled after Naděžda was lost at sea and we could finally lay the past to rest and attempt for a separate peace between us."

"She still thinks you're only here to betray her." I thought of that night in the carriage, before Amir had disappeared after Ferdy's traveling coach as it made its way to Silesia.

"Lady POW has trouble when it comes to her own heart. I don't imagine that feeling of hers will ever go away. I'm telling you to go and tend to your heart now partially because of her. I think her heart has been broken quite a bit, and I do wonder sometimes if she prefers it that way."

He patted my hand. "I do not want to see that be your fate, Eleanora. And I know for certain your mother would not want that, either."

My mother apparently would not want me in the Order at all, from what I knew. I had chased her memory, only to find myself disappointing it.

I was not the only one who had disappointed her, I thought, looking back at Amir. I did wonder why he had refused to leave the Order with her, especially given how much he clearly still loved her.

"What is it?" Amir asked.

I squeezed his hand back. "*Máma* would have been happy to meet Nassara."

Earlier, I had seen Amir fight and take down enemies, but when I said his daughter's name, he crumpled. He buried his head in his hands for a long moment. When he looked up, he was mostly back to his usual self, aside from the swelling tears in his eyes.

"Your mother wanted a different life for her children," Amir said. "She did not want to be a part of the Order. Lady POW reminded her before she went off to Prague that death or defeat is the only true way to be free."

"But she found a way," I said. "She quit."

"As I said, where your love is, your life will follow. She met your father and they married, and Ben came shortly after." Amir's light tone hid the majority of his bitterness.

" Lumiere said she stayed with my father only because of Ben."

"It was likely the truth." Amir grimaced. "She had already lost one child. She did not want to lose another. But I doubt that was her only reason. From what I know of her, I would say she did love your father."

"She still missed you." I thought of the miniature portrait of Amir I had found tucked away in my mother's locket.

"One day I will see her again. And when I do, I would be remiss if I did not help you find the life you are looking for. Naděžda would be most upset with me, and her temper is worse than your own."

Amir's attempt at levity fell flat as I thought about Ferdy. The Order was nothing like I thought it would be, but if I was loyal only to the truth, then Amir was right. And the truth was, I loved Ferdy. I had tried to forget about him, I had tried to lose him, and I had tried to protect him.

"Everyone has secrets, everyone lies, and everyone has regrets." Amir put his hand on my shoulder affectionately. "But there are some regrets you can live with, and others you can't."

He nodded toward the door. "Love is always a risk, but I don't believe you should step back from embracing it. It is a regret you will never forgive yourself over. Now, please go and tend to your beloved. It will help heal the wounds in your own heart."

He was speaking from his own experience, and I knew that in offering me the lesson of my mother's life, Amir was trying to protect me, too.

"You're right. I have to go," I said. "Excuse me."

After one last look at Ben, watching him sleep so uncomfortably in his bed with his leg wrapped up. I hurried away, allowing Amir to resume his work in peace.

He is a good doctor, I thought. A good doctor for the body as well as the soul.

I headed across the manor with quiet steps, feeling the angst in my chest. It seemed to grow and then shrink, before it dissolved and only my resolve was left behind.

The door to the room beside mine clicked gently as I opened and closed it. For a small moment, I stood there, with my back against the door as I looked at him on the bed.

He was flipping through a book, sitting propped up with a stack of pillows. He had been given a new set of clothes, and it was likely he had been able to wash up, too. His injured arm, wrapped up in thick bandages, was resting off to the side, almost as an afterthought. At my arrival, he turned to face me, giving me the same old flippant grin. "Ella."

And then, all of a sudden, I was running to him.

I nearly fell into his lap as I climbed up next to him. My lips found his as I carefully, desperately clung to him.

Ferdy responded to me at once; he wrapped his good arm around me, keeping me close as I braced my hands on his chest. His body was warm beneath his shirt. As my fingers curled into crisp fabric, I thought I could hear his heart begin to pound.

I felt him flinch as he moved his injured arm, but his mouth never left mine as we kissed, over and over and over again. For long moments, we stayed there, reveling in the certainty between us, marveling at the undeniable longing and irresistible response.

"Ferdy." His name escaped me between breaths as I pulled back from him. For a silent second I felt him still, and I could almost hear his mind wonder if I was going to pull away from him again, as I had so many times before.

THE ORDER OF THE CRYSTAL DAGGERS

Instead, I leaned into him even further. I would not leave him. I would not be able to bear that regret, and I knew it. I could no longer lie to myself about that.

"I love you," I whispered.

"I love you, too."

The wanting I had felt before, the ache I had for him, instantly transformed into need. I needed to feel the warmth of his skin, to taste the wonder of his kiss; my body shook with tension, forced between forbidden desire and moral constraints. As each second passed, I found myself drowning in flames, and more convinced I would enjoy such a fate.

It was only when Ferdy cupped my cheek, and I felt the wetness of my tears between us, that he eased back from me.

"Ella." Ferdy's voice was husky with passion as he whispered my name. "Everything is well now. We are safe. You saved us."

"No," I choked. "No, you are the one who saved me."

"I don't know if I would call getting kidnapped the same thing as saving you."

"No, that's not it." I lowered my eyes, letting my gaze fall to his bandages.

"What is it then?"

"I thought, in joining the Order, I would do something worthy. It was something my mother did once. I wanted to be free, but if I couldn't be free, fighting for her was something I could stand for."

Ferdy held on to me tightly as I continued to ramble, trying to put my muddled thoughts into a decipherable manner.

"My mother resigned from the Order because of love. I joined the Order for her, to make her proud, and to protect others."

"Which you have done," Ferdy said.

"But ..." I sighed. "If I truly want to honor her, I should leave, as she did."

My eyes met Ferdy's in the dim light. I leaned in and kissed him again, tasting the fun and freedom I had found before, even as it was buried underneath the memories of our evening and hints of lavender and mint.

Ferdy's lips grazed my neck as his hand slid down my body before resting on my hips. As the heat simmered between us, I knew why my mother

THE ORDER OF THE CRYSTAL DAGGERS

left the Order. She had wanted her freedom, but she had wanted love more. My father was not her first love, or even the most passionate. But he was the one she chose. She wanted to be with him and start a family with him, even if that meant forsaking her mother—and her mother's expectations.

I pulled back from Ferdy again, panting as I struggled to catch my breath. "Now all I want is to be with you, Ferdy. I don't want a life where I have to give you up."

"That's not true."

I stilled at his comment. "What do you mean? Of course that's true."

"Ella, *chérie*, please understand. I am flattered, but I know you want more than that. You honor your mother by choosing to follow your own heart. There is no need for you to live her life for her. But I know you want to protect others. I know you want to be there for your brother and your other friends."

"Not if it means losing you."

His fingers traced my lips tenderly. "You are not the only one that must make a sacrifice when it comes to love."

He kissed me deeply, letting his lips slide over mine once more. "Let me be with you. Let me make that sacrifice, and we can be together."

"What are you talking about?" I asked, inexplicably overwhelmed.

"I love you, Ella. I can't remember a time when I haven't. I've wanted to be with you for the longest time. Let me stay with you and keep you as mine."

"I couldn't leave you if I tried." And that was true. I had tried, and I knew it was hopeless. The days of distancing myself from him, trying to forget him, were over, like a bad dream.

Despite his injury, Ferdy bounced beneath me. "Excellent. I was legitimately worried I would have to fight Karl for the right to marry you."

"Marry me?" My mind was still full of passion's fog as Ferdy arched up against me. I gasped at the sudden movement.

"Of course I will," Ferdy said. "As soon as possible."

I held onto him. "Are you sure you want to?"

"I'm sure I want you." He cupped my cheek again, wiping away another stray tear—a happy one this time. "I want you most of all. Why do you think I've been asking if I can keep you?"

And then he kissed me again. I lost myself in it, and in him, as time slipped by in slower seconds. I barely recovered as Ben burst into the room.

At the sight of my brother, barely recovered from our earlier battle, balancing on his new crutch with his broken leg in a thick cast, I practically flew off of the bed.

"They're coming for her," he said. "They're coming for Lady POW."

Hurriedly, I smoothed down my hair and straightened out the wrinkles in my dress. "Who? Who's coming for her? And why are you out of bed? Your leg—"

"I can walk with crutches. The medicine still prevents me from feeling a lot of pain," Ben said. "This is an emergency, Ella."

My brother calling me "Ella" said everything to me about how he felt. He was upset with me, and I was unable to do anything to rectify our relationship now. Before I could say anything else, Ben glared at Ferdy.

"Your castle guards are here," Ben said flatly. "The police came too, and now they want to take her to the king. She was fighting with them when Xiana came to get me."

Ferdy sat up with a sigh. "I guess I have to give the news of my surprising return and Karl's disappearance to my parents anyway."

I nodded quickly, hurrying to grab Ferdy's coat and prepare myself. As we headed out, Ben grabbed Ferdy's injured arm.

"You can explain yourself on the way there," Ben growled.

Ferdy twitched in pain but gave my brother a smile. "*Absolument*, my good sir."

"Ben, let him go. That's where he got hurt," I said.

"He knows," Ferdy told me. "But it is better for me to forgive him. After all, we are going to be sharing a lot of adventures together from now on, *mon frère*."

Ferdy gave me that smile of his—reckless and risky, ever the irresistible man I loved. "Isn't that right, Ella?"

Ben rolled his eyes. "Just hurry up. I have to tell Harshad. You'll meet Amir and Lady POW at the stables."

Ferdy waited until he was gone from the hallway before he chuckled. "Well, I knew that wouldn't be easy. But I bet I'll still have an easier time winning him over than your grandmother."

THE ORDER OF THE CRYSTAL DAGGERS

Despite everything, I laughed. The sound was still echoing in the halls as Ferdy leaned over and kissed me again, allowing me one last reprieve from reality before we set out to face the world's trouble once more.

THE ORDER OF THE CRYSTAL DAGGERS

C. S. Johnson is the author of several young adult sci-fi and fantasy novels, including *The Starlight Chronicles* series, the *Once Upon a Princess* saga, and the *Divine Space Pirates* trilogy. With a gift for sarcasm and an apologetic heart, she currently lives in Atlanta with her family.

AUTHOR'S NOTE

Dear Reader,

As always, I am deeply touched by the time you pour into reading through my work. *Prince of Secrets and Shadows* is the second book in this trilogy, and in many ways, it took even more time to write than the first book; the theme of freedom I used as a starting point for Book 1 is a much bigger question than I thought it would be. So much about freedom is universal and personal at the same time. Working through this book, it was clear that freedom is tied to so many other ideas that it relies on, especially as it moves toward the personal side of application. So much of our freedom is only capable if there is truth and goodness, and maintaining freedom requires moral checks and balances.

With regards to this book, freedom and truth—and the trust required for it—is at the center, especially when it comes to identity. Who do you really trust? What do you really believe in? Which values are the ones that you are advocating for, and why? Such questions can be terrifying, especially if we do not want to examine our answers too closely. While Eleanora struggles with Ferdy and Ben over who she is and who she could be, she comes to face the reality of life in a fallen world, learning that sometimes people do bad things for good (or not so good) reasons, that bad things can still bring about good results, and that not everyone will agree on what is good or bad in the end.

That is a hard lesson to face on a more practical level. I'm not sure that a lot of people have truly learned it, including myself.

Freedom, truth, identity and morality. All of it matters, and all of it comes crashing together in the seconds between the choices we make when we choose to answer the question of how we should then live.

As you can see, there's still much to look forward to in Book 3! I am hoping that it will be easier to write, now that I have my sights set on the end.

Thank you again once more for joining me in this novel's adventures. I hope you will stay on for the ending of this series in the next book, *Heart of Hope and Fear*, where the fate of the empire—and the future of Eleanora and her companions—will be decided.

Until We Meet Again,

C. S. Johnson

THE ORDER OF THE CRYSTAL DAGGERS

THE ORDER OF THE CRYSTAL DAGGERS

NIGHT

of

BLOOD and BEAUTY

A COMPANION NOVELLA TO

THE ORDER OF THE CRYSTAL DAGGERS

◊   ◊   ◊   ◊

C. S. Johnson

DEDICATION

This book is first dedicated, as nearly always—at least so much that it's strange, especially if you don't see it with the spirit of my intent—to Sam.

But it is also dedicated to my good friends, Jennifer, Cathy, and Laura, whose support and enthusiasm helped bring this story into being, if for no other reason than their insistence made it so.

THE ORDER OF THE CRYSTAL DAGGERS

1

◊

"Miss Eleanor."

The desperation in his voice was only matched by his irritation, and the moment he said anything, Amir feared he had inadvertently given himself away.

The sapphire eyes he had come to both love and hate twinkled mischievously at him. "Why, Mr. Qureshi, I do believe you're quite flustered. Especially if you're going to use your manners. Where are those mongrel ways of yours? I might mistake you for a real gentleman with such a formal tone."

Her lyrical, teasing voice did nothing to lighten his mood; rather, it plucked at his heartstrings with a bittersweet twang, and Amir had to force himself to remain still as he stared down at her.

It would do nothing for his case if he showed any further sign of compromise, especially now that his partner sensed his weakness.

"It is only proper I address you as such, Miss Eleanor," Amir said, keeping his voice stripped of all his conflicting emotions. "Your mother, Her Grace, would be the first to agree with me."

At the mention of her mother, her gaze only grew bolder. "We both know my mother's favorite thing in the world is being a hypocrite," she said, crossing her arms and tapping her toe. "Call me Naděžda, as I've told you to before several times now."

Inwardly, Amir groaned. He should have known better than to say anything. If there was anything Eleanor Naděžda Ollerton-Cerná excelled at—and there was plenty—it was arguing with him. And while there was enough wrong with that in itself, it unnerved him how often he found himself losing those arguments.

"Miss Eleanor, propriety demands—"

"Is this my punishment, after all these years, to have you give me the same lecture I gave you when we first met, Amir?" Naděžda asked, arching her brow as she pouted.

Amir hated how he stared at her mouth. His Abba had always been so concerned about him looking into a woman's eyes that Amir never realized how sinful looking at a woman's lips could be. Even beneath her *yashmak,* the transparent veil worn by women on the streets of

531

Constantinople, seeing Naděžda stick out her bottom lip was like watching a rose bloom under misty moonlight.

He was secretly relieved when she crossed her arms and let out an indignant sigh, turning her face to the side; her patience was dwindling as quickly as his resolve.

All I have to do is outlast her. Amir relaxed in the slightest degree; it was always easier to outlast her than it was to outwit her.

"If I didn't know you better, I would question your intellect," she said.

"What is stopping you? You've questioned it often enough in the past several months we've been working together on the Order's missions." Amir frowned, his own patience wearing thin. "Unless, of course, you have good reason to agree with me in this case?"

"I fail to see why finding a way to engage the target would be a mistake. He's old enough to be more patient with someone of my age."

"He's old enough to see you as a nuisance."

"Doubtful. He's likely no more than ten years older than I am, probably married with a wife and an heir at home. A little flirtation from someone like me will make him feel like a young, attractive, appreciated hero. We've followed him long enough to know he's a soft touch."

Amir frowned. "Now I really don't like your idea. He could fall in love with you on sight."

"What better way to get him to slip up?" Naděžda sneered. "If anything can ruin your life, it is love."

He hated both her tone and how much he agreed with her. "Spies are not supposed to fall in love."

Though his tone did not betray it, that reminder was one that was burned into him daily, often multiple times as he worked with Naděžda.

She was a member of the Order of the Crystal Daggers, an ancient group of spies and assassins, specializing in political security and clandestine reconnaissance missions. Naděžda's mother was its leader, and Lady Penelope took great pride in her responsibilities, with an unrivaled, orderly fervor. While their adventures varied in location, task, and time, Amir always embraced the chance to work beside Naděžda. While he was not a member of the Order, he was a medical adviser and companion on many of their assignments.

THE ORDER OF THE CRYSTAL DAGGERS

Above all else, he sought to honor that trust. That was why he had to keep Naděžda safe—perhaps despite her wishes otherwise on such matters.

Amir cleared his throat cautiously. "Right now, it would be an unnecessary complication, especially if you are right about the wife and nursery at home."

"But it would be so easy." She clasped her hands together. "He's drawn to books. What better way to get his attention and earn his respect than engaging him at the book vendor?"

"No matter how much he loves books and no matter how much charm you throw his way, the Bohemian ambassador is not going to discuss business with the likes of you."

Amir glanced back at their target. They had been following him for hours now, ever since he walked through the construction site where the sultan's new Dolmabahçe Palace was being built.

Considering the crowded streets of Constantinople, and the finer points of the Bohemian's diplomacy, finding him was a miracle more than anything else. Amir did not want to lose him, and Amir especially did not want to lose him because he was too distracted from arguing with Naděžda.

And over such nonsense, too.

"I should go anyway," Naděžda murmured behind him, just loudly enough he knew she was angry enough to be serious. "You never let me do what I want."

"That's enough," Amir told her sharply. "The ambassador is the one who is supposed to meet with the merchants from the Haberecht Shipping Company, and we need to find out where they are located and why he is meeting with them. Her Grace says the company has rebellious sympathies. She suspects they could be behind the missing shipment themselves, rather than the Ottomans who supposedly took off with it."

"King Ferdinand is not concerned about the rebels. He just wants the weapons for himself."

"A king is allowed to protect his own country."

"Yes, but how can he protect himself from his own country? There is trouble brewing in Bohemia, just as there is trouble in Italy, Germany, and other Austrian principalities."

"That is why we need to find out where the shipment went."

THE ORDER OF THE CRYSTAL DAGGERS

Naděžda wrinkled her nose. "My father would likely know. If we really wanted to find out, all we would have to do is ask him."

"You know how Her Grace feels about that," Amir said quietly.

"She probably thinks he is behind it, given his own history with the League of Ungentlemanly Warfare. That's likely the main reason the Order is here, isn't it? There is nothing my mother would love more than to strike out against my father, especially now that she has the full weight of the British Empire behind her as a League member herself."

"Even if he's not behind it, we need to find the truth. Those weapons could unwittingly cause a lot of trouble for the people, even if they are the ones who end up wielding them."

"I suppose that is true," Naděžda agreed, her voice full of sad resignation.

Amir fell silent. He did not know what to say, especially since, from what he knew, Naděžda was likely correct. Ever since her parents' tumultuous affair and failed partnership, there was nothing but enmity in Lady Penelope's eyes at the mention of him.

Naděžda sighed. Seeing the soft vulnerability in her features made Amir want to reach out and comfort her.

Instead, Amir turned away, allowing her privacy while she grappled with her family's brokenness. A long moment passed in silence between them, before Naděžda sighed.

Amir took it as a sign she was ready to move on. "Right now, we just need to find the actual destination of the shipment."

"It could have been easily dispensed on the black markets already."

"That's true, but you said it yourself. This is something that is tied to the unrest in different countries, and we need to be prepared if fighting breaks out."

"Yes."

"So we need to follow the ambassador now, not flirt with him."

Naděžda whipped out a small fan from underneath the embroidered shawl she carried, fluttering it playfully in front of her half-covered face. "Well, my dear, you wouldn't be the one flirting, would you?" She straightened herself, drawing herself up to her full height, just shy of meeting him at eye level. "That is my area of expertise."

THE ORDER OF THE CRYSTAL DAGGERS

"You needn't remind me." The words came out softer much more husky, more provocative than he had intended. There was a quick, fearful gleam in her eye, and he saw she was uncomfortable, too.

She quickly played it off, snapping her fan shut and brushing off the billowing folds of her striped walking gown.

"Goodness, do all the women in this town have to be so covered up? I'm dying in these multiple layers," she said.

"The privacy of women is sacred here," Amir reminded her, more than grateful for the change in topic. "When something is sacred, it becomes law, and as such, modesty is the law of the land."

"There is no tyrant quite like one in place for one's own good, is there?"

"You should appreciate it. Wasn't your mother in Her Majesty Queen Victoria's court this past month?" Amir could not resist provoking her. "And even now you're wearing the bustle that's *à la mode*, and that seems much more troublesome than a veil."

The large, bulbous bump at the back of her gown twitched as Naděžda huffed.

"I might as well wear the Western fashions. I'm not going to blend in here," Naděžda insisted. "Even with the veil."

She was right about that, Amir thought to himself. In all the years since he had known her, she had never fit into any aspect of his life comfortably. Being so close to his childhood home, he was disheartened to see she never would.

He studied Naděžda out of the corner of his eye as she stood next to him in the small, dark corner of an alleyway. They were just outside the Court of the Mosque of Sultan Ahmed I, where tents poured out into the middle of the crowded streets and shops were tucked away behind them. The bright wooden buildings bordering the streets were interspersed with lattice-covered windows, hinting at the private sitting rooms afforded to women, allowing them a safe escape from the surrounding world of men and their markets.

Yes, Amir thought, Naděžda was indeed out of place. But knowing her as he did, he also knew she was accustomed to the experience.

"It's so hot." Naděžda waved her fan distractedly. "I'll be lucky if I don't die out here."

THE ORDER OF THE CRYSTAL DAGGERS

"You get used to the dry heat after a time," Amir told her. "And it is not all bad. It allows you to taste the salt in the air from the Bosporus, once you're close enough to the harbor, and you feel the full blessing of Allah from the wind."

"You could also assume that the heat was flying up from hell itself," Naděžda murmured, and despite his better judgment, Amir smiled.

Not one of his family members would approve of Naděžda in the slightest. She was everything he had been taught to abhor in a woman—outspoken, brash, impatient, stubborn, and at times domineering. She had an enormous awareness of propriety, if only because she learned how to break it so beautifully. Many times they had fought, on everything from customs to food to manners, to religion and politics and family.

Given his own upbringing, he should have hated it. But Naděžda was smart and passionate, and he almost always enjoyed fighting with her just to see that spark of challenge light up her eyes.

Almost always.

"As I see it, the faster we get the information we need, the sooner we can head back to the ship and report back to Uncle," she said, gathering her skirts. "Talking with the ambassador would save us time."

"Mr. Prasad would not approve of your methods," Amir countered, thinking of his mentor and sponsor.

If there was ever a man he was indebted to, it was Harshad Prasad, and he would not see Naděžda come to ruin for anything. Part of the reason Harshad insisted they work together was so Amir could protect her. With the medical training he had received as a doctor, both from his father and Harshad's patronage, and having the benefits of understanding Western and Eastern cultures, he was more than capable of seeing to Naděžda's safety as she worked for the Order of the Crystal Daggers, especially in places such as Constantinople.

In theory, anyway.

Naděžda pursed her lips, reminding Amir of her mother, and he groaned. The newly proclaimed leader of the Order, Lady Penelope Ollerton-Wellesley, the dowager duchess of Wellington, was a force of nature, and she had taught her daughter to wield chaos just as skillfully than she did, if not more so.

Queen Victoria was no doubt very fortunate to have Lady Penelope's loyalty, Amir thought. The Order of the Crystal Daggers was an ancient society, one that was originally established to protect and maintain peace

THE ORDER OF THE CRYSTAL DAGGERS

in Constantine's empire. When the Empire fell, the Order remained, quickly aligning themselves with those who were able to protect and assist them.

Which is why Harshad was here, Amir recalled. They had arrived with Harshad on the *Splendor*, one of the teak clippers from the East India Company. As an honorary member of the League of Ungentlemanly Warfare, Harshad was overseeing the fulfillment of the Treaty of Nanking, ensuring Chinese were complying with the terms of their loss. He would report back to Queen Victoria and the House of Lords when they returned to London.

It was fortunate Harshad was here, too, or they might never have realized a shipment of weapons intended to go to Prague had gone missing, or that the Bohemian ambassador had arrived for unexpected meetings with the Sultan and the Haberecht Shipping Company.

Naděžda cleared her throat, drawing Amir back to the moment.

"Are you sure it's Uncle who would not approve of my idea, Mr. Qureshi, or is it just you? Because I do believe Ambassador Svoboda would approve of me, and his approval is more important."

"What are you saying?"

Naděžda leaned toward him, batting her eyelashes flirtatiously. "I do believe you're jealous."

"Why would I be jealous?" Amir frowned, suddenly defensive. "This has nothing to do with that."

"Is that so?"

"Yes, and it never would," Amir insisted. He immediately regretted the sharpness in his voice.

Naděžda smiled bitterly, her eyes suddenly much sharper than before. "Well, then, as long as you have no claim on me, I'm overruling your order, Amir, with the stern reminder I am here as your partner, not your associate and certainly not your underling." She flipped her shawl over her shoulder proudly. "If anything, you are here under *my* seniority, given that I am the one in the Order, and you are merely here at Uncle's wishes."

"Miss Eleanor." This time, his voice came out as a hiss, but it was too late. She feinted and sidestepped him, before bustling out into the sunlight of the street, where the bazaar was full of mid-morning shoppers.

THE ORDER OF THE CRYSTAL DAGGERS

As Naděžda coyishly dabbled from vendor to vendor, Amir wondered if time had slowed merely to torment him. A woman's privacy was sacred among the streets of Constantinople, but he knew, much more than he wanted to, that the harems and concubines of the Turkish court were full of Western fashions, and as much as Naděžda might have adopted the *yashmak* to soften her charm, he had a feeling it would only enhance her appeal. He watched as she alternatively enchanted and horrified various sellers with her confident demeanor.

She could be in danger.

His hand closed around the *Wahabite Jambiya* at his side, the curved dagger his father had passed onto him before he had set out for the Western universities.

"For your protection, and the blessing of the family," his Abba had said, and Amir was more than thankful that in all his years abroad, and even during the past months working alongside Naděžda, he had never needed to use it to protect himself.

He was a doctor, after all. He worked to preserve life, not take it away.

"*Pardonnez-moi, madame.*" Naděžda's voice cut through his musings, and Amir sneaked a glance at her as she questioned a flower-seller over the different blossoms she had available.

Amir frowned, watching as Naděžda handed over her payment, recognizing his coin purse in her hand. He groaned, realizing she must have grabbed it when she had dashed past him.

"*Merci beaucoup, au revoir.*" Naděžda gave a little curtsey to the flower-seller, her arms now carrying a slightly wilting bouquet of crocus, and the gypsy woman seemed to stand much more proudly as she waved farewell to her customer. Amir did not have to ask to know she had paid full price for the flowers.

She glanced over her shoulder, pretending to adjust her veil as she winked at him.

Amir frowned in reply, but the instant she turned away, he gave her a reluctant smile. He might have hated how well she worked, but watching her do so was a thing of beauty.

He lost his grin the instant he saw her duck behind the Bohemian Ambassador, who was looking through a line of books at another vendor.

Naděžda shifted her bustle, bumping into him. The ambassador turned around, and Naděžda followed suit, smoothly enough his arm collided with hers, and her newly-purchased flowers scattered to the ground.

"Oh, dear," she said, switching to her natural Bohemian accent. "My flowers."

Amir winced. While she never said it explicitly, she hated to indulge in anything that reminded her of her father. Amir did not know the whole story of her life there, before Lady Penelope's abrupt, troublesome departure from Naděžda's father. But while she seemed to loathe the very mention of it, he had seen the light in her eyes many times when she spoke of Bohemia, and when they were alone, as they were, she always insisted upon him using her Bohemian name, even if it was against social convention.

As the man began to apologize profusely to Naděžda, Amir turned to study him, grateful for the chance for a closer look. While there was nothing wrong with him in appearance—he was clearly a man in his thirties, one who was well-read despite coming from humble means—there was something about him that Amir did not like. There were rough sores on his hands and while he had made little attempt to tame the longer locks of his coal-colored hair, his mustache seemed too trim for the streets of Constantinople.

Perhaps that was it, Amir admitted to himself. The man was a stranger here, too, and that was something Naděžda would use to her advantage—and possibly something the ambassador could use to his, if she let him.

Amir hated him for that.

He watched as Ambassador Svoboda finally finished stuttering out his speech. The man seemed to be an odd choice for a diplomat; his words came awkwardly off his tongue, as if he never said anything more than he had to.

Amir huffed disgruntledly, wondering if it was Naděžda's charm. She looked distressed and her eyes brimmed with tears—those lovely, sapphire seas—until the poor man insisted that he replace her flowers.

Naděžda skillfully slipped down her veil as she dabbed at her small tears with a handkerchief before adjusting it back into place. Amir frowned as the man did not bother to duck his head, watching as the man's face lit up with wonder.

Amir stepped closer, preparing himself to pull Naděžda away from him, inching close enough to hear their conversation.

"I assure you, Madame—"

"Please, sir, it is Miss." Her eyelashes fluttered up at him again. "It is Miss Cerná."

"Oh. Oh, I see. Yes, I assure you, Miss Cerná, you have my humblest apologies," he said. "I will replace your flowers, and if you will let me, I will do so ten times over."

"Oh, you are too much, sir." She pulled out her fan and touched it to her veiled lips thoughtfully. "What a true gentleman you are."

Amir sighed quietly. Only Naděžda could go from a damsel in distress to a smoldering temptress before turning into a shy tease within three sentences.

"Please, Miss Cerná," the man said. "Allow me to formally introduce myself. I am Adolf Svoboda, an ambassador to His Imperial Majesty, King Ferdinand V of Bohemia—though perhaps you might also know him as Emperor Ferdinand I of the Austria-Hungarian Empire."

"I was wondering if you were from Bohemia like myself," Naděžda said, her voice full of sudden excitement. "And you say you are a member of the king's court? Why, how fascinating."

Amir forced himself not to grumble as Naděžda chatted with him, apologizing for her overly suggestive remarks with the youthful, innocent naivety that never failed to make men look twice as she wound a colorful, woeful tale of getting separated from her guard and in desperate need of assistance.

The ambassador, for his part, was fully under her spell, not even thinking to question her at all, nor even considering his own plans—at least, not until he realized he had not purchased his book.

"Excuse me one moment, Miss Cerná," he said, placing his hand over hers gently. "I will pay for this book, and then I will assist you in finding your guard. I know the women in Constantinople are largely left alone, but I shudder to think of you lost on the streets here."

"Of course, sir. Why, I am surprised I forgot, but I wished to buy a book myself."

Amir crossed his arms, pretending to study the carpets on the display before him. He had been wondering if that was Naděžda's true aim all

THE ORDER OF THE CRYSTAL DAGGERS

along. He was not surprised to hear the ambassador offer to buy her a book of her choice.

"As part of my apologies for your flowers, Miss Cerná, please allow me to purchase one for you," he said, before waving his arm over the long spread of books before him.

"Oh, I could not impose, sir—"

"Nonsense, I insist."

"Well, if you insist," Naděžda replied, with just enough humility and resignation to make it sound as though she had absolutely no choice in the matter. Amir recognized it as the same voice she would use in accepting her missions for the Order, even if he knew she hated it.

He had a feeling in this case, she did not hate it at all.

It was not long before she picked one up. "How about this one?" she asked, turning back to the ambassador to look for his approval.

The searching look in her eye suddenly made Amir want to give up the charade, march over to her and haul her over his shoulder, before taking her back to their ship and paying off the captain to leave early, their mission be damned.

She never looked at him for approval like that, Amir thought bitterly. His fist tightened around the curved dagger at his side, his fingers brushing over the calligraphic inscriptions in search of comfort.

He did not find any, and he found even less when he realized Naděžda was more likely to deride his opinions in such matters. Amir remembered how appalled she was upon hearing he had never read any Shakespeare the other night, and suddenly wondered if she was purchasing the book for him.

Amir glanced back as the ambassador looked over her choice.

"I commend you on your choice, Miss Cerná," he said. "I have read several of Wordsworth's works as well."

Amir felt his heart sink.

"I've heard that *The Prelude* is a lovely preface to reading any Shakespeare," Naděžda replied.

"I thought that as well," the ambassador agreed, looking through her book. While he talked on some of the content at length, Naděžda shot Amir a triumphant look over her shoulder, and he felt a little better.

541

"What did you choose, sir, if you don't mind my asking?" Naděžda clutched the book he'd handed back to her, sneaking a peek at his own choice.

"One of Percy Shelley's works," Adolf replied, suddenly eager to talk of his love for the romantics and their style, and other things that Amir did not know of. It seemed that the man had a deep interest in books, philosophy and art, and Amir had to commend Naděžda on her luck as well as her skill; this was a target she would enjoy talking with, rather than any number of their previous informants.

Naděžda kept the ambassador in good company while Amir followed at a distance.

As the time passed, Amir started to get impatient, and he was tempted to hate the Bohemian ambassador more and more—and maybe even Naděžda, too. She clung to the man's arm more tightly than necessary, giving the illusion she was his wife far more than a grateful stranger who believed he was doing her a favor.

It was only when the *Asr* call to prayer sounded down from the mosques in the city that the ambassador seemed to wake from Naděžda's spell.

"Goodness, look at the time," he exclaimed. "I have a meeting down by the Bosporus."

"Oh, dear," Naděžda said. "I have not inconvenienced you too long, have I?"

"I will find a way to send word to him, my dear Miss Cerná," Adolf promised. "We must find your guard. Your safety is much more of a concern than my business meeting."

"Oh, well, if you are certain." Naděžda pulled out her fan again. "Where did you say your meeting was? Perhaps, if we walked toward it, we will find someone who can help me locate my guard, too."

"My meeting is down at Marmora Pier, and I regret to say, Miss Cerná, that the docks are all about business, and there is no place for a lady such as yourself to be there. Perhaps I can find you some accommodation?"

It was at that, Amir decided he'd had enough, and it was time to make his entrance. He took out his weapon and held it at the ready as he stepped forward.

"Miss Cerná," he called, purposefully thickening his Turkish accent.

THE ORDER OF THE CRYSTAL DAGGERS

At his greeting, the Bohemian ambassador whirled around, one of his hands clearly resting on the hidden sheath at his side. "Who are you?"

Naděžda offered a gasp of surprise. "Why, this is my guard," she exclaimed, managing to smile graciously up at the ambassador, who was still concerned about the interruption.

"Are you sure, miss?"

"Of course I am sure," Naděžda replied soothingly. "What a happy coincidence this turned out to be, my dear Dolf—I mean, Mr. Svoboda."

Her flirtatious blush at calling him by his Christian name allowed the ambassador to be distracted again, long enough for Amir to take another step forward. He bowed to Naděžda, hiding his face from her as much as he was avoiding her burning stare. He spoke to her in rapid Arabic, meaningless words of how her family will be upset at her disappearance and so worried—nothing that, should someone overhear them, would be anything near suspicious—before Naděžda laughed.

"I'm so sorry for the trouble." Naděžda did not look one bit sorry as she slipped her arm out of the ambassador's and into Amir's. "Thank you once more, Mr. Svoboda. I cannot thank you enough for seeing to my safety. It seems my family is waiting and I must go at once."

"I see." The ambassador frowned. "I see. Well, I am terribly sorry, Miss Cerná, that I did not get a chance to buy you the flowers I'd promised you."

"Oh, well, the book more than makes up for it," Naděžda insisted, holding up his gift. "I will have something to read while I pass the time in traveling back to London."

"You are headed for London?" he asked.

"Yes, and I will think of you the whole way there as I read through *The Prelude*," she gushed. "Perhaps before too long, I will be back in Prague, and I will be able to tell you all about it. That is, of course, so long as your wife approves."

"I regret to say so, but I do not have a wife."

For the first time, Naděžda looked truly surprised. Amir had to smother a laugh at her discomfort. He wondered if there was ever a time when she had received that particular response.

"Oh, my apologies, sir. I was certain a man of your status and knowledge must surely have a wife waiting eagerly for your return," she said, recovering nicely.

"No, I am afraid I have experienced several setbacks in my life, and I have been waiting for the right moment—and the right woman—to come along." The ambassador gave her a hopeful new look. "Perhaps, if you do come to Prague, you will call upon me? And if not there, the Emperor has sent me all over Eastern Europe, and occasionally London as well."

"Well, if that is the case, I will be sure to look you up," Naděžda said.

"Thank you, my dear," Adolf said, taking her hand and bowing over it gallantly. "And when we do meet again, I will see to it that you have all the flowers a true lady like you deserves."

Amir looked at the poor, besotted smile on the ambassador's face. Amir had to remind himself not to give away the game, and punching the ambassador senseless would most certainly do just that.

THE ORDER OF THE CRYSTAL DAGGERS

3

◊

"Amir, let me go." After a few blocks of practically dragging her behind him, it was clear Naděžda's patience had reached its limit.

Amir's grip tightened at her irritation. "No."

She pulled back, but he did not let her go until they turned down another street.

"Amir, really, what was that about? You could have let me invite myself along to his meeting, and then I would have been able to sit down in the meeting itself."

"You don't need to go prostituting yourself out like that," Amir snapped. "That man was likely one step away from proposing, and the last thing a member of the Order such as yourself needs to worry about is marriage entanglements."

She seemed surprised, but it took her less than a moment to regroup and retaliate.

"Well done, Amir. I think you have my mother's impression near perfect," she countered, her own anger creeping into her voice. "Maybe you should put on her dress and rummage around in her rouge supply to get the full effect."

"Are you even listening to me?" Amir turned her around forcing her into a small garden, one that was hidden from the street by an intricate lattice fence. "You gave that man your name and let him walk you all throughout the town. Isn't that bad enough?"

"He was a perfectly fine gentleman," Naděžda hissed. "I'm not worried about my reputation anyway. Didn't you just hear yourself? What do I have to worry about, as a spy for the Order? I'm not going to get married."

He paused for a moment, realizing she was right, but he pressed on. After all the unpleasantness he had felt at her performance, he was not about to let her escape some sort of retribution. "It's my job to protect you."

"You needn't worry about doing such a thorough job on the matter." She jerked her hands free. "You could risk the mission."

"Mr. Prasad and Her Grace will be upset with me if anything happens to you."

She put her hands on her hips. "Well, then, I guess you do have plenty of reasons to be concerned about me after all. I know I wouldn't want to be on the receiving end of their hatred."

"No, you wouldn't." Amir glared at her. "Now, before we get too distracted by your boredom and penchant for leading men on, we have to circle around and find the Marmora pier and see if we can find that missing shipment of weapons that was supposed to be headed for Prague."

"Yes, yes, by all means, let's get to business," she huffed. "Forget prostituting myself out to a man, let's get on with prostituting myself out to the Order."

She pushed past him, letting *The Prelude* fall out of her hands and onto the ground as she passed him. Amir gazed at it for a long moment, before he swiftly kicked his foot out, pushing the book under another lattice. The book disappeared underneath a curtain of twisted vines, overgrown and burned by the summer's heat.

A sense of angry righteousness blistered through him. He had dismissed Naděžda's risky ventures and chastised her as a fool, and it was only fitting that she should suffer more. All that time she had spent, and they could have just as easily followed the ambassador to the docks.

I don't need this. Amir watched as Naděžda stomped away from him.

His life had been perfectly fine before he had met Naděžda, he thought. He had grown up in a good home, not that far from the city streets of Constantinople.

He glanced down the streets; they were busier than ever, but he knew it would be easy to find his way back to his mother and father's house, if he wanted. He was even more certain his parents were at home, working diligently as ever as they attended to their duties.

He could see the picture in his mind as clearly as if it was before him. His beloved Ammi would be attending to the house, as she had done for all the years of his life, while his father would be at work, tending to patients and their medical needs. Amir could have easily gone home and joined his father. As Abba's only son and heir, Amir was expected to follow in his father's footsteps and become a doctor—a path he did not mind at all. When he had been younger, it was something he enjoyed. The first time he had feel completely happy and comfortable had been at his father's side, tending to the health of others, even the various foreigners who sought out his father's skill.

By the time his father started working under Harshad and Her Grace, Lady Penelope, unknowingly assisting the Order of the Crystal Daggers, the plan was that Amir would finish his education in the West, return home, and resume working with his father. Then he would marry and start his own family with a bride from a neighboring family.

But Amir knew he did not want to go home and see his family now.

Briefly, his eyes fell to the ground.

He loved his parents. He had always sought to do his duty to them. He did not want to upset them or disappoint them.

But all the answers to the riddles of his life became clear the instant he had laid eyes on Naděžda.

That was the moment the neat and orderly lines of his life—the boundaries between his home, work, and even his identity—suddenly faded in their sternness, overtaken by the bold stripe of irrepressible paint that Naděžda proved to be.

How did one go back to only a life of shadows after finding a rainbow, even if it was one he would never catch, but instead spend his life chasing?

She was as jarring as she was beautiful, an irresistible puzzle that left him frustrated and even more perplexed. She was rude and smart, flirtatious and vivacious and unapologetically insightful.

How could he explain to his parents how he'd felt in that moment?

And even now, he thought, when she was angry, she carried herself in a way that only made him want to apologize and beg her to smile and argue with him again.

No wonder she does not respect me. He grimaced, realizing he sounded like a fool, even to himself.

But if he was a fool, he was a fool for her. She was the answer to a question he never dared to ask, maybe even one he never wanted to ask, but one he did not dare ignore. And that made his shame a badge of honor, one he carried next to his heart.

He watched her, as she walked down through another bazaar. Her stride had slowed since she had pulled away from him.

He grinned; despite everything, she was waiting for him.

"Naděžda." Her name was a caress on the wind as he moved to catch up to her.

But before he could get far, a shadow suddenly reached out.

THE ORDER OF THE CRYSTAL DAGGERS

Darkness shifted, moving from an amorphous shape to a hand, one that wrapped around his wrist and yanked him out of the street.

Amir struggled to find his balance as his attacker slammed him into the wall of a wooden house.

"Ouch." Amir grunted as the lattice wall behind him cracked under his weight.

He quickly shrugged off his pain, moving into a fighting position. He'd been caught by surprise, but that did not mean he had none of his own.

The attacker in front of him was ready; he grabbed Amir's arm, turning and twisting it back. His enemy's hand drilled into his pressure point, making Amir grimace in silent pain.

He slid his feet out to the side, enough to make his attacker stumble.

Amir's eyes narrowed at his opponent's tiny wobble.

There it is ... an opening!

Amir lunged forward, forcing his enemy to move. He caught him off guard, long enough to force him into a new direction.

The attacker recovered, but not before Amir whirled around, slid his dagger free, and ducked low for his strike.

Amir prepared to feel the heavy impact of his dagger slicing through flesh, but his assailant was prepared for the offensive. He stepped to the side, pulled out a sword of his own, and grabbed him by the front of his shirt, and hurried to slice his throat.

Amir, completely surprised, leaned back as best as he could. It just registered inside his mind that he could die, as he felt the coolness of the sword's double-edged blade press into his neck.

There was just enough pressure to make him gulp nervously.

His attacked pulled away. "You are distracted today, Amir."

At the familiar voice, Amir almost chuckled with relief.

The sword dropped as the assailant stepped back. The mask fell away, and Amir watched as the beautiful sunstone eyes of Li Xiana glittered fiercely into his.

Seeing his old sparring partner, Amir grinned. "I should have guessed that was you, *saghira*. Even if you are set on fighting in those trousers."

She wrapped the fabric of her mask back around her neck before pulling down the turban she was wearing over her forehead, easily covering

548

the last of her silken hair. While Amir could still make out the feminine features of her eyebrows and the delicate aloofness of her chin, Amir knew no one would think she was anything but another businessman walking through the streets. She wore the loose robes and long pants of a merchant, all at once both colorful and dark in their arrangement.

The mask was a nice touch, Amir had to admit, considering there were some men who took to covering their faces as the women did.

Xiana's face tilted forward, ever so slightly in a gracious nod, but her lips tightened into a slim line. "I do wish you would stop calling me your little sister, Amir. We have both grown since Harshad finished training us."

"It appears I may need a refresher, after your near success."

"I knew you would fail to notice me," Xiana said, glancing back toward the street, where Naděžda was. "You always had a weakness for skirts on a lady."

Her tone was never more inflicted than she wanted it, and Amir did not know if she was laughing at him or if she was accusing him.

"Is that why you decided to say hello as roughly as you did? To test me?" He rubbed his shoulder, massaging the place where Xiana had drilled her pernicious fingers into his joint only a moment before.

He caught sight of her *jian* again as she sheathed it. "Or was it perhaps to test your own skills with a new sword?"

"I will not do it next time," she assured him, ignoring his comment. "You were distracted, but I can see you've managed to keep most of Harshad's lessons at the forefront of your mind with fighting, even though they did not serve you as well as they should have."

"Perhaps it is Her Grace's lessons on espionage I need to keep better," Amir conceded.

Xiana frowned. "It would be easier for you, if you did not let her daughter upset you so."

Amir coughed, trying to fight off the urge to blush. "Miss Eleanor is not accustomed to the clime of the city, I am afraid. When she is upset, it is very often that everyone else is, too."

"You are better than that."

"Most days, perhaps. But not all."

549

THE ORDER OF THE CRYSTAL DAGGERS

The two of them stepped out around the corner, watching as Naděžda continued to bustle through the marketplace, with several vendors between them. As Amir watched, she stopped to look over an array of fruit, inspecting them carefully.

"She has noticed you are not following her," Xiana said. "I should let you get back to your mission."

"You won't be joining us?"

Xiana shook her head. "Not for the moment," she said. She pulled a small pouch out from behind her and held it up. "While he is with Lady Penelope, meeting with some of the Chinese dockmasters, Harshad wanted me to get more herbs. The silver thallis supply Lady Penelope keeps is in need of replenishing."

"I thought she had a delivery of it back in her townhouse in London a few months ago. Why does she need more?"

"The silver thallis needs to be fresh when it is used," Xiana said. "If you wait too long, it loses its potency. It poisons the bloodstream but does not cause death. The body is able to remove it after a few weeks and eventually, the intended victim is able to heal."

"I see. I didn't know that."

"Many women have used it in disposing of their lovers' babes," Xiana said. Amir winced at her tone; it was entirely too straightforward, especially when considering the topic. "It seems there are many things you still have to learn about herbs and their properties."

"The silver thallis is a rare herb, and one without any healing properties. It really isn't that unusual I'd never learned about it before working with the Order."

Xiana arched a brow. "Some women would say it heals them of the shame of an unwanted pregnancy."

"But pregnancy is still a natural process, not an illness in itself." Amir held up his hands. "If the herb could cure battle wounds and venereal diseases, it would be more common knowledge among doctors such as myself."

"Once we are finished here, perhaps I will be able to teach you more."

"Are you joining us in heading back to London after we find out where the missing shipment went?" Amir asked. "I know Her Grace is eager to get back home."

THE ORDER OF THE CRYSTAL DAGGERS

"Perhaps I will come, especially if you will be going." Xiana's eyes slid over to meet his accusingly. "Why are you going back to London? What of your family here?"

She knew him too well, Amir thought with a smile. "I know it seems strange to you, but I do not like having a family all the time."

"That would be strange to me, considering I do not have a family as you do," Xiana easily agreed. "But that does not mean I am unable to understand the burdens of duty. Lady Penelope and Harshad have become my family, and I strive to do all I can to please them."

"Even if it means forgoing your own happiness?" Amir asked.

"Especially then," she said, her voice dark and almost bitter.

"Well, then, you know exactly what I feel." Amir patted her shoulder companionably. "I will see you back at the ship, *saghira.*"

"Amir." Her voice went flat. "Do not think of me as your sister. We might both share a debt to Lady Penelope and Harshad, but the last thing in this world we are is brother and sister."

Amir was struck by her harsher tone, and immediately bowed his head in apology. "If that is your wish. I beg your pardon."

"You have it," Xiana murmured. "But that is not my only wish, and I wish you would see that, as well."

"Wishes are oddly burdensome things." Amir glanced down the street at Naděžda, watching her pay for an apple at a vendor. She had used another one of his coins, he noticed.

But as she lowered her mask and took a bite out of the apple, her eyes met his in the most daring of challenges, and Amir felt it was well worth the price.

"I can see you are anxious to get back to your charge," Xiana said, her voice as stoic as ever. "Excuse me."

"Farewell," Amir replied. As Xiana pushed past him, he flinched at the sudden, sharp pain his arm. He had not been expecting her departure to be painful.

Of course, I was not expecting her arrival to be, either. He rubbed the back of his shoulder where her earlier attack did the most of its damage before checking over his throat, just to make sure her blade did not actually cut him.

He watched Xiana as she walked down the street, her gait quick and rigid—nothing like the other men surrounding them.

She was not usually so careless, Amir thought. He wondered if he was not the only one who was distracted.

He shrugged it off a moment later. There were always any number of complications that came with missions, and for all her skill and undeniable prowess, Xiana had been known to end up fighting for her results more often than not.

Amir turned back toward the market, eager to give his attention back to Naděžda.

Only to find she was nowhere in sight.

4

◊

Amir felt pure, raging panic as it flared up inside him. His vision sharpened, his eyes scourging the different vendors for a sign of Naděžda and her striped gown. As he raked his gaze over the scene before him, his nerves blistered, both in anger and fear—anger at the thought she would taunt him this way, leaving him behind as a punishment for his own neglect and their earlier disagreements, and fear that in losing sight of her, she might truly be in danger.

Where is she? Where did she go?

Amir tightened his grip on his dagger as he hurried toward the fruit vendor, weaving through the different clusters of shoppers and citizens. He had several people glance in his way, and he struggled to keep his expression calm and focused. But the more carefully he looked around, the more worried he became.

A small flicker of red caught his eye from the side of the street as he approached the corner.

Amir swallowed hard as he walked over and knelt down. It was the apple he'd seen her purchase, rolling idly on the side of the street, the missing bite she'd taken glaringly white against its distinctive redness. He picked it up, running his fingertips over it carefully, allowing himself to linger over the place where her lips had touched it.

Where could she be? Why wasn't I there to protect her?

He stood up, whirling around, desperate to find her.

"Naděžda!" The gnawing sickness in his gut grew exponentially, as she was nowhere to be found. Fear choked him as his anger was instantly forgotten.

A voice spoke up from behind him.

"Are you searching for the Western woman?"

Amir turned to see an older, dark-skinned woman on the ground, not far from the corner. He paused momentarily, recalling the inferior reputation of those who were slaves, or former slaves as this woman appeared to be. As he took in her whole appearance, he realized that there was another reason to hesitate; she was a fortune teller, and those who dabbled with devils were not to be trusted.

THE ORDER OF THE CRYSTAL DAGGERS

As if sensing his concern, the old lady laughed dryly. "Not afraid of an old negress like me more than you are of losing your lady, are you?"

Amir carefully studied the woman. He still did not trust her, but she was right about Naděžda. He had to find her, and if that meant getting help from disreputable sources, so be it.

"No," he said, stepping forward. "Please, I need your help."

"Given the fight your lady put up, I would agree," she said. "A pure-hearted man such as you is no doubt worried about recovering what is his."

Amir blushed. "She is not—"

The fortune teller arched her thin, white brows at him as she played with the cards in her hands. "Isn't she though?"

Amir said nothing to that. It was too complicated to explain to the woman, and he feared he did not have the time to indulge her.

"Please," he said. "Please tell me what you saw."

"There were some men who approached your lady. She resisted them, but when they surrounded her, she drew them into a corner."

Amir felt his hands tingle with fear and rage. "What happened?"

"Your lady is quite a fighter." The old fortune teller pointed down toward the Bosporus. "After they subdued her, they hauled her into a wagon and headed that way. I could hear the one say they were going to the docks where the other traders were."

"Do you know which ship they were on?"

She shook her head. "They are as cunning as they are varied, but they likely took your lady to the far end of the port, where the other slave traders are."

"Slave traders?" Amir felt the blood drain from his face.

"You are not from here, are you? The trade of women and children is very profitable here." The older woman's face grew more careworn as Amir's heart constricted.

The fortune teller rubbed her gnarled hands together, before laying out her pinkish palms before her apologetically. "Too many years in the British Empire, perhaps? They might have outlawed slavers, but the rest of the world continues the practice. Those in power will always want dominion those weaker than they are, and that includes the men who sell women."

554

THE ORDER OF THE CRYSTAL DAGGERS

Amir was shamed to realize how much of his own culture he had forgotten over the years.

He bowed low to the woman. "Thank you for your help," he said. "I will find a way to repay you, I promise."

The woman smiled at him, clearly delighted by his respectful manners. "You do not need to worry about it, young man. It's not as though you asked me for your fortune."

"There is no price I wouldn't pay to keep my lady safe," Amir whispered.

"Then it hardly seems fair for me to give you one, is there?" The lady's expression, hardened by years of working and disillusionment, warmed as she looked at him. "*Allah yusallmak*. If what you say is true, I suspect you know the trouble you will find as you keep your word."

"Thank you." Amir gave her one more bow and hurried off toward the docks, desperate to find Naděžda.

◊　◊　◊　◊

If Amir suspected time had slowed before out of spite, he was certain it began to speed up with a vengeance as he hurried down to the far point of the Marmora Pier. He was out of breath as he arrived, just in time to hear the *Maghrib* call to prayer ring out around him.

He stopped at the street up from the docks, looking over the area with unappreciative scrutiny. The welcoming background of the Ottoman Empire greeted the newcomers as they stepped off their ships, while the subtle dirt of the city clung to the streets. Ships of all sizes were both pulling into safe harbor and heading out to sea as merchants and more scrambled around. Several called out their sales pitches as the crowds passed by.

It could have been any ordinary afternoon, Amir thought with a grimace.

How am I supposed to find Naděžda in all of this?

He stood there, stymied, out of breath and nearly out of hope. Amir tightened his grip on his dagger, running his hands over the inscriptions once more, searching for any sign of divine assistance. There were no prayers he knew to recite that asked for such a request to be granted.

Amir closed his eyes, picturing Naděžda. Her own eyes looked back at him, full of a vulnerability he wanted to believe he was only imagining. She was only twenty, he remembered, thinking of her youthful innocence,

THE ORDER OF THE CRYSTAL DAGGERS

but he almost always forgot she was two years younger. With her spirit and stubbornness, she always seemed so much older than she was.

And much more capable, too, Amir thought bitterly. He should have known better than to let her out of his sight, even for a moment.

"Please," he prayed quietly. "Please help me find her."

An eerie silence seemed to settle around him, as the activity of the docks fell into whispers.

Was that his answer?

Amir opened his eyes, defeated, feeling more helpless and alone than ever. He slumped over, wondering if this was his punishment for loving Naděžda. It was too easy to think so. Too much of their lives would keep them apart, and it could only end badly.

"*Stop!*"

Amir's head snapped up, as he straightened. Naděžda's voice, strong and sharp, cut through the silence around him. All distractions were pushed to the side as he heard her voice.

She was nowhere in sight, but he hurried off, heading in the direction where he heard her voice. There was nothing in front of him as he stepped out in faith.

He clenched his fists as he ran, more determined than ever. There was so much that kept them apart, Amir thought. But if there was anything that could bridge the chasm between them, it was surely love.

And he loved her. Irrevocably, undeniably, he loved her, and he would find her, if only to tell her how much he needed her in his life.

Amir slowed his pace as he came up beside another teak-hulled ship designed for warmer waters. He was certain he was lost. There was no sign of Naděžda; it became increasingly obvious he had imagined her voice, driven out of his desperation.

He was about to head down the docks when he glanced saw a pair of stocks.

Slave traders.

Amir stared at the empty stocks, suddenly sickened. This was the place where they would auction off their prisoners. There was no one around— there was no sign at all that any such an event had taken place in recent hours—but as he made his way toward the stocks, he saw a man pass by.

THE ORDER OF THE CRYSTAL DAGGERS

Amir did not recognize him, but with his tunic and military-style jacket, the man wore clothes similar to the Bohemian ambassador. He seemed out of place, as if he was looking for something, too.

Instantly, a thousand different possibilities came rushing through Amir's mind, and he did not know which was worse.

Was it possible Adolf Svoboda was too enchanted with the lady with the fallen flowers? Could he have sent his guards to go and kidnap her, under the disguise slave traders?

"I knew she shouldn't have talked with him," he murmured. "I'll strangle her for this when I get her back."

Amir trailed after the man, following at a safe distance as the man came up to a warehouse. Amir watched as the man walked inside, and Amir took a deep breath.

He could follow the man, but the more that time passed, the more nervous he felt. Amir did not want to lose Naděžda. What if this was just wasting his time?

He sighed. There was nothing else to do, he thought. He would have to search the docks, one ship at a time. There was no reason he could not start where he was.

With that renewed determination, Amir made his way to the back of the warehouse.

The instant he opened the door, and the chilly shadows of the building enveloped him, chains rattled. There *was* someone there! Amir silently cheered as he squinted into the darkness.

"Naděžda?" he whispered.

The voice that greeted him squashed his fledgling hope.

"Finally!" A man huffed indignantly. "I have been waiting for someone to let me go. I can assure you, sir, your masters have made a grave mistake, and I am ecstatic to see there is someone intelligent enough among you to correct such a sinful grievance."

Amir frowned, but before he could say anything else, the man continued talking.

"Now, if you would be so good as to hurry, my good sir, and release me from these chains, I am in desperate need of refreshment. This is a silk shirt, and I can assure you, this place was not made to accommodate me at all. I need to get back to my ship."

THE ORDER OF THE CRYSTAL DAGGERS

"Which ship is yours?" Amir asked. He took a cautious step closer.

"The steamer, of course," the man replied. "I only buy the best and newest models for myself."

"If you are so rich, why are you in here?" Amir took another step closer, finally able to see the man's face.

He could see the piercing green eyes of a gentlemen, one who was educated in the best and possibly worse sort of ways; there was no room for innocence in the prisoner's gaze. He was indeed, wearing a silk shirt, and he looked as though he had been dragged out of a harem; his shirt was only buttoned halfway up his chest, and his breeches, cut in the French style, were on backwards. As Amir watched him, the man flipped a long flop of his hair upward in exasperation.

"I suppose you're after some kind of reward?" The man rolled his eyes. "Well, I suppose I can't blame you there, but really, I have to say I'm disappointed you're not going to do the right thing without financial incentive."

"I am looking for someone else," Amir said, unsure of why he was talking to this prisoner at all.

"I see. Well then, you've found the right person indeed," the man replied. "I am Lumiere Valoris, and I am more or less in charge of everything down here by the Marmora."

"How are you in charge of everything?" Amir asked. "You're not the sultan."

"Abdülmecid is terribly busy, trying to turn his Empire into Europe without anyone noticing," Lumiere scoffed. "He is like any other ruler— content to believe himself to be in charge of everything, even if he is not. I am the richest man here, thanks to my family's holdings across Europe. Tell me what you need, and I will give it to you."

"I am looking for a woman," Amir said. "She was taken, possibly by slave traders."

"Psh. There are no slave traders here while the East India Company is in port," Lumiere said. "My father's one of the people who negotiated that deal, thanks to his connections to the French and British Empires."

"France is no longer an empire."

"So you think," Lumiere said with another smirk. "Just you wait. Napoleon's legacy is not finished yet."

THE ORDER OF THE CRYSTAL DAGGERS

"I'll have to worry about that later," Amir said. He stepped back, heading toward the door, wondering if he would be able to find the Bohemian man again. "Right now, I need to find my friend. She is my business partner. I wish you well, sir."

"No, wait." Lumiere's voice was suddenly more desperate as Amir turned to leave. "They'll kill me if you leave me here."

"Why?"

"There are certain laws you can't break while you're here, and let's just say, I'm not excited about the thought of a public execution, no matter how *smashing* it might be." Lumiere's wide eyes, framed with kohl and aided by the rogue on his cheeks, seemed younger than before as he looked at Amir. "If you get me out of here, I'll help you find your partner. I promise. I will use my connections to help you."

Amir hesitated. Once more, he was faced with the thought of getting aid from someone he did not trust, and this time, it was a villain of sorts.

But as he studied Lumiere's face—seeing the pleading smolder, his roughened form, and his swaggering entitlement—Amir reluctantly softened.

He gave in, quickly using his dagger to pick through the chains, cutting them off at the manacles.

"Can't you remove these beastly things?" Lumiere complained.

"Can't you just find a way to pay someone else to do it later?" Amir asked. "Right now, you need to help me."

"I see you've failed to appreciate just how much I have suffered in the last two days," Lumiere balked. "I must get back to my father's ship if I am to return to Bohemia."

"Bohemia?" Amir quickly shook his head and dismissed the information. He did not have time to wonder about his mission now, not when Naděžda still had to be found. "What about your promise?"

Lumiere waved his arm aside, his rogued lips tightening with displeasure. "The word of a Frenchman is one thing, but his timing is another, my good sir, and you must excuse me in this manner."

"No." Amir took out his dagger, brandishing it in front of Lumiere. "This is too important."

Lumiere stared down at him for a long moment, before he growled. "Fine. Let's go. But I warn you, I must hurry. I've got a shipment of

THE ORDER OF THE CRYSTAL DAGGERS

stolen weapons heading out of port, and I don't need my father haranguing me for the delay."

"Wait." Amir grabbed Lumiere's shirt, holding his dagger up to his chest. "You have a shipment of stolen weapons?"

"Oh, goodness. Don't tell me one of the sultan's few competent policemen is my rescuer today." Lumiere grabbed Amir's wrist and stepped back, easily untangling himself. "How do you think my family got rich?"

Amir gritted his teeth together. "We can discuss it later," he snapped. "Right now, I need your help. If you're as rich and powerful as you say, you will stop all port activity until my partner is returned to me."

"We'll see about that," Lumiere murmured. "But if you want my help now, you'll have to drop your charges against me later."

"Only if you deliver," Amir warned. "Or I will make sure you suffer."

"Hey, I am *already* suffering, and of complete boredom, no less," Lumiere whined. "Let's just go. At least escaping here and looking for your partner will be more exciting that standing here and arguing with the likes of you."

THE ORDER OF THE CRYSTAL DAGGERS

5

◊

Amir did not have to question how desperate he was as he raced along the port with Lumiere behind him. As they left the building—loudly, to the objection of several of the men inside who were supposed to be guarding him—Amir was beginning to wonder if he had done the right thing in letting Lumiere go.

"Wouldn't happen to have a pistol on you, would you?" Lumiere asked, as they ran from a pair of Bohemian guards. "I'm a crack shot, and it would be easier to get rid of the king's supporters."

"No," Amir called back. "If you're going to Bohemia, why are those guards chasing you?"

"Didn't you hear me? Those are Bohemian loyalists. They came with the king's ambassador, and they think they're doing the sultan a favor by catching deviants like myself and trading me off to the local authorities. Never mind that I control half the Ottoman's profits in Constantinople."

"Those are the Bohemian ambassador's guards." Amir was grateful for the confirmation, even though he did not know what to think about it. He decided he would ask Harshad later, after he found Naděžda.

"Yes, and they're quite upset, too. Probably needed someone like me to tamper the crushing blow they're going to deliver to King Ferdinand."

"Crushing blow?"

"Let's just say not everyone in Bohemia wants a revolution, but those who are not prepared for it are going to get hit the hardest." Lumiere snorted disdainfully. "They call him 'Ferdinand the Good,' but personally, I prefer the name 'Ferdinand the Good-for-Nothing.'"

Amir said nothing; he knew there was plenty of unrest in Bohemia, same as several other nations. While there was likely to be enough blame on both sides, he had a feeling there would be no easy answer.

"Say, my good sir, what is your name, anyway?" Lumiere asked. "I'm getting tired of pretending I respect you."

Amir sniffed. "I saved your life."

"There are plenty who would say my life is of no consequence."

"My name is Amir." As they ducked around another building, Amir held out his hand in greeting. Lumiere shook it as they stopped.

561

THE ORDER OF THE CRYSTAL DAGGERS

"Good to know." Lumiere straightened as he glanced around. "I need to get back to the *Chaos*. It's nearly dark, and I need to get into my formal clothes."

"Formal clothes?"

"What am I? A commoner?" Lumiere shook his head. "I might have to work, but it's at my pleasure that I do so."

"I assume that your pleasure is the reason you were caught, too?" Amir asked.

"Don't you know me so well already?"

Amir flinched at the thought. "You can go back to your ship once I find my partner."

"Good," Lumiere said. "I'm starting to get annoyed by you. But then, men of honor are frequently annoying. And I suppose looking for a woman would do that to you."

"This is not just any woman," Amir said. "She is too important to me."

"Yes, yes, I know." Lumiere rolled his eyes. "Women. Who needs them, anyway?"

Amir frowned at him, but Lumiere grabbed his arm and tugged him down another street.

"Come, Amir," Lumiere said. "I will show you where all the contraband tends to run. If what you say is true, and she was taken by the slave traders, that is where she will be."

"I thought you said your father made it so there were no slaves at port while the British and French were around?"

"Sovereignty of nations is always a tricky thing," Lumiere said with a shrug. "Sovereignty of individuals? Even worse. Thank the good Lord for human stupidity, or I would feel the world itself would be in danger."

"As opposed to only human life?"

Lumiere grinned at Amir's irritated tone. "Of course."

Amir did his best to ignore Lumiere as they made their way through the different piers. He kept a sharp eye out for Naděžda, hoping against hope it seemed, that he would find her without needing any assistance from Lumiere. He did not want to pray for more help; he was worried that in letting Lumiere go, he had already invited the devil along with him.

THE ORDER OF THE CRYSTAL DAGGERS

"Tell me about this woman," Lumiere said, pulling Amir out of his thoughts.

"She's the daughter of a duchess." He did not want Lumiere to think this was anything he could take flippantly.

"She's the daughter of a duchess, but works with you as a partner?" Lumiere frowned. "That must mean she's actually adopted, or possibly born on the wrong side of the blanket."

Lumiere's green eyes twinkled in suspicion. "Why are you really here? What is your partner's name?"

"Her name is Eleanor Ollerton-Cerná," Amir said, struggling to keep his voice professional. "She is working with me on—"

"Ollerton? As in Ollerton-Wellesley?" Lumiere stopped short. He suddenly bent over, guffawing with laughter. "Oh, Lord, this is too precious!"

Amir stiffened. "What's so funny?"

"You." Lumiere gripped onto his stomach as he laughed uproariously. "I told you, I am the one who knows everything that goes on in this port. If you're looking for the offspring of an Ollerton and a Cerná, I'm more than willing to bet my men picked her up."

"What are you talking about?"

"I'm Lumiere *Valoris*," he said, emphasizing his last name. When Amir only gave him a blank look, he laughed harder. "You are Lady Penelope's stooge, and you've never heard of me?"

Amir frowned.

"Oh my goodness, this is so amusing." Lumiere wiped the tears from his eyes. "Well, I can't help you any further than this, I'm afraid."

"What?" Amir grabbed his arm, pushing him into the ground. "You promised me."

"I'm shocked a man working with the Order of the Crystal Daggers is so obtuse," Lumiere snapped, his tone suddenly much harder as Amir pushed him onto his knees. "Hey, watch the clothes. It would take a nice chunk out of the Iron Dowager's coffers to replace them."

Amir ignored him and, instead, tightened his grip. "How do you know about Her Grace?"

Lumiere shook his head. "Those who don't know their history are destined to make their future worse."

"What is that supposed to mean?" Amir's impatience was creeping in. "Never mind. I've had enough. Tell me where my partner is, or I will end your life here and now."

"Hardly. You're not going to do it out in public like this," Lumiere argued. He broke Amir's hold and stood up, brushing himself off indignantly. "Come. I'll take you to my father's traders. They're the ones who likely have her. They were warned the Order would try to interfere with their goals if they weren't careful."

"What are you talking about?" Amir frowned, following as Lumiere pushed himself through the crowds.

"I'm talking about a chess game," Lumiere said. "One that does not play with little pieces on a board, but one that is silently being played out between several parties, over the nation of Europe and its trading partners all around the world. I know your leader, Lady Penelope, would like to believe she's got the upper hand now that she's secured herself in working with the Order and the League, but there are plenty in the League who do not like her—perhaps especially including her former lover, Jakub Cerný, and my father, Louis Valoris."

Amir recognized the name of Naděžda's father, but the other name was foreign to him. "The League? You mean the League of Ungentlemanly Warfare?"

"Of course. She might be scheming her way in, but she will always be an outsider. Not even her former lover, Jakub Cerný, will be able to help her. In fact, he's likely a detriment now."

"Are you working with the League, too, then?"

"Ha! I am working for myself, at my pleasure, remember?" Lumiere glanced over his shoulder long enough to give Amir a sneer. "The League should be so lucky, shouldn't it?"

"You know of Her Grace, Lady Penelope."

"Yes, I do, and I would normally question anyone who works with her. In fact, why would a Turk such as yourself be content to work for a woman, and a British one at that? Especially as a babysitter for her daughter, like you've hinted?"

"I have my own reasons, just as you have your own reasons for finding pleasure in ruining others' lives," Amir retorted.

"There's no need to sound judgmental," Lumiere replied. "Suffering is supposed to be a great teacher. I am only helping the populace. They will appreciate their prosperity much more later on, thanks to my efforts."

"Ha!" Amir shook his head.

"Oh, stop," Lumiere said. "Look, I'm helping you, aren't I? And against my father's wishes, too. You should be thanking me profusely, even swearing your allegiance to me, for all I'm doing for you."

"I'm the one who saved *you*, if you'll recall."

"That happened, what? Ten minutes ago?"

"It could be an eternity at this point," Amir grumbled.

"Exactly," Lumiere said. "No need to worry about it now, do we? Especially when we have someone else to save."

"Just get us there, and then I will release you from the rest of your promise," Amir said.

"If those are your terms, I formally accept." Lumiere grinned. "Once I have my freedom, I do believe my friendship will be a much more valuable asset."

Amir did not want to believe Lumiere was serious. He was grateful that the rest of their trip was made mostly in silence, though Lumiere tried to engage Amir by making random comments from time to time. As they approached his ship, the *Chaos*, Amir coughed at the coal pouring into the air from the funnels. The smoky lines rising up from the ship clouded the skies, almost giving the impression it was nighttime.

"Keep your voice down," Lumiere said, waving his arm dismissively as they came up to a loading house.

Amir shot Lumiere an angry glare, but he said nothing else.

"Come this way." Lumiere led Amir back behind the building. He motioned to Amir to keep silent, as they hurried to the back door.

This time, the door was locked.

As Lumiere struggled to open the door in a clumsy manner, Amir groaned. He wondered if he had done the right thing again. How could he really trust Lumiere? There was nothing about him that Amir even wanted to trust him with, and yet, here he was, practically following him to the ends of the earth.

Which, Amir reminded himself, was exactly how far he would go to protect Naděžda.

What if she had escaped the men who had caught her? What if she was back with Harshad and Lady Penelope now, resting on their own ship as he searched the city for her?

The dread in his heart contradicted that vision, even if he hoped with all his soul it was true.

"Got it," Lumiere cheered, as the door opened up. He stepped back and pointed inside. "This is where we take care of the more unpleasant sides of business. If we have her, she'll be in there. Lady Penelope will be able to help you if she's not. If I ask anything of you, it is that you do not tell her you ran into me. If you want your deal to be fulfilled, actually, you will not say anything to her. She will be upset with me, as will my father, who will no doubt hear of this incident."

"Where are you going?" Amir asked, surprised to see Lumiere back away.

"I've got to get to the ship and change my clothes," he said.

"What?" Amir looked at him, incredulously. "That doesn't matter."

"Come now, I've explained this to you. These are my men, but they are paid by my father. I can't help you—not without risking my own neck and future in the process. I have paid my debt to you, and that is all I can do. If I am going to play the game here, this game of four-way or more-than-four-way chess, then I can't afford to lose, especially for something as silly as honor."

"But—"

"But nothing, Amir, my friend." Lumiere gave him a shrewd, appraising look. "It's been absolutely lovely to have a strong and loyal man such as you by my side. I hope we meet again, someday, when it will be better for us to be on the same side."

He reached out his hand, and Amir shook it politely, still dumbfounded that Lumiere was leaving him.

"Call me Lumi," Lumiere told him. "So I will know we are friends."

At the thought of being Lumiere's friend, Amir felt rather repulsed. But he nodded, despite his hesitation.

Lumiere smirked, letting his blond bangs flop forward, before his hand ran through his hair and pushed them back.

"Now, go and get your lady," Lumiere said. "I'm sure she'll be anxious to be saved. My father would be all too happy to have her in his grasp, considering how much he hates her mother. And how much he'd love to send revolutions running through Europe, too."

Before Amir could say anything else, Lumiere slipped away, strutting with pride, heading back toward his ship.

THE ORDER OF THE CRYSTAL DAGGERS

Amir did not know how to process everything. He decided a moment later to worry about it after he had Naděžda back—if, indeed, Lumiere was right about where she was.

As if on a cue, a bloodcurdling scream rang out in pain, yelling from inside the loading station.

He recognized her voice at once, much as he had recognized her the day he'd first met her.

"Naděžda." Amir breathed in deeply, both in fear and in relief. He pulled out his dagger, letting the tip of the *Wahabite Jambiya* glimmer with the fading light of day before he entered the building.

THE ORDER OF THE CRYSTAL DAGGERS

6

◊

Amir raced through the halls, the gloomy, unfamiliar atmosphere press-ing into him as he moved. The aura of grim and dirty business persisted through every inch of space around him, and he hated to think what sort of activities went on there on a regular basis.

He shook off his discomfort as much as he could, forcing himself to concentrate only on finding and rescuing Naděžda.

"You, there!" A voice called out just as Amir reached the end of the hallway. He stopped in front of a door, turning around just in time to see a pair of guards as they rushed after him. "Stop!"

He was able to briefly make out the French *fleur-de-lis* on the sleeves of their overcoats before they accosted him.

Amir allowed himself to be pushed against the doors, using their mo-mentum and flurry to gain the upper hand. He caught them off guard, and as they stumbled forward, he ducked down and slashed his dagger across the back of their knees.

The men howled in pain, both of them falling away to the side. Amir said a silent prayer for their recovery, hating how sinful men sought to de-ter him from doing right. He pushed them away before he thrust open the doors.

Stepping into the next room, Amir scrambled to block the door; there was no lock, and the men who attacked him were calling for help on the other side. Once he knew he had bought himself enough time, Amir saw he'd come right into the heart of the loading dock.

All around him, large wooden crates marked over in a variety of lan-guages were stacked high. He paused, waiting in the shadows of a tall tower of boxes, watching as a pair of men hauled another crate out of the large room. Some of the labels he recognized as part of the missing weap-ons shipment that was supposed to head to Bohemia.

Amir ran a hand over his chin ruefully. *Lumiere had been telling the truth.*

He was relieved, but he was also surprised; the incendiary Frenchman did not seem to be the type to tell the truth, unless it suited him.

Amir sighed. He would get a headache trying to figure out someone like Lumiere. He made a mental note to have Harshad send Xiana or some of their other associates over later. He gripped his dagger again, returning his focus to finding Naděžda.

As if to remind him, he heard Naděžda cry out from across the storage room.

"Stop!" Her voice was low, her teeth gritted in pain.

Amir nearly choked at the sound. He hurriedly swallowed his fear and made his way to the far end of the room, careful not to alert anyone else to his presence.

He came to the end a row of boxes, and he was suddenly able to see her.

"Naděžda."

He nearly turned away as he saw her. The sickness in his gut felt even worse.

Her hands were bound in a pair of stocks, as she knelt on the stand. The formal, striped outer layers of her gown had been stripped away along with her mask and headdress, leaving her in her petticoat and corset. The white of her pantalettes had speckles of blood that trickled down onto her garments from her back, where she had been whipped.

Amir felt the rage inside of him boil as a man stepped forward, carrying the whip in question. He wore a turban over his dark, scraggly hair, and his beard seemed to overgrow his face.

"Insolent woman!" The man cried out. "You dare mock me?"

Amir watched as Naděžda—his Naděžda, so proud and stubborn—lifted her chin defiantly to him.

"How can I resist?" she shouted back. "You have all the self-control of an infant, and the temper to go along with it. It's shameful that you should be bothered so much by a mere woman."

"You are no 'mere woman,'" the man replied, and Amir had to agree with him. "You managed to kill one of my men."

"Your man died because he couldn't swim," Naděžda shot back. "Not because I stopped him from apprehending me."

"You pushed him out of the wagon."

"It seemed prudent, considering he was the one who threw me into it against my wishes."

THE ORDER OF THE CRYSTAL DAGGERS

"What are a woman's wishes?" The foreman scoffed. "We might respect your privacy when you Western women play by our rules here, but we are still your masters."

He raised the whip to her again, and Amir couldn't watch as he brought it down on her. At her cry, Amir winced. He stepped back in horror, only to knock against a tall pile of crates.

The boxes shifted his impact, enough where they shook. Amir sized them up, while he heard Naděžda spit angrily at her opponent.

"You'll be sorry for that later," she said.

Amir prayed she would be right as he pushed on the stack of crates behind him. He felt a groan rise in his throat as he struggled to push them over.

"If you are going to try my patience, perhaps it is better I take care of breaking you before I turn you over to my captain."

Amir heard the slap of skin against tender flesh and pushed harder on the crates.

"You'll never break me," Naděžda said, her voice restrained, but lined with pain.

"We'll see about that."

Amir's eyes widened as he heard the sound of ripping fabric, and he knew Naděžda needed his help at once.

"Please," he murmured, slamming into the crates one last time.

They tumbled over, falling down and smashing open. Amir ducked behind another row as the foreman yelled and cursed, calling for his assistants. As their footsteps came closer, Amir sniffed, nearly sneezing at the dust and debris that littered the area in front of him. Careful to stay out of sight, he peeked around to see Naděžda was safe. The last of her crin petticoat had been torn away, fully exposing her pantalettes.

As the men and the foreman came closer to inspect him, Amir slipped out from his hiding place. Once he was sure they were sufficiently distracted, he quietly made his way to Naděžda.

She was breathing deeply, trying to remain calm, as he came up beside her.

Her head snapped up at his approach. "Stay away—"

Naděžda's words died on her lips as she saw him. There was nothing holding back the relief in her gaze. "Amir."

570

THE ORDER OF THE CRYSTAL DAGGERS

He nodded and put his finger to his lips, signaling her to be quiet as he used his dagger to dismantle the stocks.

"I was hoping you would come for me," she breathed. There was a dim sparkle in her eyes, and Amir was almost sickened by her doubt.

"You didn't think I would let anything happen to you, did you?" he asked.

"It was my fault for getting captured," Naděžda murmured. "You would have thought I deserved it."

Before Amir could shame her for such a thought, a shadow bore down on them.

"Watch out!" Naděžda pushed Amir away, allowing the whip to come down on her shoulder. As he rolled to his feet, Amir saw the whip lash around, cutting into her skin.

"Naděžda," he sputtered, horrified to see her bleed even more.

"So, the woman has a partner." The foreman stepped forward, holding his whip in one hand as he used his other hand to pull out a pistol. He cocked the gun and aimed it for Amir, as Naděžda screamed.

"No!" she cried, her one arm still stuck in the stock.

The foreman was distracted enough that Amir lunged at him.

The gun went off, crackling like lightning as the bullet ripped through the room. Amir felt the heat of the gun like it was a small explosion.

In that moment, he felt as though everything were happening all at once. The foreman's men behind him were rushing toward him, their own daggers high; Naděžda was still trapped, and the foreman was preparing to strike out with the whip once more.

Amir lunged forward, thrusting his dagger into the man's chest as he grabbed the hand that held the whip. Using his momentum, he whirled around, letting the whip strike his other adversaries.

The foreman's eyes went blank with death, and Amir shoved him away, pulling his blood-covered blade out of his enemy's chest. The other men backed up, faltering in their advance at the sign of their dead leader.

Amir was ready for them. He parried his dagger against the one man, while landing a kick squarely in the other man's torso, sending him falling backwards. His other opponent stepped forward, but Amir used his dagger to slice through his tunic.

The man looked at the stream of blood that spurted forward, and immediately stepped back.

"Go," Amir told him. "I am not here for you."

At his words, the two men exchanged a quick look, and then ran away.

Amir waited until they were out of the room and the door was shut behind them before he dropped his guarded stance and hurried back over to Naděžda.

She was staring at him, dumbfounded, as he severed through the last lock that held her captive. The moment she was free, she threw herself into his arms.

"Amir."

"I'm here." He tightened his arms around her and held onto her for a long moment as she fell against him. He allowed him that small moment of a reward, letting his face bury into the loosen tresses of her hair. Now that they were safe, all he wanted to do was hold her. He wanted nothing more than to run his hands all down her body and assure himself she was real and she was alive, soothing over every inch of pain with his comfort and care.

He pulled back from her more than reluctantly. He pulled off his own tunic, letting himself embrace the small warmth of the saltwater breeze through the white shirt on underneath. Once he was sure she could stand, he pulled the jacket over her.

"Let's get back to the ship," he said, his voice hoarse as he picked her up and cradled her in his arms.

"Amir, wait." She glanced around. "This is the missing shipment of weapons. We need to find out who is behind this."

Amir tightened his grip on her as he walked past the boxes he had overturned. There was a keg of gunpowder near his foot, and he was more than tempted to set the whole place on fire. He never wanted to think of Naděžda trapped there, at the mercy of some lecherous, evil man, ever again. As she opened her mouth again, no doubt to argue with him once more, Amir shook his head.

"Not now, Naděžda. I will see to it that Harshad sends someone else," he said. "Right now, I do not care about anything but you."

THE ORDER OF THE CRYSTAL DAGGERS

7

◊

Amir barely realized how much his body ached as he carried Naděžda toward the *Splendor*. He moved quickly through the port, never meeting any individual gaze, remaining focused only on getting her to a place where he could properly care for her wounds. She clung to him as he carried her, and while he reveled in the warmth of her embrace, as necessary as it was, he could feel the warmth of her blood as it oozed through his tunic.

"Amir." Her voice was a whisper as she shivered.

"Not now. We're almost to the ship."

"I can walk."

"I can carry you."

"I'm heavier than I look."

"I'm stronger than I look." He tried to give her a stern look, but his heart softened to the point of aching as he looked down at her. Her eyes were blotchy, shimmering with unshed tears. "I can carry you. So I will."

"I deserve to suffer."

Amir shifted her in his arms, bringing her further up on his chest as her legs fell back over his arm. "If you suffer, I will only suffer more."

"It was my fault they found me. It's my fault we failed in our mission."

"No," Amir whispered back. "I found out where the shipment went, and I know that the perpetrators were warned the Order was supposed to interfere."

"That's true." Naděžda gave a ladylike snort. "The men said they recognized my name from when I was talking to the ambassador. That was why I went with them at first."

Amir knew he have easily told her he had been right, but he would never be so wrong in all his life if he dared. Instead, he stopped walking and hugged her closer to him, careful not to rub up against her cuts. "Let's not talk about it anymore. You're safe now. That's what matters."

"I wish you would be upset with me. I ruined the mission, after all."

"And I saved it," Amir told her. He adjusted his grip on her again, before he resumed his trek toward the *Splendor*. "Just like I saved you."

573

Naděžda gave him a small smile. "Yes. Yes, you did." She reached up and touched his cheek, before tucking her face into the nook of his shoulder.

Amir cradled her head, his fingers lightly caressing her hair.

Despite his aching muscles, it was too soon before the *Splendor* came into sight. The sun was close to setting as Amir carried Naděžda up the gangplank.

As if he'd suspected something had gone wrong, Harshad was waiting for them. Amir did not know if he was more glad or anxious to see his mentor and patron. He did not want to distress Harshad, and he did not want to disappoint Lady Penelope. Amir also did not want to get Naděžda in trouble. Even though he was certain she would be fine, after everything that happened, he only wanted her to rest.

"My goodness, Dezda," Harshad said. His hair seemed to turn grayer as he saw her state of undress and the blood on the back of Amir's tunic. "What happened?"

Amir quickly stepped forward. Harshad listened to Amir as he spoke quickly regarding the day's adventures, briefly mentioning the Bohemian loyalists and the French ambassador's men, before informing him that the *Chaos* was carrying the missing weapons.

"Miss Eleanor has a few injuries, Mr. Prasad," Amir said dutifully. Naděžda's formal name sounded strange to his ears now; he hoped Harshad would not notice. Amir bowed his head down in both greeting and deference, as he hurried to excuse himself. "I request you allow me to see to her care."

"My God." Harshad's graying hair tussled in the salty wind as he studied Naděžda. Amir could see his ochre face blanch at the sight of her blood.

"Oh, Uncle, you needn't worry," Naděžda said with a sigh.

"Your mother will be worried when she gets back from her own meeting with the Chinese ambassadors," Harshad said.

Naděžda delicately wrinkled her nose. "Amir will take excellent care of me, just as he has so far. Mother does not need to worry about that."

Amir was gratified to see her smile in admiration as she looked at him. He had to wonder if she was being sincere, considering she would not want to put in a bad report with Harshad and her mother, either.

THE ORDER OF THE CRYSTAL DAGGERS

Harshad nodded curtly. "Take her to her room," he instructed Amir. "I will see to it that you are not disturbed."

"Thank you, Mr. Prasad," Amir replied.

"Wait." Harshad pausing, before he rubbed his chin. "Perhaps it is time for you to call me 'Harshad,' Amir. As Dezda will tell you, we are very informal with those we consider family."

"Yes, Uncle," Naděžda agreed.

"Thank you," Amir said quietly.

Harshad clasped his hands together, in a gesture of respect. "You have been working with us directly these past few months, and of course, you have known us for many years now. Surely that is enough to know your place is with us."

Amir nodded. "Yes, sir … Harshad."

"I will check in with you in a few hours, Amir. We have reports to discuss."

"Thank you." Amir quickly bowed and hurried down the deck to where Naděžda's room was located.

"It seems my mother has softened him, since they reunited," Naděžda murmured. "If that is one good thing to come out of my parents' failure of a relationship, it is Uncle."

"I'm surprised your mother could soften anyone," Amir replied, glad to see Naděžda already seemed to be recovering from the trauma of the day. When she chuckled at his comment, he was even more gratified.

Once Naděžda was settled on her bed, Amir got out his small medical kit, the one he carried with him. As he pulled out the items he needed for lacerations, she tried to make small talk with him.

He barely listened to her as he laid her across his lap, as he carefully cut and peeled off the blood-covered tunic he had used to cover her. He set about cleaning off the skin of her back, glad to see that there was only one major wound, a crude lash across her right shoulder blade. Amir could already hear Lady Penelope telling her Socialite friends how Naděžda chaffed herself on passing carriage, as she hurried to save a stray child, or some grand fabrication that would change the scar from a battle wound into a badge of valor.

She might save herself the trouble and allow Naděžda to wear more modest gowns. Even as he thought it, Amir allowed himself a moment to study Naděžda. Even with the injuries interrupting the perfect smoothness of her back,

THE ORDER OF THE CRYSTAL DAGGERS

her muscles were strong but subtle; her skin looked infinitely soft, begging for a touch.

Amir had a feeling Lady Penelope would eschew the more modest dresses. Naděžda was a wonder to work with in Society. Her charm and beauty easily made others believe her various backstories, allowing the Order to discover even the most carefully guarded secrets Society tried to hide.

Amir did his best to treat her as if she were any patient in the world, but as he stitched up the slash in her back from the foreman's whip, he had to pause several times because of his own trembling hands.

I almost lost her.

Naděžda shifted beneath him. "Amir?"

"Yes?" His tongue suddenly felt very thick.

"Are you feeling well?"

He hated lying to her, especially since he had a feeling she would know he was. "I am perfectly capable of doing my job, if you are worried about that."

"I wasn't," she replied. "I was more worried because I saw you kill the foreman. I know you very well, and such an action is contrary to your nature."

He said nothing. He only continued to thread his medical needle through the skin on her back, carefully tugging on the threat.

"I'm right, aren't I?" She glanced back at him, carefully shifting her hair behind her.

"You need to lie still," he said instead. "I only have a few stitches left."

"Amir."

"You likely don't want any worse of a scar," Amir said. "Please, hold still. For just a few moments longer."

She acquiesced, but the moment he snipped the thread and tied it off, she pushed herself up and reached for him. The gesture was so natural and smooth he never stopped to wonder or question her.

"I'm sorry you had to kill someone in order to protect me," she whispered.

"He hurt you." Amir's arms involuntarily tightened around her.

THE ORDER OF THE CRYSTAL DAGGERS

He could feel her smile into his shoulder. "Are you worried Uncle and my mother will punish you for what happened?"

Amir sighed. He did not like to think of their earlier argument. "No, Miss Eleanor."

"Stop that." Naděžda, sensing she had overstepped the limits of his patience. "I know what you're trying to do, and it won't work. I know you want to call me Naděžda, Amir. I know it, just as you surely know how much I want you to."

He said nothing, but his heart began to race. The thundering beat was pounding into him as Naděžda buried her face further into his shoulder.

"I hate this, you know," she whispered quietly, as though she was tearing the words from the deepest part of her heart, the part she never admitted aloud to anyone, possibly not even herself. Her eyes watered as she looked up at him. "I hate this life, Amir. I hate feeling like there is no true place I belong, that there is no true family for me."

"You have your mother and Mr. Prasad," Amir reminded her, tucking her hair back with one hand while wiping away a stray tear with his thumb. He caressed her cheek, reveling in the softness of her skin. Despite her toughness, she seemed so delicate to the touch.

She deserved so much more than what life had offered her, he thought.

"It's not enough," she choked out, twisting his shirt into her fingers. "I want my own family. I want my own life. I want to be free—free from my mother's expectations, and free from the Order."

Amir drew her against his chest again. He let her cry, knowing there was nothing he could say to her to make it better.

In some ways, he wished he could cry with her. Who, more than he, knew the honor required to follow a parents' wishes, even if it meant great cost? And who could know the horror of failing to live up to those expectations more than he did?

He had killed a man, even though it was to protect an innocent woman, and he worked in service to a woman, even if it was profitable.

He had fallen in love with a spy, the illegitimate daughter of his employer, a woman his family would never accept. It was all folly, all of it; there was too much keeping them apart—religion, culture, bloodlines, status, and the honor he had always striven to achieve.

"You have me, too," he whispered.

"I do?"

"Yes." He looked into her eyes and lost himself all over again, Amir knew it was more possible to stop the sun from shining than it was to stop himself from loving her. "Yes, of course you do … Naděžda."

Before the last echo of her name had begun to fade between then, Naděžda's arms were laced around his neck, her body was pressed up hard against his, and all the illusions between them were gone. All other choices between them were gone. All pretense, all innocence, all hope of any other life—no matter how orderly and neat and uncomplicated as it might have been—all of it had passed away, and only need remained.

"Amir." His name was a breath on her lips, a second before his lips were on hers.

The taste of her rushed at him and through him, penetrating into his core as she kissed him. The warm spice of her mouth, mixed with the wetness of her bitter tears, sent tremors through him, shaking his soul even as his heart reveled in the sudden security of knowing she was his, and he was hers.

No matter how much he might have imagined it, kissing Naděžda was beyond anything he'd ever experienced; it was both beyond sin and for-giveness, beyond memory and dreams. Passion, ardent and pervasive, coursed through him like fire on a fuse; the taste of her drove deeply into him, penetrating past all possible defenses, confirming his transgression even as it tasted of divine ecstasy.

Her mouth opened under his, and his body promptly rejected every last ounce of self-control he had built up over the last several months since Naděžda had become his constant companion. All he lived for in that mo-ment was to drown in her.

"Amir." His name escaped from her in a moan before she eased back, breathing heavily. "I have been trying so hard, you know, to get you to fall in love with me. Perhaps it was foolish of me."

"Yes." Amir brushed a stray lock of hair away from her face as he looked down at her. "It was."

"Well, if that's how you feel—" Naděžda began to push away from him, but Amir only pulled her close and kissed her again.

"Naděžda," he whispered. "I have been falling in love with you from the first moment we met."

"Oh." A lovely, shocked expression of wonder lit up her face as she re-laxed into him again.

"Are you finally speechless?" Amir shook his head. The muscles in his face seemed to crack as he smiled. "I should have told you sooner."

"It might have saved us several arguments." Naděžda gave him a small smile, both shy and sly as she looked up at him. "I hope you don't think this is how you'll win in the future."

"I guess we'll see."

"Amir." Naděžda's hands slid under his shirt, grasping at his shoulders as they fell back together.

Amir fell into her kiss, devastatingly overwhelmed and overly eager to claim her. Over and over their lips met in a fierce fire, his soul suturing itself into hers as he tasted and touched her. He could feel her own eagerness as her hands ran down his chest, as her kisses offered silent confessions and hinted at the desperate desires of her heart.

Amir let his hands fall to her hips, letting his hands run down her corset and his fingers fold into the ties of her pantalettes. Nothing was able to stop him from seeking out the warmth of her skin; her being called out to his, and he was just as desperate as she was to burn.

It was only when she lifted herself off his chest, pausing as she panted for breath, that he saw her apprehension.

"What is it, Naděžda? Are you afraid I will resort to my mongrel ways?" he whispered teasingly, before letting his lips linger against her temple.

"I am not afraid of you." While her words were sure, there was a new edge in her voice that told him there was something making her hesitate.

"What is it then?"

He almost did not want to know. While it seemed like a miracle that Naděžda loved him at all, there were still so many things that would keep them apart. He watched as Naděžda fidgeted with the collar of his shirt, and he mentally prepared for her list of possible objections.

He already knew them, of course. There was the issue of her mother; Amir inwardly groaned at the thought of telling Lady Penelope he wanted Naděžda for himself. She would not accept him. She saw him as an acquaintance, a necessary member of their small team of trusted people. He was breaching that trust in itself by confessing his love to Naděžda. There was no telling how much he would destroy the rest of that trust, should they act on their love.

And then there was the Order itself as well. Could they be together with the business of the Order between them? And what about a family?

Was it possible they could have children and raise them, with their lives' chosen work at risk? The Order did necessary work to keep the different corners of the world from warring with each other, even if it was distasteful and improper at times.

Amir felt his hope shrink as Naděžda finally met his eyes with hers again.

"Will I always be your only love, Amir?"

The question took him by surprise. "What are you talking about?" he asked. "There is no one but you."

"Truly?" She pressed her forehead against his. "I know things are different for us when it comes to matters like love and marriage, but I … I've never … "

For the first time in all the years he'd known her, Naděžda genuinely blushed, and Amir was touched to see it was not the small, flirtatious flush he'd seen on her cheeks many times as they interviewed informants or possible targets. Her face burned crimson all over, no longer full of shallow charm but something more than serious.

"I know that love and marriage is different in the East," she said, trying again. "I know you grew up where you can have up to four wives and any number of lovers, but—"

"You are the only one I want." He kissed her throat, enjoying how she shivered against him at the intimate caress. "You are the only one I've ever wanted, and you are the only one I will ever want. I promise."

"You do?"

"I do." He looked into her wide eyes, searching for any sign of uncertainty in her gaze, determined to scourge it from her heart and soothe any more of her silent fears. "And if anything, Eastern marriage is easier. All we have to do is sign a contract, one only between ourselves."

"No archbishop required?"

He smiled. "No."

Her eyes filled with sudden worry, and he wondered if she was thinking of her mother or the Order; she could have been wondering about the Islamic traditions of marriage, if any contract between them would hold up in the Catholic church. He reached up and cupped her chin, running his thumb over the softness of her cheek once more.

"I love you," he whispered. "Let me love you, Naděžda, as long as life allows me. Please."

THE ORDER OF THE CRYSTAL DAGGERS

"I've never loved anyone the way I love you." She hesitated for only the slightest half-second longer before she curled into his embrace, all tension gone. "I trust you, Amir."

Amir stared at her mouth, stricken. Her words were soft, laced with an intimacy he knew she had never shared with anyone else.

Later on, and multiple times, Amir would think about how he should have pushed her away—how he should have promised her the wedding he wanted to give her, how he should have done something besides sit there and embrace his doom with such self-destructive relish.

How they should have talked about leaving the Order.

How they should have talked about their future with a family.

How they should have done anything but choose to throw their fate into passion's perilous winds.

But before Amir could say or do anything else, Naděžda leaned over and kissed him again, moving her body against his, pushing back all barriers between them. Amir groaned as he felt the last of his restraint crumble inside of him; he could not stop himself from choosing her, even if it was reckless, even if it was all folly.

The last thing he heard himself say as he gave himself over to the darkness and light of her love was her name.

"Naděžda."

THE ORDER OF THE CRYSTAL DAGGERS

C. S. Johnson is an award-winning, genre-hopping author of several novels, including *The Starlight Chronicles* series, the *Once Upon a Princess* saga, and the *Divine Space Pirates* trilogy. With a gift for sarcasm and an apologetic heart, she currently lives in Atlanta with her family.

AUTHOR'S NOTE

Dear Reader,

As always, I am deeply indebted to the people who spend their time inside my work, and I think this story in particular is a sign of your dedication. For those of you who are reading this because of *Kingdom of Ash and Soot* or the other books from The Order of the Crystal Daggers, you likely know most of what happens to Amir and Nadĕžda—and all the others who get name-dropped and cameos in here—after this.

Amir and Nadĕžda's story is a tragic tale, one of so many boundaries and barricades that it is almost more painful to know that while they manage to overcome all of them, it is only for a short time.

Can there be beauty despite an unhappy ending? Or can the tragedy enhance the beauty found within the brokenness?

That's one of those tricky questions we can ask ourselves about life, and it's never an easy one to tackle. Can there be good that shines through the overwhelmingly bad?

While I was writing this novel, the idea that kept coming into my head was the story of Hudson Taylor. For those of you who know me so well, Taylor's story is a large part of the reason I became a Christian. At the young age of seven, I went to my Good News Club during the summer— which, lucky for me, was held in my own basement—and I heard Taylor's tale. He was a missionary in the 1800s who went to China to spread the gospel. Once he got there, he began to realize the people there did not understand him. So he let his skin grow dark, he dyed his hair, he learned the language of the Chinese, and he wore their clothes. He did everything he could to earn the people's trust and communicate the gospel.

I remember that day and that story so clearly. I remember thinking of all the things he did, and how Jesus did even more to find a way to communicate God's truth. Jesus came to this world wrapped in the flesh of a human, donning the lungs and eyes and heart of man, putting on hair— even armpit hair, and likely a beard—he learned to speak our language, he wore the clothes spun from wool and wore the sandals made by human hands. Taylor could have lived a far more comfortable life in Europe, and Jesus did not have to come down to this world from Heaven.

This, to me, at a young age of seven, was truly life-changing, and I remember asking Jesus to come and live in my heart that day. I even remember feeling the rush of wind inside of me as I did, and I distinctively remember this because I tried asking him a second time and nothing happened.

And now, more than two decades of backsliding and rededication and doubting and wrestling and learning later, I sit here, typing out the question that's most likely on your mind: What does this have to do with this story?

It turns out that there is much more to the story of Hudson Taylor, which I did not learn until nearly a year ago. Taylor was faithful as a missionary for many years, but at the end of his life, he fell into a deep depression, noting that he was even too depressed to pray. He died very quietly, and no one thought to highlight the very anti-climactic and somewhat depressing last days of his life.

Despite all the years of service and winning souls through his work, he still experienced depression's depths—depths I am more familiar with than I would like—and so great was his despair that he seemed to have given up.

Does this mean my own life is destined to end in despair, too? Am I wasting my life on something that is largely wind and shadow to this world?

Uncomfortable questions, for sure, and those are only followed by more.

Is there still redemption and hope for Hudson Taylor, in light of the great darkness he faced at the end? Is there some beauty for Amir and Naděžda, although they were tragically parted and their love was left largely unresolved?

I like to think so. And not just because I am a hopeless romantic, but also because I am a hopeful believer.

God might be the god of irony to me, the god of laughter and cunning, but I also see him as the Grand Storyteller, and I know from my own life story that he is able to redeem my darkest moments and use them to shed light on others' lives. Time and time again, I have seen the restoration, the reclamation that God does to his children's lives, and I am encouraged to think that where emptiness now lies, one day it will be overflowing with revealed beauty.

That does not mean those painful moments means permanent breaks, that those difficult situations become magically easy to bear. "Beauty" is not always synonymous with "happy," and perhaps that is the greatest discomfort we must face as humans fallen under time's power.

I am sure you will find similar questions and similar themes in my other work—such as in my novella, *The Princess and the Peacock*. There is a sample following this note, and I hope you will read on to see it.

It is always a beautiful thing for me, to see familiar readers looking forward to finding another piece of my heart.

Until We Meet Again,

C. S. Johnson

THE ORDER OF THE CRYSTAL DAGGERS

HEART

of

HOPE and FEAR

BOOK THREE OF *THE ORDER OF THE CRYSTAL DAGGERS*

◊   ◊   ◊   ◊

C. S. Johnson

THE ORDER OF THE CRYSTAL DAGGERS

Psalm 111:10, NIV

The fear of the Lord is the beginning of wisdom;
  all who follow his precepts have good understanding.

To him belongs eternal praise.

·

587

THE ORDER OF THE CRYSTAL DAGGERS

DEDICATION

This book is dedicated with much love to Sam, as always. I always wonder what you'll think if you read it, and then I am terrified that you actually will.

Second, this is for my own little prince and princess. You will not always be so little, but there will always be a crown in the kingdom of my heart just for you. I may write legends, but I gave birth to them, too.

Third, this is for Terri, who did everything short of holding me at gunpoint to make sure this book was finished, and Cathy, who dragged me through my points of depression and uncertainty as I made my way through the book. Without Cathy pulling me through and Terri pushing from behind, I wouldn't have made it, and I wouldn't have made it as well as I did.

Fourth, this is for Faith. In a world of princesses, you reign as queen, and I am honored to call you my friend.

Fifth, I live in a world of half-imagination and half-reality, but it is all wonder thanks to my family, friends, and fans. I owe so much to each person who has touched my life, and I am grateful for the chance to be a part of each of yours, even if it is only through the magic of a book—and the magic you sense, as such it is, is only a small pittance of the love and joy that lies beneath.

And finally, this book is also dedicated especially to my favorite friends and fans who made sure that I finished this book. The road has been very long and as cumbersome as tiresome, and I am eternally grateful for those who have given me their company and goodwill.

My (Almost) Famous Readers:

Bryn S.
Cathy H.
Jennifer S.
Laura P.
Krissy F.

Rebecca B.
Priscila P.
Malissa P.
Rebecca L.
Beth C.
Darla A.
Donna S.
David S.
David W.
Daniel S.
Terri R.
Tina M.
Christian S.
Jacob A.
Natalia K.
Jerilyn B.
Marty H.
Crystal M.
Ani S.
Marty H.
Jeremy R.
Mary S.
G. E.
Kara G.
Stephen D.
Jan K.

THE ORDER OF THE CRYSTAL DAGGERS

1

◊

"Eleanora."

Against the darkness of the lingering night, I heard my grandmother calling for me from the other side of my bedroom door.

It could've just as easily been the other side of the world, and I still would've heard her, I thought groggily.

Even though I had not known her long, I knew there was no ignoring Lady Penelope Ollerton-Wellesley—especially when she demanded my attention.

The shadows of her toes began to tap impatiently from the other side of the door. It was too easy to believe St. Peter would simply open the pearly gates at her command, rather than calling her into heaven himself.

"Eleanora, I know you're awake. This is no time to languish."

I frowned at her sharp tone. *Assuming she makes it into heaven.*

Frustrated, I shifted my weight onto my elbows and eased myself up from the softness of my mattress.

"What is it?" I flinched at the stark sound of my voice as it cut through the early morning air. I did not want to wake yet, but between Lady POW and the wintry chill, I knew there was little hope of finding sleep again.

"You have training this morning. And you are late." Lady Penelope's sour tone hardened, as if she sensed my resistance.

I stifled a groan. She only ever seemed pleased when I was miserable, and in the month since our meeting with Empress Maria Anna, the former ruler of the Austria-Hungarian Empire, pleasing her was more than impossible.

"I will be there in a few moments," I promised.

"See that you are. Also, I need you to tend to Lumiere. He's been drinking the absinthe again."

At the mention of the infuriating, incorrigible Frenchman who was currently our prisoner, I clenched my fists into the folds of my blankets. Lumiere had been drinking in excess since his arrival, and it was a miracle the rest of us hadn't followed suit. He regularly insisted that if he was stuck here, he'd make sure we were fully aware of it every cursed moment of our lives.

So far, I was the only one who had any success when it came to shaming him. Even Tulia could not stop him, and she'd never had any trouble getting anyone to heed her orders, even as a mute. Yet Lumiere only laughed at Tulia's silent chiding, calling her his favorite old crone and insisting her ugliness kept the devil at bay. Seeing Tulia so uncharacteristically helpless disturbed me far more than I wanted to admit.

Perhaps it was because Lumiere was more than a legitimate threat. Quite proudly, he'd admitted to orchestrating the attack on Tulia's house before the Advent Ball and organizing several other murders around Prague. He never repented of those transgressions, either; instead, he insisted everything he did was supposedly under the direction of his father, and he even assured me I would thank him if I knew the whole truth. But when I would ask what he meant, he only devolved into a fit of laughter.

Lady Penelope reprimanded me for paying any attention to him at all, and this made me even more upset.

How could I be anything but horrified at Lumiere's delighted confessions?

Tulia was severely burned because of his orders. Outside my family, others were dead, and the future of the kingdom was more uncertain than ever.

And after all that, why should I have to be the one bringing him to heel, as if he was a wild dog?

"I need you to hurry." Lady Penelope let out a long sigh, forcing me back to the moment at hand.

I unclenched my fists, letting the feeling come back into my fingertips. Lady Penelope could have sent anyone else to fetch me—Xiana, Amir, or Tulia, or one of her maidservants; if she had come for me, there was a good chance she hadn't been able to sleep herself.

As much as I suffered because of it, I could understand her restlessness. So much had happened after the *Salacia* had blown up in the harbor.

"All right," I replied carefully.

"Fine. Do not disappoint me, Eleanor."

I winced as she called me by my mother's name. Before I could correct her, Lady Penelope's shadow whirled around and disappeared down the

THE ORDER OF THE CRYSTAL DAGGERS

hall. As she turned down the corner, I could hear her skirts fluttering angrily.

"Thank you, Lord." I let out a quiet sigh of relief before slumping back onto my bed.

An arm reached out from the shadows beside me and curled me into a tight embrace. I smiled as the scent of lavender and mint flickered around me, hinting of musk and carrying the warmth of flesh.

"Why is she bothering us this early in the morning?" Ferdy's voice was muffled by his pillow.

"It's Lumiere. He needs to be subdued, apparently."

"I would've happily taken care of him for you, if I'd been allowed."

I grimaced at his dark tone, recalling how often in the last few weeks Ferdy had fought with Lumiere. "Lady POW told you to stay away from him if all you were going to do was argue."

"I'm happy to do more than argue." He shifted closer to me. "Besides, I don't take orders from your grandmother."

"Then think of it as a request from me." I patted his arm gently. "I don't like seeing you get hurt. Besides, Lumiere enjoys getting you into trouble. He doesn't deserve such happiness."

"What of my happiness?"

I leaned into him. "You must find it elsewhere for now."

"It's no wonder why I love you." Ferdy chuckled before his lips touched my shoulder. My skin tingled with the whisper of heightened awareness.

"You know I need to train this morning." My heart beat in warning and anticipation. "Our position with Lady Penelope is tenuous enough. For now, I'd rather you not risk her wrath."

"I wouldn't dare," Ferdy playfully assured me as he pressed another kiss on my neck.

"Ferdy." My voice was full of warning, but he was eager to ignore me.

"Come now, you already trained plenty last night." Ferdy drew me even closer to him. "Lady Penelope should appreciate enthusiastic *training* such as ours."

Even in the dark, I blushed. "Ferdy."

THE ORDER OF THE CRYSTAL DAGGERS

"Ah, *chérie*, you know I love hearing you say my name. Such a ploy is sure to make me spill all my secrets." His voice was still slightly slurred with sleep, but I knew he was stirring awake as his lips found mine.

His mouth was irresistibly warm. I twined my arms around his neck, moaning softly in momentary surrender. My lips were still swollen with his kisses from the night before, but the more I had of him, the more I wanted.

Ferdy, for his part, seemed to be in complete agreement. His one arm kept me pinned next to him, while his other held my head closer to his.

I giggled, reluctantly pulling away from him as the stubble of his beard tickled my neck. "Come, now. You know Lady Penelope is the leader of the Order, and I have to listen to her."

"You're my bride, and I'm your master now." As if to prove it, he rolled over and tugged me underneath him. The heat between the two of us crackled like lightning through the room, made more clear and certain as it met February's bristling chill.

"You might be the master, but she's still the spymaster." It was so hard to remain resolved. I let him kiss me a few more times before I slid out from under him.

"Now you're just torturing me."

"*Absolument.*" I freed myself from his grasp and rolled off the bed to grab my chemise. As I dressed for training with Harshad and Xiana, I could see Ferdy's cheeky smile in the dim morning light.

I climbed into a pair of breeches; I usually trained in my stealth habit, but with the colder weather of setting in, I opted for warmer clothes.

"You get such joy out of wounding me like this, Ella." Ferdy sat up and crossed his arms over his chest, watching me. He was clearly enjoying himself, even if he insisted on making everything harder. "Weren't you the one, just a few weeks ago, who tried to convince me that parting was such sweet sorrow, and then promptly fell into inconsolable despair after leaving me?"

Recalling the incident he was referring to, I almost smacked him.

"There is quite a difference in believing you're dead and knowing you're just a few corridors away," I retorted. Despite the flare of my temper, I was glad for his goading. There was no doubt Ferdy was infuriating at times, but that was all the more reason to make him suffer—and it would help me keep my promise to Lady Penelope. "Besides, you know this is important. I'm certain Lady POW would've shot Lumiere herself by now

THE ORDER OF THE CRYSTAL DAGGERS

if he wasn't our best lead on Lord Maximillian, and we need to find him if we're going to save Karl."

Ferdy groaned. "If there's one thing that will kill the mood, it's mentioning my wayward brother." He climbed out of bed, wrapping a sheet around himself. "But then, I suppose I have things to attend to, as well."

"What do you have to do?" I asked, genuinely curious. Ferdy was not a member of the League of Ungentlemanly Warfare, nor was he a member of the Order of the Crystal Daggers, as I was. He chose to remain at my side, even standing against his mother and Lady Penelope to do so, but he had no official orders.

"Oh, nothing much," he assured me, his tone too casual for comfort. "But if you must know, I've decided to use my time on a few special projects."

I frowned, suddenly suspicious. "What does that mean?"

"Just that if Clavan and Jarl don't see me at the Cabal every once in a while, they'll be concerned."

My cheeks filled with heat, recalling my more recent, embarrassing moments there. "Especially after I thought you were dead?"

"Especially now that I'm married," Ferdy said with a gentle chuckle.

I could almost smile back at him.

"Don't tell me Jarl is listening to your advice," I warned, thinking of our friends down at the publican house. "I won't let Faye suffer because of your antics."

"Never," Ferdy promised, once more making me suspicious with his quick appeasement. "Remember, Jarl happens to know his fiancée is not a spy or an assassin. Since that's the first rule for finding a bride, I'm willing to gamble he'll be fine in the end."

"We're *not* assassins," I murmured, knowing my objection was useless. Ferdy and I would likely never see things the same way; he observed the Order from the outside, while I was a member on the inside.

That was not all he was observing, either, I noticed, watching as his eyes followed the shadowy outline of my form as I dressed.

I pretended to ignore him, letting the next few moments pass in tense, mutual silence.

"You shouldn't worry about Karl." Ferdy finally spoke again, surprising me as he returned to our initial argument.

"Why not?" I asked, genuinely flustered. "The former empress told us Lord Maximillian's guest house had been abandoned, Karl hasn't contacted her, and even Harshad's informants haven't found a lead on their whereabouts. Aren't you worried?"

"Karl is resourceful, and if he's capable of threatening Lady Penelope, he's more than capable of taking care of himself," Ferdy pointed out. "Even if he's been kidnapped."

"If that's really what you think, then it's no wonder why I'm worried. You don't really care about him at all, do you?"

Ferdy scowled. "Of course I care, but he's stuck in a situation of his own doing. This is how justice works. Should I have endless amounts of compassion when it's better that he's gotten his comeuppance?"

"He's still your brother."

"Yes, but my brother is not your brother."

I stepped back, stricken at his words. Of all the recent shadows that had been cast over my father's manor, it was the distance I felt between myself and my older brother that haunted me the most.

"Ella." Ferdy softened at my sudden silence. "Karl's not Ben, and you shouldn't compare them in this case. Your brother is upset with me, but he hasn't tried to dislodge the kingdom from the empire or framed anyone for murder."

"I know," I murmured, still despondent even if Ferdy was right. Ben would always be a weakness of mine, and in more ways than one; it was hard for me to imagine hating my own brother. "But we're not sure what Lord Maximillian will do with Karl."

"What does it matter? It's unlikely he'll kill him. The worse that can happen is Karl will be held prisoner until his Tripartite Council convenes. And despite what Lumiere says, we all know excessive boredom isn't the same as death or torture."

"Ferdy! That's still not good enough," I objected. "Besides, what of your mother? She wants him back, and it's already been weeks. I don't want her to be even more upset with us."

"And so what if she is?" Ferdy shrugged. "There's nothing she can do, now that we're married. Even she's not able to nullify our vows."

I said nothing at his remark; instead, I began to pull my hair back.

While I was still irritated at Ferdy's flippancy regarding Karl's fate and his mother's distress, I was torn between my greatest joy and deepest pain.

It was still a miracle to me that in the past few weeks, Ferdy's cheeky grin and irreverent comments had become as necessary to me as his searing hot kisses and sincere moments of kindness. After everything we had been through, even though I did not deserve him, I could not stop myself from embracing him, especially when he made it clear he was determined to marry me.

And I truly was so happy we were married. I'd found a kind of freedom in our love, one that I never even imagined possible. It gave me security in the midst of adventure, and it was a place of arrival, as much as the milestone on the way to a greater destination.

Even if coming home from the castle as his bride had soured the already-salted wounds between me and my brother.

My fingers slipped; my hair tie fell to the floor as I stood there, remembering the look of angry shock on Ben's face when I told him the news.

"Let me help," Ferdy offered.

"I don't need your help," I snapped, my voice surprisingly harsh. "I just need to do what I am supposed to do and then everything will be fine."

The tense silence returned briefly, before Ferdy let out a sigh. "Do you know, Ella, that despite everything, I can't feel the smallest measure of remorse for the trouble we're in?"

I scowled, keeping my face hidden from his. "What Karl did isn't your fault."

"Well, that's certainly true, and you know I'd never take on the burden of guilt when it's not mine. But I'm here, just as you are." His voice was just shy of cheerful, but still deeply sincere. "Once we find Karl and appease my mother, I'll do whatever I can to make this up to you."

"It's not me you'll have to make amends with," I murmured, thinking of Lady POW's soured expression and recalling Ben's ire. Ferdy was not the only one who was wondering how to find a way to get his brother back, even if he was considerably less eager to do so.

"Anyway, Karl will be all right, Ella." Ferdy sat down on the bed again. "Lord Maximillian needs him to secure the Bohemian throne, so he'll be fine. And Karl deserves to be frightened for at least a few weeks."

"But—"

"But nothing," Ferdy insisted. "He kidnapped your grandmother to force you to marry him."

"Yes, but your mother—"

597

"No mother wants to see her child suffer, but no mother wants to believe he might deserve it, either." Ferdy frowned, and all trace of cheerfulness disappeared. In the morning shadows, he suddenly seemed so much older. "Karl's the reason Lumi hired assassins and attacked my friends."

"Oh, Ferdy." I sat down and draped my arm around his shoulder, pushing aside my anger as I sought to comfort him.

After the ballroom walls of Prague Castle had fallen, back when I first doubted Ferdy, I woke to find I was trapped in his room, and I was equally trapped in my doubt. I had left, torn between the love of my heart and the logic of my mind. That pain was only resolved when he earned my trust and I embraced my love for him.

But while we had a new life together, we still had the past to face. Now was not the time to distance myself from my greatest ally.

"I'm sorry." At my apology, crushing agony shot through me, and I tightened my grip on him. "I didn't mean to sound so upset. I'm just worried."

Ferdy drew my hand into his and kissed it, before holding it over his heart. In the dim lighting, I could see all of his usual mockery and irreverence was gone from his eyes.

"I'm sorry, too. I know how much you strive to honor and serve those you love, *chérie*, and I would do anything to keep you safe," Ferdy said.

"I feel the same for you," I whispered back.

"I know. But you don't have to fear my mother's disappointment—or your own mother's, either."

At the mention of my mother, my heart stilled, overwhelmed with a sudden mix of shame and despair.

"The promise she made to my mother was kept, remember?" Ferdy smiled at me. "You saved my life at the Advent Ball."

"Thank you." I pressed into him gratefully, as my heart began to beat regularly again. His assurance, even if it was misplaced, was more comforting than I could say.

"I love you, Ella." Ferdy pulled me into his arms. "That love has saved me more than once."

"It would have to; I can't bear to lose you." I trembled, recalling just how close I had come to that fate in recent weeks.

THE ORDER OF THE CRYSTAL DAGGERS

An overwhelming flood of love washed through me. The instinctive drive to comfort and protect was at once so primal and yet supernatural; I longed to offer him every ounce of goodness inside of me, all with the hope of pushing back against the pain he carried.

Before I knew it, we were falling back onto the bed behind us.

The second before passion consumed me, I sighed. "Lady POW is not going to like it if I'm late."

"Please don't leave me," Ferdy whispered, his voice desperate and his hands already seeking the warmth of my skin. "I'll write the apology letter for you myself."

"I suppose that's fair." My response was slightly muffled as his mouth covered mine.

2

◊

It was roughly an hour later when I finally headed for the west parlor. I was late for my training, but I had difficulty caring. My body was still tingling from my husband's touch, and I was amazed all over again that such marital joy was not only sanctioned by God, but encouraged.

A pair of servants rushed past me, careful not to call attention to themselves. I slowed my steps a little, thinking of how things had changed so drastically in such a short amount of time.

After the Advent Ball, Lumiere had captured my family's household, and then stationed them aboard the *Salacia*. They had served as working hostages during the holidays and the new year celebration. Now that they were back at the manor, they avoided me and the others under Lady Penelope. Even my friends, Betsy and Mavis, seemed unsure of whether or not to approach me.

At first, their distance felt strange, but after my hasty wedding, it was easier to accept; it was even a relief not to have to explain certain things.

And Ferdy was far from the only thing I did not want to explain; there were others I did not even want to think about.

Such as my mother's promise to Empress Maria Anna.

My steps slowed, thinking how Ferdy mentioned her promise.

From what I knew, *Máma* had come back to her childhood home of Bohemia in 1847 as unrest threatened King Ferdinand and Empress Maria Anna. She vowed to protect them and their family. Not long after that, my father saved the king when he was attacked by an unknown assailant.

My mother's promise to protect Ferdy's family was one I could wholeheartedly embrace—even if I was a little unnerved by it, as well.

That was one of the main reasons I stayed in the Order, despite my mother's wishes for a better life for me and Ben, and despite my own uncertainties.

And because Lady POW hasn't dismissed me for all my failures—yet.

Perhaps that was why *Máma's* promise bothered me so.

Such a promise was no easy undertaking, and thanks to Karl's disappearance, I'd already failed to keep it.

600

I slowed to a stop and leaned against the wall in the middle of the empty hallway. I put my head in my hands as I relived the most intense hours of our adventure—the ones I spent in Prague Castle, speaking with Ferdy's mother.

◊ ◊ ◊ ◊

"Ella."

Ferdy said my name quietly as he squeezed my hand, attempting to comfort me. But neither his encouragement, nor Lady Penelope's calm demeanor or Amir's presence, could give me any peace as we stood there, waiting.

We had just been escorted into a private throne room, similar to the one I'd seen the day of the Advent Ball. We were there to prove Lady POW was innocent of killing Ferdy—a relatively easy task, as he was standing next to me—but then we had to explain Karl's abduction and Lord Maximillian's treachery. Thanks to Harshad's contacts, we knew that they had been last seen heading east from the Vltava, but no other sign of either man had been confirmed in the hours since; we had nothing hopeful to offer the former rulers.

Finally, seemingly endless moments later, Empress Maria Anna came into the room and made her way to the throne. She was younger than Lady Penelope, but she seemed so much older, even since the Advent Ball. Her downcast eyes carried the weight of grief, and all her jewelry and ornate trimmings only seemed to add to her weariness.

She waved to the guards as she entered, a telltale sign that King Ferdinand, Ferdy's father, would not be joining us. Briefly, I wondered if he was feeling well. The former emperor had a history of physical ailments, and the events of the past few days were no doubt strenuous for him.

I tightened my grip on Ferdy, but with my other hand, I held onto the hilt of my mother's dagger, the one I carried as a member of the Order. It was hidden away between the layers of my skirts, and I was never more aware of it than when I needed to remind myself to be brave.

Máma told before me that my life could change in a moment, if I was brave enough to let it. As I stood there, I could only think of how life could change in the worst sort of ways.

Lady Penelope cleared her throat and scowled at me and Ferdy, before nodding toward our joined hands.

Quickly, I looked to Amir for guidance. He'd seen Lady Penelope in trouble before, and after all we had been through together, I could trust him to tell me if Lady Penelope was overreacting or not.

So I was surprised when he nodded curtly. I gave Amir a questioning look in return, and only when he indicated he would explain later did I acquiesce.

Ferdy frowned at me as I let him go, but before he could argue, Empress Maria Anna gasped.

"Ferdinand," she cried, realizing it was her son who stood before her.

Given Ferdy was dressed in one of Ben's older shirts and his right arm was bound up in bandages, I doubted I would've recognized him myself, especially if I was used to seeing him in his princely apparel.

"Mother." Ferdy stepped forward and opened his arms as he hurried up to her.

The former empress collapsed into him. Ferdy flinched as she brushed against his wound, yet he said nothing as her arms wrapped around him in a very ardent and tender manner. She spoke softly with him, and while I was not able to hear her words, a moment later Ferdy gestured toward me.

I felt the heat rise in my cheeks as Empress Maria Anna glowered at me. She signaled to the guards again, and they marched us forward. Ferdy took his place beside his mother as she gave us a chilly welcome.

"As you can see, Your Imperial Highness, I clearly did not murder your son," Lady Penelope said.

Empress Maria Anna's frown deepened, no doubt impugned by Lady Penelope's manners. But then, Lady POW had been imprisoned at Karl's insistence, and my grandmother had her own dignity to defend—even if she defended it poorly.

"You have my sincerest apologies, Lady Penelope," Empress Maria Anna said ruefully. "My oldest son has a rather large imagination at times, and it seems his rigorous education has only worked against me in this instance."

"That's certainly putting it mildly," Ferdy retorted, and his mother gave him a sharp, silencing glare.

THE ORDER OF THE CRYSTAL DAGGERS

"I must agree with your younger heir," Lady Penelope replied, taking another step forward. She unsheathed her dagger and held it before her as both part of her identity and her fealty. "Prince Karl's fevered imaginings of taking back the Bohemian throne have led to disaster several times in recent weeks, and it is time to put a stop to it."

She nodded toward Amir, who stepped up next to the queen and knelt as he held out a bundle of letters. I could not read the different scrawlings from where I stood, but I had a feeling the letter Lumiere had demanded of Lord Maximillian was among them.

As much as I did not trust Lumiere, there was no denying he made securing proof of treason much easier on us.

"It seems Prince Karl has been involved in several disruptive activities in the last several months," Lady Penelope said. "He is leading a political coup with the hope of overturning the emperor's authority and freeing Bohemia from the empire."

"That is not possible." Empress Maria Anna's brown eyes flooded with tears.

"I'm afraid it is," Lady Penelope said, her voice lacking any sympathy at all. "The Emperor is holding the Tripartite Council to discuss Bohemia's place in the empire, thanks to Karl's push for Bohemia's sovereignty."

The former empress shook her head in disbelief. "There is no isolating our country as we might have in the past. Karl knows this."

"Does he believe it, though? He is quite ambitious," I said.

"I am relieved to hear that you have made such a thorough study of my sons of late, Lady Eleanora." Ferdy's mother narrowed her eyes at me. "I must confess, given our last conversation, I was surprised to hear of your engagement to Karl through the papers."

My face burned with stinging heat. "I regret to inform you, Your Highness, that Karl made the arrangements with the papers. I did not agree to an engagement."

"Well, that's not entirely true," Ferdy interjected. "Ella has agreed to marry me."

His mother gasped. "What?"

Everyone turned to look at me, while I could only gape at Ferdy.

This is not the best time to discuss this.

THE ORDER OF THE CRYSTAL DAGGERS

I wanted to shout my silent words, but I wasn't capable of speaking at all.

"I love her, and she loves me," Ferdy said, ignoring my stunned look.

My heart began to race inside my chest. Each second of silence was more unbearable than the last. It was scandalous that Ferdy would love me at all, but the way in which he presented his claim on my heart was more than inappropriate—especially given that in the eyes of Society, Karl was the one who was rightfully engaged to me.

Ferdy cleared his throat. "We would like to speak with the archbishop while we are here."

"Today?" The former empress stared at him, still clearly stricken.

"Yes." Ferdy stepped down from beside the throne to stand beside me. He took my hand and brought it to his lips.

"Ferdinand … " Empress Maria Anna looked from Ferdy to me, and then back at her son. She seemed aghast, and I did not know what would calm her fears, if such a thing could be done at all. My own stomach was turning and twisting into tight knots.

"I have fallen deeply under her spell, Mother, and I would hate to fall even further into scandal and temptation," Ferdy continued, his eyes sparkling with mischief and amusement. "It would be such a stain on our family's virtuous history."

The former empress flushed as she turned back to me, and I was still too shocked to assure her Ferdy and I were not engaged in an affair.

But even if I did say anything, I worried Ferdy would only speak more about our stolen moments together, vaguely enough that everyone would assume the worst.

Some measure of relief came as Amir gave me a small smirk; it seemed he approved of Ferdy, and I was glad for that.

But as for Lady Penelope …

In that moment, I did not know what she was thinking, nor did I want to. I deliberately kept my face turned away from hers as Ferdy continued.

"It was only a few days ago that my life was endangered as I made my way back to Silesia," Ferdy said, so smoothly I did not even call him out on his lie. "Life is so fragile, Mother, and I have been waiting for Ella for so long."

THE ORDER OF THE CRYSTAL DAGGERS

He looked back up at his mother, resolved and proud but still pleading for her approval.

Ferdy had told me before that I was the more determined one between us, but as his fingers curled into mine, in a manner so seductive, yet so innocent, I wondered if he'd been lying.

Empress Maria Anna shook her head. "But your duty to the kingdom—"

"There is no better way to serve the kingdom, and show it my love, than by marrying Ella." Ferdy held steady as she looked down her nose at us, clearly skeptical.

Once more, I began to feel uncertain. I knew we would face some adversity if Ferdy and I remained together, but I never considered what he would have to give up for me.

I did not want to be the reason his family disowned him.

"What of your brother and his claim on her hand?" Empress Maria Anna asked.

"Karl is not here to object," Ferdy pointed out. "And considering his own villainous behavior of late, I know he would take Ella as his bride if he were in my position."

I tightened my grip on Ferdy's hand, sickened by the thought of Karl's manipulative behavior.

It would also be much easier for me to refuse.

Lady Penelope stepped forward. "If I may speak, Your Imperial Highness. I would prefer Eleanora to stay under my custody." She looked over at Ferdy with a slanted gaze. "The Order requires her service, and I would not want to interrupt any newlywed bliss, Prince Ferdinand."

Ferdy gave her a calculated, saccharine smile. "I assure you, Madame, you would only add to my joy. After all, I know how fond Ella is of you and the rest of your cohorts. And as for the Order, what better way to explain Karl and Ella's sudden disappearance from Society than an actual wedding?"

"What of your father's approval?" Lady Penelope argued. "Perhaps the question is better left to him."

"Excellent idea," Ferdy agreed. "As it happens, I have already secured his approval. I told him of my intent to marry Ella the night of the Advent Ball."

THE ORDER OF THE CRYSTAL DAGGERS

"That was before you knew about me and the Order," I whispered.

"Nothing has changed my feelings for you, Ella. Not even that." Ferdy looked back at his mother. "And just think, Mother. Soon, you could even be a grandmother—possibly even by the end of the year."

Empress Maria Anna's face went white, while Lady Penelope's sharp gaze traveled down my midsection, as if her squinting would allow her to see if there was indeed a baby already growing inside my womb. It dawned on me belatedly that the dress I was wearing, with its plain, simple fabric and unfashionable cut, was exactly the sort of dress I would wear if I was trying to hide a pregnancy.

The former empress' voice croaked with disbelief. "I suppose if it's too late ... to ... to prevent you from manifesting your affections, and your father has already given his blessing, I am unable to stop you."

"Are you saying you would, if you could?" I asked.

"I want only what is best for my sons." Her eyes frosted over. "This will hurt my Karl, even if it makes my Ferdinand happy. How can a mother willingly choose between her children?"

I swallowed hard, unable to think of a suitable answer.

That did not stop Ferdy, of course.

"That's simple. You can let them choose for themselves." Ferdy gave her a cheeky grin, but I frowned.

"Ferdy," I hissed.

"Oh, Ferdinand." Empress Maria Anna sighed. "At least I can take comfort that he has chosen you as his bride, Lady Eleanora. I trust your mother's promise to my family will remain intact?"

"My mother's promise? What promise?"

Empress Maria Anna frowned at me, more irritated at my ignorance. "She promised me when I was carrying Karl that her family would always protect mine."

"She did?" I blinked in surprise. There had been no hint of guile or deceit in the Empress' words as she spoke. I looked to Lady Penelope, whose expression was full of withering disdain.

The Order must not have sanctioned her promise, I realized.

"I'm surprised you've never heard the story," Empress Maria Anna said. "Before my husband abdicated, I found her promise somewhat naive, but then your father saved my husband from an assassin, and Lady Eleanor's promise proved useful."

Lady Penelope groaned. I did not have to glance behind me to know she was growing more agitated by the minute.

Still, hearing of my mother's promise of protection from the former empress made me feel proud, as though God in all his wisdom had woven these precious moments together, just for me. I took it as a sign that I was walking in the right footsteps afforded to my fate.

Empress Maria Anna cleared her throat. "If I give you my blessing, I want your oath that you will uphold her vow."

"You have it," I promised, smiling over at Ferdy. I already wanted to protect him.

He reached over and took both of my hands, a devoted look in his silver eyes.

"You will protect my family," Empress Maria Anna insisted. "And that would include Karl."

Ferdy squeezed his fingers around mine. "She already knows that," he said, failing to notice I had indeed forgotten about Karl in those few moments.

But I quickly nodded in agreement. If I worked with the Order to save Karl, keep Ferdy safe, and secure the kingdom, not only would I earn the Empress' approval, I would also honor my mother.

It was everything I could ever hope for, and everything I wanted.

"Yes, I will protect Karl, too," I vowed. "We will find him and return him to you."

"Then you can see he is adequately punished," Ferdy added, as his mother scowled at him again.

"Come here, Ferdinand," she said, beckoning him forward.

Ferdy let his hand linger around mine as long as possible before letting me go. The moment he began talking with his mother, Lady POW scooted over to speak with me.

"This is unacceptable, Eleanora," she hissed. "I didn't come here to discuss marriage."

"You didn't object to the thought of Ferdy wanting to marry me while we were on the *Salacia*," I reminded her.

"I'll humor ideas to get where we need to go, but this is ridiculous." She shook her head. "Should I remind you that you specifically told me you did not want to end up married before?"

"I did not want to be married as a bargaining chip." I did not want to argue with her, but I would fight for Ferdy. "And, well … I really do love him."

"There is no room for love in the life of a spy."

Off to the side, I saw Amir flinch. His pain strengthened my conviction.

"I will make room for it, then," I insisted, annoyed by Lady Penelope's stringency.

Why did Lady POW even have such rigid, unbending rules? There was nothing in her own life that seemed worth the price of giving up Ferdy. She had Harshad's contentious friendship, but she never allowed herself to love him more than the mission would let her; she'd supposedly trusted Amir, but at the first sign he had stepped out of line, she condemned him; and even now I knew my own mother had deserted the Order quickly enough after being freed from Lady Penelope's oversight.

"Eleanora." Lady Penelope's eyes were a chilly blue as we stared down at each other. "Are you to end up like your mother? Giving up the security of nations and the lives of others, all for your own selfish happiness?"

I gulped. It was almost as if she knew I was thinking of *Máma* in that moment.

"This would be her revenge against me, wouldn't it?" Lady POW's lips curled into a snarl. She glared over at Amir, who quickly looked away. "Perhaps you have gotten too close with your mother's former lover?"

"Amir is a good man, and he loved my mother very much."

"I'm not a fool, Eleanora. Even though she's been gone nearly fifteen years, I can see Amir still loves her," Lady Penelope murmured quietly. "But that is another reason why you should reconsider the younger prince's offer. There is no room for love in the life of a spy, because the instant you have it, you suddenly fear losing it. Can you imagine the pain you would feel if the younger prince were to die—especially if it was your fault?"

A thousand moments of terror hit me all at once; my heart leaped into my throat and I struggled to breathe, recalling how I'd felt when I thought Ferdy had been killed.

THE ORDER OF THE CRYSTAL DAGGERS

I couldn't lose him.

But I couldn't let him go, either.

Hadn't that exact truth been proven to me in the last several hours?

At my silence, Lady Penelope's frown deepened. "We can't be allowed the luxury of love; we can't be compromised by loss. So much depends on us. If you marry him, you will only put him—and others—in more danger."

I stood there, silently fuming, barely able to breathe. Lady POW was right, but she was also wrong—even if I couldn't exactly explain why.

Before I could say or do anything else, Ferdy kissed his mother's cheek, hurried back over to me, and grabbed my hand.

"Mother told me Archbishop Filak is in the *Hradčany*, over at *Katedrála svatého Víta*, St. Vitus," he said. "Come with me, Ella."

After only a second of hesitation, I nodded.

Barely ignoring Lady Penelope's red-faced fury, I bowed again to the Empress, who waved us off with a disappointed look on her face.

It was only when we were alone that I voiced my uncertainty.

"Are you sure about this, Ferdy?" I asked as he led me down through the myriad of palace hallways. "Your mother is not happy."

And neither is Lady Penelope.

"Mother's always been worried about me. And Karl, too." He paused for a moment. "It makes sense she would object to this, even if it would ensure my happiness. Karl and I weren't supposed to be born, you see."

There was nothing more antithetical to my world than that statement; Ferdy was supposed to be here, just as I was.

Of course, given my mother's history, it might have been that we were so well suited to each other precisely because neither of us would have existed had things happened differently.

"Because of your father's illnesses?" I asked, tentative but still curious.

"I shouldn't say anything, but you might as well know. My parents had an arranged marriage, like most royals. While they're friends now, my mother was very lonely early on in their marriage. She grew quite desperate for a child to love. But my father couldn't give her one. So she looked for a physician willing to help them conceive outside the accepted

practice," Ferdy explained. "The physician she eventually found was a
protégé of John Hunter and one of King George III's best surgeons."

"I can see why you're not supposed to say anything," I murmured,
thinking of the man who had championed artificial insemination in animal
husbandry. "The church doesn't look kindly on unnatural birthing methods."

"If they could look on them at all." Ferdy started laughing as I groaned.
"Come on, Ella. Those of us born into this world don't get to choose our
families, or how we are conceived. I certainly didn't choose to be born a
prince. But if there is any chance in this life for me to choose my princess,
then I choose you."

I knew at that moment I had no choice but to follow him through the
chapel doors.

Ferdy let me wait in the chapel's foyer as he set off to speak with the
chaplains.

The next several moments passed as I remained still, letting the enormity and gravity of the situation wrap itself around me. The majestic sanctuary was a source of both suffocation and comfort, and I was only truly
relieved when Amir quietly appeared at my side.

He stood with the practiced ease of a soldier, his feet positioned
straight and his arms held behind him. There was a tiredness anchored in
his deep brown irises. The previous night he had likely gotten only a little
sleep, if any at all, thanks to the work he had done in taking care of Ben
and the others.

I did not know what to say, if there was anything I could say at all, and
I was glad when Amir spoke first.

"Your beloved is right to do this."

"Do you really think so?" I asked.

"Yes." Amir's answer was quick and sure, forthright in its insistence,
but still gentle in its delivery. "If you truly love him, and you love him too
much to let him go, then don't step back from him now."

"I'm worried he will regret this," I admitted softly; I did not want even
the angels in the vespers to hear me. "He is really too good for me,
Amir."

"There is always a risk when it comes to commitment. But if you falter
now, Lady Penelope will not allow you to reconsider." Amir placed his
hands on my shoulders. "The former empress is not eager for the union,

either. If your beloved had not already received the blessing of the king, you would not be able to marry him tonight."

"I don't know about that. It seems Ferdy's mother is worried I'm carrying her grandchild."

"Lady Penelope would not see that as an issue." Amir shook his head. "Xiana told me a long time ago that there are herbs women can take to rid themselves of an unwanted babe; in fact, it's the Order's silver thallis that is used in one such mixture."

Lady Penelope's words, seemingly from a lifetime ago, echoed in my memory.

"The Order is sworn to serve the truth and protect the innocent. That includes our children. I would hate to have you live up to our family's reputation in this matter."

My eyes went wide. "My mother didn't do that, did she?"

Amir looked shocked at my question, and I immediately regretted saying anything.

"I'm sorry." I quickly stammered out my apologies, terrified I might have hurt him. "I'm sorry. I didn't mean to say that. I am so sorry, Amir … Amir?"

He stepped away from me and hid his face, much as he had when Lumiere had brought up Nassara during their scuffle.

I was terrified I'd hurt him, and then I was suddenly even more horrified I had stumbled upon the truth.

In the background, I could hear Ferdy, talking with a man who could only be Archbishop Filak, but my world was slipping away as Amir's silence dragged on.

"Eleanora." Amir's expression was grim as he finally spoke. "I apologize for my comments. I only wanted to let you know that if you want to marry your beloved, this is the only chance you will get."

I noticed he refrained from mentioning my mother, and I was more relieved than I felt comfortable admitting. I clung to his lead and focused on the question of my marriage.

"What about the Order?" I hesitated to ask, knowing Amir had painful memories of his own. "I wanted to be free before. Lady Penelope pointed out that this is the opposite of what I wanted. I can't help but feel she is right."

"Wanting to be free is not a sin in itself," Amir told me softly. "Only when that is everything and held to the highest priority is it so. We are loyal to the truth, Eleanora, but the truth is complicated, and freedom can be painful."

I couldn't stop myself from wondering if he was talking about my mother when he said that.

Still, I gave him a half-smile. "I suppose you'll tell me that good things are often painful, won't you?"

His eyes twinkled, and it was enough to give me hope. "Yes. But there is pleasure, too. Truth must stem from love, and love gives us freedom; and freedom leads to so much more." Amir looked around us, clearly marveling at the details enshrined in the church's design. He closed his eyes, as if to let the heavenly comfort surround him and embrace him. "Part of the pain, just as its pleasure, is found in freedom's limits."

"Harshad would approve of that," I said. "Paradoxes are not the same as contradictions."

"That is how life is." Amir's mustache twitched in tired, unspoken amusement. "If we truly want to be free, we must learn to govern ourselves and recognize outside influences that work against us. It is not enough to have the power to go and the choice to do so; we must step out in faith and hold onto the goodness we fight for—even if it means, on occasion, tempering that power."

I could not find any place where I disagreed with him.

"If you want to be with your beloved, you will benefit from having the full authority of the church behind you in marriage," Amir continued. "Had your mother and I had that, Lady Penelope might not have come between us."

It was not shock but curiosity that compelled me to ask the question burning inside of me. "Why would Lady Penelope do that?"

"Your mother and I were married according to the Islamic tradition when we … fell in love," he said. There was no shame in his gaze, but there was a distinct crimson shadow to his cheeks. "A *mutah* marriage does not carry the same weight as one from the Church of England or Catholic Rome. It is one that is easily dissolved."

"But you could have—"

"Please." Amir shook his head. "After all these years, I know every alternative path I could have taken. It is one thing to look back on it, and another thing to live through it. When Lady Penelope confronted us, and

THE ORDER OF THE CRYSTAL DAGGERS

then Naděžda lost our Nassara, and then everything else … I did not want to fight any longer."

"And that was when you stepped back from the Order?"

He nodded. "After … after the last time I saw her, Naděžda agreed to stay with the Order. For a few years, I went back to Constantinople and joined the military, still passing information to Harshad. The Ottomans hesitated to trust me, as a convert to Christianity, but they appreciated my skill as a doctor. I did not hear from Naděžda ever again. Lady Penelope informed me of her marriage to your father, citing her letters, and blamed me for Naděžda's decision to leave. I did my best to push aside her memory for good, but after I learned of Naděžda's passing, I returned to the Order."

"I'm sorry," I whispered, comforting him now. He'd carried so many secrets, and this was one burden we could share.

"Harshad was the one who told me," Amir said. "He was always Naděžda's champion. I went to investigate his claims. She died traveling across the North Sea. There is a small memorial at Rotterdam for the crew. It was constructed after Maas merchants discovered pieces of the wreck."

I clasped his hand in silent comfort.

"I carved her name in the gravestone there." Amir pulled back from me as he looked away, lost in his own memories. "You and Ben are not alone in seeing the Order as a way to connect with her."

Ben?

After all this time, it was strange to think of Ben missing *Máma* as I did, but I remembered how after she'd passed, *Táta* began neglecting him, and Lumiere had insisted rather callously that my mother initially stayed with my father only because she was pregnant with Ben.

Perhaps my father's assertation that I was proof of my mother's love was not so far off, after all.

Tears stung my eyes, and I was heartbroken for Ben. I cursed my own self-preoccupation, and my shame only grew as I watched Amir's face fill with years of lingering grief.

Neither of us seemed to notice Ferdy's irrepressible cheer and the foot-steps of an aged holy man until they were directly upon us.

"It is time, Eleanora." Amir cleared his throat. "You are free to make your choice, though your choice will bind you."

THE ORDER OF THE CRYSTAL DAGGERS

"Her choice has already been made," Ferdy said, giving me a quick kiss on the cheek.

"Ferdy." My cheeks grew warm at the quiet abandon of Ferdy's affection. Even if it pleased me, it contrasted sharply with the moment of mourning Amir and I had shared, and I was left disoriented from the sudden switch.

Still, I took Ferdy's arm and walked with him toward the front of the sanctuary, where Archbishop Filak was getting ready.

"Are you worried, Ella?" Ferdy brought my hand to his lips again. "You're trembling."

"After the scene you made in front of your mother, marrying you is the only way to prevent my own assassination." I straightened my shoulders, trying to compose myself. "Did you see her face when you insinuated we were having an affair?"

"Mother will be fine. She's more upset about Karl's villainy than my perceived lack of virtue."

"You promised me you wouldn't lie anymore," I reminded him.

"I said I wouldn't lie *to you*." Ferdy gave me a kind smirk. "But you have to admit, my mother wouldn't have believed you even if you'd denied any of our supposed liaisons."

"So, I should be thanking you for not ruining my reputation in the process of arranging a hasty wedding?" I raised my brow at the irony, but Ferdy only laughed.

"I would've bluntly insisted that I had thoroughly compromised you several times over if that meant I could've kept you."

"I'm glad it didn't come to that." I shuddered. "I think I would've been ill."

"Even better." Ferdy grinned. "It would have sold the illusion of a pregnancy, thus securing my success."

I nearly choked. "You are just awful."

"Awfully in love with you."

It was truly a work of art how Ferdy could make me wish to throttle him in one breath and then make me long for him in the next.

But he did not need to know that, I thought. I pulled back from him and crossed my arms instead, guarding the secret rush of pleasure I felt. "Enough to ruin my honor?"

THE ORDER OF THE CRYSTAL DAGGERS

"Enough to ruin it properly," he assured me. "I'll be happy to give you enough children to make even your grandmother blush."

"I know how to prevent that," I warned him, trying not to blush myself.

"Does this indeed mean that Eleanora is not pregnant?" Lady Penelope's voice seemed unusually loud within the large chapel. She had come up to us while I was distracted with Ferdy's abominable manners, and I nearly jumped at her question.

"I'm not," I insisted, forcing myself to meet her gaze without fear.

"Are you certain?" Lady Penelope studied my midsection carefully, before looking up at my face, searching for signs of deception as well as breeding. "I cannot be sure of your word in this matter, Eleanora, given your own tendencies toward secrets."

"A hereditary trait, I am sure, Madame," I bit back, trying not to let my anger override my good sense.

"Perhaps more than we would like," Lady POW agreed, and I flushed even more, thinking of my mother again.

"Excuse me," Ferdy interjected. "But I do believe it is time for us to be wed."

He'd wanted to keep me, and I would do everything I could to keep him safe. Surely, we would be able to find a way to face the danger before us.

He tugged on my hand, but I held back one last time.

"What is it?" he asked, his concern finally overriding his congeniality.

"Wait." I looked to Amir. "I need someone to give me away."

Amir nodded, giving me a sad, grateful look as I gripped his palm against my own.

I didn't know if *Táta* would approve or not, but I had a feeling my mother would. I was certain of this all the more as I watched Lady Penelope's lips wrinkle with displeasure.

Thankfully, she did not stop us. She remained quiet through the short, simple ceremony, like a demon banished just outside the bounds of holy joy.

But I forgot all about her soon enough.

Standing there, I pledged my heart and body to the man I loved, standing between him and the man my mother had loved. And as Ferdy kissed me, claiming his right to keep me, I felt the world shift around us.

It was a moment where the past, present, and future came together, baptizing me in its timelessness. It seemed that I could hear all of heaven applauding, led by my mother's cheering, as I grew into more of my true self in that moment—as I stepped into something that was both myself and greater than myself.

It was a new beginning, and all of the rest of my life was before me. I stepped back from Ferdy and saw him—truly saw him in that moment, recognizing him as my own. He looked at me the same way, as we were surrounded by an aura of contented surprise.

Ferdy reached forward as the archbishop kept praying, and drew me in for another kiss.

"Finally," he whispered against my lips. "Finally, I am yours, and you are mine."

"*Absolument*," I whispered back, unable to stop the rush of happy tears that suddenly clouded my vision.

3

◊

The gravity my wedding wielded over my thoughts was deep and seductive, much like the passion that resonated between me and my new husband. Our marriage was a shield around my heart, securing my joy in light of the future's uncertainty.

And there was plenty to be uncertain about.

I straightened my shoulders as I turned down the next corridor; if we were going to succeed in rescuing Karl, I had to take my duties to the Order seriously, no matter how mystifying and tempting Ferdy proved to be.

Despite myself, I smiled; I'd already failed at resisting him, and it was the one failure of mine I would enjoy repeating.

The clock struck a new hour just as I stepped inside the west parlor. I'd arrived late, as I'd anticipated, but still later than I'd intended. I prepared for the coming reprimand.

And it came as expected—but then, Lady POW was always more dependable than me in that respect.

"I was just wondering if I would have to come and drag you away from Ferdinand," Lady Penelope scoffed. She stood in front of the fireplace, looking like a divine judge full of sanctimonious power. The temptation to apologize was stronger than ever, and I only just managed to resist the impulse.

"There's no need, Madame," I murmured, refusing to let myself blush. "I'm here now."

"Married life has agreed with you." Her eyes darkened contemptuously. "You're much better about standing your ground, even when you're wrong."

"You are correct, even if you're displeased."

"I am displeased, and more so than you'd think. Since you neglected to rein in Lumiere as I requested, I had to take care of the matter myself."

I arched an eyebrow at her. "Never say Lumiere was too much for you to handle."

"I'm too much for anyone to handle, *chérie*."

617

I groaned at the sound of Lumiere's voice, unable to hide my disgust as I whirled around to face him.

He was lounging on a settee in the far corner of the room. The tired, bloodshot red of his eyes only sharpened their emerald brilliance, while his vibrant blonde hair was crimped stylishly. Much of his luxurious array of clothes and possessions had disappeared under the Vltava's waters, but he still dressed as finely as a prince—which, I supposed, given his own self-assigned title as the prince of secrets and shadows, was only appropriate.

It was then I caught sight of the iron bands around his wrists. They locked his hands together with a chain link between them, allowing only a shoulder's width of give.

"What did you say to Lady Penelope that condemned you to wear shackles?" I asked.

"Oh, these?" Lumiere chuckled. "They're mine. I wear them at my pleasure as much as for the pleasure of others."

"Unless Lady Penelope has the key, I doubt anyone is truly safe."

"We should be fine," Lady Penelope said. "He says he's willing to talk."

"He's always eager to do that." I wrinkled my nose. "Is he going to tell us anything useful?"

"Oh, *je n'ai sais quoi*." Lumiere playfully shrugged. "But after all the excruciating *ennui* I have faced, even my father would forgive me for divulging his secrets, and he never forgives anyone."

Lady Penelope crossed her arms over her chest. "As you can see, he's still somewhat drunk, but I think he's sober enough to know when to stop playing his games."

"Ah, but I do so enjoy my games," Lumiere replied with a soft hiccup. "There is a certain amount of pleasure to be had in drawing out these violent delights."

"I assure you, Lumiere, much like your father, you give no pleasure," Lady Penelope retorted.

"There is often more pleasure in pain than pleasure itself." He stretched, putting his shackled hands behind his head. "As you will no doubt find out when the baby comes, Ella."

"What?" My face filled with heat as Lady POW immediately turned to stare at my midsection.

THE ORDER OF THE CRYSTAL DAGGERS

"There's no reason to be concerned about that," I objected vehemently, even as I hurried to calculate when my most recent monthly course began. Once I was certain Ferdy and I had been careful enough, my anger at Lumiere intensified. "Why would you say such a thing?"

"And why would I *not* say such a thing, Madame?"

I clenched my fists. "Propriety, for one."

"Propriety be damned. One does what one can, after all, *n'est-ce pas?*"

He gave me a wink, and I wrinkled my nose, quickly rejecting his charm and good humor.

"It's 'one does what one *must*,' not 'one does what one *can*,'" I snapped, infuriated by his presumptuous behavior.

"Eleanora is correct," Lady Penelope said. "Liberty is not the same as license."

"Yes, but there's also 'duty until death or defeat,' isn't there, Pepé?" Lumiere rolled his eyes and scoffed, clearly slighted by our joint rejection. "Those in power are quick to determine which rules are too sacred to be broken."

"You have enough power if you're able to break them," I started to point out, but Lady Penelope stepped between us.

"I will give you one last warning, Lumiere. If you want to experience any sort of pleasure ever again, we will see to business first, once Harshad arrives," Lady Penelope said.

I didn't know why Lady POW thought he was drunk, even if he had been drinking absinthe in excess of late. As I stared at him, I could only see how his mood was too calculating and mocking; it was more like he was pretending to be drunk, rather than actually intoxicated.

He is indeed playing his games, as he openly admitted.

"Where is Harshad?" I looked around and noticed for the first time that he was not with us.

"He is gathering his reports," Lady Penelope informed me. "He's eager to go through the available information we have. Especially given that *someone* here hasn't been as useful as we'd like."

She narrowed her eyes over at Lumiere, who only yawned dramatically.

"You always were too serious for me, Pepé. I had so hoped age would soften you, yet experience has only hardened you." Lumiere cocked an eyebrow at her. "Is there no room for nuance and fun in your life?"

Lady Penelope said nothing; her scowl only deepened.

"My father is the same, you know. If you ask me, that is largely why you never did get along with him. You are too much alike." Lumiere let out a soft chuckle. "Jakub often wondered if you harbored a *tendre* for him."

"Me? A *tendre* for Louis Valoris? Ha!" Lady Penelope let out a scraggly cough. "The very idea is beyond revolting."

While I had not yet met Lumiere's father, I easily agreed with Lady POW.

Louis Valoris was the current leader of the League of Ungentlemanly Warfare, a title that once belonged to my maternal grandfather. He had used his connections to bring Lord Maximillian and Karl together, and then assisted them with their *coup d'état*. Several lives had been lost at his direction, including Ferdy's friends, a few politicians, and my father's old physician, Dr. Artha.

When I pictured Louis inside my mind, I could only see a stark, devilish face stretched over a thin mask of flesh, his eyes glowing red with blood and fire—his monstrous visage matched only by the ugliness of his twisted soul. Anyone who could willingly unleash such chaos without concern for human life had to be grotesquely appalling.

"What foolishness." Lady Penelope shook her head at Lumiere. "Your father taught you well, I see; you certainly know how to distract the enemy."

"Perhaps you are just easily distracted, Madame." Lumiere smiled back. "But you should pay better attention, as things are only going to get worse. It's been getting worse since Constantinople."

Lady Penelope's fingers twitched, almost as if she wanted to strangle Lumiere—which she probably did, in all fairness. "We do not discuss that mission."

"Why not? It was because of Constantinople that Jakub sought reconciliation with you. He even admitted he'd been wrong about my father after the Spring Revolution," Lumiere said.

Lady Penelope scowled. "Jakub knew it was too late to reconcile with me, long before the Revolution began."

"But one would think you would enjoy such a memory. You have so few happy ones."

As much as I found him beyond abhorrent, I had to admire Lumiere's tenacity; seeing Lady Penelope's bitter expression, I knew Lumiere was gambling with his life as he kept talking. But I was also grateful for him, since then I wouldn't have to ask as many questions later.

Jakub Cerný, my mother's father, had partnered with Lady Penelope and the Order before my mother was born. Along with Louis, they had been close friends and trusted allies—until Louis turned Jakub against her, and she'd fled to London when my mother was just a child. Once there, Lady Penelope married Arthur Wellesley, the Duke of Wellington.

I paused, thinking of my own married bliss, and I felt a surprise pang of sympathy for Lady POW. It was unfortunate her marriage hadn't lasted.

"I suppose that's old history anyway, and history is boring, except where I'm involved." Lumiere laughed. "Still, everyone has regrets, *non*? And it's hardly pleasant to think of them, even if you can learn from them now, Pepé."

"You can think on your own regrets later, Lumiere," Lady Penelope warned. "If you want me to learn something so badly, why don't you tell us where Max is keeping Karl?"

"Yes," I agreed. "Tell us what you know."

"I can't tell you exactly where he is. That is my official position, and it's one I've maintained since you locked me up here like an exotic bird." Lumiere ran his hand through his hair in an impertinent, graceful manner. The elegance of the movement was disrupted by his manacles, but his grin only widened. "And for the sake of your precious propriety, I dare not even hint at my unofficial positions."

"You have contingencies," Lady Penelope pressed, ignoring his banter. "I know you do."

"I doubt Amir has said anything to you about my contingencies, Madame."

"Amir?" I blinked, more intrigued than I wanted to admit.

"Of course. Did he not tell you the story of how we met?" Lumiere clapped playfully before I could answer him. "How I envy you, as you're in for a treat. I have other plans, but I must say, given what I've done for Amir, I'm disappointed he didn't rescue me this time. I'd been so hoping to spend more time with him."

I was torn between insisting that Amir would never help him and assuring Lumiere that any past goodwill he might've accumulated was gone. But before I could speak, a new voice spoke up from the back of the room.

"Amir does not owe you anything."

I whirled around to see Xiana standing against the back wall. She wore a long tunic, and there was a small sword, carefully sheathed on her back, and her ebony hair was impeccably braided. I had not heard her arrive, but I was not surprised by that; Xiana was a longtime pupil of Harshad's, and one of the best.

As she stood there, her sunstone eyes gleamed with cold fire, sending an involuntary shudder down my spine.

"My apologies, fair lady." Lumiere's voice purred with cruel pleasure. "I hadn't realized you joined us."

"You should stay away from Amir." Xiana ignored his mocking gallantry and lowered her eyes, seeming to regret the attention she'd called to herself. In the weeks since my training began, she only enjoyed speaking with Harshad and Lady POW, and Amir, if he was around. Even at Lumiere's provocation, I was surprised she had spoken at all. "It is prudent Lady Penelope is keeping him from you."

"Well, we all know how you feel about Her Ladyship's commands." Lumiere smirked. "You'd think she was at the right hand of God the way you listen to her. After all, you were always trying so hard to be just like Nadĕžda, *n'est-ce pas*? And you succeeded, too. Except in all the ways that actually count, of course."

Xiana's hand reached up and flexed around the hilt of her sword, but Lumiere was again right in his observations. Xiana had her *jian*, her sword, but despite her tutelage under Harshad in the past, she was not granted the same privilege as me and my mother—she did not carry a dagger of the Order.

I saw Xiana's eyes narrow at me briefly, as if she had read my thoughts, and I hurriedly looked away.

"Now that I am here, you know there is danger in acting like the clown you wish you were, Lumiere." Xiana whipped her sword out of its sheath; the firelight reflected off the double-edged blade, gleaming with deadly power. "It would be best if you simply answered the questions."

"Yes. We've had enough," I said, stepping between them. "Tell us what you know about Karl."

"Please," Lumiere scoffed. "It's not hard to see Karl was a fool."

"Was?" My eyes went wide, and I felt my heart pound in my chest. Panic strangled me, paralyzing me momentarily with despair and hopelessness. "Karl is dead?"

"Oh, calm down. I didn't mean that." Lumiere rolled his eyes. "Why would Max bother going through all that trouble to find him, and then just kill him?"

"I can think of a good reason," Lady Penelope offered. "Lord Maximillian, as a cousin to Emperor Franz Joseph, could more easily claim he deserves the Bohemian throne without Karl around."

"If that was his plan, he must be incredibly foolish—or truly a madman."

"It's been said that it takes a thief to catch a thief." I glared at him accusingly. "Perhaps it takes a madman to catch a madman."

"*Tsk, tsk*, Ella," Lumiere tutted. "All thieves are alike, because they are all unhappy in their envy. But there's no end to the diversity of madmen. Some revel in it, while others despair, and still others seek to remedy themselves by making others miserable."

"I guess we know which one you are."

"Of course. I'm not one at all." Lumiere smirked. "But I do like to pretend so. It's a great thing to be underestimated."

"You might not be a madman, Lumiere, but you know of Max's plans. Otherwise, you wouldn't have murdered so many people like Dr. Artha," Lady Penelope said as she crossed her arms. "You do not engage in murder blindly, especially when the victims are your known allies."

He shrugged. "Perhaps I am getting sloppy and indifferent in my old age."

"Perhaps. You are over forty now, and your best years are most certainly behind you," Lady Penelope retorted.

Lumiere dropped all pretense of charm as he glared at her. "You would certainly be the one to know that, Madame."

"Wait, I don't understand," I said. "Why did you kill Dr. Artha, and Father Novak, too? They were your informants." I thought back to the letter we'd found in the Church of Our Lady of the Snows, the one the dead priest had tucked away inside his Bible.

"Killing Father Novak was easy; despite his uses, we have a bit of a painful history, but that's a story I'll spare you, Ella. Holy men can still have their faults, and I am happy to give such men the divine justice they deserve," Lumiere said, his words laced with acrimony. "But Dr. Artha was just a bit harder to kill. He and my father were longtime allies. And, of course, Tulia was quite upset with me over his death."

I closed my eyes, picturing Dr. Artha at my father's funeral as he rushed to help King Ferdinand through a seizure. Lumiere's father was not the only one who'd had a history with him, I thought. He'd been the one to declare my father dead.

Lumiere's sigh cut through my memories. "But believe me, it was an act of kindness for me to take care of him now, especially if Max and my father get their way. Dr. Artha was loyal to the Emperor, and he would not want to see the empire fall into war and chaos."

My fingers curled into fists. "Why you—"

"I see," Lady Penelope swiftly interrupted me. "So, Louis is bringing war to the Austria-Hungarian Empire, is he?"

I blinked, and then I realized more fully what Lumiere said, instead of just his callous disregard for human life. From the look on his face, he was not displeased by Lady POW's conclusion, and I was suddenly even more disgusted than before.

"War?" I repeated. "I thought Louis was the head of the League. Queen Victoria wanted peace in this part of the continent, not war."

"The Queen would not want war, but Louis wouldn't mind it." Lady Penelope sighed. "He has a history of causing chaos, and he's serious if he is murdering those he once considered loyal."

"People can only be so loyal, and war has been looming for years now. My father is only setting up the right conditions which will benefit him the most."

"Oh, Lumiere." I shook my head; I wasn't even sure why I felt disappointed in him.

"Oh, Ella, don't be foolish. It's a miracle that man is capable of mercy, not that he is able to kill," Lumiere insisted. "Remember, I could've killed Tulia before, too. But I spared her, and she knows she's lucky I did."

"You mean *you're* lucky you spared her," I muttered darkly, reaching for the dagger at my side.

"But are *you* lucky I did?" Lumiere arched his brow at me. "Perhaps you'll wish I'd killed her at some point."

"I would never!"

"We'll see." Lumiere shrugged. "My father would've killed her if he thought it more efficient to do so. He is not as forgiving as I am—and I know this well, being the one person he will never forgive—but I suppose that's another story, and one more appropriate for a confessional."

624

THE ORDER OF THE CRYSTAL DAGGERS

"Lumiere." Lady Penelope's voice was full of warning, and I was secretly relieved she took control of the conversation once more. "What does Louis' war have to do with Karl?"

"*C'est facile.*" Lumiere relaxed into the settee cushions, resuming his aura of merriment. "Like all the Hapsburgs, Karl suffers from impairments too great to be listed in polite company. He believes himself to be the true ruler of Bohemia, and he'll welcome war if it means he gets a crown in the end. He's a useful idiot, and he'll remain one."

My fists balled up in anger. Lumiere wasn't wrong, but still, I hated how his eyes lit up with joyful sadism as he sat there, amused at the thought of widespread destruction and death.

"I see. Karl is a front for Louis to start a war in Bohemia," Lady Penelope surmised. "What's in it for him?"

"I've already told you, Pepé. War is for the poor to suffer through and maybe even survive. But for the rich? We not only thrive, but we get richer, especially if we know how to place our bets." Lumiere smiled at me. "And I'm willing to bet Karl's death, should it be warranted, will be a grand spectacle."

"What? Why?" I asked angrily, barely able to speak. "Why would Karl have to die?"

"I didn't say he would, just that if he does, it's nothing personal. Well, perhaps a little personal. Death has to be, you know. But that's just the business of men like my father, Ella." Lumiere sneered angrily. "They get rich by promising to solve problems, and they stay in business by creating more problems to solve. We're almost fortunate for the excessive bureaucracy in our governments, or we'd be taken over by mobs every other month."

"That's terrible," I whispered.

"That's politics, *chérie*, and there is nothing good about remaining an innocent when the world will only make you pay more dearly for your ignorance."

The more Lumiere spoke, the more anger stirred inside of me. I looked over at Lady Penelope for help, but she only began pacing in front of the fire.

"Louis will profit off the chaos," she said. "The more chaos there is, the more profit he'll get. It won't even matter if Karl or Lord Maximillian rules Bohemia in the end. He will have his contingencies, too. Correct, Lumiere?"

"*Oui, oui*, Madame," Lumiere said. "*Mon père* is getting older, but he is still excited to play a new game with you, and I can see why. You know him so well."

"He would enjoy risking the future of an entire nation to prove himself against me," Lady Penelope muttered bitterly.

My fingers went numb as I gripped the hilt of my mother's dagger. Louis would willingly bring war to my country, and sacrifice Karl to get it—and all for what? Money? Chaos? Power? The thrill of facing off with my grandmother?

"We will defeat him," I declared.

"He will enjoy watching you try." Lumiere smiled. "As will I."

"Assuming you survive. Such violent delights have violent ends, as you've already noted." Lady Penelope stopped pacing. "Well then, it seems right now, the quickest way to stop Louis is to find Karl. Since Eleanora has already promised to return him to his mother, our goal has not changed."

I was enormously gratified that Lady Penelope was happier about my promise, even if it was only to stop Louis. Still, it gave me hope like nothing else to see her approve of me and my decisions.

"But our search has become more urgent," Lady Penelope continued wearily. "If we can find Karl, Louis will have a harder time starting his war."

"But what else can we do?" I asked. "We've already been looking for Karl for almost two months now. The former empress has no lead on him, and neither do any of Harshad's contacts."

"Oh, I'm sure you'll find him soon, Ella. Destiny practically demands it. Pride deserves one hell of a fall, and if anyone should get one, it's that little princeling." Lumiere cheerfully grinned, his eyes shining over with absurd delight. "I happen to like his younger brother much better, don't you?"

A protective flare lit up inside me. "Forget about Ferdy, Lumiere. I don't want you near him ever again."

"Oh, don't be such a nagging fishwife. Let him have a little fun. He and I are friends, you know."

"*Were* friends," I corrected. "After your henchmen killed his traveling party, you should consider yourself fortunate to be alive."

THE ORDER OF THE CRYSTAL DAGGERS

"As he's mentioned to me, several times," Lumiere said. "Still, we'll be fine in the end. He's someone who can handle the full truth, even if he doesn't like it."

I scowled. "What are you talking about now?"

"I'm talking about how some lives must be lost in order to save others. Ferdy would agree with me, and Tulia does, too, for that matter. After all, she certainly didn't try to stop me when I showed up at your house, and she also didn't mind taking care of your father, did she, Ella?"

"What?" I crossed my arms defiantly. "What about my father—"

"Eleanora." Lady Penelope scowled. "You're letting him distract you."

She was right, but I wanted to object regardless. What did Lumiere know about Tulia and my father?

He doesn't mean that … that Tulia actually killed Táta, *does he?*

The door suddenly opened, and Harshad appeared with a bundle of papers in his hand. He made his pleasantries and apologies before Lady Penelope began to speak with him in muttered tones, no doubt catching him up on what we'd learned from Lumiere's supposedly drunken revelations.

There was nothing I could do but glare down at Lumiere as he contentedly relaxed back into the cushions. I was about to ask him my questions when he sighed and turned to me with remorse in his large, tired eyes.

"I should apologize for teasing you, *chérie*."

I rolled my eyes. "You should, but you won't."

"You must have patience. It is not yet the right time for me to reveal anything."

"And just when is the right time, Lumiere?" I grumbled softly. "It never seems to come for you."

"You see, you have to *find* it." Lumiere pulled out his pocket watch and held it out to me. "Perhaps you'd like to take a look?"

I frowned at him, but as the fire winked off the golden watch, I was taken aback.

At second glance, I saw the elegant design, with its pierced gold carved with a *fleur-de-lis* on the cover—in a very familiar pattern.

It's the same design as the one on my father's watch.

The full force of my realization struck me again as I looked over to see Lumiere. All pretension and playfulness were gone from his face.

627

THE ORDER OF THE CRYSTAL DAGGERS

"You look so much like your mother," Lumiere told me softly. "But I'd rather hoped you would remember that you are your father's daughter, too. Especially since my father is eager to start another war with your family."

*4

◊

"What are … why?" As I stared at Lumiere, my lips struggled to form the right question. There were so many I wanted to ask, and each one seemed more impossible to voice than the last.

"Find the right time, Ella." He plucked the watch from my hand and pocketed it before he gave me another smirk. "If you can."

I could only frown at him, unsure of anything in that moment.

Was he lying?

Was he joking?

Was he … telling the truth?

Maybe Lumiere was legitimately trying to befriend me, but I never wanted to examine that as a real possibility; the thought was as repulsive as the man himself.

I was still reeling from Lumiere's sincerity when Lady Penelope let out a loud curse.

"*Merde!*"

I turned around just in time to see her face scrunch up with displeasure. She began yelling at Harshad, speaking in an unfamiliar language, but I didn't have to know exactly what she was saying to know she was upset.

Harshad's ochre cheeks were wan and weathered, the paleness drawing out the liver spots and leathery pockmarks on his face. His condition could've been due to the weather, but I was certain the past several weeks had strained him as much as everyone else.

Perhaps even more than the others, I thought, studying the deeply furrowed, frustrated lines in his brow.

"What is the news, Harshad?" I asked, as Lady Penelope stormed back toward the mantle, furious and frustrated. "Has something happened with Karl?"

"No. But I am afraid our mission has become more complicated." Harshad walked back to the small writing desk at the back of the room and sat down. "The Prussians have captured Napoleon III just as the French government is preparing for war against the German Confederacy."

629

I bit down on my lip. "That doesn't sound good." I was not very well versed in international conflict, but even I knew war was never good news.

"It is not, no." He shuffled his notes as Lady Penelope let out an indignant huff.

"Of course it's not," she said. "It means Lumiere isn't lying to us. For once."

"For once," Lumiere conceded with a disingenuous giggle.

"There is more," Harshad said. "The Emperor has appointed a new Minister-President. Count Potocki has been retired earlier than he'd expected."

"Yes, yes, I've already heard from him." Lady Penelope waved her hand dismissively. "The Count believes his association with me has caused his dismissal, especially after your outrageous affair and elopement, Eleanora. He's even rescinded my invitation to his wife's ball this weekend because of all the rumors."

"It's not like you were going to go." Discreetly, I rolled my eyes, embittered by her blame and irritated at the mention of the rumors.

Ever since Karl's disappearance, and subsequently mine, whispers raged throughout Prague. There were any number of people prattling on how Karl and I were touring the ruins in Rome, attending the Opera in Paris, and strolling through Hyde Park in London. Lady Penelope had only fueled them by turning away all visitors, insisting she had taken to her bed in the throes of "irredeemable scandal."

In a very small, petty way, I imagined this was her way of punishing Ferdy for marrying me. While I doubted Ferdy was truly bothered by the rumors, it was still a callous move. When I confronted Lady Penelope about it, she only said I ought to be grateful Karl wasn't parading around with Lady Teresa Marie, before explaining to me how the rumors allowed us to work freely in the shadows. That gave us an important advantage, even if it kept us from walking out in the open.

Reluctantly, I'd decided to trust her judgment.

For now.

"If Count Potocki has been dismissed, is Karl the new Minister-President?" I asked. "The night of our so-called engagement, he announced his intent to secure the position."

THE ORDER OF THE CRYSTAL DAGGERS

Harshad shook his head. "No. The Emperor has appointed Lord Hohenwart."

I was only a little familiar with Lord Hohenwart; his wife was more memorable, with her plump figure, her voluminous gowns, and her pleasant if persistent chitter-chatter. It had been at their ball that I had been formally introduced to Prague's Society—and to Karl, too.

"That's good news," Lady Penelope said approvingly. "Hohenwart has a history of compromise. With France and Germany engaging in warfare, his appointment will help stabilize the region, even if the Emperor agreed to call for the Tripartite Council."

"With Karl missing and Count Potocki replaced, why is the Emperor still holding the council?" I asked. "There's no need to decide whether or not Bohemia should be its own kingdom now. And what about Louis?"

"The Emperor agreed to the council so he could appear to be a fair ruler, one concerned for his people. But with Hohenwart's appointment, he's shifted the players so he controls the outcome," Lady Penelope explained. "He's bought himself some time, too, no doubt in hope Karl's movement will fade out on its own."

"With Karl's disappearance, it is likely that will happen," Harshad agreed.

"Or another problem will rise to take precedence." Lady Penelope sighed. "Either way, it's political theater for the masses."

"Oh." I didn't know if I liked Franz Joseph more or less after hearing that.

"The Council is scheduled for early spring, although it's likely to be held off until September," Lady Penelope added. "Count Potocki commissioned Roman Szapira to renovate his manor before then, and he's upset that he's paying him for nothing now."

"Oh, what a shame!" Lumiere cried out, clearly enjoying himself. "A man's pride is one thing, and his job another, but his home décor? Surely that is too much to ask of him."

As Lady POW and Harshad reined in Lumiere, I could only think of Karl.

Karl will be upset Lord Hohenwart is the new Minister-President.

I clasped my hands together with grateful resolve. We would still have to save him to stop Louis, but Karl's moment to gain power had passed—

THE ORDER OF THE CRYSTAL DAGGERS

and he'd failed. With the real power behind the council stripped away, Karl's own quest for power was over.

Good.

Karl spoke to our countrymen with high platitudes, but when he was with me, he callously dismissed human life and dignity. He'd been willing to kill Ferdy to secure my hand in marriage, and he was working with Lord Maximillian and Louis Valoris to gain the Bohemian throne, even if it meant war.

He wanted to be a ruler, not a leader, and any power he would've been given would have only made others more miserable.

"The news of Hohenwart's advancement will gratify Queen Victoria." Harshad folded his hands together on top of his pile of papers. "But I still have my concerns."

"Of course, and you should. After all, there is war and rumors of war, and Karl is still missing," Lumiere said. "And then, worst of all, I have been captured by Pepé, the great enemy of *mon père*, and I am now being tortured with unrelenting disdain while I only give you information."

Lady Penelope's eyes narrowed. "Is this another game for you, Lumiere?"

"Game?" Lumiere's voice was painfully insincere. "Whatever could you mean?"

"I have been wondering why you came to Prague at all. If you had stayed away and out of sight, it was always possible we wouldn't have discovered the League's rogue members and Louis's involvement."

"I do enjoy coming—and going, too," Lumiere said with a large grin.

"I see." Lady Penelope sighed. "So, you wanted this."

"Wanted what?" I asked, confused.

"He wanted us to capture him." Lady Penelope's eyes scorched into Lumiere, and he blinked at her innocently for a long moment.

And then his lips curved into a sinister smirk, before he fell into another fit of laughter.

"Well, I guess you caught me. You're right; I'm here largely of my own choosing. And I can leave whenever I want, too."

"Is that something we should worry about?" Lady Penelope arched her brow at him skeptically.

632

"Why would you worry? Jakub always insisted Adolf's taste in books was only rivaled by his collection of alcohol. So long as I have both, I imagine I'll be content to stay," Lumiere said. "You must admit, it was an ingenious move, to use your manor as an inn."

"And all at my own insistence," Lady Penelope grumbled.

"And your own expense, too. But don't worry, Ella." Lumiere smiled again as he turned back to me. "As long as I am entertained or drunk, it's doubtful I'll try to leave. Of course, you never know when I might feel the full weight of conviction of the Holy Ghost and run for the closest monastery."

"I should've known Louis would send you here to cause me trouble," Lady Penelope grumbled.

"I'll have you know, *I* decided to let you capture me. My father will be horrified to learn what happened. Perhaps it will hurry him along," Lumiere said. "You know, not all trouble is bad for you, Pepé. Naděžda would agree with me, as would Amir."

It seemed I only blinked, and Xiana lunged across the room, grabbed Lumiere, and hauled him up out of his seat by his belt.

Lumiere looked down with rare, authentic shock, as Xiana thrust him against the wall; less than a second later, her blade swung out in a perfect arc before pressing against his throat.

Everyone went perfectly still.

Lumiere did not even breathe. I gasped as the air rushed out of my lungs as the smallest line of blood trickled down the length of Xiana's sword.

Lumiere gave Xiana a tight-lipped smile, squashing himself against the wall behind him as much as possible. "I'll have you know I've already shaved this morning."

"Amusing … you are always so amusing, Lumiere. Why not give us another laugh?"

"Xiana," Harshad said. "That is enough."

Her eyes flickered over to Harshad, briefly, before she narrowed her gaze at Lumiere once more. "Even a little chuckle will be enough to kill you, and considering it is you, it would be an appropriate death."

Lumiere cocked an eyebrow, his drunken façade finally depleted. "It's not fair of you to tempt me like that."

THE ORDER OF THE CRYSTAL DAGGERS

"I would say it is not fair for *you* to tempt *me*," Xiana hissed.

"What can I say, *Saghira?*" Lumiere's voice growled softly, his animosity reminding me of when he'd fought with Amir on the *Salacia*. "Light shines in darkness; and the darkness comprehends it not; and all deeds done in the dark will come to light."

Her muscles tightened, as if she was about to launch another attack against him. But Lumiere shook his head, and Xiana only stared at him angrily.

He gave her a venomous smile. "Killing me would only lead to more death, and you have enough blood on your hands."

"Xiana, I said enough," Harshad repeated, this time his voice edged with rebuke.

Xiana finally released Lumiere. "Killing you would be too kind—and too quick."

"I quite understand your temptation, Xiana, and I commend you on your impressive skill and restraint, as always." Lady Penelope gave Xiana a bright smile—one I'd rarely, if ever, seen for myself. "Unfortunately, Lumiere is right; for now, we need him alive. Louis will be looking for him when he arrives. However, it would be best if Lumiere is retired back to his room. See to his care, won't you?"

"Yes, Madame." Xiana nodded curtly. Lumiere had upset her, but she was once more as emotionless, methodical, and cold as ever.

"You don't have to be so stiff." Lumiere waggled his chains along in the loudest, most obnoxious way possible as Xiana tugged him out of the room.

"Make sure you lock his door," Lady Penelope added. "And take his alcohol. No need for us to bankroll his addictions while we're stuck with him."

Lumiere glared over at Lady POW, his expression full of visceral hatred and just enough panic to make me want to giggle.

"I have my own ways of getting around you, Pepé," Lumiere warned. "I trust you would not deny me my pleasures."

"I have it on good authority that such pleasure is often found in pain," Lady POW snapped, waving him away.

Lumiere's scowl deepened with bitterness, and then he turned to me. "What can I say? Our time here is at an end. Perhaps we will find more time in the future, *chérie.*"

634

THE ORDER OF THE CRYSTAL DAGGERS

I turned my nose up at him. I was still angered and frustrated by his varied and strange behavior.

Strange behavior appears to be his normal behavior.

Lady Penelope shooed him away. "Drag him out by his hair if needed, Xiana."

"There is no need for that," Lumiere assured her. "It will be good to be free from your lies again, and what luck, that I even escaped with my life. Others have not been so lucky in that regard—including members of your own family, Madame."

He looked back at me one last time, with no trace of insincerity or mockery in his expression. And then his nose twitched, and he looked down at my midsection.

That's right—Nassara is dead, too.

Sadness stung inside of me at the thought of Amir's daughter, the one my mother had lost; dark uncertainty broiled as I recalled Amir's expression back in the church when I'd asked if my mother had intentionally killed her baby.

I looked back at Lady POW, who looked uncharacteristically stricken.

Before I could say anything, she hurried Xiana and Lumiere out the door and slammed it shut. The force of its impact sent a sharp breeze into the room and made Harshad's pile of papers flutter off his desk.

I waited a full moment before I put my hands on my hips and faced my grandmother. She had a right to her secrets, but I would not stand for her lies.

"What did Lumiere mean by that?" I asked.

"It means you will be training with Xiana in the afternoon instead of this morning." Lady Penelope was clearly just as upset as Xiana had been by Lumiere's commentary.

"But Lumiere—"

"Pay him no heed, Eleanora. I should've left him in his room earlier; I don't know why I thought he might be of some use today. Of course, I thought you would put in some actual work, too."

Harshad cleared his throat. "Pepé, there is no need to be so upset. I was late, too—"

"Harshad and I wish to review through our notes," Lady Penelope continued, overruling him. "There must be other ways to find Karl we

635

THE ORDER OF THE CRYSTAL DAGGERS

haven't thought of yet. We need to find him before Louis gets here and carries out the rest of his plans."

"I can help," I offered, but she shook her head.

"No. Why don't you be a good little wife and see to your husband's needs?" she snapped. "This is serious business, and I cannot have you around right now. You are a disappointment to the Order."

"So was my mother, as I understand it."

"It is better to leave Dezda out of this," Harshad said, speaking up much more forcefully this time. "She is gone, but there is still much pain at her passing."

"I want to know what Lumiere was talking about." I knew I was over-stepping myself, but if Lumiere could spend all morning doing it, why couldn't I? "Why would he bring up Nassara?"

"To distract you, if nothing else." Lady Penelope's reddened cheeks blistered into a violet crimson as she brushed off her skirts. "Enough of this. Leave, Eleanora. Need I remind you if you'd come and dealt with Lumiere earlier, he wouldn't have been here at all?"

"You're the one who brought him," I reminded her. "You said he wanted to talk."

"And so he did, and now we can see Lumiere will use what he can to sow discord among our ranks," Lady Penelope insisted. "You must re-member there is nothing we can do about the past, and you cannot let it interfere with our current mission."

"Even if it will help you learn?" I asked tenuously, echoing Lumiere's earlier taunting.

"How can you learn anything when your emotions only hinder your fo-cus?" Lady Penelope pursed her lips, clearly displeased. "You're dis-missed, Eleanora."

I bit down on the inside of my cheek, forcing myself to keep silent.

Just as I stepped out of the parlor, Lady POW called back to me.

"One last thing, Eleanora: Louis Valoris is not an enemy one should underestimate. He has avoided justice in the British courts for decades now. He is cunning and ruthless, and he is always playing a deep game. As much as Lumiere says they have a tumultuous relationship, he is also Louis' most trusted associate. You can be sure that both of them already have several pieces in play—and that includes Karl."

THE ORDER OF THE CRYSTAL DAGGERS

"I know there is great risk," I said.

"But do you have any idea just how big the risk we face is? Bohemia is in the middle of the Austria-Hungarian Empire, which has treaties with nearly every major imperial force on the continent. Trade routes intersect and connect the East to the West. Civil war is possible, but with France and Germany fighting and Napoleon III's capture, it's clear Louis is setting the stage for a war larger than this world has ever seen."

Such an idea seemed too impossible to imagine, but Lady POW said it with such conviction that I could not dismiss it.

"So, Karl's fate, Bohemia's future, the threat of global war, and your mother's honor—all are at risk." She glared at me pointedly. "And all of that is easily forgotten, I assume, with a lover's kiss?"

My heart began to pound more ominously inside my chest, but I did not retreat from the confrontation. It was becoming more clear I would have to defend my husband at every turn. "I don't know why you're so upset over Ferdy. He's done nothing wrong, and he's even helped us out on more than one occasion."

"Perhaps I would be less preoccupied with him if you weren't," Lady Penelope retorted. "If you wanted him to be left alone, you shouldn't have married him."

"Well, I did marry him, and I don't regret it. And I will not let you come between us." I crossed my arms over my chest again. "Especially after the way you destroyed my mother and Amir's relationship."

"Ha." She snorted disdainfully. "Eleanor ruined it herself."

"Pepé." Harshad jumped up from his seat, his tan cheeks blanched over in horror.

"She was the one who brought it up, Harshad, and if she wants to know about Nassara so much—"

"Pepé, stop!" At the uncharacteristically angry snap of Harshad's voice, Lady POW dutifully shut her mouth.

My eyes widened as a large lump formed in my throat. I was suddenly afraid as the room went deadly silent. I didn't know if it was bravery or curiosity that kept me from running away.

"Eleanora." Harshad's voice was back to its normal volume, but I still heard a slight waver in its commanding tenor. "Please, take your leave. Xiana will meet with you for training later this afternoon."

"But what about—"

THE ORDER OF THE CRYSTAL DAGGERS

"No." Harshad straightened his shoulders and pointed to the door. "You will leave now."

Slowly, I looked back and forth between Harshad and Lady POW, and, seeing no support, I nodded.

As I left, the sense of discomfort I'd felt earlier came back, stronger and more vicious than ever.

Everyone has secrets.

Lady Penelope's words burned into me like never before.

Yes, everyone has secrets, I mused. My mother would have had hers, too—secrets regarding Nassara, her involvement with the Order, and her promise to Empress Maria Anna.

But at that moment, I had absolutely no desire to learn them.

THE ORDER OF THE CRYSTAL DAGGERS

5

◊

My footsteps echoed loudly across the floor as I headed for the library.

I did not want to think of the Order's mission or my mother's past, and between Lumiere's childish hunger for attention, Lady POW's disdain, Xiana's quick temper, and even Harshad's wispy sadness, it had been a long, lonely morning. My mood brightened considerably at the thought of leaving the world and falling into a new, fictional world, one far less complicated than my own.

More than ever, the library was a place of refuge—a place of books and love, family and freedom.

But just as I reached its door, it flung open, and Tulia angrily stalked out of the room.

"Tulia."

She stopped short, glaring at me, her topaz eyes full of contempt. Briefly, I wondered if she felt guilty, or even unsure like the rest of the staff. But a second later, she shook her head, brushed me aside, and resumed her determined march down the hall.

"Wait." I reached for her. "What's wrong?"

Tulia didn't answer as she slid back from me.

"Please, stop," I begged. It was clear from the scowl on her face she didn't want to talk with me, and I was suddenly afraid she hated me.

Tulia had been my mother's companion, and she was my grandfather's illegitimate half-sister. Even her alliance with Lumiere was not enough to make me doubt her; after all, I'd known her all my life and I loved her like a second mother.

"What's wrong? Tell me." I tugged at her sleeve gently. "You know I've forgiven you for working with Lumiere."

You're too kind. She signaled out a sarcastic reply as her lips twisted into a painful, amused look.

"I know you well enough to know when you regret something." I softened a little, watching her brush a stray lock of grayish white hair away from her face. Thanks to Lumiere and his hired henchman, she was covered in scrapes and small burns, adding a maimed grotesqueness to her ancient features.

639

Tulia pointed down each of her arms and around her face and winced in pain, before sticking out her tongue, speaking in the same language I'd known from her all my life.

You think I'm ugly, don't you?

"No."

Tulia snorted at my quick lie. *I'm not the only one who's changed. You have, too.*

"Is that why you're upset? Because I'm married now?" I asked, dreading the thought of having to defend Ferdy again. "I'm still the same person I always was, just more so."

She rolled her eyes and shook her head.

"Then what is it?" I stared at her expectantly and incredulously, starting to feel annoyed myself. Out of the two of us, I had more cause to be upset.

To answer me, Tulia jerked open the door to the library again. I peeked inside just in time to hear Cecilia's scathing voice.

"Is that you, Tulia? Did you come back with the tea, or is the Iron Dowager seeking new ways to punish me and my daughter?"

At my stepmother's screeching, I involuntarily flinched, remembering the damage she'd inflicted on both me and Ben with her wagging tongue. I quickly slammed the door shut.

"I can see why you're upset," I said, more apologetic this time.

When Lumiere "borrowed" the manor's workers to work on the *Salacia*, he'd coerced the staff into following his orders by telling them Lady Penelope would be sailing to England and dragging Cecilia to court there. Not everyone believed him, but when Lumiere instructed Tulia to keep Cecilia and my stepsister, Priscilla, locked inside the cargo hold, no one objected, either.

And then I arrived and rescued them. I'd gone directly against Tulia, who was frustrated with me for freeing them—even though if I hadn't, they would've died when the explosives went off.

"Are you there or not?" Cecilia's voice, muffled from the other side of the library door, was still as sharp and unforgiving as ever.

Tulia made a rude gesture toward the door in reply.

Despite her anger, I laughed. I stopped when she shot me another furious look.

THE ORDER OF THE CRYSTAL DAGGERS

In her own way, Tulia explained how Lady Penelope assigned her to guard my stepfamily; it was the same assignment Lumiere had given her on the ship, and she was eager to be rid of such a job.

There was nothing I could do about that. Since returning to the manor, everyone was on strict house arrest while "new plans for the future were considered," according to Lady Penelope. My stepfamily was required to remain under constant watch, and no one was allowed to go out without her direct approval—including me.

"I'm sorry you're upset," I said to Tulia. "But we need to make sure she's safe. It's unpleasant, but it's understandable."

Tulia flicked her fingers around. *An understandable punishment, you mean.*

"I'm sure it's not a punishment," I said, but as soon as I finished saying the words, I had a feeling Tulia was right. She had her own unpleasant history with Lady POW, and it would not be above my grandmother to plan something like this for the sake of efficiency.

Both Lumiere and Lady POW are good at finding ways to use people as much as punish them.

Tulia put her hands around her eyes again, making a hooded expression. Then she threw up her hands, clearly disgusted.

"Well ... " I bit down on the inside of my cheek and muted a regrettable sigh. "If you'd like a break, I can take over for a bit."

Tulia's hardened expression softened, ever so slightly, before she moved her fingers in a questioning manner.

"I mean it," I told her. "It's not a trick. And I'll take care of Lady POW if she says anything."

When Tulia only seemed even more suspicious, I clasped her hands in mine. "I don't know why you think I hate you. I don't. You were the only one Ben and I could trust after Cecilia married *Táta*. And *Máma* loved you, too."

Tulia hung her head. Confused, I watched her hands as her fingers spelled out a new message.

It's better if you hate me.

"It's not like I haven't tried," I admitted softly. "I haven't forgotten how you kept us from Lady POW because of the Order, and I still don't understand why you helped Lumiere. But I know you, and I know you did what you thought was best, even if you were wrong. So I've forgiven you."

THE ORDER OF THE CRYSTAL DAGGERS

Tulia looked heavenward, before she slumped forward, took my hand, and tried to explain things to me. She was rambling silently; all I could get was how she was saying I shouldn't forgive her so easily and that I knew nothing of the depths of her sins.

Before I could ask her to slow down, the library door opened once more.

"What could possibly be—" Cecilia poked her bird-like nose out of the room as she seethed with impatience, and then immediately fell silent. From the disgusted look on her face, I could not say if she was more enraged or surprised to see me.

"Well," Cecilia finally scoffed a moment later, before giving me the slightest of curtsies. "Your Highness. So nice of you to come and see us."

Your Highness? I glanced around, looking for Ferdy before I remembered that, as his wife, I was now a member of the royal family, too.

As much as I tried to stop myself, I blushed. "I'm not a real princess," I murmured, enormously grateful Ferdy wasn't around. He would've laughed at me, especially given how much I argued with him over his official titles in the past.

Clearing my throat, I turned to Tulia. "Go and rest. I'll see to my stepmother's care for now."

"Ha." Cecilia crossed her arms and scowled. "She couldn't at least get us the tea first, could she? Oh, never mind. After everything we've been through, she'd likely poison it."

I had to give Cecilia some credit; I wouldn't have been surprised to learn Tulia had thought about doing just that. But when I looked back at Tulia, she was stunned, with her eyes wide and full of horror as she stared at me.

"Tulia?" I was suddenly afraid that had actually been her plan.

"Just send her away," Cecilia said as Tulia backed away from me. "Normally, I'd ask why someone with Lady Penelope's rank and privilege would even deign to keep her around, but there's no need to ask in this case. The mute has always been quite manipulative; Adolf didn't question her at all when she stayed at the cottage nearby."

I watched as Tulia's steps faltered at the mention of my father, and a sick feeling welled up inside my stomach as I remembered Lumiere's taunting, about Tulia taking care of my father, and how I might not feel lucky with Tulia still alive.

THE ORDER OF THE CRYSTAL DAGGERS

Is it possible … ?

Unfortunately, it was possible.

Táta had been poisoned with the silver thallis herb, which the Order used as their deadliest weapon. If Father Novak had been poisoned by either someone in the Order or the League, Tulia could have known who killed my father.

Or she could've done it herself.

I rubbed my forehead, my eyes burning as I willfully pushed that thought away.

Quickly, I shuffled Cecilia back into the library, regretting my kindness, as I was the one stuck watching over her now.

A single spark of comfort settled into my heart as I saw my mother's portrait hanging above the fireplace. I sat down and looked at it, remembering how *Táta* told me he'd commissioned it shortly after they were married. Her black hair was down, her straight locks dangling over a prim, white gown. Her raspberry lips were curved into a smile, and her sapphire eyes were full of mystery and kindness.

But as the time passed, and the more I studied her, the more my mother became a stranger to me. Her shoulders were too straight, her pose too practiced, her cheeks too rosy. Her face was more heart-shaped than mine, and her smile, while at first it seemed sweet, turned strangely bitter.

"Everyone has secrets, and everyone has regrets."

Amir's words, spoken to me on the night of our battle aboard the *Salacia*, took on a more haunting quality as I looked up at my mother's picture.

So much was restored of late, but so much had been destroyed, too. I had a child's memory of *Máma*; I saw her as a daughter would see her mother. But who she was, and what she wanted, seemed to shift and change the more I learned about her. I'd already lost part of her when Lady Penelope told me the truth about her and the Order of the Crystal Daggers; I did not want to lose any more of her, even if it wasn't really her.

Distractedly, I stood up and walked back to the bookshelves. I ran my hand along their spines, remembering Amir once told me my mother's handwriting filled several of their margins. Silently, I promised myself that I would look through them all and catalogue my findings one day.

"So, Your Highness, have you come to tell us what our fate will be?"

It seemed like hours had passed when Cecilia's shrilly voice called to me from nearly a world away, and I said a silent prayer for strength as I answered her.

"No. I'm only here to watch you right now." When I saw Cecilia was not impressed, I added, "I'll give Lady Penelope my report later."

The mention of my grandmother made Cecilia shudder with visible pain, and I held back a laugh.

A small movement shuffled off to the side. Priscilla was curled up by the window, with her hands folded in her lap, and a small blanket placed over her skirts. Her face was very pale, while her eyes looked tired; her hair was done up for the day, all tied back in an intricate bun, save for one long, stylish curl that fell to her collarbone. From the reflection on the glass, I could see her frown.

"Your hair looks lovely today, Prissy," I said, keeping my tone light. Priscilla was my age, but it was hard to believe I had anything in common with my stepsister; I stood before her wearing trousers, while she was dolled up like the younger version of Empress Elisabeth she yearned to be.

Priscilla had always been quick to present herself as my better, but ever since Lady Penelope's arrival, she hardly bothered to speak at all. With Alex dead, and especially having witnessed his death myself, I was not sure if we could ever be friends.

But I did hope we could get along.

"Miss Amelia did my hair this morning," Priscilla finally replied quietly. "Marguerite told her to style it the way they do in Paris."

"Paris?" I was surprised she answered me at all, but I imagined it would get quite boring if I only had Cecilia to entertain me, too.

"Yes," Priscilla said, the barest gleam of excitement lighting up her eyes. "Vienna is the music capital of the world, but Paris is where one goes for fashion. Marguerite has been showing me some of the designs from her seamstress book. She has a sister who lives in Paris who sends her new designs."

"It sounds like their whole family knows about fashion," I said.

"Yes, it is so fascinating. It's really the only part of the day I enjoy," Priscilla said, a little miffed. "I hate it when she goes off with Ben."

"Ben?"

THE ORDER OF THE CRYSTAL DAGGERS

Her eyes suddenly went wide, and she quickly clamped her mouth shut. "I forgot I wasn't supposed to say anything."

"Why not?"

Prissy stiffened. "He didn't want me to mention Marguerite was helping him. He thought you would get upset over it."

I was not sure why Ben was with Marguerite, but as I thought about it, I remembered she'd assisted Amir with Ben's leg after I'd caused his fall on the *Salacia*. Perhaps Marguerite was still tending to his injury.

"Marguerite seems nice, and she seems like a good companion. I imagine Tulia's not the best company." I was careful to keep my tone neutral as I shifted the focus away from the topic of my brother.

Slowly, Priscilla nodded. "Yes. I like Marguerite very much."

"She seems to know a lot about Paris."

"It's where her family lives. One day I'd like to go there." Priscilla hesitated. "Do you think we'll be able to, after your grandmother finds Lord Maximillian?"

"I … I don't know," I admitted.

What would happen to me and Ben, and Ferdy, too, after all the Order's business in Prague was over? Would we go back to London to await Queen Victoria's next order? Or would we stay here?

I thought back to the early days of Lady Penelope's arrival, thinking of the mission details she'd shared. Maybe we would even go all the way over to the West Indies.

"That's enough, Priscilla," Cecilia snapped. "You shouldn't talk to Eleanora. She'll only be happy when we're gone, and when we are, it won't be because we're going to Paris. We're more likely to be going to the poorhouse."

Priscilla stiffened and went back to staring out the window. As I tried to object, she primly jutted her chin into the air and ignored me.

Alex had been a terror all his own, but in seeing Priscilla's sad defeat, I was more sympathetic to her plight.

I turned back to Cecilia. "You know, you don't have to be so antagonistic."

"What nonsense," Cecilia muttered. "I'm being held here as a prisoner, after all. I'm under no obligation to befriend you."

"But you might want to help yourself, and your daughter, too." As I watched her scowl deepen, I was suddenly inspired. "If you know anything about where Lord Maximillian might be, perhaps we can work out a deal."

I felt clever, having thought of a way to get answers. I hoped it would please Lady POW. But Cecilia was quick to cut down my enthusiasm.

"I have already told your grandmother I have nothing to say to any of you." Cecilia stood up from her chair, keeping her posture rigid as she faced me. "I have no idea where Max is, or what he wants now."

"You knew he was after the king's heir," I pointed out. "I heard you talking about it with Alex before."

"But that doesn't matter now. He found him, didn't he? Who can say what his plans are now?" Cecilia crossed her arms over her chest. "And anyway, Alex is dead because of him."

Briefly, I saw the quiet sparkle of tears in her eyes. She let out a loud sniff, and she hurriedly straightened her skirts with a rough determination.

"I don't know why you're worried, either. You found the Bohemian prince first," Cecilia continued, poised again. "I suppose I shouldn't be surprised. You are your father's daughter, after all."

"What's that supposed to mean?" I frowned. Cecilia had never mourned for my father, only that he hadn't left her more money when he'd died.

"He was the one who found out about the former Empress' son in the first place," Cecilia explained. "Adolf was quite the researcher, and he was highly regarded even among King Ferdinand and Empress Maria Anna's circle of Bohemian Loyalists."

"Why did he tell Lord Maximillian about Karl?" I did not mean for my voice to raise, but I refused to believe *Táta* had ever helped Lord Maximillian.

"It was a mistake. Max couldn't get Adolf to admit to anything further, except that the heir was born close to the same time as Benedict. Fatherly pride did him in, in the end." Cecilia wrinkled her nose in disdain. "Or perhaps it was fatherly shame, since Adolf was complaining about Benedict falling off the barn roof. And who could blame him for that?"

As Cecilia started to complain about her various husbands and the difficulties a woman without a husband or true son faced—circumstances she faced again, with Alex dead—I ignored her.

THE ORDER OF THE CRYSTAL DAGGERS

Lord Maximillian, the Duke of Moravia, was a cousin to Ferdy's father, and he'd been in line for the throne of the Austria-Hungarian Empire before the Revolution of 1848. From what I knew, he'd originally planned for Karl to marry his daughter; that way, he could gain control of the kingdom, if indirectly. If Karl was not embraced as the proper Bohemian king, Lord Maximillian's status as a former heir to the throne could have been used to win over more votes from the Diets and the *Reichsrat*.

Suddenly, I understood why I had been a complication for Lord Maximillian; Karl's attraction to me had been ardent enough he'd tried to renegotiate with Lord Maximillian plans. Karl thought I would win him a lot of support and goodwill, given how my father saved King Ferdinand.

I frowned.

It was strange that Karl had gone silent, and wasn't, as Lady POW had suggested, carting Teresa Marie around after learning of my deception, but I was still more concerned with my father's murder.

"Did Lord Maximillian kill my father, Cecilia?" The question left my mouth before I realized it, but I didn't regret it.

I knew *Táta* had been murdered; I did not know who did it, or why. Lord Maximillian had the motive and possible opportunity—and I wanted him to be the killer, too, if that meant Tulia was innocent.

I could already hate him for kidnapping Karl; I did not want to hate Tulia.

"What?" Cecilia nearly choked at my question. "The doctor said your father's heart gave out after a fit of apoplexy. Adolf was old, Eleanora. He worked all his life, traveled all over, and he was more than a decade older than your mother. No one killed him."

I hated Cecilia talking about my father, but her mention of my mother was even more egregious.

"Are you absolutely certain of that?" I put my hand on the hilt of my mother's dagger as I stepped closer to her.

"There's no need for such hysterics." She swallowed hard, clearly scared, but still angry. "Why would Max kill Adolf, if he still didn't know who Karl was until last year?"

We faced each other in a silent war; I watched her carefully, taking note of every twitch in her wrinkled face. As much as I hated how she'd treated me, I did not see any inkling of deceit. And her logic was sound, as much as I hated to admit it.

Slowly, I moved my hand off my dagger, and Cecilia let out an exhale in quiet, desperate relief.

And then a gunshot resounded from outside the manor.

At once, Cecilia let out a bloodcurdling scream, while Priscilla jumped out of her seat so fast, she tumbled to the floor.

"What was that?" My tongue was thick with instant fear, and it was hard to say anything as I stood there, stricken and unsure of what to do.

Another shot went off.

This time, I hurried to the window and searched for any sign of intruders or attack.

No one would think to ambush us here, would they?

A third gunshot rang out. The sound came from outside the other wing of the manor, and I knew it was time to see for myself what was going on.

"Stay here," I said, giving Cecilia and Priscilla a stern look before I headed out of the library.

"What is going on?" Cecilia cried, her cranky voice breaking with fear.

"I don't know," I said, sounding much braver than I felt at the moment. I took one last look at my mother's portrait, praying for her courage as I fully brandished my dagger. "But I'm going to find out."

THE ORDER OF THE CRYSTAL DAGGERS

6

◊

If there was anyone Karl should have wanted to kill, it was me.

There was another shot fired, and I wondered if it was possible he'd arrived to do just that. Or maybe it was Louis, searching for his vexing son?

I slowed my pace a little. Tulia told me before the Order had a lot of enemies. What if an entirely new foe had come to take care of Lady Penelope?

As I turned down another hall, I suddenly heard Ferdy and Ben both yelling.

"Oh, no!" I forgot all about everything else, as I was consumed by the determination to save my brother and husband.

I ran outside, heading toward them, as the chilly bluster slapped against me. The stunning frost was enough to leave me momentarily blindsided. My hair, already loosened by my run, danced in the wind and obscured my vision as my feet stumbled through the mushy, snow-dusted grass.

"Ben!" My voice was muffled by my windblown curls. As I drew closer, I could finally make out the words they were saying.

"That one was my shot," I heard Ferdy say.

"That one was your shot on my target," Ben argued. "You're awful at this."

I stopped short, watching the scene before me as the wind died down. My heart was pounding in my chest, and I was breathing too fast, but relief flooded through me; no one was attacking us—and Ben and Ferdy were not dueling with each other, either.

The two of them were yelling at each other as they held a matching pair of dueling pistols. Beyond us, there were two squares of wood on display, each with a crudely carved target in the center.

I faltered again, seeing Ben. His stance was oddly shifted, with his right leg wrapped up in an extra layer of bandages and his foot sticking out in the cold. Nearby on the ground lay a pair of crutches.

A few days after our night on the *Salacia*, Amir told me Ben's injury was mild compared to the break he'd experienced as a child, the one he'd gotten falling off the barn roof. Amir had said he would even be able to straighten the leg a little more, though it would still pain Ben for the rest of his life.

Amir had been both kind and honest to me, but it still hurt knowing I'd caused my brother such agony, especially for a second time.

I did not think it was good for him to be outside in the middle of winter, arguing with my husband while both of them held a gun in their hands.

"Lady Ella."

I jerked around to see Lumiere's companion, Didier, standing out like a still shadow against the wintery background. Didier was a French name, and with his dark skin, it was easy to think he came from the Senegalese trading posts. But from what I'd seen of him, and from how he talked, I was more willing to believe he was actually from America. Though I had not spent much time with him, Didier seemed to be Lumiere's opposite in many instances; he was quiet, thoughtful, a little blunt, and even had a calming presence. His black hair was short and cut close, and his eyes were a dark, bark-colored brown.

As Ferdy and Ben continued their argument, Didier bowed in greeting and gave me a slow, welcoming smile as he straightened.

"Gentlemen, please," he said, stepping between Ben and Ferdy. "We have an audience."

At the interruption, both of them looked over at me. Ferdy gave me a charming grin, while Ben only scowled.

My brother was more than content to avoid me of late; the one time I tried to check in on him in his room, he'd locked me out and ignored me for a good hour before I gave up and left.

"Great. She's come here to mother us," he said.

"I have not," I argued, trying to hide my discomfort. "But now that I'm here, what do you think you're doing?"

"Ben and I have reached an agreement," Ferdy explained. "Didier offered to teach us how to shoot, so if I ever break your heart or make him too angry, Ben can challenge me to a proper duel."

"That's terrible," I said, but I was warmed knowing Ben still cared about me enough to threaten Ferdy.

Ben scoffed. "If he doesn't accidentally kill himself first. Your husband is a terrible shot, Ella."

THE ORDER OF THE CRYSTAL DAGGERS

The warmth of the previous moment evaporated. Ben had always called me "Nora," until we came back from the *Salacia*. As I watched him now, there seemed to be very little I could do to earn his trust back.

Didier cleared his throat. "Would you like to try as well, Lady Ella?"

His voice was deep and low but still friendly as he held out his revolver to me.

"I don't know how," I admitted.

Didier nodded. "Trying is part of learning. You will likely have to learn at some point, given you are a member of the Order of the Crystal Daggers."

He was right about that. I thought of how Lady Penelope had shot her pistol while we fought on the *Salacia*.

"Go ahead," Didier said. "Take it. I can show you how to use it. I am a proficient shot, and I will make sure it's safe for you to use."

"I have no doubt of that," I murmured, still embarrassed. "But … "

My voice trailed off as I looked toward Ferdy and Ben, who were in deep discussion with each other. From the snippets of their conversation I could hear, I realized Ferdy was doing his best to befriend my brother.

I was unable to talk with Ben, but Ferdy was making sure I still had a voice in our relationship.

"They will not mind if you join us," Didier assured me. "Both your husband and brother have had quite a bit of fun getting the basics incorrect for the last several moments."

"It's not that." My voice did not sound convincing to me, and I'm sure he didn't believe me, either.

"You're not scared, are you?" Didier put the pistol back into the holster inside his coat. "But then, I suppose some are not inclined to use guns. Lumiere does not enjoy using them, either."

"Really?" I thought of how Lumiere had killed Alex on the *Salacia*. He did not seem so averse to guns.

"Of course. He doesn't like the mess they cause. Between the gunpowder and the scorch marks, there are plenty of reasons he uses them only when he has to."

I gave Didier a reluctant half-smile. "Now, *that* sounds like Lumiere."

Didier grinned. "Still, he knows I prefer them. He had these engraved especially for me shortly after we became friends."

I took another look at Didier's weapon. From the markings, I saw it was a Remington 1858 model, with gilt intricately engraved into the grip and cylinder. They were indeed beautifully made, so far as I could see.

"Perhaps I will try next time," I said. If Ferdy was trying to bond with Ben, I did not want to interrupt them. "I should go back in and see to Cecilia and my stepsister. We were worried when we heard the gunshots."

"I will make sure they stay alive," Didier promised, nodding back to Ben and Ferdy.

I was inclined to believe him; Didier was every bit as sincere and polite as Lumiere was loud and boisterous, and while I had to question his taste in friends, Didier had done nothing to alienate me. On more than one occasion, he'd even apologized for Lumiere's drunken crudeness or his unrelenting mockery.

"When you change your mind about shooting, come and join us. I will be working with both of them as we have time," Didier said, gesturing toward Ben and Ferdy.

"Thank you." I gave him a small curtsy before I headed back to the house. I glanced over my shoulder just in time to see Ferdy blow me a quick kiss, while Ben turned back to face the makeshift targets.

He shifted his weight on his crutches, and I decided I would ask Amir if Ben was able to work outside without hurting himself.

As I walked back into the house, there was a small shuffling noise to the side; I blinked in surprise as I saw Marguerite standing just beyond the window's light.

"Nora." She greeted me with kindness, but I saw her clasp her hands together nervously. "Is everything all right?"

"Everything is fine," I said. "Were you worried we were being attacked, too?"

She shook her head. "No, I was just … you don't think Ben is pushing himself too hard out there, do you?"

I stared at her. For the first time, I noticed Marguerite was close to me in age, although she was likely a little older; I also saw she was quite pretty, with her blond hair pulled back from her forehead, highlighting the intelligence and gentleness in her green eyes.

THE ORDER OF THE CRYSTAL DAGGERS

As she gazed back outside, staring at my brother, a sudden, deep concern settled inside of me.

"He's well enough," I said, suddenly eager to close that subject of discussion. "Did Lady Penelope send you to find me? I've been taking care of my stepmother in the library."

"Oh, no." She cleared her throat. "I only thought to check on Ben, that's all. I wasn't sure if he should be out there like that, no matter how much he insists he can do—"

"I'm sure Amir and Lady Penelope are well aware of his activities," I said brusquely. "Excuse me."

Marguerite nodded. "Certainly, Nora."

"Thank you." I bit down on the inside of my cheek. Nora was Ben's name for me, and as Marguerite glanced out the window again, I decided I didn't really like how she was so concerned about my brother.

That was *my* job, after all.

And it hurt; I was upset from hearing the gunshots and dealing with my brother's lingering hostility, and worrying that Ben and Ferdy were fighting over who had the better chances in a duel; I wasn't eager to discover my brother had an admirer, too.

"Actually, Marguerite, wait." I felt a little guilty as I saw her eyes light up with hope.

I didn't have the courage to ask her what her feelings were for Ben.

Just like I don't have the courage to face the other questions about Lumiere, Tulia, and my mother.

The thought pressed into me painfully, but I hurriedly pushed it aside as I faced Marguerite.

"Why don't you see to Lady Cecilia and Priscilla?" I asked. "My stepsister told me how much she enjoys your company."

If Marguerite suspected I was uncomfortable, she did not show any sign of it.

"Of course," she agreed. "I can get my sewing kit. I've been teaching her how to do some stitching."

"Thank you." Priscilla and Cecilia were a distraction that would keep her away from my brother, and I knew firsthand they were an effective one.

THE ORDER OF THE CRYSTAL DAGGERS

Realizing I was using the same reasoning Lady POW likely had when she'd sent Tulia to watch over them, I groaned and my fingers tightened into fists.

Sometimes, I really was too much like my grandmother for comfort.

Looking back, I saw Marguerite's gaze linger on Ben one last time, before she hurried away.

Wearily, I unclenched my fists.

"Please, Lord," I whispered desperately, lifting my palms upward in tired expectation. "Help me."

My voice echoed softly in the hallway, but there was no other indication my prayer had been heard. No peace enveloped me, no whisper of wings stirred my soul, no blessings filled my open hands.

My head dropped to my chest as my arms fell limply to my sides.

I was still in a fight with myself, at war with the enemy within, and there was no relief.

I was suddenly very grateful I would be working with Xiana shortly; between my thoughts and the weight in my heart, I welcomed the distraction.

7

◊

It wasn't long after my training started that I changed my mind. The melancholy weight on my heart was nothing compared to the screaming pain coursing through my body, courtesy of Xiana's instruction.

"Ground in your stance." Xiana's tone was tight and tense as she glared down at me disapprovingly.

Sweat pooled on my face, adding to its warmth as I blushed. I struggled to remain standing as I shifted my weight more into my feet.

I was more than sorry that Harshad wasn't with us, even if he would've had to witness my poor footwork. Without his supervision, Xiana did not hesitate to push me harder than usual, and since I had missed our earlier training session, it was in her right to do so. I did my best to make up for my absence, and I met her expectations most of the time, but Xiana still seemed more angry than pleased by my efforts.

Perhaps she is still upset because of Lumiere.

I couldn't blame her for that, even if I was the one who would suffer because of it.

"You are still not centered." Xiana feinted an attack to my right; I twisted around to avoid her and staggered off balance.

My fingernails scraped the sweat off the inside of my palms as I tried to show patience. "Can you show me how to fix it?"

"I have shown you." Xiana shook her head. "It is time you started seeing this as serious business. Harshad is too easy on you."

I bit down on my cheek to stop myself from replying. If anything, Harshad pushed me just as much, but he had been much kinder regarding my mistakes and missteps. My complaints had no such effect on Xiana.

Instead, I took a deep breath and shifted my weight again, resolving to meet her challenge.

If Lady Penelope had intended Xiana's training to be a kind of revenge for me, she'd done well.

I gritted my teeth at the thought, but still, I put my fists up, ready for the next round.

Without hesitation, Xiana lunged forward, and once more, we began to spar.

At first, I blocked her attacks successfully. Xiana was a skilled fighter, surpassing me in technique, speed, and experience. But I was younger than she was, and while I was a little shorter, I also had a wider build; if I took careful aim and waited for the right moment, my attack could do more damage—assuming I attacked at all.

Harshad had mentioned my tendency to start on the defensive more than once, and I had to play to my strengths against Xiana if I was going to survive.

"Focus," Xiana snapped as I retreated again, still looking for an opening.

I was suddenly very grateful I'd changed into my stealth habit for our session; if I had worn my skirts, or even my trousers, it would've been a lot more difficult to keep up. In some ways, our fight reminded me of a very violent dance, one in which precise movements were mandated as much as the manners that preceded it.

Perhaps that was a weakness of mine in this regard, too; after all, I was used to following the lead and never dared to tread on another's toes—unless it was warranted.

But my goal was not to be a good follower; it was to be a competent leader—one who did what was right in the face of evil, who would hold onto hope in the reality of despair, and who would fight for those she loved.

"Ow!" I yelped as Xiana landed a punch to my side.

"You are still not good enough." Xiana smacked my arms, forcing me back into position, and I could almost hear her silent, celebratory chiding as I whimpered in pain. "I have been instructing you for weeks now."

Swiftly, I held up my fists again. This time, her attack came just slightly slower; I managed to avoid it with a profound sense of relief.

Xiana had very little patience in dealing with me, but if I was careful, I knew I could outlast her in terms of energy. And there were other strategies I could try, too.

"Did Lumiere offend you earlier?" I asked.

"No. Lumiere is less than nothing." Despite the quick dismissal, Xiana's eyes flashed furiously, and I knew she was lying.

Everyone lies about something.

656

THE ORDER OF THE CRYSTAL DAGGERS

I hid a smile; Ferdy and Lady POW had made sure I'd learned that lesson. And in many ways, I did not blame Xiana for her frustration. She was usually quiet and reserved, and if Lumiere was able to irritate her in such a noticeable way, it would be something that would bother her.

I dodged another blow, but Xiana reversed and feinted. I yelped as she shoved her full weight against me; the force of her movement combined with the momentum sent me tumbling over, right into the floor.

"Ouch," I grumbled, barely catching myself. I fell hard on my hip, the one that bore the weight of my mother's dagger. I reached down to adjust it, but Xiana slapped my hand out the way.

"Get up," she ordered. "No weapons."

"I wasn't going to use it," I tried to explain, but she cut me off.

"Do not lie to me."

"I wasn't," I nearly shouted, trying to hide my growing frustration.

"If you try to use it on me, you will be sorry," Xiana warned.

"I wasn't going to; I was just trying to adjust it," I insisted, ducking my head down onto my chest.

"No." She stepped directly in front of me, her fists still balled up and ready to strike.

"Harshad would give me time to fix it." I hated how weak I sounded. It was one thing to be a noble warrior in theory; it was much more painful in practice.

A long moment of stillness passed before Xiana relaxed her stance.

"He is not here, but I will allow you to rest just this once," she conceded reluctantly.

I frowned. I had already disappointed Lady POW today; failing to meet Xiana's expectations should've been a given.

"Is Lumiere the reason Harshad is not here?" I asked, tugging the small scabbard at my side as I recalled Harshad's unusual outburst. "Or was it because of what Lady Penelope said earlier?"

I almost asked if Harshad had heard news about Karl when Xiana's eyes narrowed.

"What did Lady Penelope say?" Xiana's tone shifted immediately, and seeing her interest, I saw my chance and took it.

Quickly—but not too quickly, since I still craved a break from our battle—I explained how Lady Penelope and I had argued about my mother, and how Harshad had snapped at her.

As I spoke, I watched Xiana's stoic face carefully, looking for any small change or inflection. There was no sign of any surprise as I told her the story. When I was finished, she only nodded.

"Harshad would stop her from saying anything. He does not like to be reminded of Naděžda's great sin," Xiana said, her voice back to its usual, detached tone.

"Nassara was not my mother's sin," I snapped, standing up angrily. "No child is a mistake in God's eyes."

"In God's eyes, perhaps, but what of the world's?" Xiana's nose twitched in unspoken annoyance. "Had Nassara been born, she might've become as unhinged as Lumiere, and you might have had to kill her at some point."

Xiana's words were eerily similar to Lumiere's assertion I might one day regret he'd allowed Tulia to live, and they were no less infuriating. Tulia's actions on the *Salacia* made it clear she was not innocent, and it angered me to hear Xiana compare her with my unborn sister.

Inconvenience and innocence were different matters, and Xiana should've known better.

"Are you saying it was good my mother lost her?" I brushed a loose lock of hair out of my eyes, trying to steady myself.

"You must stay calm. Your mother is a weakness of yours," Xiana said.

"She is not a weakness." I gritted my teeth again, tempted to scream in fury, before I straightened my shoulders and composed myself. "If anything, she is a source of strength."

Xiana shook her head disdainfully. "That explains why you are so weak, then."

"I will not allow you to dishonor my mother's memory," I insisted, resuming my fighting stance.

"Eleanora, you cannot hold her up as though she was Madonna. You barely knew her, and you do not know how differently you would feel if she had lived," Xiana said. "That is the truth."

"I knew her better than you did," I objected.

THE ORDER OF THE CRYSTAL DAGGERS

"Oh, did you?" Xiana glared at me this time, furious but still unmoved. "Then you should know that Naděžda was the one who got rid of her baby."

"My mother didn't … " I swallowed the lump in my throat and tried to speak again, suddenly feeling sick and angry and full of hatred. "She didn't … "

All too clearly, I remembered the night Lady Penelope gave me *Máma's* dagger, and then Amir's words in the cathedral before my wedding. I blinked to see Xiana's glittering eyes glaring down into me, forcing me to face the earlier darkness I'd only vaguely sensed.

Máma could've taken the silver thallis herb, enough to get rid of the baby.

"She did," Xiana said, as if she could see into my thoughts. "I saw her drink the poison myself."

I couldn't say anything as her words, sharp as a dagger, sank into my heart and twisted violently.

I thought of my mother, combing my hair, cupping my cheek, kissing my forehead. Tucking me into bed, reading with me. Hearing her laugh. Seeing her smile.

"No." I shook my head as I found my voice again. "No, that's not true. Something else had to have happened."

Perhaps Xiana expected me to give up again, or to fall back in my fighting; I could see the spark of surprise briefly in her eyes as my fists balled up, and I launched forward in my first real offensive.

While I didn't mean to catch her off guard, it worked; Xiana only just barely slipped to the side.

"Do not be so naïve, Eleanora." Xiana grabbed my arm and twisted away, before her leg swept under mine, knocking me down again. "You have never known your mother or what kind of misery she was capable of inflicting on others."

Scrambling to my feet, I was unable to successfully retaliate at that poisonous, pernicious thought. Xiana threw out a hard, direct punch, hitting me square in the chest.

I could do nothing as my head fell back and I slammed into the hard floor. The wind rushed out of me, and I coughed at the pain.

"Get up," Xiana snapped. "We are still fighting."

Her words were muffled inside my mind as my body seemed to fight with itself.

"It's not possible," I wheezed out, struggling to move, still winded from Xiana's attack. "My mother wouldn't do that."

"She did do it." Xiana's lips thinned. "Harshad will not discuss it because she was under pressure from Lady Penelope to dispose of the baby."

"What?" My mouth barely formed the word as my hands grappled with hers. I blinked as sweat trickled down my brow, struggling to keep my vision clear; it was still clouded with memories of my mother—holding my hand, walking beside me, hugging Ben, welcoming my father home …

"That is the truth, Eleanora, and if you are smart, you will never speak of it again," Xiana said as she lashed out another attack. "Lady Penelope was most displeased when she discovered Amir and your mother were having an affair—"

"They were married," I objected, though it affected neither her argument nor her determination.

"—and she became pregnant. Naděžda was a great beauty, and she could have had any suitor she wanted. She could have had a prince, just as you do now."

At the mention of Ferdy, I jumped up, holding my fists up to guard my face with renewed vigor. I would not let Xiana use Ferdy against me, as Lady Penelope had earlier.

"Naturally, Lady Penelope was quite upset, especially while the Order was in the middle of an important mission." Xiana's eyes narrowed into slits as we circled each other. "Lady Penelope objected to their union, and she wanted the baby gone, so Naděžda took care of it. It was an easy solution."

"Eleanor ruined it herself."

Lady Penelope's words from earlier hit me even harder this time, and tears welled up in my eyes as my mind filled up with memories.

Disbelief and shock finally gave way to fury, and I was screaming as I grabbed Xiana's collar.

I hauled her over my shoulder, and tossed her down forcefully.

Slowly but triumphantly, breathing hard, I finally managed to gain the advantage.

THE ORDER OF THE CRYSTAL DAGGERS

"I don't believe you," I told her, as she grappled wildly underneath my hold. "You're lying."

My mother had wanted children. She'd left the Order and married my father, and she not only had Ben, but she had me as well. And even before then, I knew she'd loved Amir and Nassara.

Conviction settled inside my heart like a protective cloak.

Máma would not have done anything to risk the life of her baby. It simply did not make sense, even if Xiana did see her drink the poison.

"Why would I lie?" Xiana's voice was slightly stilted as she struggled against me. "I have only told you what Lady Penelope and Harshad will not say themselves. Naděžda knew about the silver thallis herb and its capabilities, and she drank it."

Just as I started to reply, Xiana freed herself and struck out a vengeful kick.

But this time, I was ready.

I grabbed hold of her, and I forced her under my shoulder, then rolled with her and pinned her down on the floor.

"No," I said, more to myself than to her, much more determined this time. My knuckles landed hard against her jaw, and I could feel the warmth of blood.

I was shocked—but I didn't stop.

Our battle was charged with power and intent, and I was as dazzled by our mutual strength and endurance as I was befuddled by our differences.

Our deadly dance showed our distinct rivalry; it was beautiful and intense, and then it was over.

My fist was steady at her neck; Xiana's eyes widened with confused shock as I stood over her.

But my success was short-lived; she recovered in the next instant, rolling back over her shoulder and onto her feet again, reaching for my dagger. She deftly slid it out of my scabbard, and slid the blade across my armor.

I jerked back at the surprising pain. "Stop!"

I rolled to the side and clutched at my chest, feeling for any slits in the leather or any blood spilling on my skin. My lungs were on fire and my chest burned, and I was afraid, but there was no permanent damage to my person.

THE ORDER OF THE CRYSTAL DAGGERS

"As I said, you are weak." Xiana's voice was an angry hiss, even more so as she wiped the blood from her lip. "You may have had a hard life, but so did I. My parents died when I was just a child, and Harshad took me in after he lost his own family to cholera. I was raised alongside Naděžda, and I could do nothing as she endangered Amir, upset your grandmother, and betrayed the Order."

"Betrayed?" I repeated, surprised, but Xiana ignored me.

"No one even tried to stop her, either." Xiana shook her head, letting her black braid snap through the air like a whip, before she leaped toward me again, light glinting off my mother's violet-colored dagger.

"What are you doing?" I cried, watching her body tense up with deadly resolve.

Suddenly, I was terrified I'd miscalculated and greatly overestimated her integrity.

A string of half-formed words sputtered out of me as I tried to scurry away, but it was useless; she caught me, threw me onto the floor, pinned me down, and slammed the dagger down toward my heart.

I squeezed my eyes shut, scrunching up my face, angry and terrified at facing death, but determined not to scream.

And then there was a great clash, and Xiana let out the smallest gasp.

"That's enough, Xiana."

Amir's voice was harder than I'd ever heard it.

As I tentatively opened my eyes, I saw him standing above me. His own small dagger, the *Wahabite Jambiya*, was locked firmly against Xiana's attack.

"Amir." The fire I'd seen in Xiana's eyes quickly dissolved into suspicion and fear as she looked up at him.

"You were about to kill her," Amir accused, his voice full of steady vitriol.

"She has to learn how to lose, Amir," Xiana told him, her voice tight and her bloody lips sharply drawn across her face. Her cheeks were red from exertion, but there was a slight shadow of shame in her expression, one that reminded me of Cecilia in that moment.

She did not regret pushing me; she only regretted that she'd been caught.

"No." Amir's eyes were full of disappointment. "Eleanora has to learn to keep going after a loss. That's not the same thing, and you know it."

Xiana frowned, and then, in a flash of movement, she pulled back my mother's dagger, and then thrust its blade into the floor, just a hair away from my cheek.

Before I could scream, Amir was already shoving her away. Xiana began to fight back, tangling herself around his arm, but Amir shook his head.

"Xiana." Amir stood firm. "Enough."

They both stared at each other with searching gazes, reminding me of Lady POW and Harshad. They were having a silent conversation, one of hope and resentment, of admiration and admonishment.

Watching them, I kept silent; another world lay between them, and I had no notion of what they were debating with each other.

Then, reluctantly, Xiana let go and stepped away. Their eyes never left each other's; Amir looked on her with sorrow and regret, while Xiana's gaze was flat, full of forced nothingness—the gaze of a killer.

But was she really going to kill me?

I sat up, beyond befuddled. My body was numb with shock and betrayal; belatedly, I saw I was not injured beyond my pride, but my body was crying out for rest. I pulled my mother's dagger out of the floor, angered as I saw my fingers were trembling.

"You did well, Eleanora." Amir finally turned and held out his hand to me, and I took it with gratitude. "We still have plenty of time for higher levels of instruction."

"Enough, Amir. Times have changed, and so has the Order." Xiana wiped her hands off on her tunic briskly. "You cannot allow her to remain weak."

"We all have our weaknesses, regardless of how strong we are." His words were firm but soft, and I saw her give the slightest flinch at his tone. "This is not how we train."

"Then she will die."

Amir's hand constricted against mine, as if to rebuke her statement, but before either of us could say anything, Xiana shook her head.

"I was merely attending to my duties, as Madame has instructed me," she said, her voice emotionless and mechanical once more. "If you are going to prevent me from doing so, I will take my leave."

She bowed, her form as stiff and formal as ever, and turned away from both of us.

"Xiana." Amir called out to her again as she reached the door. "I would like to talk with you later. There are some things I wish to discuss."

"No, thank you. I have nothing to say to you," Xiana replied curtly. "I have been talking to you for years, Amir, wishing you would listen to me. But you have never bothered to listen, and it is too late to change anything now."

"Xiana." His expression grew forlorn. "Wishes are oddly burdensome things."

"Yes, they are, especially when such wishes go overlooked and unfulfilled," she snapped, whirling around to face him. Her eyes rippled with unspoken emotion. "After all this time, I can only return the courtesy you have shown me. Excuse me."

Then she blinked, and her expression was once more flat and impassive.

Amir and I did not say anything as she left the room.

I listened for the echo of her nearly silent footsteps as they disappeared, feeling strangely sympathetic for her. She might have won our battle, but she'd lost something more in doing so.

"How much of our conversation did you overhear?" My voice was thick as I finally broke the silence between me and Amir.

"Enough," he replied, a vacant look in his eyes.

"I'm sorry."

"It's not your fault," Amir said. "And besides, I should thank you."

"Thank me?"

"Yes." He gave me a sad, grateful look. "I am sure your mother is happy to know you will defend her honor."

"So she didn't … ?" My whisper trailed off into nothing; I still could not bear to say it.

THE ORDER OF THE CRYSTAL DAGGERS

"If she did, she certainly fooled me. Naděžda was about twenty weeks along when she went into early labor. Before that, she was always talking about being a mother."

"And leaving the Order?"

"Death or defeat is the only way to truly leave the Order." Amir's moustache twitched as he grimaced. "Or so Lady POW would say."

"That's awful," I said.

"Only if you make it awful. Any commitment is an act of both hope and fear, of courage and faith," Amir replied. "Such a pledge binds us to our choices. In the Order's case, there is room for adjustments. Remember, Lady POW allowed you and Ben to join her, and even she didn't leave the Order when she was pregnant with Naděžda."

"Why was my mother having a baby such an inconvenience, then?" I asked. "If Lady POW did it, shouldn't my mother have been able to do it, too?"

Amir shifted uncomfortably. "I suppose there were a few reasons Lady POW objected to the situation. She and your grandfather were better off financially, for one. I had just been disowned by my family a few weeks prior to Nassara's arrival. My hand was still bandaged when I held her for the first time."

"Amir." I put my hand on his, not wanting to hear any more, knowing it would only hurt him. "You don't have to say anything else if you don't want to."

But he shook his head. "For the longest time, I wondered where Lady Penelope had gotten the notion that I'd poisoned Naděžda, or if it was even true. Now I know there was at least one witness."

Both of us looked back at the empty doorway where Xiana had disappeared.

"You didn't notice anything strange when Nassara was born?" I thought of the bluish tint to my father's lips the day of his funeral. I hadn't known about the silver thallis herb at the time, nor had I known about the Order.

"No. I only saw how beautiful she was." Amir sighed. "I told myself she was too good for this world, and for me, and her death was a sign I was unfit to be a father and a husband. And perhaps I was; I wasn't much help when Nassara arrived so unexpectedly. Another doctor tended to Naděžda after her labor. He told us she would likely never conceive again."

Amir smirked as he looked over at me again. "But we know now that's not true."

I laughed a little to ease the grief that had settled in my heart. I was surprised to feel a small tear trickling down my cheek. "I'm sorry."

"Don't be," Amir replied. "As I said, you defended her honor. Naděžda will be grateful for that."

I squeezed Amir's hand, acutely aware of the scarred flesh underneath mine. "She wouldn't have done anything to hurt Nassara. We will find out the truth," I vowed.

"If we can." He was hesitant, and I could see he was only appeasing me.

"We are loyal to the truth," I reminded him.

"Yes, we are. Truth is born of love and leads us to freedom, and freedom gives us the key to beauty. In its absence, we hold on to hope, and we wait for it faithfully, with fear and trembling." Amir patted my head affectionately. "But we must realize there are limitations this side of eternity."

I was about to argue when he shook his head again.

"You will have to excuse me, Eleanora. I have an appointment with Ben. We are going to work on his Arabic today while I check his leg."

"Perhaps Ferdy will join you," I said.

"He has in the past," Amir said, surprising me. "Ben seems to enjoy having someone distract him from grammar work. It also makes our small breaks between lessons more interesting."

"Do I even want to know how they're getting along?" I grimaced, recalling how Ben and Ferdy had been arguing with each other earlier. I looked at Amir's dagger.

"I imagine you can guess." Amir patted his blade, as if to confirm guns weren't the only weapons Ben and Ferdy were bonding over. "But don't worry. I can take care of them, and Marguerite is there to help, too."

"Why is she there?" I bit my lip, unable to conceal my frustration.

"Women tame men and civilize them in miraculous ways," Amir explained. "Lady Penelope told her to see to Ben's care, but it's also nice she can help me with bandages, and stitches, if need be. She is an impressive seamstress."

THE ORDER OF THE CRYSTAL DAGGERS

"I guess I won't worry if you're there. I can trust you." I briefly thought of asking Amir about Ben and Marguerite, but I decided to save that line of inquiry for later. There were still things I wanted to say to Amir about my mother.

"Amir?" I cleared my throat, silently praying I wasn't overstepping myself. "Just so you know, I am sure my mother still loved you, even after she married my father."

I knew this to be true; in my mother's locket, a small picture of Amir had been tucked away behind my father's portrait. For the first time, I wondered if Amir had bought my mother the locket himself.

I will give it to him later.

Amir gave me his tired smile. "After all these years, my love for Naděžda has not waned, and I have not moved my heart to make room for a beauty I know will never compare to hers." He glanced back in the direction Xiana had gone, and I realized there was more to their earlier exchange than I'd thought.

"I know Xiana's not usually this hard on me," I said. "But I am glad you came to my rescue. I can't seem to win against her."

Amir nodded. "She's a tough opponent. If force doesn't work, the only way to win against her is by surprise."

"She doesn't seem to like surprises," I agreed, recalling her argument with Lumiere. "That's probably why Lumiere made her upset earlier."

"He is good at that," Amir agreed easily enough. He put his *Wahabite Jambiya* back in its scabbard. "But I am surprised she was upset at all, and to the point where others would notice. Xiana has always been very disciplined, even when we were younger."

"How long have you known her?" I asked, suddenly very curious.

"We have known each other for a very long time. She was a young orphan when Harshad took her in, and we studied under him together. Later, she worked with Naděžda and me on several missions, and of course, she taught me about the Order's use of herbs," Amir said. "We were all quite close. Naděžda and I called her *Saghira* for many years. It means 'little sister,' in Arabic."

I bit my cheek. I could understand why Xiana was so reluctant to talk with Amir, given what I knew now. "Lumiere called her that earlier," I said, remembering how Xiana had fought with him. "He doesn't seem to share her friendship."

THE ORDER OF THE CRYSTAL DAGGERS

"The French and Chinese have a contemptuous history." Amir shrugged. "But it took a while for me to see Lumi as a friend, too. I can see where she would not appreciate his style. And Lumi has always let it be known how he preferred Naděžda over her."

And he was not the only one.

My thoughts went unspoken, but Amir gave me a small nod. "She would not forgive him easily for that."

His voice was full of sadness as he spoke, and I could see he'd never fully realized that Xiana, for all her toughness, had a weakness of her own he'd missed.

Amir was a good man—I could see why Lady Penelope would want him around, and she would trust him with her life, even if she didn't trust him with her loyalty. Amir would be the kind of person to save her, even if he hated her; and my mother had loved him enough to marry him, even if their marriage did not last. And even though he'd rejected her, Xiana would know he was worthy of her affections.

"You know, there are different kinds of beauty in this world, and if you wanted to fall in love again, I don't think *Máma* would want you to deny yourself that freedom."

It was not necessary to remind Amir that my mother had given herself that freedom, too, in marrying my father.

"She would not." Amir nodded. "But I have already left her once, and I cannot seem to do it again. Others have offered me their hearts, but I'm afraid I have nothing left to give."

He was kind enough not to mention Xiana by name, and I appreciated his concern for her. Amir clearly still had a great deal of respect for her, and he would not present her as my enemy.

"But aren't you lonely?" I asked.

"Of course I am, Eleanora. But what I lack here one day will be complete. And that is what sustains me. There is also the good company I've found with Harshad and Lady POW—and yourself and your family, too." Amir paused and then laughed a little. "Even Lumiere is not so much of a burden to me as you'd think. He loved your mother, and during our time together she called him her cousin when we would meet."

"I think he sees her when he looks at me," I confessed, slightly embarrassed; Amir and I both knew Lumiere was not the only one who was guilty of that.

668

"It is very hard not to." His tone was apologetic, but no apology followed; I knew it was somewhat foolish to object to such a circumstance, anyway, especially when I liked being similar to my mother.

Amir held out his hand to me. "Lumi was the one who helped Naděžda and Xiana save me after my father disowned me and my cousins gave me this."

The Arabic *noon*, the one that marked him as a Christian convert and an outsider to his family, was carved into his flesh. Though it had been done decades before, every inch of its deadly cut still displayed pure pain. I shuddered, unwilling to imagine what they would have done to Amir if he hadn't escaped.

"He was docked at Constantinople that night," Amir explained. "Lumi took us to London right away, back to the Order, even though it was dangerous for him. I did not make it easy for him, either; I was suffering from blood loss and calling for Halal as we left port."

I grimaced; Amir had told me before that his older sister had been killed for helping him escape.

"I was yelling rather loudly, too. Your mother told me Lumiere used chloroform to knock me out. Later, he tried to charge me for it."

I imagined Lumiere running around his ship, preparing them to set sail, all for Amir's sake. He would've enjoyed the chaos and the thrill of risk.

"It's hard to believe Lumiere was ever good for anything," I finally murmured.

"He's a handful. But he has never failed me, even if he has always inconvenienced me." Amir put his scarred hand on his dagger's hilt.

"He said you were one of his contingencies. Is that why?"

"I don't know about any secret plans he might have," Amir said. "But I'm sure our past would be enough for him to believe I would help him if he needed it. He saved my life."

"I'll try to remember that next time Lumiere irritates me," I said. I kept my tone sincere instead of cynical; it was my turn to appease Amir.

He laughed; he seemed to know I was being kind to him. "God makes things possible, but that does not mean he makes them easy. Lumiere is on our side, even if he is reluctant to admit it, or even if we are horrified to embrace it."

"I'm quite horrified, that's for certain."

669

I thought of Lumiere telling me to find the right time to come and talk with him.

I was still unsure if I wanted to hear what he had to say. I didn't just want answers; I wanted the truth, and I wasn't sure Lumiere was the kind of person who would give it to me.

"He is still the one most likely to know where Karl is, even if he hasn't said anything yet. He's probably just waiting for the right time to ensure he'll get what he wants out of the situation. That's how he usually works," Amir said, reminding me of our current mission.

I was glad for Amir's encouragement. His companionship comforted me, leaving my heart encouraged, even as we parted ways.

Just as he was about to leave the room, I called out to him again.

"What is it, Eleanora?" Amir was tired, and I knew he was busy, but it warmed me that he did not seem to mind my constant cries for attention.

Still, I could feel the sweat on my palms as I asked the most intrusive question that burdened my heart.

"I wanted to ask … if my mother did … take the poison, as Xiana said, would you still love her?"

Society did not allow for the discussion of such private matters, and even between family and friends it was hard to talk of such impropriety. I didn't want to know if my mother had purposefully poisoned Nassara, but if she did—even though it was inconceivable to me, and antithetical to all the memories I had of my mother—I wanted to know if there was still a chance that I could love her.

Amir went quiet for a long moment. I could see him thinking hard, honestly searching for an answer to give me.

At last, he spoke.

"I would still love her," he agreed. "And I would forgive her, too. But I would not be as apt to forgive myself for leaving her in a position where she believed there was no other choice. If what Xiana said was true, I could not live with such a regret."

With that, Amir excused himself, and we said nothing else. But as I watched him go, a new peace settled around me.

Even if it was unpleasant, I knew I could face the truth.

THE ORDER OF THE CRYSTAL DAGGERS

There was nothing brave or kind about feeling sorry for myself or waiting around for the right time to act. Amir deserved peace, and I wanted it for him even more than I wanted it for myself.

I rested my hand on my mother's dagger, feeling a renewed sense of urgency as I headed out of the room to go and find Lumiere. Lady Penelope had said it was more imperative than ever to find Karl, and I would no longer wait for Lumiere to find the right time.

Just as in the case with fighting and dancing, it was time to take the lead.

THE ORDER OF THE CRYSTAL DAGGERS

8

◊

"Lumiere."

I knocked hard on his door, briefly pouting as pain stung across my knuckles. After all the time I'd spent training and fighting with Xiana, my body was starting to protest at any movement at all.

"Lumiere, open up," I called again. For a brief second, I considered giving up and going to my room.

I didn't really want to deal with Lumiere. What I really wanted was a warm bath and a large supper, and then I wanted to go to bed.

But I was desperate, and curious, and left without answers—answers I suspected Lumiere could provide. Even if I couldn't trust him completely, I wanted to hear what he had to say.

After all, Lumiere knew of my mother; he'd known her before the Revolution of 1848, and he knew about my father, too. He knew about Ferdy and Karl, having met with them abroad, and he knew about the Order, and Xiana's past with Amir and Nassara.

I couldn't trust him.

But surely, if he'd loved my mother as much as everyone else did, he would give me the answers I sought.

I knocked again, this time even harder. "Lumiere, I've made the time to be here, whether it's right or not. Let me in."

There was no reply.

I pressed my ear against the door, listening for any sound at all. It was strangely quiet, and the earlier sense of regret I'd felt in deciding to talk with him suddenly increased exponentially.

"Lumiere, this is important!" I tapped my foot against the floor, waiting.

Interminably long seconds passed, and still, nothing happened. There was no answer.

Quickly but tentatively, I glanced down each side of the hallway. I checked to make sure I was in the right place, and then I looked to see no one was around as I fiddled with the lock on his door.

Lady Penelope didn't need another reason to distrust me, and I didn't need Ben to lament my poor lock-picking skills.

I bit my lip. Even if Ben did see me, I didn't think he would chide me; after all the years he'd spent building his leg braces, Ben knew he was the better mechanic between the two of us. And if he were here, he would've helped me, just as he always had.

I was the one who had trouble when it came to helping *him*—and others, too. Momentarily, my hands stilled and my eyes closed in shame; it was pure agony to remember how Alex had shot Ferdy when he'd cornered us on the *Salacia*, all because of my mistakes.

There was a small click, as the lock tumbled open.

"Oh, thank you." I opened the door, pushing my past guilt into the back of my mind. "All right, Lumiere, I'm coming in. You'd better be decent."

I was fully expecting him to assure me he was only ever decent.

But when I walked across the threshold, I was only met with cold emptiness, and my irritation turned into sincere alarm.

"Lumiere?"

The room was quiet and dark; even after I quickly drew back the curtains, the last of the day's light was barely enough to fill the room. Lumiere's effervescent personality hung in the air, and its ghostly remains lingered in the various piles of small trinkets, fine clothes, empty liquor containers.

But the man himself was stripped away.

On the bedspread, a twinkle of light sparkled like a golden flame. I already knew what it was, even before I picked it up: it was Lumiere's pocket watch, the one that he'd held up to me only hours before.

I examined it again. I could still see the similarities it held to my father's watch—the muted gold, simple design, the inlaid pierced markings. I opened it to see the elegant *fleur-de-lis* design on its clock face, encircled by a bronzed bezel. All three hands were still and silent, ominously pointing to midnight.

But for the first time, I saw the *fleur-de-lis* motif matched the princess hair combs Ferdy had given me before. It was a symbol of the Kingdom of Bohemia.

"Of course," I whispered. *Táta* had been given his watch by King Ferdinand. He'd been an ambassador, working closely with the king.

But why did Lumiere have a watch like this, too?

I looked down at the bed. There had been another item there, staring up at me, lying beside the watch.

My heart skipped a beat at the sight of my mother's journal, the one carved with the same Arabic *noon* that Amir bore on his hand.

It was a piece of her heart I never expected to find, a wish I hadn't known until I saw it.

Lumiere was the one who'd taken it, to absolutely no earth-shattering shock.

Slowly and reverently, I picked it up. Lumiere had helped *Máma* save Amir before. He would've known about the mark, and he wouldn't have had any qualms about taking the journal when he'd captured Cecilia and the others.

I leafed through the pages, momentarily awed at the neatness of my mother's handwriting. The foreign scrawl was written so smooth and straight, I could've sworn it was printed when I'd first seen it. Even the little marks and scribbles in the margins were so carefully added, it seemed to be by design rather than a doodle. My own loopy penmanship was slanted and sloppy by comparison.

There were no ripped pages, no frayed sheets, and nothing that suggested it had been waterlogged from the *Salacia*. There were a few dotted sheets with smudges, and I did not know if they were tears from my mother or someone else. I kept turning the pages, not seeing anything unusual until close to the end.

There was a small fold on the top of a page. Perhaps it was Amir's; it seemed too polite to be Lumiere's mark of progress, and its crease too sharp and fresh to be more than a few months old.

I shut the book quietly and held it against my chest. After one last fleeting glance around the room, I headed off to find Amir again.

Lumiere was missing, but my mother's journal had been found; despair and excitement both welled up inside me, and I bounced between dread and hope in a rhythm that only matched the pounding of my heart.

After awkwardly questioning a few of the staff members, I finally found Amir and Ben working in the barn. As I walked outside, the cold winter air bristled against me, but I welcomed its chilliness. My body was still sore, and walking out to the barn was like pressing my body next to a block of ice.

THE ORDER OF THE CRYSTAL DAGGERS

I paused as I reached the barn door; I could hear Ben's voice, and he sounded almost happy.

"That's what I've been wondering about ever since the night of the Advent Ball and the fire," Ben was saying. "Can you hand me that hammer, Amir? I need that one, not this one."

"Here you go," Amir answered. "What do you think? How would you go about causing such an explosion?"

"I was really worried, so I didn't think about it much at the time." Ben began to hammer at something, and it was harder for me to hear. I leaned against the door as Amir and Ben talked about the incident at Prague Castle.

"I've been trying to narrow down the list of possibilities. I thought it was nitroglycerin," Ben said. "I'd heard Mr. Nobel learned how to make it less volatile after his brother died using it, but it would be easy enough to change it back. Then the trick would be keeping it cool."

"Perhaps that was why it was in the wine cellar," Amir suggested.

"That would make sense. And it would explain Ferdy's carriage fire. As the nitroglycerin warmed, it would be more likely to detonate."

I leaned against the door, curious to hear any animosity in Ben's voice as he talked about Ferdy.

But then the door abruptly opened, and I stumbled forward.

"Ouch." I nearly dropped the journal and Lumiere's pocket watch as I struggled to keep my balance.

"Eleanora?" Amir looked over at me. He was sitting beside Ben on a workbench. From the firepit and the tools scattered around them, I could see they had been working together on a new brace for Ben and his leg.

"What are you doing here, Ella?" Ben eyed me suspiciously.

"Lumiere's gone." I came forward, desperate to cover up my insecurity and embarrassment as I handed the journal to Amir. I kept Lumiere's pocket watch in my other hand, tucked away, deciding I would worry about that on my own. "I found this in his room. I guess he had it all this time."

"I see." Amir's voice was edged with irritation as he took the journal from my hands. I was about to ask him what was wrong before he let out a sigh. "Perhaps he didn't know how much I wanted it back."

THE ORDER OF THE CRYSTAL DAGGERS

"I doubt that," Ben and I said at the same time. As we looked at each other in surprise, I wondered how much Lumiere had been bothering Ben—and what he'd been bothering him about, too.

"Thank you for this, Eleanora. I will examine it later," Amir said. "But we should find Lumiere. He was supposed to remain locked up for the rest of the day."

Dread gnawed at me from inside my stomach.

If Lumiere was missing, I wouldn't be able to ask him my questions, both about my mother's past secrets and Karl's present location.

But he might have gone to meet with his father, too—and that was even more frightening.

I shivered, but I tried to be optimistic.

"Perhaps he's with Lady POW, and they're trying their hardest to punish each other," I suggested.

Amir let out a muffled laugh, but Ben only shook his head.

"It's more likely Ferdy let him out," Ben said, carefully putting his new brace down on his worktable before reaching for his crutches.

"Ferdy wouldn't do that." My voice was harsher than I'd meant, but I was getting very tired of defending Ferdy to my family.

"So you think." Ben rolled his eyes.

"What do you mean by that?"

"I told you before, he's hardly serious about anything in particular." Ben shrugged. "It wouldn't surprise me if Ferdy thought it would be fun to let the Order's greatest asset out of his dungeon for a night."

I bit the inside of my cheek, hurt by Ben's callous tone. "I thought you were getting along with him."

"I am," Ben replied. "But he gets along with everyone until he doesn't. It's in my best interest to humor him for now, just as it's in his to befriend me. It doesn't mean we're actually friends."

I didn't like how dismissive he was, even if Ben was right about Ferdy's temperament. "You're too cynical."

"And you're too trusting."

"Ferdy is loyal to us," I insisted. "If he did let Lumiere out for any reason, it's more likely to fight with him than anything else."

THE ORDER OF THE CRYSTAL DAGGERS

Ben arched his brow at me, while my heart skipped another beat. We both knew it was too easy to believe Ferdy would do just that.

Amir cleared his throat. "Please stop arguing. You're not children anymore."

Ben and I exchanged the same guilty, knowing look. We'd hardly fought when we'd been younger, unless it was for play.

"Now," Amir said, "let's go. I believe I have some more questions for Lumiere myself."

Together we headed out of the barn and back toward the house. Ben was still using his crutches, even though his bandages had been replaced from the ones I'd seen earlier. As we walked, I peeked up at his face, happy to see that while he wore a frustrated look, it was not one of pain.

My happiness did not last.

As our search continued, there was still no sign of Lumiere. His bedroom, my father's study, and the parlor were all empty. With each empty room, my dread exponentially increased.

I couldn't help but notice that not only was Lumiere gone, but there was no sign of Ferdy, either.

"Amir, what happens if we can't find him?" There was a lump in my throat, and my lips felt very dry as I spoke. I could already guess that Lady Penelope would blame me for this, somehow—and that was just the beginning of our problems if Lumiere had indeed escaped. "What do we do?"

"We'll inform Lady POW." Amir's cool reserve steadied me, even as I saw his grip tighten around my mother's journal.

"Let's separate," Ben suggested. "I'll go check the library and see if I can talk with some of the others."

"Including Marguerite?" I asked.

Ben's jaw tightened. "Perhaps, if I see her."

I was a little gratified that, while he was annoyed at my inquiry, there was nothing in his voice that hinted at a deep, hidden affection.

"We would cover more ground more efficiently if we separate," Amir agreed. "I'll take the kitchens and the wine cellar; it wouldn't be out of character for Lumi to get himself locked in there. Ben, you should go alert the others. What about you, Eleanora?"

My fingers tightened around Lumiere's pocket watch. "I'm going to go out and look in the city. If he's already gone, surely someone would've noticed him. And depending on how long it's been since he's escaped, I might even be able to catch up to him."

"Lady POW won't like that." Ben crossed his arms. "She told you not to leave the grounds. You're supposed to be on your honeymoon with Karl, remember? The town doesn't need to know it's all a lie."

"She's already disappointed in me," I said with a shrug. "This shouldn't surprise her; in fact, given what she's told me about trusting people before, she's probably expecting me to disobey her."

"She still won't be happy when she finds out," Ben argued.

"She's never happy anyway."

"Eleanora." Amir glanced up at the windows. "It's nearly nightfall. If you are intent on leaving, you should go now."

"You're not just going to let her out of the house, are you?" Ben asked, his expression incredulous. "What about our orders? And we're not done searching here yet."

"We can take care of the grounds here while Eleanora searches the city," Amir told him. "Lumiere might have left, and she will have better luck in getting him to come back if that's the case."

"But she shouldn't go out alone. I'll go with her."

"No," I said, trying to be tactful. "Amir just said you can help him here. I'll draw less attention if I'm by myself."

He glanced down at his leg. "Well, that's true enough, isn't it?"

"You know that's not what I meant." I felt the blood drain from my face, as though I'd hurt him all over again.

"Come." Amir put his hand on Ben's shoulder. "We're wasting time. Eleanora will do her part, while we do ours."

There was a small pause, but Ben finally nodded, resigned. "Just promise me you'll be careful, Ella."

"Of course I will," I promised, giving him a brave smile. His concern was touching, even if he wasn't calling me Nora anymore.

"And don't forget to look for Ferdy, too."

My smile disappeared; I could feel my nostrils flare in anger and my fingers curled into fists. I didn't know if Ben was teasing me more out of

THE ORDER OF THE CRYSTAL DAGGERS

contempt or concern, but I hated to even give him the benefit of the doubt.

As they headed off and moved out of sight, I steadied myself.

It was time to go.

I pushed away my anger, and embraced my chance for freedom once more.

9

◊

Moonlight was shining at its fullest by the time I reached the Vltava's riverbank. The small waves and the soft lull of wispy winds carried the unspoken promise of adventure, while the starlight hummed a melody all its own.

I had spent years peeking out from my windows, watching the city skyline, wondering at the majestic walls of Prague Castle and the buildings my ancestors built and sculpted hundreds of years before. The tall, sprouting trees of the city softened its edges. Now I knew more of the sadness of its streets and the strife it carried in its quarters; I knew of the places poisoned by sin and tainted beyond mortal repair. In that way, it reminded me of Moses' burning bush: the fire's bright destruction, coexisting with nature's subtle power, in an ongoing battle both constrained and encouraged by heavenly forces.

I was still mesmerized by the majestic sight as I crossed the Stone Bridge and the Prague astronomical clock began to ring. The tolling of the bells added a new depth to the darkness, while the resplendent towers of St. Vitus Cathedral, where Ferdy and I had been wed only weeks ago, called for reckoning and judgment.

I shuddered, suddenly grateful I'd thought to wear my cloak. It was too thin to keep all the winter chill away, but it had been a gift from my friend Faye. It was a reminder to me that I was not alone, and that I did not have to be afraid.

But it was not enough to be unafraid, I thought, aspiring to be brave as I reached for my mother's dagger.

That was when a voice spoke to me from the shadows.

"It is no coincidence you are captivated, Madame."

"Excuse me?" I was surprised to see an older man standing just off to the side behind me.

"This city is full of beauty," the man explained. "And it is no coincidence that you are captivated by it."

The older man was carrying a small box and a pile of papers, and his one hand was smudged with ink and charcoal from his sketching. From his plain, orderly cloak, I guessed him to be one of Prague's many resident artists.

THE ORDER OF THE CRYSTAL DAGGERS

The assessment fit; with his neatly combed, white hair, receding in some areas, he reminded me a little of Harshad. His boots were black and clean, and the only touch of color I saw on him was a patch on his sleeve, one that bore the signet of the University.

"This is one of the most magnificent places in all of Prague." The man gestured toward the top of St. Vitus, and then to the Old Town Tower on the Stone Bridge. "On nights like this, the moon sets behind the top of the main tower. It shines down on this whole bridge, illuminating it with heaven's light and calling dead souls to their eternal rest."

"Oh, yes. It is really beautiful," I agreed, noticing the man was alone, just as I was. He seemed harmless enough, if a little lonely, and eager to speak with another soul.

He pulled out one of his drawings and held it out to me. Inspecting it, I saw a sketch of the cathedral and the bridge, and I was taken aback at its lines of confident simplicity.

"Petr Parléř built both this bridge and the cathedral," the older man continued. "He took great care in his calculations. Do you know why that number is on the tower there?"

He pointed to the east end of the bridge, where the number "135797531" was carved in the stone.

"It's when they started building it," I said, surprised I remembered *Táta* had told me about it once before as we crossed the bridge to go into the city.

"Yes. The number is a palindrome, the same backward or forward. It was meant to be a blessing," the man said. "So you see? Nothing this captivating happens randomly. It is all by design and care, and any artist who wishes to capture even a hint of its beauty must be attentive, precise, and decisive, without regret or remorse."

"Your picture is lovely." I examined the drawing again. Even from where I was, even in the poor lighting, it truly was brilliant; the lines were straight and its shadows aligned perfectly to the scene before us. "You are a talented artist. This is perfect."

"Well, not quite perfect," he said with an amused half-smile. "As beautiful as it is, there are still imperfections, and they must not be ignored or overlooked."

"But it looks just like the city," I insisted, looking back at the church and the bridge and the moon, unable to see any deviation.

681

"The city itself has its defects. See the water line? And this slope along the wall here?" He pointed down to every flaw on his paper before looking back out to the city. "This city was designed for beauty, but it was not built on a sufficiently firm foundation. You can see the erosion of time and circumstance the more you study it ... Such defects ultimately cause rot and undermine the glory of a master's design."

"Perhaps the imperfections serve to make things more beautiful," I said, looking back over at St. Vitus and the bridge and the river. I was unable to stop my smile, remembering Ferdy and our wedding. Prague was part of my history as much as I was part of its memory.

Perhaps the defects of my soul and my city were reminders of our struggles and triumphs over the years, and perhaps we should be grateful for any beauty at all in a fallen world such as ours.

"Oh, gracious, no." The man shook his head with a small laugh. "One must never indulge such thoughts. Complacency only leads to irreverence and destruction. If the foundation is not properly built, no matter how beautiful it is, it will not endure."

"Perhaps." I did not agree with him, even if I was unable to articulate why. "But I fear that means even a talented artist like yourself will be forced to remain a student forever."

"Yes. Still, such a position has its advantages." His light-colored eyes twinkled at me playfully. "We have an appreciation for history few can rival. Even if we are not the best conversationalists, perhaps?"

His smile was wrinkled and teasing, and we shared a small, sweet laugh. Then the older man folded up his sketch, and I winced at the creases in his beautiful work.

"Wait," I said. "If you're only going to dispose of it, I'd be happy to take it."

Without hesitation, he handed it to me. "It would be my pleasure, Madame."

I smoothed the drawing out, before rolling it up into a scroll. I thanked him for it, and then I quickly curtsied and excused myself.

"My apologies for keeping you," he said. "Where are you headed?"

As I held the picture, I decided it wouldn't hurt to tell him the truth. "I am going to the Cabal, a publican house near the *Josefká*. They have meetings where they discuss all sorts of topics, including history and art and politics. Perhaps as a University student, you would enjoy it, too."

682

THE ORDER OF THE CRYSTAL DAGGERS

"I know of the place," the man said. "It's been several years since I've visited, but I see I will have to go back. For now, I must return to the University."

He held up his box of tools, as if to explain.

"Farewell, Madame," he said, giving me a formal bow. "You are just as captivating and beautiful as this city."

"Thank you." I was gratified by his kindness. He seemed like a lonely man, and I was glad he had his art to keep him company.

As we parted ways, I tried tucking his drawing into my cloak. When it wouldn't fit there, I put it into the pocket inside my tunic, underneath my corset. It was a little itchy so close to my skin, but it was safe.

I resumed my quest. Soon, the light emitting from the Cabal's windows was cozy and welcoming, as was its chatter and laughter; I even listened for Lumiere's voice, expecting to hear him making a fool of himself or someone else.

My hope quickly withered away once I was inside. There were plenty of patrons around. Clavan was pouring wine and drinks, and Helen, his wife, was talking with the customers as she wiped down the bar.

But Lumiere was not among them.

Jarl called to me from the far corner of the room, and my disappointment faded.

"It's good to see you, Ella." He showed me the stack of papers in his hand. "I'm glad the crowd will be a friendly one. I'm supposed to lead one of the talks tonight."

"What will you be discussing?" I asked.

"The ethics of politics." Jarl tapped his pipe between his teeth. "So you know I'm prepared."

"Yes," said Faye as she came up behind me, balancing three cups in her hands. "You'd never guess he's been fretting over his papers for days now."

It was then I saw the papers in Jarl's hands and noticed they were all blank. "You've been working on that for weeks?"

"Yes," Jarl replied proudly as he held them up proudly. "Perhaps it will make a good book one day, don't you think?"

Faye giggled. "I'm sure it'll be a bestseller."

THE ORDER OF THE CRYSTAL DAGGERS

"It should be, if you're the one who's proofing the final manuscript for the publisher," Jarl replied. He took a sip from his cup and grimaced. "I wanted whisky, not tea."

Faye only laughed as she handed me a cup, too, and she gestured for me to join them.

I gave in and sat down, letting Jarl and Faye share the latest news and gossip around the city. Thankfully, they avoided rumors about me and Karl; Ferdy had told them about my fake scandal, but I didn't want them to worry about the Order, or what it demanded.

Every so often I would look for Lumiere, hoping he would make his appearance. I began to wish for Ferdy to arrive, too, as Faye started talking of their wedding plans.

"It's just a few weeks away now, and Dad is inviting the whole town. I'm sure this place will be packed," she said. "Did Ferdy tell you? I invited you both to come and celebrate with us, if you are able to."

"I am excited for you and your wedding. We should be able to attend," I said, although I didn't actually know if that was true. Still, I did want to go.

"Good. I'm happy you'll be there." Faye gave Jarl a loving look. "I know you must be busy, especially since your own wedding happened so quickly."

"Yes, it did." I blushed, but I hid behind my teacup as I took another gulp.

Marriage was a serious business in Society, and that was as true in Prague as it was in London and Paris and other places. Some unions were arranged by parents since the birth of their children, and others were left to the deciding factors of titles and money. Few married for love, as Ferdy and I had, and even fewer did so in such a quick manner.

Of course, I suspected I was alone in marrying a hidden prince in haste because of Bohemia's secret *coup d'état.* The people who enjoyed clutching their pearls and crying "Scandal!" would be perpetually appalled if they knew how scandalous my marriage actually was.

I almost laughed at the thought, but then Eliezer arrived, and I could hear him starting to argue with some of the other patrons.

"I'm going to remind him that he promised to let me talk tonight," Jarl said, excusing himself. Faye and I took our empty teacups to the bar, and while she talked with her mom, I looked over at Clavan.

684

He was as patient and welcoming as ever. "Lady Ella, welcome. It's good to see you're here to join us," he said, smiling at me.

"Thank you." I had come to find Lumiere, and even though he wasn't there, I was truly happy I was. "It's a good crowd tonight."

"An early judgment, perhaps." Clavan gave me a playful wink. "Eliezer's about to inform Jarl he's going to discuss Count Potocki's dismissal from his position as the Minister-President and the future of the Diets."

"I have heard there is unrest abroad, too," I said, thinking of Harshad's news of war and the rumors of war across Europe.

"War in France has been coming for a long time," Clavan said. "Many of their institutions have broken down, and that which has not the will to survive, won't. Jarl's Uncle Rhys arrived from Berlin recently, and he says there's plenty of rot in the German Confederacy, too."

"What of the Austria-Hungarian Empire?" I asked, genuinely curious as I pulled out Lumiere's watch.

"Well, no one knows the future," Clavan said. "But if I were to speculate, I would say only trouble is certain. The American Civil War has ended, and it will take time for healing. But ever since America's creation, Europeans have such a mutual disdain and envy for it, I can't help but feel they will try to follow them."

"You believe a civil war is in our future?" My hand tightened around the pocket watch in my hand.

"There has always been war, Ella. Ever since the fall of man, we have known conflict, and we either must fight to overcome it, or it will overcome us." Clavan leaned forward on his elbows. "That is why freedom is only truly found in the present. You cannot be trapped in the past, nor cast too far away into the perceived future—for one is a memory, and the other a dream. But the question of what will happen, for certain, in specific terms, remains hidden until the time of revelation."

"You could just say you don't know," I replied, making him laugh.

"Oh, but where is the fun in that?" Clavan smiled. "You know this is true of your own life. You seek out freedom, but not freedom from struggle; rather, freedom is only found through struggle."

"That all sounds so complicated," I said, suddenly feeling weary.

THE ORDER OF THE CRYSTAL DAGGERS

"Still, there should be plenty of fun to balance out the struggle freedom requires. And speaking of which, where is your rascal of a rogue tonight?" Clavan looked around.

"I came alone. I wanted to ask you about this," I said as I presented him with Lumiere's watch.

Clavan's eyes, hidden behind his small, golden spectacles, gleamed in recognition and he reached out his palm. Without a word, I handed it over to him, studying him as he examined it.

"This is the pocket watch of a Bohemian Loyalist," he said.

"Bohemian Loyalist?" I repeated the words carefully, recalling Cecilia had mentioned it only this morning.

"Yes," Clavan said. "Before he abdicated the throne, King Ferdinand V was attacked at the beginning of the Spring Revolutions of 1848. While he survived the encounter, it was said to be a significant failure of his own guards and officials, many of whom he'd erroneously trusted for years."

"My father was one," I murmured.

"And more importantly, your father remained one," Clavan continued. Since he didn't ask me any questions about *Táta*, I assumed he'd already known. "This watch was made in the early 1840s, as part of a small collection. They were a special gift for those the king considered trustworthy. They were also given plaques, which are on display at the University's *Karolinum*. After the attack, King Ferdinand sentenced the traitors to death. Their watches were collected and destroyed. Only a handful remain."

He held the watch out to me. "So you have quite a gift here."

"Is there anything else you can tell me about it?" I asked. As much as I was enormously grateful to hear of my father's honor, nothing Clavan told me gave me insight into Lumiere's thinking or his possible whereabouts.

"Nothing particularly useful, although this one seems to be broken. With the wind-up mechanism locked, it's not good for telling time. If you'd like to have it fixed, I can see about getting it done for you." He gestured toward the crowd in the Cabal, which had steadily grown. "I know a few people."

Despite my disappointment, I laughed and eagerly handed him the pocket watch again. "Thank you. Please send me a message when it's ready, and I'll come over with the payment."

"Consider it a belated wedding present for you and Ferdy," Clavan said. "It's a pleasure to help you with your questions. And as it happens, despite some of the difficulties I've had in living in Prague, it's my home, and I feel a debt toward loyal men like your father who helped it get here. Even if it's still working out some of its issues," he added, as Eliezer began challenging Jarl's arguments and Faye looked on the scene, clearly a little distressed.

"Mr. Clavan," I said carefully, "have you heard anything about Karl Marcelin of late?"

"You mean, anything official, especially regarding how you don't want it known you've refused his hand in marriage, all for the heart of a street urchin?" Clavan gave me a conspiring look. "No, he's still keeping out of the public eye. But since you're here tonight, perhaps he'll soon feel compelled to leave his castle and rejoin Society, too."

"Castle?" I asked.

Clavan frowned. "Didn't Ferdy tell you? I sent him a message two weeks ago that he was right. Karl Marcelin has taken up residence at *Vyšehrad*. He's trying to keep his presence quiet, but there are always a few guards eager to brag about such things after a few drinks."

My heart felt hollow as I struggled to speak. "I see. So Karl is at *Vyšehrad*."

Prague Castle was the primary residence for royalty in Bohemia, but other castles were scattered throughout the kingdom that were available to them. *Vyšehrad* was one, and it was not just a castle, either, I remembered. It was also a military fort—making it an ideal location where Lord Maximillian could wait for Louis' arrival.

Ferdy lied to me. He lied to me!

Ferdy had known about Karl all this time—and he'd kept it from me.

Anger stirred deep inside of me as I sat there, dumbfounded and deceived.

"If you will excuse me," I said, cutting Clavan off mid-sentence. Briefly, I folded Clavan's hands tightly in mine, trying to silently convey just how grateful I was to him for his help and kindness. "I have to go home. Thank you so much for your help."

And then I left, letting the crowds and their commentary blur into background noise. I couldn't even look up from the ground as I walked out the door.

Tears stung my eyes, but I refused to cry. Another trance of sorts now mesmerized me—but this time, I was not overwhelmed by beauty and mystery, but rather heartbreak and agony.

"Ella."

I stopped in my tracks as the spell was broken, and there was Ferdy, standing there, outside the Cabal. I blinked, wondering if my despair had somehow summoned him.

Ferdy's hand reached for mine, and he wore one of his charming smiles on his face. It could've been the same as any one of our other encounters in the city.

If only he hadn't lied to me.

His fingertips had just grazed my arm when I flinched and stepped back.

He looked confused. "Ella?"

I shook my head and turned away. I began to walk quickly, heading back toward the manor, torn between my desire to fight him and escape him.

"Where are you going?" Ferdy followed me. His voice was full of concern—and maybe, just maybe, a small measure of guilt. "What's wrong?"

"What's wrong?" I whirled around, no longer uncertain. I was ready to fight now. "What's wrong? You found out where Karl was and you didn't tell me."

Ferdy's smile disappeared, and then he sighed. "I was hoping you wouldn't find out."

If I'd harbored any hope that he would tell me I was mistaken, that I was rushing to judgment, or that there was some kind of misunderstanding, it died in that moment.

"I can't believe you did this," I hissed. "You promised me you wouldn't lie to me again."

"And I didn't," Ferdy said. "I just didn't tell you the truth."

"That's the same thing!"

"Secrets and lies are not the same thing." He reached for me again, but I slapped his hand back.

"Don't touch me," I yelled, turning away from him and heading down the street. "I can't even look at you. After all the pains I've endured for your sake, how can you betray me like this?"

"Betray you?" Ferdy finally dropped any pretense of cordiality. He caught up to me and forced me to face him. "Are you mad? I'll admit I knew where Karl was, but I'm not about to apologize for keeping you safe!"

"Keeping me safe? By lying to me?" I tried to move out of his way, but Ferdy stayed firmly in front of me. "You didn't like it when others did that to you."

"It's not the same thing."

"Of course it is." I put my hands on my hips. "How long have you imagined me a fool?"

"There's nothing to imagine," Ferdy grumbled. "You didn't know about Karl until today, and he's just fine. He's stuck at *Vyšehrad*, watched over by Lord Maximillian, and nothing has happened. Nothing. He's being punished, effectively, and I say he's earned it."

"What about the Order?"

"I'm not your lapdog, nor the Order's," Ferdy snapped.

"You're my *family*."

"And you're mine," he argued back. "It's my job to keep you safe, Ella."

"And it's my job to return Karl to his mother," I countered.

"Why? She can't stop him." Ferdy's scowl deepened with impatience. "That's the reason we're in this situation in the first place. If you free him, he's not going to give up trying to regain Bohemia for himself. At least now, he's unable to make things worse."

I shook my head. "I can't believe you don't see how wrong all of this is."

"And I can't believe you're so upset." Ferdy's eyes sparkled with fierce lightning. "Karl murdered my friends, Ella. He's working with insurrectionists to disrupt the kingdom. He hired someone to kill me, his own brother. And who knows what he would do to you if he ever got his hands on you? He's not a prodigal son who needs to go home, Ella. He's a willing agent of evil who needs to be brought to justice."

"At the cost of my mother's honor?" I studied his face carefully. "And the word of the Order?"

"Yes," Ferdy insisted angrily. "Karl can't hurt you now."

"Yes, you're doing that well enough on your own."

"How am I wrong?" Ferdy asked. "Tell me. He's fine, you're safe, and the Order is on alert, watching for Louis Valoris and his grand appearance. We couldn't ask for better circumstances."

Pressure built up behind my forehead painfully, and I finally turned my back to him and walked away.

"I was going to tell you eventually," Ferdy said, softening his tone only a little as he spoke. "I was just waiting for enough time to pass to ensure his failure."

It was more than a chore to speak as I stopped in my tracks. "And when was that supposed to be?"

"After the Tripartite Council. Once Cousin Franz rejects reforms, Karl won't be able to do anything else. His dignity will never be salvaged, his ambition will be neutered, and then we can take him back to Mother." Ferdy put his hands on my shoulders. "Don't you see? All we have to do is wait, Ella, and everything will be fine. Trust me."

His hands reached up and caressed my cheeks, and he touched his forehead against mine. Staggering intimacy flushed through me, but instead of reassuring me of his love, it only strengthened my revulsion.

"No." Briefly, I saw the surprised look on his face and felt even angrier.

He'd been expecting me to soften against him, to minimize his sins and rationalize his trespasses against me; he might've even believed I would assure him that he was right, all for the sake of wanting a kiss and his declaration of love.

"Stay away from me." I pushed myself away from him again.

"Ella—"

"No! You lied to me, after you promised you wouldn't lie to me ever again. Don't you remember that?"

I met his gaze now, and I thought back to the morning I'd woken up after the Advent Ball, when Ferdy and I had finally seen each other for who we were: a spy, and a prince, with a world of differences and dishonesty between us. We had known, back then, that the only way we could be together was through love and trust—and he'd just broken my trust.

690

THE ORDER OF THE CRYSTAL DAGGERS

Ferdy looked away in shame. "I had good reason to lie to you this time."

"That's not good enough." I shook my head. "How can I trust you?"

When he had no answer, I finally turned and hurried away from him. This time, he didn't try to stop me.

Desperately confused and angry and sad and upset, I made my way down the alleyway and turned onto a new street. I barely paid attention to where I was going until I realized I was making a large circle around the *Josefkà*. Anger and humiliation burned even further into me.

Quickly, I righted myself and headed back towards home.

It wasn't until I crossed the Stone Bridge that I stopped and looked around.

This was where I'd been standing earlier, I realized. It was the place where I'd seen the older man sketching the city, and I'd been caught up in the magic of the night.

Could it have been only an hour ago that my life seemed so much brighter?

An hour ago, I was a happily married woman, and a determined spy, on a quest to find a roguish runaway. True, I wanted to find him more for past, personal reasons than anything that had to do with the Order's mission, but I'd had a clear objective.

And now I was not only alone, but I'd failed to find Lumiere, and I was fighting with Ferdy.

I walked over to one side and put my elbows on the stone barrier that lined the bridge. My body ached more than ever as I watched the water below. It was too far down and dark for me to see my reflection, and I was relieved; I did not want my mother's ghost to stare back at me, not when I was consumed by another failure.

And then it struck me—Lady Penelope had been right.

Oh, my goodness, Lady POW was right.

She'd said Ferdy was a complication, and he would betray my trust at some point. I could almost see her gloating now, and my knees buckled; I was more horrified than ever. Was I going to face another round of disappointment if it was indeed Ferdy who let Lumiere go free?

691

I looked back at the city; moonlight now seemed to highlight its flaws, and I couldn't help but wonder if the foundation between me and Ferdy was just as scarred and eroding with hidden decay.

"Ella!"

Ferdy called for me, as a rush of silent wind flew behind me.

I was going to tell him to go away again when I saw Ferdy was calling me from downriver, from off to the side where the city was—but the steps were behind me.

I spun around just in time to see a figure, dressed all in black.

A shadowed fist lashed out, hitting me directly in my heart, all before I could prepare to fight.

The air rushed out of my lungs, and my lingering pain reawakened in full force. I slammed backward and then slumped against the stone partition, unable to even scream as I choked.

My enemy attacked again, this time pushing me hard and sending me flying backward over the edge.

I was still fighting for breath as I fell, headfirst, down into the stinging cold river.

THE ORDER OF THE CRYSTAL DAGGERS

10

◊

I hit the waves of the Vltava with a devastating splash. Immediately, the weight of my cloak drew me further down into the river's unforgiving embrace. Pain bounded through me, baptizing me in panic. I floundered, looking for the surface, unable to determine up from down, all while I couldn't breathe, and there was nothing but darkness around.

My body was trapped, tangled up in the folds of my cloak; my skin was tingling with weakness and numbness. As seconds passed and death drew closer, I swore I could almost feel my mother there in the water beside me.

This was how she'd died.

I shivered, too cold and afraid to move otherwise.

"Ella."

I heard Ferdy calling out to me from far off, just the same as he had the night of the Advent Ball. His voice was only a muffled whisper against the tides, but it was enough. My eyes squinted open under the waves, and I saw a sliver of moonlight push through the clouded water. It seemed so far away.

My ears popped, and new pain split across my temples, while I was still trembling and already nearly frozen.

But I began to fight.

I reached down for my mother's dagger. The blade sliced through my cloak as I made slow, staggered cuts through the drenched fabric. I mourned the loss of Faye's gift while I sliced at my skirts, wishing I hadn't given in to wearing them. They no longer offered me any extra warmth as they dragged me further down into the water.

Once I had my weapon secure, I swam furiously for the surface, even as my consciousness began slipping away.

Just as my vision blurred over, a pair of hands caught me and hauled me upward.

The air struck me hard and fast as we breached the surface. Water sputtered out my mouth.

"Ella. Oh, thank God you're all right."

693

THE ORDER OF THE CRYSTAL DAGGERS

Ferdy was beside me in the water, his voice frantic with worry as he held onto me with one arm while he swam with the other. I tried to tell him I could swim, but I was coughing uncontrollably.

"We're over here," he called toward the shore, waving his arm. The movement, combined with my weight, sent him under the surface again, but he bubbled up just as I blinked the last of the water out of my eyes.

My stomach lurched as the city lights blended together in my vision, and I struggled to reorient myself.

Gradually, we made it to the riverbank. Ferdy was still talking, though if it was to me or someone else, I couldn't say. Between my constant coughing and water-logged ears, I couldn't hear him properly.

A new pair of hands took hold of me and lay me down on the hard, frozen ground.

My lungs were on fire, my body was imbued with frost; my coughing slowed as I lay there.

"We've got her," an unfamiliar man said to my right. He turned back toward the bridge. "She's breathing!"

I was able to hear a small murmur of approval from out in the distance; apparently there were some onlookers by the bridge who'd watched my dramatic rescue, and my cheeks flushed with cold embarrassment.

"Can you help me get her home?" Ferdy's voice was shaking as much as my body was, now that we were out of the water.

"I'll talk to Eliezer," Jarl offered. "He's got a carriage we might be able to use."

"Of course he does," the first voice said. "But let's see if he'll let you use it."

"Uncle, please don't underestimate Elie's capabilities for charity," Jarl admonished, and I saw the man was Jarl's Uncle Rhys. I'd only briefly seen him before; he was a bigger man, with a burly stature and a gruff face. His voice held hints of the many nights he'd spent smoking his cheroots and drinking hard liquor.

"It's not his charity I would question, but his inclination to humor you," Rhys explained. "After tonight's debate, I'm not even sure you'll be allowed back in the Cabal."

"Clavan won't let him refuse," Jarl said.

"I'll pay him if needed," Ferdy offered.

THE ORDER OF THE CRYSTAL DAGGERS

"That sounds like a better deal," Rhys said.

While Jarl laughed and the two talked with each other in their familiar ways, Ferdy pulled off his shirt and thrust it over my head.

"Sorry it's cold," Ferdy whispered to me. "But I don't have anything else to cover you."

I felt myself nod limply, before I coughed again and shivered even more. My fingers were frozen as I reached for my mother's dagger again. Once I found it was still there, secured to my side, I relaxed and allowed myself to rest.

Another jacket was tucked around me. I coughed again, flooded by the smell of pipe tobacco—Jarl's coat, I realized.

The dizziness returned, amplified by the cold. Ferdy called out my name again, but I didn't answer him this time.

Instead, my thoughts turned to my mother—to her death, to how lonely I felt without her. And then the last of my reality disappeared, and my consciousness fell away.

In the world between dreams and memories, everything felt real, just as real as it had been when I was a child.

I was a child again, sitting with *Máma* in her bedroom, as she carefully brushed my hair. There was a mirror in front of me, and my five-year-old self blinked back at me with large, innocent eyes.

"Grandmother would simply adore your curls, Eleanora," *Máma* said.

Through the mirror's reflection, I drank in the sight of my mother, seeing her own ebony locks elegantly brushed back for the day. Her locket, the one hidden in my room along with my father's pocket watch, was tucked just underneath the lacy edge of her bodice. Her eyes were just like mine, but for the first time, I saw the hidden depth of their secrets and shadows.

She was everything I remembered, and everything I'd forgotten.

The door to her bedroom opened. I blinked, surprised to see *Táta* come into the room.

695

"Dolf." *Máma*'s lips turned up into a genuine smile and lit up her eyes. "Were you looking for me?"

"Only all of my life." My father stood straight and tall; his coal-black hair was as ruffled and messy as the rest of him, but his eyes were cheerful and his step was energetic as he kissed *Máma*'s hand.

He picked me up and held me close to his heart. I cried happily for my *Táta*, though my voice seemed much more hollow; my older self still knew how he would neglect Ben, plunge himself into his work, and marry again after losing my mother. But my small body stayed there, curled against him, listening as he told *Máma* he'd been called to represent the king— Ferdy's father—on another trip to Constantinople.

"Oh, Dolf," *Máma* murmured, clearly dismayed by the news. "Must you go?"

"I'm sorry, my love," he replied. "But it's my duty. And I'll get to practice more of my Arabic."

"Duty to family should come before duty to the kingdom."

"Duty to family is only possible through duty to the kingdom." My father sighed. "I am the king's ambassador. I warned you when we were married this would happen."

"And I warned you I would still complain."

"Eleanor." My father sounded heartbroken, and I remembered how he never liked to see her sad. I glanced over to see my mother's nose twitch, and then a second later, she masked her face with a large smile.

"I am only teasing," she said, her tone both apologetic and dishonest. "You are a good man, Dolf. The world doesn't deserve you, and I hate to have to share you. Especially as often as I do. It is very lonely at times."

I could still see her as my head leaned on *Táta*'s shoulder. Ben had been right about her melancholy. As much as she loved my father, and her family, I could see now there were secrets in her past that isolated and imprisoned her.

"Your cousin is still here," *Táta* replied. "Unless he's decided to end his stay early?"

My mother chuckled at his hopeful tone. "Lumiere always stays until he is escorted out. I'm sure my father will take care of him soon."

"Take care of Lumiere? You don't happen to mean Jakub will murder him for me, do you?" My father let out a jovial laugh.

THE ORDER OF THE CRYSTAL DAGGERS

I understood he was making a joke, and on any other given day, I could offer him my sincere sympathies and perverse pleasure. But this time, I could only frown at his remark; I didn't know why. I only knew the words struck me much more harshly and more familiar than I would've liked.

"No, but you needn't worry about seeing him out." *Máma's* fingers curled around her locket again. "You can stay as pure and as kind as you've always been, my dear husband. Let others sully their hands with such unpleasantries."

"First Jakub gives me permission to marry you, and now he will handle Lumiere? He spoils me with his graciousness."

"He was always very grateful for how you saved me that day in Constantinople," *Máma* said softly. "And how you've been so good to me every day since we reunited."

"It is a joy and privilege I seek to honor every day that I am home." He touched her locket delicately. "I will bring you home an even more extravagant necklace."

"You know I prefer books, Dolf." *Máma* smiled sadly. "Besides, you gave me this when we were engaged, and I would be devastated at its loss."

She took me from his arms, and then *Táta* leaned in and kissed her on the forehead.

"You think me pure and kind, but I am nowhere near as perfect as you, Madame wife," he said as he left the room.

Once my father was gone, my mother put me down again. I watched as she put her hand over her locket and fumbled with it anxiously. Her eyes clouded over with a vision I couldn't see as she let out a small, forlorn whisper and clasped her hands together in a quick, fervent prayer.

I reached for her. "*Máma.*"

"Eleanora." She bit down on her lower lip and then tucked her locket back beside her heart in a dutiful manner.

As she positioned me in front of the mirror, I blinked to see my face in the mirror had changed. I was no longer a child, but a grown woman.

But *Máma* did not change. She only patted my curls down again and sifted my curls through her fingers. "What is it?"

"What should I do?" I asked.

THE ORDER OF THE CRYSTAL DAGGERS

"Why, Eleanora, what we must do what we must." She let out a sad sigh, but she was resolved, steady, and firm. "We must be kind, and we must be brave."

I looked at her expectantly. "And then what?"

"We must have faith we made the right choices."

"And if we didn't?"

Máma looked away from me as her confidence faded and weariness shadowed her eyes; she toyed with the locket around her neck again. "Everyone has regrets, darling."

"That doesn't help." I frowned. "This is too hard."

Máma laughed softly and gathered me into her arms. "Well, don't lose hope. After all, my dear Eleanora, my lovely one, your life can change at any moment; you need only be brave enough to let it."

I was hoping for a better answer.

Ferdy had willfully kept vital information from me regarding the Order's mission, to punish Karl while also protecting me. For as little as he thought of the Order in general, he was certainly willing to act in a way that Lady POW would applaud, if only he were on her side.

I would've loved to talk with *Máma* about anything and everything, but especially about Ferdy. How I loved him, how I couldn't trust him, and how I couldn't live without him—quite literally, thanks to our current circumstance.

Of course, she'd had her own secrets, and she might've felt more sympathetic toward Ferdy than I would've liked.

My vision swam out of focus as *Máma* leaned her head down on mine. "There's still reason to hold on," she whispered.

Tearfully, I clung to her, even as I fell back into dreamlessness.

◊　　◊　　◊　　◊

As I slept, the darkness felt long but familiar, and the more I slept, the more I began to fear waking.

It was only when I heard Ben yelling angrily that reality forcefully dragged me back to the present moment.

698

"What did you do to my sister?"

I stirred; I was in my room, in my bed, with multiple layers of bedsheets on top of me. I had my nightdress on, though it was loose and the ribbons were all tied incorrectly. My hair was unbound and free, and full of sweat, all while my body ached with pain and frost and my forehead was continuously burning.

"I didn't do this," I heard Ferdy reply, and I knew both of them were in my room along with me. "She was standing on the bridge, and there was a man who came by all dressed in black and pushed her into the river."

"And where were you? Out drinking with Lumiere?"

"What? No." Ferdy scoffed. "You know, if you want to be mad at someone, you should be mad at yourself. I would've never noticed her at all that day if it hadn't been for you."

"What are you talking about?" Ben asked, still fuming as he demanded answers.

Yes, I wondered, still half-asleep and feverishly dreaming. What was he talking about?

"The first time I saw Ella in Prague," Ferdy snapped, moving back quickly as Ben advanced on him. "That day, the two of you were waiting around outside Wickward's, debating over which books of yours to sell. You were loud enough that it wasn't hard for me to listen. She wanted to keep one of them, and you said no, and then you went inside to pawn that one with the rest. The book had a red leather binding."

He could have been describing several of our trips into the city to sell *Táta*'s books. But I had a feeling I knew which trip he was talking about.

"You were spying on us?" Ben's voice was getting louder, and so far, neither of them had noticed I was waking up.

"No," Ferdy said. "I was dressed as a street urchin. I was only a few weeks into my charade back then. I'd managed to steal an apple from one of the vendors in Market Square when I heard you arguing and headed over. Being poor can be boring at times, so I went over to see what was going on. And there was Ella, making a fuss, with all her soft, pretty tears, begging you to let her keep the book. But you didn't."

"No, I didn't," Ben said. "Cecilia wanted money and would've beat her again if we didn't get it. As it was, we nearly didn't get enough."

My eyes were closed, but I still felt the world start to spin all around me as I recalled that day, nearly two years before.

699

That was the day Ben and I had to sell *Táta*'s copy of *Morte d'Arthur*, one of our favorites. I'd been devastated at the loss; it was akin to losing our father all over again, but Ben remained firm.

"I knew you were unhappy with the price Wickward gave you for it," Ferdy said. "I could see it on your face when you walked out. And Ella saw it, too. But she ran up to you and hugged you, and when I saw her smile up at you, I ... "

"I recognized you."

I could hear the words, even if he didn't say them aloud. The memory of Ferdy's tenderness on the night he first kissed me hit me hard and left me breathless.

Ferdy wasn't going to say that to Ben; there was no need to explain how he'd remembered me from my father's funeral.

Instead, he cleared his throat. "Well, that was when I started spying on you more, I guess."

After he returned from dealing with Wickward, Ben promised that one day he would get the book back for me, and when Liberté was finally established, it would be in our freedom to decide to sell it or not. I hadn't known Cecilia had threatened to have me beaten again; Ben never said anything about it. But that made it even more appropriate how I'd hugged him and told him he was a good man, and he was the kind of person who did what was right even though it was difficult—and even if I was the one making it difficult.

"I didn't have any money on me at the time," Ferdy continued. "So I wasn't able to buy your book before it was resold. But I did look for better book dealers and collectors. That's how I found Clavan, and when I finally did get to meet Ella last year, everything came together in a way I'd always dreamed, but still never expected."

"I wasn't with her that time." Ben's voice was full of grim defeat.

Ferdy chuckled. "As I said, just as I'd dreamed."

When Ferdy stopped laughing rather abruptly a second later, I didn't have to look to know Ben had glared at him threateningly.

"But you do see, don't you?" Ferdy whispered, his voice much more hoarse and weighed down with worry. "I love her, too. And I can't lose her, either."

There was a long pause between them, or perhaps I imagined it; my forehead was full of drilling pain, and I couldn't keep track of the time.

THE ORDER OF THE CRYSTAL DAGGERS

It could've been hours later when Ben finally replied.

"You should just be grateful you're still alive," Ben grumbled. "Especially now that she's come home like this."

"I didn't do this to her." Ferdy's voice was much more unsure this time. "I wasn't with her when it happened. I was nearby and when I saw her fall, I was able to get some friends of mine to help me save her."

I heard Ben let out a long, unhappy sigh. "She's all the family I have left, Ferdy."

"I know you're not happy with me," Ferdy said. "And I'm sorry if you feel like you've been cast aside or forgotten. But I promise you're not losing your sister. We are brothers now. And I'd like to be friends, one day, too."

I had to remind Ferdy he was part of my family earlier, and I suddenly wondered if he'd changed his mind about keeping Karl's location a secret. Hope fluttered through me.

"One day, perhaps," Ben retorted. "But not today. Prince or not, you're still not worthy of her."

"On that point, *mon frère*, we are in full agreement."

"This isn't a joke," Ben snapped. "You need to take this seriously. And if anything happens to her, you and I will face each other with pistols at dawn."

"If anything happens to her, I'll let you shoot me." Ferdy shuffled his feet. "I was supposed to keep her safe. The instant I found out she'd left for the city, I hurried after her. I might not have pushed her off the bridge, but it's still my fault she was almost … she was almost … "

Ferdy's voice trailed off, and in the several moments of silence that followed, I knew he was thinking of Philip, and his other friends Lumiere's henchman had killed. He seemed unable to make out the words properly, and my heart caught in my throat. Ferdy was always so irreverent; he enjoyed a good laugh, and he eagerly brushed aside the gravity of a situation with a quip. But this time he was too hurt and traumatized to even speak the truth, let alone make fun of it.

I wondered how I'd failed to see just how afraid Ferdy was. He'd been angry over Karl's actions, and while our wedding might have offered him some distraction, it was clear when he'd found out I'd gone out earlier, he'd been terrified.

There was a small knock at the door, and it opened. I half-opened one eye and saw it was Marguerite. She peeked in and looked at Ben, but he quickly shook his head. She nodded and then quietly left.

Ferdy laughed softly. "She's been standing outside for a while now. I wondered how long she was going to wait for you."

"Shut up," Ben growled.

"Just an observation," Ferdy replied, amusement still in his voice. "I happen to know how she prefers waiting with you."

I recalled the time I'd gone to Ben's room to talk with him, and he'd locked me out and told me to go away. I'd stayed there an hour waiting, but he still hadn't budged.

Was Marguerite in there with him?

As if he could sense my curious displeasure, Ben shifted toward the door.

"I'm tired of dealing with you," he told Ferdy. "Keep watch over Ella. I'm going to go talk with Amir and see about Lumiere, or if there's any other news yet."

I held my breath, waiting for Ferdy to tell Ben that Karl was at *Vyšehrad* with Lord Maximillian. He didn't even have to say when he'd learned about them, I just wanted him to say something.

But Ferdy said nothing.

As Ben hobbled out of the room, I felt my heart sicken even further as my earlier hope died.

I wanted to scream, to sob, to cry out, but I didn't move. I couldn't speak; there were too many things to say, and I wanted to say them all at once. Ferdy didn't want to help me get Karl back, and he didn't want to help me honor my mother's promise.

Suddenly, I felt trapped.

Ben was barely out of the room before Ferdy gently slid down onto the bed next to me.

Weakly, I turned away, but he only pulled me up into the crook of his shoulder and wrapped his arms around me protectively.

"I love you." He pressed a kiss on my shoulder. While his touch radiated with love, I could also sense his hesitancy. "I'm sorry about before."

THE ORDER OF THE CRYSTAL DAGGERS

"I know." I managed to croak out a reply, and I cringed, hearing how unintelligible it sounded.

"I did promise you I would do whatever possible to make this up to you," he reminded me, but I said nothing back.

Was there anything I could say to this man—this man whom I loved but couldn't trust, this man who loved me but didn't understand me?

After several long moments, Ferdy shifted away. Perhaps he seemed to realize my heart had hardened toward him, or that as much as I was grateful he'd saved me, we had once more come to an impasse.

In truth, I wasn't sure I would be able to say anything else anyway. I was already feeling sick and disoriented again, and as I lay there, I suddenly and desperately hoped I wasn't pregnant.

"Get some rest," Ferdy whispered beside me. "I'll be back to check on you soon."

He kissed me softly on my forehead, and before I could object or say anything else, he was gone.

And then I was alone.

11

◊

It was hard to say how long it was before I slipped into sleep, or when I began to emerge from it. But when I did wake up again, I was certain I was not alone.

When I blinked my eyes open, I was not surprised to see Amir was keeping watch beside my bed. He was sitting in a chair, peacefully dozing; one hand was on his cheek, and the other was tucked inside my mother's journal on his lap. There was a small light beside me, with the wick flickering brightly against the darkness of night.

"Amir." My voice came out as a hoarse croak, and I cleared my throat to try again. "Amir."

Guilt trickled through me as he jolted awake. I had no notion of how long I'd been asleep, and it was still dark outside. But there was enough light in my room I could see the traces of silver winking at Amir's temples and the ragged shadows under his eyes. He seemed much more frail of late, weary and restless at the same time.

Still, he smiled as he saw I was awake, and his countenance cheered me considerably.

"Eleanora." He shifted in his seat, clearly uncomfortable. "Pardon me. I did not mean to fall asleep. How are you feeling?"

"Cold," I admitted weakly. "Did we find Lumiere?"

Amir's smile disappeared as he rose out of the chair, walked to my wardrobe, and pulled out another blanket. As he tucked it around me, he shook his head. "No, we did not."

"Was it Ferdy who let him go free?" My voice remained weak, but this time it was not because of the chill in the air.

"No," Amir said. "Didier is still here, and he's insistent that Lumiere told him only that he was going outside to smoke."

I closed my eyes and fell back against my pillow. "So I failed again."

"No." Amir took my hand. "Lady Penelope actually blames Xiana this time. She was supposed to ensure his door was securely locked while she trained you."

"I'm surprised. I didn't think Lady POW ever got angry with her." I bit my lip, not wanting to overstep myself. I also didn't want to admit I'd

704

THE ORDER OF THE CRYSTAL DAGGERS

struggled with the lock on Lumiere's door myself, so I knew Xiana wasn't as guilty as Lady Penelope thought her to be. "You didn't tell Lady POW about what happened at my training session, did you?"

Amir shook his head again. It seemed Ferdy wasn't the only one keeping information to himself, although in this case, I could excuse Amir's decision more easily. I imagined he wanted Xiana to save face in front of the others, and he likely didn't want to discuss her unrequited affections, either.

"She did stop by earlier to apologize, to the both of us. She even brought some tea, but she took it away when I told her that you were asleep."

"I'm glad," I said. And I was glad.

Glad she apologized to Amir and me, and glad I didn't have to talk to her about it.

At last, I squeezed his hand and then let him go. "How long have I been indisposed?"

"Not long. It's nearly sunrise, although it may snow yet." Amir reached over and felt my forehead. "Your fever has improved."

Just then, my stomach rumbled loudly.

"That's also a good sign." Amir let out a quiet laugh while I politely excused myself. "The others will be happy to see you awake. Plenty have come to check in on you since your return."

"I'll wager Lady POW didn't," I murmured darkly. "She would've seen what happened to me as divine justice for going against her orders."

"Providence is full of divine mercy, too," Amir reminded me. "And as it happens, Lady Penelope did come to see you. She didn't even try to wake you up, either."

"Where's Ferdy?" I asked, trying to keep evidence of my lingering hurt out of my voice.

"He was in his old room, last I saw him." Amir gave me a thoughtful look. "He thinks he's to blame for your fall into the river."

"Unless he was the one who pushed me, he wasn't," I said with a small, disdainful snort. "But I know he feels terrible about what happened."

"Any husband would be alarmed for the fate of his wife."

"No, it's different than that." I shook my head. "He knows where Karl is. And he's known for the last fortnight."

705

THE ORDER OF THE CRYSTAL DAGGERS

There was a long pause between us before Amir simply nodded. "I see. Tell me what happened."

It wasn't hard to talk with Amir. His presence was a remedy in itself. He sat next to me, calmly listening as I explained what happened at the Cabal, and then at the bridge. Sometimes he asked questions, and I did my best to answer them. I told him about Clavan's information about Lumiere's watch and the Bohemian Loyalists, about Faye and Jarl's approaching wedding, what Ferdy had told me about Karl, and I described what I could of my attacker.

When I was done, I looked at him expectantly.

Amir put his hand on his chin thoughtfully. "It's good you left Lumiere's watch with Clavan. Otherwise you might've lost it."

"Oh, yes. I guess so." I shrugged. "But what about Ferdy?"

"What about him?" Amir shifted in his chair again, looking uncomfortable.

"He knew where Karl was and didn't tell me. And he hid the information from the Order, too."

"Do you suspect he's working with the League against Lady Penelope, or others?"

"No, of course not." I sighed. "But … he didn't tell me."

I knew I was being silly the moment I said it, but I couldn't stop myself from feeling so blindsided and betrayed.

"What were his reasons for keeping it a secret?" Amir asked.

"He said it was to keep me safe," I grumbled. "And that it would be better for Karl to be stuck at *Vyšehrad* until the Tripartite Council was over. He was quite content to keep the Order from interfering."

"Does your beloved have a reason to distrust the Order?"

"No. I mean, he thinks we're assassins," I said. "But he said he would help me as I worked with the Order. And even the Empress said *Máma* had promised to keep her family safe, remember?"

"I do not believe your mother promised that for the Order. If it was after her arrival in Prague, and her marriage to your father, she might have been promising that on her own behalf—or more on behalf of your father's oath, if he truly was a Bohemian Loyalist. It would mark a turn in her allegiance, and in her life." Amir pulled out her journal to show me the little he had left. "I am making progress in my reading."

706

THE ORDER OF THE CRYSTAL DAGGERS

I nodded in approval. "Thank you."

"And as for what to do about your beloved, the only suggestion I can give you would be that you speak with him. You see this as a breach of trust between you, and that should be mended first," Amir said. "It helps that he is right about Karl being unable to do much otherwise."

"Hey!"

"I can agree with his reasoning at that point, even if his actions have hurt you," Amir said. "Karl's ambitions have been interrupted, but most believe it is because of marriage. If the truth were to come out, his reputation would be tainted with truly irredeemable scandal. Your beloved makes a good case for keeping him under guard, even if it's the enemy that's watching him. Karl is likely upset with both of you, and there's no telling what he would do to you if he could get a hold of you."

"I didn't want you to take Ferdy's side," I groaned. "I don't care if he thinks he's protecting me. If our positions had been reversed, I wouldn't have done this to him."

"It is uncharitable to condemn others for their worst failings while we judge ourselves by our best intentions."

"Well, what about Louis?" I asked, quickly changing my approach. "Lady POW said we need to keep Karl away from him."

"Louis is playing a deep game with the monarchy and other surrounding nations," Amir agreed. "But Ferdy wouldn't have known that before yesterday, same as you. In fact, I'm not certain he even knows about it now."

I swallowed a groan; Amir was right, of course. Ferdy wouldn't have known about Louis or his plans, but he'd still known what it meant to me for us to return Karl to his mother—and that was why I'd been so upset with him.

"All right, I don't want to talk about this anymore," I said.

Amir gave me a sad smile. "Are you sorry you asked for my opinion now? Perhaps next time you will save yourself the disappointment."

"I was hoping for a better answer." I rolled my eyes, before ruefully smiling back at him. "But it seems even now, you and *Máma* are of the same mind."

"What do you mean?"

"I had a dream about her." I looked down at my hands as I clasped them together in my lap. "It felt like a memory of sorts, but I was living it again. She was talking with my father, and he had to go on a trip, and ... "

My voice trailed off, and as much as I was mortified of giving credence to a dream, I couldn't stop myself from believing it had been real.

"Eleanora." Amir moved his chair in closer to me. "Tell me something. If you had to choose between Ferdinand and the Order, which would you choose?"

"What does that have to do with my dream?" I asked, slightly irritated.

I had already been disappointed with his answers once; did he really need to upset me again?

"Be patient with me," Amir said. "Tell me your choice."

I crossed my arms, feeling a little flustered. Ferdy had deceived me, even if he hadn't technically lied, and I was angry at him for being hypocritical and high-handed. But as for the Order, it might be better for them if I stepped back. Hadn't I failed them numerous times already?

"I would choose Ferdy," I said. "But I'd at least like to finish this mission first. For *Máma*'s sake."

"I thought as much," Amir said. "This is about Naděžda more than anything else, isn't it?"

"Why wouldn't it be?" I scoffed. "That was the promise of the Order to begin with—that I would learn the truth about her."

"Eleanora, as much as I love Naděžda, I would not want you to be her," Amir told me quietly. "I beg you, do not carry her mission as your own mantle. She would not want you to."

"Because she left the Order?" I snapped back, angry Amir had seen through my façade.

"No." Amir put his hand on my shoulder gently. "Because she loved you. She would not want to burden you with her failures, real or imagined or otherwise. I have no doubt her spirit will carry you throughout your own mission, but you must not confuse it with hers."

"If she loved me so much, then why did she leave me?"

Amir gave me a pained smile as I realized what I'd said. He shook his head before I could apologize. "She has never left us, Eleanora. We still remember her; we still love her. And we will carry her in here, until we meet again." He placed his hand over his heart. "You have her spirit, but you have your own life to live. And I am here, as are the others, to help you as you do so. She loved you—as do I, and as your brother and husband do."

"What about Lady POW?" I asked, brushing the tears back into my eyes.

"I have learned not to speak for her." Amir gave me a rueful smile.

"Probably for the best."

"She has to learn, too. She has to learn to see who you are beyond Naděžda's shadow." Amir's hand tightened on my shoulder. "Don't hold back on who you are, Eleanora. You are your mother's daughter—and your father's too, if Lumiere is to be believed."

"What do you mean by that?" I asked.

"I knew of Adolf Svoboda," Amir said. "He was enchanted by your mother, as any man with seeing eyes and a beating heart would be."

"You don't have to be so kind," I whispered. "He had his faults, too."

As if Amir and I had the same thought, we both glanced off to the side, in the direction of Ben's room.

"That is true," Amir continued slowly. "And some part of that, I wonder if it wasn't my fault."

"Did *Táta* know about you?" I asked.

"I cannot say for certain. But I wouldn't be surprised." Amir gestured toward *Máma*'s journal, and my mouth went dry as I thought back to my dream. *Táta* had been learning Arabic. If he'd been able to decipher her code, he would've been able to read it.

While it had been a dream, I was still certain it held some truth.

Amir sighed. "Naděžda was … captivating, illuminating, invigorating. Her humor was infectious. But there was a darkness inside her, too. And as bright and lovely as she was, there were times when I saw it slip through. I imagine after a time, your father likely figured out she wasn't quite the person he had fallen in love with. People change, sometimes even while you get to know them, but you also find they reveal themselves more; they change, even as they stay the same."

"I'll wager Harshad taught you that."

"You're already changing yourself by adopting more of Ferdy's gambling predilections," Amir pointed out. "So you know it's true. Although if anything, Harshad is the exception that proves the rule."

709

I let out a sigh. "Ben told me he remembers *Máma* was melancholic."

All the light and humor in Amir's eyes flickered away. "Undoubtedly, she was, after everything that happened ... "

His voice drifted off, and then he cleared his throat.

"But as I was saying, regarding your father ... From what I know, he was very loyal to Bohemia. He worked with Jakub Cerný, your grandfather, to protect Prague from Louis Valoris and his previous attempts to weaken the Empire. Back in 1845, in Constantinople, Louis ordered his men to steal a shipment of weapons. They were to go to revolutionary leaders in different countries, including Bohemia."

"Lady Penelope doesn't like to talk about Constantinople," I murmured, thinking of her anger over the topic.

"She has a lot of reasons for hating that particular mission." Amir's tone was easy and light, but I could see his expression was full of longing. "Lumiere being one of them, of course. It was then we met, and I saved his life."

"You saved his life?" I asked.

"Yes." Amir smiled as I made a face. "In return, he helped us find the missing weapons. It was easy, since he was the one in charge of stealing them. In the end, Lumiere got away, of course, but that is when we first became friends."

"I can see why Lady POW doesn't like Lumiere, but why would she have a problem discussing that? It doesn't sound that bad."

"There are other reasons." Amir looked away from me again. "After we left port, we found out I'd saved Lumiere from a group of Bohemian Loyalists your grandfather had sent to find the same weapons."

"This is really complicated," I murmured.

"International politics always are," Amir replied. "The League is British, even if it has members from other nations, but the Order is now largely working under Queen Victoria, too."

"Why have two groups working like that?" I asked. "Don't they do the same thing?"

"They gain power and money by rather sundry and ill-advised means. In some ways, it is ingenious to have two sides fighting each other, while their master watches and pulls the strings from the shadows."

THE ORDER OF THE CRYSTAL DAGGERS

I grimaced at the thought. Ferdy had always seen the Order as a group of assassins, and perhaps I should not have brushed the accusations aside so quickly.

But I'm not an assassin, and Ferdy knows that.

Amir cleared his throat and continued. "Jakub eventually figured out there was a split in the League, and Louis was working to undermine the ruling elite all over Europe. Louis had cast Lady Penelope as the villain before, and Jakub finally reached out to her to make peace. She rejected his offer and refused to forgive him."

"That sounds like her. She would hold a grudge."

"As much as she tries to hide it, your grandmother is a very loyal woman, even stubbornly so at times," Amir said. "The worst thing such a person can experience is being wrongfully accused of harmful intent or selfish ambition."

"Like the time she accused you of poisoning *Máma?*"

Amir only nodded, and I felt ashamed again. I was about to apologize for overstepping myself when I remembered *Máma's* locket.

"Amir? Would you open that for me?" I pointed to the drawer that held my father's watch, my mother's locket, and the set of royal hair combs Ferdy had given to me.

Amir opened it and picked up the pocket watch. "I thought you gave this to Clavan?"

"No. The one he has is Lumiere's; that one is my father's," I said. "Can you hand me the locket?"

Amir handed it to me graciously, and then I opened it for him. Inside there was the small miniature of him, and I smiled as I gave it to him. "My mother wore this in her dream," I said. "And I remember it from the past, too. It was hers."

"Thank you, Eleanora." Amir swallowed hard as he gazed down at it. He turned it around carefully in his hand, looking at the date and the small picture *Máma* had drawn on the back.

I didn't tell him it was tucked behind the pictures of *Táta* and me and Ben, but the picture was the smallest thing I could give him.

Or so I thought.

"Eleanora, may I see your dagger, please?" Amir barely looked up at me as he held out his other hand.

711

"Sure." I looked around, puzzled, before I saw my mother's dagger on the night table. I reached for it and handed it to Amir without hesitation.

Only to object when he twisted the hilt and dislodged it from the blade.

"What are you doing? Stop!" I protested, although it was too late.

I was about to yell at him, but then Amir carefully tugged on a folded sheet of parchment, and I realized why he'd broken my weapon.

I leaned forward. "What is that?"

"Naděžda's last letter to me," he whispered as he took it and unfolded it carefully.

There were lines of English faded with age and blurry with water damage, but I could still read some of it from where I sat. I watched as Amir's face lit up with remorse and regret and wonder, and I knew the exact instant he was finished reading it.

He pushed it toward me. "Here. You can read it."

"Are you certain?" I held the thin, moist paper with trembling hands. By the time Amir nodded, I was already halfway through reading it.

My mother's voice echoed along inside my mind as I tried not to cry at seeing her true self come out.

Dearest Mr. Qureshi, devoted doctor, sweet Othello, and my darling mongrel,

After all these years, and despite our history, I still smile as I write these words and think of you. Of course, I think of you quite often. Every day, in fact. While it has been nearly two years since I have seen you, I only need to close my eyes to find solace in your memory.

After everything that has happened, I fear I have done more than a disservice to you with my silence and my secrecy. I am determined in part to correct that with this letter, as cowardly and unkind as it may seem if it ever does find its way to you.

You have no doubt heard what has happened to me by now. Uncle has always been good about seeing to your care, whether you knew it or not. It seems he suspected all along you and I would find a way to be together, even if we were not destined to stay together, and I know his love for you is the same as a father's for his son.

I found a good man to marry—one you would even recognize. It seems Sir Dolf the Bohemian is good at keeping his word, even though it has been several years since we last saw him in Constantinople. I met him on the way to Prague, and we have since then become engaged and wed. He is a good friend of my father's, and it has been nice seeing him again without the colorful lens provided by my mother.

THE ORDER OF THE CRYSTAL DAGGERS

Admittedly, I am a little disappointed to find that rather than a half-demon, my father is fully human, and thus more sympathetic in his failings. He and I have reconciled since my arrival, and he is delighted to have met my son as well.

Yes, I am a mother now—or at least, I have a son.

And this is perhaps my greatest failing to you. Once more, I have believed that I deserved to suffer without you, that I deserved to suffer my life alone after the loss of our beloved Nassara.

It seems that God in his grace did not deem that to be my fate, but in my foolishness—of which you know well—I truly believed it was justice to let you go. But now, even as I see my son grow, as my belly rounds with another child, and as much as I love them, I cannot help but think of you.

In some ways, I wish I could forget you; longing for you poisons what I have now, and I do promise Dolf is a very loving husband. He suspects I do not love him as much as he loves me, but he loves me nonetheless. I want to be a good wife to him and a good mother to my children more than anything.

But I keep remembering you, and above all else, I fear losing you.

There are unspeakable wishes in every human heart, and you know mine as no one else will, just as we both know life is not so kind to our hearts' wishes.

For now, I am letting the Order go, as my father desires, and of which my husband remains ignorant. But I know, even as I tuck my heart away and fulfill my duty to my family, of which there is no greater joy in my life, I am not letting you go. As surely as I secure this letter inside my dagger's hilt, you will remain with me all of my days, and I will never stop looking for you.

Even if death should separate us, your face will be the last one I see as I die and the first one I see in heaven. Until then, my heart remains faithfully yours, and I will ever be

Your Naděžda

As I looked up from the parchment, Amir gave me my mother's dagger back, its hilt fully restored and secured in place. There was a new glumness in his eyes as he held out his hand, silently asking for the letter back. I gave it to him at once, letting my eyes linger on my mother's ever-prim penmanship until he refolded it and tucked it into his jacket.

"Are you all right?" I bit my lip, worried I'd made him unhappy, when I'd only meant to do the opposite.

"Yes."

He was lying, and he was tired, but he still put effort into making it seem like his assertion was the truth; perhaps he was even hoping it was, or hoping that it would be.

"Then go rest." I made no attempt to hide a yawn. "I need to sleep, too. Especially if I need to be well enough to go looking for Lumiere again soon."

Amir nodded. As he reached my bedroom door, he paused. "Have you decided what to do about your beloved?"

I shrugged.

"Would you prefer I keep our conversation tonight between us while you decide?"

From the way he looked at me, I could tell he seemed to know the answer to that question, and I was more than grateful for it. Amir was willing to let me take the lead on an issue that directly impacted our mission. Ferdy thought I was a fool when it came to being a member of the Order, and perhaps he was right; but Amir believed that even if I was a fool, I should have the chance to learn from my mistakes.

"Yes, please don't say anything. I'm not sure what to do right now," I said. "But I'm sure I'll make up my mind soon."

"Of course you will." Amir bowed his head as he excused himself.

Once he was gone, I leaned back against my pillows and curled into my sheets, wrestling inwardly with myself, bound to complete agony as I was divided over what to do—about Ferdy, about my mother, about my mission.

For a long time, I lay there, wide awake, lonely and angry and frustrated, thinking and not thinking at the same time. Part of me kept waiting for Ferdy to return, and when he didn't, I only grew more frustrated.

And then all at once, I fell asleep.

THE ORDER OF THE CRYSTAL DAGGERS

12

◊

The next time I woke, there were no more dreams left. There was only the harsh reality of the present day, where all the complications of the past collided with the uncertainties of the future.

My fever was gone, or enough so that I was able to get out of bed and dress myself, even if my movements were clumsy and stiff. There was a small ringing in my ears as I worked through the motions methodically and patiently.

Everything took twice as long to complete, but as soon as I was ready, I had a plan—and this time, I decided I would talk with Lady Penelope.

I took a deep breath as I left my room. I was ready, even if I didn't feel prepared.

As I passed by Ferdy's door, I paused to listen for any sound or movement. I was still angry with him, but I hoped he was recovering, too. When I didn't hear anything, I squeezed my eyes shut and pushed myself away from his room, further resolved to find my grandmother and do my best to forget about him for a little while.

Amir had given me his counsel, and I sincerely took it to heart. But my heart was broken, both by Ferdy's overprotective callousness and a sorely renewed sense of abandonment by my mother. I loved them, and like all mortal love, the abundance in its certainty was only rivaled by the emptiness in its brokenness. It was too painful for me to fully contemplate, and in the meantime, there were other things I needed to do.

Such as find Karl and return him to his mother.

If I did that, I would fulfill my mother's promise and uphold her honor, and if I wanted, I could quit the Order and go in peace.

We would stop Karl, we would stop Louis, and I would stop being a failure.

Sunlight and silence followed my steps as I walked through the halls of my home. I couldn't tell if it was a blessing, allowing me to go over my plan in peace, or if it was an ominous omen, one that allowed dread and fear to grow inside of me. I was even willing to bet it was both, a test to see if I could cling to the good and eschew the bad.

I almost smiled; Amir was right about Ferdy's gambling habits growing on me.

But I didn't have to be a gambler to know Lady Penelope would be in an unpleasant mood when I found her in the west parlor.

What I wasn't counting on was that she was not alone.

"—cannot believe you would be so irresponsible," Lady Penelope was saying harshly. "This is too important, Xiana. Louis Valoris has come once again to ruin everything, and we were so close to gaining the upper hand. We had Lumiere in our grasp, for goodness' sake."

I inched closer to the door, slowing down and eventually stopping so I could listen.

"He did say he could leave when he wanted," Xiana objected. "I did just as you asked. You know I have always worked so hard to make you happy."

"I don't need you to make me happy; I need to be able to trust you," Lady Penelope snapped.

For all I winced at her tone, I agreed with her logic.

"Is there reason you believe I might have made this error on purpose?" Xiana asked.

There was a lingering moment of silence, and I could almost see Lady Penelope shocked that Xiana would question her reasoning.

"Harshad and I have no reason to doubt you."

That was all she said, and I wondered if Lady Penelope knew what happened at my training session.

Amir had told me he hadn't talked about it with Lady POW, but maybe he'd mentioned it to Harshad.

Neither of the women said anything else, until Xiana brusquely apologized and excused herself.

As quickly and quietly as I could, I scrambled back down the hall and pretended I was just coming around the corner. Xiana saw me as she left the west parlor. She scowled at me as I waved to her in greeting, and then she turned and headed off in the other direction.

I headed back to the parlor door. When I peeked inside, Lady Penelope was alone, and she was her usual, surly self, seated by the fire and sipping on her tea.

I approached her, reluctantly admiring how even sitting in a chair, she could look down her nose at me.

THE ORDER OF THE CRYSTAL DAGGERS

"I'm surprised you're out of bed, Eleanora." Her voice was tart but tired, and I worked hard to remember she came to check on me while I was sick, and my mind was foggy and feverish.

Perhaps because of my mother, or because of my own expectations of her as my grandmother, I was inclined to be upset with her at times. But she was the first one who had, as the leader of the Order, reaffirmed my dignity and gave me a new sense of purpose.

And as repulsive as some of her advice was to me, I now knew there was good reason for it.

After all, she'd told me to trust people only to the point where I knew they would betray me. I'd rejected the notion, seeing it as too cynical.

But she'd been right. The stinging soreness in my chest wasn't just from my attacker on the bridge.

"Eleanora? Are you well?" Lady Penelope glanced over at me quizzically.

"Oh, yes." My cheeks grew hot as I pushed my heart's humiliation away once more; Ferdy knew me well enough to believe I would break down, cry, and eventually beg for his forgiveness. And perhaps I would've, too, if I didn't feel so betrayed and insulted by the expectation.

"I figured you would require a day or two to recover, so you don't have training today. I've just sent Xiana out into the city to continue searching for Lumiere."

"Perhaps Didier could teach me about guns," I offered.

"Hmph." Lady Penelope wrinkled her nose. "Didier is taking on Lumiere's sins as his own, and he is refusing to leave his own locked room. He no doubt believes I will assume he is on our side if he behaves in such a manner."

Everything I had seen of him demonstrated his quiet thoughtfulness, but I knew Lady Penelope would never trust Didier after Lumiere's disappearance.

"What about Harshad?" I asked.

She took another sip of tea. "Harshad went out during the night, while Amir fussed over you. He is resting now."

Resting, I noticed. *Not sleeping.*

From the large, drooping bags under her own eyes, I had a feeling Harshad wasn't the only one who'd failed to sleep last night.

"That's probably for the best." I clasped my hands together behind my back. "May I join you, Madame?"

"There's no need for formalities." Lady Penelope gestured for me to sit down in the chair next to hers as she poured a cup of tea and handed it to me. "May I assume you've come to apologize for your recent reckless-ness?"

"No." I held my cup of tea with a delicate but determined sense of dar-ing. "You've said yourself I'm getting better at standing up to you," I re-minded her with a small smile.

She did not smile back. "Let me hear your excuses about what hap-pened, and we'll be done with it, then."

I sat down and explained what happened, without telling her quite eve-rything; I still wasn't sure what I would do about Ferdy, but for now I de-cided to leave him out of the Order's business. "Lumiere was missing, and I went out to see if I could find him. I didn't set out to get attacked."

"I gave you strict rules about remaining here, and you know why."

"Yes, I know." I kept my tone as light as possible. "That's actually what I came to discuss with you."

"Oh?" She arched her brow at me.

I swallowed the nervous lump in my throat. "I say we venture out into Society this weekend. If Karl still needs my cooperation to maintain sup-port for his council, his plans would be disrupted if I openly rejected him ... wouldn't they?"

Hearing myself say it aloud suddenly made me feel extra senseless, es-pecially given my numerous and recent failures.

"You must still be feverish. That is foolish." Lady Penelope's gaze nar-rowed, and my palms began to sweat.

"Well, yes," I admitted. "But if I am bound to secrecy and silence be-cause of reputation and propriety, surely Karl is, too."

"He is bound by different standards; men must keep their finances pure and pristine, while women guard their virtue. You will be ruined if people find out the truth."

"But my virtue has not been lost," I murmured as my cheeks warmed over. "If anything, it has been secured."

"In the eyes of God, perhaps, but not in the eyes of Society, and Soci-ety is a much crueler god." Lady Penelope sniffed indignantly and shook her head. "After all the scandal with your supposed elopement, we must tread more carefully than ever. The elites will not excuse many trespasses, even with money and connections."

"I still think my idea has merit. That was part of my original role, wasn't it? To distract our audience. And with Lumiere gone, we need to find Karl more than ever."

"Hopefully Lumiere will be back shortly." Her voice was curt, devoid of hope. "And all Karl would have to do is show up to discredit or discard you, and you will never be allowed to go out in Society ever again."

"But we will be able to capture him." I clasped my hands more tightly around my teacup. "One does what one must, propriety be damned, remember?"

"Propriety still has its place, as damned as it may be."

"I understand the risks." I held my ground.

Lady Penelope gave me a calculating gaze. "Are you that tired of being stuck indoors, Eleanora, that you would put yourself in such danger?"

"If I am tired of being stuck waiting, I imagine Karl is, too."

She looked back toward the fire. For long moments, we sank into a contemplative silence. I watched every miniscule movement on her face, studying each pinched lip and twisted wrinkle, waiting for her final judgment.

"I don't suppose you think this course of action will make up for your mistakes yesterday, do you?" she finally asked, arching her brow at me.

"My mistakes are in the past, and there's nothing I can do about the past." My tone was too matter of fact for her taste, but she couldn't deny my logic—after all, it was the same as her own.

"It is good to see you're learning something from all your failures at least." She set down her teacup lightly. "I will call Marguerite and tell her to prepare a new dress for you, and Amelia and Jaqueline can get one for me, too. We should go out shopping while they work."

"So, you agree with me?" I asked, leaning forward in excitement.

"Yes. Perhaps you are right. It is feasible we can draw Karl out." She nodded once, quickly and decisively, and then stood up. "We have worked too long in the shadows if we are afraid of the light."

Hope stirred within me. My struggle had led to triumph. Lady POW had resisted my idea, but in the end, I'd made my case for it—and I'd won.

"But if we are going to do this, you can't reject Karl," she said, and immediately my heart sank and my stomach turned. "While we are out, you'll have to act the part of his completely devoted wife."

"Ugh, please no." I moaned. "Why can't I reject him and tell everyone what he's doing with the League and Louis Valoris and everything else?"

"Don't be this naïve. They will not believe you," Lady Penelope said dismissively. "These are people completely obsessed with gossip—money, sex, and power. They live in an imaginary world where real life never has a say, and I'm afraid Karl's plan is all too real for them to handle. It's best we keep them in the comfort of their illusions and the safety of their ignorance."

"But they should know," I argued.

"Even if they did know, would they care? And if they do, what can they do about it? They would be trapped by helplessness until mass hysteria or mob rule ensued. And we cannot allow that, especially when innocent people are the ones who would suffer."

I swallowed hard, thinking of how I'd been appalled at Lady Penelope's previous advice. True, it had been too harsh for me to take, and it would have been better if I'd listened more carefully.

Slowly, I nodded. "All right. If you think it's best."

"I do." She ignored my gagging. "Lumiere might be with Karl, and he will not be expecting us to ignore his disappearance."

"But we're not, though."

"The others will keep looking for him, but Lumiere and his father will be more worried about what we're doing." Lady Penelope said. "So, are we agreed, then?"

My fingers curled into my palms. The thought of playing Karl's smitten wife before the world still made me feel absolutely sick inside. "Yes."

Lady Penelope placed herself between me and the fireplace, blocking me in my seat. "You didn't come up with this plan after learning Karl is at *Vyšehrad*, did you?"

At her question, the disgust I'd felt at the idea of pretending to be Karl's blushing bride instantly transformed into blunt shame. It festered inside my stomach, twisting into knots.

THE ORDER OF THE CRYSTAL DAGGERS

I quickly took a sip of tea to disguise my discomfort.

"It's a good enough plan, if a risky one, so long as we know he's trapped where he's at," Lady Penelope continued. "But certainly you knew that already, didn't you?"

I had to swallow my tea carefully to stop myself from choking. It was too tempting to squirm in my seat like a child as Lady POW looked down at me.

"How did you find out?" I asked, my voice soft and weak.

"I imagine you can guess." Lady Penelope crossed her arms over her chest. "This morning Ferdinand and I had a very lively discussion before he left."

"Left?" My palms clasped around my cup as they began to shake, as I thought of how I'd stood outside his room earlier. It hadn't even crossed my mind that he wouldn't have been in there at all.

Lady Penelope nodded. "Yes. It seems he is rather annoyed with all our spy business, and he eagerly stormed out of here after we were finished talking. I'm not sure he'll be back."

"He'll come back."

She arched her brow at me. "Are you sure?"

"Yes." My heart was racing as my mouth went dry.

A moment passed, and then she shrugged. "Perhaps you are right."

"He will," I insisted, as my temper flared in anger.

"Well then, I envy your certainty." She crossed her arms over her chest. "Men are such odd creatures, aren't they? But we should be grateful for that; it makes them easy to manipulate. They are easy to lie to, and they are too quick to fall in love with an illusion. Especially an ideal one."

She turned to me with a small smirk. "It seems our family has a history of taking advantage of this male deficiency in particular."

I was already angry, so I was ready to argue with her; so many of my own illusions about my mother had been smashed of late, it did not make sense only men overindulged in idealism. But then, I realized she was likely talking about Ferdy, or possibly even my father, especially given what Amir had told me about *Máma* and her secrets.

I stirred my tea around in my cup, furious and frustrated as I struggled to control myself.

THE ORDER OF THE CRYSTAL DAGGERS

"I know you didn't approve of my mother's marriage, or mine, but you don't need to insult my family," I finally said.

She blinked in mild surprise. "It was not my intent to cause offense; I was merely stating a fact. It does no good to deny the reality around us, no matter how grim and bleak it may be."

I bit down on my lip. She was right, but she was also rude, and the remark seemed to be too insulting for me to easily dismiss.

"I imagine Jakub was fairly relieved when we parted ways. I know Arthur was glad to be done with me. That's how I managed to get a good amount of his money, even if the title has gone on to his sons." Her smirk softened into a genuinely amused look. "I have my own legacy to contend with, Eleanor."

"Eleanora," I corrected.

"Yes, yes, of course," she murmured. "Forgive me. You remind me of her so much—reckless, willful, dutiful … deceitful, secretive, strangely optimistic. She was better about obeying me, however."

"Not all the time," I said. "I wouldn't be here if she had listened to you, after all. She got her way when she wanted to."

"That is sadly the truth." Lady Penelope sat down next to me again, and before I could argue, I saw her eyes shift into a more melancholic mood, reminding me of *Máma* from my dream. "I knew she didn't want to be part of the Order, you know. She was very happy about the baby."

"Well, I know you weren't."

"You're certainly right about that."

"My goodness, how can you be so callous?" It was my turn to stand up, ready to leave at her remark. "Were you happy when Nassara died, and Amir and my mother split up, too?"

"Eleanora!" Lady Penelope shot up out of her seat and followed after me as I made my way to the exit. For an older lady, she was quick when she wanted to be, and she managed to cut me off. "Stop. You don't understand."

"Yes, I do," I said, tears filling my eyes. "You were the one who poisoned her, weren't you?"

"What? No. Never. That's not part of the Order's code." She reached forward and put her hand on my arm, almost like she wanted to comfort me—or capture me. "I told you that we protect the innocent the night I gave you your mother's dagger."

"It's the Order that's always more important with you." I pulled away. "Family should come first."

"Really? And should freedom take precedence over truth?"

I scowled at her in silence.

"Or what of love? Should that be first?" she pressed.

"What about love, indeed? It's clear that you've forgotten all about love. You're just as bad as Louis, aren't you? You're incapable of seeing anyone's value outside of their use." Despite the uncertainty I felt in accusing her, I remained still as Lady Penelope's nostrils flared dangerously. "That is what's wrong with you, isn't it? You only care about yourself."

"That's enough," Lady Penelope hissed as she stepped back from me, and for a moment, I thought she would order me to be beaten, just as Cecilia had done before. But she only backed away from me. I could see her hands, wrinkled as they were, grasping tightly at her skirts, and I knew then that I had pushed her beyond her usual limits.

"Eleanora, you don't understand," she finally said. "You do not know what it is like to live in the world as I have. You've been very fortunate to have grown up here."

"You mean away from you?"

"No." Her lips tightened into a pinched line. "The losses you have suffered are nothing compared to my own."

"I lost *Máma*, too."

"Eleanor is my greatest loss, but far from my only one," Lady Penelope said firmly. "I grew up in a harsher world, and perhaps you can tell. But I believe in love, and truth, and freedom; I believe in a higher calling and a duty that is honorable—precisely because I come from a world without any of that."

Harshad had told me before about some of my grandmother's past and how she'd grown up in a brothel.

"Repeatedly, my belief in each of those things has been tested by the world, and often at the expense of each other. I lost Jakub when he became blind to the truth of Louis' betrayal. I lost my marriage to Arthur when I realized safety and security was not a suitable replacement for love and affection. And I lost my family, to time and chance, and others' interference."

She glanced down at my midsection, and I was surprised to see the regret and shame in her gaze. It was shocking to see that *Máma* losing

Nassara had been hard for Lady Penelope, too, even if she had not wanted her in the beginning.

I exhaled a soft sigh of relief; she hadn't been the one who'd poisoned my mother.

"I have spent years working for the Order in hopes of bringing the world into a better place for my family, only to lose them in the end," Lady Penelope said quietly. "And the largest reason I have failed in this is mostly because of Louis Valoris."

I said nothing, but my anger diminished at her admission of failure, too.

"You might as well know." Lady Penelope pursed her lips. "Years ago, several works of art went missing in London, and Queen Victoria asked me to step in to find them. Art is at the heart of a culture, and it's easy to demoralize a nation if their art is compromised or destroyed. Eleanor was supposed to distract Society—"

"Much like we'd planned here in Prague," I said.

She nodded. "But then she was pregnant, and Amir objected to her going out at all. And then, of course, after she miscarried ... well, she was too distraught, and there was a lot of fighting."

"Do you really believe my mother miscarried?" I asked quietly.

The silence hung in the air between us like a shroud. There was only the small flicker of flames, and I felt the heat in the room exponentially increase as I waited on her answer.

"Belief in these instances is a matter of choice." She wrinkled her nose. "She wrote to me a few times after she married your father, you know. She said she had reason to believe that I'd poisoned her. I suspect she'd imagined these things, out of guilt or regret."

"She didn't do it herself," I insisted, unable to stop myself.

"As I said earlier, it's no good to ignore reality around us, no matter how grim and bleak it may be." Lady Penelope looked at me somberly. "Harshad told me much later that he saw her teacup that day, full of silver thallis residue. It turns blue in the blood, but it has a silver sheen on its herb. Eleanor would've known how much to mix in so she wouldn't die, just the baby. I can't say what the truth is for certain."

I frowned. I still didn't believe her, but I couldn't deny her logic. "It had to be someone else. Like how my father died."

Lady Penelope's eyebrows shot up in surprise, but she frowned a moment later. "Perhaps. Maybe I will ask Tulia about it."

THE ORDER OF THE CRYSTAL DAGGERS

"Tulia?"

"She was here around the time of your father's death, and she might remember something," Lady Penelope explained. "But never mind that for now. Regarding your mother, Harshad and I don't talk about what happened. There are many reasons it upsets us. After Harshad told me, I accused Amir of it instead, for obvious reasons, though of course he wouldn't do such a thing. But Harshad thought of your mother as his own daughter in many ways, and after his discovery, he couldn't look at her quite the same, devastated by what we believed she'd done. He feels awful at her death, especially because they did not reconcile before she passed."

I recalled Harshad's outburst the other day, when Lady Penelope had almost told me the truth, and I nodded slowly. His eyes had been raw with hurt and anger, and I recognized it now for what it was—a heartbreak that had never quite healed.

"What happened to the art thieves?" I asked, changing the subject. I couldn't think about everything all at once; it was too overwhelming, and Lady POW was right: it was in the past, and I wasn't able to change the past.

She seemed grateful for the change in conversation, too.

"Because our attention was divided, most of them ended up dying." Lady Penelope's eyes went dark. "Louis sent assassins to kill those who had evidence against him. It's hard to kill someone with my connections, but for those poor souls, they relied on the income from working with him. He took advantage of their poverty and talent. He was always good about finding others' weaknesses and exploiting them in his favor."

"I'm sorry." She was being open and vulnerable with me, but I saw how much of her strength came from dehumanizing herself. She seemed weak and lonely as she spoke, enough to where I was tempted to reach over and pat her hand.

"It wasn't the first time he'd gotten away from me, of course." Lady POW shook her head. "Eleanor knew what she'd cost me at the end. That was why she agreed to go to Prague, to investigate the growing revolutionary movement."

"She had other reasons for leaving." I thought of Amir divorcing her, of Harshad believing the worst of her, and of Lady Penelope furious at failing in her mission.

Máma would've wanted to escape such a prison.

"Of course. But Louis managed to slip away from justice, again, and I ruthlessly blamed her. So you must forgive me, Eleanora, if I am not entirely pleasant with you at times. This mission is deeply personal to me now that he's involved. I lost that which I have loved most because of him. Nothing would give me more pleasure than to shoot the man dead. But thinking about the past won't help me bring him to justice now."

"It might help me to trust you more," I offered, and she snorted back a laugh.

"I doubt it. Harshad was right; you are Dezda's avenging angel, not her redeemer."

"Of course I wouldn't be her redeemer," I said. "She might have quit the Order, but that doesn't mean she failed. She had her own losses, but she still got what she wanted. And even if I am here in her place, I am still myself."

Lady Penelope eyed me carefully. "Tell me then, Eleanora. Do you regret joining the Order?"

"No."

And that was the truth. I didn't regret it. I had a new family, new friends, and new skills. I was stronger and freer, more of myself, and more of who I wanted to be. I had an intimate connection to my mother's life, and I had a new foundation for my future.

If I did regret anything, it was my own failures.

Failing to see Ferdy for who he was, in more ways than one.

Failing to save Ben from more pain.

Failing to stop Karl, then failing to save him.

Failing to navigate my questions and fears and feelings, only to flounder in doubt.

But even with all that, if my failures meant progress, I would relive them a thousand times over.

"Good." Her tired, sad eyes shimmered. "Now tell me, Eleanora, can you believe in something even if it brings you loss? Even if it fails you? Even if you are not able to articulate its importance properly? Even if you only understand why it is so important once it's gone?"

I hesitated and then gave the only answer I could muster. "I guess it would depend on what it is I believe in."

THE ORDER OF THE CRYSTAL DAGGERS

Lady Penelope pursed her lips together. "You say Louis and I are similar, and you're not wrong. We are powerful people with connections, and we've had our share of losses, both incidental and intentional. We are both determined, smart, and ambitious people. But … "

She turned away from me again.

"But you're not a monster," I said quietly, feeling foolish for so much in that moment.

"Oh, I wouldn't say that," Lady Penelope said. "I do not happen to enjoy being a monster, but I am one."

"I don't think you are."

"Sure you do," Lady Penelope replied easily enough. "You've said so in different ways before, how I do not allow myself to be vulnerable or give my heart away or completely trust my friends."

"Well—"

"But I would rather be a monster a hundred times over than let the true monsters in this world win."

I swallowed. "I do not think it's wise to become like the people you hate."

"Wise? No. Necessary? That's a different question," Lady Penelope put her hands on my shoulders and patted my curls affectionately. "We do not live in a world of easy choices. We live in a world where we get to choose which side we will fight for, and which side we will fight against. But how we fight is a different matter, Eleanora. I chose to become a monster to stop other monsters, and I did so willingly, so you may also choose your own way to fight."

I stood there, speechless, as her eyes shined with unshed tears.

Not for the first time, I was tempted to hate Louis for all he'd done. I didn't want to disappoint Lady Penelope, or fail my mother; I wanted to protect others from his villainy, so that no one else would face the losses my family had borne.

In that moment, I silently vowed I would kill him myself, if necessary.

Lady Penelope cleared her throat, and sniffed indignantly. A second later, the tears were gone, and her eyes were hard again. "Either way, I should have earned your trust by now."

THE ORDER OF THE CRYSTAL DAGGERS

I hesitated, and then I held my hand out to her. "Trust is something built between people, Madame. Both sides must work together, and I'm willing to do that—if you are."

Lady Penelope looked at my hand. After a moment, she took it and held on firmly.

"I will hold you to that." She nodded soberly. "Now, let's get going. If we are going back into Society, we should see about adorning the proper armor."

Almost reluctantly, I smiled, glad I would get the chance to get out of the house.

I would draw Karl out, and I would use my charade as a way to find Ferdy and Lumiere.

I paused, briefly wondering if Ferdy had really deserted me.

What if he doesn't love me anymore?

All too clearly, I remembered how Ferdy had told Ben about finding me again, thanks to our arguments outside Wickward's, and I worried for a moment that Lady Penelope had a point about falling in love with illusions and ideals. Ferdy had been so surprised and dismayed to see me when we'd found each other the night of the Advent Ball when I'd come to rescue him.

Was it possible he had been in love with who he thought I was, instead of who I actually was?

A moment later, I dismissed the thought. Ferdy and I had fought each other in a small fight, a disagreement, and the perfect trust and faith I'd had in him was broken. But it was still there, and we could rebuild it.

And we will, I thought with renewed determination. If I could find a way to make peace with Lady POW, surely, I could do so with Ferdy, too.

All I have to do is find him.

THE ORDER OF THE CRYSTAL DAGGERS

13

◊

If the best part of going back out into Society was knowing Ferdy and Karl were both going to be upset with me, the worst part was knowing I was making a spectacle of myself, and it was no longer one of goodwill.

All day and nearly all night, Lady Penelope and I went from shop to shop, and then ball to ball, party to party, and so on and so forth, whether we were invited or not.

I was polite but memorable, dignified even when I was disparaging.

But a foreboding sense of the inescapable followed me as we moved through the crowds of the people we did and did not know. It did not matter if I was laughing or dancing, or pretending to drink champagne; the more I tried to hide my despair, the more hopeless everything seemed—even if my plan was working. By the time the clocks chimed midnight in Prague, it was universally accepted Karl and I were more than happily married.

Even if Karl himself had not made an appearance.

It was nearly dawn as we made our way out of Lady Taaffe's house party. As we waited for the carriage to be brought around, I caught sight of myself in a large mirror in the hall.

I watched my reflection with a growing sense of regret and shame.

The light reflected off the princess combs in my hair, as taunting as it was elegant. They perfectly matched my sapphire gown with its ruffles, cuffs, and simple stitching, and the soft dancing slippers that covered my chilly feet. A new cloak lined with fur was draped across my shoulders, and muted rouge was spread across my lips and cheeks. Yet still my eyes were hollow and full of worry, and any attempt I made to smile only seemed to mock all that was sacred and holy.

Quickly, I looked away; I was all dressed for a night of ballrooms and dancing and lively discussions, but my heart was still crushed by the weight of forced enthusiasm.

"You did very well tonight," Lady Penelope told me. "Hopefully it won't take long for our prey to hear of our return, thanks to your acting skills."

729

"Thanks." I tightened my grip on my cloak, wistfully thinking of the one I'd lost in the Vltava. "If this doesn't work out, I suppose I can still have a career on the stage."

"So far our charade is working just fine."

"If you say so." I watched a footman lead Lady Penelope's carriage closer to the exit, still feeling like a fool.

There had been no sign of Karl, no sign of Ferdy, and even Lumiere failed to make a surprise entrance; I honestly couldn't say who disappointed me the most.

"Are you well, Eleanora? You aren't still upset at what those women were saying at the milliner shop earlier, are you?" Lady Penelope asked.

"No, I'm not upset about that," I muttered.

Before, when we were shopping—and sending the large bills to Karl's former residence at Roman Szapira's house—we had run into several ladies of Society, including some of Lady Hohenwart's friends, each one more gossip-hungry than the last.

Their greeting was full of cynical excitement, and I could see their disappointment as I began rhapsodizing over my marriage. I lauded over how happy I was, and how Karl and I would soon leave Prague for another tour of the continent. After I convinced them my virtue and good name were intact, they were visibly eager to spread the news, even if it was not as scandalous as they'd hoped.

I wrinkled my nose distastefully. "I'm just tired."

Lady Penelope nodded. "It's been more than a fortnight since we've been out in public. We are out of practice."

"Thank goodness we're finished for tonight." I glanced outside again, staring at the cityscape before me. When I'd gone out looking for Lumiere the night before, I was free, and the city was full of beauty and truth. Now I was back to donning another mask, and Prague became a world of lies and uncertainty.

Lady Penelope chuckled lightly. "Navigating Society's treacherous waters can be difficult, but you have a natural instinct for it."

"Navigating the waters is preferable to drowning," I replied before I remembered my mother, and guilt plagued me.

"True." Lady POW thankfully ignored my tasteless jesting. "Still, you could have been a very successful Original."

THE ORDER OF THE CRYSTAL DAGGERS

"I think I've just read too many books." I gave her a tired smile. "Though perhaps not *The Ladies Guide to Excellence and Etiquette.*"

She chuckled. "You would've had your pick of husbands and prospects if you hadn't joined the Order."

"I'm not worried about my choice of husband," I said, this time through gritted teeth. Until that point, I would've said Lady POW and I were getting along, but Ferdy was still a point of contention between us.

"Eleanora, hush." Lady Penelope hurriedly stepped in front of me and squared her shoulders, turning her full, blistering attention onto the man suddenly standing before us. Disappointment struck me hard as I saw it was Lord Maximillian, instead of Karl. "I wish I could say what a pleasure it is to see you again, Your Grace. Alas, there are no words to do it justice."

His large, fluffy mustache twitched with an amused grimace. "I feel the same way about your manners, Lady Wellington."

Watching his practiced gallantry, I decided disappointment suited him.

"Mrs. Marcelin." The way he said it made what little warmth there was in the air disappear entirely. "What a lovely surprise to find you here."

I scowled back. "We are more surprised to see you, as opposed to rotting in prison after all your treachery against the Bohemian Crown."

"You might have captured Lumiere, but any evidence he's given you can easily be discounted as fraud," Lord Maximillian argued.

"Yet you still have not been out in Society either of late," Lady POW reminded him. "And neither has Karl, we've noticed."

"I regret to say he is indisposed tonight." Lord Maximillian exhaled sharply. "Rumor says he is fatigued from fawning over his beloved bride, but I personally know he has other reasons for taking to his bed."

"What have you done with him?" I hissed.

"I'm merely here to tell you he will be at the Potocki ball tomorrow, to honor our great friend the Count."

"Oh, really? You wouldn't be lying, would you?" Lady Penelope looked doubtful. "But then I suppose you wouldn't want Eleanora to inform the public Karl has decided to retire from public service now that he's a happily married man."

"Such a truth could have easily been a reality, had Karl bothered to marry my daughter instead of chasing after you." Lord Maximillian gave

731

us a quick, mocking bow as our carriage pulled up to the house. "He will be there tomorrow. Now, excuse me."

Lady Penelope curtly nodded. "You should go, before the former Empress learns of your presence here."

"She can't do anything to me," Lord Maximillian snapped, but I saw him grip the folds of his coat nervously.

I didn't know why he was worried; Karl wasn't concerned about her at all, from what Ferdy had told me.

"Eleanora." Lady Penelope tugged me along into the carriage, even though I wanted nothing more than to push Lord Maximillian into the coat room and force him to tell us all his plans.

"Why did you let him go?" My voice nearly cracked in anger.

"We did enough," Lady Penelope explained. "We know where Karl will be tomorrow night, and even better, we know where he is tonight. We can easily make the arrangements to intercept him."

I frowned. "I still don't see why we couldn't capture Lord Maximillian, too. He could be a good source to incriminate Louis."

"I know," Lady Penelope said grimly. "But if he doesn't return to *Vyšehrad* tonight, Karl will undoubtedly fail to show tomorrow. Let him believe we are letting him go as a measure of thanks. He'll be more likely to make mistakes in our favor if he thinks he's in control."

Once more, I felt trapped. I wanted all of this to be over and settled, and my heart ached knowing I would be stuck waiting again.

But I nodded glumly. "Yes, Madame."

As we drove through the city, I looked out the windows, searching for any sign of Ferdy. I was still mad at him, just as he still likely believed I was a fool.

At least if I am following Lady Penelope's orders, he can't say I'm a fool.

Unless he thought her to be one, too.

"I'll get Ben to come along with us tomorrow," Lady Penelope said, interrupting my thoughts.

"I don't know if he should be out of the house just yet," I murmured, knowing Ben wouldn't appreciate my objection.

"He can ride on the top box with Harshad," Lady POW said, pointing to the top of the carriage. "We'll benefit from another pair of eyes at

THE ORDER OF THE CRYSTAL DAGGERS

Count Potocki's tomorrow night. Xiana already has her assignments, searching the city in the daytime and making some antidote for us."

"Antidote?"

"Yes, to counteract the Order's poison," she explained. "Harshad and Amir are out looking for Lumiere as well as your attacker."

"My attacker?" My tongue felt thick as I dully repeated her words. All my weariness caught up with me, and I didn't seem to be able to do much of anything other than repeat the words I heard.

"Yes. Given Lumiere's involvement, I believe your attacker is a sign that Louis is either here or nearly here in Prague."

"I didn't think of that," I admitted.

"Who else would attack you?" She shook her head. "It's the same with the attack at Prague Castle, and the man who burned Tulia's house. There's a pattern to these things that cannot be overlooked or deemed merely a coincidence."

"How would anyone know it was me, though?" I wondered, trying to picture my attacker again. I couldn't see anything but a small, black blur inside my head and feel the echoes of small, powerful punches on my chest. I laid my hand softly over my heart. "Ferdy saw everything that happened. He might be able to tell us something else."

"I doubt it." Lady POW frowned. "I do not think he will be back when we get home, Eleanora."

I felt my nostrils flare in anger.

"We will see, Madame." I looked away from her and kept my tone as light as possible. I did not want her to be right, and I was appalled how she instinctively assumed the worst.

But when we arrived at the manor, Ferdy was still nowhere to be found.

Between his absence and all the lies and stress from my performance, I was grateful I was too tired to cry myself to sleep.

I couldn't help but feel like my faith had been misplaced, and I'd failed all over again.

THE ORDER OF THE CRYSTAL DAGGERS

14

◊

"Ella."

Ben's voice would've been more welcome if he'd only called me Nora as he used to, and then it would've been easier to pretend I only had a day of chores and errands to complete—although, that was about the truth, except Lady Penelope was in charge instead of Cecilia.

I grumbled out a barely intelligible response before burying my face under my pillow even further. I reached over beside me, feeling the empty bed where Ferdy should have been. I already knew he was still missing, but I still felt disappointed.

It was all too easy to imagine him back down at the Port of Prague, entertaining himself with fist fights or gambling, or back at the Cabal, where Clavan and Jarl and Eliezer would argue over what to do with him. Or he could have gone back to Prague Castle, too, where the former Empress would self-righteously chide him for marrying me.

I shuddered. Such thoughts were worse than nightmares.

"Come on, you need to get up." Ben put his hand on my shoulder and shook me, harder than he had to, but still more gently than he could have; it was his form of brotherly kindness, and it was because of that I finally rolled over and sat up.

"What time is it?" I asked, rubbing the bleariness out of my eyes.

"Nearly four in the afternoon."

"That late?"

Though I had not drunk any champagne the previous night, I felt groggy and sick and sluggish. Still, I was surprised Lady Penelope had allowed me to sleep without interruption.

"It's time to get ready to go to your party." Ben flopped down on the bed beside me, clearly much more excited about the mission than I was.

"Watch your leg, *brácha*. I don't want you to get hurt," I mumbled out my concern, and predictably, Ben frowned.

"My leg is doing fine." He stood up again to show me how he could move around without his crutches. "Amir and I finished the new brace, and he says my leg's even a little straighter now. I might be able to get by with just a walking stick when it's stronger."

734

THE ORDER OF THE CRYSTAL DAGGERS

"He told me that might happen." I curled my hands around my sheets, feeling guilty. Ben's leg had broken close to the knee, right about where it had broken before. Nothing that would stop him from living a normal life otherwise, but Ben would never walk without a limp.

"I'm just going to ride up on the top box tonight," Ben said. "So you see, Ella? It'll be fine."

"Does this mean you'll forgive me?"

The question was meant to be more of a jest than a serious inquiry, but when Ben sat down and put his arm around my shoulders, I almost caved into the temptation to cry.

Ben knew me better than anyone, and he knew what I needed.

"I'll forgive you for my leg before I forgive you for Ferdy," he said.

I peeked over toward the empty space beside me on the bed. "That's fair."

Ben snorted back a laugh, and I felt much better.

"Well, forgiving you is easier than forgiving him," Ben said. "He knows what will happen to him if anything happens to you, Ella."

"If you do forgive me, why don't you call me Nora?" I felt my nostrils flare slightly in helpless frustration.

"Ella is who you are now," Ben replied, much more easily than I'd expected. "As much as I might disagree with his tactics, Ferdy is right; it's a name that suits you."

"I am still your sister."

"Yes, but you have a duty to others, now, too, and I've never wanted to hold you back from being who you wanted to be." He looked out into the distance thoughtfully. "And you should be the one to choose that."

"Ferdy chose the name, truth be told."

"And you chose him." Ben rolled his eyes, before his mood turned darker and more serious. "But you know, Lady POW calls *Máma* Eleanor, and Harshad says Dezda, and Amir calls her Naděžda. I remember her when she would have sad days. Sometimes now I wonder if she just didn't know who she was."

"She still loved us," I insisted, putting my hand on his.

Ben nodded. "I know. But that's not enough. Human love has its limits."

He stood up again. "Anyway, you're stuck with me, just as I know there's no escaping you, and Amir is right; you are family, and I might as well forgive you and move on. It's better if we can work together for the Order."

"I guess that's what he does with Lady POW."

"For all the good it does him some days." Ben shrugged. "I should have better luck with you than he has with her."

A knock sounded at the door, and I heard Marguerite calling to me from the other side.

"Nora? Madame sent me to dress your hair for the evening."

I saw Ben's mouth twist into a grimace. "What is it?" I asked. "Tell me."

He seemed unwilling to say anything, but perhaps in light of our awkward truce, he answered me.

"She calls you Nora. I wish she wouldn't, that's all."

"I like it when you call me Nora. And I wish you would, too. It'll remind me of who I was, and where I came from." I curled my hands around my blankets. "So much of *Máma*'s past seems like a dream now that we know the truth. If she'd have had a brother who was as good as you are to me, I'll bet she wouldn't have suffered as much."

"It's no wonder you and Ferdy get along so well," Ben grumbled. "You're both good at manipulating people when you want to."

I smirked to hide my sadness. "It's a family trait, remember?"

Ben rolled his eyes, but he patted me on the head playfully. "I guess we'll see after tonight, *ségra*."

I'd hoped he would agree with me, but I was satisfied. He was still calling me *ségra*, even if he didn't want to call me Nora.

"Hello, Nora? Are you awake yet?" Marguerite's voice sounded out patiently from the other side of the door.

"I'd better let her in," Ben said gruffly. "We need to hurry if we're going to capture Karl."

"Ben?"

He shot me an irritated look over his shoulder. "What is it?"

I bit my lip and then decided to confess. "I was awake when you and Ferdy were arguing before. After he brought me home the other night."

736

THE ORDER OF THE CRYSTAL DAGGERS

"So?"

"So … that doesn't mean it'll always be just us. You can still find someone, too."

I glanced back at the door meaningfully, and then back to Ben.

But he only shook his head. "I doubt I'll ever be in a favorable position where a woman will want to consider marriage."

"If she loves you, I'm sure an unfavorable position would be fine with her." I blushed, thinking of the night of the Advent Ball. "I was in love with Ferdy before I knew he was a prince."

"Nora?" Marguerite called louder and knocked louder from outside the room. "Can you let me in, please?"

"We don't have time to talk about this now. Just worry about the mission for now."

Ben opened the door and excused himself brusquely as he walked by Marguerite. I saw her eyes dart down briefly, before her cheeks turned pink and she smiled to herself.

As she hurried to my side to help me out of bed, Ben paused at the door. I was just about to ask him if there was something else, when I saw he wasn't looking at me; he was watching Marguerite, in a sad, lovely sort of way.

I was stunned; I would've thought their relationship was all one-sided if I hadn't seen that look of soft longing on his face.

Ben saw me, and in a blink of the eye, he slammed the door carelessly. I could hear his uneven footsteps echo down the hallway as he hurried away.

My cheeks flustered, both in anger and sisterly protectiveness, as I saw there was indeed some spark of feeling there between them. What the exact nature of it was, I couldn't be sure.

And I didn't like that.

Ferdy had known about that, too, I remembered angrily, thinking of his earlier remark to Ben.

All the more reason to find him. All the more reason to punish him.

But first, I had to save Karl.

THE ORDER OF THE CRYSTAL DAGGERS

15

◊

From the top of the carriage, the gentle *pat-pat-pat* sound pounded like a quickening heartbeat as we rode toward Count Potocki's mansion. It agitated me, but I also smiled at its music.

Ben was tapping his foot as he rode on the top box. Weeks had passed since the accident on the *Salacia*, and this was the first time he was allowed out into the city since then. From the sound of things, he was excited for our mission tonight, and I envied his enjoyment.

As the Potocki mansion appeared in the distance, I could only pray nothing would happen that would make his leg worse.

And that was only one reason I was anxious tonight; I had plenty of others, too.

"Are you listening to me, Eleanora?"

"Huh? Oh, um … yes, Madame." I blushed.

From the look on her face, I knew Lady Penelope didn't believe me. She was sitting on the opposite bench, and as I met her gaze, I could tell she knew I was lying.

Thankfully we'd already gone over tonight's plan several times.

We were to infiltrate Count Potocki's party; she would take the lead, claiming she would "forget" she'd been uninvited, while I would look for Karl, continually announcing to any and every person alive that we were beyond happy in our marriage.

It was a simple plan, and I didn't think we would have a problem carrying it out once we got there, even if I was uneasy about seeing Karl again.

"Are you afraid?" Lady Penelope asked me.

"No. I mean, I have plenty of questions," I replied, more honestly this time. "But I'm too nervous to think of them."

"There's nothing to be nervous about."

"I'm afraid that's not how nerves work, Madame."

She gave me an amused smile. "If everything goes well, Amir or Xiana should have Karl in custody before he gets here. They'll send us a message if they get him first. And if he manages to slip by them, we will get him here."

THE ORDER OF THE CRYSTAL DAGGERS

"Yes." My tone and thoughts were glum as we pulled up to the front of the Potocki mansion.

Lady Penelope patted my arm reassuringly. "Think of it this way, Eleanora; if he shows up, we will be able to leave early."

I laughed, feeling a little better at her attempt to comfort me, and also pleased she'd called me by my proper name, and not my mother's. "That does sound good to me."

Ben helped me down out of the carriage. He was donned in bright-colored livery for the night, as was Harshad, who was still sitting up on the top box, watching the others who were arriving. I wanted to say something to Ben, something that would make me feel better, but I could barely speak.

"You'll be fine," Ben said instead. His voice was steady and calming. "We'll be here if you need us."

While I felt better at his kindness, I still could only give him a nod before Lady Penelope called for me to follow her.

"I'm glad you and Benedict seem to be getting along again," Lady Penelope remarked on our way into the house.

"Even if we weren't, we would still work for the good of the mission," I insisted sullenly, thinking of how Amir had forgiven Lady POW for their past struggles. She might have never forgotten his supposed sins against her, but they could still work together for the good of others.

They were still like family in that way.

Even if their bond was overshadowed by the past.

Lady Penelope and I were ushered into Count Potocki's party, and once we were inside, I was momentarily swept up in another world.

It was too easy to think of my first ball, where I'd felt a similar sensation. Everyone was sparkling with jewels and dressed in rich fabrics, and the music was a stream of magic and moonlight. But a moment later, the luster faded, and I was able to see the defects as well as the delights. The walls were covered in a ghastly dark green silk; there were places where I could see it had been hastily adhered to the wall. The newer curtains on the windows and several mirrors looked grand, but they were randomly placed around the room. There were candelabras covered with flowers, but the winter bluster already left them wilting.

I could almost hear Lumiere's voice inside my head, mocking the choice of décor. When I let out a nervous chuckle, Lady Penelope arched her brow at me.

"What is it?" she asked.

I could tell from her sharp, impatient tone she was just as tense and anxious as I was, though she was better at hiding it; after all her years of experience, it was nice to see her façade of perfectionism slip, even if it was just a little.

"Lumiere was right," I said. "Count Potocki should pay Roman Szapira to remodel his house anyway."

"Oh. I hate to give Lumiere any credit, but he's certainly not wrong in this instance." She nodded, ever so slightly, and then went back to scanning the crowds. A moment later, she nudged me with her reticule. "Stand up straight. Here comes Lady Hohenwart."

The cheery, plump woman I'd met seemingly ages ago sauntered over to us. She was wearing another one of her large turbans, and it jiggled on her head ever so slightly as she made her way through the crowd.

"Penelope! So good to see you again." She gave Lady POW a cordial hello before turning to me. There was a smug look in her eye as she assessed me. "Oh, my dear, I'm sure you know what a great deal of trouble you've given your grandmother. It is good to see you and your husband have returned or I'd fear the worst."

"Oh, yes," I murmured delicately, dismayed at the possibility of another passive-aggressive conversation. "Well, the course of true love never runs smooth, as Shakespeare said."

Lady Hohenwart chuckled. "No wonder you and Mr. Marcelin get along so well. You're both so good with your words. Wouldn't want to be overtly scandalous, would we?"

"No, of course not, Madame." I cleared my throat to stop myself from rolling my eyes.

I knew I was supposed to be lying to everyone, and well enough they believed what we needed them to believe, but it was irritating to hear people agree Karl and I were perfect for each other.

It was also irritating because Lady Hohenwart's comment was so close to Ben's earlier observation about me and Ferdy.

"How is your own husband doing of late? Will he be joining us here? I do not imagine he and Alfred get along since he took over his position as

Minister-President." Lady Penelope stepped in to give me some cover with Lady Hohenwart.

"Oh, nonsense. The Count is always a gracious host," Lady Hohenwart said, waving away her concern. "He's standing over there with my husband and some other gentlemen."

She pointed to the far corner of the room, where there were several men gathered together, each of them more finely dressed than the last. I only just recognized our host as he was drinking champagne from a glass as others talked; I thought he seemed bored.

It was then I noticed Lord Maximillian was standing beside Count Potocki. I tugged on Lady Penelope's skirt lightly, and we exchanged a quick look; we both knew if he was here, Karl had to be on his way.

"Excuse me, ladies," a voice spoke up from behind us.

Speak of the devil.

My stomach sank as my spine tingled and my body went cold.

Karl's voice had very little of the enchanting charm it used to, but it was still able to command attention.

I forced myself to keep smiling as I turned around, but it was harder to do so when I finally saw him again.

I'd thought Count Potocki's house lacked the proper care it needed, but Karl was in a much worse condition. His hair was loosely brushed back in the current style, and while his clothes were as fine as ever with their silk lining and velvet trim, they seemed a size too large, as though he'd lost weight since we'd last met.

All in all, Karl was clearly miserable, and it was evident enough that I even felt a little sorry for him.

But I still couldn't let his pitiful state interrupt our plans, I reminded myself. He'd already gotten past Amir and Xiana somehow, so Lady Penelope and I had to ensure we captured him. If we didn't, all our plans would have been for nothing, and I would miss my best chance to fulfill my promise to the former Empress.

"Oh, there you are, Karl," I said brightly. Before he could say anything, I grabbed his arm and dragged him toward the dancing floor, moving so fast I nearly tripped on my skirts.

"Your manners have devolved since we last met, Madame." Karl snorted disdainfully. "Is that Ferdinand's doing?"

I whirled around at once. "Excuse us, please," I called back to Lady Hohenwart, who was clearly both pleased and insulted by my lack of proper etiquette. I saw Lady POW's smirk of approval, and I pushed forward.

"You might already know this, but I'd rather not dance with you," Karl muttered as he trailed behind me.

"Would you prefer to leave with Lord Maximillian?" I asked through gritted teeth as I took his hand and forced him to join the promenade of dancers. "I'm sure he wouldn't mind retiring for the night, given your mother is calling for his return as well as yours."

Karl flushed, but he reluctantly took my hand and began to dance. Briefly, I saw him scowl over in Lord Maximillian's direction.

"Mother will have to wait," Karl said as he twirled me around in such a painstakingly graceful way, I could only think of Ferdy. "I know it distresses her that I am putting myself at risk, but things will get better in the long run. She is not used to seeing a strong sense of leadership."

I did my best to remain smiling, even if I only wanted to shake him. "You're a fool if you believe that."

"You're the fool for not joining me," Karl snapped bitterly. He cleared his throat, looking shocked he'd said such harsh words to me. "I still believe my brother has blinded you, Ella."

I frowned, tempted to point out he'd just insulted me. "Do you really think I'd be happier with you?"

"Of course. I know Ferdinand quite well, even if we fundamentally disagree on certain topics. Ferdinand is far too idealistic; he sees you as who he wants you to be," Karl said as he pulled me around into another turn. "But I see you for who you are. I know you've lived in poverty and service, and you've faced unjust hardship. Yet you still are your father's daughter."

I didn't know whether or not I should be insulted, but I wasn't happy to hear him talk of *Táta*.

"Your father was loyal to mine," Karl reminded me. "If Bohemia regained its sovereignty, and I was crowned king, we could honor your father's legacy and make life better for everyone in the kingdom. Can't you see it? No more Nationalists fighting to keep hold of their heritage. No more politicians buying votes and trading favors. No more trade issues that the Diets have to argue over, or send to the *Reichsrat* for a vote. We can do a lot of good, and the kingdom will benefit from our loyalty, to it and each other. No one who hates this nation can take care of it properly."

I drew back, uncomfortable at how true his words were, not just about Ferdy and myself, but my father, too.

For a moment—just a moment—I thought about what Karl was offering.

Lady Penelope and Harshad had come to Bohemia to make the region stable for trade and travel; Karl had gotten a lot of support in recent months, and he was partially right; there were things about the country that could be adjusted and fixed, and it was possible to make things better for more people. And I wouldn't be opposed to that, if they were indeed fair and just changes.

But I had seen Karl, and I had seen his mask slip; he was content to say these things and not really mean them. He was also condoning violence when deemed necessary, as a means to his end, and I couldn't stand by that—especially since Ferdy had nearly been killed twice by his plans. And while I did think Karl was happy to proclaim his love and adoration for me, I didn't really think he was in love with me.

For all his talk of Ferdy's idealism, Karl too failed to see me for who I truly was; he only saw me as the person I could be if I was with him.

"No." I shook my head. "You've been working with people who do not think twice before poisoning and killing their opponents."

"You don't think the Order of the Crystal Daggers has done that, too?" Karl asked. At my surprise, he sneered at me. "Oh, yes, Lord Maximillian and I have talked at length about your secret organization and how they tried to kill my father during the Spring Revolution."

"That's not true," I objected fiercely, thinking of my mother. She had come to save the former rulers, and even protected Karl himself before he was born.

"It's dangerous to be so naive," Karl warned. "You're a part of the group, and you should know what it's capable of."

"I know what we're capable of, just as I know the Order protected you and your family," I argued.

"Your father protected mine," Karl said. "Not the Order. They have their own history full of lies and secrets, and they've only survived as long as they have by pandering to the powerful and lying to the gullible."

I scowled. "We are loyal to the truth, if you must know."

THE ORDER OF THE CRYSTAL DAGGERS

"Ha." Karl sniffed disdainfully as we headed into a final lap around the room. The music was drawing to a close, and I was grateful. "What is truth?"

"The truth is that everyone is capable of good and evil, and we all need to decide to stand up for what is good, and stand against what is evil," I said. "I see the Order as a way to help people."

"Yes, they help the people who pay their bills and keep them in power."

I bit down on my lip to keep myself from arguing with him. I already knew that if I let him, he would spend the rest of our time pointing out my side's flaws and imperfections while ignoring his own hypocrisies.

My hand brushed against my side, where my mother's dagger was securely hidden, and I felt braver knowing it was there.

I took a deep breath. It was time to regain control of the current situation.

"If you're that concerned about the Order, I'm surprised you haven't tried to kill me," I said.

"I'd still rather not," Karl said, ominously enough that I suddenly felt afraid. I stumbled as we turned, nearly falling over before Karl caught my hand at the last possible second. He pulled me tight against him as he whispered into my ear. "And between you and me, I am hoping to win you over yet."

I pushed him away and quickly turned it into a flirtatious movement, laughing as we moved together with the dying musical current. "Oh, Karl, you're so funny," I said, loudly enough others could hear me. Softening my voice, I added, "That will never happen."

"Honestly, I do not understand the appeal Ferdinand has," Karl muttered. "Why would you want a harder life, with little safety and comfort?"

"I am better served having one with freedom and truth." I pulled away from him as the music faded into its dénouement. "And your brother's not the only one who struggles with illusions. Your plans to take Bohemia back will only cause more chaos, and you're doing it for yourself."

"They are not mutually exclusive." Karl blushed as the dance ended. "But I do wish for you to come with me tonight."

"Where?" I asked, glancing around. "I doubt Count Potocki has his gardens open this time of the year."

"No, come with me back to my quarters." Karl gave me a bold look, assessing me from the hem of my gown to the top of the jeweled princess

744

THE ORDER OF THE CRYSTAL DAGGERS

combs twisted up in my hair. "Give me one last chance to convince you that my side is the winning one. I've convinced Lord Maximillian we still need you."

"No, thank you." I smiled my most bitter smile as the music ended with a small round of applause.

Karl inhaled deeply. "May I ask what your objections are?"

"I've already given them," I said. "But more to the point, Ferdy and I are married now."

"What?" Karl blanched before his face mixed over with crimson and scarlet. He looked sick, and I almost enjoyed his sudden discomfort.

"Your father approved it," I added. "And your mother couldn't stop it."

Karl took a long moment to compose himself, long enough I could hear the whispers starting to stir around us. He then straightened his waist coat, before he finally shook his head. "Then you are truly lost to me."

I shook my head and lost my smile. "You never had me."

Karl's scowl deepened. "Well then, it is time I departed. I suppose I can, in good conscience, leave you here to die and rot with the rest of them."

In the middle of the ballroom, he gave me a curt bow before he turned on his heel and walked away. I heard a few gasps as gossip flooded over the crowd's waggling tongues.

"Wait," I said, leaping after him and grabbing onto his sleeve. "What do you mean?"

"What I mean is farewell," Karl snarled, slapping my hand sharply before he smoothed out his jacket. "And hopefully for good. You can take comfort knowing I will celebrate your death with a toast, dear *sister*."

His words were laced with hurt and anger, and they stung more than I expected. For a moment, I could only stare at him as he headed toward the exit.

But I swiftly regained my senses. Karl never worried about the people he might hurt, and while he had never done the work of killing his opposition himself, he did not deserve my remorse.

I glanced around for Lady POW. When I didn't see her—and when I saw the various other people giving me side-glances and speaking in soft, speculative tones—I hurried after Karl.

745

"Karl!" The instant I was free of the eyes from the crowd, I hiked up my skirts and chased him down a darkened hallway until I caught up to him.

"Leave me be," he snapped, trying to push me aside.

"No." I grabbed his arm and twisted it behind him, making him gasp in surprise at the aggressive move. He fell to his knees in pain. He tried to shift away from me, but his whimpering only increased. I held on firmly. "Your mother wanted me to bring you home. And I intend to keep that promise."

"Let me go," Karl demanded. I pulled harder on his wrist, making him cry in pain. "You'll kill us both."

I was just about to ask him how that could happen when a new pair of hands grabbed me from behind.

Before I could protest, a handkerchief was plastered over my mouth, and I could smell a sweet-smelling foulness.

Chloroform.

Panic set in fast. My arms and legs began to fight back, but pressure came down hard around my neck, and I could feel weakness pouring through me.

"I'm really getting tired of rescuing you, Prince Karl," Lord Maximillian scoffed.

Thinking quickly, I fell forward, forcing him to carry my full weight. I heard his grunts and groans, and I did my best to hold my breath.

When he finally dropped me to the floor, I gasped for breath and crawled away from him as fast as I could.

I'd been shaken by the surprise attack. Lord Maximillian was considerably bigger than me, and my evening gown added an unwieldly quality to my weight, even if it provided enough padding to keep him from fully choking me.

Nausea rippled through me as they began to argue.

"I told you it was a waste of time to court her," Lord Maximillian said to Karl.

Karl stood up hastily and brushed himself off. "Did you light the fuse?"

My eyes went wide, and I coughed in disbelief at what I was hearing.

"Of course I did," Lord Maximillian replied. "Unlike you, I'm reliable."

THE ORDER OF THE CRYSTAL DAGGERS

"And I am the one properly in line to the throne," Karl snapped back. "If you want me to marry your daughter, you'll do as I say."

"If you want to get the throne at all, you'll do as *I* say." Lord Maximillian scowled with displeasure. "Now, help me with her."

He stepped toward me again, slamming his booted foot on my skirts as I fumbled for my dagger. I was still a little light-headed from the chloroform, and I desperately wondered where Lady Penelope had gone.

"No." Karl stopped Lord Maximillian. "We can leave her here."

"What?" he asked.

"Leave her here," Karl repeated, clearly irritated. "I'll get public sympathy sooner."

"Killing her at the Tripartite Council would leave a greater impact." Lord Maximillian's mustache fluttered as he exhaled sharply. "Besides, if we take her now, you can finally have her the way you always wanted."

Even in my compromised condition, I heard the threat behind Lord Maximillian's words, and I struggled harder to back away as he stood over me.

"She's a lovely young lady, as you've always said. Surely you still want such a prize?" The dark tone in Lord Maximillian's voice mirrored his morbid amusement as he looked at me. "You'd already deemed her more important than my financial support. Besides, perhaps forcing yourself on her might convince her to give up on the Order."

"No," Karl said. "I am not going to do that."

I was grateful Karl seemed to have some sense of honor, even if it was only enough to stop himself from defiling his brother's wife. I was about to commend him, but then he continued talking.

"It's better to have her die tonight, anyway."

"Die?" I feigned more shock than I felt as I moved slowly, struggling with the damask layers of my dress, grabbing for my dagger. I had to keep them talking if I was going to free myself.

Karl cleared his throat. "Lord Maximillian and I have been at odds before, but we are in complete agreement regarding the future of Bohemia. And there cannot be any great victory without great loss."

"Yes." Lord Maximillian gave me a menacing stare. "As it happens, I've been developing a weapon to make the progress we desire a reality. You've already seen its work for yourself."

Fire filled my memory; I pictured the dark wine cellar in Prague Castle, of Tulia's house, and even the carriage moving Ferdy's friends back to Silesia. And then I thought back to Ben's observations in the barn.

"Nitroglycerin." I barely whispered the word as I felt the blood drain out of my face.

"Not quite, but close," Lord Maximillian corrected. "Nobel holds the patent for dynamite, but I've determined my recipe is close enough to his that it'll work the same, if not better."

"Yes, and thanks to me, Count Potocki imported several barrels of it into his pantry tonight, just like Mother did for the Advent Ball," Karl boasted. "It won't be long before it explodes. All we had to do was light the fuse."

"Why?" I looked from Karl to Lord Maximillian, unable to comprehend how little they cared for the lives they were about to destroy. "Why are you doing this?"

"What do you mean, 'why?'" Lord Maximillian scorned me. "A better question is 'why not,' don't you think?"

"After people die here, Bohemians will see they need new leadership," Karl said. "The Emperor doesn't care for us, and the Nationalists will rise up and propel me back to the throne."

"And then you will marry my daughter," Lord Maximillian finished.

As Karl nodded glumly, I saw my moment—and I took it.

I whipped out my mother's dagger, leaned forward, and plunged the blade into Lord Maximillian's leg.

The larger man jumped back and hollered in surprise and pain; he struggled to stay balanced, and in all the confusion, I pulled my skirts out from underneath his foot.

"Why did you do that?" At the sight of blood and violence, Karl scampered back several steps, looking ill. He put his hand over his mouth, as if he was about vomit.

While the two of them yelled, I escaped down the hall. The chloroform had not worn off entirely; I ran for several large steps, and then stumbled and crashed into a crevice near a door. My one hand steadied me against the wall as my body shook. I breathed deeply, carrying my dagger in my other hand as Lord Maximillian cursed at me.

"I can only hope you'll die quickly!" he yelled back at me while Karl supported him.

THE ORDER OF THE CRYSTAL DAGGERS

"Who's worried about poor manners now?" I murmured, flinching as I saw Lord Maximillian's leg was bleeding out in small spurts.

Together with Karl, he limped away in the other direction.

Where is Lady POW when I need her?

She had said we would leave early if Karl showed up, but she wasn't supposed to leave me behind. Without her, I couldn't do anything to gain the upper hand against them both.

I could only hope Harshad and Ben would catch them as they left.

"Not again," I muttered, as another wave of dizziness took over me. Feeling hopeless, I slid onto the floor as they disappeared from my sight.

I was stuck there, my body shaking with stunned rage and weakness.

I wanted to cry at the unfairness of it all. They were so close, and yet still out of my reach, and my own body was incapable of capturing them. The only thing I could do was follow them, but that would mean the people in Count Potocki's mansion would die from their trap.

A hand reached out and took hold of my shoulder. I jerked around, ready to stab anyone who would dare try to stop me. The shadow behind me avoided my attack and then knocked my dagger from my still-trembling hands a second later. I was reaching for it again, terrified my attacker from the bridge had come back, when the figure spoke out from the darkness.

"I'd rather hoped you'd forgiven me enough not to try to kill me, *chérie.*"

It was Ferdy.

THE ORDER OF THE CRYSTAL DAGGERS

16

◊

Ferdy.

Shock and anger flooded through me, mixing into relief and even hope, before transforming into its final, aggravated form.

He smelled of the streets, of pipe tobacco, river water, and kitchen smoke. In the dim lighting, I could see he was wearing a set of livery easily two sizes too small. I could only wonder what he'd been doing, and I honestly didn't really even want to know.

Ferdy had returned to me at last—just in time to be put back in danger. After several days of silence, here he was right in front of me, just as explosives were set to go off.

Will this man ever stop frustrating me so?

"What are you doing here?" My voice was cold as he pulled me up off the floor and returned my dagger to me. Forcefully, I shoved my blade back into its sheath. "Lady Penelope said she wasn't sure you would come back."

"Well, that was always a possibility," Ferdy replied cheerfully, making me even angrier.

"Oh, so I should be grateful that you've come back at all?" I put my hands on my hips. "That you've only left me for a few days instead of years or perhaps the rest of your life?"

"What?" Ferdy looked surprised.

"If you've changed your mind about our marriage or realized I'm not the woman you thought I was, you should just tell me and be done with it."

"Ella, are you listening to yourself?" Ferdy frowned at me. "I went looking for Lumiere. I was going to come back once I found him."

I felt flustered and foolish, but I wasn't going to let that stop me. "Well, did you actually find him?"

"No … not exactly." Ferdy shrugged. "But I got a lead. It shouldn't take me much longer to track him down."

"I must say, it's so very nice you're letting me know you're leaving beforehand this time," I snapped.

750

"I told your grandmother I was leaving," he said. "She should've told you."

"No, *you* should've told me." I did not like defending Lady POW, especially when she had chosen not to tell me why Ferdy had gone. But he couldn't put all the blame on her.

"Now you know how I felt the other night when you went into the city without me, and how I had to come track you down here tonight," he argued.

"Excuse me? I was doing what I had to do!"

"And I thought if I could find Lumiere, that would keep you safe and make you happy."

"I don't need you to do things to make me happy!" I threw up my hands angrily, secretly groaning at the memory of Lady POW fighting with Xiana. "I need to be able to trust you."

Ferdy took me by the shoulders. "I can't do anything about that, but I've trusted you for a long time. Remember the night you saved me at the castle? You protected me, even to the point you risked your life, and I knew then I really was in love with you, without a doubt—the real you, not one I'd imagined. Even if you were a spy and assassin."

"Oh, please, we're not arguing about that now." I glared at him. "You knew I didn't want you to leave the house after what happened to me on the bridge."

"Of course I knew that," Ferdy agreed. "But you were sick, and that was part of the deal: I told Lady Penelope where Karl was and then I left to get Lumiere back. She was supposed to make sure you were safe while I was gone."

He gestured down the hall where Karl had made his exit. "I guess I shouldn't be surprised to find you in danger again. She didn't keep her word."

"It probably depends on your perspective," I murmured. Lady POW hadn't been eager for my plan, but she had given in to my reasoning. I could only assume she'd meant to keep me safe, even if she didn't keep me at the manor. "Besides, you're in danger now, too. Lord Maximillian and Karl are eager to repeat the events of the Advent Ball. They've already got explosives planted and the fuse is lit."

"Leave it to Karl to ruin things." Ferdy groaned and looked for an exit. "We need to get out of here."

THE ORDER OF THE CRYSTAL DAGGERS

"Wait," I said. "We have to save the others first."

Ferdy's hands tightened around me. I knew he was wrestling over what to do, and I felt my heart soften at his torment. He wanted to protect me, but he couldn't ignore my reasoning, either.

"Ferdy, please," I whispered. "We can't just leave them to die."

"I know, I know." Ferdy's angry expression crumbled into despair. "But my goodness, Ella, do you just hate me? I almost lost you twice already. I can't lose you now. Why are you making me suffer like this?"

"You know I don't hate you." I put my hands on his chest, bracing myself against him. As we stood there, I thought of all the times I'd been worried for him, fearing the worst—even before I really knew I was in love with him. I recalled hoping he was safe after learning of Dr. Artha's murder, how I'd looked for him in town after joining the Order, and how I'd surprised even myself by admitting I was in love with him at the Advent Ball. "And I've almost lost you before, too, remember?"

Ferdy shook his head. "It seems we are destined to make each other suffer."

"*Absolument.*" I pressed my forehead against his to encourage him. "But we'll have to do that later. We have work to do right now. If we won't save these people, who will?"

"Do you really believe we can?" Ferdy asked softly, and I could hear the slight tremor in his voice.

"We can, if we trust each other," I said. "I know you think I am a fool—"

"Oh, Ella. You might be a fool, but I am a fool for you." Ferdy crushed me against him. My arms slid up and wrapped around his neck instinctively, and I inwardly reveled as the full force of his warmth washed over me.

It felt so good to be back in his arms. I almost couldn't believe it had been two whole days since I'd seen him.

"Maybe you should leave," I whispered, suddenly more afraid of losing him, too. "It might be too much if both of us are acting foolish."

"No. We'll stay together and work together." He looked at me and tried to smile. "Just as we promised. For better, for worse, for richer, for poorer—and in magic and madness, in spy work and in civilian life, right?"

THE ORDER OF THE CRYSTAL DAGGERS

"Until death do we part." I curled into him briefly, listening to the beat of his heart as it pounded. I wanted him to trust me, and I had to trust him, too. I wasn't sure why, but hearing him joke irreverently about our wedding vows gave me a strange sense of peace.

"All right." Ferdy let me go, looking unhappy but resolved. "What's your plan?"

I bit my lip. It was the worst time to hesitate, but I couldn't risk failing again—not with so many lives at stake.

"Go find Ben," I said. "He came with us tonight. He'll know more about the explosives than me."

"All right," Ferdy agreed. "And then you will get out of here?"

He was hopeful, but I knew he was not expecting me to be so sensible.

"No, I'll find Lady POW, and we'll get the people out of the house," I said. "I don't know where she went, but this was definitely the worst time for her to leave."

"She's outside by now. Amir sent for her," Ferdy told me. "He ran into me as I arrived to come and rescue you."

"Amir is here? Why?"

"Lumiere sent a runner to let Amir know Karl was out for the night," Ferdy explained. "I offered to pose as the messenger boy, and then I stayed in the kitchens as a charity case—"

"—and when they weren't looking, you stole a footman's uniform and came to find me," I finished, looking down at his tightly fitting tunic with a newfound amusement.

It was almost like the time at the Hohenwart Ball. He'd been rescuing me from Karl back then, too.

"Ah, you know me so well, *chérie*." Ferdy grinned, the first genuinely happy smile I'd seen from him all night.

"And yet I love you anyway." I picked up my skirts in one hand and blew him a kiss with the other. "Go. I'm going to get these people out of here, and then I'll meet you in a bit."

"Do I know we will meet again?" Ferdy's words harkened back to that night outside the *Stavovské divadlo*, and if I had more time, I might have boxed his ears.

"Of course we will," I said through gritted teeth. "How else will I be able to punish you for distracting me right now?"

THE ORDER OF THE CRYSTAL DAGGERS

"Well, that's fair." Ferdy let out a quick laugh, and I could still hear him as he headed out to retrieve Ben.

Watching him leave felt painful and frightening, as though my skin was being ripped off my chest.

I shook my head to clear my mind. Lady POW was likely with Ben and Amir, and Ferdy was on his way to them; now, it was my job to save everyone else.

It was hard to feel brave as I looked out at the ballroom again; I saw all the beautifully clad people so happy and so ignorant and felt overwhelmed.

But how? How do I get all these people out of the house?

It didn't seem prudent to reveal myself as a member of the Order of the Crystal Daggers, especially to a large crowd; as Lady Penelope told me before, it was possible they wouldn't believe me, either about my mission or the danger.

And it would be too scandalous if they learned the truth about Karl. I'd spent the last two days establishing our overly romantic narrative, I realized with dismay. I'd spent all my goodwill on them, and they would rightfully reject me now.

Some of the guests waved to me, but I couldn't move, not even to wave back; I was stuck in an indecisive trance.

Until I caught sight of the wallpaper again.

Just off to the side, there was a small strip of it hanging loose in one corner of the room. To help hide it, a candelabra and a pedestal with a vase of flowers had been strategically placed in front of it.

An idea took hold inside of me—one I did not like.

But I liked everyone dying inside the house even less, and I could even hear Lumiere cheering me on inside my head as I moved forward.

"Come now, he was going to get Roman to redo the house anyway ... go ahead and give him some flaming incentive ... might do us a world of good, too, before other people start ordering such a grisly color ..."

At the memory of Lumiere's rampant laughter, I didn't hesitate.

I approached the curling wallpaper, grabbing a glass of champagne as a server passed by. As I pretended to examine the flowers and gaze at the candelabra, I glanced to the side, watching the crowd as nonchalantly as possible.

THE ORDER OF THE CRYSTAL DAGGERS

No one was paying attention to me.

I took a deep breath, praying my plan would work.

And then I threw the champagne onto the wilting flowers and the wall, and shoved myself into the candelabra hard enough it fell over.

The sparks flew all around and caught, and as the crowd took notice, I screamed and pointed at the spurting flames.

"Fire!" I pretended to slap at the flames, but I was only intent on spreading them.

Several in the crowd seemed confused, and I clenched my fists.

Don't they know they need to get out of here? What are they waiting for?

To hinder my apparent incompetence, several footmen were running with water and wet towels. They began beating the flames out, and I suddenly wished I'd lit the whole hallway on fire.

"It's too much!" I cried. "We need to leave!"

"Madame, we can stop it," a footman said, but I began shrieking hysterically.

"Everyone, get out," I yelled, wildly gesturing for people to leave. Some of them scowled and dutifully moved out of the room. Others stood there, drunkenly staring at me, as I hurried around in circles and pushed them toward the exit.

I never felt so embarrassed in all my life, acting like a foolish madwoman. As I continued to usher people out the door, I had to remind myself over and over that it was for their own good, that I would worry about the fallout later—or, preferably, I would never think of this moment ever again.

"I sure hope the house doesn't fall," I hollered, and more whispers erupted into shouts.

"The house is going to fall!" Lady Hohenwart screamed as she rushed by me, holding down her purple turban with one hand and barely holding onto her skirts in the other. She stumbled toward the exit, and I was grateful to see others follow her.

We might save them yet.

It helped that the fire was still spreading, and the wallpaper was falling down in sweeping lines, as though offering itself up as kindling.

755

I was just helping a gentleman stand up after he'd been knocked down when I saw Ben waving at me from the other side of the room.

"Ben!"

He looked at the fire behind me. "What did you do?"

Despite the footmen working hard to slow the spread, it had crawled toward the ceiling and extended across the wall. Some of the wallpaper was falling on the floor, too, lighting up smaller piles of fires.

"Reality needed to get too real for the crowd," I hastily explained. "Where's Ferdy?"

"He and the others are helping the guests outside into their carriages," Ben told me. "He offered to carry me inside, and I told him no. I figured you would be happy about that."

"Thank you." I could barely whisper out the words, but Ben nodded in understanding, and then I hurried to describe what had happened with Lord Maximillian and Karl. I told Ben how they'd planned to set off dynamite to gain sympathy for their political cause, and his eyes lit up in recognition.

"Dynamite?" Ben scowled. "I had a feeling about the time in Prague Castle. It couldn't have been just fire and wine that made the ballroom collapse."

"They said it was in the wine cellar," I said.

"We have to find it then." Ben grimaced. "And we'll need to hurry."

Together, Ben and I made our way down into the servants' hallways. I told the workers I saw about the fire. I ordered them to get out while they could, while Ben asked for directions to the wine cellar. It didn't take long for us to arrive at our destination.

And as we walked into the wine cellar, I already knew something was wrong.

"It's too warm in here," I murmured, and Ben nodded in agreement.

"Look!" he pointed toward the back of the room, and a small rise of smoke rose up from one of the wine barrels.

We made our way over, and Ben carefully pulled the cork out of the barrel. More smoke and the smell of oil immediately poured out.

"There's something burning inside," I said, trying not to cough. I glanced around at the other barrels nearby.

THE ORDER OF THE CRYSTAL DAGGERS

Ben eyed the smoking barrel and then the others alongside it. "This barrel was meant to be kindling."

"This must be the fuse Lord Maximillian was talking about," I said, as Ben knocked on the barrel next to him, listening intently. I didn't know what he was doing until he rapped his knuckles against the wood again.

"Whatever's in this barrel, it's not wine. It's more solid," Ben said.

"It can't be frozen."

"Yes," Ben agreed. "From what I've read, Nobel mixed the nitroglycerin with some earth and minerals to make his dynamite. It's similar to gunpowder, only stronger."

"So, it will explode."

"Yes, just like it happened at the Advent Ball." Ben tapped the barrel again. "This likely has powder inside."

"Are you sure?"

"Best guess." Ben gave me a teasing smirk. "But Ferdy might not want to bet on it."

"I'm not sure. He seems to think he's pretty lucky when it comes to gambling." I eyed the barrel nervously. "Can you stop it from going off?"

"Yes. And if we stop the fire in here, we can stop everything." He pointed to the barrel that was leaking out smoke and fumes.

"I hope you're right. Please hurry."

Ben took hold of the top of the smoking barrel. "It's better to be right than fast."

"It's best to be right *and* fast," I argued.

"That's why I'm doing it, not you."

I groaned, but he laughed, and I felt a little better. My nerves were already shattered for the night, and things couldn't be all bad if Ben was trying to get me to relax a little, even if this was absolutely not the right time for it.

It was not the right time to panic, either, I reminded myself as Ben started trying to smash open the cover. I winced at the loud noises and kept looking over at the door, almost expecting someone to come and try to stop us.

After a few more blows, the wood appeared only slightly cracked.

That's when I pulled out our mother's dagger.

"Here," I said, offering it to Ben. "Pry it open."

"Thanks." His voice was gruff, and I could tell he was hiding his own nervousness. "If you want to help some more, you can stop tapping your foot, too."

"Huh?" I'd barely noticed I was fidgeting.

"Actually, go see if there are any other barrels we need to check," Ben ordered. "That'll help us, and I won't have to worry about you distracting me, either."

As he began digging the dagger's blade around the edge of the barrel top, I looked through each line of barrels carefully. I leaned down close to smell for fire, and I knocked on the barrels, just as Ben had, to hear what was inside.

At the last one, I let out a sigh of relief. "There's no more fire," I called.

"Good." Ben pried the wooden top of his barrel off, and several oily, burning swaths emptied out onto the floor. Ben smothered the flames with his boots as I ran back to him.

"Ouch."

I saw him crouch over and back away; a spark had caught onto his brace and burned him. I hurried over, trying to ground the fire into the stone floor. My dress burned in some areas, but my skirts were thick enough I didn't feel it.

The fumes made us cough as the smell of burning oil filled the room. I tore off a section of my petticoats to tie over my mouth. I offered one to Ben, but he declined.

My skin was cold, even as we stood there next to the flames. I couldn't escape the feeling that trouble was coming, and I wouldn't be able to stop it or save anyone.

But after the fire dwindled down, I let out a shaky laugh and collapsed onto the ground in relief.

"Oh, thank you, Lord," I whispered.

"Are there anymore?" Ben asked, looking around again.

I shook my head. "No."

"All right." He nodded, clearly pleased by my report. Using my dagger again, he opened the barrel next to us. He was right; the barrel was full of a strange, brownish powder. He sniffed at it, and then shook his head. "It's different from gunpowder, but it's close."

I scanned the room. "Either way, it definitely doesn't belong here. If it went off, the wine would add to the flames, too."

"You mean like it did upstairs with your fire?" Ben was more relaxed as he teased me.

I ignored him, even if I was grateful. "What do we do now?"

"We'll have to remove the powder barrels out of the manor." Ben eyed the cellar's entrance with a calculating look. "I think that's a problem for Lady POW. She'll need Potocki's cooperation."

"I agree." My nerves were more than strained, and I welcomed the chance to hand responsibility over to someone else.

"Here." Ben held out my dagger. "Thanks. I'll have to get one for myself, one day."

I stepped back, realizing I'd forgotten how much Ben missed our mother, too. "Maybe we can share it."

"No." He shook his head and pushed the dagger back toward me. "It belongs to you. You should be the one to uphold *Máma*'s legacy; I'm the one responsible for redeeming *Otec*'s."

"We are both their children," I said, suddenly feeling apologetic. "I know you miss her, too. So we should share it."

"And we will, when we can. Like we did now." Ben placed my dagger back in my hand, and I finally put it away, only a little reluctantly; I was still grateful it was mine, and I was glad Ben was content to leave it in my care.

We headed out to find Lady POW, and that was when I remembered Ferdy was back, too.

"Did you see that Ferdy's here?" I asked. "He went out looking for Lumiere. That's why he was missing these last couple of days."

"Really?" Ben gave me a skeptical look. "Did he find him?"

"No. But he said he was close."

"Maybe it takes a rogue to find a rogue." Ben shrugged. "I'll admit I'm not eager to deal with Lumiere again so soon, but it'll be better if we get him back, especially if we weren't able to get Karl tonight."

"Oh, no, you're right." I wrinkled my nose. "I forgot about that."

759

"How could you forget something like that?"

"You know, I'm not entirely sure." I waved my arm back toward the cellar, stocked full of explosive powder. "There must be something else on my mind."

Despite the danger we'd faced, Ben and I shared a laugh, and for once I felt as though I had succeeded in an important mission—not just in saving lives, but rebuilding the trust between me and my brother.

I looked down at my mother's dagger, tucked away just at the side of my soot-covered dress. I felt much better as we walked outside. This time, even though it was chilly, I felt only warmth.

Máma would be proud of us.

17

◊

The fire was still smoldering inside Count Potocki's ballroom as Ben and I walked out toward the stables. A small spout of smoke fluttered out of the mansion's roof, its pale, wispy tail wafting upward into the wintery night.

I grimaced at the scene before us. "I was hoping that the fire wouldn't make things worse."

"I just hope no one saw you start it." Ben's voice was light, even though it was concerned. "And that they can stop it before it reaches the wine cellar."

"At least most of the people seem to be outside," I said, glancing around at the fairly large crowd. Many eyed the house with grim expressions on their faces. Several men offered their greatcoats to the ladies standing around in the cold, while others called out for their friends and companions.

I was still a little afraid about the fire, but a sense of satisfaction swelled up within me as I surveyed the scene.

Karl failed—again.

"There you are, Eleanora." Lady Penelope made her way over to us; there was enough worry in her irritated gaze that I could tell she was glad to see us. "I must apologize for my disappearance earlier."

"You should also apologize for failing to tell me why Ferdy really left," I retorted. She could've eased my doubt if only she'd explained everything to me, but she'd chosen not to.

"I was legitimately concerned he wouldn't come back." Lady Penelope did not look sorry at all, and I didn't know why I was surprised. "You must realize that I had to make sure you would still be able to work on the mission, even if he did leave for good."

"Ferdy wouldn't do that," I insisted.

"Maybe not this time," she snapped back. "But what of next time, or others, Eleanora? Will you be able to keep your resolve to finish the mission if I disappear? Or Benedict? Or any of the others in your life? This is the price you pay for your love."

She narrowed her eyes behind me, and I turned to see Ferdy. He was still in his stolen livery, leading horses toward the waiting carriages. No one seemed to realize he wasn't really part of the Potocki household.

"Well, I guess you'll never have to worry about facing such conditions," I scoffed, turning back to Lady POW.

Ben stepped between us, and I was both grateful and angry for his interruption. "Were you able to capture Karl on his way out?"

"No." She crossed her arms. "But we know where he is. We will go to *Vyšehrad* tomorrow night. Right now, we still have work to do here."

"We need Count Potocki's help to empty out his wine cellar," Ben said. "Especially if Ella's fire isn't put out."

"Hey, it's not my fire," I tried to argue.

"Don't worry about that. It's already been largely taken care of," Lady Penelope said. "The smoke will take some time to disappear."

As angry with her as I was, I was relieved by her assessment. "So the house will stand?"

"Yes."

"Assuming we get the dynamite out," Ben murmured beside me.

Lady Penelope nodded brusquely. "I will speak with the Count about that. He was eager for renovations; now he has the perfect excuse to pour even more money into his house. But you should be especially proud of yourselves tonight."

I looked back to the smoke-filled night doubtfully. "Why?"

"Karl's plan was to destroy the mansion and harm those inside. With your fire, you took something meant for evil and used it as a way to save others," Lady POW explained. "True justice always results in mercy for the innocent."

"Thank you." I clenched my jaw, hating how much I enjoyed her approval. "But don't think you can get away with insulting me by giving me compliments."

Lady Penelope rolled her eyes. "You should go home, Eleanora. Clearly your nerves are overwrought. You've done your job, and you've done it well. There's no use pretending you'll be needed now."

"We still have our own business to settle, Madame. I want to know why you didn't tell me about Ferdy—"

"You have your orders." Lady Penelope glared down at me and then turned to my brother. "Benedict, come follow me; we will see to the explosives. Eleanora, you can see to yourself."

Ben gave me an apologetic look, but I waved him on. He was still excited to be here, in the middle of the action, and Lady Penelope was right. I was tired and my nerves were strained, and I did want to go home.

Especially before I ended up fighting with Lady POW all over again.

"I know that look," Amir said, as he appeared at my side. "It is best to forgive her, Eleanora."

I crossed my arms. "I hate how she keeps undermining my trust in Ferdy."

Ferdy himself was also good at undermining my trust, but that was for the two of us to discuss, not for Lady POW to further damage.

"It is still best to forgive her."

I scowled. "I'd think of all people, you would know how it hurts to deal with her vitriol."

"Yes, and of all people, I know it is best to forgive her for it." Amir's soft rebuke stung even more than Lady Penelope's scorn. "You have to be able to stand up for yourself, Eleanora, no matter your choices. And to be fair, at least you know she doesn't want you to get hurt."

"I don't think she cares if I'm upset, so long as I'll keep working through it."

"Even if it's more because of the mission, she is still trying to protect you."

"I don't want her to." Angrily, I stomped my foot. "It's *not* fair."

"Life isn't fair," Amir agreed. "But Lady Penelope knows what it's like to be hurt, too, remember?"

I looked back at the mansion, where the smoke was dying down. "But no one's died here—so far, anyway."

"I know." Amir put one hand on my shoulder and the other on the hilt of his own dagger. "And thankfully, from the way she's talking with Ben and the others, I doubt we'll have to worry about it tonight. But there are other ways to lose people."

I nodded silently, unable to do anything else. Amir was right, of course.

"You should go home and rest," Amir continued. "If Lady Penelope let you have a break, you should take it."

I glanced back at Ben, watching him hobble after Lady POW. He was talking with Ferdy as I watched them, and they seemed to be getting along.

Amir cleared his throat. "I'll stay and watch over Ben for you. After we're done here, I'll take him on a round through the city."

"He seems tired."

"He still needs to build up his strength. Lady POW wants you to work despite your emotional burdens; Ben needs to work even in light of his physical ones."

As we approached Lady Penelope's carriage, I remembered what Ferdy had told me inside the house. "Ferdy said you received a letter from Lumiere."

Amir nodded. "He wanted me to know Karl was heading toward the Potocki mansion using the secret tunnels that run throughout the city."

"Secret tunnels?" I repeated the words, but didn't fully understand them. "What did he mean by that?"

"Everyone has secrets, even the city, it seems." Amir gave me an amused smile. "After Karl I, the first king of Bohemia, was crowned, he began to construct a secret underground. He wanted them in case of a coup. Over the years, some of them have caved in due to erosion and the city's weakened foundation in different places, but they are still there."

"I never knew about them." I wrinkled my nose. "If they were built to stop a coup, it's ironic this Karl is using them."

"Yes, and it's disquieting that Lumiere knows of them," Amir agreed. "But it does explain why Xiana and I did not intercept him on his way over."

"Where is Xiana?" I glanced around, but didn't see her. I hadn't seen her since I talked with Lady Penelope the morning after the bridge attack. Part of me wanted to confide in Amir how I felt she was upset with me, but I didn't want him to think I was imagining it, either.

"I am not sure," he admitted. "I tried to find her before I came here, but she'd already moved from her post. I imagine she saw something and took off to investigate. Have you heard anything from Xiana, Harshad?"

I looked up to the top box, where Harshad was waiting and watching over the scene patiently. He seemed more alive in the night, as if he was infinitely more comfortable.

"No, I've received nothing from her," he said. "But it could be as you say. We'll surely see her back at the manor within a few hours."

"Ben and I will look around for Xiana on our rounds," Amir told Harshad. "Lady Penelope wants Eleanora to go home."

"I'll drop her off and return for Pepé." Harshad gave Amir a concerned look. "Don't be out too late. And don't draw any attention to yourself. There are rumors about murder again."

I recalled that a Turk was to blame for the murder of Ferdy's friends. Even without a deadly ending, tonight could cause a lot more trouble yet.

Amir assured Harshad he would be fine, and then he nudged me up into the carriage. "Go home and rest."

I didn't fight back. I climbed up into the carriage, and once the door was shut and we began to move, I collapsed against the cushions.

Only to fly out of my seat as the other door of the carriage whooshed open again, and Ferdy appeared, half-hanging out the door.

"You weren't going to leave without me, were you?" he asked, trying to stay calm as he reached for me.

I saw he'd scrambled to climb inside as we moved, but he'd lost his footing.

"Oh my goodness, Ferdy." Quickly, I hurried to help, grabbing him and pulling on his arms. Less than gracefully, we fell back together, and he landed on top of me. The carriage door slammed shut, and the sounds of the streets became more muffled.

Ferdy smiled. "It's nice to see you'll still fall for me, Ella."

"Falling for you is one thing." Immediately, I pushed him off and swiftly moved away to shut the carriage curtains. "But I'd rather not fall for your lies."

Ferdy sighed dejectedly as he scooted back onto the other bench. "Why are you upset again? I was doing what I was supposed to do, just as you were. And we did work together back there."

"I'm glad you were able to help back there," I said. "But after everything that nearly happened, I want to make sure you know not to lie to me—even if it's to keep me safe."

"I'm supposed to keep you safe."

"No, you're supposed to keep me," I retorted. "That's what you said before. I didn't know what you meant when you said it, exactly, before we got married, but I certainly didn't think you were going to try to imprison me. Otherwise, I would've said no. I've lived enough of my life being trapped by others."

"I didn't tell you about Karl because I was trying to keep him imprisoned, not you," Ferdy argued. "I did apologize, and I did my best to make it up to you."

I crossed my arms and slumped over, looking away from him. Every unrealized fear I'd had in the last hour started raging inside of me, even if my anger seemed easier to handle.

"You look beautiful tonight," Ferdy said after a while. "I always thought you would look perfect in the princess combs. I was right."

I gave him a quick nod and then turned back to the window.

"You're welcome, by the way."

"For what?"

"For not telling you the truth," Ferdy said, giving me one of his charming smiles.

The last of my self-control suddenly snapped; I could almost hear it breaking as I glared back at him. "Don't do that. Lumiere says things like that, you know. He gives me nothing but trouble, and then he assumes I'm thankful for it, and I'd rather you not resemble him right now." I wrinkled my nose. "Or ever, really."

"He has his moments."

"Why aren't you going after him now?" I asked, thinking back to the small moments we'd been able to talk inside the Potocki mansion. "You said you were close to finding him."

"I'll follow up on my lead later. I'd rather spend the time with you."

I snorted disdainfully. "Well, everyone has regrets."

"I don't. Not where you're concerned." Ferdy suddenly leaned forward, snatched me right off my seat, and pulled me into his lap.

"Ferdy!" I objected. "What are you—"

My words fell away as he pressed his lips against mine.

THE ORDER OF THE CRYSTAL DAGGERS

For only a moment, I mindlessly kissed him back. Whatever anger I felt at him, I'd missed him, and no matter how tired I was, I still ached for him.

But soon, I came back to my senses and pulled away. "No. Not if you don't trust me."

"I do," Ferdy insisted.

"Fine. Then not if I can't trust you."

"You can."

"Then why didn't you tell me about Karl?" My fingers dug into his chest as we once more came to the impasse between us. "You said it was to keep me safe. That's not good enough, Ferdy. What kind of woman do you take me for? You know we are going to face trouble at some point. The fact that it's from your brother means very little to me right now."

"It was for your benefit—"

"No, it wasn't. What are we going to do when we have to spend the holidays with your family? What about if we go abroad?" I suddenly clung to him even more tightly. "What about when I find myself pregnant?"

"Are you?" he asked, glancing down at my midsection briefly.

"No." I narrowed my eyes. "But I need you to tell me the truth, no matter what it is. And I need you to be there for me."

"Ella, please ... I didn't keep the truth about Karl from you because I didn't trust you," Ferdy said quietly.

"Oh, really?" I arched my brow at him. "It sure seems like it."

"No, I promise, that's not it." He sighed. "I didn't say anything because I didn't want to force you to choose between me and the Order. If I'd told you about Karl, and gave all the reasons for leaving him alone, you would've fretted over whether or not to say something to your grandmother. Even if I asked you not to."

I tried to imagine how things would've happened if he'd told me. He wasn't wrong; even Amir had said Ferdy's reasons for keeping Karl locked away under Lord Maximillian's watch were sensible enough, and I hadn't been willing to tell Lady POW the truth even after learning it, even knowing about the danger Louis posed.

"Were you worried I would choose her over you?" I asked slowly.

He'd told me before he knew of the Order, and while he didn't think I would kill him, he was adamant the Order had its history of assassinations; yet he still insisted he loved me and wanted to be with me.

"No," Ferdy said, surprising me. "But if my plan failed, you would have blamed yourself. And, knowing you as I do, I also knew you wouldn't forgive yourself if you failed."

Tenderness suddenly filled my heart where all the anger had been simmering. I softened against him, and he quickly drew me closer to himself.

"I thought it might be easier for you to forgive me," he said. "A foolish thought, perhaps."

No, it wasn't.

I couldn't bring myself to say it, but he knew. How could he not? He knew me so well.

I buried my head into his shoulder. "Where was this calm, rational Ferdinand the other night?"

"You'll have to forgive me for that, too. You said we would have trouble, and some of it is bound to come from either one of us." Ferdy cupped my cheek and smiled at me. "I was especially upset when I found you were gone from the manor the other night; I was blindsided by your absence. So I was not at my most reasonable."

"I wasn't, either."

"No, you weren't," Ferdy agreed with a small chuckle. I started to object, but he ran his fingers reverently down my face, and I leaned into his touch. "But that's fine. I can love you within reason as much as without."

The last of any resistance I'd intended to keep gave way, and I leaned up and kissed him with renewed, fervent desperation.

He met me in the middle with equal passion. I felt the rest of the world disappear as his mouth moved over mine possessively. Soon the chill of winter was forgotten as we held onto each other.

"Loving you is magic," Ferdy whispered, pulling back from me only to catch his breath.

"I thought it was madness," I murmured back, too lost in him to be playful as I wrapped my arms around his neck.

"No," Ferdy said. "It's the thought of losing you that's madness. I'm certain of that now."

THE ORDER OF THE CRYSTAL DAGGERS

I met his gaze with mine. "I don't think there can be one without the other."

"I know." He kissed me again. "But if the cost of loving you is losing my sanity, it's a price I'll pay."

"I don't think that's the right way of putting it," I started to say before his hands moved down my body and I lost all but the most basic semblance of thought. "Ferdy, Harshad is outside and I don't think—"

"I don't think we'll make that much noise," he assured me with a mischievous grin. "I'll even bet on it."

Before I could argue any further, his lips found mine again, and I ceased thinking entirely.

◊　　◊　　◊　　◊

Hours drifted by before I stirred awake in my bed. As I stretched, my hand bumped against the small table beside my bed, carelessly knocking my mother's dagger onto the floor.

"Ugh." I cringed at the scuffling sound. It seemed louder than it was against the dark, early morning stillness.

"What is it?" Ferdy's slurred and sleepy voice was muffled from underneath his pillow.

"Nothing, my love," I said, pulling the sheet over top of him.

He mumbled out some unclear words before burying himself even further under the covers.

Ferdy had promised me that he would resume his quest to find Lumiere after he tucked me into bed, but two days of running around the city, searching through nearby ports, napping in alleyways, and questioning different runners had all taken their toll on him.

He meant to tuck me in, but it seemed better for me to put him to bed.

"Ella." Ferdy was still half-asleep as he reached for me.

At first, I resisted; I wanted to retrieve my mother's dagger and see if Lady POW and Ben and the others had made it home yet.

But Ferdy persisted, and I gave in.

769

THE ORDER OF THE CRYSTAL DAGGERS

Time deepened, pulling us into a small pocket of memory all our own as I lay beside him. My fingers trailed down his arms, feeling the strength and tenderness there. How strange and splendid it was that this person I loved so much loved me back so potently, yet still so imperfectly.

Paradoxes are not the same as contradictions.

For a small moment, I thought of his deception and felt the dull heartache of disappointment.

I'd trusted him so completely, and it seemed wrong how loving someone meant they could cause pain that would otherwise be impossible. I grimaced as my heart clenched up like a fist, jealously grasping at my inner bitterness.

The rush of righteous pain, self-righteous or not, was intoxicating at first, but the longer I clung to it, the more hollow I felt. If I let it fester like an open wound, it would only grow bigger and more painful as time went by.

I let out a long, slow exhale, forcing my heart to open again. It was like chiseling away a layer of rock and stone, desperately digging and hammering away inside of me, all in hopes of finding underneath it all, I would still be able to go on and live.

"I forgive you." My voice was barely audible, and I was sure Ferdy was asleep, but I needed to say the words, almost as if I needed to hear them to believe them.

And I needed to let him know our impasse was over, so we could move forward—together.

His heart was beating steadily and his breathing was even, but a moment later, he shifted over and kissed my shoulder. "Thank you, Ella."

I drifted back to sleep, still smiling as Ferdy held me.

THE ORDER OF THE CRYSTAL DAGGERS

18

◊

It wasn't much longer before I woke up again, but this time I jolted awake, already searching for Ferdy. My hands reached over into the sheets, where only a small shadow of his warmth remained.

Ferdy was gone.

I sat up and put my head in my hands; it was almost like a premonition of the worst sort. Despite the rest we'd had, I felt a dark cloud hanging over me, as though something bad was just on the verge of happening.

"Sorry if I woke you."

My head jerked up and there he was, dressing in the far corner of the room.

I exhaled deeply and almost laughed at my fretfulness. "I thought you'd left."

"I thought it would be best to tell you myself when I'm leaving," he replied, his voice lighthearted and teasing, before coming over and pressing a kiss to my forehead. I grabbed his hands and clung to him, reaching up for a true kiss.

I desperately wanted more time with him. "Let me get dressed and eat breakfast with you," I said, already moving out of bed.

"If you hurry," Ferdy said with a hint of challenge in his eyes as he grabbed his boots. "After all the excitement of last night, I'm starving."

I blushed, thinking of how Ferdy and I had excused ourselves to our room when we'd arrived back to the manor. I didn't have time to see Harshad's face as we ran away, but my appetite dried up at the memory.

I put on my housedress and reached down for my fallen dagger on the floor. As I grabbed it, I saw a flicker of white.

There, on the floor, hiding just underneath my bed, along with my still-soggy tunic, was the water-damaged sketch I'd received from the older man on the bridge.

I picked up the paper and unfolded it carefully. I could still see it as clearly as I had in the moonlight, even where the older man had pointed out its imperfections.

The city of Prague was majestic and sad, yet still full of hope and promises.

I glanced over at Ferdy, who was still putting on his boots.

Even if our relationship had its imperfections, I thought, it would be wrong of me to abandon him. It was too easy to leave, to tear down in temporal rage what I'd pledged myself to in hope; it was an act of love and trust to remain and rebuild the broken parts.

Did I really love him if I wasn't willing to sacrifice something of myself, especially in hopes of bettering both of us?

"Are you ready?" Ferdy asked me.

"Almost." Delicately, I put the sketch down on my night table again and reached for a band to tie back my hair.

"Aw, you're not wearing the princess combs today?" Ferdy teased.

I smiled. "No. They're very lovely, but they're heavy. And they really should only be for you."

"I like the idea of you wearing only them for me." Ferdy tussled my hair and kissed me before I could say anything about that.

Hand in hand, we walked down the quiet, empty halls of my home, heading for the kitchen as we talked in soft tones. We were passing the library when Cecilia's voice cut through the air like a knife.

"Is that you, Tulia? What could possibly be taking you so long this morning? All we wanted was tea!"

Ferdy let go of my hand to cover his ears. "I didn't know your stepmother was part banshee."

I gave him a sympathetic look. "Give me a moment. I'll take care of her."

"If you're going to kill her, you shouldn't tell me about it first. I might feel compelled to stop you," he said.

I held back a laugh as I walked into the library. "What is wrong, Cecilia?"

My stepmother jumped up from her chair at my entrance. She was visibly irritated, much like the last time I saw her.

"Your Highness," she hissed in greeting. "You'll have to excuse my trespasses. Priscilla and I have been waiting for some time for our

THE ORDER OF THE CRYSTAL DAGGERS

morning tea. But your crippled prison keeper seems to think it's funny to make us wait."

"You should be grateful you're here, and not under Lord Maximillian's watch. He is not a kind host; I have seen the evidence myself." I scowled, thinking of Karl's ragged appearance the night before. He seemed angry and more than humiliated by his forced performance at Potocki's ball. After our encounter last night, I had to wonder if Karl was relieved to be back in his own fortified prison this morning.

"Cruelty is in the eye of the beholder." Cecilia crossed her arms against her chest. "I was not so cruel to you and your brother when I was in charge."

"No, you were much worse, Madame," I assured her, wondering if she'd truly forgotten how she'd treated us.

"I could've turned you out at any time once your father died," she snapped. "Yet I gave you a room and a job."

"Would you like a job, too, Madame? Is that what you're telling me?" I was amused at the thought of her scrubbing the floors or attempting to do the laundry.

"Why, you spiteful child. You should have understood where I was coming from, in my position. I still did my Christian duty."

"Christian duty is nothing without Christian love," I retorted. "And by your logic, you should understand where I am coming from in my position now."

I bit back a sigh. There was no point in reasoning with the unreasonable. Cecilia had been a tyrant in our home, and now, as its displaced ruler, she was upset she was no longer in her seat of privilege and power. To make it worse, she was still unapologetic regarding her past actions, and she had nowhere else to go.

"When this mission is over, I will make sure you are taken care of," I promised. "And Prissy, too."

"You mean to have us murdered?" Cecilia looked shocked.

"What? No." I shook my head. As cruel as she'd been to me, I did not want to be like Cecilia; I didn't want to keep her here and make her suffer, even if I was amused by it. Truth be told, I didn't even want to really see her at all. "No, I meant I'll figure something out for you. I'll see if I can find a place for you to go and live."

THE ORDER OF THE CRYSTAL DAGGERS

I wondered if I could get a small cottage for her, and have Lady POW send her a quarterly allowance through the bank. That way we could both be rid of each other, even if she wouldn't live in the grandeur she'd always wanted.

Or maybe she'll get married again and I won't have to worry about her at all …

I could only hope for that.

"I'll check on Tulia for you." I excused myself.

Ferdy was still waiting for me outside. "I'm glad I didn't have to stop you from killing her," he joked.

"I don't want to kill her," I murmured. I couldn't bring myself to hate her enough to kill her. "I don't know what to do with her, either."

"If you'd like, I can see about getting her a room in my mother's service. She could use another lady-in-waiting."

"I don't know if being kind to Cecilia means I should be unkind to your mother," I said, but the more I thought about it, the more tempting the offer became. "Still, thank you. I appreciate it. Especially since she doesn't deserve it."

"Well, I don't deserve you." Ferdy kissed the back of my hand gallantly. "You are too kind, Ella."

"I'm not always kind." I shook my head. "*Máma* once said it takes more courage to be kind. Cecilia doesn't make me feel very brave, that's for sure."

"Still, you owe her nothing, not even kindness," Ferdy reminded me. "And if you ask me, it means less if kindness is the default and one is incapable of cruelty."

I nodded, grateful for his support. "I'm sure Lady POW can find a way to deal with her. She's still useful to us in that regard."

I was just about to share my cottage idea with him when we rounded the corner, and I ran into Betsy.

"Betsy!" I was happy to see my friend, but I quickly lost my smile when I saw her tear-filled eyes and her quivering lip. "What's wrong?"

"Oh, Nora, it's terrible," Betsy murmured, barely able to speak.

A shiver went down my spine as I suddenly smelled blood in the air. "What happened?"

THE ORDER OF THE CRYSTAL DAGGERS

"It's Tulia. She's hurt, and it's bad," Betsy whispered, and then she ducked her head and cried. Her blonde curls bounced with shame and horror, and as much as I wanted to comfort her, I needed to remain calm myself.

Gently, I put my hands on Betsy's shoulders, trying to project an aura of strength even though I was suddenly terrified.

"Go and rouse Graves," I told her. "He'll know what to do. And if not, he can find Lady Penelope and Mr. Harshad and they'll know what to do."

"Yes, Your Highness," Betsy mumbled, bowing and scrambling down the hall before I could tell her this was not the time to worry about etiquette.

"You should go with her." Ferdy's voice was full of worry as he glanced toward the kitchen.

"No." I pulled out my mother's dagger and shook my head at him. "We work together, remember?"

He said nothing, but I knew he wasn't happy as we walked into the kitchen.

My stomach turned at the sight.

There was a mess of overturned pots scattered on the floor. Bread was thrown all over, while baskets of vegetables and fruits were on their sides, spilling onto the counter.

The only thing in order was a tray of tea, still warm, that was set out and ready to be served—and just below it, on the floor, was Tulia.

Her face was splattered with blood, her gray hair was wild and frazzled—and a large knife was lodged inside her chest, all the way down to the hilt.

"Tulia!" I hurried and kneeled down next to her. Carefully, I cradled her against my legs as I watched, horrified, as her topaz eyes glazed over with tears and approaching death. "What happened?"

I wanted to ask if there had been an accident, but I also knew it was foolish to be so naïve.

I glanced down at Tulia's fingers, which were moving as they spelled out a response.

I killed him.

775

THE ORDER OF THE CRYSTAL DAGGERS

"You killed him?" I watched as she nodded. "Who? Who are you talking about?"

Your father.

"What?" My mouth dropped open in shock, and I nearly lost my grip on her.

"What did she say?" Ferdy asked, but I ignored him.

She looked up at me, and I couldn't be sure if she was telling me the truth or if she was lost in some hallucination brought on by her injuries.

But she weakly reached up and took hold of my hand.

Forgive me.

I sat there, still and unmoving, watching as blood trickled down her front, and she struggled to breathe.

Nothing was going to stop her from dying now.

Forgive me. Her hand curled in mine; her silent words were sure, and her dying wish was unmistakable.

"Nora."

I looked up as Marguerite came down to kneel by Tulia's other side.

"Marguerite?" My voice was scratchy as my throat constricted with fear—and something beyond fear. She held out a towel and pressed it down gently on Tulia's wound. The cloth was quickly drenched in blood.

"I can't do anything for her," Marguerite whispered sadly. "I don't even think Mr. Qureshi could save her now."

Her words were muffled inside my mind; I could barely process what was happening. My lovely morning with Ferdy had transformed into something beyond surreal, and as I sat there, thinking through all the times Tulia and I had shared as friends, it was impossible to imagine her killing my father.

Tulia weakly poked at me. *Forgive me.*

"Why?" I murmured. "Why did you kill my father?"

"What was that?" Ferdy asked.

But I ignored him, focusing all my attention on Tulia. She was fading fast—but I had to know.

Jakub. I promised Jakub.

"My grandfather?" I frowned in confusion.

The last of the light in her eyes went dim, and Tulia's head slumped over. Her fingers twitched again.

I'm sorry.

I shook my head, crumbling as I began to weep. I took her into my arms and held her, wishing I had more time with her. I wanted to ask her questions, to speak with her, to let her know how I felt, assuming I could even understand how I even felt.

It was all so complicated.

Tulia was my friend, my companion, one of the last links to my mother—but she was a kidnapper, a conspirator, and now a murderer?

How could I mourn for her loss? And yet, how could I not cry at losing her?

"I forgive you." I whispered the words as I held her; I felt her lips smile one last time against my cheek, and then her breathing stopped along with her heartbeat.

And then all I could see were my tears, and all I could feel was my heart screaming in agony.

She was gone.

Ferdy put his arm around me, keeping me warm as Tulia's body went cold.

I didn't know if I truly forgave her, but there was nothing to be done now that she was dead.

"I'm sorry, Ella." Ferdy leaned against me in comfort. "Did you see what happened, Marguerite?"

"There was a commotion, and when I came in here, she was on the floor like this." Marguerite looked down at the floor. "I went to see if Mr. Qureshi had returned. When I couldn't find him, I came back here with a towel. But it was too late."

"Did you see anyone else?" Ferdy asked.

"Some of the maids and cooks," Marguerite said. "They came rushing in here after me, and I told them to leave."

"Thank you," I whispered. My voice was as scraggly as ever, but I was grateful for Marguerite's kindness. Betsy and my other friends had already seen too much horror at the world's hands, and I was glad they'd been spared.

"There was something else," Marguerite said. "As I was heading here, I saw someone dressed all in black turning down the other hallway."

"In black?" Ferdy's voice was full of hidden fear as he squeezed my shoulders.

I barely understood that Tulia's killer might have been my attacker from the bridge.

"Yes. At first, I wasn't sure if what I was seeing was really there, since it's still dark out. But I'm certain I saw someone." Marguerite looked down at Tulia. "Do you think it was really her killer?"

In response to her question, Lady Penelope spoke up from behind us. "We will find out."

All of us turned to see her standing in the doorway. She looked distressed as she came forward. Harshad and Ben were both behind her. I noticed Ben was watching Marguerite with a worried expression on his face; when he saw me looking at him, he frowned.

"What happened?" he asked.

"Tulia killed *Táta*," I blurted out. I knew that wasn't what he'd wanted to know, but I needed to tell him.

Ben looked shocked. "What?"

I couldn't look at him as I spoke. "She told me before … before … "

The last time we had been together, I remembered Tulia insisting that it would be better for me to hate her, and how horror-stricken her face had been when Cecilia accused her of wanting to poison them.

She'd wanted to tell me. But why now?

I still clung to her, unable to discern anything from her chilly flesh. Maybe she supposed I'd find out soon enough and thought I truly would've hated her for her deception. Or maybe after our arguments on the *Salacia*, she might have felt some measure of guilt.

My tears slowed, but my heart ached with fresh pain and betrayal, mixed with the weight of loss and grief. Beside me, Ben was still and silent, and I was just grateful he and Ferdy were both there for me. Carefully, I moved Tulia off my lap and wiped my eyes with the back of my hand.

Harshad stepped forward. "Was this tea sitting here like this when you arrived, Miss Marguerite?"

"Yes, sir," she answered. "I didn't touch anything when I saw her. I just got the towel, and that's all, I promise."

"The tea is for Cecilia," I said, as Ferdy and Ben both helped me up from my position on the floor. "She's waiting for it in the library with Priscilla."

"There's a note here," Lady Penelope said, picking up a small, folded sheet of paper from under the teapot. "It says the tea was for you, Eleanora. You ordered it."

"No, I didn't." I reached for it, and she gave it to me. I was shocked to see there was indeed a small scribble that resembled my own writing, calling for tea to be sent up to my room. "I didn't write this."

Harshad poured the tea into a cup and sniffed it. After careful examination, he put it down with a somber look. "This tea is poisoned."

"Poisoned?" I looked over at the pots and pans which were overturned. "Tulia was fighting with someone. Maybe she saw the person who did it."

"The man in black," Marguerite whispered. "That has to be who it was."

Which means Tulia was protecting me.

Just then, I was glad I'd forgiven her. Tulia hadn't wanted me and Ben to know of my mother's history with the Order, and she'd objected to Lady Penelope's tutelage—and to be fair, she likely had her reasons against trusting Lady POW to see to our wellbeing.

I still couldn't understand why Tulia had killed my father, forcing me and Ben under Cecilia's care, or lack thereof, but I believed she did her best to look out for us after he died.

As for my grandfather, I couldn't imagine why he would want Tulia to kill my father. Jakub was a Bohemian Loyalist and a member of the League, and he had died a year after *Máma*.

My thoughts circled back to Lumiere. He knew of the Bohemian Loyalists, and if he was the true owner of his pocket watch, he would know why my grandfather would tell Tulia to do such a thing.

We have to find him.

THE ORDER OF THE CRYSTAL DAGGERS

Lumiere could have left to meet up with Louis, to stay with Karl, or even to just run away. But once more, I wanted to find him, and it was mostly for personal reasons.

"This is the Order's poison."

I glanced up in surprise, both at Harshad's hard tone and his words. The rest of us turned to face him, but he only looked to Lady Penelope.

Together, the two of them had another one of their silent conversations, and then Lady Penelope's expression soured.

"Where is Amir?" she asked.

Harshad shook his head, and I immediately objected.

"Amir wouldn't do this," I exclaimed.

Ben nodded. "She's right. Amir and I just came home a little while ago. He wouldn't have had time to do this."

"Go and get him. If he is innocent, I will need him to mix up some more antidote. I don't think we have any more now." She gestured to the pots on the ground, where a small puddle of silvery liquid shimmered against the floor.

"Amir is innocent," I insisted.

Lady Penelope and Harshad exchanged another glance, but neither of them seemed willing to explain anything to me.

"We will talk about this again later, Eleanora," Lady Penelope said. "We have other things to do now. We need to see to Tulia's burial."

She began issuing orders. Ben headed out to get Amir, and Marguerite quickly followed him. As they left, I saw her reach for his hand, and I even saw him let her take it.

I was about to tell him to wait for me, but Ferdy put his hand on my arm.

"It's fine, Ella," Ferdy whispered softly to me, as if he could see what I was thinking. "She really does care for your brother, even if he doesn't believe it, and you don't need to fear being replaced, just as I didn't replace Ben in your eyes."

I still didn't really know what to think about Marguerite and Ben; she was a sweet young lady, and Ben had wanted a unique wife, I remembered, thinking of our conversation months ago.

So why didn't he seem excited that he'd possibly found one? He seemed a little uncertain of his ability to provide for her—but I thought he was even more unwilling to believe he was worthy of her.

When I looked over at Ferdy, I understood how Ben felt.

"We will need more herbs for an antidote," Lady Penelope spoke up a moment later.

"Ferdy and I will get them from Eliezer's wife again," I volunteered, eager to get away from the house. The thought of going back to the Cabal cheered me some, if only a little. "We were going to go out and look for Lumiere anyway."

Lady Penelope looked irritated, but she only nodded. "Let me give you a list before you leave."

As she began scribbling on the back of the fake note, Amir came in, followed closely by Ben.

"You sent for me, Madame?" he inquired, and I saw the grim resolution on his face.

"Yes." Lady Penelope gestured down to Tulia. "Did you do this?"

"Of course he didn't!" I insisted, angry all over again. "Why are you so cruel?"

Amir shook his head. "It's all right."

"No, it's not," I objected. "She can't just accuse you of something like this—"

"Eleanora." Amir's tone was hard but sure. "Lady Penelope and I have worked together for years, long before you entered our lives. Please calm yourself."

"Why?" I pouted. "I'm on your side."

"Should there be a fight, I will only lay down my arms," Amir told me quietly. "But there is no need for fighting, is there, Madame?"

Lady Penelope shook her head. "No. Of course not."

"Then I trust you will forgive Eleanora for her interruption," he said, making me frown further.

"I have never trusted you with my affections, Amir, but I have always trusted you with my life." Lady Penelope gave me a slanted look, and then gestured down to Tulia's corpse. "Did you do this?"

"No." Amir's voice was thick with emotional upheaval, but there was nothing uncertain in his response. I watched as he clasped his hands together, his left hand covering the mark of the *noon* on his right.

The sight of it brought tears to my eyes. Amir really had given up so much for my mother. After breaking away from his family, I had no doubt he was prepared to stand up to Lady Penelope and the Order, too.

"Then you know what this means," Lady Penelope said, looking over at Harshad, and then back to Amir.

Once more, I was excluded from their conversation.

"We will need to take care of the matter at once," Lady Penelope said, her voice uncharacteristically soft.

"You will have to excuse me." Harshad's head fell to his chest. "I do not believe I can assist you in this matter. I would only hinder your work."

"Harshad." Lady Penelope put her hand on his arm. "We all have our weaknesses. You must forgive yourself."

"If only I could." He shook his head again and left.

There was a moment of silence, and then Amir reached for his dagger. "Thank you for saying that, Madame."

"It doesn't matter." She wrinkled her nose. "There's nothing we can do."

"It matters more than you know," Amir said. "I have never forgiven myself for leaving Naděžda; I only wanted her happiness, and I thought leaving was best. But I was wrong. And I can forgive you, Madame, for all your crimes against me, however horrible or slight they might have been, because they are nothing compared to mine against her. There is nothing we can do about the past, but for the present, it is good we acknowledge the truth. And that includes our weaknesses."

Lady POW gave him the slightest nod, before clearing her throat. "Go with Eleanora and Ferdinand and retrieve Lumiere. I will feel much better if he can give us some corresponding proof regarding this development."

"What development?" I asked, but no one answered me.

Instead, Lady POW merely handed me the list of herbs we needed from Zipporah. "After we have Lumiere, we will march on *Vyšehrad* and retrieve Karl, and then use him as bait to find Louis."

She excused herself and I said nothing as she headed out in the same direction as Harshad.

THE ORDER OF THE CRYSTAL DAGGERS

I wanted answers, but no one seemed to care.

Ferdy took my hand. "Are you sure you want to go with me?" he asked.

"Yes." I nodded. "You heard Lady POW. We'll get Lumiere, and then we'll get Karl later tonight."

"Lumi sent me a message last night," Amir said. "I know he is not with Karl or Lord Maximillian."

"I have my lead," Ferdy said. "We'll find him."

"Good," I said. "He's the only one who can tell me why Tulia would kill my father. We can stop at the Cabal on the way back and get the herbs from Eliezer's wife."

"Assuming she has them." Ferdy looked grim. "And assuming we won't run into more trouble along the way."

"There will be more, I'm afraid." Amir looked back over at me apologetically. "There are other, unexpected matters we must attend to now."

"Like what?" I asked.

Amir looked back at the tea set on the counter. "Like finding Nassara's true killer."

19

◊

"Are you sure this is the right place?" Ferdy looked at the Church of Our Lady of the Snows with doubt. "Lumiere seems more suited to gaming hells or clubs or taverns … or brothels."

"The Church of Our Lady of the Snows is where Dr. Artha was killed," Amir reminded us. "And Father Novak, too. Lumiere would know this place."

"That's what the runner meant by 'the church of the light.' There aren't any other places known by that name," I said. "Light" was the code name Lumiere used for himself.

Standing there, I remembered Tulia had her own code name, too— *Míra*, meaning "peace."

At my sudden sadness, I could only hope Tulia truly was at peace. Maybe she was with Dr. Artha now, I mused, before I stopped myself. It was still too hard for me to think about her in the afterlife. Not when I'd seen her body go limp with death only this morning.

"Let's go. There's no reason to stand here." I pulled my bonnet further down over my face and quickly traced a small cross over my heart in prayer—not just for Tulia, but for answers, too.

Despite his insistence that Nassara's killer was on the loose, Amir would not explain himself without proof. He said we would get it when we found Lumiere.

And that wasn't all we would get. My hands tingled with the memory of Tulia's last, silent words to me.

I would get more information about my father's murder, too.

"Well, the runner didn't seem like he was lying," Ferdy said as he took hold of my hand. "If you're both certain."

Walking into the church, I saw it was no less grand to me than it had been the night of Father Novak's murder. The foyer opened into the presbytery, where I turned up my face to see the high vault; its patterned supports zigzagged all across the ceiling, like a puzzling labyrinth.

It stirred hope in my soul that, as complicated and chaotic as life could be, I was secure in my hope that every question had an answer, and all the

784

questions I had would lead me to where I was supposed to be and help me do what I was supposed to do.

The organ music played in the sanctuary as we began to walk through the pews. I saw Amir's smile, and then I recognized the music's tune of "Amazing Grace," John Newton's work. Amir had told me once how he loved music, even though he had grown up believing it to be *haram*, a sinful indulgence.

Suddenly, I was very aware of so much I took for granted.

"Would you like to go pray?" I asked Amir quietly. "Ferdy and I can look around on our own."

I could see the tired gratitude in his eyes as he nodded. "I would like that. Thank you."

As Amir excused himself, I scanned the alcoves, looking for signs of Lumiere's bright, golden locks.

There were scattered sets of people, here and there and all around; some were lighting candles at the front, others were kneeling in the pews; others were simply sitting down, looking up at the majestic altar with varied expressions ranging from listlessness to feigned interest to holy wonder.

It was only when I caught sight of the closed confessionals that I paused. "Huh."

"What is it?" Ferdy asked.

"Lumiere was joking the other day about how he'd wanted Lady POW to capture him," I explained. "I guess he wasn't really joking. But he said he'd stay until he was unable to bear his guilt. Then he would head straight for the nearest monastery to confess his sins. I didn't think he meant it."

Ferdy followed my gaze. "I could try stealing a set of priestly robes."

"I don't think you'll have to. Look." I nudged his hand toward a small area behind the confessionals, where several altar boys and a priest were hauling a swaggering body away from the sanctuary. Even from where we stood, there was a fineness of the cloak and a cleanliness to the boots I knew all too well.

Ferdy and I moved as quickly and quietly as possible. We caught up with them just as they reached the side door.

"Come now, Father," Lumiere's voice was muffled. "I didn't intend to get drunk on the communion wine."

785

"Where is your self-control, sir? This is the second church you've disgraced yourself in this week," one of the boys said. "I heard Father Bercik at St. Cyril tried to perform an exorcism on you, but I admit I didn't believe it at first."

"Hey, your priests aren't supposed to be sharing my list of sins," Lumiere reprimanded. "I don't care how entertaining I am, nor do I care how boring your life is. I sin for my own pleasure, not yours."

Another altar boy sniggered into his sleeve. "Sorry," he said as the others glared at him. "But I heard he went to *Týnem*, asking for asylum and vowing to dedicate his life to the service of God, and then he got thrown out two days later for poor behavior."

I glanced over at Ferdy. "Should we stop them from tossing him out, or just get him outside?" I whispered.

There was no hesitation in his answer. "Outside."

We enjoyed a quiet laugh before we headed out to retrieve Lumiere's disgraced form. He was on the ground in the alleyway, facedown and defeated, as I came up beside him.

"Lumiere." I shook his shoulder hard as Ferdy kept watch and guarded us.

"*Oui, c'est moi, chérie*," Lumiere greeted me with a happy, drunken slur. "Are you here for me at last?"

"Yes, unfortunately," I said. "You've been misbehaving again, by the sound of it."

"Did you really do all those things they were talking about in there?" Ferdy asked.

"What? Never!" Lumiere let out a loud hiccup, his expression shocked and horrified, and then he grinned up at me, still playful. "I was at *Týnem* for three days, not two. I counted very carefully, you know. I might enjoy pretending to be mad, but I do so very much want to emulate my Lord and Savior."

I hauled him up into a sitting position. The streets were extra cold, and it spoke to the high degree of Lumiere's torment that he allowed himself to sit neatly on a pile of slush and garbage. "From what I've seen, your messiah is Bacchus, not Jesus."

"Even Bacchus would have approved of Jesus after he turned the water into wine." Lumiere gave me a half-hearted smile, before he sighed dejectedly. "But Christ had no beauty or majesty to attract us to him; there was nothing in his appearance that we should desire him. Seeing as how I am shamefully pure charisma, it's a doomed hope that I should be like him, right from the very beginning."

"Oh, my goodness, Lumiere … " I sighed and rubbed my temples in exasperation.

How could I have missed such a monster?

"Anyway, it's not my fault I got thrown out of the churches," Lumiere muttered. "I couldn't achieve the first requirement of my stay. They set me up for failure."

"What was it? Donning the plain robes of a monk?"

Lumiere shuddered. "Don't even jest about such things, Ella. That's the least funny thing I've ever heard."

"What was it then?"

"As my primary penitence, I had to receive your forgiveness for my great transgression against you."

"What?" I was tempted to laugh, but then I saw the stark, deadly serious look on his face. There were too many ills and inconveniences Lumiere had given me in our short time of acquaintance, and while they were all annoying, there was nothing I could imagine that would cause him such misery. "You're serious?"

"I am." His green eyes were blurred over, but the thought behind them was as sharp and clear as ever. "Do you know how it feels to wish so badly to be someone the opposite of yourself?"

I watched him carefully, unsure if I should say anything at all. And when I didn't reply, he waved me away.

"Of course you don't," he said, taking my hand before I could scoot away from him. "You're just like Naděžda, really. She was funny and smart and effortlessly lovely."

"She had her flaws, too."

"She certainly did." He drew up his knees to his chin and curled his arms around himself protectively. He looked like a small, princely child, sitting on his throne of garbage. "I told her not to go, you know."

"Go where?"

"To London. To see Lady Penelope and Amir again." He watched me as I felt my breathing grow shallow. "It's my fault she died."

THE ORDER OF THE CRYSTAL DAGGERS

At first, I could only hope he was joking. But I saw Lumiere's face—his proud, haughty, luminous face. In place of his usual effervescence and vitality, I only saw repentant despair.

Shock rushed through me first, followed quickly by anger. "What are you talking about?"

"The poison," he finally said. "I was the one who told her she'd been poisoned. I found out my father had made the arrangements. When I came to visit her and your grandfather, she confessed about Nassara—and I wasn't expecting it at all, and then, of course, it's no easy thing, to get a woman to open up about her sadness. Why women like to believe their suffering will go away if they just ignore it, I'll never—"

"Lumiere!" I snapped, practically strangling him. "Are you telling me that you killed my mother?"

"Ella? Are you all right?" Ferdy asked, inching closer to us.

Lumiere and I both ignored him, even though I was grateful for his presence. He would stop me from doing anything too drastic.

And as good as it might have felt, I did not want to kill Lumiere.

Not yet, anyway.

"What? No, never." Lumiere shook his head fiercely, his hair flinging out in a thrashing wave of blonde. "*Non, chérie.* I loved her dearly. She was my sister in all but blood. I used to imagine she really was, you know, even if it meant Pepé was my mother. But I so loved her and Jakub that I could pretend even that ... my father was just as awful as you might've guessed, and ... "

"How did you find out she was poisoned?" I asked slowly.

"My father and your grandmother were fighting over Europe's favorite art collection when your mother was pregnant with Nassara."

"I heard about that," I said. That was the mission Lady POW had told me my mother caused her to lose to Louis.

"Yes, well, you probably didn't know your grandmother was very close to winning," Lumiere said. "And that it would have been the end of him. So he did something very naughty—and very shocking, even for him."

He looked up at me, and then at my stomach. He shook his head, and a knot of pain twisted inside me.

Louis knew about Nassara—and he killed her.

"He didn't do it himself, of course; he found an accomplice to give her the poison. I wasn't around to stop him; I didn't even learn of it until much later, after Naděžda told me what had happened and I asked *mon père* about it." Lumiere scowled. "He was quite proud of it by then."

"Where were you when … ?" I didn't finish the question. I could barely speak. Even Lumiere was having trouble telling me what happened.

"I was … rather indisposed, if you must know."

"In prison?" My brow furrowed in impatience.

"That's one way to describe Ireland." Lumiere snorted disdainfully. "I suppose that's the other reason you irritate me at times—all that Catholicism. Protestants won't pay money to assuage their consciences, so they channel their guilt into evangelizing. But Catholics pay their indulgences and gain interest in guilting others. It's one thing to convince a man of his need for the Lord Jesus and his sacrifice, and then it's another to constantly remind him of his sin."

"Please, Lumiere, we don't have time to go through any catechisms." All over again, I was realizing how much he just wanted attention, and I hated him for it. We had just been reunited and already I wanted to scream in frustration, and for more than one reason, too. "Tell me why I should forgive you."

"You shouldn't." Lumiere laughed all of a sudden. "There is never a right time for conversations such as this, Ella, no matter where life finds us."

Ferdy sat down beside me, and without saying a word, he took hold of my other hand. At his touch, I remembered Tulia.

"Tulia's dead," I said.

"Oh." Lumiere didn't seem surprised to hear of her death.

"You didn't do it, did you? Someone spotted a man dressed all in black at the manor," Ferdy said.

"No, it wasn't me," Lumiere replied glumly. "I adore black, but it's far too colorless for me to enjoy wearing it. Especially if it's the only color." He glanced down at his ermine-lined crimson cloak, his bright leather shoes, and his gold-embroidered jacket, before he grimaced. "But I've instructed several of my henchmen to wear it, as has my father. Of course, that just means I shouldn't wear it all the more. I'm not the help, after all; I'm the second-in-command."

THE ORDER OF THE CRYSTAL DAGGERS

I ignored his narcissistic rambling. "I can't see you using a knife, either. You killed Alex without a qualm back on the *Salacia*, but you used a gun then."

"Yes, well, the bastard deserved it from all the rumors I'd heard," Lumiere said. "And Tulia deserved to die, too. I told you so myself, though I can see you're not happy about it."

"No. Of course not." I swallowed hard. "She told me she killed my father."

"She told you?" Lumiere huffed. "Well, I lost that bet. At least she's dead and I don't have to pay her now."

"You knew? Why did she do it?" I held my breath, unsure of how I would feel about his answer. "Tell me."

"He deserved it, really, that's why."

"Lumiere!"

"Calm down, Ella. Adolf was not fond of me, and I didn't like him— God, I hated him, if truth be told; he was a poor substitute for Amir, who is still a prince among men."

My jaw clenched with impatience. I should've known he would enjoy taking as long as possible with his story. "Tulia said she killed him because of my grandfather."

"Yes." Lumiere sighed. "You see, Jakub was a good and honorable man. His only defect in the League was that he was a very loyal Bohemian. When Naděžda returned to Prague in 1847, and met her Dolf again—"

"Again?"

"They met before in Constantinople," Lumiere explained quickly. "Naděžda flirted with him for information, and he was easily besotted. When they met again, he proposed, and since he was one of King Ferdinand V's closest advisors, she accepted for the sake of the mission."

I frowned. It was hard to think of my mother as a practiced flirt; I also didn't like how pragmatically she'd agreed to marriage to my father. The thought left a bad taste in my mouth.

"Then my mother got pregnant with Karl," Ferdy said.

"And soon enough, Naděžda got pregnant, too," Lumiere agreed. "At Jakub's prodding, she resigned from the Order, but Adolf didn't know about her past."

THE ORDER OF THE CRYSTAL DAGGERS

"I see," I said. My mother had grown to love my father after they married, and then he'd grown to resent her after she died.

Lumiere's drunkenness began to wane. "When she told me about Nassara, Naděžda wondered aloud if she'd been poisoned. She'd sought answers and sent out letters to Pepé, in hopes she would come here to Prague. Your grandmother predictably refused, even though she sent money and anything else asked of her. Naděžda planned to tell her about you and Benedict when everything was settled."

"But *Máma* went to see her after you told her the truth about Nassara's death." I slumped over. "And then her ship was lost at sea."

"Afterward, your grandfather asked Tulia and me to make sure that Adolf never learned about the Order."

"But my father did find out." I thought about my dream, the one where I'd remembered how my father was learning Arabic.

Lumiere nodded. "Yes, so it appears. And then because of his carelessness, Max found out about Karl, and so here we are. Tulia was right to kill him before he made it worse."

"Lumiere." I shook my head. "That's not fair of you to say."

"What kind of person would I be if I didn't say it anyway? Don't be like that, Ella. You know life is not fair, and there's no use pretending niceties and euphemisms somehow make it easier." Lumiere's head sank even further against his chest. "Jakub died less than a year after your mother. He was devastated at her loss, you know. And so was I. Just like you, I lost my family—or at least, the one of my own choosing."

We sat there, surrounded by snow and garbage, with the echo of church hymns and liturgies. Ferdy held onto me, and I even held Lumiere's hand tightly in reluctant solidarity and sympathy.

A few moments passed before Lumiere brightened a little and nudged Ferdy's shoulder companionably. "The former empress liked the promise that Adolf—and Naděžda herself—would protect her family, but she hid her second pregnancy even more than the first."

"How did you find out, then?" Ferdy asked. "You knew about it before we were even introduced."

"If you haven't noticed, I have a way with getting information from various sources, including priests and other clergymen," Lumiere said, nodding back towards the closed church doors behind us. "They remember my antics more than my questions, and since I am an egregious sinner beyond repair, they frequently forget about me if I am quiet enough."

791

THE ORDER OF THE CRYSTAL DAGGERS

He laughed, but it was hollow and dry, reminding me of how cold I felt.

I didn't know what I could really do for him, any more than I really knew what to do with him. Lumiere was a strange man, shameless but full of guilt, a victim as much as a victimizer, and as fake as he was genuine, trapped in a world in which he imagined himself free.

Perhaps that was the reason he'd found such a refuge in my mother's friendship; they were the same.

Wordlessly, I could only pray.

Many times in my life, I had prayed for a sign or a specific outcome; I had been certain of what I'd wanted, and I'd asked for it with the childlike faith that confounds the adult. I'd had moments when the heavenly bowers went silent, and my faith seemed to waver. But I also knew that there were times when no such sign was warranted at all; I did not need a sign or a specific answer to know what to do.

And right now, I had to be brave, I had to be kind, and I had to be steady. My mother wasn't here, but I knew she did not want Lumiere to carry the burden of a sin he was only guilty of covering up, not of committing.

"I forgive you," I said. The words still felt harsh and foreign as I said them for the second time that day, to a person I didn't truly know if I could just simply forgive. Lumiere was another soul I would have to forgive again and again, perhaps on a daily basis, until the habit was woven into the very fabric of my soul.

Lumiere crumpled. "I need a drink."

At that moment, I knew it was time to leave. Together, Ferdy and I hauled Lumiere to his feet; he seemed more stable as we walked.

"We've got to head to the Cabal first," Ferdy reminded me. "Lady Penelope wants more herbs for the antidote."

I nodded in agreement. "Perhaps Clavan can get Lumiere settled, too."

My heart, nestled inside its crater of fear and grief, cheered a little as Lumiere began to fume over his dirty clothes. I envied his self-concern; it was as admirable in its breadth as much as it was lamentable in its depth. But he didn't seem to let the past bother him.

Well, but then it wouldn't, I thought. He'd just settled it with me. He'd gotten what he wanted—perhaps even what he needed.

THE ORDER OF THE CRYSTAL DAGGERS

Lumiere brightened as Amir came outside to meet us, and even raced to hug him. I smiled as Amir made no objection at Lumiere's show of friendship, even if another wave of weariness took hold of me.

"Ella?" Ferdy took hold of my hand again. "Are you able to keep going?"

"We have no choice. But I can do it."

He pressed a kiss on my cheek. "There is no need for you to do so alone."

More than gratefully, I clung to him.

Lumiere and Amir talked companionably as we made our way through the city toward the *Josefkà*. Ferdy and I followed them, keeping a close watch. Now that we'd found Lumiere again, I was determined that we weren't going to let him get away.

We were almost to the Cabal when they stopped short, and Ferdy and I came to a quick halt behind them.

"What is it?" I asked.

"What else would it be, *chérie?*" Lumiere pointed ahead. "Trouble."

That was when I heard glass breaking and tasted a whisper of smoke on the wind.

The Cabal was under attack.

20

◊

"Ella." Ferdy clutched my hand even more firmly, and I couldn't say whether it was to steady me or hold me back.

A sadistic, musical barrage of destruction emitted from the small publican house as flames appeared and smoke poured out of the roof.

"Ugh," Lumiere groaned. "Look. Here comes even more trouble."

I followed his gaze up the street, surprised to see Lady Penelope climbing down from her carriage. Ben quickly jumped down from the top box, and even Marguerite followed after him.

"Why did they come?" Amir asked Lumiere, who only grimaced.

Another crackle of broken glass made me look back to the Cabal. My fear grew, but I could no longer stand around and do nothing.

Amir and Lumiere could worry about the others, I decided. I headed into the building as Ferdy followed close behind me.

A small group of annoyed patrons filed past us as we entered, with several of them still carrying their mugs.

Behind me, I could hear Lady Penelope calling for me, but I ignored her.

"Faye!" I yelled into the emptying pub, desperate to locate my friends. I pushed my bonnet back, letting it fall to the floor as I called out again. "Jarl? Mr. Clavan?"

"Let's check in the back," Ferdy suggested, as he pulled me into the kitchen.

"Faye?" I called again, much more hesitantly this time. "Mr. Clavan?"

"Back here. This way." Ferdy said as he headed toward the back room and the street exit. I followed after him closely, my eyes already stinging at the clouds of smoke as a new dread settled inside me.

Are Karl and Lord Maximillian behind this?

They didn't know about Ferdy's trips here, or our friends, or how I enjoyed my visits. Lumiere was the only one outside the Order's circle who knew about the Cabal, and he'd been terrorizing churches for the past several days.

THE ORDER OF THE CRYSTAL DAGGERS

I frowned. There was nothing I could think of that would point them to this place, and that only made me more confused and angry.

Then I saw Clavan kneeling on the floor, a line of blood dripping down his forehead. He was holding onto Helen, who was unconscious.

"Mr. Clavan." I saw he had another array of cuts on one of his arms, and his shirt was torn at the elbow. "What happened?"

"Never mind that," Clavan said, looking down at his wife. "We need to get her out of here."

Ferdy knelt down on the other side of Helen's unconscious form and carefully looped her arm around his neck.

"She's bleeding," I said, noticing the blood pooling from the back of her head.

"We can take care of it outside," Ferdy said, but I was already pulling out my dagger and cutting strips from the bottom of my dress.

"Here." I handed them to Clavan.

At first, he didn't take them; he was staring at my dagger with an intrigued wariness on his face.

"It seems you have quite the adventurous life, Ella," he said, as he finally took the cloth from my hand. "Especially if you are truly a member of the Order of the Crystal Daggers."

For some reason, I felt flustered. His observation was without admiration, nor condemnation; it was a fact, and from the way he spoke, it was a foreboding one.

I looked to Ferdy, who turned away from me, and I decided we would have to worry about it later.

"Where's Faye?" I asked.

"Faye went upstairs," Clavan said. "To get her dress."

It took me a second to remember Faye's wedding, and then I bit down on my cheek. She'd been so happy, looking forward to it, and I didn't want to think how the Cabal could burn down.

But for the safety of everyone involved, I had to face the reality that it was possible.

While Ferdy helped Clavan carefully arrange Helen's body across his back, I watched the smoke build up. I relaxed only in the slightest to see it was burning white; I knew from Ben that the dynamite concoction at the Potocki mansion would burn black.

Faye suddenly appeared at the bottom of the stairs, carrying her copy of *Jane Eyre* and a large ball of fabric that could only be her wedding dress.

"I'm here," she said, and despite the danger, she gave me a smile. There was a grim, resigned quality to it, but Faye was still hopeful and determined; she had the best of her father as well as the loveliness and grace of her mother.

Helen was finally secure in Clavan's arms. Thanks to Ferdy's help, his wound wasn't being further exasperated, and we were ready to leave.

We headed for the back door—only to see it was blocked.

Not by the fire, but by a figure, all dressed in black.

A hood covered his face, but I still felt the shock of recognition.

I felt the blood drain from my face. "You're the one who pushed me off the bridge."

There was no reply from under the hood. Instead, his hands only moved to a fighting position.

I gripped my dagger and swallowed hard. "You killed Tulia, too, didn't you?"

No response.

"Ella." Ferdy's whisper was one of fear and warning.

But I shook my head. "Get them out of the building. Use the side door up front. I'll take care of this."

My voice sounded unusually calm, even though I was terrified.

Ferdy shook his head. "No."

"Yes," I insisted. "I'm trained for this. And I have to protect you."

I thought back to that night at the port, where I'd told him before that I wouldn't die for a prince, but I would die for him.

The time had come for me to prove myself.

In the end, Ferdy gave in. There was no way for him to stop me without letting go of Helen, and neither of us wanted our friends to be harmed.

"Fine," he said. "But I'll come back for you."

THE ORDER OF THE CRYSTAL DAGGERS

"Be careful," Faye whispered as they left.

I was about to promise her I would be quick as well as careful, but the figure in black was already lunging forward. His first attack lashed out with lightning speed, right at my chest.

I only just managed to dodge it, and rebound into a defensive stance.

And then the battle truly began.

Our movements were swift, but familiar. I was grateful for this; it allowed me to be more prepared than I'd expected.

Dodging another blow, I slipped under his arm and shoved into his chest this time, crying out as I slammed the full weight of my body into his. He fell back into the door, and I landed a left hook on his face. Despite the circumstance, I was thankful I'd cut off a portion of my skirts for Helen's injuries; I was able to move much more freely without their full length, and even though I was still at a disadvantage, I'd been practicing enough to know I could win.

We battled with each other's punches in a synchronized harmony as the smoke worsened, and my eyes grew wet with grief, fear, and determination.

It was too easy to block out the rest of the world in those moments; perhaps it was the real sense of danger, or maybe it was how I wanted to protect Ferdy and my friends, or it could have even been my grief over Tulia's loss.

But no matter what it was, I kept my eyes on my enemy, and I set my heart on victory.

Finally, I grappled with his arm, yanked it close to me, and pulled him down to the floor as I slashed out with my dagger. I shouted in horrified triumph as the blade struck true and drew blood as it sliced through his shoulder.

The smallest gasp of surprise sounded out from underneath the hood. I pulled back briefly, struggling with an unbelievable thought as I stood there, struck by the sudden familiarity.

Is it possible ... ?

The figure suddenly pushed me back hard, grabbing my dagger and forcing it out my hand. Another kick landed on my chest, sending me flying into the wall by the stairs. The last of my breath flew out of my lungs.

I couldn't stop staring at my attacker—even as my own dagger was turned against me and thrust toward my face with headlong speed.

Finally, I shut my eyes, unable to do anything else.

Only to hear a familiar *clash*—the sound of metal scraping against metal.

My heart was pounding as I looked up at my rescuer.

"Amir." I gasped, feeling winded and beyond relieved that he'd saved me again.

Amir didn't appear to hear me. His *Wahabite Jambiya* glimmered as it held back my own dagger's deadly blade.

"That's enough," Amir said quietly. "You can stop now, Xiana."

"Xiana?" I looked back at the figure in black, and the earlier dread I'd felt flashed through me again.

It couldn't really be Xiana ... could it?

A long moment passed as the hooded figure stepped from us, staying back out of reach, outlined by rising flames and flowing smoke.

And then, in a graceful, sweeping move, the hood came down, and Xiana stood before us in silence. Through the smoke, her eyes spoke of hatred and anger and shame.

What had been unthinkable was suddenly inevitably true.

"Why?" I wailed, unable to understand it and unwilling to believe it. "Why did you do this?"

"She was manipulated into doing it," Amir said. "She tried to poison you earlier, and then she was forced to kill Tulia."

"You are wrong." Xiana scowled at him. Her voice sounded hoarse as she spoke, and she turned her blazing eyes on me. "I sought to kill Eleanora on my own. Louis said her death would not affect Madame quite as much as he'd hoped, so he would allow it."

"Louis?" I blinked. "You're working with Louis?"

And then I shook my head.

Of course she is.

Lumiere had told me earlier that Louis had poisoned my mother with the help of an accomplice. And Xiana had seen *Máma* take it firsthand—though my mother hadn't known herself.

"Xiana." Amir shook his head. "No matter what has happened, Nassara did not deserve death by your hand, and neither does Eleanora."

He knows.

Amir had finally found out the truth of Nassara's death, and I could only envy his calm composure at the news.

"And did I deserve such anguish by your own hand?" Xiana's uncharacteristic cry was as jarring as her sudden bloodlust. She lunged at him again, still armed with my dagger.

Amir expertly parried his weapon against my mother's blade. "Suffering in this world is unavoidable, Xiana. We may experience it differently, but we are all able to decide to inflict it on others or not."

"Then what is your choice now, Amir?" Xiana glared up at him. "Will you inflict even more suffering on me?"

"I will not allow you to hurt Eleanora," he said firmly. "But you've already hurt yourself more than I ever could. You've killed my daughter, broke my wife's trust, and worked against your friends by siding with the enemy. As much as I've lost, you've lost even more. You might have felt alone before, but now you are more alone than you've ever been."

His voice was breaking as he finished, and my tears began to fall at the sadness he carried.

"In truth, I pity you—for you truly do not know what you've done, or even what you are doing now." Amir shook his head. "I will pity you even more if you really believe there's no hope for forgiveness and reconciliation."

Amir was struggling to speak now, and she pulled back from him.

"I do not want you to forgive me," Xiana growled as she resumed her fighting stance. "I only want you to suffer now. It is too late for us to reconcile."

Amir stood his ground, and I could only watch.

But I barely blinked, and then Amir grabbed her arm, hit her hand with his knee, and freed my mother's dagger from her grasp. After he shoved her backward, he nudged the dagger back in my direction.

"Go see Lady Penelope," he ordered, his *Wahabite Jambiya* ready as Xiana pulled out her *jian* from the hidden sheath on her back.

"Are you certain?" I whispered, suddenly feeling sick as I inched back toward the front room.

"Yes." He gave me the briefest smile. "Thank you, Eleanora."

My heart had been pounding nearly the entire time I'd been at the Cabal, but as I grabbed my dagger and slid past Amir, I felt it stop, and then fall into despair.

THE ORDER OF THE CRYSTAL DAGGERS

21

◊

·Guilt hounded me as I hurried back to the front of the Cabal.

I did not want to leave Amir. He'd told me before Xiana was hard to defeat. She'd seemed angrier and more emotional than ever, and I could only hope Amir would find a way to overcome her.

I tucked my mother's dagger back into its sheath, and wiped my eyes.

The menacing fire slowly filled the publican house. The place was empty like a tomb as I stood there.

Suddenly, I realized Ferdy hadn't come back to find me, and my dread increased exponentially.

Where was he?

"Ferdy?" I called. "Faye? Mr. Clavan?"

A soft, familiar voice spoke up from behind me.

"Everyone is preoccupied at the moment, and it is no coincidence they are busy. But I'd be happy to help you if I can, Madame."

I whirled around to see an old man sitting at a table near the door. He was calmly sipping at a teacup, as though he was used to surrounding himself with chaos.

At once, I recognized him. With his pristine white hair, his cloak, with the University patch on the side, it was the old man from the bridge.

I wasn't sure why I felt nervous. I swallowed hard. "What are you doing here?"

"Enjoying a nice cup of tea." His voice was easy and light, and he seemed amused by my concern. "My dormitory is well furnished, but the tea here has always been unmatched in my esteem."

Lady Penelope suddenly burst through the door.

"Eleanora." Lady Penelope was more than capable of ignoring the condition of the Cabal as she glared at me. "I've been waiting for you outside."

"Lady Penelope." My mouth felt dry as I forced myself to speak. I was about to warn her about Amir and Xiana when she handed me a paper.

I looked down to see it was the sketch from the old man—the same old man who sat before us now, surrounded by oncoming death and destruction, as calmly as though he was on holiday by the sea.

"Where did you get this? Tell me," Lady Penelope demanded.

"Where else would she have gotten it, Pepé?" The old man shifted in his seat behind us, clearly pleased. "She got it from me."

Lady Penelope turned toward him with a bitter look on her face. "So, you have arrived."

I examined the paper again. At the corner on the front, just under the drawing, there was a small name scribbled—small enough I'd missed it, and large enough I shouldn't have ignored it.

L. Valoris.

It was then I understood.

"I've been here for some time now, Pepé." Louis Valoris chuckled as he stirred his tea with a spoon. "I do believe it is time we were formally introduced, Lady Eleanora."

"It's you," I whispered, shaking my head in shame.

"I must say, you look so much like your mother. Even in the moonlight, I could've sworn you were her ghost, the first time I saw you for myself."

"Eleanora." Lady Penelope gave me a deadly scowl.

I gave her an apologetic look, but I knew it wouldn't do any good. She'd warned me before Louis was crafty and full of cunning, and I'd been completely caught off guard.

"I must commend you on her progress, Pepé," Louis continued. "But she's still very naïve, and that's dangerous, especially for one who carries the weapon of the Order. How do you know she won't betray you when she learns all your secrets?"

"Eleanora is a loyal member of the Order," Lady Penelope said, her voice full of resignation instead of pride. "She will not betray me."

"Oh, that's a shame. It would be nice to see her live up to her mother's legacy."

At his disparaging tone, a heady, hateful fury rocked me to my core. Lumiere had told me less than an hour ago how Louis had a hand in poisoning my mother and killing Nassara—and now I knew he'd used Xiana to carry out his plans.

THE ORDER OF THE CRYSTAL DAGGERS

"The dead deserve some respect, Louis." Lady Penelope put a hand on my shoulder, as though she knew I'd wanted to attack him. "I'd rather talk of the present, now that we've come to our final rendezvous."

She let me go to pull out her own violet-colored dagger in one hand and a pistol in the other.

"I regret to inform you that this is not our last reunion," Louis said calmly. "I merely stopped by because I was invited."

He looked to me again and winked. Shame sliced through me.

"There is nothing to stop me from killing you, even if it's not in your plans." Lady Penelope cocked her gun at him, and I pulled out my dagger, too.

"Oh, I wouldn't say that. I do have my contingencies." His green eyes glimmered spitefully in the growing firelight. "After all, Maximillian Chotek is eager for his bloodline to reclaim the Bohemian throne. There's no telling how long Prince Karl will last if I am not there to stop the Duke from disposing of him."

"You wouldn't kill Karl," I said, suddenly feeling as naïve as he'd asserted earlier.

Louis laughed. "As it happens, I prefer he remains alive. For now."

"Do you actually believe he will be king of Bohemia one day?" I asked. "The people will not accept him."

"We'll worry about that if we need to," Louis assured me. "Either way, it's best for him if you leave me alive this time, Pepé. Put the gun down."

I didn't know how much he was bluffing, but I looked back to Lady POW with pleading eyes. As upset as I was at Louis, I still needed to return Karl to his mother.

"Please," I whispered softly.

Lady Penelope scowled at me with a ferocity I'd never seen as her finger slipped back from the trigger ever so slightly.

It was the smallest act of surrender she would give.

"You never had any respect for national sovereignty," Lady Penelope said, turning her attention back to Louis. "I can't imagine why you would start now."

"Change is part of life, my dear Penelope," he replied, giving her name a caressing French accent. "And conflict is as inevitable as change. Look around—conflict is already here, *n'est-ce pas?*"

803

THE ORDER OF THE CRYSTAL DAGGERS

"Only because of you."

"I have helped it along a little, yes." He beamed with pride. "But it is a *good* thing. The world is getting smaller, and as it shrinks, it grows weaker. Look at the Hapsburgs; scattered throughout European royalty, yet all of them are weak. They've been made soft by traditions they no longer understand, strangled by the bureaucracy they'd imagined would make life easier. How can they fight for their own slow, inevitable suicide? It's better for the world to tear down the weakened institutions of the past."

He gestured around us, as the fire and smoke muted the air, proud of his handiwork, and happier still to show it off.

"I didn't want to believe you're this intent on sending the continent into war," Lady Penelope said. "You're even more foolish than I'd thought. Perhaps you are getting senile in your old age."

"I'm not senile; you're just shortsighted," Louis replied. "My plan will send the world around us into the fire of war, perhaps—but a new, stronger, better empire can be reborn in its ashes."

I glanced nervously at Lady Penelope; Louis wasn't exactly wrong or delusional, even if he was dangerous—and just like before on the bridge, I couldn't articulate my disagreement with him.

"You might be right, but you are also wrong," Lady Penelope said. "It's true our leaders are weak. But tearing down corruption only works when corruption is complete; we need to repair and build up the good."

"How can it be good when the foundations are imperfect?" Louis shook his head. "You waste time on repairs and rebuilding. A new beginning is much more efficient."

"Patience has its place, and its reward. Anything worth having requires time," Lady Penelope countered. "Recklessness like yours will lead to war, and despite what you believe, war throughout Europe will not reinvigorate the nations. It would only destroy the people and their spirit."

"Have you seen these people in question, Pepé? How many of them are content to be loathsome quislings, proud of their narcissism and ignorance, or boasting of their worldly incompetence and meaningless arrogance? Even Queen Victoria herself vaunts her pitiful failures and her deference to her advisors—men who are beholden to their egos and purse strings more than national pride." Louis sniffed, disgusted at the thought. "Such specimens are better off in the grave. It is no wonder that empires and their foundations are rotting. The Order would not disagree with me, given its own darker histories."

THE ORDER OF THE CRYSTAL DAGGERS

Lady Penelope shook her head. "The Order is called to protect and preserve our rulers—yes, sometimes at the cost of human life. But we seek a better future. We don't burn everything to the ground."

She glanced around at the Cabal as it continued to fill with smoke and flames, giving him a pointed look.

But Louis only shrugged.

"You're still standing here," he replied easily enough as he stood up from his chair. "And you've allowed your family and allies to remain inside here, too. You can't be too worried."

I couldn't speak for Lady POW, but I was certainly nervous. I was just about to suggest we move out of the burning building and let Louis leave when I heard Ferdy call for me.

"Ella!"

His voice made me feel both more alive and more sick than ever. I felt even worse as Louis sneered at me with sinister pleasure.

"Are you going to ignore a cry from your prince, Lady Eleanora?" he asked me. "He's always been good to you, from what I've heard. When he lies to you, it's only because he loves you, and he wants to protect you from the pain of the truth."

"Leave him alone," I snapped, determined not to allow him to intimidate me over Ferdy. My throat was getting sore from the smoke, but I held firm. "He's fine outside with the others."

"Are you certain?"

The confident amusement in his voice sent another wave of nausea through me.

"Eleanora, get away from him." Lady Penelope took a step forward and raised her gun again. I could hear the soft *click* of a new bullet entering its chamber.

"There's no need for that. I don't intend to stay for much longer," Louis said, gesturing toward the smoke rising out of the kitchen. "I have what I came for."

"Oh? And what is that, exactly?" Lady Penelope asked.

Louis was against the far wall, and there was no room for him to make his escape; the pistol in Lady Penelope's hand remained unwavering, and her own dagger still gleamed with malicious intent.

THE ORDER OF THE CRYSTAL DAGGERS

"*Moi,* of course," Lumiere said as he walked inside, with Ferdy just behind him. We all turned to look at them, and I was shocked to see Ferdy shaking with anger.

I didn't understand. "Ferdy, what—"

And then Louis caught me from behind.

His arm suddenly clutched around my neck, choking me with more strength than I'd thought possible for a man his age. I dropped my dagger in surprise, and I heard Lady Penelope and Ferdy both yell in anger before Lumiere fired his gun.

The bullet shot into the ceiling—a warning shot. He did not look happy as I watched him.

Louis scoffed. "I never appreciate your late entrances, Lumiere, but at least they are predictable these days."

"Ella!" Ferdy reached for me, but Lumiere caught him by the neck.

"Now, now, that's not what we agreed, *mon ami,*" Lumiere admonished him, as he put his still-smoking gun to Ferdy's forehead.

"Lumiere, stop," Ferdy snapped, wrestling against him.

"Come now." Lumiere held onto him firmly. "Be a good little prince as I deliver you to my father. Just as I promised I would."

And then I realized Louis had me, while Lumiere had Ferdy. Lady Penelope was caught in the middle, unable to do anything.

Louis knew our weaknesses.

"I'm disappointed, *chérie.*" Lumiere looked back at me with an arrogant sneer. "It was too pitifully easy to let you think I was your captive."

Panic threatened me like never before, and I thrashed with anger and fear. I struggled to breathe as Louis tightened his grip on my neck. Pain laced through my head and spots began to appear before my eyes.

"Ferdy." I gasped out his name, feeling more helpless than ever.

"Is this necessary, Lumiere?" Lady Penelope asked, scowling at him as she put down her pistol.

"What do you think?" Lumiere squealed with delight. "After all these weeks of torment, you are finally getting your comeuppance, Pepé! *Mon père* wanted both princes, and now he'll get them, thanks to my undying loyalty and selflessness."

No.

THE ORDER OF THE CRYSTAL DAGGERS

My heart was weak, and my mind was muddled, but I continued to fight against Louis' hold with renewed anger and desperation. I looked down at my dagger powerlessly, as it lay on the floor in front of me.

"It's been a pleasure, my dear Penelope," Louis purred. "But don't fear. We will meet again. I always enjoy watching you fail."

"Why not just kill me now and be done with it, then?" Lady Penelope arched her brow, practically daring him to do it.

"I might be a monster, but I'm a very organized one," he said. "And your part in my play is not over yet. But don't worry. It's worth the delay. Patience has its own reward."

He pressed harder around my throat, unleashing pain down my spine. I yelped with pain as Ferdy struggled against Lumiere again.

"Please, stop," Ferdy pleaded. "You can have me. Just let Ella go."

"You're already my prisoner," Louis told him. "I knew I would be able to get you if I had her. By all accounts, you've been quite smitten with your princess for years now."

"Hard to blame him," Lumiere said. "Eleanora is very much her mother's daughter."

"It would be a shame for you to see her die, young prince." Louis tightened his grip on me again; the bones in my neck crackled in warning. "What do you say, Penelope? Let us go, and you'll have your Eleanora back, and before I break her neck. I might be old, but I've still got a few tricks left."

Before I could hear Lady Penelope's response, my body went limp; I fell forward as the world spun, before dissolving into an ocean of gray spots and swirling colors.

Louis' grip on me lessened as I rested inside the whirlwind, as everything spun out of control and into chaos.

But I heard the click of a trigger, and blood rushed back into my head. As everything began to return to normal, I saw Lady Penelope was pulling me up from the floor.

"What happened?" I coughed as my throat stung with smoke and pain.

"Oh, Eleanora," Lady Penelope murmured. "I told you marrying him wasn't a good idea."

THE ORDER OF THE CRYSTAL DAGGERS

I didn't know if she was insulting me intentionally or not, but I pushed back against her. I rubbed my neck, massaging it, as I slowly looked toward the door.

"Ferdy." My voice croaked as I said his name.

"We have to let him go for now." Lady Penelope grabbed my arm as my balance faltered. "I promise you, Eleanora, I hate to see Louis win as much as you do."

Through the smoky windows, I watched Louis step in front of two carriages. Lumiere and Ferdy climbed into the one in front, while Louis headed for the other one.

"Wait!" Tears stung my eyes as I ran outside.

I was still weak and disoriented from nearly being strangled, and I couldn't let him win.

I could not let him hurt my family.

Not again.

"Ferdy!" I raced to reach him, nearly slipping, still too dizzy and out of breath to run properly. I ended up clinging to Ben, who was suddenly at my side, helping me stay on my feet.

"What's wrong, Ella?" Ben asked, but I ignored him as Louis nodded his head to me.

"It was lovely meeting you, but I've got to get back to Karl now, before he's killed," Louis said as he climbed up into the carriage. "You remind me so much of your mother, Lady Eleanora."

"Why, you bastard!" I balled my fists as Lady Penelope held me back. "I'll kill you!"

"Still, you have my thanks." Louis only laughed. "And in more ways than one. You know, Naděžda was sent to kill King Ferdinand V during the Revolution. It's fitting that you would be the one who delivered his last heir to me."

"Excuse me?" I stopped fighting against Lady Penelope as shock overwhelmed even my hate and grief. "What?"

"Your mother was sent by the Order to kill the king," Louis repeated. "Isn't fate just so amusing—and just so cruel? Call me a perfectionist, but I do love to see a job finished, even if it has been grossly delayed and mismanaged."

My mind scrambled to make sense of his words.

THE ORDER OF THE CRYSTAL DAGGERS

But all I could think of was Ferdy telling me the Order was full of assassins; Karl asserting the Order wanted his father dead; and I even recalled the look Clavan had given me after seeing my weapon, just moments ago.

And as I looked up at Lady Penelope for her denial, another memory stirred again—Lady Penelope telling me about my mother's last mission in Prague.

"Your father was part of her last assignment," Lady Penelope said. *"She was supposed to come down here with some others and take care of King Ferdinand V during the Revolution of 1848."*

"Take care of … " I said the words aloud—the same group of words I'd heard *Táta* use as he joked with my mother about Jakub murdering Lumiere.

"Oh, Eleanora." Lady Penelope sighed.

That was the moment I knew that Louis was right.

There was no denial coming.

I closed my eyes, stunned and betrayed—stupefied and unable to live with the truth.

"Ella." Ferdy called out to me as the carriages rolled away, but I only shook my head. I couldn't face him.

Not when he'd been right about the Order—and not when my own mother had been called to assassinate his father.

"Ella, I'll be fine," Ferdy shouted back. "I still love you."

"Our time together was very enjoyable, *chérie*." Lumiere waved back at me as their carriage sped off, closely followed by the one Louis was riding in. "We will see you again, when the time is right."

"Stop them," I begged Lady Penelope, but it was too late.

The carriages took off, and sped away.

I watched them move bluntly through the crowded streets. Their drivers had no concern for human life, and all I could think about was how Lumiere betrayed us.

Lumiere betrayed me.

I clenched my fists. He'd insisted he wanted to be like Christ, but he was more like Judas.

Lumiere's carriage turned down one street, and Louis' carriage went onto another street. I kept looking for Ferdy, hoping against hope he would escape.

Please, God. Let him break free. Let him come back to me …

Once more I felt my prayers went unanswered.

"Ella?"

I looked to the side, looking at my brother with blinking, disbelieving eyes. There was blood all down Ben's front.

"Ben! What happened? Are you all right?" I gasped, suddenly afraid again.

He nodded and quickly explained how he'd helped Clavan and some of the others. Marguerite was still tending to some minor injuries.

I was glad he was all right, but I barely heard him. I wiped my tears off and reached down my side for my mother's dagger—only to remember I'd dropped it inside after Louis had grabbed me.

"Good. You've stopped your blubbering," Lady Penelope said. "It's quite embarrassing."

"You!" I scrambled to face her, angry and vengeful, and more upset than ever. I couldn't believe I'd listened to her, after she'd lied so many times. "You are no monster, Madame—you are the very devil incarnate. How could you do this to me? How could you lie to me about *Máma* and let Louis take Ferdy hostage?"

Lady Penelope held firm. "Your mother's mission is in the past. Clearly, she didn't go through with it, so I don't see why you're upset about it—"

I leapt at her, eager to inflict her with all the damage and pain I felt. I screamed, but Ben grabbed me before I could do anything too damaging.

"Eleanora, calm yourself," Lady Penelope ordered as she sidestepped my clumsy rage. "This is just what Louis wants—he wants you to hate me. You're just going to let him win again if you can't control yourself."

My head pounded with renewed pain. Ben put his hand on my shoulder, trying to reassure me, but all I could do was just stand there and stare at Lady Penelope.

How could she really think I was upset that Louis had won this round? How could she truly believe I cared about his supposed victory more than Ferdy's life?

"Well, Louis got what he wanted," I finally shouted. "Now it's time for me to get what I want. I want Ferdy back!"

"You heard Louis." Lady Penelope grimaced. "He'll meet with us again."

"When?" I hollered. "Where? There were two carriages and they went in different directions. Where did Lumiere and Ferdy go?"

"Louis is likely heading back to *Vyšehrad*, where Karl is being held. I'm not sure where Lumiere took Ferdinand, but we'll find them soon enough," Lady Penelope insisted. "Louis said I still have a role to fulfill in his little play, remember?"

"But why did he want Ferdy?" Ben asked, distracting me momentarily. "He's already got Karl."

"I'm not certain." For once, Lady POW seemed willing to admit the truth. "But we should get to work. If he thinks I'll just wait around by the fire at home for him to come knocking on my door, he's dead wrong."

"If only he were dead," I muttered darkly, before pulling free of Ben and heading back into the Cabal.

"Where are you going, Eleanora?" Lady Penelope asked me brusquely. "The building's going to come down."

"I need my mother's dagger," I snapped back.

"Oh, yes. Go and get it." She nodded approvingly, and I scowled back at her.

I didn't need her patronizing looks right now. I turned back toward the door and took one last breath of fresh air before stepping inside.

"We need to go back to the manor and prepare to go to *Vyšehrad*," I heard Lady Penelope say. "If we're going to win against Louis, we can't leave it to chance. Where is Amir?"

I froze.

And then, as if to answer her question, a loud cry came out from behind the bar.

My breath left me in a sharp exhale. "Oh, no!"

THE ORDER OF THE CRYSTAL DAGGERS

22

◊

Stinging heat cloaked me as I raced inside the Cabal. In the few moments since I'd been outside, the smoke had grown into dark, deadly clouds, and fire framed the building.

But that didn't matter to me. Not now.

Ashes danced in the air, and fire simmered all around, but I swiped my dagger off the floor, thankful Louis and Lumiere had ignored it earlier, and hurried to the back room where I'd left Amir.

Only to stop when I saw he was still alive.

"Thank you, Lord," I whispered.

Amir was standing in the middle of the room, while Xiana was supporting herself against the burnt, blackened wall. Neither of them appeared to have noticed me, or the fire that was creeping up from all around them.

"Attack me properly," she yelled at Amir, clearly upset. "You cannot avoid me forever."

"I do not wish to fight with you," Amir insisted.

"You will fight me!" Xiana launched into another attack.

Amir parried with her thrusts expertly, managing to throw off her footwork in the process.

Her eyes were wild with their sun-colored fire, with hate and sorrow burning up from inside her very soul as she stumbled back.

"Xiana, please stop." Amir took hold of her hand and stopped her.

"No," she yelled back.

"You have always been driven to succeed," Amir told her quietly. "But this is not a victory you truly want."

"Eleanora." Lady Penelope appeared behind me. "What are you ... "

Her voice faded as she saw the scene before me; she uncharacteristically faltered at the sight of Xiana dressed in her full form as an agent of the enemy.

Even in the fire, I saw her eyes glisten, and then she set her jaw and moved between them.

I didn't see that her gun was back in her hand until the very last second. Lady Penelope took aim and fired.

My eyes squeezed shut in horror, but I opened them a second later, curious and terrified of what had happened.

Xiana and Amir were both still; neither of them had been shot, and even with all the ash in the air, I breathed a deep sigh of relief.

"That's enough," Lady Penelope said. "Amir. We have work to do. And Xiana, you're dismissed from my presence—for good, this time."

"Madame." Xiana looked at her, stricken. "You would dismiss me after all the training I took on? After all the work, after all I have learned?"

Lady Penelope only paused for a small second, before she nodded. "Harshad and I have given you what we could, but after what we know you've done, you should be grateful I'm not here to kill you."

"All I have ever wanted was your love and to be part of your family!"

"You were part of my family, until you decided your own happiness was more important." Lady Penelope shook her head scornfully. "I would kill you myself, and quite cheerfully, too, if it weren't for Harshad. For the sake of his love for you, I'll spare you, just this once."

At once, Xiana's shoulders dropped, and she lowered the sword in her hand.

"Now, depart from me; I see now that you never really knew me." Lady Penelope waved her away.

Amir bowed his head to Xiana, and then he spoke to her.

"I forgive you." There was pain and agony laced in every word.

I looked down at the floor, hoping Amir truly had peace at last.

Together, Lady Penelope and Amir walked toward the exit where I was waiting. Amir gave me a small, tired smile, but I knew he was miserable.

A board from the ceiling broke and crashed down around us. Xiana remained standing in the fire, unaffected by the destruction and fire around her.

She wanted to stay and burn, and I was content to let her.

But I reached for Amir, wanting to comfort him. He'd saved me, again, and after Ferdy's capture, I was so glad Amir was still with me.

But then I blinked, and Xiana moved with deadly precision—aiming her sword not at me, not at Amir, but at Lady Penelope.

THE ORDER OF THE CRYSTAL DAGGERS

I cried out in warning, but it was already too late.

Time slowed and stretched, filling me with even more horror and agony, as Amir pushed Lady Penelope into me and stepped in front of her to shield her from Xiana's attack.

I couldn't hear anything else as I screamed. I saw Xiana's eyes widen with anger and shock and horror, and Lady Penelope gasped; I could even hear her berate Amir for saving her as he fell to his knees, Xiana's *jian* still lodged deep into his stomach.

"Amir!" I screamed. "No!"

Xiana jerked her sword free from Amir, and he writhed and groaned with renewed pain.

"He's going to die," she told me bitterly. "I put the Order's poison on my sword. There is no antidote left. I made sure of that."

Her eyes looked up from his fallen form to Lady Penelope. Xiana glanced at the gun still in Lady Penelope's hand, and I realized what Xiana wanted.

She wanted Lady Penelope to shoot her.

She wanted to die.

But instead, Lady Penelope only knelt down on the other side of Amir's body and took him in her arms, letting him fall against her knees, much like I'd held Tulia in her last moments.

She ignored Xiana entirely.

I wanted to yell at Lady Penelope, to tell her to shoot Xiana. I grabbed my dagger, ready to give Xiana the death she so desperately wanted.

But at my approach, Xiana finally turned and left. She leapt through the labyrinth of fire and broken boards, and then disappeared. I saw one last glint of light on her sword's poisoned blade as she disappeared into the darkness.

I had no words to say; I was beyond rage, shaking my fists at heaven for Amir's fate, cursing Lady Penelope's foolish weakness, and crumbling under the weight of another failure.

I fell to my knees, sobbing with rage as I took Amir's hand.

Amir squeezed my hand in return. Already I could feel his weakness. Warm blood splashed between our palms, and I couldn't find my voice; my throat seemed clogged, and my tongue felt too thick and dry to say anything.

THE ORDER OF THE CRYSTAL DAGGERS

"Ella, what happened?" Ben's voice seemed to call to me from miles away, and I barely looked as he appeared beside me.

"Oh, Ben." My lips quivered, and I couldn't say anything.

Lady Penelope pulled Amir's head up onto her lap. "My son."

Her voice broke, and she finally began to cry.

Amir used his other hand—the one marked with the *noon*—to embrace her. He whispered something I couldn't hear in her ears, and she only shook her head and buried her face into his shoulder.

"Ben." Amir's voice was stalling, but it was still sure. He groaned as he reached for his *Wahabite Jambiya*. He was breathing heavily, with sweat streaming down his brow, as he handed it to my brother. "Here. I need you to be strong and brave now, for my sake, and for theirs, too."

Ben took the dagger with shaking hands, and the two men exchanged a look—one I hadn't seen on my brother's face since *Máma* was alive, and *Táta* was still pure in Ben's eyes.

Amir was giving Ben more than a weapon; he was giving him a legacy, one a father would give to a son out of reverence and love.

"I will." Ben's voice was shaking, but it was still strong.

Amir's breathing went ragged as he looked up at me.

"I'm sorry," I finally blubbered out. "I'm so sorry."

Why was saying "I'm sorry" so insufficient, and yet it was the only thing I could hope to say?

I loved Amir, and I hated how my life had served to only make his more miserable, whether it was the constant reminder of my mother, or my own insolence at learning the waltz, or cutting into his soul with my carelessness a thousand times over.

"Oh, Eleanora," Amir gasped through strangling breaths. "Naděžda imagined herself too cowardly to live, but I am not afraid to die."

"I'm afraid of losing you," I whispered back.

"You won't," he promised. "We will all be together again one day. And you'll get to meet Nassara."

I tried to smile, but I couldn't. Even dying, Amir was the one comforting me. A fresh set of tears streamed down my cheeks.

The fire was still growing around us, and I could barely breathe, but I refused to leave Amir's side.

815

He turned to look up at me and smiled brightly, one last time. He no longer looked so tired, even if his body seemed much weaker. And then his head dropped back, and his hand fell out of mine.

"Naděžda."

He spoke my mother's name like a song, and then, as the sound died on the air between us, so did he.

For a long moment, with the fire eagerly blazing around us and the building slowly collapsing around us, we said nothing.

It seemed like a long time later when Lady Penelope eased Amir back down to the floor and wiped her eyes. "We have to leave," she said.

I barely felt anything at all as Ben hauled me to my feet and Lady Penelope led us out of the kitchen.

I looked back at Amir, just in time to see his body catch fire.

As we made it outside again, the taste of ash and soot clung to my dried lips. It served as a bitter reminder that I was alive and alone—and that I'd failed all over again, and more spectacularly than ever.

23

◊

Time passed in a slow, grueling fashion, dragging and pushing me against every bit of anguish inside of me as the Cabal finished burning down.

I couldn't do anything but stand and watch as it burned. It felt as though my own world was burning down, too—and not only had I failed to save it, but I'd hastened its demise.

I forced myself to watch the flames as they rose higher, and I did not look away until the fire gradually recoiled into itself, like a snake curling up to die.

The flame-tipped ashes wafted away in the wind, taking Amir with them.

After fearing dynamite and nitroglycerin, it was hard to admit I'd forgotten how a simple fire could cause such damage all on its own—and how swiftly, too.

It was only hours ago my life had been so very different. Lumiere was almost a friend, Amir was alive, and Ferdy had been at my side.

But now, Louis had earned another victory.

Ferdy was captured, Amir was gone, and Lumiere had betrayed us; and in addition to that, I was left without trust in Lady Penelope's leadership, Karl was still kidnapped, and I had no more admiration for my mother's role in the Order.

There was no certainty of truth, and I was numb from pain too great for me to bear.

I was angry beyond rage and tired beyond belief. I could only cry.

Lady Penelope was much more productive than me. She had sent a runner to retrieve Harshad, while Marguerite helped take care of our collective injuries. Ben stood beside me, until I made him help Marguerite instead.

I wanted to be alone.

I *was* alone.

I was so alone that I didn't see Faye as she came up beside me. It was only when she took hold of my hand I noticed her. Together, we stood there; she was mourning her losses, with the death of her dreams and the destruction of her home, while I was just lost.

"I'm sorry." I whispered the words after what seemed to be a lifetime. I couldn't find the courage to admit I'd been the one to lead Louis to the Cabal. "I'm sorry about your wedding."

"Ella." Faye put her arm around my shoulders. "Look."

She nodded toward the alleyway, where Jarl was currently helping some of the others squelch out some of the smaller piles of flames. He'd come after hearing the news and quickly started running around, issuing orders to volunteers and even assisting Lady POW.

"We might be down for a bit. But life will go on, and we will rebuild," she explained. "So this is not the end. Even if it feels like it."

She gave me a brave smile, even if her eyes were still full of tears. "Not everything is always as it appears."

I nodded in easy, tepid agreement. My throat was scratchy and sore from inhaling all that smoke, and I didn't want to say anything else.

I was glad when Jarl called over to her and Faye left me by myself. She gave me one last hug before she headed off, promising me that she would let me know what would happen with her wedding.

Faye couldn't comfort me, and Ben couldn't comfort me, either. From time to time, he stopped working with Marguerite to check on me. But I just shook my head at him, and he went back to work.

After a while, he seemed to understand that I didn't want to be consoled.

I wanted blood.

I wanted to give into my anger and hate and rage.

I wanted to kill Xiana, I wanted to kill Louis, and I wanted to kill Lumiere, and maybe even Karl, too.

It was so antithetical to who I believed myself to be, it was all I could do to just stand there and suffer, to try to hold onto the good and not to let evil consume me.

I had already lost Amir; I did not want to lose myself, too.

It was only when Clavan came up to me that my inner warfare called a momentary cease-fire.

THE ORDER OF THE CRYSTAL DAGGERS

"Ella." He gave me a respectful nod, wincing briefly at his wounds. "Thank you for your help today."

"How is your wife doing?"

I was happy to play along and be polite, even if I couldn't feel the depth and breadth of my emotions. It was too draining, and too tempting to give in against my baser instincts for blood.

"She's well enough," Clavan told me. "We were in the kitchen when that intruder came in and lit the fire. As bad as things look, it's fortunate that it wasn't worse."

I swallowed the lump in my throat and only nodded. Clavan likely knew someone had died, but I doubted he truly knew how much of a loss Amir was to the world, and to me.

"Here. I wanted to give this back to you." Clavan reached into his back pocket and pulled out Lumiere's watch.

Gently, I took hold of it. Some part of me wanted to smash it into the ground and spit on it, but the delicate outline of the *fleur-de-lis* reminded me too much of my father's watch.

I couldn't punish Lumiere without blemishing my father's memory.

"My friend wasn't able to fix it," Clavan said as I opened the watch and saw it was still set to midnight. "Apparently, it broke some number of years ago, and there's quite a bit of rust. He offered to replace the parts, but I said I would talk with you first. It's a rare item, and one that seems to be more sentimental than functional in its use."

"Thank you." Mindlessly, I ran my ashen palms over the golden design, before I saw Clavan looking at the dagger at my side. I put the watch away and held my weapon out to him. "Did you want to look at this, too?"

Wariness briefly lit up into his eyes again, but he took it a moment later. He lifted his small eyeglasses up and studied it carefully; he tested its weight and its balance and swung it through the air with a few moves.

"It's been well-preserved," he said. "The alloy is unique to the Middle East, but its rarity only contributes to half its value. Hardly anything made today would be able to compare with its craftsmanship."

"Thank you." I gazed at the Cabal, my eyes already tearing up again. "For all the good it did me today."

"You helped save Helen," he reminded me softly.

"I know. But it wasn't enough to save everyone," I whispered, putting my hands over my eyes.

Nothing I had done was enough to save Amir, and nothing I'd done was enough to stop Louis.

"You can't save everyone, you know," Clavan replied. "And not everyone wants to be saved, either. But the important thing is that you do what you can, and hope some are saved in the end."

I shook my head. I wanted to explain that everything I did only seemed to make things worse. Xiana escaped, Louis walked out, while Lumiere had Ferdy at his mercy.

Why was it that only the worst sort of people were the ones who survived?

"Here." Clavan gently pried one hand away from my face and gently pressed my dagger's hilt into my palm. I looked down at it through tear-soaked eyes.

"Fighting, and then losing, is not the same thing as surrender, Ella," he told me. "You've fought the good fight, and you've seen failure. But you've never seen a self-defeat, and I pray you will not start now."

My mother's dagger was usually a source of comfort as well as courage, but I felt nothing as I stood there and held it—nothing but disgust and disbelief, and even betrayal.

"I don't know," I mumbled, feeling as weak as Louis believed the nations to be.

It was possible he was right; if I was this pathetic, how could an entire nation of people be strong enough to stop him and others like him?

"Yes, you do," Clavan said. "And since you are a member of the Order, you know what's at stake, especially with the Emperor on his way here."

My mind was muddled with grief and anger, and it took me a moment to respond. "What?"

"The Emperor is coming to Prague. His ship is due to arrive later today at the fort at *Vyšehrad*. He's called for the Tripartite Council to commence this week at Prague Castle."

"But it's not supposed to happen until March, or even until later this year," I said, recalling what Lady Penelope had said, only days ago.

"Something's happened that made him move it up." Clavan glanced around. "At first, I thought it was the war between France and Germany.

THE ORDER OF THE CRYSTAL DAGGERS

But now I suspect it's something more personal—perhaps an issue with succession?"

He looked at me intently, and at first, I couldn't imagine what it was that he was trying to tell me. But when I realized he meant Ferdy, or Karl, or maybe even both now that Louis had them, I coughed in surprise.

"Um, I don't know." I stuttered out the words, unwilling to ask him directly if he knew the truth about Ferdy; I preferred to leave that as a mystery, and I had a feeling he did, too.

"It might be best to find out," Clavan replied gently. "The Order is known for its courage and determination—*In Hoc Signo Vinces.*"

"With this sign, you shall win." I repeated the words that formed the motto of the Order, feeling further away from anything even resembling victory than ever.

"You should know it's not the sword, or even the wielder, that leads to victory, but the faith behind it." Clavan gave me another smile. "It takes courage to believe in truth, and even more to live a life dedicated to it."

I tightened my grip on my mother's dagger. As much as I felt conflicted over her past and her choices, there was nothing conflicted about how much I wanted Ferdy back, and how I wanted him safe from the likes of Louis Valoris.

"Ella."

Ben called out to me, and when I looked over at him, he pointed down the street.

As I watched, Harshad and Didier climbed out of Lady Penelope's carriage.

I didn't see what difference it would make at this point if they were here or not, but when Ben waved for me to come over, I nodded and excused myself to Clavan.

"Thank you, for everything—again," I whispered. "I must go now."

Clavan graciously bowed his head to me, and as we parted ways, I couldn't help but envy him; he was going off to his family, and they would survive this difficult time together. He seemed to be the kind of person who had things figured out, and even if he didn't, he had enough peace about the possibilities that would allow him to recover from life's brutalities.

THE ORDER OF THE CRYSTAL DAGGERS

My steps slowed as I saw Lady Penelope speak with Harshad. While I couldn't hear the words they spoke, I knew she was telling him about Amir's death and Xiana's treachery.

As I watched, Harshad drew her into a slight embrace. For a long moment, he held her there, and she seemed to weaken only slightly against him. In contrast, he stood there, still and strong, unmoved by the worst of circumstances.

I wondered how he could be so blasé about everything, but then I remembered how he'd excused himself after seeing the poison.

He probably knew what Xiana had done.

I approached them and I heard him speak to Lady Penelope.

"I am sorry I was not here," he said to her. "But thank you. You did all you could."

My mouth dropped open in shock. "Excuse me?"

Both of them looked at me, and at that moment, all the fury I'd been trying to control raged inside of me with renewed vigor; all the words I couldn't speak earlier came rushing out all at once.

"What do you mean, she did all she could?" I pointed at Lady Penelope, adamant I would not say her name or give any indication I considered her even the slightest bit human. "She didn't kill Louis when she had the chance, and she let Lumiere take Ferdy away. She did *nothing.*"

"Need I remind you that I saved your life and Ferdinand's by allowing Louis to leave?" Lady Penelope's jaw clenched. "I understand your grief, Eleanora. But don't be ridiculous."

"I'm ridiculous?" I could barely believe her. "You could've killed Xiana, before *and* after she stabbed Amir. I saw her; she *wanted* you to kill her. She was daring you to do it, and you ignored her, just like a coward."

"Eleanora." Lady Penelope sighed. "There are times when life is much more of a punishment than death—and there are times when some things are more important than justice. Don't forget your mother did the same."

"What are you talking about?"

Lady Penelope crossed her arms over her chest. "She didn't kill Ferdinand's father, after all."

I was disoriented at her mention of King Ferdinand, but I would not let her win this argument. Lady POW was wrong, and not even my mother's past would stop my tirade.

"How dare you mention her at all," I hissed. "Especially after you lied to me about her mission."

"I didn't lie—"

"You misled me, and Ben, too." My voice was getting louder and stronger as my anger boiled over.

"Stop yelling," Lady Penelope hissed. "Look, Eleanor wasn't under direct orders to kill him. But it was the first option on a very short list; honestly, if you know history at all, you know it was a miracle the issue was resolved without his permanent disposal. It would have been easier to poison him, allow others to believe it was a natural death, and then discuss the line of succession with more optimism."

"That doesn't matter," I yelled. "You still didn't tell me the truth."

"The truth is complicated, Eleanora," Lady Penelope retorted.

"Yes, and now Amir is dead, and Ferdy's gone," I shouted back. I whipped out my dagger and took a menacing step forward. "All of this is your fault, Madame, and I will never, ever forgive you for this! Not that you would ever ask for it yourself."

"Eleanora." Harshad stepped between me and Lady Penelope. "Please … I am sorry I was not here for you."

Harshad was old, and tired, and just barely taller than I was, but he still remained an imposing figure; I didn't know if he was protecting me from Lady POW, or the other way around—but I lost all my bluster as he stood there before me.

He took my shoulders and hugged me close, but I couldn't embrace him back.

His affection was nothing like Amir's had been. Standing there, I felt empty and absent of true warmth. But Harshad was still trying, and because Lady Penelope was still watching me, I stopped myself from crying again.

He let go, and I stepped back, sheathed my dagger, and turned away from both of them.

"I'm sorry," he said again.

I crossed my arms as a new lump formed in my throat. "It's not your fault. You didn't know what … what Xiana would do."

"Nevertheless, I taught you about weaknesses, and it's my own that has brought us to this point." Harshad sighed. "It is always much easier to teach the lesson than it is to learn it, and I have failed to live up to my own standards in this regard."

"No." I narrowed my eyes, murderously glaring at Lady Penelope. "It wasn't your weakness that led to this. It was *hers*. She let Xiana leave."

"Xiana will face her fate at the appointed time," Harshad said solemnly. "But she was as much a daughter to me as your mother was, and I am as grateful as I am conflicted that she did not die."

Especially by Lady Penelope's hand.

The words were unspoken, but I knew what he meant.

I shook my head. "I don't care. I can't forgive her. And I *won't*."

"It may be easier to forgive Xiana after she receives justice for her sins," Harshad replied neutrally. "In the meantime, we cannot do anything for Amir any longer. We can rescue your beloved Ferdinand, and his brother, too. Once we have them back, we will see to Louis and his plans for Prague."

"Fine." My eyes fell to the ground.

Harshad was right, even if I was still in pain.

Xiana wasn't the only one who had to face justice, I thought, thinking of the old man who'd seemed so harmless before.

I should tell them about the Emperor.

I whirled around, ready to tell them what Clavan told me. But Harshad was already talking to Ben, hesitating just the slightest as the sight of Amir's dagger in my brother's hand.

A slight shadow came up from behind me.

If I wasn't so despondent, I might've jumped at the sudden sight of Didier.

"What are you doing here?" I asked, unable to hide the bitterness in my voice. "Why aren't you still locked up in Lumiere's bedroom, worried about earning Lady POW's trust?"

"I've never been fond of an exercise in futility," he replied, almost making me smile. "When she called for Harshad to come here, I had a feeling it was time."

"Time for what?"

"Lumiere told me that if trouble should come, I was to give these to Ben and Ferdy." He pulled out a pair of dueling pistols, just like the ones they'd been working with the day I'd stumbled outside, worried the manor was being attacked.

"Lumiere's a traitor." I practically spat out the words as I thought of how pathetic I'd thought him to be only this morning. "He took Ferdy as his prisoner."

"Lumiere is indeed a traitor," Didier agreed. "But not to you. He's on your side."

"Ha." I sniffed, my nose drippling with snot from all my earlier tears. "He's on his own side."

"Well … that is a better way of saying it," Didier agreed. "But right now, your goals are aligned. He might have Ferdy, but I know he will keep him safe from Louis."

Hope briefly stirred inside of me. I didn't know if I could trust it to be true, but if I was going to save Ferdy, I had to believe it was possible— until it wasn't.

"Where are they going?" I asked. "There were two carriages. Lady POW says Louis went to *Vyšehrad*, where Karl is being kept. But where did Lumiere go? Surely you have some idea?"

"I've known Lumi for many years, but the man is still an enigma." Didier smiled. "However, he did tell me that he trusts you to find the right place and time for the knowledge you seek."

"He also said it was too easy to fool me." I crossed my arms over my chest glumly, thinking of how miserable Lumiere had been earlier, when he told me there was no proper place and time for some conversations.

But then I stopped.

I pulled out the pocket watch Clavan had given back to me, and I thought back to its connections with the Bohemian Loyalists.

Lumiere's watch … and Louis' patch on his sleeve.

"The University." I heard myself say the words more than I said them, but it was the only sensible answer.

Louis was staying at a dormitory, posing as an art student. In the University's *Karolinum*, there was a display for the Bohemian Loyalists—and there was more than that, I thought, recalling what Amir had said about the secrets of the city.

The tunnels.

THE ORDER OF THE CRYSTAL DAGGERS

There were secret tunnels under the city from *Vyšehrad*. There was no telling where they all went, but there had to be one that led to the University.

"Harshad?" I stepped up beside him. "I have to talk with you."

"What is it now?" Lady Penelope asked, her blatant bitterness clear despite her curiosity.

I frowned at her. "I want to talk to Harshad, not you. I have a plan."

Quickly, I explained what I'd found out, and all the clues I'd put together.

As I finished, Lady Penelope sighed.

"Oh, Eleanora," she groaned. "Louis is right about you. You're naïve and too idealistic by far."

"I know," I snapped, my voice harder this time. With renewed determination, I gripped my mother's dagger in my hand. "But don't worry, Madame. After this mission is over, you will never have to deal with my naivety and idealism ever again."

"We'll see," she muttered.

"No." I straightened my shoulders. "*You'll* see."

THE ORDER OF THE CRYSTAL DAGGERS

24

◊

Much like I'd felt earlier, standing before the Church of Our Lady of the Snows, I felt very small and uncertain as I looked up at the large, rounded entrance of the University's *Karolinum*.

I could only hope I would have better luck finding Ferdy than I'd had trying to find Karl—and Lumiere, and Louis, too.

"Are you sure he's here?" Ben asked, as if he knew I was suddenly doubting myself.

"Shhh … " I put my finger to my lips.

Ben's question was reasonable enough, but I didn't particularly want to answer him.

Lumiere was not a creature I considered beholden to reason. His little quips and barbs over the past weeks could've been clues—or merely the half-drunken ramblings of a madman still lucid enough to believe himself sane.

I was gambling on the former, but the odds were the same for the latter.

I bit back a smile, and then forced myself not to tear up again. Ferdy would approve, and not just because he was the one we were trying to save.

"It's been about two hours since we left the Cabal," Ben said. "Harshad and Lady POW should be near *Vyšehrad* by now."

"If you wanted to go with them, you should've said something," I whispered back.

"I'm only letting you know. Clavan said Emperor Franz Joseph is expected to arrive before the end of the day, if he's not there already. If you want your plan to work, we need to hurry."

"I know."

"And anyway, I'm not leaving you. We're family."

"Then it'll either be easier or harder to forgive me if I'm wrong about this."

"I've forgiven you for much worse," Ben said, provoking me as well as comforting me.

A little reluctantly, I smiled. Ben's loyalty was touching, even in light of his impatience. "Well, thank you, *brácha*."

"Ben." Marguerite appeared at his side and tugged on his sleeve. "Be nice to your sister."

"I wasn't trying to be mean," Ben objected.

"We're fine." I didn't mind that Marguerite had joined our group to come to the University, but I didn't need her to defend me; Ben and I had grown up knowing hurting each other and helping each other were not mutually exclusive.

Still, it was difficult to soften my sarcasm. "Perhaps I'm more worried about forgiving myself."

"You told Lady Penelope that you knew what you were about." Didier shuffled next to me, his large form cloaking me in an extra shadow; his dark eyes twinkled down at me. "I'd hate to think you would doubt yourself now."

"That's part of my naïve charm." I glanced up at the sky, realizing there was more than one reason to hurry. It was getting darker, and it looked like it might rain. The clouds were gray and feathery, as uncertain of themselves as I was of myself and Lumiere. "Come on."

The old door to the University was off to the side of one of the city's markets, and the busy streets were enough to give us sufficient cover as we crossed into the building's threshold.

Stepping inside, I tripped on my skirts. I grimaced as I stopped myself from falling. I regretted not wearing my stealth habit. The bright morning I'd had with Ferdy seemed like a lifetime ago as my day increasingly devolved into madness, fear, and death.

As one of the university's oldest sections, the *Karolinum* often housed both the German and Bohemian Diets, along with the *Reichsrat*, and it was still a place of reception for foreign leaders, ambassadors, and diplomats. It had been born of a coming together of nations, with Czechs, the Bavarians, the Polish, the Slavs, the Saxons, and more. As we made our way through the outer rooms, I saw the long history of Bohemia and its people was housed there. Some of the architecture was rough and pagan, while others were Christianized, but all of it showed Bohemia's complicated history, both in its conquests, and even its current struggles to maintain the unity in the diversity of its ethnic roots.

The University was a place of both chaos and order, ideas and histories, and histories revisited in light of new ideas; it was a place of judgment and record, a place of destiny, death, and rebirth.

Yes, I thought, Louis would appreciate such a place—and Karl would, too.

We entered into the vestibule of the Great Hall, where the walls were lined with paintings enshrined in elaborate and elegant frames; their painted eyes all looked down at me and offered up their varied, silent judgments.

"We don't have time to linger," Ben reminded me.

"The dormitories are upstairs." Marguerite gestured toward a staircase down the hall. "Maybe we should look there."

"That's likely where Louis has been staying," I said. "But I don't think Lumiere will be there."

"Where do you think he is, then?" Ben asked.

"The Great Hall." I nodded toward the doors in front of us and then looked back at Didier. "I can't imagine Lumiere would settle for anything less than greatness. Would you?"

Didier gave me a smile. "It depends on what you mean by greatness."

"So much depends on so much," I murmured, pushing the doors open.

Inside, flags adorned the walls along with paintings and elegant architectural décor, and the room was capped with a dome ceiling. There were two lines of chairs circled around a podium, and in the middle was a chair, where the leader of the room would sit.

I was surprised to see it was empty; I'd been expecting Lumiere to have claimed it for his own.

My shoulders slumped. I'd been wrong.

"Ella!"

My heart leapt as Ferdy called for me. I whirled around to see him sitting down on a chair, just tucked into a far alcove, near the entrance to the small chapel of St. Margaret.

"Oh, thank you, Lord," I whispered, hurrying over.

Only to stop abruptly in my tracks, as Xiana stepped directly in front of me.

"Be careful," Ferdy warned, his voice full of glum fear.

829

THE ORDER OF THE CRYSTAL DAGGERS

Xiana was still in her ash-covered cloak, the white and gray specks clinging to the cloth, covered in little splashes of Amir's blood. Her eyes were still full of fire and vengeance, but I could see the regret in her gaze.

She was not nearly as calm as she appeared. And—to my great relief—I saw she was not armed. I still had my mother's dagger, and as long as I kept it this time, I could win against her.

"Ella." Ben came up beside me and held up his fists, too. "We can do this together."

I nodded. Ben and I had both lost so much with Amir's death; it was in his right to be there alongside me.

I couldn't say who took the first step, but soon, Ben and I were locked in combat with Xiana.

The sounds of our battle muffled out the rest of the world; Xiana's breathing increased as my own heart thundered, complemented by the *click-clack* of Ben's brace as we fought.

I watched her moves, the feints, the ducks, and rolls, and I saw her weaken briefly as I went to the defensive, and Ben whipped out Amir's dagger.

The *Wahabite Jambiya* surprised both me and Xiana, and Ben used that against her.

A long streak of blood appeared on her chest, and her eyes narrowed even further as she retreated.

"I see Amir managed to slip one more surprise by me." Xiana finally spoke as she glared at Ben with malice. "But it will be his last."

She lunged off to the side, away from us, and I was momentarily puzzled—until I saw she meant to attack Marguerite.

"Marguerite, watch out," I called, but Ben was already moving.

He dipped down low and fell forward, deliberately intercepting Xiana's attack. His movement awkwardly propelled himself into her. The two of them tumbled over. I heard Ben's brace *clank* against the floor. His leg came free, but he still managed to trap her.

I was about to hurry over when suddenly Lumiere's laughter rang out from behind us.

"Ah, Ella, there you are. I was just beginning to wonder if you would show at all, *chérie*."

I froze and whirled around to face him.

THE ORDER OF THE CRYSTAL DAGGERS

Lumiere was sitting at the front of the altar by St. Margaret's chapel, calm and smiling.

I could've sworn the chapel was empty besides Ferdy just a moment ago, but I was breathing too hard to say anything.

"Not now, Lumiere." Xiana kicked herself free from Ben's hold, and he grabbed at his leg where she'd struck him. "This is not a good time."

"*Oui, oui, j'accord*," Lumiere muttered as he came over to stand in front of Xiana. "But we will make it better, *non*? Where are our good manners?"

"I can't imagine what you mean," I muttered, struggling not to curse Lumiere as he gave Marguerite a curtsy and bowed to Ben on the floor.

Xiana and I both scowled at him.

"Ah, *mon ami*, it is good to see you again." Lumiere put his hand on Didier's shoulder. "I trust you will forgive me for my sudden departure?"

"Of course." Didier clasped his arm in return. "You can count on me to forgive you, just as I can count on you to be unpredictable."

Lumiere shrugged. "I'm not as unpredictable as you'd think."

"Lumiere," Xiana's voice growled. "This is—"

"*Pardonnez-moi*, Xiana, but surely you must know how I've always hated your poor manners." Lumiere's bubbly, dulcet tones went low and deadly as he jerked away from Didier and whirled around to face her.

I gasped at the sudden sight of the gun in his hand. Lumiere had pilfered it from Didier's front coat.

It's just like before, on the Salacia. *He's going to—*

I didn't have time to finish my thought as Lumiere squeezed the trigger and shot Xiana straight through the chest.

Blood rained out from her wound, and she was too taken aback to do anything but drop to her knees in shock.

"That was for Amir," Lumiere told her, his tone full of condemnation. "It turns out he had an additional last surprise for you, *Saghira*. But that should have been expected. For what fellowship can light have with darkness?"

Xiana began to choke; she fought death, even as any movement only hastened her inevitable fate.

"Just so you know, my father would shoot you, too, just like a horse with a broken leg."

"I am … not … " Xiana seethed, barely able to move her lips.

"Please. You're just a tool to get work done. My father offered you apples and sugar cubes for your tasks, but now you're really no longer useful to him—or, more importantly, to me." Lumiere gave her a cruel smirk. "Am I not such a good actor? Blackmailing you into helping me was fun, but I must admit, it feels good to shoot you now."

Xiana's lips quivered, and, before she could try to say anything else, Lumiere shot her twice more—once in the stomach, and then straight through the head.

"That's for Nassara and Naděžda." Lumiere's eyes lit up with wicked pleasure as Xiana fell forward. Her body began twitching as he laughed. "Yes, it's *very* good to shoot you—a most impure delight. Now I'm only sorry I didn't do it earlier after our little *tête-à-tête* in the west parlor back at Pepé's house."

"Lumiere!" I was taken aback by his violent delight. "That's enough."

"*Pourquoi?* Should I not have my own surprises?"

"You always do," Didier said. "I'm surprised you used the gun this time."

Lumiere grinned. "Oh, I know. It'll be a dreadful mess to clean all the gunpowder off my sleeves. But I didn't have any poison, and swords are too hard to conceal. And I do rather like how quick and painful it was for her. It really adds to the surprise."

Xiana's body lay on the floor, her blood gathering in scarlet pools.

"Lumiere," I muttered.

There was no cheery smile on his face, no hint of remorse; his green eyes were filled with expectancy and satisfaction.

"You're welcome," Lumiere told me, gesturing toward Xiana's body, and then to Ferdy. "A punished murderer, and a saved prince. And you needn't worry about his condition; I strapped him down myself so she wouldn't suspect I had other plans."

He turned back to Didier. "Thank you for bringing the guns. I'll be sure to get you more in the near future, and some nice bullets to go along with them, too."

"I would like my stock replenished," Didier agreed.

"You still have extra rounds on you, *oui?*"

THE ORDER OF THE CRYSTAL DAGGERS

The two of them were talking so normally, and it was all the more jarring. They chatted amicably as I struggled to find the words I wanted to say—if I could even think of what to say. It was good to see Xiana dead, but I still didn't appreciate Lumiere's style.

"Ella." Ferdy said my name, and the spell was broken; he was still stuck in his chair.

"Oh, yes." Lumiere gestured toward Ferdy. "Please, finish rescuing him now, Ella. I'm done."

"Done?" I gritted my teeth.

"You didn't have to be so loud about it, Lumiere," Ben said from behind us. I noticed he was leaning against Marguerite as he stood. "What if someone else comes in here?"

"I reserved this room for a special chapel time, in memory of the Bohemian Loyalists," Lumiere said. "But we should hope others will arrive soon. We'll need someone to clean up this mess. Even God himself didn't want to do it. Why else do you think she fell forward away from St. Margaret's alcove?"

Ben and I exchanged an irritated look, and then he shrugged. I bit down on my cheek as Didier and Lumiere went back to chatting with each other.

I went to see to Ferdy's care. After I unceremoniously stepped over Xiana's corpse, I saw he was tied down to his chair with thick ropes.

"I'm glad you're here." Ferdy gave me an irreverent grin as he held up his wrists. I saw he was wearing a familiar pair of manacles. "I may need to make a stop at the men's withdrawing room before we leave."

He was trying to make me laugh, and I almost hated how kind he was being to me.

"I'm just glad you're all right," I whispered. "I was so worried when … "

My voice trailed off as I thought of Louis revealing my mother's past, and how afraid I'd been at Ferdy's loss.

My fingers seemed numb and weak as I stood there, realizing I didn't deserve Ferdy's forgiveness. My vision was once more blurred with tears, and my hands were now shaking as I was unable to look at him.

Ferdy put his hand on mine. "Ella—I'm sorry about Amir."

He knew I was upset.

"Xiana came here a little while ago, and Lumiere more or less guessed what happened," Ferdy continued. "I wasn't surprised Lumiere killed her, really. I was more surprised he let her live as long as he did."

I nodded, still unable to say anything. I knelt down and tried to untangle the knots at his feet. I thought about using my mother's dagger, but I didn't even want to think of her in that moment.

"Ella." Ferdy reached for me. Even wearing Lumiere's iron shackles, he pulled me close and held onto me tightly. "What's wrong?"

Once more, someone who I should have been taking care of was the one taking care of me.

"I'm sorry," I whispered, my voice breaking.

I thought of my own mother being sent to kill his father, how I'd doubted Ferdy when he'd told me the Order was full of assassins—and how I'd been so content to believe that since I was a member of the Order, they were all like me, instead of acknowledging I was on my way to becoming like them.

I'd been content to be ignorant, and now I was truly so undeserving of Ferdy and his love.

Shamefully, I bowed my head down onto my chest. "I'm so sorry."

"This is hardly your fault." Ferdy lay my head onto his lap, running his hands through my curls with loving care.

"I meant … I mean, I'm sorry about my mother … and your father." I barely whispered the words. I didn't want to look up at him as I asked the question that burned through my soul. "Can you still love me?"

"Oh, Ella." Ferdy cradled my face in his hands and smiled down at me, tenderly amused. "You are your mother's daughter, but don't forget, you are your father's daughter, too."

He nodded toward the far wall of the chapel, and I glanced behind me. On a small plaque, my father's name was carved in gilded lettering, with an embossed *fleur-de-lis* underneath.

That's right, I thought, turning back to Ferdy with widened eyes.

My father saved King Ferdinand.

"I didn't doubt for a minute that you would come for me this time. But no matter your family's history, you are your own self. And you've never backed down from trying to save me." Ferdy chuckled lightly and then,

THE ORDER OF THE CRYSTAL DAGGERS

leaning down, he pressed his forehead against mine. "How could I not love you?"

"You are too wonderful for me." After a long day of tragedy and loss, I felt truly hopeful again. I felt warmth and love, and I knew I didn't deserve anything as good and perfect as what I had.

"We can revisit that topic later," Ferdy said. "Can you get me out of these ropes first?"

I wiped my eyes with the back of my hand and gave him a tremulous smile. "*Absolument.*"

Soon, Ferdy was free of his ropes.

The instant he stood up, he kissed me. His mouth was firm, yet patient, against my own and I succumbed to the pleasure of holding him again.

I'd been so afraid I'd lost him, and I kissed him back, letting the downpour of love in my heart wash away all my fear.

It was only when both Lumiere and Ben groaned that I pulled back.

"Ferdy." I was a little embarrassed, even if I was still pleased. "This isn't the right time."

"That is a matter of opinion." Ferdy grinned at me.

He looked so adorable and handsome, I had to busy myself with his shackles to stop myself from kissing him again.

I was about to call Ben over to see about picking the locks on the manacles, but I saw Marguerite was helping him tighten up his brace. She was being so careful, and Ben was being so patient. He'd risked injury for her wellbeing, and I couldn't bring myself to interrupt them.

Thankfully, Lumiere held out the key.

"I'd offer to let you keep my manacles if I didn't think we'd need them later." Lumiere gave me a playful wink. "They're quite a pleasure for nighttime activities, even if they are a little painful to wear."

"I'd rather you offer to wear them," I shot back, still irritated with him for kidnapping Ferdy earlier.

"Now, now, I'm sure your husband wouldn't be happy about that," Lumiere replied. "He means to keep you all to himself, and I'm not particularly interested in such an invitation. No offense, Madame."

"What?" I suddenly blushed as I realized what he'd meant.

"You're right, Lumi." Ferdy took the key and unlocked the manacles. Once he removed them, he rubbed his wrists. "I do mean to keep her all to myself. But we should keep a hold of the handcuffs for Karl, after we get to *Vyšehrad.*"

"Yes," I agreed quickly. "Once we get Karl free and stop Louis, we can deal with your transgressions, Lumiere."

I'd rescued Ferdy, even if he wasn't in as much danger as I'd thought, and Lumiere had, as he'd said, paid for his earlier betrayal.

Now all I had left to do was rescue Karl, and then stop Louis.

Preferably killing him after all the losses he'd caused me.

"There's no need for you to deal with my sins." Lumiere pointed to Xiana's motionless figure on the floor behind us. "I've paid you for them—and now, I even will gladly help you force my father to pay for his."

"Oh, really?" I crossed my arms, skeptical. "Are you sure you're not going to betray me again?"

"No, I'm done with that. Now, I'm going to tell you what to do." He gave me a wicked grin. "I'm second-in-command, remember?"

"Dare we even ask what you have planned, Lumiere?" Ben grumbled.

"Since you're here, I can guess Pepé's gone ahead to *Vyšehrad* with her Indian manservant running at her heels, hasn't she?"

I nodded. "Yes. I sent her there to take care of the Emperor while we saved Ferdy."

Lumiere cocked his brow at me. "What? *You* sent her? No wonder that's a foolish plan, then."

"Hey!"

"Oh, Ella, my father is there, waiting for her. That's all he needs to frame the Order for the death of the Emperor, and blame her for the resulting war." Lumiere sighed. "All of you will be hunted down while he puts Karl or Max on the throne. He'll probably favor Max, since he can take the dynamite as payment and then sell it to both sides."

All of the pieces of Louis' plan suddenly came together in a devastating moment.

Lord Maximillian wanted the throne, as did Karl. They were working with Louis to cause enough chaos for the Emperor to come to Prague. Using the Tripartite Council as a front, and Ferdy and Karl as hostages,

THE ORDER OF THE CRYSTAL DAGGERS

Louis would murder him, blame the Order, and start another war across Europe—one that would destroy the old, weak foundations of the past and allow him to rebuild a new world using his wartime profits.

"But your father wouldn't really kill Karl, would he?" I asked.

"Karl would deserve it." Lumiere sniffed indignantly. "All of his recent bluster about freeing Bohemia from the Empire seems to have paid off, but when you appeal to a tyrant for your own purposes, you're only digging your own grave."

"Lumiere," I growled in warning.

"Ella, you know *mon père* and your grandmother are monsters of the worst sort. They only understand honor when it concerns their own, and they forget it easily enough when they want to destroy each other."

"We still need to work with Lady Penelope if we're going to stop Louis," I said.

"Oh, *chérie*, please. Naděžda discovered long ago what you should know now: You are far, far too good for their world, and they do not deserve you. And both of them know it. But both of them will still feast on your soul. It gives them new purpose, like vampires sucking the life from their victims. Sure, some of their intentions sound noble, and perhaps their cause is justified; but so what? Can anything be worth the loss of your own soul? The loss of your own freedom?"

I bit my lip. "And what if something is worth it?"

"If it is, then only you should truly make that decision," Lumiere told me. "It is your choice, and the consequences that follow will belong to you—even if they befall others besides you."

Both of us looked over at Ferdy, who shook his head.

"I'm not leaving Ella's side," he said firmly.

"Oh, you foolish children." Lumiere took me by the hand, and then Ferdy, too. "Several times, I have learned—and relearned—that the whole world wants to tell you what to do. Each person wants to tell you what to feel, how to act, what to believe. They will try to persuade you, berate you, threaten you. But you will be free if you stand up for yourself, if you take your proper place in standing against them—even if you end up agreeing with them in the end. You must listen to the voice of truth, and you must be willing to count the cost of your choices, your failures as well as victories.

THE ORDER OF THE CRYSTAL DAGGERS

"So now, I will tell you what you need to do, Ella—and that is to betray Pepé, as I will betray my father. They have led us into ruin, in the soul if not the body."

"Maybe." I squeezed Lumiere's hand, still conflicted. At the sight of Xiana's bloodied body on the floor, I remembered Amir's voice, telling me Lumi was a friend, how he'd been my mother's brotherly companion, and a victim of his father's neglect and abuse—as well as an abuser himself. He was a captive soul tormented further by his own debilitating choices. "But if I did betray her, I'd be doing what Louis wanted. He said my mother betrayed her, too."

"And Naděžda was right to." Lumiere shook his head. "The legacy we inherit doesn't have to be the one we leave behind. Of all people, your mother and I would be the ones who know this best."

In the distance, I could hear the soft chimes of the *Pražský orloj* ringing, as if to remind me time was not forgiving in either its pleasures or its pains.

"We have to hurry." Ben was full of impatience as I looked over at him. Marguerite had stepped back and he was walking again on his own.

"I know." Finally, I sighed. "I promised Empress Maria Anna I'd return him to her. This is a matter of my mother's honor, too."

"That's right," Ferdy spoke up. "Ella's mother didn't kill my father; and even more, she sent Ella's father to save mine. There's still plenty of good in the past. You can help us save it, Lumiere."

I gave Ferdy a grateful look.

Lumiere's expression softened, and then he sighed reluctantly. "You're right about that. I will do what I can to honor Naděžda. Even if it means following your orders when I agree with them."

I gave him a reluctant half-smile. "Thank you. Now, we've got to move if we're going to stop Louis. You know of the tunnels under the city. Use them and take us to *Vyšehrad.*"

Lumiere scoffed. "I'll take you. That was part of my plan anyway. However, I have one condition."

"What is it?" I asked, exasperated.

"I will do this, but only if you make me, Ella." Lumiere nodded to Didier, who held out Ferdy's dueling pistol to me. "Who knows if I will truly have the courage to follow through or not? It's best to keep me at gunpoint."

"I won't argue with you." I took the gun carefully. It felt heavier in my hands than I'd expected, and I was suddenly afraid of its power. "It's a deal."

"*C'est parfait.* A deal between the prince of secrets and shadows, and the princess of Prague—ooh, how I love it!" Lumiere squealed with glee and then held out his wrists to me. "Handcuffs, please."

"Good idea." Ferdy quickly obliged, locking Lumiere in his own manacles. "Even I know some gambles are safer than others."

"So far, I like your plan, Lumiere," I admitted. "What happens after we get to *Vyšehrad?*"

"You'll see." Lumiere smirked as he looked back at Xiana's lifeless form. "But I can promise it'll be even more fun."

25

◊

"Why am I the one who has to do this, again?" I held the barrel of Ferdy's dueling pistol steady behind Lumiere's back as we walked through the *Karolinum* toward the tunnel entrance. "I don't even know how to use a gun."

I wished I could use my dagger to keep Lumiere in line. I had a long way to go in learning to use it effectively, but I had more experience with its use.

I felt better since Didier checked the gun to make sure it was properly loaded and ready to fire; if Lumiere had been the one to fiddle with it, I would've suspected him of setting me up for failure, even if he'd insisted he wasn't going to betray me again.

That's exactly what someone going to betray me would say.

"No time like the present to learn." Lumiere practically sang out the words before breaking out into obnoxious laughter. "Makes you wish you'd taken Didier up on his offer before, *ne c'est pas?* Anyway, this will convince *mon père* that you are serious. It's my brilliance at work with your own, which is what you wanted."

"You don't need to sound so pleased with yourself," I said through gritted teeth, watching as he secured his pocket watch back onto his vest. He seemed glad to have it back. "I'm the one who's supposed to make you suffer."

"*Chérie*, we are allies now, and that means we compromise on how much we make each other suffer. Almost like marriage."

"You might not want to tempt me any further then." I poked the barrel of the gun against his back, and he scowled at me.

"Watch how eagerly you ruin my cloak," he warned. "I'll make you pay for it. I made Xiana pay for nicking me the other day."

He rubbed his neck where she'd held him up against the parlor wall, but I only rolled my eyes. I was about to assure him I was already paying for my restraint when Ben interrupted us.

"Let's just focus on getting to the tunnels." Ben was clearly annoyed with Lumiere's behavior, but he didn't say anything in my defense, either. "I don't want someone to see us and wonder why we have a hostage."

"At this point, I'd say Lumiere enjoys it," I muttered.

"I'm sure he does," Ferdy agreed. "But that's all the more reason to make sure we don't let anyone else find out we have him. He likes the attention, remember? And there's hardly a surplus for it here."

Ferdy was right. We'd walked through several other rooms of the *Karolinum*, but they were largely empty.

There was an echo of organ music whispering around us as we turned down another hall and entered into the library of the National Hall. The room was two stories high and lined with books. There was a small set of stairs that enabled eager readers to easily navigate the collection. I smiled to be surrounded by music and books.

"Mr. Clavan would like this place." A new wave of guilt washed through me as I thought of the books back at the Cabal; while Faye had been able to escape with her copy of *Jane Eyre*, I doubted Clavan had saved any of his own.

Ferdy nodded. "He might be able to come here one day."

"No," Lumiere said. "This room was special to the king, and it's held in reserve for the Emperor now. Of course, since it's *moi*, you know I'm good at getting into places where I shouldn't be—right, Didier?"

Didier nodded. "We've certainly had some adventures."

Lumiere's manacles clinked together as he turned and faced a shelf of no particular distinction. He reached out and grabbed onto something in front of him, something I couldn't see, and twisted it. From the sound I heard, I would've said he was winding up a watch.

Then he stepped back down with a proud look on his face, and we waited expectantly.

For several long seconds, nothing happened. I was about to tell him he must've been wrong when there was a loud creak, and the bookshelf pressed inward, opening to a secret stairway that headed downward.

I could feel the dank chill in its air, and I could taste the musky scent of its fog.

"Don't be afraid," Lumiere said teasingly. "The music is what is making it worse right now. The organ pipes reach up to heaven, but they also remind the listener that death is but one breath away for all of us in the end."

"It's dark in there." I hurriedly gathered up my skirts and cut them up again, before grabbing a flag nearby and stripping off its colored fabric.

841

"What are you doing?" Ben asked as I broke the pole in two.

"Making a *flambeau*," I said. "It's not like we have a lot of candlesticks available right now, and it doesn't look like it's lit."

"I approve of torches," Lumiere agreed.

"I don't think one will be enough for all of us. Marguerite? Can you give me some of your skirt fabric?"

"No." Ben stepped in front of her. "No, she's not going with us."

Marguerite was just as surprised as I was by his statement.

"Why not?" she asked, looking indignant and hurt. "I have been with Lady Penelope for several years now. I can handle walking around in the dark."

"No." Ben's voice was hard. "You already almost got hurt back there, and you should go home now."

"You saved me."

"Yes, but now I'd rather you wait at the manor."

Ben had always been a perfect gentleman with Betsy and Mavis, and our other friends who'd worked under Cecilia. He was naturally protective, but I was still surprised at how brusquely he spoke to Marguerite.

I knew there was something between them, but I still couldn't say what, other than I could tell she was smitten with him.

Didn't he like her in the same way?

I'd caught him staring at her before. Had I been mistaken about his affections?

"Ella, let me help you with that," Ferdy offered, rolling up the fabric around the broken flagpole more tightly. "Why don't you go find a fireplace, and we can borrow some fire from it?"

He was practically pushing me out of the room, but he was also right.

"Watch Lumiere for me," I muttered reluctantly as Lumiere began betting Didier on who would win between Ben and Marguerite. I didn't have to look at Ferdy to know he was aching to put in his own wager.

Hurriedly, I located a fireplace and lit the torch. When I returned to the library, I slowed my steps to listen.

Ben and Marguerite were still whispering furiously with each other.

"I want to help you," I heard her argue.

I stopped moving, pressed my body against the wall, and cocked an ear toward their conversation. The flagpole in my hand continued to burn as I eavesdropped.

"I don't need your help. I need your cooperation," Ben insisted. "Please, go back to the manor. You shouldn't have come with us."

"I volunteered," Marguerite reminded him. "You can't order me around. Nora will let me come, just as Lady POW said I could come with you earlier."

Ben stifled a groan. "Marguerite ... I don't want you to be in danger."

"Why not?"

"Because that's a very sensible position."

"But I don't want you to be in danger, either."

I smiled; Marguerite was good at holding her own against him. I didn't know if Ben would like that or not.

"I know we're not going to agree on this." From Ben's voice, I knew he was annoyed. "What can I give you, if you promise to go home and stay there and wait for me?"

"I can have anything?"

I held my breath as Ben paused.

"If you're sure you want it," he finally replied. "And if I can give it—then yes."

There was another scuffle of movement, and I finally glanced into the room as Marguerite wrapped her arms around Ben's neck, leaned up, and kissed him.

My eyes went wide as I stood there, watching as Ben softened against her, ever so slightly before he quickly—but gently—untangled himself from her.

"Thank you," Marguerite said. "We have a deal. But fair warning—this is the last time I'm stepping back, Ben."

"Thank you." Ben's cheeks were a light red as he saw me watching them.

I was stupefied at what I'd witnessed, but Ben glanced over at Didier.

"Can you take her home?" he asked.

"I will be glad to protect Miss Marguerite," Didier said. "Assuming Lumiere won't need me."

"We always need those who are loyal to us, and we'll miss you, but it's for the best you go," Lumiere replied. "You've seen only a sample of what my father is capable of doing. It's best if you're safe from him, too, this one, last time. This is no time for weakness, *mon ami*, my own included."

As Lumiere gave Didier another set of cryptic instructions for his contingencies, I walked up and stood beside Ben. "Well, I guess my prayers didn't work."

When he arched his brow at me, I smiled. "Marguerite's quite pretty, and you said you'd wanted an odd wife."

"Oh, Ella … I'm not talking about this with you. Besides," he muttered, "I said 'unique,' not 'odd.'"

"God knows what I meant." I watched as Marguerite headed out the door behind Didier. She turned back one last time to smile at Ben.

As I let out a small chuckle, Ben shook his head. "I'm still not talking about this with you."

"And that's for the best," Ferdy agreed. "We must go now. We've already been delayed long enough. Right, *mon frère?*"

Ben gave Ferdy a gruff nod, and I smiled; my brother knew Ferdy was rescuing him at that moment, and Ben was eager to embrace the offer.

"Lead the way, Lumiere." I handed the torch off to Ferdy as I picked up the gun again. "You should go first since you enjoy being such a *light* to others."

"Your jesting pains me more than bullets," Lumiere scoffed.

"You aren't going to be arguing all the way to the fort, are you?" Ben asked. "Maybe I should go with Marguerite."

"No, it's better you're here with us. Now we can tease you about her in person," Lumiere said.

Despite the tension surrounding us, I was grateful for the distracting banter as we headed down below the University and walked toward *Vyšeh-rad*.

The chill came up and settled around my exposed ankles, and the tunnels were narrow and cramped. The path was lined with stones and cement from ages before, and I had to breathe deep breaths to stay calm in the small, dark space.

844

THE ORDER OF THE CRYSTAL DAGGERS

This will all be over soon.

We would save Karl. Lord Maximillian would go to prison. Louis would be stopped. The kingdom would know peace, and I would defend my mother's honor.

Or at least, I hoped so.

26

◊

It seemed like a long time passed as we walked under the city. I heard the gentle *splish-splash* of the Vltava's waves through the walls until we came to a stairway.

We climbed upward, and Ferdy stepped forward to open up a hidden gate.

And then we were free.

"Thank you, Lord." I was grateful to be back outside, even if it was dark now. The air was still cold, but it was much more pungent and fresh, and I could breathe much more easily. I tossed my makeshift torch into the water eagerly.

I looked around to see we came out on a stone path on the riverbanks, far down below the actual fort of *Vyšehrad*.

"Hold up." Ben held up his arm, and the rest of us went still.

Two pairs of guards appeared, walking across the battlements above us.

"We should head for the fort's cemetery," Ferdy whispered as they walked by. "There's an entrance there that no one guards."

"How do you know?" I asked.

"My parents often brought me and Karl to *Vyšehrad* when we were younger. I didn't ever imagine I'd try sneaking into it. But I remember enough to know this is the southeast side."

It was too easy to forget sometimes that Ferdy had grown up as a hidden prince of Bohemia. I glanced down at the common street clothes he wore. His copper hair was more red than ever against the wintery background, and his eyes twinkled with silver mischief as he smiled at me.

Ferdy craned his neck toward the gatehouse. "If I had to guess, Karl's going to be in his assigned chambers here, or Lord Maximillian might have even put him in the king's rooms. I'm not sure where Louis would be."

"We'll get Karl first," I said. "That's the most important part of all of this."

It was what I'd been working toward for the last several weeks, and if it hadn't been for all the anguish I'd suffered so far today, I would've almost been excited to be there.

Ferdy took the lead, and the rest of us followed without issue—even Lumiere who seemed oddly quiet as we climbed up stairs, hid in alcoves, and ducked down on the ground as we made our way toward the keep.

As we came to the top of the bailey, we passed by a cellar. Inside the large stone chambers were a number of barrels and boxes. Behind them, several doors were on the other side, and Ferdy nodded when I asked him if they led out to the landing port.

"In times of war, this area would be filled with weapons and supplies," Ferdy said. "These barrels are likely full of food and water and other supplies for the castle's occupants."

"I doubt it. Look at the ground. Several barrels have been brought in and out of here recently," Ben said, pointing at tracks on the ground. There were several footsteps and scratches where large items had been moved.

Using Amir's dagger, he pried open one that was nearby. Inside, there was a large quantity of the sand-colored powder I'd seen at Count Potocki's house.

"Looks like Lord Maximillian has already paid Louis for his services," Ben said in a disgusted voice.

"Louis wants the dynamite to sell to both sides of the war." I glanced over at Lumiere. "Isn't that what you said?"

"Yes, but I don't know if they've officially concluded their arrangements or not." Lumiere shrugged, before he nodded to Ferdy. "You can probably make the guards tell us. They are Bohemian, and they should listen to you."

I brightened. "We could try that."

"No." Ferdy's face blanched over before he shook his head. "I'm not really a prince, Ella."

"But what if you could stop this now?" I asked.

"I doubt I could. Karl hasn't been able to leave this place. He only came out for Count Potocki's ball," Ferdy reminded me. "If Karl's not in charge, I can't see why I would be able to order anyone around here, either."

"We could still try."

"When we were younger, Karl would always play the crown prince in here, terrorizing the guards," Ferdy said, looking up at the twin bell towers of the basilica before us, and then to the yard full of graves off to its side. "But not me. I've never wanted a prince's power or authority."

"But—"

"No," he insisted, more sharply this time. "Some men need a king to follow, but no man deserves to be a king. It's too much for me, Ella, and it's too tempting—"

"You can do so much good with it, though. And it would help us now," I argued. "Don't be such a coward."

"I'd rather be a coward than a tyrant," Ferdy shot back, surprising me with the sudden flare of his temper. He glanced over at Lumiere, and his eyes went dark with vengeful lightning. "My brother tried to kill me, and he succeeded in killing my friends. It's already too tempting to use any means for my own satisfaction."

"Oh, Ferdy." My heart ached at his sadness and anger. I'd known that feeling myself earlier.

Lumiere let out a loud, disgruntled sigh as I passed Ben the gun, and I slipped into Ferdy's arms.

"Do you know why I love you?" I asked him.

Ferdy attempted to smile. "My charm, my wit, my good looks?" His joking fell flat, but I still smiled.

"No. I love you because you give me such hope." I rested my head on his shoulder, willing him to be comforted. "Even now, when you're afraid and you suffer, you don't stop me from doing what ought to be done. And even more, you come with me and stand beside me, trying to protect me."

"I'm not that scared," Ferdy muttered, irritated more than angry now. "Just cautious, and rightly so, given my brother's tendency toward despotism."

"You are not your brother," I reminded him, keeping my voice kind. "You are your own self—just as I am, remember?"

Ferdy paused for a moment, and then he gave me a small, rueful smile. "Well, I can see why we're perfect for each other."

"Because you remind me who I am, and I tell you who you're not?"

THE ORDER OF THE CRYSTAL DAGGERS

"No," Ferdy said with a soft chuckle. "Because you make me afraid like nothing else."

"You want to know what I'm afraid of?" Lumiere asked from behind us. "That you'll mess this up, and all because you always stare into each other's eyes and moan about how much you're in love. That's not going to stop *mon père*."

I wrinkled my nose at Lumiere. "You're just jealous."

Ferdy laughed, and he seemed to be back to more of his usual self. But then he tightened his grip on me. "I've already lost so much. I can't lose you, Ella. If I lose you, I'll lose myself, too."

"You won't lose me," I promised.

"Are you done now?" Lumiere huffed. "I'm getting tired of sappy speeches."

"You've had your own share of them," I reminded him.

"I still wouldn't count on any of my supposed princely authority." Ferdy interrupted our fighting by returning us back to our earlier concern. "We don't know who's really in charge, and I don't exactly look like a Bohemian prince right now."

"Would that really be an issue?" Ben asked skeptically.

"Probably." Ferdy gave him a sheepish look. "More than once, Philip took my place here while I snuck out to the city."

"If you don't want the authority, you should've started with that argument. No one wants to take orders from a beggar or a farmer, unless they're American." Lumiere eyed Ferdy's attire disdainfully before turning back to me. "If you're done playing the role of the good wife, take the gun back from Ben. I don't want him holding me hostage."

"Why not?" I asked with a renewed sense of suspicion.

"He's the better shot, and he's much better than your husband, too." Lumiere scowled. "But also, you'll need to be in control when we run into *mon père*, Ella. He needs to see you're in charge, and the person in charge is usually the one who's got the most threatening weapon."

"Usually?"

"You have to consider that I'm the one telling you to keep it," Lumiere said, sneering with snide pleasure. "I just hope I don't have to tell you when to use it, too."

It was tempting to ask him if that meant I should use it on him, but I resisted it and focused on what needed to be done. "Where are Karl's rooms located, Ferdy?"

"In the keep."

"What do we do about the dynamite powder?" Ben asked, gesturing toward the small collection of barrels. "We can't just leave it here."

"We're not going to be able to do anything about it now," I said. "We need to get Karl first."

"We can come back for it later," Ferdy said. "For now, follow me."

Ben was reluctant to leave the barrels, but Karl needed to be rescued first.

Ferdy led us through the last hidden trails of the graveyard, walked through a small vineyard, slipped through the basilica, and headed inside the fortified keep.

Immediately, we all scrambled to hide in a courtyard bower as another pair of guards passed by.

They'd just missed seeing us, but they were busy talking about the "little prince" who was fortunately imprisoned in his room.

Finally.

Ferdy smiled as we slid out from our dark hiding spot. "For once, I'm glad Karl likes to talk so much."

"Me, too." I thought about how it was too easy to coax information from Karl when I'd danced with him.

After that, all of us were able to get to Karl's door without trouble. There were guards that patrolled through the hallway, but none that were standing in front of his room.

There was no obstacle to freeing Karl—other than his locked door.

"Ben?" I was about to ask him to pick the lock when Karl started pounding on the door.

"Hello? Hello, guards? I can hear you, and I demand you let me free at once," Karl called out. His voice was a little hoarse, as though he'd been yelling for some time. "I know you're there."

Lumiere groaned. "Do we have to free him?"

Before I could answer, Karl began ranting and raving about why he shouldn't be locked up when the Emperor was coming to visit, and how

850

THE ORDER OF THE CRYSTAL DAGGERS

he and Lord Maximilian were equal partners in their political arrangements.

Karl was in full tantrum mode, but at least we'd found him, and he was alive.

"Doesn't sound like an equal partnership to me," Ben grumbled. "Keep watch for us, Ferdy."

"I'm good at that." Ferdy grinned.

"Yes," Ben said tersely. "I know."

"Of course, *mon frère*," Ferdy said, as I held back a giggle. It was too easy to recall Ben's objection to Ferdy spying on us after seeing us outside Wickward's shop.

A moment later, thanks to Ben's handywork, the knob clicked open, and Karl yanked open the door.

"Finally, it's about time you … "

His voice trailed off as he stared at all of us.

I imagined the sight surprised him as much as it angered him. All of us were tired and ragged, covered in dirt and sweat, and my arm ached as I still held the gun to Lumiere's back.

Karl was a little surprising himself. While he wore the formal jacket of a king, with its gold braid and shining buttons paired down the front, I could see stray threads peeking out from the frayed cuffs and collar. His gray eyes were darkened from stress, while his cheeks were hollow and thin. His jaw was tight, his hair needed a trim, and there were even a few strands of light grey in his ebony locks.

He had been miserable at the Potocki ball, but I could now see it wasn't just because he'd dreaded seeing me again.

Karl remained speechless as Ferdy motioned to Ben that the guards were coming, and Ben quickly ushered all of us into the room and shut the door again.

It was very nice, with large windows and elegant furniture. The floor was graced with Oriental rugs, and the room was covered in a much nicer green-colored silk wallpaper. A desk was off to the side, littered with papers and ink and books, and further off to the side, there was an alcove in the back for sleeping.

Karl might have been held against his will, but he was still surrounded by comfort and security.

"Why are you here?" Karl finally found his voice again as he glared at us in disbelief. "If you've come to take the throne away from me, you're not going to succeed."

"The idea that we're 'taking the throne' from you implies you have it in the first place," Ferdy argued.

"You're happy to be a pauper. You can't imagine the loss I feel. If you weren't my brother, I would challenge you to a duel!"

"You've already tried to have me killed. That would be a step up for you and your so-called notions of honor."

"You don't deserve honor," Karl hissed. "You stole Ella from me and you've twisted her mind, and now you want Bohemia to suffer."

"Bohemia would suffer if you were its king."

"Stop," I ordered, stepping between them. "Karl, Bohemia is part of the Empire now. Nothing you do can—"

"I refuse to believe that," Karl snapped.

Lumiere chuckled. "This is exactly why I told *mon père* that it would be much better to keep you two separate."

"Be quiet, Lumiere," I snapped.

"You know I'm right, Ella. They'll always have their little squabbles, over you as well as the throne. Can you believe my father didn't agree with me at first? It took me some time to convince him otherwise, too. He's getting old."

Ferdy and Karl began arguing again as I thought about Louis' appearance in the Cabal. He was calm and even very polite, but when Lumiere appeared with Ferdy in hand, he'd seemed largely unimpressed and even expressed derision toward his son. "He likely has good reasons to disagree with you at times."

"Good reasons, no. His own reasons? Yes."

"You're just as bad as he is when you say it that way."

"Wisdom is seen in how you use knowledge, just as virtue is how you choose to contend with opportunities," Lumiere drawled. "I'm working toward my goals while he has his own end in mind."

"And what are your goals, exactly?" I asked, suddenly curious.

"His end, of course." His eyes glimmered. "I should thank him, really. Thanks to my father's investments—the more legitimate ones—all I have

852

THE ORDER OF THE CRYSTAL DAGGERS

to do is secure his arrest and trials, and I'll have enough money to live out the rest of my days as I see fit. And while he's all excited at the thought of profiting off worldwide warfare, I prefer to be left alone."

"You wish for freedom." I suddenly wondered how I'd never realized it before.

"Of course I do. Men like my father want power—the ability to determine truth and its meaning, and how it should be used. What a waste of a life, if you ask me." Lumiere eyed Karl with clear disgust. "And look at this one here. The promise of power seduces the worst sort of men, and somehow manages to make them even more repulsive."

"Excuse me?" Karl took a break from arguing with Ferdy to scowl at Lumiere.

"Cloaking your degeneracy in decency never works, young princeling." Lumiere smirked. "That's why I've always worn my sins so well. I don't have to lie about them in addition to covering them up."

"You are clearly a deviant, sir, and I will not be lectured by the likes of you." Karl was incensed. "I don't have to guess to know this is all your doing, Eleanora. Is the Order here to kill me if I don't cooperate?"

"No," I said. "I promised your mother I would bring you back to her. Given your current circumstances, it might be the best option for you right now."

"That is preposterous."

"All of us heard you yelling just now," I told him. "You're stuck as a prisoner here, and you're not going to tell me that you agreed to it?"

"I did at first." Karl flustered. "It seemed sensible. Max was compromised, and I couldn't afford the scandal of a broken engagement—"

"Especially when you'd lost your bride to your own brother, no less," Ferdy interrupted with a smug grin, and I shook my head at him in warning.

Karl's mouth twisted in displeasure. "And certainty not when the public was so enthralled with Eleanora."

"They'll soon forget about me," I said. "I was a sensation, but I wasn't that popular. And Society will forget me soon enough."

"They'll remember you longer than you think. If I was to free Bohemia from the Empire, I needed money, and I needed Society's blessing. It was the perfect time to act, and you would've helped me," Karl said. "You provided the social influence—intrigue, connections, money, and historical prestige. It was perfect. Until I found out you lied to me."

"Lord Maximillian killed people with his dynamite at the Advent Ball, and you're complicit in his crimes. And you tried to kill me, and everyone else, at Count Potocki's. I ruined your plans to kill people, and that was a good thing," I said, much more calmly than I felt. "You're lucky I'm not here to kill you after all of that."

"Your death would have been a point of sympathy," Karl explained, as if I'd be honored by his self-concerned intentions. "It was Max's idea to build on the outrage of the Advent Ball incident. But Louis said we should wait until you were here along with the Emperor. He said if we killed you here, it would anger the Bohemians even more."

I glanced over at Lumiere, who nodded. "*C'est vrai, chérie.* You make a good prize, dead or alive."

"Ella's not going to die," Ben said. "And we're not leaving here without you, Karl."

Karl eyed Ben carefully. He'd only seen him a handful of times, if that, and when I saw Karl look at Ben's brace and wrinkle his brow in disdain, I almost hit him.

"So are you going to come with us to go see your mother, or are we going to drag you out of here?" Ben's tone was a bit harsher as he spoke this time, and I knew he'd seen Karl's judgmental assessment.

"Do I have a choice?" Karl scowled.

"Do you?" I asked. "Louis and Lord Maximillian don't seem eager to let you do as you'd like."

Karl's wan face blushed over crimson again. "I suppose you have a point."

"I think you should stay here," Ferdy said, before I could tell him to stop aggravating his brother. "Your handlers wouldn't like it if you disobeyed them."

"I'll go where I want, *brother.* You can't tell me to stay," Karl snarled. "If you've unlocked the doors, we can leave now."

He marched toward the door as Ferdy gave me a quick wink and one of his charming grins. I could almost hear him bragging about manipulating Karl. I bit back a smile, before turning to Lumiere.

"All right, Lumiere, let's—"

THE ORDER OF THE CRYSTAL DAGGERS

I was suddenly interrupted by the sound of a trumpet and marching soldiers, followed by a lone gunshot that crackled like lightning.

Terror ran down my spine, and I could feel the tension around us thicken with the threat of danger.

All of us headed for the windows.

"Look, Ella," Ben whispered, pointing down toward the riverbank. I followed the direction he indicated to see a small line of palace soldiers heading toward *Vyšehrad*. "It looks like Harshad and Lady POW were able to do what you wanted."

A rush of happiness overwhelmed me.

Lady Penelope and I had agreed we would get more done if we split up our party; I went after Ferdy and Lumiere, and she'd gone to catch Louis. But before heading out for *Vyšehrad*, I'd wanted her to go see Empress Maria Anna and inform her about Louis' plans.

Even if we hadn't yet rescued Karl, I'd suspected the former Empress would be willing to aid us if she could. Ferdy offered to write a letter to his mother himself.

And now, thanks to the approaching regiment of soldiers, even if Louis had sought to trap us, he was the one who was now trapped.

"This is good." Ferdy exhaled with relief. "It'll be better having my parents' guard here."

"Yes, they know you and your real face better," Lumiere remarked from behind us.

"We should still get Karl out of here," I said. "It'll be safer for him if he's further away from both Louis and Lord Maximillian. Come on, Lumiere."

"Try to make it more convincing, would you?"

"Fine." I held the gun up to his chest. "Let's go get Karl, Lumiere, or I'll shoot you."

"That's an improvement, but I think you can still do better. It's not like I want to go on a nice jaunt around the fort here."

I gritted my teeth. "You've been sitting or lying around the manor for weeks now, drinking an excess of alcohol and spirits. You should thank me for making you move your bloated form along. You need the exercise."

"Are you calling me fat?"

"I didn't say that. Specifically." It was hard not to laugh at the horrified look on his face, but he'd wanted me to be more convincing, and his vanity was an easy target.

It helped that he did seem to be a little more robust since I first saw him in the Cabal, or even when he'd donned Hawaiian coconuts and colorful flowers at the Estates Theatre. It could've been his clothes, but as I examined his midsection, I wondered if I'd been right.

And then I felt bad, because I remembered how Lady Penelope would stare at my stomach for any signs of pregnancy or laziness.

Thinking of her, I gripped the gun in one hand and pulled out my mother's dagger with the other.

I hated how alike we were at times, but in this one instance, it was to my advantage.

Lumiere crossed his arms. "That was better. I'll humor you for your efforts."

"Thank you for your cooperation," I murmured, prodding him with the gun again; in spite of his egregious graciousness, I figured he could use the extra incentive to move.

"Ella." Ben took my arm briefly. "I'm going to go to the front and see if I can find Lady Penelope and Harshad. I'll let them know you've got Karl so she can concentrate on finding Louis, and maybe Harshad and I can do something about the dynamite powder."

I didn't like the thought of separating from Ben this time; if we had run into this situation back when we first started training, I wouldn't have let him go.

"I'll be all right," Ben promised. "My leg's doing well enough. I also have the other gun and Amir's dagger."

It was touching and insulting that he knew me so well, especially my weaknesses.

Reluctantly, I nodded. "That's probably a good idea," I conceded. "Be careful."

"I will."

Ben walked away, wincing as his limp was a little exaggerated because of the fort's stony floors. I almost called him back, but Ferdy brushed up beside me.

"Your brother will be fine," he said. "My brother, on the other hand … "

Karl sniffed loudly from behind us. "I'd rather you stop talking about me as though I'm not present. I can hear you just fine."

"I'm sorry." I apologized without thinking, making Lumiere laugh at me.

Ferdy frowned at Karl. "Stop talking to my wife."

Karl eyed him maliciously. "*Your wife* can handle me speaking to her."

"I don't care. You stop talking to her, or I'll—"

"You'll what?" Karl sneered, his voice suddenly more vicious than I'd ever heard it before. "Kill me?"

"You'd be so lucky," Ferdy snapped back.

"Please stop." I didn't want to beg them to behave, but I could see Karl had less incentive than ever to help us out. He'd been gallant enough to refrain from forcing himself on me, but he was starting to realize his plans had all failed. "You're family, for goodness' sake."

I took Ferdy's arm. "You told me that Karl always looked out for you when you were younger," I reminded him. "He saw to your well-being."

"If only to keep him from embarrassing me and the rest of our royal heritage," Karl snapped.

"And you," I said, trying not to let my anger overtake my voice. "You should realize that Ferdy is not the one at fault because your father favored him over you."

Karl's face turned purple. "Is that what he told you?" Karl sputtered; he was so angry, I knew I'd spoken the raw truth. "What utter rubbish. My father was a king, and he was an awful one. I shouldn't have lost the crown because of his incompetency. I don't care if he liked Ferdinand better."

"You shouldn't get a crown just because of your bloodline, either," Ferdy said, and I shot him another warning look.

"You're still brothers, and you're still family," I repeated, more angrily this time. "You might not trust each other, but you should still have some affection for one another."

There was nothing repentant on either Ferdy or Karl's face, and I sighed, eager to give up.

THE ORDER OF THE CRYSTAL DAGGERS

Reconciliation was a dream, and just then, I could only hope we would be able to contain Karl's anger long enough to get out of *Vyšehrad* safely.

I only had one gun, and I needed it to move Lumiere along.

At the thought of him, I turned to see he was staring out the window now with a look of interest on his face. "What is it, Lumiere?"

"We'd better hurry if we're going to leave," Lumiere said. "It's getting dark, but I can still see it."

"See what?" Ferdy asked, moving over beside him.

"The Emperor's flagship."

Just as he spoke, a round of gunfire sounded out from near the entrance of the fort.

A sinking feeling tore through my knotted stomach. I didn't know how, but I knew we needed to get out of there. And fast.

Quickly, I gathered up Ferdy, Karl, and Lumiere, and we ran out into the open air of the courtyard.

The fort's guardsmen were running and gathering in small groups, heading for the battlements as the sounds of battle began increasing from the front.

"What are Lady POW and Harshad doing?" I wondered aloud. "They should be able to get in with the former Empress' soldiers coming, shouldn't they?"

A new voice answered my question.

"The guards here are under my orders." Lord Maximillian's voice was precise and formal as I whirled around to face him. "And I've told them not to let anyone else in, especially now that you are here, Lady Eleanora."

THE ORDER OF THE CRYSTAL DAGGERS

27

◊

"Karl." Lord Maximillian stared down at Karl angrily. "Why are you out of your room?"

"I didn't have much of a choice." Karl clutched at his fraying sleeves as he gestured to me and the weapons I held. "Besides, if you hadn't locked me up, we wouldn't have such an issue."

"That's no way for a man to talk to his future father-in-law—or his future king."

"I'm the one who will be the king," Karl insisted. "Not you."

"You're not in charge here," Lord Maximillian reminded him. "You've already caused me too much trouble in Bohemia. Now that Louis and I have finalized our deal, you will serve me and follow my orders—or you will die."

Lord Maximillian had said before he would gain power when Lady Teresa Marie married Karl. Now it was clear that he intended to rule himself.

Beside me, Karl stiffened with fear. I held my breath, while Ferdy looked worried and Lumiere yawned.

"But you're not the king, or even an immediate heir," I said to Lord Maximillian. "Why would Bohemia accept you as their king?"

I was stalling for time, desperate to think of something.

Lady POW and Harshad were still outside *Vyšehrad*. Ben had gone off to find them. I didn't think I'd be able to shoot him, and I didn't actually want to kill him. Lord Maximillian was a witness to Louis' crimes in Prague and Silesia, and he had also implicated himself with the development of a dynamite-like weapon that could be used for war.

At least he wasn't armed, I noticed.

"They know a respectable leader when they see one." Lord Maximillian sneered at me and stepped forward carefully. I noticed he was limping a little, thanks to how I'd managed to injure him the other night.

"Do they?" I asked quietly.

"Lady Eleanora has an excellent point, Maximillian."

All of us turned toward the sound of Louis Valoris' voice.

859

The evening starlight reflected off the pristine white of his hair and the little golden threads in his embroidered tunic. Louis was stylish and stately, calm and in charge, ever the master of both chaos and order.

Behind me, I heard Lumiere shuffle, and I quickly held my gun at the level of his heart.

Louis didn't seem to mind. "*Bon nuit* to you, my honored guests. I know we had such a lovely time earlier, but I'll admit I didn't prepare for your arrival quite this soon. I pray you'll forgive me."

I was about to tell him he should pray for something else when he turned back to Lord Maximillian.

"I'd like to hear your answer to Lady Eleanora's question. Do Bohemians truly know a respectable leader when they see him?"

"Excuse me?" Lord Maximillian was caught off guard by Louis' question.

Ferdy tugged my arm, trying to pull me back toward a stairway, where there was an alcove, one that we could use for cover.

"I wouldn't move if I were you, Lady Eleanora." Louis spoke firmly, leaving our small group frozen where we stood. "You want to know the answer to your question, don't you? You asked for it, after all."

"Well, Maximillian?" Louis looked at him expectantly.

"I am a duke," Lord Maximillian finally answered. "I am rich, and I've worked with weaponry and warfare for years. I own my own land, and I have grown my vineyards, made my own wine, and sold it for profits to fund my research for years."

"That describes you; it says nothing of Bohemia, or its people." Louis smirked. "I think you'll find much more resistance than you'd like to believe.

"Take the guardsmen here for example. You may believe they'll listen to you, but they've worked for me for years already." Louis gestured toward the battlements. "They're enjoying their playtime with you here, but they all know who they answer to in the end."

Before Lord Maximillian could reply, Louis pulled out a gun of his own and shot him.

I swallowed the scream in my throat as Lord Maximillian fell to the ground, writhing in pain as he clutched at his torso.

THE ORDER OF THE CRYSTAL DAGGERS

Louis laughed. "I'll admit, I must thank you, Maximillian. Your explosives will greatly profit me now that France and Germany are at war, and soon the rest of Europe will be too, including Bohemia, and all the countries in the Austria-Hungarian Empire."

So that's what he wanted.

Louis didn't care about Bohemia's kingdom, or its ruler. He just wanted war across the continent.

"I'll kill you for this," Lord Maximillian hissed angrily, still grappling with the pain in his side.

"We've had a very good partnership. But now that your weapon is being mixed up in more factories, and all your research is in my hands, I don't need you anymore. You're just a broken man."

"No more good to me than a horse with a broken leg," Lumiere whispered behind me.

"No more good to me than a horse with a broken leg," Louis continued, walking closer to Lord Maximillian's fallen form.

He shot his gun again, and this time, Lord Maximillian grabbed his leg. His shrieks of pain echoed throughout the courtyard as blood poured out, and Louis shot him in the other leg.

"Stop it," I cried, unable to bear Lord Maximillian's screams any longer.

"It's not me doing this." Louis was still as calm as ever as he smiled at me. "Why would you and the Order of the Crystal Daggers take care of a duke like Lord Maximillian like this?"

"But the Order's not—" I stopped, shutting my mouth as I realized Louis didn't need Lady Penelope to frame the Order for any crimes.

I was present—and armed with a gun.

Louis was amused as he turned his gun on Ferdy, and then he moved it to Karl. "What do you think? Who should die for the Order next?"

"No." My nerves shattered with dread. I stood there, unable to move, barely able to breathe.

From the look on Karl's face, he was in just as much turmoil as I was. Ferdy looked on Louis' steady figure with a grim expression, but all elements of his irreverence and lightheartedness were gone.

Gunshots and fighting was still going on from the entrance, and Lord Maximillian was whimpering as he crawled away from the courtyard.

THE ORDER OF THE CRYSTAL DAGGERS

"Come now," Louis persisted. "I'll even let you choose, Eleanora. Which prince would you save? The man you love, who's been hidden even more carefully from the public eye, or the prince willing to destroy the world to restore Bohemia's national pride? I only need one of them alive to get the Emperor to realize cooperation with me is not optional."

I swallowed hard. "You can't kill either of them."

"That's not very fun," Louis said.

"I can't choose between the two of them." I shook my head. Ferdy was my heart's future, and Karl was my mother's past. "But I have a better idea."

Louis laughed. "The Emperor isn't here yet. Who would I kill instead?"

I lowered the gun I held. "Take me instead."

"Oh?" Louis arched his brow at me. "I'd rather not kill you. I like having a scapegoat alive. It's rather fun to watch them squirm."

Lumiere cleared his throat behind me.

"Ella," Lumiere whispered, deliberately interrupting me as I was trying to save Ferdy and Karl.

"Lumiere." I hissed through gritted teeth. "What is it?"

"The gun he's using is a Smith & Wesson Model 3. It has five shots before he needs to reload."

"So?" I barely registered his words; I had no idea what he meant.

And then Lumiere suddenly burst into tears.

"Oh, *Papa!*" Lumiere cried out in sniveling relief. "I am so glad you're here. Ella has captured me, and she's going to kill me next if you don't save me!"

I saw the slightest twitch along Louis' jaw. "Not now, Lumiere."

He was enough of a distraction that even if I lost my composure, I was able to regain my resolve.

"Lumiere is not wrong." I held up my gun again, pointing it carefully at Lumiere's heart. "But not for the reason you might think."

Louis arched his brow. "You're quite bold, Eleanora, but you're also naïve and innocent. I'm not interested in a trade for him, and I know you'd never kill him."

"I would if I had to," I said, doing my best to keep the nervousness out of my voice. "And that's why you should take me instead of killing Karl or Ferdy. Take me as your apprentice."

I saw the flicker of surprise on his face.

"You're right about me, Mr. Valoris," I told him, my eyes filling with tears. "I am idealistic and inexperienced, and I don't have the confidence like you. But I would do anything to save Ferdy. And Karl, too."

"Ella. What are you doing?" Ferdy asked.

"The only thing I can do," I said, keeping my gaze on Louis. "I've thought about it, and you've been right about me, and so much more, in the short time I've known you, Mr. Valoris."

He was watching me with interest now. "Such as?"

"Such as weakness, and how imperfections can ruin everything." I swallowed hard, but I straightened my shoulders.

I had to do this, I told myself.

I had to.

It was the only way.

"I've seen that Lady Penelope is unfit to instruct me as her pupil, and my mother was right to leave her."

"That's enough out of you, Eleanora." Lady Penelope's voice called out from off to the side, but it never sounded more grating. "Stop this foolishness."

She appeared in the east side entrance to the courtyard. Harshad was close behind her. Both of them were armed with guns, and Lady Penelope was carrying the dagger of the Order in her left hand. There were still gunshots ringing around us, and I figured she'd left the palace guards to fight off Louis' men as she made her way here. Quickly, I looked for Ben, but I didn't see him.

"No, that's enough of you, Madame," I snapped. "You say I'm a disappointment to you, but what of yourself? You failed to kill Louis when we met in the Cabal earlier—

"You asked me not to," Lady Penelope interrupted, but I kept talking over her.

"—and you didn't shoot Xiana after she killed Amir—"

"I can kill Louis now," she offered harshly, but I intentionally moved and stepped in front of Louis.

Lady Penelope and Harshad both looked shocked, and I could almost feel Louis' amused approval from behind me.

"No," I said. "You are a coward. You've always blamed me for our troubles. But now I know you're the one who is weak. You can't even keep your own family safe!"

Lady Penelope's eyes suddenly shimmered with angry tears.

"Eleanora," Harshad said. "Please stop."

"But I'm right!" I insisted.

"That's true," Louis agreed cheerfully. "I may have lost money and investments throughout our history together, but I have taken what you love most, Penelope."

I turned toward Louis. "You've said I've made good progress in my learning. Well, if I'm going to be better, I need a good teacher, Mr. Valoris. One who is accomplished and successful. Lady Penelope is unfit for the job, and a failure."

"That is also true." Louis nodded.

"So if you will keep Ferdy and Karl safe, I will pledge myself to your tutelage and work to become worthy as your partner, your right-hand man."

Louis looked at me, maliciously pleased and impressed. "Your offer is enticing."

"That's enough of this, Eleanora." Lady Penelope's voice trembled as she scolded me.

I would not let her deter me. I would not give into guilt, I vowed, as I scowled back at her.

"I'm tired of your failure. You ruined Amir's life, and my mother's, too. And because you couldn't see Xiana's treachery, I lost a sister."

"Louis is the one who's responsible for her death," Lady Penelope reminded me.

"Only because you failed to stop him," I pressed. "You've always hated Louis Valoris because he was the successful victor, and now, I will serve him. Even at the cost of my honor. It's clear to me that your honor only serves you, Madame. That will not be my fate. I'm not like you—and that's the greatest failure you could ever have."

"Death or defeat, Eleanora!" Lady Penelope insisted. She pulled her gun level up to me, and I couldn't say if she would shoot me or not. "That is the only way a member of the Order leaves."

My knees buckled, but I couldn't back down now.

"No, Ella," Ferdy insisted. "What are you doing?"

"I love you," I told him. "And I can't lose you."

Lady Penelope looked stricken, and Louis only laughed.

I turned to face Louis. "I will do anything it takes to keep my family safe. Even if it means betraying you. Even if I have to kill for it."

"I must admit, I wasn't expecting this when I arrived here," he said.

Lumiere groaned loudly. "I'll agree it's been fun, but if you are going to accept her offer, will you have Ella release me or not, *Papa*?"

Louis gave me a thoughtful look. "Your offer is a good one, but I already have Lumiere for my second-in-command."

"I must inform you, sir, that Lumiere is not a good partner for you." Slowly, I secured my finger around the gun's trigger. "My offer will be more enticing to you after I tell you Lumiere is a traitor. He's been giving Lady Penelope information, and he only pretended to kidnap Ferdy earlier. He also killed Xiana."

Louis gave Lumiere a questioning look. "Well, Lumiere?" His voice was still cheerful and amused. He didn't seem bothered at all by my news, until Lumiere smirked back at him.

Slowly, Lumiere moved backward and stood in front of the wall of the courtyard. He held up his hands in surrender.

"Ella is right," Lumiere said, the easy pride in his voice full of amusement. "I guess it's for the best I tell you the truth at last, Old Man. I'm done following your orders, and I've decided to defect to Lady Penelope's side—officially, of course. I have been undermining you for years already. And I know I'm perfectly safe, since you will always protect me, *ne c'est pas*?"

There was absolute silence as Louis' expression completely lost its good humor.

"You see?" I said. "I've seen it myself, and I know how you feel about imperfections like this, Mr. Valoris. I used him to find you, but I will turn him over to you now as proof of my desire to serve you."

Louis's lips thinned into a barely perceivable line.

865

"I know I'm not your flesh and blood," I continued, my resolve strengthening. "But that's even better, isn't it? I'm Lady Penelope's granddaughter, and Jakub's, too. I would serve under you, and my blood would give you both her disdain and his approval. My family has suffered from opposing you for years, and it's time I make that right—especially if I want to save my own family now."

I glanced at Ferdy, meeting his eyes with mine. He shook his head, and I had to look away.

"What do you say?" I asked. "Do you accept my deal? Will you let Karl and Ferdy go?"

The whole world seemed to hang on my question; I could almost see Louis thinking over my offer. Lady Penelope seethed behind me, and Karl was back to whimpering, while Ferdy's eyes were full of disappointment.

"This isn't right," Ferdy objected. "Don't do this, Ella. You'll only hurt me if you forfeit your honor."

"I would do anything to keep you safe. How could I live if I lost you? And don't you want to have a family one day?"

"Well, yes, but—

"Then this is my only choice," I told him. My voice was full of resignation. "And I'm not sorry in the least."

"That's a good start," Louis said. "I will agree to your offer, Lady Eleanora."

I let out a sigh of relief, while Ferdy's face crumpled in despair.

"For your first assignment, you must kill Lumiere for me."

My skin began to tingle with disgust and uncertainty, but I swallowed hard and turned toward Lumiere.

"Come now, *Papa*, this is ridiculous," Lumiere scoffed. "She's wanted to kill me ever since she found out I admitted I was the masked assailant who nearly killed King Ferdinand."

"What? You were the one who attacked my father?" Ferdy stepped toward Lumiere threateningly, but Louis stopped him with a look of warning.

"Now, now. Eleanora is the one who has the decision to make. You're still my captive till then, little prince." Louis looked over at me. "Well?"

"Shoot him, Eleanora," Ferdy snarled.

THE ORDER OF THE CRYSTAL DAGGERS

I thought back to Ferdy's vehemence at the Order's history with his family, and his anger at Lumiere, even though he insisted Lumiere was a friend.

Lumiere must've caused the attack to fail.

"Yes." Louis grimaced. "Shoot him."

Despite the sickness I felt, I nodded and tightened my grip around the gun, and turned back to Lumiere.

"You've asked for this, Lumiere," I said bitterly.

"Please. If it's one thing I'm familiar with, it's giving into temptation. You're enjoying this moment." Lumiere sneered as he gracefully ran one of his shackled hands through his blond hair.

He wasn't wrong. Once I might've enjoyed this moment, I thought. But just then, I didn't know how to feel, other than awful and unsure.

Carefully, I aimed for Lumiere's heart and looked into his green eyes.

His gaze was steady and peaceful, and I almost wondered if he was giving me his blessing. My finger seemed stuck as I tried to squeeze the trigger.

But there came a point where there was the distinctive *click*, and the bullet surged forward out of the shaft.

The sound echoed all around us, filling the courtyard like a demon's cry.

My eyes flew shut as the bullet shot out of its chamber, and I only opened them in time to see Lumiere's eyes widen with shock and pain.

Time seemed to slow, as he grabbed his chest, fell to his knees, and then slumped forward.

His cloak fluttered peacefully around him, gently falling over his still form like the wings of a bird wrapping around its body before it sleeps. When he finally settled to the ground—the dirty, sullen ground—I lowered my head to my chest.

Tears shot to my eyes, and I felt my lip blubber out in regret and self-disgust.

What have I done?

As if to answer me, Louis clapped. "Well done, my new protégé. I wasn't sure you would do it. But you have proven you're willing to kill for those you love, and that's a fine start."

"Thank you, sir." I did my best to compose myself, and I turned to Lady Penelope. "At last, I am free of you, Madame."

Her mouth was hanging open in shock. "You've betrayed me," she gasped.

"You only have yourself to blame." I held up the gun again, this time aiming at her. "Perhaps I should kill you next? Or should I leave you alive to suffer?"

Louis came up beside me. "I must say, you are quite an impressive creature. But now, we will need her alive just a little longer. The Emperor will be here, and that's when we will frame Pepé for his murder."

At the mention of the Emperor, Karl finally spoke up again. "What of my kingdom?" he yelled. "If you kill Franz Joseph, the Empire will go to Prince Rupert."

Louis waved him away. "We can draw up a treaty first." He started to explain more of his intentions to Karl, but I could only stare at Lumiere's corpse.

Then the sound of marching soldiers rang from the courtyard entrance.

Ben burst through the courtyard archway. "Get away from the southwest wall, everyone. The cellar is going to explode!"

I looked over to where Lord Maximillian had been shot earlier.

His body was gone, but there was a steady trail of blood on the ground. It led to a doorway down near the riverbank, where the cellars were located.

They were still likely full of dynamite powder.

"Ella." Ferdy and I exchanged a quick look. "Do you think—"

The rest of his words were cut off as a large, loud explosion of fire and stone rippled through the fort.

THE ORDER OF THE CRYSTAL DAGGERS

28

◊

Instinctively, I reached out and took hold of Ferdy. We gripped onto each other, just as we had the night of the Advent Ball.

Together, we fell to the ground.

Smoke and flames appeared along the far wall, and the doorway through which Lord Maximillian had escaped through was now a firepit of flame and death.

"Ella?" Ferdy whispered.

"I'm here," I said, feeling dizzy as we sat up. My voice was a whisper, but I felt as though I was screaming.

Everyone else around us was on the ground.

The tremendous force had sent everyone reeling. Lumiere's body hadn't moved much, but Harshad knelt beside Lady Penelope as she smothered small flames on her skirts. Ben was using a courtyard pillar to pull himself back up to his feet, and his brace seemed a little bent from the sudden force.

Ferdy let go of me to haul Karl up from the ground, but Karl was already shoving him away.

I forced myself up off the ground. My sleeves were torn and my hands were bloodied from my fall, and I'd dropped my gun. I looked around before I saw it laying on the ground nearby.

I let it stay there, too preoccupied with the scene around me. There was fire and death and blood, and it was all chaos—but not by Louis' hand, this time.

Lord Maximillian had gotten his revenge against Louis.

Louis.

He was on the ground, too, and it was the first time I'd ever seen him so disheveled.

His perfectly combed hair was all blown out, and the white tips were covered with ash and dirt. Of all the people around us, he was the only one unable to get up. He grabbed at his side, biting his lip in pain.

"Eleanora." Louis stared up at me as I stood over him. I think he expected me to help him.

Is he injured? What happened to him?

And then, behind us, Lumiere's laughter rang out. "Oh, no, *mon père!* Tell me you didn't break your hip."

Ferdy, Karl, and all of us turned around to see Lumiere stand up, still laughing as he took off his manacles and walked toward us.

Relief washed over me, and I almost ran to hug him.

Louis looked savagely stricken as Lumiere approached us. "You're alive."

"Of course I am," Lumiere said. "Ella doesn't know how to use a gun properly."

"Lumiere," I growled at him, but he only laughed harder.

"It also helps that I wore some plate armor," he said, pulling up his tunic a little to show me the thick layer of metal that covered his skin around his torso. "Of course, you missed me anyway."

I frowned at him, but I didn't say anything, either.

That explains why he looks so much thicker.

"Eleanora." Lady Penelope called over to me as she limped over to us.

Lumiere smiled. "Don't tell me you're suffering from the same fate, too, Pepé? I suppose you've both had a good run of things after all these decades, and it's only fitting that you should be forced from the front line."

"I can still walk," Lady Penelope snapped at Lumiere. She held out her gun and pointed it down at Louis. "And I can still shoot you."

"Good," I said, enjoying the surprise I saw in Louis' expression. "Shoot him."

"Ah, but that's not part of my plan." Lumiere handed his handcuffs to Lady Penelope as he picked his father up off the ground. "It's time for *mon père* to face the ultimate suffering: Paying for his crimes against humanity in court—while I live off his hard-won labor."

"Lumiere!" Louis barked. There was a thick undertone of pain in his voice, and he was still holding his hip with both hands.

Lumiere laughed at him. "I've waited a long time for this day. Let me enjoy it, *Papa*—goodness knows you've robbed me of so much enjoyment in my life, you'd think you'd allow your one and only son to have some happiness. Even if it's at your own spectacular failure."

THE ORDER OF THE CRYSTAL DAGGERS

"Yes, and it is a complete failure," Harshad agreed. "Benedict warned us about the dynamite, and the palace guards have your men in custody by now. Also, because of the fire now, the Emperor will not dare arrive at *Vyšehrad*."

"And both Karl and Ferdy are safe," I added, beaming with pride.

Louis was beyond weary as he looked at me.

"You don't really think I was serious about joining you, do you?" I crossed my arms over my chest. "I might be naïve and inexperienced, but I'm good at manipulating others when I want to."

"And that's why we're so good together," Ferdy agreed.

All the heat around us was nothing compared to the burning fire I saw in his gaze as we looked at each other.

Lady Penelope cleared her throat. "You didn't have to be so convincing, Eleanora. I didn't know if you were telling the truth or not, given some of our recent conversations."

"It wasn't hard to hate you. You're just fortunate that I hate Louis more." I turned away from her abruptly, eager to see the end of Louis. "Now, Louis, you can die, knowing all your plans have failed."

"I already said no, *chérie*." Lumiere shook his head. "I need him for the courts."

"But she said she could shoot him." I looked at Lady Penelope expectantly.

Anger boiled up inside of me again as she only sighed.

"I'm not going to do it, Eleanora," she said, putting her gun away.

I gaped at her. "What?"

"I hate it, but Lumiere is right," she said through gritted teeth. She'd told me before how much she loathed to give Lumiere any credit, and I felt more offended than ever at her bitterness. "I can't do it."

"This is the man who killed my sister, used Xiana against my mother and Amir, and laughed at causing you pain," I shouted, angrier than ever. "He's Lumiere's father, and he's escaped justice for years. He has contingencies, remember? How can you let him live? Shoot him! It's a matter of justice as much as security."

"There is more at stake than justice," Lumiere said. "His crime syndicate workers are all over the world. We need his cooperation to get all the information out of him, so we can prevent even more damage from being done."

"What?" I shook my head. "I don't believe this."

"Ella, please." Ferdy's soft whisper made me even more upset.

Everyone seemed to think it was just fine to leave Louis alive after all the terrible things he'd done.

After all the disgusting things I'd said to trick him.

After I'd nearly sacrificed myself and Lumiere for the chance to stop him.

After all the sadness and sorrow I felt.

All I wanted was some peace. And I wouldn't have it.

"I was right about you!" I shoved Lady Penelope in anger. "I can't believe this. I can't believe how weak and cowardly and foolish you are."

"You don't see things the way I do," Lady Penelope argued back. "We can't sacrifice long-term good for short-term pleasure."

"Speak for yourself," Lumiere muttered, but no one paid him any attention as I battled with Lady Penelope.

"You've always done this," I shouted. "You've always regretted it, too. He's killed *our family*, and he's gotten away. Can't you see this is one time when you should do things differently?"

"As I said, Lumiere is right. Louis' cooperation can help prevent other people's further troubles," Lady Penelope said. "This is not just about you, or me, or even about your mother, Eleanora."

"Lumiere." Louis let out a gasp, and we all turned to look at him.

Louis had lost his balance, and he was falling forward out of Lumiere's grip—or so I thought.

Time seemed to slow down as I suddenly saw the gun hidden away in his left hand. He took aim for Ferdy as he pretended to fall.

"No!" I shouted, and I lunged forward into Louis.

There was one shot, and then I had my hand around his wrist. Louis grappled with me, twisting me against him and choking me again.

Behind me, Lady Penelope struggled as she and Lumiere were caught off balance.

"This is the end," Louis huffed beside me.

THE ORDER OF THE CRYSTAL DAGGERS

"For you," I growled back. I was stronger, younger, and less injured than he was, and now I was more experienced in fighting with him, too. I pulled out my mother's dagger, and sliced the blade into his other side.

He gasped in renewed pain, and I slipped free of his grip.

But then my shoe tripped over a stone, and I fell forward.

I glanced back just as Louis once more aimed his gun.

One shot left.

"Ella," Ferdy cried out.

Out of the corner of my eye, I saw Karl grab onto him. "Let her die," Karl said. "I can still use her death—"

The next second of my life blurred over as Ferdy pushed Karl away from him—right into Louis' path.

The bullet left his gun in a deadly echo and caught Karl directly in the chest.

Blood surged out where he was struck.

I screamed, while Ferdy grabbed hold of me and dragged me away from danger.

Lumiere took hold of his father again. The gun was empty, and Louis had no choice but to be shackled. Lady Penelope looked confused as to what had happened in the last few seconds, while I pushed away from Ferdy's hold.

"No, Ella," Ferdy told me.

"Why did you do that?" I yelled at him, pounding my fists against him. "I was supposed to protect Karl. I was supposed to take him back to your mother."

Ferdy braced himself, keeping his hold on me firm. "I didn't shoot him," he said. "But either way, I won't let you die for a prince, Ella. Even if it's supposed to be me."

I finally wriggled out of his grasp and went over to Karl's body. I shifted him onto my lap as my tears began rolling down my cheeks all over again.

Karl's listless eyes narrowed at me, and then at Ferdy.

"Karl?" I whispered. Hope fluttered up inside me. Maybe he would be all right.

"I … hate you," Karl moaned, before his eyes turned sightless and his body went limp.

All I could do was sit there, more helpless than ever. Ferdy sat beside me, but I didn't want him to touch me; I was devastated.

I cried as the rest of the world faded away, and I was left all alone with my failure.

Even my mother's memory was of no comfort to me as I sat there, completely shattered.

A few moments, or perhaps an eternity, passed before a shadow fell over me.

I looked up, surprised to see Lady Penelope standing over me. The fires were still burning high around us, and in that moment, she reminded me of a demon.

And that was how I saw her.

"Stay away." I shook my head, desperate to ignore her, wishing she was just a figment of my imagination. I bowed my head over Karl's dead body. "Stay away from me."

"I'm sorry, Eleanora," she said.

"No, you're not," I snapped, still crying. "You could have just killed Louis like I wanted, but no. You had to break *Máma*'s promise to the former Empress and dishonor her memory one last time."

"These things happen," Lady Penelope tried to explain carefully, but I shook my head.

"It doesn't matter now," I said. "Get away from me. I'll never forgive you for this. I don't want to see you or talk to you, ever again."

She grimaced. "Yes, I know, so you've told me."

"Just go then," I screamed. "Go!"

I don't know how long I was there, or how long the chaos raged around me. I just knew the night was still full of burning flames when an elegant pair of Hessians stood before me.

"Huh?" I looked up to see a familiar-looking man in front of me. I said nothing as I stared up at him; my mouth couldn't seem to make words.

"Cousin Franz," Ferdy whispered. He hurriedly stood up and bowed.

The Emperor looked back at me. "Are you Lady Eleanora of Bohemia?"

THE ORDER OF THE CRYSTAL DAGGERS

My eyes were still full of tears as I nodded glumly.

He didn't smile, nor did his expression change, but for some reason he seemed pleased all of a sudden. "I have been looking forward to meeting you."

29

◊

The Emperor was much more kind and gracious than I'd expected.

Shortly after we introduced ourselves, Lady Penelope and Harshad explained what had happened, while Lumiere lent his support to their claims where needed.

The Emperor nodded and asked questions, and when it was all over, he offered to send Karl's body to Prague Castle with a small escort of troops.

Several pairs of hands came forward, presenting a board transformed into a makeshift litter. Together, they pried Karl's body from my stiff, bloodied hands.

"No," I whispered, knowing my objection was futile.

There was nothing I could do now.

Karl was dead.

Louis was captured, Lord Maximillian was gone, and the Emperor was safe—and the Tripartite Council was likely canceled, or indefinitely postponed.

But Karl was dead, and I'd failed in my most important task.

I'd failed Karl, the former empress, and my mother, too.

I'd failed.

"Ella."

I shook my head, but Ferdy took my hand.

He pulled me up from the ground and held me.

I let him. I was still angry with him, even though I knew that was senseless, too.

It had been a very long day, full of hours of fighting and tears and walking and sadness.

"Come with me," Ferdy said, and soon we were walking back to Prague Castle with Karl's body.

It was just like my father's funeral, I thought.

THE ORDER OF THE CRYSTAL DAGGERS

There were pallbearers and a royal escort forming a procession, and though the night had settled in over Prague, along with its cloudy skies, we gathered at the gates of *Vyšehrad*.

"Lady Eleanora." Franz Joseph appeared before me again, just before we were about to leave. This time, without Karl's body on top of me, I was able to give him a proper curtsy, even if I still couldn't smile.

"Your Imperial Highness." I mumbled the words, wishing I had more energy to care as much as I perhaps should have about my poor manners.

Franz Joseph didn't seem to mind. He had been trained in war, and as I looked back up at him, he seemed to recognize how much the day had drained me.

"I must commend you on your efforts today," the Emperor said. "You and the Order have been of service to my empire, and our country."

"Thank you."

I glanced behind the Emperor to see another group of guards put Louis on a chair and use it to carry him. He seemed to be in considerable pain, but he didn't make a move to stop them or fight back. There was a thick bandage around his hips, and one side was red from where I'd stabbed him.

I wondered if Louis was silent with shock; I was half-hoping to see him realize he was defeated.

"I also understand that I should welcome you to my family," Franz Joseph continued, nodding toward Ferdy. "Though we have not known each other long, I am glad to meet you, and I am hoping you'll join us at court. I would be grateful for you to remain in service to the empire, as your father had done for my great uncle."

I swallowed the lump in my throat as I nodded. "Yes. *Táta* always was good to King Ferdinand. He would have been good to you, too, especially if you had been coronated here, Majesty."

"I have offered to get coronated here before," Franz Joseph said quietly. "But empty gestures and performances won't be enough to convince the people I am now their king, even with my great uncle still alive."

"I doubt it would be seen as an empty gesture." I glanced around. "Not like the Tripartite Council you've arranged."

"Fortunately, we don't have to worry about the Tripartite Council as much as it seems," he said, confirming my suspicions before giving me a tired smile. "But I will share a secret with you. I believe there are things

877

more important than making people happy, all in hopes of securing their acceptance. I'd rather honor King Ferdinand during his life, and I hope I'll be assessed by what I do as an emperor than be judged for what I didn't do as king."

"History will judge both aspects of your reign," I said, still blushing as I spoke candidly with him.

"Perhaps it will judge me more kindly if I have your allegiance," Franz Joseph replied.

From his voice, I knew he didn't want to hear any more arguments, and I didn't really want to make them, anyway.

I merely nodded, and then I bowed again. "If you are certain, Your Imperial Highness."

"I am."

I didn't have the heart or energy to explain the Order's loyalties or exact history or our skill sets. But perhaps he already knew. Either way, I was glad when he spoke with Ferdy instead, confirming we would attend a commendation ceremony in the near future.

We parted ways shortly after Franz Joseph congratulated Ferdy on securing me as his bride.

Once he was done thanking Ferdy for his own service, Franz Joseph headed back down to his ship.

We made our way out of *Vyšehrad*, walking through the streets of Prague, still escorting Karl's body to Prague Castle. I heard from Ferdy that Franz Joseph was heading back to his ship, and then he would pull into the Port of Prague. After that, he would be taken to the castle by carriage once he landed on shore again.

The Emperor seemed sincere as a ruler, and thoughtful as a man. Karl died believing him to be an obstacle, someone to dethrone, but I mostly pitied Franz Joseph.

My sympathy grew as I saw the people watching us as we made our way to the castle.

Even if Louis had not succeeded in murdering the Emperor, there would likely be others who were just as discontent with his rule. Karl's death would be hard for those like him, and it could possibly raise another usurper—one who might even fulfill Louis' dream of a global war.

I shuddered at the thought.

THE ORDER OF THE CRYSTAL DAGGERS

We might have delayed such a fate, but it was awful to think it was still possible.

Ferdy and I walked in mostly silence for the rest of the trip, until we came up to Prague Castle's grand entrance.

"Ella." Ferdy squeezed my hand. "Don't let go of my hand this time."

I didn't even consider the possibility—until we met with Empress Maria Anna.

When Karl's fallen form was gently laid before her, the cry that left her lips was utterly inhuman in its agony.

She fell beside his corpse as she wept. Her large skirts billowed out around her, and her headdress shifted dangerously on her head until she finally tugged it free and let down her limp, thin, gray-black hair. She had none of the calm repose I'd always associated with Mary, the Mother of Jesus; instead she wept so hard that her cheeks swelled with her salty tears and her nose ran.

It was then that I tried to rush forward to comfort her, but Ferdy held me back. His own silver eyes were full of regret and shame, and he could only shake his head.

We both knew there was no comfort we could offer her that would heal her broken heart; it was the same for any mother who lost a child.

When Ferdy did speak several long moments later, all he said was, "I'm sorry, Mother."

Her eyes snapped up, and she pointed at me accusingly. "You were supposed to protect him. You promised me!"

"I … I don't … I'm sorry—"

I tried to say something, but there was nothing I could say. I wanted to believe it wasn't my fault Karl was dead, but I didn't even believe that.

I replayed the whole scene out in my head, wishing I'd stabbed Louis harder, or knocked him out, or held onto Lumiere's gun.

I wished I'd have done anything else, rather than face such dreadful failure.

"This is all your fault," Empress Maria Anna wailed at me.

"No, Mother." Ferdy stepped forward to defend me, still holding onto my hand. "It's my fault that he's dead. I'm the one who caused him to die."

"Ferdinand." Empress Maria Anna gasped out his name, and then she howled again.

"Ferdy," I whispered, but he shook his head at me.

His mother sobbed. "How could you do this to your only brother? How could you do this to me?"

Ferdy looked down at the ground. "I pray you will forgive me, Mother," he said. "I did not want him to die."

Her face scrunched up as she began weeping again, and she wasn't able to say anything I could understand clearly.

Finally, she waved us away. "Leave us. Leave me."

Ferdy bowed, and I followed in suit. He had to lead me out of the room; I still wanted to say something else—that I was sorry, that I'd tried, that I didn't mean for it to end this way.

But, of course, I couldn't.

Once we were out of the throne room, Ferdy tugged me down the long hallway.

I didn't know where we were going at first, but then I recognized a little bit of the castle. I could see the ballroom where the Advent Ball had taken place months before; it was still in disrepair, but it didn't look as bad as I remembered it.

Perhaps Faye had been right, I thought. Life would go on, and we could still rebuild.

"This is where I told you I loved you for the first time," I said as we turned down another hall.

Ferdy nodded. "I'd already fallen in love with you several times over before then. But there was nothing like catching you when you fell."

For the first time in what felt like a long time, a small smile managed to curl on my cheeks. My face was full of pain and my expression felt stiff, but the anguish in my heart felt a little lighter.

"Where are we going?" I asked.

"To see my father." Ferdy turned us down another corridor, and then he pushed open a door and led me into the indoor garden where Karl had once taken me.

THE ORDER OF THE CRYSTAL DAGGERS

I stopped as we entered inside. It was chilly, and the lack of sunlight had caused the flowers and plants to wilt since I'd last been there. Many of them were brown with death.

That was when I noticed the smell of rotting leaves in the air.

"This is my father's favorite place," Ferdy told me as he walked down a row of small succulents, which were somehow still alive. "I'd come here sometimes and help him plant new seeds. We would spend hours in here, sometimes just in silence. Karl never liked it much in here after he started school, even though we would play here sometimes if I begged him. He preferred his study; once he went away for schooling, he would stay in his room to write letters to his friends and instructors."

Ferdy's voice thickened as he spoke. He still didn't really feel like Karl was gone for good, I realized.

"Ah, Ferdinand."

Ferdy and I looked up to see his father, King Ferdinand V, appear at the far door ahead of us. The older man looked weak and small, with his large robes wrapped all around him, and he leaned heavily on his cane. But there was a broad smile on his large face as he made his way over to us.

"You're back," he said. "Come to help me with the weeding?"

Ferdy gave him a small smile. "There's not much left to do here, I'm afraid."

The king nodded. "You're right. There's a hole in the roof near here. All the heat is leaving the room."

"Will it be fixed?" I asked, looking around the desolate garden.

"Perhaps." The king shrugged. "When the rest of the castle is, likely."

He reached out a ring-covered hand to poke at some of the different plants and walked slowly but steadily around the garden.

"Father." Ferdy cleared his throat. "Karl died."

His father didn't look up from his plants. "When?"

"Earlier today," Ferdy told him. "He was shot by Louis Valoris."

I held my breath, waiting for the king to dissolve into tears like Empress Maria Anna had, or for him to possibly have a seizure.

But he didn't do either of those. He only shrugged. "His mother will be sad."

"Will you be all right?" I asked, coming up beside him.

He smiled down at me with a simple, gentle expression. "Eleanora. I didn't mean to ignore you. You are tired today."

"Yes. I'm sad about Karl," I said, trying to redirect him back to our conversation. "Aren't you?"

"I am." He shrugged again. "But I never knew him very well. And he didn't know me very well, either."

King Ferdinand looked back over to Ferdy. "Have you come to help me in the garden today?"

"No." Ferdy took my hand. "I wanted to show Ella your flowers."

"They're not in good condition right now." The king tapped one of the shelves with his cane. "But neither am I."

"You're still the father I remember," Ferdy replied, and the king grinned.

"Not the king, but a father." He nodded, and then he sighed. "Karl never saw me as a father. He only saw me as a deposed king."

I gave Ferdy a questioning look, and he said nothing. His father was nowhere near as upset at Karl's death as Empress Maria Anna.

Soon after that, Ferdy excused both of us.

"Ferdinand. Don't come back until your mother summons you," King Ferdinand told us. "She won't want to see visitors for a while."

"Yes, sire." Ferdy gave his father a quick hug. The king patted him in a mechanical sort of fashion, but I saw his eyes shimmer with tears as we left.

"Your father loves you," I said. "And he loves you as a father loves his son."

Ferdy nodded. "He says he didn't know Karl very well. I don't think he knows me very well, either."

"But he loves you." I took his hand and leaned against him. "I don't think it's easy for children to know their parents. I imagine it's hard to see them as real people. I would've never guessed some things about my mother, or my father, either."

"Yes, that's true." Ferdy gave me an irreverent smile. "I'm glad your mother decided not to murder my father."

"Ferdy."

THE ORDER OF THE CRYSTAL DAGGERS

"It's fine," he told me. "I'm sorry if it's too soon to joke about it. But as I said before, your father saved mine. So it all worked out in the end."

I pursed my lips together for a moment. "Was it really Lumiere that attacked the king when my father saved him?"

"Assuming he wasn't lying when he told me, then yes," Ferdy said, his voice full of irritation again. "He told me a few years ago when we met. He also told me some of the more nasty truths about the Order, and his own involvement on the continent with his father. Lumi seemed to want to impress me. But after everything that's happened this week, I think maybe he wanted out, and he saw me as a friend who would help him."

My hand tightened around his. "You would be a good person to trust with that."

"So you think." Ferdy smiled a little. "He worked with your mother to make sure my father survived."

"I'm surprised he told you." I wrinkled my nose. "He arranged for your friends to be murdered."

"He explained that by telling me how Louis had been unhappy with his recent performances, and especially in the last few years when Lumiere 'accidentally' freed Didier in America," Ferdy said. "He said it was good my friends died, so it looked like he was still competent."

"What?" I clenched my jaw. "That's awful. About your friends, I mean. But I'm glad about Didier. And Lumiere's still pretty callous."

"There are a lot of stories he should tell you," Ferdy said. "I guess he needs a few successes here and there to keep his father from finding out the truth. Or at least, he did. Hopefully he will stop now that he's openly betrayed Louis."

I nodded and then blinked. "Where are we?" I asked, looking around. "We're supposed to leave the castle, aren't we?"

"We just have to stay out of my mother's way for a while," Ferdy said. "And it's cold, and it looks like rain, and it's past nightfall. So I thought, well … "

He looked toward a long flight of stairs, and suddenly I knew where we were going.

Ferdy reached his bedroom door and opened it, and I welcomed the familiar sight.

THE ORDER OF THE CRYSTAL DAGGERS

The candles on the candelabras were smaller, and there was a small layer of dust, but the books were still all over the floors and shelves, and there was a lingering scent of lavender and mint.

This was the room he'd brought me to after the Advent Ball had rendered me unconscious.

"Come on," he said, before leading me to the bed and pulling down the covers. "You deserve to rest now, my princess."

"I won't argue about that." My body's guard dropped, and I let myself fall into bed next to him. I was already asleep by the time my head hit the pillow.

30

◊

I didn't know if hours or days had passed when I finally shifted out of sleep completely. There was no way to tell for sure, since it was raining when I sat up in Ferdy's bed.

I didn't bother trying to find out, either; I was too enchanted at the sight of my husband sitting down on the window seat, looking through a pile of books.

He didn't notice I was awake. The way he thumbed through the pages, looking them over before stacking them up quietly, made me think of my mother's journal.

Maybe Ferdy can teach me and Ben Arabic so we can read it, I thought, suddenly dreading having to search through Amir's room and his possessions when we got back to the manor.

"What are you looking for?" My voice was harsh and low against the silence around us.

"Ella." Ferdy looked back and smiled at me.

He was still sad, but he was much more energetic, and I was glad to see he'd been able to rest. I'd had a few nightmares, but I was too tired and sad to do anything but wait until they passed.

I had a feeling some of my nightmares would return.

Ferdy briefly put the books aside. "Go back to sleep. We're not going to be able to leave until the rain's finished."

"Why not?" I asked. "It's just rain."

He gestured toward a stack of books and patted them affectionately. "I was going to take those to Clavan. To see if he wants any, to start a new collection, or sell some, so he'll have some money to rebuild the Cabal."

"That's very kind of you." I chuckled a little. "Although I doubt he would be able to sell any to Wickard. Not for profit, anyway."

"I don't want the books damaged by the rain," Ferdy continued, gazing at them and then looking all around the room. "And I don't imagine I'll be coming back here any time soon. If at all."

At his sudden despondency, I got out of the bed and went to sit down next to him. Distractedly, I rummaged through another small pile of books he had been sorting through. There were several with the same title, and I picked one up with loving hands.

"How many copies do you have of *Le Morte d'Arthur*, exactly?" I asked.

"What does that matter, if it's not the right book?" Ferdy replied. "I know the one Ben sold was red. That's all I know for sure, other than the title."

"There's an inscription in the cover." I opened the book, trying to remember it. "It was originally for Ben, you know. *Táta* gave it to him the birthday before he broke his leg, I think. I didn't want Ben to lose it. The book was a reminder of better times, when we had a better father, and I didn't want Ben to forget that."

"He didn't," Ferdy said.

"How do you know?"

"I can tell." Ferdy shrugged. "That's why he's sour toward him. It's easier to hate someone if they've always been awful to you. But if you know there's some good, and it's just been taken away, it hurts so much more."

I wondered if he was thinking of Karl when he spoke, and I decided I didn't want to contemplate that.

For reasons I hated, I was already thinking of Lady Penelope, too, and I wanted to think of her even less.

Ferdy sighed. "Anyway, go back to bed. Get some more sleep."

I put his book down on the window seat again, and then I cradled his face in my hands. "I'll go back to bed if you come with me."

I leaned over and kissed him, and soon Ferdy was kissing me back.

We were still kissing each other as I led him to the large bed and pulled him down on top of me.

THE ORDER OF THE CRYSTAL DAGGERS

31

◊

Ferdy and I waited until the rain stopped to return to the manor, but no one was waiting for me as they had been the last time I'd come home from the castle.

Days of colorless grief settled around us, and while I had my husband, my brother, and plenty of friends, I felt numb and bland as the long days slowly passed, an impasse between listlessness and restlessness.

Franz Joseph had ordered Louis to pay for his crimes in Bohemia; all of his assets within the country and the Empire's territories would be confiscated and turned over to the imperial authorities.

After that, Louis was to be sent off to London to be tried in Queen Victoria's courts. Didier told me that Lumiere would be going with Lady Penelope, and while they were away, Didier would stay here and help Harshad and some of the others keep an eye on Prague.

There was still the possibility of turmoil, with the fights breaking out between the Bohemian and German Diets more frequently after the news of Karl's death.

It wasn't the first time in recent weeks that the rumors made me furious. Rumors said it was possible he'd been killed by a German Confederacy supporter, or even a Jewish anarchist.

It angered me even more that the truth wouldn't come out, and more people had the chance to believe whatever they wanted, no matter how wrong or depraved or irrational it was.

And then I saw Lady Penelope, one last time, before she was to return to London with Louis and Lumiere.

Shortly after Ferdy and I returned to the manor, she arrived to pick up her luggage.

She called me and Ben to the west parlor to say goodbye, but I didn't go.

Instead, I crossed my arms and stood on the manor's battlements, the same one I'd beaten Alex on, the day she'd arrived on the manor's doorstop.

I watched her as she headed toward her carriage.

I didn't exactly know how I felt about her departure.

THE ORDER OF THE CRYSTAL DAGGERS

I was happy to see her gone.

I was angry she would leave me here now.

I was puzzled when she didn't insist that I come along with her.

And I hated how she didn't fight with me any longer.

As I watched her step into the carriage, she glanced up my way.

I froze.

From where I was, I could see her nostrils flaring, and as much as I hated her, I think that was the moment I realized I hated myself for what had happened, too.

But everyone lies, and everyone has secrets, and everyone has regrets— and sometimes the most egregious lies, the most treacherous secrets, and the hardest regrets we have are the ones about ourselves.

I buried that last little bit of hatred inside of me, and despite my better judgment, I was determined to nurture it, and yet still forget about Lady Penelope entirely.

I decided I didn't care, but I cared too much to let myself truly know how conflicted I was.

She entered the carriage, and then she was gone.

Good.

Then Lumiere appeared behind her, and he looked up at me, just as she had.

"Goodbye, Ella!" he called, waving up to me. He blew me several kisses. "Don't get too pudgy while we're away! And make sure you let Didier teach you how to use a gun. I'll be eager to see your improvement when I get back!"

I shook my head and walked inside, heading for the library.

Once I got there, I saw my mother's portrait looking at me again. She was my mother, and as much as I'd loved her, I needed to accept that some part of her would always be a mystery.

"I'm not going to miss Lumiere that much," I told her. "I don't care if you loved him like a brother. To me, he's just an infuriating clown."

"You'll miss him more than you'll admit, *ségra.*" Ben appeared behind me and put his hand on my shoulder. He had a new scabbard for Amir's dagger on his side, and along with that, and a bath and some food, Ben appeared much more healthy and cheerful. "He's a strange man, but there's bound to be some good in him."

"Ferdy and I have a bet about how long it will take before Lady POW throws him overboard," I said, and Ben and I shared a much-needed laugh.

By the time we stopped, the carriage was already far off down the road.

"Where's Marguerite?" I asked, looking behind him.

Ben lost his smile. "She's not going to follow me around all day, like you do to Ferdy. She's still here, working with Prissy, and Betsy and Mavis, too."

"Really?"

"Well, since Amelia and Jaqueline are with Lady Penelope, Marguerite is teaching the other girls how to sew like she can." Ben frowned. "So they can replace her in Lady POW's service when she gets back. That will free Marguerite up so she can stay with me."

"Since you're getting married, that'll be good," I said. "She doesn't need to work with our grandmother."

"I'm not thrilled that she's not interested in setting up a household of her own," Ben admitted. "She wants to go on missions with me."

"Well, we don't have any missions right now," I said. "And it'll take some time for Lady Penelope to return here. Longer, if court drags on for Louis. Perhaps by then she'll be more eager to settle down with you and start a family."

Ben sighed. "I don't know why I agreed to this."

"You promised. And you do love her, don't you?" I was certain he did love her, otherwise I knew he would've found a way to wiggle out of their previous agreement.

"Yes." Ben scowled at me. "You have it easy with Ferdy, you know. He doesn't have to be here with us. He's a prince. He can provide for you without trouble."

"He was born a prince, and he'll always be one to me." Momentarily, I slumped forward and put my head in my hands. "But you should've seen Empress Maria Anna's face, Ben. After what happened to Karl, I don't know if Ferdy will ever see her again. I think he's more content to be here than at the castle anyway."

"He still doesn't have a bad leg to stop him from a regular income."

THE ORDER OF THE CRYSTAL DAGGERS

I gave him an irritated look. "Your leg won't stop you from getting your inheritance from *Táta*, now that Lady POW and her man of affairs took care of it."

"It's not the money—"

"And you've more than proven you can handle your leg," I reminded him. "Even better, Harshad told me that Cecilia is going with Lady POW to London. She'll be working in the household of the new Duke of Wellington. Lady Penelope's stepson had an opening for a lady's companion for his spinster aunt, apparently. So she'll be gone, even if she deserves much more of a punishment."

"She might deserve less, but Marguerite deserves more."

"Well, I can't argue with that," I said with a smile. The way Ben asserted that fact made me so proud to be his sister.

"I don't want her helping with the Order," Ben said. "I've been hurt before, but I don't want to see her injured, either. And being a spy is not a respectable job."

"I know Society feels that way. But you can at least look on the bright side," I said.

"What's that?" Ben asked.

I grinned playfully. "You'll be able to commiserate with Ferdy much better now. He says the same thing about me."

Ben only groaned as I laughed, and I was still chuckling as he left me and went off to the kitchen for some food.

I thought about following him, but in the aftermath of everything that had happened, my appetite was practically non-existent.

Instead, I looked around for a book, and then sat down and curled up to read it. Hours might have passed before I heard Harshad say my name.

"Eleanora."

I looked up as he appeared in the room.

I was shocked to see the broken quality of his gaze.

He had always seemed so solid, so unmoved by the world, but as I watched him sit in Lady Penelope's usual seat in the library, as I saw him gaze at my mother's portrait and then out the window, I saw that his pain was ongoing, universal in both his movements and his moments.

THE ORDER OF THE CRYSTAL DAGGERS

"Harshad?" I put down my book and stood up, moving closer to him even though I was uncertain of what I should do—or if I should do anything at all. "Are you well?"

He surely couldn't be this lost without Lady POW, could he?

"Grief is a masterful devil in its own right; it does not want to take a final shape, only allowing us to see its presence is marked by the absence of our loved ones." Harshad sighed and shook his head.

My eyes filled with tears, and I tried to push back the memory of Amir's hand in mine. I tried to picture Amir at his best, when he was helping me waltz, teaching me to fight, when he would talk with me and share with me some part of my mother's secret lives.

I didn't know if remembering Amir like that helped or not, because I knew the ending.

I was surprised when Harshad's hand touched mine. I was even more surprised when I fell into his arms and cried.

This time, I didn't hesitate to embrace Harshad.

"This is not the end, Eleanora. Amir is at peace, just as Dezda is," he told me, as he held me. "We are the ones who mourn for our loss, and the world's. But we do not mourn for them."

"You have a bigger heart than me," I said, as my tears finally slipped free. "I'd rather the world suffer if it meant I didn't have to lose them."

"There are some philosophies in this world that say all life is suffering—that love is an act of violence upon the soul. To love is to have something so good that everything else is able to be seen for the tragedy it truly is." Harshad squeezed his hand over mine. "I have seen this in my own life. And this is why I believe what I believe, and more importantly, I know whom I have believed. God is merciful in our most vulnerable moments; not that he takes away our pain, but that he took on that pain himself."

"I know death makes us turn toward God, but I can't help but feel he's deserted me." I buried my face into Harshad's shoulder.

I did not really want to talk about Amir and the others. It was too painful.

"On the contrary." Harshad paused. "If you think of how God experiences time, he sees it all at once, like a line of blood on a paper. And so, he is always able to see the cross. He is always on the cross.

"God is love, and he suffers for it—he suffers for me. And so I, in turn, must suffer, too."

Harshad stepped back from me, but he still held onto my hands with his. "In all the world, in all the places I have been and the people I have met, I have never seen such an answer to suffering as this. God remembers the cross and experiences it each day. Right now, we carry those we love, as he does; we experience that pain we feel, that sharp absence of love. You've carried your mother this far, as I have, and you've honored her in your memory. Now, you will go on and carry Amir, as will I. That loss is part of our cross to bear."

"I am too weak to carry such a loss."

Amir had spent so much of the last months of my life teaching me to be strong. It broke me even further to know I couldn't do what he'd sought to teach me.

I'd failed him all over again.

Harshad let go of me, and I expected his rebuke.

But Harshad was not Lady Penelope, and he gave me a small kiss on the top of my head, reminding me of *Táta*. "Then I will help you carry it, as much as I can. And so will the others who love you."

When Harshad finally stepped back from me, I felt a curious warmth; some people would mistake it for distance, but I knew it was an act of trust.

My hand went to my mother's dagger at my side. I took the weapon with a small sense of resolve. Amir had warned me once not to make my mother's mantle my mission in life. We were different people, and after all that had transpired, I knew this was true more than I would've liked at times.

But I had a better life, too, that she'd helped to give me—both in my own life, and in giving me Ben as a brother. My mother had never had a brother like him.

I thought of how Amir had passed his dagger onto him. I hoped Ben would be sure not to let himself get caught up in pleasing Amir the way one would please a false and truly faceless idol; but then, Ben had me, too, and now he also had Marguerite, half of Lumiere, and perhaps even Lady Penelope, and most certainly Harshad … there were more of us than ever in our lives.

Perhaps we would never establish Liberté, I thought. But I could rest easy knowing Ben and I were free in a way we never had been before.

892

THE ORDER OF THE CRYSTAL DAGGERS

Now, we only have to keep it that way …

I wiped my eyes with the back of my hand before I straightened my shoulders. "I'll be here if there's a new assignment," I told Harshad.

Harshad nodded. "Your new assignment right now is to recover from the previous one. Pepé and Lumiere and the others are with Louis, who is in chains and under tight guard, and they'll be sailing off in the morning. Everyone needs time, Eleanora."

"Including me."

"Including both of us." He nodded, and then his eyes cleared of their sadness; it was time for us to return to business. "I know you do not wish to work with your grandmother again. For now, until there is a change, I will manage your assignments, and I will be keeping you here in Prague as much as possible."

"I can go other places," I told him. "I'm sure Ferdy won't mind."

"But I do." Harshad clasped his hands together. "As much as you might disagree, you are a princess now, and you have a country as well as a family to oversee. I heard you speak with Franz Joseph the other night in *Vyšehrad*. You agreed to become part of his court."

"But that doesn't really mean anything—"

"Yes, Eleanora, it does," he said, surprising me by his interruption. "Even if the kingdom does not know about you, you should still be here for them. Your beloved Ferdinand belongs here, too."

My heart fluttered; I was grateful Harshad approved of Ferdy.

"One day you might be called away, but this is your home, and you should stay here when you can. You should protect and provide for it as much as you can, for as long as you can."

"At least Louis is on his way to court, and then jail," I said. "He can't do anything too upsetting from where he is now."

"He's always had his contingencies." Harshad frowned. "While Louis did not succeed in starting all the wars he'd planned, he was successful in showing us how weak and divided the people are. He's left a path of destruction in his wake, and if we are not careful to rebuild the good, and create new life where there was only death, he will still win in the end."

I shivered at the thought. "I hope that day never comes."

Louis was not a madman, even if he was ambitious. He'd wanted to orchestrate wars across Europe, all for his own profit, prestige, and amusement. And he was right; Bohemia and other smaller countries were at the mercy of their neighbors' continued benevolence and honor. It wouldn't take much to bring us down, and using our own principles to do so.

"I pray that, too," Harshad agreed with another weary sigh. "But I pray more that if it does come, we will survive and learn to do better. The past is full of blood and tears, and the future is likely to be much of the same. Even if it's different, there will always be poverty and depravity."

"But there will still be good people, too," I said, thinking of Ferdy and Clavan and Amir—and my mother and father, and Harshad and Ben and even myself, and my other friends and associates who would stand up against evil and stand up for truth and justice.

Perhaps I could even include Lady Penelope in that list, but I didn't want to give her any credit; any good she was capable of seemed more like a divine accident than her direct intention.

"Yes." Harshad agreed.

I smiled, looking back at my mother's portrait. "There are reasons to hold on."

"Yes, there are reasons to have hope, despite the temptation to despair. Hope is like happiness in this regard; we see it better when we give it away." He gave me another small smile. "You have learned well, Eleanora."

"I've been taught well."

"I will tell you a secret, Eleanora," Harshad said. "You can have the best teacher and still fail to learn, just as you can show up and make all the right choices and still lose. So it is something special when you do learn, and when what you've learned leads to victory."

"I will try to remember that," I promised. Learning things was hard, but relearning things seemed even more painful. "Thank you."

"You're welcome." He nodded toward the door. "Go and rest now. Louis is taken care of. You have your friend's wedding in a few days, and you should be ready to go."

I was surprised he'd known about Faye's wedding, but I nodded.

But before I left, I gave Harshad another quick hug, surprising him right back.

THE ORDER OF THE CRYSTAL DAGGERS

◊   ◊   ◊   ◊

Hours later, Ferdy and Ben headed out to practice shooting with Didier, and I made my way back to the library again, eager to read a book and escape from reality for a little while.

But when I entered, I saw Harshad was still there, standing by the window, looking outside despondently. He had his hands tucked behind him as he stoically faced the world outside, and inside of one hand was a bright, white scroll with Lady Penelope's signature on it.

I bit my lip before I gave into my curiosity. "What is it?"

Harshad didn't flinch or move. "Louis is gone."

"Gone?" I felt the blood rush out of my head. "You mean, he escaped?"

"No. He is dead. He poisoned himself."

"Was it the silver thallis poison?" When Harshad nodded, I hesitated for only a moment. "Are you sure Lady Penelope or Lumiere aren't responsible?"

"Fairly. He had the poison hidden away in a small packet, sewn into the inside of his jacket."

"Oh. I guess he was the kind of man who would have everything in order."

"His last contingency, and it was a cowardly one." Harshad shook his head.

There wasn't much else I could say.

I couldn't say if Harshad believed Lady Penelope or Lumiere was responsible, but even if he did, I doubted he would tell me. Eventually, silence between us spoke of shared frustration, even if there was firmer foundation for trust.

We stood there, together, facing the known and the unknown before us.

"So at long last, Louis Valoris is gone." Harshad shook his head. "And he managed to escape justice. After all these years and all our losses, he will not endure punishment for his crimes or face the people he has hurt."

I came to stand next to him. "He will have divine condemnation, if not earthly judgment."

"Yes." Harshad nodded grimly. "But I fear the world will face more trouble by his hand now. There's no telling how many of his projects and investments remain active, or how many of his underlings will seek to take his place."

Briefly, I thought of Lady Penelope, telling me about Louis' attempts to steal art from all over Europe, and then I recalled Louis himself telling us about his various investments in war and medicine.

Eventually, I put my hand on Harshad's arm, attempting to comfort him as well as steady myself. "The Order will stand for justice, and it will stand against them, too."

He patted my hand gratefully, and then we both turned and stared out the window for a long time after that, eventually listening to Ferdy and Ben as they argued between taking turns shooting the targets outside.

After a while, I excused myself, forgetting about my books, and headed outside to join them.

The Order was ready to stand against evil, but if we were going to do it effectively and efficiently, I figured it was time I learned how to use a gun properly.

32

◊

An ominous, eerie calmness settled over the house as the next weeks passed. I aimlessly moved through the various routines of my life.

Even with Louis dead, Lady Penelope was off for London with Lumiere, Cecilia, and her traveling company; she seemed to take the bitter fire inside of me along with her, and I once more hated how I was indebted to her in that way.

Harshad had ordered me to recover from my mission, but such a recovery was largely a mystery, one I had to solve all on my own.

Not that I was alone in doing so.

Ferdy seemed quiet and contemplative by his standards, but he still teased me, talked with me, and tenderly held me, and I responded to him in love, patience, and passion.

To help pass the time during the day, Ben offered to work with me on our fighting skills. He was getting much stronger, and said he wouldn't hold back any longer, as long as I didn't either.

Even if I lost, I was just grateful we'd been able to grow back together.

Ben would always be one of my weaknesses, but it was a weakness that would grow smaller over the years, even if my love for my brother would grow deeper into my heart.

He didn't seem to mind losing to me as much, either; Marguerite was there to help take care of him, and it didn't take me long to see she'd been just as diligent in healing his physical injuries as she was in healing the wounds in his heart.

For her part, Marguerite kept her promise; I never saw her step back from Ben's side.

Despite all the things I had to be grateful for, there were still random moments when I only felt numb inside.

I'd never imagined before how nothing could feel so heavy.

Perhaps holding Karl as he died had made some of me die, too.

It was only when I got a new invitation for Faye's wedding that something dead inside me began to stir alive again.

Harshad quickly insisted Ferdy, Ben, Marguerite, and I attend.

He didn't have to work too hard to force us out of the house. Spring was well on its way, and we were eager to leave the house, even if I still had to be discreet about my appearances in the city. Karl's tragic death left me as his widow in Society's narrative, and that meant I was unable to rejoin them. I didn't know if it was a permanent retreat, but I had a feeling things would change once more when I was called to Franz Joseph's court in Vienna.

The worst part of the journey was walking across the Stone Bridge to get there. While I hated thinking of Louis practicing his sketching on the bridge, it was even more irritating since after Karl's passing, a new ordinance had passed, and the Stone Bridge had been renamed as the Charles Bridge.

While it was the anglicized pronunciation of his name, and not quite the honor Karl sought, it was the one he'd received—and unfittingly so. I was glad people ignorantly credited the name to Bohemia's first crowned king instead.

The second worst part of getting to the wedding was passing by the burnt remains of the Cabal.

It was still a long way from reconstruction, but Jarl's Uncle Rhys had purchased a modest townhouse near Market Square, and Faye and Jarl made the official ceremony arrangements with a church nearby.

I felt much better as we walked into the *Kostel Matky Boží před Týnem*, the Church of Týn. Its tall towers reached upward in an effort to touch heaven—a goal that was beyond reach, but not beyond wonder.

"You're here," Faye called out to us.

She was radiant in her lovely cream-colored dress; it complemented the light in her eyes and contrasted with the curls of her hair. She gathered me into a hug, much as she had the last time we'd met, and I could feel her delight.

She was full of joy as she and Jarl finally spoke their vows, and their two souls were knit together, in hopes they would create a new, blessed legacy.

My eyes filled up with tears again, and I was full of wonder and humility. For the last few months, I'd been immersed in a world all about the people and the physical realm in which they existed, and where they died and fell into depravity and disillusionment.

But as I saw Faye and Jarl walk down the aisle as husband and wife, I felt the pull of heaven.

THE ORDER OF THE CRYSTAL DAGGERS

There was another way to see the world from outside of this one, and I only needed to look around me to see it.

Prague was my home, but it was not made of mere walls and lumber, paint and bricks and fabric and gold; it was a city I could see as just that, but I knew it to be so much more.

And just as Prague was more than the physical, so was I, and so was my marriage; it was a home that would be fruitful and multiply, and bring joy into my heart that my soul magnify; and even after all the physical things had passed away, I would be left as mirror for God's graciousness and mercy, a memory that embodied hope and sought to stir it in others.

Ferdy took my hand as we stood and the music rang out from the organ pipes behind us. "I am sorry if you didn't get the wedding you wanted, Ella," he said. "This one was very beautiful."

"It's all right." I smiled up at him as I wiped the tears off my cheeks. "I got the groom I wanted."

"You don't regret anything, then?" he asked. "I was worried you were upset we didn't have a lovely wedding such as this one."

"No, I'm not upset."

"Those are happy tears, then?"

Clavan came up behind us. "Of course they are," he said to Ferdy, while dabbing at the moisture in his own eyes. "For we are free men, and in moments like these, while freedom is found in truth and the struggle for it, we celebrate the victory that is already here, as well as the one to come."

"Is that so?" Ferdy chuckled. "I thought it was just a very nice wedding, with a very happy bride and groom."

I nodded. "After fighting as much as I have, I am glad to celebrate something good."

"As it will be at the final wedding feast in the new heaven," Clavan said. "Much sorrow often lies in waiting for us, and our scars will still stand out brightly on our hearts long after we find rest. But only a free man can weep at the thought of an enslaved one, and only a free man can weep with joy in knowing freedom itself."

He was swept away by the crowd, and soon, I was swept up in the glory and the beauty of everything, too.

899

THE ORDER OF THE CRYSTAL DAGGERS

As the wedding finished and the celebration began, I watched as Helen cheerfully chatted with Eliezer and Zipporah; I danced with Ferdy, I joked with Ben, and I hugged Faye.

As the night went on, I thought of my mother and father, I thought of Amir with Nassara, I thought of all the good and beautiful and true things I had ever known. It was much easier to bear my losses in light of joy, and I found my appetite again.

And at the end of the celebration, I saw goodness, beauty, and truth were still there, even if they were hidden by the world's darkness. Seeing them, and realizing their staying power, I knew that despite my sadness and frustration over the last few weeks, I could go on and I could endure, too.

"Are you ready to go home, *chérie?*" Ferdy asked, taking my hand as it grew late. He was still full of energy and overly cheerful as he called for Ben and Marguerite.

"Yes." I tightened my fingers around his and gave him a kiss on the cheek. I looked at my friends and the beauty around us, and conviction settled deep inside of me.

I had hope.

I would continue on, and I would endure, and I would not do it alone.

In that moment, I was truly loved—and I was truly free.

Epilogue

◊

Vienna, 1875

"Ferdy."

His name was less than a whisper on my lips as I stood beside him, at the back of the grand resting place of Ferdy's family.

At the front altar, the reverend of the Capuchin Church recited the final funeral liturgy of the night.

Ferdy's eyes were fixed forward, his gaze empty and distant. The familiar silver sparkle in his eyes was dimmed by sorrow and tainted by loss.

For a moment, I wondered if he did not hear me, but I knew after the past four years of our lives, his heart was always so well attuned to mine— even if he did not hear me, he would know I was waiting for him.

When he turned to face me a moment later and gave me a half-hearted smile, I could only squeeze his hand in comfort.

"Are you trying to be brave?" I asked.

"I'm not sure." Briefly, his smile curled into a half-smirk, and he leaned over and kissed my forehead. "But if I succeed, it's likely because I have you to inspire me."

"I'm worried for you." I watched the priest as he flicked holy water over the coffin, cleansing it of this world's impurities, even though the stench of death would never leave the body inside.

"My father was a good, honorable man. And he had a good life. He had my mother, and Karl and me, too, even if it was just for a time." Ferdy watched the front of the sanctuary, where the coffin was on display for all to see. "He is with Karl now."

Assuming Karl made it to heaven.

The thought was sharp and clear inside of me, so persistent I barely managed to stop myself from saying it aloud. It spoke to the finest elements of Ferdy's character that he believed Karl to be in heaven, even as it demonstrated the worst of mine.

Ferdy sighed. "You might be worried for me, but I am more worried for my mother. She has already buried one child and lost another. I don't know how hard she is taking the loss of my father."

901

I looked forward and peeked through the various heads of the vast audience before us. In the very front, Empress Maria Anna stood, facing the altar.

"She has not lost you," I said, keeping my tone as kind and quiet as possible.

As if she had heard me, Empress Maria Anna turned her head ever so slightly. The large headdress, covered with a black veil and decorated with more pearls than seemed feasible, wobbled and clinked awkwardly with her movements. She had to be uncomfortable, this time in June, both because of her gown's dark colors and the heavy fabric.

Her outfit made me think of the one Cecilia wore on the day of my father's funeral. Just as before, I felt more than ragged in comparison.

I will need to get some new clothes soon.

I held back a smile, thinking of the horrifying things Lumiere would say at the sight of me. My gown was an older one, made of a deep purple damask and trimmed with black lace, while the stays were currently pulled tightly across my body. I always thought the violet went well with my dagger; I still wore it at my side, tucking it between the hidden slits of my skirts.

The pearls and heavy fabric jostled again, and I looked to see Empress Maria Anna glancing over her shoulder. Her eyes searched the sea of faces in the church as she held her rosary and crucifix.

I held my breath, waiting to see if she would spot us. Even tucked near the back of the crowded sanctuary, I could hear her movements, and I suddenly wondered if she could hear me, too. When she reverted her gaze back to the front of the church, I exhaled in relief.

As much as I was sure King Ferdinand would've been happy to have Ferdy at his funeral, there was no sure way of knowing how the former empress would feel about seeing Ferdy and me.

I could still perfectly remember Karl's dead body lying before her, and I'm sure she could, too.

"Mother." Ferdy's whisper was soft and warm, and I nearly teared up at his pained gentleness.

"Are you going to see her?" It was a question I'd held off on asking Ferdy as we traveled to Vienna from Prague, following behind the king's body on the way to its final resting place.

THE ORDER OF THE CRYSTAL DAGGERS

"I want to," he admitted. "But it might cause problems now. There are many details to attend to when a ruler dies, even a former one. When everything is more settled, I will go and see her."

If she will allow me to see her.

The words were left unspoken, but I heard them nonetheless.

Ferdy had called me kind after watching me at my own father's funeral, and I wish I could believe it after watching him. He was hurting at the loss of his father, and it seemed so wrong that his mother might still turn him away. But he was still so understanding and patient, I wanted to curse the unfairness of the world all over again.

"I am sorry you have to wonder about that at all," I said. "It's all my fault."

"You know after Karl's death my parents rightfully disowned me."

"They still should not have done that," I said, keeping my tone light. I was appalled by his parents' decision, and even in that moment, I would've let Empress Maria Anna know of my displeasure if I had the proper chance.

Ferdy said nothing; he only glanced at me, allowing our eyes to meet for the smallest second before he turned back to face the front.

Karl should not have died, either.

Once more, words passed unspoken between us, and I was grateful I did not have to hear them.

We watched as the casket carrying the king was arranged on a pedestal at the front of the sanctuary.

I studied the altar of the church, awed over the eternal good of God and his providence, and I thought back to those dark hours and lonely moments when I used to look on the city of Prague in the distance from my home.

As I stood beside Ferdy in Vienna's finest church, baptized in the holy atmosphere, I knew I had been too focused on the city instead of the god behind it.

Even if my fairy tale kingdom would one day fall due to the deterioration of its roots and the crippled lines of its imperfect foundation, I knew there was good that would last; all of my life I had known that, even if I had just recently realized it.

Such constancy was built up with truth and everlasting love, and at its beauty, I knew we were not alone in our suffering and sorrow.

I did not like to think of the night Karl died, and I knew Ferdy did not, either. Over the past four years, the memories of Karl's untimely end had faded; Ferdy drowned out my guilt with his lovingkindness and his steadfastness. Every time I had nightmares, he held me and kept me close, keeping true to his promises that he would keep me, and he would keep me safe and only for himself.

I responded in kind, soothing his heartache as much as I could; I was his family, and while I was grateful when my own finally and fully embraced him, I knew Ben's gruff approval and Harshad's acceptance meant less to Ferdy than it did to me.

"Truth be told, I was worried for you, too, Ella," Ferdy murmured quietly. "I did not want this to bring up sad memories of Amir."

Hearing his name was both poignant and painful. I swallowed hard. My nose prickled, and my eyes were suddenly wet with tears at the mention of my friend and mentor.

But a moment later, I shook my head. Amir was home with my mother, and their daughter, too. Maybe he had even met my father and found a way to befriend the man who convinced my mother to give love another chance.

My lips trembled as I tried to give Ferdy my own brave smile. I found it much more difficult than I remembered it being when I was a child. "We have both lost so many."

"Death is an expected part of life." Ferdy wrapped his arm around me, letting his hand rest at my waist. "But I would rather stare down a thousand deaths than face this life without you."

"You should feel fortunate then," I said. "You get to do both, with all the Order does to keep us busy."

A gleam of amusement crept into his eye, and had we been anywhere else, I suspected he might've laughed.

"I have always been lucky when it comes to you," he agreed.

"Is that so? It seems that our rendezvous have only ever caused us more trouble." I glanced at his arm, where Alex had shot him so many years before. Though his formal jacket hid his scar, I could still picture the large, red divot running up his shoulder.

THE ORDER OF THE CRYSTAL DAGGERS

"Still, I have never lost a gamble when it comes to you." He smiled. "I am indeed extraordinarily blessed, far beyond even my luck's capabilities."

It was true that the Order kept us busy, but we were never too busy to love each other in a way that pushed back against the trials we faced.

We lived in a fallen world, but we had also fallen in love, and there was nothing more freeing than finding a home in each other's heart.

I was about to kiss him when I saw it.

A small, distinct glimmer of violet light flashed across the far corner of my eye, and even though it had been years, I stiffened.

"What is it?" Ferdy asked.

"Nothing."

"Ella." He raised his brow. I had spoken too softly and too swiftly, and he knew I was lying. "Tell me."

I gave in reluctantly. While we were risking a scene by coming to Vienna, I did not actually want to engage in one.

"*She's* here," I grumbled, nodding my head toward an alcove at the back of the church.

"Then why don't you go and see her?" His tone was serious, before he gave me a playful smirk. "Maybe on your way to the ladies' withdrawing room to take care of a personal matter?"

Ferdy was trying to lighten the mood with his levity, but I was not inclined to let him do so. "No. I don't want to leave you."

"I'll be fine for the next several moments, while the priest has another round of blessings and the choir has some Latin to recite," Ferdy assured me. "Go. You should talk to her regardless, just as I should talk with my mother."

He was not wrong about that.

"You should also go," he said quietly, "because it is something your mother would want. She would not want your heart to turn to stone all because of the Iron Dowager."

"All right," I agreed bitterly. "I won't be long."

"I'll be here for you when you're finished, *chérie*."

Awkwardly, I shuffled out of the pew. Several others looked at me with half-disapproving stares as I left during the formal prayers for King Ferdinand, but I ignored them.

905

"Eleanora."

I nearly flinched as my estranged grandmother greeted me for the first time in four years.

While her authoritative tone had remained the same during our time apart, I was surprised to see how much the rest of her had changed.

The wrinkles lining her cheeks had increased, both in number and in depth. Her hair seemed to be a shade whiter than the last time, even though her cheeks and eyes were sharper. Her lips were thinner, giving her a more sour expression than I remembered. Her impeccable appearance seemed to be just slightly less so, with her hair bundled up with a wig to give an added layer.

"Lady Penelope." I gave her the smallest curtsy I could manage. "How do you do, Madame?"

"You can drop the act, same as before. I do not need your manners."

"Manners make matters such as this more—"

"More what?" Lady POW raised an eyebrow at me. "More comfortable? Hardly. I'll grant you they can make things more quiet and constrained, but you should be disciplined enough to manage that, even without the manners."

"Why are you here, then?" I asked, allowing my initial sympathy to wane. "I didn't think someone like you would be able to walk on hallowed ground."

At my jab, Lady Penelope smiled. "Good. Much better. Honesty is good between allies."

"I do not like to think of us as allies."

The truth was, I did not like to think of her at all. Even if I still did, and more frequently than I would've liked.

She seemed to sense my weakness in that regard, too, which only made me more disgruntled. "Ah, but we are. There is no denying the truth, no matter how grim and dark it may be."

"Just tell me why you're here."

That time, I saw her hesitate. "I must admit, I am surprised you came over to see me," she said.

"I'm surprised I managed to surprise you," I retorted.

THE ORDER OF THE CRYSTAL DAGGERS

"As you've no doubt already noticed, I'm getting older. It's actually somewhat refreshing, you should know, to find that life can still surprise me—even if it is not always enjoyable." She shrugged. "Old age makes one see things differently from time to time, with death nearing the horizon."

I bit my lip. I did not really want to antagonize her. She was still, after all, my grandmother.

I reached for the comfort and strength my mother's dagger had to offer.

"There is no need for violence," Lady Penelope said quietly. "I am merely here to pay my respects to the king."

"Even if you wanted him killed?"

She pursed her lips into an odd little smile. "Yes. Your husband is right. He was a good man, if a terrible ruler."

I softened, but only slightly. "I am sure Ferdy will agree his father had his faults."

"His favoritism was easily such an example," Lady Penelope agreed. "We might've avoided the whole Karl debacle itself if the king had only bonded with his eldest son. But then, I know from my own observations that terrible parents are not an absolute condemnation for life, even if the likelihood of suffering is more certain."

I noticed that she'd said observations, not experiences, and I might have slapped her for my mother's sake if we were not inside a church.

"I do not want to talk about this with you. I am not sure I want to talk with you at all."

"You don't. I saw Ferdinand push you to come see me." She crossed her arms. "I suppose he really does love you, to know how to manipulate you so."

"Sometimes it is good to be encouraged to do right, just as we need people to dissuade us from doing wrong."

I thought of my mother again.

Ben had told me, after learning more Arabic and deciphering more of her journal, she'd worked with Lumiere's plan to attempt to kill the emperor, and she was the one who convinced my father to go save him during the Spring Revolution.

THE ORDER OF THE CRYSTAL DAGGERS

So much of fate was a tangle. It was not unlike freedom, in that so much of it relied on so many other elements; between the timing, the indomitability of the human will, and the tendency of nature toward self-destruction, I was unable to believe fate was merely a sequence of coincidences.

It was indeed something greater, something so much greater, than I could fully contemplate—greater than my sadness, greater than my joy.

"I suppose you are correct," Lady Penelope said. "But no matter. To business, then."

"To business?"

"Whether or not you want to believe it, I have missed you, Eleanora."

My heart stung with hidden pain. I did not want to admit that I'd missed her, too, over the past several years.

Working with the Order, coordinating messages to Harshad and Lumiere and several others now, tracking down hostages and villains, recovering missing items, and gathering information—all of it was much less exciting than my first mission, even if it was safer than going after assassins and traitors.

Reporting on it to Franz Joseph was equally as cumbersome now, too.

Lady POW had once said she would never understand my generation's obsession with bureaucracy, and I was finally old enough and experienced enough I could agree.

"Her Majesty Queen Victoria has given me and Harshad another mission," Lady Penelope said. "You must know Her Majesty is greatly concerned with her new country."

"Yes, the Empress of India," I murmured, recalling the news with a nod. Just last month, Queen Victoria had been given the title, and it would be made official at the start of the coming year. "It seems while your mission to stabilize this region was a success, India still did not make it on its own."

"It will improve," Lady Penelope said. "Her Majesty has requested Harshad and I step in."

I did not believe for one moment that "stepping in" was all that was required to help a country.

But I did not question it.

THE ORDER OF THE CRYSTAL DAGGERS

I'd learned sometimes it was better not to ask questions, especially in matters involving my grandmother.

"I came here because I wanted to see if you and Ferdinand would come with us. We could use Ferdy's charm and your beauty as a cover," Lady Penelope said. "I know Lumiere has agreed to stay in Prague while you are here in Vienna. Why not just ask him to keep up the good work? I'm sure Didier wouldn't mind. He's become quite the beer enthusiast of late."

"He is enjoying his membership to the Cabal, now that it has been rebuilt," I agreed. "But … "

In that moment, I hated how hard it was to still hate her. Lady Penelope, while she had added significantly to my mother's misery and Amir's, not to mention my own, had never been my true enemy.

It was almost too painful to acknowledge that. I felt a gnawing pit in my stomach as I realized I still did not want to disappoint her.

But I also knew I was going to do just that.

She pursed her lips again, this time more tightly, in that surly way she had. "You're not going to say yes, are you?"

"No. Not today." I clasped my hands in front of me.

"No apology, either?" Lady Penelope nodded. "Good."

This time, I didn't stop my smile. I enjoyed earning her approval, even if I no longer needed it.

"It has been nice seeing you again, Eleanora. Perhaps we can do it again in the future."

Lady Penelope nodded curtly and then walked past me. I could feel the tension increase at our nearness.

She was the one who taught me that everyone had secrets and everyone lied.

But there were so many other things I'd learned, and as I stood there, watching her pass me, I thought of the many unspoken dreams and wishes of every human heart.

Ferdy showed me that everyone kept secrets, even from themselves; Ben had taught me everyone had pain, secret or not; Harshad taught me that learning often required failure; and Amir was the one who taught me that everyone carried regrets, sometimes throughout our lives.

909

And I was a better person, and more of myself, both because of and in spite of Lady Penelope, too.

I took a deep breath. "Wait."

Lady Penelope glanced over her shoulder. "What is it, Eleanora? Feeling sentimental? It's not a good feature for a spy."

"I am more than a spy. Just as you are more than a spymaster."

She blinked, and I knew I caught her off guard with the truth.

"You are also my grandmother," I continued. "So before you go, I have two things for you."

"Is that so?" Lady Penelope's lips curled in false amusement, and I wondered if she was thinking of the night of the Advent Ball as she glanced at my dagger.

"Yes," I said. "My gifts may not be as meaningful as my mother's dagger, or as practical as your … special instructions. But I'd like to give them nevertheless."

"I appreciate your candor and bravery." Lady POW arched her brow, wryly amused.

Her mockery was a little infuriating. I could've used the time to satisfy all the rage and hurt inside of me I'd carried since our last meeting, and she was entertained to see me rise above my baser emotions.

I stood, reconsidering my intent, but I remembered how Lady Penelope had pulled out my mother's dagger.

She'd offered me freedom—freedom from servanthood—and gave me the tools I needed to find truth and fight against doubt. I had embraced her gifts, with all the blessings and burdens that came with them.

With the truth, I had a way to reach my mother—and embrace her, as a real person rather than a wraith of a memory.

But with her, I had embraced the past, and the past was gone. It had taken me a long time to forgive myself for Karl's death—and it was possible I would still need to forgive myself again in the future. But I would have to find a new way forward if I was going to honor my mother's legacy.

There was no freedom in being trapped in the past.

Louis had conspired against many nations, Xiana had been the one who had poisoned my mother, making her miscarry Nassara, and Tulia had been the one responsible for my father's death. I believed justice had been done where it could be, and I felt no need to hold their sins against them—at least, not to the degree I felt compelled to do so with my grandmother.

But I would not honor the hate I had inside of me. It was time to lay it down and let it go.

I blinked back the sudden rush of tears and clenched my fingers around the hilt of my dagger.

This was what Amir had told me all those years ago, as we stood together in the church where I'd married Ferdy. He'd told me that freedom had its limits, both from the outside and from within.

I had not known exactly what he'd meant, but I did now.

Amir had always been the better one between us; even now he was still teaching me. He had never let his own desires or delusions enslave him. He carried his disappointments in his heart and learned from them, never letting go of the beauty of my mother's memory as he clung to his faith, hoping above all else he would see her again.

"The first gift I have for you," I said to Lady POW through gritted teeth, "is my forgiveness."

She did not move as she continued staring at me; it was hard to determine if what I said had any effect on her at all.

I swallowed hard, trying to keep myself composed, even as there was nothing I wanted more than to fall to my knees and weep.

I was truly free in that moment, as the last of the poison in my heart against her was uprooted.

I'd needed to forgive her, just as I'd needed to forgive myself.

It wasn't enough to move on and keep carrying a burden I was trying to ignore.

"I hated you for so long for what happened before. But I know you are a woman of freedom. If liberty is the power to do what we ought to do, we can still fail to honor that power. When we met, you said there was a cost to knowing the truth. I didn't see it then, but I do now. And I know now that you and I will continue paying for that price for the rest of our lives."

The amusement in her eyes faded. "Yes," she agreed. "We will pay for it."

"I refuse to let unforgiveness rob me of even more of my life."

911

"A wise move," she intoned blandly.

I decided to hold back in reminding her about the church's teachings on the matter; she was not responding to me, and I did not think she would willingly reply to God either.

But after a moment passed between us, she cleared her throat, and I wondered if God had not spoken to her himself anyway.

"Amir taught you well, didn't he?" Lady Penelope whispered. Her voice was steady, but I saw she was struggling to remain composed. "You know, when he died, he asked me to forgive him."

I thought of that moment, before Amir had turned to Ben and me, when he'd whispered something to Lady POW.

She gave me another bitter smile. "But it was I who should have been asking for his forgiveness, wasn't it?"

"Yes." I almost smiled when she blinked; she had not expected me to reply aloud. "Yes, Amir did teach me well."

She rolled her eyes.

"The second gift I have for you is much like the first one," I said, changing the subject. "I wanted to tell you that you were wrong."

She laughed mirthlessly. "Oh, is that it? What was I wrong about?"

"You were wrong about how this will end. You said before that life as a spy would only end in death or defeat. You may be partially right. No one is getting out of this life alive. But my mother is proof that you were wrong, and I am now proof, too."

"You are quitting the Order?" She raised her brow in surprise. "I figured you wouldn't want to go to India, but I didn't think you'd let go of your mother's legacy."

"No, it's not that." I shook my head. "My mother quit, and she lived. She found my father, and found love, even if it was not the yearning she felt for another. She had Ben and me, and Tulia came back to her, too. She spent the last years of her life building a new one—even to the extent she wanted to see you again. And she was right to do that."

"Is that so? Not biased at all, are you?"

I ignored the sharp retort. "It does us no good to let the kingdoms around us burn down. We might start the fire and celebrate the sight of the ashes, but we will never truly live if we don't build up the good. So I choose freedom, which is only possible with truth and goodness, and I choose to build up a better future."

I paused for a long moment before I added, "Starting with my own children."

Silence fell between us as her eyes squinted at my midsection more carefully.

"Well, well … I suppose congratulations are in order," Lady Penelope said quietly. "And here I just thought you were getting fat."

The slight bulge was barely noticeable behind the dark colors of my gown, even if the fabric was drawn tight across my breasts and hips, but the proof of my growing baby was getting harder to hide every week.

I bit down on the inside of my cheek as I placed a hand on my stomach.

It was not easy to tell her the truth. Originally, I didn't want her to know about my offspring at all, but I remembered too clearly the night that she found out the truth about me.

I would not repeat my mother's choices, even if I truly understood them.

"I suppose I am getting old," Lady Penelope murmured, "if you are four months along and I did not realize it sooner. But then, I did see that your husband is still quite relentlessly cheerful, even at his father's funeral."

"Yes." I blushed, still unnerved by her bluntness after all these years. "Ferdy is quite excited about being a father."

I did not want to hide the truth, but I did not see a reason to tell her about his announcement to the Cabal, his staggering kisses as he told me he could not wait to meet his son or daughter, or how he promised to get started on a list of names and decorate a nursery.

"So, you say I am wrong." Lady Penelope shrugged. "In the end, maybe that is a good thing. I was sure you would give me your mother's dagger back."

"It is my dagger now, Madame."

And it was true. I felt a new bond with my weapon as I let the last piece of vengeance for my mother leave my heart.

THE ORDER OF THE CRYSTAL DAGGERS

Maybe that was the real reason I wanted nothing to do with Lady Penelope in the end. Forgiving her fulfilled my mother's last mission, and I did not want to say goodbye to *Máma* again.

But I knew *Máma* had never really left, either. She was with me, in me, and part of me. And what she'd left me, I would assess what was good, repair what had been damaged, and build on a new legacy for my own children one day.

After all, the legacy we inherit is not the one we have to leave behind.

"We can fight in other ways besides maintaining the status quo and protecting royals and statesmen," I said. "There is more to the Order's calling than to protect the present. We must prepare those who come after us, too."

"You are a wise young lady, Eleanora. You should know I am proud to call you my family, even if I have not earned that right." She cleared her throat. "Harshad and I will be leaving in a few hours for Delhi. Any message you would like to pass along to him? I'm sure he would be concerned to hear how pudgy you're getting, but at least you have a valid excuse."

"Give Harshad my best. He deserves it, that poor man, working with you."

"He will need it," Lady Penelope agreed. She paused for a moment; I could see her mind weighing her options, and I knew the instant she made her decision. "We have decided to marry."

My mouth dropped open in shock, before I quickly composed myself. "I assume because it is good for the mission?"

"Well, yes."

It was a little disappointing to see her swift agreement, but then I saw her smile—a real, genuine smile of happiness, one I had rarely, if ever, seen before.

I smiled back. "And because it is good for you, too?"

"Yes." She nodded and then actually laughed, letting the almost musical sound ring through the church alcove. "It seems you were right about things like love, Eleanora. Life is full of loss, but you can't lose what you never claim to have in the first place."

I nodded. "That is what *Máma* would want."

"She always called him 'Uncle,'" Lady Penelope said softly. She looked at me, and then past me; and then she nodded. "Eleanor loved him as much as her own *Táta*."

914

THE ORDER OF THE CRYSTAL DAGGERS

"Then please don't give Harshad a reason to regret his decision."

"I will have to do my best, and he'll have to accept that my best is not good enough some days," she said, waving the matter aside. "Perhaps we will see you on our way back to London, whenever the Queen calls us to return. Your son should be here by then."

"How do you know it's a boy?" My fingers tightened on my belly, protective and full of awe at the thought of Ferdy's son.

Would he have silver eyes like his father? That irreverent smirk, the pointed nose? Would he get my ebony curls, or Ferdy's wispy, copper-colored locks?

Lady Penelope smirked. "I told you a long time ago, Eleanora. You have good birthing hips. It'll be a boy."

I flushed over, half pleased and half embarrassed.

"Oh, come now. It's close enough to Christmas that he'll make a nice gift for Ferdinand. And Benedict will enjoy having a new pupil to teach when he gets back from Paris; after all, Harshad is getting older, too."

"Have you heard from Ben?" I asked.

"Yes." She smiled. "Marguerite still writes to me quite often."

"Their third anniversary is next month."

"I haven't forgotten." Lady POW lifted her skirts to show me the uneven hem of her underskirt. "How could I? I'm still looking for a seamstress with her level of talent. I know Betsy and Mavis are your friends, Eleanora, but as her replacements, they have been quite a disappointment."

I was tempted to argue with her, again, but outside the alcove, the music began to swell.

"They're almost finished with the service," Lady Penelope said. "You'd better get back to your husband. Assuming you don't actually need to use the ladies' withdrawing room?"

"Goodbye, Lady Penelope." I ignored her taunt and gave her another small curtsy. "I wish you all the best for your work in India."

She pursed her lips and then nodded. "All right. Farewell, Eleanora. For now."

She reached out her hand toward me; after only a moment, I reached out and took it.

THE ORDER OF THE CRYSTAL DAGGERS

We clasped each other tightly, knowing we were family, and we would continue working on building up the trust between us. No matter how slowly, progress was progress. With one hand, I held onto her, and with the other, I put my hand over my growing child.

And then we let go.

I watched as she walked away from me.

I kept my eye on her as she slipped into the main sanctuary. In the second I blinked, she managed to slide out of the church through one of the side doors.

And then she was gone.

For now.

I gripped my dagger at my side with one hand, pressing my other hand protectively against my stomach, unable to stop myself from smiling.

Even Lady Penelope was capable of change. There was truly hope to be had in this world after all.

My steps were quiet as I made my way back to Ferdy's side.

"Ella?" he whispered as he took my hand. "I'm here. Everything will be all right."

"Are you sure?" My voice was quiet and shaky, but I already felt a little better.

There would be trouble ahead. There would be sad days and lost battles and fearful nights. Such were the risks and realities of life and freedom. Yet I had survived everything life had brought me so far—and I wouldn't face the rest of it alone.

"Of course it will." Ferdy gave me a small grin. "We're going to live happily ever after."

"Oh?" I gave him a playful smirk. "How do you know?"

"Clavan once said that if you want proof that something is true, you only have to see how your joy is multiplied over time. There is no need to keep lying if there is joy." He reached down between us, letting his hand rest on my stomach. "And there is no greater joy I have than the joy I've found here with you."

Our baby—perhaps our son?—wriggled underneath Ferdy's touch, as if to prove his words true.

THE ORDER OF THE CRYSTAL DAGGERS

A new kind of wonder lit up in Ferdy's eyes as the church around us glowed with peace. My soul was never more firmly anchored at the foot of the cross as I stood there, caught between heaven and hell, life and death, between the past, present, and future.

"Clavan always seems to have the right answers," I said, smiling brightly, and happy tears swelled up in my eyes. I put my hand on top of his. "Lady Penelope says he'll be a boy."

"I'm glad," Ferdy said. "We won't have to wonder about naming him after her, then."

We shared a soft laugh. I looked back up at the altar, and then back at Ferdy. "I think I'd like to name him Nicholas."

My baby moved inside of me again, a small little flutter that echoed with the same hope and fear inside my heart.

"He seems to like it," Ferdy agreed. "As he should. He is our gift of wonder."

"Yes." I smiled at the thought of my son. Did he already know how much he was mine? How much I loved him, and what I would do to keep him safe?

My stomach lurched at the thought; all of my choices in the last several weeks—from traveling out to Vienna, to wearing restrictive clothing, to sleeping on my side—all of them came rushing at me, and I gripped my stomach, suddenly more afraid than I had ever been in my life.

"I love you." I opened my arms and fully embraced Ferdy, drawing his lips down onto mine.

It was the wrong time, the wrong place, and I knew we were going to get evil looks from any pearl-clutching spectators.

But I loved him. I wanted him, I needed him, I loved him.

And I loved him so much.

"Ella." Ferdy gripped me close. He knew as I did that we both wanted comfort, standing there in the ornate church, surrounded by the pain and the memories and the path we carried and the ones we wound not escape. "I love you. And you can bet on that."

"Is that so?" I asked, already knowing what his answer would be as I wiped the tears out of my eyes.

He grinned. "*Absolument.*"

C. S. Johnson is the award-winning, genre-hopping author of several young adult sci-fi and fantasy novels, including *The Starlight Chronicles* series, the *Once Upon a Princess* saga, and the *Divine Space Pirates* trilogy. With a gift for sarcasm and an apologetic heart, she currently lives in Atlanta with her family.

AUTHOR'S NOTE

Dear Reader,

If you're like me, there is always something a little bittersweet about coming to the end of a book series. I have traveled many roads and dreamed so many possibilities for my characters, so when we have come to the end of our time together, to the point where the dreaming must continue on without me, I always feel a little bereft. I am greatly comforted in knowing that you are the ones who continue on with them, and I know if you've read this far, they are in good hands. Thankfully, too, in this case, I am sure Ella and Ferdy, and all the others, have more than enough determination to survive if they so choose.

But in this case, I feel there is more of a sense of "finality for now" with this series. When I started these books, I was partially inspired to write this series, as some of you know, because I had heard Nabeel Qureshi, a favorite, beloved author of mine, had been diagnosed with stomach cancer. I was absolutely devastated by his death, believing as I had that he would be healed and allowed to continue his life here on earth as a testimony to God's healing and mercy. Before I could publish the first book, he had passed on.

I mourned for quite some time. It is only as I write this that I can smile at the thought of him in heaven. His voice, along with many others, have lent their insights into this series, and now I can really only continue on in my grief and joy. Both life and death have marked me, and now I rejoice as much as I grieve; and I must smile even more, because paradoxes are not the same as contradictions, after all.

I will be alright, but I will never be the same.

But for now, I must go on. I take great comfort in knowing I must go on, and that I am not alone.

In keeping with this, in this last book of the series, I wanted to tackle the question of freedom, and I always enjoy getting to see what I learn along the way as much as I enjoy the story. There is so much that goes into this book, and I am not apologetic in the slightest how it has a lot to offer for the one who is seeking for it. Life is full of surprises and questions, and there are complicated questions that can only require complicated answers.

For this book, I wanted to take a look at maintaining freedom. With its dependency on so much—both personal and universal aspects of morality, goodness, and perhaps especially identity—I wanted to see what it would take to not only secure it, but to keep it, and to keep ourselves from letting it slip away. The only way to do this is with power, love, and goodness; power without love is corrosive to the human heart, and

THE ORDER OF THE CRYSTAL DAGGERS

goodness without love is feeling without meaning, and love cannot exist in its purest form without goodness.

I feel this is the same way about friends sometimes; it is easy to want friends, but harder to become friends, and sometimes, harder still to keep them.

While I heavily favor literary aspects, I am not a complete plot-hater, either, and I also wanted to bring up elements of forgiveness, hope, and fear. The trick is in the title, as always, because hope is both a gift and something to be born, and fear is grounded in respect for power, but only the fear of the Lord can be seen as the beginning of wisdom. This is reflected in the hero's journey, as the character's life includes innocence, trust—sometimes false trust—and wisdom.

That is where the paradox of freedom is. It gives power, but requires power, too, including the power (and goodness) to constrain itself.

We must be like Ella when it comes to such things as freedom, faith, and friendship: Determined, resolved, and intentional—and humble or hapless enough to lay down our arms when the battle we are fighting turns out to be one that is destroying us. We may not be armed with a crystal dagger at our side, but we can carry so much power in our hearts through love and truth; it is really only truth that can link hope and fear and allow for true love to shine through.

Before you go, I have promised my most ardent fans to let you know that Amir is perfectly content with his fate, and that, to me at least, he is in story heaven with Naděžda, Nassara, and even Dolf is laughing with him as they celebrate the strange overlappings of their lives.

If you've enjoyed this book, I hope you will take a look at my other work, to come and find me again, and let me entertain you; I tend to genre-hop but I can promise you, my Shakespearean-Machiavellian-Khardashian influences all run through my stories, juxtaposing character with complicated fun, mixing the wisdom with the winsome and wonderous.

My books are not just words on a page or stories from inside; they are a piece of my heart, full of blood and sweat and tears, restless nights and ceaseless prayers, and so many words beyond all possible words. And with that, I can only thank you for the gift of your time. It truly is appreciated.

Until We Meet Again,

C. S. Johnson

THE ORDER OF THE CRYSTAL DAGGERS

P. S. If you do not know Jesus as your Lord and Savior, I pray that you will seek him and that you will find him. Death is a stark reality, a perpetual shadow on our souls. Many people object to religion, and several times, I have found their reasonings to be understandable, especially when we talk of religious people. But I do think Jesus himself should be taken more than seriously and I know he welcomes such scrutiny, especially if a relationship with you is the final prize. Risking your heart and pride is a great price, but the prize is more than worth the while. So in this regard, I hope you have yourself a bit of a gamble, as Ferdy might say.

Also: If you've enjoyed this series, look for the second companion novella to The Order of the Crystal Daggers, *City of Light and Sun*. It's a short novella featuring Ben and Marguerite on a new mission together in Paris.

922

THE ORDER OF THE CRYSTAL DAGGERS

AUTHOR'S ACKNOWLEDGEMENTS

EDITOR

Jennifer C. Sell

Jennifer Clark Sell is a professional book editor and proofreader. She works from her home in Southern California. With her years of professional and personal experience, she offers several quality packages for authors. Find her at https://www.facebook.com/JenniferSellEditingService.

Photo Credit: Savannah Sell

C. S. JOHNSON

AUTHOR'S ACKNOWLEDGEMENTS

COVER ILLUSTRATOR

Amalia Chitulescu

Amalia Iuliana Chitulescu is a digital artist from Campina, Romania. Raised in a small town, this self-taught artist has a technique which is delineated by the contrast between obscurity and enlightenment, using dark elements in a dreamy world. Her areas of expertise include the use of theatrical concepts to create a macabre and surrealistic world that still maintains a highly recognizable attachment to reality. Bridging a diaphanous environment with light elements, an eerie view, she creates a dream world of dark beauty, done with a blend of photography and digital painting. Find her at <u>https://www.facebook.com/Amalia.Chitulescu.Digital.Art</u>

Photo Credit: Amalia Chitulescu

CITY

OF

LIGHT AND SUN

A COMPANION NOVELLA TO

THE ORDER OF THE CRYSTAL DAGGERS

◊   ◊   ◊   ◊

C. S. Johnson

1st Edition.
eBook ISBN: 978-1-948464-69-7
Paperback ISBN: 978-1-948464-70-3
Hardback ISBN: 978-1-948464-71-0

AUTHOR'S QUICK NOTE:

This book is set after the story and before the epilogue in *Heart of Hope and Fear*, Book 3 of The Order of the Crystal Daggers, but it can be read as a standalone adventure for Ben and Marguerite.

This book is first dedicated to Sam. It might be tradition at this point, but the point is still there, and I still know why it's there, too.

Second, this book is for my dear friend Kevin, and his soon-to-be-wife, Laura! *Cảm ơn,* for the help with the translation work, *ban.*

Finally, this book is also dedicated to all the people who, like me, where unwilling to let the series go without one last huzzah: Terri, Laura, Gay, Anne, Pat-Charis, William, Jennifer, and Cathy, Rebecca, Priscila, Darla, Donna, Rebecca B., Priscila, Tina, and Carla, and Anne.

THE ORDER OF THE CRYSTAL DAGGERS

THE ORDER OF THE CRYSTAL DAGGERS

1

◊

Paris, 1874

"Ben."

It was always an exceptional case when I failed to hear Marguerite calling for me. In the short years since we'd met, my wife's voice had become a necessary sound to my world; it was music to my soul, a bulwark against all the darkness and pain in the world as much as it was a foretaste of heavenly pleasure.

I did not ignore it lightly.

But at just that moment, I found myself in the middle of a grand Parisian bookshop, and my attention was understandably divided. I glanced upward, scanning the high, wooden shelves around me, and gazing at the upper levels of bookcases, all housed underneath a high vaulted ceiling. After days traveling at sea, it was not only the books that captivated and steadied me.

Standing there, I was transfixed by a ghostly, otherworldly sense, one full of certainty and strength.

I closed my eyes and let the wonder wash over me.

Somehow, unexplainably, I knew my mother had once been in this shop.

Máma.

My mother had been lost at sea when I was just a boy. Since then, I clung to what I could remember of her.

I could picture her in my mind, with her hair long and dark, smooth and straight. Against fashion and convention, she'd often worn it down, letting it frame her face and fall behind her. I could see her eyes, blue as the sky, as they clouded over with secrets.

I never quite knew what she was thinking, but never did I question her love for me—or her love for my sister, Ella, or her love for my father. It was a constant light, hovering over us, all throughout our time together. After she died, that essence remained, its presence as real and certain as her absence.

She loved us with that same, supernatural assurance I felt standing in the small, cluttered bookshop.

I opened my eyes, both elevated and deflated; it was though I'd been welcomed home, only to find myself more homesick than ever.

I bit back a sigh. I'd lost more than my mother when she died.

"Ben."

Marguerite tugged on my sleeve, and I turned to face her.

Despite my mood, I gave her a small smile. There was a poetic symmetry in her delicacy, one that contrasted sharply with her assertive nose, her green-glittered eyes, and her loose, persistent blonde curls. She was in many ways the perfect counterpart for me; she had optimism to battle my cynicism, and sweetness to balance out my surliness.

"What is it?" I asked.

"Is this the one you were looking for?" She held out a copy of *Morte d'Arthur*, and the familiarity of the bright scarlet cover immediately caught my attention.

At once, an old memory came to mind.

I could see the same book in *Máma*'s hand as she pleaded with *Otec* to read it aloud to the rest of us. Cheerfully, as much as reluctantly, he read at her insistence, ruffling his mustache as he flipped through the pages. I sat in *Máma*'s lap as Ella squirmed in front of us on the library floor.

After *Máma* died, *Otec*'s approval of me seemed to die along with her. He no longer read much, except when Ella asked. He never willingly denied my mother anything, and Ella looked so much like her, I imagined the habit was too hard for him to break.

And after I broke my leg, leaving me with a permanent limp, what had been broken between me and my father further shattered into dust.

Still, as Marguerite pressed the book into my hands, I touched the leather cover reverently. Taking a deep breath, I opened it up, and there, inside the back cover, was my father's firm penmanship.

"To Benedict, who I am proud—"

I exhaled sharply.

A new layer of stitching had been added to the cover, likely in the last year or two. The lining's small little strips of thread obscured the rest of the inscription, although I could still recite the words by heart:

"to call my son. May the blessings of strength, wisdom, and courage follow you throughout life. Your Father, Adolf Svoboda."

THE ORDER OF THE CRYSTAL DAGGERS

The dedication was brief before it was cut off, and then, the pain of the past was covered and tended to by others' hands; *Otec* and his affection for me had suffered a similar fate. In the end, it was disappointing, but also fitting.

Marguerite cleared her throat behind me. "Is it the right one?"

"This is it." I nodded, both grateful and conflicted by its rediscovery. "This is the one I promised my sister I would find."

"Wonderful." Marguerite's smile lit up like the sun. "Nora will be so happy. And Ferdy will be glad, too."

"I suppose." My jaw tightened at the mention of my brother-in-law. In one of his rare moments of blunt, unrehearsed honesty, he'd confessed to becoming enchanted with my sister the day we had to sell this particular book. At that memory, a small amount of petty pleasure washed over me; I was happy that I'd found it before he had. "It's something unexpected, that's for sure."

"Can you really expect the unexpected?" Marguerite gave me a flirtatious look.

She was pleased, too, for having pleased me, and her selflessness made me feel even more petty.

"If you've taught me nothing else, it's to be more prepared for life's surprises."

"Surely that's not the only thing I've taught you?" Marguerite gave me a playful wink.

Discretely, I glanced around. We were hidden by the surrounding bookcases, so I leaned forward and brushed a quick kiss across her lips, watching as Marguerite's eyes lit up with pleasure.

The taste of her was minimal and fleeting, but I was both nourished and left wanting more.

Marguerite always enjoyed it when I flirted with her, even if I didn't do it often, especially in public.

She gave me a brilliant smile. "Nora would approve."

"It's not her approval I seek."

"Ah, so it's Ferdy's you look for, then?" Marguerite ran her hands down my cheeks coyishly. "His beard is getting quite thick, too, now that I think of it."

THE ORDER OF THE CRYSTAL DAGGERS

I wrinkled my nose, but didn't say anything in reply as I caught sight of the *Wahabite Jambiya* at my side.

There was no man alive whose approval I sought, but I did want to honor the man who'd given his life and happiness to save my family.

At my sudden sadness, Marguerite laid her lily hand on mine. "My apologies for your pain, *mon amour.*"

"There's no need to apologize." I struggled to keep my tone light. Years of working with Lady Penelope had made Marguerite more intuitive than I would've liked. "Honoring Amir means I must remember him. And … well, he was the closest thing I've had to a father in years," I said softly. "I miss that."

"I know," Marguerite said. "But he is beyond pain now, and I am here to attend to yours."

I frowned. "Lady Penelope didn't assign you to come with me so you could take care of me."

"That is true." Marguerite kept her tone light, too, but underneath her pleasant tone, her patience was dwindling. "But she wouldn't be able to stop me from doing so, either."

There was nothing I could say at her familiar words.

Instead, I glanced around, pretending to look for my stepsister. "Where's Priscilla?"

"Prissy said she would join us at the front of the shop." Marguerite gestured toward the bookcases around us. "She told me she wanted to purchase a few new novels."

I'd never cared for Prissy much, but I was actually glad she had come with us. Once she was established as an apprentice seamstress under Marguerite's sister, Priscilla would have a new home, one free of her pernicious mother. To me, it seemed like an odd, unsavory fate for my long-pampered stepsister, but she was excited to be on her own, and she'd embraced the chance to live in Paris.

"What about your sister?" I asked. "Aren't we supposed to meet her soon?"

"Yes, but not until three o'clock. We have a little time yet." Marguerite gazed outside a nearby window, and I saw the worry in her eyes. "Paris is surprisingly lovely right now, and Madame Phénix's shop is blooming with service, no doubt."

THE ORDER OF THE CRYSTAL DAGGERS

I knew of her past, just as she knew of mine, but neither of us enjoyed discussing such topics if we could avoid it. There were a number of reasons Marguerite had wanted to leave Paris and travel abroad with Lady Penelope.

"Were you worried about coming back here?"

She paused as she pursed her lips. "A little."

"Just a little?" I asked, trying to be gentle.

"I was not sure about the political clime. It has only been a year since Napoleon III died," she murmured noncommittally. "Lumiere had mentioned how displeased he was over the matter."

"I assumed Lumiere meant that his father would be upset, not that he was himself." I wrinkled my nose at the mention of Lumiere. Ella had a soft spot for that grating, overly self-absorbed degenerate, but at best, I only saw him as an unreliable ally. "Maybe Lumiere was just angry Napoleon was allowed to live after being dethroned. He would see it as a missed opportunity for a good beheading."

"I'm not so sure."

"Well, it is Lumiere we're talking about. Nothing is ever certain when it concerns him."

"True." Marguerite gave me an amused smile. "But he was quite certain that Napoleon was going to shape France's future."

"If he was, it's hard to imagine how it would be better than it is now," I said, gesturing toward the window again.

Outside, the city bustled with energy. After docking at the Port of Paris this morning, we had seen ladies in their bright walking dresses and men sauntering down the streets with hopeful steps. Horses and carriages jostled over the cobblestones, while merchants busily sold their goods. Even common workers seemed full of enthusiasm as we made our way through the shopping district.

"Perhaps you are right," Marguerite said.

"Well, perhaps I'm wrong." I studied the scene before us with new eyes, worried I'd missed something, and that I'd only been too eager to see what was good. "We both know things aren't always what they seem."

"Oh, Ben, please. Harshad and Lady Penelope both said this would be a simple mission."

"If it's just a simple mission, then you should've stayed home."

THE ORDER OF THE CRYSTAL DAGGERS

The instant I spoke the words, I knew I shouldn't have said them at all.

"That's not fair." Marguerite's objection was both swift and full of hurt. "I'm always left at home when you go somewhere."

"It's not like I travel frequently—"

"There was that delivery you made to Brussels two years ago, and you went with Nora to Vienna to report to Franz Joseph, and then you escorted an ambassador to Prussia … " Marguerite counted off my past assignments on her fingers. "Last winter, you were in Berlin for an extra month."

"That one wasn't my fault," I argued. "The snow—"

"That's not my point." Marguerite turned away from me. "You regularly leave me behind. Perhaps you don't realize this, but waiting for you to come home is actually quite tiresome. And though I love your sister, it is vexing to watch her cling to Ferdy so much. I'm convinced he likes having you home since it gives him a break from all her attention."

"I doubt that." I held back a groan, thinking of all the times I'd caught them stealing away to indulge in their passionate embraces. "He's happy to keep her within his reach when I'm home, too."

"Then they're probably happy I'm here so they can be together more." Marguerite crossed her arms over her chest. "Nora's delighted to have her library project, too."

"She would be," I agreed.

Before his death, Amir had mentioned my mother would make notes along the margins of various books as she read. In between her own work for Franz Joseph and the Order, Ella had started going through the manor's library. She'd made slow progress over the years, but considering how slowly I made my own way through *Máma*'s journal, I could understand. There was a trepidation that accompanied the anticipation as we worked, and our reactions ranged from wonder to despair to confusion after all we'd learned about our mother since Lady Penelope and the others had entered our lives.

Thinking of *Máma* reminded me of how sad she'd been when *Otec* would leave. Eventually, she'd had Ella and me to keep her company, but I knew it wasn't enough for her.

I looked down at the book in my hands again and sighed. "I'm sorry for what I said. I am glad you're here with me."

She arched her brow at me, unmoved by my apology, even though it was a rare occurrence between us.

"Please, Marguerite." I bit back a groan. Marguerite was one of the few people with whom I could be vulnerable, but that didn't mean I did it often, and that didn't mean I enjoyed it. "I've lost a lot of people in my life. And I … I can't bear the thought of losing you, too."

"I'm not as frail as you seem to think I am."

"*I* am."

"No, you're not—" Marguerite glanced down at my crooked leg, looking horrified. "I've told you before you're not frail because of your leg."

"No, not that." I stopped myself from rolling my eyes. It was exactly that sort of reason I didn't like to say anything; pity, whether it was my own or someone else's, never did any good. "I'm used to the pain in my leg. I meant I don't like risking your safety or your discomfort."

Marguerite softened. "I can handle the danger and the discomfort."

"I know. But I still don't like it," I grumbled. "And, I don't want to fail the Order, either."

"There's no need to worry about the Order," Marguerite said gently. "Amir and Harshad have taught you well. Lady Penelope has mentioned she would like you to take on more duties."

"I have plenty of duties."

"She'd like you train some new recruits. Lady Penelope and Harshad aren't getting any younger, and you would make a good mentor."

"Well, I don't know about that, but I still don't want to be caught off guard." I paused meaningfully, as she'd just proved my point. "And you do have a way of bringing about the unexpected."

"I do not see you as someone who would step back from a challenge, nor shirk your responsibilities, *mon amour*, even if I am around and making it more difficult for you." Marguerite leaned over and placed a small kiss on my cheek. "If that's all that worries you, then we have nothing to worry about. I trust you, and others do, too."

There was something depressingly familiar about the determined twinkle in her eyes. "Have you been taking lessons on arguing from Lumiere?" I asked.

At my question, she only smirked and pulled away. "Come, now. We have what we were looking for."

935

THE ORDER OF THE CRYSTAL DAGGERS

The change of subject was sudden enough to let me know we were done arguing, but it was gracious enough that we could both move on. I had a feeling if I was the winner of our disagreement, it was only on Marguerite's terms.

And for now, her terms were acceptable.

I followed closely behind her, keeping the copy of *Morte d'Arthur* secure in my hands.

"Thank you for finding this," I said. "This means a lot to me, and Ella, too."

"And you found it before Ferdy, so that should please you even more." She tossed me a shrewd look over her shoulder. "You know, I'm surprised you don't get along with him better. You're actually quite similar."

"No, we're not," I scoffed. "I wouldn't set out to seduce a naïve girl over a book."

Marguerite laughed. At once, the cheerful sound strengthened both my heart and my resolve. I didn't want her to remain mad at me, even if I understood her anger.

"Well, that's true." Marguerite smiled at me, and I was smiling back as she added, "You prefer to be the one who's seduced."

This time, I didn't bother to ensure we had any privacy; I jerked her back, pulling her against me as I kissed her.

"*Ben.*"

I swallowed her small gasp of surprise, even as she clung to me in that heated, intense moment.

I'd meant to make her fall under my spell, but I only succeeded in falling under hers more deeply. She tasted of springtime and softness, and I found myself wanting not only to fall, but to drown in her essence.

We were both very well kissed before I finally released her.

"I might prefer to be seduced, but I'll participate in a seduction in either role, provided it's with you." I grinned, seeing her eyes glazed over with passion and excitement. "I want you to be safe, Marguerite, but I still want you."

Before she could recover enough to reply, I tucked her arm underneath mine like a proper gentleman, even as other store patrons looked on in disapproval. "Now, let's find Prissy, pay for our purchases, send this book home to Ella, and go meet your family."

2

◊

"Did you see all the books in there? And they had such an adorable little arrangement in their window," Priscilla chattered, as lively as ever while we walked along the Seine River, and even I had to admit it was nice our luggage from the ship would be delivered separately. It was a beautiful day for a walk.

Prissy pointed over to Notre Dame Cathedral. "Oh, look over there! Isn't that just so beautiful? Have you ever seen such a sight?"

"Of course, I have," Marguerite said with a giggle. "I grew up here, after all."

"Oh, that's right! Yes, I nearly forgot."

"Still, Notre Dame is one of the most beautiful places in all the world. I would like to take Ben there one day." Marguerite gave me an eager look, and I didn't resist giving into her silent plea.

"We'll get there soon," I promised. "If that's what you truly want."

"It's all I've ever wanted, *mon amour*."

"Really?" I was genuinely surprised. When Lady POW had hired her, Marguerite was all too eager to escape Paris. Even now, I didn't think she had any desire to return other than to see her sister.

"Really." Marguerite's smile radiated with joy. "I would have insisted we go there first, but I know you were so happy to visit another bookshop after so many days at sea."

"That's true." I tightened my hand around the book we'd just purchased. Long before Lady Penelope had entered our lives, Ella and I used to plan for Liberté, the name of our own intended bookshop in Prague.

We never did achieve our dream of setting up our own shop, but we both found freedom in other ways.

"How can you be content with just a simple bookshop when we have all of Paris before us?" Priscilla let out a jubilant sigh as Marguerite began to point out other famous places Priscilla had inquired of during our trip, while I studied our surroundings with care.

I was to oversee the signing of the Philastre treaty, but I still wanted to make sure things went smoothly, and that meant I had to research the relationship between the French and the Kingdom of Annam. My progress

937

had been slow as I had to relearn much of the French I'd forgotten over the years.

Tulia would not be pleased.

I smiled a little, thinking back to how she'd taught me and Ella. Tulia had been a hard instructor, rapping my knuckles more than once, and she would have been disappointed at how little I'd remembered from her lessons.

I didn't want to miss her, but sometimes I did.

Tulia was always seemed to know when I was feeling down; she once told me we were alike, since I was crippled with my leg and she was mute and old, but we still did our best to protect Ella from the rest of the world. Tulia had that kind of blunt, unapologetic honesty that was refreshing as much as irritating.

But she was also the one who'd murdered my father, to prevent him from learning of the Order and my mother's participation in it. And when he died, Ella and I had been constantly abused by our stepmother.

Three years later, it was easy to miss the good Tulia brought me, though it was hard to forget the trouble she'd caused.

A foreign voice, just a little way behind us, pulled me out of my thoughts.

"Pardonne, Monsieur? Ou … est … la shoppe de … "

I almost winced at the rough-sounding French. When I looked back, there was a woman standing just a little way from us, talking to a police guard.

I slowed my steps as I looked at the woman. She looked to be close to my age, although it was hard to be sure; she had tan skin, a flat nose, and very large, very brown eyes. She reminded me of both Harshad and Xiana in some ways, and even a little bit like Amir. I was almost certain at the sight of her that she was from the far East, perhaps from the Southeast Asian region, and the longer I saw her, the more I wondered if she'd come with the Annam ambassador. She was dressed in a respectable walking dress, but she seemed unaccustomed to the heavy fabric of the tiered ruffles as she struggled to communicate with the policeman.

"Ben?" Marguerite had noticed my delay. "What is it?"

"She's asking for directions to Madame Phénix's shop," I explained, pointing to the woman. "She looks like she might be a lady from the kingdom of Annam."

THE ORDER OF THE CRYSTAL DAGGERS

Marguerite listened as the lady, who was clearly struggling with the language, attempted to speak in French again.

"Yes," Marguerite agreed. "Poor dear."

Before I could stop her, Marguerite left my side and hurried over to the woman.

"*Xin lỗi?*"

"*Anh có thể giúp em được không?*" The woman eyed her warily, and she seemed even more skeptical as Marguerite nodded.

I was about to call for Marguerite to return when the woman's frustration won over her suspicion. She began to speak with Marguerite, and my wife nodded in empathy, and then blinked in surprise.

"What is it, Marguerite?" I looked back at the policeman for help, but found none.

Clearly relieved Marguerite had stepped in to assist the woman, he slouched back from them and walked away, glad it wasn't a matter that required him to act.

"Marguerite?"

Marguerite didn't answer me but continued speaking to the lady and pointing down the streets as she talked.

For some reason, I didn't like how the woman kept glancing around. She didn't seem that interested in Marguerite's assistance.

"Marguerite," I called again, waving at her. "Come back here."

Priscilla stepped up next to me. "Are you in pain, Ben?"

"What?" I frowned. "No. Why?"

"I … I just thought you might have needed her help," Priscilla murmured apologetically. She blushed, and I could only guess that she was recalling all the times her brother, Alex, had made fun of me for my right leg's crooked bend when we were younger. "She's just trying to help the lady. I don't think it'll take that long."

"It's not that." I didn't explain to Priscilla that the woman's lack of interest in Marguerite's help made me uneasy.

The woman then dipped her chin, muttered something that sounded like a goodbye, and waved Marguerite away. Almost glad for her rudeness, I was even more relieved when the woman headed off down a different street from the one my wife had pointed out.

939

THE ORDER OF THE CRYSTAL DAGGERS

"Wait!" Marguerite called. "That's the wrong way!"

I reached out and took her arm. "Let her go."

"She's not from here, Ben. She doesn't know where to go."

"She was hardly listening to you as you spoke to her."

"She was looking for my sister's shop," Marguerite explained. "I was just about to invite her to join us when she left."

"Do you think we should go after her?" Priscilla asked, clearly unsure of whether she should speak up again.

"That's a good idea," Marguerite began, but I shook my head.

"No," I objected. "Let her go for now."

"We ought to help her," Marguerite pressed. "We are used to being in different cities, Ben. I doubt she is."

"And I doubt she was really interested in your help. You probably shouldn't have said anything in the first place." Marguerite scowled at me, but I stood my ground. "If she does find trouble, she'll be more willing to listen to the next person who offers assistance."

Priscilla shuffled her feet. "Maybe we can just follow after her for a block or two?"

I waited for Marguerite to agree with her and beg me to give in. But instead, she slowly shook her head.

"No. Ben's likely correct. Besides, Hélène is waiting for us. If that woman is looking for her shop, perhaps we will see her soon."

Priscilla bit her lip like she wanted to protest, but as Marguerite and I began walking again, she fell into step beside us.

We were silent as we crossed the Seine River, but once we were on the other side, I pressed a kiss to Marguerite's palm.

"Thank you," I whispered.

"For what?"

"For agreeing with me back there."

She gave me a sidelong look. "You could've been nicer about it, but I do agree with you. The lady was definitely distracted while I was talking with her."

"Is that your way of admitting that I was right?" I teased and brushed up against her lightly.

940

THE ORDER OF THE CRYSTAL DAGGERS

She rolled her eyes, but she still gave me a smile. "You would be such a good teacher, *mon amour*, if only you were a little more humble. You forget that I was right, too, and Hélène is waiting for us. We are late."

As if to confirm her statement, the bells of Notre Dame rang out, striking three times to mark the hour.

"Where is your sister's shop, Marguerite?" Priscilla asked as we passed by the gardens and turned down onto another street.

I caught a glimpse of the *Palais de Louvre* and the *Palais de la Cité*. Both castles spoke of France's long and rich history and reminded me of *Vyšehrad*, the fortress-castle up the Vltava River back in Bohemia. Further up ahead, I could see the signs for shops, for the *patisseries* and the *boulangeries*, a milliner's shop and flower stations optimally positioned for sales.

"It's not too much further," Marguerite answered. "Hélène works by the Latin Quarter, just off the main strip."

"Madame Phénix, you mean."

Marguerite chuckled. "Hélène can change her name all she'd like, but she's still my sister, no matter how famous she is."

"The name is part of the reason she's so famous, no doubt," I said.

A modiste as famous and financially successful as Hélène would need a reputation for exclusive and upscale services. The name and persona she'd established had lent that illusion long enough for it to become a reality.

"Yes," Marguerite agreed, but the cheerfulness in her voice instantly faded. "She learned that much from our mother."

Marguerite and Hélène were the illegitimate offspring of the owner of *Salon Angelique*, a prestigious Parisian brothel, and her unnamed lover. The two girls had been raised to take over the brothel one day, but when their mother unexpectedly died, Marguerite and Hélène discovered the true, dire state of their finances. Faced with the possibility of losing their home, Marguerite suggested using their patrons as sources of information and blackmail. Her idea worked, and although their financial situation improved, money was not enough to lift their spirits. Marguerite sank into a deep melancholy, while Hélène poured all her anxiety and extra energy into designing clothes. Soon after that, Lady Penelope met them while on an assignment in Paris. Thanks to Marguerite and Hélène's illicit information, my grandmother completed her mission. As a gesture of gratitude, Lady POW became their principal investor in a new business venture. *Salon Angelique* burned to the ground, and Madame Phénix's shop made its grand opening. For all her hardness towards others, Lady POW

THE ORDER OF THE CRYSTAL DAGGERS

still had a soft heart, no matter how much Ella said otherwise, as her treatment of Hélène and Marguerite proved.

I reached over and took hold of my wife's hand, reassuring her without words her past didn't affect how I felt about her.

"*Arrêtez, voleur!*"

At the angry shout, I blinked, suddenly aware of footsteps pounding behind me. I glanced around, looking for what was wrong—only to spy a swiftly moving shadow making its way through the crowd.

The strained voice full of authority and anger called out again. "*Larron!*"

"'*Thief.*'" Marguerite's eyes went wide as she translated the yelling.

But I was already moving. "Get over," I ordered, pushing Marguerite off to the side.

The shadow darted around and slipped through the crowd with expert grace. I caught a brief glimpse of a distinctively male face under a bowler hat, then positioned myself in his path.

Just as he moved to avoid me, I stepped into him.

We collided, hard and fast, forcefully propelling us to the ground. He was a short, young man, likely only a few years younger than I. He wore the clothes of a street urchin, but dealing with Ferdy had taught me to take a closer look, which vindicated my suspicions. Under his ragged collar, the bright white of a proper shirt peeked out, and his shoes were in good condition, even if I didn't recognize the design. His skin tone was similar to the woman Marguerite had tried to help earlier, and he had straight, black hair. His broad, flat nose was covered in blood. The bowler hat might have hidden his face, but there was no mistaking his anger as he glared at me.

He'd been caught off guard by my movement as I was by the pain, but thanks to speed and youth on his part and training on mine, we recovered quickly.

Marguerite called for me, but I ignored her.

"*Arrêtez!*" The voice from earlier filled the street, and seconds later, a familiar-looking policemen came around the corner.

"*Ngu thê!*" The apparent thief, still bleeding, yelled at me, no doubt cursing me in his native language, but, as he brushed away the blood on his face, I saw what the policeman was after.

THE ORDER OF THE CRYSTAL DAGGERS

A large, bulky package was strapped to his back, a small case that didn't fit with the rest of his outfit; I grabbed for it, but it was tied around the thief's shoulders.

The rope around the package snapped, further infuriating the thief.

"*Mày khùng tới nơi*," he shouted as he tried to swat me away, but I didn't let go.

Out of the corner of my eye, I could see the policeman approach. I tightened my hold on the case, determined to keep the thief from break away. If he couldn't leave, he would be arrested.

I was just feeling victorious, when all of a sudden, he let go.

Immediately, I went flying backward, lost my balance, and dropped the case in surprise.

The thief didn't waste his time. He snatched up the box again and sneered. I braced for another attack, but he merely tossed his hat at me as I sat on the ground.

The policeman cut through the crowd just as I stood up.

"*Arrêtez-vous,*" he yelled, grabbing my shoulder. "*Larron!*"

"No, wait. It's not him you're after," Marguerite cried out.

Dealing with a street thief was not part of my job for the Order. I could let him go and let the police handle it.

But I wouldn't.

"Marguerite, stay with Prissy," I ordered, scrambling out of the policeman's reach. "I'll meet up with you later."

"Ben!"

I glanced over my shoulder just as Marguerite stepped forward and blocked the policeman from grabbing me a second time. As she explained the situation and he argued back, I slipped away, following after the real thief.

Pushing Marguerite's worried voice out of my head, I ran down the street and turned the corner into an alleyway. My right leg was still weak, and the rest of my body was still stinging from its earlier impact, but I pressed on.

I would not let my pain get the best of me—not when I had a job to do.

3

◊

By the time the thief reached the end of the block, he'd noticed I was following him. No doubt I was hard to miss; due to my leg, I limped as I ran, even if it was a little less noticeable than when I walked.

I saw him glance behind himself more than a few times, watching as I followed after him. His curiosity allowed me to advance on his lead, and even with the limp, I knew it would be only a matter of time before I caught up with him.

But as I turned the corner at the second block, I quickly skidded to a halt.

A large vase flew through the air toward me.

I barely managed to dodge it. Jumping to the side, I used my good leg and arm to ricochet off a nearby wall, and the vase smashed to the ground and broke into shards.

Regaining my footing, I resumed the chase, drawing even with a flower saleslady who was yelling and throwing pots at the thief. If he'd stolen the vase from her, she was understandably upset.

Inspired, I grabbed a pot myself and took careful aim.

Crash!

I smiled a little as the pot smashed right on top of his head, and he pitched forward onto the ground.

The saleslady grinned at me, clearly grateful and amused, but in the blink of an eye, the thief got up, scowled at us, and then resumed his running.

At that point, there was no doubt in my mind that he was younger than I. It was obvious in the way he sped through the streets, practically dancing between pedestrians and weaving his way between wagons and carriages, and in how he could keep going whatever other obstacles were in his way. Reluctantly, I admired how he seemed just as agile with his mind as he was with his feet. And then I ran after him again, too.

My discomfort increased with each step. I was running out of strength, but despite the pain, I pressed forward, forcing myself to run even faster.

He slithered up to a hackney, only to steal a cloak from the carriage box and wrap it around himself. Twisting the collar to hide his face, he walked away at a normal pace, trying to melt into the crowd.

I paused and pretended to look around, confused and lost, letting him think he'd tricked me. My ruse gave me a moment to catch my breath and steady myself, and it gave him the chance to make a mistake.

Out of the corner of my eye, I watched as a Parisian man hailed the thief and asked him for a ride, believing him to be the carriage driver.

It was then, while he was distracted by the man's request, that I leaped at him.

"I can still see your shoes," I yelled as I tackled him. "I know you're the thief!"

He shouted back at me in his native language, but even if I didn't know what he was saying, at least the people around us would know what was happening.

The cloak twitched and fell, revealing his face. Clearly, he'd been caught, and he'd been caught off guard, too.

Before I could celebrate, he slid out of the cloak, leaving the material in my hand even as he slipped from my grasp and rolled away.

My mouth dropped open in surprise. I was even more disgruntled, however, when the cloak caught on his bag, and I was jerked off to the side.

I still held onto the cloak, while he tried to free the package from the material. Quickly, I pulled out my *Wahabite Jambiya* and slashed through the cloth, cutting the bulky package from its belt. He went flying backward.

There was a sickening *crunch* as his head slammed into the ground, and he lay very still.

"Oh, great," I muttered while I sheathed my blade, hoping I wouldn't be arrested for murder as well as burglary.

I let go of the cloak and the package and carefully pushed myself up. I could feel the stinging shadow of bitter work, but I wanted to make sure he was still alive.

His eyes were closed and his jaw was slack, but I felt a pulse at his neck and his breathing was there, even if it seemed shallow.

Relieved, I sat for a moment, catching my breath, and tried to remember what I'd learned about treating injuries. Marguerite had tried to teach me what she'd learned under Amir, and I had great respect for her skills, especially when it was my own pain she tended. Nothing helpful came to mind. I sighed.

"You've caused me quite a bit of trouble today," I muttered to the young man.

Carefully and reluctantly, I hoisted him off the ground and placed him on my shoulders. He was shorter than I, but young and muscular. Gritting my teeth, I resolved to carry him, no matter how long it took or how heavy he was, but his leg twitched.

He jolted, rocking my balance again, and pushed himself from my shoulders. He grabbed at his head and groaned in pain, before covering his eyes with his hands.

"Are you hurt?" I asked carefully. "I mean, very badly?"

His eyes peeked at me through his fingers.

And then he lunged forward, kneed me in the gut, and threw me down to the ground.

I yelped as I landed hard on my back. He was already running as I pulled myself up into a sitting position.

But this time, he didn't take his bag with him.

He'd left it on the ground, just a few feet from me.

"Well, at least there's that," I muttered, picking myself up off the street and brushing myself off. My whole body screamed at me, angry and in agony.

"Ben!"

I turned around to see Marguerite. She was running toward me, holding up her skirts, concern etched into her lovely features. She stopped just shy of embracing me, and I was relieved. I doubt I could have withstood the pressure of her embrace, and we already had an audience.

"What happened? Are you all right?" Marguerite looked me over as carefully as she could in public.

"I'm fine," I replied, shooing her back. "I didn't catch him."

"Can you walk still?" Marguerite leaned over and placed my arm on her shoulder.

THE ORDER OF THE CRYSTAL DAGGERS

"I'm fine." I was lying, but only a little. "Anyway, where is Prissy? You didn't leave her with the policeman, did you?"

"She was right behind me a moment ago." Marguerite squinted down the lane, and then pointed. "There she is. She's coming."

"I told you to stay with her," I muttered. "Not drag her here."

"The policeman wanted to know more about you," Marguerite said. "So, I thought it was best to leave. And I didn't want you to come back to deal with him. He insisted that you were the real guilty one, although I'll never understand why."

"I can guess." The policeman been only too happy to let Marguerite take care of the foreign lady before; with my limp, I was willing to gamble that he thought I'd be the easier one to catch.

"Oh, Ben." Marguerite softened as she realized what I'd meant, but I bristled.

"I don't want or need your pity," I grumbled. "As you well know. Or you should, after all these years."

"I have no pity for you, *mon amour*. You are not a victim." Marguerite scowled back at me, her indignation a rebuke. She had always tended to me in genuine care, not sympathy, and we both knew it. "If I do have any pity, it's for him, if that's what he truly thinks. And if I have anything, it's contempt for your poor logic in this case than anything else."

"*My* poor logic? What are you talking about? I already know I didn't have to go after the thief."

"It's not that you chased him," Marguerite argued. "It's that you left me and Prissy behind."

"I couldn't wait for you both." I gestured back toward the top of the street, where Prissy was still making her way toward us. "Not if I was going to catch him."

"You said you'd meet up with us later. But you don't know where my sister's shop is, and you could've gotten lost."

"Even if I did get lost," I said, "I know how to retrace my steps."

"And by the time you did that, Prissy and I would've been arrested ourselves."

I arched my brow. "I doubt that."

"Well, we weren't, because we came after you," Marguerite insisted. "And I knew you wouldn't want me to get into any trouble."

"I would've preferred you waited."

She gave me an overly sweet smile. "I didn't know how long you would take."

"Ben! Marguerite! Oh, thank goodness I found you."

Marguerite and I went silent as Prissy finally joined us. There was no point in arguing over what should have or could have happened, and we both knew it.

"Did you catch him, Ben?" Prissy asked. She was panting hard, but she looked at both of us in eager expectation.

I almost groaned. I didn't need her obsessing over any part of my mission, or even any side events I chose to undertake. It was bad enough Marguerite wanted to do more; I didn't need Prissy acting up, too.

Instead, I only shook my head. "No, I didn't catch him. But I did get him to drop the case he was carrying. So at least we'll be able to return whatever he stole." I walked over to the case and picked it up; it looked heavy, but it was much lighter than I'd anticipated. "I wonder what it is."

"Let's take it to Hélène's," Marguerite suggested. "We'll have more room to better examine it there."

"Yes." I nodded, already hauling the thief's case onto my back. "But I'll return it myself. I don't want either of you to worry about it."

"But we might be able to help," Marguerite said.

I shook my head. "Not now, please. We can discuss it later, if you like."

The barest hint of a pout appeared on Marguerite's face, but she said nothing.

She had come with me to Paris because of her sister. She was not working for the Order, as I was. I did not want her to get into any more trouble, and I didn't want her to think she ought to join me on more of my missions in the future.

"Come," I said, hoping to cheer her up some. "Hélène is waiting for us."

4

◊

We were just about to enter Hélène's shop near the Latin Quarter when its door burst open and a woman who was undeniably related to Marguerite appeared in our path. She was nearly identical to her sister, with delicate hands and the same blunt nose, kind smile, and sharp emerald eyes. She wore a dress of several bright, jewel-tone colors, and her own mop of curly hair was braided and hung down her back.

"Marguerite! You're here." She opened her arms wide as she embraced Marguerite. "I have been waiting all day for your arrival."

"Hélène." Marguerite's smile was warm. "It's so good to see you again. It has been too long."

Hélène pulled back from her and glanced over at me. "It has been too long for certain. But at least I can see for myself my baby sister is in good hands."

"Very good hands." Marguerite gave me a flirtatious look as Hélène continued to scrutinize me.

"It is lovely to formally meet you, Miss Hélène," I said, taking her hand and bowing over it gallantly. It was no small feat, with my leg in pain and the thief's large package hanging over my shoulder, but I could see her appreciation for my effort.

Hélène curtsied back. "I do regret I wasn't able to make it to the wedding," she said apologetically. "But to be fair, I should have had better notice."

I said nothing to that; I had offered to Marguerite to wait to get married, letting her invite others and pull a reception and a wedding together. She didn't like the idea of waiting long, even if it was just until traveling was easier, and when my friends from The Cabal, Clavan, Eliezer, and Jarl, all set up a small reception for us, neither of us could say no.

Neither of us wanted to, either.

We were married a few short weeks after Lady Penelope had given us her permission and blessing, and that was all I really wanted before we were wed. I didn't need her approval, but I felt it was honorable and right to ask for it; she was my grandmother, after all. Still, I doubted she was excited to see the news of our nuptials so soon.

THE ORDER OF THE CRYSTAL DAGGERS

Marguerite finished introducing Prissy to Hélène, and they were all talking excitedly when I heard a small scrape behind us.

I looked around, narrowing my eyes.

I couldn't explain it, but I suddenly felt as though we were being watched.

Is the thief back? Did he follow us?

"Oh, listen to me just chatting incessantly. Come on in," Hélène insisted, pulling on my sleeve. "You will not believe what I have for you. I've been working on some really special projects of late, and I just must show them off."

Before I knew it, we were pushed through the doorway and thrust into an entirely new world. There were piles of cloth on shelves and chairs; large mirrors were placed behind tall privacy screens, and everywhere I looked, it was clean and shining. There were even some gowns hanging up, each one more elaborate than the last.

"Your shop is so lovely," Prissy said shyly, blushing a little. "I don't know if my work will be good enough for you."

"My seamstresses and I will get you there," Hélène promised her. "Now, don't worry about that. Instead, look here. I designed it for you to wear tomorrow."

She reached out for a gown. I liked the look of it; a claret-colored gown would look wonderful on my wife. But I was confused when Hélène grabbed the skirts and pulled them out.

"Oh, wow," Marguerite said. "That's amazing, Hélène."

"What is it?" I didn't see anything but a skirt.

"She's added another layer into it, so there are shadow pockets," Marguerite explained. She stood up and pulled the fabric a little tighter, and I could see the folds a little more clearly; they were perfectly placed for collecting small objects and hiding them discreetly. "This is brilliant."

"What's it for?" I asked, still confused.

"What's it for? Why, what else? It's for espionage," Hélène said with a small laugh. "Come on, *mon frère*, don't tell me you didn't think I would want to help you and Marguerite on your job."

I'd hoped to discourage Marguerite from accompanying me on my future missions.

THE ORDER OF THE CRYSTAL DAGGERS

I thought visiting with her sister would offer her a nice, happy distraction while I figured out what to do with the thief and his mystery case and still make it to the treaty signing.

Unfortunately, I suspected Hélène did not share in my hopes.

"We're just going to the Philastre treaty signing," I said uneasily. "Lady Penelope only wanted us to observe and suggest policies for the Order regarding the Kingdom of Annam and Far East."

"Come now, what's wrong with a well-armored attire, even if it's a gown?"

"Nora would love to see some of these, too," Marguerite reminded me, as she and Prissy began looking over the other dresses.

The two of them fawned over the different items Hélène had prepared. There was a bonnet that carried hair pins and lock picks, a feathered fan that concealed daggers, and even a reticule that could easily hold a revolver and some extra bullets.

As I watched them, my uneasiness grew. I loved my wife; I loved her smile, her laugh, and even her gentle stubbornness. I loved the two of us, and how we were together, and I loved how she loved me.

I did not want trouble between us.

Hélène was a clever woman, and one just as beautiful as her sister, she could be a bad influence on Marguerite—and that worried me.

"There's more in the back," Hélène said. "I even have a walking stick that conceals a rapier for you, Benedict, and I just finished up a design for a tall hat, just like the one Mr. Lincoln used to wear. I heard he liked to use it so he could keep his notes nearby. Isn't that so thoughtful? I'm trying to figure out how to make sure nothing falls when the hat is pulled off, but I daresay it'll be a great asset to you once I'm finished with it."

"Ben might be able to help you," Marguerite said. "He's great with designs like that."

I felt a little embarrassed as Marguerite listed off several examples of my technical skills, including my leg brace, my lock picks, and even some of the ways I'd worked on concealing my own weapons as I traveled.

"If you don't mind, I'd like to wait on things like that. Right now, we have a bit of a mystery to solve," I said, grabbing the thief's case. I held it up to show her. "I'd like to see what's inside this package."

"Is that not your luggage?" Hélène frowned. "Perhaps I should check with my housekeeper. Mrs. DeSaille had mentioned that your luggage had arrived earlier, but she was supposed to see to your rooms."

"This isn't mine," I explained.

"Oh, yes," Marguerite said. "Hélène, you won't believe what happened to us on our way here."

Hélène handed me a pair of shears as Marguerite and Prissy took turns telling her the tale of my heroism and noble quest to stop the passing thief. I almost rolled my eyes at their exaggerations, but I knew their account was one of goodwill, so I said nothing.

"Ben didn't have to step in at all, either," Marguerite said with a beaming smile. "But he still recovered the package."

"And the police officer didn't arrest him," Prissy added.

"I see." Hélène watched me as I cut the rest of the rope away from the case. "Well, it's good to know that some true gentlemen are still out there, *n'est-pas?* To think, you must be the most noble man I've ever met. No wonder Margie decided to marry you, Benedict."

Her words were hardened, but not with malice, and I remembered that Hélène had been a prostitute in *Salon Angelique* longer than her sister, before my grandmother had intervened and burned down their past.

So instead of engaging with her bitterness, I simply looked up. "Margie?" I repeated innocently.

Marguerite giggled. "You know she means me, Ben."

"I know, but I thought it was a silly name for you." I turned back to the case, opening it up. "Well, look at this."

Inside the thief's package was a folded canvas. Even without unfolding it, I knew it was a large one, taller than me and much wider, too.

"It's a painting," Marguerite said. "Prissy, will you help us?"

"Certainly."

Together, we gently unfolded it. It was old, and there was something familiar about it, too. A half-nude woman warrior held up a large French flag. Several bodies lay on the ground, and fighting raged while the woman led men into battle.

"*Mon Dieu.*" Hélène gasped. Her hand covered her open mouth in shock. "It's Marianne—Lady Liberty herself."

"Who is she?" Prissy asked, looking the woman over carefully.

"She is the spirit of the French people," Hélène explained quickly. "This is simply amazing. This painting is a legendary piece of artwork. It was supposedly destroyed in 1855, after it caused a stir at a Salon. The artist himself, the great painter, Delacroix, said it was best hidden away from all of history, given what rebellion and revolution has done to our country."

"If it was supposed to be destroyed, how did a regular thief acquire it?" Prissy asked.

"I doubt he was a regular thief," I murmured, recalling the determined look on the young man's face. "But I'm not sure we'll be able to find him again."

"If he's looking for this painting, perhaps we will see him again," Marguerite said.

"In the meantime, at least I know where to return it," I said. "I can take it to a museum. They should know how to take care of such a painting."

I looked around for agreement, and all of them seemed to think that was the right course to take. I felt much better, even if I was uneasy about having such a rare artifact on hand.

"Perhaps I should take it over now." I motioned to Prissy and Marguerite, and they began to help me fold it back up, as it had been in the case.

"*Non*, not now," Hélène said. "You have only just arrived. There is no need to rush right now, is there?"

"No, there's not." Marguerite looked at me with pleading eyes.

"It would be just a quick trip," I said, keeping my tone light.

"Would it? I doubt that," Marguerite said. "What if the police comes back for you? And who knows how long it will take you to find a museum curator at this hour?"

"She is right," Hélène agreed. "The *Palais de Louvre* is the best option for such a place, and their art exhibitions will be closed to the public soon."

"I could take it to a Salon," I suggested. "That's probably where it came from, right? It seems fitting for it to have been in a smaller place, with hidden or rare paintings like these that are only open to a high-paying or select audience."

"Ben, let's just save it for tomorrow," Marguerite begged. "We have the signing tomorrow, after all, and we don't want to miss that. That's the whole reason we came."

"*Excusez-moi?*" Hélène lifted her brow and crossed her arms. "Am I nothing, then?"

"No, of course not," Prissy said. "I had to come and see you, too. And Marguerite has been talking of little else but you and Paris since we left Prague."

As they began to argue, I could only sigh.

"I'll hold off on dealing with this with tomorrow, if that is your wish," I said, speaking loudly enough to overrun their conversation. "I don't like the idea of it being here, though. I wasn't able to catch the thief."

"It'll be fine for one day," Hélène said. "I have my own guards positioned around the shop if needed."

"You do?" Prissy's eyes went wide. Why?"

Hélène gave Prissy a generic reply, saying as one of Paris' most famous modistes, she had a duty to keep her high-paying clients safe as well as her own person, but I knew the real reason; Hélène and Marguerite had a past, and it was a dangerous one.

I relaxed a little. Hélène was telling the truth, and that was likely why I'd felt like we were being watched earlier; we probably were, but there was no reason to think we were being watched by the young thief.

"Ben?"

Marguerite glanced over at me, and we exchanged a look.

And then I put the canvas back inside the case and secured the ties again. "You asked me to leave it until tomorrow," I said. "Very well. Tonight is for our family."

Hélène looked pleased, and Prissy smiled, and Marguerite's eyes glistened with delight.

"Thank you, *mon amour*," Marguerite whispered.

"Well, I think it's time we reacquainted ourselves, my baby sister." Hélène clapped her hands, and her housekeeper, an older lady named Mrs. DeSaille, appeared in the doorway. "Let's go to the parlor for tea, shall we? Oh, and I'll give you a tour of the shop and my rooms upstairs. I did get your rooms all nice and ready to go for you tonight. And there's more! While I must work some while you're here, I do promise, I will take you

954

THE ORDER OF THE CRYSTAL DAGGERS

on a tour of Paris you will never forget. There's just so much to do, and so much for you to see. So much has changed since you've been here last …"

Hélène was still prattling on as Marguerite and I reached for each other. I took her hand in mine, and she tightened her grip on me.

"Thank you," she whispered again, pressing a quick kiss onto my cheek. "This means a lot to me."

"I know."

I said nothing else as we fell into step behind Hélène and Prissy; but, really, what else was there that could I say?

Marguerite was likely right that it would take a longer time than we would both like for me to return the painting, and we didn't have much time before Lady Penelope would send us back to Prague. I could wait for now. And it was something Marguerite had asked of me. I couldn't say no to her, not when it was unreasonable to do so.

THE ORDER OF THE CRYSTAL DAGGERS

5

◊

Whether it was from our prolonged walk through Paris, the several previous days at sea, or just the general exhaustion that came with traveling, I was more than grateful when Marguerite was finally ready to retire for the night. For hours, we had talked with Hélène about her business, the gossip around the city, and the various rumors of war and intrigue surrounding the world.

When I was growing up, after *Máma* passed, I'd wondered why *Otec* had never bothered to go out much. He would travel frequently, as I did, but he always came home and read through his books or kept busy with his work. As an ambassador for the king, there was plenty he had to do. He would further check on our farmland and the small cluster of animals we kept, and there were always accounts to balance. When he married Cecilia, my first thought was he'd done so in order to have help with running our household.

Hélène's rooms above her shop were elegant, if cluttered. Prissy wasn't the only seamstress staying with her, though. Several other apprentices— young girls who looked as if Hélène had brought them in off the street— would not look me in the eye as Hélène introduced them to us. Prissy went with them and Mrs. DeSaille, the housekeeper, to get settled in her room, but Marguerite and I had a room just down the hall from Hélène's quarters.

Marguerite tripped. I grabbed hold of her, steadying her as we walked toward our room.

"You probably shouldn't have had the champagne," I told her.

She giggled. "I don't drink it very often. And Hélène wanted to toast our wedding. That was kind of her. You didn't have to make her feel awkward by refusing it."

"And you didn't have to try to make her feel better by drinking my share." I raised a brow. "You know I'm not fond of champagne. If I'm going to drink, I prefer brandy. It dulls the pain in my leg."

"But it also dulls your mind." Marguerite nodded. "And you don't want to worry about that."

"Yes."

"You have other things to worry about."

956

THE ORDER OF THE CRYSTAL DAGGERS

"Yes." I looked at her pointedly. "I do."

She sighed. "You don't have to worry about me so much, you know. It's so very tiresome, Ben."

"My concern for you is not turned off and on at your whim, Madame. That's not how it works."

"It's not a matter of working or not," she replied. "It's a matter of trust, between us, and a matter of faith, should things go awry."

I said nothing. Instead, I opened the door to the room and found everything in order. The curtains were pulled back, and from where we were, the city shone like the night sky. There were streets of lights, all of them twinkling and sparkling, as the darkness settled in around it.

"Paris suits you," I told Marguerite, as she came to stand beside me. "It's playful, energetic, and much … softer, I would say. Prague always felt stilted to me. Ella says she sees the city as a fairy tale, but this place is more like a dream."

"I have enjoyed forgetting Paris," Marguerite admitted. "If only because it means I get to experience it anew this time. I did not see much that has changed since I was last here; but I can almost feel the difference. The people here now are more hopeful for the future."

"Well, no wonder it suits you, then," I said, pressing a kiss to her forehead. "That's how I feel when you're around."

She pouted. "I wouldn't know it, seeing how often you seem to wish I wasn't."

A new wave of weariness washed over me. "What of when we have children, Marguerite?" I asked. "What will you do then?"

"Yes, Ben, what of when we have children?" Marguerite looked back at me with calculated consideration. "Would you prefer to leave them at home with me and keep them from knowing their legacy, as you were?"

"I'd rather have that, than thrust them into something they're not prepared for, as you were."

I'm not sure why she was shocked at my reply; her own jab was just as stinging.

I loved Marguerite, and really, I did not want to hurt her. I knew, in bringing up her own mother's legacy, I was only anxious for her to see reason.

"I already know better than my mother did," Marguerite said slowly, her voice edged with bitterness, even as she seemed resigned. "And you ought to know better than yours, too."

I crossed my arms over my chest. "I do."

"Well, then let us prove we're both better than our parents."

"We're already better than our parents." I gestured out the window. "We're married, we're together, and we know all of each other's secrets."

Marguerite bit her lip. "I suppose that's mostly true."

"Mostly?"

"Never mind." Marguerite shrugged. "I meant we ought to work out a compromise. It seems reasonable to say that we'll likely have some more disagreements over the years."

"I'd rather not."

"Of course we will, Ben. You don't want a wife who will blindly follow you."

"Oh, you mean I don't?" I gave her a teasing smile.

"No." She put her arms around my neck. "You want one who will challenge you and fight to be by your side in all things."

"I guess it's fair to say we've had our share of challenges." I put my hands on her hips and she stepped closer into me. "Honestly, if Lady POW is not enough to scare you away from me, surely our fights won't, either."

She gave me a playful smile. "Even when I'm arguing with you over the Order's missions?"

"Even then," I agreed, grinning. "Especially since I win those arguments."

"You do not," Marguerite objected. "I just let you think you do."

"Fortunately for us, there are ways we can both win," I said, as I pulled her close and finally kissed her again.

Marguerite could only murmur in agreement as we pressed closer to each other. The earlier rush I'd felt in kissing her came back, more potent and captivating than ever. Marguerite made love the same way she loved me; she tenderly massaged away my pains as she stirred my heart to life. I responded with passion and desperation, eager to impress myself upon her.

958

THE ORDER OF THE CRYSTAL DAGGERS

It was hard to believe there was ever a time I didn't need her as ardently as I did now.

When we'd first met, Marguerite had been quick to flirt with me—something I disdained initially. I didn't need her sympathy, fake or otherwise, and I told her so, in no uncertain terms.

She surprised me by readily agreeing with me.

"Everyone pities a victim, but a man who overcomes his pain and fights injustice is to be admired." She remained steadfast and held her ground. "And I do not believe you are a victim."

Considering how angry, bitter, and impolite I'd been to her up until that point, I had to respect her for dealing with my churlishness with aplomb. She could have easily slapped me for my rudeness and I wouldn't have blamed her for doing so. Instead, she excused herself and left me standing there, dumbstruck and dumbfounded, just staring after her.

After that, I started to like her.

Our stolen glances soon turned into stolen moments, and our stolen moments soon gave way to stolen kisses.

I would look for her after my training sessions, and even Ella's despair during the winter of our first mission wasn't enough to keep me from looking for Marguerite.

When we had the chance, we would talk about everything from our favorite books and hobbies to our pasts and even some of our secrets; I remembered the moments where I would just watch her speak, feeling as though every word was an antidote to the old pains in my heart. She was a little older than me, but both of us had experienced profound suffering, and it was a revelation to find my company was just as healing to her as hers was to me.

But then my leg broke for the second time on the *Salacia*, and I discovered Lady POW had instructed her to see to my care—even my *intimate* care, if needed. Angry and betrayed, I confronted Marguerite about it.

I crumpled when she did not deny her orders.

Just as I intended to turn her away for good, Marguerite, in a rare moment of anger, refused to let me push her away. She insisted Lady Penelope wouldn't be able to order her away from me and then declared she was in love with me.

After my shock wore off, I told Marguerite she sounded ridiculous, and she agreed with me.

Our stolen kisses reverted back to stolen glances, but even during our confrontation, I knew it was too late; she had managed to steal my heart, too.

The happiest moment of my life was when Lady Penelope reluctantly agreed to our marriage. I never felt more alive than when I had Marguerite with me.

"Ben."

Marguerite murmured my name as she lay down on my shoulder, and I held onto her.

The last thing I saw before my eyes closed to sleep was her lovely face, framed by her sprawled-out curls.

◊　◊　◊　◊

By the time the morning light crept in, she was on her own side of our bed, curled into the soft covers, as cozy as a kitten.

I watched her for a few moments, awed at the feeling of perfect contentedness I felt.

When Ella and I had been younger, and our parents were gone, she'd promised that I was all the family she needed. I'd told her she would feel differently one day, and she had told me I'd given up on the prospect of having a wife too early. It turned out we were both right about each other; even if I'd felt more than a little rebuffed when Ferdy wedged his way into our family, I could not imagine my life without Marguerite.

And I was more than blessed, too, to have a wife who not only loved me, but she didn't mind how I made a living—in fact, she was eager to join me in my work at every opportunity.

"Marguerite?" I whispered, tucking a loose curl behind her ear. "Are you awake?"

She shook her head and buried her face into the covers. I smiled; it seemed I wasn't the only one who was tired from our recent ventures. When her breathing returned to its steady rhythm, I decided to let her sleep.

She had come to spend some time with Hélène, and I would let her attend to her family while I took care of my mission.

THE ORDER OF THE CRYSTAL DAGGERS

I got up and moved as silently as I could, wincing at the pain in my crooked leg. All the running had been far from kind to it, but I would recover. It would just take time.

I was nearly out the door when I heard Hélène's voice from behind me.

"Does my sister know you're leaving?"

I turned around. Hélène was wearing a morning dress, and her hair was loose; she was clearly comfortable being the queen in her own quarters, even with guests present. She had a teacup and a saucer in her hand as she stood by the parlor door.

"Marguerite knows I have work here," I replied neutrally. "I told you about the treaty signing last night."

"Yes, yes, I know," Hélène smiled and waved her hand, as if to dismiss her concerns. "Lady Penelope is a fine patron, and I would not want to disappoint her. I am glad to see that our late hours did not keep you down."

I noticed she did not say anything about Marguerite, and I gave her a polite nod.

Perhaps we were not as opposed to each other's ideals as I'd thought.

"Please let her rest," I said. "She's had a hard night."

"So I have heard, *mon frère*. But not to worry. Hard nights can be enjoyable in their own way." Hélène gave me a smirk as she stirred her tea.

She pretended to ignore me as I blushed.

"Thank you," I muttered back. "I'll be back later. Excuse me."

"Enjoy the ceremony," Hélène replied. "This is the second treaty we've had with Annam, is it not? Perhaps we'll have a third, even. But given our history, it'll still be a decade before it comes around again."

"Let's hope it'll be the last, and this one will work."

"Hope? Yes. Trust? No." Hélène gave me another smirk. "But that's good for you, if it fails, *n'est-pas*? Repeat business."

"There's no need to hope for a repeat of unpleasant business."

Hélène gave me an approving look. "I can see why my sister loves you. You are a man of honor first, and then a man of action."

"I'd hardly call myself a man of action."

"Well, that's another noble trait of yours. Humility." Hélène looked me over. "Combine that with your honor and integrity, and I assume your reliability, and that is all my sister and I have ever wanted in a man."

I frowned a little, frustrated at her goading. I didn't know why she would say such a thing or what her point was in doing so. Was she trying to test me?

She cocked her head to the side a little. "Did it bother you to learn of her past? There is plenty of scandal in both our lives."

"Marguerite is my wife," I answered, more than a little irritated. I also knew Marguerite herself would be appalled and embarrassed by Hélène's remarks. "I'm more concerned with her future than her past."

"What about her heritage?" Hélène pressed.

"What's wrong with her heritage?"

"So you don't know?" She bit her lip, much as Marguerite had done the night before.

"Marguerite told me about your mother, and her Salon," I said. "If that's what you mean."

Hélène shrugged, and then laughed a bit. "Never mind," she said, waving her hand and brushing the matter aside. "I was more interested to see if you indeed had any flaws at all. But I guess not, *n'est-pas?*"

"I'm sure Marguerite will tell you I have plenty, especially if you wait until after I give her orders to follow."

I turned to walk away, but as I glanced back, I was surprised to see Hélène looked glum.

"What is it?" I asked, frowning. "Do you have a problem with me, Hélène? I'd rather things be plain between us. We are adults; we can still maintain pleasantries in public, and you don't need to worry about Marguerite."

"Oh, I don't worry for her," Hélène said. "She has you. Rather, I'm quite jealous."

"Jealous?"

"Yes," Hélène said with a sigh. "I imagine it's not very likely there will be another such a man as yourself out there for me. Marguerite is truly a lucky woman to have found you."

THE ORDER OF THE CRYSTAL DAGGERS

Hélène had a prosperous career and she lived in Paris, a city with everything she could ever need, no more than a few blocks away. And she had come a long way from her roots and made a respectable life for herself.

I could say nothing to that. Instead, I merely bowed my head to her again in farewell. "I must be going. Good day, Hélène."

She waved, and despite her clear bitterness, she smiled at me. "Good day, Ben."

THE ORDER OF THE CRYSTAL DAGGERS

6

◊

By the time I arrived at the *Palais du Luxembourg*, I was grateful to be alone and back to work. Hélène's morning conversation had been strangely unsettling, and I was glad to have a distraction.

Even though it was a relatively short walk from the Latin Quarter, I hailed a carriage. Dirtying my formal suit dirty by walking would not leave a good impression, and a carriage ride would allow me to use the time to go over the notes I'd made over the last few weeks.

When I walked through the palace entrance, I regretted leaving Marguerite behind. I knew enough French to get by, though, and the one benefit of listening to Hélène and Marguerite talk for hours last night was that I was better able to listen and understand French by the time we retired. But learning a new language required extensive practice, and I would need more to master it yet.

As I jumped down from the carriage, plenty of people had already gathered outside the palace. The small crowd milled around, hoping to get a glimpse of history in the making. A wave of whispers suddenly shot through the crowd, and I turned to see where everyone's attention had shifted.

Coming down the street was a large litter bearing a small, ornately decorated chair, half-covered by a silk canopy. Several men carried it using the large, wooden poles at the sides. They each had dark skin and black hair and wore longer tunics—and familiar-looking shoes.

The thief wore similar shoes.

I frowned, trying to recall exactly how tall he'd been. I looked from each man to the next, searching for any sign of recognition, but I was too far away to get a good look. I would need to get closer.

A nice springtime breeze blew softly, and the silk canopy shifted, revealing the solitary figure in the chair. The wind ruffled his small fan and the turban on his head, but he remained still.

"Nguyễn Văn Tường," I whispered, no doubt butchering the language. "The one who's supposed to meet with Philastre to sign the treaty."

As the litter made its way into the palace, I saw the French government officials and several military men preparing to greet Nguyễn.

964

THE ORDER OF THE CRYSTAL DAGGERS

Two maidservant women pulled the canopy back for their leader. Briefly, I saw their large, formal dresses of silk, with all their delicate designs of embroidery.

Hélène would have liked seeing them.

All of them had come together in their polite, stern circle, and then Nguyễn disembarked from his litter. I strode forward along with the rest of them; thanks to the Order and Lady Penelope, I was acting as Queen Victoria's selected representative. I pulled out the papers that gave me the official invitation, and the palace guards let me inside.

The palace itself was full of business and history, and I felt all the hallowed quality that came with age and prestige as I walked to the signing room.

Nguyễn and Philastre greeted each other in the signing room, and the service began.

Overall, it was relatively quiet. The next hour was spent going over the various details of the treaty. From what I could translate, that included the formal recognition of Annam as a kingdom, France's role in protecting it from its warring neighbors, and guaranteeing trade rights. There were a few questions and replies, but then they signed their documents, and then it was time for the procession to leave.

I watched as all of this happened, and I was about to hail another carriage back to Hélène's quarters, satisfied with the calm turnout, when I saw him.

The thief from the day before was among those walking behind the Nguyễn's litter; I'd missed him on the way in, but as he passed me, his slanted eyes narrowed into angry slits, and he slowed in his pace, melting back into his native crowd.

I clenched my fists; I would have to find a way to capture him, and I would have to do it discretely. This was not the time to cause trouble, when representatives from two countries were watching.

I kept my eye firmly on the thief as I began to move forward. I walked briskly, not too fast, not too slow, but consistently; once the litter turned down the road toward the Port of Paris, I would make my move then.

The thief and I were of the same mind; the second the last carrier's shadow disappeared around the corner, we both took off.

"Not again," I grumbled under my breath.

Once more we raced through the streets. He was wearing the formal white robes of his country, so it was easy to spot him for a good while. By the time we reached the riverbanks, I saw he was trying to shed his outer robe gradually, letting himself fade into the rest of the crowds.

"Stop!" I called out.

It felt useless to say anything, and I felt even more discouraged when I passed by the same policeman from yesterday, and he began to call at me to stop, too.

"*Arrêtez!*"

Out the corner of my eye, I saw the thief stiffen; he recognized the policeman, too.

We raced ahead, just as the noontime church bells rang out through the city streets.

The bells must have given the thief an idea or two though, because he headed for the church entrance.

I was just thinking it was a shame Marguerite was not here when a horse neighed loudly.

Turning around, I was shocked to see Marguerite was riding atop the horse—and it was headed my way.

"Marguerite!" I scowled up at her. "What do you think you are doing?"

"Good morning to you, sir," Marguerite responded as I jumped aside to avoid getting run over. She wore her riding gown and bonnet with ease, and even from where I was, I could see her gloved hands had a firm, yet delicate grip on the reigns as she caught up to the thief.

He wasn't expecting her any more than I'd been.

She whirled the horse around in front of him. He tried to avoid it, but he ran right into the horse instead. As he strained to regain his balance, Marguerite jumped down from her sidesaddle.

As she landed squarely on top of him, I only wanted to grab her by the shoulders and scream at her for her recklessness.

Her horse was clearly uneasy by her sudden movement. It sidestepped, and the reins dragged along the ground.

I wanted to grab her by the shoulders and scream at her for her recklessness. Running up, I hauled Marguerite off the thief and both gently and angrily stood her on her feet.

"Marguerite," I growled. "Are you trying to give me a fit of apoplexy?"

"I was stopping him for you," Marguerite replied, fixing her bonnet, which had fallen askew when she'd jumped down. "And look, I got him—"

She was cut off as the thief jumped up, pushed himself between us, and shoved me down.

He grabbed Marguerite and held his arm around her throat dangerously.

She gasped in surprise as I scraped my leg on the cobblestone street.

"Marguerite!" I was screaming now with urgency as the thief held my wife hostage; no policeman was in sight, and people nearby scurried away as I feared the theif would strangle Marguerite. "Let her go—"

But Marguerite pulled out her fan; in the blink of an eye, she opened it up to reveal there were several long daggers hidden in the feathery folds. She stabbed him in the side.

He tightened his grip on her, but then he let her go as his side began to bleed significantly.

A moment later, he fell to the ground on his knees, and Marguerite knelt down next to him.

"Would you please stop?" I asked her. "You've done enough damage."

"I regret that I had to injure him," she said tightly. "But if you didn't want me to be here, you should've woken me up."

"You'd had a long night, and I didn't want you to worry about the treaty," I said. "You're here to see your sister. I figured you'd like the rest and you would appreciate the time with her."

"She's working this morning," Marguerite told me. "She's seeing to Prissy's training and getting her started with some basic rips and seams. She also has appointments with the ladies and courtesans of the city for measurements and fittings."

"Well, I didn't know that." I rolled my eyes. "She didn't mention that when I talked with her earlier."

Marguerite frowned. "You spoke to her this morning?"

"Yes. She was having a cup of tea when I left."

Marguerite scowled, and I didn't really think that mattered too much, but at the groan from below us, I remembered the thief.

"Let's take care of him, and then we can finish up this discussion later," I said to Marguerite.

"I'm the better doctor."

"I know, but I don't want him to hurt you. And after what he tried to do to you, he doesn't even deserve my help, little as it is." I pressed down on the thief's injury, trying to stop the bleeding. He squirmed and shouted at me angrily in his native tongue; after the signing, I knew he was from the Kingdom of Annam. "Do you know what he's saying?" I asked Marguerite.

"Nothing kind," she replied in a curt tone. "And I can't blame him. You're not going to stop the bleeding like that. In fact, I wouldn't be surprised if—"

She broke off as the thief collapsed into unconsciousness.

Marguerite and I exchanged a glance with each other, and she shrugged. "Well, I was about to say I wouldn't be surprised if he fainted."

"He's been quite the headache for us, but at least he's getting it as much as he'd giving it," I said.

"Ben, that is not kind."

I wanted to remind her that she was the one who'd nearly run him down with a horse, but I only shrugged. "What do you suggest?"

"Let's take him back to Hélène's." Marguerite skipped over to where the horse she'd been riding had gone. It was only a little way from us.

I looked back at her horse, which seemed docile enough. "Where did you get the horse?"

"I borrowed him from Hélène's neighbor, once I realized I was late to the signing," she said.

"He let you borrow it?"

"That's what I said, *mon amour.*" Marguerite gave me a cool smile. "I thought it would be rather unexpected. Don't you agree?"

I decided not say anything. I did wonder if Hélène's neighbor knew that she'd borrowed the horse or not, but either way, I was actually secretly pleased she did. That meant I wouldn't be forced to carry the bleeding thief on my own.

We loaded the thief up onto the saddle carefully, and then each of us took a side as we headed back toward Hélène's shop.

THE ORDER OF THE CRYSTAL DAGGERS

"We'll go around the back," Marguerite said as we headed down a block further than we needed. "That way I can return the horse while you get him up to bed."

I didn't think the thief needed the comfort of a bed, but I didn't say anything to Marguerite. She would only object, saying he needed care, and we would have to tend to him if we wanted to learn why he stole the painting, and she probably did feel bad about hurting him, even if he'd tried to hurt her first.

"Do you think it's a good idea to take him back to Hélène's when we still have the painting there?" I asked Marguerite.

"What choice do we have, Ben?" She looked back at the unconscious man on the horse. "We can't leave him. His wound needs treated."

His wound that you caused, I wanted to say, but I refrained.

"Now that the signing is over, I'll go and take the painting to the Louvre," I said. "That way, we won't be risking the painting's theft a second time."

"And what should I do?" Marguerite asked.

"You stay and watch over him," I grumbled, barely hiding my frustration. It looked like Marguerite had managed to find a way to work with me on my mission after all. "I'll tie him down before I leave, so you'll be safe if he wakes up while I'm gone."

Marguerite gave me a dazzling smile. "Sounds good, *mon amour.*"

"Yes," I said. "It sounds good—to you, at least."

THE ORDER OF THE CRYSTAL DAGGERS

7

◊

I was worried that the thief would wake up again before I left. It had been easy for him to escape me the first time he'd passed out, and I was not angling for a repeat experience.

This time, it appeared he was in much worse condition; after Marguerite and I had him tied down firmly to a spare bed, he still hadn't woken up.

So, I packed up the painting he'd been carrying and I headed out, once more hailing a carriage as I headed to the Louvre. I wasn't happy about leaving Marguerite, but I did want to clear my name and make sure the painting was secured. And it was nice to get a bit more of a rest in after chasing the thief from the Luxembourg Palace to Notre Dame. It had been several blocks, and I hadn't fully recovered from the previous day's run.

The Louvre had been one of France's finest palaces before it had been transformed into a museum. Several hallways and adjoining buildings were part of the palace but not part of the public display, and a number of construction projects had been underway for decades now, in efforts to take surrounding buildings and join them in with the Louvre. While there were various historical reasons for the project, and I could see it was all very grand; I was glad that I was able to find the service entrance without much difficulty.

After the chase yesterday, and then this morning, it unnerved me that so many policemen lined the hallways, but at least none of them looked familiar. Still, I kept an eye on them as I walked to meet with the curator, a man named Phillippe de Marsden.

He was a bright, energetic-looking man, with a flop of gray-speckled brown hair and a matching mustache that was neatly trimmed. He was wearing a suit that was professional, but it was covered with grime and paint at various spots. I didn't mind; he greeted me with warmth, and then suspicion, as I explained to him the unique situation.

"Well," he said eagerly, "I can see why they let you in, if it's truly Delacroix's Marianne. I have heard some concerns about your person, but since you mean to give me the painting, and you're not asking for money, I am willing to inspect your claims."

"Thank you," I said. I didn't like that my integrity was questioned, but it wasn't as if the man knew me, or even knew of me.

With the help of de Marsden and his assistants, I pulled out the painting carefully. He glanced it over and pulled out a large glass, examining different portions of the canvas.

"How did you come to own this?" he asked, frowning as he moved. His earlier excitement was gone, and his eyes were full of concern.

"I stole it from a thief," I admitted.

"A thief?"

"I figure it's not wrong to steal something that's been stolen, as long as it goes back to its rightful owner."

"Is that so?" de Marsden's scowl deepened. "I've been told the rumors about a thief with a crippled leg, who was stealing this from a rather popular Salon."

"I'm not the thief," I scoffed. "Or at least, not the original one. I just told you so."

"Yes, you did admit you stole it," de Marsden said angrily. "And I suspect, with that kind of caviler attitude, I have very little hope you're not here to try to claim some reward after all."

"What do you mean?" I asked. "This is the painting I found, and I told you I'm here to return it."

"Do you think I'm a fool? I am the curator here at the Louvre, the most acclaimed museum and collection of art in the modern world!" Phillippe looked indignant as he shook his head and gestured toward one of the guards at the door. "And this is a forgery."

"A fake?" I repeated. "But—"

"It's a very good one, sir, and one of the better ones, for certain," he continued, as the guard came up behind me. "But this is not Delacroix's true work."

"Why would I lie to you?" I asked, pushing back.

"Well, if you have nothing to hide, you wouldn't run away, for one," Phillippe said. "And another, I suspect this is a forgery that you intended to turn over to us, and, when you and your thieving cohorts went to sell the original, we would assume this one is the real one. But you underestimate us, sir."

THE ORDER OF THE CRYSTAL DAGGERS

"I didn't know it was a fake," I insisted, ducking as another guard tried to catch me.

"You're a very good actor, but just like this painting, it's all falsehoods and lies in the end." Phillippe shook his head. "For shame, too. Have you no decency, sir?"

It was more than ironic, I thought. I was trying to return a painting that had been presumed lost, only to find out it was a forgery, and then get accused of working with the original thief.

"There were rumors of art thieves decades ago," Phillippe continued. "They were ambitious, wanting to secure and replace the world's most treasured pieces with their own fakes. France has always been the envy of the world; but it is precisely because of that, I have made a most meticulous study, and I will not be misled."

"This was just a mistake," I reiterated, but it was to no avail. Phillippe wouldn't listen to me.

"Didn't you hear me?" Phillippe scoffed. "I will not be made a fool over this. Guards, arrest him, and then escort my assistants to the junk pile. This forgery needs to be burned with the rest of our discards at the end of the day."

Phillippe would not listen; I had no choice but to run for it.

As I made my escape, I sincerely hoped our thief would be awake by the time I got back to Marguerite and her sister. I needed some answers, and it was clear he was the only one who could give them to me.

8

◊

"Marguerite, come quickly." I stepped into Hélène's house, eager to find a place to sit down and rest.

Not without some difficulty, I had escaped the Louvre, and made the long way back to Hélène's shop. The run home had been long and spread out, and while I'd been able to take more breaks than when I had been chasing after the thief, I was still exhausted, and I wanted nothing more than to rest my feet.

I didn't hear a response, so I headed toward the parlor, wondering if perhaps she was talking with Hélène or even Prissy some.

I was surprised to see all of them sitting there, nervously looking at each other in silence.

"Hello, ladies," I said, suddenly realizing something was dreadfully wrong. "What is—?"

At the small, familiar *click* of a bullet entering the shaft chamber, I froze and went silent, too.

I glanced to the side, expecting to see the thief we'd caught earlier.

But to my surprise, it wasn't him.

It was a woman—the same woman Marguerite had tried to help the previous day.

"I see you found Madame Phénix's shop," I said dryly.

"Be quiet," the woman muttered in English. "I have come here for my brother—and our painting. I want them now."

"Your painting?" I needed to keep her talking, distracting her as my fingers slid down to the dagger at my side. "You mean the fake painting? The forgery of Delacroix's *Liberty Leading the People?*"

She went quiet for a long moment, before I realized she was trying to translate my words in her head. I thought about repeating myself, but she eventually nodded.

"Yes. It is our painting." She held the gun up more firmly to my temple. "I demand you give it to me along with my brother."

"Who are you?" I asked, stepping back.

973

"You don't know?" she huffed. "I should not be surprised to see that the family of Louis Valoris does not recognize me. They do not acknowledge their victims."

"What?" My jaw tightened. "We're not part of the Valoris family. Why would you think that? We're nothing like that lying, murderous—"

I was about to tell her she had her information wrong, and that she was mistaken—and unlike Phillippe de Marsden, I would be willing to hear her side of the story.

But just at that moment, Marguerite let out a frightened moan, and I turned to look at her.

And this time, I *really* looked at her.

For all the years of our marriage, I'd never before noticed how some of her features—even the more prominent ones, like her crystalline green eyes or her blond curls—suddenly reminded me of Lumiere.

Before, I'd never noticed it; and now, it was uncanny.

My jaw went slack as the truth struck me hard, and my heart sank.

All other thoughts—the foreign woman, her injured brother, the painting, the gun—fled.

How could my sweet, beloved Marguerite be related to the insidious Louis Valoris—the same Louis Valoris who was a murderer, the mastermind behind the world's end, and the one who'd damaged and destroyed so much of my family?

"I told you to tell him the truth," Hélène whispered.

I turned to glare over at her, wanting to rebuke her for doubting me; but then I saw the similarity in her distinctive eyebrows and her pouted lips, and it struck me hard that I'd married into Louis and Lumiere's family.

"How?" I finally asked.

"Louis was our father," Marguerite whispered quietly, as her eyes fill with tears. "We are his illegitimate offspring. We didn't know until our mother died. She must have suspected he might come after her at some point, because she named him in her will."

"We think he had her killed," Hélène added. "Although there is no way to prove it now. But our mother was a shrewd, ruthless woman of business herself, and she knew too much about his ambitions."

"What of Lumiere?" I asked. "Does he know?"

974

THE ORDER OF THE CRYSTAL DAGGERS

"He is our half-brother. He doesn't know. Or at least, we don't think so," Marguerite admitted, glancing over at Hélène, who nodded in agreement. "We only truly know the power and reputation behind Louis Valoris' name, which is why we vowed never to speak of it."

"What about Lady Penelope?" I asked, suddenly curious. It did seem very strange my grandmother, Louis' long-time rival and archenemy, would be the very person to save his illegitimate daughters from a life of professional prostitution and never mention it to me. "Does she know?"

"No." Marguerite shook her head. "Neither of us ever mentioned it to her."

I didn't know what to think of that; I was more willing to bet Lady Penelope *did* know.

All of my earlier desire to learn of the painting and its origins had been summarily dismissed inside my mind; I was flustered and unexpectedly caught off guard by the revelation.

But the woman pressed the barrel of her gun into my temple again, once more demanding our attention.

"I want my brother, and our painting," she insisted. She seemed to realize I was stunned by the revelation of Marguerite's lineage, and that she had missed something after all. "I waited for you to return; I will not wait any longer now that you can see I will kill you and your family if you do not give me what I want."

"Your brother, or the man I assume to be your brother, is upstairs resting," I said. "I ran into him earlier. He did not escape unscathed."

She paused again, and I clarified, "He's hurt."

"What happened?" she asked. "Did you hurt him?"

"Yes, but I did not mean to." I heard Marguerite whimper again; she knew I was protecting her from the woman's anger. "My wife has been caring for him."

The woman looked crushed, and her aim faltered as her shoulders slumped forward in despair.

"Please," Marguerite said as she stood up.

The woman jerked back up her gun in Marguerite's direction, and I couldn't risk it; I whipped out my dagger, letting the blade of the *Wahabite Jambiya* strike; the gun fell out of the woman's grasp, and I hurried to kick it away from her.

THE ORDER OF THE CRYSTAL DAGGERS

The woman screamed in frustration as Hélène grabbed the fallen gun, and Marguerite pulled her toward the small couch. I sat down on her one side and gripped her arm, while Marguerite sat down on the other side; much as we had earlier with the thief on the horse, we secured her between us.

"Hélène," I said. "Go and see if her brother is awake."

"Prissy is tending to him," Marguerite told me. "I had her stay upstairs when Hélène called me."

Hélène nodded toward the woman. "She told me she was an ambassador for Nguyễn Văn Tường. She wanted me to see about creating a style for the Kingdom of Annam, making dresses and *ao dai*, their traditional formal wear."

"I saw your brother with Nguyễn earlier," I said, surprising the woman. "He was one of his servants."

The woman nodded. "Yes. We both work for Nguyễn. It was the only way we could come to Paris."

"Why did you want to come here?" Marguerite looked at her curiously. "Was it because of Louis Valoris?"

The woman glared at her and went silent.

"I am sorry," Marguerite said, her eyes on the ground. "But I vow, my sister and I are not like our father. We do not support him or anything that he has done. We do not even know what he did in many instances."

"You are lying."

"No, we're not," Marguerite insisted. "We will prove it to you. We will let you go, and we will give you your brother, and your painting, too."

I cleared my throat. "Well, actually—"

Before I could tell them what happened to the painting, Hélène came down the stairs with the thief behind her. Prissy was behind him, helping him stay upright. I noticed his nose had a small scratch on it, and there was a large bandage wrapped around his torso.

I didn't need to ask; I could guess that Marguerite and Prissy had patched him up after my lackluster job earlier.

When the thief saw his sister, he immediately brightened up. "Thuy!"

We all exchanged looks, but the woman jumped up from between me and Marguerite, and she went running up to him.

THE ORDER OF THE CRYSTAL DAGGERS

"Tho," she exclaimed happily. "I am so happy you are alive. I thought they would kill you."

"They helped me with my wounds," Tho replied. He glared over at me. "But they also caused them."

"I was only trying to stop you from getting away with thievery," I explained.

"Ben, say you're sorry," Prissy insisted. "He's a nice young man and he's injured, too."

"Yes, Mr. Ben," Tho said. "Say you're sorry."

If I had been less shocked by Marguerite's secret, I might have been amused by the entire situation. Thuy's determination for justice was understandable, Tho's battered state could have been avoided, but I was baffled by Prissy's assertiveness. It seemed my stepsister had been charmed by her patient, and at a most inconvenient time.

Tho and Thuy turned to look at me.

Now that I saw them together, I realized they were likely twins; they were around the same age, height, and learning, and they even seemed more coordinated in their movements and mannerisms than most individuals.

If I knew anything about siblings on mission, they were to be taken seriously.

"I'm Benedict Svoboda," I said, giving them a formal introduction. "I am a member of the Order of the Crystal Daggers, and I came here to oversee the signing of the Philastre Treaty. This is my wife, Marguerite, and her sister, Hélène."

"Madame Phénix," Thuy murmured, and I nodded.

"This is also my stepsister, Priscilla," I said, gesturing toward her.

"We've met," Tho replied, making me scowl as Prissy smiled.

"I am Khang Von Thuy, and this is my brother, Khang Von Tho," Thuy said. "Now, where is our painting?"

"I took it to the Louvre," I said. "It is an art museum. The curator is the one who told me it is a fake."

Tho and Thuy did not look surprised in the least.

"We know," Tho said. "Our mother was the one who painted it."

THE ORDER OF THE CRYSTAL DAGGERS

I looked back to Marguerite and Hélène, and I started to realize how everything was connected. I thought back to what Ella had told me about our mother's last mission to Prague, about Louis' devious plans involving an art ring, and even Phillippe de Marsden's earlier tale of forgeries.

"Your mother was one of Louis Valoris' artists," I said. "He used a lot of them to make forgeries of famous works throughout Europe and the known world."

Thuy and Tho nodded in unison.

"The Order worked against him," I said quietly. "My own mother worked on such a case."

"Our mother was a great talent," Thuy said. "Louis Valoris brought the original of our painting to her in Saigon, and she painted it. It was a perfect match."

"Some of the paint compositions must have been different, and perhaps the canvas material, too," I said, thinking of how de Marsden had examined the painting. "But if it was in its frame, no one would be able to tell."

"Yes." Tho nodded. "She died many years ago; we suspect one of her rivals killed her, or even because of Louis Valoris himself. We have been struggling to find all her paintings. The one I stole earlier was her first forgery. There are several others around Europe that are hers, too."

I glanced over at Marguerite. If what they were saying was true—and it seemed like it was—then it was certainly something the Order should investigate.

She nodded in agreement, but then she looked down in shame.

"We want her work back," Thuy continued. "They are the only things we have left of her now. It is hard for others to understand our desires, but we want them to remind us of her."

"My mother died a long time ago, too." I heard myself say the words before I realized I was speaking. Quickly, I brushed aside my embarrassment and stepped forward. "I understand you more than you can ever know."

I thought back to the book Marguerite had found for me just the day before; I thought of how happy Ella would be to know we'd found it. Holding it had been holding onto a piece of my past, and a piece of our family history.

THE ORDER OF THE CRYSTAL DAGGERS

Yes, I understood Tho and Thuy very well in that moment. I could even understand their hatred of Louis Valoris, knowing how he'd tormented Lady Penelope and my mother over the years before his suicide.

Long silence passed between us, and then Thuy reached out her hand.

"We would like our painting now."

I cringed. "I told you, I don't have it. I would give it to you, but I left it at the Louvre when they accused me of working with a gang of art thieves."

Tho and Thuy both frowned.

"You do not have it?" Tho asked again, as if he had not understood me.

I shook my head. "No. But I will do everything I can to help you get it back. If you will come with me now, we will get it back before the day is over."

And we will have to. Otherwise, their painting will burn.

"What do you want us to do?" Tho asked. He inhaled sharply. "I may not be much good."

"I will hire a carriage," Hélène said before she rushed from the room.

"I will help with Tho's injuries," Prissy volunteered.

"And I will follow your directions," Marguerite promised.

Her comment made me pause; I could tell from her expression she was still unsure of how shocked I was, and she didn't want to cross me. I wanted to talk to her, to ask questions, and try to figure things out.

But there were more pressing matters to attend to. If my mother's book was about to get burned, as Tho and Thuy's mother's painting was, I would not want anything to stop me. As we all lined up to load into a carriage, I pulled her aside.

"We will talk later," I said. "For now, stay where I can see you."

"I wouldn't let you down," Marguerite insisted. "And I wouldn't betray you."

I put my hands on her shoulders. "We will talk later," I reiterated. "We have a job to do."

"We?"

I was at least a little gratified to see she was not certain how to take the news that she would be joining me on our outing, even if I still worried for her safety.

Grimly, I nodded. "Yes."

Even before we arrived at the Louvre, I knew getting inside would be much harder, especially since I'd run away earlier, and there were still guards around. Whether they recognized me or not, I was certain that it wasn't common for a "crippled thief" to bring in a painting, expect no compensation, and then fight to take his leave.

"Listen," I said. "The Louvre is a big palace. I'm not sure where they took your painting. We'll have to make a plan."

"Why can we not run in?" Tho asked.

"They think your painting was from a criminal art forgery ring," I tried to explain. "They will think you're the villain."

Just as I did, until about an hour ago.

I did not say that part aloud.

I glanced over at Marguerite, who was huddled in the seat next to me, still unwilling to meet my gaze. She was the one who taught me I could never expect the unexpected. I was starting to realize that in expecting the unexpected anyway, the unexpected only became more absurd.

Here I was, teaming up with twins, helping them recover their mother's painting, which was linked all the way back to Louis Valoris and my own mother's memory, too.

"Here's what we're going to do," I said. "Tho, you're injured, so you're going to walk toward the servant's entrance in the back, the one where I went in earlier. Prissy, you walk with him."

"That's fine with me," Prissy agreed, tightening her arm around Tho's.

"You're going to walk until you're about halfway between the street and the door," I said to Tho. "Then, I want you to pretend that you're sick and you need help. You need to faint. I know you can manage that."

Tho made a face at me, but he nodded.

"Then, Prissy, you start crying and get them to come and help you pick Tho up."

"Yes," Prissy agreed. "I can do that."

"Are you sure?" I'd never seen her cry before, but I wasn't about to assign Marguerite the role instead.

She squared her shoulders with pride. "Yes. I'm good at looking help-less."

I wasn't going to argue with her.

"Thuy," I said, turning to her. "You're going to go to the front. You'll pretend to be the ambassador for Nguyễn Văn Tường again. I know you can do that well."

"So do I," Hélène agreed with a begrudging smile.

I ignored her, as I pointed to Thuy's gun, the one she'd tried to use on us earlier. "Once you're inside, you—"

"What do I do? Do I shoot someone?" Thuy asked.

She reminded me of Ella so much in that moment, and while I knew my sister was a weakness, it was such a weakness that gave me the strength to fight harder. It was understood between us that we were no longer enemies, but allies. As I met Thuy's gaze, I had the feeling it was possible we might even be friends one day, if our mission went well.

"Hopefully not." I almost smiled. "Pretend that you're here for your scheduled tour, and that Nguyễn Văn Tường has personally requested Phillippe de Marsden, the curator, as your guide. Hélène, you go with her as her translator. See if you can find out where the burning pile is located. I heard Phillippe de Marsden say he wanted to burn your mother's paint-ing, since it was such an excellent forgery."

After another long moment, Thuy nodded, and then I looked to Mar-guerite.

"You and I will sneak in after the others provide the distraction," I said. "Go follow Prissy and Tho, and sneak in the back."

"What should we do after the guards come?" Prissy asked.

"Have them take you and Tho to a room inside the Louvre," I said. "That way, they can provide him with medical treatment. If they won't do that, have them escort you to a carriage again, and go home. We will meet you later. There's nothing else the rest of us will be able to help you."

"You seem to have all of this planned out," Hélène said, amused. "It seems that you've inherited Lady Penelope's famed intellect."

"Well, Ella got my mother's looks; I had to get something from the family, too," I replied, watching as Marguerite smiled. I could almost see her thoughts; we both knew if I'd waited to return the painting, none of our planning would be necessary. "Now, does anyone have any ques-tions?"

A moment passed in silence before my wife spoke up.

"If we find the painting, how do we get out?" Marguerite asked.

"As fast as you can." I tried to give her a smile, but it was impossible to smile when she seemed so miserable.

Instead, I took a deep breath and shifted my focus.

I would talk with her later. I had more pressing concerns at the moment. Once I solved the problem I'd helped cause, I could move on to the next bit of trouble without worry.

◊   ◊   ◊   ◊

The plan seemed simple enough, but it wasn't flawless. I'd taken everyone's strengths and weaknesses into consideration, and I'd given them the push to do what they did best.

I'd planned it all out, and now I had to hope for the best, and then leave it at that.

Hélène and Thuy alighted down from the carriage first, since we were passing by the main entrance. I decided to wait until everyone else had gone to their assigned locations to loop around and follow after Hélène and Thuy. I watched as they went down and headed off, and I had to fight the urge not to yell out further instructions before the carriage rolled on.

When Prissy and Tho left next, it was just me and Marguerite left.

I looked at her, but she still did not want to look at me.

Is she worried I'll only think of Lumiere when I see her? Or maybe I'd think of how much I hate Louis for all his cruelty?

I couldn't imagine what was going on inside her mind. I would just have to wait and talk with her later.

"Marguerite." I took her hands in mine, but she jerked away from me. I sighed and let her go, as it was time for us to move, too. "Please be safe."

"I will." She finally gave me a small glimpse, before she nodded.

"Once we get the painting, we can leave and go home," I said.

She only winced, and I didn't know what else to say.

I got down from our carriage, paid the driver, and then we also sped off.

Already, I could hear Prissy wailing at the top of her lungs, as Tho twitched on the ground, grabbing his side and crying out in pain. It looked like they were both eager for careers on the stage, should the occasion call for it.

I almost said this to Marguerite, but she was already gone, slipping inside the servant door I'd walked through earlier, as the guards tried to pacify both Prissy and Tho.

I disappeared down an alleyway, looking for a way inside. I tripped and fell by accident as my bad leg caught on a garbage bin lid. It was then I thought of Ferdy and his clever use of disguises, and I rubbed more grime on my clothes, and walked out, exaggerating my limp.

"Help," I whimpered, engaging in my own acting abilities with a sense of personal humiliation. "I've been robbed."

Some of the guards came to see me, and it wasn't long before I'd managed to talk my way inside the Louvre—and once I was inside, I followed up my act using my sister's favorite trick.

"I need to excuse myself," I said. "I fear I need to use the washroom."

No one bothered to question me.

I made my way through the large palace, looking for different rooms, wondering where the painting could have gone. It was a very large, grueling job, and my leg ached again with overuse; I would need to rest, and really rest, before I did any strenuous exercise.

It was only when I heard Phillippe de Marsden's voice again that I cheered up. I could hear him talking to Hélène while Thuy was speaking in her native language fervently. Beside her, Hélène gave her best charming act to Phillippe, who looked absolutely dazzled by her attentions, as she pretended to translate Thuy's words.

"My client heard that you had some of Delacroix's work here," Hélène said. "She is most interested in his Lady Liberty."

"That's so strange," Phillippe said, but he brightened up as Hélène let him take her arm and escort her more closely. "I specifically had a fake version of that painting taken out back to the gardens. As it is a fake, it's not right to let it remain; others would get confused. In fact, I'm certain that you must have heard that from one of the worker boys here; they're ignorant and they know nothing of true art, let alone how to identify a forgery."

"So it is a forgery?" Hélène pressed. "How do you know?"

THE ORDER OF THE CRYSTAL DAGGERS

"Why, I examined it myself, and while the painting was excellent, and the quality was high, the canvas was made of rice leaves," he explained. "Papyrus was the main paper of the Egyptians, and the Far East has rice plants. You can tell a culture by its paper, you know."

"Oh, do go on," Hélène said, as Thuy went quiet. She had a look of pride on her face as they continued to walk down the hall.

"Good," I muttered under my breath. "The painting is in the back gardens."

Quietly as possible, I signaled Thuy. She saw me at once, and gave me an almost imperceivable nod.

Even without knowing her long, I knew she had gotten my message. She was doing a good job at distracting the curator, and we knew where to look—and that was where I was headed.

As I made my way there, I overheard servants complaining about "the spoiled little rich girl" and her "foreign husband" who was clearly hoping to die thanks to how tightly she clung to him.

I grinned; Prissy was playing her part well, too.

I was just wondering where Marguerite was when we both stepped into the back gardens; she came from the east side, and I came from the west.

Her face lit up briefly. "Ben."

I gave her a slight bow. "Madame."

"You heard that the painting was here, too, did you?"

I nodded. "Let's find it and get out of here, shall we?"

She smiled. "I think I've seen enough art today."

Together, it didn't take the two of us long to find the painting. It had been thrown in a pile of other items; dirty curtains, stained, incomplete canvasses, and even some damaged frames.

It was strange to see such damaged beauty in a garden that was full of lovely plants and just-blooming bushes and flowers.

Without a word, Marguerite and I pulled the fake painting from the pile, smoothed it out, and folded it carefully. She then handed it to me.

"Thank you," I said, as we turned back to leave.

"Did I listen to you?" Marguerite asked, her voice full of hesitation. "Are you pleased?"

"I think everyone did a good job so far," I said. "See if you can let them know we got it, and they can leave now. I'll sneak out and get a carriage. And then we can go home."

"I will do that," Marguerite said. Her voice was still gloomy, and I knew she was still unsure of how I felt.

I wasn't entirely sure of that myself, but I was certain that Louis Valoris would never bother to steal a fake painting from a secure museum, nor would he make friends with the people he'd chased all over the city the day before.

And knowing that, it gave me hope.

10

◊

Not for the first time, it was pure relief to get back to Hélène's shop.

Tho and Thuy were very pleased to have their mother's painting back; Hélène and Prissy were lively, excited to have been helpful in a real spy mission. Marguerite was the only one who seemed distant, but even she answered questions and told the others about how she'd listened to my instructions perfectly.

Everyone else seemed eager to exchange stories and hear what had happened in the museum. While I was just happy no one had been caught, arrested, or killed, all the running around and the stress had worn me out.

I was nodding off as the carriage rolled up to the shop.

"I know we said we would talk later," I said to Marguerite. "But it has been a very long day, and I am tired. We can talk in the morning, if that suits you."

She paused for a moment, and then nodded. "If that is your wish."

I arched my brow at her again. "I thought you said I wouldn't want a wife who would follow me blindly."

"My faith in you is not blind," Marguerite said quietly, though there was a depressed quality to her expression. "I do want to say something first. I want you to know that I'm aware I broke the trust between us by not telling you the truth about my father. I do hope you'll be able to forgive me for that. But I still love you and I want to remain your wife, even though I know your family hates mine."

"Marguerite, don't—"

I reached for her, but she shook her head. She stepped back, gave me a quick curtsy, and then excused herself.

"I'll see you in the morning," she murmured, before she left.

Before I could follow her, I felt a tug on my other sleeve.

I turned to see Tho there. He was still holding his side a little uneasily, but he was smiling.

"Mr. Ben," he said. "My sister and I have been talking, and we would like to work with you."

"Work with me?" I repeated, as though I wasn't sure I'd heard him correctly.

"Yes. You know a lot about this spy business. And we can help the Order you were talking about, too. We have some of our mother's notes about her paintings. If we work together, we might be able to find more."

"Yes," Thuy agreed. "And you could teach us more. We do not know how to do spy work like you do. Would the Order accept orphans such as us?"

I looked at Thuy's young face, and Tho's eager expression.

I thought back to my own early days working with Lady Penelope, and Amir, and Harshad, and how I'd longed for a place to belong and a purpose to serve.

I knew what it was like to be in their position. They were orphaned, alone except each other, determined to honor their mother's legacy.

Who could teach them better than me?

"Well … " I glanced back toward the door Marguerite had disappeared through. She'd told me before that Lady Penelope would like to see me progress in the Order, and pass on what I'd learned.

It looked like I would be able to not only be a mentor, but I would be able to find my own students, too—starting with two of them.

In some ways, I could almost see Ella's smile twinkling through Thuy's bright brown eyes. And it wasn't hard for me to remember my own resolve to succeed when I'd first started; looking at Tho, it was clear he had that same determination, too.

"I would be honored to teach you," I finally said.

They both bowed to me, and then they both reached out and took hold of my hands.

Thuy smiled reverently. "Thank you, Teacher."

Tho glanced up. "We welcome your instruction. We promise to do well, in honor of our mother."

I gripped their hands back tightly in my own, truly touched by the gift of their time and their trust.

I had a feeling the next few weeks would be hard on them, and maybe on me, too.

THE ORDER OF THE CRYSTAL DAGGERS

All of us would be squashed into Hélène's quarters—but we could make ourselves a home here.

Yes. Everything will be fine. We can make it work. I can just think of it as another new mission.

I looked up at Thuy and Tho. "You're welcome. We'll start training tomorrow afternoon. Before we begin, I have to draw up some plans, and I should write a letter to Lady Penelope, to let her know we will be staying in Paris a little while longer." I glanced behind me again, looking for Marguerite, even though I knew she'd gone up to bed. "And there's something important that I need to take care of tomorrow morning, too."

989

THE ORDER OF THE CRYSTAL DAGGERS

11

◊

I fell asleep fast, but the next morning, when I woke up, I found I'd been dreaming of *Otec* and *Máma*, of Ella and Ferdy; I thought about Lady POW and Harshad, of Hélène and Prissy, and Marguerite, too, and I thought about how my family had done a fair job of growing in the last few years.

In the distance, I could hear the sound of the Cathedral's church bells.

Was it really Sunday already?

I opened my eyes to see my wife sleeping peacefully on the bed, curled away from me. Her hair was a tangled mess of curls as she breathed in deeply and peacefully. I pushed a curl back from her forehead, watching her in wonder. Watching her was magic, and hearing the call of the day's beginning felt like the spell was breaking—but it was only breaking into something more beautiful.

I reached over, pulling Marguerite against me.

"What is it?" she murmured sleepily.

"Get up and get dressed," I whispered. "And hurry. We have to get going."

"Do we have a mission today?"

"Yes," I said. "We do."

Marguerite finally opened her eyes; she was more than a little confused, but she still did as I requested.

Quietly, the two of us made our way through Hélène's house and sneaked out the back door; I was in a good mood, and enough so that even my leg didn't seem quite so painful this morning.

We began to walk, and Marguerite asked me all sorts of questions before she gave up.

I kept my silence; I wouldn't tell her where we were going.

It was only when the Notre Dame Cathedral came into view, and we began to walk up to its majestic entrance that Marguerite fell completely silent. I held onto her hand, which was trembling, and I was surprised to see her eyes filling with tears as we entered into the sacred building.

"What is it?" I lowered my voice. "Did I do something wrong?"

990

THE ORDER OF THE CRYSTAL DAGGERS

"No. It's just … I have been wanting to come here with you," Marguerite whispered. "More than anything. With everything that happened since we've come, I almost forgot."

"It's no matter. I remembered." I tightened her hand in mine as we entered into the sanctuary of the Notre Dame Cathedral. Its grand buttresses, the high vaulted ceilings, and the delicately ornate altar immersed us in an otherworldly setting. There were people in the pews, preparing for the morning mass, and several of the church's priests and attendants were scurrying around as they prepared for service.

"After my mother died, I used to come here when I couldn't sleep," Marguerite confessed.

"Back when you and Hélène were still running your mother's … business?"

She nodded, even as she shivered. A brothel was a sordid business, even if it was still a "business."

"I used to cry and pray to be rescued from my troubles. I used to dream that despite the obstacles I had from my birth and background, I would be able to find a husband who could love me."

"Of course, you would." I could hardly believe that it was a point of pain for her to believe herself unlovable, especially since I, as her husband, got to love her as no one else would. "Who could resist loving you?"

"Are you certain you should ask me that?" Marguerite asked. "I know of plenty who can resist; some of the people Hélène and I blackmailed wanted us dead. Men don't actually want to marry prostitutes. And of course, my own father, whether I knew him or not, was a monster and a murderer."

"You are not who he is, Marguerite," I told her. "That's why I brought you here."

She looked around. "What?"

"I wanted to tell you, on hallowed, sacred ground, that I still love you, and I still want you to be my wife," I said. "It's true our families have complicated histories; but why should that stop us from finding love, especially among all the hate? That is what love does, after all."

Marguerite finally smiled at me—that smile I loved, the one bursting with sunlight and joy.

991

"You know, when Hélène was all finished setting her new identity and her shop, I left Paris with Lady Penelope. I'd never felt so free in all my life. But I did feel bad. I had to stop coming here, to this place, to wish away my shame, even if I still carried it, and soon enough, I forgot my dreams."

She looked all around, taking in the brilliantly lit windows, full of light and sunshine. I could almost see her memories, as she remembered how desperate she'd felt as she lit a candle by the altar, praying for a future she found unattainable.

"You can't understand how wonderful I feel, standing here beside you, Ben." When she turned back to face me, her eyes were shining with happy tears. "You are a miracle—a miracle to me, and a miracle for me. Even when we were first together, you didn't have to marry me; I would have taken any position to be with you—lover, mistress, nurse, student. Anything at all."

I took both her hands in mine. "It's not just your prayer that has been answered; I don't think I ever even dared to voice mine. I am glad I have you as my wife."

Discreetly as possible, I leaned over. The whole room lit, blazing with the colors of the rose window, as I kissed her softly on the lips.

I closed my eyes at the taste of her, and my vision swirled with light and color, falling into love's messy, warm, and radiant embrace. My heart felt as dazzling and deep as any impressionist work of art, and Marguerite was twice as captivating—and in that moment, I knew that I would only be drawn more in as the years passed and we faced down all our days together.

"I love you," I whispered.

"I love you, too." Marguerite pulled away and smiled up at me, bright enough to rival the sun itself. "And no one will ever be able to stop me from doing so."

"That's just as well, since I don't intend to let you stop." I leaned in to kiss her.

"Wait," Marguerite said, putting her finger over my lips. "Does this mean you'll let me come on more missions with you now? Now you know I have a stellar spy pedigree, in addition to Lady Penelope's training."

She was teasing me, but just like Ella, Marguerite was a weakness in my heart that compelled me to become stronger.

THE ORDER OF THE CRYSTAL DAGGERS

"I think I will have to bring you along now," I said. "We can't have someone like you left to her own devices for too long without supervision. But you must promise me two things."

"Yes. Anything."

"We have no more secrets between us," I said.

"That's fair."

"And you'll follow my directions."

"As long as you answer all my questions, I will agree to that." Marguerite's mischievousness lit up her emerald eyes as the morning sunshine blazed through the rose-stained glass and baptized us in a sea of color and light.

"We'll work it out," I said, unable to stop myself from leaning in.

The church bells began to ring again, and their music was a resounding, heavenly harkening, only perfected all the more by Marguerite's muted laughter as I kissed her.

THE ORDER OF THE CRYSTAL DAGGERS

C. S. Johnson is an award-winning, genre-hopping author of several novels, including *The Starlight Chronicles* series, the *Once Upon a Princess* saga, and the *Divine Space Pirates* trilogy. With a gift for sarcasm and an apologetic heart, she currently lives in Atlanta with her family.

AUTHOR'S NOTE

Dear Reader,

I hope you don't mind my indulgence in this matter. Leaving The Order of the Crystal Daggers behind was difficult for me, and I am not really that surprised to find myself writing this companion novella—especially since I started writing it before *Heart of Hope and Fear* was even finished.

There were a few things that went into this one with the rawness of an open wound.

A few years ago, in 2019, I watched in horror as Notre Dame Cathedral began to burn. Eventually the spire collapsed and the roof, centuries old and its secrets well-guarded, collapsed. I am truly grateful for the French fire department workers who sought to save it, including the relics, but as I watched it burn I felt as though a part of my own heart was on fire. I wept at the loss, and later, I wept out of gratefulness for what was saved. I couldn't stop the pain or the change, but I am grateful for what is left, and what can be sustained.

At the heart of this novel, I think that this is what Ben also realizes.

There is good in tearing down tyranny, if it is all tyranny; but something better still must be built up in its place. While Ben's pain at the loss of his mother, father, and Amir is still there, he realizes without those losses, he never would have met Marguerite, and that good is not something to let go of despite the scars and wounds he's accumulated throughout his life. Her love, tender and meticulous, has strengthened him in ways that, even with his crooked leg, he will be able to better face the challenges of his life—and help teach others to do the same.

And challenges will come; the world doesn't wait for change, after all, and I think that's the hardest thing for me to put down in this novella. Ben is healing from the past, and looking forward to the future, but the present is full of changes that might seem good or bad, but either way, they can still bring us the best blessings.

When you are caught behind in your struggles, it can be hard to move along with time, and that's why unchanging things of truth, beauty, and goodness are so critical to use as mile markers, as well as progress. The world is changing, yet we still must find the good, the beautiful, and the true, and cling to it even as our ability to do just that wanes and waxes.

I truly hope you have enjoyed this series, and I love to think that leaving you here will give you plenty of ideas for your own stories of Ben and Marguerite going on missions with Tho and Thuy, and perhaps Ella, Ferdy, and all the others, too.

I hope you will look forward to my next series. It is always a miracle to me, to find familiar eyes on my work.

Until We Meet Again,

C. S. Johnson

SAMPLE READING

Chapter 1 *from*

DRAGON TEARS

A COMPANION NOVELLA TO

THE ALLIANCE OF THE DRAGON SWORD

❋ ❋ ❋ ❋

C. S. Johnson

CHAPTER ONE

No one ever paid attention to a Ghost.

By the time I was twelve, I was used to how often eyes slid over me and the others as we went about our work. We were considered an essential, if regrettable, part of life in Laena, but as odd as that may sound, that was just how things were. In many ways, it was an understandable situation, too.

The Ghost Children of the Laenite Tribe were children who were born out of wedlock, orphaned at a young age, or even on the rare occasion, abandoned by our parents. The "Ghost" moniker was rumored to have been a jest originally, but as we were the remnants of incomplete lives, forgotten dreams, or abandoned mistakes, it was a label that carried a cruel truth.

In our community, where faith came first and family came second, Ghost Children were largely an afterthought.

However, the others and I did not allow this to be a point of contention between us and other Laenites. It wasn't as though the world and its realities left us unprepared. The Creator had given us a beautiful place to live and thrive, but because of sin, darkness, and despair, imperfections and abuses, there was an endless, growing chasm between humanity and divinity—all of this was unable to be ignored or denied. Our religion taught us to embrace our positions as the invisible shadows of our society, and through our work, even if it was not acknowledged, we kept the light burning ever more brightly.

To us, this was only right, since we were the adopted children of Ceru, the Great Sea Serpent and the Water Dragon Guardian of Laena.

Like the other Ghosts, Ceru took me in as an abandoned baby and gave me a bed, clothes, food, and a traditional education. It was thanks to Ceru that I had grown up surrounded by the hills of my home, where snowy mountains bled into waterfalls like open wounds and flowers dotted the ravines all throughout spring.

The arrangement had a sacred name in the ancient tongue, but the Laenites often referred to it as a Life Debt. Ceru saved my life when he adopted me, so it was my duty to serve and honor him.

Since I was a baby when my parents left me, I would be released from my Life Debt in my seventeenth year; if he'd saved my life as a grown adult, I would have been honor-bound to serve him for seven years or until he released me from my debt.

On my fourteenth Adoption Day—a Ghost Child's equivalent of a birthday—I received my main job assignment with the medic healers of Cathedral City. One year had passed since then, and ever since I started, I had enjoyed learning all I could about tending to different wounds and injuries, caring dutifully to the last moments of a dying life, and educating my patients on their recovery needs and expectations. Much like how I'd been drawn to Ceru's underground nest, I felt drawn toward my work as a healer.

Even when we lost a community member to disease or old age, I was greatly comforted by Ceru's assurance that such souls had entered into a better place; it was said the Dragon of Death would carry faithful souls to the Eternal Hall of the Creator, where we would live in endless joy. In this way, our grief was not without hope, and even in our sadness, I still found a gleam of goodness.

By far my favorite part of the job was helping the new mothers. I envied them the most, despite their obvious discomfort and their childbearing pain. The babies I helped birth made my heart flutter and ache at the same time, and while I had no husband to marry or admirer to court, I imagined falling in love wasn't so different from how I felt seeing that first glimpse of new, created life.

Each time I handed a mother her new baby, I felt a spark of fulfillment as much as a twang of longing.

I was grateful for what I had been given, I truly was; but as much as I loved Ceru and my home, my job, and my friends, I desperately wanted a family of my own.

There was something so alluring about the thought of running my own household, having a husband coming home to my hugs and kisses, and adding children to the world who were born out of the mutual adoration in my marriage.

It was so easy to picture that perfection inside my mind, even if I didn't have any idea what my future husband would look like.

Still, that only added to some of the mysterious allure. One day my husband could be tall and tan, with a large frame and soft eyes; the next he could have long hair and dimples that hugged his smiles. I didn't mind if he was long and lanky, or if he was short and stocky; as long as he loved me, I would love him more than anything else in the world, and we would never be happy unless we were together.

"Thessa! What are you doing?"

At the sound of Mother Nia's voice, I blinked, and my daydreams blurred into the scene before me, where I was tending to a sleeping patient. I was using a damp cloth to cool down a man's feverish brow, but I'd been caught up in thinking of tending to my own children in such a loving manner that I'd failed to notice the water was being so thickly applied, it was soaking his pillow.

"Oh." I quickly stepped away and gave Mother Nia a sheepish look.

"You're going to drown him if you're not careful." Her mouth was firmly set, but her ancient eyes lit up with a hidden laugh as she moved to adjust her habit.

"Well, it wouldn't be the worst thing to happen to him today," I replied with a joking smile.

Mother Nia clicked her tongue. "Impertinent girl," she murmured, but I saw her struggle to compose herself; I counted my retort as a win when she turned away from me.

From across the room, another voice spoke up in scolding tones. "If you ask me, Thessa's too distracted to work tonight."

I glared over at Kana, not surprised to see the disapproval on her otherwise perfect face. Kana was another Ghost who worked with me in the healer station. She was a little younger than me by a few months, but despite our similarities, I knew we would never be friends. We got along out of ritualistic necessity, even when I could see the underlying hints of her animosity.

Times like this.

"Forgive me, Mother Nia," I replied dutifully, lowering my eyes until I was absolved for my inattention.

No one ever paid attention to a Ghost—not unless we were doing something wrong. In my case, it did not help that Kana was quick to point out my shortcomings.

"Yes, yes, child." Mother Nia's normal reserved expression had returned by the time she waved away my meaningless apology. "Now, hurry. The pillow needs to be changed out quickly. We don't want Zebedee to get a cold."

"I will." I shot Kana a determined look.

"Perhaps I should take over for her tonight," Kana offered. "It is Thessa's Adoption Day, after all."

"That's true," I said, keeping my tone agreeable but not affirming. "But I can still work. My meeting with Father Ephyras isn't for another hour at least."

Kana held steady. "But if you're endangering the patients—"

"I'm sure Thessa won't let it happen again," Mother Nia said with a small, labored sigh. "And she's hardly endangering Zebedee, Kana. Honestly, if a man his age can survive falling into a ravine during combat drills, I'm sure a little extra water won't bother him. Now, be silent, girls, and get back to the tasks you've been assigned."

Mother Nia's face wrinkled as she gave us a warning glance and then shuffled out of the room.

Kana sneered at me before she went back to changing the bedsheets of another empty cot.

I felt heavy-hearted as Kana ignored me. I wasn't sure why we always seemed to have such trouble between us.

Kana was well-known for her good looks and intelligence. She had a larger group of friends than I did, and despite the rule of forbidden favorites, many of the priests and nuns around Cathedral City gushed over her more often than not.

Pia once told me that Kana hated being younger than me, and while I thought that was just silly, it was technically the one thing she would never accomplish over me—she could easily do a better job with our studies and accomplish more in the medical station. When it came to looking the part, Kana was organized, put-together, and always on time. I was always running a little late, my robes were a little wrinkled from sleeping in Ceru's mountain nest, and cleaning my room was a chore and a half.

"Did I hear that girl right? It's your Adoption Day?"

Zebedee stirred in his bed, and as I turned to face him, I saw him looking up at me with wonder.

"Yes, sir." I was glad he was awake; I wouldn't have to work as hard to get the pillow out from underneath him. "I'll be headed to the Cathedral after I'm done here."

"You should go then." Zebedee gave me a half-smile, one that looked painful from underneath the thick bandage on his head. "It's your fifteenth year, isn't it? Some young man will surely be ecstatic to have you as his bride."

Since we had been friendly for months, I gave Zebedee a quick kiss on the cheek. "I'm sure I can make an old man happy that I'm his medic."

Kana let out a discreet cough, and without looking, I knew she was rolling her eyes at me as Zebedee laughed.

"I'm surprised you're feeling so well. Especially since you had a rough tumble," I said. "Your first commander was horrified by the sight of you falling off the rocks."

"Ah, well ... I should've been expecting it," Zebedee said. "Ceru's getting old, too, Thessa. His city and Laena itself are starting to crumble."

I felt a lump in my throat. The High Priests taught us through their records of history and prophecies that one day, the Age of Dragons would be over, and a new order would begin through bloodshed and sacrifice.

There was not much I doubted Ceru could handle—but the word of the Creator was not to be ignored, either.

But surely, I told myself, there were times when it was best to ignore such theories? Ceru, while he was old, had me and the other Ghosts by his side. We loved him, and I knew we would continue taking care of him for many years to come.

On the other hand, Zebedee was an old man, and perhaps he was just trying to massage his own ego by saying the main island of Laena was starting to weaken.

"Now, now," I said calmly, "Saying such things won't push Ceru to love you any more than he already does. I'm sure you'll get a dragon tear if he hears you need it."

"I doubt I'll need it. Ceru likely needs them more than I do, the way things are looking," Zebedee said, grimacing with pain. "But I'll take some painkillers if you have them ready."

I did my best to brush off his concern for Ceru. Zebedee was an older man, and stubborn, too. I wouldn't be able to convince him Ceru was fine, no matter how long I spent arguing with him.

But if nothing else, Zebedee was right. Painkillers would help. "I'll go and retrieve them for you."

Zebedee nodded. "After that, promise me you'll go and see Father Ephyras. I know you're eager to have your marriage arranged, but the community wants to hear who the very lucky man will be just as much as you do."

"All right." My cheeks flushed over with humbled pleasure, even if I doubted he was correct on that point, too. "Thank you, Zebedee."

True to my word, I finished my last chore for the night and headed out. Even Mother Nia seemed glad Zebedee had gotten me to agree to leave early. Both of them offered their blessings as I left, and the memory of their quiet, sincere affection kept me warm as I moved through the streets of Cathedral City.

A few others waved at me, and I waved back, surprised by the attention.

Maybe Zebedee wasn't entirely incorrect.

I was still a Ghost, but now that I was fifteen, and it was my Adoption Day, I was starting to become more of a real person in the eyes of the community.

The sun was still high enough in the sky I could see clearly all the way to the top of the Hallowed Mountain. As I walked down from the medic station, I sighed contentedly at the sights before me.

The market in the city was bustling with a lively energy, like the invisible echoes of a song, and its rhythm was one with the beat of my own heart.

The Cathedral of the Great Sea Serpent was a massive building, built at the bottom of the Hallowed Mountain, where Ceru resided and labyrinthian springs of water kept him connected to the rest of the world. On either side of the mountain, a crescent arm of land curled around, making a natural harbor, where community members would keep their fishing ships and other seacraft. Behind the mountain, there was the forest of Laena, with its various trails, and then even further back, there was mostly farmland where the people of Laena peacefully resided. There were some other mountains, too, and then at the back of the island, there was the Great Waterfall of Laena. It was at the opposite end of the island from the Cathedral, running down the middle of the island's natural plateau.

At the bottom of the waterfall was marked the border between us and the home of Fuergo, the Fire Dragon Republic of Kator. They filled in a large chunk of the rest of the main continent, though there were several ongoing border disputes and historical claims with the Earth Dragon, Yla, and her nation, Atlaris, or so I'd heard.

The leaders of the Laenite Tribe had long ago decided not to interfere with the affairs of the world, and it was precisely because of Yla and Fuergo's various forms of warfare that history could attest to the wisdom of that decision.

"Thessa, there you are! Good heavens, did you hear?"

I barely had time to prepare myself before I found Philia rushing into me. She embraced me in a quick, sisterly hug, which I tried to reciprocate before she began jumping up and down.

"What is it?" I asked, laughing at her wild enthusiasm before catching some myself. "Did you hear something about me for my Adoption Day?"

"Oh, that's right. That's today, too." Philia's pretty face ducked down in apologetic shame. "I forgot."

"There's no issue," I assured her, even though I felt a little disappointed. I hid my hurt from her and gripped her hands with some measure of excitement. "Tell me what's happening."

"Oh, Thessa, an Arian ship is pulling into the harbor." Philia grinned. "And it's a big one, too. Perhaps we will get to hear another concert, maybe? What do you think?"

"I don't know," I admitted, although I was intrigued.

The Arian Islands were our neighbors from across the Western Seas. They served under Aria, the Dragon of Air, and their kingdom was made on artificially connected islands. They were full of talented artists and musicians, known for their appreciation and desire for beauty throughout the rest of the world. Occasionally, they would visit other regions of the world to showcase their talents or expand their trade routes.

"Come and see," Philia said, tugging on my hands. "They should be at port in a few moments."

I hesitated only for a moment; I wanted to go to the Hallowed Mountain, back to where Father Siah and the High Priest would be waiting for me, along with a message from Ceru regarding my Adoption Day—a message which possibly would inform me of who I was to marry after my Life Debt was over.

But Philia kept pulling on me, and after I took a look at the water clock set up in front of the Cathedral, I saw I had a little time to indulge my friend.

"Come on, Thessa," Philia insisted. "Pia's already down there, and Davar and Edmun are headed that way, too. They were told to report there for their soldier training in full uniform, so you know it has to be something important."

"They were?" I began walking with Philia, watching as she bubbled over with pleasure. She was a little over a year younger than me, and I couldn't help but feel old as she tried to hold my hand and skip down the street.

"Oh, yeah," Philia said. "Pia's already down there because of her job, but she'll be let out by the time we get there. And I was let out of work early today since one of the younglings spit up on me."

"Ew." I shook her off my arm. "You should've told me that earlier."

"I was wearing an apron." Philia nearly doubled over in laughter as I let out a silent prayer of thanks that I'd been appointed to work with the healers.

My friends and fellow Ghosts were old enough that each had been assigned a job, but I loved mine the most. Philia worked with the younger children as an assistant teacher; she would be promoted to a primary teacher in a few more years, and then she would work until she was married. Pia, her twin sister, worked down by Cathedral City's main port, overseeing fisherman and food production. I still saw them frequently, despite my longer shifts, but it was harder to keep up with my friends Davar and Edmun, since in addition to their jobs, boys were called to train as part of the Laenite Tribe's armed forces, but when we had a chance to meet, we did. As much as it interrupted my Adoption Day, I smiled at the thought of seeing them again.

"Ooh, Thessa, remember last time the Arians came? They brought us spools of fine cloth and those lovely shoes," Philia gushed. "And that jewelry, too!"

"You know Ghosts like us aren't supposed to draw attention to ourselves," I reminded her. "Why get so excited?"

"I'm more excited for you," Philia said. "Your Adoption Day is today. Surely, you'll get your marriage arranged, and as a bride, you can be as extravagant as you'd like."

As we made our way down to the port, Philia continued to babble, filling my head with even more daydreams and ideas. I couldn't help but allow her ideas to whisk my imagination away into another world, and even the sight of the Arian ship tying off into port couldn't fully bring me back to attention.

"Philia, Thessa, over here!"

Over the gathering crowds, I heard Davar calling out to us from the adjacent dock. I could see the dark burgundy of his hair sticking out from his helm. Philia had been right, it seemed; Davar was in his full armor, decked out in his gilded breastplate and the formal, silver-embroidered leather underneath his chainmail.

We made our way over to the adjacent dock as the Arian ship crept closer to shore.

"Where's Edmun?" I asked as we approached.

"He went to go with some of the other Ghosts," Davar said. "Father Piet ordered him to get Cathedral City's best guesthouses ready."

"So you know who's coming? What have you heard?" Philia asked Davar as we greeted each other.

"You wouldn't believe me if I told you." Davar straightened with pride, clearly enjoying having the upper hand over us; it was a rare occasion. "I've heard some of the port keepers talking about it."

"Well, tell us, then," Philia insisted. "Don't be cruel and make us wait. Is it another concert tour?"

"No, and praise the Creator for that." Davar stuck out his tongue in light disgust. He had no patience for music, although I had to wonder if that was intentional. Thanks to Philia, who often took to gossiping, we knew that Davar's father had likely been an Arian singer.

"Word has it that the Arian king has sent his highest-ranking ambassador here, and the ship's marking proves it," Davar said. He pointed toward the mast, where a royal purple flag waved in the breeze. "See the silver design on it? That's the coat of arms for the Rico family."

"It's so elegant," Philia said with a happy sigh. "I wonder what they've brought us? Maybe a new flag for Cathedral City's public square? That would be lovely. Father Dion was just mentioning about seeing to the City's upgrades."

"I don't know," I said, suddenly noticing the small legion of troops standing on the top deck. "They've come with soldiers."

"Well, I doubt it's an invasion if you're worried about that. They wouldn't be that foolish," Philia said. "Laena is very self-sufficient, and that's largely because our troops help protect us."

Davar grinned. "Of course we do, so you're welcome."

"Who says I was talking about you?" Philia teased. "You're still at a minor rank."

"Still better than you," Davar snapped back.

"Well, it's not my fault that women don't fight, is it?"

"Women like you are the reason we fight. We protect the rest of the world from having to deal with the likes of you."

I bit back a sigh as I ignored them. Philia and Davar had always been close, and with each passing year, I often wondered if they fought to prove they weren't secretly in love. Due to the mysterious nature of their heritage, Ghost Children were not often allowed to marry each other. Ceru would be the one who would have the final say in that matter, but given the odds, I couldn't blame Philia and Davar for their squabbles. Smaller pains in the present helped to possibly avoid larger ones in the future.

That was part of the reason the Laenites did not encourage some of the courting rituals many of the other countries and nations had, too. From what I knew of other nations' temporal relationships, divorces, and dating disasters, I was honestly relieved. I wanted a lasting love, a love that I could rely on to strengthen and support me; something I could add to and something that could give back something even more beautiful.

As Davar and Philia continued to tease and taunt each other, I kept my eyes on the approaching ship. It was a grand one, with silk-lined sails and intricate carvings along both sides. The Arians were known for their spectacle as much as their presentation.

I squinted as I saw a soldier moving across the ship, headed for the point of the bow.

The sun's setting light flickered over his helmed brow like a kiss of lightning. I watched, intrigued, as he took out a small flute and began to play.

The trill of the music fluttered down from on high in a lovely wave, making my heart lurch inside my chest.

I had always adored music. Both in my darkest midnights and my bright moments of joy, I would sing songs and find strength and sustenance.

I looked for the source of the song, and found myself staring at a man near the maidenhead of the ship.

The flute player held himself upright with confidence and flare, and as I watched him play, I almost wished I'd learned how to play an instrument, too. I was part of the worship choir as a singer, but I had no great talent.

I decided right then and there that if I ever had the time, I would write Ceru a song I could sing while another played the flute.

"Oh, that's beautiful." Philia leaned against my shoulder as she finally took notice of the music.

"Please, he's not that good," Davar argued, which sparked another argument with Philia.

I heard another shout from behind the flute player, and the music halted in mid-song.

A breath of stillness and silence took over.

And then, in the blink of an eye, the Arian boat suddenly slammed against the receiving dock.

The dock's wooden titles snapped. Ropes alternatively tightened and lagged, while several others called out everything from orders to screams of horror.

My eyes widened in shock as I watched the flute player. He wobbled dangerously atop the maidenhead of the ship, and just like before, a long, seemingly endless moment passed as we watched, transfixed by the danger.

And then fate finally gave its verdict.

Philia gasped, and even Davar's mouth dropped open as the flute player lost his battle with his balance, and he fell forward off the ship.

I closed my eyes as he met the water's surface in a devastating *splash*.

C. S. JOHNSON

Thank you for reading!

Please leave a review for this book and check my other books
for more complicated, meaningful fun!